CW00540852

Charles John Huffam Dickens (7 February 1812 – 9 June 1870) was an English writer and social critic. He created some of the world's best-known fictional characters and is regarded by many as the greatest novelist of the Victorian era. His works enjoyed unprecedented popularity during his lifetime, and by the 20th century critics and scholars had recognised him as a literary genius. His novels and short stories are still widely read today.

Born in Portsmouth, Dickens left school to work in a factory when his father was incarcerated in a debtors' prison. Despite his lack of formal education, he edited a weekly journal for 20 years, wrote 15 novels, five novellas, hundreds of short stories and non-fiction articles, lectured and performed readings extensively, was an indefatigable letter writer, and campaigned vigorously for children's rights, education, and other social reforms. (Source: Wikipedia)

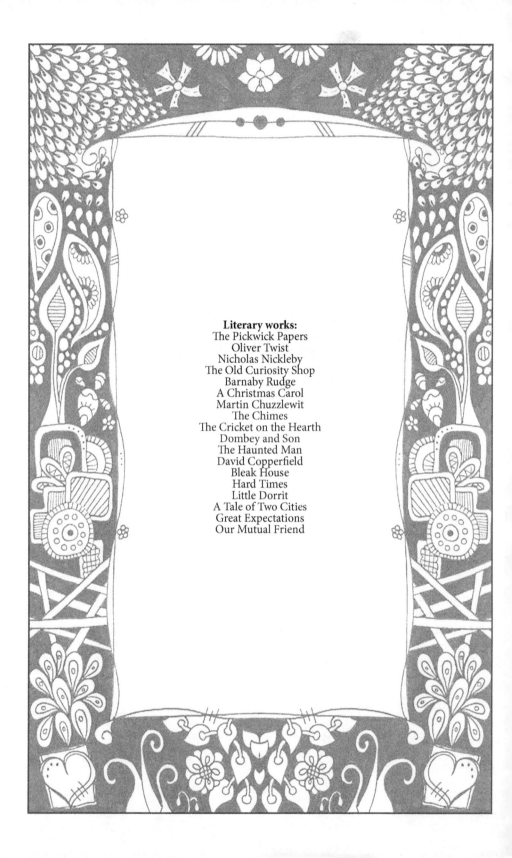

Literary works:
The Pickwick Papers
Oliver Twist
Nicholas Nickleby
The Old Curiosity Shop
Barnaby Rudge
A Christmas Carol
Martin Chuzzlewit
The Chimes
The Cricket on the Hearth
Dombey and Son
The Haunted Man
David Copperfield
Bleak House
Hard Times
Little Dorrit
A Tale of Two Cities
Great Expectations
Our Mutual Friend

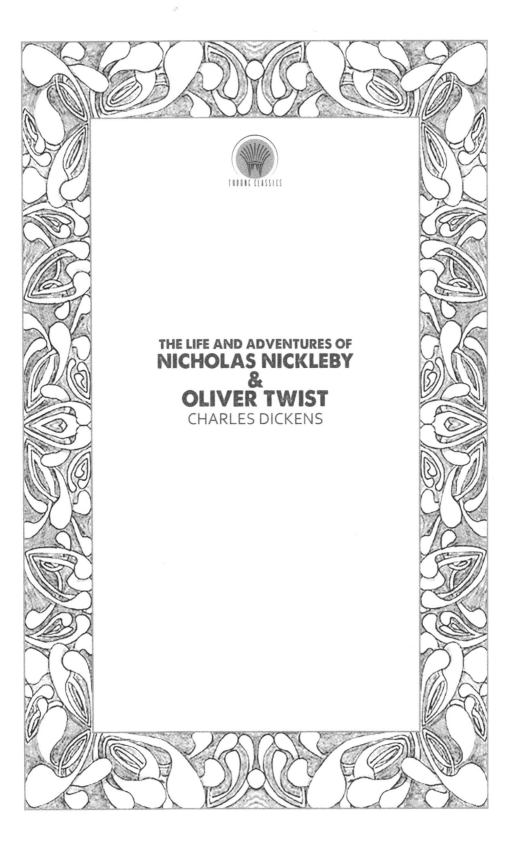

THRONE CLASSICS

THE LIFE AND ADVENTURES OF
NICHOLAS NICKLEBY
&
OLIVER TWIST
CHARLES DICKENS

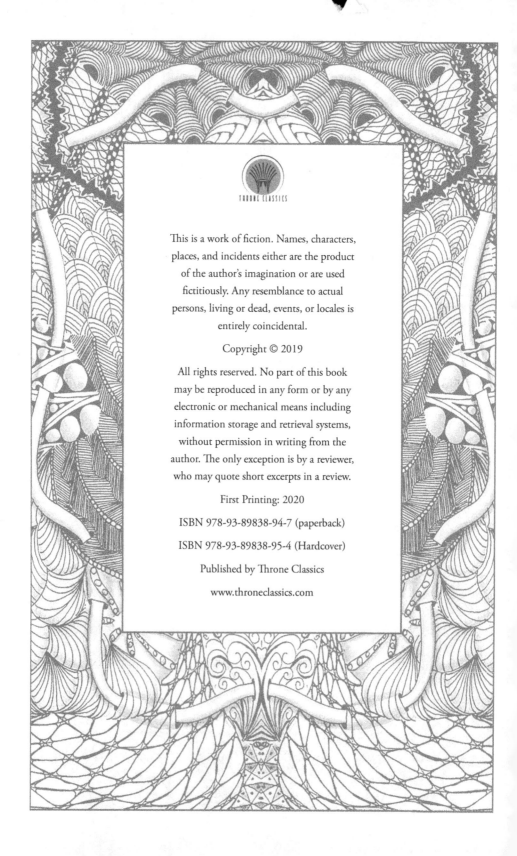

First Printing: 2020

ISBN 978-93-89838-94-7 (paperback)

ISBN 978-93-89838-95-4 (Hardcover)

Published by Throne Classics

www.throneclassics.com

Contents

THE LIFE AND ADVENTURES OF
NICHOLAS NICKLEBY
&
OLIVER TWIST

THE LIFE AND ADVENTURES OF NICHOLAS NICKLEBY

AUTHOR'S PREFACE

This story was begun, within a few months after the publication of the completed "Pickwick Papers." There were, then, a good many cheap Yorkshire schools in existence. There are very few now.

Of the monstrous neglect of education in England, and the disregard of it by the State as a means of forming good or bad citizens, and miserable or happy men, private schools long afforded a notable example. Although any man who had proved his unfitness for any other occupation in life, was free, without examination or qualification, to open a school anywhere; although preparation for the functions he undertook, was required in the surgeon who assisted to bring a boy into the world, or might one day assist, perhaps, to send him out of it; in the chemist, the attorney, the butcher, the baker, the candlestick maker; the whole round of crafts and trades, the schoolmaster excepted; and although schoolmasters, as a race, were the blockheads and impostors who might naturally be expected to spring from such a state of things, and to flourish in it; these Yorkshire schoolmasters were the lowest and most rotten round in the whole ladder. Traders in the avarice, indifference, or imbecility of parents, and the helplessness of children; ignorant, sordid, brutal men, to whom few considerate persons would have entrusted the board and lodging of a horse or a dog; they formed the worthy cornerstone of a structure, which, for absurdity and a magnificent high-minded Laissez-Aller neglect, has rarely been exceeded in the world.

We hear sometimes of an action for damages against the unqualified medical practitioner, who has deformed a broken limb in pretending to heal it. But, what of the hundreds of thousands of minds that have been deformed for ever by the incapable pettifoggers who have pretended to form them!

I make mention of the race, as of the Yorkshire schoolmasters, in the past tense. Though it has not yet finally disappeared, it is dwindling daily. A long day's work remains to be done about us in the way of education, Heaven knows; but great improvements and facilities towards the attainment of a good one, have been furnished, of late years.

I cannot call to mind, now, how I came to hear about Yorkshire schools when I was a not very robust child, sitting in bye-places near Rochester Castle, with a head full of Partridge, Strap, Tom Pipes, and Sancho Panza; but I know that my first impressions of them were picked up at that time, and that they were somehow or other connected with a suppurated abscess that some boy had come home with, in consequence of his Yorkshire guide, philosopher, and friend, having ripped it open with an inky pen-knife. The impression made upon me, however made, never left me. I was always curious about Yorkshire schools—fell, long afterwards and at sundry times, into the way of hearing more about them—at last, having an audience, resolved to write about them.

With that intent I went down into Yorkshire before I began this book, in very severe winter time which is pretty faithfully described herein. As I wanted to see a schoolmaster or two, and was forewarned that those gentlemen might, in their modesty, be shy of receiving a visit from the author of the "Pickwick Papers," I consulted with a professional friend who had a Yorkshire connexion, and with whom I concerted a pious fraud. He gave me some letters of introduction, in the name, I think, of my travelling companion; they bore reference to a supposititious little boy who had been left with a widowed mother who didn't know what to do with him; the poor lady had thought, as a means of thawing the tardy compassion of her relations in his behalf, of sending him to a Yorkshire school; I was the poor lady's friend, travelling that way; and if the recipient of the letter could inform me of a school in his neighbourhood, the writer would be very much obliged.

I went to several places in that part of the country where I understood the schools to be most plentifully sprinkled, and had no occasion to deliver a letter until I came to a certain town which shall be nameless. The person to whom it was addressed, was not at home; but he came down at night, through the snow, to the inn where I was staying. It was after dinner; and he needed little persuasion to sit down by the fire in a warm corner, and take his share of the wine that was on the table.

I am afraid he is dead now. I recollect he was a jovial, ruddy, broad-faced man; that we got acquainted directly; and that we talked on all kinds of subjects, except the school, which he showed a great anxiety to avoid. "Was there any large school near?" I asked him, in reference to the letter. "Oh yes," he said; "there was a pratty big 'un." "Was it a good one?" I asked. "Ey!" he said, "it was as good as anoother; that was a' a matther of opinion"; and fell to looking at the fire, staring round the room, and whistling a little. On my reverting to some other topic that we had been discussing, he recovered immediately; but, though I tried him again and again, I never approached the question of the school, even if he were in the middle of a laugh, without observing that his countenance fell, and that he became uncomfortable. At last, when we had passed a couple of hours or so, very agreeably, he suddenly took up his hat, and leaning over the table and looking me full in the face, said, in a low voice: "Weel, Misther, we've been vara pleasant toogather, and ar'll spak' my moind tiv'ee. Dinnot let the weedur send her lattle boy to yan o' our school-measthers, while there's a harse to hoold in a' Lunnun, or a gootther to lie asleep in. Ar wouldn't mak' ill words amang my neeburs, and ar speak tiv'ee quiet loike. But I'm dom'd if ar can gang to bed and not tellee, for weedur's sak', to keep the lattle boy from a' sike scoondrels while there's a harse to hoold in a' Lunnun, or a gootther to lie asleep in!" Repeating these words with great heartiness, and with a solemnity on his jolly face that made it look twice as large as before, he shook hands and went away. I never saw him afterwards, but I sometimes imagine that I descry a faint reflection of him in John Browdie.

In reference to these gentry, I may here quote a few words from the original preface to this book.

"It has afforded the Author great amusement and satisfaction, during the progress of this work, to learn, from country friends and from a variety of ludicrous statements concerning himself in provincial newspapers, that more than one Yorkshire schoolmaster lays claim to being the original of Mr. Squeers. One worthy, he has reason to believe, has actually consulted authorities learned in the law, as to his having good grounds on which to rest an action for libel; another, has meditated a journey to London, for the express purpose of committing an assault and battery on his traducer; a third, perfectly remembers being waited on, last January twelve-month, by two gentlemen, one of whom held him in conversation while the other took his likeness; and, although Mr. Squeers has but one eye, and he has two, and the published sketch does not resemble him (whoever he may be) in any other respect, still he and all his friends and neighbours know at once for whom it is meant, because—the character is so like him.

"While the Author cannot but feel the full force of the compliment thus conveyed to him, he ventures to suggest that these contentions may arise from the fact, that Mr. Squeers is the representative of a class, and not of an individual. Where imposture, ignorance, and brutal cupidity, are the stock in trade of a small body of men, and one is described by these characteristics, all his fellows will recognise something belonging to themselves, and each will have a misgiving that the portrait is his own.

"The Author's object in calling public attention to the system would be very imperfectly fulfilled, if he did not state now, in his own person, emphatically and earnestly, that Mr. Squeers and his school are faint and feeble pictures of an existing reality, purposely subdued and kept down lest they should be deemed impossible. That there are, upon record, trials at law in which damages have been sought as a poor recompense for lasting agonies and disfigurements inflicted upon children by the treatment of the master in these places, involving such offensive and foul details of neglect, cruelty, and disease, as no writer of fiction would have the boldness to imagine. And that, since he has been engaged upon these Adventures, he has received, from private quarters far beyond the reach of suspicion or distrust, accounts of atrocities, in the perpetration of which upon neglected or repudiated children, these schools have been the main instruments, very far exceeding any that appear in these pages."

This comprises all I need say on the subject; except that if I had seen occasion, I had resolved to reprint a few of these details of legal proceedings, from certain old newspapers.

One other quotation from the same Preface may serve to introduce a fact that my readers may think curious.

"To turn to a more pleasant subject, it may be right to say, that there are two characters in this book which are drawn from life. It is remarkable that what we call the world, which is so very credulous in what professes to be true, is most incredulous in what professes to be imaginary; and that, while, every day in real life, it will allow in one man no blemishes, and in another no virtues, it will seldom admit a very strongly-marked character, either good or bad, in a fictitious narrative, to be within the limits of probability. But those who take an interest in this tale, will be glad to learn that the Brothers Cheeryble live; that their liberal charity, their singleness of heart, their noble nature, and their unbounded benevolence, are no creations of the Author's brain; but are prompting every day (and oftenest by stealth) some munificent and generous deed in that town of which they are the pride and honour."

If I were to attempt to sum up the thousands of letters, from all sorts of people in all sorts of latitudes and climates, which this unlucky paragraph brought down upon me, I should get into an arithmetical difficulty from which I could not easily extricate myself. Suffice it to say, that I believe the applications for loans, gifts, and offices of profit that I have been requested to forward to the originals of the Brothers Cheeryble (with whom I never interchanged any communication in my life) would have exhausted the combined patronage of all the Lord

Chancellors since the accession of the House of Brunswick, and would have broken the Rest of the Bank of England.

The Brothers are now dead.

There is only one other point, on which I would desire to offer a remark. If Nicholas be not always found to be blameless or agreeable, he is not always intended to appear so. He is a young man of an impetuous temper and of little or no experience; and I saw no reason why such a hero should be lifted out of nature.

CHAPTER 1
Introduces all the Rest

There once lived, in a sequestered part of the county of Devonshire, one Mr. Godfrey Nickleby: a worthy gentleman, who, taking it into his head rather late in life that he must get married, and not being young enough or rich enough to aspire to the hand of a lady of fortune, had wedded an old flame out of mere attachment, who in her turn had taken him for the same reason. Thus two people who cannot afford to play cards for money, sometimes sit down to a quiet game for love.

Some ill-conditioned persons who sneer at the life-matrimonial, may perhaps suggest, in this place, that the good couple would be better likened to two principals in a sparring match, who, when fortune is low and backers scarce, will chivalrously set to, for the mere pleasure of the buffeting; and in one respect indeed this comparison would hold good; for, as the adventurous pair of the Fives' Court will afterwards send round a hat, and trust to the bounty of the lookers-on for the means of regaling themselves, so Mr. Godfrey Nickleby and his partner, the honeymoon being over, looked out wistfully into the world, relying in no inconsiderable degree upon chance for the improvement of their means. Mr. Nickleby's income, at the period of his marriage, fluctuated between sixty and eighty pounds per annum.

There are people enough in the world, Heaven knows! and even in London (where Mr. Nickleby dwelt in those days) but few complaints prevail, of the population being scanty. It is extraordinary how long a man may look among the crowd without discovering the face of a friend, but it is no less true. Mr. Nickleby looked, and looked, till his eyes became sore as his heart, but no friend appeared; and when, growing tired of the search, he turned his eyes homeward, he saw very little there to relieve his weary vision. A painter who has gazed too long upon some glaring colour, refreshes his dazzled sight by looking upon a darker and more sombre tint; but everything that met Mr. Nickleby's gaze wore so black and gloomy a hue, that he would have been beyond description refreshed by the very reverse of the contrast.

At length, after five years, when Mrs. Nickleby had presented her husband with a couple of sons, and that embarrassed gentleman, impressed with the necessity of making some provision for his family, was seriously revolving in his mind a little commercial speculation of insuring his life next quarter-day, and then falling from the top of the Monument by accident, there came, one morning, by the general post, a black-bordered letter to inform him how his uncle, Mr. Ralph Nickleby, was dead, and had left him the bulk of his little property, amounting in all to five thousand pounds sterling.

As the deceased had taken no further notice of his nephew in his lifetime, than sending to his eldest boy (who had been christened after him, on desperate speculation) a silver spoon in a morocco case, which, as he had not too much to eat with it, seemed a kind of satire upon his having been born without that useful article of plate in his mouth, Mr. Godfrey Nickleby could, at first, scarcely believe the tidings thus conveyed to him. On examination, however, they turned out to be strictly correct. The amiable old gentleman, it seemed, had intended to leave the whole to the Royal Humane Society, and had indeed executed a will to that effect; but the Institution, having been unfortunate enough, a few months before, to save the life of a poor relation to whom he paid a weekly allowance of three shillings and sixpence, he had, in a fit of very natural exasperation, revoked the bequest in a codicil, and left it all to Mr Godfrey Nickleby; with a special mention of his indignation, not only against the society for saving the poor relation's life, but against the poor relation also, for allowing himself to be saved.

With a portion of this property Mr. Godfrey Nickleby purchased a small farm, near Dawlish in Devonshire, whither he retired with his wife and two children, to live upon the best interest he could get for the rest of his money, and the little produce he could raise from his land. The two prospered so well together that, when he died, some fifteen years after this period, and some five after his wife, he was enabled to leave, to his eldest son, Ralph, three thousand pounds in cash, and to his youngest son, Nicholas, one thousand and the farm, which was as small a landed estate as one would desire to see.

These two brothers had been brought up together in a school at Exeter; and, being accustomed to go home once a week, had often heard, from their mother's lips, long accounts of their father's sufferings in his days of poverty, and of their deceased uncle's importance in his days of affluence: which recitals produced a very different impression on the two: for, while the younger, who was of a timid and retiring disposition, gleaned from thence nothing but forewarnings to shun the great world and attach himself to the quiet routine of a country life, Ralph, the elder, deduced from the often-repeated tale the two great morals that riches are the only true source of happiness and power, and that it is lawful and just to compass their acquisition by all means short of felony. 'And,' reasoned Ralph with himself, 'if no good came of my uncle's money when he was alive, a great deal of good came of it after he was dead, inasmuch as my father has got it now, and is saving it up for me, which is a highly virtuous purpose; and, going back to the old gentleman, good did come of it to him too, for he had the pleasure of thinking of it all his life long, and of being envied and courted by all his family besides.' And Ralph always wound up these mental soliloquies by arriving at the conclusion, that there was nothing like money.

Not confining himself to theory, or permitting his faculties to rust, even at that early age, in mere abstract speculations, this promising lad commenced usurer on a limited scale at school; putting out at good interest a small capital of slate-pencil and marbles, and gradually extending his operations until they aspired to the copper coinage of this realm, in which he speculated to considerable advantage. Nor did he trouble his borrowers with abstract calculations of figures, or references to ready-reckoners; his simple rule of interest being all comprised in the one golden sentence, 'two-pence for every half-penny,' which greatly simplified the accounts, and which, as a familiar precept, more easily acquired and retained in the memory than any known rule of arithmetic, cannot be too strongly recommended to the notice of capitalists, both large and small, and more especially of money-brokers and bill-discounters. Indeed, to do these gentlemen justice, many of them are to this day in the frequent habit of adopting it, with eminent success.

In like manner, did young Ralph Nickleby avoid all those minute and intricate calculations of odd days, which nobody who has worked sums in simple-interest can fail to have found most embarrassing, by establishing the one general rule that all sums of principal and interest should be paid on pocket-money day, that is to say, on Saturday: and that whether a loan were contracted on the Monday, or on the Friday, the amount of interest should be, in both cases, the same. Indeed he argued, and with great show of reason, that it ought to be rather more for one day than for five, inasmuch as the borrower might in the former case be very fairly presumed to be in great extremity, otherwise he would not borrow at all with such odds against him. This fact is interesting, as illustrating the secret connection and sympathy which always exist between great minds. Though Master Ralph Nickleby was not at that time aware of it, the class of gentlemen before alluded to, proceed on just the same principle in all their transactions.

From what we have said of this young gentleman, and the natural admiration the reader will immediately conceive of his character, it may perhaps be inferred that he is to be the hero of the work which we shall presently begin. To set this point at rest, for once and for ever, we hasten to undeceive them, and stride to its commencement.

On the death of his father, Ralph Nickleby, who had been some time before placed in a mercantile house in London, applied himself passionately to his old pursuit of money-getting, in which he speedily became so buried and absorbed, that he quite forgot his brother for many years; and if, at times, a recollection of his old playfellow broke upon him through the haze in which he lived—for gold conjures up a mist about a man, more destructive of all his old senses and lulling to his feelings than the fumes of charcoal—it brought along with it a companion thought, that if they were intimate he would want to borrow money of him. So, Mr. Ralph Nickleby shrugged his shoulders, and said things were better as they were.

As for Nicholas, he lived a single man on the patrimonial estate until he grew tired of living alone, and then he took to wife the daughter of a neighbouring gentleman with a dower of one thousand pounds. This good lady bore him two children, a son and a daughter, and when the son was about nineteen, and the daughter fourteen, as near as we can guess—impartial records of young ladies' ages being, before the passing of the new act, nowhere preserved in the registries of this country—Mr. Nickleby looked about him for the means of repairing his capital, now sadly reduced by this increase in his family, and the expenses of their education.

'Speculate with it,' said Mrs. Nickleby.

'Spec—u—late, my dear?' said Mr. Nickleby, as though in doubt.

'Why not?' asked Mrs. Nickleby.

'Because, my dear, if we should lose it,' rejoined Mr. Nickleby, who was a slow and time-taking speaker, 'if we should lose it, we shall no longer be able to live, my dear.'

'Fiddle,' said Mrs. Nickleby.

'I am not altogether sure of that, my dear,' said Mr. Nickleby.

'There's Nicholas,' pursued the lady, 'quite a young man—it's time he was in the way of doing something for himself; and Kate too, poor girl, without a penny in the world. Think of your brother! Would he be what he is, if he hadn't speculated?'

'That's true,' replied Mr. Nickleby. 'Very good, my dear. Yes. I will speculate, my dear.'

Speculation is a round game; the players see little or nothing of their cards at first starting; gains may be great—and so may losses. The run of luck went against Mr. Nickleby. A mania prevailed, a bubble burst, four stock-brokers took villa residences at Florence, four hundred nobodies were ruined, and among them Mr. Nickleby.

'The very house I live in,' sighed the poor gentleman, 'may be taken from me tomorrow.

Not an article of my old furniture, but will be sold to strangers!'

The last reflection hurt him so much, that he took at once to his bed; apparently resolved to keep that, at all events.

'Cheer up, sir!' said the apothecary.

'You mustn't let yourself be cast down, sir,' said the nurse.

'Such things happen every day,' remarked the lawyer.

'And it is very sinful to rebel against them,' whispered the clergyman.

'And what no man with a family ought to do,' added the neighbours.

Mr. Nickleby shook his head, and motioning them all out of the room, embraced his wife and children, and having pressed them by turns to his languidly beating heart, sunk exhausted on his pillow. They were concerned to find that his reason went astray after this; for he babbled, for a long time, about the generosity and goodness of his brother, and the merry old times when they were at school together. This fit of wandering past, he solemnly commended them to One who never deserted the widow or her fatherless children, and, smiling gently on them, turned upon his face, and observed, that he thought he could fall asleep.

CHAPTER 2

Of Mr. Ralph Nickleby, and his Establishments, and his Undertakings, and of a great Joint Stock Company of vast national Importance

Mr. Ralph Nickleby was not, strictly speaking, what you would call a merchant, neither was he a banker, nor an attorney, nor a special pleader, nor a notary. He was certainly not a tradesman, and still less could he lay any claim to the title of a professional gentleman; for it would have been impossible to mention any recognised profession to which he belonged. Nevertheless, as he lived in a spacious house in Golden Square, which, in addition to a brass plate upon the street-door, had another brass plate two sizes and a half smaller upon the left hand door-post, surrounding a brass model of an infant's fist grasping a fragment of a skewer, and displaying the word 'Office,' it was clear that Mr. Ralph Nickleby did, or pretended to do, business of some kind; and the fact, if it required any further circumstantial evidence, was abundantly demonstrated by the diurnal attendance, between the hours of half-past nine and five, of a sallow-faced man in rusty brown, who sat upon an uncommonly hard stool in a species of butler's pantry at the end of the passage, and always had a pen behind his ear when he answered the bell.

Although a few members of the graver professions live about Golden Square, it is not exactly in anybody's way to or from anywhere. It is one of the squares that have been; a quarter of the town that has gone down in the world, and taken to letting lodgings. Many of its first and second floors are let, furnished, to single gentlemen; and it takes boarders besides. It is a great resort of foreigners. The dark-complexioned men who wear large rings, and heavy watch-guards, and bushy whiskers, and who congregate under the Opera Colonnade, and about the box-office in the season, between four and five in the afternoon, when they give away the orders,—all live in Golden Square, or within a street of it. Two or three violins and a wind instrument from the Opera band reside within its precincts. Its boarding-houses are musical, and the notes of pianos and harps float in the evening time round the head of the mournful statue, the guardian genius of a little wilderness of shrubs, in the centre of the square. On a summer's night, windows are thrown open, and groups of swarthy moustached men are seen by the passer-by, lounging at the casements, and smoking fearfully. Sounds of gruff voices practising vocal music invade the evening's silence; and the fumes of choice tobacco scent the air. There, snuff and cigars, and German pipes and flutes, and violins and violoncellos, divide the supremacy between them. It is the region of song and smoke. Street bands are on their mettle in Golden Square; and itinerant glee-singers quaver involuntarily as they raise their voices within its boundaries.

This would not seem a spot very well adapted to the transaction of business; but Mr. Ralph Nickleby had lived there, notwithstanding, for many years, and uttered no complaint on that score. He knew nobody round about, and nobody knew him, although he enjoyed the reputation of being immensely rich. The tradesmen held that he was a sort of lawyer, and the other neighbours opined that he was a kind of general agent; both of which guesses were as correct and definite as guesses about other people's affairs usually are, or need to be.

Mr. Ralph Nickleby sat in his private office one morning, ready dressed to walk abroad. He wore a bottle-green spencer over a blue coat; a white waistcoat, grey mixture pantaloons, and Wellington boots drawn over them. The corner of a small-plaited shirt-frill struggled out, as if insisting to show itself, from between his chin and the top button of his spencer; and the latter garment was not made low enough to conceal a long gold watch-chain, composed of a series of plain rings, which had its beginning at the handle of a gold repeater in Mr. Nickleby's pocket, and its termination in two little keys: one belonging to the watch itself, and the other to some patent padlock. He wore a sprinkling of powder upon his head, as if to make himself look benevolent; but if that were his purpose, he would perhaps have done better to powder his countenance also, for there was something in its very wrinkles, and in his cold restless eye, which seemed to tell of cunning that would announce itself in spite of him. However this might be, there he was; and as he was all alone, neither the powder, nor the wrinkles, nor the eyes, had the smallest effect, good or bad, upon anybody just then, and are consequently no business of ours just now.

Mr. Nickleby closed an account-book which lay on his desk, and, throwing himself back in his chair, gazed with an air of abstraction through the dirty window. Some London houses have a melancholy little plot of ground behind them, usually fenced in by four high whitewashed walls, and frowned upon by stacks of chimneys: in which there withers on, from year to year, a crippled tree, that makes a show of putting forth a few leaves late in autumn when other trees shed theirs, and, drooping in the effort, lingers on, all crackled and smoke-dried, till the following season, when it repeats the same process, and perhaps, if the weather be particularly genial, even tempts some rheumatic sparrow to chirrup in its branches. People sometimes call these dark yards 'gardens'; it is not supposed that they were ever planted, but rather that they are pieces of unreclaimed land, with the withered vegetation of the original brick-field. No man thinks of walking in this desolate place, or of turning it to any account. A few hampers, half-a-dozen broken bottles, and such-like rubbish, may be thrown there, when the tenant first moves in, but nothing more; and there they remain until he goes away again: the damp straw taking just as long to moulder as it thinks proper: and mingling with the scanty box, and stunted everbrowns, and broken flower-pots, that are scattered mournfully about—a prey to 'blacks' and dirt.

It was into a place of this kind that Mr. Ralph Nickleby gazed, as he sat with his hands in his pockets looking out of the window. He had fixed his eyes upon a distorted fir tree, planted by some former tenant in a tub that had once been green, and left there, years before, to rot away piecemeal. There was nothing very inviting in the object, but Mr. Nickleby was wrapt in a brown study, and sat contemplating it with far greater attention than, in a more conscious mood, he would have deigned to bestow upon the rarest exotic. At length, his eyes wandered to a little dirty window on the left, through which the face of the clerk was dimly visible; that worthy chancing to look up, he beckoned him to attend.

In obedience to this summons the clerk got off the high stool (to which he had communicated a high polish by countless gettings off and on), and presented himself in Mr. Nickleby's room. He was a tall man of middle age, with two goggle eyes whereof one was a fixture, a rubicund nose, a cadaverous face, and a suit of clothes (if the term be allowable when they suited him not at all) much the worse for wear, very much too small, and placed upon such a short allowance of buttons that it was marvellous how he contrived to keep them on.

'Was that half-past twelve, Noggs?' said Mr. Nickleby, in a sharp and grating voice.

'Not more than five-and-twenty minutes by the—' Noggs was going to add public-house clock, but recollecting himself, substituted 'regular time.'

'My watch has stopped,' said Mr. Nickleby; 'I don't know from what cause.'

'Not wound up,' said Noggs.

'Yes it is,' said Mr. Nickleby.

'Over-wound then,' rejoined Noggs.

'That can't very well be,' observed Mr. Nickleby.

'Must be,' said Noggs.

'Well!' said Mr. Nickleby, putting the repeater back in his pocket; 'perhaps it is.'

Noggs gave a peculiar grunt, as was his custom at the end of all disputes with his master, to imply that he (Noggs) triumphed; and (as he rarely spoke to anybody unless somebody spoke to him) fell into a grim silence, and rubbed his hands slowly over each other: cracking the joints of his fingers, and squeezing them into all possible distortions. The incessant performance of this routine on every occasion, and the communication of a fixed and rigid look to his unaffected eye, so as to make it uniform with the other, and to render it impossible for anybody to determine where or at what he was looking, were two among the numerous peculiarities of Mr Noggs, which struck an inexperienced observer at first sight.

'I am going to the London Tavern this morning,' said Mr. Nickleby.

'Public meeting?' inquired Noggs.

Mr. Nickleby nodded. 'I expect a letter from the solicitor respecting that mortgage of Ruddle's. If it comes at all, it will be here by the two o'clock delivery. I shall leave the city about that time and walk to Charing Cross on the left-hand side of the way; if there are any letters, come and meet me, and bring them with you.'

Noggs nodded; and as he nodded, there came a ring at the office bell. The master looked up from his papers, and the clerk calmly remained in a stationary position.

'The bell,' said Noggs, as though in explanation. 'At home?'

'Yes.'

'To anybody?'

'Yes.'

'To the tax-gatherer?'

'No! Let him call again.'

Noggs gave vent to his usual grunt, as much as to say 'I thought so!' and, the ring being repeated, went to the door, whence he presently returned, ushering in, by the name of Mr. Bonney, a pale gentleman in a violent hurry, who, with his hair standing up in great disorder all over his head, and a very narrow white cravat tied loosely round his throat, looked as if he had been knocked up in the night and had not dressed himself since.

'My dear Nickleby,' said the gentleman, taking off a white hat which was so full of papers that it would scarcely stick upon his head, 'there's not a moment to lose; I have a cab at the door. Sir Matthew Pupker takes the chair, and three members of Parliament are positively coming. I have seen two of them safely out of bed. The third, who was at Crockford's all night, has just gone home to put a clean shirt on, and take a bottle or two of soda water, and will certainly be with us, in time to address the meeting. He is a little excited by last night, but never mind that; he always speaks the stronger for it.'

'It seems to promise pretty well,' said Mr. Ralph Nickleby, whose deliberate manner was strongly opposed to the vivacity of the other man of business.

'Pretty well!' echoed Mr. Bonney. 'It's the finest idea that was ever started. "United Metropolitan Improved Hot Muffin and Crumpet Baking and Punctual Delivery Company. Capital, five millions, in five hundred thousand shares of ten pounds each." Why the very name will get the shares up to a premium in ten days.'

'And when they are at a premium,' said Mr. Ralph Nickleby, smiling.

'When they are, you know what to do with them as well as any man alive, and how to back quietly out at the right time,' said Mr. Bonney, slapping the capitalist familiarly on the shoulder. 'By-the-bye, what a very remarkable man that clerk of yours is.'

'Yes, poor devil!' replied Ralph, drawing on his gloves. 'Though Newman Noggs kept his horses and hounds once.'

'Ay, ay?' said the other carelessly.

'Yes,' continued Ralph, 'and not many years ago either; but he squandered his money, invested it anyhow, borrowed at interest, and in short made first a thorough fool of himself, and then a beggar. He took to drinking, and had a touch of paralysis, and then came here to borrow a pound, as in his better days I had—'

'Done business with him,' said Mr. Bonney with a meaning look.

'Just so,' replied Ralph; 'I couldn't lend it, you know.'

'Oh, of course not.'

'But as I wanted a clerk just then, to open the door and so forth, I took him out of charity, and he has remained with me ever since. He is a little mad, I think,' said Mr. Nickleby, calling up a charitable look, 'but he is useful enough, poor creature—useful enough.'

The kind-hearted gentleman omitted to add that Newman Noggs, being utterly destitute, served him for rather less than the usual wages of a boy of thirteen; and likewise failed to mention in his hasty chronicle, that his eccentric taciturnity rendered him an especially valuable person in a place where much business was done, of which it was desirable no mention should be made out of doors. The other gentleman was plainly impatient to be gone, however, and as they hurried into the hackney cabriolet immediately afterwards, perhaps Mr. Nickleby forgot to mention circumstances so unimportant.

There was a great bustle in Bishopsgate Street Within, as they drew up, and (it being a windy day) half-a-dozen men were tacking across the road under a press of paper, bearing gigantic announcements that a Public Meeting would be holden at one o'clock precisely, to take into consideration the propriety of petitioning Parliament in favour of the United Metropolitan Improved Hot Muffin and Crumpet Baking and Punctual Delivery Company, capital five millions, in five hundred thousand shares of ten pounds each; which sums were duly set forth in fat black figures of considerable size. Mr. Bonney elbowed his way briskly upstairs, receiving in his progress many low bows from the waiters who stood on the landings to show the way; and, followed by Mr. Nickleby, dived into a suite of apartments behind the great public room: in the second of which was a business-looking table, and several business-looking people.

'Hear!' cried a gentleman with a double chin, as Mr. Bonney presented himself. 'Chair, gentlemen, chair!'

The new-comers were received with universal approbation, and Mr. Bonney bustled up to the top of the table, took off his hat, ran his fingers through his hair, and knocked a hackney-coachman's knock on the table with a little hammer: whereat several gentlemen cried 'Hear!' and nodded slightly to each other, as much as to say what spirited conduct that was. Just at this moment, a waiter, feverish with agitation, tore into the room, and throwing the door open with a crash, shouted 'Sir Matthew Pupker!'

The committee stood up and clapped their hands for joy, and while they were clapping them, in came Sir Matthew Pupker, attended by two live members of Parliament, one Irish and one Scotch, all smiling and bowing, and looking so pleasant that it seemed a perfect marvel how any man could have the heart to vote against them. Sir Matthew Pupker especially, who had a little round head with a flaxen wig on the top of it, fell into such a paroxysm of bows, that the wig threatened to be jerked off, every instant. When these symptoms had in some degree subsided, the gentlemen who were on speaking terms with Sir Matthew Pupker, or the two other members, crowded round them in three little groups, near one or other of which the gentlemen who were not on speaking terms with Sir Matthew Pupker or the two other members, stood lingering, and smiling, and rubbing their hands, in the desperate hope of something turning up which might bring them into notice. All this time, Sir Matthew Pupker and the two other members were relating to their separate circles what the intentions of government were, about taking up the bill; with a full account of what the government had said in a whisper the last time they dined with it, and how the government had been observed to wink when it said so; from which premises they were at no loss to draw the conclusion, that if the government had one object more at heart than another, that one object was the welfare and advantage of the United Metropolitan Improved Hot Muffin and Crumpet Baking and Punctual Delivery Company.

Meanwhile, and pending the arrangement of the proceedings, and a fair division of the speechifying, the public in the large room were eyeing, by turns, the empty platform, and the ladies in the Music Gallery. In these amusements the greater portion of them had been occupied for a couple of hours before, and as the most agreeable diversions pall upon the taste on a too protracted enjoyment of them, the sterner spirits now began to hammer the floor with their boot-heels, and to express their dissatisfaction by various hoots and cries. These vocal exertions, emanating from the people who had been there longest, naturally proceeded from those who were nearest to the platform and furthest from the policemen in attendance, who having no great mind to fight their way through the crowd, but entertaining nevertheless a praiseworthy desire to do something to quell the disturbance, immediately began to drag forth, by the coat tails and collars, all the quiet people near the door; at the same time dealing out various smart and tingling blows with their truncheons, after the manner of that ingenious actor, Mr. Punch: whose brilliant example, both in the fashion of his weapons and their use, this branch of the executive occasionally follows.

Several very exciting skirmishes were in progress, when a loud shout attracted the attention even of the belligerents, and then there poured on to the platform, from a door at the side, a long line of gentlemen with their hats off, all looking behind them, and uttering vociferous cheers; the cause whereof was sufficiently explained when Sir Matthew Pupker and the two other real members of Parliament came to the front, amidst deafening shouts, and testified to each other in dumb motions that they had never seen such a glorious sight as that, in the whole course of their public career.

At length, and at last, the assembly left off shouting, but Sir Matthew Pupker being voted into the chair, they underwent a relapse which lasted five minutes. This over, Sir Matthew Pupker went on to say what must be his feelings on that great occasion, and what must be that occasion in the eyes of the world, and what must be the intelligence of his fellow-countrymen before him, and what must be the wealth and respectability of his honourable friends behind him, and lastly, what must be the importance to the wealth, the happiness, the comfort, the liberty, the very existence of a free and great people, of such an Institution as the United Metropolitan Improved Hot Muffin and Crumpet Baking and Punctual Delivery Company!

Mr. Bonney then presented himself to move the first resolution; and having run his right hand through his hair, and planted his left, in an easy manner, in his ribs, he consigned his hat to the care of the gentleman with the double chin (who acted as a species of bottle-holder to the orators generally), and said he would read to them the first resolution—'That this meeting views with alarm and apprehension, the existing state of the Muffin Trade in this Metropolis and its neighbourhood; that it considers the Muffin Boys, as at present constituted, wholly underserving the confidence of the public; and that it deems the whole Muffin system alike prejudicial to the health and morals of the people, and subversive of the best interests of a great commercial and mercantile community.' The honourable gentleman made a speech which drew tears from the eyes of the ladies, and awakened the liveliest emotions in every individual present. He had visited the houses of the poor in the various districts of London, and had found them destitute of the slightest vestige of a muffin, which there appeared too much reason to believe some of these indigent persons did not taste from year's end to year's end. He had found that among muffin-sellers there existed drunkenness, debauchery, and profligacy, which he attributed to the debasing nature of their employment as at present exercised; he had found the same vices among the poorer class of people who ought to be muffin consumers;

and this he attributed to the despair engendered by their being placed beyond the reach of that nutritious article, which drove them to seek a false stimulant in intoxicating liquors. He would undertake to prove before a committee of the House of Commons, that there existed a combination to keep up the price of muffins, and to give the bellmen a monopoly; he would prove it by bellmen at the bar of that House; and he would also prove, that these men corresponded with each other by secret words and signs as 'Snooks,' 'Walker,' 'Ferguson,' 'Is Murphy right?' and many others. It was this melancholy state of things that the Company proposed to correct; firstly, by prohibiting, under heavy penalties, all private muffin trading of every description; secondly, by themselves supplying the public generally, and the poor at their own homes, with muffins of first quality at reduced prices. It was with this object that a bill had been introduced into Parliament by their patriotic chairman Sir Matthew Pupker; it was this bill that they had met to support; it was the supporters of this bill who would confer undying brightness and splendour upon England, under the name of the United Metropolitan Improved Hot Muffin and Crumpet Baking and Punctual Delivery Company; he would add, with a capital of Five Millions, in five hundred thousand shares of ten pounds each.

Mr. Ralph Nickleby seconded the resolution, and another gentleman having moved that it be amended by the insertion of the words 'and crumpet' after the word 'muffin,' whenever it occurred, it was carried triumphantly. Only one man in the crowd cried 'No!' and he was promptly taken into custody, and straightway borne off.

The second resolution, which recognised the expediency of immediately abolishing 'all muffin (or crumpet) sellers, all traders in muffins (or crumpets) of whatsoever description, whether male or female, boys or men, ringing hand-bells or otherwise,' was moved by a grievous gentleman of semi-clerical appearance, who went at once into such deep pathetics, that he knocked the first speaker clean out of the course in no time. You might have heard a pin fall—a pin! a feather—as he described the cruelties inflicted on muffin boys by their masters, which he very wisely urged were in themselves a sufficient reason for the establishment of that inestimable company. It seemed that the unhappy youths were nightly turned out into the wet streets at the most inclement periods of the year, to wander about, in darkness and rain—or it might be hail or snow—for hours together, without shelter, food, or warmth; and let the public never forget upon the latter point, that while the muffins were provided with warm clothing and blankets, the boys were wholly unprovided for, and left to their own miserable resources. (Shame!) The honourable gentleman related one case of a muffin boy, who having been exposed to this inhuman and barbarous system for no less than five years, at length fell a victim to a cold in the head, beneath which he gradually sunk until he fell into a perspiration and recovered; this he could vouch for, on his own authority, but he had heard (and he had no reason to doubt the fact) of a still more heart-rending and appalling circumstance. He had heard of the case of an orphan muffin boy, who, having been run over by a hackney carriage, had been removed to the hospital, had undergone the amputation of his leg below the knee, and was now actually pursuing his occupation on crutches. Fountain of justice, were these things to last!

This was the department of the subject that took the meeting, and this was the style of speaking to enlist their sympathies. The men shouted; the ladies wept into their pocket-handkerchiefs till they were moist, and waved them till they were dry; the excitement was tremendous; and Mr Nickleby whispered his friend that the shares were thenceforth at a premium of five-and-twenty per cent.

The resolution was, of course, carried with loud acclamations, every man holding up both hands in favour of it, as he would in his enthusiasm have held up both legs also, if he could have conveniently accomplished it. This done, the draft of the proposed petition was read at length: and the petition said, as all petitions do say, that the petitioners were very humble, and the petitioned very honourable, and the object very virtuous; therefore (said the petition) the bill ought to be passed into a law at once, to the everlasting honour and glory of that most honourable and glorious Commons of England in Parliament assembled.

Then, the gentleman who had been at Crockford's all night, and who looked something the worse about the eyes in consequence, came forward to tell his fellow-countrymen what a speech he meant to make in favour of that petition whenever it should be presented, and how desperately he meant to taunt the parliament if they rejected the bill; and to inform them also, that he regretted his honourable friends had not inserted a clause rendering the purchase of muffins and crumpets compulsory upon all classes of the community, which he—opposing all half-measures, and preferring to go the extreme animal—pledged himself to propose and divide upon, in committee. After announcing this determination, the honourable gentleman grew jocular; and as patent boots, lemon-coloured kid gloves, and a fur coat collar, assist jokes materially, there was immense laughter and much cheering, and moreover such a brilliant display of ladies' pocket-handkerchiefs, as threw the grievous gentleman quite into the shade.

And when the petition had been read and was about to be adopted, there came forward the Irish member (who was a young gentleman of ardent temperament,) with such a speech as only an Irish member can make, breathing the true soul and spirit of poetry, and poured forth with such fervour, that it made one warm to look at him; in the course whereof, he told them how he would demand the extension of that great boon to his native country; how he would claim for her equal rights in the muffin laws as in all other laws; and how he yet hoped to see the day when crumpets should be toasted in her lowly cabins, and muffin bells should ring in her rich green valleys. And, after him, came the Scotch member, with various pleasant allusions to the probable amount of profits, which increased the good humour that the poetry had awakened; and all the speeches put together did exactly what they were intended to do, and established in the hearers' minds that there was no speculation so promising, or at the same time so praiseworthy, as the United Metropolitan Improved Hot Muffin and Crumpet Baking and Punctual Delivery Company.

So, the petition in favour of the bill was agreed upon, and the meeting adjourned with acclamations, and Mr. Nickleby and the other directors went to the office to lunch, as they did every day at half-past one o'clock; and to remunerate themselves for which trouble, (as the company was yet in its infancy,) they only charged three guineas each man for every such attendance.

CHAPTER 3
Mr. Ralph Nickleby receives Sad Tidings of his Brother, but bears up nobly against the Intelligence communicated to him. The Reader is informed how he liked Nicholas, who is herein introduced, and how kindly he proposed to

make his Fortune at once.

Having rendered his zealous assistance towards dispatching the lunch, with all that promptitude and energy which are among the most important qualities that men of business can possess, Mr. Ralph Nickleby took a cordial farewell of his fellow-speculators, and bent his steps westward in unwonted good humour. As he passed St Paul's he stepped aside into a doorway to set his watch, and with his hand on the key and his eye on the cathedral dial, was intent upon so doing, when a man suddenly stopped before him. It was Newman Noggs.

'Ah! Newman,' said Mr. Nickleby, looking up as he pursued his occupation. 'The letter about the mortgage has come, has it? I thought it would.'

'Wrong,' replied Newman.

'What! and nobody called respecting it?' inquired Mr. Nickleby, pausing. Noggs shook his head.

'What has come, then?' inquired Mr. Nickleby.

'I have,' said Newman.

'What else?' demanded the master, sternly.

'This,' said Newman, drawing a sealed letter slowly from his pocket. 'Post-mark, Strand, black wax, black border, woman's hand, C. N. in the corner.'

'Black wax?' said Mr. Nickleby, glancing at the letter. 'I know something of that hand, too. Newman, I shouldn't be surprised if my brother were dead.'

'I don't think you would,' said Newman, quietly.

'Why not, sir?' demanded Mr. Nickleby.

'You never are surprised,' replied Newman, 'that's all.'

Mr. Nickleby snatched the letter from his assistant, and fixing a cold look upon him, opened, read it, put it in his pocket, and having now hit the time to a second, began winding up his watch.

'It is as I expected, Newman,' said Mr. Nickleby, while he was thus engaged. 'He is dead. Dear me! Well, that's sudden thing. I shouldn't have thought it, really.' With these touching expressions of sorrow, Mr Nickleby replaced his watch in his fob, and, fitting on his gloves to a nicety, turned upon his way, and walked slowly westward with his hands behind him.

'Children alive?' inquired Noggs, stepping up to him.

'Why, that's the very thing,' replied Mr. Nickleby, as though his thoughts were about them at that moment. 'They are both alive.'

'Both!' repeated Newman Noggs, in a low voice.

'And the widow, too,' added Mr. Nickleby, 'and all three in London, confound them; all three here, Newman.'

Newman fell a little behind his master, and his face was curiously twisted as by a spasm; but whether of paralysis, or grief, or inward laughter, nobody but himself could possibly explain. The expression of a man's face is commonly a help to his thoughts, or glossary on his speech; but the countenance of Newman Noggs, in his ordinary moods, was a problem which no stretch of ingenuity could solve.

'Go home!' said Mr. Nickleby, after they had walked a few paces: looking round at the clerk as if he were his dog. The words were scarcely uttered when Newman darted across the road, slunk among the crowd, and disappeared in an instant.

'Reasonable, certainly!' muttered Mr. Nickleby to himself, as he walked on, 'very reasonable! My brother never did anything for me, and I never expected it; the breath is no sooner out of his body than I am to be looked to, as the support of a great hearty woman, and a grown boy and girl. What are they to me! I never saw them.'

Full of these, and many other reflections of a similar kind, Mr. Nickleby made the best of his way to the Strand, and, referring to his letter as if to ascertain the number of the house he wanted, stopped at a private door about half-way down that crowded thoroughfare.

A miniature painter lived there, for there was a large gilt frame screwed upon the street-door, in which were displayed, upon a black velvet ground, two portraits of naval dress coats with faces looking out of them, and telescopes attached; one of a young gentleman in a very vermilion uniform, flourishing a sabre; and one of a literary character with a high forehead, a pen and ink, six books, and a curtain. There was, moreover, a touching representation of a young lady reading a manuscript in an unfathomable forest, and a charming whole length of a large-headed little boy, sitting on a stool with his legs fore-shortened to the size of salt-spoons. Besides these works of art, there were a great many heads of old ladies and gentlemen smirking at each other out of blue and brown skies, and an elegantly written card of terms with an embossed border.

Mr. Nickleby glanced at these frivolities with great contempt, and gave a double knock, which, having been thrice repeated, was answered by a servant girl with an uncommonly dirty face.

'Is Mrs. Nickleby at home, girl?' demanded Ralph sharply.

'Her name ain't Nickleby,' said the girl, 'La Creevy, you mean.'

Mr. Nickleby looked very indignant at the handmaid on being thus corrected, and demanded with much asperity what she meant; which she was about to state, when a female voice proceeding from a perpendicular staircase at the end of the passage, inquired who was wanted.

'Mrs. Nickleby,' said Ralph.

'It's the second floor, Hannah,' said the same voice; 'what a stupid thing you are! Is the second floor at home?'

'Somebody went out just now, but I think it was the attic which had been a cleaning of himself,' replied the girl.

'You had better see,' said the invisible female. 'Show the gentleman where the bell is, and tell him he mustn't knock double knocks for the second floor; I can't allow a knock except when the bell's broke, and then it must be two single ones.'

'Here,' said Ralph, walking in without more parley, 'I beg your pardon; is that Mrs. La what's-her-name?'

'Creevy—La Creevy,' replied the voice, as a yellow headdress bobbed over the banisters.

'I'll speak to you a moment, ma'am, with your leave,' said Ralph.

The voice replied that the gentleman was to walk up; but he had walked up before it spoke, and stepping into the first floor, was received by the wearer of the yellow head-dress, who had a gown to correspond, and was of much the same colour herself. Miss La Creevy was a mincing young lady of fifty, and Miss La Creevy's apartment was the gilt frame downstairs on a larger scale and something dirtier.

'Hem!' said Miss La Creevy, coughing delicately behind her black silk mitten. 'A miniature, I presume. A very strongly-marked countenance for the purpose, sir. Have you ever sat before?'

'You mistake my purpose, I see, ma'am,' replied Mr. Nickleby, in his usual blunt fashion. 'I have no money to throw away on miniatures, ma'am, and nobody to give one to (thank God) if I had. Seeing you on the stairs, I wanted to ask a question of you, about some lodgers here.'

Miss La Creevy coughed once more—this cough was to conceal her disappointment—and said, 'Oh, indeed!'

'I infer from what you said to your servant, that the floor above belongs to you, ma'am,' said Mr. Nickleby.

Yes it did, Miss La Creevy replied. The upper part of the house belonged to her, and as she had no necessity for the second-floor rooms just then, she was in the habit of letting them. Indeed, there was a lady from the country and her two children in them, at that present speaking.

'A widow, ma'am?' said Ralph.

'Yes, she is a widow,' replied the lady.

'A poor widow, ma'am,' said Ralph, with a powerful emphasis on that little adjective which conveys so much.

'Well, I'm afraid she is poor,' rejoined Miss La Creevy.

'I happen to know that she is, ma'am,' said Ralph. 'Now, what business has a poor widow in such a house as this, ma'am?'

'Very true,' replied Miss La Creevy, not at all displeased with this implied compliment to the apartments. 'Exceedingly true.'

'I know her circumstances intimately, ma'am,' said Ralph; 'in fact, I am a relation of the family; and I should recommend you not to keep them here, ma'am.'

'I should hope, if there was any incompatibility to meet the pecuniary obligations,' said Miss La Creevy with another cough, 'that the lady's family would—'

'No they wouldn't, ma'am,' interrupted Ralph, hastily. 'Don't think it.'

'If I am to understand that,' said Miss La Creevy, 'the case wears a very different appearance.'

'You may understand it then, ma'am,' said Ralph, 'and make your arrangements accordingly. I am the family, ma'am—at least, I believe I am the only relation they have, and I think it right that you should know I can't support them in their extravagances. How long have they taken these lodgings for?'

'Only from week to week,' replied Miss La Creevy. 'Mrs. Nickleby paid the first week in advance.'

'Then you had better get them out at the end of it,' said Ralph. 'They can't do better than go back to the country, ma'am; they are in everybody's way here.'

'Certainly,' said Miss La Creevy, rubbing her hands, 'if Mrs. Nickleby took the apartments without the means of paying for them, it was very unbecoming a lady.'

'Of course it was, ma'am,' said Ralph.

'And naturally,' continued Miss La Creevy, 'I who am, at present—hem—an unprotected female, cannot afford to lose by the apartments.'

'Of course you can't, ma'am,' replied Ralph.

'Though at the same time,' added Miss La Creevy, who was plainly wavering between her good-nature and her interest, 'I have nothing whatever to say against the lady, who is extremely pleasant and affable, though, poor thing, she seems terribly low in her spirits; nor against the young people either, for nicer, or better-behaved young people cannot be.'

'Very well, ma'am,' said Ralph, turning to the door, for these encomiums on poverty irritated him; 'I have done my duty, and perhaps more than I ought: of course nobody will thank me for saying what I have.'

'I am sure I am very much obliged to you at least, sir,' said Miss La Creevy in a gracious manner. 'Would you do me the favour to look at a few specimens of my portrait painting?'

'You're very good, ma'am,' said Mr. Nickleby, making off with great speed; 'but as I have a visit to pay upstairs, and my time is precious, I really can't.'

'At any other time when you are passing, I shall be most happy,' said Miss La Creevy. 'Perhaps you will have the kindness to take a card of terms with you? Thank you—good-morning!'

'Good-morning, ma'am,' said Ralph, shutting the door abruptly after him to prevent any further conversation. 'Now for my sister-in-law. Bah!'

Climbing up another perpendicular flight, composed with great mechanical ingenuity of nothing but corner stairs, Mr. Ralph Nickleby stopped to take breath on the landing, when he was overtaken by the handmaid, whom the politeness of Miss La Creevy had dispatched to announce him, and who had apparently been making a variety of unsuccessful attempts, since their last interview, to wipe her dirty face clean, upon an apron much dirtier.

'What name?' said the girl.

'Nickleby,' replied Ralph.

'Oh! Mrs. Nickleby,' said the girl, throwing open the door, 'here's Mr Nickleby.'

A lady in deep mourning rose as Mr. Ralph Nickleby entered, but appeared incapable of advancing to meet him, and leant upon the arm of a slight but very beautiful girl of about seventeen, who had been sitting by her. A youth, who appeared a year or two older, stepped forward and saluted Ralph as his uncle.

'Oh,' growled Ralph, with an ill-favoured frown, 'you are Nicholas, I suppose?'

'That is my name, sir,' replied the youth.

'Put my hat down,' said Ralph, imperiously. 'Well, ma'am, how do you do? You must bear up against sorrow, ma'am; I always do.'

'Mine was no common loss!' said Mrs. Nickleby, applying her handkerchief to her eyes.

'It was no uncommon loss, ma'am,' returned Ralph, as he coolly unbuttoned his spencer. 'Husbands die every day, ma'am, and wives too.'

'And brothers also, sir,' said Nicholas, with a glance of indignation.

'Yes, sir, and puppies, and pug-dogs likewise,' replied his uncle, taking a chair. 'You didn't mention in your letter what my brother's complaint was, ma'am.'

'The doctors could attribute it to no particular disease,' said Mrs Nickleby; shedding tears. 'We have too much reason to fear that he died of a broken heart.'

'Pooh!' said Ralph, 'there's no such thing. I can understand a man's dying of a broken neck, or suffering from a broken arm, or a broken head, or a broken leg, or a broken nose; but a broken heart!—nonsense, it's the cant of the day. If a man can't pay his debts, he dies of a broken heart, and his widow's a martyr.'

'Some people, I believe, have no hearts to break,' observed Nicholas, quietly.

'How old is this boy, for God's sake?' inquired Ralph, wheeling back his chair, and surveying his nephew from head to foot with intense scorn.

'Nicholas is very nearly nineteen,' replied the widow.

'Nineteen, eh!' said Ralph; 'and what do you mean to do for your bread, sir?'

'Not to live upon my mother,' replied Nicholas, his heart swelling as he spoke.

'You'd have little enough to live upon, if you did,' retorted the uncle, eyeing him contemptuously.

'Whatever it be,' said Nicholas, flushed with anger, 'I shall not look to you to make it more.'

'Nicholas, my dear, recollect yourself,' remonstrated Mrs. Nickleby.

'Dear Nicholas, pray,' urged the young lady.

'Hold your tongue, sir,' said Ralph. 'Upon my word! Fine beginnings, Mrs Nickleby—fine beginnings!'

Mrs. Nickleby made no other reply than entreating Nicholas by a gesture to keep silent; and the uncle and nephew looked at each other for some seconds without speaking. The face of the old man was stern, hard-featured, and forbidding; that of the young one, open, handsome, and ingenuous. The old man's eye was keen with the twinklings of avarice and cunning; the young man's bright with the light of intelligence and spirit. His figure was somewhat slight, but manly and well formed; and, apart from all the grace of youth and comeliness, there was an emanation from the warm young heart in his look and bearing which kept the old man down.

However striking such a contrast as this may be to lookers-on, none ever feel it with half the keenness or acuteness of perfection with which it strikes to the very soul of him whose inferiority it marks. It galled Ralph to the heart's core, and he hated Nicholas from that hour.

The mutual inspection was at length brought to a close by Ralph withdrawing his eyes, with a great show of disdain, and calling Nicholas 'a boy.' This word is much used as a term of reproach by elderly gentlemen towards their juniors: probably with the view of deluding society into the belief that if they could be young again, they wouldn't on any account.

'Well, ma'am,' said Ralph, impatiently, 'the creditors have administered, you tell me, and there's nothing left for you?'

'Nothing,' replied Mrs. Nickleby.

'And you spent what little money you had, in coming all the way to London, to see what I could do for you?' pursued Ralph.

'I hoped,' faltered Mrs. Nickleby, 'that you might have an opportunity of doing something for your brother's children. It was his dying wish that I should appeal to you in their behalf.'

'I don't know how it is,' muttered Ralph, walking up and down the room, 'but whenever a man dies without any property of his own, he always seems to think he has a right to dispose of other people's. What is your daughter fit for, ma'am?'

'Kate has been well educated,' sobbed Mrs. Nickleby. 'Tell your uncle, my dear, how far you went in French and extras.'

The poor girl was about to murmur something, when her uncle stopped her, very unceremoniously.

'We must try and get you apprenticed at some boarding-school,' said Ralph. 'You have not been brought up too delicately for that, I hope?'

'No, indeed, uncle,' replied the weeping girl. 'I will try to do anything that will gain me a home and bread.'

'Well, well,' said Ralph, a little softened, either by his niece's beauty or her distress (stretch a point, and say the latter). 'You must try it, and if the life is too hard, perhaps dressmaking or tambour-work will come lighter. Have you ever done anything, sir?' (turning to his nephew.)

'No,' replied Nicholas, bluntly.

'No, I thought not!' said Ralph. 'This is the way my brother brought up his children, ma'am.'

'Nicholas has not long completed such education as his poor father could give him,' rejoined Mrs. Nickleby, 'and he was thinking of—'

'Of making something of him someday,' said Ralph. 'The old story; always thinking, and never doing. If my brother had been a man of activity and prudence, he might have left you a rich woman, ma'am: and if he had turned his son into the world, as my father turned me, when I wasn't as old as that boy by a year and a half, he would have been in a situation to help you, instead of being a burden upon you, and increasing your distress. My brother was a thoughtless, inconsiderate man, Mrs. Nickleby, and nobody, I am sure, can have better reason to feel that, than you.'

This appeal set the widow upon thinking that perhaps she might have made a more successful venture with her one thousand pounds, and then she began to reflect what a comfortable sum it would have been just then; which dismal thoughts made her tears flow faster, and in the excess of these griefs she (being a well-meaning woman enough, but weak withal) fell first to deploring her hard fate, and then to remarking, with many sobs, that to be sure she had been a slave to poor Nicholas, and had often told him she might have married better (as indeed she had, very often), and that she never knew in his lifetime how the money went, but that if he had confided in her they might all have been better off that day; with other bitter recollections common to most married ladies, either during their coverture, or afterwards, or at both periods. Mrs. Nickleby concluded by lamenting that the dear departed had never deigned to profit by her advice, save on one occasion; which was a strictly veracious statement, inasmuch as he had only acted upon it once, and had ruined himself in consequence.

Mr. Ralph Nickleby heard all this with a half-smile; and when the widow had finished, quietly took up the subject where it had been left before the above outbreak.

'Are you willing to work, sir?' he inquired, frowning on his nephew.

'Of course I am,' replied Nicholas haughtily.

'Then see here, sir,' said his uncle. 'This caught my eye this morning, and you may thank your stars for it.'

With this exordium, Mr. Ralph Nickleby took a newspaper from his pocket, and after unfolding it, and looking for a short time among the advertisements, read as follows:

'"Education.—At Mr. Wackford Squeers's Academy, Dotheboys Hall, at the delightful village of Dotheboys, near Greta Bridge in Yorkshire, Youth are boarded, clothed, booked, furnished with pocket-money, provided with all necessaries, instructed in all languages living and dead, mathematics, orthography, geometry, astronomy, trigonometry, the use of the globes, algebra, single stick (if required), writing, arithmetic, fortification, and every other branch of classical literature. Terms, twenty guineas per annum. No extras, no vacations, and diet unparalleled. Mr. Squeers is in town, and attends daily, from one till four, at the Saracen's Head, Snow Hill. N.B. An able assistant wanted. Annual salary 5 pounds. A Master of Arts would be preferred."

'There!' said Ralph, folding the paper again. 'Let him get that situation, and his fortune is made.'

'But he is not a Master of Arts,' said Mrs. Nickleby.

'That,' replied Ralph, 'that, I think, can be got over.'

'But the salary is so small, and it is such a long way off, uncle!' faltered Kate.

'Hush, Kate my dear,' interposed Mrs. Nickleby; 'your uncle must know best.'

'I say,' repeated Ralph, tartly, 'let him get that situation, and his fortune is made. If he don't like that, let him get one for himself. Without friends, money, recommendation, or knowledge of business of any kind, let him find honest employment in London, which will keep him in shoe leather, and I'll give him a thousand pounds. At least,' said Mr Ralph Nickleby, checking himself, 'I would if I had it.'

'Poor fellow!' said the young lady. 'Oh! uncle, must we be separated so soon!'

'Don't tease your uncle with questions when he is thinking only for our good, my love,' said Mrs. Nickleby. 'Nicholas, my dear, I wish you would say something.'

'Yes, mother, yes,' said Nicholas, who had hitherto remained silent and absorbed in thought. 'If I am fortunate enough to be appointed to this post, sir, for which I am so imperfectly qualified, what will become of those I leave behind?'

'Your mother and sister, sir,' replied Ralph, 'will be provided for, in that case (not otherwise), by me, and placed in some sphere of life in which they will be able to be independent. That will be my immediate care; they will not remain as they are, one week after your departure, I will undertake.'

'Then,' said Nicholas, starting gaily up, and wringing his uncle's hand, 'I am ready to do anything you wish me. Let us try our fortune with Mr Squeers at once; he can but refuse.'

'He won't do that,' said Ralph. 'He will be glad to have you on my recommendation. Make yourself of use to him, and you'll rise to be a partner in the establishment in no time. Bless me, only think! if he were to die, why your fortune's made at once.'

'To be sure, I see it all,' said poor Nicholas, delighted with a thousand visionary ideas, that his good spirits and his inexperience were conjuring up before him. 'Or suppose some young nobleman who is being educated at the Hall, were to take a fancy to me, and get his father to appoint me his travelling tutor when he left, and when we come back from the continent, procured me some handsome appointment. Eh! uncle?'

'Ah, to be sure!' sneered Ralph.

'And who knows, but when he came to see me when I was settled (as he would of course), he might fall in love with Kate, who would be keeping my house, and—and marry her, eh! uncle? Who knows?'

'Who, indeed!' snarled Ralph.

'How happy we should be!' cried Nicholas with enthusiasm. 'The pain of parting is nothing to the joy of meeting again. Kate will be a beautiful woman, and I so proud to hear them say so, and mother so happy to be with us once again, and all these sad times forgotten, and—' The picture was too bright a one to bear, and Nicholas, fairly overpowered by it, smiled faintly, and burst into tears.

This simple family, born and bred in retirement, and wholly unacquainted with what is called the world—a conventional phrase which, being interpreted, often signifieth all the rascals in it—mingled their tears together at the thought of their first separation; and, this first gush of feeling over, were proceeding to dilate with all the buoyancy of untried hope on the bright prospects before them, when Mr. Ralph Nickleby suggested, that if they lost time, some more fortunate candidate might deprive Nicholas of the stepping-stone to fortune which the advertisement pointed out, and so undermine all their air-built castles. This timely reminder effectually stopped the conversation. Nicholas, having carefully copied the address of Mr. Squeers, the uncle and nephew issued forth together in quest of that accomplished gentleman; Nicholas firmly persuading himself that he had done his relative great injustice in disliking him at first sight; and Mrs. Nickleby being at some pains to inform her daughter that she was sure he was a much more kindly disposed person than he seemed; which, Miss Nickleby dutifully remarked, he might very easily be.

To tell the truth, the good lady's opinion had been not a little influenced by her brother-in-law's appeal to her better understanding, and his implied compliment to her high deserts; and although she had dearly loved her husband, and still doted on her children, he had struck so successfully on one of those little jarring chords in the human heart (Ralph was well acquainted with its worst weaknesses, though he knew nothing of its best), that she had already begun seriously to consider herself the amiable and suffering victim of her late husband's imprudence.

CHAPTER 4
Nicholas and his Uncle (to secure the Fortune without loss of time) wait upon Mr. Wackford Squeers, the Yorkshire Schoolmaster

Snow Hill! What kind of place can the quiet townspeople who see the words emblazoned, in all the legibility of gilt letters and dark shading, on the north-country coaches, take Snow Hill to be? All people have some undefined and shadowy notion of a place whose name is frequently before their eyes, or often in their ears. What a vast number of random ideas there must be perpetually floating about, regarding this same Snow Hill. The name is such a good one. Snow Hill—Snow Hill too, coupled with a Saracen's Head: picturing to us by a double association of ideas, something stern and rugged! A bleak desolate tract of country, open to piercing blasts and fierce wintry storms—a dark, cold, gloomy heath, lonely by day, and scarcely to be thought of by honest folks at night—a place which solitary wayfarers shun, and where desperate robbers congregate;—this, or something like this, should be the prevalent notion of Snow Hill, in those remote and rustic parts, through which the Saracen's Head, like some grim apparition, rushes each day and night with mysterious and ghost-like punctuality; holding its swift and headlong course in all weathers, and seeming to bid defiance to the very elements themselves.

The reality is rather different, but by no means to be despised notwithstanding. There, at the very core of London, in the heart of its business and animation, in the midst of a whirl of noise and motion: stemming as it were the giant currents of life that flow ceaselessly on from different quarters, and meet beneath its walls: stands Newgate; and in that crowded street on which it frowns so darkly—within a few feet of the squalid tottering houses—upon the very spot on which the vendors of soup and fish and damaged fruit are now plying their trades—scores of human beings, amidst a roar of sounds to which even the tumult of a great city is as nothing, four, six, or eight strong men at a time, have been hurried violently and swiftly from the world, when the scene has been rendered frightful with excess of human life; when curious eyes have glared from casement and house-top, and wall and pillar; and when, in the mass of white and upturned faces, the dying wretch, in his all-comprehensive look of agony, has met not one—not one—that bore the impress of pity or compassion.

Near to the jail, and by consequence near to Smithfield also, and the Compter, and the bustle and noise of the city; and just on that particular part of Snow Hill where omnibus horses going eastward seriously think of falling down on purpose, and where horses in hackney cabriolets going westward not unfrequently fall by accident, is the coach-yard of the Saracen's Head Inn; its portal guarded by two Saracens' heads and shoulders, which it was once the pride and glory of the choice spirits of this metropolis to pull down at night, but which have for some time remained in undisturbed tranquillity; possibly because this species of humour is now confined to St James's parish, where door knockers are preferred as being more portable, and bell-wires esteemed as convenient toothpicks. Whether this be the reason or not, there they are, frowning upon you from each side of the gateway. The inn itself garnished with another Saracen's Head, frowns upon you from the top of the yard; while from the door of the hind boot of all the red coaches that are standing therein, there glares a small Saracen's Head, with a twin expression to the large Saracens' Heads below, so that the general appearance of the pile is decidedly of the Saracenic order.

When you walk up this yard, you will see the booking-office on your left, and the tower of St Sepulchre's church, darting abruptly up into the sky, on your right, and a gallery of bedrooms on both sides. Just before you, you will observe a long window with the words 'coffee-room' legibly painted above it; and looking out of that window, you would have seen in addition, if you had gone at the right time, Mr. Wackford Squeers with his hands in his pockets.

Mr. Squeers's appearance was not prepossessing. He had but one eye, and the popular prejudice runs in favour of two. The eye he had, was unquestionably useful, but decidedly not ornamental: being of a greenish grey, and in shape resembling the fan-light of a street door. The blank side of his face was much wrinkled and puckered up, which gave him a very sinister appearance, especially when he smiled, at which times his expression bordered closely on the villainous. His hair was very flat and shiny, save at the ends, where it was brushed stiffly up from a low protruding forehead, which assorted well with his harsh voice and coarse manner. He was about two or three and fifty, and a trifle below the middle size; he wore a white neckerchief with long ends, and a suit of scholastic black; but his coat sleeves being a great deal too long, and his trousers a great deal too short, he appeared ill at ease in his clothes, and as if he were in a perpetual state of astonishment at finding himself so respectable.

Mr. Squeers was standing in a box by one of the coffee-room fire-places, fitted with one such table as is usually seen in coffee-rooms, and two of extraordinary shapes and dimensions made to suit the angles of the partition. In a corner of the seat, was a very small deal trunk, tied round with a scanty piece of cord; and on the trunk was perched—his lace-up half-boots and corduroy trousers dangling in the air—a diminutive boy, with his shoulders drawn up to his ears, and his hands planted on his knees, who glanced timidly at the schoolmaster, from time to time, with evident dread and apprehension.

'Half-past three,' muttered Mr. Squeers, turning from the window, and looking sulkily at the coffee-room clock. 'There will be nobody here today.'

Much vexed by this reflection, Mr. Squeers looked at the little boy to see whether he was doing anything he could beat him for. As he happened not to be doing anything at all, he merely boxed his ears, and told him not to do it again.

'At Midsummer,' muttered Mr. Squeers, resuming his complaint, 'I took down ten boys; ten twenties is two hundred pound. I go back at eight o'clock tomorrow morning, and have got only three—three oughts is an ought—three twos is six—sixty pound. What's come of all the boys? what's parents got in their heads? what does it all mean?'

Here the little boy on the top of the trunk gave a violent sneeze.

'Halloa, sir!' growled the schoolmaster, turning round. 'What's that, sir?'

'Nothing, please sir,' replied the little boy.

'Nothing, sir!' exclaimed Mr. Squeers.

'Please sir, I sneezed,' rejoined the boy, trembling till the little trunk shook under him.

'Oh! sneezed, did you?' retorted Mr. Squeers. 'Then what did you say "nothing" for, sir?'

In default of a better answer to this question, the little boy screwed a couple of knuckles into each of his eyes and began to cry, wherefore Mr Squeers knocked him off the trunk with a blow on one side of the face, and knocked him on again with a blow on the other.

'Wait till I get you down into Yorkshire, my young gentleman,' said Mr Squeers, 'and then I'll give you the rest. Will you hold that noise, sir?'

'Ye—ye—yes,' sobbed the little boy, rubbing his face very hard with the Beggar's Petition in printed calico.

'Then do so at once, sir,' said Squeers. 'Do you hear?'

As this admonition was accompanied with a threatening gesture, and uttered with a savage aspect, the little boy rubbed his face harder, as if to keep the tears back; and, beyond alternately sniffing and choking, gave no further vent to his emotions.

'Mr. Squeers,' said the waiter, looking in at this juncture; 'here's a gentleman asking for you at the bar.'

'Show the gentleman in, Richard,' replied Mr. Squeers, in a soft voice. 'Put your handkerchief in your pocket, you little scoundrel, or I'll murder you when the gentleman goes.'

The schoolmaster had scarcely uttered these words in a fierce whisper, when the stranger entered. Affecting not to see him, Mr. Squeers feigned to be intent upon mending a pen, and offering benevolent advice to his youthful pupil.

'My dear child,' said Mr. Squeers, 'all people have their trials. This early trial of yours that is fit to make your little heart burst, and your very eyes come out of your head with crying, what is it? Nothing; less than nothing. You are leaving your friends, but you will have a father in me, my dear, and a mother in Mrs. Squeers. At the delightful village of Dotheboys, near Greta Bridge in Yorkshire, where youth are boarded, clothed, booked, washed, furnished with pocket-money, provided with all necessaries—'

'It is the gentleman,' observed the stranger, stopping the schoolmaster in the rehearsal of his advertisement. 'Mr. Squeers, I believe, sir?'

'The same, sir,' said Mr. Squeers, with an assumption of extreme surprise.

'The gentleman,' said the stranger, 'that advertised in the Times newspaper?'

'—Morning Post, Chronicle, Herald, and Advertiser, regarding the Academy called Dotheboys Hall at the delightful village of Dotheboys, near Greta Bridge in Yorkshire,' added Mr. Squeers. 'You come on business, sir. I see by my young friends. How do you do, my little gentleman? and how do you do, sir?' With this salutation Mr. Squeers patted the heads of two hollow-eyed, small-boned little boys, whom the applicant had brought with him, and waited for further communications.

'I am in the oil and colour way. My name is Snawley, sir,' said the stranger.

Squeers inclined his head as much as to say, 'And a remarkably pretty name, too.'

The stranger continued. 'I have been thinking, Mr. Squeers, of placing my two boys at your school.'

'It is not for me to say so, sir,' replied Mr. Squeers, 'but I don't think you could possibly do a better thing.'

'Hem!' said the other. 'Twenty pounds per annewum, I believe, Mr. Squeers?'

'Guineas,' rejoined the schoolmaster, with a persuasive smile.

'Pounds for two, I think, Mr. Squeers,' said Mr. Snawley, solemnly.

'I don't think it could be done, sir,' replied Squeers, as if he had never considered the proposition before. 'Let me see; four fives is twenty, double that, and deduct the—well, a pound either way shall not stand betwixt us. You must recommend me to your connection, sir, and make it up that way.'

'They are not great eaters,' said Mr. Snawley.

'Oh! that doesn't matter at all,' replied Squeers. 'We don't consider the boys' appetites at our establishment.' This was strictly true; they did not.

'Every wholesome luxury, sir, that Yorkshire can afford,' continued Squeers; 'every beautiful moral that Mrs. Squeers can instil; every—in short, every comfort of a home that a boy could wish for, will be theirs, Mr. Snawley.'

'I should wish their morals to be particularly attended to,' said Mr Snawley.

'I am glad of that, sir,' replied the schoolmaster, drawing himself up. 'They have come to the right shop for morals, sir.'

'You are a moral man yourself,' said Mr. Snawley.

'I rather believe I am, sir,' replied Squeers.

'I have the satisfaction to know you are, sir,' said Mr. Snawley. 'I asked one of your references, and he said you were pious.'

'Well, sir, I hope I am a little in that line,' replied Squeers.

'I hope I am also,' rejoined the other. 'Could I say a few words with you in the next box?'

'By all means,' rejoined Squeers with a grin. 'My dears, will you speak to your new playfellow a minute or two? That is one of my boys, sir. Belling his name is,—a Taunton boy that, sir.'

'Is he, indeed?' rejoined Mr. Snawley, looking at the poor little urchin as if he were some extraordinary natural curiosity.

'He goes down with me tomorrow, sir,' said Squeers. 'That's his luggage that he is a sitting upon now. Each boy is required to bring, sir, two suits of clothes, six shirts, six pair of stockings, two nightcaps, two pocket-handkerchiefs, two pair of shoes, two hats, and a razor.'

'A razor!' exclaimed Mr. Snawley, as they walked into the next box. 'What for?'

'To shave with,' replied Squeers, in a slow and measured tone.

There was not much in these three words, but there must have been something in the manner in which they were said, to attract attention; for the schoolmaster and his companion looked steadily at each other for a few seconds, and then exchanged a very meaning smile. Snawley was a sleek, flat-nosed man, clad in sombre garments, and long black gaiters, and bearing in his countenance an expression of much mortification and sanctity; so, his smiling without any obvious reason was the more remarkable.

'Up to what age do you keep boys at your school then?' he asked at length.

'Just as long as their friends make the quarterly payments to my agent in town, or until such time as they run away,' replied Squeers. 'Let us understand each other; I see we may safely do so. What are these boys;—natural children?'

'No,' rejoined Snawley, meeting the gaze of the schoolmaster's one eye. 'They ain't.'

'I thought they might be,' said Squeers, coolly. 'We have a good many of them; that boy's one.'

'Him in the next box?' said Snawley.

Squeers nodded in the affirmative; his companion took another peep at the little boy on the trunk, and, turning round again, looked as if he were quite disappointed to see him so much like other boys, and said he should hardly have thought it.

'He is,' cried Squeers. 'But about these boys of yours; you wanted to speak to me?'

'Yes,' replied Snawley. 'The fact is, I am not their father, Mr. Squeers. I'm only their father-in-law.'

'Oh! Is that it?' said the schoolmaster. 'That explains it at once. I was wondering what the devil you were going to send them to Yorkshire for. Ha! ha! Oh, I understand now.'

'You see I have married the mother,' pursued Snawley; 'it's expensive keeping boys at home, and as she has a little money in her own right, I am afraid (women are so very foolish, Mr. Squeers) that she might be led to squander it on them, which would be their ruin, you know.'

'I see,' returned Squeers, throwing himself back in his chair, and waving his hand.

'And this,' resumed Snawley, 'has made me anxious to put them to some school a good distance off, where there are no holidays—none of those ill-judged coming home twice a year that unsettle children's minds so—and where they may rough it a little—you comprehend?'

'The payments regular, and no questions asked,' said Squeers, nodding his head.

'That's it, exactly,' rejoined the other. 'Morals strictly attended to, though.'

'Strictly,' said Squeers.

'Not too much writing home allowed, I suppose?' said the father-in-law, hesitating.

'None, except a circular at Christmas, to say they never were so happy, and hope they may never be sent for,' rejoined Squeers.

'Nothing could be better,' said the father-in-law, rubbing his hands.

'Then, as we understand each other,' said Squeers, 'will you allow me to ask you whether you consider me a highly virtuous, exemplary, and well-conducted man in private life; and whether, as a person whose business it is to take charge of youth, you place the strongest confidence in my unimpeachable integrity, liberality, religious principles, and ability?'

'Certainly I do,' replied the father-in-law, reciprocating the schoolmaster's grin.

'Perhaps you won't object to say that, if I make you a reference?'

'Not the least in the world.'

'That's your sort!' said Squeers, taking up a pen; 'this is doing business, and that's what I like.'

Having entered Mr. Snawley's address, the schoolmaster had next to perform the still

40

more agreeable office of entering the receipt of the first quarter's payment in advance, which he had scarcely completed, when another voice was heard inquiring for Mr. Squeers.

'Here he is,' replied the schoolmaster; 'what is it?'

'Only a matter of business, sir,' said Ralph Nickleby, presenting himself, closely followed by Nicholas. 'There was an advertisement of yours in the papers this morning?'

'There was, sir. This way, if you please,' said Squeers, who had by this time got back to the box by the fire-place. 'Won't you be seated?'

'Why, I think I will,' replied Ralph, suiting the action to the word, and placing his hat on the table before him. 'This is my nephew, sir, Mr Nicholas Nickleby.'

'How do you do, sir?' said Squeers.

Nicholas bowed, said he was very well, and seemed very much astonished at the outward appearance of the proprietor of Dotheboys Hall: as indeed he was.

'Perhaps you recollect me?' said Ralph, looking narrowly at the schoolmaster.

'You paid me a small account at each of my half-yearly visits to town, for some years, I think, sir,' replied Squeers.

'I did,' rejoined Ralph.

'For the parents of a boy named Dorker, who unfortunately—'

'—unfortunately died at Dotheboys Hall,' said Ralph, finishing the sentence.

'I remember very well, sir,' rejoined Squeers. 'Ah! Mrs. Squeers, sir, was as partial to that lad as if he had been her own; the attention, sir, that was bestowed upon that boy in his illness! Dry toast and warm tea offered him every night and morning when he couldn't swallow anything—a candle in his bedroom on the very night he died—the best dictionary sent up for him to lay his head upon—I don't regret it though. It is a pleasant thing to reflect that one did one's duty by him.'

Ralph smiled, as if he meant anything but smiling, and looked round at the strangers present.

'These are only some pupils of mine,' said Wackford Squeers, pointing to the little boy on the trunk and the two little boys on the floor, who had been staring at each other without uttering a word, and writhing their bodies into most remarkable contortions, according to the custom of little boys when they first become acquainted. 'This gentleman, sir, is a parent who is kind enough to compliment me upon the course of education adopted at Dotheboys Hall, which is situated, sir, at the delightful village of Dotheboys, near Greta Bridge in Yorkshire, where youth are boarded, clothed, booked, washed, furnished with pocket-money—'

'Yes, we know all about that, sir,' interrupted Ralph, testily. 'It's in the advertisement.'

'You are very right, sir; it is in the advertisement,' replied Squeers.

'And in the matter of fact besides,' interrupted Mr. Snawley. 'I feel bound to assure you, sir, and I am proud to have this opportunity of assuring you, that I consider Mr. Squeers a gentleman highly virtuous, exemplary, well conducted, and—'

'I make no doubt of it, sir,' interrupted Ralph, checking the torrent of recommendation; 'no doubt of it at all. Suppose we come to business?'

'With all my heart, sir,' rejoined Squeers. '"Never postpone business," is the very first lesson we instil into our commercial pupils. Master Belling, my dear, always remember that; do you hear?'

'Yes, sir,' repeated Master Belling.

'He recollects what it is, does he?' said Ralph.

'Tell the gentleman,' said Squeers.

'"Never,"' repeated Master Belling.

'Very good,' said Squeers; 'go on.'

'Never,' repeated Master Belling again.

'Very good indeed,' said Squeers. 'Yes.'

'P,' suggested Nicholas, good-naturedly.

'Perform—business!' said Master Belling. 'Never—perform—business!'

'Very well, sir,' said Squeers, darting a withering look at the culprit. 'You and I will perform a little business on our private account by-and-by.'

'And just now,' said Ralph, 'we had better transact our own, perhaps.'

'If you please,' said Squeers.

'Well,' resumed Ralph, 'it's brief enough; soon broached; and I hope easily concluded. You have advertised for an able assistant, sir?'

'Precisely so,' said Squeers.

'And you really want one?'

'Certainly,' answered Squeers.

'Here he is!' said Ralph. 'My nephew Nicholas, hot from school, with everything he learnt there, fermenting in his head, and nothing fermenting in his pocket, is just the man you want.'

'I am afraid,' said Squeers, perplexed with such an application from a youth of Nicholas's figure, 'I am afraid the young man won't suit me.'

'Yes, he will,' said Ralph; 'I know better. Don't be cast down, sir; you will be teaching all the young noblemen in Dotheboys Hall in less than a week's time, unless this gentleman is more obstinate than I take him to be.'

'I fear, sir,' said Nicholas, addressing Mr. Squeers, 'that you object to my youth, and to my not being a Master of Arts?'

'The absence of a college degree is an objection,' replied Squeers, looking as grave as he could, and considerably puzzled, no less by the contrast between the simplicity of the nephew and the worldly manner of the uncle, than by the incomprehensible allusion to the young noblemen under his tuition.

'Look here, sir,' said Ralph; 'I'll put this matter in its true light in two seconds.'

'If you'll have the goodness,' rejoined Squeers.

'This is a boy, or a youth, or a lad, or a young man, or a hobbledehoy, or whatever you like to call him, of eighteen or nineteen, or thereabouts,' said Ralph.

'That I see,' observed the schoolmaster.

'So do I,' said Mr. Snawley, thinking it as well to back his new friend occasionally.

'His father is dead, he is wholly ignorant of the world, has no resources whatever, and wants something to do,' said Ralph. 'I recommend him to this splendid establishment of yours, as an opening which will lead him to fortune if he turns it to proper account. Do you see that?'

'Everybody must see that,' replied Squeers, half imitating the sneer with which the old gentleman was regarding his unconscious relative.

'I do, of course,' said Nicholas, eagerly.

'He does, of course, you observe,' said Ralph, in the same dry, hard manner. 'If any caprice of temper should induce him to cast aside this golden opportunity before he has brought it to perfection, I consider myself absolved from extending any assistance to his mother and sister. Look at him, and think of the use he may be to you in half-a-dozen ways! Now, the question is, whether, for some time to come at all events, he won't serve your purpose better than twenty of the kind of people you would get under ordinary circumstances. Isn't that a question for consideration?'

'Yes, it is,' said Squeers, answering a nod of Ralph's head with a nod of his own.

'Good,' rejoined Ralph. 'Let me have two words with you.'

The two words were had apart; in a couple of minutes Mr. Wackford Squeers announced that Mr. Nicholas Nickleby was, from that moment, thoroughly nominated to, and installed in, the office of first assistant master at Dotheboys Hall.

'Your uncle's recommendation has done it, Mr. Nickleby,' said Wackford Squeers.

Nicholas, overjoyed at his success, shook his uncle's hand warmly, and could almost have worshipped Squeers upon the spot.

'He is an odd-looking man,' thought Nicholas. 'What of that? Porson was an odd-looking man, and so was Doctor Johnson; all these bookworms are.'

'At eight o'clock tomorrow morning, Mr. Nickleby,' said Squeers, 'the coach starts. You must be here at a quarter before, as we take these boys with us.'

'Certainly, sir,' said Nicholas.

'And your fare down, I have paid,' growled Ralph. 'So, you'll have nothing to do but keep yourself warm.'

Here was another instance of his uncle's generosity! Nicholas felt his unexpected kindness so much, that he could scarcely find words to thank him; indeed, he had not found half enough, when they took leave of the schoolmaster, and emerged from the Saracen's Head gateway.

'I shall be here in the morning to see you fairly off,' said Ralph. 'No skulking!'

'Thank you, sir,' replied Nicholas; 'I never shall forget this kindness.'

'Take care you don't,' replied his uncle. 'You had better go home now, and pack up what you have got to pack. Do you think you could find your way to Golden Square first?'

'Certainly,' said Nicholas. 'I can easily inquire.'

'Leave these papers with my clerk, then,' said Ralph, producing a small parcel, 'and tell him to wait till I come home.'

Nicholas cheerfully undertook the errand, and bidding his worthy uncle an affectionate farewell, which that warm-hearted old gentleman acknowledged by a growl, hastened away to execute his commission.

He found Golden Square in due course; Mr. Noggs, who had stepped out for a minute or so to the public-house, was opening the door with a latch-key, as he reached the steps.

'What's that?' inquired Noggs, pointing to the parcel.

'Papers from my uncle,' replied Nicholas; 'and you're to have the goodness to wait till he comes home, if you please.'

'Uncle!' cried Noggs.

'Mr. Nickleby,' said Nicholas in explanation.

'Come in,' said Newman.

Without another word he led Nicholas into the passage, and thence into the official pantry at the end of it, where he thrust him into a chair, and mounting upon his high stool, sat, with his arms hanging, straight down by his sides, gazing fixedly upon him, as from a tower of observation.

'There is no answer,' said Nicholas, laying the parcel on a table beside him.

Newman said nothing, but folding his arms, and thrusting his head forward so as to obtain a nearer view of Nicholas's face, scanned his features closely.

'No answer,' said Nicholas, speaking very loud, under the impression that Newman Noggs was deaf.

Newman placed his hands upon his knees, and, without uttering a syllable, continued the same close scrutiny of his companion's face.

This was such a very singular proceeding on the part of an utter stranger, and his appearance was so extremely peculiar, that Nicholas, who had a sufficiently keen sense of the ridiculous, could not refrain from breaking into a smile as he inquired whether Mr. Noggs had any commands for him.

Noggs shook his head and sighed; upon which Nicholas rose, and remarking that he required no rest, bade him good-morning.

It was a great exertion for Newman Noggs, and nobody knows to this day how he ever came to make it, the other party being wholly unknown to him, but he drew a long breath and actually said, out loud, without once stopping, that if the young gentleman did not object to tell, he should like to know what his uncle was going to do for him.

Nicholas had not the least objection in the world, but on the contrary was rather pleased to have an opportunity of talking on the subject which occupied his thoughts; so, he sat down again, and (his sanguine imagination warming as he spoke) entered into a fervent and glowing description of all the honours and advantages to be derived from his appointment at that seat of learning, Dotheboys Hall.

'But, what's the matter—are you ill?' said Nicholas, suddenly breaking off, as his companion, after throwing himself into a variety of uncouth attitudes, thrust his hands under the stool, and cracked his finger-joints as if he were snapping all the bones in his hands.

Newman Noggs made no reply, but went on shrugging his shoulders and cracking his finger-joints; smiling horribly all the time, and looking steadfastly at nothing, out of the tops of his eyes, in a most ghastly manner.

At first, Nicholas thought the mysterious man was in a fit, but, on further consideration, decided that he was in liquor, under which circumstances he deemed it prudent to make off at once. He looked back when he had got the street-door open. Newman Noggs was still indulging in the same extraordinary gestures, and the cracking of his fingers sounded louder that ever.

CHAPTER 5
Nicholas starts for Yorkshire. Of his Leave-taking and his Fellow-Travellers, and what befell them on the Road

If tears dropped into a trunk were charms to preserve its owner from sorrow and misfortune, Nicholas Nickleby would have commenced his expedition under most happy auspices. There was so much to be done, and so little time to do it in; so many kind words to be spoken, and such bitter pain in the hearts in which they rose to impede their utterance; that the little preparations for his journey were made mournfully indeed. A hundred things which the anxious care of his mother and sister deemed indispensable for his comfort, Nicholas insisted on leaving behind, as they might prove of some after use, or might be convertible into money if occasion required. A hundred affectionate contests on such points as these, took place on the sad night which preceded his departure; and, as the termination of every angerless dispute brought them nearer and nearer to the close of their slight preparations, Kate grew busier and busier, and wept more silently.

The box was packed at last, and then there came supper, with some little delicacy provided for the occasion, and as a set-off against the expense of which, Kate and her mother had feigned to dine when Nicholas was out. The poor lad nearly choked himself by attempting to partake of it, and almost suffocated himself in affecting a jest or two, and forcing a melancholy laugh. Thus, they lingered on till the hour of separating for the night was long past; and then they found that they might as well have given vent to their real feelings before, for they could not suppress them, do what they would. So, they let them have their way, and even that was a relief.

Nicholas slept well till six next morning; dreamed of home, or of what was home once—no matter which, for things that are changed or gone will come back as they used to be, thank God! in sleep—and rose quite brisk and gay. He wrote a few lines in pencil, to say the goodbye which he was afraid to pronounce himself, and laying them, with half his scanty stock of money, at his sister's door, shouldered his box and crept softly downstairs.

'Is that you, Hannah?' cried a voice from Miss La Creevy's sitting-room, whence shone the light of a feeble candle.

'It is I, Miss La Creevy,' said Nicholas, putting down the box and looking in.

'Bless us!' exclaimed Miss La Creevy, starting and putting her hand to her curl-papers.

'You're up very early, Mr. Nickleby.'

'So are you,' replied Nicholas.

'It's the fine arts that bring me out of bed, Mr. Nickleby,' returned the lady. 'I'm waiting for the light to carry out an idea.'

Miss La Creevy had got up early to put a fancy nose into a miniature of an ugly little boy, destined for his grandmother in the country, who was expected to bequeath him property if he was like the family.

'To carry out an idea,' repeated Miss La Creevy; 'and that's the great convenience of living in a thoroughfare like the Strand. When I want a nose or an eye for any particular sitter, I have only to look out of window and wait till I get one.'

'Does it take long to get a nose, now?' inquired Nicholas, smiling.

'Why, that depends in a great measure on the pattern,' replied Miss La Creevy. 'Snubs and Romans are plentiful enough, and there are flats of all sorts and sizes when there's a meeting at Exeter Hall; but perfect aquilines, I am sorry to say, are scarce, and we generally use them for uniforms or public characters.'

'Indeed!' said Nicholas. 'If I should meet with any in my travels, I'll endeavour to sketch them for you.'

'You don't mean to say that you are really going all the way down into Yorkshire this cold winter's weather, Mr. Nickleby?' said Miss La Creevy. 'I heard something of it last night.'

'I do, indeed,' replied Nicholas. 'Needs must, you know, when somebody drives. Necessity is my driver, and that is only another name for the same gentleman.'

'Well, I am very sorry for it; that's all I can say,' said Miss La Creevy; 'as much on your mother's and sister's account as on yours. Your sister is a very pretty young lady, Mr. Nickleby, and that is an additional reason why she should have somebody to protect her. I persuaded her to give me a sitting or two, for the street-door case. 'Ah! she'll make a sweet miniature.' As Miss La Creevy spoke, she held up an ivory countenance intersected with very perceptible sky-blue veins, and regarded it with so much complacency, that Nicholas quite envied her.

'If you ever have an opportunity of showing Kate some little kindness,' said Nicholas, presenting his hand, 'I think you will.'

'Depend upon that,' said the good-natured miniature painter; 'and God bless you, Mr. Nickleby; and I wish you well.'

It was very little that Nicholas knew of the world, but he guessed enough about its ways to think, that if he gave Miss La Creevy one little kiss, perhaps she might not be the less kindly disposed towards those he was leaving behind. So, he gave her three or four with a kind of jocose gallantry, and Miss La Creevy evinced no greater symptoms of displeasure than declaring, as she adjusted her yellow turban, that she had never heard of such a thing, and couldn't have believed it possible.

Having terminated the unexpected interview in this satisfactory manner, Nicholas hastily withdrew himself from the house. By the time he had found a man to carry his box it was only seven o'clock, so he walked slowly on, a little in advance of the porter, and very probably with not half as light a heart in his breast as the man had, although he had no waistcoat to cover it with, and had evidently, from the appearance of his other garments, been spending the night in a stable, and taking his breakfast at a pump.

Regarding, with no small curiosity and interest, all the busy preparations for the coming day which every street and almost every house displayed; and thinking, now and then, that it seemed rather hard that so many people of all ranks and stations could earn a livelihood in London, and that he should be compelled to journey so far in search of one; Nicholas speedily arrived at the Saracen's Head, Snow Hill. Having dismissed his attendant, and seen the box safely deposited in the coach-office, he looked into the coffee-room in search of Mr. Squeers.

He found that learned gentleman sitting at breakfast, with the three little boys before noticed, and two others who had turned up by some lucky chance since the interview of the previous day, ranged in a row on the opposite seat. Mr. Squeers had before him a small measure of coffee, a plate of hot toast, and a cold round of beef; but he was at that moment intent on preparing breakfast for the little boys.

'This is twopenn'orth of milk, is it, waiter?' said Mr. Squeers, looking down into a large blue mug, and slanting it gently, so as to get an accurate view of the quantity of liquid contained in it.

'That's twopenn'orth, sir,' replied the waiter.

'What a rare article milk is, to be sure, in London!' said Mr. Squeers, with a sigh. 'Just fill that mug up with lukewarm water, William, will you?'

'To the wery top, sir?' inquired the waiter. 'Why, the milk will be drownded.'

'Never you mind that,' replied Mr. Squeers. 'Serve it right for being so dear. You ordered that thick bread and butter for three, did you?'

'Coming directly, sir.'

'You needn't hurry yourself,' said Squeers; 'there's plenty of time. Conquer your passions, boys, and don't be eager after vittles.' As he uttered this moral precept, Mr. Squeers took a large bite out of the cold beef, and recognised Nicholas.

'Sit down, Mr. Nickleby,' said Squeers. 'Here we are, a breakfasting you see!'

Nicholas did not see that anybody was breakfasting, except Mr. Squeers; but he bowed with all becoming reverence, and looked as cheerful as he could.

'Oh! that's the milk and water, is it, William?' said Squeers. 'Very good; don't forget the bread and butter presently.'

At this fresh mention of the bread and butter, the five little boys looked very eager, and followed the waiter out, with their eyes; meanwhile Mr Squeers tasted the milk and water.

'Ah!' said that gentleman, smacking his lips, 'here's richness! Think of the many beggars and orphans in the streets that would be glad of this, little boys. A shocking thing hunger, isn't it, Mr. Nickleby?'

'Very shocking, sir,' said Nicholas.

'When I say number one,' pursued Mr. Squeers, putting the mug before the children, 'the boy on the left hand nearest the window may take a drink; and when I say number two, the boy next him will go in, and so till we come to number five, which is the last boy. Are you ready?'

'Yes, sir,' cried all the little boys with great eagerness.

'That's right,' said Squeers, calmly getting on with his breakfast; 'keep ready till I tell you to begin. Subdue your appetites, my dears, and you've conquered human natur. This is the way we inculcate strength of mind, Mr. Nickleby,' said the schoolmaster, turning to Nicholas, and speaking with his mouth very full of beef and toast.

Nicholas murmured something—he knew not what—in reply; and the little boys, dividing their gaze between the mug, the bread and butter (which had by this time arrived), and every morsel which Mr. Squeers took into his mouth, remained with strained eyes in torments of expectation.

'Thank God for a good breakfast,' said Squeers, when he had finished. 'Number one may take a drink.'

Number one seized the mug ravenously, and had just drunk enough to make him wish for more, when Mr. Squeers gave the signal for number two, who gave up at the same interesting moment to number three; and the process was repeated until the milk and water terminated with number five.

'And now,' said the schoolmaster, dividing the bread and butter for three into as many portions as there were children, 'you had better look sharp with your breakfast, for the horn will blow in a minute or two, and then every boy leaves off.'

Permission being thus given to fall to, the boys began to eat voraciously, and in desperate haste: while the schoolmaster (who was in high good humour after his meal) picked his teeth with a fork, and looked smilingly on. In a very short time, the horn was heard.

'I thought it wouldn't be long,' said Squeers, jumping up and producing a little basket from under the seat; 'put what you haven't had time to eat, in here, boys! You'll want it on the road!'

Nicholas was considerably startled by these very economical arrangements; but he had no time to reflect upon them, for the little boys had to be got up to the top of the coach, and their boxes had to be brought out and put in, and Mr. Squeers's luggage was to be seen carefully deposited in the boot, and all these offices were in his department. He was in the full heat and bustle of concluding these operations, when his uncle, Mr. Ralph Nickleby, accosted him.

'Oh! here you are, sir!' said Ralph. 'Here are your mother and sister, sir.'

'Where?' cried Nicholas, looking hastily round.

'Here!' replied his uncle. 'Having too much money and nothing at all to do with it, they were paying a hackney coach as I came up, sir.'

'We were afraid of being too late to see him before he went away from us,' said Mrs. Nickleby, embracing her son, heedless of the unconcerned lookers-on in the coach-yard.

'Very good, ma'am,' returned Ralph, 'you're the best judge of course. I merely said that you were paying a hackney coach. I never pay a hackney coach, ma'am; I never hire one. I haven't been in a hackney coach of my own hiring, for thirty years, and I hope I shan't be for thirty more, if I live as long.'

'I should never have forgiven myself if I had not seen him,' said Mrs Nickleby. 'Poor dear boy—going away without his breakfast too, because he feared to distress us!'

'Mighty fine certainly,' said Ralph, with great testiness. 'When I first went to business, ma'am, I took a penny loaf and a ha'porth of milk for my breakfast as I walked to the city every morning; what do you say to that, ma'am? Breakfast! Bah!'

'Now, Nickleby,' said Squeers, coming up at the moment buttoning his greatcoat; 'I think you'd better get up behind. I'm afraid of one of them boys falling off and then there's twenty pound a year gone.'

'Dear Nicholas,' whispered Kate, touching her brother's arm, 'who is that vulgar man?'

'Eh!' growled Ralph, whose quick ears had caught the inquiry. 'Do you wish to be introduced to Mr. Squeers, my dear?'

'That the schoolmaster! No, uncle. Oh no!' replied Kate, shrinking back.

'I'm sure I heard you say as much, my dear,' retorted Ralph in his cold sarcastic manner. 'Mr. Squeers, here's my niece: Nicholas's sister!'

'Very glad to make your acquaintance, miss,' said Squeers, raising his hat an inch or two. 'I wish Mrs. Squeers took gals, and we had you for a teacher. I don't know, though, whether she mightn't grow jealous if we had. Ha! ha! ha!'

If the proprietor of Dotheboys Hall could have known what was passing in his assistant's breast at that moment, he would have discovered, with some surprise, that he was as near being soundly pummelled as he had ever been in his life. Kate Nickleby, having a quicker perception of her brother's emotions, led him gently aside, and thus prevented Mr. Squeers from being impressed with the fact in a peculiarly disagreeable manner.

'My dear Nicholas,' said the young lady, 'who is this man? What kind of place can it be that you are going to?'

'I hardly know, Kate,' replied Nicholas, pressing his sister's hand. 'I suppose the Yorkshire folks are rather rough and uncultivated; that's all.'

'But this person,' urged Kate.

'Is my employer, or master, or whatever the proper name may be,' replied Nicholas quickly; 'and I was an ass to take his coarseness ill. They are looking this way, and it is time I was in my place. Bless you, love, and goodbye! Mother, look forward to our meeting again someday! Uncle, farewell! Thank you heartily for all you have done and all you mean to do. Quite ready, sir!'

With these hasty adieux, Nicholas mounted nimbly to his seat, and waved his hand as gallantly as if his heart went with it.

At this moment, when the coachman and guard were comparing notes for the last time before starting, on the subject of the way-bill; when porters were screwing out the last reluctant sixpences, itinerant newsmen making the last offer of a morning paper, and the horses giving the last impatient rattle to their harness; Nicholas felt somebody pulling softly at his leg. He looked down, and there stood Newman Noggs, who pushed up into his hand a dirty letter.

'What's this?' inquired Nicholas.

'Hush!' rejoined Noggs, pointing to Mr. Ralph Nickleby, who was saying a few earnest words to Squeers, a short distance off: 'Take it. Read it. Nobody knows. That's all.'

'Stop!' cried Nicholas.

'No,' replied Noggs.

Nicholas cried stop, again, but Newman Noggs was gone.

A minute's bustle, a banging of the coach doors, a swaying of the vehicle to one side, as the heavy coachman, and still heavier guard, climbed into their seats; a cry of all right, a few notes from the horn, a hasty glance of two sorrowful faces below, and the hard features of Mr. Ralph Nickleby—and the coach was gone too, and rattling over the stones of Smithfield.

The little boys' legs being too short to admit of their feet resting upon anything as they sat, and the little boys' bodies being consequently in imminent hazard of being jerked off the coach, Nicholas had enough to do over the stones to hold them on. Between the manual exertion and the mental anxiety attendant upon this task, he was not a little relieved when the coach stopped at the Peacock at Islington. He was still more relieved when a hearty-looking gentleman, with a very good-humoured face, and a very fresh colour, got up behind, and proposed to take the other corner of the seat.

'If we put some of these youngsters in the middle,' said the new-comer, 'they'll be safer in case of their going to sleep; eh?'

'If you'll have the goodness, sir,' replied Squeers, 'that'll be the very thing. Mr. Nickleby, take three of them boys between you and the gentleman. Belling and the youngest Snawley can sit between me and the guard. Three children,' said Squeers, explaining to the stranger, 'books as two.'

'I have not the least objection I am sure,' said the fresh-coloured gentleman; 'I have a brother who wouldn't object to book his six children as two at any butcher's or baker's in the kingdom, I dare say. Far from it.'

'Six children, sir?' exclaimed Squeers.

'Yes, and all boys,' replied the stranger.

'Mr. Nickleby,' said Squeers, in great haste, 'catch hold of that basket. Let me give you a card, sir, of an establishment where those six boys can be brought up in an enlightened, liberal, and moral manner, with no mistake at all about it, for twenty guineas a year each—twenty guineas, sir—or I'd take all the boys together upon a average right through, and say a hundred pound a year for the lot.'

'Oh!' said the gentleman, glancing at the card, 'you are the Mr. Squeers mentioned here, I presume?'

'Yes, I am, sir,' replied the worthy pedagogue; 'Mr. Wackford Squeers is my name, and I'm very far from being ashamed of it. These are some of my boys, sir; that's one of my assistants, sir—Mr. Nickleby, a gentleman's son, and a good scholar, mathematical, classical, and commercial. We don't do things by halves at our shop. All manner of learning my boys take down, sir; the expense is never thought of; and they get paternal treatment and washing in.'

'Upon my word,' said the gentleman, glancing at Nicholas with a half-smile, and a more than half expression of surprise, 'these are advantages indeed.'

'You may say that, sir,' rejoined Squeers, thrusting his hands into his great-coat pockets. 'The most unexceptionable references are given and required. I wouldn't take a reference with any boy, that wasn't responsible for the payment of five pound five a quarter, no, not if you went down on your knees, and asked me, with the tears running down your face, to do it.'

'Highly considerate,' said the passenger.

'It's my great aim and end to be considerate, sir,' rejoined Squeers. 'Snawley, junior, if you don't leave off chattering your teeth, and shaking with the cold, I'll warm you with a severe thrashing in about half a minute's time.'

'Sit fast here, genelmen,' said the guard as he clambered up.

'All right behind there, Dick?' cried the coachman.

'All right,' was the reply. 'Off she goes!' And off she did go—if coaches be feminine—amidst a loud flourish from the guard's horn, and the calm approval of all the judges of coaches and coach-horses congregated at the Peacock, but more especially of the helpers, who stood, with the cloths over their arms, watching the coach till it disappeared, and then lounged admiringly stablewards, bestowing various gruff encomiums on the beauty of the turn-out.

When the guard (who was a stout old Yorkshireman) had blown himself quite out of breath, he put the horn into a little tunnel of a basket fastened to the coach-side for the purpose, and giving himself a plentiful shower of blows on the chest and shoulders, observed it was uncommon cold; after which, he demanded of every person separately whether he was going right through, and if not, where he was going. Satisfactory replies being made to these queries, he surmised that the roads were pretty heavy arter that fall last night, and took the liberty of asking whether any of them gentlemen carried a snuff-box. It happening that nobody did, he remarked with a mysterious air that he had heard a medical gentleman as went down to Grantham last week, say how that snuff-taking was bad for the eyes; but for his part he had never found it so, and what he said was, that everybody should speak as they found. Nobody attempting to controvert this position, he took a small brown-paper parcel out of his hat, and putting on a pair of horn spectacles (the writing being crabbed) read the direction half-a-dozen times over; having done which, he consigned the parcel to its old place, put up his spectacles again, and stared at everybody in turn. After this, he took another blow at the horn by way of refreshment; and, having now exhausted his usual topics of conversation, folded his arms as well as he could in so many coats, and falling into a solemn silence, looked carelessly at the familiar objects which met his eye on every side as the coach rolled on; the only things he seemed to care for, being horses and droves of cattle, which he scrutinised with a critical air as they were passed upon the road.

The weather was intensely and bitterly cold; a great deal of snow fell from time to time; and the wind was intolerably keen. Mr. Squeers got down at almost every stage—to stretch his legs as he said—and as he always came back from such excursions with a very red nose, and composed himself to sleep directly, there is reason to suppose that he derived great benefit from the process. The little pupils having been stimulated with the remains of their breakfast, and further invigorated by sundry small cups of a curious cordial carried by Mr. Squeers, which tasted very like toast-and-water put into a brandy bottle by mistake, went to sleep, woke, shivered, and cried, as their feelings prompted. Nicholas and the good-tempered man found so many things to talk about, that between conversing together, and cheering up the boys, the time passed with them as rapidly as it could, under such adverse circumstances.

So the day wore on. At Eton Slocomb there was a good coach dinner, of which the box, the four front outsides, the one inside, Nicholas, the good-tempered man, and Mr. Squeers, partook; while the five little boys were put to thaw by the fire, and regaled with sandwiches. A stage or two further on, the lamps were lighted, and a great to-do occasioned by the taking up, at a roadside inn, of a very fastidious lady with an infinite variety of cloaks and small parcels, who loudly lamented, for the behoof of the outsides, the non-arrival of her own carriage which was to have taken her on, and made the guard solemnly promise to stop every green chariot he saw coming; which, as it was a dark night and he was sitting with his face the other way, that officer undertook, with many fervent asseverations, to do. Lastly, the fastidious lady, finding there was a solitary gentleman inside, had a small lamp lighted which she carried in reticule, and being after much trouble shut in, the horses were put into a brisk canter and the coach was once more in rapid motion.

The night and the snow came on together, and dismal enough they were. There was no sound to be heard but the howling of the wind; for the noise of the wheels, and the tread of the horses' feet, were rendered inaudible by the thick coating of snow which covered the ground, and was fast increasing every moment. The streets of Stamford were deserted as they passed through the town; and its old churches rose, frowning and dark, from the whitened ground. Twenty miles further on, two of the front outside passengers, wisely availing themselves of their arrival at one of the best inns in England, turned in, for the night, at the George at Grantham. The remainder wrapped themselves more closely in their coats and cloaks, and leaving the light and warmth of the town behind them, pillowed themselves against the luggage, and prepared, with many half-suppressed moans, again to encounter the piercing blast which swept across the open country.

They were little more than a stage out of Grantham, or about halfway between it and Newark, when Nicholas, who had been asleep for a short time, was suddenly roused by a violent jerk which nearly threw him from his seat. Grasping the rail, he found that the coach had sunk greatly on one side, though it was still dragged forward by the horses; and while—confused by their plunging and the loud screams of the lady inside—he hesitated, for an instant, whether to jump off or not, the vehicle turned easily over, and relieved him from all further uncertainty by flinging him into the road.

CHAPTER 6

In which the Occurrence of the Accident mentioned in the last Chapter, affords an Opportunity to a couple of Gentlemen to tell Stories against each other

'Wo ho!' cried the guard, on his legs in a minute, and running to the leaders' heads. 'Is there ony genelmen there as can len' a hond here? Keep quiet, dang ye! Wo ho!'

'What's the matter?' demanded Nicholas, looking sleepily up.

'Matther mun, matter eneaf for one neight,' replied the guard; 'dang the wall-eyed bay, he's gane mad wi' glory I think, carse t'coorch is over. Here, can't ye len' a hond? Dom it, I'd ha' dean it if all my boans were brokken.'

'Here!' cried Nicholas, staggering to his feet, 'I'm ready. I'm only a little abroad, that's all.'

'Hoold 'em toight,' cried the guard, 'while ar coot treaces. Hang on tiv'em sumhoo. Well deane, my lod. That's it. Let'em goa noo. Dang 'em, they'll gang whoam fast eneaf!'

In truth, the animals were no sooner released than they trotted back, with much deliberation, to the stable they had just left, which was distant not a mile behind.

'Can you blo' a harn?' asked the guard, disengaging one of the coach-lamps.

'I dare say I can,' replied Nicholas.

'Then just blo' away into that 'un as lies on the grund, fit to wakken the deead, will'ee,' said the man, 'while I stop sum o' this here squealing inside. Cumin', cumin'. Dean't make that noise, wooman.'

As the man spoke, he proceeded to wrench open the uppermost door of the coach, while Nicholas, seizing the horn, awoke the echoes far and wide with one of the most extraordinary performances on that instrument ever heard by mortal ears. It had its effect, however, not only in rousing such of their fall, but in summoning assistance to their relief; for lights gleamed in the distance, and people were already astir.

In fact, a man on horseback galloped down, before the passengers were well collected together; and a careful investigation being instituted, it appeared that the lady inside had broken her lamp, and the gentleman his head; that the two front outsides had escaped with black eyes; the box with a bloody nose; the coachman with a contusion on the temple; Mr Squeers with a portmanteau bruise on his back; and the remaining passengers without any injury at all—thanks to the softness of the snow-drift in which they had been overturned. These facts were no sooner thoroughly ascertained, than the lady gave several indications of fainting, but being forewarned that if she did, she must be carried on some gentleman's shoulders to the nearest public-house, she prudently thought better of it, and walked back with the rest.

They found on reaching it, that it was a lonely place with no very great accommodation in the way of apartments—that portion of its resources being all comprised in one public room with a sanded floor, and a chair or two. However, a large faggot and a plentiful supply of coals being heaped upon the fire, the appearance of things was not long in mending; and, by the time they had washed off all effaceable marks of the late accident, the room was warm and light, which was a most agreeable exchange for the cold and darkness out of doors.

'Well, Mr. Nickleby,' said Squeers, insinuating himself into the warmest corner, 'you did very right to catch hold of them horses. I should have done it myself if I had come to in time, but I am very glad you did it. You did it very well; very well.'

'So well,' said the merry-faced gentleman, who did not seem to approve very much of the patronising tone adopted by Squeers, 'that if they had not been firmly checked when they were, you would most probably have had no brains left to teach with.'

This remark called up a discourse relative to the promptitude Nicholas had displayed, and he was overwhelmed with compliments and commendations.

'I am very glad to have escaped, of course,' observed Squeers: 'every man is glad when he escapes from danger; but if any one of my charges had been hurt—if I had been prevented from restoring any one of these little boys to his parents whole and sound as I received him—

what would have been my feelings? Why the wheel a-top of my head would have been far preferable to it.'

'Are they all brothers, sir?' inquired the lady who had carried the 'Davy' or safety-lamp.

'In one sense they are, ma'am,' replied Squeers, diving into his greatcoat pocket for cards. 'They are all under the same parental and affectionate treatment. Mrs. Squeers and myself are a mother and father to every one of 'em. Mr. Nickleby, hand the lady them cards, and offer these to the gentleman. Perhaps they might know of some parents that would be glad to avail themselves of the establishment.'

Expressing himself to this effect, Mr. Squeers, who lost no opportunity of advertising gratuitously, placed his hands upon his knees, and looked at the pupils with as much benignity as he could possibly affect, while Nicholas, blushing with shame, handed round the cards as directed.

'I hope you suffer no inconvenience from the overturn, ma'am?' said the merry-faced gentleman, addressing the fastidious lady, as though he were charitably desirous to change the subject.

'No bodily inconvenience,' replied the lady.

'No mental inconvenience, I hope?'

'The subject is a very painful one to my feelings, sir,' replied the lady with strong emotion; 'and I beg you as a gentleman, not to refer to it.'

'Dear me,' said the merry-faced gentleman, looking merrier still, 'I merely intended to inquire—'

'I hope no inquiries will be made,' said the lady, 'or I shall be compelled to throw myself on the protection of the other gentlemen. Landlord, pray direct a boy to keep watch outside the door—and if a green chariot passes in the direction of Grantham, to stop it instantly.'

The people of the house were evidently overcome by this request, and when the lady charged the boy to remember, as a means of identifying the expected green chariot, that it would have a coachman with a gold-laced hat on the box, and a footman, most probably in silk stockings, behind, the attentions of the good woman of the inn were redoubled. Even the box-passenger caught the infection, and growing wonderfully deferential, immediately inquired whether there was not very good society in that neighbourhood, to which the lady replied yes, there was: in a manner which sufficiently implied that she moved at the very tiptop and summit of it all.

'As the guard has gone on horseback to Grantham to get another coach,' said the good-tempered gentleman when they had been all sitting round the fire, for some time, in silence, 'and as he must be gone a couple of hours at the very least, I propose a bowl of hot punch. What say you, sir?'

This question was addressed to the broken-headed inside, who was a man of very genteel appearance, dressed in mourning. He was not past the middle age, but his hair was grey; it seemed to have been prematurely turned by care or sorrow. He readily acceded to the proposal, and appeared to be prepossessed by the frank good-nature of the individual from whom it emanated.

This latter personage took upon himself the office of tapster when the punch was ready, and after dispensing it all round, led the conversation to the antiquities of York, with which both he and the grey-haired gentleman appeared to be well acquainted. When this topic flagged, he turned with a smile to the grey-headed gentleman, and asked if he could sing.

'I cannot indeed,' replied gentleman, smiling in his turn.

'That's a pity,' said the owner of the good-humoured countenance. 'Is there nobody here who can sing a song to lighten the time?'

The passengers, one and all, protested that they could not; that they wished they could; that they couldn't remember the words of anything without the book; and so forth.

'Perhaps the lady would not object,' said the president with great respect, and a merry twinkle in his eye. 'Some little Italian thing out of the last opera brought out in town, would be most acceptable I am sure.'

As the lady condescended to make no reply, but tossed her head contemptuously, and murmured some further expression of surprise regarding the absence of the green chariot, one or two voices urged upon the president himself, the propriety of making an attempt for the general benefit.

'I would if I could,' said he of the good-tempered face; 'for I hold that in this, as in all other cases where people who are strangers to each other are thrown unexpectedly together, they should endeavour to render themselves as pleasant, for the joint sake of the little community, as possible.'

'I wish the maxim were more generally acted on, in all cases,' said the grey-headed gentleman.

'I'm glad to hear it,' returned the other. 'Perhaps, as you can't sing, you'll tell us a story?'

'Nay. I should ask you.'

'After you, I will, with pleasure.'

'Indeed!' said the grey-haired gentleman, smiling, 'Well, let it be so. I fear the turn of my thoughts is not calculated to lighten the time you must pass here; but you have brought this upon yourselves, and shall judge. We were speaking of York Minster just now. My story shall have some reference to it. Let us call it

THE FIVE SISTERS OF YORK

After a murmur of approbation from the other passengers, during which the fastidious lady drank a glass of punch unobserved, the grey-headed gentleman thus went on:

'A great many years ago—for the fifteenth century was scarce two years old at the time, and King Henry the Fourth sat upon the throne of England—there dwelt, in the ancient city of York, five maiden sisters, the subjects of my tale.

'These five sisters were all of surpassing beauty. The eldest was in her twenty-third year, the second a year younger, the third a year younger than the second, and the fourth a year younger than the third. They were tall stately figures, with dark flashing eyes and hair of jet; dignity and grace were in their every movement; and the fame of their great beauty had spread through all the country round.

'But, if the four elder sisters were lovely, how beautiful was the youngest, a fair creature of sixteen! The blushing tints in the soft bloom on the fruit, or the delicate painting on the flower, are not more exquisite than was the blending of the rose and lily in her gentle face, or the deep blue of her eye. The vine, in all its elegant luxuriance, is not more graceful than were the clusters of rich brown hair that sported round her brow.

'If we all had hearts like those which beat so lightly in the bosoms of the young and beautiful, what a heaven this earth would be! If, while our bodies grow old and withered, our hearts could but retain their early youth and freshness, of what avail would be our sorrows and sufferings! But, the faint image of Eden which is stamped upon them in childhood, chafes and rubs in our rough struggles with the world, and soon wears away: too often to leave nothing but a mournful blank remaining.

'The heart of this fair girl bounded with joy and gladness. Devoted attachment to her sisters, and a fervent love of all beautiful things in nature, were its pure affections. Her gleesome voice and merry laugh were the sweetest music of their home. She was its very light and life. The brightest flowers in the garden were reared by her; the caged birds sang when they heard her voice, and pined when they missed its sweetness. Alice, dear Alice; what living thing within the sphere of her gentle witchery, could fail to love her!

'You may seek in vain, now, for the spot on which these sisters lived, for their very names have passed away, and dusty antiquaries tell of them as of a fable. But they dwelt in an old wooden house—old even in those days—with overhanging gables and balconies of rudely-carved oak, which stood within a pleasant orchard, and was surrounded by a rough stone wall, whence a stout archer might have winged an arrow to St Mary's Abbey. The old abbey flourished then; and the five sisters, living on its fair domains, paid yearly dues to the black monks of St Benedict, to which fraternity it belonged.

'It was a bright and sunny morning in the pleasant time of summer, when one of those black monks emerged from the abbey portal, and bent his steps towards the house of the fair sisters. Heaven above was blue, and earth beneath was green; the river glistened like a path of diamonds in the sun; the birds poured forth their songs from the shady trees; the lark soared high above the waving corn; and the deep buzz of insects filled the air. Everything looked gay and smiling; but the holy man walked gloomily on, with his eyes bent upon the ground. The beauty of the earth is but a breath, and man is but a shadow. What sympathy should a holy preacher have with either?

'With eyes bent upon the ground, then, or only raised enough to prevent his stumbling over such obstacles as lay in his way, the religious man moved slowly forward until he reached a small postern in the wall of the sisters' orchard, through which he passed, closing it behind him. The noise of soft voices in conversation, and of merry laughter, fell upon his ears ere he had advanced many paces; and raising his eyes higher than was his humble wont, he descried, at no great distance, the five sisters seated on the grass, with Alice in the centre: all busily plying their customary task of embroidering.

'"Save you, fair daughters!" said the friar; and fair in truth they were. Even a monk might have loved them as choice masterpieces of his Maker's hand.

'The sisters saluted the holy man with becoming reverence, and the eldest motioned him to a mossy seat beside them. But the good friar shook his head, and bumped himself down on a very hard stone,—at which, no doubt, approving angels were gratified.

"'Ye were merry, daughters," said the monk.

"'You know how light of heart sweet Alice is," replied the eldest sister, passing her fingers through the tresses of the smiling girl.

"'And what joy and cheerfulness it wakes up within us, to see all nature beaming in brightness and sunshine, father," added Alice, blushing beneath the stern look of the recluse.

'The monk answered not, save by a grave inclination of the head, and the sisters pursued their task in silence.

"'Still wasting the precious hours," said the monk at length, turning to the eldest sister as he spoke, "still wasting the precious hours on this vain trifling. Alas, alas! that the few bubbles on the surface of eternity—all that Heaven wills we should see of that dark deep stream—should be so lightly scattered!"

"'Father," urged the maiden, pausing, as did each of the others, in her busy task, "we have prayed at matins, our daily alms have been distributed at the gate, the sick peasants have been tended,—all our morning tasks have been performed. I hope our occupation is a blameless one?'

"'See here," said the friar, taking the frame from her hand, "an intricate winding of gaudy colours, without purpose or object, unless it be that one day it is destined for some vain ornament, to minister to the pride of your frail and giddy sex. Day after day has been employed upon this senseless task, and yet it is not half accomplished. The shade of each departed day falls upon our graves, and the worm exults as he beholds it, to know that we are hastening thither. Daughters, is there no better way to pass the fleeting hours?"

'The four elder sisters cast down their eyes as if abashed by the holy man's reproof, but Alice raised hers, and bent them mildly on the friar.

"'Our dear mother," said the maiden; "Heaven rest her soul!"

"'Amen!" cried the friar in a deep voice.

"'Our dear mother," faltered the fair Alice, "was living when these long tasks began, and bade us, when she should be no more, ply them in all discretion and cheerfulness, in our leisure hours; she said that if in harmless mirth and maidenly pursuits we passed those hours together, they would prove the happiest and most peaceful of our lives, and that if, in later times, we went forth into the world, and mingled with its cares and trials—if, allured by its temptations and dazzled by its glitter, we ever forgot that love and duty which should bind, in holy ties, the children of one loved parent—a glance at the old work of our common girlhood would awaken good thoughts of bygone days, and soften our hearts to affection and love."

"'Alice speaks truly, father," said the elder sister, somewhat proudly. And so saying she resumed her work, as did the others.

'It was a kind of sampler of large size, that each sister had before her; the device was of a complex and intricate description, and the pattern and colours of all five were the same. The sisters bent gracefully over their work; the monk, resting his chin upon his hands, looked from one to the other in silence.

"'How much better," he said at length, "to shun all such thoughts and chances, and, in the peaceful shelter of the church, devote your lives to Heaven! Infancy, childhood, the prime of life, and old age, wither as rapidly as they crowd upon each other. Think how human dust rolls onward to the tomb, and turning your faces steadily towards that goal, avoid the cloud which takes its rise among the pleasures of the world, and cheats the senses of their votaries. The veil, daughters, the veil!"

'"Never, sisters," cried Alice. "Barter not the light and air of heaven, and the freshness of earth and all the beautiful things which breathe upon it, for the cold cloister and the cell. Nature's own blessings are the proper goods of life, and we may share them sinlessly together. To die is our heavy portion, but, oh, let us die with life about us; when our cold hearts cease to beat, let warm hearts be beating near; let our last look be upon the bounds which God has set to his own bright skies, and not on stone walls and bars of iron! Dear sisters, let us live and die, if you list, in this green garden's compass; only shun the gloom and sadness of a cloister, and we shall be happy."

'The tears fell fast from the maiden's eyes as she closed her impassioned appeal, and hid her face in the bosom of her sister.

'"Take comfort, Alice," said the eldest, kissing her fair forehead. "The veil shall never cast its shadow on thy young brow. How say you, sisters? For yourselves you speak, and not for Alice, or for me."

'The sisters, as with one accord, cried that their lot was cast together, and that there were dwellings for peace and virtue beyond the convent's walls.

'"Father," said the eldest lady, rising with dignity, "you hear our final resolve. The same pious care which enriched the abbey of St Mary, and left us, orphans, to its holy guardianship, directed that no constraint should be imposed upon our inclinations, but that we should be free to live according to our choice. Let us hear no more of this, we pray you. Sisters, it is nearly noon. Let us take shelter until evening!" With a reverence to the friar, the lady rose and walked towards the house, hand in hand with Alice; the other sisters followed.

'The holy man, who had often urged the same point before, but had never met with so direct a repulse, walked some little distance behind, with his eyes bent upon the earth, and his lips moving as if in prayer. As the sisters reached the porch, he quickened his pace, and called upon them to stop.

'"Stay!" said the monk, raising his right hand in the air, and directing an angry glance by turns at Alice and the eldest sister. "Stay, and hear from me what these recollections are, which you would cherish above eternity, and awaken—if in mercy they slumbered—by means of idle toys. The memory of earthly things is charged, in after life, with bitter disappointment, affliction, death; with dreary change and wasting sorrow. The time will one day come, when a glance at those unmeaning baubles will tear open deep wounds in the hearts of some among you, and strike to your inmost souls. When that hour arrives—and, mark me, come it will— turn from the world to which you clung, to the refuge which you spurned. Find me the cell which shall be colder than the fire of mortals grows, when dimmed by calamity and trial, and there weep for the dreams of youth. These things are Heaven's will, not mine," said the friar, subduing his voice as he looked round upon the shrinking girls. "The Virgin's blessing be upon you, daughters!"

'With these words he disappeared through the postern; and the sisters hastening into the house were seen no more that day.

'But nature will smile though priests may frown, and next day the sun shone brightly, and on the next, and the next again. And in the morning's glare, and the evening's soft repose, the five sisters still walked, or worked, or beguiled the time by cheerful conversation, in their quiet orchard.

'Time passed away as a tale that is told; faster indeed than many tales that are told, of which number I fear this may be one. The house of the five sisters stood where it did, and the same trees cast their pleasant shade upon the orchard grass. The sisters too were there, and lovely as at first, but a change had come over their dwelling. Sometimes, there was the clash of armour, and the gleaming of the moon on caps of steel; and, at others, jaded coursers were spurred up to the gate, and a female form glided hurriedly forth, as if eager to demand tidings of the weary messenger. A goodly train of knights and ladies lodged one night within the abbey walls, and next day rode away, with two of the fair sisters among them. Then, horsemen began to come less frequently, and seemed to bring bad tidings when they did, and at length they ceased to come at all, and footsore peasants slunk to the gate after sunset, and did their errand there, by stealth. Once, a vassal was dispatched in haste to the abbey at dead of night, and when morning came, there were sounds of woe and wailing in the sisters' house; and after this, a mournful silence fell upon it, and knight or lady, horse or armour, was seen about it no more.

'There was a sullen darkness in the sky, and the sun had gone angrily down, tinting the dull clouds with the last traces of his wrath, when the same black monk walked slowly on, with folded arms, within a stone's-throw of the abbey. A blight had fallen on the trees and shrubs; and the wind, at length beginning to break the unnatural stillness that had prevailed all day, sighed heavily from time to time, as though foretelling in grief the ravages of the coming storm. The bat skimmed in fantastic flights through the heavy air, and the ground was alive with crawling things, whose instinct brought them forth to swell and fatten in the rain.

'No longer were the friar's eyes directed to the earth; they were cast abroad, and roamed from point to point, as if the gloom and desolation of the scene found a quick response in his own bosom. Again he paused near the sisters' house, and again he entered by the postern.

'But not again did his ear encounter the sound of laughter, or his eyes rest upon the beautiful figures of the five sisters. All was silent and deserted. The boughs of the trees were bent and broken, and the grass had grown long and rank. No light feet had pressed it for many, many a day.

'With the indifference or abstraction of one well accustomed to the change, the monk glided into the house, and entered a low, dark room. Four sisters sat there. Their black garments made their pale faces whiter still, and time and sorrow had worked deep ravages. They were stately yet; but the flush and pride of beauty were gone.

'And Alice—where was she? In Heaven.

'The monk—even the monk—could bear with some grief here; for it was long since these sisters had met, and there were furrows in their blanched faces which years could never plough. He took his seat in silence, and motioned them to continue their speech.

'"They are here, sisters," said the elder lady in a trembling voice. "I have never borne to look upon them since, and now I blame myself for my weakness. What is there in her memory that we should dread? To call up our old days shall be a solemn pleasure yet."

'She glanced at the monk as she spoke, and, opening a cabinet, brought forth the five frames of work, completed long before. Her step was firm, but her hand trembled as she produced the last one; and, when the feelings of the other sisters gushed forth at sight of it, her pent-up tears made way, and she sobbed "God bless her!"

'The monk rose and advanced towards them. "It was almost the last thing she touched in health," he said in a low voice.

'"It was," cried the elder lady, weeping bitterly.

'The monk turned to the second sister.

'"The gallant youth who looked into thine eyes, and hung upon thy very breath when first he saw thee intent upon this pastime, lies buried on a plain whereof the turf is red with blood. Rusty fragments of armour, once brightly burnished, lie rotting on the ground, and are as little distinguishable for his, as are the bones that crumble in the mould!"

'The lady groaned, and wrung her hands.

'"The policy of courts," he continued, turning to the two other sisters, "drew ye from your peaceful home to scenes of revelry and splendour. The same policy, and the restless ambition of—proud and fiery men, have sent ye back, widowed maidens, and humbled outcasts. Do I speak truly?"

'The sobs of the two sisters were their only reply.

'"There is little need," said the monk, with a meaning look, "to fritter away the time in gewgaws which shall raise up the pale ghosts of hopes of early years. Bury them, heap penance and mortification on their heads, keep them down, and let the convent be their grave!"

'The sisters asked for three days to deliberate; and felt, that night, as though the veil were indeed the fitting shroud for their dead joys. But, morning came again, and though the boughs of the orchard trees drooped and ran wild upon the ground, it was the same orchard still. The grass was coarse and high, but there was yet the spot on which they had so often sat together, when change and sorrow were but names. There was every walk and nook which Alice had made glad; and in the minster nave was one flat stone beneath which she slept in peace.

'And could they, remembering how her young heart had sickened at the thought of cloistered walls, look upon her grave, in garbs which would chill the very ashes within it? Could they bow down in prayer, and when all Heaven turned to hear them, bring the dark shade of sadness on one angel's face? No.

'They sent abroad, to artists of great celebrity in those times, and having obtained the church's sanction to their work of piety, caused to be executed, in five large compartments of richly stained glass, a faithful copy of their old embroidery work. These were fitted into a large window until that time bare of ornament; and when the sun shone brightly, as she had so well loved to see it, the familiar patterns were reflected in their original colours, and throwing a stream of brilliant light upon the pavement, fell warmly on the name of Alice.

'For many hours in every day, the sisters paced slowly up and down the nave, or knelt by the side of the flat broad stone. Only three were seen in the customary place, after many years; then but two, and, for a long time afterwards, but one solitary female bent with age. At length she came no more, and the stone bore five plain Christian names.

'That stone has worn away and been replaced by others, and many generations have come and gone since then. Time has softened down the colours, but the same stream of light still falls upon the forgotten tomb, of which no trace remains; and, to this day, the stranger is shown in York Cathedral, an old window called the Five Sisters.'

'That's a melancholy tale,' said the merry-faced gentleman, emptying his glass.

'It is a tale of life, and life is made up of such sorrows,' returned the other, courteously, but in a grave and sad tone of voice.

'There are shades in all good pictures, but there are lights too, if we choose to contemplate them,' said the gentleman with the merry face. 'The youngest sister in your tale was always light-hearted.'

'And died early,' said the other, gently.

'She would have died earlier, perhaps, had she been less happy,' said the first speaker, with much feeling. 'Do you think the sisters who loved her so well, would have grieved the less if her life had been one of gloom and sadness? If anything could soothe the first sharp pain of a heavy loss, it would be—with me—the reflection, that those I mourned, by being innocently happy here, and loving all about them, had prepared themselves for a purer and happier world. The sun does not shine upon this fair earth to meet frowning eyes, depend upon it.'

'I believe you are right,' said the gentleman who had told the story.

'Believe!' retorted the other, 'can anybody doubt it? Take any subject of sorrowful regret, and see with how much pleasure it is associated. The recollection of past pleasure may become pain—'

'It does,' interposed the other.

'Well; it does. To remember happiness which cannot be restored, is pain, but of a softened kind. Our recollections are unfortunately mingled with much that we deplore, and with many actions which we bitterly repent; still in the most chequered life I firmly think there are so many little rays of sunshine to look back upon, that I do not believe any mortal (unless he had put himself without the pale of hope) would deliberately drain a goblet of the waters of Lethe, if he had it in his power.'

'Possibly you are correct in that belief,' said the grey-haired gentleman after a short reflection. 'I am inclined to think you are.'

'Why, then,' replied the other, 'the good in this state of existence preponderates over the bad, let miscalled philosophers tell us what they will. If our affections be tried, our affections are our consolation and comfort; and memory, however sad, is the best and purest link between this world and a better. But come! I'll tell you a story of another kind.'

After a very brief silence, the merry-faced gentleman sent round the punch, and glancing slyly at the fastidious lady, who seemed desperately apprehensive that he was going to relate something improper, began

THE BARON OF GROGZWIG

'The Baron Von Koeldwethout, of Grogzwig in Germany, was as likely a young baron as you would wish to see. I needn't say that he lived in a castle, because that's of course; neither need I say that he lived in an old castle; for what German baron ever lived in a new one? There were many strange circumstances connected with this venerable building, among which, not the least startling and mysterious were, that when the wind blew, it rumbled in the chimneys, or even howled among the trees in the neighbouring forest; and that when the moon shone, she found her way through certain small loopholes in the wall, and actually made some parts of the wide halls and galleries quite light, while she left others in gloomy shadow. I believe that one of the baron's ancestors, being short of money, had inserted a dagger in a gentleman who called one night to ask his way, and it was supposed that these miraculous occurrences took place in consequence. And yet I hardly know how that could have been, either, because the baron's ancestor, who was an amiable man, felt very sorry afterwards for having been so rash, and laying violent hands upon a quantity of stone and timber which belonged to a weaker baron, built a chapel as an apology, and so took a receipt from Heaven, in full of all demands.

'Talking of the baron's ancestor puts me in mind of the baron's great claims to respect, on the score of his pedigree. I am afraid to say, I am sure, how many ancestors the baron had; but I know that he had a great many more than any other man of his time; and I only wish that he had lived in these latter days, that he might have had more. It is a very hard thing upon the great men of past centuries, that they should have come into the world so soon, because a man who was born three or four hundred years ago, cannot reasonably be expected to have had as many relations before him, as a man who is born now. The last man, whoever he is—and he may be a cobbler or some low vulgar dog for aught we know—will have a longer pedigree than the greatest nobleman now alive; and I contend that this is not fair.

'Well, but the Baron Von Koeldwethout of Grogzwig! He was a fine swarthy fellow, with dark hair and large moustachios, who rode a-hunting in clothes of Lincoln green, with russet boots on his feet, and a bugle slung over his shoulder like the guard of a long stage. When he blew this bugle, four-and-twenty other gentlemen of inferior rank, in Lincoln green a little coarser, and russet boots with a little thicker soles, turned out directly: and away galloped the whole train, with spears in their hands like lacquered area railings, to hunt down the boars, or perhaps encounter a bear: in which latter case the baron killed him first, and greased his whiskers with him afterwards.

'This was a merry life for the Baron of Grogzwig, and a merrier still for the baron's retainers, who drank Rhine wine every night till they fell under the table, and then had the bottles on the floor, and called for pipes. Never were such jolly, roystering, rollicking, merry-making blades, as the jovial crew of Grogzwig.

'But the pleasures of the table, or the pleasures of under the table, require a little variety; especially when the same five-and-twenty people sit daily down to the same board, to discuss the same subjects, and tell the same stories. The baron grew weary, and wanted excitement. He took to quarrelling with his gentlemen, and tried kicking two or three of them every day after dinner. This was a pleasant change at first; but it became monotonous after a week or so, and the baron felt quite out of sorts, and cast about, in despair, for some new amusement.

'One night, after a day's sport in which he had outdone Nimrod or Gillingwater, and slaughtered "another fine bear," and brought him home in triumph, the Baron Von Koeldwethout sat moodily at the head of his table, eyeing the smoky roof of the hall with a discontented aspect. He swallowed huge bumpers of wine, but the more he swallowed, the more he frowned. The gentlemen who had been honoured with the dangerous distinction of sitting on his right and left, imitated him to a miracle in the drinking, and frowned at each other.

'"I will!" cried the baron suddenly, smiting the table with his right hand, and twirling his moustache with his left. "Fill to the Lady of Grogzwig!"

'The four-and-twenty Lincoln greens turned pale, with the exception of their four-and-twenty noses, which were unchangeable.

'"I said to the Lady of Grogzwig," repeated the baron, looking round the board.

'"To the Lady of Grogzwig!" shouted the Lincoln greens; and down their four-and-twenty throats went four-and-twenty imperial pints of such rare old hock, that they smacked their eight-and-forty lips, and winked again.

'"The fair daughter of the Baron Von Swillenhausen," said Koeldwethout, condescending to explain. "We will demand her in marriage of her father, ere the sun goes down tomorrow. If he refuse our suit, we will cut off his nose."

'A hoarse murmur arose from the company; every man touched, first the hilt of his sword, and then the tip of his nose, with appalling significance.

'What a pleasant thing filial piety is to contemplate! If the daughter of the Baron Von Swillenhausen had pleaded a preoccupied heart, or fallen at her father's feet and corned them in salt tears, or only fainted away, and complimented the old gentleman in frantic ejaculations, the odds are a hundred to one but Swillenhausen Castle would have been turned out at window, or rather the baron turned out at window, and the castle demolished. The damsel held her peace, however, when an early messenger bore the request of Von Koeldwethout next morning, and modestly retired to her chamber, from the casement of which she watched the coming of the suitor and his retinue. She was no sooner assured that the horseman with the large moustachios was her proffered husband, than she hastened to her father's presence, and expressed her readiness to sacrifice herself to secure his peace. The venerable baron caught his child to his arms, and shed a wink of joy.

'There was great feasting at the castle, that day. The four-and-twenty Lincoln greens of Von Koeldwethout exchanged vows of eternal friendship with twelve Lincoln greens of Von Swillenhausen, and promised the old baron that they would drink his wine "Till all was blue"—meaning probably until their whole countenances had acquired the same tint as their noses. Everybody slapped everybody else's back, when the time for parting came; and the Baron Von Koeldwethout and his followers rode gaily home.

'For six mortal weeks, the bears and boars had a holiday. The houses of Koeldwethout and Swillenhausen were united; the spears rusted; and the baron's bugle grew hoarse for lack of blowing.

'Those were great times for the four-and-twenty; but, alas! their high and palmy days had taken boots to themselves, and were already walking off.

'"My dear," said the baroness.

'"My love," said the baron.

'"Those coarse, noisy men—"

'"Which, ma'am?" said the baron, starting.

'The baroness pointed, from the window at which they stood, to the courtyard beneath, where the unconscious Lincoln greens were taking a copious stirrup-cup, preparatory to issuing forth after a boar or two.

'"My hunting train, ma'am," said the baron.

'"Disband them, love," murmured the baroness.

'"Disband them!" cried the baron, in amazement.

'"To please me, love," replied the baroness.

'"To please the devil, ma'am," answered the baron.

'Whereupon the baroness uttered a great cry, and swooned away at the baron's feet.

'What could the baron do? He called for the lady's maid, and roared for the doctor; and then, rushing into the yard, kicked the two Lincoln greens who were the most used to it, and cursing the others all round, bade them go—but never mind where. I don't know the German for it, or I would put it delicately that way.

'It is not for me to say by what means, or by what degrees, some wives manage to keep down some husbands as they do, although I may have my private opinion on the subject, and may think that no Member of Parliament ought to be married, inasmuch as three married members out of every four, must vote according to their wives' consciences (if there be such things), and not according to their own. All I need say, just now, is, that the Baroness Von Koeldwethout somehow or other acquired great control over the Baron Von Koeldwethout, and that, little by little, and bit by bit, and day by day, and year by year, the baron got the worst of some disputed question, or was slyly unhorsed from some old hobby; and that by the time he was a fat hearty fellow of forty-eight or thereabouts, he had no feasting, no revelry, no hunting train, and no hunting—nothing in short that he liked, or used to have; and that, although he was as fierce as a lion, and as bold as brass, he was decidedly snubbed and put down, by his own lady, in his own castle of Grogzwig.

'Nor was this the whole extent of the baron's misfortunes. About a year after his nuptials, there came into the world a lusty young baron, in whose honour a great many fireworks were let off, and a great many dozens of wine drunk; but next year there came a young baroness, and next year another young baron, and so on, every year, either a baron or baroness (and one year both together), until the baron found himself the father of a small family of twelve. Upon every one of these anniversaries, the venerable Baroness Von Swillenhausen was nervously sensitive for the well-being of her child the Baroness Von Koeldwethout; and although it was not found that the good lady ever did anything material towards contributing to her child's recovery, still she made it a point of duty to be as nervous as possible at the castle of Grogzwig, and to divide her time between moral observations on the baron's housekeeping, and bewailing the hard lot of her unhappy daughter. And if the Baron of Grogzwig, a little hurt and irritated at this, took heart, and ventured to suggest that his wife was at least no worse off than the wives of other barons, the Baroness Von Swillenhausen begged all persons to take notice, that nobody but she, sympathised with her dear daughter's sufferings; upon which, her relations and friends remarked, that to be sure she did cry a great deal more than her son-in-law, and that if there were a hard-hearted brute alive, it was that Baron of Grogzwig.

'The poor baron bore it all as long as he could, and when he could bear it no longer lost his appetite and his spirits, and sat himself gloomily and dejectedly down. But there were worse troubles yet in store for him, and as they came on, his melancholy and sadness increased. Times changed. He got into debt. The Grogzwig coffers ran low, though the Swillenhausen family had looked upon them as inexhaustible; and just when the baroness was on the point of making a thirteenth addition to the family pedigree, Von Koeldwethout discovered that he had no means of replenishing them.

"'I don't see what is to be done," said the baron. "I think I'll kill myself."

'This was a bright idea. The baron took an old hunting-knife from a cupboard hard by, and having sharpened it on his boot, made what boys call "an offer" at his throat.

"'Hem!" said the baron, stopping short. "Perhaps it's not sharp enough."

'The baron sharpened it again, and made another offer, when his hand was arrested by a loud screaming among the young barons and baronesses, who had a nursery in an upstairs tower with iron bars outside the window, to prevent their tumbling out into the moat.

"'If I had been a bachelor," said the baron sighing, "I might have done it fifty times over, without being interrupted. Hallo! Put a flask of wine and the largest pipe in the little vaulted room behind the hall."

'One of the domestics, in a very kind manner, executed the baron's order in the course of half an hour or so, and Von Koeldwethout being apprised thereof, strode to the vaulted room, the walls of which, being of dark shining wood, gleamed in the light of the blazing logs which were piled upon the hearth. The bottle and pipe were ready, and, upon the whole, the place looked very comfortable.

"'Leave the lamp," said the baron.

"'Anything else, my lord?" inquired the domestic.

"'The room," replied the baron. The domestic obeyed, and the baron locked the door.

"'I'll smoke a last pipe," said the baron, "and then I'll be off." So, putting the knife upon the table till he wanted it, and tossing off a goodly measure of wine, the Lord of Grogzwig threw himself back in his chair, stretched his legs out before the fire, and puffed away.

'He thought about a great many things—about his present troubles and past days of bachelorship, and about the Lincoln greens, long since dispersed up and down the country, no one knew whither: with the exception of two who had been unfortunately beheaded, and four who had killed themselves with drinking. His mind was running upon bears and boars, when, in the process of draining his glass to the bottom, he raised his eyes, and saw, for the first time and with unbounded astonishment, that he was not alone.

'No, he was not; for, on the opposite side of the fire, there sat with folded arms a wrinkled hideous figure, with deeply sunk and bloodshot eyes, and an immensely long cadaverous face, shadowed by jagged and matted locks of coarse black hair. He wore a kind of tunic of a dull bluish colour, which, the baron observed, on regarding it attentively, was clasped or ornamented down the front with coffin handles. His legs, too, were encased in coffin plates as though in armour; and over his left shoulder he wore a short dusky cloak, which seemed made of a remnant of some pall. He took no notice of the baron, but was intently eyeing the fire.

"'Halloa!" said the baron, stamping his foot to attract attention.

"'Halloa!" replied the stranger, moving his eyes towards the baron, but not his face or himself "What now?"

"'What now!" replied the baron, nothing daunted by his hollow voice and lustreless eyes. "I should ask that question. How did you get here?"

"'Through the door," replied the figure.

"'What are you?" says the baron.

"'A man," replied the figure.

"'I don't believe it," says the baron.

"'Disbelieve it then," says the figure.

"'I will," rejoined the baron.

'The figure looked at the bold Baron of Grogzwig for some time, and then said familiarly,

"'There's no coming over you, I see. I'm not a man!"

"'What are you then?" asked the baron.

"'A genius," replied the figure.

"'You don't look much like one," returned the baron scornfully.

"'I am the Genius of Despair and Suicide," said the apparition. "Now you know me."

'With these words the apparition turned towards the baron, as if composing himself for a talk—and, what was very remarkable, was that he threw his cloak aside, and displaying a stake, which was run through the centre of his body, pulled it out with a jerk, and laid it on the table, as composedly as if it had been a walking-stick.

"'Now," said the figure, glancing at the hunting-knife, "are you ready for me?"

"'Not quite," rejoined the baron; "I must finish this pipe first."

"'Look sharp then," said the figure.

"'You seem in a hurry," said the baron.

"'Why, yes, I am," answered the figure; "they're doing a pretty brisk business in my way, over in England and France just now, and my time is a good deal taken up."

"'Do you drink?" said the baron, touching the bottle with the bowl of his pipe.

"'Nine times out of ten, and then very hard," rejoined the figure, drily.

"'Never in moderation?" asked the baron.

"'Never," replied the figure, with a shudder, "that breeds cheerfulness."

'The baron took another look at his new friend, whom he thought an uncommonly queer customer, and at length inquired whether he took any active part in such little proceedings as that which he had in contemplation.

"'No," replied the figure evasively; "but I am always present."

"'Just to see fair, I suppose?" said the baron.

"'Just that," replied the figure, playing with his stake, and examining the ferule. "Be as quick as you can, will you, for there's a young gentleman who is afflicted with too much money and leisure wanting me now, I find."

"'Going to kill himself because he has too much money!" exclaimed the baron, quite tickled. "Ha! ha! that's a good one." (This was the first time the baron had laughed for many a long day.)

"'I say,' expostulated the figure, looking very much scared; "don't do that again."

"'Why not?" demanded the baron.

"'Because it gives me pain all over,' replied the figure. "Sigh as much as you please: that does me good."

'The baron sighed mechanically at the mention of the word; the figure, brightening up again, handed him the hunting-knife with most winning politeness.

"'It's not a bad idea though,' said the baron, feeling the edge of the weapon; "a man killing himself because he has too much money."

"'Pooh!' said the apparition, petulantly, "no better than a man's killing himself because he has none or little."

'Whether the genius unintentionally committed himself in saying this, or whether he thought the baron's mind was so thoroughly made up that it didn't matter what he said, I have no means of knowing. I only know that the baron stopped his hand, all of a sudden, opened his eyes wide, and looked as if quite a new light had come upon him for the first time.

"'Why, certainly,' said Von Koeldwethout, "nothing is too bad to be retrieved."

"'Except empty coffers,' cried the genius.

"'Well; but they may be one day filled again,' said the baron.

"'Scolding wives,' snarled the genius.

"'Oh! They may be made quiet,' said the baron.

"'Thirteen children,' shouted the genius.

"'Can't all go wrong, surely,' said the baron.

'The genius was evidently growing very savage with the baron, for holding these opinions all at once; but he tried to laugh it off, and said if he would let him know when he had left off joking he should feel obliged to him.

"'But I am not joking; I was never farther from it,' remonstrated the baron.

"'Well, I am glad to hear that,' said the genius, looking very grim, "because a joke, without any figure of speech, is the death of me. Come! Quit this dreary world at once."

"'I don't know,' said the baron, playing with the knife; "it's a dreary one certainly, but I don't think yours is much better, for you have not the appearance of being particularly comfortable. That puts me in mind—what security have I, that I shall be any the better for going out of the world after all!" he cried, starting up; "I never thought of that."

"'Dispatch,' cried the figure, gnashing his teeth.

"'Keep off!' said the baron. 'I'll brood over miseries no longer, but put a good face on the matter, and try the fresh air and the bears again; and if that don't do, I'll talk to the baroness soundly, and cut the Von Swillenhausens dead.' With this the baron fell into his chair, and laughed so loud and boisterously, that the room rang with it.

'The figure fell back a pace or two, regarding the baron meanwhile with a look of intense terror, and when he had ceased, caught up the stake, plunged it violently into its body, uttered a frightful howl, and disappeared.

'Von Koeldwethout never saw it again. Having once made up his mind to action, he soon brought the baroness and the Von Swillenhausens to reason, and died many years afterwards: not a rich man that I am aware of, but certainly a happy one: leaving behind him a numerous family, who had been carefully educated in bear and boar-hunting under his own personal eye. And my advice to all men is, that if ever they become hipped and melancholy from similar causes (as very many men do), they look at both sides of the question, applying a magnifying-glass to the best one; and if they still feel tempted to retire without leave, that they smoke a large pipe and drink a full bottle first, and profit by the laudable example of the Baron of Grogzwig.'

'The fresh coach is ready, ladies and gentlemen, if you please,' said a new driver, looking in.

This intelligence caused the punch to be finished in a great hurry, and prevented any discussion relative to the last story. Mr. Squeers was observed to draw the grey-headed gentleman on one side, and to ask a question with great apparent interest; it bore reference to the Five Sisters of York, and was, in fact, an inquiry whether he could inform him how much per annum the Yorkshire convents got in those days with their boarders.

The journey was then resumed. Nicholas fell asleep towards morning, and, when he awoke, found, with great regret, that, during his nap, both the Baron of Grogzwig and the grey-haired gentleman had got down and were gone. The day dragged on uncomfortably enough. At about six o'clock that night, he and Mr. Squeers, and the little boys, and their united luggage, were all put down together at the George and New Inn, Greta Bridge.

CHAPTER 7
Mr. and Mrs. Squeers at Home

Mr. Squeers, being safely landed, left Nicholas and the boys standing with the luggage in the road, to amuse themselves by looking at the coach as it changed horses, while he ran into the tavern and went through the leg-stretching process at the bar. After some minutes, he returned, with his legs thoroughly stretched, if the hue of his nose and a short hiccup afforded any criterion; and at the same time there came out of the yard a rusty pony-chaise, and a cart, driven by two labouring men.

'Put the boys and the boxes into the cart,' said Squeers, rubbing his hands; 'and this young man and me will go on in the chaise. Get in, Nickleby.'

Nicholas obeyed. Mr. Squeers with some difficulty inducing the pony to obey also, they started off, leaving the cart-load of infant misery to follow at leisure.

'Are you cold, Nickleby?' inquired Squeers, after they had travelled some distance in silence.

'Rather, sir, I must say.'

'Well, I don't find fault with that,' said Squeers; 'it's a long journey this weather.'

'Is it much farther to Dotheboys Hall, sir?' asked Nicholas.

'About three mile from here,' replied Squeers. 'But you needn't call it a Hall down here.'

Nicholas coughed, as if he would like to know why.

'The fact is, it ain't a Hall,' observed Squeers drily.

'Oh, indeed!' said Nicholas, whom this piece of intelligence much astonished.

'No,' replied Squeers. 'We call it a Hall up in London, because it sounds better, but they don't know it by that name in these parts. A man may call his house an island if he likes; there's no act of Parliament against that, I believe?'

'I believe not, sir,' rejoined Nicholas.

Squeers eyed his companion slyly, at the conclusion of this little dialogue, and finding that he had grown thoughtful and appeared in nowise disposed to volunteer any observations, contented himself with lashing the pony until they reached their journey's end.

'Jump out,' said Squeers. 'Hallo there! Come and put this horse up. Be quick, will you!'

While the schoolmaster was uttering these and other impatient cries, Nicholas had time to observe that the school was a long, cold-looking house, one storey high, with a few straggling out-buildings behind, and a barn and stable adjoining. After the lapse of a minute or two, the noise of somebody unlocking the yard-gate was heard, and presently a tall lean boy, with a lantern in his hand, issued forth.

'Is that you, Smike?' cried Squeers.

'Yes, sir,' replied the boy.

'Then why the devil didn't you come before?'

'Please, sir, I fell asleep over the fire,' answered Smike, with humility.

'Fire! what fire? Where's there a fire?' demanded the schoolmaster, sharply.

'Only in the kitchen, sir,' replied the boy. 'Missus said as I was sitting up, I might go in there for a warm.'

'Your missus is a fool,' retorted Squeers. 'You'd have been a deuced deal more wakeful in the cold, I'll engage.'

By this time Mr. Squeers had dismounted; and after ordering the boy to see to the pony, and to take care that he hadn't any more corn that night, he told Nicholas to wait at the front-door a minute while he went round and let him in.

A host of unpleasant misgivings, which had been crowding upon Nicholas during the whole journey, thronged into his mind with redoubled force when he was left alone. His great distance from home and the impossibility of reaching it, except on foot, should he feel ever so anxious to return, presented itself to him in most alarming colours; and as he looked up at the dreary house and dark windows, and upon the wild country round, covered with snow, he felt a depression of heart and spirit which he had never experienced before.

'Now then!' cried Squeers, poking his head out at the front-door. 'Where are you, Nickleby?'

'Here, sir,' replied Nicholas.

'Come in, then,' said Squeers 'the wind blows in, at this door, fit to knock a man off his legs.'

Nicholas sighed, and hurried in. Mr. Squeers, having bolted the door to keep it shut, ushered him into a small parlour scantily furnished with a few chairs, a yellow map hung against the wall, and a couple of tables; one of which bore some preparations for supper; while, on the other, a tutor's assistant, a Murray's grammar, half-a-dozen cards of terms, and a worn letter directed to Wackford Squeers, Esquire, were arranged in picturesque confusion.

They had not been in this apartment a couple of minutes, when a female bounced into the room, and, seizing Mr. Squeers by the throat, gave him two loud kisses: one close after the other, like a postman's knock. The lady, who was of a large raw-boned figure, was about half a head taller than Mr Squeers, and was dressed in a dimity night-jacket; with her hair in papers; she had also a dirty nightcap on, relieved by a yellow cotton handkerchief which tied it under the chin.

'How is my Squeery?' said this lady in a playful manner, and a very hoarse voice.

'Quite well, my love,' replied Squeers. 'How's the cows?'

'All right, every one of 'em,' answered the lady.

'And the pigs?' said Squeers.

'As well as they were when you went away.'

'Come; that's a blessing,' said Squeers, pulling off his great-coat. 'The boys are all as they were, I suppose?'

'Oh, yes, they're well enough,' replied Mrs. Squeers, snappishly. 'That young Pitcher's had a fever.'

'No!' exclaimed Squeers. 'Damn that boy, he's always at something of that sort.'

'Never was such a boy, I do believe,' said Mrs. Squeers; 'whatever he has is always catching too. I say it's obstinacy, and nothing shall ever convince me that it isn't. I'd beat it out of him; and I told you that, six months ago.'

'So you did, my love,' rejoined Squeers. 'We'll try what can be done.'

Pending these little endearments, Nicholas had stood, awkwardly enough, in the middle of the room: not very well knowing whether he was expected to retire into the passage, or to remain where he was. He was now relieved from his perplexity by Mr. Squeers.

'This is the new young man, my dear,' said that gentleman.

'Oh,' replied Mrs. Squeers, nodding her head at Nicholas, and eyeing him coldly from top to toe.

'He'll take a meal with us tonight,' said Squeers, 'and go among the boys tomorrow morning. You can give him a shake-down here, tonight, can't you?'

'We must manage it somehow,' replied the lady. 'You don't much mind how you sleep, I suppose, sir?'

No, indeed,' replied Nicholas, 'I am not particular.'

'That's lucky,' said Mrs. Squeers. And as the lady's humour was considered to lie chiefly in retort, Mr. Squeers laughed heartily, and seemed to expect that Nicholas should do the same.

After some further conversation between the master and mistress relative to the success of Mr. Squeers's trip and the people who had paid, and the people who had made default in payment, a young servant girl brought in a Yorkshire pie and some cold beef, which being set upon the table, the boy Smike appeared with a jug of ale.

Mr. Squeers was emptying his great-coat pockets of letters to different boys, and other small documents, which he had brought down in them. The boy glanced, with an anxious and timid expression, at the papers, as if with a sickly hope that one among them might relate to him. The look was a very painful one, and went to Nicholas's heart at once; for it told a long and very sad history.

It induced him to consider the boy more attentively, and he was surprised to observe the extraordinary mixture of garments which formed his dress. Although he could not have been less than eighteen or nineteen years old, and was tall for that age, he wore a skeleton suit, such as is usually put upon very little boys, and which, though most absurdly short in the arms and legs, was quite wide enough for his attenuated frame. In order that the lower part of his legs might be in perfect keeping with this singular dress, he had a very large pair of boots, originally made for tops, which might have been once worn by some stout farmer, but were now too patched and tattered for a beggar. Heaven knows how long he had been there, but he still wore the same linen which he had first taken down; for, round his neck, was a tattered child's frill, only half concealed by a coarse, man's neckerchief. He was lame; and as he feigned to be busy in arranging the table, glanced at the letters with a look so keen, and yet so dispirited and hopeless, that Nicholas could hardly bear to watch him.

'What are you bothering about there, Smike?' cried Mrs. Squeers; 'let the things alone, can't you?'

'Eh!' said Squeers, looking up. 'Oh! it's you, is it?'

'Yes, sir,' replied the youth, pressing his hands together, as though to control, by force, the nervous wandering of his fingers. 'Is there—'

'Well!' said Squeers.

'Have you—did anybody—has nothing been heard—about me?'

'Devil a bit,' replied Squeers testily.

The lad withdrew his eyes, and, putting his hand to his face, moved towards the door.

'Not a word,' resumed Squeers, 'and never will be. Now, this is a pretty sort of thing, isn't it, that you should have been left here, all these years, and no money paid after the first six— nor no notice taken, nor no clue to be got who you belong to? It's a pretty sort of thing that I should have to feed a great fellow like you, and never hope to get one penny for it, isn't it?'

The boy put his hand to his head as if he were making an effort to recollect something, and then, looking vacantly at his questioner, gradually broke into a smile, and limped away.

'I'll tell you what, Squeers,' remarked his wife as the door closed, 'I think that young chap's turning silly.'

'I hope not,' said the schoolmaster; 'for he's a handy fellow out of doors, and worth his meat and drink, anyway. I should think he'd have wit enough for us though, if he was. But come; let's have supper, for I am hungry and tired, and want to get to bed.'

This reminder brought in an exclusive steak for Mr. Squeers, who speedily proceeded to do it ample justice. Nicholas drew up his chair, but his appetite was effectually taken away.

'How's the steak, Squeers?' said Mrs. S.

'Tender as a lamb,' replied Squeers. 'Have a bit.'

'I couldn't eat a morsel,' replied his wife. 'What'll the young man take, my dear?'

'Whatever he likes that's present,' rejoined Squeers, in a most unusual burst of generosity.

'What do you say, Mr. Knuckleboy?' inquired Mrs. Squeers.

'I'll take a little of the pie, if you please,' replied Nicholas. 'A very little, for I'm not hungry.'

Well, it's a pity to cut the pie if you're not hungry, isn't it?' said Mrs Squeers. 'Will you try a bit of the beef?'

'Whatever you please,' replied Nicholas abstractedly; 'it's all the same to me.'

Mrs. Squeers looked vastly gracious on receiving this reply; and nodding to Squeers, as much as to say that she was glad to find the young man knew his station, assisted Nicholas to a slice of meat with her own fair hands.

'Ale, Squeery?' inquired the lady, winking and frowning to give him to understand that the question propounded, was, whether Nicholas should have ale, and not whether he (Squeers) would take any.

'Certainly,' said Squeers, re-telegraphing in the same manner. 'A glassful.'

So Nicholas had a glassful, and being occupied with his own reflections, drank it, in happy innocence of all the foregone proceedings.

'Uncommon juicy steak that,' said Squeers, as he laid down his knife and fork, after plying it, in silence, for some time.

'It's prime meat,' rejoined his lady. 'I bought a good large piece of it myself on purpose for—'

'For what!' exclaimed Squeers hastily. 'Not for the—'

'No, no; not for them,' rejoined Mrs. Squeers; 'on purpose for you against you came home. Lor! you didn't think I could have made such a mistake as that.'

'Upon my word, my dear, I didn't know what you were going to say,' said Squeers, who had turned pale.

'You needn't make yourself uncomfortable,' remarked his wife, laughing heartily. 'To think that I should be such a noddy! Well!'

This part of the conversation was rather unintelligible; but popular rumour in the neighbourhood asserted that Mr. Squeers, being amiably opposed to cruelty to animals, not unfrequently purchased for boy consumption the bodies of horned cattle who had died a natural death; possibly he was apprehensive of having unintentionally devoured some choice morsel intended for the young gentlemen.

Supper being over, and removed by a small servant girl with a hungry eye, Mrs. Squeers retired to lock it up, and also to take into safe custody the clothes of the five boys who had just arrived, and who were half-way up the troublesome flight of steps which leads to death's door, in consequence of exposure to the cold. They were then regaled with a light supper of porridge, and stowed away, side by side, in a small bedstead, to warm each other, and dream of a substantial meal with something hot after it, if their fancies set that way: which it is not at all improbable they did.

Mr. Squeers treated himself to a stiff tumbler of brandy and water, made on the liberal half-and-half principle, allowing for the dissolution of the sugar; and his amiable helpmate mixed Nicholas the ghost of a small glassful of the same compound. This done, Mr. and Mrs. Squeers drew close up to the fire, and sitting with their feet on the fender, talked confidentially in whispers; while Nicholas, taking up the tutor's assistant, read the interesting legends in the miscellaneous questions, and all the figures into the bargain, with as much thought or consciousness of what he was doing, as if he had been in a magnetic slumber.

At length, Mr. Squeers yawned fearfully, and opined that it was high time to go to bed; upon which signal, Mrs. Squeers and the girl dragged in a small straw mattress and a couple of blankets, and arranged them into a couch for Nicholas.

'We'll put you into your regular bedroom tomorrow, Nickelby,' said Squeers. 'Let me see! Who sleeps in Brooks's bed, my dear?'

'In Brooks's,' said Mrs. Squeers, pondering. 'There's Jennings, little Bolder, Graymarsh, and what's his name.'

'So there is,' rejoined Squeers. 'Yes! Brooks is full.'

'Full!' thought Nicholas. 'I should think he was.'

'There's a place somewhere, I know,' said Squeers; 'but I can't at this moment call to mind where it is. However, we'll have that all settled tomorrow. Good-night, Nickleby. Seven o'clock in the morning, mind.'

'I shall be ready, sir,' replied Nicholas. 'Good-night.'

'I'll come in myself and show you where the well is,' said Squeers. 'You'll always find a little bit of soap in the kitchen window; that belongs to you.'

Nicholas opened his eyes, but not his mouth; and Squeers was again going away, when he once more turned back.

'I don't know, I am sure,' he said, 'whose towel to put you on; but if you'll make shift with something tomorrow morning, Mrs. Squeers will arrange that, in the course of the day. My dear, don't forget.'

'I'll take care,' replied Mrs. Squeers; 'and mind you take care, young man, and get first wash. The teacher ought always to have it; but they get the better of him if they can.'

Mr. Squeers then nudged Mrs. Squeers to bring away the brandy bottle, lest Nicholas should help himself in the night; and the lady having seized it with great precipitation, they retired together.

Nicholas, being left alone, took half-a-dozen turns up and down the room in a condition of much agitation and excitement; but, growing gradually calmer, sat himself down in a chair, and mentally resolved that, come what come might, he would endeavour, for a time, to bear whatever wretchedness might be in store for him, and that remembering the helplessness of his mother and sister, he would give his uncle no plea for deserting them in their need. Good resolutions seldom fail of producing some good effect in the mind from which they spring. He grew less desponding, and—so sanguine and buoyant is youth—even hoped that affairs at Dotheboys Hall might yet prove better than they promised.

He was preparing for bed, with something like renewed cheerfulness, when a sealed letter fell from his coat pocket. In the hurry of leaving London, it had escaped his attention, and had not occurred to him since, but it at once brought back to him the recollection of the mysterious behaviour of Newman Noggs.

'Dear me!' said Nicholas; 'what an extraordinary hand!'

It was directed to himself, was written upon very dirty paper, and in such cramped and crippled writing as to be almost illegible. After great difficulty and much puzzling, he contrived to read as follows:—

My dear young Man.

I know the world. Your father did not, or he would not have done me a kindness when there was no hope of return. You do not, or you would not be bound on such a journey.

If ever you want a shelter in London (don't be angry at this, I once thought I never should), they know where I live, at the sign of the Crown, in Silver Street, Golden Square. It is at the corner of Silver Street and James Street, with a bar door both ways. You can come at night. Once, nobody was ashamed—never mind that. It's all over.

Excuse errors. I should forget how to wear a whole coat now. I have forgotten all my old ways. My spelling may have gone with them.

NEWMAN NOGGS.

P.S. If you should go near Barnard Castle, there is good ale at the King's Head. Say you know me, and I am sure they will not charge you for it. You may say Mr. Noggs there, for I was a gentleman then. I was indeed.

It may be a very undignified circumstances to record, but after he had folded this letter and placed it in his pocket-book, Nicholas Nickleby's eyes were dimmed with a moisture that might have been taken for tears.

CHAPTER 8
Of the Internal Economy of Dotheboys Hall

A ride of two hundred and odd miles in severe weather, is one of the best softeners of a hard bed that ingenuity can devise. Perhaps it is even a sweetener of dreams, for those which hovered over the rough couch of Nicholas, and whispered their airy nothings in his ear, were of an agreeable and happy kind. He was making his fortune very fast indeed, when the faint glimmer of an expiring candle shone before his eyes, and a voice he had no difficulty in recognising as part and parcel of Mr. Squeers, admonished him that it was time to rise.

'Past seven, Nickleby,' said Mr. Squeers.

'Has morning come already?' asked Nicholas, sitting up in bed.

'Ah! that has it,' replied Squeers, 'and ready iced too. Now, Nickleby, come; tumble up, will you?'

Nicholas needed no further admonition, but 'tumbled up' at once, and proceeded to dress himself by the light of the taper, which Mr. Squeers carried in his hand.

'Here's a pretty go,' said that gentleman; 'the pump's froze.'

'Indeed!' said Nicholas, not much interested in the intelligence.

'Yes,' replied Squeers. 'You can't wash yourself this morning.'

'Not wash myself!' exclaimed Nicholas.

'No, not a bit of it,' rejoined Squeers tartly. 'So you must be content with giving yourself a dry polish till we break the ice in the well, and can get a bucketful out for the boys. Don't stand staring at me, but do look sharp, will you?'

Offering no further observation, Nicholas huddled on his clothes. Squeers, meanwhile, opened the shutters and blew the candle out; when the voice of his amiable consort was heard in the passage, demanding admittance.

'Come in, my love,' said Squeers.

Mrs. Squeers came in, still habited in the primitive night-jacket which had displayed the symmetry of her figure on the previous night, and further ornamented with a beaver bonnet of some antiquity, which she wore, with much ease and lightness, on the top of the nightcap before mentioned.

'Drat the things,' said the lady, opening the cupboard; 'I can't find the school spoon anywhere.'

'Never mind it, my dear,' observed Squeers in a soothing manner; 'it's of no consequence.'

'No consequence, why how you talk!' retorted Mrs. Squeers sharply; 'isn't it brimstone morning?'

'I forgot, my dear,' rejoined Squeers; 'yes, it certainly is. We purify the boys' bloods now and then, Nickleby.'

'Purify fiddlesticks' ends,' said his lady. 'Don't think, young man, that we go to the expense of flower of brimstone and molasses, just to purify them; because if you think we carry on the business in that way, you'll find yourself mistaken, and so I tell you plainly.'

'My dear,' said Squeers frowning. 'Hem!'

'Oh! nonsense,' rejoined Mrs. Squeers. 'If the young man comes to be a teacher here, let him understand, at once, that we don't want any foolery about the boys. They have the brimstone and treacle, partly because if they hadn't something or other in the way of medicine they'd be always ailing and giving a world of trouble, and partly because it spoils their appetites and comes cheaper than breakfast and dinner. So, it does them good and us good at the same time, and that's fair enough I'm sure.'

Having given this explanation, Mrs. Squeers put her head into the closet and instituted a stricter search after the spoon, in which Mr. Squeers assisted. A few words passed between them while they were thus engaged, but as their voices were partially stifled by the cupboard, all that Nicholas could distinguish was, that Mr. Squeers said what Mrs. Squeers had said, was injudicious, and that Mrs. Squeers said what Mr. Squeers said, was 'stuff.'

A vast deal of searching and rummaging ensued, and it proving fruitless, Smike was called in, and pushed by Mrs. Squeers, and boxed by Mr. Squeers; which course of treatment brightening his intellects, enabled him to suggest that possibly Mrs. Squeers might have the spoon in her pocket, as indeed turned out to be the case. As Mrs. Squeers had previously protested, however, that she was quite certain she had not got it, Smike received another box on the ear for presuming to contradict his mistress, together with a promise of a sound thrashing if he were not more respectful in future; so that he took nothing very advantageous by his motion.

'A most invaluable woman, that, Nickleby,' said Squeers when his consort had hurried away, pushing the drudge before her.

'Indeed, sir!' observed Nicholas.

'I don't know her equal,' said Squeers; 'I do not know her equal. That woman, Nickleby, is always the same—always the same bustling, lively, active, saving creetur that you see her now.'

Nicholas sighed involuntarily at the thought of the agreeable domestic prospect thus opened to him; but Squeers was, fortunately, too much occupied with his own reflections to perceive it.

'It's my way to say, when I am up in London,' continued Squeers, 'that to them boys she is a mother. But she is more than a mother to them; ten times more. She does things for them boys, Nickleby, that I don't believe half the mothers going, would do for their own sons.'

'I should think they would not, sir,' answered Nicholas.

Now, the fact was, that both Mr. and Mrs. Squeers viewed the boys in the light of their proper and natural enemies; or, in other words, they held and considered that their business and profession was to get as much from every boy as could by possibility be screwed out of him. On this point they were both agreed, and behaved in unison accordingly. The only difference between them was, that Mrs. Squeers waged war against the enemy openly and fearlessly, and that Squeers covered his rascality, even at home, with a spice of his habitual deceit; as if he really had a notion of someday or other being able to take himself in, and persuade his own mind that he was a very good fellow.

'But come,' said Squeers, interrupting the progress of some thoughts to this effect in the mind of his usher, 'let's go to the schoolroom; and lend me a hand with my school-coat, will you?'

Nicholas assisted his master to put on an old fustian shooting-jacket, which he took down from a peg in the passage; and Squeers, arming himself with his cane, led the way across a yard, to a door in the rear of the house.

'There,' said the schoolmaster as they stepped in together; 'this is our shop, Nickleby!'

It was such a crowded scene, and there were so many objects to attract attention, that, at first, Nicholas stared about him, really without seeing anything at all. By degrees, however, the place resolved itself into a bare and dirty room, with a couple of windows, whereof a tenth part might be of glass, the remainder being stopped up with old copy-books and paper. There were a couple of long old rickety desks, cut and notched, and inked, and damaged, in every possible way; two or three forms; a detached desk for Squeers; and another for his assistant.

The ceiling was supported, like that of a barn, by cross-beams and rafters; and the walls were so stained and discoloured, that it was impossible to tell whether they had ever been touched with paint or whitewash.

But the pupils—the young noblemen! How the last faint traces of hope, the remotest glimmering of any good to be derived from his efforts in this den, faded from the mind of Nicholas as he looked in dismay around! Pale and haggard faces, lank and bony figures, children with the countenances of old men, deformities with irons upon their limbs, boys of stunted growth, and others whose long meagre legs would hardly bear their stooping bodies, all crowded on the view together; there were the bleared eye, the hare-lip, the crooked foot, and every ugliness or distortion that told of unnatural aversion conceived by parents for their offspring, or of young lives which, from the earliest dawn of infancy, had been one horrible endurance of cruelty and neglect. There were little faces which should have been handsome, darkened with the scowl of sullen, dogged suffering; there was childhood with the light of its eye quenched, its beauty gone, and its helplessness alone remaining; there were vicious-faced boys, brooding, with leaden eyes, like malefactors in a jail; and there were young creatures on whom the sins of their frail parents had descended, weeping even for the mercenary nurses they had known, and lonesome even in their loneliness. With every kindly sympathy and affection blasted in its birth, with every young and healthy feeling flogged and starved down, with every revengeful passion that can fester in swollen hearts, eating its evil way to their core in silence, what an incipient Hell was breeding here!

And yet this scene, painful as it was, had its grotesque features, which, in a less interested observer than Nicholas, might have provoked a smile. Mrs. Squeers stood at one of the desks, presiding over an immense basin of brimstone and treacle, of which delicious compound she administered a large instalment to each boy in succession: using for the purpose a common wooden spoon, which might have been originally manufactured for some gigantic top, and which widened every young gentleman's mouth considerably: they being all obliged, under heavy corporal penalties, to take in the whole of the bowl at a gasp. In another corner, huddled together for companionship, were the little boys who had arrived on the preceding night, three of them in very large leather breeches, and two in old trousers, a something tighter fit than drawers are usually worn; at no great distance from these was seated the juvenile son and heir of Mr Squeers—a striking likeness of his father—kicking, with great vigour, under the hands of Smike, who was fitting upon him a pair of new boots that bore a most suspicious resemblance to those which the least of the little boys had worn on the journey down—as the little boy himself seemed to think, for he was regarding the appropriation with a look of most rueful amazement. Besides these, there was a long row of boys waiting, with countenances of no pleasant anticipation, to be treacled; and another file, who had just escaped from the infliction, making a variety of wry mouths indicative of anything but satisfaction. The whole were attired in such motley, ill-assorted, extraordinary garments, as would have been irresistibly ridiculous, but for the foul appearance of dirt, disorder, and disease, with which they were associated.

'Now,' said Squeers, giving the desk a great rap with his cane, which made half the little boys nearly jump out of their boots, 'is that physicking over?'

'Just over,' said Mrs. Squeers, choking the last boy in her hurry, and tapping the crown of his head with the wooden spoon to restore him. 'Here, you Smike; take away now. Look sharp!'

Smike shuffled out with the basin, and Mrs. Squeers having called up a little boy with a curly head, and wiped her hands upon it, hurried out after him into a species of wash-house, where there was a small fire and a large kettle, together with a number of little wooden bowls which were arranged upon a board.

Into these bowls, Mrs. Squeers, assisted by the hungry servant, poured a brown composition, which looked like diluted pincushions without the covers, and was called porridge. A minute wedge of brown bread was inserted in each bowl, and when they had eaten their porridge by means of the bread, the boys ate the bread itself, and had finished their breakfast; whereupon Mr. Squeers said, in a solemn voice, 'For what we have received, may the Lord make us truly thankful!'—and went away to his own.

Nicholas distended his stomach with a bowl of porridge, for much the same reason which induces some savages to swallow earth—lest they should be inconveniently hungry when there is nothing to eat. Having further disposed of a slice of bread and butter, allotted to him in virtue of his office, he sat himself down, to wait for school-time.

He could not but observe how silent and sad the boys all seemed to be. There was none of the noise and clamour of a schoolroom; none of its boisterous play, or hearty mirth. The children sat crouching and shivering together, and seemed to lack the spirit to move about. The only pupil who evinced the slightest tendency towards locomotion or playfulness was Master Squeers, and as his chief amusement was to tread upon the other boys' toes in his new boots, his flow of spirits was rather disagreeable than otherwise.

After some half-hour's delay, Mr. Squeers reappeared, and the boys took their places and their books, of which latter commodity the average might be about one to eight learners. A few minutes having elapsed, during which Mr. Squeers looked very profound, as if he had a perfect apprehension of what was inside all the books, and could say every word of their contents by heart if he only chose to take the trouble, that gentleman called up the first class.

Obedient to this summons there ranged themselves in front of the schoolmaster's desk, half-a-dozen scarecrows, out at knees and elbows, one of whom placed a torn and filthy book beneath his learned eye.

'This is the first class in English spelling and philosophy, Nickleby,' said Squeers, beckoning Nicholas to stand beside him. 'We'll get up a Latin one, and hand that over to you. Now, then, where's the first boy?'

'Please, sir, he's cleaning the back-parlour window,' said the temporary head of the philosophical class.

'So he is, to be sure,' rejoined Squeers. 'We go upon the practical mode of teaching, Nickleby; the regular education system. C-l-e-a-n, clean, verb active, to make bright, to scour. W-i-n, win, d-e-r, der, winder, a casement. When the boy knows this out of book, he goes and does it. It's just the same principle as the use of the globes. Where's the second boy?'

'Please, sir, he's weeding the garden,' replied a small voice.

'To be sure,' said Squeers, by no means disconcerted. 'So he is. B-o-t, bot, t-i-n, tin, bottin, n-e-y, ney, bottinney, noun substantive, a knowledge of plants. When he has learned that bottinney means a knowledge of plants, he goes and knows 'em. That's our system, Nickleby: what do you think of it?'

'It's very useful one, at any rate,' answered Nicholas.

'I believe you,' rejoined Squeers, not remarking the emphasis of his usher. 'Third boy, what's horse?'

'A beast, sir,' replied the boy.

'So it is,' said Squeers. 'Ain't it, Nickleby?'

'I believe there is no doubt of that, sir,' answered Nicholas.

'Of course there isn't,' said Squeers. 'A horse is a quadruped, and quadruped's Latin for beast, as everybody that's gone through the grammar knows, or else where's the use of having grammars at all?'

'Where, indeed!' said Nicholas abstractedly.

'As you're perfect in that,' resumed Squeers, turning to the boy, 'go and look after my horse, and rub him down well, or I'll rub you down. The rest of the class go and draw water up, till somebody tells you to leave off, for it's washing-day tomorrow, and they want the coppers filled.'

So saying, he dismissed the first class to their experiments in practical philosophy, and eyed Nicholas with a look, half cunning and half doubtful, as if he were not altogether certain what he might think of him by this time.

'That's the way we do it, Nickleby,' he said, after a pause.

Nicholas shrugged his shoulders in a manner that was scarcely perceptible, and said he saw it was.

'And a very good way it is, too,' said Squeers. 'Now, just take them fourteen little boys and hear them some reading, because, you know, you must begin to be useful. Idling about here won't do.'

Mr. Squeers said this, as if it had suddenly occurred to him, either that he must not say too much to his assistant, or that his assistant did not say enough to him in praise of the establishment. The children were arranged in a semicircle round the new master, and he was soon listening to their dull, drawling, hesitating recital of those stories of engrossing interest which are to be found in the more antiquated spelling-books.

In this exciting occupation, the morning lagged heavily on. At one o'clock, the boys, having previously had their appetites thoroughly taken away by stir-about and potatoes, sat down in the kitchen to some hard salt beef, of which Nicholas was graciously permitted to take his portion to his own solitary desk, to eat it there in peace. After this, there was another hour of crouching in the schoolroom and shivering with cold, and then school began again.

It was Mr. Squeer's custom to call the boys together, and make a sort of report, after every half-yearly visit to the metropolis, regarding the relations and friends he had seen, the news he had heard, the letters he had brought down, the bills which had been paid, the accounts which had been left unpaid, and so forth. This solemn proceeding always took place in the afternoon of the day succeeding his return; perhaps, because the boys acquired strength of mind from the suspense of the morning, or, possibly, because Mr. Squeers himself acquired greater sternness and inflexibility from certain warm potations in which he was wont to indulge after his early dinner. Be this as it may, the boys were recalled from house-window, garden, stable, and cow-yard, and the school were assembled in full conclave, when Mr. Squeers, with a small bundle of papers in his hand, and Mrs. S. following with a pair of canes, entered the room and proclaimed silence.

'Let any boy speak a word without leave,' said Mr. Squeers mildly, 'and I'll take the skin off his back.'

This special proclamation had the desired effect, and a deathlike silence immediately prevailed, in the midst of which Mr. Squeers went on to say:

'Boys, I've been to London, and have returned to my family and you, as strong and well as ever.'

According to half-yearly custom, the boys gave three feeble cheers at this refreshing intelligence. Such cheers! Sights of extra strength with the chill on.

'I have seen the parents of some boys,' continued Squeers, turning over his papers, 'and they're so glad to hear how their sons are getting on, that there's no prospect at all of their going away, which of course is a very pleasant thing to reflect upon, for all parties.'

Two or three hands went to two or three eyes when Squeers said this, but the greater part of the young gentlemen having no particular parents to speak of, were wholly uninterested in the thing one way or other.

'I have had disappointments to contend against,' said Squeers, looking very grim; 'Bolder's father was two pound ten short. Where is Bolder?'

'Here he is, please sir,' rejoined twenty officious voices. Boys are very like men to be sure.

'Come here, Bolder,' said Squeers.

An unhealthy-looking boy, with warts all over his hands, stepped from his place to the master's desk, and raised his eyes imploringly to Squeers's face; his own, quite white from the rapid beating of his heart.

'Bolder,' said Squeers, speaking very slowly, for he was considering, as the saying goes, where to have him. 'Bolder, if you father thinks that because—why, what's this, sir?'

As Squeers spoke, he caught up the boy's hand by the cuff of his jacket, and surveyed it with an edifying aspect of horror and disgust.

'What do you call this, sir?' demanded the schoolmaster, administering a cut with the cane to expedite the reply.

'I can't help it, indeed, sir,' rejoined the boy, crying. 'They will come; it's the dirty work I think, sir—at least I don't know what it is, sir, but it's not my fault.'

'Bolder,' said Squeers, tucking up his wristbands, and moistening the palm of his right hand to get a good grip of the cane, 'you're an incorrigible young scoundrel, and as the last thrashing did you no good, we must see what another will do towards beating it out of you.'

With this, and wholly disregarding a piteous cry for mercy, Mr. Squeers fell upon the boy and caned him soundly: not leaving off, indeed, until his arm was tired out.

'There,' said Squeers, when he had quite done; 'rub away as hard as you like, you won't rub that off in a hurry. Oh! you won't hold that noise, won't you? Put him out, Smike.'

The drudge knew better from long experience, than to hesitate about obeying, so he bundled the victim out by a side-door, and Mr. Squeers perched himself again on his own stool, supported by Mrs. Squeers, who occupied another at his side.

'Now let us see,' said Squeers. 'A letter for Cobbey. Stand up, Cobbey.'

Another boy stood up, and eyed the letter very hard while Squeers made a mental abstract of the same.

'Oh!' said Squeers: 'Cobbey's grandmother is dead, and his uncle John has took to drinking, which is all the news his sister sends, except eighteenpence, which will just pay for that broken square of glass. Mrs Squeers, my dear, will you take the money?'

The worthy lady pocketed the eighteenpence with a most business-like air, and Squeers passed on to the next boy, as coolly as possible.

'Graymarsh,' said Squeers, 'he's the next. Stand up, Graymarsh.'

Another boy stood up, and the schoolmaster looked over the letter as before.

'Graymarsh's maternal aunt,' said Squeers, when he had possessed himself of the contents, 'is very glad to hear he's so well and happy, and sends her respectful compliments to Mrs. Squeers, and thinks she must be an angel. She likewise thinks Mr. Squeers is too good for this world; but hopes he may long be spared to carry on the business. Would have sent the two pair of stockings as desired, but is short of money, so forwards a tract instead, and hopes Graymarsh will put his trust in Providence. Hopes, above all, that he will study in everything to please Mr. and Mrs Squeers, and look upon them as his only friends; and that he will love Master Squeers; and not object to sleeping five in a bed, which no Christian should. Ah!' said Squeers, folding it up, 'a delightful letter. Very affecting indeed.'

It was affecting in one sense, for Graymarsh's maternal aunt was strongly supposed, by her more intimate friends, to be no other than his maternal parent; Squeers, however, without alluding to this part of the story (which would have sounded immoral before boys), proceeded with the business by calling out 'Mobbs,' whereupon another boy rose, and Graymarsh resumed his seat.

'Mobbs's step-mother,' said Squeers, 'took to her bed on hearing that he wouldn't eat fat, and has been very ill ever since. She wishes to know, by an early post, where he expects to go to, if he quarrels with his vittles; and with what feelings he could turn up his nose at the cow's-liver broth, after his good master had asked a blessing on it. This was told her in the London newspapers—not by Mr. Squeers, for he is too kind and too good to set anybody against anybody—and it has vexed her so much, Mobbs can't think. She is sorry to find he is discontented, which is sinful and horrid, and hopes Mr. Squeers will flog him into a happier state of mind; with which view, she has also stopped his halfpenny a week pocket-money, and given a double-bladed knife with a corkscrew in it to the Missionaries, which she had bought on purpose for him.'

'A sulky state of feeling,' said Squeers, after a terrible pause, during which he had moistened the palm of his right hand again, 'won't do. Cheerfulness and contentment must be kept up. Mobbs, come to me!'

Mobbs moved slowly towards the desk, rubbing his eyes in anticipation of good cause for doing so; and he soon afterwards retired by the side-door, with as good cause as a boy need have.

Mr. Squeers then proceeded to open a miscellaneous collection of letters; some enclosing money, which Mrs. Squeers 'took care of;' and others referring to small articles of apparel, as caps and so forth, all of which the same lady stated to be too large, or too small, and calculated for nobody but young Squeers, who would appear indeed to have had most accommodating limbs, since everything that came into the school fitted him to a nicety. His head, in particular, must have been singularly elastic, for hats and caps of all dimensions were alike to him.

This business dispatched, a few slovenly lessons were performed, and Squeers retired to his fireside, leaving Nicholas to take care of the boys in the school-room, which was very cold, and where a meal of bread and cheese was served out shortly after dark.

There was a small stove at that corner of the room which was nearest to the master's desk, and by it Nicholas sat down, so depressed and self-degraded by the consciousness of his position, that if death could have come upon him at that time, he would have been almost happy to meet it. The cruelty of which he had been an unwilling witness, the coarse and ruffianly behaviour of Squeers even in his best moods, the filthy place, the sights and sounds about him, all contributed to this state of feeling; but when he recollected that, being there as an assistant, he actually seemed—no matter what unhappy train of circumstances had brought him to that pass—to be the aider and abettor of a system which filled him with honest disgust and indignation, he loathed himself, and felt, for the moment, as though the mere consciousness of his present situation must, through all time to come, prevent his raising his head again.

But, for the present, his resolve was taken, and the resolution he had formed on the preceding night remained undisturbed. He had written to his mother and sister, announcing the safe conclusion of his journey, and saying as little about Dotheboys Hall, and saying that little as cheerfully, as he possibly could. He hoped that by remaining where he was, he might do some good, even there; at all events, others depended too much on his uncle's favour, to admit of his awakening his wrath just then.

One reflection disturbed him far more than any selfish considerations arising out of his own position. This was the probable destination of his sister Kate. His uncle had deceived him, and might he not consign her to some miserable place where her youth and beauty would prove a far greater curse than ugliness and decrepitude? To a caged man, bound hand and foot, this was a terrible idea—but no, he thought, his mother was by; there was the portrait-painter, too—simple enough, but still living in the world, and of it. He was willing to believe that Ralph Nickleby had conceived a personal dislike to himself. Having pretty good reason, by this time, to reciprocate it, he had no great difficulty in arriving at this conclusion, and tried to persuade himself that the feeling extended no farther than between them.

As he was absorbed in these meditations, he all at once encountered the upturned face of Smike, who was on his knees before the stove, picking a few stray cinders from the hearth and planting them on the fire. He had paused to steal a look at Nicholas, and when he saw that he was observed, shrunk back, as if expecting a blow.

'You need not fear me,' said Nicholas kindly. 'Are you cold?'

'N-n-o.'

'You are shivering.'

'I am not cold,' replied Smike quickly. 'I am used to it.'

There was such an obvious fear of giving offence in his manner, and he was such a timid, broken-spirited creature, that Nicholas could not help exclaiming, 'Poor fellow!'

If he had struck the drudge, he would have slunk away without a word. But, now, he burst into tears.

'Oh dear, oh dear!' he cried, covering his face with his cracked and horny hands. 'My heart will break. It will, it will.'

'Hush!' said Nicholas, laying his hand upon his shoulder. 'Be a man; you are nearly one by years, God help you.'

'By years!' cried Smike. 'Oh dear, dear, how many of them! How many of them since I was a little child, younger than any that are here now! Where are they all!'

'Whom do you speak of?' inquired Nicholas, wishing to rouse the poor half-witted creature to reason. 'Tell me.'

'My friends,' he replied, 'myself—my—oh! what sufferings mine have been!'

'There is always hope,' said Nicholas; he knew not what to say.

'No,' rejoined the other, 'no; none for me. Do you remember the boy that died here?'

'I was not here, you know,' said Nicholas gently; 'but what of him?'

'Why,' replied the youth, drawing closer to his questioner's side, 'I was with him at night, and when it was all silent he cried no more for friends he wished to come and sit with him, but began to see faces round his bed that came from home; he said they smiled, and talked to him; and he died at last lifting his head to kiss them. Do you hear?'

'Yes, yes,' rejoined Nicholas.

'What faces will smile on me when I die!' cried his companion, shivering. 'Who will talk to me in those long nights! They cannot come from home; they would frighten me, if they did, for I don't know what it is, and shouldn't know them. Pain and fear, pain and fear for me, alive or dead. No hope, no hope!'

The bell rang to bed: and the boy, subsiding at the sound into his usual listless state, crept away as if anxious to avoid notice. It was with a heavy heart that Nicholas soon afterwards— no, not retired; there was no retirement there—followed—to his dirty and crowded dormitory.

CHAPTER 9
Of Miss Squeers, Mrs. Squeers, Master Squeers, and Mr. Squeers; and of various Matters and Persons connected no less with the Squeerses than Nicholas Nickleby

When Mr. Squeers left the schoolroom for the night, he betook himself, as has been before remarked, to his own fireside, which was situated—not in the room in which Nicholas had supped on the night of his arrival, but in a smaller apartment in the rear of the premises, where his lady wife, his amiable son, and accomplished daughter, were in the full enjoyment of each other's society; Mrs. Squeers being engaged in the matronly pursuit of stocking-darning; and the young lady and gentleman being occupied in the adjustment of some youthful differences, by means of a pugilistic contest across the table, which, on the approach of their honoured parent, subsided into a noiseless exchange of kicks beneath it.

And, in this place, it may be as well to apprise the reader, that Miss Fanny Squeers was in her three-and-twentieth year. If there be any one grace or loveliness inseparable from that particular period of life, Miss Squeers may be presumed to have been possessed of it, as there is no reason to suppose that she was a solitary exception to an universal rule. She was not tall like her mother, but short like her father; from the former she inherited a voice of harsh quality; from the latter a remarkable expression of the right eye, something akin to having none at all.

Miss Squeers had been spending a few days with a neighbouring friend, and had only just returned to the parental roof. To this circumstance may be referred, her having heard nothing of Nicholas, until Mr. Squeers himself now made him the subject of conversation.

'Well, my dear,' said Squeers, drawing up his chair, 'what do you think of him by this time?'

'Think of who?' inquired Mrs. Squeers; who (as she often remarked) was no grammarian, thank Heaven.

'Of the young man—the new teacher—who else could I mean?'

'Oh! that Knuckleboy,' said Mrs. Squeers impatiently. 'I hate him.'

'What do you hate him for, my dear?' asked Squeers.

'What's that to you?' retorted Mrs. Squeers. 'If I hate him, that's enough, ain't it?'

'Quite enough for him, my dear, and a great deal too much I dare say, if he knew it,' replied Squeers in a pacific tone. 'I only ask from curiosity, my dear.'

'Well, then, if you want to know,' rejoined Mrs. Squeers, 'I'll tell you. Because he's a proud, haughty, consequential, turned-up-nosed peacock.'

Mrs. Squeers, when excited, was accustomed to use strong language, and, moreover, to make use of a plurality of epithets, some of which were of a figurative kind, as the word peacock, and furthermore the allusion to Nicholas's nose, which was not intended to be taken in its literal sense, but rather to bear a latitude of construction according to the fancy of the hearers.

Neither were they meant to bear reference to each other, so much as to the object on whom they were bestowed, as will be seen in the present case: a peacock with a turned-up nose being a novelty in ornithology, and a thing not commonly seen.

'Hem!' said Squeers, as if in mild deprecation of this outbreak. 'He is cheap, my dear; the young man is very cheap.'

'Not a bit of it,' retorted Mrs. Squeers.

'Five pound a year,' said Squeers.

'What of that; it's dear if you don't want him, isn't it?' replied his wife.

'But we do want him,' urged Squeers.

'I don't see that you want him any more than the dead,' said Mrs. Squeers. 'Don't tell me. You can put on the cards and in the advertisements, "Education by Mr. Wackford Squeers and able assistants," without having any assistants, can't you? Isn't it done every day by all the masters about? I've no patience with you.'

'Haven't you!' said Squeers, sternly. 'Now I'll tell you what, Mrs Squeers. In this matter of having a teacher, I'll take my own way, if you please. A slave driver in the West Indies is allowed a man under him, to see that his blacks don't run away, or get up a rebellion; and I'll have a man under me to do the same with our blacks, till such time as little Wackford is able to take charge of the school.'

'Am I to take care of the school when I grow up a man, father?' said Wackford junior, suspending, in the excess of his delight, a vicious kick which he was administering to his sister.

'You are, my son,' replied Mr. Squeers, in a sentimental voice.

'Oh my eye, won't I give it to the boys!' exclaimed the interesting child, grasping his father's cane. 'Oh, father, won't I make 'em squeak again!'

It was a proud moment in Mr. Squeers's life, when he witnessed that burst of enthusiasm in his young child's mind, and saw in it a foreshadowing of his future eminence. He pressed a penny into his hand, and gave vent to his feelings (as did his exemplary wife also), in a shout of approving laughter. The infantine appeal to their common sympathies, at once restored cheerfulness to the conversation, and harmony to the company.

'He's a nasty stuck-up monkey, that's what I consider him,' said Mrs Squeers, reverting to Nicholas.

'Supposing he is,' said Squeers, 'he is as well stuck up in our schoolroom as anywhere else, isn't he?—especially as he don't like it.'

'Well,' observed Mrs. Squeers, 'there's something in that. I hope it'll bring his pride down, and it shall be no fault of mine if it don't.'

Now, a proud usher in a Yorkshire school was such a very extraordinary and unaccountable thing to hear of,—any usher at all being a novelty; but a proud one, a being of whose existence the wildest imagination could never have dreamed—that Miss Squeers, who seldom troubled herself with scholastic matters, inquired with much curiosity who this Knuckleboy was, that gave himself such airs.

'Nickleby,' said Squeers, spelling the name according to some eccentric system which prevailed in his own mind; 'your mother always calls things and people by their wrong names.'

'No matter for that,' said Mrs. Squeers; 'I see them with right eyes, and that's quite enough for me. I watched him when you were laying on to little Bolder this afternoon. He looked as black as thunder, all the while, and, one time, started up as if he had more than got it in his mind to make a rush at you. I saw him, though he thought I didn't.'

'Never mind that, father,' said Miss Squeers, as the head of the family was about to reply. 'Who is the man?'

'Why, your father has got some nonsense in his head that he's the son of a poor gentleman that died the other day,' said Mrs. Squeers.

'The son of a gentleman!'

'Yes; but I don't believe a word of it. If he's a gentleman's son at all, he's a fondling, that's my opinion.'

'Mrs. Squeers intended to say 'foundling,' but, as she frequently remarked when she made any such mistake, it would be all the same a hundred years hence; with which axiom of philosophy, indeed, she was in the constant habit of consoling the boys when they laboured under more than ordinary ill-usage.

'He's nothing of the kind,' said Squeers, in answer to the above remark, 'for his father was married to his mother years before he was born, and she is alive now. If he was, it would be no business of ours, for we make a very good friend by having him here; and if he likes to learn the boys anything besides minding them, I have no objection I am sure.'

'I say again, I hate him worse than poison,' said Mrs. Squeers vehemently.

'If you dislike him, my dear,' returned Squeers, 'I don't know anybody who can show dislike better than you, and of course there's no occasion, with him, to take the trouble to hide it.'

'I don't intend to, I assure you,' interposed Mrs. S.

'That's right,' said Squeers; 'and if he has a touch of pride about him, as I think he has, I don't believe there's woman in all England that can bring anybody's spirit down, as quick as you can, my love.'

Mrs. Squeers chuckled vastly on the receipt of these flattering compliments, and said, she hoped she had tamed a high spirit or two in her day. It is but due to her character to say, that in conjunction with her estimable husband, she had broken many and many a one.

Miss Fanny Squeers carefully treasured up this, and much more conversation on the same subject, until she retired for the night, when she questioned the hungry servant, minutely, regarding the outward appearance and demeanour of Nicholas; to which queries the girl returned such enthusiastic replies, coupled with so many laudatory remarks touching his beautiful dark eyes, and his sweet smile, and his straight legs—upon which last-named articles she laid particular stress; the general run of legs at Dotheboys Hall being crooked— that Miss Squeers was not long in arriving at the conclusion that the new usher must be a very remarkable person, or, as she herself significantly phrased it, 'something quite out of the common.' And so Miss Squeers made up her mind that she would take a personal observation of Nicholas the very next day.

In pursuance of this design, the young lady watched the opportunity of her mother being engaged, and her father absent, and went accidentally into the schoolroom to get a pen mended: where, seeing nobody but Nicholas presiding over the boys, she blushed very deeply, and exhibited great confusion.

'I beg your pardon,' faltered Miss Squeers; 'I thought my father was—or might be—dear me, how very awkward!'

'Mr. Squeers is out,' said Nicholas, by no means overcome by the apparition, unexpected though it was.

'Do you know will he be long, sir?' asked Miss Squeers, with bashful hesitation.

'He said about an hour,' replied Nicholas—politely of course, but without any indication of being stricken to the heart by Miss Squeers's charms.

'I never knew anything happen so cross,' exclaimed the young lady. 'Thank you! I am very sorry I intruded, I am sure. If I hadn't thought my father was here, I wouldn't upon any account have—it is very provoking—must look so very strange,' murmured Miss Squeers, blushing once more, and glancing, from the pen in her hand, to Nicholas at his desk, and back again.

'If that is all you want,' said Nicholas, pointing to the pen, and smiling, in spite of himself, at the affected embarrassment of the schoolmaster's daughter, 'perhaps I can supply his place.'

Miss Squeers glanced at the door, as if dubious of the propriety of advancing any nearer to an utter stranger; then round the schoolroom, as though in some measure reassured by the presence of forty boys; and finally sidled up to Nicholas and delivered the pen into his hand, with a most winning mixture of reserve and condescension.

'Shall it be a hard or a soft nib?' inquired Nicholas, smiling to prevent himself from laughing outright.

'He has a beautiful smile,' thought Miss Squeers.

'Which did you say?' asked Nicholas.

'Dear me, I was thinking of something else for the moment, I declare,' replied Miss Squeers. 'Oh! as soft as possible, if you please.' With which words, Miss Squeers sighed. It might be, to give Nicholas to understand that her heart was soft, and that the pen was wanted to match.

Upon these instructions Nicholas made the pen; when he gave it to Miss Squeers, Miss Squeers dropped it; and when he stooped to pick it up, Miss Squeers stooped also, and they knocked their heads together; whereat five-and-twenty little boys laughed aloud: being positively for the first and only time that half-year.

'Very awkward of me,' said Nicholas, opening the door for the young lady's retreat.

'Not at all, sir,' replied Miss Squeers; 'it was my fault. It was all my foolish—a—a—good-morning!'

'Goodbye,' said Nicholas. 'The next I make for you, I hope will be made less clumsily. Take care! You are biting the nib off now.'

'Really,' said Miss Squeers; 'so embarrassing that I scarcely know what I—very sorry to give you so much trouble.'

'Not the least trouble in the world,' replied Nicholas, closing the schoolroom door.

'I never saw such legs in the whole course of my life!' said Miss Squeers, as she walked away.

In fact, Miss Squeers was in love with Nicholas Nickleby.

To account for the rapidity with which this young lady had conceived a passion for Nicholas, it may be necessary to state, that the friend from whom she had so recently returned, was a miller's daughter of only eighteen, who had contracted herself unto the son of a small corn-factor, resident in the nearest market town. Miss Squeers and the miller's daughter, being fast friends, had covenanted together some two years before, according to a custom prevalent among young ladies, that whoever was first engaged to be married, should straightway confide the mighty secret to the bosom of the other, before communicating it to any living soul, and bespeak her as bridesmaid without loss of time; in fulfilment of which pledge the miller's daughter, when her engagement was formed, came out express, at eleven o'clock at night as the corn-factor's son made an offer of his hand and heart at twenty-five minutes past ten by the Dutch clock in the kitchen, and rushed into Miss Squeers's bedroom with the gratifying intelligence. Now, Miss Squeers being five years older, and out of her teens (which is also a great matter), had, since, been more than commonly anxious to return the compliment, and possess her friend with a similar secret; but, either in consequence of finding it hard to please herself, or harder still to please anybody else, had never had an opportunity so to do, inasmuch as she had no such secret to disclose. The little interview with Nicholas had no sooner passed, as above described, however, than Miss Squeers, putting on her bonnet, made her way, with great precipitation, to her friend's house, and, upon a solemn renewal of divers old vows of secrecy, revealed how that she was—not exactly engaged, but going to be—to a gentleman's son—(none of your corn-factors, but a gentleman's son of high descent)—who had come down as teacher to Dotheboys Hall, under most mysterious and remarkable circumstances—indeed, as Miss Squeers more than once hinted she had good reason to believe, induced, by the fame of her many charms, to seek her out, and woo and win her.

'Isn't it an extraordinary thing?' said Miss Squeers, emphasising the adjective strongly.

'Most extraordinary,' replied the friend. 'But what has he said to you?'

'Don't ask me what he said, my dear,' rejoined Miss Squeers. 'If you had only seen his looks and smiles! I never was so overcome in all my life.'

'Did he look in this way?' inquired the miller's daughter, counterfeiting, as nearly as she could, a favourite leer of the corn-factor.

'Very like that—only more genteel,' replied Miss Squeers.

'Ah!' said the friend, 'then he means something, depend on it.'

Miss Squeers, having slight misgivings on the subject, was by no means ill pleased to be confirmed by a competent authority; and discovering, on further conversation and comparison of notes, a great many points of resemblance between the behaviour of Nicholas, and that of the corn-factor, grew so exceedingly confidential, that she intrusted her friend with a vast number of things Nicholas had not said, which were all so very complimentary as to be quite conclusive. Then, she dilated on the fearful hardship of having a father and mother strenuously opposed to her intended husband; on which unhappy circumstance she dwelt at great length; for the friend's father and mother were quite agreeable to her being married, and the whole courtship was in consequence as flat and common-place an affair as it was possible to imagine.

'How I should like to see him!' exclaimed the friend.

'So you shall, 'Tilda,' replied Miss Squeers. 'I should consider myself one of the most ungrateful creatures alive, if I denied you. I think mother's going away for two days to fetch some boys; and when she does, I'll ask you and John up to tea, and have him to meet you.'

This was a charming idea, and having fully discussed it, the friends parted.

It so fell out, that Mrs. Squeers's journey, to some distance, to fetch three new boys, and dun the relations of two old ones for the balance of a small account, was fixed that very afternoon, for the next day but one; and on the next day but one, Mrs. Squeers got up outside the coach, as it stopped to change at Greta Bridge, taking with her a small bundle containing something in a bottle, and some sandwiches, and carrying besides a large white top-coat to wear in the night-time; with which baggage she went her way.

Whenever such opportunities as these occurred, it was Squeers's custom to drive over to the market town, every evening, on pretence of urgent business, and stop till ten or eleven o'clock at a tavern he much affected. As the party was not in his way, therefore, but rather afforded a means of compromise with Miss Squeers, he readily yielded his full assent thereunto, and willingly communicated to Nicholas that he was expected to take his tea in the parlour that evening, at five o'clock.

To be sure Miss Squeers was in a desperate flutter as the time approached, and to be sure she was dressed out to the best advantage: with her hair—it had more than a tinge of red, and she wore it in a crop—curled in five distinct rows, up to the very top of her head, and arranged dexterously over the doubtful eye; to say nothing of the blue sash which floated down her back, or the worked apron or the long gloves, or the green gauze scarf worn over one shoulder and under the other; or any of the numerous devices which were to be as so many arrows to the heart of Nicholas. She had scarcely completed these arrangements to her entire satisfaction, when the friend arrived with a whity-brown parcel—flat and three-cornered—containing sundry small adornments which were to be put on upstairs, and which the friend put on, talking incessantly. When Miss Squeers had 'done' the friend's hair, the friend 'did' Miss Squeers's hair, throwing in some striking improvements in the way of ringlets down the neck; and then, when they were both touched up to their entire satisfaction, they went downstairs in full state with the long gloves on, all ready for company.

'Where's John, 'Tilda?' said Miss Squeers.

'Only gone home to clean himself,' replied the friend. 'He will be here by the time the tea's drawn.'

'I do so palpitate,' observed Miss Squeers.

'Ah! I know what it is,' replied the friend.

'I have not been used to it, you know, 'Tilda,' said Miss Squeers, applying her hand to the left side of her sash.

'You'll soon get the better of it, dear,' rejoined the friend. While they were talking thus, the hungry servant brought in the tea-things, and, soon afterwards, somebody tapped at the room door.

'There he is!' cried Miss Squeers. 'Oh 'Tilda!'

'Hush!' said 'Tilda. 'Hem! Say, come in.'

'Come in,' cried Miss Squeers faintly. And in walked Nicholas.

'Good-evening,' said that young gentleman, all unconscious of his conquest. 'I understood from Mr. Squeers that—'

'Oh yes; it's all right,' interposed Miss Squeers. 'Father don't tea with us, but you won't mind that, I dare say.' (This was said archly.)

Nicholas opened his eyes at this, but he turned the matter off very coolly—not caring, particularly, about anything just then—and went through the ceremony of introduction to the miller's daughter with so much grace, that that young lady was lost in admiration.

'We are only waiting for one more gentleman,' said Miss Squeers, taking off the teapot lid, and looking in, to see how the tea was getting on.

It was matter of equal moment to Nicholas whether they were waiting for one gentleman or twenty, so he received the intelligence with perfect unconcern; and, being out of spirits, and not seeing any especial reason why he should make himself agreeable, looked out of the window and sighed involuntarily.

As luck would have it, Miss Squeers's friend was of a playful turn, and hearing Nicholas sigh, she took it into her head to rally the lovers on their lowness of spirits.

'But if it's caused by my being here,' said the young lady, 'don't mind me a bit, for I'm quite as bad. You may go on just as you would if you were alone.'

''Tilda,' said Miss Squeers, colouring up to the top row of curls, 'I am ashamed of you;' and here the two friends burst into a variety of giggles, and glanced from time to time, over the tops of their pocket-handkerchiefs, at Nicholas, who from a state of unmixed astonishment, gradually fell into one of irrepressible laughter—occasioned, partly by the bare notion of his being in love with Miss Squeers, and partly by the preposterous appearance and behaviour of the two girls. These two causes of merriment, taken together, struck him as being so keenly ridiculous, that, despite his miserable condition, he laughed till he was thoroughly exhausted.

'Well,' thought Nicholas, 'as I am here, and seem expected, for some reason or other, to be amiable, it's of no use looking like a goose. I may as well accommodate myself to the company.'

We blush to tell it; but his youthful spirits and vivacity getting, for the time, the better of his sad thoughts, he no sooner formed this resolution than he saluted Miss Squeers and the friend with great gallantry, and drawing a chair to the tea-table, began to make himself more at home than in all probability an usher has ever done in his employer's house since ushers were first invented.

The ladies were in the full delight of this altered behaviour on the part of Mr. Nickleby, when the expected swain arrived, with his hair very damp from recent washing, and a clean shirt, whereof the collar might have belonged to some giant ancestor, forming, together with a white waistcoat of similar dimensions, the chief ornament of his person.

'Well, John,' said Miss Matilda Price (which, by-the-bye, was the name of the miller's daughter).

'Weel,' said John with a grin that even the collar could not conceal.

'I beg your pardon,' interposed Miss Squeers, hastening to do the honours. 'Mr. Nickleby—Mr. John Browdie.'

'Servant, sir,' said John, who was something over six feet high, with a face and body rather above the due proportion than below it.

'Yours to command, sir,' replied Nicholas, making fearful ravages on the bread and butter.

Mr. Browdie was not a gentleman of great conversational powers, so he grinned twice more, and having now bestowed his customary mark of recognition on every person in company, grinned at nothing in particular, and helped himself to food.

'Old wooman awa', bean't she?' said Mr. Browdie, with his mouth full.

Miss Squeers nodded assent.

Mr. Browdie gave a grin of special width, as if he thought that really was something to laugh at, and went to work at the bread and butter with increased vigour. It was quite a sight to behold how he and Nicholas emptied the plate between them.

'Ye wean't get bread and butther ev'ry neight, I expect, mun,' said Mr Browdie, after he had sat staring at Nicholas a long time over the empty plate.

Nicholas bit his lip, and coloured, but affected not to hear the remark.

'Ecod,' said Mr. Browdie, laughing boisterously, 'they dean't put too much intiv'em. Ye'll be nowt but skeen and boans if you stop here long eneaf. Ho! ho! ho!'

'You are facetious, sir,' said Nicholas, scornfully.

'Na; I dean't know,' replied Mr. Browdie, 'but t'oother teacher, 'cod he wur a learn 'un, he wur.' The recollection of the last teacher's leanness seemed to afford Mr. Browdie the most exquisite delight, for he laughed until he found it necessary to apply his coat-cuffs to his eyes.

'I don't know whether your perceptions are quite keen enough, Mr. Browdie, to enable you to understand that your remarks are offensive,' said Nicholas in a towering passion, 'but if they are, have the goodness to—'

'If you say another word, John,' shrieked Miss Price, stopping her admirer's mouth as he was about to interrupt, 'only half a word, I'll never forgive you, or speak to you again.'

'Weel, my lass, I dean't care aboot 'un,' said the corn-factor, bestowing a hearty kiss on Miss Matilda; 'let 'un gang on, let 'un gang on.'

It now became Miss Squeers's turn to intercede with Nicholas, which she did with many symptoms of alarm and horror; the effect of the double intercession was, that he and John Browdie shook hands across the table with much gravity; and such was the imposing nature of the ceremonial, that Miss Squeers was overcome and shed tears.

'What's the matter, Fanny?' said Miss Price.

'Nothing, 'Tilda,' replied Miss Squeers, sobbing.

'There never was any danger,' said Miss Price, 'was there, Mr. Nickleby?'

'None at all,' replied Nicholas. 'Absurd.'

'That's right,' whispered Miss Price, 'say something kind to her, and she'll soon come round. Here! Shall John and I go into the little kitchen, and come back presently?'

'Not on any account,' rejoined Nicholas, quite alarmed at the proposition. 'What on earth should you do that for?'

'Well,' said Miss Price, beckoning him aside, and speaking with some degree of contempt—'you are a one to keep company.'

'What do you mean?' said Nicholas; 'I am not a one to keep company at all—here at all events. I can't make this out.'

'No, nor I neither,' rejoined Miss Price; 'but men are always fickle, and always were, and always will be; that I can make out, very easily.'

'Fickle!' cried Nicholas; 'what do you suppose? You don't mean to say that you think—'

'Oh no, I think nothing at all,' retorted Miss Price, pettishly. 'Look at her, dressed so beautiful and looking so well—really almost handsome. I am ashamed at you.'

'My dear girl, what have I got to do with her dressing beautifully or looking well?' inquired Nicholas.

'Come, don't call me a dear girl,' said Miss Price—smiling a little though, for she was pretty, and a coquette too in her small way, and Nicholas was good-looking, and she supposed him the property of somebody else, which were all reasons why she should be gratified to think she had made an impression on him,—'or Fanny will be saying it's my fault. Come; we're going to have a game at cards.' Pronouncing these last words aloud, she tripped away and rejoined the big Yorkshireman.

This was wholly unintelligible to Nicholas, who had no other distinct impression on his mind at the moment, than that Miss Squeers was an ordinary-looking girl, and her friend Miss Price a pretty one; but he had not time to enlighten himself by reflection, for the hearth being by this time swept up, and the candle snuffed, they sat down to play speculation.

'There are only four of us, 'Tilda,' said Miss Squeers, looking slyly at Nicholas; 'so we had better go partners, two against two.'

'What do you say, Mr. Nickleby?' inquired Miss Price.

'With all the pleasure in life,' replied Nicholas. And so saying, quite unconscious of his heinous offence, he amalgamated into one common heap those portions of a Dotheboys Hall card of terms, which represented his own counters, and those allotted to Miss Price, respectively.

'Mr. Browdie,' said Miss Squeers hysterically, 'shall we make a bank against them?'

The Yorkshireman assented—apparently quite overwhelmed by the new usher's impudence—and Miss Squeers darted a spiteful look at her friend, and giggled convulsively.

The deal fell to Nicholas, and the hand prospered.

'We intend to win everything,' said he.

''Tilda has won something she didn't expect, I think, haven't you, dear?' said Miss Squeers, maliciously.

'Only a dozen and eight, love,' replied Miss Price, affecting to take the question in a literal sense.

'How dull you are tonight!' sneered Miss Squeers.

'No, indeed,' replied Miss Price, 'I am in excellent spirits. I was thinking you seemed out of sorts.'

'Me!' cried Miss Squeers, biting her lips, and trembling with very jealousy. 'Oh no!'

'That's well,' remarked Miss Price. 'Your hair's coming out of curl, dear.'

'Never mind me,' tittered Miss Squeers; 'you had better attend to your partner.'

'Thank you for reminding her,' said Nicholas. 'So she had.'

The Yorkshireman flattened his nose, once or twice, with his clenched fist, as if to keep his hand in, till he had an opportunity of exercising it upon the features of some other gentleman; and Miss Squeers tossed her head with such indignation, that the gust of wind raised by the multitudinous curls in motion, nearly blew the candle out.

'I never had such luck, really,' exclaimed coquettish Miss Price, after another hand or two. 'It's all along of you, Mr. Nickleby, I think. I should like to have you for a partner always.'

'I wish you had.'

'You'll have a bad wife, though, if you always win at cards,' said Miss Price.

'Not if your wish is gratified,' replied Nicholas. 'I am sure I shall have a good one in that case.'

To see how Miss Squeers tossed her head, and the corn-factor flattened his nose, while this conversation was carrying on! It would have been worth a small annuity to have beheld that; let alone Miss Price's evident joy at making them jealous, and Nicholas Nickleby's happy unconsciousness of making anybody uncomfortable.

'We have all the talking to ourselves, it seems,' said Nicholas, looking good-humouredly round the table as he took up the cards for a fresh deal.

'You do it so well,' tittered Miss Squeers, 'that it would be a pity to interrupt, wouldn't it, Mr. Browdie? He! he! he!'

'Nay,' said Nicholas, 'we do it in default of having anybody else to talk to.'

'We'll talk to you, you know, if you'll say anything,' said Miss Price.

'Thank you, 'Tilda, dear,' retorted Miss Squeers, majestically.

'Or you can talk to each other, if you don't choose to talk to us,' said Miss Price, rallying her dear friend. 'John, why don't you say something?'

'Say summat?' repeated the Yorkshireman.

'Ay, and not sit there so silent and glum.'

'Weel, then!' said the Yorkshireman, striking the table heavily with his fist, 'what I say's this—Dang my boans and boddy, if I stan' this ony longer. Do ye gang whoam wi' me, and do yon loight an' toight young whipster look sharp out for a brokken head, next time he cums under my hond.'

'Mercy on us, what's all this?' cried Miss Price, in affected astonishment.

'Cum whoam, tell 'e, cum whoam,' replied the Yorkshireman, sternly. And as he delivered the reply, Miss Squeers burst into a shower of tears; arising in part from desperate vexation, and in part from an impotent desire to lacerate somebody's countenance with her fair finger-nails.

This state of things had been brought about by divers means and workings. Miss Squeers had brought it about, by aspiring to the high state and condition of being matrimonially engaged, without good grounds for so doing; Miss Price had brought it about, by indulging in three motives of action: first, a desire to punish her friend for laying claim to a rivalship in dignity, having no good title: secondly, the gratification of her own vanity, in receiving the compliments of a smart young man: and thirdly, a wish to convince the corn-factor of the great danger he ran, in deferring the celebration of their expected nuptials; while Nicholas had brought it about, by half an hour's gaiety and thoughtlessness, and a very sincere desire to avoid the imputation of inclining at all to Miss Squeers. So the means employed, and the end produced, were alike the most natural in the world; for young ladies will look forward to being married, and will jostle each other in the race to the altar, and will avail themselves of all opportunities of displaying their own attractions to the best advantage, down to the very end of time, as they have done from its beginning.

'Why, and here's Fanny in tears now!' exclaimed Miss Price, as if in fresh amazement. 'What can be the matter?'

'Oh! you don't know, miss, of course you don't know. Pray don't trouble yourself to inquire,' said Miss Squeers, producing that change of countenance which children call making a face.

'Well, I'm sure!' exclaimed Miss Price.

'And who cares whether you are sure or not, ma'am?' retorted Miss Squeers, making another face.

'You are monstrous polite, ma'am,' said Miss Price.

'I shall not come to you to take lessons in the art, ma'am!' retorted Miss Squeers.

'You needn't take the trouble to make yourself plainer than you are, ma'am, however,' rejoined Miss Price, 'because that's quite unnecessary.'

Miss Squeers, in reply, turned very red, and thanked God that she hadn't got the bold faces of some people. Miss Price, in rejoinder, congratulated herself upon not being possessed of the envious feeling of other people; whereupon Miss Squeers made some general remark touching the danger of associating with low persons; in which Miss Price entirely coincided: observing that it was very true indeed, and she had thought so a long time.

''Tilda,' exclaimed Miss Squeers with dignity, 'I hate you.'

'Ah! There's no love lost between us, I assure you,' said Miss Price, tying her bonnet strings with a jerk. 'You'll cry your eyes out, when I'm gone; you know you will.'

'I scorn your words, Minx,' said Miss Squeers.

'You pay me a great compliment when you say so,' answered the miller's daughter, curtseying very low. 'Wish you a very good-night, ma'am, and pleasant dreams attend your sleep!'

With this parting benediction, Miss Price swept from the room, followed by the huge Yorkshireman, who exchanged with Nicholas, at parting, that peculiarly expressive scowl with which the cut-and-thrust counts, in melodramatic performances, inform each other they will meet again.

They were no sooner gone, than Miss Squeers fulfilled the prediction of her quondam friend by giving vent to a most copious burst of tears, and uttering various dismal lamentations and incoherent words. Nicholas stood looking on for a few seconds, rather doubtful what to do, but feeling uncertain whether the fit would end in his being embraced, or scratched, and considering that either infliction would be equally agreeable, he walked off very quietly while Miss Squeers was moaning in her pocket-handkerchief.

'This is one consequence,' thought Nicholas, when he had groped his way to the dark sleeping-room, 'of my cursed readiness to adapt myself to any society in which chance carries me. If I had sat mute and motionless, as I might have done, this would not have happened.'

He listened for a few minutes, but all was quiet.

'I was glad,' he murmured, 'to grasp at any relief from the sight of this dreadful place, or the presence of its vile master. I have set these people by the ears, and made two new enemies, where, Heaven knows, I needed none. Well, it is a just punishment for having forgotten, even for an hour, what is around me now!'

So saying, he felt his way among the throng of weary-hearted sleepers, and crept into his poor bed.

CHAPTER 10
How Mr. Ralph Nickleby provided for his Niece and Sister-in-Law

On the second morning after the departure of Nicholas for Yorkshire, Kate Nickleby sat in a very faded chair raised upon a very dusty throne in Miss La Creevy's room, giving that lady a sitting for the portrait upon which she was engaged; and towards the full perfection of which, Miss La Creevy had had the street-door case brought upstairs, in order that she might be the better able to infuse into the counterfeit countenance of Miss Nickleby, a bright salmon flesh-tint which she had originally hit upon while executing the miniature of a young officer therein contained, and which bright salmon flesh-tint was considered, by Miss La Creevy's chief friends and patrons, to be quite a novelty in art: as indeed it was.

'I think I have caught it now,' said Miss La Creevy. 'The very shade! This will be the sweetest portrait I have ever done, certainly.'

'It will be your genius that makes it so, then, I am sure,' replied Kate, smiling.

'No, no, I won't allow that, my dear,' rejoined Miss La Creevy. 'It's a very nice subject—a very nice subject, indeed—though, of course, something depends upon the mode of treatment.'

'And not a little,' observed Kate.

'Why, my dear, you are right there,' said Miss La Creevy, 'in the main you are right there; though I don't allow that it is of such very great importance in the present case. Ah! The difficulties of Art, my dear, are great.'

'They must be, I have no doubt,' said Kate, humouring her good-natured little friend.

'They are beyond anything you can form the faintest conception of,' replied Miss La Creevy. 'What with bringing out eyes with all one's power, and keeping down noses with all one's force, and adding to heads, and taking away teeth altogether, you have no idea of the trouble one little miniature is.'

'The remuneration can scarcely repay you,' said Kate.

'Why, it does not, and that's the truth,' answered Miss La Creevy; 'and then people are so dissatisfied and unreasonable, that, nine times out of ten, there's no pleasure in painting them. Sometimes they say, "Oh, how very serious you have made me look, Miss La Creevy!" and at others, "La, Miss La Creevy, how very smirking!" when the very essence of a good portrait is, that it must be either serious or smirking, or it's no portrait at all.'

'Indeed!' said Kate, laughing.

'Certainly, my dear; because the sitters are always either the one or the other,' replied Miss La Creevy. 'Look at the Royal Academy! All those beautiful shiny portraits of gentlemen in black velvet waistcoats, with their fists doubled up on round tables, or marble slabs, are serious, you know; and all the ladies who are playing with little parasols, or little dogs, or little children—it's the same rule in art, only varying the objects—are smirking. In fact,' said Miss La Creevy, sinking her voice to a confidential whisper, 'there are only two styles of portrait painting; the serious and the smirk; and we always use the serious for professional people (except actors sometimes), and the smirk for private ladies and gentlemen who don't care so much about looking clever.'

Kate seemed highly amused by this information, and Miss La Creevy went on painting and talking, with immovable complacency.

'What a number of officers you seem to paint!' said Kate, availing herself of a pause in the discourse, and glancing round the room.

'Number of what, child?' inquired Miss La Creevy, looking up from her work. 'Character portraits, oh yes—they're not real military men, you know.'

'No!'

'Bless your heart, of course not; only clerks and that, who hire a uniform coat to be painted in, and send it here in a carpet bag. Some artists,' said Miss La Creevy, 'keep a red coat, and charge seven-and-sixpence extra for hire and carmine; but I don't do that myself, for I don't consider it legitimate.'

Drawing herself up, as though she plumed herself greatly upon not resorting to these lures to catch sitters, Miss La Creevy applied herself, more intently, to her task: only raising her head occasionally, to look with unspeakable satisfaction at some touch she had just put in: and now and then giving Miss Nickleby to understand what particular feature she was at work upon, at the moment; 'not,' she expressly observed, 'that you should make it up for painting, my dear, but because it's our custom sometimes to tell sitters what part we are upon, in order that if there's any particular expression they want introduced, they may throw it in, at the time, you know.'

'And when,' said Miss La Creevy, after a long silence, to wit, an interval of full a minute and a half, 'when do you expect to see your uncle again?'

'I scarcely know; I had expected to have seen him before now,' replied Kate. 'Soon I hope, for this state of uncertainty is worse than anything.'

'I suppose he has money, hasn't he?' inquired Miss La Creevy.

'He is very rich, I have heard,' rejoined Kate. 'I don't know that he is, but I believe so.'

'Ah, you may depend upon it he is, or he wouldn't be so surly,' remarked Miss La Creevy, who was an odd little mixture of shrewdness and simplicity. 'When a man's a bear, he is generally pretty independent.'

'His manner is rough,' said Kate.

'Rough!' cried Miss La Creevy, 'a porcupine's a featherbed to him! I never met with such a cross-grained old savage.'

'It is only his manner, I believe,' observed Kate, timidly; 'he was disappointed in early life, I think I have heard, or has had his temper soured by some calamity. I should be sorry to think ill of him until I knew he deserved it.'

'Well; that's very right and proper,' observed the miniature painter, 'and Heaven forbid that I should be the cause of your doing so! But, now, mightn't he, without feeling it himself, make you and your mama some nice little allowance that would keep you both comfortable until you were well married, and be a little fortune to her afterwards? What would a hundred a year for instance, be to him?'

'I don't know what it would be to him,' said Kate, with energy, 'but it would be that to me I would rather die than take.'

'Heyday!' cried Miss La Creevy.

'A dependence upon him,' said Kate, 'would embitter my whole life. I should feel begging a far less degradation.'

'Well!' exclaimed Miss La Creevy. 'This of a relation whom you will not hear an indifferent person speak ill of, my dear, sounds oddly enough, I confess.'

'I dare say it does,' replied Kate, speaking more gently, 'indeed I am sure it must. I—I—only mean that with the feelings and recollection of better times upon me, I could not bear to live on anybody's bounty—not his particularly, but anybody's.'

Miss La Creevy looked slyly at her companion, as if she doubted whether Ralph himself were not the subject of dislike, but seeing that her young friend was distressed, made no remark.

'I only ask of him,' continued Kate, whose tears fell while she spoke, 'that he will move so little out of his way, in my behalf, as to enable me by his recommendation—only by his recommendation—to earn, literally, my bread and remain with my mother. Whether we shall ever taste happiness again, depends upon the fortunes of my dear brother; but if he will do this, and Nicholas only tells us that he is well and cheerful, I shall be contented.'

As she ceased to speak, there was a rustling behind the screen which stood between her and the door, and some person knocked at the wainscot.'

'Come in, whoever it is!' cried Miss La Creevy.

The person complied, and, coming forward at once, gave to view the form and features of no less an individual than Mr. Ralph Nickleby himself.

'Your servant, ladies,' said Ralph, looking sharply at them by turns. 'You were talking so loud, that I was unable to make you hear.'

When the man of business had a more than commonly vicious snarl lurking at his heart, he had a trick of almost concealing his eyes under their thick and protruding brows, for an instant, and then displaying them in their full keenness. As he did so now, and tried to keep down the smile which parted his thin compressed lips, and puckered up the bad lines about his mouth, they both felt certain that some part, if not the whole, of their recent conversation, had been overheard.

'I called in, on my way upstairs, more than half expecting to find you here,' said Ralph, addressing his niece, and looking contemptuously at the portrait. 'Is that my niece's portrait, ma'am?'

'Yes it is, Mr. Nickleby,' said Miss La Creevy, with a very sprightly air, 'and between you and me and the post, sir, it will be a very nice portrait too, though I say it who am the painter.'

'Don't trouble yourself to show it to me, ma'am,' cried Ralph, moving away, 'I have no eye for likenesses. Is it nearly finished?'

'Why, yes,' replied Miss La Creevy, considering with the pencil end of her brush in her mouth. 'Two sittings more will—'

'Have them at once, ma'am,' said Ralph. 'She'll have no time to idle over fooleries after tomorrow. Work, ma'am, work; we must all work. Have you let your lodgings, ma'am?'

'I have not put a bill up yet, sir.'

'Put it up at once, ma'am; they won't want the rooms after this week, or if they do, can't pay for them. Now, my dear, if you're ready, we'll lose no more time.'

With an assumption of kindness which sat worse upon him even than his usual manner, Mr. Ralph Nickleby motioned to the young lady to precede him, and bowing gravely to Miss La Creevy, closed the door and followed upstairs, where Mrs. Nickleby received him with many expressions of regard. Stopping them somewhat abruptly, Ralph waved his hand with an impatient gesture, and proceeded to the object of his visit.

'I have found a situation for your daughter, ma'am,' said Ralph.

'Well,' replied Mrs. Nickleby. 'Now, I will say that that is only just what I have expected of you. "Depend upon it," I said to Kate, only yesterday morning at breakfast, "that after your uncle has provided, in that most ready manner, for Nicholas, he will not leave us until he has done at least the same for you." These were my very words, as near as I remember. Kate, my dear, why don't you thank your—'

'Let me proceed, ma'am, pray,' said Ralph, interrupting his sister-in-law in the full torrent of her discourse.

'Kate, my love, let your uncle proceed,' said Mrs. Nickleby.

'I am most anxious that he should, mama,' rejoined Kate.

'Well, my dear, if you are anxious that he should, you had better allow your uncle to say what he has to say, without interruption,' observed Mrs Nickleby, with many small nods and frowns. 'Your uncle's time is very valuable, my dear; and however desirous you may be—and naturally desirous, as I am sure any affectionate relations who have seen so little of your uncle as we have, must naturally be to protract the pleasure of having him among us, still, we are bound not to be selfish, but to take into consideration the important nature of his occupations in the city.'

'I am very much obliged to you, ma'am,' said Ralph with a scarcely perceptible sneer. 'An absence of business habits in this family leads, apparently, to a great waste of words before business—when it does come under consideration—is arrived at, at all.'

'I fear it is so indeed,' replied Mrs. Nickleby with a sigh. 'Your poor brother—'

'My poor brother, ma'am,' interposed Ralph tartly, 'had no idea what business was—was unacquainted, I verily believe, with the very meaning of the word.'

'I fear he was,' said Mrs. Nickleby, with her handkerchief to her eyes. 'If it hadn't been for me, I don't know what would have become of him.'

What strange creatures we are! The slight bait so skilfully thrown out by Ralph, on their first interview, was dangling on the hook yet. At every small deprivation or discomfort which presented itself in the course of the four-and-twenty hours to remind her of her straitened and altered circumstances, peevish visions of her dower of one thousand pounds had arisen before Mrs. Nickleby's mind, until, at last, she had come to persuade herself that of all her late husband's creditors she was the worst used and the most to be pitied. And yet, she had loved him dearly for many years, and had no greater share of selfishness than is the usual lot of mortals. Such is the irritability of sudden poverty. A decent annuity would have restored her thoughts to their old train, at once.

'Repining is of no use, ma'am,' said Ralph. 'Of all fruitless errands, sending a tear to look after a day that is gone is the most fruitless.'

'So it is,' sobbed Mrs. Nickleby. 'So it is.'

'As you feel so keenly, in your own purse and person, the consequences of inattention to business, ma'am,' said Ralph, 'I am sure you will impress upon your children the necessity of attaching themselves to it early in life.'

'Of course I must see that,' rejoined Mrs. Nickleby. 'Sad experience, you know, brother-in-law.—Kate, my dear, put that down in the next letter to Nicholas, or remind me to do it if I write.'

Ralph paused for a few moments, and seeing that he had now made pretty sure of the mother, in case the daughter objected to his proposition, went on to say:

'The situation that I have made interest to procure, ma'am, is with—with a milliner and dressmaker, in short.'

'A milliner!' cried Mrs. Nickleby.

'A milliner and dressmaker, ma'am,' replied Ralph. 'Dressmakers in London, as I need not remind you, ma'am, who are so well acquainted with all matters in the ordinary routine of life, make large fortunes, keep equipages, and become persons of great wealth and fortune.'

Now, the first idea called up in Mrs. Nickleby's mind by the words milliner and dressmaker were connected with certain wicker baskets lined with black oilskin, which she remembered to have seen carried to and fro in the streets; but, as Ralph proceeded, these disappeared, and were replaced by visions of large houses at the West end, neat private carriages, and a banker's book; all of which images succeeded each other with such rapidity, that he had no sooner finished speaking, than she nodded her head and said 'Very true,' with great appearance of satisfaction.

'What your uncle says is very true, Kate, my dear,' said Mrs. Nickleby. 'I recollect when your poor papa and I came to town after we were married, that a young lady brought me home a chip cottage-bonnet, with white and green trimming, and green persian lining, in her own carriage, which drove up to the door full gallop;—at least, I am not quite certain whether it was her own carriage or a hackney chariot, but I remember very well that the horse dropped down dead as he was turning round, and that your poor papa said he hadn't had any corn for a fortnight.'

This anecdote, so strikingly illustrative of the opulence of milliners, was not received with any great demonstration of feeling, inasmuch as Kate hung down her head while it was relating, and Ralph manifested very intelligible symptoms of extreme impatience.

'The lady's name,' said Ralph, hastily striking in, 'is Mantalini—Madame Mantalini. I know her. She lives near Cavendish Square. If your daughter is disposed to try after the situation, I'll take her there directly.'

'Have you nothing to say to your uncle, my love?' inquired Mrs. Nickleby.

'A great deal,' replied Kate; 'but not now. I would rather speak to him when we are alone;—it will save his time if I thank him and say what I wish to say to him, as we walk along.'

With these words, Kate hurried away, to hide the traces of emotion that were stealing down her face, and to prepare herself for the walk, while Mrs. Nickleby amused her brother-in-law by giving him, with many tears, a detailed account of the dimensions of a rosewood cabinet piano they had possessed in their days of affluence, together with a minute description of eight drawing-room chairs, with turned legs and green chintz squabs to match the curtains, which had cost two pounds fifteen shillings apiece, and had gone at the sale for a mere nothing.

These reminiscences were at length cut short by Kate's return in her walking dress, when Ralph, who had been fretting and fuming during the whole time of her absence, lost no time, and used very little ceremony, in descending into the street.

'Now,' he said, taking her arm, 'walk as fast as you can, and you'll get into the step that you'll have to walk to business with, every morning.' So saying, he led Kate off, at a good round pace, towards Cavendish Square.

'I am very much obliged to you, uncle,' said the young lady, after they had hurried on in silence for some time; 'very.'

'I'm glad to hear it,' said Ralph. 'I hope you'll do your duty.'

'I will try to please, uncle,' replied Kate: 'indeed I—'

'Don't begin to cry,' growled Ralph; 'I hate crying.'

'It's very foolish, I know, uncle,' began poor Kate.

'It is,' replied Ralph, stopping her short, 'and very affected besides. Let me see no more of it.'

Perhaps this was not the best way to dry the tears of a young and sensitive female, about to make her first entry on an entirely new scene of life, among cold and uninterested strangers; but it had its effect notwithstanding. Kate coloured deeply, breathed quickly for a few moments, and then walked on with a firmer and more determined step.

It was a curious contrast to see how the timid country girl shrunk through the crowd that hurried up and down the streets, giving way to the press of people, and clinging closely to Ralph as though she feared to lose him in the throng; and how the stern and hard-featured man of business went doggedly on, elbowing the passengers aside, and now and then exchanging a gruff salutation with some passing acquaintance, who turned to look back upon his pretty charge, with looks expressive of surprise, and seemed to wonder at the ill-assorted companionship. But, it would have been a stranger contrast still, to have read the hearts that were beating side by side; to have laid bare the gentle innocence of the one, and the rugged villainy of the other; to have hung upon the guileless thoughts of the affectionate girl, and been amazed that, among all the wily plots and calculations of the old man, there should not be one word or figure denoting thought of death or of the grave. But so it was; and stranger still—though this is a thing of every day—the warm young heart palpitated with a thousand anxieties and apprehensions, while that of the old worldly man lay rusting in its cell, beating only as a piece of cunning mechanism, and yielding no one throb of hope, or fear, or love, or care, for any living thing.

'Uncle,' said Kate, when she judged they must be near their destination, 'I must ask one question of you. I am to live at home?'

'At home!' replied Ralph; 'where's that?'

'I mean with my mother—The Widow,' said Kate emphatically.

'You will live, to all intents and purposes, here,' rejoined Ralph; 'for here you will take your meals, and here you will be from morning till night—occasionally perhaps till morning again.'

'But at night, I mean,' said Kate; 'I cannot leave her, uncle. I must have some place that I can call a home; it will be wherever she is, you know, and may be a very humble one.'

'May be!' said Ralph, walking faster, in the impatience provoked by the remark; 'must be, you mean. May be a humble one! Is the girl mad?'

'The word slipped from my lips, I did not mean it indeed,' urged Kate.

'I hope not,' said Ralph.

'But my question, uncle; you have not answered it.'

'Why, I anticipated something of the kind,' said Ralph; 'and—though I object very strongly, mind—have provided against it. I spoke of you as an out-of-door worker; so you will go to this home that may be humble, every night.'

There was comfort in this. Kate poured forth many thanks for her uncle's consideration, which Ralph received as if he had deserved them all, and they arrived without any further conversation at the dressmaker's door, which displayed a very large plate, with Madame Mantalini's name and occupation, and was approached by a handsome flight of steps. There was a shop to the house, but it was let off to an importer of otto of roses. Madame Mantalini's shows-rooms were on the first-floor: a fact which was notified to the nobility and gentry by the casual exhibition, near the handsomely curtained windows, of two or three elegant bonnets of the newest fashion, and some costly garments in the most approved taste.

A liveried footman opened the door, and in reply to Ralph's inquiry whether Madame Mantalini was at home, ushered them, through a handsome hall and up a spacious staircase, into the show saloon, which comprised two spacious drawing-rooms, and exhibited an immense variety of superb dresses and materials for dresses: some arranged on stands, others laid carelessly on sofas, and others again, scattered over the carpet, hanging on the cheval-glasses, or mingling, in some other way, with the rich furniture of various descriptions, which was profusely displayed.

They waited here a much longer time than was agreeable to Mr. Ralph Nickleby, who eyed the gaudy frippery about him with very little concern, and was at length about to pull the bell, when a gentleman suddenly popped his head into the room, and, seeing somebody there, as suddenly popped it out again.

'Here. Hollo!' cried Ralph. 'Who's that?'

At the sound of Ralph's voice, the head reappeared, and the mouth, displaying a very long row of very white teeth, uttered in a mincing tone the words, 'Demmit. What, Nickleby! oh, demmit!' Having uttered which ejaculations, the gentleman advanced, and shook hands with Ralph, with great warmth. He was dressed in a gorgeous morning gown, with a waistcoat and Turkish trousers of the same pattern, a pink silk neckerchief, and bright green slippers, and had a very copious watch-chain wound round his body. Moreover, he had whiskers and a moustache, both dyed black and gracefully curled.

'Demmit, you don't mean to say you want me, do you, demmit?' said this gentleman, smiting Ralph on the shoulder.

'Not yet,' said Ralph, sarcastically.

'Ha! ha! demmit,' cried the gentleman; when, wheeling round to laugh with greater elegance, he encountered Kate Nickleby, who was standing near.

'My niece,' said Ralph.

'I remember,' said the gentleman, striking his nose with the knuckle of his forefinger as a chastening for his forgetfulness. 'Demmit, I remember what you come for. Step this way, Nickleby; my dear, will you follow me? Ha! ha! They all follow me, Nickleby; always did, demmit, always.'

Giving loose to the playfulness of his imagination, after this fashion, the gentleman led the way to a private sitting-room on the second floor, scarcely less elegantly furnished than the apartment below, where the presence of a silver coffee-pot, an egg-shell, and sloppy china for one, seemed to show that he had just breakfasted.

'Sit down, my dear,' said the gentleman: first staring Miss Nickleby out of countenance, and then grinning in delight at the achievement. 'This cursed high room takes one's breath away. These infernal sky parlours—I'm afraid I must move, Nickleby.'

'I would, by all means,' replied Ralph, looking bitterly round.

'What a demd rum fellow you are, Nickleby,' said the gentleman, 'the demdest, longest-headed, queerest-tempered old coiner of gold and silver ever was—demmit.'

Having complimented Ralph to this effect, the gentleman rang the bell, and stared at Miss Nickleby until it was answered, when he left off to bid the man desire his mistress to come directly; after which, he began again, and left off no more until Madame Mantalini appeared.

The dressmaker was a buxom person, handsomely dressed and rather good-looking, but much older than the gentleman in the Turkish trousers, whom she had wedded some six months before. His name was originally Muntle; but it had been converted, by an easy transition, into Mantalini: the lady rightly considering that an English appellation would be of serious injury to the business. He had married on his whiskers; upon which property he had previously subsisted, in a genteel manner, for some years; and which he had recently improved, after patient cultivation by the addition of a moustache, which promised to secure him an easy independence: his share in the labours of the business being at present confined to spending the money, and occasionally, when that ran short, driving to Mr. Ralph Nickleby to procure discount—at a percentage—for the customers' bills.

'My life,' said Mr. Mantalini, 'what a demd devil of a time you have been!'

'I didn't even know Mr. Nickleby was here, my love,' said Madame Mantalini.

'Then what a doubly demd infernal rascal that footman must be, my soul,' remonstrated Mr. Mantalini.

'My dear,' said Madame, 'that is entirely your fault.'

'My fault, my heart's joy?'

'Certainly,' returned the lady; 'what can you expect, dearest, if you will not correct the man?'

'Correct the man, my soul's delight!'

'Yes; I am sure he wants speaking to, badly enough,' said Madame, pouting.

'Then do not vex itself,' said Mr. Mantalini; 'he shall be horse-whipped till he cries out demnebly.' With this promise Mr. Mantalini kissed Madame Mantalini, and, after that performance, Madame Mantalini pulled Mr Mantalini playfully by the ear: which done, they descended to business.

'Now, ma'am,' said Ralph, who had looked on, at all this, with such scorn as few men can express in looks, 'this is my niece.'

'Just so, Mr. Nickleby,' replied Madame Mantalini, surveying Kate from head to foot, and back again. 'Can you speak French, child?'

'Yes, ma'am,' replied Kate, not daring to look up; for she felt that the eyes of the odious man in the dressing-gown were directed towards her.

'Like a demd native?' asked the husband.

Miss Nickleby offered no reply to this inquiry, but turned her back upon the questioner, as if addressing herself to make answer to what his wife might demand.

'We keep twenty young women constantly employed in the establishment,' said Madame.

'Indeed, ma'am!' replied Kate, timidly.

'Yes; and some of 'em demd handsome, too,' said the master.

'Mantalini!' exclaimed his wife, in an awful voice.

'My senses' idol!' said Mantalini.

'Do you wish to break my heart?'

'Not for twenty thousand hemispheres populated with—with—with little ballet-dancers,' replied Mantalini in a poetical strain.

'Then you will, if you persevere in that mode of speaking,' said his wife. 'What can Mr. Nickleby think when he hears you?'

'Oh! Nothing, ma'am, nothing,' replied Ralph. 'I know his amiable nature, and yours,—mere little remarks that give a zest to your daily intercourse—lovers' quarrels that add sweetness to those domestic joys which promise to last so long—that's all; that's all.'

If an iron door could be supposed to quarrel with its hinges, and to make a firm resolution to open with slow obstinacy, and grind them to powder in the process, it would emit a pleasanter sound in so doing, than did these words in the rough and bitter voice in which they were uttered by Ralph. Even Mr. Mantalini felt their influence, and turning affrighted round, exclaimed: 'What a demd horrid croaking!'

'You will pay no attention, if you please, to what Mr. Mantalini says,' observed his wife, addressing Miss Nickleby.

'I do not, ma'am,' said Kate, with quiet contempt.

'Mr. Mantalini knows nothing whatever about any of the young women,' continued Madame, looking at her husband, and speaking to Kate. 'If he has seen any of them, he must have seen them in the street, going to, or returning from, their work, and not here. He was never even in the room. I do not allow it. What hours of work have you been accustomed to?'

'I have never yet been accustomed to work at all, ma'am,' replied Kate, in a low voice.

'For which reason she'll work all the better now,' said Ralph, putting in a word, lest this confession should injure the negotiation.

'I hope so,' returned Madame Mantalini; 'our hours are from nine to nine, with extra work when we're very full of business, for which I allow payment as overtime.'

Kate bowed her head, to intimate that she heard, and was satisfied.

'Your meals,' continued Madame Mantalini, 'that is, dinner and tea, you will take here. I should think your wages would average from five to seven shillings a week; but I can't give you any certain information on that point, until I see what you can do.'

Kate bowed her head again.

'If you're ready to come,' said Madame Mantalini, 'you had better begin on Monday morning at nine exactly, and Miss Knag the forewoman shall then have directions to try you with some easy work at first. Is there anything more, Mr. Nickleby?'

'Nothing more, ma'am,' replied Ralph, rising.

'Then I believe that's all,' said the lady. Having arrived at this natural conclusion, she looked at the door, as if she wished to be gone, but hesitated notwithstanding, as though unwilling to leave to Mr. Mantalini the sole honour of showing them downstairs. Ralph relieved her from her perplexity by taking his departure without delay: Madame Mantalini making many gracious inquiries why he never came to see them; and Mr. Mantalini anathematising the stairs with great volubility as he followed them down, in the hope of inducing Kate to look round,—a hope, however, which was destined to remain ungratified.

'There!' said Ralph when they got into the street; 'now you're provided for.'

Kate was about to thank him again, but he stopped her.

'I had some idea,' he said, 'of providing for your mother in a pleasant part of the country—(he had a presentation to some almshouses on the borders of Cornwall, which had occurred to him more than once)—but as you want to be together, I must do something else for her. She has a little money?'

'A very little,' replied Kate.

'A little will go a long way if it's used sparingly,' said Ralph. 'She must see how long she can make it last, living rent free. You leave your lodgings on Saturday?'

'You told us to do so, uncle.'

'Yes; there is a house empty that belongs to me, which I can put you into till it is let, and then, if nothing else turns up, perhaps I shall have another. You must live there.'

'Is it far from here, sir?' inquired Kate.

'Pretty well,' said Ralph; 'in another quarter of the town—at the East end; but I'll send my clerk down to you, at five o'clock on Saturday, to take you there. Goodbye. You know your way? Straight on.'

Coldly shaking his niece's hand, Ralph left her at the top of Regent Street, and turned down a by-thoroughfare, intent on schemes of money-getting. Kate walked sadly back to their lodgings in the Strand.

CHAPTER 11
Newman Noggs inducts Mrs. and Miss Nickleby into their New Dwelling in the City

Miss Nickleby's reflections, as she wended her way homewards, were of that desponding nature which the occurrences of the morning had been sufficiently calculated to awaken. Her uncle's was not a manner likely to dispel any doubts or apprehensions she might have formed, in the outset, neither was the glimpse she had had of Madame Mantalini's establishment by any means encouraging. It was with many gloomy forebodings and misgivings, therefore, that she looked forward, with a heavy heart, to the opening of her new career.

If her mother's consolations could have restored her to a pleasanter and more enviable state of mind, there were abundance of them to produce the effect. By the time Kate reached home, the good lady had called to mind two authentic cases of milliners who had been possessed of considerable property, though whether they had acquired it all in business, or had had a capital to start with, or had been lucky and married to advantage, she could not exactly remember. However, as she very logically remarked, there must have been some young person in that way of business who had made a fortune without having anything to begin with, and that being taken for granted, why should not Kate do the same? Miss La Creevy, who was a member of the little council, ventured to insinuate some doubts relative to the probability of Miss Nickleby's arriving at this happy consummation in the compass of an ordinary lifetime; but the good lady set that question entirely at rest, by informing them that she had a presentiment on the subject—a species of second-sight with which she had been in the habit of clenching every argument with the deceased Mr. Nickleby, and, in nine cases and three-quarters out of every ten, determining it the wrong way.

'I am afraid it is an unhealthy occupation,' said Miss La Creevy. 'I recollect getting three young milliners to sit to me, when I first began to paint, and I remember that they were all very pale and sickly.'

'Oh! that's not a general rule by any means,' observed Mrs. Nickleby; 'for I remember, as well as if it was only yesterday, employing one that I was particularly recommended to, to make me a scarlet cloak at the time when scarlet cloaks were fashionable, and she had a very red face—a very red face, indeed.'

'Perhaps she drank,' suggested Miss La Creevy.

'I don't know how that may have been,' returned Mrs. Nickleby: 'but I know she had a very red face, so your argument goes for nothing.'

In this manner, and with like powerful reasoning, did the worthy matron meet every little objection that presented itself to the new scheme of the morning. Happy Mrs. Nickleby! A project had but to be new, and it came home to her mind, brightly varnished and gilded as a glittering toy.

This question disposed of, Kate communicated her uncle's desire about the empty house, to which Mrs. Nickleby assented with equal readiness, characteristically remarking, that, on the fine evenings, it would be a pleasant amusement for her to walk to the West end to fetch her daughter home; and no less characteristically forgetting, that there were such things as wet nights and bad weather to be encountered in almost every week of the year.

'I shall be sorry—truly sorry to leave you, my kind friend,' said Kate, on whom the good feeling of the poor miniature painter had made a deep impression.

'You shall not shake me off, for all that,' replied Miss La Creevy, with as much sprightliness as she could assume. 'I shall see you very often, and come and hear how you get on; and if, in all London, or all the wide world besides, there is no other heart that takes an interest in your welfare, there will be one little lonely woman that prays for it night and day.'

With this, the poor soul, who had a heart big enough for Gog, the guardian genius of London, and enough to spare for Magog to boot, after making a great many extraordinary faces which would have secured her an ample fortune, could she have transferred them to ivory or canvas, sat down in a corner, and had what she termed 'a real good cry.'

But no crying, or talking, or hoping, or fearing, could keep off the dreaded Saturday afternoon, or Newman Noggs either; who, punctual to his time, limped up to the door, and breathed a whiff of cordial gin through the keyhole, exactly as such of the church clocks in the neighbourhood as agreed among themselves about the time, struck five. Newman waited for the last stroke, and then knocked.

'From Mr. Ralph Nickleby,' said Newman, announcing his errand, when he got upstairs, with all possible brevity.

'We shall be ready directly,' said Kate. 'We have not much to carry, but I fear we must have a coach.'

'I'll get one,' replied Newman.

'Indeed you shall not trouble yourself,' said Mrs. Nickleby.

'I will,' said Newman.

'I can't suffer you to think of such a thing,' said Mrs. Nickleby.

'You can't help it,' said Newman.

'Not help it!'

'No; I thought of it as I came along; but didn't get one, thinking you mightn't be ready. I think of a great many things. Nobody can prevent that.'

'Oh yes, I understand you, Mr. Noggs,' said Mrs. Nickleby. 'Our thoughts are free, of course. Everybody's thoughts are their own, clearly.'

'They wouldn't be, if some people had their way,' muttered Newman.

'Well, no more they would, Mr. Noggs, and that's very true,' rejoined Mrs Nickleby. 'Some people to be sure are such—how's your master?'

Newman darted a meaning glance at Kate, and replied with a strong emphasis on the last word of his answer, that Mr. Ralph Nickleby was well, and sent his love.

'I am sure we are very much obliged to him,' observed Mrs. Nickleby.

'Very,' said Newman. 'I'll tell him so.'

It was no very easy matter to mistake Newman Noggs, after having once seen him, and as Kate, attracted by the singularity of his manner (in which on this occasion, however, there was something respectful and even delicate, notwithstanding the abruptness of his speech), looked at him more closely, she recollected having caught a passing glimpse of that strange figure before.

'Excuse my curiosity,' she said, 'but did I not see you in the coachyard, on the morning my brother went away to Yorkshire?'

Newman cast a wistful glance on Mrs. Nickleby and said 'No,' most unblushingly.

'No!' exclaimed Kate, 'I should have said so anywhere.'

'You'd have said wrong,' rejoined Newman. 'It's the first time I've been out for three weeks. I've had the gout.'

Newman was very, very far from having the appearance of a gouty subject, and so Kate could not help thinking; but the conference was cut short by Mrs. Nickleby's insisting on having the door shut, lest Mr. Noggs should take cold, and further persisting in sending the servant girl for a coach, for fear he should bring on another attack of his disorder. To both conditions, Newman was compelled to yield. Presently, the coach came; and, after many sorrowful farewells, and a great deal of running backwards and forwards across the pavement on the part of Miss La Creevy, in the course of which the yellow turban came into violent contact with sundry foot-passengers, it (that is to say the coach, not the turban) went away again, with the two ladies and their luggage inside; and Newman, despite all Mrs. Nickleby's assurances that it would be his death—on the box beside the driver.

They went into the city, turning down by the river side; and, after a long and very slow drive, the streets being crowded at that hour with vehicles of every kind, stopped in front of a large old dingy house in Thames Street: the door and windows of which were so bespattered with mud, that it would have appeared to have been uninhabited for years.

The door of this deserted mansion Newman opened with a key which he took out of his hat—in which, by-the-bye, in consequence of the dilapidated state of his pockets, he deposited everything, and would most likely have carried his money if he had had any—and the coach being discharged, he led the way into the interior of the mansion.

Old, and gloomy, and black, in truth it was, and sullen and dark were the rooms, once so bustling with life and enterprise. There was a wharf behind, opening on the Thames. An empty dog-kennel, some bones of animals, fragments of iron hoops, and staves of old casks, lay strewn about, but no life was stirring there. It was a picture of cold, silent decay.

'This house depresses and chills one,' said Kate, 'and seems as if some blight had fallen on it. If I were superstitious, I should be almost inclined to believe that some dreadful crime had been perpetrated within these old walls, and that the place had never prospered since. How frowning and how dark it looks!'

'Lord, my dear,' replied Mrs. Nickleby, 'don't talk in that way, or you'll frighten me to death.'

'It is only my foolish fancy, mama,' said Kate, forcing a smile.

'Well, then, my love, I wish you would keep your foolish fancy to yourself, and not wake up my foolish fancy to keep it company,' retorted Mrs. Nickleby. 'Why didn't you think of all this before—you are so careless—we might have asked Miss La Creevy to keep us company or borrowed a dog, or a thousand things—but it always was the way, and was just the same with your poor dear father. Unless I thought of everything—' This was Mrs. Nickleby's usual commencement of a general lamentation, running through a dozen or so of complicated sentences addressed to nobody in particular, and into which she now launched until her breath was exhausted.

Newman appeared not to hear these remarks, but preceded them to a couple of rooms on the first floor, which some kind of attempt had been made to render habitable. In one, were a few chairs, a table, an old hearth-rug, and some faded baize; and a fire was ready laid in the grate. In the other stood an old tent bedstead, and a few scanty articles of chamber furniture.

'Well, my dear,' said Mrs. Nickleby, trying to be pleased, 'now isn't this thoughtful and considerate of your uncle? Why, we should not have had anything but the bed we bought yesterday, to lie down upon, if it hadn't been for his thoughtfulness!'

'Very kind, indeed,' replied Kate, looking round.

Newman Noggs did not say that he had hunted up the old furniture they saw, from attic and cellar; or that he had taken in the halfpennyworth of milk for tea that stood upon a shelf, or filled the rusty kettle on the hob, or collected the woodchips from the wharf, or begged the coals. But the notion of Ralph Nickleby having directed it to be done, tickled his fancy so much, that he could not refrain from cracking all his ten fingers in succession: at which performance Mrs. Nickleby was rather startled at first, but supposing it to be in some remote manner connected with the gout, did not remark upon.

'We need detain you no longer, I think,' said Kate.

'Is there nothing I can do?' asked Newman.

'Nothing, thank you,' rejoined Miss Nickleby.

'Perhaps, my dear, Mr. Noggs would like to drink our healths,' said Mrs Nickleby, fumbling in her reticule for some small coin.

'I think, mama,' said Kate hesitating, and remarking Newman's averted face, 'you would hurt his feelings if you offered it.'

Newman Noggs, bowing to the young lady more like a gentleman than the miserable wretch he seemed, placed his hand upon his breast, and, pausing for a moment, with the air of a man who struggles to speak but is uncertain what to say, quitted the room.

As the jarring echoes of the heavy house-door, closing on its latch, reverberated dismally through the building, Kate felt half tempted to call him back, and beg him to remain a little while; but she was ashamed to own her fears, and Newman Noggs was on his road homewards.

CHAPTER 12

Whereby the Reader will be enabled to trace the further course of Miss Fanny Squeer's Love, and to ascertain whether it ran smooth or otherwise.

It was a fortunate circumstance for Miss Fanny Squeers, that when her worthy papa returned home on the night of the small tea-party, he was what the initiated term 'too far gone' to observe the numerous tokens of extreme vexation of spirit which were plainly visible in her countenance. Being, however, of a rather violent and quarrelsome mood in his cups, it is not impossible that he might have fallen out with her, either on this or some imaginary topic, if the young lady had not, with a foresight and prudence highly commendable, kept a boy up, on purpose, to bear the first brunt of the good gentleman's anger; which, having vented itself in a variety of kicks and cuffs, subsided sufficiently to admit of his being persuaded to go to bed. Which he did with his boots on, and an umbrella under his arm.

The hungry servant attended Miss Squeers in her own room according to custom, to curl her hair, perform the other little offices of her toilet, and administer as much flattery as she could get up, for the purpose; for Miss Squeers was quite lazy enough (and sufficiently vain and frivolous withal) to have been a fine lady; and it was only the arbitrary distinctions of rank and station which prevented her from being one.

'How lovely your hair do curl tonight, miss!' said the handmaiden. 'I declare if it isn't a pity and a shame to brush it out!'

'Hold your tongue!' replied Miss Squeers wrathfully.

Some considerable experience prevented the girl from being at all surprised at any outbreak of ill-temper on the part of Miss Squeers. Having a half-perception of what had occurred in the course of the evening, she changed her mode of making herself agreeable, and proceeded on the indirect tack.

'Well, I couldn't help saying, miss, if you was to kill me for it,' said the attendant, 'that I never see nobody look so vulgar as Miss Price this night.'

Miss Squeers sighed, and composed herself to listen.

'I know it's very wrong in me to say so, miss,' continued the girl, delighted to see the impression she was making, 'Miss Price being a friend of your'n, and all; but she do dress herself out so, and go on in such a manner to get noticed, that—oh—well, if people only saw themselves!'

'What do you mean, Phib?' asked Miss Squeers, looking in her own little glass, where, like most of us, she saw—not herself, but the reflection of some pleasant image in her own brain. 'How you talk!'

'Talk, miss! It's enough to make a Tom cat talk French grammar, only to see how she tosses her head,' replied the handmaid.

'She does toss her head,' observed Miss Squeers, with an air of abstraction.

'So vain, and so very—very plain,' said the girl.

'Poor 'Tilda!' sighed Miss Squeers, compassionately.

'And always laying herself out so, to get to be admired,' pursued the servant. 'Oh, dear! It's positive indelicate.'

'I can't allow you to talk in that way, Phib,' said Miss Squeers. ''Tilda's friends are low people, and if she don't know any better, it's their fault, and not hers.'

'Well, but you know, miss,' said Phoebe, for which name 'Phib' was used as a patronising abbreviation, 'if she was only to take copy by a friend—oh! if she only knew how wrong she was, and would but set herself right by you, what a nice young woman she might be in time!'

'Phib,' rejoined Miss Squeers, with a stately air, 'it's not proper for me to hear these comparisons drawn; they make 'Tilda look a coarse improper sort of person, and it seems unfriendly in me to listen to them. I would rather you dropped the subject, Phib; at the same time, I must say, that if 'Tilda Price would take pattern by somebody—not me particularly—'

'Oh yes; you, miss,' interposed Phib.

'Well, me, Phib, if you will have it so,' said Miss Squeers. 'I must say, that if she would, she would be all the better for it.'

'So somebody else thinks, or I am much mistaken,' said the girl mysteriously.

'What do you mean?' demanded Miss Squeers.

'Never mind, miss,' replied the girl; 'I know what I know; that's all.'

'Phib,' said Miss Squeers dramatically, 'I insist upon your explaining yourself. What is this dark mystery? Speak.'

'Why, if you will have it, miss, it's this,' said the servant girl. 'Mr John Browdie thinks as you think; and if he wasn't too far gone to do it creditable, he'd be very glad to be off with Miss Price, and on with Miss Squeers.'

'Gracious heavens!' exclaimed Miss Squeers, clasping her hands with great dignity. 'What is this?'

'Truth, ma'am, and nothing but truth,' replied the artful Phib.

'What a situation!' cried Miss Squeers; 'on the brink of unconsciously destroying the peace and happiness of my own 'Tilda. What is the reason that men fall in love with me, whether I like it or not, and desert their chosen intendeds for my sake?'

'Because they can't help it, miss,' replied the girl; 'the reason's plain.' (If Miss Squeers were the reason, it was very plain.)

'Never let me hear of it again,' retorted Miss Squeers. 'Never! Do you hear? 'Tilda Price has faults—many faults—but I wish her well, and above all I wish her married; for I think it highly desirable—most desirable from the very nature of her failings—that she should be married as soon as possible. No, Phib. Let her have Mr. Browdie. I may pity him, poor fellow; but I have a great regard for 'Tilda, and only hope she may make a better wife than I think she will.'

With this effusion of feeling, Miss Squeers went to bed.

Spite is a little word; but it represents as strange a jumble of feelings, and compound of discords, as any polysyllable in the language. Miss Squeers knew as well in her heart of hearts that what the miserable serving-girl had said was sheer, coarse, lying flattery, as did the girl herself; yet the mere opportunity of venting a little ill-nature against the offending Miss Price, and affecting to compassionate her weaknesses and foibles, though only in the presence of a solitary dependant, was almost as great a relief to her spleen as if the whole had been gospel truth. Nay, more. We have such extraordinary powers of persuasion when they are exerted over ourselves, that Miss Squeers felt quite high-minded and great after her noble renunciation of John Browdie's hand, and looked down upon her rival with a kind of holy calmness and tranquillity, that had a mighty effect in soothing her ruffled feelings.

This happy state of mind had some influence in bringing about a reconciliation; for, when a knock came at the front-door next day, and the miller's daughter was announced, Miss Squeers betook herself to the parlour in a Christian frame of spirit, perfectly beautiful to behold.

'Well, Fanny,' said the miller's daughter, 'you see I have come to see you, although we had some words last night.'

'I pity your bad passions, 'Tilda,' replied Miss Squeers, 'but I bear no malice. I am above it.'

'Don't be cross, Fanny,' said Miss Price. 'I have come to tell you something that I know will please you.'

'What may that be, 'Tilda?' demanded Miss Squeers; screwing up her lips, and looking as if nothing in earth, air, fire, or water, could afford her the slightest gleam of satisfaction.

'This,' rejoined Miss Price. 'After we left here last night John and I had a dreadful quarrel.'

'That doesn't please me,' said Miss Squeers—relaxing into a smile though.

'Lor! I wouldn't think so bad of you as to suppose it did,' rejoined her companion. 'That's not it.'

'Oh!' said Miss Squeers, relapsing into melancholy. 'Go on.'

'After a great deal of wrangling, and saying we would never see each other any more,' continued Miss Price, 'we made it up, and this morning John went and wrote our names down to be put up, for the first time, next Sunday, so we shall be married in three weeks, and I give you notice to get your frock made.'

There was mingled gall and honey in this intelligence. The prospect of the friend's being married so soon was the gall, and the certainty of her not entertaining serious designs upon Nicholas was the honey. Upon the whole, the sweet greatly preponderated over the bitter, so Miss Squeers said she would get the frock made, and that she hoped 'Tilda might be happy, though at the same time she didn't know, and would not have her build too much upon it, for men were strange creatures, and a great many married women were very miserable, and wished themselves single again with all their hearts; to which condolences Miss Squeers added others equally calculated to raise her friend's spirits and promote her cheerfulness of mind.

'But come now, Fanny,' said Miss Price, 'I want to have a word or two with you about young Mr. Nickleby.'

'He is nothing to me,' interrupted Miss Squeers, with hysterical symptoms. 'I despise him too much!'

'Oh, you don't mean that, I am sure?' replied her friend. 'Confess, Fanny; don't you like him now?'

Without returning any direct reply, Miss Squeers, all at once, fell into a paroxysm of spiteful tears, and exclaimed that she was a wretched, neglected, miserable castaway.

'I hate everybody,' said Miss Squeers, 'and I wish that everybody was dead—that I do.'

'Dear, dear,' said Miss Price, quite moved by this avowal of misanthropical sentiments. 'You are not serious, I am sure.'

'Yes, I am,' rejoined Miss Squeers, tying tight knots in her pocket-handkerchief and clenching her teeth. 'And I wish I was dead too. There!'

'Oh! you'll think very differently in another five minutes,' said Matilda. 'How much better to take him into favour again, than to hurt yourself by going on in that way. Wouldn't it be much nicer, now, to have him all to yourself on good terms, in a company-keeping, love-making, pleasant sort of manner?'

'I don't know but what it would,' sobbed Miss Squeers. 'Oh! 'Tilda, how could you have acted so mean and dishonourable! I wouldn't have believed it of you, if anybody had told me.'

'Heyday!' exclaimed Miss Price, giggling. 'One would suppose I had been murdering somebody at least.'

'Very nigh as bad,' said Miss Squeers passionately.

'And all this because I happen to have enough of good looks to make people civil to me,' cried Miss Price. 'Persons don't make their own faces, and it's no more my fault if mine is a good one than it is other people's fault if theirs is a bad one.'

'Hold your tongue,' shrieked Miss Squeers, in her shrillest tone; 'or you'll make me slap you, 'Tilda, and afterwards I should be sorry for it!'

It is needless to say, that, by this time, the temper of each young lady was in some slight degree affected by the tone of her conversation, and that a dash of personality was infused into the altercation, in consequence. Indeed, the quarrel, from slight beginnings, rose to a considerable height, and was assuming a very violent complexion, when both parties, falling into a great passion of tears, exclaimed simultaneously, that they had never thought of being spoken to in that way: which exclamation, leading to a remonstrance, gradually brought on an explanation: and the upshot was, that they fell into each other's arms and vowed eternal friendship; the occasion in question making the fifty-second time of repeating the same impressive ceremony within a twelvemonth.

Perfect amicability being thus restored, a dialogue naturally ensued upon the number and nature of the garments which would be indispensable for Miss Price's entrance into the holy state of matrimony, when Miss Squeers clearly showed that a great many more than the miller could, or would, afford, were absolutely necessary, and could not decently be dispensed with. The young lady then, by an easy digression, led the discourse to her own wardrobe, and after recounting its principal beauties at some length, took her friend upstairs to make inspection thereof. The treasures of two drawers and a closet having been displayed, and all the smaller articles tried on, it was time for Miss Price to return home; and as she had been in raptures with all the frocks, and had been stricken quite dumb with admiration of a new pink scarf, Miss Squeers said in high good humour, that she would walk part of the way with her, for the pleasure of her company; and off they went together: Miss Squeers dilating, as they walked along, upon her father's accomplishments: and multiplying his income by ten, to give her friend some faint notion of the vast importance and superiority of her family.

It happened that that particular time, comprising the short daily interval which was suffered to elapse between what was pleasantly called the dinner of Mr. Squeers's pupils, and their return to the pursuit of useful knowledge, was precisely the hour when Nicholas was accustomed to issue forth for a melancholy walk, and to brood, as he sauntered listlessly through the village, upon his miserable lot. Miss Squeers knew this perfectly well, but had perhaps forgotten it, for when she caught sight of that young gentleman advancing towards them, she evinced many symptoms of surprise and consternation, and assured her friend that she 'felt fit to drop into the earth.'

'Shall we turn back, or run into a cottage?' asked Miss Price. 'He don't see us yet.'

'No, 'Tilda,' replied Miss Squeers, 'it is my duty to go through with it, and I will!'

As Miss Squeers said this, in the tone of one who has made a high moral resolution, and was, besides, taken with one or two chokes and catchings of breath, indicative of feelings at a high pressure, her friend made no further remark, and they bore straight down upon Nicholas, who, walking with his eyes bent upon the ground, was not aware of their approach until they were close upon him; otherwise, he might, perhaps, have taken shelter himself.

'Good-morning,' said Nicholas, bowing and passing by.

'He is going,' murmured Miss Squeers. 'I shall choke, 'Tilda.'

'Come back, Mr. Nickleby, do!' cried Miss Price, affecting alarm at her friend's threat, but really actuated by a malicious wish to hear what Nicholas would say; 'come back, Mr. Nickleby!'

Mr. Nickleby came back, and looked as confused as might be, as he inquired whether the ladies had any commands for him.

'Don't stop to talk,' urged Miss Price, hastily; 'but support her on the other side. How do you feel now, dear?'

'Better,' sighed Miss Squeers, laying a beaver bonnet of a reddish brown with a green veil attached, on Mr. Nickleby's shoulder. 'This foolish faintness!'

'Don't call it foolish, dear,' said Miss Price: her bright eye dancing with merriment as she saw the perplexity of Nicholas; 'you have no reason to be ashamed of it. It's those who are too proud to come round again, without all this to-do, that ought to be ashamed.'

'You are resolved to fix it upon me, I see,' said Nicholas, smiling, 'although I told you, last night, it was not my fault.'

'There; he says it was not his fault, my dear,' remarked the wicked Miss Price. 'Perhaps you were too jealous, or too hasty with him? He says it was not his fault. You hear; I think that's apology enough.'

'You will not understand me,' said Nicholas. 'Pray dispense with this jesting, for I have no time, and really no inclination, to be the subject or promoter of mirth just now.'

'What do you mean?' asked Miss Price, affecting amazement.

'Don't ask him, 'Tilda,' cried Miss Squeers; 'I forgive him.'

'Dear me,' said Nicholas, as the brown bonnet went down on his shoulder again, 'this is more serious than I supposed. Allow me! Will you have the goodness to hear me speak?'

Here he raised up the brown bonnet, and regarding with most unfeigned astonishment a look of tender reproach from Miss Squeers, shrunk back a few paces to be out of the reach of the fair burden, and went on to say:

'I am very sorry—truly and sincerely sorry—for having been the cause of any difference among you, last night. I reproach myself, most bitterly, for having been so unfortunate as to cause the dissension that occurred, although I did so, I assure you, most unwittingly and heedlessly.'

'Well; that's not all you have got to say surely,' exclaimed Miss Price as Nicholas paused.

'I fear there is something more,' stammered Nicholas with a half-smile, and looking towards Miss Squeers, 'it is a most awkward thing to say—but—the very mention of such a supposition makes one look like a puppy—still—may I ask if that lady supposes that I entertain any—in short, does she think that I am in love with her?'

'Delightful embarrassment,' thought Miss Squeers, 'I have brought him to it, at last. Answer for me, dear,' she whispered to her friend.

'Does she think so?' rejoined Miss Price; 'of course she does.'

'She does!' exclaimed Nicholas with such energy of utterance as might have been, for the moment, mistaken for rapture.

'Certainly,' replied Miss Price

'If Mr. Nickleby has doubted that, 'Tilda,' said the blushing Miss Squeers in soft accents, 'he may set his mind at rest. His sentiments are recipro—'

'Stop,' cried Nicholas hurriedly; 'pray hear me. This is the grossest and wildest delusion, the completest and most signal mistake, that ever human being laboured under, or committed. I have scarcely seen the young lady half-a-dozen times, but if I had seen her sixty times, or am destined to see her sixty thousand, it would be, and will be, precisely the same. I have not one thought, wish, or hope, connected with her, unless it be—and I say this, not to hurt her feelings, but to impress her with the real state of my own—unless it be the one object, dear to my heart as life itself, of being one day able to turn my back upon this accursed place, never to set foot in it again, or think of it—even think of it—but with loathing and disgust.'

With this particularly plain and straightforward declaration, which he made with all the vehemence that his indignant and excited feelings could bring to bear upon it, Nicholas waiting to hear no more, retreated.

But poor Miss Squeers! Her anger, rage, and vexation; the rapid succession of bitter and passionate feelings that whirled through her mind; are not to be described. Refused! refused by a teacher, picked up by advertisement, at an annual salary of five pounds payable at indefinite periods, and 'found' in food and lodging like the very boys themselves; and this too in the presence of a little chit of a miller's daughter of eighteen, who was going to be married, in three weeks' time, to a man who had gone down on his very knees to ask her. She could have choked in right good earnest, at the thought of being so humbled.

But, there was one thing clear in the midst of her mortification; and that was, that she hated and detested Nicholas with all the narrowness of mind and littleness of purpose worthy a descendant of the house of Squeers. And there was one comfort too; and that was, that every hour in every day she could wound his pride, and goad him with the infliction of some slight, or insult, or deprivation, which could not but have some effect on the most insensible person, and must be acutely felt by one so sensitive as Nicholas. With these two reflections uppermost in her mind, Miss Squeers made the best of the matter to her friend, by observing that Mr. Nickleby was such an odd creature, and of such a violent temper, that she feared she should be obliged to give him up; and parted from her.

114

And here it may be remarked, that Miss Squeers, having bestowed her affections (or whatever it might be that, in the absence of anything better, represented them) on Nicholas Nickleby, had never once seriously contemplated the possibility of his being of a different opinion from herself in the business. Miss Squeers reasoned that she was prepossessing and beautiful, and that her father was master, and Nicholas man, and that her father had saved money, and Nicholas had none, all of which seemed to her conclusive arguments why the young man should feel only too much honoured by her preference. She had not failed to recollect, either, how much more agreeable she could render his situation if she were his friend, and how much more disagreeable if she were his enemy; and, doubtless, many less scrupulous young gentlemen than Nicholas would have encouraged her extravagance had it been only for this very obvious and intelligible reason. However, he had thought proper to do otherwise, and Miss Squeers was outrageous.

'Let him see,' said the irritated young lady, when she had regained her own room, and eased her mind by committing an assault on Phib, 'if I don't set mother against him a little more when she comes back!'

It was scarcely necessary to do this, but Miss Squeers was as good as her word; and poor Nicholas, in addition to bad food, dirty lodging, and the being compelled to witness one dull unvarying round of squalid misery, was treated with every special indignity that malice could suggest, or the most grasping cupidity put upon him.

Nor was this all. There was another and deeper system of annoyance which made his heart sink, and nearly drove him wild, by its injustice and cruelty.

The wretched creature, Smike, since the night Nicholas had spoken kindly to him in the schoolroom, had followed him to and fro, with an ever-restless desire to serve or help him; anticipating such little wants as his humble ability could supply, and content only to be near him. He would sit beside him for hours, looking patiently into his face; and a word would brighten up his care-worn visage, and call into it a passing gleam, even of happiness. He was an altered being; he had an object now; and that object was, to show his attachment to the only person—that person a stranger—who had treated him, not to say with kindness, but like a human creature.

Upon this poor being, all the spleen and ill-humour that could not be vented on Nicholas were unceasingly bestowed. Drudgery would have been nothing—Smike was well used to that. Buffetings inflicted without cause, would have been equally a matter of course; for to them also he had served a long and weary apprenticeship; but it was no sooner observed that he had become attached to Nicholas, than stripes and blows, stripes and blows, morning, noon, and night, were his only portion. Squeers was jealous of the influence which his man had so soon acquired, and his family hated him, and Smike paid for both. Nicholas saw it, and ground his teeth at every repetition of the savage and cowardly attack.

He had arranged a few regular lessons for the boys; and one night, as he paced up and down the dismal schoolroom, his swollen heart almost bursting to think that his protection and countenance should have increased the misery of the wretched being whose peculiar destitution had awakened his pity, he paused mechanically in a dark corner where sat the object of his thoughts.

The poor soul was poring hard over a tattered book, with the traces of recent tears still upon his face; vainly endeavouring to master some task which a child of nine years old, possessed of ordinary powers, could have conquered with ease, but which, to the addled brain of the crushed boy of nineteen, was a sealed and hopeless mystery. Yet there he sat, patiently conning the page again and again, stimulated by no boyish ambition, for he was the common jest and scoff even of the uncouth objects that congregated about him, but inspired by the one eager desire to please his solitary friend.

Nicholas laid his hand upon his shoulder.

'I can't do it,' said the dejected creature, looking up with bitter disappointment in every feature. 'No, no.'

'Do not try,' replied Nicholas.

The boy shook his head, and closing the book with a sigh, looked vacantly round, and laid his head upon his arm. He was weeping.

'Do not for God's sake,' said Nicholas, in an agitated voice; 'I cannot bear to see you.'

'They are more hard with me than ever,' sobbed the boy.

'I know it,' rejoined Nicholas. 'They are.'

'But for you,' said the outcast, 'I should die. They would kill me; they would; I know they would.'

'You will do better, poor fellow,' replied Nicholas, shaking his head mournfully, 'when I am gone.'

'Gone!' cried the other, looking intently in his face.

'Softly!' rejoined Nicholas. 'Yes.'

'Are you going?' demanded the boy, in an earnest whisper.

'I cannot say,' replied Nicholas. 'I was speaking more to my own thoughts, than to you.'

'Tell me,' said the boy imploringly, 'oh do tell me, will you go—will you?'

'I shall be driven to that at last!' said Nicholas. 'The world is before me, after all.'

'Tell me,' urged Smike, 'is the world as bad and dismal as this place?'

'Heaven forbid,' replied Nicholas, pursuing the train of his own thoughts; 'its hardest, coarsest toil, were happiness to this.'

'Should I ever meet you there?' demanded the boy, speaking with unusual wildness and volubility.

'Yes,' replied Nicholas, willing to soothe him.

'No, no!' said the other, clasping him by the hand. 'Should I—should I—tell me that again. Say I should be sure to find you.'

'You would,' replied Nicholas, with the same humane intention, 'and I would help and aid you, and not bring fresh sorrow on you as I have done here.'

The boy caught both the young man's hands passionately in his, and, hugging them to his breast, uttered a few broken sounds which were unintelligible. Squeers entered at the moment, and he shrunk back into his old corner.

116

CHAPTER 13

Nicholas varies the Monotony of Dothebys Hall by a most vigorous and remarkable proceeding, which leads to Consequences of some Importance

The cold, feeble dawn of a January morning was stealing in at the windows of the common sleeping-room, when Nicholas, raising himself on his arm, looked among the prostrate forms which on every side surrounded him, as though in search of some particular object.

It needed a quick eye to detect, from among the huddled mass of sleepers, the form of any given individual. As they lay closely packed together, covered, for warmth's sake, with their patched and ragged clothes, little could be distinguished but the sharp outlines of pale faces, over which the sombre light shed the same dull heavy colour; with, here and there, a gaunt arm thrust forth: its thinness hidden by no covering, but fully exposed to view, in all its shrunken ugliness. There were some who, lying on their backs with upturned faces and clenched hands, just visible in the leaden light, bore more the aspect of dead bodies than of living creatures; and there were others coiled up into strange and fantastic postures, such as might have been taken for the uneasy efforts of pain to gain some temporary relief, rather than the freaks of slumber. A few—and these were among the youngest of the children—slept peacefully on, with smiles upon their faces, dreaming perhaps of home; but ever and again a deep and heavy sigh, breaking the stillness of the room, announced that some new sleeper had awakened to the misery of another day; and, as morning took the place of night, the smiles gradually faded away, with the friendly darkness which had given them birth.

Dreams are the bright creatures of poem and legend, who sport on earth in the night season, and melt away in the first beam of the sun, which lights grim care and stern reality on their daily pilgrimage through the world.

Nicholas looked upon the sleepers; at first, with the air of one who gazes upon a scene which, though familiar to him, has lost none of its sorrowful effect in consequence; and, afterwards, with a more intense and searching scrutiny, as a man would who missed something his eye was accustomed to meet, and had expected to rest upon. He was still occupied in this search, and had half risen from his bed in the eagerness of his quest, when the voice of Squeers was heard, calling from the bottom of the stairs.

'Now then,' cried that gentleman, 'are you going to sleep all day, up there—'

'You lazy hounds?' added Mrs. Squeers, finishing the sentence, and producing, at the same time, a sharp sound, like that which is occasioned by the lacing of stays.

'We shall be down directly, sir,' replied Nicholas.

'Down directly!' said Squeers. 'Ah! you had better be down directly, or I'll be down upon some of you in less. Where's that Smike?'

Nicholas looked hurriedly round again, but made no answer.

'Smike!' shouted Squeers.

'Do you want your head broke in a fresh place, Smike?' demanded his amiable lady in the same key.

Still there was no reply, and still Nicholas stared about him, as did the greater part of the boys, who were by this time roused.

'Confound his impudence!' muttered Squeers, rapping the stair-rail impatiently with his cane. 'Nickleby!'

'Well, sir.'

'Send that obstinate scoundrel down; don't you hear me calling?'

'He is not here, sir,' replied Nicholas.

'Don't tell me a lie,' retorted the schoolmaster. 'He is.'

'He is not,' retorted Nicholas angrily, 'don't tell me one.'

'We shall soon see that,' said Mr. Squeers, rushing upstairs. 'I'll find him, I warrant you.'

With which assurance, Mr. Squeers bounced into the dormitory, and, swinging his cane in the air ready for a blow, darted into the corner where the lean body of the drudge was usually stretched at night. The cane descended harmlessly upon the ground. There was nobody there.

'What does this mean?' said Squeers, turning round with a very pale face. 'Where have you hid him?'

'I have seen nothing of him since last night,' replied Nicholas.

'Come,' said Squeers, evidently frightened, though he endeavoured to look otherwise, 'you won't save him this way. Where is he?'

'At the bottom of the nearest pond for aught I know,' rejoined Nicholas in a low voice, and fixing his eyes full on the master's face.

'Damn you, what do you mean by that?' retorted Squeers in great perturbation. Without waiting for a reply, he inquired of the boys whether any one among them knew anything of their missing schoolmate.

There was a general hum of anxious denial, in the midst of which, one shrill voice was heard to say (as, indeed, everybody thought):

'Please, sir, I think Smike's run away, sir.'

'Ha!' cried Squeers, turning sharp round. 'Who said that?'

'Tomkins, please sir,' rejoined a chorus of voices. Mr. Squeers made a plunge into the crowd, and at one dive, caught a very little boy, habited still in his night-gear, and the perplexed expression of whose countenance, as he was brought forward, seemed to intimate that he was as yet uncertain whether he was about to be punished or rewarded for the suggestion. He was not long in doubt.

'You think he has run away, do you, sir?' demanded Squeers.

'Yes, please sir,' replied the little boy.

'And what, sir,' said Squeers, catching the little boy suddenly by the arms and whisking up his drapery in a most dexterous manner, 'what reason have you to suppose that any boy would want to run away from this establishment? Eh, sir?'

The child raised a dismal cry, by way of answer, and Mr. Squeers, throwing himself into the most favourable attitude for exercising his strength, beat him until the little urchin in his writhings actually rolled out of his hands, when he mercifully allowed him to roll away, as he best could.

'There,' said Squeers. 'Now if any other boy thinks Smike has run away, I shall be glad to have a talk with him.'

There was, of course, a profound silence, during which Nicholas showed his disgust as plainly as looks could show it.

'Well, Nickleby,' said Squeers, eyeing him maliciously. 'You think he has run away, I suppose?'

'I think it extremely likely,' replied Nicholas, in a quiet manner.

'Oh, you do, do you?' sneered Squeers. 'Maybe you know he has?'

'I know nothing of the kind.'

'He didn't tell you he was going, I suppose, did he?' sneered Squeers.

'He did not,' replied Nicholas; 'I am very glad he did not, for it would then have been my duty to have warned you in time.'

'Which no doubt you would have been devilish sorry to do,' said Squeers in a taunting fashion.

'I should indeed,' replied Nicholas. 'You interpret my feelings with great accuracy.'

Mrs. Squeers had listened to this conversation, from the bottom of the stairs; but, now losing all patience, she hastily assumed her night-jacket, and made her way to the scene of action.

'What's all this here to-do?' said the lady, as the boys fell off right and left, to save her the trouble of clearing a passage with her brawny arms. 'What on earth are you a talking to him for, Squeery!'

'Why, my dear,' said Squeers, 'the fact is, that Smike is not to be found.'

'Well, I know that,' said the lady, 'and where's the wonder? If you get a parcel of proud-stomached teachers that set the young dogs a rebelling, what else can you look for? Now, young man, you just have the kindness to take yourself off to the schoolroom, and take the boys off with you, and don't you stir out of there till you have leave given you, or you and I may fall out in a way that'll spoil your beauty, handsome as you think yourself, and so I tell you.'

'Indeed!' said Nicholas.

'Yes; and indeed and indeed again, Mister Jackanapes,' said the excited lady; 'and I wouldn't keep such as you in the house another hour, if I had my way.'

'Nor would you if I had mine,' replied Nicholas. 'Now, boys!'

'Ah! Now, boys,' said Mrs. Squeers, mimicking, as nearly as she could, the voice and manner of the usher. 'Follow your leader, boys, and take pattern by Smike if you dare. See what he'll get for himself, when he is brought back; and, mind! I tell you that you shall have as bad, and twice as bad, if you so much as open your mouths about him.'

'If I catch him,' said Squeers, 'I'll only stop short of flaying him alive. I give you notice, boys.'

'If you catch him,' retorted Mrs. Squeers, contemptuously; 'you are sure to; you can't help it, if you go the right way to work. Come! Away with you!'

With these words, Mrs. Squeers dismissed the boys, and after a little light skirmishing with those in the rear who were pressing forward to get out of the way, but were detained for a few moments by the throng in front, succeeded in clearing the room, when she confronted her spouse alone.

'He is off,' said Mrs. Squeers. 'The cow-house and stable are locked up, so he can't be there; and he's not downstairs anywhere, for the girl has looked. He must have gone York way, and by a public road too.'

'Why must he?' inquired Squeers.

'Stupid!' said Mrs. Squeers angrily. 'He hadn't any money, had he?'

'Never had a penny of his own in his whole life, that I know of,' replied Squeers.

'To be sure,' rejoined Mrs. Squeers, 'and he didn't take anything to eat with him; that I'll answer for. Ha! ha! ha!'

'Ha! ha! ha!' laughed Squeers.

'Then, of course,' said Mrs. S., 'he must beg his way, and he could do that, nowhere, but on the public road.'

'That's true,' exclaimed Squeers, clapping his hands.

'True! Yes; but you would never have thought of it, for all that, if I hadn't said so,' replied his wife. 'Now, if you take the chaise and go one road, and I borrow Swallow's chaise, and go the other, what with keeping our eyes open, and asking questions, one or other of us is pretty certain to lay hold of him.'

The worthy lady's plan was adopted and put in execution without a moment's delay. After a very hasty breakfast, and the prosecution of some inquiries in the village, the result of which seemed to show that he was on the right track, Squeers started forth in the pony-chaise, intent upon discovery and vengeance. Shortly afterwards, Mrs. Squeers, arrayed in the white top-coat, and tied up in various shawls and handkerchiefs, issued forth in another chaise and another direction, taking with her a good-sized bludgeon, several odd pieces of strong cord, and a stout labouring man: all provided and carried upon the expedition, with the sole object of assisting in the capture, and (once caught) insuring the safe custody of the unfortunate Smike.

Nicholas remained behind, in a tumult of feeling, sensible that whatever might be the upshot of the boy's flight, nothing but painful and deplorable consequences were likely to ensue from it. Death, from want and exposure to the weather, was the best that could be expected from the protracted wandering of so poor and helpless a creature, alone and unfriended, through a country of which he was wholly ignorant. There was little, perhaps, to choose between this fate and a return to the tender mercies of the Yorkshire school; but the unhappy being had established a hold upon his sympathy and compassion, which made his heart ache at the prospect of the suffering he was destined to undergo. He lingered on, in restless anxiety, picturing a thousand possibilities, until the evening of next day, when Squeers returned, alone, and unsuccessful.

'No news of the scamp!' said the schoolmaster, who had evidently been stretching his legs, on the old principle, not a few times during the journey. 'I'll have consolation for this out of somebody, Nickleby, if Mrs Squeers don't hunt him down; so I give you warning.'

'It is not in my power to console you, sir,' said Nicholas. 'It is nothing to me.'

'Isn't it?' said Squeers in a threatening manner. 'We shall see!'

'We shall,' rejoined Nicholas.

'Here's the pony run right off his legs, and me obliged to come home with a hack cob, that'll cost fifteen shillings besides other expenses,' said Squeers; 'who's to pay for that, do you hear?'

Nicholas shrugged his shoulders and remained silent.

'I'll have it out of somebody, I tell you,' said Squeers, his usual harsh crafty manner changed to open bullying 'None of your whining vapourings here, Mr. Puppy, but be off to your kennel, for it's past your bedtime! Come! Get out!'

Nicholas bit his lip and knit his hands involuntarily, for his fingerends tingled to avenge the insult; but remembering that the man was drunk, and that it could come to little but a noisy brawl, he contented himself with darting a contemptuous look at the tyrant, and walked, as majestically as he could, upstairs: not a little nettled, however, to observe that Miss Squeers and Master Squeers, and the servant girl, were enjoying the scene from a snug corner; the two former indulging in many edifying remarks about the presumption of poor upstarts, which occasioned a vast deal of laughter, in which even the most miserable of all miserable servant girls joined: while Nicholas, stung to the quick, drew over his head such bedclothes as he had, and sternly resolved that the outstanding account between himself and Mr. Squeers should be settled rather more speedily than the latter anticipated.

Another day came, and Nicholas was scarcely awake when he heard the wheels of a chaise approaching the house. It stopped. The voice of Mrs. Squeers was heard, and in exultation, ordering a glass of spirits for somebody, which was in itself a sufficient sign that something extraordinary had happened. Nicholas hardly dared to look out of the window; but he did so, and the very first object that met his eyes was the wretched Smike: so bedabbled with mud and rain, so haggard and worn, and wild, that, but for his garments being such as no scarecrow was ever seen to wear, he might have been doubtful, even then, of his identity.

'Lift him out,' said Squeers, after he had literally feasted his eyes, in silence, upon the culprit. 'Bring him in; bring him in!'

'Take care,' cried Mrs. Squeers, as her husband proffered his assistance. 'We tied his legs under the apron and made 'em fast to the chaise, to prevent his giving us the slip again.'

With hands trembling with delight, Squeers unloosened the cord; and Smike, to all appearance more dead than alive, was brought into the house and securely locked up in a cellar, until such time as Mr. Squeers should deem it expedient to operate upon him, in presence of the assembled school.

Upon a hasty consideration of the circumstances, it may be matter of surprise to some persons, that Mr. and Mrs. Squeers should have taken so much trouble to repossess themselves of an incumbrance of which it was their wont to complain so loudly; but their surprise will cease when they are informed that the manifold services of the drudge, if performed by anybody else, would have cost the establishment some ten or twelve shillings per week in the shape of wages; and furthermore, that all runaways were, as a matter of policy, made severe examples of, at Dotheboys Hall, inasmuch as, in consequence of the limited extent of its attractions, there was but little inducement, beyond the powerful impulse of fear, for any pupil, provided with the usual number of legs and the power of using them, to remain.

The news that Smike had been caught and brought back in triumph, ran like wild-fire through the hungry community, and expectation was on tiptoe all the morning. On tiptoe it was destined to remain, however, until afternoon; when Squeers, having refreshed himself with his dinner, and further strengthened himself by an extra libation or so, made his appearance (accompanied by his amiable partner) with a countenance of portentous import, and a fearful instrument of flagellation, strong, supple, wax-ended, and new,—in short, purchased that morning, expressly for the occasion.

'Is every boy here?' asked Squeers, in a tremendous voice.

Every boy was there, but every boy was afraid to speak, so Squeers glared along the lines to assure himself; and every eye drooped, and every head cowered down, as he did so.

'Each boy keep his place,' said Squeers, administering his favourite blow to the desk, and regarding with gloomy satisfaction the universal start which it never failed to occasion. 'Nickleby! to your desk, sir.'

It was remarked by more than one small observer, that there was a very curious and unusual expression in the usher's face; but he took his seat, without opening his lips in reply. Squeers, casting a triumphant glance at his assistant and a look of most comprehensive despotism on the boys, left the room, and shortly afterwards returned, dragging Smike by the collar—or rather by that fragment of his jacket which was nearest the place where his collar would have been, had he boasted such a decoration.

In any other place, the appearance of the wretched, jaded, spiritless object would have occasioned a murmur of compassion and remonstrance. It had some effect, even there; for the lookers-on moved uneasily in their seats; and a few of the boldest ventured to steal looks at each other, expressive of indignation and pity.

They were lost on Squeers, however, whose gaze was fastened on the luckless Smike, as he inquired, according to custom in such cases, whether he had anything to say for himself.

'Nothing, I suppose?' said Squeers, with a diabolical grin.

Smike glanced round, and his eye rested, for an instant, on Nicholas, as if he had expected him to intercede; but his look was riveted on his desk.

'Have you anything to say?' demanded Squeers again: giving his right arm two or three flourishes to try its power and suppleness. 'Stand a little out of the way, Mrs. Squeers, my dear; I've hardly got room enough.'

'Spare me, sir!' cried Smike.

'Oh! that's all, is it?' said Squeers. 'Yes, I'll flog you within an inch of your life, and spare you that.'

'Ha, ha, ha,' laughed Mrs. Squeers, 'that's a good 'un!'

'I was driven to do it,' said Smike faintly; and casting another imploring look about him.

'Driven to do it, were you?' said Squeers. 'Oh! it wasn't your fault; it was mine, I suppose—eh?'

'A nasty, ungrateful, pig-headed, brutish, obstinate, sneaking dog,' exclaimed Mrs. Squeers, taking Smike's head under her arm, and administering a cuff at every epithet; 'what does he mean by that?'

'Stand aside, my dear,' replied Squeers. 'We'll try and find out.'

Mrs. Squeers, being out of breath with her exertions, complied. Squeers caught the boy firmly in his grip; one desperate cut had fallen on his body—he was wincing from the lash and uttering a scream of pain—it was raised again, and again about to fall—when Nicholas Nickleby, suddenly starting up, cried 'Stop!' in a voice that made the rafters ring.

'Who cried stop?' said Squeers, turning savagely round.

'I,' said Nicholas, stepping forward. 'This must not go on.'

'Must not go on!' cried Squeers, almost in a shriek.

'No!' thundered Nicholas.

Aghast and stupefied by the boldness of the interference, Squeers released his hold of Smike, and, falling back a pace or two, gazed upon Nicholas with looks that were positively frightful.

'I say must not,' repeated Nicholas, nothing daunted; 'shall not. I will prevent it.'

Squeers continued to gaze upon him, with his eyes starting out of his head; but astonishment had actually, for the moment, bereft him of speech.

'You have disregarded all my quiet interference in the miserable lad's behalf,' said Nicholas; 'you have returned no answer to the letter in which I begged forgiveness for him, and offered to be responsible that he would remain quietly here. Don't blame me for this public interference. You have brought it upon yourself; not I.'

'Sit down, beggar!' screamed Squeers, almost beside himself with rage, and seizing Smike as he spoke.

'Wretch,' rejoined Nicholas, fiercely, 'touch him at your peril! I will not stand by, and see it done. My blood is up, and I have the strength of ten such men as you. Look to yourself, for by Heaven I will not spare you, if you drive me on!'

'Stand back,' cried Squeers, brandishing his weapon.

'I have a long series of insults to avenge,' said Nicholas, flushed with passion; 'and my indignation is aggravated by the dastardly cruelties practised on helpless infancy in this foul den. Have a care; for if you do raise the devil within me, the consequences shall fall heavily upon your own head!'

He had scarcely spoken, when Squeers, in a violent outbreak of wrath, and with a cry like the howl of a wild beast, spat upon him, and struck him a blow across the face with his instrument of torture, which raised up a bar of livid flesh as it was inflicted. Smarting with the agony of the blow, and concentrating into that one moment all his feelings of rage, scorn, and indignation, Nicholas sprang upon him, wrested the weapon from his hand, and pinning him by the throat, beat the ruffian till he roared for mercy.

The boys—with the exception of Master Squeers, who, coming to his father's assistance, harassed the enemy in the rear—moved not, hand or foot; but Mrs. Squeers, with many shrieks for aid, hung on to the tail of her partner's coat, and endeavoured to drag him from his infuriated adversary; while Miss Squeers, who had been peeping through the keyhole in expectation of a very different scene, darted in at the very beginning of the attack, and after launching a shower of inkstands at the usher's head, beat Nicholas to her heart's content; animating herself, at every blow, with the recollection of his having refused her proffered love, and thus imparting additional strength to an arm which (as she took after her mother in this respect) was, at no time, one of the weakest.

Nicholas, in the full torrent of his violence, felt the blows no more than if they had been dealt with feathers; but, becoming tired of the noise and uproar, and feeling that his arm grew weak besides, he threw all his remaining strength into half-a-dozen finishing cuts, and flung Squeers from him with all the force he could muster. The violence of his fall precipitated Mrs. Squeers completely over an adjacent form; and Squeers striking his head against it in his descent, lay at his full length on the ground, stunned and motionless.

Having brought affairs to this happy termination, and ascertained, to his thorough satisfaction, that Squeers was only stunned, and not dead (upon which point he had had some unpleasant doubts at first), Nicholas left his family to restore him, and retired to consider what course he had better adopt. He looked anxiously round for Smike, as he left the room, but he was nowhere to be seen.

After a brief consideration, he packed up a few clothes in a small leathern valise, and, finding that nobody offered to oppose his progress, marched boldly out by the front-door, and shortly afterwards, struck into the road which led to Greta Bridge.

When he had cooled sufficiently to be enabled to give his present circumstances some little reflection, they did not appear in a very encouraging light; he had only four shillings and a few pence in his pocket, and was something more than two hundred and fifty miles from London, whither he resolved to direct his steps, that he might ascertain, among other things, what account of the morning's proceedings Mr. Squeers transmitted to his most affectionate uncle.

Lifting up his eyes, as he arrived at the conclusion that there was no remedy for this unfortunate state of things, he beheld a horseman coming towards him, whom, on nearer approach, he discovered, to his infinite chagrin, to be no other than Mr. John Browdie, who, clad in cords and leather leggings, was urging his animal forward by means of a thick ash stick, which seemed to have been recently cut from some stout sapling.

'I am in no mood for more noise and riot,' thought Nicholas, 'and yet, do what I will, I shall have an altercation with this honest blockhead, and perhaps a blow or two from yonder staff.'

In truth, there appeared some reason to expect that such a result would follow from the encounter, for John Browdie no sooner saw Nicholas advancing, than he reined in his horse by the footpath, and waited until such time as he should come up; looking meanwhile, very sternly between the horse's ears, at Nicholas, as he came on at his leisure.

'Servant, young genelman,' said John.

'Yours,' said Nicholas.

'Weel; we ha' met at last,' observed John, making the stirrup ring under a smart touch of the ash stick.

'Yes,' replied Nicholas, hesitating. 'Come!' he said, frankly, after a moment's pause, 'we parted on no very good terms the last time we met; it was my fault, I believe; but I had no intention of offending you, and no idea that I was doing so. I was very sorry for it, afterwards. Will you shake hands?'

'Shake honds!' cried the good-humoured Yorkshireman; 'ah! that I weel;' at the same time, he bent down from the saddle, and gave Nicholas's fist a huge wrench: 'but wa'at be the matther wi' thy feace, mun? it be all brokken loike.'

'It is a cut,' said Nicholas, turning scarlet as he spoke,—'a blow; but I returned it to the giver, and with good interest too.'

'Noa, did 'ee though?' exclaimed John Browdie. 'Well deane! I loike 'un for thot.'

'The fact is,' said Nicholas, not very well knowing how to make the avowal, 'the fact is, that I have been ill-treated.'

'Noa!' interposed John Browdie, in a tone of compassion; for he was a giant in strength and stature, and Nicholas, very likely, in his eyes, seemed a mere dwarf; 'dean't say thot.'

'Yes, I have,' replied Nicholas, 'by that man Squeers, and I have beaten him soundly, and am leaving this place in consequence.'

'What!' cried John Browdie, with such an ecstatic shout, that the horse quite shied at it. 'Beatten the schoolmeasther! Ho! ho! ho! Beatten the schoolmeasther! who ever heard o' the loike o' that noo! Giv' us thee hond agean, yoongster. Beatten the schoolmeasther! Dang it, I loov' thee for't.'

With these expressions of delight, John Browdie laughed and laughed again—so loud that the echoes, far and wide, sent back nothing but jovial peals of merriment—and shook Nicholas by the hand meanwhile, no less heartily. When his mirth had subsided, he inquired what Nicholas meant to do; on his informing him, to go straight to London, he shook his head doubtfully, and inquired if he knew how much the coaches charged to carry passengers so far.

'No, I do not,' said Nicholas; 'but it is of no great consequence to me, for I intend walking.'

'Gang awa' to Lunnun afoot!' cried John, in amazement.

'Every step of the way,' replied Nicholas. 'I should be many steps further on by this time, and so goodbye!'

'Nay noo,' replied the honest countryman, reining in his impatient horse, 'stan' still, tellee. Hoo much cash hast thee gotten?'

'Not much,' said Nicholas, colouring, 'but I can make it enough. Where there's a will, there's a way, you know.'

John Browdie made no verbal answer to this remark, but putting his hand in his pocket, pulled out an old purse of solid leather, and insisted that Nicholas should borrow from him whatever he required for his present necessities.

'Dean't be afeard, mun,' he said; 'tak' eneaf to carry thee whoam. Thee'lt pay me yan day, a' warrant.'

Nicholas could by no means be prevailed upon to borrow more than a sovereign, with which loan Mr. Browdie, after many entreaties that he would accept of more (observing, with a touch of Yorkshire caution, that if he didn't spend it all, he could put the surplus by, till he had an opportunity of remitting it carriage free), was fain to content himself.

'Tak' that bit o' timber to help thee on wi', mun,' he added, pressing his stick on Nicholas, and giving his hand another squeeze; 'keep a good heart, and bless thee. Beatten the schoolmeasther! 'Cod it's the best thing a've heerd this twonty year!'

So saying, and indulging, with more delicacy than might have been expected from him, in another series of loud laughs, for the purpose of avoiding the thanks which Nicholas poured forth, John Browdie set spurs to his horse, and went off at a smart canter: looking back, from time to time, as Nicholas stood gazing after him, and waving his hand cheerily, as if to encourage him on his way. Nicholas watched the horse and rider until they disappeared over the brow of a distant hill, and then set forward on his journey.

He did not travel far that afternoon, for by this time it was nearly dark, and there had been a heavy fall of snow, which not only rendered the way toilsome, but the track uncertain and difficult to find, after daylight, save by experienced wayfarers. He lay, that night, at a cottage, where beds were let at a cheap rate to the more humble class of travellers; and, rising betimes next morning, made his way before night to Boroughbridge. Passing through that town in search of some cheap resting-place, he stumbled upon an empty barn within a couple of hundred yards of the roadside; in a warm corner of which, he stretched his weary limbs, and soon fell asleep.

When he awoke next morning, and tried to recollect his dreams, which had been all connected with his recent sojourn at Dotheboys Hall, he sat up, rubbed his eyes and stared—not with the most composed countenance possible—at some motionless object which seemed to be stationed within a few yards in front of him.

'Strange!' cried Nicholas; 'can this be some lingering creation of the visions that have scarcely left me! It cannot be real—and yet I—I am awake! Smike!'

The form moved, rose, advanced, and dropped upon its knees at his feet. It was Smike indeed.

'Why do you kneel to me?' said Nicholas, hastily raising him.

'To go with you—anywhere—everywhere—to the world's end—to the churchyard grave,' replied Smike, clinging to his hand. 'Let me, oh do let me. You are my home—my kind friend—take me with you, pray.'

'I am a friend who can do little for you,' said Nicholas, kindly. 'How came you here?'

He had followed him, it seemed; had never lost sight of him all the way; had watched while he slept, and when he halted for refreshment; and had feared to appear before, lest he should be sent back. He had not intended to appear now, but Nicholas had awakened more suddenly than he looked for, and he had had no time to conceal himself.

'Poor fellow!' said Nicholas, 'your hard fate denies you any friend but one, and he is nearly as poor and helpless as yourself.'

'May I—may I go with you?' asked Smike, timidly. 'I will be your faithful hard-working servant, I will, indeed. I want no clothes,' added the poor creature, drawing his rags together; 'these will do very well. I only want to be near you.'

'And you shall,' cried Nicholas. 'And the world shall deal by you as it does by me, till one or both of us shall quit it for a better. Come!'

With these words, he strapped his burden on his shoulders, and, taking his stick in one hand, extended the other to his delighted charge; and so they passed out of the old barn, together.

CHAPTER 14
Having the Misfortune to treat of none but Common People, is necessarily of a Mean and Vulgar Character

In that quarter of London in which Golden Square is situated, there is a bygone, faded, tumble-down street, with two irregular rows of tall meagre houses, which seem to have stared each other out of countenance years ago. The very chimneys appear to have grown dismal and melancholy, from having had nothing better to look at than the chimneys over the way. Their tops are battered, and broken, and blackened with smoke; and, here and there, some taller stack than the rest, inclining heavily to one side, and toppling over the roof, seems to meditate taking revenge for half a century's neglect, by crushing the inhabitants of the garrets beneath.

The fowls who peck about the kennels, jerking their bodies hither and thither with a gait which none but town fowls are ever seen to adopt, and which any country cock or hen would be puzzled to understand, are perfectly in keeping with the crazy habitations of their owners. Dingy, ill-plumed, drowsy flutterers, sent, like many of the neighbouring children, to get a livelihood in the streets, they hop, from stone to stone, in forlorn search of some hidden eatable in the mud, and can scarcely raise a crow among them. The only one with anything approaching to a voice, is an aged bantam at the baker's; and even he is hoarse, in consequence of bad living in his last place.

To judge from the size of the houses, they have been, at one time, tenanted by persons of better condition than their present occupants; but they are now let off, by the week, in floors or rooms, and every door has almost as many plates or bell-handles as there are apartments within. The windows are, for the same reason, sufficiently diversified in appearance, being ornamented with every variety of common blind and curtain that can easily be imagined; while every doorway is blocked up, and rendered nearly impassable, by a motley collection of children and porter pots of all sizes, from the baby in arms and the half-pint pot, to the full-grown girl and half-gallon can.

In the parlour of one of these houses, which was perhaps a thought dirtier than any of its neighbours; which exhibited more bell-handles, children, and porter pots, and caught in all its freshness the first gust of the thick black smoke that poured forth, night and day, from a large brewery hard by; hung a bill, announcing that there was yet one room to let within its walls, though on what story the vacant room could be—regard being had to the outward tokens of many lodgers which the whole front displayed, from the mangle in the kitchen window to the flower-pots on the parapet—it would have been beyond the power of a calculating boy to discover.

The common stairs of this mansion were bare and carpetless; but a curious visitor who had to climb his way to the top, might have observed that there were not wanting indications of the progressive poverty of the inmates, although their rooms were shut. Thus, the first-floor lodgers, being flush of furniture, kept an old mahogany table—real mahogany—on the landing-place outside, which was only taken in, when occasion required. On the second story, the spare furniture dwindled down to a couple of old deal chairs, of which one, belonging to the back-room, was shorn of a leg, and bottomless. The story above, boasted no greater excess than a worm-eaten wash-tub; and the garret landing-place displayed no costlier articles than two crippled pitchers, and some broken blacking-bottles.

It was on this garret landing-place that a hard-featured square-faced man, elderly and shabby, stopped to unlock the door of the front attic, into which, having surmounted the task of turning the rusty key in its still more rusty wards, he walked with the air of legal owner.

This person wore a wig of short, coarse, red hair, which he took off with his hat, and hung upon a nail. Having adopted in its place a dirty cotton nightcap, and groped about in the dark till he found a remnant of candle, he knocked at the partition which divided the two garrets, and inquired, in a loud voice, whether Mr. Noggs had a light.

The sounds that came back were stifled by the lath and plaster, and it seemed moreover as though the speaker had uttered them from the interior of a mug or other drinking vessel; but they were in the voice of Newman, and conveyed a reply in the affirmative.

'A nasty night, Mr. Noggs!' said the man in the nightcap, stepping in to light his candle.

'Does it rain?' asked Newman.

'Does it?' replied the other pettishly. 'I am wet through.'

'It doesn't take much to wet you and me through, Mr. Crowl,' said Newman, laying his hand upon the lappel of his threadbare coat.

'Well; and that makes it the more vexatious,' observed Mr. Crowl, in the same pettish tone.

Uttering a low querulous growl, the speaker, whose harsh countenance was the very epitome of selfishness, raked the scanty fire nearly out of the grate, and, emptying the glass which Noggs had pushed towards him, inquired where he kept his coals.

Newman Noggs pointed to the bottom of a cupboard, and Mr. Crowl, seizing the shovel, threw on half the stock: which Noggs very deliberately took off again, without saying a word.

'You have not turned saving, at this time of day, I hope?' said Crowl.

Newman pointed to the empty glass, as though it were a sufficient refutation of the charge, and briefly said that he was going downstairs to supper.

'To the Kenwigses?' asked Crowl.

Newman nodded assent.

'Think of that now!' said Crowl. 'If I didn't—thinking that you were certain not to go, because you said you wouldn't—tell Kenwigs I couldn't come, and make up my mind to spend the evening with you!'

'I was obliged to go,' said Newman. 'They would have me.'

'Well; but what's to become of me?' urged the selfish man, who never thought of anybody else. 'It's all your fault. I'll tell you what—I'll sit by your fire till you come back again.'

Newman cast a despairing glance at his small store of fuel, but, not having the courage to say no—a word which in all his life he never had said at the right time, either to himself or anyone else—gave way to the proposed arrangement. Mr. Crowl immediately went about making himself as comfortable, with Newman Nogg's means, as circumstances would admit of his being made.

The lodgers to whom Crowl had made allusion under the designation of 'the Kenwigses,' were the wife and olive branches of one Mr. Kenwigs, a turner in ivory, who was looked upon as a person of some consideration on the premises, inasmuch as he occupied the whole of the first floor, comprising a suite of two rooms. Mrs. Kenwigs, too, was quite a lady in her manners, and of a very genteel family, having an uncle who collected a water-rate; besides which distinction, the two eldest of her little girls went twice a week to a dancing school in the neighbourhood, and had flaxen hair, tied with blue ribbons, hanging in luxuriant pigtails down their backs; and wore little white trousers with frills round the ankles—for all of which reasons, and many more equally valid but too numerous to mention, Mrs. Kenwigs was considered a very desirable person to know, and was the constant theme of all the gossips in the street, and even three or four doors round the corner at both ends.

It was the anniversary of that happy day on which the Church of England as by law established, had bestowed Mrs. Kenwigs upon Mr. Kenwigs; and in grateful commemoration of the same, Mrs. Kenwigs had invited a few select friends to cards and a supper in the first floor, and had put on a new gown to receive them in: which gown, being of a flaming colour and made upon a juvenile principle, was so successful that Mr. Kenwigs said the eight years of matrimony and the five children seemed all a dream, and Mrs Kenwigs younger and more blooming than on the very first Sunday he had kept company with her.

Beautiful as Mrs. Kenwigs looked when she was dressed though, and so stately that you would have supposed she had a cook and housemaid at least, and nothing to do but order them about, she had a world of trouble with the preparations; more, indeed, than she, being of a delicate and genteel constitution, could have sustained, had not the pride of housewifery upheld her. At last, however, all the things that had to be got together were got together, and all the things that had to be got out of the way were got out of the way, and everything was ready, and the collector himself having promised to come, fortune smiled upon the occasion.

The party was admirably selected. There were, first of all, Mr. Kenwigs and Mrs. Kenwigs, and four olive Kenwigses who sat up to supper; firstly, because it was but right that they should have a treat on such a day; and secondly, because their going to bed, in presence of the company, would have been inconvenient, not to say improper. Then, there was a young lady who had made Mrs. Kenwigs's dress, and who—it was the most convenient thing in the world—living in the two-pair back, gave up her bed to the baby, and got a little girl to watch it. Then, to match this young lady, was a young man, who had known Mr. Kenwigs when he was a bachelor, and was much esteemed by the ladies, as bearing the reputation of a rake. To these were added a newly-married couple, who had visited Mr. and Mrs Kenwigs in their courtship; and a sister of Mrs. Kenwigs's, who was quite a beauty; besides whom, there was another young man, supposed to entertain honourable designs upon the lady last mentioned; and Mr. Noggs, who was a genteel person to ask, because he had been a gentleman once. There were also an elderly lady from the back-parlour, and one more young lady, who, next to the collector, perhaps was the great lion of the party, being the daughter of a theatrical fireman, who 'went on' in the pantomime, and had the greatest turn for the stage that was ever known, being able to sing and recite in a manner that brought the tears into Mrs. Kenwigs's eyes. There was only one drawback upon the pleasure of seeing such friends, and that was, that the lady in the back-parlour, who was very fat, and turned of sixty, came in a low book-muslin dress and short kid gloves, which so exasperated Mrs. Kenwigs, that that lady assured her visitors, in private, that if it hadn't happened that the supper was cooking at the back-parlour grate at that moment, she certainly would have requested its representative to withdraw.

'My dear,' said Mr. Kenwigs, 'wouldn't it be better to begin a round game?'

'Kenwigs, my dear,' returned his wife, 'I am surprised at you. Would you begin without my uncle?'

'I forgot the collector,' said Kenwigs; 'oh no, that would never do.'

'He's so particular,' said Mrs. Kenwigs, turning to the other married lady, 'that if we began without him, I should be out of his will for ever.'

'Dear!' cried the married lady.

'You've no idea what he is,' replied Mrs. Kenwigs; 'and yet as good a creature as ever breathed.'

'The kindest-hearted man as ever was,' said Kenwigs.

'It goes to his heart, I believe, to be forced to cut the water off, when the people don't pay,' observed the bachelor friend, intending a joke.

'George,' said Mr. Kenwigs, solemnly, 'none of that, if you please.'

'It was only my joke,' said the friend, abashed.

'George,' rejoined Mr. Kenwigs, 'a joke is a wery good thing—a wery good thing—but when that joke is made at the expense of Mrs Kenwigs's feelings, I set my face against it. A man in public life expects to be sneered at—it is the fault of his elewated sitivation, and not of himself. Mrs. Kenwigs's relation is a public man, and that he knows, George, and that he can bear; but putting Mrs. Kenwigs out of the question (if I could put Mrs. Kenwigs out of the question on such an occasion as this), I have the honour to be connected with the collector by marriage; and I cannot allow these remarks in my—' Mr. Kenwigs was going to say 'house,' but he rounded the sentence with 'apartments'.

At the conclusion of these observations, which drew forth evidences of acute feeling from Mrs. Kenwigs, and had the intended effect of impressing the company with a deep sense of the collector's dignity, a ring was heard at the bell.

'That's him,' whispered Mr. Kenwigs, greatly excited. 'Morleena, my dear, run down and let your uncle in, and kiss him directly you get the door open. Hem! Let's be talking.'

Adopting Mr. Kenwigs's suggestion, the company spoke very loudly, to look easy and unembarrassed; and almost as soon as they had begun to do so, a short old gentleman in drabs and gaiters, with a face that might have been carved out of Lignum Vitae, for anything that appeared to the contrary, was led playfully in by Miss Morleena Kenwigs, regarding whose uncommon Christian name it may be here remarked that it had been invented and composed by Mrs. Kenwigs previous to her first lying-in, for the special distinction of her eldest child, in case it should prove a daughter.

'Oh, uncle, I am so glad to see you,' said Mrs. Kenwigs, kissing the collector affectionately on both cheeks. 'So glad!'

'Many happy returns of the day, my dear,' replied the collector, returning the compliment.

Now, this was an interesting thing. Here was a collector of water-rates, without his book, without his pen and ink, without his double knock, without his intimidation, kissing— actually kissing—an agreeable female, and leaving taxes, summonses, notices that he had called, or announcements that he would never call again, for two quarters' due, wholly out of the question. It was pleasant to see how the company looked on, quite absorbed in the sight, and to behold the nods and winks with which they expressed their gratification at finding so much humanity in a tax-gatherer.

'Where will you sit, uncle?' said Mrs. Kenwigs, in the full glow of family pride, which the appearance of her distinguished relation occasioned.

'Anywheres, my dear,' said the collector, 'I am not particular.'

Not particular! What a meek collector! If he had been an author, who knew his place, he couldn't have been more humble.

'Mr. Lillyvick,' said Kenwigs, addressing the collector, 'some friends here, sir, are very anxious for the honour of—thank you—Mr. and Mrs. Cutler, Mr. Lillyvick.'

'Proud to know you, sir,' said Mr. Cutler; 'I've heerd of you very often.' These were not mere words of ceremony; for, Mr. Cutler, having kept house in Mr. Lillyvick's parish, had heard of him very often indeed. His attention in calling had been quite extraordinary.

'George, you know, I think, Mr. Lillyvick,' said Kenwigs; 'lady from downstairs— Mr. Lillyvick. Mr. Snewkes—Mr. Lillyvick. Miss Green—Mr Lillyvick. Mr. Lillyvick— Miss Petowker of the Theatre Royal, Drury Lane. Very glad to make two public characters acquainted! Mrs. Kenwigs, my dear, will you sort the counters?'

Mrs. Kenwigs, with the assistance of Newman Noggs, (who, as he performed sundry little acts of kindness for the children, at all times and seasons, was humoured in his request to be taken no notice of, and was merely spoken about, in a whisper, as the decayed gentleman), did as he was desired; and the greater part of the guests sat down to speculation, while Newman himself, Mrs. Kenwigs, and Miss Petowker of the Theatre Royal Drury Lane, looked after the supper-table.

While the ladies were thus busying themselves, Mr. Lillyvick was intent upon the game in progress, and as all should be fish that comes to a water-collector's net, the dear old gentleman was by no means scrupulous in appropriating to himself the property of his neighbours, which, on the contrary, he abstracted whenever an opportunity presented itself, smiling good-humouredly all the while, and making so many condescending speeches to the owners, that they were delighted with his amiability, and thought in their hearts that he deserved to be Chancellor of the Exchequer at least.

After a great deal of trouble, and the administration of many slaps on the head to the infant Kenwigses, whereof two of the most rebellious were summarily banished, the cloth was laid with much elegance, and a pair of boiled fowls, a large piece of pork, apple-pie, potatoes and greens, were served; at sight of which, the worthy Mr. Lillyvick vented a great many witticisms, and plucked up amazingly: to the immense delight and satisfaction of the whole body of admirers.

Very well and very fast the supper went off; no more serious difficulties occurring, than those which arose from the incessant demand for clean knives and forks; which made poor Mrs. Kenwigs wish, more than once, that private society adopted the principle of schools, and required that every guest should bring his own knife, fork, and spoon; which doubtless would be a great accommodation in many cases, and to no one more so than to the lady and gentleman of the house, especially if the school principle were carried out to the full extent, and the articles were expected, as a matter of delicacy, not to be taken away again.

Everybody having eaten everything, the table was cleared in a most alarming hurry, and with great noise; and the spirits, whereat the eyes of Newman Noggs glistened, being arranged in order, with water both hot and cold, the party composed themselves for conviviality; Mr. Lillyvick being stationed in a large armchair by the fireside, and the four little Kenwigses disposed on a small form in front of the company with their flaxen tails towards them, and their faces to the fire; an arrangement which was no sooner perfected, than Mrs. Kenwigs was overpowered by the feelings of a mother, and fell upon the left shoulder of Mr. Kenwigs dissolved in tears.

'They are so beautiful!' said Mrs. Kenwigs, sobbing.

'Oh, dear,' said all the ladies, 'so they are! it's very natural you should feel proud of that; but don't give way, don't.'

'I can—not help it, and it don't signify,' sobbed Mrs. Kenwigs; 'oh! they're too beautiful to live, much too beautiful!'

On hearing this alarming presentiment of their being doomed to an early death in the flower of their infancy, all four little girls raised a hideous cry, and burying their heads in their mother's lap simultaneously, screamed until the eight flaxen tails vibrated again; Mrs. Kenwigs meanwhile clasping them alternately to her bosom, with attitudes expressive of distraction, which Miss Petowker herself might have copied.

At length, the anxious mother permitted herself to be soothed into a more tranquil state, and the little Kenwigses, being also composed, were distributed among the company, to prevent the possibility of Mrs. Kenwigs being again overcome by the blaze of their combined beauty. This done, the ladies and gentlemen united in prophesying that they would live for many, many years, and that there was no occasion at all for Mrs. Kenwigs to distress herself; which, in good truth, there did not appear to be; the loveliness of the children by no means justifying her apprehensions.

'This day eight year,' said Mr. Kenwigs after a pause. 'Dear me—ah!'

This reflection was echoed by all present, who said 'Ah!' first, and 'dear me,' afterwards.

'I was younger then,' tittered Mrs. Kenwigs.

'No,' said the collector.

'Certainly not,' added everybody.

'I remember my niece,' said Mr. Lillyvick, surveying his audience with a grave air; 'I remember her, on that very afternoon, when she first acknowledged to her mother a partiality for Kenwigs. "Mother," she says, "I love him."'

'"Adore him," I said, uncle,' interposed Mrs. Kenwigs.

'"Love him," I think, my dear,' said the collector, firmly.

'Perhaps you are right, uncle,' replied Mrs. Kenwigs, submissively. 'I thought it was "adore."'

'"Love," my dear,' retorted Mr. Lillyvick. '"Mother," she says, "I love him!" "What do I hear?" cries her mother; and instantly falls into strong conwulsions.'

A general exclamation of astonishment burst from the company.

'Into strong conwulsions,' repeated Mr. Lillyvick, regarding them with a rigid look. 'Kenwigs will excuse my saying, in the presence of friends, that there was a very great objection to him, on the ground that he was beneath the family, and would disgrace it. You remember, Kenwigs?'

'Certainly,' replied that gentleman, in no way displeased at the reminiscence, inasmuch as it proved, beyond all doubt, what a high family Mrs. Kenwigs came of.

'I shared in that feeling,' said Mr. Lillyvick: 'perhaps it was natural; perhaps it wasn't.'

A gentle murmur seemed to say, that, in one of Mr. Lillyvick's station, the objection was not only natural, but highly praiseworthy.

'I came round to him in time,' said Mr. Lillyvick. 'After they were married, and there was no help for it, I was one of the first to say that Kenwigs must be taken notice of. The family did take notice of him, in consequence, and on my representation; and I am bound to say—and proud to say—that I have always found him a very honest, well-behaved, upright, respectable sort of man. Kenwigs, shake hands.'

'I am proud to do it, sir,' said Mr. Kenwigs.

'So am I, Kenwigs,' rejoined Mr. Lillyvick.

'A very happy life I have led with your niece, sir,' said Kenwigs.

'It would have been your own fault if you had not, sir,' remarked Mr Lillyvick.

'Morleena Kenwigs,' cried her mother, at this crisis, much affected, 'kiss your dear uncle!'

The young lady did as she was requested, and the three other little girls were successively hoisted up to the collector's countenance, and subjected to the same process, which was afterwards repeated on them by the majority of those present.

'Oh dear, Mrs. Kenwigs,' said Miss Petowker, 'while Mr. Noggs is making that punch to drink happy returns in, do let Morleena go through that figure dance before Mr. Lillyvick.'

'No, no, my dear,' replied Mrs. Kenwigs, 'it will only worry my uncle.'

'It can't worry him, I am sure,' said Miss Petowker. 'You will be very much pleased, won't you, sir?'

'That I am sure I shall' replied the collector, glancing at the punch-mixer.

'Well then, I'll tell you what,' said Mrs. Kenwigs, 'Morleena shall do the steps, if uncle can persuade Miss Petowker to recite us the Blood-Drinker's Burial, afterwards.'

There was a great clapping of hands and stamping of feet, at this proposition; the subject whereof, gently inclined her head several times, in acknowledgment of the reception.

'You know,' said Miss Petowker, reproachfully, 'that I dislike doing anything professional in private parties.'

'Oh, but not here!' said Mrs. Kenwigs. 'We are all so very friendly and pleasant, that you might as well be going through it in your own room; besides, the occasion—'

'I can't resist that,' interrupted Miss Petowker; 'anything in my humble power I shall be delighted to do.'

Mrs. Kenwigs and Miss Petowker had arranged a small programme of the entertainments between them, of which this was the prescribed order, but they had settled to have a little pressing on both sides, because it looked more natural. The company being all ready, Miss Petowker hummed a tune, and Morleena danced a dance; having previously had the soles of her shoes chalked, with as much care as if she were going on the tight-rope. It was a very beautiful figure, comprising a great deal of work for the arms, and was received with unbounded applause.

'If I was blessed with a—a child—' said Miss Petowker, blushing, 'of such genius as that, I would have her out at the Opera instantly.'

Mrs. Kenwigs sighed, and looked at Mr. Kenwigs, who shook his head, and observed that he was doubtful about it.

'Kenwigs is afraid,' said Mrs. K.

'What of?' inquired Miss Petowker, 'not of her failing?'

'Oh no,' replied Mrs. Kenwigs, 'but if she grew up what she is now,—only think of the young dukes and marquises.'

'Very right,' said the collector.

'Still,' submitted Miss Petowker, 'if she took a proper pride in herself, you know—'

'There's a good deal in that,' observed Mrs. Kenwigs, looking at her husband.

'I only know—' faltered Miss Petowker,—'it may be no rule to be sure—but I have never found any inconvenience or unpleasantness of that sort.'

Mr. Kenwigs, with becoming gallantry, said that settled the question at once, and that he would take the subject into his serious consideration. This being resolved upon, Miss Petowker was entreated to begin the Blood-Drinker's Burial; to which end, that young lady let down her back hair, and taking up her position at the other end of the room, with the bachelor friend posted in a corner, to rush out at the cue 'in death expire,' and catch her in his arms when she died raving mad, went through the performance with extraordinary spirit, and to the great terror of the little Kenwigses, who were all but frightened into fits.

The ecstasies consequent upon the effort had not yet subsided, and Newman (who had not been thoroughly sober at so late an hour for a long long time,) had not yet been able to put in a word of announcement, that the punch was ready, when a hasty knock was heard at the room-door, which elicited a shriek from Mrs. Kenwigs, who immediately divined that the baby had fallen out of bed.

'Who is that?' demanded Mr. Kenwigs, sharply.

'Don't be alarmed, it's only me,' said Crowl, looking in, in his nightcap. 'The baby is very comfortable, for I peeped into the room as I came down, and it's fast asleep, and so is the girl; and I don't think the candle will set fire to the bed-curtain, unless a draught was to get into the room—it's Mr. Noggs that's wanted.'

'Me!' cried Newman, much astonished.

'Why, it is a queer hour, isn't it?' replied Crowl, who was not best pleased at the prospect of losing his fire; 'and they are queer-looking people, too, all covered with rain and mud. Shall I tell them to go away?'

'No,' said Newman, rising. 'People? How many?'

'Two,' rejoined Crowl.

'Want me? By name?' asked Newman.

'By name,' replied Crowl. 'Mr. Newman Noggs, as pat as need be.'

Newman reflected for a few seconds, and then hurried away, muttering that he would be back directly. He was as good as his word; for, in an exceedingly short time, he burst into the room, and seizing, without a word of apology or explanation, a lighted candle and tumbler of hot punch from the table, darted away like a madman.

'What the deuce is the matter with him?' exclaimed Crowl, throwing the door open. 'Hark! Is there any noise above?'

The guests rose in great confusion, and, looking in each other's faces with much perplexity and some fear, stretched their necks forward, and listened attentively.

CHAPTER 15
Acquaints the Reader with the Cause and Origin of the Interruption described in the last Chapter, and with some other Matters necessary to be known

Newman Noggs scrambled in violent haste upstairs with the steaming beverage, which he had so unceremoniously snatched from the table of Mr Kenwigs, and indeed from the very grasp of the water-rate collector, who was eyeing the contents of the tumbler, at the moment of its unexpected abstraction, with lively marks of pleasure visible in his countenance. He bore his prize straight to his own back-garret, where, footsore and nearly shoeless, wet, dirty, jaded, and disfigured with every mark of fatiguing travel, sat Nicholas and Smike, at once the cause and partner of his toil; both perfectly worn out by their unwonted and protracted exertion.

Newman's first act was to compel Nicholas, with gentle force, to swallow half of the punch at a breath, nearly boiling as it was; and his next, to pour the remainder down the throat of Smike, who, never having tasted anything stronger than aperient medicine in his whole life, exhibited various odd manifestations of surprise and delight, during the passage of the liquor down his throat, and turned up his eyes most emphatically when it was all gone.

'You are wet through,' said Newman, passing his hand hastily over the coat which

Nicholas had thrown off; 'and I—I—haven't even a change,' he added, with a wistful glance at the shabby clothes he wore himself.

'I have dry clothes, or at least such as will serve my turn well, in my bundle,' replied Nicholas. 'If you look so distressed to see me, you will add to the pain I feel already, at being compelled, for one night, to cast myself upon your slender means for aid and shelter.'

Newman did not look the less distressed to hear Nicholas talking in this strain; but, upon his young friend grasping him heartily by the hand, and assuring him that nothing but implicit confidence in the sincerity of his professions, and kindness of feeling towards himself, would have induced him, on any consideration, even to have made him acquainted with his arrival in London, Mr. Noggs brightened up again, and went about making such arrangements as were in his power for the comfort of his visitors, with extreme alacrity.

These were simple enough; poor Newman's means halting at a very considerable distance short of his inclinations; but, slight as they were, they were not made without much bustling and running about. As Nicholas had husbanded his scanty stock of money, so well that it was not yet quite expended, a supper of bread and cheese, with some cold beef from the cook's shop, was soon placed upon the table; and these viands being flanked by a bottle of spirits and a pot of porter, there was no ground for apprehension on the score of hunger or thirst, at all events. Such preparations as Newman had it in his power to make, for the accommodation of his guests during the night, occupied no very great time in completing; and as he had insisted, as an express preliminary, that Nicholas should change his clothes, and that Smike should invest himself in his solitary coat (which no entreaties would dissuade him from stripping off for the purpose), the travellers partook of their frugal fare, with more satisfaction than one of them at least had derived from many a better meal.

They then drew near the fire, which Newman Noggs had made up as well as he could, after the inroads of Crowl upon the fuel; and Nicholas, who had hitherto been restrained by the extreme anxiety of his friend that he should refresh himself after his journey, now pressed him with earnest questions concerning his mother and sister.

'Well,' replied Newman, with his accustomed taciturnity; 'both well.'

'They are living in the city still?' inquired Nicholas.

'They are,' said Newman.

'And my sister,'—added Nicholas. 'Is she still engaged in the business which she wrote to tell me she thought she should like so much?'

Newman opened his eyes rather wider than usual, but merely replied by a gasp, which, according to the action of the head that accompanied it, was interpreted by his friends as meaning yes or no. In the present instance, the pantomime consisted of a nod, and not a shake; so Nicholas took the answer as a favourable one.

'Now listen to me,' said Nicholas, laying his hand on Newman's shoulder. 'Before I would make an effort to see them, I deemed it expedient to come to you, lest, by gratifying my own selfish desire, I should inflict an injury upon them which I can never repair. What has my uncle heard from Yorkshire?'

Newman opened and shut his mouth, several times, as though he were trying his utmost to speak, but could make nothing of it, and finally fixed his eyes on Nicholas with a grim and ghastly stare.

'What has he heard?' urged Nicholas, colouring. 'You see that I am prepared to hear the very worst that malice can have suggested. Why should you conceal it from me? I must know it sooner or later; and what purpose can be gained by trifling with the matter for a few minutes, when half the time would put me in possession of all that has occurred? Tell me at once, pray.'

'Tomorrow morning,' said Newman; 'hear it tomorrow.'

'What purpose would that answer?' urged Nicholas.

'You would sleep the better,' replied Newman.

'I should sleep the worse,' answered Nicholas, impatiently. 'Sleep! Exhausted as I am, and standing in no common need of rest, I cannot hope to close my eyes all night, unless you tell me everything.'

'And if I should tell you everything,' said Newman, hesitating.

'Why, then you may rouse my indignation or wound my pride,' rejoined Nicholas; 'but you will not break my rest; for if the scene were acted over again, I could take no other part than I have taken; and whatever consequences may accrue to myself from it, I shall never regret doing as I have done—never, if I starve or beg in consequence. What is a little poverty or suffering, to the disgrace of the basest and most inhuman cowardice! I tell you, if I had stood by, tamely and passively, I should have hated myself, and merited the contempt of every man in existence. The black-hearted scoundrel!'

With this gentle allusion to the absent Mr. Squeers, Nicholas repressed his rising wrath, and relating to Newman exactly what had passed at Dotheboys Hall, entreated him to speak out without more pressing. Thus adjured, Mr Noggs took, from an old trunk, a sheet of paper, which appeared to have been scrawled over in great haste; and after sundry extraordinary demonstrations of reluctance, delivered himself in the following terms.

'My dear young man, you mustn't give way to—this sort of thing will never do, you know—as to getting on in the world, if you take everybody's part that's ill-treated—Damn it, I am proud to hear of it; and would have done it myself!'

Newman accompanied this very unusual outbreak with a violent blow upon the table, as if, in the heat of the moment, he had mistaken it for the chest or ribs of Mr. Wackford Squeers. Having, by this open declaration of his feelings, quite precluded himself from offering Nicholas any cautious worldly advice (which had been his first intention), Mr. Noggs went straight to the point.

'The day before yesterday,' said Newman, 'your uncle received this letter. I took a hasty copy of it, while he was out. Shall I read it?'

'If you please,' replied Nicholas. Newman Noggs accordingly read as follows:

'Dotheboys Hall, 'Thursday Morning. 'Sir,

'My pa requests me to write to you, the doctors considering it doubtful whether he will ever recuvver the use of his legs which prevents his holding a pen.

'We are in a state of mind beyond everything, and my pa is one mask of brooses both blue and green likewise two forms are steeped in his Goar. We were kimpelled to have him carried down into the kitchen where he now lays. You will judge from this that he has been brought very low.

'When your nevew that you recommended for a teacher had done this to my pa and jumped upon his body with his feet and also langwedge which I will not pollewt my pen with describing, he assaulted my ma with dreadful violence, dashed her to the earth, and drove her back comb several inches into her head. A very little more and it must have entered her skull. We have a medical certifiket that if it had, the tortershell would have affected the brain.

'Me and my brother were then the victims of his feury since which we have suffered very much which leads us to the arrowing belief that we have received some injury in our insides, especially as no marks of violence are visible externally. I am screaming out loud all the time I write and so is my brother which takes off my attention rather and I hope will excuse mistakes.

'The monster having sasiated his thirst for blood ran away, taking with him a boy of desperate character that he had excited to rebellyon, and a garnet ring belonging to my ma, and not having been apprehended by the constables is supposed to have been took up by some stage-coach. My pa begs that if he comes to you the ring may be returned, and that you will let the thief and assassin go, as if we prosecuted him he would only be transported, and if he is let go he is sure to be hung before long which will save us trouble and be much more satisfactory. Hoping to hear from you when convenient

'I remain 'Yours and cetrer 'FANNY SQUEERS.

'P.S. I pity his ignorance and despise him.'

A profound silence succeeded to the reading of this choice epistle, during which Newman Noggs, as he folded it up, gazed with a kind of grotesque pity at the boy of desperate character therein referred to; who, having no more distinct perception of the matter in hand, than that he had been the unfortunate cause of heaping trouble and falsehood upon Nicholas, sat mute and dispirited, with a most woe-begone and heart-stricken look.

'Mr. Noggs,' said Nicholas, after a few moments' reflection, 'I must go out at once.'

'Go out!' cried Newman.

'Yes,' said Nicholas, 'to Golden Square. Nobody who knows me would believe this story of the ring; but it may suit the purpose, or gratify the hatred of Mr. Ralph Nickleby to feign to attach credence to it. It is due—not to him, but to myself—that I should state the truth; and moreover, I have a word or two to exchange with him, which will not keep cool.'

'They must,' said Newman.

'They must not, indeed,' rejoined Nicholas firmly, as he prepared to leave the house.

'Hear me speak,' said Newman, planting himself before his impetuous young friend. 'He is not there. He is away from town. He will not be back for three days; and I know that letter will not be answered before he returns.'

'Are you sure of this?' asked Nicholas, chafing violently, and pacing the narrow room with rapid strides.

'Quite,' rejoined Newman. 'He had hardly read it when he was called away. Its contents are known to nobody but himself and us.'

'Are you certain?' demanded Nicholas, precipitately; 'not even to my mother or sister? If I thought that they—I will go there—I must see them. Which is the way? Where is it?'

'Now, be advised by me,' said Newman, speaking for the moment, in his earnestness, like any other man—'make no effort to see even them, till he comes home. I know the man. Do not seem to have been tampering with anybody. When he returns, go straight to him, and speak as boldly as you like. Guessing at the real truth, he knows it as well as you or I. Trust him for that.'

'You mean well to me, and should know him better than I can,' replied Nicholas, after some consideration. 'Well; let it be so.'

Newman, who had stood during the foregoing conversation with his back planted against the door, ready to oppose any egress from the apartment by force, if necessary, resumed his seat with much satisfaction; and as the water in the kettle was by this time boiling, made a glassful of spirits and water for Nicholas, and a cracked mug-full for the joint accommodation of himself and Smike, of which the two partook in great harmony, while Nicholas, leaning his head upon his hand, remained buried in melancholy meditation.

Meanwhile, the company below stairs, after listening attentively and not hearing any noise which would justify them in interfering for the gratification of their curiosity, returned to the chamber of the Kenwigses, and employed themselves in hazarding a great variety of conjectures relative to the cause of Mr. Noggs' sudden disappearance and detention.

'Lor, I'll tell you what,' said Mrs. Kenwigs. 'Suppose it should be an express sent up to say that his property has all come back again!'

'Dear me,' said Mr. Kenwigs; 'it's not impossible. Perhaps, in that case, we'd better send up and ask if he won't take a little more punch.'

'Kenwigs!' said Mr. Lillyvick, in a loud voice, 'I'm surprised at you.'

'What's the matter, sir?' asked Mr. Kenwigs, with becoming submission to the collector of water-rates.

'Making such a remark as that, sir,' replied Mr. Lillyvick, angrily. 'He has had punch already, has he not, sir? I consider the way in which that punch was cut off, if I may use the expression, highly disrespectful to this company; scandalous, perfectly scandalous. It may be the custom to allow such things in this house, but it's not the kind of behaviour that I've been used to see displayed, and so I don't mind telling you, Kenwigs. A gentleman has a glass of punch before him to which he is just about to set his lips, when another gentleman comes and collars that glass of punch, without a "with your leave", or "by your leave", and carries that glass of punch away. This may be good manners—I dare say it is—but I don't understand it, that's all; and what's more, I don't care if I never do. It's my way to speak my mind, Kenwigs, and that is my mind; and if you don't like it, it's past my regular time for going to bed, and I can find my way home without making it later.'

Here was an untoward event! The collector had sat swelling and fuming in offended dignity for some minutes, and had now fairly burst out. The great man—the rich relation—the unmarried uncle—who had it in his power to make Morleena an heiress, and the very baby a legatee—was offended. Gracious Powers, where was this to end!

'I am very sorry, sir,' said Mr. Kenwigs, humbly.

'Don't tell me you're sorry,' retorted Mr. Lillyvick, with much sharpness. 'You should have prevented it, then.'

The company were quite paralysed by this domestic crash. The back-parlour sat with her mouth wide open, staring vacantly at the collector, in a stupor of dismay; the other guests were scarcely less overpowered by the great man's irritation. Mr. Kenwigs, not being skilful in such matters, only fanned the flame in attempting to extinguish it.

'I didn't think of it, I am sure, sir,' said that gentleman. 'I didn't suppose that such a little thing as a glass of punch would have put you out of temper.'

'Out of temper! What the devil do you mean by that piece of impertinence, Mr. Kenwigs?' said the collector. 'Morleena, child—give me my hat.'

'Oh, you're not going, Mr. Lillyvick, sir,' interposed Miss Petowker, with her most bewitching smile.

But still Mr. Lillyvick, regardless of the siren, cried obdurately, 'Morleena, my hat!' upon the fourth repetition of which demand, Mrs Kenwigs sunk back in her chair, with a cry that might have softened a water-butt, not to say a water-collector; while the four little girls (privately instructed to that effect) clasped their uncle's drab shorts in their arms, and prayed him, in imperfect English, to remain.

'Why should I stop here, my dears?' said Mr. Lillyvick; 'I'm not wanted here.'

'Oh, do not speak so cruelly, uncle,' sobbed Mrs. Kenwigs, 'unless you wish to kill me.'

'I shouldn't wonder if some people were to say I did,' replied Mr Lillyvick, glancing angrily at Kenwigs. 'Out of temper!'

'Oh! I cannot bear to see him look so, at my husband,' cried Mrs. Kenwigs. 'It's so dreadful in families. Oh!'

'Mr. Lillyvick,' said Kenwigs, 'I hope, for the sake of your niece, that you won't object to be reconciled.'

The collector's features relaxed, as the company added their entreaties to those of his nephew-in-law. He gave up his hat, and held out his hand.

'There, Kenwigs,' said Mr. Lillyvick; 'and let me tell you, at the same time, to show you how much out of temper I was, that if I had gone away without another word, it would have made no difference respecting that pound or two which I shall leave among your children when I die.'

'Morleena Kenwigs,' cried her mother, in a torrent of affection. 'Go down upon your knees to your dear uncle, and beg him to love you all his life through, for he's more a angel than a man, and I've always said so.'

Miss Morleena approaching to do homage, in compliance with this injunction, was summarily caught up and kissed by Mr. Lillyvick; and thereupon Mrs. Kenwigs darted forward and kissed the collector, and an irrepressible murmur of applause broke from the company who had witnessed his magnanimity.

The worthy gentleman then became once more the life and soul of the society; being again reinstated in his old post of lion, from which high station the temporary distraction of their thoughts had for a moment dispossessed him. Quadruped lions are said to be savage, only when they are hungry; biped lions are rarely sulky longer than when their appetite for distinction remains unappeased. Mr. Lillyvick stood higher than ever; for he had shown his power; hinted at his property and testamentary intentions; gained great credit for disinterestedness and virtue; and, in addition to all, was finally accommodated with a much larger tumbler of punch than that which Newman Noggs had so feloniously made off with.

'I say! I beg everybody's pardon for intruding again,' said Crowl, looking in at this happy juncture; 'but what a queer business this is, isn't it? Noggs has lived in this house, now going on for five years, and nobody has ever been to see him before, within the memory of the oldest inhabitant.'

'It's a strange time of night to be called away, sir, certainly,' said the collector; 'and the behaviour of Mr. Noggs himself, is, to say the least of it, mysterious.'

'Well, so it is,' rejoined Crowl; 'and I'll tell you what's more—I think these two geniuses, whoever they are, have run away from somewhere.'

'What makes you think that, sir?' demanded the collector, who seemed, by a tacit understanding, to have been chosen and elected mouthpiece to the company. 'You have no reason to suppose that they have run away from anywhere without paying the rates and taxes due, I hope?'

Mr. Crowl, with a look of some contempt, was about to enter a general protest against the payment of rates or taxes, under any circumstances, when he was checked by a timely whisper from Kenwigs, and several frowns and winks from Mrs. K., which providentially stopped him.

'Why the fact is,' said Crowl, who had been listening at Newman's door with all his might and main; 'the fact is, that they have been talking so loud, that they quite disturbed me in my room, and so I couldn't help catching a word here, and a word there; and all I heard, certainly seemed to refer to their having bolted from some place or other. I don't wish to alarm Mrs. Kenwigs; but I hope they haven't come from any jail or hospital, and brought away a fever or some unpleasantness of that sort, which might be catching for the children.'

Mrs. Kenwigs was so overpowered by this supposition, that it needed all the tender attentions of Miss Petowker, of the Theatre Royal, Drury Lane, to restore her to anything like a state of calmness; not to mention the assiduity of Mr. Kenwigs, who held a fat smelling-bottle to his lady's nose, until it became matter of some doubt whether the tears which coursed down her face were the result of feelings or sal volatile.

The ladies, having expressed their sympathy, singly and separately, fell, according to custom, into a little chorus of soothing expressions, among which, such condolences as 'Poor dear!'—'I should feel just the same, if I was her'—'To be sure, it's a very trying thing'—and 'Nobody but a mother knows what a mother's feelings is,' were among the most prominent, and most frequently repeated. In short, the opinion of the company was so clearly manifested, that Mr. Kenwigs was on the point of repairing to Mr. Noggs's room, to demand an explanation, and had indeed swallowed a preparatory glass of punch, with great inflexibility and steadiness of purpose, when the attention of all present was diverted by a new and terrible surprise.

This was nothing less than the sudden pouring forth of a rapid succession of the shrillest and most piercing screams, from an upper story; and to all appearance from the very two-pair back, in which the infant Kenwigs was at that moment enshrined. They were no sooner audible, than Mrs Kenwigs, opining that a strange cat had come in, and sucked the baby's breath while the girl was asleep, made for the door, wringing her hands, and shrieking dismally; to the great consternation and confusion of the company.

'Mr. Kenwigs, see what it is; make haste!' cried the sister, laying violent hands upon Mrs. Kenwigs, and holding her back by force. 'Oh don't twist about so, dear, or I can never hold you.'

'My baby, my blessed, blessed, blessed, blessed baby!' screamed Mrs Kenwigs, making every blessed louder than the last. 'My own darling, sweet, innocent Lillyvick—Oh let me go to him. Let me go-o-o-o!'

Pending the utterance of these frantic cries, and the wails and lamentations of the four little girls, Mr. Kenwigs rushed upstairs to the room whence the sounds proceeded; at the door of which, he encountered Nicholas, with the child in his arms, who darted out with such violence, that the anxious father was thrown down six stairs, and alighted on the nearest landing-place, before he had found time to open his mouth to ask what was the matter.

'Don't be alarmed,' cried Nicholas, running down; 'here it is; it's all out, it's all over; pray compose yourselves; there's no harm done;' and with these, and a thousand other assurances, he delivered the baby (whom, in his hurry, he had carried upside down), to Mrs. Kenwigs, and ran back to assist Mr. Kenwigs, who was rubbing his head very hard, and looking much bewildered by his tumble.

Reassured by this cheering intelligence, the company in some degree recovered from their fears, which had been productive of some most singular instances of a total want of presence of mind; thus, the bachelor friend had, for a long time, supported in his arms Mrs. Kenwigs's sister, instead of Mrs. Kenwigs; and the worthy Mr. Lillyvick had been actually seen, in the perturbation of his spirits, to kiss Miss Petowker several times, behind the room-door, as calmly as if nothing distressing were going forward.

'It is a mere nothing,' said Nicholas, returning to Mrs. Kenwigs; 'the little girl, who was watching the child, being tired I suppose, fell asleep, and set her hair on fire.'

'Oh you malicious little wretch!' cried Mrs. Kenwigs, impressively shaking her forefinger at the small unfortunate, who might be thirteen years old, and was looking on with a singed head and a frightened face.

'I heard her cries,' continued Nicholas, 'and ran down, in time to prevent her setting fire to anything else. You may depend upon it that the child is not hurt; for I took it off the bed myself, and brought it here to convince you.'

This brief explanation over, the infant, who, as he was christened after the collector! rejoiced in the names of Lillyvick Kenwigs, was partially suffocated under the caresses of the audience, and squeezed to his mother's bosom, until he roared again. The attention of the company was then directed, by a natural transition, to the little girl who had had the audacity to burn her hair off, and who, after receiving sundry small slaps and pushes from the more energetic of the ladies, was mercifully sent home: the ninepence, with which she was to have been rewarded, being escheated to the Kenwigs family.

'And whatever we are to say to you, sir,' exclaimed Mrs. Kenwigs, addressing young Lillyvick's deliverer, 'I am sure I don't know.'

'You need say nothing at all,' replied Nicholas. 'I have done nothing to found any very strong claim upon your eloquence, I am sure.'

'He might have been burnt to death, if it hadn't been for you, sir,' simpered Miss Petowker.

142

'Not very likely, I think,' replied Nicholas; 'for there was abundance of assistance here, which must have reached him before he had been in any danger.'

'You will let us drink your health, anyvays, sir!' said Mr. Kenwigs motioning towards the table.

'—In my absence, by all means,' rejoined Nicholas, with a smile. 'I have had a very fatiguing journey, and should be most indifferent company—a far greater check upon your merriment, than a promoter of it, even if I kept awake, which I think very doubtful. If you will allow me, I'll return to my friend, Mr. Noggs, who went upstairs again, when he found nothing serious had occurred. Good-night.'

Excusing himself, in these terms, from joining in the festivities, Nicholas took a most winning farewell of Mrs. Kenwigs and the other ladies, and retired, after making a very extraordinary impression upon the company.

'What a delightful young man!' cried Mrs. Kenwigs.

'Uncommon gentlemanly, really,' said Mr. Kenwigs. 'Don't you think so, Mr Lillyvick?'

'Yes,' said the collector, with a dubious shrug of his shoulders, 'He is gentlemanly, very gentlemanly—in appearance.'

'I hope you don't see anything against him, uncle?' inquired Mrs. Kenwigs.

'No, my dear,' replied the collector, 'no. I trust he may not turn out—well—no matter— my love to you, my dear, and long life to the baby!'

'Your namesake,' said Mrs. Kenwigs, with a sweet smile.

'And I hope a worthy namesake,' observed Mr. Kenwigs, willing to propitiate the collector. 'I hope a baby as will never disgrace his godfather, and as may be considered, in arter years, of a piece with the Lillyvicks whose name he bears. I do say—and Mrs. Kenwigs is of the same sentiment, and feels it as strong as I do—that I consider his being called Lillyvick one of the greatest blessings and Honours of my existence.'

'The greatest blessing, Kenwigs,' murmured his lady.

'The greatest blessing,' said Mr. Kenwigs, correcting himself. 'A blessing that I hope, one of these days, I may be able to deserve.'

This was a politic stroke of the Kenwigses, because it made Mr. Lillyvick the great head and fountain of the baby's importance. The good gentleman felt the delicacy and dexterity of the touch, and at once proposed the health of the gentleman, name unknown, who had signalised himself, that night, by his coolness and alacrity.

'Who, I don't mind saying,' observed Mr. Lillyvick, as a great concession, 'is a good-looking young man enough, with manners that I hope his character may be equal to.'

'He has a very nice face and style, really,' said Mrs. Kenwigs.

'He certainly has,' added Miss Petowker. 'There's something in his appearance quite— dear, dear, what's that word again?'

'What word?' inquired Mr. Lillyvick.

'Why—dear me, how stupid I am,' replied Miss Petowker, hesitating. 'What do you call it, when Lords break off door-knockers and beat policemen, and play at coaches with other people's money, and all that sort of thing?'

'Aristocratic?' suggested the collector.

'Ah! aristocratic,' replied Miss Petowker; 'something very aristocratic about him, isn't there?'

The gentleman held their peace, and smiled at each other, as who should say, 'Well! there's no accounting for tastes;' but the ladies resolved unanimously that Nicholas had an aristocratic air; and nobody caring to dispute the position, it was established triumphantly.

The punch being, by this time, drunk out, and the little Kenwigses (who had for some time previously held their little eyes open with their little forefingers) becoming fractious, and requesting rather urgently to be put to bed, the collector made a move by pulling out his watch, and acquainting the company that it was nigh two o'clock; whereat some of the guests were surprised and others shocked, and hats and bonnets being groped for under the tables, and in course of time found, their owners went away, after a vast deal of shaking of hands, and many remarks how they had never spent such a delightful evening, and how they marvelled to find it so late, expecting to have heard that it was half-past ten at the very latest, and how they wished that Mr. and Mrs. Kenwigs had a wedding-day once a week, and how they wondered by what hidden agency Mrs. Kenwigs could possibly have managed so well; and a great deal more of the same kind. To all of which flattering expressions, Mr. and Mrs. Kenwigs replied, by thanking every lady and gentleman, seriatim, for the favour of their company, and hoping they might have enjoyed themselves only half as well as they said they had.

As to Nicholas, quite unconscious of the impression he had produced, he had long since fallen asleep, leaving Mr. Newman Noggs and Smike to empty the spirit bottle between them; and this office they performed with such extreme good-will, that Newman was equally at a loss to determine whether he himself was quite sober, and whether he had ever seen any gentleman so heavily, drowsily, and completely intoxicated as his new acquaintance.

CHAPTER 16
Nicholas seeks to employ himself in a New Capacity, and being unsuccessful, accepts an engagement as Tutor in a Private Family

The first care of Nicholas, next morning, was, to look after some room in which, until better times dawned upon him, he could contrive to exist, without trenching upon the hospitality of Newman Noggs, who would have slept upon the stairs with pleasure, so that his young friend was accommodated.

The vacant apartment to which the bill in the parlour window bore reference, appeared, on inquiry, to be a small back-room on the second floor, reclaimed from the leads, and overlooking a soot-bespeckled prospect of tiles and chimney-pots. For the letting of this portion of the house from week to week, on reasonable terms, the parlour lodger was empowered to treat; he being deputed by the landlord to dispose of the rooms as they became vacant, and to keep a sharp look-out that the lodgers didn't run away. As a means of securing the punctual discharge of which last service he was permitted to live rent-free, lest he should at any time be tempted to run away himself.

Of this chamber, Nicholas became the tenant; and having hired a few common articles of furniture from a neighbouring broker, and paid the first week's hire in advance, out of a small fund raised by the conversion of some spare clothes into ready money, he sat himself down to ruminate upon his prospects, which, like the prospect outside his window, were sufficiently confined and dingy. As they by no means improved on better acquaintance, and as familiarity breeds contempt, he resolved to banish them from his thoughts by dint of hard walking. So, taking up his hat, and leaving poor Smike to arrange and rearrange the room with as much delight as if it had been the costliest palace, he betook himself to the streets, and mingled with the crowd which thronged them.

Although a man may lose a sense of his own importance when he is a mere unit among a busy throng, all utterly regardless of him, it by no means follows that he can dispossess himself, with equal facility, of a very strong sense of the importance and magnitude of his cares. The unhappy state of his own affairs was the one idea which occupied the brain of Nicholas, walk as fast as he would; and when he tried to dislodge it by speculating on the situation and prospects of the people who surrounded him, he caught himself, in a few seconds, contrasting their condition with his own, and gliding almost imperceptibly back into his old train of thought again.

Occupied in these reflections, as he was making his way along one of the great public thoroughfares of London, he chanced to raise his eyes to a blue board, whereon was inscribed, in characters of gold, 'General Agency Office; for places and situations of all kinds inquire within.' It was a shop-front, fitted up with a gauze blind and an inner door; and in the window hung a long and tempting array of written placards, announcing vacant places of every grade, from a secretary's to a foot-boy's.

Nicholas halted, instinctively, before this temple of promise, and ran his eye over the capital-text openings in life which were so profusely displayed. When he had completed his survey he walked on a little way, and then back, and then on again; at length, after pausing irresolutely several times before the door of the General Agency Office, he made up his mind, and stepped in.

He found himself in a little floor-clothed room, with a high desk railed off in one corner, behind which sat a lean youth with cunning eyes and a protruding chin, whose performances in capital-text darkened the window. He had a thick ledger lying open before him, and with the fingers of his right hand inserted between the leaves, and his eyes fixed on a very fat old lady in a mob-cap—evidently the proprietress of the establishment—who was airing herself at the fire, seemed to be only waiting her directions to refer to some entries contained within its rusty clasps.

As there was a board outside, which acquainted the public that servants-of-all-work were perpetually in waiting to be hired from ten till four, Nicholas knew at once that some half-dozen strong young women, each with pattens and an umbrella, who were sitting upon a form in one corner, were in attendance for that purpose: especially as the poor things looked anxious and weary. He was not quite so certain of the callings and stations of two smart young ladies who were in conversation with the fat lady before the fire, until—having sat himself down in a corner, and remarked that he would wait until the other customers had been served—the fat lady resumed the dialogue which his entrance had interrupted.

'Cook, Tom,' said the fat lady, still airing herself as aforesaid.

'Cook,' said Tom, turning over some leaves of the ledger. 'Well!'

'Read out an easy place or two,' said the fat lady.

'Pick out very light ones, if you please, young man,' interposed a genteel female, in shepherd's-plaid boots, who appeared to be the client.

'"Mrs. Marker,"' said Tom, reading, '"Russell Place, Russell Square; offers eighteen guineas; tea and sugar found. Two in family, and see very little company. Five servants kept. No man. No followers."'

'Oh Lor!' tittered the client. 'That won't do. Read another, young man, will you?'

'"Mrs. Wrymug,"' said Tom, '"Pleasant Place, Finsbury. Wages, twelve guineas. No tea, no sugar. Serious family—"'

'Ah! you needn't mind reading that,' interrupted the client.

'"Three serious footmen,"' said Tom, impressively.

'Three? did you say?' asked the client in an altered tone.

'Three serious footmen,' replied Tom. '"Cook, housemaid, and nursemaid; each female servant required to join the Little Bethel Congregation three times every Sunday—with a serious footman. If the cook is more serious than the footman, she will be expected to improve the footman; if the footman is more serious than the cook, he will be expected to improve the cook."'

'I'll take the address of that place,' said the client; 'I don't know but what it mightn't suit me pretty well.'

'Here's another,' remarked Tom, turning over the leaves. '"Family of Mr Gallanbile, MP. Fifteen guineas, tea and sugar, and servants allowed to see male cousins, if godly. Note. Cold dinner in the kitchen on the Sabbath, Mr. Gallanbile being devoted to the Observance question. No victuals whatever cooked on the Lord's Day, with the exception of dinner for Mr. and Mrs. Gallanbile, which, being a work of piety and necessity, is exempted. Mr. Gallanbile dines late on the day of rest, in order to prevent the sinfulness of the cook's dressing herself."'

'I don't think that'll answer as well as the other,' said the client, after a little whispering with her friend. 'I'll take the other direction, if you please, young man. I can but come back again, if it don't do.'

Tom made out the address, as requested, and the genteel client, having satisfied the fat lady with a small fee, meanwhile, went away accompanied by her friend.

As Nicholas opened his mouth, to request the young man to turn to letter S, and let him know what secretaryships remained undisposed of, there came into the office an applicant, in whose favour he immediately retired, and whose appearance both surprised and interested him.

This was a young lady who could be scarcely eighteen, of very slight and delicate figure, but exquisitely shaped, who, walking timidly up to the desk, made an inquiry, in a very low tone of voice, relative to some situation as governess, or companion to a lady. She raised her veil, for an instant, while she preferred the inquiry, and disclosed a countenance of most uncommon beauty, though shaded by a cloud of sadness, which, in one so young, was doubly remarkable. Having received a card of reference to some person on the books, she made the usual acknowledgment, and glided away.

She was neatly, but very quietly attired; so much so, indeed, that it seemed as though her dress, if it had been worn by one who imparted fewer graces of her own to it, might have looked poor and shabby. Her attendant—for she had one—was a red-faced, round-eyed, slovenly girl, who, from a certain roughness about the bare arms that peeped from under her draggled shawl, and the half-washed-out traces of smut and blacklead which tattooed her countenance, was clearly of a kin with the servants-of-all-work on the form: between whom and herself there had passed various grins and glances, indicative of the freemasonry of the craft.

This girl followed her mistress; and, before Nicholas had recovered from the first effects of his surprise and admiration, the young lady was gone. It is not a matter of such complete and utter improbability as some sober people may think, that he would have followed them out, had he not been restrained by what passed between the fat lady and her book-keeper.

'When is she coming again, Tom?' asked the fat lady.

'Tomorrow morning,' replied Tom, mending his pen.

'Where have you sent her to?' asked the fat lady.

'Mrs. Clark's,' replied Tom.

'She'll have a nice life of it, if she goes there,' observed the fat lady, taking a pinch of snuff from a tin box.

Tom made no other reply than thrusting his tongue into his cheek, and pointing the feather of his pen towards Nicholas—reminders which elicited from the fat lady an inquiry, of 'Now, sir, what can we do for you?'

Nicholas briefly replied, that he wanted to know whether there was any such post to be had, as secretary or amanuensis to a gentleman.

'Any such!' rejoined the mistress; 'a-dozen-such. An't there, Tom?'

'I should think so,' answered that young gentleman; and as he said it, he winked towards Nicholas, with a degree of familiarity which he, no doubt, intended for a rather flattering compliment, but with which Nicholas was most ungratefully disgusted.

Upon reference to the book, it appeared that the dozen secretaryships had dwindled down to one. Mr. Gregsbury, the great member of parliament, of Manchester Buildings, Westminster, wanted a young man, to keep his papers and correspondence in order; and Nicholas was exactly the sort of young man that Mr. Gregsbury wanted.

'I don't know what the terms are, as he said he'd settle them himself with the party,' observed the fat lady; 'but they must be pretty good ones, because he's a member of parliament.'

Inexperienced as he was, Nicholas did not feel quite assured of the force of this reasoning, or the justice of this conclusion; but without troubling himself to question it, he took down the address, and resolved to wait upon Mr. Gregsbury without delay.

'I don't know what the number is,' said Tom; 'but Manchester Buildings isn't a large place; and if the worst comes to the worst it won't take you very long to knock at all the doors on both sides of the way till you find him out. I say, what a good-looking gal that was, wasn't she?'

'What girl?' demanded Nicholas, sternly.

'Oh yes. I know—what gal, eh?' whispered Tom, shutting one eye, and cocking his chin in the air. 'You didn't see her, you didn't—I say, don't you wish you was me, when she comes tomorrow morning?'

Nicholas looked at the ugly clerk, as if he had a mind to reward his admiration of the young lady by beating the ledger about his ears, but he refrained, and strode haughtily out of the office; setting at defiance, in his indignation, those ancient laws of chivalry, which not only made it proper and lawful for all good knights to hear the praise of the ladies to whom they were devoted, but rendered it incumbent upon them to roam about the world, and knock at head all such matter-of-fact and un-poetical characters, as declined to exalt, above all the earth, damsels whom they had never chanced to look upon or hear of—as if that were any excuse!

Thinking no longer of his own misfortunes, but wondering what could be those of the beautiful girl he had seen, Nicholas, with many wrong turns, and many inquiries, and almost as many misdirections, bent his steps towards the place whither he had been directed.

Within the precincts of the ancient city of Westminster, and within half a quarter of a mile of its ancient sanctuary, is a narrow and dirty region, the sanctuary of the smaller members of Parliament in modern days. It is all comprised in one street of gloomy lodging-houses, from whose windows, in vacation-time, there frown long melancholy rows of bills, which say, as plainly as did the countenances of their occupiers, ranged on ministerial and opposition benches in the session which slumbers with its fathers, 'To Let', 'To Let'. In busier periods of the year these bills disappear, and the houses swarm with legislators. There are legislators in the parlours, in the first floor, in the second, in the third, in the garrets; the small apartments reek with the breath of deputations and delegates. In damp weather, the place is rendered close, by the steams of moist acts of parliament and frouzy petitions; general postmen grow faint as they enter its infected limits, and shabby figures in quest of franks, flit restlessly to and fro like the troubled ghosts of Complete Letter-writers departed. This is Manchester Buildings; and here, at all hours of the night, may be heard the rattling of latch-keys in their respective keyholes: with now and then—when a gust of wind sweeping across the water which washes the Buildings' feet, impels the sound towards its entrance—the weak, shrill voice of some young member practising tomorrow's speech. All the livelong day, there is a grinding of organs and clashing and clanging of little boxes of music; for Manchester Buildings is an eel-pot, which has no outlet but its awkward mouth—a case-bottle which has no thoroughfare, and a short and narrow neck—and in this respect it may be typical of the fate of some few among its more adventurous residents, who, after wriggling themselves into Parliament by violent efforts and contortions, find that it, too, is no thoroughfare for them; that, like Manchester Buildings, it leads to nothing beyond itself; and that they are fain at last to back out, no wiser, no richer, not one whit more famous, than they went in.

Into Manchester Buildings Nicholas turned, with the address of the great Mr. Gregsbury in his hand. As there was a stream of people pouring into a shabby house not far from the entrance, he waited until they had made their way in, and then making up to the servant, ventured to inquire if he knew where Mr. Gregsbury lived.

The servant was a very pale, shabby boy, who looked as if he had slept underground from his infancy, as very likely he had. 'Mr. Gregsbury?' said he; 'Mr. Gregsbury lodges here. It's all right. Come in!'

Nicholas thought he might as well get in while he could, so in he walked; and he had no sooner done so, than the boy shut the door, and made off.

This was odd enough: but what was more embarrassing was, that all along the passage, and all along the narrow stairs, blocking up the window, and making the dark entry darker still, was a confused crowd of persons with great importance depicted in their looks; who were, to all appearance, waiting in silent expectation of some coming event. From time to time, one man would whisper to his neighbour, or a little group would whisper together, and then the whisperers would nod fiercely to each other, or give their heads a relentless shake, as if they were bent upon doing something very desperate, and were determined not to be put off, whatever happened.

As a few minutes elapsed without anything occurring to explain this phenomenon, and as he felt his own position a peculiarly uncomfortable one, Nicholas was on the point of seeking some information from the man next him, when a sudden move was visible on the stairs, and a voice was heard to cry, 'Now, gentleman, have the goodness to walk up!'

So far from walking up, the gentlemen on the stairs began to walk down with great alacrity, and to entreat, with extraordinary politeness, that the gentlemen nearest the street would go first; the gentlemen nearest the street retorted, with equal courtesy, that they couldn't think of such a thing on any account; but they did it, without thinking of it, inasmuch as the other gentlemen pressing some half-dozen (among whom was Nicholas) forward, and closing up behind, pushed them, not merely up the stairs, but into the very sitting-room of Mr. Gregsbury, which they were thus compelled to enter with most unseemly precipitation, and without the means of retreat; the press behind them, more than filling the apartment.

'Gentlemen,' said Mr. Gregsbury, 'you are welcome. I am rejoiced to see you.'

For a gentleman who was rejoiced to see a body of visitors, Mr. Gregsbury looked as uncomfortable as might be; but perhaps this was occasioned by senatorial gravity, and a statesmanlike habit of keeping his feelings under control. He was a tough, burly, thick-headed gentleman, with a loud voice, a pompous manner, a tolerable command of sentences with no meaning in them, and, in short, every requisite for a very good member indeed.

'Now, gentlemen,' said Mr. Gregsbury, tossing a great bundle of papers into a wicker basket at his feet, and throwing himself back in his chair with his arms over the elbows, 'you are dissatisfied with my conduct, I see by the newspapers.'

'Yes, Mr. Gregsbury, we are,' said a plump old gentleman in a violent heat, bursting out of the throng, and planting himself in the front.

'Do my eyes deceive me,' said Mr. Gregsbury, looking towards the speaker, 'or is that my old friend Pugstyles?'

'I am that man, and no other, sir,' replied the plump old gentleman.

'Give me your hand, my worthy friend,' said Mr. Gregsbury. 'Pugstyles, my dear friend, I am very sorry to see you here.'

'I am very sorry to be here, sir,' said Mr. Pugstyles; 'but your conduct, Mr. Gregsbury, has rendered this deputation from your constituents imperatively necessary.'

'My conduct, Pugstyles,' said Mr. Gregsbury, looking round upon the deputation with gracious magnanimity—'my conduct has been, and ever will be, regulated by a sincere regard for the true and real interests of this great and happy country. Whether I look at home, or abroad; whether I behold the peaceful industrious communities of our island home: her rivers covered with steamboats, her roads with locomotives, her streets with cabs, her skies with balloons of a power and magnitude hitherto unknown in the history of aeronautics in this or any other nation—I say, whether I look merely at home, or, stretching my eyes farther, contemplate the boundless prospect of conquest and possession—achieved by British perseverance and British valour—which is outspread before me, I clasp my hands, and turning my eyes to the broad expanse above my head, exclaim, "Thank Heaven, I am a Briton!"'

The time had been, when this burst of enthusiasm would have been cheered to the very echo; but now, the deputation received it with chilling coldness. The general impression seemed to be, that as an explanation of Mr. Gregsbury's political conduct, it did not enter quite enough into detail; and one gentleman in the rear did not scruple to remark aloud, that, for his purpose, it savoured rather too much of a 'gammon' tendency.

'The meaning of that term—gammon,' said Mr. Gregsbury, 'is unknown to me. If it means that I grow a little too fervid, or perhaps even hyperbolical, in extolling my native land, I admit the full justice of the remark. I am proud of this free and happy country. My form dilates, my eye glistens, my breast heaves, my heart swells, my bosom burns, when I call to mind her greatness and her glory.'

'We wish, sir,' remarked Mr. Pugstyles, calmly, 'to ask you a few questions.'

'If you please, gentlemen; my time is yours—and my country's—and my country's—' said Mr. Gregsbury.

This permission being conceded, Mr. Pugstyles put on his spectacles, and referred to a written paper which he drew from his pocket; whereupon nearly every other member of the deputation pulled a written paper from his pocket, to check Mr. Pugstyles off, as he read the questions.

This done, Mr. Pugstyles proceeded to business.

'Question number one.—Whether, sir, you did not give a voluntary pledge previous to your election, that in event of your being returned, you would immediately put down the practice of coughing and groaning in the House of Commons. And whether you did not submit to be coughed and groaned down in the very first debate of the session, and have since made no effort to effect a reform in this respect? Whether you did not also pledge yourself to astonish the government, and make them shrink in their shoes? And whether you have astonished them, and made them shrink in their shoes, or not?'

'Go on to the next one, my dear Pugstyles,' said Mr. Gregsbury.

'Have you any explanation to offer with reference to that question, sir?' asked Mr. Pugstyles.

'Certainly not,' said Mr. Gregsbury.

The members of the deputation looked fiercely at each other, and afterwards at the member. 'Dear Pugstyles' having taken a very long stare at Mr. Gregsbury over the tops of his spectacles, resumed his list of inquiries.

'Question number two.—Whether, sir, you did not likewise give a voluntary pledge that you would support your colleague on every occasion; and whether you did not, the night before last, desert him and vote upon the other side, because the wife of a leader on that other side had invited Mrs. Gregsbury to an evening party?'

'Go on,' said Mr. Gregsbury.

'Nothing to say on that, either, sir?' asked the spokesman.

'Nothing whatever,' replied Mr. Gregsbury. The deputation, who had only seen him at canvassing or election time, were struck dumb by his coolness. He didn't appear like the same man; then he was all milk and honey; now he was all starch and vinegar. But men are so different at different times!

'Question number three—and last,' said Mr. Pugstyles, emphatically. 'Whether, sir, you did not state upon the hustings, that it was your firm and determined intention to oppose everything proposed; to divide the house upon every question, to move for returns on every subject, to place a motion on the books every day, and, in short, in your own memorable words, to play the very devil with everything and everybody?' With this comprehensive inquiry, Mr. Pugstyles folded up his list of questions, as did all his backers.

Mr. Gregsbury reflected, blew his nose, threw himself further back in his chair, came forward again, leaning his elbows on the table, made a triangle with his two thumbs and his two forefingers, and tapping his nose with the apex thereof, replied (smiling as he said it), 'I deny everything.'

At this unexpected answer, a hoarse murmur arose from the deputation; and the same gentleman who had expressed an opinion relative to the gammoning nature of the introductory speech, again made a monosyllabic demonstration, by growling out 'Resign!' Which growl being taken up by his fellows, swelled into a very earnest and general remonstrance.

'I am requested, sir, to express a hope,' said Mr. Pugstyles, with a distant bow, 'that on receiving a requisition to that effect from a great majority of your constituents, you will not object at once to resign your seat in favour of some candidate whom they think they can better trust.'

To this, Mr. Gregsbury read the following reply, which, anticipating the request, he had composed in the form of a letter, whereof copies had been made to send round to the newspapers.

'My Dear Mr Pugstyles,

'Next to the welfare of our beloved island—this great and free and happy country, whose powers and resources are, I sincerely believe, illimitable—I value that noble independence which is an Englishman's proudest boast, and which I fondly hope to bequeath to my children, untarnished and unsullied. Actuated by no personal motives, but moved only by high and great constitutional considerations; which I will not attempt to explain, for they are really beneath the comprehension of those who have not made themselves masters, as I have, of the intricate and arduous study of politics; I would rather keep my seat, and intend doing so.

'Will you do me the favour to present my compliments to the constituent body, and acquaint them with this circumstance?

'With great esteem, 'My dear Mr. Pugstyles, '&c.&c.'

'Then you will not resign, under any circumstances?' asked the spokesman.

Mr. Gregsbury smiled, and shook his head.

'Then, good-morning, sir,' said Pugstyles, angrily.

'Heaven bless you!' said Mr. Gregsbury. And the deputation, with many growls and scowls, filed off as quickly as the narrowness of the staircase would allow of their getting down.

The last man being gone, Mr. Gregsbury rubbed his hands and chuckled, as merry fellows will, when they think they have said or done a more than commonly good thing; he was so engrossed in this self-congratulation, that he did not observe that Nicholas had been left behind in the shadow of the window-curtains, until that young gentleman, fearing he might otherwise overhear some soliloquy intended to have no listeners, coughed twice or thrice, to attract the member's notice.

'What's that?' said Mr. Gregsbury, in sharp accents.

Nicholas stepped forward, and bowed.

'What do you do here, sir?' asked Mr. Gregsbury; 'a spy upon my privacy! A concealed voter! You have heard my answer, sir. Pray follow the deputation.'

'I should have done so, if I had belonged to it, but I do not,' said Nicholas.

'Then how came you here, sir?' was the natural inquiry of Mr. Gregsbury, MP. 'And where the devil have you come from, sir?' was the question which followed it.

'I brought this card from the General Agency Office, sir,' said Nicholas, 'wishing to offer myself as your secretary, and understanding that you stood in need of one.'

'That's all you have come for, is it?' said Mr. Gregsbury, eyeing him in some doubt.

Nicholas replied in the affirmative.

'You have no connection with any of those rascally papers have you?' said Mr. Gregsbury. 'You didn't get into the room, to hear what was going forward, and put it in print, eh?'

'I have no connection, I am sorry to say, with anything at present,' rejoined Nicholas,—politely enough, but quite at his ease.

'Oh!' said Mr. Gregsbury. 'How did you find your way up here, then?'

Nicholas related how he had been forced up by the deputation.

'That was the way, was it?' said Mr. Gregsbury. 'Sit down.'

Nicholas took a chair, and Mr. Gregsbury stared at him for a long time, as if to make certain, before he asked any further questions, that there were no objections to his outward appearance.

'You want to be my secretary, do you?' he said at length.

'I wish to be employed in that capacity, sir,' replied Nicholas.

'Well,' said Mr. Gregsbury; 'now what can you do?'

'I suppose,' replied Nicholas, smiling, 'that I can do what usually falls to the lot of other secretaries.'

'What's that?' inquired Mr. Gregsbury.

'What is it?' replied Nicholas.

'Ah! What is it?' retorted the member, looking shrewdly at him, with his head on one side.

'A secretary's duties are rather difficult to define, perhaps,' said Nicholas, considering. 'They include, I presume, correspondence?'

'Good,' interposed Mr. Gregsbury.

'The arrangement of papers and documents?'

'Very good.'

'Occasionally, perhaps, the writing from your dictation; and possibly, sir,' said Nicholas, with a half-smile, 'the copying of your speech for some public journal, when you have made one of more than usual importance.'

'Certainly,' rejoined Mr. Gregsbury. 'What else?'

'Really,' said Nicholas, after a moment's reflection, 'I am not able, at this instant, to recapitulate any other duty of a secretary, beyond the general one of making himself as agreeable and useful to his employer as he can, consistently with his own respectability, and without overstepping that line of duties which he undertakes to perform, and which the designation of his office is usually understood to imply.'

Mr. Gregsbury looked fixedly at Nicholas for a short time, and then glancing warily round the room, said in a suppressed voice:

'This is all very well, Mr—what is your name?'

'Nickleby.'

'This is all very well, Mr. Nickleby, and very proper, so far as it goes—so far as it goes, but it doesn't go far enough. There are other duties, Mr Nickleby, which a secretary to a parliamentary gentleman must never lose sight of. I should require to be crammed, sir.'

'I beg your pardon,' interposed Nicholas, doubtful whether he had heard aright.

'—To be crammed, sir,' repeated Mr. Gregsbury.

'May I beg your pardon again, if I inquire what you mean, sir?' said Nicholas.

'My meaning, sir, is perfectly plain,' replied Mr. Gregsbury with a solemn aspect. 'My secretary would have to make himself master of the foreign policy of the world, as it is mirrored in the newspapers; to run his eye over all accounts of public meetings, all leading articles, and accounts of the proceedings of public bodies; and to make notes of anything which it appeared to him might be made a point of, in any little speech upon the question of some petition lying on the table, or anything of that kind. Do you understand?'

'I think I do, sir,' replied Nicholas.

'Then,' said Mr. Gregsbury, 'it would be necessary for him to make himself acquainted, from day to day, with newspaper paragraphs on passing events; such as "Mysterious disappearance, and supposed suicide of a potboy," or anything of that sort, upon which I might found a question to the Secretary of State for the Home Department. Then, he would have to copy the question, and as much as I remembered of the answer (including a little compliment about independence and good sense); and to send the manuscript in a frank to the local paper, with perhaps half-a-dozen lines of leader, to the effect, that I was always to be found in my place in parliament, and never shrunk from the responsible and arduous duties, and so forth. You see?'

Nicholas bowed.

'Besides which,' continued Mr. Gregsbury, 'I should expect him, now and then, to go through a few figures in the printed tables, and to pick out a few results, so that I might come out pretty well on timber duty questions, and finance questions, and so on; and I should like him to get up a few little arguments about the disastrous effects of a return to cash payments and a metallic currency, with a touch now and then about the exportation of bullion, and the Emperor of Russia, and bank notes, and all that kind of thing, which it's only necessary to talk fluently about, because nobody understands it. Do you take me?'

'I think I understand,' said Nicholas.

'With regard to such questions as are not political,' continued Mr Gregsbury, warming; 'and which one can't be expected to care a curse about, beyond the natural care of not allowing inferior people to be as well off as ourselves—else where are our privileges?—I should wish my secretary to get together a few little flourishing speeches, of a patriotic cast. For instance, if any preposterous bill were brought forward, for giving poor grubbing devils of authors a right to their own property, I should like to say, that I for one would never consent to opposing an insurmountable bar to the diffusion of literature among the people,—you understand?—that the creations of the pocket, being man's, might belong to one man, or one family; but that the creations of the brain, being God's, ought as a matter of course to belong to the people at large—and if I was pleasantly disposed, I should like to make a joke about posterity, and say that those who wrote for posterity should be content to be rewarded by the approbation of posterity; it might take with the house, and could never do me any harm, because posterity can't be expected to know anything about me or my jokes either—do you see?'

'I see that, sir,' replied Nicholas.

'You must always bear in mind, in such cases as this, where our interests are not affected,' said Mr. Gregsbury, 'to put it very strong about the people, because it comes out very well at election-time; and you could be as funny as you liked about the authors; because I believe the greater part of them live in lodgings, and are not voters. This is a hasty outline of the chief things you'd have to do, except waiting in the lobby every night, in case I forgot anything, and should want fresh cramming; and, now and then, during great debates, sitting in the front row of the gallery, and saying to the people about—'You see that gentleman, with his hand to his face, and his arm twisted round the pillar—that's Mr Gregsbury—the celebrated Mr. Gregsbury,'—with any other little eulogium that might strike you at the moment. And for salary,' said Mr Gregsbury, winding up with great rapidity; for he was out of breath—'and for salary, I don't mind saying at once in round numbers, to prevent any dissatisfaction—though it's more than I've been accustomed to give—fifteen shillings a week, and find yourself. There!'

With this handsome offer, Mr. Gregsbury once more threw himself back in his chair, and looked like a man who had been most profligately liberal, but is determined not to repent of it notwithstanding.

'Fifteen shillings a week is not much,' said Nicholas, mildly.

'Not much! Fifteen shillings a week not much, young man?' cried Mr Gregsbury. 'Fifteen shillings a—'

'Pray do not suppose that I quarrel with the sum, sir,' replied Nicholas; 'for I am not ashamed to confess, that whatever it may be in itself, to me it is a great deal. But the duties and responsibilities make the recompense small, and they are so very heavy that I fear to undertake them.'

'Do you decline to undertake them, sir?' inquired Mr. Gregsbury, with his hand on the bell-rope.

'I fear they are too great for my powers, however good my will may be, sir,' replied Nicholas.

'That is as much as to say that you had rather not accept the place, and that you consider fifteen shillings a week too little,' said Mr. Gregsbury, ringing. 'Do you decline it, sir?'

'I have no alternative but to do so,' replied Nicholas.

'Door, Matthews!' said Mr. Gregsbury, as the boy appeared.

'I am sorry I have troubled you unnecessarily, sir,' said Nicholas.

'I am sorry you have,' rejoined Mr. Gregsbury, turning his back upon him. 'Door, Matthews!'

'Good-morning, sir,' said Nicholas.

'Door, Matthews!' cried Mr. Gregsbury.

The boy beckoned Nicholas, and tumbling lazily downstairs before him, opened the door, and ushered him into the street. With a sad and pensive air, he retraced his steps homewards.

Smike had scraped a meal together from the remnant of last night's supper, and was anxiously awaiting his return. The occurrences of the morning had not improved Nicholas's appetite, and, by him, the dinner remained untasted. He was sitting in a thoughtful attitude, with the plate which the poor fellow had assiduously filled with the choicest morsels, untouched, by his side, when Newman Noggs looked into the room.

'Come back?' asked Newman.

'Yes,' replied Nicholas, 'tired to death: and, what is worse, might have remained at home for all the good I have done.'

'Couldn't expect to do much in one morning,' said Newman.

'Maybe so, but I am sanguine, and did expect,' said Nicholas, 'and am proportionately disappointed.' Saying which, he gave Newman an account of his proceedings.

'If I could do anything,' said Nicholas, 'anything, however slight, until Ralph Nickleby returns, and I have eased my mind by confronting him, I should feel happier. I should think it no disgrace to work, Heaven knows. Lying indolently here, like a half-tamed sullen beast, distracts me.'

'I don't know,' said Newman; 'small things offer—they would pay the rent, and more— but you wouldn't like them; no, you could hardly be expected to undergo it—no, no.'

'What could I hardly be expected to undergo?' asked Nicholas, raising his eyes. 'Show me, in this wide waste of London, any honest means by which I could even defray the weekly hire of this poor room, and see if I shrink from resorting to them! Undergo! I have undergone too much, my friend, to feel pride or squeamishness now. Except—' added Nicholas hastily, after a short silence, 'except such squeamishness as is common honesty, and so much pride as constitutes self-respect. I see little to choose, between assistant to a brutal pedagogue, and toad-eater to a mean and ignorant upstart, be he member or no member.'

'I hardly know whether I should tell you what I heard this morning, or not,' said Newman.

'Has it reference to what you said just now?' asked Nicholas.

'It has.'

'Then in Heaven's name, my good friend, tell it me,' said Nicholas. 'For God's sake consider my deplorable condition; and, while I promise to take no step without taking counsel with you, give me, at least, a vote in my own behalf.'

Moved by this entreaty, Newman stammered forth a variety of most unaccountable and entangled sentences, the upshot of which was, that Mrs Kenwigs had examined him, at great length that morning, touching the origin of his acquaintance with, and the whole life, adventures, and pedigree of, Nicholas; that Newman had parried these questions as long as he could, but being, at length, hard pressed and driven into a corner, had gone so far as to admit, that Nicholas was a tutor of great accomplishments, involved in some misfortunes which he was not at liberty to explain, and bearing the name of Johnson. That Mrs. Kenwigs, impelled by gratitude, or ambition, or maternal pride, or maternal love, or all four powerful motives conjointly, had taken secret conference with Mr. Kenwigs, and had finally returned to propose that Mr. Johnson should instruct the four Miss Kenwigses in the French language as spoken by natives, at the weekly stipend of five shillings, current coin of the realm; being at the rate of one shilling per week, per each Miss Kenwigs, and one shilling over, until such time as the baby might be able to take it out in grammar.

'Which, unless I am very much mistaken,' observed Mrs. Kenwigs in making the proposition, 'will not be very long; for such clever children, Mr Noggs, never were born into this world, I do believe.'

'There,' said Newman, 'that's all. It's beneath you, I know; but I thought that perhaps you might—'

'Might!' cried Nicholas, with great alacrity; 'of course I shall. I accept the offer at once. Tell the worthy mother so, without delay, my dear fellow; and that I am ready to begin whenever she pleases.'

Newman hastened, with joyful steps, to inform Mrs. Kenwigs of his friend's acquiescence, and soon returning, brought back word that they would be happy to see him in the first floor as soon as convenient; that Mrs Kenwigs had, upon the instant, sent out to secure a second-hand French grammar and dialogues, which had long been fluttering in the sixpenny box at the bookstall round the corner; and that the family, highly excited at the prospect of this addition to their gentility, wished the initiatory lesson to come off immediately.

And here it may be observed, that Nicholas was not, in the ordinary sense of the word, a young man of high spirit. He would resent an affront to himself, or interpose to redress a wrong offered to another, as boldly and freely as any knight that ever set lance in rest; but he lacked that peculiar excess of coolness and great-minded selfishness, which invariably distinguish gentlemen of high spirit. In truth, for our own part, we are disposed to look upon such gentleman as being rather incumbrances than otherwise in rising families: happening to be acquainted with several whose spirit prevents their settling down to any grovelling occupation, and only displays itself in a tendency to cultivate moustachios, and look fierce; and although moustachios and ferocity are both very pretty things in their way, and very much to be commended, we confess to a desire to see them bred at the owner's proper cost, rather than at the expense of low-spirited people.

Nicholas, therefore, not being a high-spirited young man according to common parlance, and deeming it a greater degradation to borrow, for the supply of his necessities, from Newman Noggs, than to teach French to the little Kenwigses for five shillings a week, accepted the offer with the alacrity already described, and betook himself to the first floor with all convenient speed.

Here, he was received by Mrs. Kenwigs with a genteel air, kindly intended to assure him of her protection and support; and here, too, he found Mr Lillyvick and Miss Petowker; the four Miss Kenwigses on their form of audience; and the baby in a dwarf porter's chair with a deal tray before it, amusing himself with a toy horse without a head; the said horse being composed of a small wooden cylinder, not unlike an Italian iron, supported on four crooked pegs, and painted in ingenious resemblance of red wafers set in blacking.

'How do you do, Mr. Johnson?' said Mrs. Kenwigs. 'Uncle—Mr. Johnson.'

'How do you do, sir?' said Mr. Lillyvick—rather sharply; for he had not known what Nicholas was, on the previous night, and it was rather an aggravating circumstance if a tax collector had been too polite to a teacher.

'Mr. Johnson is engaged as private master to the children, uncle,' said Mrs Kenwigs.

'So you said just now, my dear,' replied Mr. Lillyvick.

'But I hope,' said Mrs. Kenwigs, drawing herself up, 'that that will not make them proud; but that they will bless their own good fortune, which has born them superior to common people's children. Do you hear, Morleena?'

'Yes, ma,' replied Miss Kenwigs.

'And when you go out in the streets, or elsewhere, I desire that you don't boast of it to the other children,' said Mrs. Kenwigs; 'and that if you must say anything about it, you don't say no more than "We've got a private master comes to teach us at home, but we ain't proud, because ma says it's sinful." Do you hear, Morleena?'

'Yes, ma,' replied Miss Kenwigs again.

'Then mind you recollect, and do as I tell you,' said Mrs. Kenwigs. 'Shall Mr. Johnson begin, uncle?'

'I am ready to hear, if Mr. Johnson is ready to commence, my dear,' said the collector, assuming the air of a profound critic. 'What sort of language do you consider French, sir?'

'How do you mean?' asked Nicholas.

'Do you consider it a good language, sir?' said the collector; 'a pretty language, a sensible language?'

'A pretty language, certainly,' replied Nicholas; 'and as it has a name for everything, and admits of elegant conversation about everything, I presume it is a sensible one.'

'I don't know,' said Mr. Lillyvick, doubtfully. 'Do you call it a cheerful language, now?'

'Yes,' replied Nicholas, 'I should say it was, certainly.'

'It's very much changed since my time, then,' said the collector, 'very much.'

'Was it a dismal one in your time?' asked Nicholas, scarcely able to repress a smile.

'Very,' replied Mr. Lillyvick, with some vehemence of manner. 'It's the war time that I speak of; the last war. It may be a cheerful language. I should be sorry to contradict anybody; but I can only say that I've heard the French prisoners, who were natives, and ought to know how to speak it, talking in such a dismal manner, that it made one miserable to hear them. Ay, that I have, fifty times, sir—fifty times!'

Mr. Lillyvick was waxing so cross, that Mrs. Kenwigs thought it expedient to motion to Nicholas not to say anything; and it was not until Miss Petowker had practised several blandishments, to soften the excellent old gentleman, that he deigned to break silence by asking,

'What's the water in French, sir?'

'L'eau,' replied Nicholas.

'Ah!' said Mr. Lillyvick, shaking his head mournfully, 'I thought as much. Lo, eh? I don't think anything of that language—nothing at all.'

'I suppose the children may begin, uncle?' said Mrs. Kenwigs.

'Oh yes; they may begin, my dear,' replied the collector, discontentedly. 'I have no wish to prevent them.'

This permission being conceded, the four Miss Kenwigses sat in a row, with their tails all one way, and Morleena at the top: while Nicholas, taking the book, began his preliminary explanations. Miss Petowker and Mrs Kenwigs looked on, in silent admiration, broken only by the whispered assurances of the latter, that Morleena would have it all by heart in no time; and Mr. Lillyvick regarded the group with frowning and attentive eyes, lying in wait for something upon which he could open a fresh discussion on the language.

CHAPTER 17
Follows the Fortunes of Miss Nickleby

It was with a heavy heart, and many sad forebodings which no effort could banish, that Kate Nickleby, on the morning appointed for the commencement of her engagement with Madame Mantalini, left the city when its clocks yet wanted a quarter of an hour of eight, and threaded her way alone, amid the noise and bustle of the streets, towards the west end of London.

At this early hour many sickly girls, whose business, like that of the poor worm, is to produce, with patient toil, the finery that bedecks the thoughtless and luxurious, traverse our streets, making towards the scene of their daily labour, and catching, as if by stealth, in their hurried walk, the only gasp of wholesome air and glimpse of sunlight which cheer their monotonous existence during the long train of hours that make a working day. As she drew nigh to the more fashionable quarter of the town, Kate marked many of this class as they passed by, hurrying like herself to their painful occupation, and saw, in their unhealthy looks and feeble gait, but too clear an evidence that her misgivings were not wholly groundless.

She arrived at Madame Mantalini's some minutes before the appointed hour, and after walking a few times up and down, in the hope that some other female might arrive and spare her the embarrassment of stating her business to the servant, knocked timidly at the door: which, after some delay, was opened by the footman, who had been putting on his striped jacket as he came upstairs, and was now intent on fastening his apron.

'Is Madame Mantalini in?' faltered Kate.

'Not often out at this time, miss,' replied the man in a tone which rendered "Miss," something more offensive than "My dear."

'Can I see her?' asked Kate.

'Eh?' replied the man, holding the door in his hand, and honouring the inquirer with a stare and a broad grin, 'Lord, no.'

'I came by her own appointment,' said Kate; 'I am—I am—to be employed here.'

'Oh! you should have rung the worker's bell,' said the footman, touching the handle of one in the door-post. 'Let me see, though, I forgot—Miss Nickleby, is it?'

'Yes,' replied Kate.

'You're to walk upstairs then, please,' said the man. 'Madame Mantalini wants to see you—this way—take care of these things on the floor.'

Cautioning her, in these terms, not to trip over a heterogeneous litter of pastry-cook's trays, lamps, waiters full of glasses, and piles of rout seats which were strewn about the hall, plainly bespeaking a late party on the previous night, the man led the way to the second story, and ushered Kate into a back-room, communicating by folding-doors with the apartment in which she had first seen the mistress of the establishment.

'If you'll wait here a minute,' said the man, 'I'll tell her presently.' Having made this promise with much affability, he retired and left Kate alone.

There was not much to amuse in the room; of which the most attractive feature was, a half-length portrait in oil, of Mr. Mantalini, whom the artist had depicted scratching his head in an easy manner, and thus displaying to advantage a diamond ring, the gift of Madame Mantalini before her marriage. There was, however, the sound of voices in conversation in the next room; and as the conversation was loud and the partition thin, Kate could not help discovering that they belonged to Mr and Mrs. Mantalini.

'If you will be odiously, demnebly, outr_i_geously jealous, my soul,' said Mr. Mantalini, 'you will be very miserable—horrid miserable—demnition miserable.' And then, there was a sound as though Mr. Mantalini were sipping his coffee.

'I am miserable,' returned Madame Mantalini, evidently pouting.

'Then you are an ungrateful, unworthy, demd unthankful little fairy,' said Mr. Mantalini.

'I am not,' returned Madame, with a sob.

'Do not put itself out of humour,' said Mr. Mantalini, breaking an egg. 'It is a pretty, bewitching little demd countenance, and it should not be out of humour, for it spoils its loveliness, and makes it cross and gloomy like a frightful, naughty, demd hobgoblin.'

'I am not to be brought round in that way, always,' rejoined Madame, sulkily.

'It shall be brought round in any way it likes best, and not brought round at all if it likes that better,' retorted Mr. Mantalini, with his egg-spoon in his mouth.

'It's very easy to talk,' said Mrs. Mantalini.

'Not so easy when one is eating a demnition egg,' replied Mr. Mantalini; 'for the yolk runs down the waistcoat, and yolk of egg does not match any waistcoat but a yellow waistcoat, demmit.'

'You were flirting with her during the whole night,' said Madame Mantalini, apparently desirous to lead the conversation back to the point from which it had strayed.

'No, no, my life.'

'You were,' said Madame; 'I had my eye upon you all the time.'

'Bless the little winking twinkling eye; was it on me all the time!' cried Mantalini, in a sort of lazy rapture. 'Oh, demmit!'

'And I say once more,' resumed Madame, 'that you ought not to waltz with anybody but your own wife; and I will not bear it, Mantalini, if I take poison first.'

'She will not take poison and have horrid pains, will she?' said Mantalini; who, by the altered sound of his voice, seemed to have moved his chair, and taken up his position nearer to his wife. 'She will not take poison, because she had a demd fine husband who might have married two countesses and a dowager—'

'Two countesses,' interposed Madame. 'You told me one before!'

'Two!' cried Mantalini. 'Two demd fine women, real countesses and splendid fortunes, demmit.'

'And why didn't you?' asked Madame, playfully.

'Why didn't I!' replied her husband. 'Had I not seen, at a morning concert, the demdest little fascinator in all the world, and while that little fascinator is my wife, may not all the countesses and dowagers in England be—'

Mr. Mantalini did not finish the sentence, but he gave Madame Mantalini a very loud kiss, which Madame Mantalini returned; after which, there seemed to be some more kissing mixed up with the progress of the breakfast.

'And what about the cash, my existence's jewel?' said Mantalini, when these endearments ceased. 'How much have we in hand?'

'Very little indeed,' replied Madame.

'We must have some more,' said Mantalini; 'we must have some discount out of old Nickleby to carry on the war with, demmit.'

'You can't want any more just now,' said Madame coaxingly.

'My life and soul,' returned her husband, 'there is a horse for sale at Scrubbs's, which it would be a sin and a crime to lose—going, my senses' joy, for nothing.'

'For nothing,' cried Madame, 'I am glad of that.'

'For actually nothing,' replied Mantalini. 'A hundred guineas down will buy him; mane, and crest, and legs, and tail, all of the demdest beauty. I will ride him in the park before the very chariots of the rejected countesses. The demd old dowager will faint with grief and rage; the other two will say "He is married, he has made away with himself, it is a demd thing, it is all up!" They will hate each other demnebly, and wish you dead and buried. Ha! ha! Demmit.'

Madame Mantalini's prudence, if she had any, was not proof against these triumphal pictures; after a little jingling of keys, she observed that she would see what her desk contained, and rising for that purpose, opened the folding-door, and walked into the room where Kate was seated.

'Dear me, child!' exclaimed Madame Mantalini, recoiling in surprise. 'How came you here?'

'Child!' cried Mantalini, hurrying in. 'How came—eh!—oh—demmit, how d'ye do?'

'I have been waiting, here some time, ma'am,' said Kate, addressing Madame Mantalini. 'The servant must have forgotten to let you know that I was here, I think.'

'You really must see to that man,' said Madame, turning to her husband. 'He forgets everything.'

'I will twist his demd nose off his countenance for leaving such a very pretty creature all alone by herself,' said her husband.

'Mantalini,' cried Madame, 'you forget yourself.'

'I don't forget you, my soul, and never shall, and never can,' said Mantalini, kissing his wife's hand, and grimacing aside, to Miss Nickleby, who turned away.

Appeased by this compliment, the lady of the business took some papers from her desk which she handed over to Mr. Mantalini, who received them with great delight. She then requested Kate to follow her, and after several feints on the part of Mr. Mantalini to attract the young lady's attention, they went away: leaving that gentleman extended at full length on the sofa, with his heels in the air and a newspaper in his hand.

Madame Mantalini led the way down a flight of stairs, and through a passage, to a large room at the back of the premises where were a number of young women employed in sewing, cutting out, making up, altering, and various other processes known only to those who are cunning in the arts of millinery and dressmaking. It was a close room with a skylight, and as dull and quiet as a room need be.

On Madame Mantalini calling aloud for Miss Knag, a short, bustling, over-dressed female, full of importance, presented herself, and all the young ladies suspending their operations for the moment, whispered to each other sundry criticisms upon the make and texture of Miss Nickleby's dress, her complexion, cast of features, and personal appearance, with as much good breeding as could have been displayed by the very best society in a crowded ball-room.

'Oh, Miss Knag,' said Madame Mantalini, 'this is the young person I spoke to you about.'

Miss Knag bestowed a reverential smile upon Madame Mantalini, which she dexterously transformed into a gracious one for Kate, and said that certainly, although it was a great deal of trouble to have young people who were wholly unused to the business, still, she was sure the young person would try to do her best—impressed with which conviction she (Miss Knag) felt an interest in her, already.

'I think that, for the present at all events, it will be better for Miss Nickleby to come into the show-room with you, and try things on for people,' said Madame Mantalini. 'She will not be able for the present to be of much use in any other way; and her appearance will—'

'Suit very well with mine, Madame Mantalini,' interrupted Miss Knag. 'So it will; and to be sure I might have known that you would not be long in finding that out; for you have so much taste in all those matters, that really, as I often say to the young ladies, I do not know how, when, or where, you possibly could have acquired all you know—hem—Miss Nickleby and I are quite a pair, Madame Mantalini, only I am a little darker than Miss Nickleby, and—hem—I think my foot may be a little smaller. Miss Nickleby, I am sure, will not be offended at my saying that, when she hears that our family always have been celebrated for small feet ever since—hem—ever since our family had any feet at all, indeed, I think. I had an uncle once, Madame Mantalini, who lived in Cheltenham, and had a most excellent business as a tobacconist—hem—who had such small feet, that they were no bigger than those which are usually joined to wooden legs—the most symmetrical feet, Madame Mantalini, that even you can imagine.'

'They must have had something of the appearance of club feet, Miss Knag,' said Madame.

'Well now, that is so like you,' returned Miss Knag, 'Ha! ha! ha! Of club feet! Oh very good! As I often remark to the young ladies, "Well I must say, and I do not care who knows it, of all the ready humour—hem—I ever heard anywhere"—and I have heard a good deal; for when my dear brother was alive (I kept house for him, Miss Nickleby), we had to supper once a week two or three young men, highly celebrated in those days for their humour, Madame Mantalini—"Of all the ready humour," I say to the young ladies, "I ever heard, Madame Mantalini's is the most remarkable—hem. It is so gentle, so sarcastic, and yet so good-natured (as I was observing to Miss Simmonds only this morning), that how, or when, or by what means she acquired it, is to me a mystery indeed."'

Here Miss Knag paused to take breath, and while she pauses it may be observed—not that she was marvellously loquacious and marvellously deferential to Madame Mantalini, since these are facts which require no comment; but that every now and then, she was accustomed, in the torrent of her discourse, to introduce a loud, shrill, clear 'hem!' the import and meaning of which, was variously interpreted by her acquaintance; some holding that Miss Knag dealt in exaggeration, and introduced the monosyllable when any fresh invention was in course of coinage in her brain; others, that when she wanted a word, she threw it in to gain time, and prevent anybody else from striking into the conversation. It may be further remarked, that Miss Knag still aimed at youth, although she had shot beyond it, years ago; and that she was weak and vain, and one of those people who are best described by the axiom, that you may trust them as far as you can see them, and no farther.

'You'll take care that Miss Nickleby understands her hours, and so forth,' said Madame Mantalini; 'and so I'll leave her with you. You'll not forget my directions, Miss Knag?'

Miss Knag of course replied, that to forget anything Madame Mantalini had directed, was a moral impossibility; and that lady, dispensing a general good-morning among her assistants, sailed away.

'Charming creature, isn't she, Miss Nickleby?' said Miss Knag, rubbing her hands together.

'I have seen very little of her,' said Kate. 'I hardly know yet.'

'Have you seen Mr. Mantalini?' inquired Miss Knag.

'Yes; I have seen him twice.'

'Isn't he a charming creature?'

'Indeed he does not strike me as being so, by any means,' replied Kate.

'No, my dear!' cried Miss Knag, elevating her hands. 'Why, goodness gracious mercy, where's your taste? Such a fine tall, full-whiskered dashing gentlemanly man, with such teeth and hair, and—hem—well now, you do astonish me.'

'I dare say I am very foolish,' replied Kate, laying aside her bonnet; 'but as my opinion is of very little importance to him or anyone else, I do not regret having formed it, and shall be slow to change it, I think.'

'He is a very fine man, don't you think so?' asked one of the young ladies.

'Indeed he may be, for anything I could say to the contrary,' replied Kate.

'And drives very beautiful horses, doesn't he?' inquired another.

'I dare say he may, but I never saw them,' answered Kate.

'Never saw them!' interposed Miss Knag. 'Oh, well! There it is at once you know; how can you possibly pronounce an opinion about a gentleman—hem—if you don't see him as he turns out altogether?'

There was so much of the world—even of the little world of the country girl—in this idea of the old milliner, that Kate, who was anxious, for every reason, to change the subject, made no further remark, and left Miss Knag in possession of the field.

After a short silence, during which most of the young people made a closer inspection of Kate's appearance, and compared notes respecting it, one of them offered to help her off with her shawl, and the offer being accepted, inquired whether she did not find black very uncomfortable wear.

'I do indeed,' replied Kate, with a bitter sigh.

'So dusty and hot,' observed the same speaker, adjusting her dress for her.

Kate might have said, that mourning is sometimes the coldest wear which mortals can assume; that it not only chills the breasts of those it clothes, but extending its influence to summer friends, freezes up their sources of good-will and kindness, and withering all the buds of promise they once so liberally put forth, leaves nothing but bared and rotten hearts exposed. There are few who have lost a friend or relative constituting in life their sole dependence, who have not keenly felt this chilling influence of their sable garb. She had felt it acutely, and feeling it at the moment, could not quite restrain her tears.

'I am very sorry to have wounded you by my thoughtless speech,' said her companion. 'I did not think of it. You are in mourning for some near relation?'

'For my father,' answered Kate.

'For what relation, Miss Simmonds?' asked Miss Knag, in an audible voice.

'Her father,' replied the other softly.

'Her father, eh?' said Miss Knag, without the slightest depression of her voice. 'Ah! A long illness, Miss Simmonds?'

'Hush,' replied the girl; 'I don't know.'

'Our misfortune was very sudden,' said Kate, turning away, 'or I might perhaps, at a time like this, be enabled to support it better.'

There had existed not a little desire in the room, according to invariable custom, when any new 'young person' came, to know who Kate was, and what she was, and all about her; but, although it might have been very naturally increased by her appearance and emotion, the knowledge that it pained her to be questioned, was sufficient to repress even this curiosity; and Miss Knag, finding it hopeless to attempt extracting any further particulars just then, reluctantly commanded silence, and bade the work proceed.

In silence, then, the tasks were plied until half-past one, when a baked leg of mutton, with potatoes to correspond, were served in the kitchen. The meal over, and the young ladies having enjoyed the additional relaxation of washing their hands, the work began again, and was again performed in silence, until the noise of carriages rattling through the streets, and of loud double knocks at doors, gave token that the day's work of the more fortunate members of society was proceeding in its turn.

One of these double knocks at Madame Mantalini's door, announced the equipage of some great lady—or rather rich one, for there is occasionally a distinction between riches and greatness—who had come with her daughter to approve of some court-dresses which had been a long time preparing, and upon whom Kate was deputed to wait, accompanied by Miss Knag, and officered of course by Madame Mantalini.

Kate's part in the pageant was humble enough, her duties being limited to holding articles of costume until Miss Knag was ready to try them on, and now and then tying a string, or fastening a hook-and-eye. She might, not unreasonably, have supposed herself beneath the reach of any arrogance, or bad humour; but it happened that the lady and daughter were both out of temper that day, and the poor girl came in for her share of their revilings. She was awkward—her hands were cold—dirty—coarse—she could do nothing right; they wondered how Madame Mantalini could have such people about her; requested they might see some other young woman the next time they came; and so forth.

So common an occurrence would be hardly deserving of mention, but for its effect. Kate shed many bitter tears when these people were gone, and felt, for the first time, humbled by her occupation. She had, it is true, quailed at the prospect of drudgery and hard service; but she had felt no degradation in working for her bread, until she found herself exposed to insolence and pride. Philosophy would have taught her that the degradation was on the side of those who had sunk so low as to display such passions habitually, and without cause: but she was too young for such consolation, and her honest feeling was hurt. May not the complaint, that common people are above their station, often take its rise in the fact of uncommon people being below theirs?

In such scenes and occupations the time wore on until nine o'clock, when Kate, jaded and dispirited with the occurrences of the day, hastened from the confinement of the workroom, to join her mother at the street corner, and walk home:—the more sadly, from having to disguise her real feelings, and feign to participate in all the sanguine visions of her companion.

'Bless my soul, Kate,' said Mrs. Nickleby; 'I've been thinking all day what a delightful thing it would be for Madame Mantalini to take you into partnership—such a likely thing too, you know! Why, your poor dear papa's cousin's sister-in-law—a Miss Browndock—was taken into partnership by a lady that kept a school at Hammersmith, and made her fortune in no time at all. I forget, by-the-bye, whether that Miss Browndock was the same lady that got the ten thousand pounds prize in the lottery, but I think she was; indeed, now I come to think of it, I am sure she was. "Mantalini and Nickleby", how well it would sound!—and if Nicholas has any good fortune, you might have Doctor Nickleby, the head-master of Westminster School, living in the same street.'

'Dear Nicholas!' cried Kate, taking from her reticule her brother's letter from Dotheboys Hall. 'In all our misfortunes, how happy it makes me, mama, to hear he is doing well, and to find him writing in such good spirits! It consoles me for all we may undergo, to think that he is comfortable and happy.'

Poor Kate! she little thought how weak her consolation was, and how soon she would be undeceived.

CHAPTER 18
Miss Knag, after doting on Kate Nickleby for three whole Days, makes up her Mind to hate her for evermore. The Causes which led Miss Knag to form this Resolution

There are many lives of much pain, hardship, and suffering, which, having no stirring interest for any but those who lead them, are disregarded by persons who do not want thought or feeling, but who pamper their compassion and need high stimulants to rouse it.

There are not a few among the disciples of charity who require, in their vocation, scarcely less excitement than the votaries of pleasure in theirs; and hence it is that diseased sympathy and compassion are every day expended on out-of-the-way objects, when only too many demands upon the legitimate exercise of the same virtues in a healthy state, are constantly within the sight and hearing of the most unobservant person alive. In short, charity must have its romance, as the novelist or playwright must have his. A thief in fustian is a vulgar character, scarcely to be thought of by persons of refinement; but dress him in green velvet, with a high-crowned hat, and change the scene of his operations, from a thickly-peopled city, to a mountain road, and you shall find in him the very soul of poetry and adventure. So it is with the one great cardinal virtue, which, properly nourished and exercised, leads to, if it does not necessarily include, all the others. It must have its romance; and the less of real, hard, struggling work-a-day life there is in that romance, the better.

The life to which poor Kate Nickleby was devoted, in consequence of the unforeseen train of circumstances already developed in this narrative, was a hard one; but lest the very dulness, unhealthy confinement, and bodily fatigue, which made up its sum and substance, should deprive it of any interest with the mass of the charitable and sympathetic, I would rather keep Miss Nickleby herself in view just now, than chill them in the outset, by a minute and lengthened description of the establishment presided over by Madame Mantalini.

'Well, now, indeed, Madame Mantalini,' said Miss Knag, as Kate was taking her weary way homewards on the first night of her novitiate; 'that Miss Nickleby is a very creditable young person—a very creditable young person indeed—hem—upon my word, Madame Mantalini, it does very extraordinary credit even to your discrimination that you should have found such a very excellent, very well-behaved, very—hem—very unassuming young woman to assist in the fitting on. I have seen some young women when they had the opportunity of displaying before their betters, behave in such a—oh, dear—well—but you're always right, Madame Mantalini, always; and as I very often tell the young ladies, how you do contrive to be always right, when so many people are so often wrong, is to me a mystery indeed.'

'Beyond putting a very excellent client out of humour, Miss Nickleby has not done anything very remarkable today—that I am aware of, at least,' said Madame Mantalini in reply.

'Oh, dear!' said Miss Knag; 'but you must allow a great deal for inexperience, you know.'

'And youth?' inquired Madame.

'Oh, I say nothing about that, Madame Mantalini,' replied Miss Knag, reddening; 'because if youth were any excuse, you wouldn't have—'

'Quite so good a forewoman as I have, I suppose,' suggested Madame.

'Well, I never did know anybody like you, Madame Mantalini,' rejoined Miss Knag most complacently, 'and that's the fact, for you know what one's going to say, before it has time to rise to one's lips. Oh, very good! Ha, ha, ha!'

'For myself,' observed Madame Mantalini, glancing with affected carelessness at her assistant, and laughing heartily in her sleeve, 'I consider Miss Nickleby the most awkward girl I ever saw in my life.'

'Poor dear thing,' said Miss Knag, 'it's not her fault. If it was, we might hope to cure it; but as it's her misfortune, Madame Mantalini, why really you know, as the man said about the blind horse, we ought to respect it.'

'Her uncle told me she had been considered pretty,' remarked Madame Mantalini. 'I think her one of the most ordinary girls I ever met with.'

'Ordinary!' cried Miss Knag with a countenance beaming delight; 'and awkward! Well, all I can say is, Madame Mantalini, that I quite love the poor girl; and that if she was twice as indifferent-looking, and twice as awkward as she is, I should be only so much the more her friend, and that's the truth of it.'

In fact, Miss Knag had conceived an incipient affection for Kate Nickleby, after witnessing her failure that morning, and this short conversation with her superior increased the favourable prepossession to a most surprising extent; which was the more remarkable, as when she first scanned that young lady's face and figure, she had entertained certain inward misgivings that they would never agree.

'But now,' said Miss Knag, glancing at the reflection of herself in a mirror at no great distance, 'I love her—I quite love her—I declare I do!'

Of such a highly disinterested quality was this devoted friendship, and so superior was it to the little weaknesses of flattery or ill-nature, that the kind-hearted Miss Knag candidly informed Kate Nickleby, next day, that she saw she would never do for the business, but that she need not give herself the slightest uneasiness on this account, for that she (Miss Knag), by increased exertions on her own part, would keep her as much as possible in the background, and that all she would have to do, would be to remain perfectly quiet before company, and to shrink from attracting notice by every means in her power. This last suggestion was so much in accordance with the timid girl's own feelings and wishes, that she readily promised implicit reliance on the excellent spinster's advice: without questioning, or indeed bestowing a moment's reflection upon, the motives that dictated it.

'I take quite a lively interest in you, my dear soul, upon my word,' said Miss Knag; 'a sister's interest, actually. It's the most singular circumstance I ever knew.'

Undoubtedly it was singular, that if Miss Knag did feel a strong interest in Kate Nickleby, it should not rather have been the interest of a maiden aunt or grandmother; that being the conclusion to which the difference in their respective ages would have naturally tended. But Miss Knag wore clothes of a very youthful pattern, and perhaps her feelings took the same shape.

'Bless you!' said Miss Knag, bestowing a kiss upon Kate at the conclusion of the second day's work, 'how very awkward you have been all day.'

'I fear your kind and open communication, which has rendered me more painfully conscious of my own defects, has not improved me,' sighed Kate.

'No, no, I dare say not,' rejoined Miss Knag, in a most uncommon flow of good humour. 'But how much better that you should know it at first, and so be able to go on, straight and comfortable! Which way are you walking, my love?'

'Towards the city,' replied Kate.

'The city!' cried Miss Knag, regarding herself with great favour in the glass as she tied her bonnet. 'Goodness gracious me! now do you really live in the city?'

'Is it so very unusual for anybody to live there?' asked Kate, half smiling.

'I couldn't have believed it possible that any young woman could have lived there, under any circumstances whatever, for three days together,' replied Miss Knag.

'Reduced—I should say poor people,' answered Kate, correcting herself hastily, for she was afraid of appearing proud, 'must live where they can.'

'Ah! very true, so they must; very proper indeed!' rejoined Miss Knag with that sort of half-sigh, which, accompanied by two or three slight nods of the head, is pity's small change in general society; 'and that's what I very often tell my brother, when our servants go away ill, one after another, and he thinks the back-kitchen's rather too damp for 'em to sleep in. These sort of people, I tell him, are glad to sleep anywhere! Heaven suits the back to the burden. What a nice thing it is to think that it should be so, isn't it?'

'Very,' replied Kate.

'I'll walk with you part of the way, my dear,' said Miss Knag, 'for you must go very near our house; and as it's quite dark, and our last servant went to the hospital a week ago, with St Anthony's fire in her face, I shall be glad of your company.'

Kate would willingly have excused herself from this flattering companionship; but Miss Knag having adjusted her bonnet to her entire satisfaction, took her arm with an air which plainly showed how much she felt the compliment she was conferring, and they were in the street before she could say another word.

'I fear,' said Kate, hesitating, 'that mama—my mother, I mean—is waiting for me.'

'You needn't make the least apology, my dear,' said Miss Knag, smiling sweetly as she spoke; 'I dare say she is a very respectable old person, and I shall be quite—hem—quite pleased to know her.'

As poor Mrs. Nickleby was cooling—not her heels alone, but her limbs generally at the street corner, Kate had no alternative but to make her known to Miss Knag, who, doing the last new carriage customer at second-hand, acknowledged the introduction with condescending politeness. The three then walked away, arm in arm: with Miss Knag in the middle, in a special state of amiability.

'I have taken such a fancy to your daughter, Mrs. Nickleby, you can't think,' said Miss Knag, after she had proceeded a little distance in dignified silence.

'I am delighted to hear it,' said Mrs. Nickleby; 'though it is nothing new to me, that even strangers should like Kate.'

'Hem!' cried Miss Knag.

'You will like her better when you know how good she is,' said Mrs Nickleby. 'It is a great blessing to me, in my misfortunes, to have a child, who knows neither pride nor vanity, and whose bringing-up might very well have excused a little of both at first. You don't know what it is to lose a husband, Miss Knag.'

As Miss Knag had never yet known what it was to gain one, it followed, very nearly as a matter of course, that she didn't know what it was to lose one; so she said, in some haste, 'No, indeed I don't,' and said it with an air intending to signify that she should like to catch herself marrying anybody—no, no, she knew better than that.

'Kate has improved even in this little time, I have no doubt,' said Mrs Nickleby, glancing proudly at her daughter.

'Oh! of course,' said Miss Knag.

'And will improve still more,' added Mrs. Nickleby.

'That she will, I'll be bound,' replied Miss Knag, squeezing Kate's arm in her own, to point the joke.

'She always was clever,' said poor Mrs. Nickleby, brightening up, 'always, from a baby. I recollect when she was only two years and a half old, that a gentleman who used to visit very much at our house—Mr. Watkins, you know, Kate, my dear, that your poor papa went bail for, who afterwards ran away to the United States, and sent us a pair of snow shoes, with such an affectionate letter that it made your poor dear father cry for a week. You remember the letter? In which he said that he was very sorry he couldn't repay the fifty pounds just then, because his capital was all out at interest, and he was very busy making his fortune, but that he didn't forget you were his god-daughter, and he should take it very unkind if we didn't buy you a silver coral and put it down to his old account? Dear me, yes, my dear, how stupid you are! and spoke so affectionately of the old port wine that he used to drink a bottle and a half of every time he came. You must remember, Kate?'

'Yes, yes, mama; what of him?'

'Why, that Mr. Watkins, my dear,' said Mrs. Nickleby slowly, as if she were making a tremendous effort to recollect something of paramount importance; 'that Mr. Watkins—he wasn't any relation, Miss Knag will understand, to the Watkins who kept the Old Boar in the village; by-the-bye, I don't remember whether it was the Old Boar or the George the Third, but it was one of the two, I know, and it's much the same—that Mr. Watkins said, when you were only two years and a half old, that you were one of the most astonishing children he ever saw. He did indeed, Miss Knag, and he wasn't at all fond of children, and couldn't have had the slightest motive for doing it. I know it was he who said so, because I recollect, as well as if it was only yesterday, his borrowing twenty pounds of her poor dear papa the very moment afterwards.'

Having quoted this extraordinary and most disinterested testimony to her daughter's excellence, Mrs. Nickleby stopped to breathe; and Miss Knag, finding that the discourse was turning upon family greatness, lost no time in striking in, with a small reminiscence on her own account.

'Don't talk of lending money, Mrs. Nickleby,' said Miss Knag, 'or you'll drive me crazy, perfectly crazy. My mama—hem—was the most lovely and beautiful creature, with the most striking and exquisite—hem—the most exquisite nose that ever was put upon a human face, I do believe, Mrs Nickleby (here Miss Knag rubbed her own nose sympathetically); the most delightful and accomplished woman, perhaps, that ever was seen; but she had that one failing of lending money, and carried it to such an extent that she lent—hem—oh! thousands of pounds, all our little fortunes, and what's more, Mrs. Nickleby, I don't think, if we were to live till—till—hem—till the very end of time, that we should ever get them back again. I don't indeed.'

After concluding this effort of invention without being interrupted, Miss Knag fell into many more recollections, no less interesting than true, the full tide of which, Mrs. Nickleby in vain attempting to stem, at length sailed smoothly down by adding an under-current of her own recollections; and so both ladies went on talking together in perfect contentment; the only difference between them being, that whereas Miss Knag addressed herself to Kate, and talked very loud, Mrs. Nickleby kept on in one unbroken monotonous flow, perfectly satisfied to be talking and caring very little whether anybody listened or not.

In this manner they walked on, very amicably, until they arrived at Miss Knag's brother's, who was an ornamental stationer and small circulating library keeper, in a by-street off Tottenham Court Road; and who let out by the day, week, month, or year, the newest old novels, whereof the titles were displayed in pen-and-ink characters on a sheet of pasteboard, swinging at his door-post. As Miss Knag happened, at the moment, to be in the middle of an account of her twenty-second offer from a gentleman of large property, she insisted upon their all going in to supper together; and in they went.

'Don't go away, Mortimer,' said Miss Knag as they entered the shop. 'It's only one of our young ladies and her mother. Mrs. and Miss Nickleby.'

'Oh, indeed!' said Mr. Mortimer Knag. 'Ah!'

Having given utterance to these ejaculations with a very profound and thoughtful air, Mr. Knag slowly snuffed two kitchen candles on the counter, and two more in the window, and then snuffed himself from a box in his waistcoat pocket.

There was something very impressive in the ghostly air with which all this was done; and as Mr. Knag was a tall lank gentleman of solemn features, wearing spectacles, and garnished with much less hair than a gentleman bordering on forty, or thereabouts, usually boasts, Mrs. Nickleby whispered her daughter that she thought he must be literary.

'Past ten,' said Mr. Knag, consulting his watch. 'Thomas, close the warehouse.'

Thomas was a boy nearly half as tall as a shutter, and the warehouse was a shop about the size of three hackney coaches.

'Ah!' said Mr. Knag once more, heaving a deep sigh as he restored to its parent shelf the book he had been reading. 'Well—yes—I believe supper is ready, sister.'

With another sigh Mr. Knag took up the kitchen candles from the counter, and preceded the ladies with mournful steps to a back-parlour, where a charwoman, employed in the absence of the sick servant, and remunerated with certain eighteenpences to be deducted from her wages due, was putting the supper out.

'Mrs. Blockson,' said Miss Knag, reproachfully, 'how very often I have begged you not to come into the room with your bonnet on!'

'I can't help it, Miss Knag,' said the charwoman, bridling up on the shortest notice. 'There's been a deal o'cleaning to do in this house, and if you don't like it, I must trouble you to look out for somebody else, for it don't hardly pay me, and that's the truth, if I was to be hung this minute.'

'I don't want any remarks if you please,' said Miss Knag, with a strong emphasis on the personal pronoun. 'Is there any fire downstairs for some hot water presently?'

'No there is not, indeed, Miss Knag,' replied the substitute; 'and so I won't tell you no stories about it.'

'Then why isn't there?' said Miss Knag.

'Because there arn't no coals left out, and if I could make coals I would, but as I can't I won't, and so I make bold to tell you, Mem,' replied Mrs Blockson.

'Will you hold your tongue—female?' said Mr. Mortimer Knag, plunging violently into this dialogue.

'By your leave, Mr. Knag,' retorted the charwoman, turning sharp round. 'I'm only too glad not to speak in this house, excepting when and where I'm spoke to, sir; and with regard to being a female, sir, I should wish to know what you considered yourself?'

'A miserable wretch,' exclaimed Mr. Knag, striking his forehead. 'A miserable wretch.'

'I'm very glad to find that you don't call yourself out of your name, sir,' said Mrs. Blockson; 'and as I had two twin children the day before yesterday was only seven weeks, and my little Charley fell down a airy and put his elber out, last Monday, I shall take it as a favour if you'll send nine shillings, for one week's work, to my house, afore the clock strikes ten tomorrow.'

With these parting words, the good woman quitted the room with great ease of manner, leaving the door wide open; Mr. Knag, at the same moment, flung himself into the 'warehouse,' and groaned aloud.

'What is the matter with that gentleman, pray?' inquired Mrs. Nickleby, greatly disturbed by the sound.

'Is he ill?' inquired Kate, really alarmed.

'Hush!' replied Miss Knag; 'a most melancholy history. He was once most devotedly attached to—hem—to Madame Mantalini.'

'Bless me!' exclaimed Mrs. Nickleby.

'Yes,' continued Miss Knag, 'and received great encouragement too, and confidently hoped to marry her. He has a most romantic heart, Mrs Nickleby, as indeed—hem—as indeed all our family have, and the disappointment was a dreadful blow. He is a wonderfully accomplished man—most extraordinarily accomplished—reads—hem—reads every novel that comes out; I mean every novel that—hem—that has any fashion in it, of course. The fact is, that he did find so much in the books he read, applicable to his own misfortunes, and did find himself in every respect so much like the heroes—because of course he is conscious of his own superiority, as we all are, and very naturally—that he took to scorning everything, and became a genius; and I am quite sure that he is, at this very present moment, writing another book.'

'Another book!' repeated Kate, finding that a pause was left for somebody to say something.

'Yes,' said Miss Knag, nodding in great triumph; 'another book, in three volumes post octavo. Of course it's a great advantage to him, in all his little fashionable descriptions, to have the benefit of my—hem—of my experience, because, of course, few authors who write about such things can have such opportunities of knowing them as I have. He's so wrapped up in high life, that the least allusion to business or worldly matters—like that woman just now, for instance—quite distracts him; but, as I often say, I think his disappointment a great thing for him, because if he hadn't been disappointed he couldn't have written about blighted hopes and all that; and the fact is, if it hadn't happened as it has, I don't believe his genius would ever have come out at all.'

How much more communicative Miss Knag might have become under more favourable circumstances, it is impossible to divine, but as the gloomy one was within ear-shot, and the fire wanted making up, her disclosures stopped here. To judge from all appearances, and the difficulty of making the water warm, the last servant could not have been much accustomed to any other fire than St Anthony's; but a little brandy and water was made at last, and the guests, having been previously regaled with cold leg of mutton and bread and cheese, soon afterwards took leave; Kate amusing herself, all the way home, with the recollection of her last glimpse of Mr Mortimer Knag deeply abstracted in the shop; and Mrs. Nickleby by debating within herself whether the dressmaking firm would ultimately become 'Mantalini, Knag, and Nickleby', or 'Mantalini, Nickleby, and Knag'.

At this high point, Miss Knag's friendship remained for three whole days, much to the wonderment of Madame Mantalini's young ladies who had never beheld such constancy in that quarter, before; but on the fourth, it received a check no less violent than sudden, which thus occurred.

It happened that an old lord of great family, who was going to marry a young lady of no family in particular, came with the young lady, and the young lady's sister, to witness the ceremony of trying on two nuptial bonnets which had been ordered the day before, and Madame Mantalini announcing the fact, in a shrill treble, through the speaking-pipe, which communicated with the workroom, Miss Knag darted hastily upstairs with a bonnet in each hand, and presented herself in the show-room, in a charming state of palpitation, intended to demonstrate her enthusiasm in the cause. The bonnets were no sooner fairly on, than Miss Knag and Madame Mantalini fell into convulsions of admiration.

'A most elegant appearance,' said Madame Mantalini.

'I never saw anything so exquisite in all my life,' said Miss Knag.

Now, the old lord, who was a very old lord, said nothing, but mumbled and chuckled in a state of great delight, no less with the nuptial bonnets and their wearers, than with his own address in getting such a fine woman for his wife; and the young lady, who was a very lively young lady, seeing the old lord in this rapturous condition, chased the old lord behind a cheval-glass, and then and there kissed him, while Madame Mantalini and the other young lady looked, discreetly, another way.

But, pending the salutation, Miss Knag, who was tinged with curiosity, stepped accidentally behind the glass, and encountered the lively young lady's eye just at the very moment when she kissed the old lord; upon which the young lady, in a pouting manner, murmured something about 'an old thing,' and 'great impertinence,' and finished by darting a look of displeasure at Miss Knag, and smiling contemptuously.

'Madame Mantalini,' said the young lady.

'Ma'am,' said Madame Mantalini.

'Pray have up that pretty young creature we saw yesterday.'

'Oh yes, do,' said the sister.

'Of all things in the world, Madame Mantalini,' said the lord's intended, throwing herself languidly on a sofa, 'I hate being waited upon by frights or elderly persons. Let me always see that young creature, I beg, whenever I come.'

'By all means,' said the old lord; 'the lovely young creature, by all means.'

'Everybody is talking about her,' said the young lady, in the same careless manner; 'and my lord, being a great admirer of beauty, must positively see her.'

'She is universally admired,' replied Madame Mantalini. 'Miss Knag, send up Miss Nickleby. You needn't return.'

'I beg your pardon, Madame Mantalini, what did you say last?' asked Miss Knag, trembling.

'You needn't return,' repeated the superior, sharply. Miss Knag vanished without another word, and in all reasonable time was replaced by Kate, who took off the new bonnets and put on the old ones: blushing very much to find that the old lord and the two young ladies were staring her out of countenance all the time.

'Why, how you colour, child!' said the lord's chosen bride.

'She is not quite so accustomed to her business, as she will be in a week or two,' interposed Madame Mantalini with a gracious smile.

'I am afraid you have been giving her some of your wicked looks, my lord,' said the intended.

'No, no, no,' replied the old lord, 'no, no, I'm going to be married, and lead a new life. Ha, ha, ha! a new life, a new life! ha, ha, ha!'

It was a satisfactory thing to hear that the old gentleman was going to lead a new life, for it was pretty evident that his old one would not last him much longer. The mere exertion of protracted chuckling reduced him to a fearful ebb of coughing and gasping; it was some minutes before he could find breath to remark that the girl was too pretty for a milliner.

'I hope you don't think good looks a disqualification for the business, my lord,' said Madame Mantalini, simpering.

'Not by any means,' replied the old lord, 'or you would have left it long ago.'

'You naughty creature,' said the lively lady, poking the peer with her parasol; 'I won't have you talk so. How dare you?'

This playful inquiry was accompanied with another poke, and another, and then the old lord caught the parasol, and wouldn't give it up again, which induced the other lady to come to the rescue, and some very pretty sportiveness ensued.

'You will see that those little alterations are made, Madame Mantalini,' said the lady. 'Nay, you bad man, you positively shall go first; I wouldn't leave you behind with that pretty girl, not for half a second. I know you too well. Jane, my dear, let him go first, and we shall be quite sure of him.'

The old lord, evidently much flattered by this suspicion, bestowed a grotesque leer upon Kate as he passed; and, receiving another tap with the parasol for his wickedness, tottered downstairs to the door, where his sprightly body was hoisted into the carriage by two stout footmen.

'Foh!' said Madame Mantalini, 'how he ever gets into a carriage without thinking of a hearse, I can't think. There, take the things away, my dear, take them away.'

Kate, who had remained during the whole scene with her eyes modestly fixed upon the ground, was only too happy to avail herself of the permission to retire, and hasten joyfully downstairs to Miss Knag's dominion.

The circumstances of the little kingdom had greatly changed, however, during the short period of her absence. In place of Miss Knag being stationed in her accustomed seat, preserving all the dignity and greatness of Madame Mantalini's representative, that worthy soul was reposing on a large box, bathed in tears, while three or four of the young ladies in close attendance upon her, together with the presence of hartshorn, vinegar, and other restoratives, would have borne ample testimony, even without the derangement of the head-dress and front row of curls, to her having fainted desperately.

'Bless me!' said Kate, stepping hastily forward, 'what is the matter?'

This inquiry produced in Miss Knag violent symptoms of a relapse; and several young ladies, darting angry looks at Kate, applied more vinegar and hartshorn, and said it was 'a shame.'

'What is a shame?' demanded Kate. 'What is the matter? What has happened? tell me.'

'Matter!' cried Miss Knag, coming, all at once, bolt upright, to the great consternation of the assembled maidens; 'matter! Fie upon you, you nasty creature!'

'Gracious!' cried Kate, almost paralysed by the violence with which the adjective had been jerked out from between Miss Knag's closed teeth; 'have I offended you?'

'You offended me!' retorted Miss Knag, 'you! a chit, a child, an upstart nobody! Oh, indeed! Ha, ha!'

Now, it was evident, as Miss Knag laughed, that something struck her as being exceedingly funny; and as the young ladies took their tone from Miss Knag—she being the chief—they all got up a laugh without a moment's delay, and nodded their heads a little, and smiled sarcastically to each other, as much as to say how very good that was!

'Here she is,' continued Miss Knag, getting off the box, and introducing Kate with much ceremony and many low curtseys to the delighted throng; 'here she is—everybody is talking about her—the belle, ladies—the beauty, the—oh, you bold-faced thing!'

At this crisis, Miss Knag was unable to repress a virtuous shudder, which immediately communicated itself to all the young ladies; after which, Miss Knag laughed, and after that, cried.

'For fifteen years,' exclaimed Miss Knag, sobbing in a most affecting manner, 'for fifteen years have I been the credit and ornament of this room and the one upstairs. Thank God,' said Miss Knag, stamping first her right foot and then her left with remarkable energy, 'I have never in all that time, till now, been exposed to the arts, the vile arts, of a creature, who disgraces us with all her proceedings, and makes proper people blush for themselves. But I feel it, I do feel it, although I am disgusted.'

Miss Knag here relapsed into softness, and the young ladies renewing their attentions, murmured that she ought to be superior to such things, and that for their part they despised them, and considered them beneath their notice; in witness whereof, they called out, more emphatically than before, that it was a shame, and that they felt so angry, they did, they hardly knew what to do with themselves.

'Have I lived to this day to be called a fright!' cried Miss Knag, suddenly becoming convulsive, and making an effort to tear her front off.

'Oh no, no,' replied the chorus, 'pray don't say so; don't now!'

'Have I deserved to be called an elderly person?' screamed Miss Knag, wrestling with the supernumeraries.

'Don't think of such things, dear,' answered the chorus.

'I hate her,' cried Miss Knag; 'I detest and hate her. Never let her speak to me again; never let anybody who is a friend of mine speak to her; a slut, a hussy, an impudent artful hussy!' Having denounced the object of her wrath, in these terms, Miss Knag screamed once, hiccuped thrice, gurgled in her throat several times, slumbered, shivered, woke, came to, composed her head-dress, and declared herself quite well again.

Poor Kate had regarded these proceedings, at first, in perfect bewilderment. She had then turned red and pale by turns, and once or twice essayed to speak; but, as the true motives of this altered behaviour developed themselves, she retired a few paces, and looked calmly on without deigning a reply. Nevertheless, although she walked proudly to her seat, and turned her back upon the group of little satellites who clustered round their ruling planet in the remotest corner of the room, she gave way, in secret, to some such bitter tears as would have gladdened Miss Knag's inmost soul, if she could have seen them fall.

CHAPTER 19
Descriptive of a Dinner at Mr. Ralph Nickleby's, and of the Manner in which the Company entertained themselves, before Dinner, at Dinner, and after Dinner.

The bile and rancour of the worthy Miss Knag undergoing no diminution during the remainder of the week, but rather augmenting with every successive hour; and the honest ire of all the young ladies rising, or seeming to rise, in exact proportion to the good spinster's indignation, and both waxing very hot every time Miss Nickleby was called upstairs; it will be readily imagined that that young lady's daily life was none of the most cheerful or enviable kind. She hailed the arrival of Saturday night, as a prisoner would a few delicious hours' respite from slow and wearing torture, and felt that the poor pittance for her first week's labour would have been dearly and hardly earned, had its amount been trebled.

When she joined her mother, as usual, at the street corner, she was not a little surprised to find her in conversation with Mr. Ralph Nickleby; but her surprise was soon redoubled, no less by the matter of their conversation, than by the smoothed and altered manner of Mr. Nickleby himself.

'Ah! my dear!' said Ralph; 'we were at that moment talking about you.'

'Indeed!' replied Kate, shrinking, though she scarce knew why, from her uncle's cold glistening eye.

'That instant,' said Ralph. 'I was coming to call for you, making sure to catch you before you left; but your mother and I have been talking over family affairs, and the time has slipped away so rapidly—'

'Well, now, hasn't it?' interposed Mrs. Nickleby, quite insensible to the sarcastic tone of Ralph's last remark. 'Upon my word, I couldn't have believed it possible, that such a—Kate, my dear, you're to dine with your uncle at half-past six o'clock tomorrow.'

Triumphing in having been the first to communicate this extraordinary intelligence, Mrs. Nickleby nodded and smiled a great many times, to impress its full magnificence on Kate's wondering mind, and then flew off, at an acute angle, to a committee of ways and means.

'Let me see,' said the good lady. 'Your black silk frock will be quite dress enough, my dear, with that pretty little scarf, and a plain band in your hair, and a pair of black silk stock—Dear, dear,' cried Mrs Nickleby, flying off at another angle, 'if I had but those unfortunate amethysts of mine—you recollect them, Kate, my love—how they used to sparkle, you know—but your papa, your poor dear papa—ah! there never was anything so cruelly sacrificed as those jewels were, never!' Overpowered by this agonising thought, Mrs. Nickleby shook her head, in a melancholy manner, and applied her handkerchief to her eyes.

I don't want them, mama, indeed,' said Kate. 'Forget that you ever had them.'

'Lord, Kate, my dear,' rejoined Mrs. Nickleby, pettishly, 'how like a child you talk! Four-and-twenty silver tea-spoons, brother-in-law, two gravies, four salts, all the amethysts—necklace, brooch, and ear-rings—all made away with, at the same time, and I saying, almost on my bended knees, to that poor good soul, "Why don't you do something, Nicholas? Why don't you make some arrangement?" I am sure that anybody who was about us at that time, will do me the justice to own, that if I said that once, I said it fifty times a day. Didn't I, Kate, my dear? Did I ever lose an opportunity of impressing it on your poor papa?'

'No, no, mama, never,' replied Kate. And to do Mrs. Nickleby justice, she never had lost—and to do married ladies as a body justice, they seldom do lose—any occasion of inculcating similar golden percepts, whose only blemish is, the slight degree of vagueness and uncertainty in which they are usually enveloped.

'Ah!' said Mrs. Nickleby, with great fervour, 'if my advice had been taken at the beginning—Well, I have always done my duty, and that's some comfort.'

When she had arrived at this reflection, Mrs. Nickleby sighed, rubbed her hands, cast up her eyes, and finally assumed a look of meek composure; thus importing that she was a persecuted saint, but that she wouldn't trouble her hearers by mentioning a circumstance which must be so obvious to everybody.

'Now,' said Ralph, with a smile, which, in common with all other tokens of emotion, seemed to skulk under his face, rather than play boldly over it—'to return to the point from which we have strayed. I have a little party of—of—gentlemen with whom I am connected in business just now, at my house tomorrow; and your mother has promised that you shall keep house for me. I am not much used to parties; but this is one of business, and such fooleries are an important part of it sometimes. You don't mind obliging me?'

'Mind!' cried Mrs. Nickleby. 'My dear Kate, why—'

'Pray,' interrupted Ralph, motioning her to be silent. 'I spoke to my niece.'

'I shall be very glad, of course, uncle,' replied Kate; 'but I am afraid you will find me awkward and embarrassed.'

'Oh no,' said Ralph; 'come when you like, in a hackney coach—I'll pay for it. Good-night—a—a—God bless you.'

The blessing seemed to stick in Mr. Ralph Nickleby's throat, as if it were not used to the thoroughfare, and didn't know the way out. But it got out somehow, though awkwardly enough; and having disposed of it, he shook hands with his two relatives, and abruptly left them.

'What a very strongly marked countenance your uncle has!' said Mrs Nickleby, quite struck with his parting look. 'I don't see the slightest resemblance to his poor brother.'

'Mama!' said Kate reprovingly. 'To think of such a thing!'

'No,' said Mrs. Nickleby, musing. 'There certainly is none. But it's a very honest face.'

The worthy matron made this remark with great emphasis and elocution, as if it comprised no small quantity of ingenuity and research; and, in truth, it was not unworthy of being classed among the extraordinary discoveries of the age. Kate looked up hastily, and as hastily looked down again.

'What has come over you, my dear, in the name of goodness?' asked Mrs Nickleby, when they had walked on, for some time, in silence.

'I was only thinking, mama,' answered Kate.

'Thinking!' repeated Mrs. Nickleby. 'Ay, and indeed plenty to think about, too. Your uncle has taken a strong fancy to you, that's quite clear; and if some extraordinary good fortune doesn't come to you, after this, I shall be a little surprised, that's all.'

With this she launched out into sundry anecdotes of young ladies, who had had thousand-pound notes given them in reticules, by eccentric uncles; and of young ladies who had accidentally met amiable gentlemen of enormous wealth at their uncles' houses, and married them, after short but ardent courtships; and Kate, listening first in apathy, and afterwards in amusement, felt, as they walked home, something of her mother's sanguine complexion gradually awakening in her own bosom, and began to think that her prospects might be brightening, and that better days might be dawning upon them. Such is hope, Heaven's own gift to struggling mortals; pervading, like some subtle essence from the skies, all things, both good and bad; as universal as death, and more infectious than disease!

The feeble winter's sun—and winter's suns in the city are very feeble indeed—might have brightened up, as he shone through the dim windows of the large old house, on witnessing the unusual sight which one half-furnished room displayed. In a gloomy corner, where, for years, had stood a silent dusty pile of merchandise, sheltering its colony of mice, and frowning, a dull and lifeless mass, upon the panelled room, save when, responding to the roll of heavy waggons in the street without, it quaked with sturdy tremblings and caused the bright eyes of its tiny citizens to grow brighter still with fear, and struck them motionless, with attentive ear and palpitating heart, until the alarm had passed away—in this dark corner, was arranged, with scrupulous care, all Kate's little finery for the day; each article of dress partaking of that indescribable air of jauntiness and individuality which empty garments— whether by association, or that they become moulded, as it were, to the owner's form—will take, in eyes accustomed to, or picturing, the wearer's smartness. In place of a bale of musty goods, there lay the black silk dress: the neatest possible figure in itself. The small shoes, with toes delicately turned out, stood upon the very pressure of some old iron weight; and a pile of harsh discoloured leather had unconsciously given place to the very same little pair of black silk stockings, which had been the objects of Mrs. Nickleby's peculiar care. Rats and mice, and such small gear, had long ago been starved, or had emigrated to better quarters: and, in their stead, appeared gloves, bands, scarfs, hair-pins, and many other little devices, almost as ingenious in their way as rats and mice themselves, for the tantalisation of mankind. About and among them all, moved Kate herself, not the least beautiful or unwonted relief to the stern, old, gloomy building.

In good time, or in bad time, as the reader likes to take it—for Mrs Nickleby's impatience went a great deal faster than the clocks at that end of the town, and Kate was dressed to the very last hair-pin a full hour and a half before it was at all necessary to begin to think about it—in good time, or in bad time, the toilet was completed; and it being at length the hour agreed upon for starting, the milkman fetched a coach from the nearest stand, and Kate, with many adieux to her mother, and many kind messages to Miss La Creevy, who was to come to tea, seated herself in it, and went away in state, if ever anybody went away in state in a hackney coach yet. And the coach, and the coachman, and the horses, rattled, and jangled, and whipped, and cursed, and swore, and tumbled on together, until they came to Golden Square.

The coachman gave a tremendous double knock at the door, which was opened long before he had done, as quickly as if there had been a man behind it, with his hand tied to the latch. Kate, who had expected no more uncommon appearance than Newman Noggs in a clean shirt, was not a little astonished to see that the opener was a man in handsome livery, and that there were two or three others in the hall. There was no doubt about its being the right house, however, for there was the name upon the door; so she accepted the laced coat-sleeve which was tendered her, and entering the house, was ushered upstairs, into a back drawing-room, where she was left alone.

If she had been surprised at the apparition of the footman, she was perfectly absorbed in amazement at the richness and splendour of the furniture. The softest and most elegant carpets, the most exquisite pictures, the costliest mirrors; articles of richest ornament, quite dazzling from their beauty and perplexing from the prodigality with which they were scattered around; encountered her on every side. The very staircase nearly down to the hall-door, was crammed with beautiful and luxurious things, as though the house were brimful of riches, which, with a very trifling addition, would fairly run over into the street.

Presently, she heard a series of loud double knocks at the street-door, and after every knock some new voice in the next room; the tones of Mr Ralph Nickleby were easily distinguishable at first, but by degrees they merged into the general buzz of conversation, and all she could ascertain was, that there were several gentlemen with no very musical voices, who talked very loud, laughed very heartily, and swore more than she would have thought quite necessary. But this was a question of taste.

At length, the door opened, and Ralph himself, divested of his boots, and ceremoniously embellished with black silks and shoes, presented his crafty face.

'I couldn't see you before, my dear,' he said, in a low tone, and pointing, as he spoke, to the next room. 'I was engaged in receiving them. Now—shall I take you in?'

'Pray, uncle,' said Kate, a little flurried, as people much more conversant with society often are, when they are about to enter a room full of strangers, and have had time to think of it previously, 'are there any ladies here?'

'No,' said Ralph, shortly, 'I don't know any.'

'Must I go in immediately?' asked Kate, drawing back a little.

'As you please,' said Ralph, shrugging his shoulders. 'They are all come, and dinner will be announced directly afterwards—that's all.'

Kate would have entreated a few minutes' respite, but reflecting that her uncle might consider the payment of the hackney-coach fare a sort of bargain for her punctuality, she suffered him to draw her arm through his, and to lead her away.

Seven or eight gentlemen were standing round the fire when they went in, and, as they were talking very loud, were not aware of their entrance until Mr. Ralph Nickleby, touching one on the coat-sleeve, said in a harsh emphatic voice, as if to attract general attention—

'Lord Frederick Verisopht, my niece, Miss Nickleby.'

The group dispersed, as if in great surprise, and the gentleman addressed, turning round, exhibited a suit of clothes of the most superlative cut, a pair of whiskers of similar quality, a moustache, a head of hair, and a young face.

'Eh!' said the gentleman. 'What—the—deyvle!'

With which broken ejaculations, he fixed his glass in his eye, and stared at Miss Nickleby in great surprise.

'My niece, my lord,' said Ralph.

'Then my ears did not deceive me, and it's not wa-a-x work,' said his lordship. 'How de do? I'm very happy.' And then his lordship turned to another superlative gentleman, something older, something stouter, something redder in the face, and something longer upon town, and said in a loud whisper that the girl was 'deyvlish pitty.'

'Introduce me, Nickleby,' said this second gentleman, who was lounging with his back to the fire, and both elbows on the chimneypiece.

'Sir Mulberry Hawk,' said Ralph.

'Otherwise the most knowing card in the pa-ack, Miss Nickleby,' said Lord Frederick Verisopht.

'Don't leave me out, Nickleby,' cried a sharp-faced gentleman, who was sitting on a low chair with a high back, reading the paper.

'Mr. Pyke,' said Ralph.

'Nor me, Nickleby,' cried a gentleman with a flushed face and a flash air, from the elbow of Sir Mulberry Hawk.

'Mr. Pluck,' said Ralph. Then wheeling about again, towards a gentleman with the neck of a stork and the legs of no animal in particular, Ralph introduced him as the Honourable Mr. Snobb; and a white-headed person at the table as Colonel Chowser. The colonel was in conversation with somebody, who appeared to be a make-weight, and was not introduced at all.

There were two circumstances which, in this early stage of the party, struck home to Kate's bosom, and brought the blood tingling to her face. One was the flippant contempt with which the guests evidently regarded her uncle, and the other, the easy insolence of their manner towards herself. That the first symptom was very likely to lead to the aggravation of the second, it needed no great penetration to foresee. And here Mr. Ralph Nickleby had reckoned without his host; for however fresh from the country a young lady (by nature) may be, and however unacquainted with conventional behaviour, the chances are, that she will have quite as strong an innate sense of the decencies and proprieties of life as if she had run the gauntlet of a dozen London seasons—possibly a stronger one, for such senses have been known to blunt in this improving process.

When Ralph had completed the ceremonial of introduction, he led his blushing niece to a seat. As he did so, he glanced warily round as though to assure himself of the impression which her unlooked-for appearance had created.

'An unexpected playsure, Nickleby,' said Lord Frederick Verisopht, taking his glass out of his right eye, where it had, until now, done duty on Kate, and fixing it in his left, to bring it to bear on Ralph.

'Designed to surprise you, Lord Frederick,' said Mr. Pluck.

'Not a bad idea,' said his lordship, 'and one that would almost warrant the addition of an extra two and a half per cent.'

'Nickleby,' said Sir Mulberry Hawk, in a thick coarse voice, 'take the hint, and tack it on the other five-and-twenty, or whatever it is, and give me half for the advice.'

Sir Mulberry garnished this speech with a hoarse laugh, and terminated it with a pleasant oath regarding Mr. Nickleby's limbs, whereat Messrs Pyke and Pluck laughed consumedly.

These gentlemen had not yet quite recovered the jest, when dinner was announced, and then they were thrown into fresh ecstasies by a similar cause; for Sir Mulberry Hawk, in an excess of humour, shot dexterously past Lord Frederick Verisopht who was about to lead Kate downstairs, and drew her arm through his up to the elbow.

'No, damn it, Verisopht,' said Sir Mulberry, 'fair play's a jewel, and Miss Nickleby and I settled the matter with our eyes ten minutes ago.'

'Ha, ha, ha!' laughed the honourable Mr. Snobb, 'very good, very good.'

Rendered additionally witty by this applause, Sir Mulberry Hawk leered upon his friends most facetiously, and led Kate downstairs with an air of familiarity, which roused in her gentle breast such burning indignation, as she felt it almost impossible to repress. Nor was the intensity of these feelings at all diminished, when she found herself placed at the top of the table, with Sir Mulberry Hawk and Lord Frederick Verisopht on either side.

'Oh, you've found your way into our neighbourhood, have you?' said Sir Mulberry as his lordship sat down.

'Of course,' replied Lord Frederick, fixing his eyes on Miss Nickleby, 'how can you a-ask me?'

'Well, you attend to your dinner,' said Sir Mulberry, 'and don't mind Miss Nickleby and me, for we shall prove very indifferent company, I dare say.'

'I wish you'd interfere here, Nickleby,' said Lord Frederick.

'What is the matter, my lord?' demanded Ralph from the bottom of the table, where he was supported by Messrs Pyke and Pluck.

'This fellow, Hawk, is monopolising your niece,' said Lord Frederick.

'He has a tolerable share of everything that you lay claim to, my lord,' said Ralph with a sneer.

''Gad, so he has,' replied the young man; 'deyvle take me if I know which is master in my house, he or I.'

'I know,' muttered Ralph.

'I think I shall cut him off with a shilling,' said the young nobleman, jocosely.

'No, no, curse it,' said Sir Mulberry. 'When you come to the shilling—the last shilling—I'll cut you fast enough; but till then, I'll never leave you—you may take your oath of it.'

This sally (which was strictly founded on fact) was received with a general roar, above which, was plainly distinguishable the laughter of Mr Pyke and Mr. Pluck, who were, evidently, Sir Mulberry's toads in ordinary. Indeed, it was not difficult to see, that the majority of the company preyed upon the unfortunate young lord, who, weak and silly as he was, appeared by far the least vicious of the party. Sir Mulberry Hawk was remarkable for his tact in ruining, by himself and his creatures, young gentlemen of fortune—a genteel and elegant profession, of which he had undoubtedly gained the head. With all the boldness of an original genius, he had struck out an entirely new course of treatment quite opposed to the usual method; his custom being, when he had gained the ascendancy over those he took in hand, rather to keep them down than to give them their own way; and to exercise his vivacity upon them openly, and without reserve. Thus, he made them butts, in a double sense, and while he emptied them with great address, caused them to ring with sundry well-administered taps, for the diversion of society.

The dinner was as remarkable for the splendour and completeness of its appointments as the mansion itself, and the company were remarkable for doing it ample justice, in which respect Messrs Pyke and Pluck particularly signalised themselves; these two gentlemen eating of every dish, and drinking of every bottle, with a capacity and perseverance truly astonishing. They were remarkably fresh, too, notwithstanding their great exertions: for, on the appearance of the dessert, they broke out again, as if nothing serious had taken place since breakfast.

'Well,' said Lord Frederick, sipping his first glass of port, 'if this is a discounting dinner, all I have to say is, deyvle take me, if it wouldn't be a good pla-an to get discount every day.'

'You'll have plenty of it, in your time,' returned Sir Mulberry Hawk; 'Nickleby will tell you that.'

'What do you say, Nickleby?' inquired the young man; 'am I to be a good customer?'

'It depends entirely on circumstances, my lord,' replied Ralph.

'On your lordship's circumstances,' interposed Colonel Chowser of the Militia—and the race-courses.

The gallant colonel glanced at Messrs Pyke and Pluck as if he thought they ought to laugh at his joke; but those gentlemen, being only engaged to laugh for Sir Mulberry Hawk, were, to his signal discomfiture, as grave as a pair of undertakers. To add to his defeat, Sir Mulberry, considering any such efforts an invasion of his peculiar privilege, eyed the offender steadily, through his glass, as if astonished at his presumption, and audibly stated his impression that it was an 'infernal liberty,' which being a hint to Lord Frederick, he put up his glass, and surveyed the object of censure as if he were some extraordinary wild animal then exhibiting for the first time. As a matter of course, Messrs Pyke and Pluck stared at the individual whom Sir Mulberry Hawk stared at; so, the poor colonel, to hide his confusion, was reduced to the necessity of holding his port before his right eye and affecting to scrutinise its colour with the most lively interest.

All this while, Kate had sat as silently as she could, scarcely daring to raise her eyes, lest they should encounter the admiring gaze of Lord Frederick Verisopht, or, what was still more embarrassing, the bold looks of his friend Sir Mulberry. The latter gentleman was obliging enough to direct general attention towards her.

'Here is Miss Nickleby,' observed Sir Mulberry, 'wondering why the deuce somebody doesn't make love to her.'

'No, indeed,' said Kate, looking hastily up, 'I—' and then she stopped, feeling it would have been better to have said nothing at all.

'I'll hold any man fifty pounds,' said Sir Mulberry, 'that Miss Nickleby can't look in my face, and tell me she wasn't thinking so.'

'Done!' cried the noble gull. 'Within ten minutes.'

'Done!' responded Sir Mulberry. The money was produced on both sides, and the Honourable Mr. Snobb was elected to the double office of stake-holder and time-keeper.

'Pray,' said Kate, in great confusion, while these preliminaries were in course of completion. 'Pray do not make me the subject of any bets. Uncle, I cannot really—'

'Why not, my dear?' replied Ralph, in whose grating voice, however, there was an unusual huskiness, as though he spoke unwillingly, and would rather that the proposition had not been broached. 'It is done in a moment; there is nothing in it. If the gentlemen insist on it—'

'I don't insist on it,' said Sir Mulberry, with a loud laugh. 'That is, I by no means insist upon Miss Nickleby's making the denial, for if she does, I lose; but I shall be glad to see her bright eyes, especially as she favours the mahogany so much.'

'So she does, and it's too ba-a-d of you, Miss Nickleby,' said the noble youth.

'Quite cruel,' said Mr. Pyke.

'Horrid cruel,' said Mr. Pluck.

'I don't care if I do lose,' said Sir Mulberry; 'for one tolerable look at Miss Nickleby's eyes is worth double the money.'

'More,' said Mr. Pyke.

'Far more,' said Mr. Pluck.

'How goes the enemy, Snobb?' asked Sir Mulberry Hawk.

'Four minutes gone.'

'Bravo!'

'Won't you ma-ake one effort for me, Miss Nickleby?' asked Lord Frederick, after a short interval.

'You needn't trouble yourself to inquire, my buck,' said Sir Mulberry; 'Miss Nickleby and I understand each other; she declares on my side, and shows her taste. You haven't a chance, old fellow. Time, Snobb?'

'Eight minutes gone.'

'Get the money ready,' said Sir Mulberry; 'you'll soon hand over.'

'Ha, ha, ha!' laughed Mr. Pyke.

Mr. Pluck, who always came second, and topped his companion if he could, screamed outright.

The poor girl, who was so overwhelmed with confusion that she scarcely knew what she did, had determined to remain perfectly quiet; but fearing that by so doing she might seem to countenance Sir Mulberry's boast, which had been uttered with great coarseness and vulgarity of manner, raised her eyes, and looked him in the face. There was something so odious, so insolent, so repulsive in the look which met her, that, without the power to stammer forth a syllable, she rose and hurried from the room. She restrained her tears by a great effort until she was alone upstairs, and then gave them vent.

'Capital!' said Sir Mulberry Hawk, putting the stakes in his pocket.

'That's a girl of spirit, and we'll drink her health.'

It is needless to say, that Pyke and Co. responded, with great warmth of manner, to this proposal, or that the toast was drunk with many little insinuations from the firm, relative to the completeness of Sir Mulberry's conquest. Ralph, who, while the attention of the other guests was attracted to the principals in the preceding scene, had eyed them like a wolf, appeared to breathe more freely now his niece was gone; the decanters passing quickly round, he leaned back in his chair, and turned his eyes from speaker to speaker, as they warmed with wine, with looks that seemed to search their hearts, and lay bare, for his distempered sport, every idle thought within them.

Meanwhile Kate, left wholly to herself, had, in some degree, recovered her composure. She had learnt from a female attendant, that her uncle wished to see her before she left, and had also gleaned the satisfactory intelligence, that the gentlemen would take coffee at table. The prospect of seeing them no more, contributed greatly to calm her agitation, and, taking up a book, she composed herself to read.

She started sometimes, when the sudden opening of the dining-room door let loose a wild shout of noisy revelry, and more than once rose in great alarm, as a fancied footstep on the staircase impressed her with the fear that some stray member of the party was returning alone. Nothing occurring, however, to realise her apprehensions, she endeavoured to fix her attention more closely on her book, in which by degrees she became so much interested, that she had read on through several chapters without heed of time or place, when she was terrified by suddenly hearing her name pronounced by a man's voice close at her ear.

The book fell from her hand. Lounging on an ottoman close beside her, was Sir Mulberry Hawk, evidently the worse—if a man be a ruffian at heart, he is never the better—for wine.

'What a delightful studiousness!' said this accomplished gentleman. 'Was it real, now, or only to display the eyelashes?'

Kate, looking anxiously towards the door, made no reply.

'I have looked at 'em for five minutes,' said Sir Mulberry. 'Upon my soul, they're perfect. Why did I speak, and destroy such a pretty little picture?'

'Do me the favour to be silent now, sir,' replied Kate.

'No, don't,' said Sir Mulberry, folding his crushed hat to lay his elbow on, and bringing himself still closer to the young lady; 'upon my life, you oughtn't to. Such a devoted slave of yours, Miss Nickleby—it's an infernal thing to treat him so harshly, upon my soul it is.'

'I wish you to understand, sir,' said Kate, trembling in spite of herself, but speaking with great indignation, 'that your behaviour offends and disgusts me. If you have a spark of gentlemanly feeling remaining, you will leave me.'

'Now why,' said Sir Mulberry, 'why will you keep up this appearance of excessive rigour, my sweet creature? Now, be more natural—my dear Miss Nickleby, be more natural—do.'

Kate hastily rose; but as she rose, Sir Mulberry caught her dress, and forcibly detained her.

'Let me go, sir,' she cried, her heart swelling with anger. 'Do you hear? Instantly—this moment.'

'Sit down, sit down,' said Sir Mulberry; 'I want to talk to you.'

'Unhand me, sir, this instant,' cried Kate.

'Not for the world,' rejoined Sir Mulberry. Thus speaking, he leaned over, as if to replace her in her chair; but the young lady, making a violent effort to disengage herself, he lost his balance, and measured his length upon the ground. As Kate sprung forward to leave the room, Mr. Ralph Nickleby appeared in the doorway, and confronted her.

'What is this?' said Ralph.

'It is this, sir,' replied Kate, violently agitated: 'that beneath the roof where I, a helpless girl, your dead brother's child, should most have found protection, I have been exposed to insult which should make you shrink to look upon me. Let me pass you.'

Ralph did shrink, as the indignant girl fixed her kindling eye upon him; but he did not comply with her injunction, nevertheless: for he led her to a distant seat, and returning, and approaching Sir Mulberry Hawk, who had by this time risen, motioned towards the door.

'Your way lies there, sir,' said Ralph, in a suppressed voice, that some devil might have owned with pride.

'What do you mean by that?' demanded his friend, fiercely.

The swoln veins stood out like sinews on Ralph's wrinkled forehead, and the nerves about his mouth worked as though some unendurable emotion wrung them; but he smiled disdainfully, and again pointed to the door.

'Do you know me, you old madman?' asked Sir Mulberry.

'Well,' said Ralph. The fashionable vagabond for the moment quite quailed under the steady look of the older sinner, and walked towards the door, muttering as he went.

'You wanted the lord, did you?' he said, stopping short when he reached the door, as if a new light had broken in upon him, and confronting Ralph again. 'Damme, I was in the way, was I?'

Ralph smiled again, but made no answer.

'Who brought him to you first?' pursued Sir Mulberry; 'and how, without me, could you ever have wound him in your net as you have?'

'The net is a large one, and rather full,' said Ralph. 'Take care that it chokes nobody in the meshes.'

'You would sell your flesh and blood for money; yourself, if you have not already made a bargain with the devil,' retorted the other. 'Do you mean to tell me that your pretty niece was not brought here as a decoy for the drunken boy downstairs?'

Although this hurried dialogue was carried on in a suppressed tone on both sides, Ralph looked involuntarily round to ascertain that Kate had not moved her position so as to be within hearing. His adversary saw the advantage he had gained, and followed it up.

'Do you mean to tell me,' he asked again, 'that it is not so? Do you mean to say that if he had found his way up here instead of me, you wouldn't have been a little more blind, and a little more deaf, and a little less flourishing, than you have been? Come, Nickleby, answer me that.'

'I tell you this,' replied Ralph, 'that if I brought her here, as a matter of business—'

'Ay, that's the word,' interposed Sir Mulberry, with a laugh. 'You're coming to yourself again now.'

'—As a matter of business,' pursued Ralph, speaking slowly and firmly, as a man who has made up his mind to say no more, 'because I thought she might make some impression on the silly youth you have taken in hand and are lending good help to ruin, I knew—knowing him—that it would be long before he outraged her girl's feelings, and that unless he offended by mere puppyism and emptiness, he would, with a little management, respect the sex and conduct even of his usurer's niece. But if I thought to draw him on more gently by this device, I did not think of subjecting the girl to the licentiousness and brutality of so old a hand as you. And now we understand each other.'

'Especially as there was nothing to be got by it—eh?' sneered Sir Mulberry.

'Exactly so,' said Ralph. He had turned away, and looked over his shoulder to make this last reply. The eyes of the two worthies met, with an expression as if each rascal felt that there was no disguising himself from the other; and Sir Mulberry Hawk shrugged his shoulders and walked slowly out.

His friend closed the door, and looked restlessly towards the spot where his niece still remained in the attitude in which he had left her. She had flung herself heavily upon the couch, and with her head drooping over the cushion, and her face hidden in her hands, seemed to be still weeping in an agony of shame and grief.

Ralph would have walked into any poverty-stricken debtor's house, and pointed him out to a bailiff, though in attendance upon a young child's death-bed, without the smallest concern, because it would have been a matter quite in the ordinary course of business, and the man would have been an offender against his only code of morality. But, here was a young girl, who had done no wrong save that of coming into the world alive; who had patiently yielded to all his wishes; who had tried hard to please him—above all, who didn't owe him money—and he felt awkward and nervous.

Ralph took a chair at some distance; then, another chair a little nearer; then, moved a little nearer still; then, nearer again, and finally sat himself on the same sofa, and laid his hand on Kate's arm.

'Hush, my dear!' he said, as she drew it back, and her sobs burst out afresh. 'Hush, hush! Don't mind it, now; don't think of it.'

'Oh, for pity's sake, let me go home,' cried Kate. 'Let me leave this house, and go home.'

'Yes, yes,' said Ralph. 'You shall. But you must dry your eyes first, and compose yourself. Let me raise your head. There—there.'

'Oh, uncle!' exclaimed Kate, clasping her hands. 'What have I done—what have I done—that you should subject me to this? If I had wronged you in thought, or word, or deed, it would have been most cruel to me, and the memory of one you must have loved in some old time; but—'

'Only listen to me for a moment,' interrupted Ralph, seriously alarmed by the violence of her emotions. 'I didn't know it would be so; it was impossible for me to foresee it. I did all I could.—Come, let us walk about. You are faint with the closeness of the room, and the heat of these lamps. You will be better now, if you make the slightest effort.'

'I will do anything,' replied Kate, 'if you will only send me home.'

'Well, well, I will,' said Ralph; 'but you must get back your own looks; for those you have, will frighten them, and nobody must know of this but you and I. Now let us walk the other way. There. You look better even now.'

With such encouragements as these, Ralph Nickleby walked to and fro, with his niece leaning on his arm; actually trembling beneath her touch.

In the same manner, when he judged it prudent to allow her to depart, he supported her downstairs, after adjusting her shawl and performing such little offices, most probably for the first time in his life. Across the hall, and down the steps, Ralph led her too; nor did he withdraw his hand until she was seated in the coach.

As the door of the vehicle was roughly closed, a comb fell from Kate's hair, close at her uncle's feet; and as he picked it up, and returned it into her hand, the light from a neighbouring lamp shone upon her face. The lock of hair that had escaped and curled loosely over her brow, the traces of tears yet scarcely dry, the flushed cheek, the look of sorrow, all fired some dormant train of recollection in the old man's breast; and the face of his dead brother seemed present before him, with the very look it bore on some occasion of boyish grief, of which every minutest circumstance flashed upon his mind, with the distinctness of a scene of yesterday.

Ralph Nickleby, who was proof against all appeals of blood and kindred—who was steeled against every tale of sorrow and distress—staggered while he looked, and went back into his house, as a man who had seen a spirit from some world beyond the grave.

CHAPTER 20
Wherein Nicholas at length encounters his Uncle, to whom he expresses his Sentiments with much Candour. His Resolution.

Little Miss La Creevy trotted briskly through divers streets at the west end of the town, early on Monday morning—the day after the dinner—charged with the important commission of acquainting Madame Mantalini that Miss Nickleby was too unwell to attend that day, but hoped to be enabled to resume her duties on the morrow. And as Miss La Creevy walked along, revolving in her mind various genteel forms and elegant turns of expression, with a view to the selection of the very best in which to couch her communication, she cogitated a good deal upon the probable causes of her young friend's indisposition.

'I don't know what to make of it,' said Miss La Creevy. 'Her eyes were decidedly red last night. She said she had a headache; headaches don't occasion red eyes. She must have been crying.'

Arriving at this conclusion, which, indeed, she had established to her perfect satisfaction on the previous evening, Miss La Creevy went on to consider—as she had done nearly all night—what new cause of unhappiness her young friend could possibly have had.

'I can't think of anything,' said the little portrait painter. 'Nothing at all, unless it was the behaviour of that old bear. Cross to her, I suppose? Unpleasant brute!'

Relieved by this expression of opinion, albeit it was vented upon empty air, Miss La Creevy trotted on to Madame Mantalini's; and being informed that the governing power was not yet out of bed, requested an interview with the second in command; whereupon Miss Knag appeared.

'So far as I am concerned,' said Miss Knag, when the message had been delivered, with many ornaments of speech; 'I could spare Miss Nickleby for evermore.'

'Oh, indeed, ma'am!' rejoined Miss La Creevy, highly offended. 'But, you see, you are not mistress of the business, and therefore it's of no great consequence.'

'Very good, ma'am,' said Miss Knag. 'Have you any further commands for me?'

'No, I have not, ma'am,' rejoined Miss La Creevy.

'Then good-morning, ma'am,' said Miss Knag.

'Good-morning to you, ma'am; and many obligations for your extreme politeness and good breeding,' rejoined Miss La Creevy.

Thus terminating the interview, during which both ladies had trembled very much, and been marvellously polite—certain indications that they were within an inch of a very desperate quarrel—Miss La Creevy bounced out of the room, and into the street.

'I wonder who that is,' said the queer little soul. 'A nice person to know, I should think! I wish I had the painting of her: I'D do her justice.' So, feeling quite satisfied that she had said a very cutting thing at Miss Knag's expense, Miss La Creevy had a hearty laugh, and went home to breakfast in great good humour.

Here was one of the advantages of having lived alone so long! The little bustling, active, cheerful creature existed entirely within herself, talked to herself, made a confidante of herself, was as sarcastic as she could be, on people who offended her, by herself; pleased herself, and did no harm. If she indulged in scandal, nobody's reputation suffered; and if she enjoyed a little bit of revenge, no living soul was one atom the worse. One of the many to whom, from straitened circumstances, a consequent inability to form the associations they would wish, and a disinclination to mix with the society they could obtain, London is as complete a solitude as the plains of Syria, the humble artist had pursued her lonely, but contented way for many years; and, until the peculiar misfortunes of the Nickleby family attracted her attention, had made no friends, though brimful of the friendliest feelings to all mankind. There are many warm hearts in the same solitary guise as poor little Miss La Creevy's.

However, that's neither here nor there, just now. She went home to breakfast, and had scarcely caught the full flavour of her first sip of tea, when the servant announced a gentleman, whereat Miss La Creevy, at once imagining a new sitter transfixed by admiration at the street-door case, was in unspeakable consternation at the presence of the tea-things.

'Here, take 'em away; run with 'em into the bedroom; anywhere,' said Miss La Creevy. 'Dear, dear; to think that I should be late on this particular morning, of all others, after being ready for three weeks by half-past eight o'clock, and not a soul coming near the place!'

'Don't let me put you out of the way,' said a voice Miss La Creevy knew. 'I told the servant not to mention my name, because I wished to surprise you.'

'Mr. Nicholas!' cried Miss La Creevy, starting in great astonishment. 'You have not forgotten me, I see,' replied Nicholas, extending his hand.

'Why, I think I should even have known you if I had met you in the street,' said Miss La Creevy, with a smile. 'Hannah, another cup and saucer. Now, I'll tell you what, young man; I'll trouble you not to repeat the impertinence you were guilty of, on the morning you went away.'

'You would not be very angry, would you?' asked Nicholas.

'Wouldn't I!' said Miss La Creevy. 'You had better try; that's all!'

Nicholas, with becoming gallantry, immediately took Miss La Creevy at her word, who uttered a faint scream and slapped his face; but it was not a very hard slap, and that's the truth.

'I never saw such a rude creature!' exclaimed Miss La Creevy.

'You told me to try,' said Nicholas.

'Well; but I was speaking ironically,' rejoined Miss La Creevy.

'Oh! that's another thing,' said Nicholas; 'you should have told me that, too.'

'I dare say you didn't know, indeed!' retorted Miss La Creevy. 'But, now I look at you again, you seem thinner than when I saw you last, and your face is haggard and pale. And how come you to have left Yorkshire?'

She stopped here; for there was so much heart in her altered tone and manner, that Nicholas was quite moved.

'I need look somewhat changed,' he said, after a short silence; 'for I have undergone some suffering, both of mind and body, since I left London. I have been very poor, too, and have even suffered from want.'

'Good Heaven, Mr. Nicholas!' exclaimed Miss La Creevy, 'what are you telling me?'

'Nothing which need distress you quite so much,' answered Nicholas, with a more sprightly air; 'neither did I come here to bewail my lot, but on matter more to the purpose. I wish to meet my uncle face to face. I should tell you that first.'

'Then all I have to say about that is,' interposed Miss La Creevy, 'that I don't envy you your taste; and that sitting in the same room with his very boots, would put me out of humour for a fortnight.'

'In the main,' said Nicholas, 'there may be no great difference of opinion between you and me, so far; but you will understand, that I desire to confront him, to justify myself, and to cast his duplicity and malice in his throat.'

'That's quite another matter,' rejoined Miss La Creevy. 'Heaven forgive me; but I shouldn't cry my eyes quite out of my head, if they choked him. Well?'

'To this end, I called upon him this morning,' said Nicholas. 'He only returned to town on Saturday, and I knew nothing of his arrival until late last night.'

'And did you see him?' asked Miss La Creevy.

'No,' replied Nicholas. 'He had gone out.'

'Hah!' said Miss La Creevy; 'on some kind, charitable business, I dare say.'

'I have reason to believe,' pursued Nicholas, 'from what has been told me, by a friend of mine who is acquainted with his movements, that he intends seeing my mother and sister today, and giving them his version of the occurrences that have befallen me. I will meet him there.'

'That's right,' said Miss La Creevy, rubbing her hands. 'And yet, I don't know,' she added, 'there is much to be thought of—others to be considered.'

'I have considered others,' rejoined Nicholas; 'but as honesty and honour are both at issue, nothing shall deter me.'

'You should know best,' said Miss La Creevy.

'In this case I hope so,' answered Nicholas. 'And all I want you to do for me, is, to prepare them for my coming. They think me a long way off, and if I went wholly unexpected, I should frighten them. If you can spare time to tell them that you have seen me, and that I shall be with them in a quarter of an hour afterwards, you will do me a great service.'

'I wish I could do you, or any of you, a greater,' said Miss La Creevy; 'but the power to serve, is as seldom joined with the will, as the will is with the power, I think.'

Talking on very fast and very much, Miss La Creevy finished her breakfast with great expedition, put away the tea-caddy and hid the key under the fender, resumed her bonnet, and, taking Nicholas's arm, sallied forth at once to the city. Nicholas left her near the door of his mother's house, and promised to return within a quarter of an hour.

It so chanced that Ralph Nickleby, at length seeing fit, for his own purposes, to communicate the atrocities of which Nicholas had been guilty, had (instead of first proceeding to another quarter of the town on business, as Newman Noggs supposed he would) gone straight to his sister-in-law. Hence, when Miss La Creevy, admitted by a girl who was cleaning the house, made her way to the sitting-room, she found Mrs Nickleby and Kate in tears, and Ralph just concluding his statement of his nephew's misdemeanours. Kate beckoned her not to retire, and Miss La Creevy took a seat in silence.

'You are here already, are you, my gentleman?' thought the little woman. 'Then he shall announce himself, and see what effect that has on you.'

'This is pretty,' said Ralph, folding up Miss Squeers's note; 'very pretty. I recommend him—against all my previous conviction, for I knew he would never do any good—to a man with whom, behaving himself properly, he might have remained, in comfort, for years. What is the result? Conduct for which he might hold up his hand at the Old Bailey.'

'I never will believe it,' said Kate, indignantly; 'never. It is some base conspiracy, which carries its own falsehood with it.'

'My dear,' said Ralph, 'you wrong the worthy man. These are not inventions. The man is assaulted, your brother is not to be found; this boy, of whom they speak, goes with him—

remember, remember.'

'It is impossible,' said Kate. 'Nicholas!—and a thief too! Mama, how can you sit and hear such statements?'

Poor Mrs. Nickleby, who had, at no time, been remarkable for the possession of a very clear understanding, and who had been reduced by the late changes in her affairs to a most complicated state of perplexity, made no other reply to this earnest remonstrance than exclaiming from behind a mass of pocket-handkerchief, that she never could have believed it—thereby most ingeniously leaving her hearers to suppose that she did believe it.

'It would be my duty, if he came in my way, to deliver him up to justice,' said Ralph, 'my bounden duty; I should have no other course, as a man of the world and a man of business, to pursue. And yet,' said Ralph, speaking in a very marked manner, and looking furtively, but fixedly, at Kate, 'and yet I would not. I would spare the feelings of his—of his sister. And his mother of course,' added Ralph, as though by an afterthought, and with far less emphasis.

Kate very well understood that this was held out as an additional inducement to her to preserve the strictest silence regarding the events of the preceding night. She looked involuntarily towards Ralph as he ceased to speak, but he had turned his eyes another way, and seemed for the moment quite unconscious of her presence.

'Everything,' said Ralph, after a long silence, broken only by Mrs Nickleby's sobs, 'everything combines to prove the truth of this letter, if indeed there were any possibility of disputing it. Do innocent men steal away from the sight of honest folks, and skulk in hiding-places, like outlaws? Do innocent men inveigle nameless vagabonds, and prowl with them about the country as idle robbers do? Assault, riot, theft, what do you call these?'

'A lie!' cried a voice, as the door was dashed open, and Nicholas came into the room.

In the first moment of surprise, and possibly of alarm, Ralph rose from his seat, and fell back a few paces, quite taken off his guard by this unexpected apparition. In another moment, he stood, fixed and immovable with folded arms, regarding his nephew with a scowl; while Kate and Miss La Creevy threw themselves between the two, to prevent the personal violence which the fierce excitement of Nicholas appeared to threaten.

'Dear Nicholas,' cried his sister, clinging to him. 'Be calm, consider—'

'Consider, Kate!' cried Nicholas, clasping her hand so tight in the tumult of his anger, that she could scarcely bear the pain. 'When I consider all, and think of what has passed, I need be made of iron to stand before him.'

'Or bronze,' said Ralph, quietly; 'there is not hardihood enough in flesh and blood to face it out.'

'Oh dear, dear!' cried Mrs. Nickleby, 'that things should have come to such a pass as this!'

'Who speaks in a tone, as if I had done wrong, and brought disgrace on them?' said Nicholas, looking round.

'Your mother, sir,' replied Ralph, motioning towards her.

'Whose ears have been poisoned by you,' said Nicholas; 'by you—who, under pretence of deserving the thanks she poured upon you, heaped every insult, wrong, and indignity upon my head. You, who sent me to a den where sordid cruelty, worthy of yourself, runs wanton, and youthful misery stalks precocious; where the lightness of childhood shrinks into the heaviness of age, and its every promise blights, and withers as it grows. I call Heaven to witness,' said Nicholas, looking eagerly round, 'that I have seen all this, and that he knows it.'

'Refute these calumnies,' said Kate, 'and be more patient, so that you may give them no advantage. Tell us what you really did, and show that they are untrue.'

'Of what do they—or of what does he—accuse me?' said Nicholas.

'First, of attacking your master, and being within an ace of qualifying yourself to be tried for murder,' interposed Ralph. 'I speak plainly, young man, bluster as you will.'

'I interfered,' said Nicholas, 'to save a miserable creature from the vilest cruelty. In so doing, I inflicted such punishment upon a wretch as he will not readily forget, though far less than he deserved from me. If the same scene were renewed before me now, I would take the same part; but I would strike harder and heavier, and brand him with such marks as he should carry to his grave, go to it when he would.'

'You hear?' said Ralph, turning to Mrs. Nickleby. 'Penitence, this!'

'Oh dear me!' cried Mrs. Nickleby, 'I don't know what to think, I really don't.'

'Do not speak just now, mama, I entreat you,' said Kate. 'Dear Nicholas, I only tell you, that you may know what wickedness can prompt, but they accuse you of—a ring is missing, and they dare to say that—'

'The woman,' said Nicholas, haughtily, 'the wife of the fellow from whom these charges come, dropped—as I suppose—a worthless ring among some clothes of mine, early in the morning on which I left the house. At least, I know that she was in the bedroom where they lay, struggling with an unhappy child, and that I found it when I opened my bundle on the road. I returned it, at once, by coach, and they have it now.'

'I knew, I knew,' said Kate, looking towards her uncle. 'About this boy, love, in whose company they say you left?'

'The boy, a silly, helpless creature, from brutality and hard usage, is with me now,' rejoined Nicholas.

'You hear?' said Ralph, appealing to the mother again, 'everything proved, even upon his own confession. Do you choose to restore that boy, sir?'

'No, I do not,' replied Nicholas.

'You do not?' sneered Ralph.

'No,' repeated Nicholas, 'not to the man with whom I found him. I would that I knew on whom he has the claim of birth: I might wring something from his sense of shame, if he were dead to every tie of nature.'

'Indeed!' said Ralph. 'Now, sir, will you hear a word or two from me?'

'You can speak when and what you please,' replied Nicholas, embracing his sister. 'I take little heed of what you say or threaten.'

'Mighty well, sir,' retorted Ralph; 'but perhaps it may concern others, who may think it worth their while to listen, and consider what I tell them. I will address your mother, sir, who knows the world.'

'Ah! and I only too dearly wish I didn't,' sobbed Mrs. Nickleby.

There really was no necessity for the good lady to be much distressed upon this particular head; the extent of her worldly knowledge being, to say the least, very questionable; and so Ralph seemed to think, for he smiled as she spoke. He then glanced steadily at her and Nicholas by turns, as he delivered himself in these words:

'Of what I have done, or what I meant to do, for you, ma'am, and my niece, I say not one syllable. I held out no promise, and leave you to judge for yourself. I hold out no threat now, but I say that this boy, headstrong, wilful and disorderly as he is, should not have one penny of my money, or one crust of my bread, or one grasp of my hand, to save him from the loftiest gallows in all Europe. I will not meet him, come where he comes, or hear his name. I will not help him, or those who help him. With a full knowledge of what he brought upon you by so doing, he has come back in his selfish sloth, to be an aggravation of your wants, and a burden upon his sister's scanty wages. I regret to leave you, and more to leave her, now, but I will not encourage this compound of meanness and cruelty, and, as I will not ask you to renounce him, I see you no more.'

If Ralph had not known and felt his power in wounding those he hated, his glances at Nicholas would have shown it him, in all its force, as he proceeded in the above address. Innocent as the young man was of all wrong, every artful insinuation stung, every well-considered sarcasm cut him to the quick; and when Ralph noted his pale face and quivering lip, he hugged himself to mark how well he had chosen the taunts best calculated to strike deep into a young and ardent spirit.

'I can't help it,' cried Mrs. Nickleby. 'I know you have been very good to us, and meant to do a good deal for my dear daughter. I am quite sure of that; I know you did, and it was very kind of you, having her at your house and all—and of course it would have been a great thing for her and for me too. But I can't, you know, brother-in-law, I can't renounce my own son, even if he has done all you say he has—it's not possible; I couldn't do it; so we must go to rack and ruin, Kate, my dear. I can bear it, I dare say.' Pouring forth these and a perfectly wonderful train of other disjointed expressions of regret, which no mortal power but Mrs Nickleby's could ever have strung together, that lady wrung her hands, and her tears fell faster.

'Why do you say "if Nicholas has done what they say he has," mama?' asked Kate, with honest anger. 'You know he has not.'

'I don't know what to think, one way or other, my dear,' said Mrs Nickleby; 'Nicholas is so violent, and your uncle has so much composure, that I can only hear what he says, and not what Nicholas does. Never mind, don't let us talk any more about it. We can go to the Workhouse, or the Refuge for the Destitute, or the Magdalen Hospital, I dare say; and the sooner we go the better.' With this extraordinary jumble of charitable institutions, Mrs. Nickleby again gave way to her tears.

'Stay,' said Nicholas, as Ralph turned to go. 'You need not leave this place, sir, for it will be relieved of my presence in one minute, and it will be long, very long, before I darken these doors again.'

'Nicholas,' cried Kate, throwing herself on her brother's shoulder, 'do not say so. My dear brother, you will break my heart. Mama, speak to him. Do not mind her, Nicholas; she does not mean it, you should know her better. Uncle, somebody, for Heaven's sake speak to him.'

'I never meant, Kate,' said Nicholas, tenderly, 'I never meant to stay among you; think better of me than to suppose it possible. I may turn my back on this town a few hours sooner than I intended, but what of that? We shall not forget each other apart, and better days will come when we shall part no more. Be a woman, Kate,' he whispered, proudly, 'and do not make me one, while he looks on.'

'No, no, I will not,' said Kate, eagerly, 'but you will not leave us. Oh! think of all the happy days we have had together, before these terrible misfortunes came upon us; of all the comfort and happiness of home, and the trials we have to bear now; of our having no protector under all the slights and wrongs that poverty so much favours, and you cannot leave us to bear them alone, without one hand to help us.'

'You will be helped when I am away,' replied Nicholas hurriedly. 'I am no help to you, no protector; I should bring you nothing but sorrow, and want, and suffering. My own mother sees it, and her fondness and fears for you, point to the course that I should take. And so all good angels bless you, Kate, till I can carry you to some home of mine, where we may revive the happiness denied to us now, and talk of these trials as of things gone by. Do not keep me here, but let me go at once. There. Dear girl—dear girl.'

The grasp which had detained him relaxed, and Kate swooned in his arms. Nicholas stooped over her for a few seconds, and placing her gently in a chair, confided her to their honest friend.

'I need not entreat your sympathy,' he said, wringing her hand, 'for I know your nature. You will never forget them.'

He stepped up to Ralph, who remained in the same attitude which he had preserved throughout the interview, and moved not a finger.

'Whatever step you take, sir,' he said, in a voice inaudible beyond themselves, 'I shall keep a strict account of. I leave them to you, at your desire. There will be a day of reckoning sooner or later, and it will be a heavy one for you if they are wronged.'

Ralph did not allow a muscle of his face to indicate that he heard one word of this parting address. He hardly knew that it was concluded, and Mrs. Nickleby had scarcely made up her mind to detain her son by force if necessary, when Nicholas was gone.

As he hurried through the streets to his obscure lodging, seeking to keep pace, as it were, with the rapidity of the thoughts which crowded upon him, many doubts and hesitations arose in his mind, and almost tempted him to return. But what would they gain by this? Supposing he were to put Ralph Nickleby at defiance, and were even fortunate enough to obtain some small employment, his being with them could only render their present condition worse, and might greatly impair their future prospects; for his mother had spoken of some new kindnesses towards Kate which she had not denied. 'No,' thought Nicholas, 'I have acted for the best.'

But, before he had gone five hundred yards, some other and different feeling would come upon him, and then he would lag again, and pulling his hat over his eyes, give way to the melancholy reflections which pressed thickly upon him. To have committed no fault, and yet to be so entirely alone in the world; to be separated from the only persons he loved, and to be proscribed like a criminal, when six months ago he had been surrounded by every comfort, and looked up to, as the chief hope of his family—this was hard to bear. He had not deserved it either. Well, there was comfort in that; and poor Nicholas would brighten up again, to be again depressed, as his quickly shifting thoughts presented every variety of light and shade before him.

Undergoing these alternations of hope and misgiving, which no one, placed in a situation of ordinary trial, can fail to have experienced, Nicholas at length reached his poor room, where, no longer borne up by the excitement which had hitherto sustained him, but depressed by the revulsion of feeling it left behind, he threw himself on the bed, and turning his face to the wall, gave free vent to the emotions he had so long stifled.

He had not heard anybody enter, and was unconscious of the presence of Smike, until, happening to raise his head, he saw him, standing at the upper end of the room, looking wistfully towards him. He withdrew his eyes when he saw that he was observed, and affected to be busied with some scanty preparations for dinner.

'Well, Smike,' said Nicholas, as cheerfully as he could speak, 'let me hear what new acquaintances you have made this morning, or what new wonder you have found out, in the compass of this street and the next one.'

'No,' said Smike, shaking his head mournfully; 'I must talk of something else today.'

'Of what you like,' replied Nicholas, good-humouredly.

'Of this,' said Smike. 'I know you are unhappy, and have got into great trouble by bringing me away. I ought to have known that, and stopped behind—I would, indeed, if I had thought it then. You—you—are not rich; you have not enough for yourself, and I should not be here. You grow,' said the lad, laying his hand timidly on that of Nicholas, 'you grow thinner every day; your cheek is paler, and your eye more sunk. Indeed I cannot bear to see you so, and think how I am burdening you. I tried to go away today, but the thought of your kind face drew me back. I could not leave you without a word.' The poor fellow could say no more, for his eyes filled with tears, and his voice was gone.

'The word which separates us,' said Nicholas, grasping him heartily by the shoulder, 'shall never be said by me, for you are my only comfort and stay. I would not lose you now, Smike, for all the world could give. The thought of you has upheld me through all I have endured today, and shall, through fifty times such trouble. Give me your hand. My heart is linked to yours. We will journey from this place together, before the week is out. What, if I am steeped in poverty? You lighten it, and we will be poor together.'

CHAPTER 21
Madam Mantalini finds herself in a Situation of some Difficulty, and Miss Nickleby finds herself in no Situation at all

The agitation she had undergone, rendered Kate Nickleby unable to resume her duties at the dressmaker's for three days, at the expiration of which interval she betook herself at the accustomed hour, and with languid steps, to the temple of fashion where Madame Mantalini reigned paramount and supreme.

The ill-will of Miss Knag had lost nothing of its virulence in the interval. The young ladies still scrupulously shrunk from all companionship with their denounced associate; and when that exemplary female arrived a few minutes afterwards, she was at no pains to conceal the displeasure with which she regarded Kate's return.

'Upon my word!' said Miss Knag, as the satellites flocked round, to relieve her of her bonnet and shawl; 'I should have thought some people would have had spirit enough to stop away altogether, when they know what an incumbrance their presence is to right-minded persons. But it's a queer world; oh! it's a queer world!'

Miss Knag, having passed this comment on the world, in the tone in which most people do pass comments on the world when they are out of temper, that is to say, as if they by no means belonged to it, concluded by heaving a sigh, wherewith she seemed meekly to compassionate the wickedness of mankind.

The attendants were not slow to echo the sigh, and Miss Knag was apparently on the eve of favouring them with some further moral reflections, when the voice of Madame Mantalini, conveyed through the speaking-tube, ordered Miss Nickleby upstairs to assist in the arrangement of the show-room; a distinction which caused Miss Knag to toss her head so much, and bite her lips so hard, that her powers of conversation were, for the time, annihilated.

'Well, Miss Nickleby, child,' said Madame Mantalini, when Kate presented herself; 'are you quite well again?'

'A great deal better, thank you,' replied Kate.

'I wish I could say the same,' remarked Madame Mantalini, seating herself with an air of weariness.

'Are you ill?' asked Kate. 'I am very sorry for that.'

'Not exactly ill, but worried, child—worried,' rejoined Madame.

'I am still more sorry to hear that,' said Kate, gently. 'Bodily illness is more easy to bear than mental.'

'Ah! and it's much easier to talk than to bear either,' said Madame, rubbing her nose with much irritability of manner. 'There, get to your work, child, and put the things in order, do.'

While Kate was wondering within herself what these symptoms of unusual vexation portended, Mr. Mantalini put the tips of his whiskers, and, by degrees, his head, through the half-opened door, and cried in a soft voice—

'Is my life and soul there?'

'No,' replied his wife.

'How can it say so, when it is blooming in the front room like a little rose in a demnition flower-pot?' urged Mantalini. 'May its poppet come in and talk?'

'Certainly not,' replied Madame: 'you know I never allow you here. Go along!'

The poppet, however, encouraged perhaps by the relenting tone of this reply, ventured to rebel, and, stealing into the room, made towards Madame Mantalini on tiptoe, blowing her a kiss as he came along.

'Why will it vex itself, and twist its little face into bewitching nutcrackers?' said Mantalini, putting his left arm round the waist of his life and soul, and drawing her towards him with his right.

'Oh! I can't bear you,' replied his wife.

'Not—eh, not bear me!' exclaimed Mantalini. 'Fibs, fibs. It couldn't be. There's not a woman alive, that could tell me such a thing to my face—to my own face.' Mr. Mantalini stroked his chin, as he said this, and glanced complacently at an opposite mirror.

'Such destructive extravagance,' reasoned his wife, in a low tone.

'All in its joy at having gained such a lovely creature, such a little Venus, such a demd, enchanting, bewitching, engrossing, captivating little Venus,' said Mantalini.

'See what a situation you have placed me in!' urged Madame.

'No harm will come, no harm shall come, to its own darling,' rejoined Mr Mantalini. 'It is all over; there will be nothing the matter; money shall be got in; and if it don't come in fast enough, old Nickleby shall stump up again, or have his jugular separated if he dares to vex and hurt the little—'

'Hush!' interposed Madame. 'Don't you see?'

Mr. Mantalini, who, in his eagerness to make up matters with his wife, had overlooked, or feigned to overlook, Miss Nickleby hitherto, took the hint, and laying his finger on his lip, sunk his voice still lower. There was, then, a great deal of whispering, during which Madame Mantalini appeared to make reference, more than once, to certain debts incurred by Mr Mantalini previous to her coverture; and also to an unexpected outlay of money in payment of the aforesaid debts; and furthermore, to certain agreeable weaknesses on that gentleman's part, such as gaming, wasting, idling, and a tendency to horse-flesh; each of which matters of accusation Mr. Mantalini disposed of, by one kiss or more, as its relative importance demanded. The upshot of it all was, that Madame Mantalini was in raptures with him, and that they went upstairs to breakfast.

Kate busied herself in what she had to do, and was silently arranging the various articles of decoration in the best taste she could display, when she started to hear a strange man's voice in the room, and started again, to observe, on looking round, that a white hat, and a red neckerchief, and a broad round face, and a large head, and part of a green coat were in the room too.

'Don't alarm yourself, miss,' said the proprietor of these appearances. 'I say; this here's the mantie-making consarn, an't it?'

'Yes,' rejoined Kate, greatly astonished. 'What did you want?'

The stranger answered not; but, first looking back, as though to beckon to some unseen person outside, came, very deliberately, into the room, and was closely followed by a little man in brown, very much the worse for wear, who brought with him a mingled fumigation of stale tobacco and fresh onions. The clothes of this gentleman were much bespeckled with flue; and his shoes, stockings, and nether garments, from his heels to the waist buttons of his coat inclusive, were profusely embroidered with splashes of mud, caught a fortnight previously— before the setting-in of the fine weather.

Kate's very natural impression was, that these engaging individuals had called with the view of possessing themselves, unlawfully, of any portable articles that chanced to strike their fancy. She did not attempt to disguise her apprehensions, and made a move towards the door.

'Wait a minnit,' said the man in the green coat, closing it softly, and standing with his back against it. 'This is a unpleasant bisness. Vere's your govvernor?'

'My what—did you say?' asked Kate, trembling; for she thought 'governor' might be slang for watch or money.

'Mister Muntlehiney,' said the man. 'Wot's come on him? Is he at home?'

'He is above stairs, I believe,' replied Kate, a little reassured by this inquiry. 'Do you want him?'

'No,' replied the visitor. 'I don't ezactly want him, if it's made a favour on. You can jist give him that 'ere card, and tell him if he wants to speak to me, and save trouble, here I am; that's all.'

With these words, the stranger put a thick square card into Kate's hand, and, turning to his friend, remarked, with an easy air, 'that the rooms was a good high pitch;' to which the friend assented, adding, by way of illustration, 'that there was lots of room for a little boy to grow up a man in either on 'em, vithout much fear of his ever bringing his head into contract vith the ceiling.'

After ringing the bell which would summon Madame Mantalini, Kate glanced at the card, and saw that it displayed the name of 'Scaley,' together with some other information to which she had not had time to refer, when her attention was attracted by Mr. Scaley himself, who, walking up to one of the cheval-glasses, gave it a hard poke in the centre with his stick, as coolly as if it had been made of cast iron.

'Good plate this here, Tix,' said Mr. Scaley to his friend.

'Ah!' rejoined Mr. Tix, placing the marks of his four fingers, and a duplicate impression of his thumb, on a piece of sky-blue silk; 'and this here article warn't made for nothing, mind you.'

From the silk, Mr. Tix transferred his admiration to some elegant articles of wearing apparel, while Mr. Scaley adjusted his neckcloth, at leisure, before the glass, and afterwards, aided by its reflection, proceeded to the minute consideration of a pimple on his chin; in which absorbing occupation he was yet engaged, when Madame Mantalini, entering the room, uttered an exclamation of surprise which roused him.

'Oh! Is this the missis?' inquired Scaley.

'It is Madame Mantalini,' said Kate.

'Then,' said Mr. Scaley, producing a small document from his pocket and unfolding it very slowly, 'this is a writ of execution, and if it's not conwenient to settle we'll go over the house at wunst, please, and take the inwentory.'

Poor Madame Mantalini wrung her hands for grief, and rung the bell for her husband; which done, she fell into a chair and a fainting fit, simultaneously. The professional gentlemen, however, were not at all discomposed by this event, for Mr. Scaley, leaning upon a stand on which a handsome dress was displayed (so that his shoulders appeared above it, in nearly the same manner as the shoulders of the lady for whom it was designed would have done if she had had it on), pushed his hat on one side and scratched his head with perfect unconcern, while his friend Mr. Tix, taking that opportunity for a general survey of the apartment preparatory to entering on business, stood with his inventory-book under his arm and his hat in his hand, mentally occupied in putting a price upon every object within his range of vision.

Such was the posture of affairs when Mr. Mantalini hurried in; and as that distinguished specimen had had a pretty extensive intercourse with Mr Scaley's fraternity in his bachelor days, and was, besides, very far from being taken by surprise on the present agitating occasion, he merely shrugged his shoulders, thrust his hands down to the bottom of his pockets, elevated his eyebrows, whistled a bar or two, swore an oath or two, and, sitting astride upon a chair, put the best face upon the matter with great composure and decency.

'What's the demd total?' was the first question he asked.

'Fifteen hundred and twenty-seven pound, four and ninepence ha'penny,' replied Mr. Scaley, without moving a limb.

'The halfpenny be demd,' said Mr. Mantalini, impatiently.

'By all means if you vish it,' retorted Mr. Scaley; 'and the ninepence.'

'It don't matter to us if the fifteen hundred and twenty-seven pound went along with it, that I know on,' observed Mr. Tix.

'Not a button,' said Scaley.

'Well,' said the same gentleman, after a pause, 'wot's to be done—anything? Is it only a small crack, or a out-and-out smash? A break-up of the constitootion is it?—werry good. Then Mr. Tom Tix, esk-wire, you must inform your angel wife and lovely family as you won't sleep at home for three nights to come, along of being in possession here. Wot's the good of the lady a fretting herself?' continued Mr. Scaley, as Madame Mantalini sobbed. 'A good half of wot's here isn't paid for, I des-say, and wot a consolation oughtn't that to be to her feelings!'

With these remarks, combining great pleasantry with sound moral encouragement under difficulties, Mr. Scaley proceeded to take the inventory, in which delicate task he was materially assisted by the uncommon tact and experience of Mr. Tix, the broker.

'My cup of happiness's sweetener,' said Mantalini, approaching his wife with a penitent air; 'will you listen to me for two minutes?'

'Oh! don't speak to me,' replied his wife, sobbing. 'You have ruined me, and that's enough.'

Mr. Mantalini, who had doubtless well considered his part, no sooner heard these words pronounced in a tone of grief and severity, than he recoiled several paces, assumed an expression of consuming mental agony, rushed headlong from the room, and was, soon afterwards, heard to slam the door of an upstairs dressing-room with great violence.

'Miss Nickleby,' cried Madame Mantalini, when this sound met her ear, 'make haste, for Heaven's sake, he will destroy himself! I spoke unkindly to him, and he cannot bear it from me. Alfred, my darling Alfred.'

With such exclamations, she hurried upstairs, followed by Kate who, although she did not quite participate in the fond wife's apprehensions, was a little flurried, nevertheless. The dressing-room door being hastily flung open, Mr. Mantalini was disclosed to view, with his shirt-collar symmetrically thrown back: putting a fine edge to a breakfast knife by means of his razor strop.

'Ah!' cried Mr. Mantalini, 'interrupted!' and whisk went the breakfast knife into Mr. Mantalini's dressing-gown pocket, while Mr. Mantalini's eyes rolled wildly, and his hair floating in wild disorder, mingled with his whiskers.

'Alfred,' cried his wife, flinging her arms about him, 'I didn't mean to say it, I didn't mean to say it!'

'Ruined!' cried Mr. Mantalini. 'Have I brought ruin upon the best and purest creature that ever blessed a demnition vagabond! Demmit, let me go.' At this crisis of his ravings Mr. Mantalini made a pluck at the breakfast knife, and being restrained by his wife's grasp, attempted to dash his head against the wall—taking very good care to be at least six feet from it.

'Compose yourself, my own angel,' said Madame. 'It was nobody's fault; it was mine as much as yours, we shall do very well yet. Come, Alfred, come.'

Mr. Mantalini did not think proper to come to, all at once; but, after calling several times for poison, and requesting some lady or gentleman to blow his brains out, gentler feelings came upon him, and he wept pathetically. In this softened frame of mind he did not oppose the capture of the knife—which, to tell the truth, he was rather glad to be rid of, as an inconvenient and dangerous article for a skirt pocket—and finally he suffered himself to be led away by his affectionate partner.

After a delay of two or three hours, the young ladies were informed that their services would be dispensed with until further notice, and at the expiration of two days, the name of Mantalini appeared in the list of bankrupts: Miss Nickleby received an intimation per post, on the same morning, that the business would be, in future, carried on under the name of Miss Knag, and that her assistance would no longer be required—a piece of intelligence with which Mrs. Nickleby was no sooner made acquainted, than that good lady declared she had expected it all along and cited divers unknown occasions on which she had prophesied to that precise effect.

'And I say again,' remarked Mrs. Nickleby (who, it is scarcely necessary to observe, had never said so before), 'I say again, that a milliner's and dressmaker's is the very last description of business, Kate, that you should have thought of attaching yourself to. I don't make it a reproach to you, my love; but still I will say, that if you had consulted your own mother—'

'Well, well, mama,' said Kate, mildly: 'what would you recommend now?'

'Recommend!' cried Mrs. Nickleby, 'isn't it obvious, my dear, that of all occupations in this world for a young lady situated as you are, that of companion to some amiable lady is the very thing for which your education, and manners, and personal appearance, and everything else, exactly qualify you? Did you never hear your poor dear papa speak of the young lady who was the daughter of the old lady who boarded in the same house that he boarded in once, when he was a bachelor—what was her name again? I know it began with a B, and ended with g, but whether it was Waters or—no, it couldn't have been that, either; but whatever her name was, don't you know that that young lady went as companion to a married lady who died soon afterwards, and that she married the husband, and had one of the finest little boys that the medical man had ever seen—all within eighteen months?'

Kate knew, perfectly well, that this torrent of favourable recollection was occasioned by some opening, real or imaginary, which her mother had discovered, in the companionship walk of life. She therefore waited, very patiently, until all reminiscences and anecdotes, bearing or not bearing upon the subject, had been exhausted, and at last ventured to inquire what discovery had been made. The truth then came out. Mrs. Nickleby had, that morning, had a yesterday's newspaper of the very first respectability from the public-house where the porter came from; and in this yesterday's newspaper was an advertisement, couched in the purest and most grammatical English, announcing that a married lady was in want of a genteel young person as companion, and that the married lady's name and address were to be known, on application at a certain library at the west end of the town, therein mentioned.

'And I say,' exclaimed Mrs. Nickleby, laying the paper down in triumph, 'that if your uncle don't object, it's well worth the trial.'

Kate was too sick at heart, after the rough jostling she had already had with the world, and really cared too little at the moment what fate was reserved for her, to make any objection. Mr. Ralph Nickleby offered none, but, on the contrary, highly approved of the suggestion; neither did he express any great surprise at Madame Mantalini's sudden failure, indeed it would have been strange if he had, inasmuch as it had been procured and brought about chiefly by himself. So, the name and address were obtained without loss of time, and Miss Nickleby and her mama went off in quest of Mrs. Wititterly, of Cadogan Place, Sloane Street, that same forenoon.

Cadogan Place is the one slight bond that joins two great extremes; it is the connecting link between the aristocratic pavements of Belgrave Square, and the barbarism of Chelsea. It is in Sloane Street, but not of it. The people in Cadogan Place look down upon Sloane Street, and think Brompton low. They affect fashion too, and wonder where the New Road is. Not that they claim to be on precisely the same footing as the high folks of Belgrave Square and Grosvenor Place, but that they stand, with reference to them, rather in the light of those illegitimate children of the great who are content to boast of their connections, although their connections disavow them. Wearing as much as they can of the airs and semblances of loftiest rank, the people of Cadogan Place have the realities of middle station. It is the conductor which communicates to the inhabitants of regions beyond its limit, the shock of pride of birth and rank, which it has not within itself, but derives from a fountain-head beyond; or, like the ligament which unites the Siamese twins, it contains something of the life and essence of two distinct bodies, and yet belongs to neither.

Upon this doubtful ground, lived Mrs. Wititterly, and at Mrs. Wititterly's door Kate Nickleby knocked with trembling hand. The door was opened by a big footman with his head floured, or chalked, or painted in some way (it didn't look genuine powder), and the big footman, receiving the card of introduction, gave it to a little page; so little, indeed, that his body would not hold, in ordinary array, the number of small buttons which are indispensable to a page's costume, and they were consequently obliged to be stuck on four abreast. This young gentleman took the card upstairs on a salver, and pending his return, Kate and her mother were shown into a dining-room of rather dirty and shabby aspect, and so comfortably arranged as to be adapted to almost any purpose rather than eating and drinking.

Now, in the ordinary course of things, and according to all authentic descriptions of high life, as set forth in books, Mrs. Wititterly ought to have been in her boudoir; but whether it was that Mr. Wititterly was at that moment shaving himself in the boudoir or what not, certain it is that Mrs. Wititterly gave audience in the drawing-room, where was everything proper and necessary, including curtains and furniture coverings of a roseate hue, to shed a delicate bloom on Mrs. Wititterly's complexion, and a little dog to snap at strangers' legs for Mrs. Wititterly's amusement, and the afore-mentioned page, to hand chocolate for Mrs. Wititterly's refreshment.

The lady had an air of sweet insipidity, and a face of engaging paleness; there was a faded look about her, and about the furniture, and about the house. She was reclining on a sofa in such a very unstudied attitude, that she might have been taken for an actress all ready for the first scene in a ballet, and only waiting for the drop curtain to go up.

'Place chairs.'

The page placed them.

'Leave the room, Alphonse.'

The page left it; but if ever an Alphonse carried plain Bill in his face and figure, that page was the boy.

'I have ventured to call, ma'am,' said Kate, after a few seconds of awkward silence, 'from having seen your advertisement.'

'Yes,' replied Mrs. Wititterly, 'one of my people put it in the paper—Yes.'

'I thought, perhaps,' said Kate, modestly, 'that if you had not already made a final choice, you would forgive my troubling you with an application.'

'Yes,' drawled Mrs. Wititterly again.

'If you have already made a selection—'

'Oh dear no,' interrupted the lady, 'I am not so easily suited. I really don't know what to say. You have never been a companion before, have you?'

Mrs. Nickleby, who had been eagerly watching her opportunity, came dexterously in, before Kate could reply. 'Not to any stranger, ma'am,' said the good lady; 'but she has been a companion to me for some years. I am her mother, ma'am.'

'Oh!' said Mrs. Wititterly, 'I apprehend you.'

'I assure you, ma'am,' said Mrs. Nickleby, 'that I very little thought, at one time, that it would be necessary for my daughter to go out into the world at all, for her poor dear papa was an independent gentleman, and would have been at this moment if he had but listened in time to my constant entreaties and—'

'Dear mama,' said Kate, in a low voice.

'My dear Kate, if you will allow me to speak,' said Mrs. Nickleby, 'I shall take the liberty of explaining to this lady—'

'I think it is almost unnecessary, mama.'

And notwithstanding all the frowns and winks with which Mrs. Nickleby intimated that she was going to say something which would clench the business at once, Kate maintained her point by an expressive look, and for once Mrs. Nickleby was stopped upon the very brink of an oration.

'What are your accomplishments?' asked Mrs. Wititterly, with her eyes shut.

Kate blushed as she mentioned her principal acquirements, and Mrs. Nickleby checked them all off, one by one, on her fingers; having calculated the number before she came out. Luckily the two calculations agreed, so Mrs Nickleby had no excuse for talking.

'You are a good temper?' asked Mrs. Wititterly, opening her eyes for an instant, and shutting them again.

'I hope so,' rejoined Kate.

'And have a highly respectable reference for everything, have you?'

Kate replied that she had, and laid her uncle's card upon the table.

'Have the goodness to draw your chair a little nearer, and let me look at you,' said Mrs. Wititterly; 'I am so very nearsighted that I can't quite discern your features.'

Kate complied, though not without some embarrassment, with this request, and Mrs. Wititterly took a languid survey of her countenance, which lasted some two or three minutes.

'I like your appearance,' said that lady, ringing a little bell. 'Alphonse, request your master to come here.'

The page disappeared on this errand, and after a short interval, during which not a word was spoken on either side, opened the door for an important gentleman of about eight-and-thirty, of rather plebeian countenance, and with a very light head of hair, who leant over Mrs Wititterly for a little time, and conversed with her in whispers.

'Oh!' he said, turning round, 'yes. This is a most important matter. Mrs Wititterly is of a very excitable nature; very delicate, very fragile; a hothouse plant, an exotic.'

'Oh! Henry, my dear,' interposed Mrs. Wititterly.

'You are, my love, you know you are; one breath—' said Mr. W., blowing an imaginary feather away. 'Pho! you're gone!'

The lady sighed.

'Your soul is too large for your body,' said Mr. Wititterly. 'Your intellect wears you out; all the medical men say so; you know that there is not a physician who is not proud of being called in to you. What is their unanimous declaration? "My dear doctor," said I to Sir Tumley Snuffim, in this very room, the very last time he came. "My dear doctor, what is my wife's complaint? Tell me all. I can bear it. Is it nerves?" "My dear fellow," he said, "be proud of that woman; make much of her; she is an ornament to the fashionable world, and to you. Her complaint is soul. It swells, expands, dilates—the blood fires, the pulse quickens, the excitement increases—Whew!"' Here Mr. Wititterly, who, in the ardour of his description, had flourished his right hand to within something less than an inch of Mrs. Nickleby's bonnet, drew it hastily back again, and blew his nose as fiercely as if it had been done by some violent machinery.

'You make me out worse than I am, Henry,' said Mrs. Wititterly, with a faint smile.

'I do not, Julia, I do not,' said Mr. W. 'The society in which you move—necessarily move, from your station, connection, and endowments—is one vortex and whirlpool of the most frightful excitement. Bless my heart and body, can I ever forget the night you danced with the baronet's nephew at the election ball, at Exeter! It was tremendous.'

'I always suffer for these triumphs afterwards,' said Mrs. Wititterly.

'And for that very reason,' rejoined her husband, 'you must have a companion, in whom there is great gentleness, great sweetness, excessive sympathy, and perfect repose.'

Here, both Mr. and Mrs. Wititterly, who had talked rather at the Nicklebys than to each other, left off speaking, and looked at their two hearers, with an expression of countenance which seemed to say, 'What do you think of all this?'

'Mrs. Wititterly,' said her husband, addressing himself to Mrs. Nickleby, 'is sought after and courted by glittering crowds and brilliant circles. She is excited by the opera, the drama, the fine arts, the—the—the—'

'The nobility, my love,' interposed Mrs. Wititterly.

'The nobility, of course,' said Mr. Wititterly. 'And the military. She forms and expresses an immense variety of opinions on an immense variety of subjects. If some people in public life were acquainted with Mrs Wititterly's real opinion of them, they would not hold their heads, perhaps, quite as high as they do.'

'Hush, Henry,' said the lady; 'this is scarcely fair.'

'I mention no names, Julia,' replied Mr. Wititterly; 'and nobody is injured. I merely mention the circumstance to show that you are no ordinary person, that there is a constant friction perpetually going on between your mind and your body; and that you must be soothed and tended. Now let me hear, dispassionately and calmly, what are this young lady's qualifications for the office.'

In obedience to this request, the qualifications were all gone through again, with the addition of many interruptions and cross-questionings from Mr. Wititterly. It was finally arranged that inquiries should be made, and a decisive answer addressed to Miss Nickleby under cover of her uncle, within two days. These conditions agreed upon, the page showed them down as far as the staircase window; and the big footman, relieving guard at that point, piloted them in perfect safety to the street-door.

'They are very distinguished people, evidently,' said Mrs. Nickleby, as she took her daughter's arm. 'What a superior person Mrs. Wititterly is!'

'Do you think so, mama?' was all Kate's reply.

'Why, who can help thinking so, Kate, my love?' rejoined her mother. 'She is pale though, and looks much exhausted. I hope she may not be wearing herself out, but I am very much afraid.'

These considerations led the deep-sighted lady into a calculation of the probable duration of Mrs. Wititterly's life, and the chances of the disconsolate widower bestowing his hand on her daughter. Before reaching home, she had freed Mrs. Wititterly's soul from all bodily restraint; married Kate with great splendour at St George's, Hanover Square; and only left undecided the minor question, whether a splendid French-polished mahogany bedstead should be erected for herself in the two-pair back of the house in Cadogan Place, or in the three-pair front: between which apartments she could not quite balance the advantages, and therefore adjusted the question at last, by determining to leave it to the decision of her son-in-law.

The inquiries were made. The answer—not to Kate's very great joy—was favourable; and at the expiration of a week she betook herself, with all her movables and valuables, to Mrs. Wititterly's mansion, where for the present we will leave her.

CHAPTER 22
Nicholas, accompanied by Smike, sallies forth to seek his Fortune. He encounters Mr. Vincent Crummles; and who he was, is herein made manifest

The whole capital which Nicholas found himself entitled to, either in possession, reversion, remainder, or expectancy, after paying his rent and settling with the broker from whom he had hired his poor furniture, did not exceed, by more than a few halfpence, the sum of twenty shillings. And yet he hailed the morning on which he had resolved to quit London, with a light heart, and sprang from his bed with an elasticity of spirit which is happily the lot of young persons, or the world would never be stocked with old ones.

It was a cold, dry, foggy morning in early spring. A few meagre shadows flitted to and fro in the misty streets, and occasionally there loomed through the dull vapour, the heavy outline of some hackney coach wending homewards, which, drawing slowly nearer, rolled jangling by, scattering the thin crust of frost from its whitened roof, and soon was lost again in the cloud. At intervals were heard the tread of slipshod feet, and the chilly cry of the poor sweep as he crept, shivering, to his early toil; the heavy footfall of the official watcher of the night, pacing slowly up and down and cursing the tardy hours that still intervened between him and sleep; the rambling of ponderous carts and waggons; the roll of the lighter vehicles which carried buyers and sellers to the different markets; the sound of ineffectual knocking at the doors of heavy sleepers—all these noises fell upon the ear from time to time, but all seemed muffled by the fog, and to be rendered almost as indistinct to the ear as was every object to the sight. The sluggish darkness thickened as the day came on; and those who had the courage to rise and peep at the gloomy street from their curtained windows, crept back to bed again, and coiled themselves up to sleep.

Before even these indications of approaching morning were rife in busy London, Nicholas had made his way alone to the city, and stood beneath the windows of his mother's house. It was dull and bare to see, but it had light and life for him; for there was at least one heart within its old walls to which insult or dishonour would bring the same blood rushing, that flowed in his own veins.

He crossed the road, and raised his eyes to the window of the room where he knew his sister slept. It was closed and dark. 'Poor girl,' thought Nicholas, 'she little thinks who lingers here!'

He looked again, and felt, for the moment, almost vexed that Kate was not there to exchange one word at parting. 'Good God!' he thought, suddenly correcting himself, 'what a boy I am!'

'It is better as it is,' said Nicholas, after he had lounged on, a few paces, and returned to the same spot. 'When I left them before, and could have said goodbye a thousand times if I had chosen, I spared them the pain of leave-taking, and why not now?' As he spoke, some fancied motion of the curtain almost persuaded him, for the instant, that Kate was at the window, and by one of those strange contradictions of feeling which are common to us all, he shrunk involuntarily into a doorway, that she might not see him. He smiled at his own weakness; said

'God bless them!' and walked away with a lighter step.

Smike was anxiously expecting him when he reached his old lodgings, and so was Newman, who had expended a day's income in a can of rum and milk to prepare them for the journey. They had tied up the luggage, Smike shouldered it, and away they went, with Newman Noggs in company; for he had insisted on walking as far as he could with them, overnight.

'Which way?' asked Newman, wistfully.

'To Kingston first,' replied Nicholas.

'And where afterwards?' asked Newman. 'Why won't you tell me?'

'Because I scarcely know myself, good friend,' rejoined Nicholas, laying his hand upon his shoulder; 'and if I did, I have neither plan nor prospect yet, and might shift my quarters a hundred times before you could possibly communicate with me.'

'I am afraid you have some deep scheme in your head,' said Newman, doubtfully.

'So deep,' replied his young friend, 'that even I can't fathom it. Whatever I resolve upon, depend upon it I will write you soon.'

'You won't forget?' said Newman.

'I am not very likely to,' rejoined Nicholas. 'I have not so many friends that I shall grow confused among the number, and forget my best one.'

Occupied in such discourse, they walked on for a couple of hours, as they might have done for a couple of days if Nicholas had not sat himself down on a stone by the wayside, and resolutely declared his intention of not moving another step until Newman Noggs turned back. Having pleaded ineffectually first for another half-mile, and afterwards for another quarter, Newman was fain to comply, and to shape his course towards Golden Square, after interchanging many hearty and affectionate farewells, and many times turning back to wave his hat to the two wayfarers when they had become mere specks in the distance.

'Now listen to me, Smike,' said Nicholas, as they trudged with stout hearts onwards. 'We are bound for Portsmouth.'

Smike nodded his head and smiled, but expressed no other emotion; for whether they had been bound for Portsmouth or Port Royal would have been alike to him, so they had been bound together.

'I don't know much of these matters,' resumed Nicholas; 'but Portsmouth is a seaport town, and if no other employment is to be obtained, I should think we might get on board some ship. I am young and active, and could be useful in many ways. So could you.'

'I hope so,' replied Smike. 'When I was at that—you know where I mean?'

'Yes, I know,' said Nicholas. 'You needn't name the place.'

'Well, when I was there,' resumed Smike; his eyes sparkling at the prospect of displaying his abilities; 'I could milk a cow, and groom a horse, with anybody.'

'Ha!' said Nicholas, gravely. 'I am afraid they don't keep many animals of either kind on board ship, Smike, and even when they have horses, that they are not very particular about rubbing them down; still you can learn to do something else, you know. Where there's a will, there's a way.'

'And I am very willing,' said Smike, brightening up again.

'God knows you are,' rejoined Nicholas; 'and if you fail, it shall go hard but I'll do enough for us both.'

'Do we go all the way today?' asked Smike, after a short silence.

'That would be too severe a trial, even for your willing legs,' said Nicholas, with a good-humoured smile. 'No. Godalming is some thirty and odd miles from London—as I found from a map I borrowed—and I purpose to rest there. We must push on again tomorrow, for we are not rich enough to loiter. Let me relieve you of that bundle! Come!'

'No, no,' rejoined Smike, falling back a few steps. 'Don't ask me to give it up to you.'

'Why not?' asked Nicholas.

'Let me do something for you, at least,' said Smike. 'You will never let me serve you as I ought. You will never know how I think, day and night, of ways to please you.'

'You are a foolish fellow to say it, for I know it well, and see it, or I should be a blind and senseless beast,' rejoined Nicholas. 'Let me ask you a question while I think of it, and there is no one by,' he added, looking him steadily in the face. 'Have you a good memory?'

'I don't know,' said Smike, shaking his head sorrowfully. 'I think I had once; but it's all gone now—all gone.'

'Why do you think you had once?' asked Nicholas, turning quickly upon him as though the answer in some way helped out the purport of his question.

'Because I could remember, when I was a child,' said Smike, 'but that is very, very long ago, or at least it seems so. I was always confused and giddy at that place you took me from; and could never remember, and sometimes couldn't even understand, what they said to me. I—let me see—let me see!'

'You are wandering now,' said Nicholas, touching him on the arm.

'No,' replied his companion, with a vacant look 'I was only thinking how—' He shivered involuntarily as he spoke.

'Think no more of that place, for it is all over,' retorted Nicholas, fixing his eyes full upon that of his companion, which was fast settling into an unmeaning stupefied gaze, once habitual to him, and common even then. 'What of the first day you went to Yorkshire?'

'Eh!' cried the lad.

'That was before you began to lose your recollection, you know,' said Nicholas quietly. 'Was the weather hot or cold?'

'Wet,' replied the boy. 'Very wet. I have always said, when it has rained hard, that it was like the night I came: and they used to crowd round and laugh to see me cry when the rain fell heavily. It was like a child, they said, and that made me think of it more. I turned cold all over sometimes, for I could see myself as I was then, coming in at the very same door.'

'As you were then,' repeated Nicholas, with assumed carelessness; 'how was that?'

'Such a little creature,' said Smike, 'that they might have had pity and mercy upon me, only to remember it.'

'You didn't find your way there, alone!' remarked Nicholas.

'No,' rejoined Smike, 'oh no.'

'Who was with you?'

'A man—a dark, withered man. I have heard them say so, at the school, and I remembered that before. I was glad to leave him, I was afraid of him; but they made me more afraid of them, and used me harder too.'

'Look at me,' said Nicholas, wishing to attract his full attention. 'There; don't turn away. Do you remember no woman, no kind woman, who hung over you once, and kissed your lips, and called you her child?'

'No,' said the poor creature, shaking his head, 'no, never.'

'Nor any house but that house in Yorkshire?'

'No,' rejoined the youth, with a melancholy look; 'a room—I remember I slept in a room, a large lonesome room at the top of a house, where there was a trap-door in the ceiling. I have covered my head with the clothes often, not to see it, for it frightened me: a young child with no one near at night: and I used to wonder what was on the other side. There was a clock too, an old clock, in one corner. I remember that. I have never forgotten that room; for when I have terrible dreams, it comes back, just as it was. I see things and people in it that I had never seen then, but there is the room just as it used to be; that never changes.'

'Will you let me take the bundle now?' asked Nicholas, abruptly changing the theme.

'No,' said Smike, 'no. Come, let us walk on.'

He quickened his pace as he said this, apparently under the impression that they had been standing still during the whole of the previous dialogue. Nicholas marked him closely, and every word of this conversation remained upon his memory.

It was, by this time, within an hour of noon, and although a dense vapour still enveloped the city they had left, as if the very breath of its busy people hung over their schemes of gain and profit, and found greater attraction there than in the quiet region above, in the open country it was clear and fair. Occasionally, in some low spots they came upon patches of mist which the sun had not yet driven from their strongholds; but these were soon passed, and as they laboured up the hills beyond, it was pleasant to look down, and see how the sluggish mass rolled heavily off, before the cheering influence of day. A broad, fine, honest sun lighted up the green pastures and dimpled water with the semblance of summer, while it left the travellers all the invigorating freshness of that early time of year. The ground seemed elastic under their feet; the sheep-bells were music to their ears; and exhilarated by exercise, and stimulated by hope, they pushed onward with the strength of lions.

The day wore on, and all these bright colours subsided, and assumed a quieter tint, like young hopes softened down by time, or youthful features by degrees resolving into the calm and serenity of age. But they were scarcely less beautiful in their slow decline, than they had been in their prime; for nature gives to every time and season some beauties of its own; and from morning to night, as from the cradle to the grave, is but a succession of changes so gentle and easy, that we can scarcely mark their progress.

To Godalming they came at last, and here they bargained for two humble beds, and slept soundly. In the morning they were astir: though not quite so early as the sun: and again afoot; if not with all the freshness of yesterday, still, with enough of hope and spirit to bear them cheerily on.

It was a harder day's journey than yesterday's, for there were long and weary hills to climb; and in journeys, as in life, it is a great deal easier to go down hill than up. However, they kept on, with unabated perseverance, and the hill has not yet lifted its face to heaven that perseverance will not gain the summit of at last.

They walked upon the rim of the Devil's Punch Bowl; and Smike listened with greedy interest as Nicholas read the inscription upon the stone which, reared upon that wild spot, tells of a murder committed there by night. The grass on which they stood, had once been dyed with gore; and the blood of the murdered man had run down, drop by drop, into the hollow which gives the place its name. 'The Devil's Bowl,' thought Nicholas, as he looked into the void, 'never held fitter liquor than that!'

Onward they kept, with steady purpose, and entered at length upon a wide and spacious tract of downs, with every variety of little hill and plain to change their verdant surface. Here, there shot up, almost perpendicularly, into the sky, a height so steep, as to be hardly accessible to any but the sheep and goats that fed upon its sides, and there, stood a mound of green, sloping and tapering off so delicately, and merging so gently into the level ground, that you could scarce define its limits. Hills swelling above each other; and undulations shapely and uncouth, smooth and rugged, graceful and grotesque, thrown negligently side by side, bounded the view in each direction; while frequently, with unexpected noise, there uprose from the ground a flight of crows, who, cawing and wheeling round the nearest hills, as if uncertain of their course, suddenly poised themselves upon the wing and skimmed down the long vista of some opening valley, with the speed of light itself.

By degrees, the prospect receded more and more on either hand, and as they had been shut out from rich and extensive scenery, so they emerged once again upon the open country. The knowledge that they were drawing near their place of destination, gave them fresh courage to proceed; but the way had been difficult, and they had loitered on the road, and Smike was tired. Thus, twilight had already closed in, when they turned off the path to the door of a roadside inn, yet twelve miles short of Portsmouth.

'Twelve miles,' said Nicholas, leaning with both hands on his stick, and looking doubtfully at Smike.

'Twelve long miles,' repeated the landlord.

'Is it a good road?' inquired Nicholas.

'Very bad,' said the landlord. As of course, being a landlord, he would say.

'I want to get on,' observed Nicholas, hesitating. 'I scarcely know what to do.'

'Don't let me influence you,' rejoined the landlord. 'I wouldn't go on if it was me.'

'Wouldn't you?' asked Nicholas, with the same uncertainty.

'Not if I knew when I was well off,' said the landlord. And having said it he pulled up his apron, put his hands into his pockets, and, taking a step or two outside the door, looked down the dark road with an assumption of great indifference.

A glance at the toil-worn face of Smike determined Nicholas, so without any further consideration he made up his mind to stay where he was.

The landlord led them into the kitchen, and as there was a good fire he remarked that it was very cold. If there had happened to be a bad one he would have observed that it was very warm.

'What can you give us for supper?' was Nicholas's natural question.

'Why—what would you like?' was the landlord's no less natural answer.

Nicholas suggested cold meat, but there was no cold meat—poached eggs, but there were no eggs—mutton chops, but there wasn't a mutton chop within three miles, though there had been more last week than they knew what to do with, and would be an extraordinary supply the day after tomorrow.

'Then,' said Nicholas, 'I must leave it entirely to you, as I would have done, at first, if you had allowed me.'

'Why, then I'll tell you what,' rejoined the landlord. 'There's a gentleman in the parlour that's ordered a hot beef-steak pudding and potatoes, at nine. There's more of it than he can manage, and I have very little doubt that if I ask leave, you can sup with him. I'll do that, in a minute.'

'No, no,' said Nicholas, detaining him. 'I would rather not. I—at least—pshaw! why cannot I speak out? Here; you see that I am travelling in a very humble manner, and have made my way hither on foot. It is more than probable, I think, that the gentleman may not relish my company; and although I am the dusty figure you see, I am too proud to thrust myself into his.'

'Lord love you,' said the landlord, 'it's only Mr. Crummles; he isn't particular.'

'Is he not?' asked Nicholas, on whose mind, to tell the truth, the prospect of the savoury pudding was making some impression.

'Not he,' replied the landlord. 'He'll like your way of talking, I know. But we'll soon see all about that. Just wait a minute.'

The landlord hurried into the parlour, without staying for further permission, nor did Nicholas strive to prevent him: wisely considering that supper, under the circumstances, was too serious a matter to be trifled with. It was not long before the host returned, in a condition of much excitement.

'All right,' he said in a low voice. 'I knew he would. You'll see something rather worth seeing, in there. Ecod, how they are a-going of it!'

There was no time to inquire to what this exclamation, which was delivered in a very rapturous tone, referred; for he had already thrown open the door of the room; into which Nicholas, followed by Smike with the bundle on his shoulder (he carried it about with him as vigilantly as if it had been a sack of gold), straightway repaired.

Nicholas was prepared for something odd, but not for something quite so odd as the sight he encountered. At the upper end of the room, were a couple of boys, one of them very tall and the other very short, both dressed as sailors—or at least as theatrical sailors, with belts, buckles, pigtails, and pistols complete—fighting what is called in play-bills a terrific combat, with two of those short broad-swords with basket hilts which are commonly used at our minor theatres. The short boy had gained a great advantage over the tall boy, who was reduced to mortal strait, and both were overlooked by a large heavy man, perched against the corner of a table, who emphatically adjured them to strike a little more fire out of the swords, and they couldn't fail to bring the house down, on the very first night.

'Mr. Vincent Crummles,' said the landlord with an air of great deference. 'This is the young gentleman.'

Mr. Vincent Crummles received Nicholas with an inclination of the head, something between the courtesy of a Roman emperor and the nod of a pot companion; and bade the landlord shut the door and begone.

'There's a picture,' said Mr. Crummles, motioning Nicholas not to advance and spoil it. 'The little 'un has him; if the big 'un doesn't knock under, in three seconds, he's a dead man. Do that again, boys.'

The two combatants went to work afresh, and chopped away until the swords emitted a shower of sparks: to the great satisfaction of Mr. Crummles, who appeared to consider this a very great point indeed. The engagement commenced with about two hundred chops administered by the short sailor and the tall sailor alternately, without producing any particular result, until the short sailor was chopped down on one knee; but this was nothing to him, for he worked himself about on the one knee with the assistance of his left hand, and fought most desperately until the tall sailor chopped his sword out of his grasp. Now, the inference was, that the short sailor, reduced to this extremity, would give in at once and cry quarter, but, instead of that, he all of a sudden drew a large pistol from his belt and presented it at the face of the tall sailor, who was so overcome at this (not expecting it) that he let the short sailor pick up his sword and begin again. Then, the chopping recommenced, and a variety of fancy chops were administered on both sides; such as chops dealt with the left hand, and under the leg, and over the right shoulder, and over the left; and when the short sailor made a vigorous cut at the tall sailor's legs, which would have shaved them clean off if it had taken effect, the tall sailor jumped over the short sailor's sword, wherefore to balance the matter, and make it all fair, the tall sailor administered the same cut, and the short sailor jumped over his sword. After this, there was a good deal of dodging about, and hitching up of the inexpressibles in the absence of braces, and then the short sailor (who was the moral character evidently, for he always had the best of it) made a violent demonstration and closed with the tall sailor, who, after a few unavailing struggles, went down, and expired in great torture as the short sailor put his foot upon his breast, and bored a hole in him through and through.

'That'll be a double encore if you take care, boys,' said Mr. Crummles. 'You had better get your wind now and change your clothes.'

Having addressed these words to the combatants, he saluted Nicholas, who then observed that the face of Mr. Crummles was quite proportionate in size to his body; that he had a very full under-lip, a hoarse voice, as though he were in the habit of shouting very much, and very short black hair, shaved off nearly to the crown of his head—to admit (as he afterwards learnt) of his more easily wearing character wigs of any shape or pattern.

'What did you think of that, sir?' inquired Mr. Crummles.

'Very good, indeed—capital,' answered Nicholas.

'You won't see such boys as those very often, I think,' said Mr. Crummles.

Nicholas assented—observing that if they were a little better match—

'Match!' cried Mr. Crummles.

'I mean if they were a little more of a size,' said Nicholas, explaining himself.

'Size!' repeated Mr. Crummles; 'why, it's the essence of the combat that there should be a foot or two between them. How are you to get up the sympathies of the audience in a legitimate manner, if there isn't a little man contending against a big one?—unless there's at least five to one, and we haven't hands enough for that business in our company.'

'I see,' replied Nicholas. 'I beg your pardon. That didn't occur to me, I confess.'

'It's the main point,' said Mr. Crummles. 'I open at Portsmouth the day after tomorrow. If you're going there, look into the theatre, and see how that'll tell.'

Nicholas promised to do so, if he could, and drawing a chair near the fire, fell into conversation with the manager at once. He was very talkative and communicative, stimulated perhaps, not only by his natural disposition, but by the spirits and water he sipped very plentifully, or the snuff he took in large quantities from a piece of whitey-brown paper in his waistcoat pocket. He laid open his affairs without the smallest reserve, and descanted at some length upon the merits of his company, and the acquirements of his family; of both of which, the two broad-sword boys formed an honourable portion. There was to be a gathering, it seemed, of the different ladies and gentlemen at Portsmouth on the morrow, whither the father and sons were proceeding (not for the regular season, but in the course of a wandering speculation), after fulfilling an engagement at Guildford with the greatest applause.

'You are going that way?' asked the manager.

'Ye-yes,' said Nicholas. 'Yes, I am.'

'Do you know the town at all?' inquired the manager, who seemed to consider himself entitled to the same degree of confidence as he had himself exhibited.

'No,' replied Nicholas.

'Never there?'

'Never.'

Mr. Vincent Crummles gave a short dry cough, as much as to say, 'If you won't be communicative, you won't;' and took so many pinches of snuff from the piece of paper, one after another, that Nicholas quite wondered where it all went to.

While he was thus engaged, Mr. Crummles looked, from time to time, with great interest at Smike, with whom he had appeared considerably struck from the first. He had now fallen asleep, and was nodding in his chair.

'Excuse my saying so,' said the manager, leaning over to Nicholas, and sinking his voice, 'but what a capital countenance your friend has got!'

'Poor fellow!' said Nicholas, with a half-smile, 'I wish it were a little more plump, and less haggard.'

'Plump!' exclaimed the manager, quite horrified, 'you'd spoil it for ever.'

'Do you think so?'

'Think so, sir! Why, as he is now,' said the manager, striking his knee emphatically; 'without a pad upon his body, and hardly a touch of paint upon his face, he'd make such an actor for the starved business as was never seen in this country. Only let him be tolerably well up in the Apothecary in Romeo and Juliet, with the slightest possible dab of red on the tip of his nose, and he'd be certain of three rounds the moment he put his head out of the practicable door in the front grooves O.P.'

'You view him with a professional eye,' said Nicholas, laughing.

'And well I may,' rejoined the manager. 'I never saw a young fellow so regularly cut out for that line, since I've been in the profession. And I played the heavy children when I was eighteen months old.'

The appearance of the beef-steak pudding, which came in simultaneously with the junior Vincent Crummleses, turned the conversation to other matters, and indeed, for a time, stopped it altogether. These two young gentlemen wielded their knives and forks with scarcely less address than their broad-swords, and as the whole party were quite as sharp set as either class of weapons, there was no time for talking until the supper had been disposed of.

The Master Crummleses had no sooner swallowed the last procurable morsel of food, than they evinced, by various half-suppressed yawns and stretchings of their limbs, an obvious inclination to retire for the night, which Smike had betrayed still more strongly: he having, in the course of the meal, fallen asleep several times while in the very act of eating. Nicholas therefore proposed that they should break up at once, but the manager would by no means hear of it; vowing that he had promised himself the pleasure of inviting his new acquaintance to share a bowl of punch, and that if he declined, he should deem it very unhandsome behaviour.

'Let them go,' said Mr. Vincent Crummles, 'and we'll have it snugly and cosily together by the fire.'

Nicholas was not much disposed to sleep—being in truth too anxious—so, after a little demur, he accepted the offer, and having exchanged a shake of the hand with the young Crummleses, and the manager having on his part bestowed a most affectionate benediction on Smike, he sat himself down opposite to that gentleman by the fireside to assist in emptying the bowl, which soon afterwards appeared, steaming in a manner which was quite exhilarating to behold, and sending forth a most grateful and inviting fragrance.

But, despite the punch and the manager, who told a variety of stories, and smoked tobacco from a pipe, and inhaled it in the shape of snuff, with a most astonishing power, Nicholas was absent and dispirited. His thoughts were in his old home, and when they reverted to his present condition, the uncertainty of the morrow cast a gloom upon him, which his utmost efforts were unable to dispel. His attention wandered; although he heard the manager's voice, he was deaf to what he said; and when Mr. Vincent Crummles concluded the history of some long adventure with a loud laugh, and an inquiry what Nicholas would have done under the same circumstances, he was obliged to make the best apology in his power, and to confess his entire ignorance of all he had been talking about.

'Why, so I saw,' observed Mr. Crummles. 'You're uneasy in your mind. What's the matter?'

Nicholas could not refrain from smiling at the abruptness of the question; but, thinking

212

it scarcely worth while to parry it, owned that he was under some apprehensions lest he might not succeed in the object which had brought him to that part of the country.

'And what's that?' asked the manager.

'Getting something to do which will keep me and my poor fellow-traveller in the common necessaries of life,' said Nicholas. 'That's the truth. You guessed it long ago, I dare say, so I may as well have the credit of telling it you with a good grace.'

'What's to be got to do at Portsmouth more than anywhere else?' asked Mr Vincent Crummles, melting the sealing-wax on the stem of his pipe in the candle, and rolling it out afresh with his little finger.

'There are many vessels leaving the port, I suppose,' replied Nicholas. 'I shall try for a berth in some ship or other. There is meat and drink there at all events.'

'Salt meat and new rum; pease-pudding and chaff-biscuits,' said the manager, taking a whiff at his pipe to keep it alight, and returning to his work of embellishment.

'One may do worse than that,' said Nicholas. 'I can rough it, I believe, as well as most young men of my age and previous habits.'

'You need be able to,' said the manager, 'if you go on board ship; but you won't.'

'Why not?'

'Because there's not a skipper or mate that would think you worth your salt, when he could get a practised hand,' replied the manager; 'and they as plentiful there, as the oysters in the streets.'

'What do you mean?' asked Nicholas, alarmed by this prediction, and the confident tone in which it had been uttered. 'Men are not born able seamen. They must be reared, I suppose?'

Mr. Vincent Crummles nodded his head. 'They must; but not at your age, or from young gentlemen like you.'

There was a pause. The countenance of Nicholas fell, and he gazed ruefully at the fire.

'Does no other profession occur to you, which a young man of your figure and address could take up easily, and see the world to advantage in?' asked the manager.

'No,' said Nicholas, shaking his head.

'Why, then, I'll tell you one,' said Mr. Crummles, throwing his pipe into the fire, and raising his voice. 'The stage.'

'The stage!' cried Nicholas, in a voice almost as loud.

'The theatrical profession,' said Mr. Vincent Crummles. 'I am in the theatrical profession myself, my wife is in the theatrical profession, my children are in the theatrical profession. I had a dog that lived and died in it from a puppy; and my chaise-pony goes on, in Timour the Tartar. I'll bring you out, and your friend too. Say the word. I want a novelty.'

'I don't know anything about it,' rejoined Nicholas, whose breath had been almost taken away by this sudden proposal. 'I never acted a part in my life, except at school.'

'There's genteel comedy in your walk and manner, juvenile tragedy in your eye, and touch-and-go farce in your laugh,' said Mr. Vincent Crummles. 'You'll do as well as if you had thought of nothing else but the lamps, from your birth downwards.'

Nicholas thought of the small amount of small change that would remain in his pocket after paying the tavern bill; and he hesitated.

'You can be useful to us in a hundred ways,' said Mr. Crummles. 'Think what capital bills a man of your education could write for the shop-windows.'

'Well, I think I could manage that department,' said Nicholas.

'To be sure you could,' replied Mr. Crummles. '"For further particulars see small hand-bills"—we might have half a volume in every one of 'em. Pieces too; why, you could write us a piece to bring out the whole strength of the company, whenever we wanted one.'

'I am not quite so confident about that,' replied Nicholas. 'But I dare say I could scribble something now and then, that would suit you.'

'We'll have a new show-piece out directly,' said the manager. 'Let me see—peculiar resources of this establishment—new and splendid scenery—you must manage to introduce a real pump and two washing-tubs.'

'Into the piece?' said Nicholas.

'Yes,' replied the manager. 'I bought 'em cheap, at a sale the other day, and they'll come in admirably. That's the London plan. They look up some dresses, and properties, and have a piece written to fit 'em. Most of the theatres keep an author on purpose.'

'Indeed!' cried Nicholas.

'Oh, yes,' said the manager; 'a common thing. It'll look very well in the bills in separate lines—Real pump!—Splendid tubs!—Great attraction! You don't happen to be anything of an artist, do you?'

'That is not one of my accomplishments,' rejoined Nicholas.

'Ah! Then it can't be helped,' said the manager. 'If you had been, we might have had a large woodcut of the last scene for the posters, showing the whole depth of the stage, with the pump and tubs in the middle; but, however, if you're not, it can't be helped.'

'What should I get for all this?' inquired Nicholas, after a few moments' reflection. 'Could I live by it?'

'Live by it!' said the manager. 'Like a prince! With your own salary, and your friend's, and your writings, you'd make—ah! you'd make a pound a week!'

'You don't say so!'

'I do indeed, and if we had a run of good houses, nearly double the money.'

Nicholas shrugged his shoulders; but sheer destitution was before him; and if he could summon fortitude to undergo the extremes of want and hardship, for what had he rescued his helpless charge if it were only to bear as hard a fate as that from which he had wrested him? It was easy to think of seventy miles as nothing, when he was in the same town with the man who had treated him so ill and roused his bitterest thoughts; but now, it seemed far enough. What if he went abroad, and his mother or Kate were to die the while?

Without more deliberation, he hastily declared that it was a bargain, and gave Mr. Vincent Crummles his hand upon it.

214

CHAPTER 23
Treats of the Company of Mr. Vincent Crummles, and of his Affairs, Domestic and Theatrical

As Mr. Crummles had a strange four-legged animal in the inn stables, which he called a pony, and a vehicle of unknown design, on which he bestowed the appellation of a four-wheeled phaeton, Nicholas proceeded on his journey next morning with greater ease than he had expected: the manager and himself occupying the front seat: and the Master Crummleses and Smike being packed together behind, in company with a wicker basket defended from wet by a stout oilskin, in which were the broad-swords, pistols, pigtails, nautical costumes, and other professional necessaries of the aforesaid young gentlemen.

The pony took his time upon the road, and—possibly in consequence of his theatrical education—evinced, every now and then, a strong inclination to lie down. However, Mr. Vincent Crummles kept him up pretty well, by jerking the rein, and plying the whip; and when these means failed, and the animal came to a stand, the elder Master Crummles got out and kicked him. By dint of these encouragements, he was persuaded to move from time to time, and they jogged on (as Mr. Crummles truly observed) very comfortably for all parties.

'He's a good pony at bottom,' said Mr. Crummles, turning to Nicholas.

He might have been at bottom, but he certainly was not at top, seeing that his coat was of the roughest and most ill-favoured kind. So, Nicholas merely observed that he shouldn't wonder if he was.

'Many and many is the circuit this pony has gone,' said Mr. Crummles, flicking him skilfully on the eyelid for old acquaintance' sake. 'He is quite one of us. His mother was on the stage.'

'Was she?' rejoined Nicholas.

'She ate apple-pie at a circus for upwards of fourteen years,' said the manager; 'fired pistols, and went to bed in a nightcap; and, in short, took the low comedy entirely. His father was a dancer.'

'Was he at all distinguished?'

'Not very,' said the manager. 'He was rather a low sort of pony. The fact is, he had been originally jobbed out by the day, and he never quite got over his old habits. He was clever in melodrama too, but too broad—too broad. When the mother died, he took the port-wine business.'

'The port-wine business!' cried Nicholas.

'Drinking port-wine with the clown,' said the manager; 'but he was greedy, and one night bit off the bowl of the glass, and choked himself, so his vulgarity was the death of him at last.'

The descendant of this ill-starred animal requiring increased attention from Mr. Crummles as he progressed in his day's work, that gentleman had very little time for conversation. Nicholas was thus left at leisure to entertain himself with his own thoughts, until they arrived at the drawbridge at Portsmouth, when Mr. Crummles pulled up.

'We'll get down here,' said the manager, 'and the boys will take him round to the stable, and call at my lodgings with the luggage. You had better let yours be taken there, for the present.'

Thanking Mr. Vincent Crummles for his obliging offer, Nicholas jumped out, and, giving Smike his arm, accompanied the manager up High Street on their way to the theatre; feeling nervous and uncomfortable enough at the prospect of an immediate introduction to a scene so new to him.

They passed a great many bills, pasted against the walls and displayed in windows, wherein the names of Mr. Vincent Crummles, Mrs. Vincent Crummles, Master Crummles, Master P. Crummles, and Miss Crummles, were printed in very large letters, and everything else in very small ones; and, turning at length into an entry, in which was a strong smell of orange-peel and lamp-oil, with an under-current of sawdust, groped their way through a dark passage, and, descending a step or two, threaded a little maze of canvas screens and paint pots, and emerged upon the stage of the Portsmouth Theatre.

'Here we are,' said Mr. Crummles.

It was not very light, but Nicholas found himself close to the first entrance on the prompt side, among bare walls, dusty scenes, mildewed clouds, heavily daubed draperies, and dirty floors. He looked about him; ceiling, pit, boxes, gallery, orchestra, fittings, and decorations of every kind,—all looked coarse, cold, gloomy, and wretched.

'Is this a theatre?' whispered Smike, in amazement; 'I thought it was a blaze of light and finery.'

'Why, so it is,' replied Nicholas, hardly less surprised; 'but not by day, Smike—not by day.'

The manager's voice recalled him from a more careful inspection of the building, to the opposite side of the proscenium, where, at a small mahogany table with rickety legs and of an oblong shape, sat a stout, portly female, apparently between forty and fifty, in a tarnished silk cloak, with her bonnet dangling by the strings in her hand, and her hair (of which she had a great quantity) braided in a large festoon over each temple.

'Mr. Johnson,' said the manager (for Nicholas had given the name which Newman Noggs had bestowed upon him in his conversation with Mrs. Kenwigs), 'let me introduce Mrs. Vincent Crummles.'

'I am glad to see you, sir,' said Mrs. Vincent Crummles, in a sepulchral voice. 'I am very glad to see you, and still more happy to hail you as a promising member of our corps.'

The lady shook Nicholas by the hand as she addressed him in these terms; he saw it was a large one, but had not expected quite such an iron grip as that with which she honoured him.

'And this,' said the lady, crossing to Smike, as tragic actresses cross when they obey a stage direction, 'and this is the other. You too, are welcome, sir.'

'He'll do, I think, my dear?' said the manager, taking a pinch of snuff.

'He is admirable,' replied the lady. 'An acquisition indeed.'

As Mrs. Vincent Crummles recrossed back to the table, there bounded on to the stage from some mysterious inlet, a little girl in a dirty white frock with tucks up to the knees, short trousers, sandaled shoes, white spencer, pink gauze bonnet, green veil and curl papers; who turned a pirouette, cut twice in the air, turned another pirouette, then, looking off at the opposite wing, shrieked, bounded forward to within six inches of the footlights, and fell into a beautiful attitude of terror, as a shabby gentleman in an old pair of buff slippers came in at one powerful slide, and chattering his teeth, fiercely brandished a walking-stick.

'They are going through the Indian Savage and the Maiden,' said Mrs Crummles.

'Oh!' said the manager, 'the little ballet interlude. Very good, go on. A little this way, if you please, Mr. Johnson. That'll do. Now!'

The manager clapped his hands as a signal to proceed, and the savage, becoming ferocious, made a slide towards the maiden; but the maiden avoided him in six twirls, and came down, at the end of the last one, upon the very points of her toes. This seemed to make some impression upon the savage; for, after a little more ferocity and chasing of the maiden into corners, he began to relent, and stroked his face several times with his right thumb and four fingers, thereby intimating that he was struck with admiration of the maiden's beauty. Acting upon the impulse of this passion, he (the savage) began to hit himself severe thumps in the chest, and to exhibit other indications of being desperately in love, which being rather a prosy proceeding, was very likely the cause of the maiden's falling asleep; whether it was or no, asleep she did fall, sound as a church, on a sloping bank, and the savage perceiving it, leant his left ear on his left hand, and nodded sideways, to intimate to all whom it might concern that she was asleep, and no shamming. Being left to himself, the savage had a dance, all alone. Just as he left off, the maiden woke up, rubbed her eyes, got off the bank, and had a dance all alone too—such a dance that the savage looked on in ecstasy all the while, and when it was done, plucked from a neighbouring tree some botanical curiosity, resembling a small pickled cabbage, and offered it to the maiden, who at first wouldn't have it, but on the savage shedding tears relented. Then the savage jumped for joy; then the maiden jumped for rapture at the sweet smell of the pickled cabbage. Then the savage and the maiden danced violently together, and, finally, the savage dropped down on one knee, and the maiden stood on one leg upon his other knee; thus concluding the ballet, and leaving the spectators in a state of pleasing uncertainty, whether she would ultimately marry the savage, or return to her friends.

'Very well indeed,' said Mr. Crummles; 'bravo!'

'Bravo!' cried Nicholas, resolved to make the best of everything. 'Beautiful!'

'This, sir,' said Mr. Vincent Crummles, bringing the maiden forward, 'this is the infant phenomenon—Miss Ninetta Crummles.'

'Your daughter?' inquired Nicholas.

'My daughter—my daughter,' replied Mr. Vincent Crummles; 'the idol of every place we go into, sir. We have had complimentary letters about this girl, sir, from the nobility and gentry of almost every town in England.'

'I am not surprised at that,' said Nicholas; 'she must be quite a natural genius.'

'Quite a—!' Mr. Crummles stopped: language was not powerful enough to describe the infant phenomenon. 'I'll tell you what, sir,' he said; 'the talent of this child is not to be imagined. She must be seen, sir—seen—to be ever so faintly appreciated. There; go to your mother, my dear.'

'May I ask how old she is?' inquired Nicholas.

'You may, sir,' replied Mr. Crummles, looking steadily in his questioner's face, as some men do when they have doubts about being implicitly believed in what they are going to say. 'She is ten years of age, sir.'

'Not more!'

'Not a day.'

'Dear me!' said Nicholas, 'it's extraordinary.'

It was; for the infant phenomenon, though of short stature, had a comparatively aged countenance, and had moreover been precisely the same age—not perhaps to the full extent of the memory of the oldest inhabitant, but certainly for five good years. But she had been kept up late every night, and put upon an unlimited allowance of gin-and-water from infancy, to prevent her growing tall, and perhaps this system of training had produced in the infant phenomenon these additional phenomena.

While this short dialogue was going on, the gentleman who had enacted the savage, came up, with his walking shoes on his feet, and his slippers in his hand, to within a few paces, as if desirous to join in the conversation. Deeming this a good opportunity, he put in his word.

'Talent there, sir!' said the savage, nodding towards Miss Crummles.

Nicholas assented.

'Ah!' said the actor, setting his teeth together, and drawing in his breath with a hissing sound, 'she oughtn't to be in the provinces, she oughtn't.'

'What do you mean?' asked the manager.

'I mean to say,' replied the other, warmly, 'that she is too good for country boards, and that she ought to be in one of the large houses in London, or nowhere; and I tell you more, without mincing the matter, that if it wasn't for envy and jealousy in some quarter that you know of, she would be. Perhaps you'll introduce me here, Mr. Crummles.'

'Mr. Folair,' said the manager, presenting him to Nicholas.

'Happy to know you, sir.' Mr. Folair touched the brim of his hat with his forefinger, and then shook hands. 'A recruit, sir, I understand?'

'An unworthy one,' replied Nicholas.

'Did you ever see such a set-out as that?' whispered the actor, drawing him away, as Crummles left them to speak to his wife.

'As what?'

Mr. Folair made a funny face from his pantomime collection, and pointed over his shoulder.

'You don't mean the infant phenomenon?'

'Infant humbug, sir,' replied Mr. Folair. 'There isn't a female child of common sharpness in a charity school, that couldn't do better than that. She may thank her stars she was born a manager's daughter.'

'You seem to take it to heart,' observed Nicholas, with a smile.

'Yes, by Jove, and well I may,' said Mr. Folair, drawing his arm through his, and walking him up and down the stage. 'Isn't it enough to make a man crusty to see that little sprawler put up in the best business every night, and actually keeping money out of the house, by being forced down the people's throats, while other people are passed over? Isn't it extraordinary to see a man's confounded family conceit blinding him, even to his own interest? Why I know of fifteen and sixpence that came to Southampton one night last month, to see me dance the Highland Fling; and what's the consequence? I've never been put up in it since—never once—while the "infant phenomenon" has been grinning through artificial flowers at five people and a baby in the pit, and two boys in the gallery, every night.'

'If I may judge from what I have seen of you,' said Nicholas, 'you must be a valuable member of the company.'

'Oh!' replied Mr. Folair, beating his slippers together, to knock the dust out; 'I CAn come it pretty well—nobody better, perhaps, in my own line—but having such business as one gets here, is like putting lead on one's feet instead of chalk, and dancing in fetters without the credit of it. Holloa, old fellow, how are you?'

The gentleman addressed in these latter words was a dark-complexioned man, inclining indeed to sallow, with long thick black hair, and very evident inclinations (although he was close shaved) of a stiff beard, and whiskers of the same deep shade. His age did not appear to exceed thirty, though many at first sight would have considered him much older, as his face was long, and very pale, from the constant application of stage paint. He wore a checked shirt, an old green coat with new gilt buttons, a neckerchief of broad red and green stripes, and full blue trousers; he carried, too, a common ash walking-stick, apparently more for show than use, as he flourished it about, with the hooked end downwards, except when he raised it for a few seconds, and throwing himself into a fencing attitude, made a pass or two at the side-scenes, or at any other object, animate or inanimate, that chanced to afford him a pretty good mark at the moment.

'Well, Tommy,' said this gentleman, making a thrust at his friend, who parried it dexterously with his slipper, 'what's the news?'

'A new appearance, that's all,' replied Mr. Folair, looking at Nicholas.

'Do the honours, Tommy, do the honours,' said the other gentleman, tapping him reproachfully on the crown of the hat with his stick.

'This is Mr. Lenville, who does our first tragedy, Mr. Johnson,' said the pantomimist.

'Except when old bricks and mortar takes it into his head to do it himself, you should add, Tommy,' remarked Mr. Lenville. 'You know who bricks and mortar is, I suppose, sir?'

'I do not, indeed,' replied Nicholas.

'We call Crummles that, because his style of acting is rather in the heavy and ponderous way,' said Mr. Lenville. 'I mustn't be cracking jokes though, for I've got a part of twelve lengths here, which I must be up in tomorrow night, and I haven't had time to look at it yet; I'm a confounded quick study, that's one comfort.'

Consoling himself with this reflection, Mr. Lenville drew from his coat pocket a greasy and crumpled manuscript, and, having made another pass at his friend, proceeded to walk to and fro, conning it to himself and indulging occasionally in such appropriate action as his imagination and the text suggested.

A pretty general muster of the company had by this time taken place; for besides Mr. Lenville and his friend Tommy, there were present, a slim young gentleman with weak eyes, who played the low-spirited lovers and sang tenor songs, and who had come arm-in-arm with the comic countryman—a man with a turned-up nose, large mouth, broad face, and staring eyes. Making himself very amiable to the infant phenomenon, was an inebriated elderly gentleman in the last depths of shabbiness, who played the calm and virtuous old men; and paying especial court to Mrs. Crummles was another elderly gentleman, a shade more respectable, who played the irascible old men—those funny fellows who have nephews in the army and perpetually run about with thick sticks to compel them to marry heiresses. Besides these, there was a roving-looking person in a rough great-coat, who strode up and down in front of the lamps, flourishing a dress cane, and rattling away, in an undertone, with great vivacity for the amusement of an ideal audience. He was not quite so young as he had been, and his figure was rather running to seed; but there was an air of exaggerated gentility about him, which bespoke the hero of swaggering comedy. There was, also, a little group of three or four young men with lantern jaws and thick eyebrows, who were conversing in one corner; but they seemed to be of secondary importance, and laughed and talked together without attracting any attention.

The ladies were gathered in a little knot by themselves round the rickety table before mentioned. There was Miss Snevellicci—who could do anything, from a medley dance to Lady Macbeth, and also always played some part in blue silk knee-smalls at her benefit—glancing, from the depths of her coal-scuttle straw bonnet, at Nicholas, and affecting to be absorbed in the recital of a diverting story to her friend Miss Ledrook, who had brought her work, and was making up a ruff in the most natural manner possible. There was Miss Belvawney—who seldom aspired to speaking parts, and usually went on as a page in white silk hose, to stand with one leg bent, and contemplate the audience, or to go in and out after Mr. Crummles in stately tragedy—twisting up the ringlets of the beautiful Miss Bravassa, who had once had her likeness taken 'in character' by an engraver's apprentice, whereof impressions were hung up for sale in the pastry-cook's window, and the greengrocer's, and at the circulating library, and the box-office, whenever the announce bills came out for her annual night. There was Mrs. Lenville, in a very limp bonnet and veil, decidedly in that way in which she would wish to be if she truly loved Mr. Lenville; there was Miss Gazingi, with an imitation ermine boa tied in a loose knot round her neck, flogging Mr. Crummles, junior, with both ends, in fun. Lastly, there was Mrs. Grudden in a brown cloth pelisse and a beaver bonnet, who assisted Mrs. Crummles in her domestic affairs, and took money at the doors, and dressed the ladies, and swept the house, and held the prompt book when everybody else was on for the last scene, and acted any kind of part on any emergency without ever learning it, and was put down in the bills under any name or names whatever, that occurred to Mr. Crummles as looking well in print.

Mr. Folair having obligingly confided these particulars to Nicholas, left him to mingle with his fellows; the work of personal introduction was completed by Mr. Vincent Crummles, who publicly heralded the new actor as a prodigy of genius and learning.

'I beg your pardon,' said Miss Snevellicci, sidling towards Nicholas, 'but did you ever play at Canterbury?'

'I never did,' replied Nicholas.

'I recollect meeting a gentleman at Canterbury,' said Miss Snevellicci, 'only for a few moments, for I was leaving the company as he joined it, so like you that I felt almost certain it was the same.'

'I see you now for the first time,' rejoined Nicholas with all due gallantry. 'I am sure I never saw you before; I couldn't have forgotten it.'

'Oh, I'm sure—it's very flattering of you to say so,' retorted Miss Snevellicci with a graceful bend. 'Now I look at you again, I see that the gentleman at Canterbury hadn't the same eyes as you—you'll think me very foolish for taking notice of such things, won't you?'

'Not at all,' said Nicholas. 'How can I feel otherwise than flattered by your notice in any way?'

'Oh! you men are such vain creatures!' cried Miss Snevellicci. Whereupon, she became charmingly confused, and, pulling out her pocket-handkerchief from a faded pink silk reticule with a gilt clasp, called to Miss Ledrook—

'Led, my dear,' said Miss Snevellicci.

'Well, what is the matter?' said Miss Ledrook.

'It's not the same.'

'Not the same what?'

'Canterbury—you know what I mean. Come here! I want to speak to you.'

But Miss Ledrook wouldn't come to Miss Snevellicci, so Miss Snevellicci was obliged to go to Miss Ledrook, which she did, in a skipping manner that was quite fascinating; and Miss Ledrook evidently joked Miss Snevellicci about being struck with Nicholas; for, after some playful whispering, Miss Snevellicci hit Miss Ledrook very hard on the backs of her hands, and retired up, in a state of pleasing confusion.

'Ladies and gentlemen,' said Mr. Vincent Crummles, who had been writing on a piece of paper, 'we'll call the Mortal Struggle tomorrow at ten; everybody for the procession. Intrigue, and Ways and Means, you're all up in, so we shall only want one rehearsal. Everybody at ten, if you please.'

'Everybody at ten,' repeated Mrs. Grudden, looking about her.

'On Monday morning we shall read a new piece,' said Mr. Crummles; 'the name's not known yet, but everybody will have a good part. Mr. Johnson will take care of that.'

'Hallo!' said Nicholas, starting. 'I—'

'On Monday morning,' repeated Mr. Crummles, raising his voice, to drown the unfortunate Mr. Johnson's remonstrance; 'that'll do, ladies and gentlemen.'

The ladies and gentlemen required no second notice to quit; and, in a few minutes, the theatre was deserted, save by the Crummles family, Nicholas, and Smike.

'Upon my word,' said Nicholas, taking the manager aside, 'I don't think I can be ready by Monday.'

'Pooh, pooh,' replied Mr. Crummles.

'But really I can't,' returned Nicholas; 'my invention is not accustomed to these demands,

221

or possibly I might produce—'

'Invention! what the devil's that got to do with it!' cried the manager hastily.

'Everything, my dear sir.'

'Nothing, my dear sir,' retorted the manager, with evident impatience. 'Do you understand French?'

'Perfectly well.'

'Very good,' said the manager, opening the table drawer, and giving a roll of paper from it to Nicholas. 'There! Just turn that into English, and put your name on the title-page. Damn me,' said Mr. Crummles, angrily, 'if I haven't often said that I wouldn't have a man or woman in my company that wasn't master of the language, so that they might learn it from the original, and play it in English, and save all this trouble and expense.'

Nicholas smiled and pocketed the play.

'What are you going to do about your lodgings?' said Mr. Crummles.

Nicholas could not help thinking that, for the first week, it would be an uncommon convenience to have a turn-up bedstead in the pit, but he merely remarked that he had not turned his thoughts that way.

'Come home with me then,' said Mr. Crummles, 'and my boys shall go with you after dinner, and show you the most likely place.'

The offer was not to be refused; Nicholas and Mr. Crummles gave Mrs Crummles an arm each, and walked up the street in stately array. Smike, the boys, and the phenomenon, went home by a shorter cut, and Mrs. Grudden remained behind to take some cold Irish stew and a pint of porter in the box-office.

Mrs. Crummles trod the pavement as if she were going to immediate execution with an animating consciousness of innocence, and that heroic fortitude which virtue alone inspires. Mr. Crummles, on the other hand, assumed the look and gait of a hardened despot; but they both attracted some notice from many of the passers-by, and when they heard a whisper of 'Mr. and Mrs Crummles!' or saw a little boy run back to stare them in the face, the severe expression of their countenances relaxed, for they felt it was popularity.

Mr. Crummles lived in St Thomas's Street, at the house of one Bulph, a pilot, who sported a boat-green door, with window-frames of the same colour, and had the little finger of a drowned man on his parlour mantelshelf, with other maritime and natural curiosities. He displayed also a brass knocker, a brass plate, and a brass bell-handle, all very bright and shining; and had a mast, with a vane on the top of it, in his back yard.

'You are welcome,' said Mrs. Crummles, turning round to Nicholas when they reached the bow-windowed front room on the first floor.

Nicholas bowed his acknowledgments, and was unfeignedly glad to see the cloth laid.

'We have but a shoulder of mutton with onion sauce,' said Mrs. Crummles, in the same charnel-house voice; 'but such as our dinner is, we beg you to partake of it.'

'You are very good,' replied Nicholas, 'I shall do it ample justice.'

'Vincent,' said Mrs. Crummles, 'what is the hour?'

'Five minutes past dinner-time,' said Mr. Crummles.

Mrs. Crummles rang the bell. 'Let the mutton and onion sauce appear.'

The slave who attended upon Mr. Bulph's lodgers, disappeared, and after a short interval reappeared with the festive banquet. Nicholas and the infant phenomenon opposed each other at the pembroke-table, and Smike and the master Crummleses dined on the sofa bedstead.

'Are they very theatrical people here?' asked Nicholas.

'No,' replied Mr. Crummles, shaking his head, 'far from it—far from it.'

'I pity them,' observed Mrs. Crummles.

'So do I,' said Nicholas; 'if they have no relish for theatrical entertainments, properly conducted.'

'Then they have none, sir,' rejoined Mr. Crummles. 'To the infant's benefit, last year, on which occasion she repeated three of her most popular characters, and also appeared in the Fairy Porcupine, as originally performed by her, there was a house of no more than four pound twelve.'

'Is it possible?' cried Nicholas.

'And two pound of that was trust, pa,' said the phenomenon.

'And two pound of that was trust,' repeated Mr. Crummles. 'Mrs. Crummles herself has played to mere handfuls.'

'But they are always a taking audience, Vincent,' said the manager's wife.

'Most audiences are, when they have good acting—real good acting—the regular thing,' replied Mr. Crummles, forcibly.

'Do you give lessons, ma'am?' inquired Nicholas.

'I do,' said Mrs. Crummles.

'There is no teaching here, I suppose?'

'There has been,' said Mrs. Crummles. 'I have received pupils here. I imparted tuition to the daughter of a dealer in ships' provision; but it afterwards appeared that she was insane when she first came to me. It was very extraordinary that she should come, under such circumstances.'

Not feeling quite so sure of that, Nicholas thought it best to hold his peace.

'Let me see,' said the manager cogitating after dinner. 'Would you like some nice little part with the infant?'

'You are very good,' replied Nicholas hastily; 'but I think perhaps it would be better if I had somebody of my own size at first, in case I should turn out awkward. I should feel more at home, perhaps.'

'True,' said the manager. 'Perhaps you would. And you could play up to the infant, in time, you know.'

'Certainly,' replied Nicholas: devoutly hoping that it would be a very long time before he was honoured with this distinction.

'Then I'll tell you what we'll do,' said Mr. Crummles. 'You shall study Romeo when you've done that piece—don't forget to throw the pump and tubs in by-the-bye—Juliet Miss Snevellicci, old Grudden the nurse.—Yes, that'll do very well. Rover too;—you might get up Rover while you were about it, and Cassio, and Jeremy Diddler. You can easily knock them off; one part helps the other so much. Here they are, cues and all.'

With these hasty general directions Mr. Crummles thrust a number of little books into the faltering hands of Nicholas, and bidding his eldest son go with him and show where lodgings were to be had, shook him by the hand, and wished him good night.

There is no lack of comfortable furnished apartments in Portsmouth, and no difficulty in finding some that are proportionate to very slender finances; but the former were too good, and the latter too bad, and they went into so many houses, and came out unsuited, that Nicholas seriously began to think he should be obliged to ask permission to spend the night in the theatre, after all.

Eventually, however, they stumbled upon two small rooms up three pair of stairs, or rather two pair and a ladder, at a tobacconist's shop, on the Common Hard: a dirty street leading down to the dockyard. These Nicholas engaged, only too happy to have escaped any request for payment of a week's rent beforehand.

'There! Lay down our personal property, Smike,' he said, after showing young Crummles downstairs. 'We have fallen upon strange times, and Heaven only knows the end of them; but I am tired with the events of these three days, and will postpone reflection till tomorrow—if I can.'

CHAPTER 24
Of the Great Bespeak for Miss Snevellicci, and the first Appearance of Nicholas upon any Stage

Nicholas was up betimes in the morning; but he had scarcely begun to dress, notwithstanding, when he heard footsteps ascending the stairs, and was presently saluted by the voices of Mr. Folair the pantomimist, and Mr Lenville, the tragedian.

'House, house, house!' cried Mr. Folair.

'What, ho! within there,' said Mr. Lenville, in a deep voice.

'Confound these fellows!' thought Nicholas; 'they have come to breakfast, I suppose. I'll open the door directly, if you'll wait an instant.'

The gentlemen entreated him not to hurry himself; and, to beguile the interval, had a fencing bout with their walking-sticks on the very small landing-place: to the unspeakable discomposure of all the other lodgers downstairs.

'Here, come in,' said Nicholas, when he had completed his toilet. 'In the name of all that's horrible, don't make that noise outside.'

'An uncommon snug little box this,' said Mr. Lenville, stepping into the front room, and taking his hat off, before he could get at it all. 'Pernicious snug.'

'For a man at all particular in such matters, it might be a trifle too snug,' said Nicholas; 'for, although it is, undoubtedly, a great convenience to be able to reach anything you want from the ceiling or the floor, or either side of the room, without having to move from your chair, still these advantages can only be had in an apartment of the most limited size.'

'It isn't a bit too confined for a single man,' returned Mr. Lenville. 'That reminds me,— my wife, Mr. Johnson,—I hope she'll have some good part in this piece of yours?'

'I glanced at the French copy last night,' said Nicholas. 'It looks very good, I think.'

'What do you mean to do for me, old fellow?' asked Mr. Lenville, poking the struggling fire with his walking-stick, and afterwards wiping it on the skirt of his coat. 'Anything in the gruff and grumble way?'

'You turn your wife and child out of doors,' said Nicholas; 'and, in a fit of rage and jealousy, stab your eldest son in the library.'

'Do I though!' exclaimed Mr. Lenville. 'That's very good business.'

'After which,' said Nicholas, 'you are troubled with remorse till the last act, and then you make up your mind to destroy yourself. But, just as you are raising the pistol to your head, a clock strikes—ten.'

'I see,' cried Mr. Lenville. 'Very good.'

'You pause,' said Nicholas; 'you recollect to have heard a clock strike ten in your infancy. The pistol falls from your hand—you are overcome—you burst into tears, and become a virtuous and exemplary character for ever afterwards.'

'Capital!' said Mr. Lenville: 'that's a sure card, a sure card. Get the curtain down with a touch of nature like that, and it'll be a triumphant success.'

'Is there anything good for me?' inquired Mr. Folair, anxiously.

'Let me see,' said Nicholas. 'You play the faithful and attached servant; you are turned out of doors with the wife and child.'

'Always coupled with that infernal phenomenon,' sighed Mr. Folair; 'and we go into poor lodgings, where I won't take any wages, and talk sentiment, I suppose?'

'Why—yes,' replied Nicholas: 'that is the course of the piece.'

'I must have a dance of some kind, you know,' said Mr. Folair. 'You'll have to introduce one for the phenomenon, so you'd better make a pas de deux, and save time.'

'There's nothing easier than that,' said Mr. Lenville, observing the disturbed looks of the young dramatist.

'Upon my word I don't see how it's to be done,' rejoined Nicholas.

'Why, isn't it obvious?' reasoned Mr. Lenville. 'Gadzooks, who can help seeing the way to do it?—you astonish me! You get the distressed lady, and the little child, and the attached servant, into the poor lodgings, don't you?—Well, look here. The distressed lady sinks into a chair, and buries her face in her pocket-handkerchief. "What makes you weep, mama?" says the child. "Don't weep, mama, or you'll make me weep too!"—"And me!" says the favourite servant, rubbing his eyes with his arm. "What can we do to raise your spirits, dear mama?" says the little child. "Ay, what can we do?" says the faithful servant. "Oh, Pierre!" says the distressed lady; "would that I could shake off these painful thoughts."—"Try, ma'am, try," says the faithful servant; "rouse yourself, ma'am; be amused."—"I will," says the lady, "I will learn to suffer with fortitude. Do you remember that dance, my honest friend, which, in happier days, you practised with this sweet angel? It never failed to calm my spirits then. Oh! let me see it once again before I die!"—There it is—cue for the band, before I die,—and off they go. That's the regular thing; isn't it, Tommy?'

'That's it,' replied Mr. Folair. 'The distressed lady, overpowered by old recollections, faints at the end of the dance, and you close in with a picture.'

Profiting by these and other lessons, which were the result of the personal experience of the two actors, Nicholas willingly gave them the best breakfast he could, and, when he at length got rid of them, applied himself to his task: by no means displeased to find that it was so much easier than he had at first supposed. He worked very hard all day, and did not leave his room until the evening, when he went down to the theatre, whither Smike had repaired before him to go on with another gentleman as a general rebellion.

Here all the people were so much changed, that he scarcely knew them. False hair, false colour, false calves, false muscles—they had become different beings. Mr. Lenville was a blooming warrior of most exquisite proportions; Mr. Crummles, his large face shaded by a profusion of black hair, a Highland outlaw of most majestic bearing; one of the old gentlemen a jailer, and the other a venerable patriarch; the comic countryman, a fighting-man of great valour, relieved by a touch of humour; each of the Master Crummleses a prince in his own right; and the low-spirited lover, a desponding captive. There was a gorgeous banquet ready spread for the third act, consisting of two pasteboard vases, one plate of biscuits, a black bottle, and a vinegar cruet; and, in short, everything was on a scale of the utmost splendour and preparation.

Nicholas was standing with his back to the curtain, now contemplating the first scene, which was a Gothic archway, about two feet shorter than Mr Crummles, through which that gentleman was to make his first entrance, and now listening to a couple of people who were cracking nuts in the gallery, wondering whether they made the whole audience, when the manager himself walked familiarly up and accosted him.

'Been in front tonight?' said Mr. Crummles.

'No,' replied Nicholas, 'not yet. I am going to see the play.'

'We've had a pretty good Let,' said Mr. Crummles. 'Four front places in the centre, and the whole of the stage-box.'

'Oh, indeed!' said Nicholas; 'a family, I suppose?'

'Yes,' replied Mr. Crummles, 'yes. It's an affecting thing. There are six children, and they never come unless the phenomenon plays.'

It would have been difficult for any party, family, or otherwise, to have visited the theatre on a night when the phenomenon did not play, inasmuch as she always sustained one, and not uncommonly two or three, characters, every night; but Nicholas, sympathising with the feelings of a father, refrained from hinting at this trifling circumstance, and Mr. Crummles continued to talk, uninterrupted by him.

'Six,' said that gentleman; 'pa and ma eight, aunt nine, governess ten, grandfather and grandmother twelve. Then, there's the footman, who stands outside, with a bag of oranges and a jug of toast-and-water, and sees the play for nothing through the little pane of glass in the box-door—it's cheap at a guinea; they gain by taking a box.'

'I wonder you allow so many,' observed Nicholas.

'There's no help for it,' replied Mr. Crummles; 'it's always expected in the country. If there are six children, six people come to hold them in their laps. A family-box carries double always. Ring in the orchestra, Grudden!'

That useful lady did as she was requested, and shortly afterwards the tuning of three fiddles was heard. Which process having been protracted as long as it was supposed that the patience of the audience could possibly bear it, was put a stop to by another jerk of the bell, which, being the signal to begin in earnest, set the orchestra playing a variety of popular airs, with involuntary variations.

If Nicholas had been astonished at the alteration for the better which the gentlemen displayed, the transformation of the ladies was still more extraordinary. When, from a snug corner of the manager's box, he beheld Miss Snevellicci in all the glories of white muslin with a golden hem, and Mrs. Crummles in all the dignity of the outlaw's wife, and Miss Bravassa in all the sweetness of Miss Snevellicci's confidential friend, and Miss Belvawney in the white silks of a page doing duty everywhere and swearing to live and die in the service of everybody, he could scarcely contain his admiration, which testified itself in great applause, and the closest possible attention to the business of the scene. The plot was most interesting. It belonged to no particular age, people, or country, and was perhaps the more delightful on that account, as nobody's previous information could afford the remotest glimmering of what would ever come of it. An outlaw had been very successful in doing something somewhere, and came home, in triumph, to the sound of shouts and fiddles, to greet his wife—a lady of masculine mind, who talked a good deal about her father's bones, which it seemed were unburied, though whether from a peculiar taste on the part of the old gentleman himself, or the reprehensible neglect of his relations, did not appear. This outlaw's wife was, somehow or other, mixed up with a patriarch, living in a castle a long way off, and this patriarch was the father of several of the characters, but he didn't exactly know which, and was uncertain whether he had brought up the right ones in his castle, or the wrong ones; he rather inclined to the latter opinion, and, being uneasy, relieved his mind with a banquet, during which solemnity somebody in a cloak said 'Beware!' which somebody was known by nobody (except the audience) to be the outlaw himself, who had come there, for reasons unexplained, but possibly with an eye to the spoons. There was an agreeable little surprise in the way of certain love passages between the desponding captive and Miss Snevellicci, and the comic fighting-man and Miss Bravassa; besides which, Mr. Lenville had several very tragic scenes in the dark, while on throat-cutting expeditions, which were all baffled by the skill and bravery of the comic fighting-man (who overheard whatever was said all through the piece) and the intrepidity of Miss Snevellicci, who adopted tights, and therein repaired to the prison of her captive lover, with a small basket of refreshments and a dark lantern. At last, it came out that the patriarch was the man who had treated the bones of the outlaw's father-in-law with so much disrespect, for which cause and reason the outlaw's wife repaired to his castle to kill him, and so got into a dark room, where, after a good deal of groping in the dark, everybody got hold of everybody else, and took them for somebody besides, which occasioned a vast quantity of confusion, with some pistolling, loss of life, and torchlight; after which, the patriarch came forward, and observing, with a knowing look, that he knew all about his children now, and would tell them when they got inside, said that there could not be a more appropriate occasion for marrying the young people than that; and therefore he joined their hands, with the full consent of the indefatigable page, who (being the only other person surviving) pointed with his cap into the clouds, and his right hand to the ground; thereby invoking a blessing and giving the cue for the curtain to come down, which it did, amidst general applause.

'What did you think of that?' asked Mr. Crummles, when Nicholas went round to the stage again. Mr. Crummles was very red and hot, for your outlaws are desperate fellows to shout.

'I think it was very capital indeed,' replied Nicholas; 'Miss Snevellicci in particular was uncommonly good.'

'She's a genius,' said Mr. Crummles; 'quite a genius, that girl. By-the-bye, I've been thinking of bringing out that piece of yours on her bespeak night.'

'When?' asked Nicholas.

'The night of her bespeak. Her benefit night, when her friends and patrons bespeak the play,' said Mr. Crummles.

'Oh! I understand,' replied Nicholas.

'You see,' said Mr. Crummles, 'it's sure to go, on such an occasion, and even if it should not work up quite as well as we expect, why it will be her risk, you know, and not ours.'

'Yours, you mean,' said Nicholas.

'I said mine, didn't I?' returned Mr. Crummles. 'Next Monday week. What do you say? You'll have done it, and are sure to be up in the lover's part, long before that time.'

'I don't know about "long before,"' replied Nicholas; 'but by that time I think I can undertake to be ready.'

'Very good,' pursued Mr. Crummles, 'then we'll call that settled. Now, I want to ask you something else. There's a little—what shall I call it?—a little canvassing takes place on these occasions.'

'Among the patrons, I suppose?' said Nicholas.

'Among the patrons; and the fact is, that Snevellicci has had so many bespeaks in this place, that she wants an attraction. She had a bespeak when her mother-in-law died, and a bespeak when her uncle died; and Mrs Crummles and myself have had bespeaks on the anniversary of the phenomenon's birthday, and our wedding-day, and occasions of that description, so that, in fact, there's some difficulty in getting a good one. Now, won't you help this poor girl, Mr. Johnson?' said Crummles, sitting himself down on a drum, and taking a great pinch of snuff, as he looked him steadily in the face.

'How do you mean?' rejoined Nicholas.

'Don't you think you could spare half an hour tomorrow morning, to call with her at the houses of one or two of the principal people?' murmured the manager in a persuasive tone.

'Oh dear me,' said Nicholas, with an air of very strong objection, 'I shouldn't like to do that.'

'The infant will accompany her,' said Mr. Crummles. 'The moment it was suggested to me, I gave permission for the infant to go. There will not be the smallest impropriety—Miss

Snevellicci, sir, is the very soul of honour. It would be of material service—the gentleman from London—author of the new piece—actor in the new piece—first appearance on any boards— it would lead to a great bespeak, Mr. Johnson.'

'I am very sorry to throw a damp upon the prospects of anybody, and more especially a lady,' replied Nicholas; 'but really I must decidedly object to making one of the canvassing party.'

'What does Mr. Johnson say, Vincent?' inquired a voice close to his ear; and, looking round, he found Mrs. Crummles and Miss Snevellicci herself standing behind him.

'He has some objection, my dear,' replied Mr. Crummles, looking at Nicholas.

'Objection!' exclaimed Mrs. Crummles. 'Can it be possible?'

'Oh, I hope not!' cried Miss Snevellicci. 'You surely are not so cruel—oh, dear me!— Well, I—to think of that now, after all one's looking forward to it!'

'Mr. Johnson will not persist, my dear,' said Mrs. Crummles. 'Think better of him than to suppose it. Gallantry, humanity, all the best feelings of his nature, must be enlisted in this interesting cause.'

'Which moves even a manager,' said Mr. Crummles, smiling.

'And a manager's wife,' added Mrs. Crummles, in her accustomed tragedy tones. 'Come, come, you will relent, I know you will.'

'It is not in my nature,' said Nicholas, moved by these appeals, 'to resist any entreaty, unless it is to do something positively wrong; and, beyond a feeling of pride, I know nothing which should prevent my doing this. I know nobody here, and nobody knows me. So be it then. I yield.'

Miss Snevellicci was at once overwhelmed with blushes and expressions of gratitude, of which latter commodity neither Mr. nor Mrs. Crummles was by any means sparing. It was arranged that Nicholas should call upon her, at her lodgings, at eleven next morning, and soon after they parted: he to return home to his authorship: Miss Snevellicci to dress for the after-piece: and the disinterested manager and his wife to discuss the probable gains of the forthcoming bespeak, of which they were to have two-thirds of the profits by solemn treaty of agreement.

At the stipulated hour next morning, Nicholas repaired to the lodgings of Miss Snevellicci, which were in a place called Lombard Street, at the house of a tailor. A strong smell of ironing pervaded the little passage; and the tailor's daughter, who opened the door, appeared in that flutter of spirits which is so often attendant upon the periodical getting up of a family's linen.

'Miss Snevellicci lives here, I believe?' said Nicholas, when the door was opened.

The tailor's daughter replied in the affirmative.

'Will you have the goodness to let her know that Mr. Johnson is here?' said Nicholas.

'Oh, if you please, you're to come upstairs,' replied the tailor's daughter, with a smile.

Nicholas followed the young lady, and was shown into a small apartment on the first floor, communicating with a back-room; in which, as he judged from a certain half-subdued clinking sound, as of cups and saucers, Miss Snevellicci was then taking her breakfast in bed.

'You're to wait, if you please,' said the tailor's daughter, after a short period of absence, during which the clinking in the back-room had ceased, and been succeeded by whispering— 'She won't be long.'

As she spoke, she pulled up the window-blind, and having by this means (as she thought) diverted Mr. Johnson's attention from the room to the street, caught up some articles which were airing on the fender, and had very much the appearance of stockings, and darted off.

As there were not many objects of interest outside the window, Nicholas looked about the room with more curiosity than he might otherwise have bestowed upon it. On the sofa lay an old guitar, several thumbed pieces of music, and a scattered litter of curl-papers; together with a confused heap of play-bills, and a pair of soiled white satin shoes with large blue rosettes. Hanging over the back of a chair was a half-finished muslin apron with little pockets ornamented with red ribbons, such as waiting-women wear on the stage, and (by consequence) are never seen with anywhere else. In one corner stood the diminutive pair of top-boots in which Miss Snevellicci was accustomed to enact the little jockey, and, folded on a chair hard by, was a small parcel, which bore a very suspicious resemblance to the companion smalls.

But the most interesting object of all was, perhaps, the open scrapbook, displayed in the midst of some theatrical duodecimos that were strewn upon the table; and pasted into which scrapbook were various critical notices of Miss Snevellicci's acting, extracted from different provincial journals, together with one poetic address in her honour, commencing—

Sing, God of Love, and tell me in what dearth

Thrice-gifted Snevellicci came on earth,

To thrill us with her smile, her tear, her eye,

Sing, God of Love, and tell me quickly why.

Besides this effusion, there were innumerable complimentary allusions, also extracted from newspapers, such as—'We observe from an advertisement in another part of our paper of today, that the charming and highly-talented Miss Snevellicci takes her benefit on Wednesday, for which occasion she has put forth a bill of fare that might kindle exhilaration in the breast of a misanthrope. In the confidence that our fellow-townsmen have not lost that high appreciation of public utility and private worth, for which they have long been so pre-eminently distinguished, we predict that this charming actress will be greeted with a bumper.' 'To Correspondents.—J.S. is misinformed when he supposes that the highly-gifted and beautiful Miss Snevellicci, nightly captivating all hearts at our pretty and commodious little theatre, is not the same lady to whom the young gentleman of immense fortune, residing within a hundred miles of the good city of York, lately made honourable proposals. We have reason to know that Miss Snevellicci is the lady who was implicated in that mysterious and romantic affair, and whose conduct on that occasion did no less honour to her head and heart, than do her histrionic triumphs to her brilliant genius.' A copious assortment of such paragraphs as these, with long bills of benefits all ending with 'Come Early', in large capitals, formed the principal contents of Miss Snevellicci's scrapbook.

Nicholas had read a great many of these scraps, and was absorbed in a circumstantial and melancholy account of the train of events which had led to Miss Snevellicci's spraining her ankle by slipping on a piece of orange-peel flung by a monster in human form, (so the paper said,) upon the stage at Winchester,—when that young lady herself, attired in the coal-scuttle bonnet and walking-dress complete, tripped into the room, with a thousand apologies for having detained him so long after the appointed time.

'But really,' said Miss Snevellicci, 'my darling Led, who lives with me here, was taken so very ill in the night that I thought she would have expired in my arms.'

'Such a fate is almost to be envied,' returned Nicholas, 'but I am very sorry to hear it nevertheless.'

'What a creature you are to flatter!' said Miss Snevellicci, buttoning her glove in much confusion.

'If it be flattery to admire your charms and accomplishments,' rejoined Nicholas, laying his hand upon the scrapbook, 'you have better specimens of it here.'

'Oh you cruel creature, to read such things as those! I'm almost ashamed to look you in the face afterwards, positively I am,' said Miss Snevellicci, seizing the book and putting it away in a closet. 'How careless of Led! How could she be so naughty!'

'I thought you had kindly left it here, on purpose for me to read,' said Nicholas. And really it did seem possible.

'I wouldn't have had you see it for the world!' rejoined Miss Snevellicci. 'I never was so vexed—never! But she is such a careless thing, there's no trusting her.'

The conversation was here interrupted by the entrance of the phenomenon, who had discreetly remained in the bedroom up to this moment, and now presented herself, with much grace and lightness, bearing in her hand a very little green parasol with a broad fringe border, and no handle. After a few words of course, they sallied into the street.

The phenomenon was rather a troublesome companion, for first the right sandal came down, and then the left, and these mischances being repaired, one leg of the little white trousers was discovered to be longer than the other; besides these accidents, the green parasol was dropped down an iron grating, and only fished up again with great difficulty and by dint of much exertion. However, it was impossible to scold her, as she was the manager's daughter, so Nicholas took it all in perfect good humour, and walked on, with Miss Snevellicci, arm-in-arm on one side, and the offending infant on the other.

The first house to which they bent their steps, was situated in a terrace of respectable appearance. Miss Snevellicci's modest double-knock was answered by a foot-boy, who, in reply to her inquiry whether Mrs. Curdle was at home, opened his eyes very wide, grinned very much, and said he didn't know, but he'd inquire. With this he showed them into a parlour where he kept them waiting, until the two women-servants had repaired thither, under false pretences, to see the play-actors; and having compared notes with them in the passage, and joined in a vast quantity of whispering and giggling, he at length went upstairs with Miss Snevellicci's name.

Now, Mrs. Curdle was supposed, by those who were best informed on such points, to possess quite the London taste in matters relating to literature and the drama; and as to Mr. Curdle, he had written a pamphlet of sixty-four pages, post octavo, on the character of the Nurse's deceased husband in Romeo and Juliet, with an inquiry whether he really had been a 'merry man' in his lifetime, or whether it was merely his widow's affectionate partiality that induced her so to report him. He had likewise proved, that by altering the received mode of punctuation, any one of Shakespeare's plays could be made quite different, and the sense completely changed; it is needless to say, therefore, that he was a great critic, and a very profound and most original thinker.

'Well, Miss Snevellicci,' said Mrs. Curdle, entering the parlour, 'and how do you do?'

Miss Snevellicci made a graceful obeisance, and hoped Mrs. Curdle was well, as also Mr. Curdle, who at the same time appeared. Mrs. Curdle was dressed in a morning wrapper, with a little cap stuck upon the top of her head. Mr Curdle wore a loose robe on his back, and his right forefinger on his forehead after the portraits of Sterne, to whom somebody or other had once said he bore a striking resemblance.

'I venture to call, for the purpose of asking whether you would put your name to my bespeak, ma'am,' said Miss Snevellicci, producing documents.

'Oh! I really don't know what to say,' replied Mrs. Curdle. 'It's not as if the theatre was in its high and palmy days—you needn't stand, Miss Snevellicci—the drama is gone, perfectly gone.'

'As an exquisite embodiment of the poet's visions, and a realisation of human intellectuality, gilding with refulgent light our dreamy moments, and laying open a new and magic world before the mental eye, the drama is gone, perfectly gone,' said Mr. Curdle.

'What man is there, now living, who can present before us all those changing and prismatic colours with which the character of Hamlet is invested?' exclaimed Mrs. Curdle.

'What man indeed—upon the stage,' said Mr. Curdle, with a small reservation in favour of himself. 'Hamlet! Pooh! ridiculous! Hamlet is gone, perfectly gone.'

Quite overcome by these dismal reflections, Mr. and Mrs. Curdle sighed, and sat for some short time without speaking. At length, the lady, turning to Miss Snevellicci, inquired what play she proposed to have.

'Quite a new one,' said Miss Snevellicci, 'of which this gentleman is the author, and in which he plays; being his first appearance on any stage. Mr Johnson is the gentleman's name.'

'I hope you have preserved the unities, sir?' said Mr. Curdle.

'The original piece is a French one,' said Nicholas. 'There is abundance of incident, sprightly dialogue, strongly-marked characters—'

'—All unavailing without a strict observance of the unities, sir,' returned Mr. Curdle. 'The unities of the drama, before everything.'

'Might I ask you,' said Nicholas, hesitating between the respect he ought to assume, and his love of the whimsical, 'might I ask you what the unities are?'

Mr. Curdle coughed and considered. 'The unities, sir,' he said, 'are a completeness—a kind of universal dovetailedness with regard to place and time—a sort of a general oneness, if I may be allowed to use so strong an expression. I take those to be the dramatic unities, so far as I have been enabled to bestow attention upon them, and I have read much upon the subject, and thought much. I find, running through the performances of this child,' said Mr. Curdle, turning to the phenomenon, 'a unity of feeling, a breadth, a light and shade, a warmth of colouring, a tone, a harmony, a glow, an artistical development of original conceptions, which I look for, in vain, among older performers—I don't know whether I make myself understood?'

'Perfectly,' replied Nicholas.

'Just so,' said Mr. Curdle, pulling up his neckcloth. 'That is my definition of the unities of the drama.'

Mrs. Curdle had sat listening to this lucid explanation with great complacency. It being finished, she inquired what Mr. Curdle thought, about putting down their names.

'I don't know, my dear; upon my word I don't know,' said Mr. Curdle. 'If we do, it must be distinctly understood that we do not pledge ourselves to the quality of the performances. Let it go forth to the world, that we do not give them the sanction of our names, but that we confer the distinction merely upon Miss Snevellicci. That being clearly stated, I take it to be, as it were, a duty, that we should extend our patronage to a degraded stage, even for the sake of the associations with which it is entwined. Have you got two-and-sixpence for half-a-crown, Miss Snevellicci?' said Mr. Curdle, turning over four of those pieces of money.

Miss Snevellicci felt in all the corners of the pink reticule, but there was nothing in any of them. Nicholas murmured a jest about his being an author, and thought it best not to go through the form of feeling in his own pockets at all.

'Let me see,' said Mr. Curdle; 'twice four's eight—four shillings a-piece to the boxes, Miss Snevellicci, is exceedingly dear in the present state of the drama—three half-crowns is seven-and-six; we shall not differ about sixpence, I suppose? Sixpence will not part us, Miss Snevellicci?'

Poor Miss Snevellicci took the three half-crowns, with many smiles and bends, and Mrs. Curdle, adding several supplementary directions relative to keeping the places for them, and dusting the seat, and sending two clean bills as soon as they came out, rang the bell, as a signal for breaking up the conference.

'Odd people those,' said Nicholas, when they got clear of the house.

'I assure you,' said Miss Snevellicci, taking his arm, 'that I think myself very lucky they did not owe all the money instead of being sixpence short. Now, if you were to succeed, they would give people to understand that they had always patronised you; and if you were to fail, they would have been quite certain of that from the very beginning.'

At the next house they visited, they were in great glory; for, there, resided the six children who were so enraptured with the public actions of the phenomenon, and who, being called down from the nursery to be treated with a private view of that young lady, proceeded to poke their fingers into her eyes, and tread upon her toes, and show her many other little attentions peculiar to their time of life.

'I shall certainly persuade Mr. Borum to take a private box,' said the lady of the house, after a most gracious reception. 'I shall only take two of the children, and will make up the rest of the party, of gentlemen—your admirers, Miss Snevellicci. Augustus, you naughty boy, leave the little girl alone.'

This was addressed to a young gentleman who was pinching the phenomenon behind, apparently with a view of ascertaining whether she was real.

'I am sure you must be very tired,' said the mama, turning to Miss Snevellicci. 'I cannot think of allowing you to go, without first taking a glass of wine. Fie, Charlotte, I am ashamed of you! Miss Lane, my dear, pray see to the children.'

Miss Lane was the governess, and this entreaty was rendered necessary by the abrupt behaviour of the youngest Miss Borum, who, having filched the phenomenon's little green parasol, was now carrying it bodily off, while the distracted infant looked helplessly on.

'I am sure, where you ever learnt to act as you do,' said good-natured Mrs Borum, turning again to Miss Snevellicci, 'I cannot understand (Emma, don't stare so); laughing in one piece, and crying in the next, and so natural in all—oh, dear!'

'I am very happy to hear you express so favourable an opinion,' said Miss Snevellicci. 'It's quite delightful to think you like it.'

'Like it!' cried Mrs. Borum. 'Who can help liking it? I would go to the play, twice a week if I could: I dote upon it—only you're too affecting sometimes. You do put me in such a state—into such fits of crying! Goodness gracious me, Miss Lane, how can you let them torment that poor child so!'

The phenomenon was really in a fair way of being torn limb from limb; for two strong little boys, one holding on by each of her hands, were dragging her in different directions as a trial of strength. However, Miss Lane (who had herself been too much occupied in contemplating the grown-up actors, to pay the necessary attention to these proceedings) rescued the unhappy infant at this juncture, who, being recruited with a glass of wine, was shortly afterwards taken away by her friends, after sustaining no more serious damage than a flattening of the pink gauze bonnet, and a rather extensive creasing of the white frock and trousers.

It was a trying morning; for there were a great many calls to make, and everybody wanted a different thing. Some wanted tragedies, and others comedies; some objected to dancing; some wanted scarcely anything else. Some thought the comic singer decidedly low, and others hoped he would have more to do than he usually had. Some people wouldn't promise to go, because other people wouldn't promise to go; and other people wouldn't go at all, because other people went. At length, and by little and little, omitting something in this place, and adding something in that, Miss Snevellicci pledged herself to a bill of fare which was comprehensive enough, if it had no other merit (it included among other trifles, four pieces, divers songs, a few combats, and several dances); and they returned home, pretty well exhausted with the business of the day.

Nicholas worked away at the piece, which was speedily put into rehearsal, and then worked away at his own part, which he studied with great perseverance and acted—as the whole company said—to perfection. And at length the great day arrived. The crier was sent round, in the morning, to proclaim the entertainments with the sound of bell in all the thoroughfares; and extra bills of three feet long by nine inches wide, were dispersed in all directions, flung down all the areas, thrust under all the knockers, and developed in all the shops. They were placarded on all the walls too, though not with complete success, for an illiterate person having undertaken this office during the indisposition of the regular bill-sticker, a part were posted sideways, and the remainder upside down.

At half-past five, there was a rush of four people to the gallery-door; at a quarter before six, there were at least a dozen; at six o'clock the kicks were terrific; and when the elder Master Crummles opened the door, he was obliged to run behind it for his life. Fifteen shillings were taken by Mrs. Grudden in the first ten minutes.

Behind the scenes, the same unwonted excitement prevailed. Miss Snevellicci was in such a perspiration that the paint would scarcely stay on her face. Mrs. Crummles was so nervous that she could hardly remember her part. Miss Bravassa's ringlets came out of curl with the heat and anxiety; even Mr. Crummles himself kept peeping through the hole in the curtain, and running back, every now and then, to announce that another man had come into the pit.

At last, the orchestra left off, and the curtain rose upon the new piece. The first scene, in which there was nobody particular, passed off calmly enough, but when Miss Snevellicci went on in the second, accompanied by the phenomenon as child, what a roar of applause broke out! The people in the Borum box rose as one man, waving their hats and handkerchiefs, and uttering shouts of 'Bravo!' Mrs. Borum and the governess cast wreaths upon the stage, of which, some fluttered into the lamps, and one crowned the temples of a fat gentleman in the pit, who, looking eagerly towards the scene, remained unconscious of the honour; the tailor and his family kicked at the panels of the upper boxes till they threatened to come out altogether; the very ginger-beer boy remained transfixed in the centre of the house; a young officer, supposed to entertain a passion for Miss Snevellicci, stuck his glass in his eye as though to hide a tear. Again and again Miss Snevellicci curtseyed lower and lower, and again and again the applause came down, louder and louder. At length, when the phenomenon picked up one of the smoking wreaths and put it on, sideways, over Miss Snevellicci's eye, it reached its climax, and the play proceeded.

But when Nicholas came on for his crack scene with Mrs. Crummles, what a clapping of hands there was! When Mrs. Crummles (who was his unworthy mother), sneered, and called him 'presumptuous boy,' and he defied her, what a tumult of applause came on! When he quarrelled with the other gentleman about the young lady, and producing a case of pistols, said, that if he was a gentleman, he would fight him in that drawing-room, until the furniture was sprinkled with the blood of one, if not of two—how boxes, pit, and gallery, joined in one most vigorous cheer! When he called his mother names, because she wouldn't give up the young lady's property, and she relenting, caused him to relent likewise, and fall down on one knee and ask her blessing, how the ladies in the audience sobbed! When he was hid behind the curtain in the dark, and the wicked relation poked a sharp sword in every direction, save where his legs were plainly visible, what a thrill of anxious fear ran through the house! His air, his figure, his walk, his look, everything he said or did, was the subject of commendation. There was a round of applause every time he spoke. And when, at last, in the pump-and-tub scene, Mrs. Grudden lighted the blue fire, and all the unemployed members of the company came in, and tumbled down in various directions—not because that had anything to do with the plot, but in order to finish off with a tableau—the audience (who had by this time increased considerably) gave vent to such a shout of enthusiasm as had not been heard in those walls for many and many a day.

In short, the success both of new piece and new actor was complete, and when Miss Snevellicci was called for at the end of the play, Nicholas led her on, and divided the applause.

CHAPTER 25
Concerning a young Lady from London, who joins the Company, and an elderly Admirer who follows in her Train; with an affecting Ceremony consequent on their Arrival

The new piece being a decided hit, was announced for every evening of performance until further notice, and the evenings when the theatre was closed, were reduced from three in the week to two. Nor were these the only tokens of extraordinary success; for, on the succeeding Saturday, Nicholas received, by favour of the indefatigable Mrs. Grudden, no less a sum than thirty shillings; besides which substantial reward, he enjoyed considerable fame and honour: having a presentation copy of Mr. Curdle's pamphlet forwarded to the theatre, with that gentleman's own autograph (in itself an inestimable treasure) on the fly-leaf, accompanied with a note, containing many expressions of approval, and an unsolicited assurance that Mr. Curdle would be very happy to read Shakespeare to him for three hours every morning before breakfast during his stay in the town.

'I've got another novelty, Johnson,' said Mr. Crummles one morning in great glee.

'What's that?' rejoined Nicholas. 'The pony?'

'No, no, we never come to the pony till everything else has failed,' said Mr. Crummles. 'I don't think we shall come to the pony at all, this season. No, no, not the pony.'

'A boy phenomenon, perhaps?' suggested Nicholas.

'There is only one phenomenon, sir,' replied Mr. Crummles impressively, 'and that's a girl.'

'Very true,' said Nicholas. 'I beg your pardon. Then I don't know what it is, I am sure.'

'What should you say to a young lady from London?' inquired Mr. Crummles. 'Miss So-and-so, of the Theatre Royal, Drury Lane?'

'I should say she would look very well in the bills,' said Nicholas.

'You're about right there,' said Mr. Crummles; 'and if you had said she would look very well upon the stage too, you wouldn't have been far out. Look here; what do you think of this?'

With this inquiry Mr. Crummles unfolded a red poster, and a blue poster, and a yellow poster, at the top of each of which public notification was inscribed in enormous characters— 'First appearance of the unrivalled Miss Petowker of the Theatre Royal, Drury Lane!'

'Dear me!' said Nicholas, 'I know that lady.'

'Then you are acquainted with as much talent as was ever compressed into one young person's body,' retorted Mr. Crummles, rolling up the bills again; 'that is, talent of a certain sort—of a certain sort. "The Blood Drinker,"' added Mr. Crummles with a prophetic sigh, '"The Blood Drinker" will die with that girl; and she's the only sylph I ever saw, who could stand upon one leg, and play the tambourine on her other knee, like a sylph.'

'When does she come down?' asked Nicholas.

'We expect her today,' replied Mr. Crummles. 'She is an old friend of Mrs Crummles's. Mrs. Crummles saw what she could do—always knew it from the first. She taught her, indeed, nearly all she knows. Mrs. Crummles was the original Blood Drinker.'

'Was she, indeed?'

'Yes. She was obliged to give it up though.'

'Did it disagree with her?' asked Nicholas.

'Not so much with her, as with her audiences,' replied Mr. Crummles. 'Nobody could stand it. It was too tremendous. You don't quite know what Mrs. Crummles is yet.'

Nicholas ventured to insinuate that he thought he did.

'No, no, you don't,' said Mr. Crummles; 'you don't, indeed. I don't, and that's a fact. I don't think her country will, till she is dead. Some new proof of talent bursts from that astonishing woman every year of her life. Look at her—mother of six children—three of 'em alive, and all upon the stage!'

'Extraordinary!' cried Nicholas.

'Ah! extraordinary indeed,' rejoined Mr. Crummles, taking a complacent pinch of snuff, and shaking his head gravely. 'I pledge you my professional word I didn't even know she could dance, till her last benefit, and then she played Juliet, and Helen Macgregor, and did the skipping-rope hornpipe between the pieces. The very first time I saw that admirable woman, Johnson,' said Mr. Crummles, drawing a little nearer, and speaking in the tone of confidential friendship, 'she stood upon her head on the butt-end of a spear, surrounded with blazing fireworks.'

'You astonish me!' said Nicholas.

'She astonished me!' returned Mr. Crummles, with a very serious countenance. 'Such grace, coupled with such dignity! I adored her from that moment!'

The arrival of the gifted subject of these remarks put an abrupt termination to Mr. Crummles's eulogium. Almost immediately afterwards, Master Percy Crummles entered with a letter, which had arrived by the General Post, and was directed to his gracious mother; at sight of the superscription whereof, Mrs. Crummles exclaimed, 'From Henrietta Petowker, I do declare!' and instantly became absorbed in the contents.

'Is it—?' inquired Mr. Crummles, hesitating.

'Oh, yes, it's all right,' replied Mrs. Crummles, anticipating the question. 'What an excellent thing for her, to be sure!'

'It's the best thing altogether, that I ever heard of, I think,' said Mr Crummles; and then Mr. Crummles, Mrs. Crummles, and Master Percy Crummles, all fell to laughing violently. Nicholas left them to enjoy their mirth together, and walked to his lodgings; wondering very much what mystery connected with Miss Petowker could provoke such merriment, and pondering still more on the extreme surprise with which that lady would regard his sudden enlistment in a profession of which she was such a distinguished and brilliant ornament.

But, in this latter respect he was mistaken; for—whether Mr. Vincent Crummles had paved the way, or Miss Petowker had some special reason for treating him with even more than her usual amiability—their meeting at the theatre next day was more like that of two dear friends who had been inseparable from infancy, than a recognition passing between a lady and gentleman who had only met some half-dozen times, and then by mere chance. Nay, Miss

Petowker even whispered that she had wholly dropped the Kenwigses in her conversations with the manager's family, and had represented herself as having encountered Mr. Johnson in the very first and most fashionable circles; and on Nicholas receiving this intelligence with unfeigned surprise, she added, with a sweet glance, that she had a claim on his good nature now, and might tax it before long.

Nicholas had the honour of playing in a slight piece with Miss Petowker that night, and could not but observe that the warmth of her reception was mainly attributable to a most persevering umbrella in the upper boxes; he saw, too, that the enchanting actress cast many sweet looks towards the quarter whence these sounds proceeded; and that every time she did so, the umbrella broke out afresh. Once, he thought that a peculiarly shaped hat in the same corner was not wholly unknown to him; but, being occupied with his share of the stage business, he bestowed no great attention upon this circumstance, and it had quite vanished from his memory by the time he reached home.

He had just sat down to supper with Smike, when one of the people of the house came outside the door, and announced that a gentleman below stairs wished to speak to Mr. Johnson.

'Well, if he does, you must tell him to come up; that's all I know,' replied Nicholas. 'One of our hungry brethren, I suppose, Smike.'

His fellow-lodger looked at the cold meat in silent calculation of the quantity that would be left for dinner next day, and put back a slice he had cut for himself, in order that the visitor's encroachments might be less formidable in their effects.

'It is not anybody who has been here before,' said Nicholas, 'for he is tumbling up every stair. Come in, come in. In the name of wonder! Mr Lillyvick?'

It was, indeed, the collector of water-rates who, regarding Nicholas with a fixed look and immovable countenance, shook hands with most portentous solemnity, and sat himself down in a seat by the chimney-corner.

'Why, when did you come here?' asked Nicholas.

'This morning, sir,' replied Mr. Lillyvick.

'Oh! I see; then you were at the theatre tonight, and it was your umb—'

'This umbrella,' said Mr. Lillyvick, producing a fat green cotton one with a battered ferrule. 'What did you think of that performance?'

'So far as I could judge, being on the stage,' replied Nicholas, 'I thought it very agreeable.'

'Agreeable!' cried the collector. 'I mean to say, sir, that it was delicious.'

Mr. Lillyvick bent forward to pronounce the last word with greater emphasis; and having done so, drew himself up, and frowned and nodded a great many times.

'I say, delicious,' repeated Mr. Lillyvick. 'Absorbing, fairy-like, toomultuous,' and again Mr. Lillyvick drew himself up, and again he frowned and nodded.

'Ah!' said Nicholas, a little surprised at these symptoms of ecstatic approbation. 'Yes—she is a clever girl.'

'She is a divinity,' returned Mr. Lillyvick, giving a collector's double knock on the ground with the umbrella before-mentioned. 'I have known divine actresses before now, sir, I used to collect—at least I used to call for—and very often call for—the water-rate at the house of a divine actress, who lived in my beat for upwards of four year but never—no, never, sir of all divine creatures, actresses or no actresses, did I see a diviner one than is Henrietta Petowker.'

Nicholas had much ado to prevent himself from laughing; not trusting himself to speak, he merely nodded in accordance with Mr. Lillyvick's nods, and remained silent.

'Let me speak a word with you in private,' said Mr. Lillyvick.

Nicholas looked good-humouredly at Smike, who, taking the hint, disappeared.

'A bachelor is a miserable wretch, sir,' said Mr. Lillyvick.

'Is he?' asked Nicholas.

'He is,' rejoined the collector. 'I have lived in the world for nigh sixty year, and I ought to know what it is.'

'You ought to know, certainly,' thought Nicholas; 'but whether you do or not, is another question.'

'If a bachelor happens to have saved a little matter of money,' said Mr Lillyvick, 'his sisters and brothers, and nephews and nieces, look to that money, and not to him; even if, by being a public character, he is the head of the family, or, as it may be, the main from which all the other little branches are turned on, they still wish him dead all the while, and get low-spirited every time they see him looking in good health, because they want to come into his little property. You see that?'

'Oh yes,' replied Nicholas: 'it's very true, no doubt.'

'The great reason for not being married,' resumed Mr. Lillyvick, 'is the expense; that's what's kept me off, or else—Lord!' said Mr Lillyvick, snapping his fingers, 'I might have had fifty women.'

'Fine women?' asked Nicholas.

'Fine women, sir!' replied the collector; 'ay! not so fine as Henrietta Petowker, for she is an uncommon specimen, but such women as don't fall into every man's way, I can tell you. Now suppose a man can get a fortune in a wife instead of with her—eh?'

'Why, then, he's a lucky fellow,' replied Nicholas.

'That's what I say,' retorted the collector, patting him benignantly on the side of the head with his umbrella; 'just what I say. Henrietta Petowker, the talented Henrietta Petowker has a fortune in herself, and I am going to—'

'To make her Mrs. Lillyvick?' suggested Nicholas.

'No, sir, not to make her Mrs. Lillyvick,' replied the collector. 'Actresses, sir, always keep their maiden names—that's the regular thing—but I'm going to marry her; and the day after tomorrow, too.'

'I congratulate you, sir,' said Nicholas.

'Thank you, sir,' replied the collector, buttoning his waistcoat. 'I shall draw her salary, of course, and I hope after all that it's nearly as cheap to keep two as it is to keep one; that's a consolation.'

'Surely you don't want any consolation at such a moment?' observed Nicholas.

'No,' replied Mr. Lillyvick, shaking his head nervously: 'no—of course not.'

'But how come you both here, if you're going to be married, Mr. Lillyvick?' asked Nicholas.

'Why, that's what I came to explain to you,' replied the collector of water-rate. 'The fact is, we have thought it best to keep it secret from the family.'

'Family!' said Nicholas. 'What family?'

'The Kenwigses of course,' rejoined Mr. Lillyvick. 'If my niece and the children had known a word about it before I came away, they'd have gone into fits at my feet, and never have come out of 'em till I took an oath not to marry anybody—or they'd have got out a commission of lunacy, or some dreadful thing,' said the collector, quite trembling as he spoke.

'To be sure,' said Nicholas. 'Yes; they would have been jealous, no doubt.'

'To prevent which,' said Mr. Lillyvick, 'Henrietta Petowker (it was settled between us) should come down here to her friends, the Crummleses, under pretence of this engagement, and I should go down to Guildford the day before, and join her on the coach there, which I did, and we came down from Guildford yesterday together. Now, for fear you should be writing to Mr. Noggs, and might say anything about us, we have thought it best to let you into the secret. We shall be married from the Crummleses' lodgings, and shall be delighted to see you—either before church or at breakfast-time, which you like. It won't be expensive, you know,' said the collector, highly anxious to prevent any misunderstanding on this point; 'just muffins and coffee, with perhaps a shrimp or something of that sort for a relish, you know.'

'Yes, yes, I understand,' replied Nicholas. 'Oh, I shall be most happy to come; it will give me the greatest pleasure. Where's the lady stopping—with Mrs. Crummles?'

'Why, no,' said the collector; 'they couldn't very well dispose of her at night, and so she is staying with an acquaintance of hers, and another young lady; they both belong to the theatre.'

'Miss Snevellicci, I suppose?' said Nicholas.

'Yes, that's the name.'

'And they'll be bridesmaids, I presume?' said Nicholas.

'Why,' said the collector, with a rueful face, 'they will have four bridesmaids; I'm afraid they'll make it rather theatrical.'

'Oh no, not at all,' replied Nicholas, with an awkward attempt to convert a laugh into a cough. 'Who may the four be? Miss Snevellicci of course—Miss Ledrook—'

'The—the phenomenon,' groaned the collector.

'Ha, ha!' cried Nicholas. 'I beg your pardon, I don't know what I'm laughing at—yes, that'll be very pretty—the phenomenon—who else?'

'Some young woman or other,' replied the collector, rising; 'some other friend of Henrietta Petowker's. Well, you'll be careful not to say anything about it, will you?'

'You may safely depend upon me,' replied Nicholas. 'Won't you take anything to eat or drink?'

'No,' said the collector; 'I haven't any appetite. I should think it was a very pleasant life, the married one, eh?'

'I have not the least doubt of it,' rejoined Nicholas.

'Yes,' said the collector; 'certainly. Oh yes. No doubt. Good night.'

With these words, Mr. Lillyvick, whose manner had exhibited through the whole of this interview a most extraordinary compound of precipitation, hesitation, confidence and doubt, fondness, misgiving, meanness, and self-importance, turned his back upon the room, and left Nicholas to enjoy a laugh by himself if he felt so disposed.

Without stopping to inquire whether the intervening day appeared to Nicholas to consist of the usual number of hours of the ordinary length, it may be remarked that, to the parties more directly interested in the forthcoming ceremony, it passed with great rapidity, insomuch that when Miss Petowker awoke on the succeeding morning in the chamber of Miss Snevellicci, she declared that nothing should ever persuade her that that really was the day which was to behold a change in her condition.

'I never will believe it,' said Miss Petowker; 'I cannot really. It's of no use talking, I never can make up my mind to go through with such a trial!'

On hearing this, Miss Snevellicci and Miss Ledrook, who knew perfectly well that their fair friend's mind had been made up for three or four years, at any period of which time she would have cheerfully undergone the desperate trial now approaching if she could have found any eligible gentleman disposed for the venture, began to preach comfort and firmness, and to say how very proud she ought to feel that it was in her power to confer lasting bliss on a deserving object, and how necessary it was for the happiness of mankind in general that women should possess fortitude and resignation on such occasions; and that although for their parts they held true happiness to consist in a single life, which they would not willingly exchange—no, not for any worldly consideration—still (thank God), if ever the time should come, they hoped they knew their duty too well to repine, but would the rather submit with meekness and humility of spirit to a fate for which Providence had clearly designed them with a view to the contentment and reward of their fellow-creatures.

'I might feel it was a great blow,' said Miss Snevellicci, 'to break up old associations and what-do-you-callems of that kind, but I would submit, my dear, I would indeed.'

'So would I,' said Miss Ledrook; 'I would rather court the yoke than shun it. I have broken hearts before now, and I'm very sorry for it: for it's a terrible thing to reflect upon.'

'It is indeed,' said Miss Snevellicci. 'Now Led, my dear, we must positively get her ready, or we shall be too late, we shall indeed.'

This pious reasoning, and perhaps the fear of being too late, supported the bride through the ceremony of robing, after which, strong tea and brandy were administered in alternate doses as a means of strengthening her feeble limbs and causing her to walk steadier.

'How do you feel now, my love?' inquired Miss Snevellicci.

'Oh Lillyvick!' cried the bride. 'If you knew what I am undergoing for you!'

'Of course he knows it, love, and will never forget it,' said Miss Ledrook.

'Do you think he won't?' cried Miss Petowker, really showing great capability for the stage. 'Oh, do you think he won't? Do you think Lillyvick will always remember it—always, always, always?'

There is no knowing in what this burst of feeling might have ended, if Miss Snevellicci had not at that moment proclaimed the arrival of the fly, which so astounded the bride that she shook off divers alarming symptoms which were coming on very strong, and running to the glass adjusted her dress, and calmly declared that she was ready for the sacrifice.

She was accordingly supported into the coach, and there 'kept up' (as Miss Snevellicci said) with perpetual sniffs of sal volatile and sips of brandy and other gentle stimulants, until they reached the manager's door, which was already opened by the two Master Crummleses, who wore white cockades, and were decorated with the choicest and most resplendent waistcoats in the theatrical wardrobe. By the combined exertions of these young gentlemen and the bridesmaids, assisted by the coachman, Miss Petowker was at length supported in a condition of much exhaustion to the first floor, where she no sooner encountered the youthful bridegroom than she fainted with great decorum.

'Henrietta Petowker!' said the collector; 'cheer up, my lovely one.'

Miss Petowker grasped the collector's hand, but emotion choked her utterance.

'Is the sight of me so dreadful, Henrietta Petowker?' said the collector.

'Oh no, no, no,' rejoined the bride; 'but all the friends—the darling friends—of my youthful days—to leave them all—it is such a shock!'

With such expressions of sorrow, Miss Petowker went on to enumerate the dear friends of her youthful days one by one, and to call upon such of them as were present to come and embrace her. This done, she remembered that Mrs. Crummles had been more than a mother to her, and after that, that Mr. Crummles had been more than a father to her, and after that, that the Master Crummleses and Miss Ninetta Crummles had been more than brothers and sisters to her. These various remembrances being each accompanied with a series of hugs, occupied a long time, and they were obliged to drive to church very fast, for fear they should be too late.

The procession consisted of two flys; in the first of which were Miss Bravassa (the fourth bridesmaid), Mrs. Crummles, the collector, and Mr Folair, who had been chosen as his second on the occasion. In the other were the bride, Mr. Crummles, Miss Snevellicci, Miss Ledrook, and the phenomenon. The costumes were beautiful. The bridesmaids were quite covered with artificial flowers, and the phenomenon, in particular, was rendered almost invisible by the portable arbour in which she was enshrined. Miss Ledrook, who was of a romantic turn, wore in her breast the miniature of some field-officer unknown, which she had purchased, a great bargain, not very long before; the other ladies displayed several dazzling articles of imitative jewellery, almost equal to real, and Mrs Crummles came out in a stern and gloomy majesty, which attracted the admiration of all beholders.

But, perhaps the appearance of Mr. Crummles was more striking and appropriate than that of any member of the party. This gentleman, who personated the bride's father, had, in pursuance of a happy and original conception, 'made up' for the part by arraying himself in a theatrical wig, of a style and pattern commonly known as a brown George, and moreover assuming a snuff-coloured suit, of the previous century, with grey silk stockings, and buckles to his shoes. The better to support his assumed character he had determined to be greatly overcome, and, consequently, when they entered the church, the sobs of the affectionate parent were so heart-rending that the pew-opener suggested the propriety of his retiring to the vestry, and comforting himself with a glass of water before the ceremony began.

The procession up the aisle was beautiful. The bride, with the four bridesmaids, forming a group previously arranged and rehearsed; the collector, followed by his second, imitating his walk and gestures to the indescribable amusement of some theatrical friends in the gallery; Mr Crummles, with an infirm and feeble gait; Mrs. Crummles advancing with that stage walk, which consists of a stride and a stop alternately—it was the completest thing ever witnessed. The ceremony was very quickly disposed of, and all parties present having signed the register (for which purpose, when it came to his turn, Mr. Crummles carefully wiped and put on an immense pair of spectacles), they went back to breakfast in high spirits. And here they found Nicholas awaiting their arrival.

'Now then,' said Crummles, who had been assisting Mrs. Grudden in the preparations, which were on a more extensive scale than was quite agreeable to the collector. 'Breakfast, breakfast.'

No second invitation was required. The company crowded and squeezed themselves at the table as well as they could, and fell to, immediately: Miss Petowker blushing very much when anybody was looking, and eating very much when anybody was not looking; and Mr. Lillyvick going to work as though with the cool resolve, that since the good things must be paid for by him, he would leave as little as possible for the Crummleses to eat up afterwards.

'It's very soon done, sir, isn't it?' inquired Mr. Folair of the collector, leaning over the table to address him.

'What is soon done, sir?' returned Mr. Lillyvick.

'The tying up—the fixing oneself with a wife,' replied Mr. Folair. 'It don't take long, does it?'

'No, sir,' replied Mr. Lillyvick, colouring. 'It does not take long. And what then, sir?'

'Oh! nothing,' said the actor. 'It don't take a man long to hang himself, either, eh? ha, ha!'

Mr. Lillyvick laid down his knife and fork, and looked round the table with indignant astonishment.

'To hang himself!' repeated Mr. Lillyvick.

A profound silence came upon all, for Mr. Lillyvick was dignified beyond expression.

'To hang himself!' cried Mr. Lillyvick again. 'Is any parallel attempted to be drawn in this company between matrimony and hanging?'

'The noose, you know,' said Mr. Folair, a little crest-fallen.

'The noose, sir?' retorted Mr. Lillyvick. 'Does any man dare to speak to me of a noose, and Henrietta Pe—'

'Lillyvick,' suggested Mr. Crummles.

'—And Henrietta Lillyvick in the same breath?' said the collector. 'In this house, in the presence of Mr. and Mrs. Crummles, who have brought up a talented and virtuous family, to be blessings and phenomenons, and what not, are we to hear talk of nooses?'

'Folair,' said Mr. Crummles, deeming it a matter of decency to be affected by this allusion to himself and partner, 'I'm astonished at you.'

'What are you going on in this way at me for?' urged the unfortunate actor. 'What have

I done?'

'Done, sir!' cried Mr. Lillyvick, 'aimed a blow at the whole framework of society—'

'And the best and tenderest feelings,' added Crummles, relapsing into the old man.

'And the highest and most estimable of social ties,' said the collector. 'Noose! As if one was caught, trapped into the married state, pinned by the leg, instead of going into it of one's own accord and glorying in the act!'

'I didn't mean to make it out, that you were caught and trapped, and pinned by the leg,' replied the actor. 'I'm sorry for it; I can't say any more.'

'So you ought to be, sir,' returned Mr. Lillyvick; 'and I am glad to hear that you have enough of feeling left to be so.'

The quarrel appearing to terminate with this reply, Mrs. Lillyvick considered that the fittest occasion (the attention of the company being no longer distracted) to burst into tears, and require the assistance of all four bridesmaids, which was immediately rendered, though not without some confusion, for the room being small and the table-cloth long, a whole detachment of plates were swept off the board at the very first move. Regardless of this circumstance, however, Mrs. Lillyvick refused to be comforted until the belligerents had passed their words that the dispute should be carried no further, which, after a sufficient show of reluctance, they did, and from that time Mr. Folair sat in moody silence, contenting himself with pinching Nicholas's leg when anything was said, and so expressing his contempt both for the speaker and the sentiments to which he gave utterance.

There were a great number of speeches made; some by Nicholas, and some by Crummles, and some by the collector; two by the Master Crummleses in returning thanks for themselves, and one by the phenomenon on behalf of the bridesmaids, at which Mrs. Crummles shed tears. There was some singing, too, from Miss Ledrook and Miss Bravassa, and very likely there might have been more, if the fly-driver, who stopped to drive the happy pair to the spot where they proposed to take steamboat to Ryde, had not sent in a peremptory message intimating, that if they didn't come directly he should infallibly demand eighteen-pence over and above his agreement.

This desperate threat effectually broke up the party. After a most pathetic leave-taking, Mr. Lillyvick and his bride departed for Ryde, where they were to spend the next two days in profound retirement, and whither they were accompanied by the infant, who had been appointed travelling bridesmaid on Mr. Lillyvick's express stipulation: as the steamboat people, deceived by her size, would (he had previously ascertained) transport her at half-price.

As there was no performance that night, Mr. Crummles declared his intention of keeping it up till everything to drink was disposed of; but Nicholas having to play Romeo for the first time on the ensuing evening, contrived to slip away in the midst of a temporary confusion, occasioned by the unexpected development of strong symptoms of inebriety in the conduct of Mrs. Grudden.

To this act of desertion he was led, not only by his own inclinations, but by his anxiety on account of Smike, who, having to sustain the character of the Apothecary, had been as yet wholly unable to get any more of the part into his head than the general idea that he was very hungry, which—perhaps from old recollections—he had acquired with great aptitude.

244

'I don't know what's to be done, Smike,' said Nicholas, laying down the book. 'I am afraid you can't learn it, my poor fellow.'

'I am afraid not,' said Smike, shaking his head. 'I think if you—but that would give you so much trouble.'

'What?' inquired Nicholas. 'Never mind me.'

'I think,' said Smike, 'if you were to keep saying it to me in little bits, over and over again, I should be able to recollect it from hearing you.'

'Do you think so?' exclaimed Nicholas. 'Well said. Let us see who tires first. Not I, Smike, trust me. Now then. Who calls so loud?'

'"Who calls so loud?"' said Smike.

'"Who calls so loud?"' repeated Nicholas.

'"Who calls so loud?"' cried Smike.

Thus they continued to ask each other who called so loud, over and over again; and when Smike had that by heart Nicholas went to another sentence, and then to two at a time, and then to three, and so on, until at midnight poor Smike found to his unspeakable joy that he really began to remember something about the text.

Early in the morning they went to it again, and Smike, rendered more confident by the progress he had already made, got on faster and with better heart. As soon as he began to acquire the words pretty freely, Nicholas showed him how he must come in with both hands spread out upon his stomach, and how he must occasionally rub it, in compliance with the established form by which people on the stage always denote that they want something to eat. After the morning's rehearsal they went to work again, nor did they stop, except for a hasty dinner, until it was time to repair to the theatre at night.

Never had master a more anxious, humble, docile pupil. Never had pupil a more patient, unwearying, considerate, kindhearted master.

As soon as they were dressed, and at every interval when he was not upon the stage, Nicholas renewed his instructions. They prospered well. The Romeo was received with hearty plaudits and unbounded favour, and Smike was pronounced unanimously, alike by audience and actors, the very prince and prodigy of Apothecaries.

CHAPTER 26
Is fraught with some Danger to Miss Nickleby's Peace of Mind

The place was a handsome suite of private apartments in Regent Street; the time was three o'clock in the afternoon to the dull and plodding, and the first hour of morning to the gay and spirited; the persons were Lord Frederick Verisopht, and his friend Sir Mulberry Hawk.

These distinguished gentlemen were reclining listlessly on a couple of sofas, with a table between them, on which were scattered in rich confusion the materials of an untasted breakfast. Newspapers lay strewn about the room, but these, like the meal, were neglected and unnoticed; not, however, because any flow of conversation prevented the attractions of the journals from being called into request, for not a word was exchanged between the two, nor was any sound uttered, save when one, in tossing about to find an easier resting-place for his aching head, uttered an exclamation of impatience, and seemed for a moment to communicate a new restlessness to his companion.

These appearances would in themselves have furnished a pretty strong clue to the extent of the debauch of the previous night, even if there had not been other indications of the amusements in which it had been passed. A couple of billiard balls, all mud and dirt, two battered hats, a champagne bottle with a soiled glove twisted round the neck, to allow of its being grasped more surely in its capacity of an offensive weapon; a broken cane; a card-case without the top; an empty purse; a watch-guard snapped asunder; a handful of silver, mingled with fragments of half-smoked cigars, and their stale and crumbled ashes;—these, and many other tokens of riot and disorder, hinted very intelligibly at the nature of last night's gentlemanly frolics.

Lord Frederick Verisopht was the first to speak. Dropping his slippered foot on the ground, and, yawning heavily, he struggled into a sitting posture, and turned his dull languid eyes towards his friend, to whom he called in a drowsy voice.

'Hallo!' replied Sir Mulberry, turning round.

'Are we going to lie here all da-a-y?' said the lord.

'I don't know that we're fit for anything else,' replied Sir Mulberry; 'yet awhile, at least. I haven't a grain of life in me this morning.'

'Life!' cried Lord Verisopht. 'I feel as if there would be nothing so snug and comfortable as to die at once.'

'Then why don't you die?' said Sir Mulberry.

With which inquiry he turned his face away, and seemed to occupy himself in an attempt to fall asleep.

His hopeful friend and pupil drew a chair to the breakfast-table, and essayed to eat; but, finding that impossible, lounged to the window, then loitered up and down the room with his hand to his fevered head, and finally threw himself again on his sofa, and roused his friend once more.

'What the devil's the matter?' groaned Sir Mulberry, sitting upright on the couch.

Although Sir Mulberry said this with sufficient ill-humour, he did not seem to feel himself quite at liberty to remain silent; for, after stretching himself very often, and declaring with a shiver that it was 'infernal cold,' he made an experiment at the breakfast-table, and proving more successful in it than his less-seasoned friend, remained there.

'Suppose,' said Sir Mulberry, pausing with a morsel on the point of his fork, 'suppose we go back to the subject of little Nickleby, eh?'

'Which little Nickleby; the money-lender or the ga-a-l?' asked Lord Verisopht.

'You take me, I see,' replied Sir Mulberry. 'The girl, of course.'

'You promised me you'd find her out,' said Lord Verisopht.

'So I did,' rejoined his friend; 'but I have thought further of the matter since then. You distrust me in the business—you shall find her out yourself.'

'Na-ay,' remonstrated Lord Verisopht.

'But I say yes,' returned his friend. 'You shall find her out yourself. Don't think that I mean, when you can—I know as well as you that if I did, you could never get sight of her without me. No. I say you shall find her out—shall—and I'll put you in the way.'

'Now, curse me, if you ain't a real, deyvlish, downright, thorough-paced friend,' said the young lord, on whom this speech had produced a most reviving effect.

'I'll tell you how,' said Sir Mulberry. 'She was at that dinner as a bait for you.'

'No!' cried the young lord. 'What the dey—'

'As a bait for you,' repeated his friend; 'old Nickleby told me so himself.'

'What a fine old cock it is!' exclaimed Lord Verisopht; 'a noble rascal!'

'Yes,' said Sir Mulberry, 'he knew she was a smart little creature—'

'Smart!' interposed the young lord. 'Upon my soul, Hawk, she's a perfect beauty—a—a picture, a statue, a—a—upon my soul she is!'

'Well,' replied Sir Mulberry, shrugging his shoulders and manifesting an indifference, whether he felt it or not; 'that's a matter of taste; if mine doesn't agree with yours, so much the better.'

'Confound it!' reasoned the lord, 'you were thick enough with her that day, anyhow. I could hardly get in a word.'

'Well enough for once, well enough for once,' replied Sir Mulberry; 'but not worth the trouble of being agreeable to again. If you seriously want to follow up the niece, tell the uncle that you must know where she lives and how she lives, and with whom, or you are no longer a customer of his. He'll tell you fast enough.'

'Why didn't you say this before?' asked Lord Verisopht, 'instead of letting me go on burning, consuming, dragging out a miserable existence for an a-age!'

'I didn't know it, in the first place,' answered Sir Mulberry carelessly; 'and in the second, I didn't believe you were so very much in earnest.'

Now, the truth was, that in the interval which had elapsed since the dinner at Ralph Nickleby's, Sir Mulberry Hawk had been furtively trying by every means in his power to discover whence Kate had so suddenly appeared, and whither she had disappeared. Unassisted by Ralph, however, with whom he had held no communication since their angry parting on that occasion, all his efforts were wholly unavailing, and he had therefore arrived at the determination of communicating to the young lord the substance of the admission he had gleaned from that worthy. To this he was impelled by various considerations; among which the certainty of knowing whatever the weak young man knew was decidedly not the least, as the desire of encountering the usurer's niece again, and using his utmost arts to reduce her pride, and revenge himself for her contempt, was uppermost in his thoughts. It was a politic course of proceeding, and one which could not fail to redound to his advantage in every point of view, since the very circumstance of his having extorted from Ralph Nickleby his real design in introducing his niece to such society, coupled with his extreme disinterestedness in communicating it so freely to his friend, could not but advance his interests in that quarter, and greatly facilitate the passage of coin (pretty frequent and speedy already) from the pockets of Lord Frederick Verisopht to those of Sir Mulberry Hawk.

Thus reasoned Sir Mulberry, and in pursuance of this reasoning he and his friend soon afterwards repaired to Ralph Nickleby's, there to execute a plan of operations concerted by Sir Mulberry himself, avowedly to promote his friend's object, and really to attain his own.

They found Ralph at home, and alone. As he led them into the drawing-room, the recollection of the scene which had taken place there seemed to occur to him, for he cast a curious look at Sir Mulberry, who bestowed upon it no other acknowledgment than a careless smile.

They had a short conference upon some money matters then in progress, which were scarcely disposed of when the lordly dupe (in pursuance of his friend's instructions) requested with some embarrassment to speak to Ralph alone.

'Alone, eh?' cried Sir Mulberry, affecting surprise. 'Oh, very good. I'll walk into the next room here. Don't keep me long, that's all.'

So saying, Sir Mulberry took up his hat, and humming a fragment of a song disappeared through the door of communication between the two drawing-rooms, and closed it after him.

'Now, my lord,' said Ralph, 'what is it?'

'Nickleby,' said his client, throwing himself along the sofa on which he had been previously seated, so as to bring his lips nearer to the old man's ear, 'what a pretty creature your niece is!'

'Is she, my lord?' replied Ralph. 'Maybe—maybe—I don't trouble my head with such matters.'

'You know she's a deyvlish fine girl,' said the client. 'You must know that, Nickleby. Come, don't deny that.'

'Yes, I believe she is considered so,' replied Ralph. 'Indeed, I know she is. If I did not, you are an authority on such points, and your taste, my lord—on all points, indeed—is undeniable.'

Nobody but the young man to whom these words were addressed could have been deaf to the sneering tone in which they were spoken, or blind to the look of contempt by which they were accompanied. But Lord Frederick Verisopht was both, and took them to be complimentary.

'Well,' he said, 'p'raps you're a little right, and p'raps you're a little wrong—a little of both, Nickleby. I want to know where this beauty lives, that I may have another peep at her, Nickleby.'

'Really—' Ralph began in his usual tones.

'Don't talk so loud,' cried the other, achieving the great point of his lesson to a miracle. 'I don't want Hawk to hear.'

'You know he is your rival, do you?' said Ralph, looking sharply at him.

'He always is, d-a-amn him,' replied the client; 'and I want to steal a march upon him. Ha, ha, ha! He'll cut up so rough, Nickleby, at our talking together without him. Where does she live, Nickleby, that's all? Only tell me where she lives, Nickleby.'

'He bites,' thought Ralph. 'He bites.'

'Eh, Nickleby, eh?' pursued the client. 'Where does she live?'

'Really, my lord,' said Ralph, rubbing his hands slowly over each other, 'I must think before I tell you.'

'No, not a bit of it, Nickleby; you mustn't think at all,' replied Verisopht. 'Where is it?'

'No good can come of your knowing,' replied Ralph. 'She has been virtuously and well brought up; to be sure she is handsome, poor, unprotected! Poor girl, poor girl.'

Ralph ran over this brief summary of Kate's condition as if it were merely passing through his own mind, and he had no intention to speak aloud; but the shrewd sly look which he directed at his companion as he delivered it, gave this poor assumption the lie.

'I tell you I only want to see her,' cried his client. 'A ma-an may look at a pretty woman without harm, mayn't he? Now, where does she live? You know you're making a fortune out of me, Nickleby, and upon my soul nobody shall ever take me to anybody else, if you only tell me this.'

'As you promise that, my lord,' said Ralph, with feigned reluctance, 'and as I am most anxious to oblige you, and as there's no harm in it—no harm—I'll tell you. But you had better keep it to yourself, my lord; strictly to yourself.' Ralph pointed to the adjoining room as he spoke, and nodded expressively.

The young lord, feigning to be equally impressed with the necessity of this precaution, Ralph disclosed the present address and occupation of his niece, observing that from what he heard of the family they appeared very ambitious to have distinguished acquaintances, and that a lord could, doubtless, introduce himself with great ease, if he felt disposed.

'Your object being only to see her again,' said Ralph, 'you could effect it at any time you chose by that means.'

Lord Verisopht acknowledged the hint with a great many squeezes of Ralph's hard, horny hand, and whispering that they would now do well to close the conversation, called to Sir Mulberry Hawk that he might come back.

'I thought you had gone to sleep,' said Sir Mulberry, reappearing with an ill-tempered air.

'Sorry to detain you,' replied the gull; 'but Nickleby has been so ama-azingly funny that I couldn't tear myself away.'

'No, no,' said Ralph; 'it was all his lordship. You know what a witty, humorous, elegant, accomplished man Lord Frederick is. Mind the step, my lord—Sir Mulberry, pray give way.'

With such courtesies as these, and many low bows, and the same cold sneer upon his face all the while, Ralph busied himself in showing his visitors downstairs, and otherwise than by the slightest possible motion about the corners of his mouth, returned no show of answer to the look of admiration with which Sir Mulberry Hawk seemed to compliment him on being such an accomplished and most consummate scoundrel.

There had been a ring at the bell a few minutes before, which was answered by Newman Noggs just as they reached the hall. In the ordinary course of business Newman would have either admitted the new-comer in silence, or have requested him or her to stand aside while the gentlemen passed out. But he no sooner saw who it was, than as if for some private reason of his own, he boldly departed from the established custom of Ralph's mansion in business hours, and looking towards the respectable trio who were approaching, cried in a loud and sonorous voice, 'Mrs. Nickleby!'

'Mrs. Nickleby!' cried Sir Mulberry Hawk, as his friend looked back, and stared him in the face.

It was, indeed, that well-intentioned lady, who, having received an offer for the empty house in the city directed to the landlord, had brought it post-haste to Mr. Nickleby without delay.

'Nobody you know,' said Ralph. 'Step into the office, my—my—dear. I'll be with you directly.'

'Nobody I know!' cried Sir Mulberry Hawk, advancing to the astonished lady. 'Is this Mrs. Nickleby—the mother of Miss Nickleby—the delightful creature that I had the happiness of meeting in this house the very last time I dined here? But no;' said Sir Mulberry, stopping short. 'No, it can't be. There is the same cast of features, the same indescribable air of—But no; no. This lady is too young for that.'

'I think you can tell the gentleman, brother-in-law, if it concerns him to know,' said Mrs. Nickleby, acknowledging the compliment with a graceful bend, 'that Kate Nickleby is my daughter.'

'Her daughter, my lord!' cried Sir Mulberry, turning to his friend. 'This lady's daughter, my lord.'

'My lord!' thought Mrs. Nickleby. 'Well, I never did—'

'This, then, my lord,' said Sir Mulberry, 'is the lady to whose obliging marriage we owe so much happiness. This lady is the mother of sweet Miss Nickleby. Do you observe the extraordinary likeness, my lord? Nickleby—introduce us.'

Ralph did so, in a kind of desperation.

'Upon my soul, it's a most delightful thing,' said Lord Frederick, pressing forward. 'How de do?'

Mrs. Nickleby was too much flurried by these uncommonly kind salutations, and her regrets at not having on her other bonnet, to make any immediate reply, so she merely continued to bend and smile, and betray great agitation.

'A—and how is Miss Nickleby?' said Lord Frederick. 'Well, I hope?'

'She is quite well, I'm obliged to you, my lord,' returned Mrs. Nickleby, recovering. 'Quite well. She wasn't well for some days after that day she dined here, and I can't help thinking, that she caught cold in that hackney coach coming home. Hackney coaches, my lord, are such nasty things, that it's almost better to walk at any time, for although I believe a hackney coachman can be transported for life, if he has a broken window, still they are so reckless, that they nearly all have broken windows. I once had a swelled face for six weeks, my lord, from riding in a hackney coach—I think it was a hackney coach,' said Mrs. Nickleby reflecting, 'though I'm not quite certain whether it wasn't a chariot; at all events I know it was a dark green, with a very long number, beginning with a nought and ending with a nine—no, beginning with a nine, and ending with a nought, that was it, and of course the stamp-office people would know at once whether it was a coach or a chariot if any inquiries were made there—however that was, there it was with a broken window and there was I for six weeks with a swelled face—I think that was the very same hackney coach, that we found out afterwards, had the top open all the time, and we should never even have known it, if they hadn't charged us a shilling an hour extra for having it open, which it seems is the law, or was then, and a most shameful law it appears to be—I don't understand the subject, but I should say the Corn Laws could be nothing to that act of Parliament.'

Having pretty well run herself out by this time, Mrs. Nickleby stopped as suddenly as she had started off; and repeated that Kate was quite well. 'Indeed,' said Mrs. Nickleby, 'I don't think she ever was better, since she had the hooping-cough, scarlet-fever, and measles, all at the same time, and that's the fact.'

'Is that letter for me?' growled Ralph, pointing to the little packet Mrs Nickleby held in her hand.

'For you, brother-in-law,' replied Mrs. Nickleby, 'and I walked all the way up here on purpose to give it you.'

'All the way up here!' cried Sir Mulberry, seizing upon the chance of discovering where Mrs. Nickleby had come from. 'What a confounded distance! How far do you call it now?'

'How far do I call it?' said Mrs. Nickleby. 'Let me see. It's just a mile from our door to the Old Bailey.'

'No, no. Not so much as that,' urged Sir Mulberry.

'Oh! It is indeed,' said Mrs. Nickleby. 'I appeal to his lordship.'

'I should decidedly say it was a mile,' remarked Lord Frederick, with a solemn aspect.

'It must be; it can't be a yard less,' said Mrs. Nickleby. 'All down Newgate Street, all down Cheapside, all up Lombard Street, down Gracechurch Street, and along Thames Street, as far as Spigwiffin's Wharf. Oh! It's a mile.'

'Yes, on second thoughts I should say it was,' replied Sir Mulberry. 'But you don't surely mean to walk all the way back?'

'Oh, no,' rejoined Mrs. Nickleby. 'I shall go back in an omnibus. I didn't travel about in omnibuses, when my poor dear Nicholas was alive, brother-in-law. But as it is, you know—'

'Yes, yes,' replied Ralph impatiently, 'and you had better get back before dark.'

'Thank you, brother-in-law, so I had,' returned Mrs. Nickleby. 'I think I had better say goodbye, at once.'

'Not stop and—rest?' said Ralph, who seldom offered refreshments unless something was to be got by it.

'Oh dear me no,' returned Mrs. Nickleby, glancing at the dial.

'Lord Frederick,' said Sir Mulberry, 'we are going Mrs. Nickleby's way. We'll see her safe to the omnibus?'

'By all means. Ye-es.'

'Oh! I really couldn't think of it!' said Mrs. Nickleby.

But Sir Mulberry Hawk and Lord Verisopht were peremptory in their politeness, and leaving Ralph, who seemed to think, not unwisely, that he looked less ridiculous as a mere spectator, than he would have done if he had taken any part in these proceedings, they quitted the house with Mrs Nickleby between them; that good lady in a perfect ecstasy of satisfaction, no less with the attentions shown her by two titled gentlemen, than with the conviction that Kate might now pick and choose, at least between two large fortunes, and most unexceptionable husbands.

As she was carried away for the moment by an irresistible train of thought, all connected with her daughter's future greatness, Sir Mulberry Hawk and his friend exchanged glances over the top of the bonnet which the poor lady so much regretted not having left at home, and proceeded to dilate with great rapture, but much respect on the manifold perfections of Miss Nickleby.

'What a delight, what a comfort, what a happiness, this amiable creature must be to you,' said Sir Mulberry, throwing into his voice an indication of the warmest feeling.

'She is indeed, sir,' replied Mrs. Nickleby; 'she is the sweetest-tempered, kindest-hearted creature—and so clever!'

'She looks clayver,' said Lord Verisopht, with the air of a judge of cleverness.

'I assure you she is, my lord,' returned Mrs. Nickleby. 'When she was at school in Devonshire, she was universally allowed to be beyond all exception the very cleverest girl there, and there were a great many very clever ones too, and that's the truth—twenty-five young ladies, fifty guineas a year without the et-ceteras, both the Miss Dowdles the most accomplished, elegant, fascinating creatures—Oh dear me!' said Mrs. Nickleby, 'I never shall forget what pleasure she used to give me and her poor dear papa, when she was at that school, never—such a delightful letter every half-year, telling us that she was the first pupil in the whole establishment, and had made more progress than anybody else! I can scarcely bear to think of it even now. The girls wrote all the letters themselves,' added Mrs. Nickleby, 'and the writing-master touched them up afterwards with a magnifying glass and a silver pen; at least I think they wrote them, though Kate was never quite certain about that, because she didn't know the handwriting of hers again; but anyway, I know it was a circular which they all copied, and of course it was a very gratifying thing—very gratifying.'

With similar recollections Mrs. Nickleby beguiled the tediousness of the way, until they reached the omnibus, which the extreme politeness of her new friends would not allow them to leave until it actually started, when they took their hats, as Mrs. Nickleby solemnly assured her hearers on many subsequent occasions, 'completely off,' and kissed their straw-coloured kid gloves till they were no longer visible.

Mrs. Nickleby leant back in the furthest corner of the conveyance, and, closing her eyes, resigned herself to a host of most pleasing meditations. Kate had never said a word about having met either of these gentlemen; 'that,' she thought, 'argues that she is strongly prepossessed in favour of one of them.' Then the question arose, which one could it be. The lord was the youngest, and his title was certainly the grandest; still Kate was not the girl to be swayed by such considerations as these. 'I will never put any constraint upon her inclinations,' said Mrs. Nickleby to herself; 'but upon my word I think there's no comparison between his lordship and Sir Mulberry—Sir Mulberry is such an attentive gentlemanly creature, so much manner, such a fine man, and has so much to say for himself. I hope it's Sir Mulberry—I think it must be Sir Mulberry!' And then her thoughts flew back to her old predictions, and the number of times she had said, that Kate with no fortune would marry better than other people's daughters with thousands; and, as she pictured with the brightness of a mother's fancy all the beauty and grace of the poor girl who had struggled so cheerfully with her new life of hardship and trial, her heart grew too full, and the tears trickled down her face.

Meanwhile, Ralph walked to and fro in his little back-office, troubled in mind by what had just occurred. To say that Ralph loved or cared for—in the most ordinary acceptation of those terms—any one of God's creatures, would be the wildest fiction. Still, there had somehow stolen upon him from time to time a thought of his niece which was tinged with compassion and pity; breaking through the dull cloud of dislike or indifference which darkened men and women in his eyes, there was, in her case, the faintest gleam of light—a most feeble and sickly ray at the best of times—but there it was, and it showed the poor girl in a better and purer aspect than any in which he had looked on human nature yet.

'I wish,' thought Ralph, 'I had never done this. And yet it will keep this boy to me, while there is money to be made. Selling a girl—throwing her in the way of temptation, and insult, and coarse speech. Nearly two thousand pounds profit from him already though. Pshaw! match-making mothers do the same thing every day.'

He sat down, and told the chances, for and against, on his fingers.

'If I had not put them in the right track today,' thought Ralph, 'this foolish woman would have done so. Well. If her daughter is as true to herself as she should be from what I have seen, what harm ensues? A little teasing, a little humbling, a few tears. Yes,' said Ralph, aloud, as he locked his iron safe. 'She must take her chance. She must take her chance.'

CHAPTER 27
Mrs. Nickleby becomes acquainted with Messrs Pyke and Pluck, whose Affection and Interest are beyond all Bounds

Mrs. Nickleby had not felt so proud and important for many a day, as when, on reaching home, she gave herself wholly up to the pleasant visions which had accompanied her on her way thither. Lady Mulberry Hawk—that was the prevalent idea. Lady Mulberry Hawk!—On Tuesday last, at St George's, Hanover Square, by the Right Reverend the Bishop of Llandaff, Sir Mulberry Hawk, of Mulberry Castle, North Wales, to Catherine, only daughter of the late Nicholas Nickleby, Esquire, of Devonshire. 'Upon my word!' cried Mrs. Nicholas Nickleby, 'it sounds very well.'

Having dispatched the ceremony, with its attendant festivities, to the perfect satisfaction of her own mind, the sanguine mother pictured to her imagination a long train of honours and distinctions which could not fail to accompany Kate in her new and brilliant sphere. She would be presented at court, of course. On the anniversary of her birthday, which was upon the nineteenth of July ('at ten minutes past three o'clock in the morning,' thought Mrs. Nickleby in a parenthesis, 'for I recollect asking what o'clock it was'), Sir Mulberry would give a great feast to all his tenants, and would return them three and a half per cent on the amount of their last half-year's rent, as would be fully described and recorded in the fashionable intelligence, to the immeasurable delight and admiration of all the readers thereof. Kate's picture, too, would be in at least half-a-dozen of the annuals, and on the opposite page would appear, in delicate type, 'Lines on contemplating the Portrait of Lady Mulberry Hawk. By Sir Dingleby Dabber.' Perhaps some one annual, of more comprehensive design than its fellows, might even contain a portrait of the mother of Lady Mulberry Hawk, with lines by the father of Sir Dingleby Dabber. More unlikely things had come to pass. Less interesting portraits had appeared. As this thought occurred to the good lady, her countenance unconsciously assumed that compound expression of simpering and sleepiness which, being common to all such portraits, is perhaps one reason why they are always so charming and agreeable.

With such triumphs of aerial architecture did Mrs. Nickleby occupy the whole evening after her accidental introduction to Ralph's titled friends; and dreams, no less prophetic and equally promising, haunted her sleep that night. She was preparing for her frugal dinner next day, still occupied with the same ideas—a little softened down perhaps by sleep and daylight— when the girl who attended her, partly for company, and partly to assist in the household affairs, rushed into the room in unwonted agitation, and announced that two gentlemen were waiting in the passage for permission to walk upstairs.

'Bless my heart!' cried Mrs. Nickleby, hastily arranging her cap and front, 'if it should be—dear me, standing in the passage all this time—why don't you go and ask them to walk up, you stupid thing?'

While the girl was gone on this errand, Mrs. Nickleby hastily swept into a cupboard all vestiges of eating and drinking; which she had scarcely done, and seated herself with looks as collected as she could assume, when two gentlemen, both perfect strangers, presented themselves.

'How do you do?' said one gentleman, laying great stress on the last word of the inquiry.

'How do you do?' said the other gentleman, altering the emphasis, as if to give variety to the salutation.

Mrs. Nickleby curtseyed and smiled, and curtseyed again, and remarked, rubbing her hands as she did so, that she hadn't the—really—the honour to—

'To know us,' said the first gentleman. 'The loss has been ours, Mrs Nickleby. Has the loss been ours, Pyke?'

'It has, Pluck,' answered the other gentleman.

'We have regretted it very often, I believe, Pyke?' said the first gentleman.

'Very often, Pluck,' answered the second.

'But now,' said the first gentleman, 'now we have the happiness we have pined and languished for. Have we pined and languished for this happiness, Pyke, or have we not?'

'You know we have, Pluck,' said Pyke, reproachfully.

'You hear him, ma'am?' said Mr. Pluck, looking round; 'you hear the unimpeachable testimony of my friend Pyke—that reminds me,—formalities, formalities, must not be neglected in civilised society. Pyke—Mrs Nickleby.'

Mr. Pyke laid his hand upon his heart, and bowed low.

'Whether I shall introduce myself with the same formality,' said Mr. Pluck—'whether I shall say myself that my name is Pluck, or whether I shall ask my friend Pyke (who being now regularly introduced, is competent to the office) to state for me, Mrs. Nickleby, that my name is Pluck; whether I shall claim your acquaintance on the plain ground of the strong interest I take in your welfare, or whether I shall make myself known to you as the friend of Sir Mulberry Hawk—these, Mrs. Nickleby, are considerations which I leave to you to determine.'

'Any friend of Sir Mulberry Hawk's requires no better introduction to me,' observed Mrs. Nickleby, graciously.

'It is delightful to hear you say so,' said Mr. Pluck, drawing a chair close to Mrs. Nickleby, and sitting himself down. 'It is refreshing to know that you hold my excellent friend, Sir Mulberry, in such high esteem. A word in your ear, Mrs. Nickleby. When Sir Mulberry knows it, he will be a happy man—I say, Mrs. Nickleby, a happy man. Pyke, be seated.'

'My good opinion,' said Mrs. Nickleby, and the poor lady exulted in the idea that she was marvellously sly,—'my good opinion can be of very little consequence to a gentleman like Sir Mulberry.'

'Of little consequence!' exclaimed Mr. Pluck. 'Pyke, of what consequence to our friend, Sir Mulberry, is the good opinion of Mrs. Nickleby?'

'Of what consequence?' echoed Pyke.

'Ay,' repeated Pluck; 'is it of the greatest consequence?'

'Of the very greatest consequence,' replied Pyke.

'Mrs. Nickleby cannot be ignorant,' said Mr. Pluck, 'of the immense impression which that sweet girl has—'

'Pluck!' said his friend, 'beware!'

'Pyke is right,' muttered Mr. Pluck, after a short pause; 'I was not to mention it. Pyke is very right. Thank you, Pyke.'

'Well now, really,' thought Mrs. Nickleby within herself. 'Such delicacy as that, I never saw!'

Mr. Pluck, after feigning to be in a condition of great embarrassment for some minutes, resumed the conversation by entreating Mrs. Nickleby to take no heed of what he had inadvertently said—to consider him imprudent, rash, injudicious. The only stipulation he would make in his own favour was, that she should give him credit for the best intentions.

'But when,' said Mr. Pluck, 'when I see so much sweetness and beauty on the one hand, and so much ardour and devotion on the other, I—pardon me, Pyke, I didn't intend to resume that theme. Change the subject, Pyke.'

'We promised Sir Mulberry and Lord Frederick,' said Pyke, 'that we'd call this morning and inquire whether you took any cold last night.'

'Not the least in the world last night, sir,' replied Mrs. Nickleby, 'with many thanks to his lordship and Sir Mulberry for doing me the honour to inquire; not the least—which is the more singular, as I really am very subject to colds, indeed—very subject. I had a cold once,' said Mrs. Nickleby, 'I think it was in the year eighteen hundred and seventeen; let me see, four and five are nine, and—yes, eighteen hundred and seventeen, that I thought I never should get rid of; actually and seriously, that I thought I never should get rid of. I was only cured at last by a remedy that I don't know whether you ever happened to hear of, Mr. Pluck. You have a gallon of water as hot as you can possibly bear it, with a pound of salt, and sixpen'orth of the finest bran, and sit with your head in it for twenty minutes every night just before going to bed; at least, I don't mean your head—your feet. It's a most extraordinary cure—a most extraordinary cure. I used it for the first time, I recollect, the day after Christmas Day, and by the middle of April following the cold was gone. It seems quite a miracle when you come to think of it, for I had it ever since the beginning of September.'

'What an afflicting calamity!' said Mr. Pyke.

'Perfectly horrid!' exclaimed Mr. Pluck.

'But it's worth the pain of hearing, only to know that Mrs. Nickleby recovered it, isn't it, Pluck?' cried Mr. Pyke.

'That is the circumstance which gives it such a thrilling interest,' replied Mr. Pluck.

'But come,' said Pyke, as if suddenly recollecting himself; 'we must not forget our mission in the pleasure of this interview. We come on a mission, Mrs. Nickleby.'

'On a mission,' exclaimed that good lady, to whose mind a definite proposal of marriage for Kate at once presented itself in lively colours.

'From Sir Mulberry,' replied Pyke. 'You must be very dull here.'

'Rather dull, I confess,' said Mrs. Nickleby.

'We bring the compliments of Sir Mulberry Hawk, and a thousand entreaties that you'll take a seat in a private box at the play tonight,' said Mr Pluck.

'Oh dear!' said Mrs. Nickleby, 'I never go out at all, never.'

'And that is the very reason, my dear Mrs. Nickleby, why you should go out tonight,' retorted Mr. Pluck. 'Pyke, entreat Mrs. Nickleby.'

'Oh, pray do,' said Pyke.

'You positively must,' urged Pluck.

'You are very kind,' said Mrs. Nickleby, hesitating; 'but—'

'There's not a but in the case, my dear Mrs. Nickleby,' remonstrated Mr Pluck; 'not such a word in the vocabulary. Your brother-in-law joins us, Lord Frederick joins us, Sir Mulberry joins us, Pyke joins us—a refusal is out of the question. Sir Mulberry sends a carriage for you—twenty minutes before seven to the moment—you'll not be so cruel as to disappoint the whole party, Mrs. Nickleby?'

'You are so very pressing, that I scarcely know what to say,' replied the worthy lady.

'Say nothing; not a word, not a word, my dearest madam,' urged Mr. Pluck. 'Mrs. Nickleby,' said that excellent gentleman, lowering his voice, 'there is the most trifling, the most excusable breach of confidence in what I am about to say; and yet if my friend Pyke there overheard it—such is that man's delicate sense of honour, Mrs. Nickleby—he'd have me out before dinner-time.'

Mrs. Nickleby cast an apprehensive glance at the warlike Pyke, who had walked to the window; and Mr. Pluck, squeezing her hand, went on:

'Your daughter has made a conquest—a conquest on which I may congratulate you. Sir

Mulberry, my dear ma'am, Sir Mulberry is her devoted slave. Hem!'

'Hah!' cried Mr. Pyke at this juncture, snatching something from the chimney-piece with a theatrical air. 'What is this! what do I behold!'

'What do you behold, my dear fellow?' asked Mr. Pluck.

'It is the face, the countenance, the expression,' cried Mr. Pyke, falling into his chair with a miniature in his hand; 'feebly portrayed, imperfectly caught, but still the face, the countenance, the expression.'

'I recognise it at this distance!' exclaimed Mr. Pluck in a fit of enthusiasm. 'Is it not, my dear madam, the faint similitude of—'

'It is my daughter's portrait,' said Mrs. Nickleby, with great pride. And so it was. And little Miss La Creevy had brought it home for inspection only two nights before.

Mr. Pyke no sooner ascertained that he was quite right in his conjecture, than he launched into the most extravagant encomiums of the divine original; and in the warmth of his enthusiasm kissed the picture a thousand times, while Mr. Pluck pressed Mrs. Nickleby's hand to his heart, and congratulated her on the possession of such a daughter, with so much earnestness and affection, that the tears stood, or seemed to stand, in his eyes. Poor Mrs. Nickleby, who had listened in a state of enviable complacency at first, became at length quite overpowered by these tokens of regard for, and attachment to, the family; and even the servant girl, who had peeped in at the door, remained rooted to the spot in astonishment at the ecstasies of the two friendly visitors.

By degrees these raptures subsided, and Mrs. Nickleby went on to entertain her guests with a lament over her fallen fortunes, and a picturesque account of her old house in the country: comprising a full description of the different apartments, not forgetting the little store-room, and a lively recollection of how many steps you went down to get into the garden, and which way you turned when you came out at the parlour door, and what capital fixtures there were in the kitchen. This last reflection naturally conducted her into the wash-house, where she stumbled upon the brewing utensils, among which she might have wandered for an hour, if the mere mention of those implements had not, by an association of ideas, instantly reminded Mr. Pyke that he was 'amazing thirsty.'

'And I'll tell you what,' said Mr. Pyke; 'if you'll send round to the public-house for a pot of milk half-and-half, positively and actually I'll drink it.'

And positively and actually Mr. Pyke did drink it, and Mr. Pluck helped him, while Mrs. Nickleby looked on in divided admiration of the condescension of the two, and the aptitude with which they accommodated themselves to the pewter-pot; in explanation of which seeming marvel it may be here observed, that gentlemen who, like Messrs Pyke and Pluck, live upon their wits (or not so much, perhaps, upon the presence of their own wits as upon the absence of wits in other people) are occasionally reduced to very narrow shifts and straits, and are at such periods accustomed to regale themselves in a very simple and primitive manner.

'At twenty minutes before seven, then,' said Mr. Pyke, rising, 'the coach will be here. One more look—one little look—at that sweet face. Ah! here it is. Unmoved, unchanged!' This, by the way, was a very remarkable circumstance, miniatures being liable to so many changes of expression—'Oh, Pluck! Pluck!'

Mr. Pluck made no other reply than kissing Mrs. Nickleby's hand with a great show of feeling and attachment; Mr. Pyke having done the same, both gentlemen hastily withdrew.

Mrs. Nickleby was commonly in the habit of giving herself credit for a pretty tolerable share of penetration and acuteness, but she had never felt so satisfied with her own sharp-sightedness as she did that day. She had found it all out the night before. She had never seen Sir Mulberry and Kate together—never even heard Sir Mulberry's name—and yet hadn't she said to herself from the very first, that she saw how the case stood? and what a triumph it was, for there was now no doubt about it. If these flattering attentions to herself were not sufficient proofs, Sir Mulberry's confidential friend had suffered the secret to escape him in so many words. 'I am quite in love with that dear Mr. Pluck, I declare I am,' said Mrs. Nickleby.

There was one great source of uneasiness in the midst of this good fortune, and that was the having nobody by, to whom she could confide it. Once or twice she almost resolved to walk straight to Miss La Creevy's and tell it all to her. 'But I don't know,' thought Mrs. Nickleby; 'she is a very worthy person, but I am afraid too much beneath Sir Mulberry's station for us to make a companion of. Poor thing!' Acting upon this grave consideration she rejected the idea of taking the little portrait painter into her confidence, and contented herself with holding out sundry vague and mysterious hopes of preferment to the servant girl, who received these obscure hints of dawning greatness with much veneration and respect.

Punctual to its time came the promised vehicle, which was no hackney coach, but a private chariot, having behind it a footman, whose legs, although somewhat large for his body, might, as mere abstract legs, have set themselves up for models at the Royal Academy. It was quite exhilarating to hear the clash and bustle with which he banged the door and jumped up behind after Mrs. Nickleby was in; and as that good lady was perfectly unconscious that he applied the gold-headed end of his long stick to his nose, and so telegraphed most disrespectfully to the coachman over her very head, she sat in a state of much stiffness and dignity, not a little proud of her position.

At the theatre entrance there was more banging and more bustle, and there were also Messrs Pyke and Pluck waiting to escort her to her box; and so polite were they, that Mr. Pyke threatened with many oaths to 'smifligate' a very old man with a lantern who accidentally stumbled in her way—to the great terror of Mrs. Nickleby, who, conjecturing more from Mr. Pyke's excitement than any previous acquaintance with the etymology of the word that smifligation and bloodshed must be in the main one and the same thing, was alarmed beyond expression, lest something should occur. Fortunately, however, Mr. Pyke confined himself to mere verbal smifligation, and they reached their box with no more serious interruption by the way, than a desire on the part of the same pugnacious gentleman to 'smash' the assistant box-keeper for happening to mistake the number.

Mrs. Nickleby had scarcely been put away behind the curtain of the box in an armchair, when Sir Mulberry and Lord Verisopht arrived, arrayed from the crowns of their heads to the tips of their gloves, and from the tips of their gloves to the toes of their boots, in the most elegant and costly manner. Sir Mulberry was a little hoarser than on the previous day, and Lord Verisopht looked rather sleepy and queer; from which tokens, as well as from the circumstance of their both being to a trifling extent unsteady upon their legs, Mrs. Nickleby justly concluded that they had taken dinner.

'We have been—we have been—toasting your lovely daughter, Mrs Nickleby,' whispered Sir Mulberry, sitting down behind her.

'Oh, ho!' thought that knowing lady; 'wine in, truth out.—You are very kind, Sir Mulberry.'

'No, no upon my soul!' replied Sir Mulberry Hawk. 'It's you that's kind, upon my soul it is. It was so kind of you to come tonight.'

'So very kind of you to invite me, you mean, Sir Mulberry,' replied Mrs Nickleby, tossing her head, and looking prodigiously sly.

'I am so anxious to know you, so anxious to cultivate your good opinion, so desirous that there should be a delicious kind of harmonious family understanding between us,' said Sir Mulberry, 'that you mustn't think I'm disinterested in what I do. I'm infernal selfish; I am—upon my soul I am.'

'I am sure you can't be selfish, Sir Mulberry!' replied Mrs. Nickleby. 'You have much too open and generous a countenance for that.'

'What an extraordinary observer you are!' said Sir Mulberry Hawk.

'Oh no, indeed, I don't see very far into things, Sir Mulberry,' replied Mrs. Nickleby, in a tone of voice which left the baronet to infer that she saw very far indeed.

'I am quite afraid of you,' said the baronet. 'Upon my soul,' repeated Sir Mulberry, looking round to his companions; 'I am afraid of Mrs. Nickleby. She is so immensely sharp.'

Messrs Pyke and Pluck shook their heads mysteriously, and observed together that they had found that out long ago; upon which Mrs. Nickleby tittered, and Sir Mulberry laughed, and Pyke and Pluck roared.

'But where's my brother-in-law, Sir Mulberry?' inquired Mrs. Nickleby. 'I shouldn't be here without him. I hope he's coming.'

'Pyke,' said Sir Mulberry, taking out his toothpick and lolling back in his chair, as if he were too lazy to invent a reply to this question. 'Where's Ralph Nickleby?'

'Pluck,' said Pyke, imitating the baronet's action, and turning the lie over to his friend, 'where's Ralph Nickleby?'

Mr. Pluck was about to return some evasive reply, when the hustle caused by a party entering the next box seemed to attract the attention of all four gentlemen, who exchanged glances of much meaning. The new party beginning to converse together, Sir Mulberry suddenly assumed the character of a most attentive listener, and implored his friends not to breathe—not to breathe.

'Why not?' said Mrs. Nickleby. 'What is the matter?'

'Hush!' replied Sir Mulberry, laying his hand on her arm. 'Lord Frederick, do you recognise the tones of that voice?'

'Deyvle take me if I didn't think it was the voice of Miss Nickleby.'

'Lor, my lord!' cried Miss Nickleby's mama, thrusting her head round the curtain. 'Why actually—Kate, my dear, Kate.'

'You here, mama! Is it possible!'

'Possible, my dear? Yes.'

'Why who—who on earth is that you have with you, mama?' said Kate, shrinking back as she caught sight of a man smiling and kissing his hand.

'Who do you suppose, my dear?' replied Mrs. Nickleby, bending towards Mrs Wititterly, and speaking a little louder for that lady's edification. 'There's Mr. Pyke, Mr. Pluck, Sir Mulberry Hawk, and Lord Frederick Verisopht.'

'Gracious Heaven!' thought Kate hurriedly. 'How comes she in such society?'

Now, Kate thought thus so hurriedly, and the surprise was so great, and moreover brought back so forcibly the recollection of what had passed at Ralph's delectable dinner, that she turned extremely pale and appeared greatly agitated, which symptoms being observed by Mrs. Nickleby, were at once set down by that acute lady as being caused and occasioned by violent love. But, although she was in no small degree delighted by this discovery, which reflected so much credit on her own quickness of perception, it did not lessen her motherly anxiety in Kate's behalf; and accordingly, with a vast quantity of trepidation, she quitted her own box to hasten into that of Mrs. Wititterly. Mrs. Wititterly, keenly alive to the glory of having a lord and a baronet among her visiting acquaintance, lost no time in signing to Mr. Wititterly to open the door, and thus it was that in less than thirty seconds Mrs. Nickleby's party had made an irruption into Mrs. Wititterly's box, which it filled to the very door, there being in fact only room for Messrs Pyke and Pluck to get in their heads and waistcoats.

'My dear Kate,' said Mrs. Nickleby, kissing her daughter affectionately. 'How ill you looked a moment ago! You quite frightened me, I declare!'

'It was mere fancy, mama,—the—the—reflection of the lights perhaps,' replied Kate, glancing nervously round, and finding it impossible to whisper any caution or explanation.

'Don't you see Sir Mulberry Hawk, my dear?'

Kate bowed slightly, and biting her lip turned her head towards the stage.

But Sir Mulberry Hawk was not to be so easily repulsed, for he advanced with extended hand; and Mrs. Nickleby officiously informing Kate of this circumstance, she was obliged to extend her own. Sir Mulberry detained it while he murmured a profusion of compliments, which Kate, remembering what had passed between them, rightly considered as so many aggravations of the insult he had already put upon her. Then followed the recognition of Lord Verisopht, and then the greeting of Mr. Pyke, and then that of Mr. Pluck, and finally, to complete the young lady's mortification, she was compelled at Mrs. Wititterly's request to perform the ceremony of introducing the odious persons, whom she regarded with the utmost indignation and abhorrence.

'Mrs. Wititterly is delighted,' said Mr. Wititterly, rubbing his hands; 'delighted, my lord, I am sure, with this opportunity of contracting an acquaintance which, I trust, my lord, we shall improve. Julia, my dear, you must not allow yourself to be too much excited, you must not. Indeed you must not. Mrs. Wititterly is of a most excitable nature, Sir Mulberry. The snuff of a candle, the wick of a lamp, the bloom on a peach, the down on a butterfly. You might blow her away, my lord; you might blow her away.'

Sir Mulberry seemed to think that it would be a great convenience if the lady could be blown away. He said, however, that the delight was mutual, and Lord Verisopht added that it was mutual, whereupon Messrs Pyke and Pluck were heard to murmur from the distance that it was very mutual indeed.

'I take an interest, my lord,' said Mrs. Wititterly, with a faint smile, 'such an interest in the drama.'

'Ye—es. It's very interesting,' replied Lord Verisopht.

'I'm always ill after Shakespeare,' said Mrs. Wititterly. 'I scarcely exist the next day; I find the reaction so very great after a tragedy, my lord, and Shakespeare is such a delicious creature.'

'Ye—es!' replied Lord Verisopht. 'He was a clayver man.'

'Do you know, my lord,' said Mrs. Wititterly, after a long silence, 'I find I take so much more interest in his plays, after having been to that dear little dull house he was born in! Were you ever there, my lord?'

'No, nayver,' replied Verisopht.

'Then really you ought to go, my lord,' returned Mrs. Wititterly, in very languid and drawling accents. 'I don't know how it is, but after you've seen the place and written your name in the little book, somehow or other you seem to be inspired; it kindles up quite a fire within one.'

'Ye—es!' replied Lord Verisopht, 'I shall certainly go there.'

'Julia, my life,' interposed Mr. Wititterly, 'you are deceiving his lordship—unintentionally, my lord, she is deceiving you. It is your poetical temperament, my dear—your ethereal soul—your fervid imagination, which throws you into a glow of genius and excitement. There is nothing in the place, my dear—nothing, nothing.'

'I think there must be something in the place,' said Mrs. Nickleby, who had been listening in silence; 'for, soon after I was married, I went to Stratford with my poor dear Mr. Nickleby, in a post-chaise from Birmingham—was it a post-chaise though?' said Mrs. Nickleby, considering; 'yes, it must have been a post-chaise, because I recollect remarking at the time that the driver had a green shade over his left eye;—in a post-chaise from Birmingham, and after we had seen Shakespeare's tomb and birthplace, we went back to the inn there, where we slept that night, and I recollect that all night long I dreamt of nothing but a black gentleman, at full length, in plaster-of-Paris, with a lay-down collar tied with two tassels, leaning against a post and thinking; and when I woke in the morning and described him to Mr. Nickleby, he said it was Shakespeare just as he had been when he was alive, which was very curious indeed. Stratford—Stratford,' continued Mrs. Nickleby, considering. 'Yes, I am positive about that, because I recollect I was in the family way with my son Nicholas at the time, and I had been very much frightened by an Italian image boy that very morning. In fact, it was quite a mercy, ma'am,' added Mrs. Nickleby, in a whisper to Mrs. Wititterly, 'that my son didn't turn out to be a Shakespeare, and what a dreadful thing that would have been!'

When Mrs. Nickleby had brought this interesting anecdote to a close, Pyke and Pluck, ever zealous in their patron's cause, proposed the adjournment of a detachment of the party into the next box; and with so much skill were the preliminaries adjusted, that Kate, despite all she could say or do to the contrary, had no alternative but to suffer herself to be led away by Sir Mulberry Hawk. Her mother and Mr. Pluck accompanied them, but the worthy lady, pluming herself upon her discretion, took particular care not so much as to look at her daughter during the whole evening, and to seem wholly absorbed in the jokes and conversation of Mr. Pluck, who, having been appointed sentry over Mrs. Nickleby for that especial purpose, neglected, on his side, no possible opportunity of engrossing her attention.

Lord Frederick Verisopht remained in the next box to be talked to by Mrs Wititterly, and Mr. Pyke was in attendance to throw in a word or two when necessary. As to Mr. Wititterly, he was sufficiently busy in the body of the house, informing such of his friends and acquaintance as happened to be there, that those two gentlemen upstairs, whom they had seen in conversation with Mrs. W., were the distinguished Lord Frederick Verisopht and his most intimate friend, the gay Sir Mulberry Hawk—a communication which inflamed several respectable house-keepers with the utmost jealousy and rage, and reduced sixteen unmarried daughters to the very brink of despair.

The evening came to an end at last, but Kate had yet to be handed downstairs by the detested Sir Mulberry; and so skilfully were the manoeuvres of Messrs Pyke and Pluck conducted, that she and the baronet were the last of the party, and were even—without an appearance of effort or design—left at some little distance behind.

'Don't hurry, don't hurry,' said Sir Mulberry, as Kate hastened on, and attempted to release her arm.

She made no reply, but still pressed forward.

'Nay, then—' coolly observed Sir Mulberry, stopping her outright.

'You had best not seek to detain me, sir!' said Kate, angrily.

'And why not?' retorted Sir Mulberry. 'My dear creature, now why do you keep up this show of displeasure?'

'Show!' repeated Kate, indignantly. 'How dare you presume to speak to me, sir—to address me—to come into my presence?'

'You look prettier in a passion, Miss Nickleby,' said Sir Mulberry Hawk, stooping down, the better to see her face.

'I hold you in the bitterest detestation and contempt, sir,' said Kate. 'If you find any attraction in looks of disgust and aversion, you—let me rejoin my friends, sir, instantly. Whatever considerations may have withheld me thus far, I will disregard them all, and take a course that even you might feel, if you do not immediately suffer me to proceed.'

Sir Mulberry smiled, and still looking in her face and retaining her arm, walked towards the door.

'If no regard for my sex or helpless situation will induce you to desist from this coarse and unmanly persecution,' said Kate, scarcely knowing, in the tumult of her passions, what she said,—'I have a brother who will resent it dearly, one day.'

'Upon my soul!' exclaimed Sir Mulberry, as though quietly communing with himself; passing his arm round her waist as he spoke, 'she looks more beautiful, and I like her better in this mood, than when her eyes are cast down, and she is in perfect repose!'

How Kate reached the lobby where her friends were waiting she never knew, but she hurried across it without at all regarding them, and disengaged herself suddenly from her companion, sprang into the coach, and throwing herself into its darkest corner burst into tears.

Messrs Pyke and Pluck, knowing their cue, at once threw the party into great commotion by shouting for the carriages, and getting up a violent quarrel with sundry inoffensive bystanders; in the midst of which tumult they put the affrighted Mrs. Nickleby in her chariot, and having got her safely off, turned their thoughts to Mrs. Wititterly, whose attention also they had now effectually distracted from the young lady, by throwing her into a state of the utmost bewilderment and consternation. At length, the conveyance in which she had come rolled off too with its load, and the four worthies, being left alone under the portico, enjoyed a hearty laugh together.

'There,' said Sir Mulberry, turning to his noble friend. 'Didn't I tell you last night that if we could find where they were going by bribing a servant through my fellow, and then established ourselves close by with the mother, these people's honour would be our own? Why here it is, done in four-and-twenty hours.'

'Ye—es,' replied the dupe. 'But I have been tied to the old woman all ni-ight.'

'Hear him,' said Sir Mulberry, turning to his two friends. 'Hear this discontented grumbler. Isn't it enough to make a man swear never to help him in his plots and schemes again? Isn't it an infernal shame?'

Pyke asked Pluck whether it was not an infernal shame, and Pluck asked Pyke; but neither answered.

'Isn't it the truth?' demanded Verisopht. 'Wasn't it so?'

'Wasn't it so!' repeated Sir Mulberry. 'How would you have had it? How could we have got a general invitation at first sight—come when you like, go when you like, stop as long as you like, do what you like—if you, the lord, had not made yourself agreeable to the foolish mistress of the house? Do I care for this girl, except as your friend? Haven't I been sounding your praises in her ears, and bearing her pretty sulks and peevishness all night for you? What sort of stuff do you think I'm made of? Would I do this for every man? Don't I deserve even gratitude in return?'

'You're a deyvlish good fellow,' said the poor young lord, taking his friend's arm. 'Upon my life you're a deyvlish good fellow, Hawk.'

'And I have done right, have I?' demanded Sir Mulberry.

'Quite ri-ght.'

'And like a poor, silly, good-natured, friendly dog as I am, eh?'

'Ye—es, ye—es; like a friend,' replied the other.

'Well then,' replied Sir Mulberry, 'I'm satisfied. And now let's go and have our revenge on the German baron and the Frenchman, who cleaned you out so handsomely last night.'

With these words the friendly creature took his companion's arm and led him away, turning half round as he did so, and bestowing a wink and a contemptuous smile on Messrs Pyke and Pluck, who, cramming their handkerchiefs into their mouths to denote their silent enjoyment of the whole proceedings, followed their patron and his victim at a little distance.

CHAPTER 28

Miss Nickleby, rendered desperate by the Persecution of Sir Mulberry Hawk, and the Complicated Difficulties and Distresses which surround her, appeals, as a last resource, to her Uncle for Protection

The ensuing morning brought reflection with it, as morning usually does; but widely different was the train of thought it awakened in the different persons who had been so unexpectedly brought together on the preceding evening, by the active agency of Messrs Pyke and Pluck.

The reflections of Sir Mulberry Hawk—if such a term can be applied to the thoughts of the systematic and calculating man of dissipation, whose joys, regrets, pains, and pleasures, are all of self, and who would seem to retain nothing of the intellectual faculty but the power to debase himself, and to degrade the very nature whose outward semblance he wears—the reflections of Sir Mulberry Hawk turned upon Kate Nickleby, and were, in brief, that she was undoubtedly handsome; that her coyness must be easily conquerable by a man of his address and experience, and that the pursuit was one which could not fail to redound to his credit, and greatly to enhance his reputation with the world. And lest this last consideration—no mean or secondary one with Sir Mulberry—should sound strangely in the ears of some, let it be remembered that most men live in a world of their own, and that in that limited circle alone are they ambitious for distinction and applause. Sir Mulberry's world was peopled with profligates, and he acted accordingly.

Thus, cases of injustice, and oppression, and tyranny, and the most extravagant bigotry, are in constant occurrence among us every day. It is the custom to trumpet forth much wonder and astonishment at the chief actors therein setting at defiance so completely the opinion of the world; but there is no greater fallacy; it is precisely because they do consult the opinion of their own little world that such things take place at all, and strike the great world dumb with amazement.

The reflections of Mrs. Nickleby were of the proudest and most complacent kind; and under the influence of her very agreeable delusion she straightway sat down and indited a long letter to Kate, in which she expressed her entire approval of the admirable choice she had made, and extolled Sir Mulberry to the skies; asserting, for the more complete satisfaction of her daughter's feelings, that he was precisely the individual whom she (Mrs. Nickleby) would have chosen for her son-in-law, if she had had the picking and choosing from all mankind. The good lady then, with the preliminary observation that she might be fairly supposed not to have lived in the world so long without knowing its ways, communicated a great many subtle precepts applicable to the state of courtship, and confirmed in their wisdom by her own personal experience. Above all things she commended a strict maidenly reserve, as being not only a very laudable thing in itself, but as tending materially to strengthen and increase a lover's ardour. 'And I never,' added Mrs Nickleby, 'was more delighted in my life than to observe last night, my dear, that your good sense had already told you this.' With which sentiment, and various hints of the pleasure she derived from the knowledge that her daughter inherited so large an instalment of her own excellent sense and discretion (to nearly the full measure of which she might hope, with care, to succeed in time), Mrs. Nickleby concluded a very long and rather illegible letter.

Poor Kate was well-nigh distracted on the receipt of four closely-written and closely-crossed sides of congratulation on the very subject which had prevented her closing her eyes all night, and kept her weeping and watching in her chamber; still worse and more trying was the necessity of rendering herself agreeable to Mrs. Wititterly, who, being in low spirits after the fatigue of the preceding night, of course expected her companion (else wherefore had she board and salary?) to be in the best spirits possible. As to Mr. Wititterly, he went about all day in a tremor of delight at having shaken hands with a lord, and having actually asked him to come and see him in his own house. The lord himself, not being troubled to any inconvenient extent with the power of thinking, regaled himself with the conversation of Messrs Pyke and Pluck, who sharpened their wit by a plentiful indulgence in various costly stimulants at his expense.

It was four in the afternoon—that is, the vulgar afternoon of the sun and the clock—and Mrs. Wititterly reclined, according to custom, on the drawing-room sofa, while Kate read aloud a new novel in three volumes, entitled 'The Lady Flabella,' which Alphonse the doubtful had procured from the library that very morning. And it was a production admirably suited to a lady labouring under Mrs. Wititterly's complaint, seeing that there was not a line in it, from beginning to end, which could, by the most remote contingency, awaken the smallest excitement in any person breathing.

Kate read on.

"'Cherizette,' said the Lady Flabella, inserting her mouse-like feet in the blue satin slippers, which had unwittingly occasioned the half-playful half-angry altercation between herself and the youthful Colonel Befillaire, in the Duke of Mincefenille's Salon De Danse on the previous night. "Cherizette, Ma Chere, Donnez-Moi De L'eau-De-Cologne, S'il Vous Plait, Mon Enfant."

"'Mercie—thank you,' said the Lady Flabella, as the lively but devoted Cherizette plentifully besprinkled with the fragrant compound the Lady Flabella's MOUCHOIR of finest cambric, edged with richest lace, and emblazoned at the four corners with the Flabella crest, and gorgeous heraldic bearings of that noble family. "Mercie—that will do."

'At this instant, while the Lady Flabella yet inhaled that delicious fragrance by holding the mouchoir to her exquisite, but thoughtfully-chiselled nose, the door of the boudoir (artfully concealed by rich hangings of silken damask, the hue of Italy's firmament) was thrown open, and with noiseless tread two valets-de-chambre, clad in sumptuous liveries of peach-blossom and gold, advanced into the room followed by a page in bas de soie—silk stockings—who, while they remained at some distance making the most graceful obeisances, advanced to the feet of his lovely mistress, and dropping on one knee presented, on a golden salver gorgeously chased, a scented billet.

'The Lady Flabella, with an agitation she could not repress, hastily tore off the envelope and broke the scented seal. It was from Befillaire—the young, the slim, the low-voiced—her own Befillaire.'

'Oh, charming!' interrupted Kate's patroness, who was sometimes taken literary. 'Poetic, really. Read that description again, Miss Nickleby.'

Kate complied.

'Sweet, indeed!' said Mrs. Wititterly, with a sigh. 'So voluptuous, is it not—so soft?'

'Yes, I think it is,' replied Kate, gently; 'very soft.'

'Close the book, Miss Nickleby,' said Mrs. Wititterly. 'I can hear nothing more today; I should be sorry to disturb the impression of that sweet description. Close the book.'

Kate complied, not unwillingly; and, as she did so, Mrs. Wititterly raising her glass with a languid hand, remarked, that she looked pale.

'It was the fright of that—that noise and confusion last night,' said Kate.

'How very odd!' exclaimed Mrs. Wititterly, with a look of surprise. And certainly, when one comes to think of it, it was very odd that anything should have disturbed a companion. A steam-engine, or other ingenious piece of mechanism out of order, would have been nothing to it.

'How did you come to know Lord Frederick, and those other delightful creatures, child?' asked Mrs. Wititterly, still eyeing Kate through her glass.

'I met them at my uncle's,' said Kate, vexed to feel that she was colouring deeply, but unable to keep down the blood which rushed to her face whenever she thought of that man.

'Have you known them long?'

'No,' rejoined Kate. 'Not long.'

'I was very glad of the opportunity which that respectable person, your mother, gave us of being known to them,' said Mrs. Wititterly, in a lofty manner. 'Some friends of ours were on the very point of introducing us, which makes it quite remarkable.'

This was said lest Miss Nickleby should grow conceited on the honour and dignity of having known four great people (for Pyke and Pluck were included among the delightful creatures), whom Mrs. Wititterly did not know. But as the circumstance had made no impression one way or other upon Kate's mind, the force of the observation was quite lost upon her.

'They asked permission to call,' said Mrs. Wititterly. 'I gave it them of course.'

'Do you expect them today?' Kate ventured to inquire.

Mrs. Wititterly's answer was lost in the noise of a tremendous rapping at the street-door, and before it had ceased to vibrate, there drove up a handsome cabriolet, out of which leaped Sir Mulberry Hawk and his friend Lord Verisopht.

'They are here now,' said Kate, rising and hurrying away.

'Miss Nickleby!' cried Mrs. Wititterly, perfectly aghast at a companion's attempting to quit the room, without her permission first had and obtained. 'Pray don't think of going.'

'You are very good!' replied Kate. 'But—'

'For goodness' sake, don't agitate me by making me speak so much,' said Mrs. Wititterly, with great sharpness. 'Dear me, Miss Nickleby, I beg—'

It was in vain for Kate to protest that she was unwell, for the footsteps of the knockers, whoever they were, were already on the stairs. She resumed her seat, and had scarcely done so, when the doubtful page darted into the room and announced, Mr. Pyke, and Mr. Pluck, and

Lord Verisopht, and Sir Mulberry Hawk, all at one burst.

'The most extraordinary thing in the world,' said Mr. Pluck, saluting both ladies with the utmost cordiality; 'the most extraordinary thing. As Lord Frederick and Sir Mulberry drove up to the door, Pyke and I had that instant knocked.'

'That instant knocked,' said Pyke.

'No matter how you came, so that you are here,' said Mrs. Wititterly, who, by dint of lying on the same sofa for three years and a half, had got up quite a little pantomime of graceful attitudes, and now threw herself into the most striking of the whole series, to astonish the visitors. 'I am delighted, I am sure.'

'And how is Miss Nickleby?' said Sir Mulberry Hawk, accosting Kate, in a low voice— not so low, however, but that it reached the ears of Mrs Wititterly.

'Why, she complains of suffering from the fright of last night,' said the lady. 'I am sure I don't wonder at it, for my nerves are quite torn to pieces.'

'And yet you look,' observed Sir Mulberry, turning round; 'and yet you look—'

'Beyond everything,' said Mr. Pyke, coming to his patron's assistance. Of course Mr. Pluck said the same.

'I am afraid Sir Mulberry is a flatterer, my lord,' said Mrs. Wititterly, turning to that young gentleman, who had been sucking the head of his cane in silence, and staring at Kate.

'Oh, deyvlish!' replied Verisopht. Having given utterance to which remarkable sentiment, he occupied himself as before.

'Neither does Miss Nickleby look the worse,' said Sir Mulberry, bending his bold gaze upon her. 'She was always handsome, but upon my soul, ma'am, you seem to have imparted some of your own good looks to her besides.'

To judge from the glow which suffused the poor girl's countenance after this speech, Mrs. Wititterly might, with some show of reason, have been supposed to have imparted to it some of that artificial bloom which decorated her own. Mrs. Wititterly admitted, though not with the best grace in the world, that Kate did look pretty. She began to think, too, that Sir Mulberry was not quite so agreeable a creature as she had at first supposed him; for, although a skilful flatterer is a most delightful companion if you can keep him all to yourself, his taste becomes very doubtful when he takes to complimenting other people.

'Pyke,' said the watchful Mr. Pluck, observing the effect which the praise of Miss Nickleby had produced.

'Well, Pluck,' said Pyke.

'Is there anybody,' demanded Mr. Pluck, mysteriously, 'anybody you know, that Mrs. Wititterly's profile reminds you of?'

'Reminds me of!' answered Pyke. 'Of course there is.'

'Who do you mean?' said Pluck, in the same mysterious manner. 'The D. of B.?'

'The C. of B.,' replied Pyke, with the faintest trace of a grin lingering in his countenance. 'The beautiful sister is the countess; not the duchess.'

'True,' said Pluck, 'the C. of B. The resemblance is wonderful!'

'Perfectly startling,' said Mr. Pyke.

Here was a state of things! Mrs. Wititterly was declared, upon the testimony of two veracious and competent witnesses, to be the very picture of a countess! This was one of the consequences of getting into good society. Why, she might have moved among grovelling people for twenty years, and never heard of it. How could she, indeed? what did they know about countesses?

The two gentlemen having, by the greediness with which this little bait was swallowed, tested the extent of Mrs. Wititterly's appetite for adulation, proceeded to administer that commodity in very large doses, thus affording to Sir Mulberry Hawk an opportunity of pestering Miss Nickleby with questions and remarks, to which she was absolutely obliged to make some reply. Meanwhile, Lord Verisopht enjoyed unmolested the full flavour of the gold knob at the top of his cane, as he would have done to the end of the interview if Mr. Wititterly had not come home, and caused the conversation to turn to his favourite topic.

'My lord,' said Mr. Wititterly, 'I am delighted—honoured—proud. Be seated again, my lord, pray. I am proud, indeed—most proud.'

It was to the secret annoyance of his wife that Mr. Wititterly said all this, for, although she was bursting with pride and arrogance, she would have had the illustrious guests believe that their visit was quite a common occurrence, and that they had lords and baronets to see them every day in the week. But Mr. Wititterly's feelings were beyond the power of suppression.

'It is an honour, indeed!' said Mr. Wititterly. 'Julia, my soul, you will suffer for this tomorrow.'

'Suffer!' cried Lord Verisopht.

'The reaction, my lord, the reaction,' said Mr. Wititterly. 'This violent strain upon the nervous system over, my lord, what ensues? A sinking, a depression, a lowness, a lassitude, a debility. My lord, if Sir Tumley Snuffim was to see that delicate creature at this moment, he would not give a—a—this for her life.' In illustration of which remark, Mr. Wititterly took a pinch of snuff from his box, and jerked it lightly into the air as an emblem of instability.

'Not that,' said Mr. Wititterly, looking about him with a serious countenance. 'Sir Tumley Snuffim would not give that for Mrs. Wititterly's existence.'

Mr. Wititterly told this with a kind of sober exultation, as if it were no trifling distinction for a man to have a wife in such a desperate state, and Mrs. Wititterly sighed and looked on, as if she felt the honour, but had determined to bear it as meekly as might be.

'Mrs. Wititterly,' said her husband, 'is Sir Tumley Snuffim's favourite patient. I believe I may venture to say, that Mrs. Wititterly is the first person who took the new medicine which is supposed to have destroyed a family at Kensington Gravel Pits. I believe she was. If I am wrong, Julia, my dear, you will correct me.'

'I believe I was,' said Mrs. Wititterly, in a faint voice.

As there appeared to be some doubt in the mind of his patron how he could best join in this conversation, the indefatigable Mr. Pyke threw himself into the breach, and, by way of saying something to the point, inquired—with reference to the aforesaid medicine—whether it was nice.

'No, sir, it was not. It had not even that recommendation,' said Mr. W.

'Mrs. Wititterly is quite a martyr,' observed Pyke, with a complimentary bow.

'I think I am,' said Mrs. Wititterly, smiling.

'I think you are, my dear Julia,' replied her husband, in a tone which seemed to say that he was not vain, but still must insist upon their privileges. 'If anybody, my lord,' added Mr. Wititterly, wheeling round to the nobleman, 'will produce to me a greater martyr than Mrs. Wititterly, all I can say is, that I shall be glad to see that martyr, whether male or female—that's all, my lord.'

Pyke and Pluck promptly remarked that certainly nothing could be fairer than that; and the call having been by this time protracted to a very great length, they obeyed Sir Mulberry's look, and rose to go. This brought Sir Mulberry himself and Lord Verisopht on their legs also. Many protestations of friendship, and expressions anticipative of the pleasure which must inevitably flow from so happy an acquaintance, were exchanged, and the visitors departed, with renewed assurances that at all times and seasons the mansion of the Wititterlys would be honoured by receiving them beneath its roof.

That they came at all times and seasons—that they dined there one day, supped the next, dined again on the next, and were constantly to and fro on all—that they made parties to visit public places, and met by accident at lounges—that upon all these occasions Miss Nickleby was exposed to the constant and unremitting persecution of Sir Mulberry Hawk, who now began to feel his character, even in the estimation of his two dependants, involved in the successful reduction of her pride—that she had no intervals of peace or rest, except at those hours when she could sit in her solitary room, and weep over the trials of the day—all these were consequences naturally flowing from the well-laid plans of Sir Mulberry, and their able execution by the auxiliaries, Pyke and Pluck.

And thus for a fortnight matters went on. That any but the weakest and silliest of people could have seen in one interview that Lord Verisopht, though he was a lord, and Sir Mulberry Hawk, though he was a baronet, were not persons accustomed to be the best possible companions, and were certainly not calculated by habits, manners, tastes, or conversation, to shine with any very great lustre in the society of ladies, need scarcely be remarked. But with Mrs. Wititterly the two titles were all sufficient; coarseness became humour, vulgarity softened itself down into the most charming eccentricity; insolence took the guise of an easy absence of reserve, attainable only by those who had had the good fortune to mix with high folks.

If the mistress put such a construction upon the behaviour of her new friends, what could the companion urge against them? If they accustomed themselves to very little restraint before the lady of the house, with how much more freedom could they address her paid dependent! Nor was even this the worst. As the odious Sir Mulberry Hawk attached himself to Kate with less and less of disguise, Mrs. Wititterly began to grow jealous of the superior attractions of Miss Nickleby. If this feeling had led to her banishment from the drawing-room when such company was there, Kate would have been only too happy and willing that it should have existed, but unfortunately for her she possessed that native grace and true gentility of manner, and those thousand nameless accomplishments which give to female society its greatest charm; if these be valuable anywhere, they were especially so where the lady of the house was a mere animated doll. The consequence was, that Kate had the double mortification of being an indispensable part of the circle when Sir Mulberry and his friends were there, and of being exposed, on that very account, to all Mrs. Wititterly's ill-humours and caprices when they were gone. She became utterly and completely miserable.

Mrs. Wititterly had never thrown off the mask with regard to Sir Mulberry, but when she was more than usually out of temper, attributed the circumstance, as ladies sometimes do, to nervous indisposition. However, as the dreadful idea that Lord Verisopht also was somewhat taken with Kate, and that she, Mrs. Wititterly, was quite a secondary person, dawned upon that lady's mind and gradually developed itself, she became possessed with a large quantity of highly proper and most virtuous indignation, and felt it her duty, as a married lady and a moral member of society, to mention the circumstance to 'the young person' without delay.

Accordingly Mrs. Wititterly broke ground next morning, during a pause in the novel-reading.

'Miss Nickleby,' said Mrs. Wititterly, 'I wish to speak to you very gravely. I am sorry to have to do it, upon my word I am very sorry, but you leave me no alternative, Miss Nickleby.' Here Mrs. Wititterly tossed her head—not passionately, only virtuously—and remarked, with some appearance of excitement, that she feared that palpitation of the heart was coming on again.

'Your behaviour, Miss Nickleby,' resumed the lady, 'is very far from pleasing me—very far. I am very anxious indeed that you should do well, but you may depend upon it, Miss Nickleby, you will not, if you go on as you do.'

'Ma'am!' exclaimed Kate, proudly.

'Don't agitate me by speaking in that way, Miss Nickleby, don't,' said Mrs Wititterly, with some violence, 'or you'll compel me to ring the bell.'

Kate looked at her, but said nothing.

'You needn't suppose,' resumed Mrs. Wititterly, 'that your looking at me in that way, Miss Nickleby, will prevent my saying what I am going to say, which I feel to be a religious duty. You needn't direct your glances towards me,' said Mrs. Wititterly, with a sudden burst of spite; 'I am not Sir Mulberry, no, nor Lord Frederick Verisopht, Miss Nickleby, nor am I Mr Pyke, nor Mr. Pluck either.'

Kate looked at her again, but less steadily than before; and resting her elbow on the table, covered her eyes with her hand.

'If such things had been done when I was a young girl,' said Mrs Wititterly (this, by the way, must have been some little time before), 'I don't suppose anybody would have believed it.'

'I don't think they would,' murmured Kate. 'I do not think anybody would believe, without actually knowing it, what I seem doomed to undergo!'

'Don't talk to me of being doomed to undergo, Miss Nickleby, if you please,' said Mrs. Wititterly, with a shrillness of tone quite surprising in so great an invalid. 'I will not be answered, Miss Nickleby. I am not accustomed to be answered, nor will I permit it for an instant. Do you hear?' she added, waiting with some apparent inconsistency for an answer.

'I do hear you, ma'am,' replied Kate, 'with surprise—with greater surprise than I can express.'

'I have always considered you a particularly well-behaved young person for your station in life,' said Mrs. Wititterly; 'and as you are a person of healthy appearance, and neat in your dress and so forth, I have taken an interest in you, as I do still, considering that I owe a sort of duty to that respectable old female, your mother. For these reasons, Miss Nickleby, I must tell you once for all, and begging you to mind what I say, that I must insist upon your immediately altering your very forward behaviour to the gentlemen who visit at this house. It really is not becoming,' said Mrs. Wititterly, closing her chaste eyes as she spoke; 'it is improper—quite improper.'

'Oh!' cried Kate, looking upwards and clasping her hands; 'is not this, is not this, too cruel, too hard to bear! Is it not enough that I should have suffered as I have, night and day; that I should almost have sunk in my own estimation from very shame of having been brought into contact with such people; but must I also be exposed to this unjust and most unfounded charge!'

'You will have the goodness to recollect, Miss Nickleby,' said Mrs Wititterly, 'that when you use such terms as "unjust", and "unfounded", you charge me, in effect, with stating that which is untrue.'

'I do,' said Kate with honest indignation. 'Whether you make this accusation of yourself, or at the prompting of others, is alike to me. I say it is vilely, grossly, wilfully untrue. Is it possible!' cried Kate, 'that anyone of my own sex can have sat by, and not have seen the misery these men have caused me? Is it possible that you, ma'am, can have been present, and failed to mark the insulting freedom that their every look bespoke? Is it possible that you can have avoided seeing, that these libertines, in their utter disrespect for you, and utter disregard of all gentlemanly behaviour, and almost of decency, have had but one object in introducing themselves here, and that the furtherance of their designs upon a friendless, helpless girl, who, without this humiliating confession, might have hoped to receive from one so much her senior something like womanly aid and sympathy? I do not—I cannot believe it!'

If poor Kate had possessed the slightest knowledge of the world, she certainly would not have ventured, even in the excitement into which she had been lashed, upon such an injudicious speech as this. Its effect was precisely what a more experienced observer would have foreseen. Mrs Wititterly received the attack upon her veracity with exemplary calmness, and listened with the most heroic fortitude to Kate's account of her own sufferings. But allusion being made to her being held in disregard by the gentlemen, she evinced violent emotion, and this blow was no sooner followed up by the remark concerning her seniority, than she fell back upon the sofa, uttering dismal screams.

'What is the matter?' cried Mr. Wititterly, bouncing into the room. 'Heavens, what do I see? Julia! Julia! look up, my life, look up!'

But Julia looked down most perseveringly, and screamed still louder; so Mr Wititterly rang the bell, and danced in a frenzied manner round the sofa on which Mrs. Wititterly lay; uttering perpetual cries for Sir Tumley Snuffim, and never once leaving off to ask for any explanation of the scene before him.

'Run for Sir Tumley,' cried Mr. Wititterly, menacing the page with both fists. 'I knew it, Miss Nickleby,' he said, looking round with an air of melancholy triumph, 'that society has been too much for her. This is all soul, you know, every bit of it.' With this assurance Mr.

Wititterly took up the prostrate form of Mrs. Wititterly, and carried her bodily off to bed.

Kate waited until Sir Tumley Snuffim had paid his visit and looked in with a report, that, through the special interposition of a merciful Providence (thus spake Sir Tumley), Mrs. Wititterly had gone to sleep. She then hastily attired herself for walking, and leaving word that she should return within a couple of hours, hurried away towards her uncle's house.

It had been a good day with Ralph Nickleby—quite a lucky day; and as he walked to and fro in his little back-room with his hands clasped behind him, adding up in his own mind all the sums that had been, or would be, netted from the business done since morning, his mouth was drawn into a hard stern smile; while the firmness of the lines and curves that made it up, as well as the cunning glance of his cold, bright eye, seemed to tell, that if any resolution or cunning would increase the profits, they would not fail to be excited for the purpose.

'Very good!' said Ralph, in allusion, no doubt, to some proceeding of the day. 'He defies the usurer, does he? Well, we shall see. "Honesty is the best policy," is it? We'll try that too.'

He stopped, and then walked on again.

'He is content,' said Ralph, relaxing into a smile, 'to set his known character and conduct against the power of money—dross, as he calls it. Why, what a dull blockhead this fellow must be! Dross to, dross! Who's that?'

'Me,' said Newman Noggs, looking in. 'Your niece.'

'What of her?' asked Ralph sharply.

'She's here.'

'Here!'

Newman jerked his head towards his little room, to signify that she was waiting there.

'What does she want?' asked Ralph.

'I don't know,' rejoined Newman. 'Shall I ask?' he added quickly.

'No,' replied Ralph. 'Show her in! Stay.' He hastily put away a padlocked cash-box that was on the table, and substituted in its stead an empty purse. 'There,' said Ralph. 'Now she may come in.'

Newman, with a grim smile at this manoeuvre, beckoned the young lady to advance, and having placed a chair for her, retired; looking stealthily over his shoulder at Ralph as he limped slowly out.

'Well,' said Ralph, roughly enough; but still with something more of kindness in his manner than he would have exhibited towards anybody else. 'Well, my—dear. What now?'

Kate raised her eyes, which were filled with tears; and with an effort to master her emotion strove to speak, but in vain. So drooping her head again, she remained silent. Her face was hidden from his view, but Ralph could see that she was weeping.

'I can guess the cause of this!' thought Ralph, after looking at her for some time in silence. 'I can—I can—guess the cause. Well! Well!' thought Ralph—for the moment quite disconcerted, as he watched the anguish of his beautiful niece. 'Where is the harm? only a few tears; and it's an excellent lesson for her, an excellent lesson.'

'What is the matter?' asked Ralph, drawing a chair opposite, and sitting down.

He was rather taken aback by the sudden firmness with which Kate looked up and answered him.

'The matter which brings me to you, sir,' she said, 'is one which should call the blood up into your cheeks, and make you burn to hear, as it does me to tell. I have been wronged; my feelings have been outraged, insulted, wounded past all healing, and by your friends.'

'Friends!' cried Ralph, sternly. 'I have no friends, girl.'

'By the men I saw here, then,' returned Kate, quickly. 'If they were no friends of yours, and you knew what they were,—oh, the more shame on you, uncle, for bringing me among them. To have subjected me to what I was exposed to here, through any misplaced confidence or imperfect knowledge of your guests, would have required some strong excuse; but if you did it—as I now believe you did—knowing them well, it was most dastardly and cruel.'

Ralph drew back in utter amazement at this plain speaking, and regarded Kate with the sternest look. But she met his gaze proudly and firmly, and although her face was very pale, it looked more noble and handsome, lighted up as it was, than it had ever appeared before.

'There is some of that boy's blood in you, I see,' said Ralph, speaking in his harshest tones, as something in the flashing eye reminded him of Nicholas at their last meeting.

'I hope there is!' replied Kate. 'I should be proud to know it. I am young, uncle, and all the difficulties and miseries of my situation have kept it down, but I have been roused today beyond all endurance, and come what may, I will not, as I am your brother's child, bear these insults longer.'

'What insults, girl?' demanded Ralph, sharply.

'Remember what took place here, and ask yourself,' replied Kate, colouring deeply. 'Uncle, you must—I am sure you will—release me from such vile and degrading companionship as I am exposed to now. I do not mean,' said Kate, hurrying to the old man, and laying her arm upon his shoulder; 'I do not mean to be angry and violent—I beg your pardon if I have seemed so, dear uncle,—but you do not know what I have suffered, you do not indeed. You cannot tell what the heart of a young girl is—I have no right to expect you should; but when I tell you that I am wretched, and that my heart is breaking, I am sure you will help me. I am sure, I am sure you will!'

Ralph looked at her for an instant; then turned away his head, and beat his foot nervously upon the ground.

'I have gone on day after day,' said Kate, bending over him, and timidly placing her little hand in his, 'in the hope that this persecution would cease; I have gone on day after day, compelled to assume the appearance of cheerfulness, when I was most unhappy. I have had no counsellor, no adviser, no one to protect me. Mama supposes that these are honourable men, rich and distinguished, and how can I—how can I undeceive her—when she is so happy in these little delusions, which are the only happiness she has? The lady with whom you placed me, is not the person to whom I could confide matters of so much delicacy, and I have come at last to you, the only friend I have at hand—almost the only friend I have at all—to entreat and implore you to assist me.'

'How can I assist you, child?' said Ralph, rising from his chair, and pacing up and down the room in his old attitude.

'You have influence with one of these men, I know,' rejoined Kate, emphatically. 'Would not a word from you induce them to desist from this unmanly course?'

'No,' said Ralph, suddenly turning; 'at least—that—I can't say it, if it would.'

'Can't say it!'

'No,' said Ralph, coming to a dead stop, and clasping his hands more tightly behind him. 'I can't say it.'

Kate fell back a step or two, and looked at him, as if in doubt whether she had heard aright.

'We are connected in business,' said Ralph, poising himself alternately on his toes and heels, and looking coolly in his niece's face, 'in business, and I can't afford to offend them. What is it after all? We have all our trials, and this is one of yours. Some girls would be proud to have such gallants at their feet.'

'Proud!' cried Kate.

'I don't say,' rejoined Ralph, raising his forefinger, 'but that you do right to despise them; no, you show your good sense in that, as indeed I knew from the first you would. Well. In all other respects you are comfortably bestowed. It's not much to bear. If this young lord does dog your footsteps, and whisper his drivelling inanities in your ears, what of it? It's a dishonourable passion. So be it; it won't last long. Some other novelty will spring up one day, and you will be released. In the mean time—'

'In the mean time,' interrupted Kate, with becoming pride and indignation, 'I am to be the scorn of my own sex, and the toy of the other; justly condemned by all women of right feeling, and despised by all honest and honourable men; sunken in my own esteem, and degraded in every eye that looks upon me. No, not if I work my fingers to the bone, not if I am driven to the roughest and hardest labour. Do not mistake me. I will not disgrace your recommendation. I will remain in the house in which it placed me, until I am entitled to leave it by the terms of my engagement; though, mind, I see these men no more. When I quit it, I will hide myself from them and you, and, striving to support my mother by hard service, I will live, at least, in peace, and trust in God to help me.'

With these words, she waved her hand, and quitted the room, leaving Ralph Nickleby motionless as a statue.

The surprise with which Kate, as she closed the room-door, beheld, close beside it, Newman Noggs standing bolt upright in a little niche in the wall like some scarecrow or Guy Faux laid up in winter quarters, almost occasioned her to call aloud. But, Newman laying his finger upon his lips, she had the presence of mind to refrain.

'Don't,' said Newman, gliding out of his recess, and accompanying her across the hall. 'Don't cry, don't cry.' Two very large tears, by-the-bye, were running down Newman's face as he spoke.

'I see how it is,' said poor Noggs, drawing from his pocket what seemed to be a very old duster, and wiping Kate's eyes with it, as gently as if she were an infant. 'You're giving way now. Yes, yes, very good; that's right, I like that. It was right not to give way before him. Yes, yes! Ha, ha, ha! Oh, yes. Poor thing!'

274

With these disjointed exclamations, Newman wiped his own eyes with the afore-mentioned duster, and, limping to the street-door, opened it to let her out.

'Don't cry any more,' whispered Newman. 'I shall see you soon. Ha! ha! ha! And so shall somebody else too. Yes, yes. Ho! ho!'

'God bless you,' answered Kate, hurrying out, 'God bless you.'

'Same to you,' rejoined Newman, opening the door again a little way to say so. 'Ha, ha, ha! Ho! ho! ho!'

And Newman Noggs opened the door once again to nod cheerfully, and laugh—and shut it, to shake his head mournfully, and cry.

Ralph remained in the same attitude till he heard the noise of the closing door, when he shrugged his shoulders, and after a few turns about the room—hasty at first, but gradually becoming slower, as he relapsed into himself—sat down before his desk.

It is one of those problems of human nature, which may be noted down, but not solved;—although Ralph felt no remorse at that moment for his conduct towards the innocent, true-hearted girl; although his libertine clients had done precisely what he had expected, precisely what he most wished, and precisely what would tend most to his advantage, still he hated them for doing it, from the very bottom of his soul.

'Ugh!' said Ralph, scowling round, and shaking his clenched hand as the faces of the two profligates rose up before his mind; 'you shall pay for this. Oh! you shall pay for this!'

As the usurer turned for consolation to his books and papers, a performance was going on outside his office door, which would have occasioned him no small surprise, if he could by any means have become acquainted with it.

Newman Noggs was the sole actor. He stood at a little distance from the door, with his face towards it; and with the sleeves of his coat turned back at the wrists, was occupied in bestowing the most vigorous, scientific, and straightforward blows upon the empty air.

At first sight, this would have appeared merely a wise precaution in a man of sedentary habits, with the view of opening the chest and strengthening the muscles of the arms. But the intense eagerness and joy depicted in the face of Newman Noggs, which was suffused with perspiration; the surprising energy with which he directed a constant succession of blows towards a particular panel about five feet eight from the ground, and still worked away in the most untiring and persevering manner, would have sufficiently explained to the attentive observer, that his imagination was thrashing, to within an inch of his life, his body's most active employer, Mr. Ralph Nickleby.

CHAPTER 29

Of the Proceedings of Nicholas, and certain Internal Divisions in the Company of Mr. Vincent Crummles

The unexpected success and favour with which his experiment at Portsmouth had been received, induced Mr. Crummles to prolong his stay in that town for a fortnight beyond the period he had originally assigned for the duration of his visit, during which time Nicholas personated a vast variety of characters with undiminished success, and attracted so many people to the theatre who had never been seen there before, that a benefit was considered by the manager a very promising speculation. Nicholas assenting to the terms proposed, the benefit was had, and by it he realised no less a sum than twenty pounds.

Possessed of this unexpected wealth, his first act was to enclose to honest John Browdie the amount of his friendly loan, which he accompanied with many expressions of gratitude and esteem, and many cordial wishes for his matrimonial happiness. To Newman Noggs he forwarded one half of the sum he had realised, entreating him to take an opportunity of handing it to Kate in secret, and conveying to her the warmest assurances of his love and affection. He made no mention of the way in which he had employed himself; merely informing Newman that a letter addressed to him under his assumed name at the Post Office, Portsmouth, would readily find him, and entreating that worthy friend to write full particulars of the situation of his mother and sister, and an account of all the grand things that Ralph Nickleby had done for them since his departure from London.

'You are out of spirits,' said Smike, on the night after the letter had been dispatched.

'Not I!' rejoined Nicholas, with assumed gaiety, for the confession would have made the boy miserable all night; 'I was thinking about my sister, Smike.'

'Sister!'

'Ay.'

'Is she like you?' inquired Smike.

'Why, so they say,' replied Nicholas, laughing, 'only a great deal handsomer.'

'She must be very beautiful,' said Smike, after thinking a little while with his hands folded together, and his eyes bent upon his friend.

'Anybody who didn't know you as well as I do, my dear fellow, would say you were an accomplished courtier,' said Nicholas.

'I don't even know what that is,' replied Smike, shaking his head. 'Shall I ever see your sister?'

'To be sure,' cried Nicholas; 'we shall all be together one of these days—when we are rich, Smike.'

'How is it that you, who are so kind and good to me, have nobody to be kind to you?' asked Smike. 'I cannot make that out.'

'Why, it is a long story,' replied Nicholas, 'and one you would have some difficulty in comprehending, I fear. I have an enemy—you understand what that is?'

'Oh, yes, I understand that,' said Smike.

'Well, it is owing to him,' returned Nicholas. 'He is rich, and not so easily punished as your old enemy, Mr. Squeers. He is my uncle, but he is a villain, and has done me wrong.'

'Has he though?' asked Smike, bending eagerly forward. 'What is his name? Tell me his name.'

'Ralph—Ralph Nickleby.'

'Ralph Nickleby,' repeated Smike. 'Ralph. I'll get that name by heart.'

He had muttered it over to himself some twenty times, when a loud knock at the door disturbed him from his occupation. Before he could open it, Mr Folair, the pantomimist, thrust in his head.

Mr. Folair's head was usually decorated with a very round hat, unusually high in the crown, and curled up quite tight in the brims. On the present occasion he wore it very much on one side, with the back part forward in consequence of its being the least rusty; round his neck he wore a flaming red worsted comforter, whereof the straggling ends peeped out beneath his threadbare Newmarket coat, which was very tight and buttoned all the way up. He carried in his hand one very dirty glove, and a cheap dress cane with a glass handle; in short, his whole appearance was unusually dashing, and demonstrated a far more scrupulous attention to his toilet than he was in the habit of bestowing upon it.

'Good-evening, sir,' said Mr. Folair, taking off the tall hat, and running his fingers through his hair. 'I bring a communication. Hem!'

'From whom and what about?' inquired Nicholas. 'You are unusually mysterious tonight.'

'Cold, perhaps,' returned Mr. Folair; 'cold, perhaps. That is the fault of my position— not of myself, Mr. Johnson. My position as a mutual friend requires it, sir.' Mr. Folair paused with a most impressive look, and diving into the hat before noticed, drew from thence a small piece of whity-brown paper curiously folded, whence he brought forth a note which it had served to keep clean, and handing it over to Nicholas, said—

'Have the goodness to read that, sir.'

Nicholas, in a state of much amazement, took the note and broke the seal, glancing at Mr. Folair as he did so, who, knitting his brow and pursing up his mouth with great dignity, was sitting with his eyes steadily fixed upon the ceiling.

It was directed to blank Johnson, Esq., by favour of Augustus Folair, Esq.; and the astonishment of Nicholas was in no degree lessened, when he found it to be couched in the following laconic terms:—

"Mr. Lenville presents his kind regards to Mr. Johnson, and will feel obliged if he will inform him at what hour tomorrow morning it will be most convenient to him to meet Mr. L. at the Theatre, for the purpose of having his nose pulled in the presence of the company.

"Mr. Lenville requests Mr. Johnson not to neglect making an appointment, as he has invited two or three professional friends to witness the ceremony, and cannot disappoint them upon any account whatever.

"PORTSMOUTH, TUESDAY NIGHT."

Indignant as he was at this impertinence, there was something so exquisitely absurd in such a cartel of defiance, that Nicholas was obliged to bite his lip and read the note over two or three times before he could muster sufficient gravity and sternness to address the hostile messenger, who had not taken his eyes from the ceiling, nor altered the expression of his face in the slightest degree.

'Do you know the contents of this note, sir?' he asked, at length.

'Yes,' rejoined Mr. Folair, looking round for an instant, and immediately carrying his eyes back again to the ceiling.

'And how dare you bring it here, sir?' asked Nicholas, tearing it into very little pieces, and jerking it in a shower towards the messenger. 'Had you no fear of being kicked downstairs, sir?'

Mr. Folair turned his head—now ornamented with several fragments of the note—towards Nicholas, and with the same imperturbable dignity, briefly replied 'No.'

'Then,' said Nicholas, taking up the tall hat and tossing it towards the door, 'you had better follow that article of your dress, sir, or you may find yourself very disagreeably deceived, and that within a dozen seconds.'

'I say, Johnson,' remonstrated Mr. Folair, suddenly losing all his dignity, 'none of that, you know. No tricks with a gentleman's wardrobe.'

'Leave the room,' returned Nicholas. 'How could you presume to come here on such an errand, you scoundrel?'

'Pooh! pooh!' said Mr. Folair, unwinding his comforter, and gradually getting himself out of it. 'There—that's enough.'

'Enough!' cried Nicholas, advancing towards him. 'Take yourself off, sir.'

'Pooh! pooh! I tell you,' returned Mr. Folair, waving his hand in deprecation of any further wrath; 'I wasn't in earnest. I only brought it in joke.'

'You had better be careful how you indulge in such jokes again,' said Nicholas, 'or you may find an allusion to pulling noses rather a dangerous reminder for the subject of your facetiousness. Was it written in joke, too, pray?'

'No, no, that's the best of it,' returned the actor; 'right down earnest—honour bright.'

Nicholas could not repress a smile at the odd figure before him, which, at all times more calculated to provoke mirth than anger, was especially so at that moment, when with one knee upon the ground, Mr. Folair twirled his old hat round upon his hand, and affected the extremest agony lest any of the nap should have been knocked off—an ornament which it is almost superfluous to say, it had not boasted for many months.

'Come, sir,' said Nicholas, laughing in spite of himself. 'Have the goodness to explain.'

'Why, I'll tell you how it is,' said Mr. Folair, sitting himself down in a chair with great coolness. 'Since you came here Lenville has done nothing but second business, and, instead of having a reception every night as he used to have, they have let him come on as if he was nobody.'

'What do you mean by a reception?' asked Nicholas.

'Jupiter!' exclaimed Mr. Folair, 'what an unsophisticated shepherd you are, Johnson! Why, applause from the house when you first come on. So he has gone on night after night, never getting a hand, and you getting a couple of rounds at least, and sometimes three, till at length he got quite desperate, and had half a mind last night to play Tybalt with a real sword, and pink you—not dangerously, but just enough to lay you up for a month or two.'

'Very considerate,' remarked Nicholas.

'Yes, I think it was under the circumstances; his professional reputation being at stake,' said Mr. Folair, quite seriously. 'But his heart failed him, and he cast about for some other way of annoying you, and making himself popular at the same time—for that's the point. Notoriety, notoriety, is the thing. Bless you, if he had pinked you,' said Mr. Folair, stopping to make a calculation in his mind, 'it would have been worth—ah, it would have been worth eight or ten shillings a week to him. All the town would have come to see the actor who nearly killed a man by mistake; I shouldn't wonder if it had got him an engagement in London. However, he was obliged to try some other mode of getting popular, and this one occurred to him. It's a clever idea, really. If you had shown the white feather, and let him pull your nose, he'd have got it into the paper; if you had sworn the peace against him, it would have been in the paper too, and he'd have been just as much talked about as you—don't you see?'

'Oh, certainly,' rejoined Nicholas; 'but suppose I were to turn the tables, and pull his nose, what then? Would that make his fortune?'

'Why, I don't think it would,' replied Mr. Folair, scratching his head, 'because there wouldn't be any romance about it, and he wouldn't be favourably known. To tell you the truth though, he didn't calculate much upon that, for you're always so mild-spoken, and are so popular among the women, that we didn't suspect you of showing fight. If you did, however, he has a way of getting out of it easily, depend upon that.'

'Has he?' rejoined Nicholas. 'We will try, tomorrow morning. In the meantime, you can give whatever account of our interview you like best. Good-night.'

As Mr. Folair was pretty well known among his fellow-actors for a man who delighted in mischief, and was by no means scrupulous, Nicholas had not much doubt but that he had secretly prompted the tragedian in the course he had taken, and, moreover, that he would have carried his mission with a very high hand if he had not been disconcerted by the very unexpected demonstrations with which it had been received. It was not worth his while to be serious with him, however, so he dismissed the pantomimist, with a gentle hint that if he offended again it would be under the penalty of a broken head; and Mr. Folair, taking the caution in exceedingly good part, walked away to confer with his principal, and give such an account of his proceedings as he might think best calculated to carry on the joke.

He had no doubt reported that Nicholas was in a state of extreme bodily fear; for when that young gentleman walked with much deliberation down to the theatre next morning at the usual hour, he found all the company assembled in evident expectation, and Mr. Lenville, with his severest stage face, sitting majestically on a table, whistling defiance.

Now the ladies were on the side of Nicholas, and the gentlemen (being jealous) were on the side of the disappointed tragedian; so that the latter formed a little group about the redoubtable Mr. Lenville, and the former looked on at a little distance in some trepidation and anxiety. On Nicholas stopping to salute them, Mr. Lenville laughed a scornful laugh, and made some general remark touching the natural history of puppies.

'Oh!' said Nicholas, looking quietly round, 'are you there?'

'Slave!' returned Mr. Lenville, flourishing his right arm, and approaching Nicholas with a theatrical stride. But somehow he appeared just at that moment a little startled, as if Nicholas did not look quite so frightened as he had expected, and came all at once to an awkward halt, at which the assembled ladies burst into a shrill laugh.

'Object of my scorn and hatred!' said Mr. Lenville, 'I hold ye in contempt.'

Nicholas laughed in very unexpected enjoyment of this performance; and the ladies, by way of encouragement, laughed louder than before; whereat Mr Lenville assumed his bitterest smile, and expressed his opinion that they were 'minions'.

'But they shall not protect ye!' said the tragedian, taking an upward look at Nicholas, beginning at his boots and ending at the crown of his head, and then a downward one, beginning at the crown of his head, and ending at his boots—which two looks, as everybody knows, express defiance on the stage. 'They shall not protect ye—boy!'

Thus speaking, Mr. Lenville folded his arms, and treated Nicholas to that expression of face with which, in melodramatic performances, he was in the habit of regarding the tyrannical kings when they said, 'Away with him to the deepest dungeon beneath the castle moat;' and which, accompanied with a little jingling of fetters, had been known to produce great effects in its time.

Whether it was the absence of the fetters or not, it made no very deep impression on Mr. Lenville's adversary, however, but rather seemed to increase the good-humour expressed in his countenance; in which stage of the contest, one or two gentlemen, who had come out expressly to witness the pulling of Nicholas's nose, grew impatient, murmuring that if it were to be done at all it had better be done at once, and that if Mr. Lenville didn't mean to do it he had better say so, and not keep them waiting there. Thus urged, the tragedian adjusted the cuff of his right coat sleeve for the performance of the operation, and walked in a very stately manner up to Nicholas, who suffered him to approach to within the requisite distance, and then, without the smallest discomposure, knocked him down.

Before the discomfited tragedian could raise his head from the boards, Mrs Lenville (who, as has been before hinted, was in an interesting state) rushed from the rear rank of ladies, and uttering a piercing scream threw herself upon the body.

'Do you see this, monster? Do you see this?' cried Mr. Lenville, sitting up, and pointing to his prostrate lady, who was holding him very tight round the waist.

'Come,' said Nicholas, nodding his head, 'apologise for the insolent note you wrote to me last night, and waste no more time in talking.'

'Never!' cried Mr. Lenville.

'Yes—yes—yes!' screamed his wife. 'For my sake—for mine, Lenville—forego all idle forms, unless you would see me a blighted corse at your feet.'

'This is affecting!' said Mr. Lenville, looking round him, and drawing the back of his hand across his eyes. 'The ties of nature are strong. The weak husband and the father—the father that is yet to be—relents. I apologise.'

'Humbly and submissively?' said Nicholas.

'Humbly and submissively,' returned the tragedian, scowling upwards. 'But only to save her,—for a time will come—'

'Very good,' said Nicholas; 'I hope Mrs. Lenville may have a good one; and when it does come, and you are a father, you shall retract it if you have the courage. There. Be careful, sir, to what lengths your jealousy carries you another time; and be careful, also, before you venture too far, to ascertain your rival's temper.' With this parting advice Nicholas picked up Mr. Lenville's ash stick which had flown out of his hand, and breaking it in half, threw him the pieces and withdrew, bowing slightly to the spectators as he walked out.

The profoundest deference was paid to Nicholas that night, and the people who had been most anxious to have his nose pulled in the morning, embraced occasions of taking him aside, and telling him with great feeling, how very friendly they took it that he should have treated that Lenville so properly, who was a most unbearable fellow, and on whom they had all, by a remarkable coincidence, at one time or other contemplated the infliction of condign punishment, which they had only been restrained from administering by considerations of mercy; indeed, to judge from the invariable termination of all these stories, there never was such a charitable and kind-hearted set of people as the male members of Mr Crummles's company.

Nicholas bore his triumph, as he had his success in the little world of the theatre, with the utmost moderation and good humour. The crestfallen Mr. Lenville made an expiring effort to obtain revenge by sending a boy into the gallery to hiss, but he fell a sacrifice to popular indignation, and was promptly turned out without having his money back.

'Well, Smike,' said Nicholas when the first piece was over, and he had almost finished dressing to go home, 'is there any letter yet?'

'Yes,' replied Smike, 'I got this one from the post-office.'

'From Newman Noggs,' said Nicholas, casting his eye upon the cramped direction; 'it's no easy matter to make his writing out. Let me see—let me see.'

By dint of poring over the letter for half an hour, he contrived to make himself master of the contents, which were certainly not of a nature to set his mind at ease. Newman took upon himself to send back the ten pounds, observing that he had ascertained that neither Mrs. Nickleby nor Kate was in actual want of money at the moment, and that a time might shortly come when Nicholas might want it more. He entreated him not to be alarmed at what he was about to say;—there was no bad news—they were in good health—but he thought circumstances might occur, or were occurring, which would render it absolutely necessary that Kate should have her brother's protection, and if so, Newman said, he would write to him to that effect, either by the next post or the next but one.

Nicholas read this passage very often, and the more he thought of it the more he began to fear some treachery upon the part of Ralph. Once or twice he felt tempted to repair to London at all hazards without an hour's delay, but a little reflection assured him that if such a step were necessary, Newman would have spoken out and told him so at once.

'At all events I should prepare them here for the possibility of my going away suddenly,' said Nicholas; 'I should lose no time in doing that.' As the thought occurred to him, he took up his hat and hurried to the green-room.

'Well, Mr. Johnson,' said Mrs. Crummles, who was seated there in full regal costume, with the phenomenon as the Maiden in her maternal arms, 'next week for Ryde, then for Winchester, then for—'

'I have some reason to fear,' interrupted Nicholas, 'that before you leave here my career with you will have closed.'

'Closed!' cried Mrs. Crummles, raising her hands in astonishment.

'Closed!' cried Miss Snevellicci, trembling so much in her tights that she actually laid her hand upon the shoulder of the manageress for support.

'Why he don't mean to say he's going!' exclaimed Mrs. Grudden, making her way towards Mrs. Crummles. 'Hoity toity! Nonsense.'

The phenomenon, being of an affectionate nature and moreover excitable, raised a loud cry, and Miss Belvawney and Miss Bravassa actually shed tears. Even the male performers stopped in their conversation, and echoed the word 'Going!' although some among them (and they had been the loudest in their congratulations that day) winked at each other as though they would not be sorry to lose such a favoured rival; an opinion, indeed, which the honest Mr. Folair, who was ready dressed for the savage, openly stated in so many words to a demon with whom he was sharing a pot of porter.

Nicholas briefly said that he feared it would be so, although he could not yet speak with any degree of certainty; and getting away as soon as he could, went home to con Newman's letter once more, and speculate upon it afresh.

How trifling all that had been occupying his time and thoughts for many weeks seemed to him during that sleepless night, and how constantly and incessantly present to his imagination was the one idea that Kate in the midst of some great trouble and distress might even then be looking—and vainly too—for him!

CHAPTER 30
Festivities are held in honour of Nicholas, who suddenly withdraws himself from the Society of Mr. Vincent Crummles and his Theatrical Companions

Mr. Vincent Crummles was no sooner acquainted with the public announcement which Nicholas had made relative to the probability of his shortly ceasing to be a member of the company, than he evinced many tokens of grief and consternation; and, in the extremity of his despair, even held out certain vague promises of a speedy improvement not only in the amount of his regular salary, but also in the contingent emoluments appertaining to his authorship. Finding Nicholas bent upon quitting the society—for he had now determined that, even if no further tidings came from Newman, he would, at all hazards, ease his mind by repairing to London and ascertaining the exact position of his sister—Mr. Crummles was fain to content himself by calculating the chances of his coming back again, and taking prompt and energetic measures to make the most of him before he went away.

'Let me see,' said Mr. Crummles, taking off his outlaw's wig, the better to arrive at a cool-headed view of the whole case. 'Let me see. This is Wednesday night. We'll have posters out the first thing in the morning, announcing positively your last appearance for tomorrow.'

'But perhaps it may not be my last appearance, you know,' said Nicholas. 'Unless I am summoned away, I should be sorry to inconvenience you by leaving before the end of the week.'

'So much the better,' returned Mr. Crummles. 'We can have positively your last appearance, on Thursday—re-engagement for one night more, on Friday—and, yielding to the wishes of numerous influential patrons, who were disappointed in obtaining seats, on Saturday. That ought to bring three very decent houses.'

'Then I am to make three last appearances, am I?' inquired Nicholas, smiling.

'Yes,' rejoined the manager, scratching his head with an air of some vexation; 'three is not enough, and it's very bungling and irregular not to have more, but if we can't help it we can't, so there's no use in talking. A novelty would be very desirable. You couldn't sing a comic song on the pony's back, could you?'

'No,' replied Nicholas, 'I couldn't indeed.'

'It has drawn money before now,' said Mr. Crummles, with a look of disappointment. 'What do you think of a brilliant display of fireworks?'

'That it would be rather expensive,' replied Nicholas, drily.

'Eighteen-pence would do it,' said Mr. Crummles. 'You on the top of a pair of steps with the phenomenon in an attitude; "Farewell!" on a transparency behind; and nine people at the wings with a squib in each hand—all the dozen and a half going off at once—it would be very grand—awful from the front, quite awful.'

As Nicholas appeared by no means impressed with the solemnity of the proposed effect, but, on the contrary, received the proposition in a most irreverent manner, and laughed at it very heartily, Mr. Crummles abandoned the project in its birth, and gloomily observed that they must make up the best bill they could with combats and hornpipes, and so stick to the legitimate drama.

For the purpose of carrying this object into instant execution, the manager at once repaired to a small dressing-room, adjacent, where Mrs Crummles was then occupied in exchanging the habiliments of a melodramatic empress for the ordinary attire of matrons in the nineteenth century. And with the assistance of this lady, and the accomplished Mrs. Grudden (who had quite a genius for making out bills, being a great hand at throwing in the notes of admiration, and knowing from long experience exactly where the largest capitals ought to go), he seriously applied himself to the composition of the poster.

'Heigho!' sighed Nicholas, as he threw himself back in the prompter's chair, after telegraphing the needful directions to Smike, who had been playing a meagre tailor in the interlude, with one skirt to his coat, and a little pocket-handkerchief with a large hole in it, and a woollen nightcap, and a red nose, and other distinctive marks peculiar to tailors on the stage. 'Heigho! I wish all this were over.'

'Over, Mr. Johnson!' repeated a female voice behind him, in a kind of plaintive surprise.

'It was an ungallant speech, certainly,' said Nicholas, looking up to see who the speaker was, and recognising Miss Snevellicci. 'I would not have made it if I had known you had been within hearing.'

'What a dear that Mr. Digby is!' said Miss Snevellicci, as the tailor went off on the opposite side, at the end of the piece, with great applause. (Smike's theatrical name was Digby.)

'I'll tell him presently, for his gratification, that you said so,' returned Nicholas.

'Oh you naughty thing!' rejoined Miss Snevellicci. 'I don't know though, that I should much mind his knowing my opinion of him; with some other people, indeed, it might be—' Here Miss Snevellicci stopped, as though waiting to be questioned, but no questioning came, for Nicholas was thinking about more serious matters.

'How kind it is of you,' resumed Miss Snevellicci, after a short silence, 'to sit waiting here for him night after night, night after night, no matter how tired you are; and taking so much pains with him, and doing it all with as much delight and readiness as if you were coining gold by it!'

'He well deserves all the kindness I can show him, and a great deal more,' said Nicholas. 'He is the most grateful, single-hearted, affectionate creature that ever breathed.'

'So odd, too,' remarked Miss Snevellicci, 'isn't he?'

'God help him, and those who have made him so; he is indeed,' rejoined Nicholas, shaking his head.

'He is such a devilish close chap,' said Mr. Folair, who had come up a little before, and now joined in the conversation. 'Nobody can ever get anything out of him.'

'What should they get out of him?' asked Nicholas, turning round with some abruptness.

'Zooks! what a fire-eater you are, Johnson!' returned Mr. Folair, pulling up the heel of his dancing shoe. 'I'm only talking of the natural curiosity of the people here, to know what he has been about all his life.'

'Poor fellow! it is pretty plain, I should think, that he has not the intellect to have been about anything of much importance to them or anybody else,' said Nicholas.

'Ay,' rejoined the actor, contemplating the effect of his face in a lamp reflector, 'but that involves the whole question, you know.'

'What question?' asked Nicholas.

'Why, the who he is and what he is, and how you two, who are so different, came to be such close companions,' replied Mr. Folair, delighted with the opportunity of saying something disagreeable. 'That's in everybody's mouth.'

'The "everybody" of the theatre, I suppose?' said Nicholas, contemptuously.

'In it and out of it too,' replied the actor. 'Why, you know, Lenville says—'

'I thought I had silenced him effectually,' interrupted Nicholas, reddening.

'Perhaps you have,' rejoined the immovable Mr. Folair; 'if you have, he said this before he was silenced: Lenville says that you're a regular stick of an actor, and that it's only the mystery about you that has caused you to go down with the people here, and that Crummles keeps it up for his own sake; though Lenville says he don't believe there's anything at all in it, except your having got into a scrape and run away from somewhere, for doing something or other.'

'Oh!' said Nicholas, forcing a smile.

'That's a part of what he says,' added Mr. Folair. 'I mention it as the friend of both parties, and in strict confidence. I don't agree with him, you know. He says he takes Digby to be more knave than fool; and old Fluggers, who does the heavy business you know, he says that when he delivered messages at Covent Garden the season before last, there used to be a pickpocket hovering about the coach-stand who had exactly the face of Digby; though, as he very properly says, Digby may not be the same, but only his brother, or some near relation.'

'Oh!' cried Nicholas again.

'Yes,' said Mr. Folair, with undisturbed calmness, 'that's what they say. I thought I'd tell you, because really you ought to know. Oh! here's this blessed phenomenon at last. Ugh, you little imposition, I should like to—quite ready, my darling,—humbug—Ring up, Mrs. G., and let the favourite wake 'em.'

Uttering in a loud voice such of the latter allusions as were complimentary to the unconscious phenomenon, and giving the rest in a confidential 'aside' to Nicholas, Mr. Folair followed the ascent of the curtain with his eyes, regarded with a sneer the reception of Miss Crummles as the Maiden, and, falling back a step or two to advance with the better effect, uttered a preliminary howl, and 'went on' chattering his teeth and brandishing his tin tomahawk as the Indian Savage.

'So these are some of the stories they invent about us, and bandy from mouth to mouth!' thought Nicholas. 'If a man would commit an inexpiable offence against any society, large or small, let him be successful. They will forgive him any crime but that.'

'You surely don't mind what that malicious creature says, Mr. Johnson?' observed Miss Snevellicci in her most winning tones.

'Not I,' replied Nicholas. 'If I were going to remain here, I might think it worth my while to embroil myself. As it is, let them talk till they are hoarse. But here,' added Nicholas, as Smike approached, 'here comes the subject of a portion of their good-nature, so let he and I say good night together.'

'No, I will not let either of you say anything of the kind,' returned Miss Snevellicci. 'You must come home and see mama, who only came to Portsmouth today, and is dying to behold you. Led, my dear, persuade Mr. Johnson.'

'Oh, I'm sure,' returned Miss Ledrook, with considerable vivacity, 'if you can't persuade him—' Miss Ledrook said no more, but intimated, by a dexterous playfulness, that if Miss Snevellicci couldn't persuade him, nobody could.

'Mr. and Mrs. Lillyvick have taken lodgings in our house, and share our sitting-room for the present,' said Miss Snevellicci. 'Won't that induce you?'

'Surely,' returned Nicholas, 'I can require no possible inducement beyond your invitation.'

'Oh no! I dare say,' rejoined Miss Snevellicci. And Miss Ledrook said, 'Upon my word!' Upon which Miss Snevellicci said that Miss Ledrook was a giddy thing; and Miss Ledrook said that Miss Snevellicci needn't colour up quite so much; and Miss Snevellicci beat Miss Ledrook, and Miss Ledrook beat Miss Snevellicci.

'Come,' said Miss Ledrook, 'it's high time we were there, or we shall have poor Mrs. Snevellicci thinking that you have run away with her daughter, Mr Johnson; and then we should have a pretty to-do.'

'My dear Led,' remonstrated Miss Snevellicci, 'how you do talk!'

Miss Ledrook made no answer, but taking Smike's arm in hers, left her friend and Nicholas to follow at their pleasure; which it pleased them, or rather pleased Nicholas, who had no great fancy for a tete-a-tete under the circumstances, to do at once.

There were not wanting matters of conversation when they reached the street, for it turned out that Miss Snevellicci had a small basket to carry home, and Miss Ledrook a small bandbox, both containing such minor articles of theatrical costume as the lady performers usually carried to and fro every evening. Nicholas would insist upon carrying the basket, and Miss Snevellicci would insist upon carrying it herself, which gave rise to a struggle, in which

Nicholas captured the basket and the bandbox likewise. Then Nicholas said, that he wondered what could possibly be inside the basket, and attempted to peep in, whereat Miss Snevellicci screamed, and declared that if she thought he had seen, she was sure she should faint away. This declaration was followed by a similar attempt on the bandbox, and similar demonstrations on the part of Miss Ledrook, and then both ladies vowed that they wouldn't move a step further until Nicholas had promised that he wouldn't offer to peep again. At last Nicholas pledged himself to betray no further curiosity, and they walked on: both ladies giggling very much, and declaring that they never had seen such a wicked creature in all their born days—never.

Lightening the way with such pleasantry as this, they arrived at the tailor's house in no time; and here they made quite a little party, there being present besides Mr. Lillyvick and Mrs. Lillyvick, not only Miss Snevellicci's mama, but her papa also. And an uncommonly fine man Miss Snevellicci's papa was, with a hook nose, and a white forehead, and curly black hair, and high cheek bones, and altogether quite a handsome face, only a little pimply as though with drinking. He had a very broad chest had Miss Snevellicci's papa, and he wore a threadbare blue dress-coat buttoned with gilt buttons tight across it; and he no sooner saw Nicholas come into the room, than he whipped the two forefingers of his right hand in between the two centre buttons, and sticking his other arm gracefully a-kimbo seemed to say, 'Now, here I am, my buck, and what have you got to say to me?'

Such was, and in such an attitude sat Miss Snevellicci's papa, who had been in the profession ever since he had first played the ten-year-old imps in the Christmas pantomimes; who could sing a little, dance a little, fence a little, act a little, and do everything a little, but not much; who had been sometimes in the ballet, and sometimes in the chorus, at every theatre in London; who was always selected in virtue of his figure to play the military visitors and the speechless noblemen; who always wore a smart dress, and came on arm-in-arm with a smart lady in short petticoats,—and always did it too with such an air that people in the pit had been several times known to cry out 'Bravo!' under the impression that he was somebody. Such was Miss Snevellicci's papa, upon whom some envious persons cast the imputation that he occasionally beat Miss Snevellicci's mama, who was still a dancer, with a neat little figure and some remains of good looks; and who now sat, as she danced,—being rather too old for the full glare of the foot-lights,—in the background.

To these good people Nicholas was presented with much formality. The introduction being completed, Miss Snevellicci's papa (who was scented with rum-and-water) said that he was delighted to make the acquaintance of a gentleman so highly talented; and furthermore remarked, that there hadn't been such a hit made—no, not since the first appearance of his friend Mr. Glavormelly, at the Coburg.

'You have seen him, sir?' said Miss Snevellicci's papa.

'No, really I never did,' replied Nicholas.

'You never saw my friend Glavormelly, sir!' said Miss Snevellicci's papa. 'Then you have never seen acting yet. If he had lived—'

'Oh, he is dead, is he?' interrupted Nicholas.

'He is,' said Mr. Snevellicci, 'but he isn't in Westminster Abbey, more's the shame. He was a—. Well, no matter. He is gone to that bourne from whence no traveller returns. I hope he is appreciated there.'

So saying Miss Snevellicci's papa rubbed the tip of his nose with a very yellow silk handkerchief, and gave the company to understand that these recollections overcame him.

'Well, Mr. Lillyvick,' said Nicholas, 'and how are you?'

'Quite well, sir,' replied the collector. 'There is nothing like the married state, sir, depend upon it.'

'Indeed!' said Nicholas, laughing.

'Ah! nothing like it, sir,' replied Mr. Lillyvick solemnly. 'How do you think,' whispered the collector, drawing him aside, 'how do you think she looks tonight?'

'As handsome as ever,' replied Nicholas, glancing at the late Miss Petowker.

'Why, there's air about her, sir,' whispered the collector, 'that I never saw in anybody. Look at her now she moves to put the kettle on. There! Isn't it fascination, sir?'

'You're a lucky man,' said Nicholas.

'Ha, ha, ha!' rejoined the collector. 'No. Do you think I am though, eh? Perhaps I may be, perhaps I may be. I say, I couldn't have done much better if I had been a young man, could I? You couldn't have done much better yourself, could you—eh—could you?' With such inquires, and many more such, Mr. Lillyvick jerked his elbow into Nicholas's side, and chuckled till his face became quite purple in the attempt to keep down his satisfaction.

By this time the cloth had been laid under the joint superintendence of all the ladies, upon two tables put together, one being high and narrow, and the other low and broad. There were oysters at the top, sausages at the bottom, a pair of snuffers in the centre, and baked potatoes wherever it was most convenient to put them. Two additional chairs were brought in from the bedroom: Miss Snevellicci sat at the head of the table, and Mr Lillyvick at the foot; and Nicholas had not only the honour of sitting next Miss Snevellicci, but of having Miss Snevellicci's mama on his right hand, and Miss Snevellicci's papa over the way. In short, he was the hero of the feast; and when the table was cleared and something warm introduced, Miss Snevellicci's papa got up and proposed his health in a speech containing such affecting allusions to his coming departure, that Miss Snevellicci wept, and was compelled to retire into the bedroom.

'Hush! Don't take any notice of it,' said Miss Ledrook, peeping in from the bedroom. 'Say, when she comes back, that she exerts herself too much.'

Miss Ledrook eked out this speech with so many mysterious nods and frowns before she shut the door again, that a profound silence came upon all the company, during which Miss Snevellicci's papa looked very big indeed—several sizes larger than life—at everybody in turn, but particularly at Nicholas, and kept on perpetually emptying his tumbler and filling it again, until the ladies returned in a cluster, with Miss Snevellicci among them.

'You needn't alarm yourself a bit, Mr. Snevellicci,' said Mrs. Lillyvick. 'She is only a little weak and nervous; she has been so ever since the morning.'

'Oh,' said Mr. Snevellicci, 'that's all, is it?'

'Oh yes, that's all. Don't make a fuss about it,' cried all the ladies together.

Now this was not exactly the kind of reply suited to Mr. Snevellicci's importance as a man and a father, so he picked out the unfortunate Mrs Snevellicci, and asked her what the devil she meant by talking to him in that way.

'Dear me, my dear!' said Mrs. Snevellicci.

'Don't call me your dear, ma'am,' said Mr. Snevellicci, 'if you please.'

'Pray, pa, don't,' interposed Miss Snevellicci.

'Don't what, my child?'

'Talk in that way.'

'Why not?' said Mr. Snevellicci. 'I hope you don't suppose there's anybody here who is to prevent my talking as I like?'

'Nobody wants to, pa,' rejoined his daughter.

'Nobody would if they did want to,' said Mr. Snevellicci. 'I am not ashamed of myself, Snevellicci is my name; I'm to be found in Broad Court, Bow Street, when I'm in town. If I'm not at home, let any man ask for me at the stage-door. Damme, they know me at the stage-door I suppose. Most men have seen my portrait at the cigar shop round the corner. I've been mentioned in the newspapers before now, haven't I? Talk! I'll tell you what; if I found out that any man had been tampering with the affections of my daughter, I wouldn't talk. I'd astonish him without talking; that's my way.'

So saying, Mr. Snevellicci struck the palm of his left hand three smart blows with his clenched fist; pulled a phantom nose with his right thumb and forefinger, and swallowed another glassful at a draught. 'That's my way,' repeated Mr. Snevellicci.

Most public characters have their failings; and the truth is that Mr Snevellicci was a little addicted to drinking; or, if the whole truth must be told, that he was scarcely ever sober. He knew in his cups three distinct stages of intoxication,—the dignified—the quarrelsome—the amorous. When professionally engaged he never got beyond the dignified; in private circles he went through all three, passing from one to another with a rapidity of transition often rather perplexing to those who had not the honour of his acquaintance.

Thus Mr. Snevellicci had no sooner swallowed another glassful than he smiled upon all present in happy forgetfulness of having exhibited symptoms of pugnacity, and proposed 'The ladies! Bless their hearts!' in a most vivacious manner.

'I love 'em,' said Mr. Snevellicci, looking round the table, 'I love 'em, every one.'

'Not every one,' reasoned Mr. Lillyvick, mildly.

'Yes, every one,' repeated Mr. Snevellicci.

'That would include the married ladies, you know,' said Mr. Lillyvick.

'I love them too, sir,' said Mr. Snevellicci.

The collector looked into the surrounding faces with an aspect of grave astonishment, seeming to say, 'This is a nice man!' and appeared a little surprised that Mrs. Lillyvick's manner yielded no evidences of horror and indignation.

'One good turn deserves another,' said Mr. Snevellicci. 'I love them and they love me.' And as if this avowal were not made in sufficient disregard and defiance of all moral obligations, what did Mr. Snevellicci do? He winked—winked openly and undisguisedly; winked with his right eye—upon Henrietta Lillyvick!

The collector fell back in his chair in the intensity of his astonishment. If anybody had winked at her as Henrietta Petowker, it would have been indecorous in the last degree; but as Mrs. Lillyvick! While he thought of it in a cold perspiration, and wondered whether it was possible that he could be dreaming, Mr. Snevellicci repeated the wink, and drinking to Mrs Lillyvick in dumb show, actually blew her a kiss! Mr. Lillyvick left his chair, walked straight up to the other end of the table, and fell upon him—literally fell upon him—instantaneously. Mr. Lillyvick was no light weight, and consequently when he fell upon Mr. Snevellicci, Mr. Snevellicci fell under the table. Mr. Lillyvick followed him, and the ladies screamed.

'What is the matter with the men! Are they mad?' cried Nicholas, diving under the table, dragging up the collector by main force, and thrusting him, all doubled up, into a chair, as if he had been a stuffed figure. 'What do you mean to do? What do you want to do? What is the matter with you?'

While Nicholas raised up the collector, Smike had performed the same office for Mr. Snevellicci, who now regarded his late adversary in tipsy amazement.

'Look here, sir,' replied Mr. Lillyvick, pointing to his astonished wife, 'here is purity and elegance combined, whose feelings have been outraged—violated, sir!'

'Lor, what nonsense he talks!' exclaimed Mrs. Lillyvick in answer to the inquiring look of Nicholas. 'Nobody has said anything to me.'

'Said, Henrietta!' cried the collector. 'Didn't I see him—' Mr Lillyvick couldn't bring himself to utter the word, but he counterfeited the motion of the eye.

'Well!' cried Mrs. Lillyvick. 'Do you suppose nobody is ever to look at me? A pretty thing to be married indeed, if that was law!'

'You didn't mind it?' cried the collector.

'Mind it!' repeated Mrs. Lillyvick contemptuously. 'You ought to go down on your knees and beg everybody's pardon, that you ought.'

'Pardon, my dear?' said the dismayed collector.

'Yes, and mine first,' replied Mrs. Lillyvick. 'Do you suppose I ain't the best judge of what's proper and what's improper?'

'To be sure,' cried all the ladies. 'Do you suppose we shouldn't be the first to speak, if there was anything that ought to be taken notice of?'

'Do you suppose they don't know, sir?' said Miss Snevellicci's papa, pulling up his collar, and muttering something about a punching of heads, and being only withheld by considerations of age. With which Miss Snevellicci's papa looked steadily and sternly at Mr. Lillyvick for some seconds, and then rising deliberately from his chair, kissed the ladies all round, beginning with Mrs. Lillyvick.

The unhappy collector looked piteously at his wife, as if to see whether there was any one trait of Miss Petowker left in Mrs. Lillyvick, and finding too surely that there was not, begged pardon of all the company with great humility, and sat down such a crest-fallen, dispirited, disenchanted man, that despite all his selfishness and dotage, he was quite an object of compassion.

Miss Snevellicci's papa being greatly exalted by this triumph, and incontestable proof of his popularity with the fair sex, quickly grew convivial, not to say uproarious; volunteering more than one song of no inconsiderable length, and regaling the social circle between-whiles with recollections of divers splendid women who had been supposed to entertain a passion for himself, several of whom he toasted by name, taking occasion to remark at the same time that if he had been a little more alive to his own interest, he might have been rolling at that moment in his chariot-and-four. These reminiscences appeared to awaken no very torturing pangs in the breast of Mrs. Snevellicci, who was sufficiently occupied in descanting to Nicholas upon the manifold accomplishments and merits of her daughter. Nor was the young lady herself at all behind-hand in displaying her choicest allurements; but these, heightened as they were by the artifices of Miss Ledrook, had no effect whatever in increasing the attentions of Nicholas, who, with the precedent of Miss Squeers still fresh in his memory, steadily resisted every fascination, and placed so strict a guard upon his behaviour that when he had taken his leave the ladies were unanimous in pronouncing him quite a monster of insensibility.

Next day the posters appeared in due course, and the public were informed, in all the colours of the rainbow, and in letters afflicted with every possible variation of spinal deformity, how that Mr. Johnson would have the honour of making his last appearance that evening, and how that an early application for places was requested, in consequence of the extraordinary overflow attendant on his performances,—it being a remarkable fact in theatrical history, but one long since established beyond dispute, that it is a hopeless endeavour to attract people to a theatre unless they can be first brought to believe that they will never get into it.

Nicholas was somewhat at a loss, on entering the theatre at night, to account for the unusual perturbation and excitement visible in the countenances of all the company, but he was not long in doubt as to the cause, for before he could make any inquiry respecting it Mr. Crummles approached, and in an agitated tone of voice, informed him that there was a London manager in the boxes.

'It's the phenomenon, depend upon it, sir,' said Crummles, dragging Nicholas to the little hole in the curtain that he might look through at the London manager. 'I have not the smallest doubt it's the fame of the phenomenon—that's the man; him in the great-coat and no shirt-collar. She shall have ten pound a week, Johnson; she shall not appear on the London boards for a farthing less. They shan't engage her either, unless they engage Mrs. Crummles too—twenty pound a week for the pair; or I'll tell you what, I'll throw in myself and the two boys, and they shall have the family for thirty. I can't say fairer than that. They must take us all, if none of us will go without the others. That's the way some of the London people do, and it always answers. Thirty pound a week—it's too cheap, Johnson. It's dirt cheap.'

Nicholas replied, that it certainly was; and Mr. Vincent Crummles taking several huge pinches of snuff to compose his feelings, hurried away to tell Mrs. Crummles that he had quite settled the only terms that could be accepted, and had resolved not to abate one single farthing.

When everybody was dressed and the curtain went up, the excitement occasioned by the presence of the London manager increased a thousand-fold. Everybody happened to know that the London manager had come down specially to witness his or her own performance, and all were in a flutter of anxiety and expectation. Some of those who were not on in the first scene, hurried to the wings, and there stretched their necks to have a peep at him; others stole up into the two little private boxes over the stage-doors, and from that position reconnoitred the London manager. Once the London manager was seen to smile—he smiled at the comic countryman's pretending to catch a blue-bottle, while Mrs. Crummles was making her greatest effect. 'Very good, my fine fellow,' said Mr. Crummles, shaking his fist at the comic countryman when he came off, 'you leave this company next Saturday night.'

In the same way, everybody who was on the stage beheld no audience but one individual; everybody played to the London manager. When Mr. Lenville in a sudden burst of passion called the emperor a miscreant, and then biting his glove, said, 'But I must dissemble,' instead of looking gloomily at the boards and so waiting for his cue, as is proper in such cases, he kept his eye fixed upon the London manager. When Miss Bravassa sang her song at her lover, who according to custom stood ready to shake hands with her between the verses, they looked, not at each other, but at the London manager. Mr. Crummles died point blank at him; and when the two guards came in to take the body off after a very hard death, it was seen to open its eyes and glance at the London manager. At length the London manager was discovered to be asleep, and shortly after that he woke up and went away, whereupon all the company fell foul of the unhappy comic countryman, declaring that his buffoonery was the sole cause; and Mr. Crummles said, that he had put up with it a long time, but that he really couldn't stand it any longer, and therefore would feel obliged by his looking out for another engagement.

All this was the occasion of much amusement to Nicholas, whose only feeling upon the subject was one of sincere satisfaction that the great man went away before he appeared. He went through his part in the two last pieces as briskly as he could, and having been received with unbounded favour and unprecedented applause—so said the bills for next day, which had been printed an hour or two before—he took Smike's arm and walked home to bed.

With the post next morning came a letter from Newman Noggs, very inky, very short, very dirty, very small, and very mysterious, urging Nicholas to return to London instantly; not to lose an instant; to be there that night if possible.

'I will,' said Nicholas. 'Heaven knows I have remained here for the best, and sorely against my own will; but even now I may have dallied too long. What can have happened? Smike, my good fellow, here—take my purse. Put our things together, and pay what little debts we owe—quick, and we shall be in time for the morning coach. I will only tell them that we are going, and will return to you immediately.'

So saying, he took his hat, and hurrying away to the lodgings of Mr Crummles, applied his hand to the knocker with such hearty good-will, that he awakened that gentleman, who was still in bed, and caused Mr. Bulph the pilot to take his morning's pipe very nearly out of his mouth in the extremity of his surprise.

The door being opened, Nicholas ran upstairs without any ceremony, and bursting into the darkened sitting-room on the one-pair front, found that the two Master Crummleses had sprung out of the sofa-bedstead and were putting on their clothes with great rapidity, under the impression that it was the middle of the night, and the next house was on fire.

Before he could undeceive them, Mr. Crummles came down in a flannel gown and nightcap; and to him Nicholas briefly explained that circumstances had occurred which rendered it necessary for him to repair to London immediately.

'So goodbye,' said Nicholas; 'goodbye, goodbye.'

He was half-way downstairs before Mr. Crummles had sufficiently recovered his surprise to gasp out something about the posters.

'I can't help it,' replied Nicholas. 'Set whatever I may have earned this week against them, or if that will not repay you, say at once what will. Quick, quick.'

'We'll cry quits about that,' returned Crummles. 'But can't we have one last night more?'

'Not an hour—not a minute,' replied Nicholas, impatiently.

'Won't you stop to say something to Mrs. Crummles?' asked the manager, following him down to the door.

'I couldn't stop if it were to prolong my life a score of years,' rejoined Nicholas. 'Here, take my hand, and with it my hearty thanks.—Oh! that I should have been fooling here!'

Accompanying these words with an impatient stamp upon the ground, he tore himself from the manager's detaining grasp, and darting rapidly down the street was out of sight in an instant.

'Dear me, dear me,' said Mr. Crummles, looking wistfully towards the point at which he had just disappeared; 'if he only acted like that, what a deal of money he'd draw! He should have kept upon this circuit; he'd have been very useful to me. But he don't know what's good for him. He is an impetuous youth. Young men are rash, very rash.'

Mr. Crummles being in a moralising mood, might possibly have moralised for some minutes longer if he had not mechanically put his hand towards his waistcoat pocket, where he was accustomed to keep his snuff. The absence of any pocket at all in the usual direction, suddenly recalled to his recollection the fact that he had no waistcoat on; and this leading him to a contemplation of the extreme scantiness of his attire, he shut the door abruptly, and retired upstairs with great precipitation.

Smike had made good speed while Nicholas was absent, and with his help everything was soon ready for their departure. They scarcely stopped to take a morsel of breakfast, and in less than half an hour arrived at the coach-office: quite out of breath with the haste they had made to reach it in time. There were yet a few minutes to spare, so, having secured the places, Nicholas hurried into a slopseller's hard by, and bought Smike a great-coat. It would have been rather large for a substantial yeoman, but the shopman averring (and with considerable truth) that it was a most uncommon fit, Nicholas would have purchased it in his impatience if it had been twice the size.

As they hurried up to the coach, which was now in the open street and all ready for starting, Nicholas was not a little astonished to find himself suddenly clutched in a close and violent embrace, which nearly took him off his legs; nor was his amazement at all lessened by hearing the voice of Mr. Crummles exclaim, 'It is he—my friend, my friend!'

'Bless my heart,' cried Nicholas, struggling in the manager's arms, 'what are you about?'

The manager made no reply, but strained him to his breast again, exclaiming as he did so, 'Farewell, my noble, my lion-hearted boy!'

In fact, Mr. Crummles, who could never lose any opportunity for professional display, had turned out for the express purpose of taking a public farewell of Nicholas; and to render it the more imposing, he was now, to that young gentleman's most profound annoyance, inflicting upon him a rapid succession of stage embraces, which, as everybody knows, are performed by the embracer's laying his or her chin on the shoulder of the object of affection, and looking over it. This Mr. Crummles did in the highest style of melodrama, pouring forth at the same time all the most dismal forms of farewell he could think of, out of the stock pieces. Nor was this all, for the elder Master Crummles was going through a similar ceremony with Smike; while Master Percy Crummles, with a very little second-hand camlet cloak, worn theatrically over his left shoulder, stood by, in the attitude of an attendant officer, waiting to convey the two victims to the scaffold.

The lookers-on laughed very heartily, and as it was as well to put a good face upon the matter, Nicholas laughed too when he had succeeded in disengaging himself; and rescuing the astonished Smike, climbed up to the coach roof after him, and kissed his hand in honour of the absent Mrs Crummles as they rolled away.

CHAPTER 31
Of Ralph Nickleby and Newman Noggs, and some wise Precautions, the success or failure of which will appear in the Sequel

In blissful unconsciousness that his nephew was hastening at the utmost speed of four good horses towards his sphere of action, and that every passing minute diminished the distance between them, Ralph Nickleby sat that morning occupied in his customary avocations, and yet unable to prevent his thoughts wandering from time to time back to the interview which had taken place between himself and his niece on the previous day. At such intervals, after a few moments of abstraction, Ralph would mutter some peevish interjection, and apply himself with renewed steadiness of purpose to the ledger before him, but again and again the same train of thought came back despite all his efforts to prevent it, confusing him in his calculations, and utterly distracting his attention from the figures over which he bent. At length Ralph laid down his pen, and threw himself back in his chair as though he had made up his mind to allow the obtrusive current of reflection to take its own course, and, by giving it full scope, to rid himself of it effectually.

'I am not a man to be moved by a pretty face,' muttered Ralph sternly. 'There is a grinning skull beneath it, and men like me who look and work below the surface see that, and not its delicate covering. And yet I almost like the girl, or should if she had been less proudly and squeamishly brought up. If the boy were drowned or hanged, and the mother dead, this house should be her home. I wish they were, with all my soul.'

Notwithstanding the deadly hatred which Ralph felt towards Nicholas, and the bitter contempt with which he sneered at poor Mrs. Nickleby—notwithstanding the baseness with which he had behaved, and was then behaving, and would behave again if his interest prompted him, towards Kate herself—still there was, strange though it may seem, something humanising and even gentle in his thoughts at that moment. He thought of what his home might be if Kate were there; he placed her in the empty chair, looked upon her, heard her speak; he felt again upon his arm the gentle pressure of the trembling hand; he strewed his costly rooms with the hundred silent tokens of feminine presence and occupation; he came back again to the cold fireside and the silent dreary splendour; and in that one glimpse of a better nature, born as it was in selfish thoughts, the rich man felt himself friendless, childless, and alone. Gold, for the instant, lost its lustre in his eyes, for there were countless treasures of the heart which it could never purchase.

A very slight circumstance was sufficient to banish such reflections from the mind of such a man. As Ralph looked vacantly out across the yard towards the window of the other office, he became suddenly aware of the earnest observation of Newman Noggs, who, with his red nose almost touching the glass, feigned to be mending a pen with a rusty fragment of a knife, but was in reality staring at his employer with a countenance of the closest and most eager scrutiny.

Ralph exchanged his dreamy posture for his accustomed business attitude: the face of Newman disappeared, and the train of thought took to flight, all simultaneously, and in an instant.

After a few minutes, Ralph rang his bell. Newman answered the summons, and Ralph raised his eyes stealthily to his face, as if he almost feared to read there, a knowledge of his recent thoughts.

There was not the smallest speculation, however, in the countenance of Newman Noggs. If it be possible to imagine a man, with two eyes in his head, and both wide open, looking in no direction whatever, and seeing nothing, Newman appeared to be that man while Ralph Nickleby regarded him.

'How now?' growled Ralph.

'Oh!' said Newman, throwing some intelligence into his eyes all at once, and dropping them on his master, 'I thought you rang.' With which laconic remark Newman turned round and hobbled away.

'Stop!' said Ralph.

Newman stopped; not at all disconcerted.

'I did ring.'

'I knew you did.'

'Then why do you offer to go if you know that?'

'I thought you rang to say you didn't ring,' replied Newman. 'You often do.'

'How dare you pry, and peer, and stare at me, sirrah?' demanded Ralph.

'Stare!' cried Newman, 'at you! Ha, ha!' which was all the explanation Newman deigned to offer.

'Be careful, sir,' said Ralph, looking steadily at him. 'Let me have no drunken fooling here. Do you see this parcel?'

'It's big enough,' rejoined Newman.

'Carry it into the city; to Cross, in Broad Street, and leave it there—quick. Do you hear?'

Newman gave a dogged kind of nod to express an affirmative reply, and, leaving the room for a few seconds, returned with his hat. Having made various ineffective attempts to fit the parcel (which was some two feet square) into the crown thereof, Newman took it under his arm, and after putting on his fingerless gloves with great precision and nicety, keeping his eyes fixed upon Mr. Ralph Nickleby all the time, he adjusted his hat upon his head with as much care, real or pretended, as if it were a bran-new one of the most expensive quality, and at last departed on his errand.

He executed his commission with great promptitude and dispatch, only calling at one public-house for half a minute, and even that might be said to be in his way, for he went in at one door and came out at the other; but as he returned and had got so far homewards as the Strand, Newman began to loiter with the uncertain air of a man who has not quite made up his mind whether to halt or go straight forwards. After a very short consideration, the former inclination prevailed, and making towards the point he had had in his mind, Newman knocked a modest double knock, or rather a nervous single one, at Miss La Creevy's door.

It was opened by a strange servant, on whom the odd figure of the visitor did not appear to make the most favourable impression possible, inasmuch as she no sooner saw him than she very nearly closed it, and placing herself in the narrow gap, inquired what he wanted. But Newman merely uttering the monosyllable 'Noggs,' as if it were some cabalistic word, at sound of which bolts would fly back and doors open, pushed briskly past and gained the door of Miss La Creevy's sitting-room, before the astonished servant could offer any opposition.

'Walk in if you please,' said Miss La Creevy in reply to the sound of Newman's knuckles; and in he walked accordingly.

'Bless us!' cried Miss La Creevy, starting as Newman bolted in; 'what did you want, sir?'

'You have forgotten me,' said Newman, with an inclination of the head. 'I wonder at that. That nobody should remember me who knew me in other days, is natural enough; but there are few people who, seeing me once, forget me now.' He glanced, as he spoke, at his shabby clothes and paralytic limb, and slightly shook his head.

'I did forget you, I declare,' said Miss La Creevy, rising to receive Newman, who met her half-way, 'and I am ashamed of myself for doing so; for you are a kind, good creature, Mr. Noggs. Sit down and tell me all about Miss Nickleby. Poor dear thing! I haven't seen her for this many a week.'

'How's that?' asked Newman.

'Why, the truth is, Mr. Noggs,' said Miss La Creevy, 'that I have been out on a visit—the first visit I have made for fifteen years.'

'That is a long time,' said Newman, sadly.

'So it is a very long time to look back upon in years, though, somehow or other, thank Heaven, the solitary days roll away peacefully and happily enough,' replied the miniature painter. 'I have a brother, Mr. Noggs—the only relation I have—and all that time I never saw him once. Not that we ever quarrelled, but he was apprenticed down in the country, and he got married there; and new ties and affections springing up about him, he forgot a poor little woman like me, as it was very reasonable he should, you know. Don't suppose that I complain about that, because I always said to myself, "It is very natural; poor dear John is making his way in the world, and has a wife to tell his cares and troubles to, and children now to play about him, so God bless him and them, and send we may all meet together one day where we shall part no more." But what do you think, Mr. Noggs,' said the miniature painter, brightening up and clapping her hands, 'of that very same brother coming up to London at last, and never resting till he found me out; what do you think of his coming here and sitting down in that very chair, and crying like a child because he was so glad to see me—what do you think of his insisting on taking me down all the way into the country to his own house (quite a sumptuous place, Mr. Noggs, with a large garden and I don't know how many fields, and a man in livery waiting at table, and cows and horses and pigs and I don't know what besides), and making me stay a whole month, and pressing me to stop there all my life—yes, all my life—and so did his wife, and so did the children—and there were four of them, and one, the eldest girl of all, they—they had named her after me eight good years before, they had indeed. I never was so happy; in all my life I never was!' The worthy soul hid her face in her handkerchief, and sobbed aloud; for it was the first opportunity she had had of unburdening her heart, and it would have its way.

'But bless my life,' said Miss La Creevy, wiping her eyes after a short pause, and cramming her handkerchief into her pocket with great bustle and dispatch; 'what a foolish creature I must seem to you, Mr. Noggs! I shouldn't have said anything about it, only I wanted to explain to you how it was I hadn't seen Miss Nickleby.'

'Have you seen the old lady?' asked Newman.

'You mean Mrs. Nickleby?' said Miss La Creevy. 'Then I tell you what, Mr Noggs, if you want to keep in the good books in that quarter, you had better not call her the old lady any more, for I suspect she wouldn't be best pleased to hear you. Yes, I went there the night before last, but she was quite on the high ropes about something, and was so grand and mysterious, that I couldn't make anything of her: so, to tell you the truth, I took it into my head to be grand too, and came away in state. I thought she would have come round again before this, but she hasn't been here.'

'About Miss Nickleby—' said Newman.

'Why, she was here twice while I was away,' returned Miss La Creevy. 'I was afraid she mightn't like to have me calling on her among those great folks in what's-its-name Place, so I thought I'd wait a day or two, and if I didn't see her, write.'

'Ah!' exclaimed Newman, cracking his fingers.

'However, I want to hear all the news about them from you,' said Miss La Creevy. 'How is the old rough and tough monster of Golden Square? Well, of course; such people always are. I don't mean how is he in health, but how is he going on: how is he behaving himself?'

'Damn him!' cried Newman, dashing his cherished hat on the floor; 'like a false hound.'

'Gracious, Mr. Noggs, you quite terrify me!' exclaimed Miss La Creevy, turning pale.

'I should have spoilt his features yesterday afternoon if I could have afforded it,' said Newman, moving restlessly about, and shaking his fist at a portrait of Mr. Canning over the mantelpiece. 'I was very near it. I was obliged to put my hands in my pockets, and keep 'em there very tight. I shall do it some day in that little back-parlour, I know I shall. I should have done it before now, if I hadn't been afraid of making bad worse. I shall double-lock myself in with him and have it out before I die, I'm quite certain of it.'

'I shall scream if you don't compose yourself, Mr. Noggs,' said Miss La Creevy; 'I'm sure I shan't be able to help it.'

'Never mind,' rejoined Newman, darting violently to and fro. 'He's coming up tonight: I wrote to tell him. He little thinks I know; he little thinks I care. Cunning scoundrel! he don't think that. Not he, not he. Never mind, I'll thwart him—I, Newman Noggs. Ho, ho, the rascal!'

Lashing himself up to an extravagant pitch of fury, Newman Noggs jerked himself about the room with the most eccentric motion ever beheld in a human being: now sparring at the little miniatures on the wall, and now giving himself violent thumps on the head, as if to heighten the delusion, until he sank down in his former seat quite breathless and exhausted.

'There,' said Newman, picking up his hat; 'that's done me good. Now I'm better, and I'll tell you all about it.'

It took some little time to reassure Miss La Creevy, who had been almost frightened out of her senses by this remarkable demonstration; but that done, Newman faithfully related all that had passed in the interview between Kate and her uncle, prefacing his narrative with a statement of his previous suspicions on the subject, and his reasons for forming them; and concluding with a communication of the step he had taken in secretly writing to Nicholas.

Though little Miss La Creevy's indignation was not so singularly displayed as Newman's, it was scarcely inferior in violence and intensity. Indeed, if Ralph Nickleby had happened to make his appearance in the room at that moment, there is some doubt whether he would not have found Miss La Creevy a more dangerous opponent than even Newman Noggs himself.

'God forgive me for saying so,' said Miss La Creevy, as a wind-up to all her expressions of anger, 'but I really feel as if I could stick this into him with pleasure.'

It was not a very awful weapon that Miss La Creevy held, it being in fact nothing more nor less than a black-lead pencil; but discovering her mistake, the little portrait painter exchanged it for a mother-of-pearl fruit knife, wherewith, in proof of her desperate thoughts, she made a lunge as she spoke, which would have scarcely disturbed the crumb of a half-quartern loaf.

'She won't stop where she is after tonight,' said Newman. 'That's a comfort.'

'Stop!' cried Miss La Creevy, 'she should have left there, weeks ago.'

'—If we had known of this,' rejoined Newman. 'But we didn't. Nobody could properly interfere but her mother or brother. The mother's weak—poor thing—weak. The dear young man will be here tonight.'

'Heart alive!' cried Miss La Creevy. 'He will do something desperate, Mr Noggs, if you tell him all at once.'

Newman left off rubbing his hands, and assumed a thoughtful look.

'Depend upon it,' said Miss La Creevy, earnestly, 'if you are not very careful in breaking out the truth to him, he will do some violence upon his uncle or one of these men that will bring some terrible calamity upon his own head, and grief and sorrow to us all.'

'I never thought of that,' rejoined Newman, his countenance falling more and more. 'I came to ask you to receive his sister in case he brought her here, but—'

'But this is a matter of much greater importance,' interrupted Miss La Creevy; 'that you might have been sure of before you came, but the end of this, nobody can foresee, unless you are very guarded and careful.'

'What can I do?' cried Newman, scratching his head with an air of great vexation and perplexity. 'If he was to talk of pistoling 'em all, I should be obliged to say, "Certainly—serve 'em right.'"

Miss La Creevy could not suppress a small shriek on hearing this, and instantly set about extorting a solemn pledge from Newman that he would use his utmost endeavours to pacify the wrath of Nicholas; which, after some demur, was conceded. They then consulted together on the safest and surest mode of communicating to him the circumstances which had rendered his presence necessary.

'He must have time to cool before he can possibly do anything,' said Miss La Creevy. 'That is of the greatest consequence. He must not be told until late at night.'

'But he'll be in town between six and seven this evening,' replied Newman. 'I can't keep it from him when he asks me.'

'Then you must go out, Mr. Noggs,' said Miss La Creevy. 'You can easily have been kept away by business, and must not return till nearly midnight.'

'Then he will come straight here,' retorted Newman.

'So I suppose,' observed Miss La Creevy; 'but he won't find me at home, for I'll go straight to the city the instant you leave me, make up matters with Mrs. Nickleby, and take her away to the theatre, so that he may not even know where his sister lives.'

Upon further discussion, this appeared the safest and most feasible mode of proceeding that could possibly be adopted. Therefore it was finally determined that matters should be so arranged, and Newman, after listening to many supplementary cautions and entreaties, took his leave of Miss La Creevy and trudged back to Golden Square; ruminating as he went upon a vast number of possibilities and impossibilities which crowded upon his brain, and arose out of the conversation that had just terminated.

CHAPTER 32

Relating chiefly to some remarkable Conversation, and some remarkable Proceedings to which it gives rise

'London at last!' cried Nicholas, throwing back his greatcoat and rousing Smike from a long nap. 'It seemed to me as though we should never reach it.'

'And yet you came along at a tidy pace too,' observed the coachman, looking over his shoulder at Nicholas with no very pleasant expression of countenance.

'Ay, I know that,' was the reply; 'but I have been very anxious to be at my journey's end, and that makes the way seem long.'

'Well,' remarked the coachman, 'if the way seemed long with such cattle as you've sat behind, you must have been most uncommon anxious;' and so saying, he let out his whip-lash and touched up a little boy on the calves of his legs by way of emphasis.

They rattled on through the noisy, bustling, crowded street of London, now displaying long double rows of brightly-burning lamps, dotted here and there with the chemists' glaring lights, and illuminated besides with the brilliant flood that streamed from the windows of the shops, where sparkling jewellery, silks and velvets of the richest colours, the most inviting delicacies, and most sumptuous articles of luxurious ornament, succeeded each other in rich and glittering profusion. Streams of people apparently without end poured on and on, jostling each other in the crowd and hurrying forward, scarcely seeming to notice the riches that surrounded them on every side; while vehicles of all shapes and makes, mingled up together in one moving mass, like running water, lent their ceaseless roar to swell the noise and tumult.

As they dashed by the quickly-changing and ever-varying objects, it was curious to observe in what a strange procession they passed before the eye. Emporiums of splendid dresses, the materials brought from every quarter of the world; tempting stores of everything to stimulate and pamper the sated appetite and give new relish to the oft-repeated feast; vessels of burnished gold and silver, wrought into every exquisite form of vase, and dish, and goblet; guns, swords, pistols, and patent engines of destruction; screws and irons for the crooked, clothes for the newly-born, drugs for the sick, coffins for the dead, and churchyards for the buried—all these jumbled each with the other and flocking side by side, seemed to flit by in motley dance like the fantastic groups of the old Dutch painter, and with the same stern moral for the unheeding restless crowd.

Nor were there wanting objects in the crowd itself to give new point and purpose to the shifting scene. The rags of the squalid ballad-singer fluttered in the rich light that showed the goldsmith's treasures, pale and pinched-up faces hovered about the windows where was tempting food, hungry eyes wandered over the profusion guarded by one thin sheet of brittle glass—an iron wall to them; half-naked shivering figures stopped to gaze at Chinese shawls and golden stuffs of India. There was a christening party at the largest coffin-maker's and a funeral hatchment had stopped some great improvements in the bravest mansion. Life and death went hand in hand; wealth and poverty stood side by side; repletion and starvation laid them down together.

But it was London; and the old country lady inside, who had put her head out of the coach-window a mile or two this side Kingston, and cried out to the driver that she was sure he must have passed it and forgotten to set her down, was satisfied at last.

Nicholas engaged beds for himself and Smike at the inn where the coach stopped, and repaired, without the delay of another moment, to the lodgings of Newman Noggs; for his anxiety and impatience had increased with every succeeding minute, and were almost beyond control.

There was a fire in Newman's garret; and a candle had been left burning; the floor was cleanly swept, the room was as comfortably arranged as such a room could be, and meat and drink were placed in order upon the table. Everything bespoke the affectionate care and attention of Newman Noggs, but Newman himself was not there.

'Do you know what time he will be home?' inquired Nicholas, tapping at the door of Newman's front neighbour.

'Ah, Mr. Johnson!' said Crowl, presenting himself. 'Welcome, sir. How well you're looking! I never could have believed—'

'Pardon me,' interposed Nicholas. 'My question—I am extremely anxious to know.'

'Why, he has a troublesome affair of business,' replied Crowl, 'and will not be home before twelve o'clock. He was very unwilling to go, I can tell you, but there was no help for it. However, he left word that you were to make yourself comfortable till he came back, and that I was to entertain you, which I shall be very glad to do.'

In proof of his extreme readiness to exert himself for the general entertainment, Mr. Crowl drew a chair to the table as he spoke, and helping himself plentifully to the cold meat, invited Nicholas and Smike to follow his example.

Disappointed and uneasy, Nicholas could touch no food, so, after he had seen Smike comfortably established at the table, he walked out (despite a great many dissuasions uttered by Mr. Crowl with his mouth full), and left Smike to detain Newman in case he returned first.

As Miss La Creevy had anticipated, Nicholas betook himself straight to her house. Finding her from home, he debated within himself for some time whether he should go to his mother's residence, and so compromise her with Ralph Nickleby. Fully persuaded, however, that Newman would not have solicited him to return unless there was some strong reason which required his presence at home, he resolved to go there, and hastened eastwards with all speed.

Mrs. Nickleby would not be at home, the girl said, until past twelve, or later. She believed Miss Nickleby was well, but she didn't live at home now, nor did she come home except very seldom. She couldn't say where she was stopping, but it was not at Madame Mantalini's. She was sure of that.

With his heart beating violently, and apprehending he knew not what disaster, Nicholas returned to where he had left Smike. Newman had not been home. He wouldn't be, till twelve o'clock; there was no chance of it. Was there no possibility of sending to fetch him if it were only for an instant, or forwarding to him one line of writing to which he might return a verbal reply? That was quite impracticable. He was not at Golden Square, and probably had been sent to execute some commission at a distance.

Nicholas tried to remain quietly where he was, but he felt so nervous and excited that he could not sit still. He seemed to be losing time unless he was moving. It was an absurd fancy, he knew, but he was wholly unable to resist it. So, he took up his hat and rambled out again.

He strolled westward this time, pacing the long streets with hurried footsteps, and agitated by a thousand misgivings and apprehensions which he could not overcome. He passed into Hyde Park, now silent and deserted, and increased his rate of walking as if in the hope of leaving his thoughts behind. They crowded upon him more thickly, however, now there were no passing objects to attract his attention; and the one idea was always uppermost, that some stroke of ill-fortune must have occurred so calamitous in its nature that all were fearful of disclosing it to him. The old question arose again and again—What could it be? Nicholas walked till he was weary, but was not one bit the wiser; and indeed he came out of the Park at last a great deal more confused and perplexed than when he went in.

He had taken scarcely anything to eat or drink since early in the morning, and felt quite worn out and exhausted. As he returned languidly towards the point from which he had started, along one of the thoroughfares which lie between Park Lane and Bond Street, he passed a handsome hotel, before which he stopped mechanically.

'An expensive place, I dare say,' thought Nicholas; 'but a pint of wine and a biscuit are no great debauch wherever they are had. And yet I don't know.'

He walked on a few steps, but looking wistfully down the long vista of gas-lamps before him, and thinking how long it would take to reach the end of it and being besides in that kind of mood in which a man is most disposed to yield to his first impulse—and being, besides, strongly attracted to the hotel, in part by curiosity, and in part by some odd mixture of feelings which he would have been troubled to define—Nicholas turned back again, and walked into the coffee-room.

It was very handsomely furnished. The walls were ornamented with the choicest specimens of French paper, enriched with a gilded cornice of elegant design. The floor was covered with a rich carpet; and two superb mirrors, one above the chimneypiece and one at the opposite end of the room reaching from floor to ceiling, multiplied the other beauties and added new ones of their own to enhance the general effect. There was a rather noisy party of four gentlemen in a box by the fire-place, and only two other persons present—both elderly gentlemen, and both alone.

Observing all this in the first comprehensive glance with which a stranger surveys a place that is new to him, Nicholas sat himself down in the box next to the noisy party, with his back towards them, and postponing his order for a pint of claret until such time as the waiter and one of the elderly gentlemen should have settled a disputed question relative to the price of an item in the bill of fare, took up a newspaper and began to read.

He had not read twenty lines, and was in truth himself dozing, when he was startled by the mention of his sister's name. 'Little Kate Nickleby' were the words that caught his ear. He raised his head in amazement, and as he did so, saw by the reflection in the opposite glass, that two of the party behind him had risen and were standing before the fire. 'It must have come from one of them,' thought Nicholas. He waited to hear more with a countenance of some indignation, for the tone of speech had been anything but respectful, and the appearance of the individual whom he presumed to have been the speaker was coarse and swaggering.

This person—so Nicholas observed in the same glance at the mirror which had enabled him to see his face—was standing with his back to the fire conversing with a younger man, who stood with his back to the company, wore his hat, and was adjusting his shirt-collar by the aid of the glass. They spoke in whispers, now and then bursting into a loud laugh, but Nicholas could catch no repetition of the words, nor anything sounding at all like the words, which had attracted his attention.

At length the two resumed their seats, and more wine being ordered, the party grew louder in their mirth. Still there was no reference made to anybody with whom he was acquainted, and Nicholas became persuaded that his excited fancy had either imagined the sounds altogether, or converted some other words into the name which had been so much in his thoughts.

'It is remarkable too,' thought Nicholas: 'if it had been "Kate" or "Kate Nickleby," I should not have been so much surprised: but "little Kate Nickleby!"'

The wine coming at the moment prevented his finishing the sentence. He swallowed a glassful and took up the paper again. At that instant—

'Little Kate Nickleby!' cried the voice behind him.

'I was right,' muttered Nicholas as the paper fell from his hand. 'And it was the man I supposed.'

'As there was a proper objection to drinking her in heel-taps,' said the voice, 'we'll give her the first glass in the new magnum. Little Kate Nickleby!'

'Little Kate Nickleby,' cried the other three. And the glasses were set down empty.

Keenly alive to the tone and manner of this slight and careless mention of his sister's name in a public place, Nicholas fired at once; but he kept himself quiet by a great effort, and did not even turn his head.

'The jade!' said the same voice which had spoken before. 'She's a true Nickleby—a worthy imitator of her old uncle Ralph—she hangs back to be more sought after—so does he; nothing to be got out of Ralph unless you follow him up, and then the money comes doubly welcome, and the bargain doubly hard, for you're impatient and he isn't. Oh! infernal cunning.'

'Infernal cunning,' echoed two voices.

Nicholas was in a perfect agony as the two elderly gentlemen opposite, rose one after the other and went away, lest they should be the means of his losing one word of what was said. But the conversation was suspended as they withdrew, and resumed with even greater freedom when they had left the room.

'I am afraid,' said the younger gentleman, 'that the old woman has grown jea-a-lous, and locked her up. Upon my soul it looks like it.'

'If they quarrel and little Nickleby goes home to her mother, so much the better,' said the first. 'I can do anything with the old lady. She'll believe anything I tell her.'

'Egad that's true,' returned the other voice. 'Ha, ha, ha! Poor deyvle!'

The laugh was taken up by the two voices which always came in together, and became general at Mrs. Nickleby's expense. Nicholas turned burning hot with rage, but he commanded himself for the moment, and waited to hear more.

What he heard need not be repeated here. Suffice it that as the wine went round he heard enough to acquaint him with the characters and designs of those whose conversation he overhead; to possess him with the full extent of Ralph's villainy, and the real reason of his own presence being required in London. He heard all this and more. He heard his sister's sufferings derided, and her virtuous conduct jeered at and brutally misconstrued; he heard her name bandied from mouth to mouth, and herself made the subject of coarse and insolent wagers, free speech, and licentious jesting.

The man who had spoken first, led the conversation, and indeed almost engrossed it, being only stimulated from time to time by some slight observation from one or other of his companions. To him then Nicholas addressed himself when he was sufficiently composed to stand before the party, and force the words from his parched and scorching throat.

'Let me have a word with you, sir,' said Nicholas.

'With me, sir?' retorted Sir Mulberry Hawk, eyeing him in disdainful surprise.

'I said with you,' replied Nicholas, speaking with great difficulty, for his passion choked him.

'A mysterious stranger, upon my soul!' exclaimed Sir Mulberry, raising his wine-glass to his lips, and looking round upon his friends.

'Will you step apart with me for a few minutes, or do you refuse?' said Nicholas sternly.

Sir Mulberry merely paused in the act of drinking, and bade him either name his business or leave the table.

Nicholas drew a card from his pocket, and threw it before him.

'There, sir,' said Nicholas; 'my business you will guess.'

A momentary expression of astonishment, not unmixed with some confusion, appeared in the face of Sir Mulberry as he read the name; but he subdued it in an instant, and tossing the card to Lord Verisopht, who sat opposite, drew a toothpick from a glass before him, and very leisurely applied it to his mouth.

'Your name and address?' said Nicholas, turning paler as his passion kindled.

'I shall give you neither,' replied Sir Mulberry.

'If there is a gentleman in this party,' said Nicholas, looking round and scarcely able to make his white lips form the words, 'he will acquaint me with the name and residence of this man.'

There was a dead silence.

'I am the brother of the young lady who has been the subject of conversation here,' said Nicholas. 'I denounce this person as a liar, and impeach him as a coward. If he has a friend here, he will save him the disgrace of the paltry attempt to conceal his name—and utterly useless one—for I will find it out, nor leave him until I have.'

Sir Mulberry looked at him contemptuously, and, addressing his companions, said—

'Let the fellow talk, I have nothing serious to say to boys of his station; and his pretty sister shall save him a broken head, if he talks till midnight.'

'You are a base and spiritless scoundrel!' said Nicholas, 'and shall be proclaimed so to the world. I will know you; I will follow you home if you walk the streets till morning.'

Sir Mulberry's hand involuntarily closed upon the decanter, and he seemed for an instant about to launch it at the head of his challenger. But he only filled his glass, and laughed in derision.

Nicholas sat himself down, directly opposite to the party, and, summoning the waiter, paid his bill.

'Do you know that person's name?' he inquired of the man in an audible voice; pointing out Sir Mulberry as he put the question.

Sir Mulberry laughed again, and the two voices which had always spoken together, echoed the laugh; but rather feebly.

'That gentleman, sir?' replied the waiter, who, no doubt, knew his cue, and answered with just as little respect, and just as much impertinence as he could safely show: 'no, sir, I do not, sir.'

'Here, you sir,' cried Sir Mulberry, as the man was retiring; 'do you know that person's name?'

'Name, sir? No, sir.'

'Then you'll find it there,' said Sir Mulberry, throwing Nicholas's card towards him; 'and when you have made yourself master of it, put that piece of pasteboard in the fire—do you hear me?'

The man grinned, and, looking doubtfully at Nicholas, compromised the matter by sticking the card in the chimney-glass. Having done this, he retired.

Nicholas folded his arms, and biting his lip, sat perfectly quiet; sufficiently expressing by his manner, however, a firm determination to carry his threat of following Sir Mulberry home, into steady execution.

It was evident from the tone in which the younger member of the party appeared to remonstrate with his friend, that he objected to this course of proceeding, and urged him to comply with the request which Nicholas had made. Sir Mulberry, however, who was not quite sober, and who was in a sullen and dogged state of obstinacy, soon silenced the representations of his weak young friend, and further seemed—as if to save himself from a repetition of them—to insist on being left alone. However this might have been, the young gentleman and the two who had always spoken together, actually rose to go after a short interval, and presently retired, leaving their friend alone with Nicholas.

It will be very readily supposed that to one in the condition of Nicholas, the minutes appeared to move with leaden wings indeed, and that their progress did not seem the more rapid from the monotonous ticking of a French clock, or the shrill sound of its little bell which told the quarters. But there he sat; and in his old seat on the opposite side of the room reclined Sir Mulberry Hawk, with his legs upon the cushion, and his handkerchief thrown negligently over his knees: finishing his magnum of claret with the utmost coolness and indifference.

Thus they remained in perfect silence for upwards of an hour—Nicholas would have thought for three hours at least, but that the little bell had only gone four times. Twice or thrice he looked angrily and impatiently round; but there was Sir Mulberry in the same attitude, putting his glass to his lips from time to time, and looking vacantly at the wall, as if he were wholly ignorant of the presence of any living person.

At length he yawned, stretched himself, and rose; walked coolly to the glass, and having surveyed himself therein, turned round and honoured Nicholas with a long and contemptuous stare. Nicholas stared again with right good-will; Sir Mulberry shrugged his shoulders, smiled slightly, rang the bell, and ordered the waiter to help him on with his greatcoat.

The man did so, and held the door open.

'Don't wait,' said Sir Mulberry; and they were alone again.

Sir Mulberry took several turns up and down the room, whistling carelessly all the time; stopped to finish the last glass of claret which he had poured out a few minutes before, walked again, put on his hat, adjusted it by the glass, drew on his gloves, and, at last, walked slowly out. Nicholas, who had been fuming and chafing until he was nearly wild, darted from his seat, and followed him: so closely, that before the door had swung upon its hinges after Sir Mulberry's passing out, they stood side by side in the street together.

There was a private cabriolet in waiting; the groom opened the apron, and jumped out to the horse's head.

'Will you make yourself known to me?' asked Nicholas in a suppressed voice.

'No,' replied the other fiercely, and confirming the refusal with an oath. 'No.'

'If you trust to your horse's speed, you will find yourself mistaken,' said Nicholas. 'I will accompany you. By Heaven I will, if I hang on to the foot-board.'

'You shall be horsewhipped if you do,' returned Sir Mulberry.

'You are a villain,' said Nicholas.

'You are an errand-boy for aught I know,' said Sir Mulberry Hawk.

'I am the son of a country gentleman,' returned Nicholas, 'your equal in birth and education, and your superior I trust in everything besides. I tell you again, Miss Nickleby is my sister. Will you or will you not answer for your unmanly and brutal conduct?'

'To a proper champion—yes. To you—no,' returned Sir Mulberry, taking the reins in his hand. 'Stand out of the way, dog. William, let go her head.'

'You had better not,' cried Nicholas, springing on the step as Sir Mulberry jumped in, and catching at the reins. 'He has no command over the horse, mind. You shall not go—you shall not, I swear—till you have told me who you are.'

The groom hesitated, for the mare, who was a high-spirited animal and thorough-bred, plunged so violently that he could scarcely hold her.

'Leave go, I tell you!' thundered his master.

The man obeyed. The animal reared and plunged as though it would dash the carriage into a thousand pieces, but Nicholas, blind to all sense of danger, and conscious of nothing but his fury, still maintained his place and his hold upon the reins.

'Will you unclasp your hand?'

'Will you tell me who you are?'

'No!'

'No!'

In less time than the quickest tongue could tell it, these words were exchanged, and Sir Mulberry shortening his whip, applied it furiously to the head and shoulders of Nicholas. It was broken in the struggle; Nicholas gained the heavy handle, and with it laid open one side of his antagonist's face from the eye to the lip. He saw the gash; knew that the mare had darted off at a wild mad gallop; a hundred lights danced in his eyes, and he felt himself flung violently upon the ground.

He was giddy and sick, but staggered to his feet directly, roused by the loud shouts of the men who were tearing up the street, and screaming to those ahead to clear the way. He was conscious of a torrent of people rushing quickly by—looking up, could discern the cabriolet whirled along the foot-pavement with frightful rapidity—then heard a loud cry, the smashing of some heavy body, and the breaking of glass—and then the crowd closed in in the distance, and he could see or hear no more.

The general attention had been entirely directed from himself to the person in the carriage, and he was quite alone. Rightly judging that under such circumstances it would be madness to follow, he turned down a bye-street in search of the nearest coach-stand, finding after a minute or two that he was reeling like a drunken man, and aware for the first time of a stream of blood that was trickling down his face and breast.

CHAPTER 33

In which Mr. Ralph Nickleby is relieved, by a very expeditious Process, from all Commerce with his Relations

Smike and Newman Noggs, who in his impatience had returned home long before the time agreed upon, sat before the fire, listening anxiously to every footstep on the stairs, and the slightest sound that stirred within the house, for the approach of Nicholas. Time had worn on, and it was growing late. He had promised to be back in an hour; and his prolonged absence began to excite considerable alarm in the minds of both, as was abundantly testified by the blank looks they cast upon each other at every new disappointment.

At length a coach was heard to stop, and Newman ran out to light Nicholas up the stairs. Beholding him in the trim described at the conclusion of the last chapter, he stood aghast in wonder and consternation.

'Don't be alarmed,' said Nicholas, hurrying him back into the room. 'There is no harm done, beyond what a basin of water can repair.'

'No harm!' cried Newman, passing his hands hastily over the back and arms of Nicholas, as if to assure himself that he had broken no bones. 'What have you been doing?'

'I know all,' interrupted Nicholas; 'I have heard a part, and guessed the rest. But before I remove one jot of these stains, I must hear the whole from you. You see I am collected. My resolution is taken. Now, my good friend, speak out; for the time for any palliation or concealment is past, and nothing will avail Ralph Nickleby now.'

'Your dress is torn in several places; you walk lame, and I am sure you are suffering pain,' said Newman. 'Let me see to your hurts first.'

'I have no hurts to see to, beyond a little soreness and stiffness that will soon pass off,' said Nicholas, seating himself with some difficulty. 'But if I had fractured every limb, and still preserved my senses, you should not bandage one till you had told me what I have the right to know. Come,' said Nicholas, giving his hand to Noggs. 'You had a sister of your own, you told me once, who died before you fell into misfortune. Now think of her, and tell me, Newman.'

'Yes, I will, I will,' said Noggs. 'I'll tell you the whole truth.'

Newman did so. Nicholas nodded his head from time to time, as it corroborated the particulars he had already gleaned; but he fixed his eyes upon the fire, and did not look round once.

His recital ended, Newman insisted upon his young friend's stripping off his coat and allowing whatever injuries he had received to be properly tended. Nicholas, after some opposition, at length consented, and, while some pretty severe bruises on his arms and shoulders were being rubbed with oil and vinegar, and various other efficacious remedies which Newman borrowed from the different lodgers, related in what manner they had been received. The recital made a strong impression on the warm imagination of Newman; for when Nicholas came to the violent part of the quarrel, he rubbed so hard, as to occasion him the most exquisite pain, which he would not have exhibited, however, for the world, it being perfectly clear that, for the moment, Newman was operating on Sir Mulberry Hawk, and had quite lost sight of his real patient.

This martyrdom over, Nicholas arranged with Newman that while he was otherwise occupied next morning, arrangements should be made for his mother's immediately quitting her present residence, and also for dispatching Miss La Creevy to break the intelligence to her. He then wrapped himself in Smike's greatcoat, and repaired to the inn where they were to pass the night, and where (after writing a few lines to Ralph, the delivery of which was to be intrusted to Newman next day), he endeavoured to obtain the repose of which he stood so much in need.

Drunken men, they say, may roll down precipices, and be quite unconscious of any serious personal inconvenience when their reason returns. The remark may possibly apply to injuries received in other kinds of violent excitement: certain it is, that although Nicholas experienced some pain on first awakening next morning, he sprung out of bed as the clock struck seven, with very little difficulty, and was soon as much on the alert as if nothing had occurred.

Merely looking into Smike's room, and telling him that Newman Noggs would call for him very shortly, Nicholas descended into the street, and calling a hackney coach, bade the man drive to Mrs. Witterly's, according to the direction which Newman had given him on the previous night.

It wanted a quarter to eight when they reached Cadogan Place. Nicholas began to fear that no one might be stirring at that early hour, when he was relieved by the sight of a female servant, employed in cleaning the door-steps. By this functionary he was referred to the doubtful page, who appeared with dishevelled hair and a very warm and glossy face, as of a page who had just got out of bed.

By this young gentleman he was informed that Miss Nickleby was then taking her morning's walk in the gardens before the house. On the question being propounded whether he could go and find her, the page desponded and thought not; but being stimulated with a shilling, the page grew sanguine and thought he could.

'Say to Miss Nickleby that her brother is here, and in great haste to see her,' said Nicholas.

The plated buttons disappeared with an alacrity most unusual to them, and Nicholas paced the room in a state of feverish agitation which made the delay even of a minute insupportable. He soon heard a light footstep which he well knew, and before he could advance to meet her, Kate had fallen on his neck and burst into tears.

'My darling girl,' said Nicholas as he embraced her. 'How pale you are!'

'I have been so unhappy here, dear brother,' sobbed poor Kate; 'so very, very miserable. Do not leave me here, dear Nicholas, or I shall die of a broken heart.'

'I will leave you nowhere,' answered Nicholas—'never again, Kate,' he cried, moved in spite of himself as he folded her to his heart. 'Tell me that I acted for the best. Tell me that we parted because I feared to bring misfortune on your head; that it was a trial to me no less than to yourself, and that if I did wrong it was in ignorance of the world and unknowingly.'

'Why should I tell you what we know so well?' returned Kate soothingly. 'Nicholas—dear Nicholas—how can you give way thus?'

'It is such bitter reproach to me to know what you have undergone,' returned her brother; 'to see you so much altered, and yet so kind and patient—God!' cried Nicholas, clenching his fist and suddenly changing his tone and manner, 'it sets my whole blood on fire again. You must leave here with me directly; you should not have slept here last night, but that I knew all this too late. To whom can I speak, before we drive away?'

This question was most opportunely put, for at that instant Mr. Wititterly walked in, and to him Kate introduced her brother, who at once announced his purpose, and the impossibility of deferring it.

'The quarter's notice,' said Mr. Wititterly, with the gravity of a man on the right side, 'is not yet half expired. Therefore—'

'Therefore,' interposed Nicholas, 'the quarter's salary must be lost, sir. You will excuse this extreme haste, but circumstances require that I should immediately remove my sister, and I have not a moment's time to lose. Whatever she brought here I will send for, if you will allow me, in the course of the day.'

Mr. Wititterly bowed, but offered no opposition to Kate's immediate departure; with which, indeed, he was rather gratified than otherwise, Sir Tumley Snuffim having given it as his opinion, that she rather disagreed with Mrs. Wititterly's constitution.

'With regard to the trifle of salary that is due,' said Mr. Wititterly, 'I will'—here he was interrupted by a violent fit of coughing—'I will—owe it to Miss Nickleby.'

Mr. Wititterly, it should be observed, was accustomed to owe small accounts, and to leave them owing. All men have some little pleasant way of their own; and this was Mr. Wititterly's.

'If you please,' said Nicholas. And once more offering a hurried apology for so sudden a departure, he hurried Kate into the vehicle, and bade the man drive with all speed into the city.

To the city they went accordingly, with all the speed the hackney coach could make; and as the horses happened to live at Whitechapel and to be in the habit of taking their breakfast there, when they breakfasted at all, they performed the journey with greater expedition than could reasonably have been expected.

Nicholas sent Kate upstairs a few minutes before him, that his unlooked-for appearance might not alarm his mother, and when the way had been paved, presented himself with much duty and affection. Newman had not been idle, for there was a little cart at the door, and the effects were hurrying out already.

Now, Mrs. Nickleby was not the sort of person to be told anything in a hurry, or rather to comprehend anything of peculiar delicacy or importance on a short notice. Wherefore, although the good lady had been subjected to a full hour's preparation by little Miss La Creevy, and was now addressed in most lucid terms both by Nicholas and his sister, she was in a state of singular bewilderment and confusion, and could by no means be made to comprehend the necessity of such hurried proceedings.

'Why don't you ask your uncle, my dear Nicholas, what he can possibly mean by it?' said Mrs. Nickleby.

'My dear mother,' returned Nicholas, 'the time for talking has gone by. There is but one step to take, and that is to cast him off with the scorn and indignation he deserves. Your own honour and good name demand that, after the discovery of his vile proceedings, you should not be beholden to him one hour, even for the shelter of these bare walls.'

308

'To be sure,' said Mrs. Nickleby, crying bitterly, 'he is a brute, a monster; and the walls are very bare, and want painting too, and I have had this ceiling whitewashed at the expense of eighteen-pence, which is a very distressing thing, considering that it is so much gone into your uncle's pocket. I never could have believed it—never.'

'Nor I, nor anybody else,' said Nicholas.

'Lord bless my life!' exclaimed Mrs. Nickleby. 'To think that that Sir Mulberry Hawk should be such an abandoned wretch as Miss La Creevy says he is, Nicholas, my dear; when I was congratulating myself every day on his being an admirer of our dear Kate's, and thinking what a thing it would be for the family if he was to become connected with us, and use his interest to get you some profitable government place. There are very good places to be got about the court, I know; for a friend of ours (Miss Cropley, at Exeter, my dear Kate, you recollect), he had one, and I know that it was the chief part of his duty to wear silk stockings, and a bag wig like a black watch-pocket; and to think that it should come to this after all—oh, dear, dear, it's enough to kill one, that it is!' With which expressions of sorrow, Mrs. Nickleby gave fresh vent to her grief, and wept piteously.

As Nicholas and his sister were by this time compelled to superintend the removal of the few articles of furniture, Miss La Creevy devoted herself to the consolation of the matron, and observed with great kindness of manner that she must really make an effort, and cheer up.

'Oh I dare say, Miss La Creevy,' returned Mrs. Nickleby, with a petulance not unnatural in her unhappy circumstances, 'it's very easy to say cheer up, but if you had as many occasions to cheer up as I have had—and there,' said Mrs. Nickleby, stopping short. 'Think of Mr. Pyke and Mr. Pluck, two of the most perfect gentlemen that ever lived, what am I too say to them—what can I say to them? Why, if I was to say to them, "I'm told your friend Sir Mulberry is a base wretch," they'd laugh at me.'

'They will laugh no more at us, I take it,' said Nicholas, advancing. 'Come, mother, there is a coach at the door, and until Monday, at all events, we will return to our old quarters.'

'—Where everything is ready, and a hearty welcome into the bargain,' added Miss La Creevy. 'Now, let me go with you downstairs.'

But Mrs. Nickleby was not to be so easily moved, for first she insisted on going upstairs to see that nothing had been left, and then on going downstairs to see that everything had been taken away; and when she was getting into the coach she had a vision of a forgotten coffee-pot on the back-kitchen hob, and after she was shut in, a dismal recollection of a green umbrella behind some unknown door. At last Nicholas, in a condition of absolute despair, ordered the coachman to drive away, and in the unexpected jerk of a sudden starting, Mrs. Nickleby lost a shilling among the straw, which fortunately confined her attention to the coach until it was too late to remember anything else.

Having seen everything safely out, discharged the servant, and locked the door, Nicholas jumped into a cabriolet and drove to a bye place near Golden Square where he had appointed to meet Noggs; and so quickly had everything been done, that it was barely half-past nine when he reached the place of meeting.

'Here is the letter for Ralph,' said Nicholas, 'and here the key. When you come to me this evening, not a word of last night. Ill news travels fast, and they will know it soon enough. Have you heard if he was much hurt?'

Newman shook his head.

'I will ascertain that myself without loss of time,' said Nicholas.

'You had better take some rest,' returned Newman. 'You are fevered and ill.'

Nicholas waved his hand carelessly, and concealing the indisposition he really felt, now that the excitement which had sustained him was over, took a hurried farewell of Newman Noggs, and left him.

Newman was not three minutes' walk from Golden Square, but in the course of that three minutes he took the letter out of his hat and put it in again twenty times at least. First the front, then the back, then the sides, then the superscription, then the seal, were objects of Newman's admiration. Then he held it at arm's length as if to take in the whole at one delicious survey, and then he rubbed his hands in a perfect ecstasy with his commission.

He reached the office, hung his hat on its accustomed peg, laid the letter and key upon the desk, and waited impatiently until Ralph Nickleby should appear. After a few minutes, the well-known creaking of his boots was heard on the stairs, and then the bell rung.

'Has the post come in?'

'No.'

'Any other letters?'

'One.' Newman eyed him closely, and laid it on the desk.

'What's this?' asked Ralph, taking up the key.

'Left with the letter;—a boy brought them—quarter of an hour ago, or less.'

Ralph glanced at the direction, opened the letter, and read as follows:—

'You are known to me now. There are no reproaches I could heap upon your head which would carry with them one thousandth part of the grovelling shame that this assurance will awaken even in your breast.

'Your brother's widow and her orphan child spurn the shelter of your roof, and shun you with disgust and loathing. Your kindred renounce you, for they know no shame but the ties of blood which bind them in name with you.

'You are an old man, and I leave you to the grave. May every recollection of your life cling to your false heart, and cast their darkness on your death-bed.'

Ralph Nickleby read this letter twice, and frowning heavily, fell into a fit of musing; the paper fluttered from his hand and dropped upon the floor, but he clasped his fingers, as if he held it still.

Suddenly, he started from his seat, and thrusting it all crumpled into his pocket, turned furiously to Newman Noggs, as though to ask him why he lingered. But Newman stood unmoved, with his back towards him, following up, with the worn and blackened stump of an old pen, some figures in an Interest-table which was pasted against the wall, and apparently quite abstracted from every other object.

CHAPTER 34

Wherein Mr. Ralph Nickleby is visited by Persons with whom the Reader has been already made acquainted

'What a demnition long time you have kept me ringing at this confounded old cracked tea-kettle of a bell, every tinkle of which is enough to throw a strong man into blue convulsions, upon my life and soul, oh demmit,'—said Mr. Mantalini to Newman Noggs, scraping his boots, as he spoke, on Ralph Nickleby's scraper.

'I didn't hear the bell more than once,' replied Newman.

'Then you are most immensely and outr-i-geously deaf,' said Mr. Mantalini, 'as deaf as a demnition post.'

Mr. Mantalini had got by this time into the passage, and was making his way to the door of Ralph's office with very little ceremony, when Newman interposed his body; and hinting that Mr. Nickleby was unwilling to be disturbed, inquired whether the client's business was of a pressing nature.

'It is most demnebly particular,' said Mr. Mantalini. 'It is to melt some scraps of dirty paper into bright, shining, chinking, tinkling, demd mint sauce.'

Newman uttered a significant grunt, and taking Mr. Mantalini's proffered card, limped with it into his master's office. As he thrust his head in at the door, he saw that Ralph had resumed the thoughtful posture into which he had fallen after perusing his nephew's letter, and that he seemed to have been reading it again, as he once more held it open in his hand. The glance was but momentary, for Ralph, being disturbed, turned to demand the cause of the interruption.

As Newman stated it, the cause himself swaggered into the room, and grasping Ralph's horny hand with uncommon affection, vowed that he had never seen him looking so well in all his life.

'There is quite a bloom upon your demd countenance,' said Mr. Mantalini, seating himself unbidden, and arranging his hair and whiskers. 'You look quite juvenile and jolly, demmit!'

'We are alone,' returned Ralph, tartly. 'What do you want with me?'

'Good!' cried Mr. Mantalini, displaying his teeth. 'What did I want! Yes. Ha, ha! Very good. What did I want. Ha, ha. Oh dem!'

'What do you want, man?' demanded Ralph, sternly.

'Demnition discount,' returned Mr. Mantalini, with a grin, and shaking his head waggishly.

'Money is scarce,' said Ralph.

'Demd scarce, or I shouldn't want it,' interrupted Mr. Mantalini.

'The times are bad, and one scarcely knows whom to trust,' continued Ralph. 'I don't want to do business just now, in fact I would rather not; but as you are a friend—how many bills have you there?'

'Two,' returned Mr. Mantalini.

'What is the gross amount?'

'Demd trifling—five-and-seventy.'

'And the dates?'

'Two months, and four.'

'I'll do them for you—mind, for you; I wouldn't for many people—for five-and-twenty pounds,' said Ralph, deliberately.

'Oh demmit!' cried Mr. Mantalini, whose face lengthened considerably at this handsome proposal.

'Why, that leaves you fifty,' retorted Ralph. 'What would you have? Let me see the names.'

'You are so demd hard, Nickleby,' remonstrated Mr. Mantalini.

'Let me see the names,' replied Ralph, impatiently extending his hand for the bills. 'Well! They are not sure, but they are safe enough. Do you consent to the terms, and will you take the money? I don't want you to do so. I would rather you didn't.'

'Demmit, Nickleby, can't you—' began Mr. Mantalini.

'No,' replied Ralph, interrupting him. 'I can't. Will you take the money—down, mind; no delay, no going into the city and pretending to negotiate with some other party who has no existence, and never had. Is it a bargain, or is it not?'

Ralph pushed some papers from him as he spoke, and carelessly rattled his cash-box, as though by mere accident. The sound was too much for Mr Mantalini. He closed the bargain directly it reached his ears, and Ralph told the money out upon the table.

He had scarcely done so, and Mr. Mantalini had not yet gathered it all up, when a ring was heard at the bell, and immediately afterwards Newman ushered in no less a person than Madame Mantalini, at sight of whom Mr Mantalini evinced considerable discomposure, and swept the cash into his pocket with remarkable alacrity.

'Oh, you are here,' said Madame Mantalini, tossing her head.

'Yes, my life and soul, I am,' replied her husband, dropping on his knees, and pouncing with kitten-like playfulness upon a stray sovereign. 'I am here, my soul's delight, upon Tom Tiddler's ground, picking up the demnition gold and silver.'

'I am ashamed of you,' said Madame Mantalini, with much indignation.

'Ashamed—of me, my joy? It knows it is talking demd charming sweetness, but naughty fibs,' returned Mr. Mantalini. 'It knows it is not ashamed of its own popolorum tibby.'

Whatever were the circumstances which had led to such a result, it certainly appeared as though the popolorum tibby had rather miscalculated, for the nonce, the extent of his lady's affection. Madame Mantalini only looked scornful in reply; and, turning to Ralph, begged him to excuse her intrusion.

'Which is entirely attributable,' said Madame, 'to the gross misconduct and most improper behaviour of Mr. Mantalini.'

'Of me, my essential juice of pineapple!'

312

'Of you,' returned his wife. 'But I will not allow it. I will not submit to be ruined by the extravagance and profligacy of any man. I call Mr Nickleby to witness the course I intend to pursue with you.'

'Pray don't call me to witness anything, ma'am,' said Ralph. 'Settle it between yourselves, settle it between yourselves.'

'No, but I must beg you as a favour,' said Madame Mantalini, 'to hear me give him notice of what it is my fixed intention to do—my fixed intention, sir,' repeated Madame Mantalini, darting an angry look at her husband.

'Will she call me "Sir"?' cried Mantalini. 'Me who dote upon her with the demdest ardour! She, who coils her fascinations round me like a pure angelic rattlesnake! It will be all up with my feelings; she will throw me into a demd state.'

'Don't talk of feelings, sir,' rejoined Madame Mantalini, seating herself, and turning her back upon him. 'You don't consider mine.'

'I do not consider yours, my soul!' exclaimed Mr. Mantalini.

'No,' replied his wife.

And notwithstanding various blandishments on the part of Mr. Mantalini, Madame Mantalini still said no, and said it too with such determined and resolute ill-temper, that Mr. Mantalini was clearly taken aback.

'His extravagance, Mr. Nickleby,' said Madame Mantalini, addressing herself to Ralph, who leant against his easy-chair with his hands behind him, and regarded the amiable couple with a smile of the supremest and most unmitigated contempt,—'his extravagance is beyond all bounds.'

'I should scarcely have supposed it,' answered Ralph, sarcastically.

'I assure you, Mr. Nickleby, however, that it is,' returned Madame Mantalini. 'It makes me miserable! I am under constant apprehensions, and in constant difficulty. And even this,' said Madame Mantalini, wiping her eyes, 'is not the worst. He took some papers of value out of my desk this morning without asking my permission.'

Mr. Mantalini groaned slightly, and buttoned his trousers pocket.

'I am obliged,' continued Madame Mantalini, 'since our late misfortunes, to pay Miss Knag a great deal of money for having her name in the business, and I really cannot afford to encourage him in all his wastefulness. As I have no doubt that he came straight here, Mr. Nickleby, to convert the papers I have spoken of, into money, and as you have assisted us very often before, and are very much connected with us in this kind of matters, I wish you to know the determination at which his conduct has compelled me to arrive.'

Mr. Mantalini groaned once more from behind his wife's bonnet, and fitting a sovereign into one of his eyes, winked with the other at Ralph. Having achieved this performance with great dexterity, he whipped the coin into his pocket, and groaned again with increased penitence.

'I have made up my mind,' said Madame Mantalini, as tokens of impatience manifested themselves in Ralph's countenance, 'to allowance him.'

'To do that, my joy?' inquired Mr. Mantalini, who did not seem to have caught the words.

'To put him,' said Madame Mantalini, looking at Ralph, and prudently abstaining from the slightest glance at her husband, lest his many graces should induce her to falter in her resolution, 'to put him upon a fixed allowance; and I say that if he has a hundred and twenty pounds a year for his clothes and pocket-money, he may consider himself a very fortunate man.'

Mr. Mantalini waited, with much decorum, to hear the amount of the proposed stipend, but when it reached his ears, he cast his hat and cane upon the floor, and drawing out his pocket-handkerchief, gave vent to his feelings in a dismal moan.

'Demnition!' cried Mr. Mantalini, suddenly skipping out of his chair, and as suddenly skipping into it again, to the great discomposure of his lady's nerves. 'But no. It is a demd horrid dream. It is not reality. No!'

Comforting himself with this assurance, Mr. Mantalini closed his eyes and waited patiently till such time as he should wake up.

'A very judicious arrangement,' observed Ralph with a sneer, 'if your husband will keep within it, ma'am—as no doubt he will.'

'Demmit!' exclaimed Mr. Mantalini, opening his eyes at the sound of Ralph's voice, 'it is a horrid reality. She is sitting there before me. There is the graceful outline of her form; it cannot be mistaken—there is nothing like it. The two countesses had no outlines at all, and the dowager's was a demd outline. Why is she so excruciatingly beautiful that I cannot be angry with her, even now?'

'You have brought it upon yourself, Alfred,' returned Madame Mantalini—still reproachfully, but in a softened tone.

'I am a demd villain!' cried Mr. Mantalini, smiting himself on the head. 'I will fill my pockets with change for a sovereign in halfpence and drown myself in the Thames; but I will not be angry with her, even then, for I will put a note in the twopenny-post as I go along, to tell her where the body is. She will be a lovely widow. I shall be a body. Some handsome women will cry; she will laugh demnebly.'

'Alfred, you cruel, cruel creature,' said Madame Mantalini, sobbing at the dreadful picture.

'She calls me cruel—me—me—who for her sake will become a demd, damp, moist, unpleasant body!' exclaimed Mr. Mantalini.

'You know it almost breaks my heart, even to hear you talk of such a thing,' replied Madame Mantalini.

'Can I live to be mistrusted?' cried her husband. 'Have I cut my heart into a demd extraordinary number of little pieces, and given them all away, one after another, to the same little engrossing demnition captivater, and can I live to be suspected by her? Demmit, no I can't.'

'Ask Mr. Nickleby whether the sum I have mentioned is not a proper one,' reasoned Madame Mantalini.

'I don't want any sum,' replied her disconsolate husband; 'I shall require no demd allowance. I will be a body.'

On this repetition of Mr. Mantalini's fatal threat, Madame Mantalini wrung her hands, and implored the interference of Ralph Nickleby; and after a great quantity of tears and talking, and several attempts on the part of Mr. Mantalini to reach the door, preparatory to straightway committing violence upon himself, that gentleman was prevailed upon, with difficulty, to promise that he wouldn't be a body. This great point attained, Madame Mantalini argued the question of the allowance, and Mr. Mantalini did the same, taking occasion to show that he could live with uncommon satisfaction upon bread and water, and go clad in rags, but that he could not support existence with the additional burden of being mistrusted by the object of his most devoted and disinterested affection. This brought fresh tears into Madame Mantalini's eyes, which having just begun to open to some few of the demerits of Mr. Mantalini, were only open a very little way, and could be easily closed again. The result was, that without quite giving up the allowance question, Madame Mantalini, postponed its further consideration; and Ralph saw, clearly enough, that Mr. Mantalini had gained a fresh lease of his easy life, and that, for some time longer at all events, his degradation and downfall were postponed.

'But it will come soon enough,' thought Ralph; 'all love—bah! that I should use the cant of boys and girls—is fleeting enough; though that which has its sole root in the admiration of a whiskered face like that of yonder baboon, perhaps lasts the longest, as it originates in the greater blindness and is fed by vanity. Meantime the fools bring grist to my mill, so let them live out their day, and the longer it is, the better.'

These agreeable reflections occurred to Ralph Nickleby, as sundry small caresses and endearments, supposed to be unseen, were exchanged between the objects of his thoughts.

'If you have nothing more to say, my dear, to Mr. Nickleby,' said Madame Mantalini, 'we will take our leaves. I am sure we have detained him much too long already.'

Mr. Mantalini answered, in the first instance, by tapping Madame Mantalini several times on the nose, and then, by remarking in words that he had nothing more to say.

'Demmit! I have, though,' he added almost immediately, drawing Ralph into a corner. 'Here's an affair about your friend Sir Mulberry. Such a demd extraordinary out-of-the-way kind of thing as never was—eh?'

'What do you mean?' asked Ralph.

'Don't you know, demmit?' asked Mr. Mantalini.

'I see by the paper that he was thrown from his cabriolet last night, and severely injured, and that his life is in some danger,' answered Ralph with great composure; 'but I see nothing extraordinary in that—accidents are not miraculous events, when men live hard, and drive after dinner.'

'Whew!' cried Mr. Mantalini in a long shrill whistle. 'Then don't you know how it was?'

'Not unless it was as I have just supposed,' replied Ralph, shrugging his shoulders carelessly, as if to give his questioner to understand that he had no curiosity upon the subject.

'Demmit, you amaze me,' cried Mantalini.

Ralph shrugged his shoulders again, as if it were no great feat to amaze Mr. Mantalini, and cast a wistful glance at the face of Newman Noggs, which had several times appeared behind a couple of panes of glass in the room door; it being a part of Newman's duty, when unimportant people called, to make various feints of supposing that the bell had rung for him to show them out: by way of a gentle hint to such visitors that it was time to go.

'Don't you know,' said Mr. Mantalini, taking Ralph by the button, 'that it wasn't an accident at all, but a demd, furious, manslaughtering attack made upon him by your nephew?'

'What!' snarled Ralph, clenching his fists and turning a livid white.

'Demmit, Nickleby, you're as great a tiger as he is,' said Mantalini, alarmed at these demonstrations.

'Go on,' cried Ralph. 'Tell me what you mean. What is this story? Who told you? Speak,' growled Ralph. 'Do you hear me?'

''Gad, Nickleby,' said Mr. Mantalini, retreating towards his wife, 'what a demneble fierce old evil genius you are! You're enough to frighten the life and soul out of her little delicious wits—flying all at once into such a blazing, ravaging, raging passion as never was, demmit!'

'Pshaw,' rejoined Ralph, forcing a smile. 'It is but manner.'

'It is a demd uncomfortable, private-madhouse-sort of a manner,' said Mr Mantalini, picking up his cane.

Ralph affected to smile, and once more inquired from whom Mr. Mantalini had derived his information.

'From Pyke; and a demd, fine, pleasant, gentlemanly dog it is,' replied Mantalini. 'Demnition pleasant, and a tip-top sawyer.'

'And what said he?' asked Ralph, knitting his brows.

'That it happened this way—that your nephew met him at a coffeehouse, fell upon him with the most demneble ferocity, followed him to his cab, swore he would ride home with him, if he rode upon the horse's back or hooked himself on to the horse's tail; smashed his countenance, which is a demd fine countenance in its natural state; frightened the horse, pitched out Sir Mulberry and himself, and—'

'And was killed?' interposed Ralph with gleaming eyes. 'Was he? Is he dead?'

Mantalini shook his head.

'Ugh,' said Ralph, turning away. 'Then he has done nothing. Stay,' he added, looking round again. 'He broke a leg or an arm, or put his shoulder out, or fractured his collar-bone, or ground a rib or two? His neck was saved for the halter, but he got some painful and slow-healing injury for his trouble? Did he? You must have heard that, at least.'

'No,' rejoined Mantalini, shaking his head again. 'Unless he was dashed into such little pieces that they blew away, he wasn't hurt, for he went off as quiet and comfortable as—as—as demnition,' said Mr Mantalini, rather at a loss for a simile.

'And what,' said Ralph, hesitating a little, 'what was the cause of quarrel?'

'You are the demdest, knowing hand,' replied Mr. Mantalini, in an admiring tone, 'the cunningest, rummest, superlativest old fox—oh dem!—to pretend now not to know that it was the little bright-eyed niece—the softest, sweetest, prettiest—'

'Alfred!' interposed Madame Mantalini.

316

'She is always right,' rejoined Mr. Mantalini soothingly, 'and when she says it is time to go, it is time, and go she shall; and when she walks along the streets with her own tulip, the women shall say, with envy, she has got a demd fine husband; and the men shall say with rapture, he has got a demd fine wife; and they shall both be right and neither wrong, upon my life and soul—oh demmit!'

With which remarks, and many more, no less intellectual and to the purpose, Mr. Mantalini kissed the fingers of his gloves to Ralph Nickleby, and drawing his lady's arm through his, led her mincingly away.

'So, so,' muttered Ralph, dropping into his chair; 'this devil is loose again, and thwarting me, as he was born to do, at every turn. He told me once there should be a day of reckoning between us, sooner or later. I'll make him a true prophet, for it shall surely come.'

'Are you at home?' asked Newman, suddenly popping in his head.

'No,' replied Ralph, with equal abruptness.

Newman withdrew his head, but thrust it in again.

'You're quite sure you're not at home, are you?' said Newman.

'What does the idiot mean?' cried Ralph, testily.

'He has been waiting nearly ever since they first came in, and may have heard your voice—that's all,' said Newman, rubbing his hands.

'Who has?' demanded Ralph, wrought by the intelligence he had just heard, and his clerk's provoking coolness, to an intense pitch of irritation.

The necessity of a reply was superseded by the unlooked-for entrance of a third party—the individual in question—who, bringing his one eye (for he had but one) to bear on Ralph Nickleby, made a great many shambling bows, and sat himself down in an armchair, with his hands on his knees, and his short black trousers drawn up so high in the legs by the exertion of seating himself, that they scarcely reached below the tops of his Wellington boots.

'Why, this is a surprise!' said Ralph, bending his gaze upon the visitor, and half smiling as he scrutinised him attentively; 'I should know your face, Mr. Squeers.'

'Ah!' replied that worthy, 'and you'd have know'd it better, sir, if it hadn't been for all that I've been a-going through. Just lift that little boy off the tall stool in the back-office, and tell him to come in here, will you, my man?' said Squeers, addressing himself to Newman. 'Oh, he's lifted his-self off. My son, sir, little Wackford. What do you think of him, sir, for a specimen of the Dotheboys Hall feeding? Ain't he fit to bust out of his clothes, and start the seams, and make the very buttons fly off with his fatness? Here's flesh!' cried Squeers, turning the boy about, and indenting the plumpest parts of his figure with divers pokes and punches, to the great discomposure of his son and heir. 'Here's firmness, here's solidness! Why you can hardly get up enough of him between your finger and thumb to pinch him anywheres.'

In however good condition Master Squeers might have been, he certainly did not present this remarkable compactness of person, for on his father's closing his finger and thumb in illustration of his remark, he uttered a sharp cry, and rubbed the place in the most natural manner possible.

'Well,' remarked Squeers, a little disconcerted, 'I had him there; but that's because we breakfasted early this morning, and he hasn't had his lunch yet. Why you couldn't shut a bit of him in a door, when he's had his dinner. Look at them tears, sir,' said Squeers, with a triumphant air, as Master Wackford wiped his eyes with the cuff of his jacket, 'there's oiliness!'

'He looks well, indeed,' returned Ralph, who, for some purposes of his own, seemed desirous to conciliate the schoolmaster. 'But how is Mrs Squeers, and how are you?'

'Mrs. Squeers, sir,' replied the proprietor of Dotheboys, 'is as she always is—a mother to them lads, and a blessing, and a comfort, and a joy to all them as knows her. One of our boys—gorging his-self with vittles, and then turning in; that's their way—got a abscess on him last week. To see how she operated upon him with a pen-knife! Oh Lor!' said Squeers, heaving a sigh, and nodding his head a great many times, 'what a member of society that woman is!'

Mr. Squeers indulged in a retrospective look, for some quarter of a minute, as if this allusion to his lady's excellences had naturally led his mind to the peaceful village of Dotheboys near Greta Bridge in Yorkshire; and then looked at Ralph, as if waiting for him to say something.

'Have you quite recovered that scoundrel's attack?' asked Ralph.

'I've only just done it, if I've done it now,' replied Squeers. 'I was one blessed bruise, sir,' said Squeers, touching first the roots of his hair, and then the toes of his boots, 'from here to there. Vinegar and brown paper, vinegar and brown paper, from morning to night. I suppose there was a matter of half a ream of brown paper stuck upon me, from first to last. As I laid all of a heap in our kitchen, plastered all over, you might have thought I was a large brown-paper parcel, chock full of nothing but groans. Did I groan loud, Wackford, or did I groan soft?' asked Mr Squeers, appealing to his son.

'Loud,' replied Wackford.

'Was the boys sorry to see me in such a dreadful condition, Wackford, or was they glad?' asked Mr. Squeers, in a sentimental manner.

'Gl—'

'Eh?' cried Squeers, turning sharp round.

'Sorry,' rejoined his son.

'Oh!' said Squeers, catching him a smart box on the ear. 'Then take your hands out of your pockets, and don't stammer when you're asked a question. Hold your noise, sir, in a gentleman's office, or I'll run away from my family and never come back any more; and then what would become of all them precious and forlorn lads as would be let loose on the world, without their best friend at their elbers?'

'Were you obliged to have medical attendance?' inquired Ralph.

'Ay, was I,' rejoined Squeers, 'and a precious bill the medical attendant brought in too; but I paid it though.'

Ralph elevated his eyebrows in a manner which might be expressive of either sympathy or astonishment—just as the beholder was pleased to take it.

'Yes, I paid it, every farthing,' replied Squeers, who seemed to know the man he had to deal with, too well to suppose that any blinking of the question would induce him to subscribe towards the expenses; 'I wasn't out of pocket by it after all, either.'

318

'No!' said Ralph.

'Not a halfpenny,' replied Squeers. 'The fact is, we have only one extra with our boys, and that is for doctors when required—and not then, unless we're sure of our customers. Do you see?'

'I understand,' said Ralph.

'Very good,' rejoined Squeers. 'Then, after my bill was run up, we picked out five little boys (sons of small tradesmen, as was sure pay) that had never had the scarlet fever, and we sent one to a cottage where they'd got it, and he took it, and then we put the four others to sleep with him, and they took it, and then the doctor came and attended 'em once all round, and we divided my total among 'em, and added it on to their little bills, and the parents paid it. Ha! ha! ha!'

'And a good plan too,' said Ralph, eyeing the schoolmaster stealthily.

'I believe you,' rejoined Squeers. 'We always do it. Why, when Mrs. Squeers was brought to bed with little Wackford here, we ran the hooping-cough through half-a-dozen boys, and charged her expenses among 'em, monthly nurse included. Ha! ha! ha!'

Ralph never laughed, but on this occasion he produced the nearest approach to it that he could, and waiting until Mr. Squeers had enjoyed the professional joke to his heart's content, inquired what had brought him to town.

'Some bothering law business,' replied Squeers, scratching his head, 'connected with an action, for what they call neglect of a boy. I don't know what they would have. He had as good grazing, that boy had, as there is about us.'

Ralph looked as if he did not quite understand the observation.

'Grazing,' said Squeers, raising his voice, under the impression that as Ralph failed to comprehend him, he must be deaf. 'When a boy gets weak and ill and don't relish his meals, we give him a change of diet—turn him out, for an hour or so every day, into a neighbour's turnip field, or sometimes, if it's a delicate case, a turnip field and a piece of carrots alternately, and let him eat as many as he likes. There an't better land in the country than this perwerse lad grazed on, and yet he goes and catches cold and indigestion and what not, and then his friends brings a lawsuit against me! Now, you'd hardly suppose,' added Squeers, moving in his chair with the impatience of an ill-used man, 'that people's ingratitude would carry them quite as far as that; would you?'

'A hard case, indeed,' observed Ralph.

'You don't say more than the truth when you say that,' replied Squeers. 'I don't suppose there's a man going, as possesses the fondness for youth that I do. There's youth to the amount of eight hundred pound a year at Dotheboys Hall at this present time. I'd take sixteen hundred pound worth if I could get 'em, and be as fond of every individual twenty pound among 'em as nothing should equal it!'

'Are you stopping at your old quarters?' asked Ralph.

'Yes, we are at the Saracen,' replied Squeers, 'and as it don't want very long to the end of the half-year, we shall continney to stop there till I've collected the money, and some new boys too, I hope. I've brought little Wackford up, on purpose to show to parents and guardians. I shall put him in the advertisement, this time. Look at that boy—himself a pupil. Why he's a miracle of high feeding, that boy is!'

'I should like to have a word with you,' said Ralph, who had both spoken and listened mechanically for some time, and seemed to have been thinking.

'As many words as you like, sir,' rejoined Squeers. 'Wackford, you go and play in the back office, and don't move about too much or you'll get thin, and that won't do. You haven't got such a thing as twopence, Mr. Nickleby, have you?' said Squeers, rattling a bunch of keys in his coat pocket, and muttering something about its being all silver.

'I—think I have,' said Ralph, very slowly, and producing, after much rummaging in an old drawer, a penny, a halfpenny, and two farthings.

'Thankee,' said Squeers, bestowing it upon his son. 'Here! You go and buy a tart—Mr. Nickleby's man will show you where—and mind you buy a rich one. Pastry,' added Squeers, closing the door on Master Wackford, 'makes his flesh shine a good deal, and parents thinks that a healthy sign.'

With this explanation, and a peculiarly knowing look to eke it out, Mr Squeers moved his chair so as to bring himself opposite to Ralph Nickleby at no great distance off; and having planted it to his entire satisfaction, sat down.

'Attend to me,' said Ralph, bending forward a little.

Squeers nodded.

'I am not to suppose,' said Ralph, 'that you are dolt enough to forgive or forget, very readily, the violence that was committed upon you, or the exposure which accompanied it?'

'Devil a bit,' replied Squeers, tartly.

'Or to lose an opportunity of repaying it with interest, if you could get one?' said Ralph.

'Show me one, and try,' rejoined Squeers.

'Some such object it was, that induced you to call on me?' said Ralph, raising his eyes to the schoolmaster's face.

'N-n-no, I don't know that,' replied Squeers. 'I thought that if it was in your power to make me, besides the trifle of money you sent, any compensation—'

'Ah!' cried Ralph, interrupting him. 'You needn't go on.'

After a long pause, during which Ralph appeared absorbed in contemplation, he again broke silence by asking:

'Who is this boy that he took with him?'

Squeers stated his name.

'Was he young or old, healthy or sickly, tractable or rebellious? Speak out, man,' retorted Ralph.

'Why, he wasn't young,' answered Squeers; 'that is, not young for a boy, you know.'

'That is, he was not a boy at all, I suppose?' interrupted Ralph.

'Well,' returned Squeers, briskly, as if he felt relieved by the suggestion, 'he might have been nigh twenty. He wouldn't seem so old, though, to them as didn't know him, for he was a little wanting here,' touching his forehead; 'nobody at home, you know, if you knocked ever so often.'

'And you did knock pretty often, I dare say?' muttered Ralph.

'Pretty well,' returned Squeers with a grin.

'When you wrote to acknowledge the receipt of this trifle of money as you call it,' said Ralph, 'you told me his friends had deserted him long ago, and that you had not the faintest clue or trace to tell you who he was. Is that the truth?'

'It is, worse luck!' replied Squeers, becoming more and more easy and familiar in his manner, as Ralph pursued his inquiries with the less reserve. 'It's fourteen years ago, by the entry in my book, since a strange man brought him to my place, one autumn night, and left him there; paying five pound five, for his first quarter in advance. He might have been five or six year old at that time—not more.'

'What more do you know about him?' demanded Ralph.

'Devilish little, I'm sorry to say,' replied Squeers. 'The money was paid for some six or eight year, and then it stopped. He had given an address in London, had this chap; but when it came to the point, of course nobody knowed anything about him. So I kept the lad out of—out of—'

'Charity?' suggested Ralph drily.

'Charity, to be sure,' returned Squeers, rubbing his knees, 'and when he begins to be useful in a certain sort of way, this young scoundrel of a Nickleby comes and carries him off. But the most vexatious and aggeravating part of the whole affair is,' said Squeers, dropping his voice, and drawing his chair still closer to Ralph, 'that some questions have been asked about him at last—not of me, but, in a roundabout kind of way, of people in our village. So, that just when I might have had all arrears paid up, perhaps, and perhaps—who knows? such things have happened in our business before—a present besides for putting him out to a farmer, or sending him to sea, so that he might never turn up to disgrace his parents, supposing him to be a natural boy, as many of our boys are—damme, if that villain of a Nickleby don't collar him in open day, and commit as good as highway robbery upon my pocket.'

'We will both cry quits with him before long,' said Ralph, laying his hand on the arm of the Yorkshire schoolmaster.

'Quits!' echoed Squeers. 'Ah! and I should like to leave a small balance in his favour, to be settled when he can. I only wish Mrs. Squeers could catch hold of him. Bless her heart! She'd murder him, Mr. Nickleby—she would, as soon as eat her dinner.'

'We will talk of this again,' said Ralph. 'I must have time to think of it. To wound him through his own affections and fancies—. If I could strike him through this boy—'

'Strike him how you like, sir,' interrupted Squeers, 'only hit him hard enough, that's all—and with that, I'll say good-morning. Here!—just chuck that little boy's hat off that corner peg, and lift him off the stool will you?'

Bawling these requests to Newman Noggs, Mr. Squeers betook himself to the little back-office, and fitted on his child's hat with parental anxiety, while Newman, with his pen behind his ear, sat, stiff and immovable, on his stool, regarding the father and son by turns with a broad stare.

'He's a fine boy, an't he?' said Squeers, throwing his head a little on one side, and falling back to the desk, the better to estimate the proportions of little Wackford.

'Very,' said Newman.

'Pretty well swelled out, an't he?' pursued Squeers. 'He has the fatness of twenty boys, he has.'

'Ah!' replied Newman, suddenly thrusting his face into that of Squeers, 'he has;—the fatness of twenty!—more! He's got it all. God help that others. Ha! ha! Oh Lord!'

Having uttered these fragmentary observations, Newman dropped upon his desk and began to write with most marvellous rapidity.

'Why, what does the man mean?' cried Squeers, colouring. 'Is he drunk?'

Newman made no reply.

'Is he mad?' said Squeers.

But, still Newman betrayed no consciousness of any presence save his own; so, Mr. Squeers comforted himself by saying that he was both drunk and mad; and, with this parting observation, he led his hopeful son away.

In exact proportion as Ralph Nickleby became conscious of a struggling and lingering regard for Kate, had his detestation of Nicholas augmented. It might be, that to atone for the weakness of inclining to any one person, he held it necessary to hate some other more intensely than before; but such had been the course of his feelings. And now, to be defied and spurned, to be held up to her in the worst and most repulsive colours, to know that she was taught to hate and despise him: to feel that there was infection in his touch, and taint in his companionship—to know all this, and to know that the mover of it all was that same boyish poor relation who had twitted him in their very first interview, and openly bearded and braved him since, wrought his quiet and stealthy malignity to such a pitch, that there was scarcely anything he would not have hazarded to gratify it, if he could have seen his way to some immediate retaliation.

But, fortunately for Nicholas, Ralph Nickleby did not; and although he cast about all that day, and kept a corner of his brain working on the one anxious subject through all the round of schemes and business that came with it, night found him at last, still harping on the same theme, and still pursuing the same unprofitable reflections.

'When my brother was such as he,' said Ralph, 'the first comparisons were drawn between us—always in my disfavour. he was open, liberal, gallant, gay; I a crafty hunks of cold and stagnant blood, with no passion but love of saving, and no spirit beyond a thirst for gain. I recollected it well when I first saw this whipster; but I remember it better now.'

He had been occupied in tearing Nicholas's letter into atoms; and as he spoke, he scattered it in a tiny shower about him.

'Recollections like these,' pursued Ralph, with a bitter smile, 'flock upon me—when I resign myself to them—in crowds, and from countless quarters. As a portion of the world affect to despise the power of money, I must try and show them what it is.'

And being, by this time, in a pleasant frame of mind for slumber, Ralph Nickleby went to bed.

CHAPTER 35
Smike becomes known to Mrs. Nickleby and Kate. Nicholas also meets with new Acquaintances. Brighter Days seem to dawn upon the Family

Having established his mother and sister in the apartments of the kind-hearted miniature painter, and ascertained that Sir Mulberry Hawk was in no danger of losing his life, Nicholas turned his thoughts to poor Smike, who, after breakfasting with Newman Noggs, had remained, in a disconsolate state, at that worthy creature's lodgings, waiting, with much anxiety, for further intelligence of his protector.

'As he will be one of our own little household, wherever we live, or whatever fortune is in reserve for us,' thought Nicholas, 'I must present the poor fellow in due form. They will be kind to him for his own sake, and if not (on that account solely) to the full extent I could wish, they will stretch a point, I am sure, for mine.'

Nicholas said 'they', but his misgivings were confined to one person. He was sure of Kate, but he knew his mother's peculiarities, and was not quite so certain that Smike would find favour in the eyes of Mrs. Nickleby.

'However,' thought Nicholas as he departed on his benevolent errand; 'she cannot fail to become attached to him, when she knows what a devoted creature he is, and as she must quickly make the discovery, his probation will be a short one.'

'I was afraid,' said Smike, overjoyed to see his friend again, 'that you had fallen into some fresh trouble; the time seemed so long, at last, that I almost feared you were lost.'

'Lost!' replied Nicholas gaily. 'You will not be rid of me so easily, I promise you. I shall rise to the surface many thousand times yet, and the harder the thrust that pushes me down, the more quickly I shall rebound, Smike. But come; my errand here is to take you home.'

'Home!' faltered Smike, drawing timidly back.

'Ay,' rejoined Nicholas, taking his arm. 'Why not?'

'I had such hopes once,' said Smike; 'day and night, day and night, for many years. I longed for home till I was weary, and pined away with grief, but now—'

'And what now?' asked Nicholas, looking kindly in his face. 'What now, old friend?'

'I could not part from you to go to any home on earth,' replied Smike, pressing his hand; 'except one, except one. I shall never be an old man; and if your hand placed me in the grave, and I could think, before I died, that you would come and look upon it sometimes with one of your kind smiles, and in the summer weather, when everything was alive—not dead like me—I could go to that home almost without a tear.'

'Why do you talk thus, poor boy, if your life is a happy one with me?' said Nicholas.

'Because I should change; not those about me. And if they forgot me, I should never know it,' replied Smike. 'In the churchyard we are all alike, but here there are none like me. I am a poor creature, but I know that.'

'You are a foolish, silly creature,' said Nicholas cheerfully. 'If that is what you mean, I grant you that. Why, here's a dismal face for ladies' company!—my pretty sister too, whom you have so often asked me about. Is this your Yorkshire gallantry? For shame! for shame!'

Smike brightened up and smiled.

'When I talk of home,' pursued Nicholas, 'I talk of mine—which is yours of course. If it were defined by any particular four walls and a roof, God knows I should be sufficiently puzzled to say whereabouts it lay; but that is not what I mean. When I speak of home, I speak of the place where—in default of a better—those I love are gathered together; and if that place were a gypsy's tent, or a barn, I should call it by the same good name notwithstanding. And now, for what is my present home, which, however alarming your expectations may be, will neither terrify you by its extent nor its magnificence!'

So saying, Nicholas took his companion by the arm, and saying a great deal more to the same purpose, and pointing out various things to amuse and interest him as they went along, led the way to Miss La Creevy's house.

'And this, Kate,' said Nicholas, entering the room where his sister sat alone, 'is the faithful friend and affectionate fellow-traveller whom I prepared you to receive.'

Poor Smike was bashful, and awkward, and frightened enough, at first, but Kate advanced towards him so kindly, and said, in such a sweet voice, how anxious she had been to see him after all her brother had told her, and how much she had to thank him for having comforted Nicholas so greatly in their very trying reverses, that he began to be very doubtful whether he should shed tears or not, and became still more flurried. However, he managed to say, in a broken voice, that Nicholas was his only friend, and that he would lay down his life to help him; and Kate, although she was so kind and considerate, seemed to be so wholly unconscious of his distress and embarrassment, that he recovered almost immediately and felt quite at home.

Then, Miss La Creevy came in; and to her Smike had to be presented also. And Miss La Creevy was very kind too, and wonderfully talkative: not to Smike, for that would have made him uneasy at first, but to Nicholas and his sister. Then, after a time, she would speak to Smike himself now and then, asking him whether he was a judge of likenesses, and whether he thought that picture in the corner was like herself, and whether she didn't think it would have looked better if she had made herself ten years younger, and whether he didn't think, as a matter of general observation, that young ladies looked better not only in pictures, but out of them too, than old ones; with many more small jokes and facetious remarks, which were delivered with such good-humour and merriment, that Smike thought, within himself, she was the nicest lady he had ever seen; even nicer than Mrs. Grudden, of Mr. Vincent Crummles's theatre; and she was a nice lady too, and talked, perhaps more, but certainly louder, than Miss La Creevy.

At length the door opened again, and a lady in mourning came in; and Nicholas kissing the lady in mourning affectionately, and calling her his mother, led her towards the chair from which Smike had risen when she entered the room.

'You are always kind-hearted, and anxious to help the oppressed, my dear mother,' said Nicholas, 'so you will be favourably disposed towards him, I know.'

'I am sure, my dear Nicholas,' replied Mrs. Nickleby, looking very hard at her new friend, and bending to him with something more of majesty than the occasion seemed to require:

'I am sure any friend of yours has, as indeed he naturally ought to have, and must have, of course, you know, a great claim upon me, and of course, it is a very great pleasure to me to be introduced to anybody you take an interest in. There can be no doubt about that; none at all; not the least in the world,' said Mrs. Nickleby. 'At the same time I must say, Nicholas, my dear, as I used to say to your poor dear papa, when he would bring gentlemen home to dinner, and there was nothing in the house, that if he had come the day before yesterday—no, I don't mean the day before yesterday now; I should have said, perhaps, the year before last—we should have been better able to entertain him.'

With which remarks, Mrs. Nickleby turned to her daughter, and inquired, in an audible whisper, whether the gentleman was going to stop all night.

'Because, if he is, Kate, my dear,' said Mrs. Nickleby, 'I don't see that it's possible for him to sleep anywhere, and that's the truth.'

Kate stepped gracefully forward, and without any show of annoyance or irritation, breathed a few words into her mother's ear.

'La, Kate, my dear,' said Mrs. Nickleby, shrinking back, 'how you do tickle one! Of course, I understand that, my love, without your telling me; and I said the same to Nicholas, and I am very much pleased. You didn't tell me, Nicholas, my dear,' added Mrs. Nickleby, turning round with an air of less reserve than she had before assumed, 'what your friend's name is.'

'His name, mother,' replied Nicholas, 'is Smike.'

The effect of this communication was by no means anticipated; but the name was no sooner pronounced, than Mrs. Nickleby dropped upon a chair, and burst into a fit of crying.

'What is the matter?' exclaimed Nicholas, running to support her.

'It's so like Pyke,' cried Mrs. Nickleby; 'so exactly like Pyke. Oh! don't speak to me—I shall be better presently.'

And after exhibiting every symptom of slow suffocation in all its stages, and drinking about a tea-spoonful of water from a full tumbler, and spilling the remainder, Mrs. Nickleby was better, and remarked, with a feeble smile, that she was very foolish, she knew.

'It's a weakness in our family,' said Mrs. Nickleby, 'so, of course, I can't be blamed for it. Your grandmama, Kate, was exactly the same—precisely. The least excitement, the slightest surprise—she fainted away directly. I have heard her say, often and often, that when she was a young lady, and before she was married, she was turning a corner into Oxford Street one day, when she ran against her own hairdresser, who, it seems, was escaping from a bear;—the mere suddenness of the encounter made her faint away directly. Wait, though,' added Mrs. Nickleby, pausing to consider. 'Let me be sure I'm right. Was it her hairdresser who had escaped from a bear, or was it a bear who had escaped from her hairdresser's? I declare I can't remember just now, but the hairdresser was a very handsome man, I know, and quite a gentleman in his manners; so that it has nothing to do with the point of the story.'

Mrs. Nickleby having fallen imperceptibly into one of her retrospective moods, improved in temper from that moment, and glided, by an easy change of the conversation occasionally, into various other anecdotes, no less remarkable for their strict application to the subject in hand.

'Mr. Smike is from Yorkshire, Nicholas, my dear?' said Mrs. Nickleby, after dinner, and when she had been silent for some time.

'Certainly, mother,' replied Nicholas. 'I see you have not forgotten his melancholy history.'

'O dear no,' cried Mrs. Nickleby. 'Ah! melancholy, indeed. You don't happen, Mr. Smike, ever to have dined with the Grimbles of Grimble Hall, somewhere in the North Riding, do you?' said the good lady, addressing herself to him. 'A very proud man, Sir Thomas Grimble, with six grown-up and most lovely daughters, and the finest park in the county.'

'My dear mother,' reasoned Nicholas, 'do you suppose that the unfortunate outcast of a Yorkshire school was likely to receive many cards of invitation from the nobility and gentry in the neighbourhood?'

'Really, my dear, I don't know why it should be so very extraordinary,' said Mrs. Nickleby. 'I know that when I was at school, I always went at least twice every half-year to the Hawkinses at Taunton Vale, and they are much richer than the Grimbles, and connected with them in marriage; so you see it's not so very unlikely, after all.'

Having put down Nicholas in this triumphant manner, Mrs. Nickleby was suddenly seized with a forgetfulness of Smike's real name, and an irresistible tendency to call him Mr. Slammons; which circumstance she attributed to the remarkable similarity of the two names in point of sound both beginning with an S, and moreover being spelt with an M. But whatever doubt there might be on this point, there was none as to his being a most excellent listener; which circumstance had considerable influence in placing them on the very best terms, and inducing Mrs. Nickleby to express the highest opinion of his general deportment and disposition.

Thus, the little circle remained, on the most amicable and agreeable footing, until the Monday morning, when Nicholas withdrew himself from it for a short time, seriously to reflect upon the state of his affairs, and to determine, if he could, upon some course of life, which would enable him to support those who were so entirely dependent upon his exertions.

Mr. Crummles occurred to him more than once; but although Kate was acquainted with the whole history of his connection with that gentleman, his mother was not; and he foresaw a thousand fretful objections, on her part, to his seeking a livelihood upon the stage. There were graver reasons, too, against his returning to that mode of life. Independently of those arising out of its spare and precarious earnings, and his own internal conviction that he could never hope to aspire to any great distinction, even as a provincial actor, how could he carry his sister from town to town, and place to place, and debar her from any other associates than those with whom he would be compelled, almost without distinction, to mingle? 'It won't do,' said Nicholas, shaking his head; 'I must try something else.'

It was much easier to make this resolution than to carry it into effect. With no greater experience of the world than he had acquired for himself in his short trials; with a sufficient share of headlong rashness and precipitation (qualities not altogether unnatural at his time of life); with a very slender stock of money, and a still more scanty stock of friends; what could he do? 'Egad!' said Nicholas, 'I'll try that Register Office again.'

He smiled at himself as he walked away with a quick step; for, an instant before, he had been internally blaming his own precipitation. He did not laugh himself out of the intention, however, for on he went: picturing to himself, as he approached the place, all kinds of splendid possibilities, and impossibilities too, for that matter, and thinking himself, perhaps with good reason, very fortunate to be endowed with so buoyant and sanguine a temperament.

The office looked just the same as when he had left it last, and, indeed, with one or two exceptions, there seemed to be the very same placards in the window that he had seen before. There were the same unimpeachable masters and mistresses in want of virtuous servants, and the same virtuous servants in want of unimpeachable masters and mistresses, and the same magnificent estates for the investment of capital, and the same enormous quantities of capital to be invested in estates, and, in short, the same opportunities of all sorts for people who wanted to make their fortunes. And a most extraordinary proof it was of the national prosperity, that people had not been found to avail themselves of such advantages long ago.

As Nicholas stopped to look in at the window, an old gentleman happened to stop too; and Nicholas, carrying his eye along the window-panes from left to right in search of some capital-text placard which should be applicable to his own case, caught sight of this old gentleman's figure, and instinctively withdrew his eyes from the window, to observe the same more closely.

He was a sturdy old fellow in a broad-skirted blue coat, made pretty large, to fit easily, and with no particular waist; his bulky legs clothed in drab breeches and high gaiters, and his head protected by a low-crowned broad-brimmed white hat, such as a wealthy grazier might wear. He wore his coat buttoned; and his dimpled double chin rested in the folds of a white neckerchief—not one of your stiff-starched apoplectic cravats, but a good, easy, old-fashioned white neckcloth that a man might go to bed in and be none the worse for. But what principally attracted the attention of Nicholas was the old gentleman's eye,—never was such a clear, twinkling, honest, merry, happy eye, as that. And there he stood, looking a little upward, with one hand thrust into the breast of his coat, and the other playing with his old-fashioned gold watch-chain: his head thrown a little on one side, and his hat a little more on one side than his head, (but that was evidently accident; not his ordinary way of wearing it,) with such a pleasant smile playing about his mouth, and such a comical expression of mingled slyness, simplicity, kind-heartedness, and good-humour, lighting up his jolly old face, that Nicholas would have been content to have stood there and looked at him until evening, and to have forgotten, meanwhile, that there was such a thing as a soured mind or a crabbed countenance to be met with in the whole wide world.

But, even a very remote approach to this gratification was not to be made, for although he seemed quite unconscious of having been the subject of observation, he looked casually at Nicholas; and the latter, fearful of giving offence, resumed his scrutiny of the window instantly.

Still, the old gentleman stood there, glancing from placard to placard, and Nicholas could not forbear raising his eyes to his face again. Grafted upon the quaintness and oddity of his appearance, was something so indescribably engaging, and bespeaking so much worth, and there were so many little lights hovering about the corners of his mouth and eyes, that it was not a mere amusement, but a positive pleasure and delight to look at him.

This being the case, it is no wonder that the old man caught Nicholas in the fact, more than once. At such times, Nicholas coloured and looked embarrassed: for the truth is, that he had begun to wonder whether the stranger could, by any possibility, be looking for a clerk or secretary; and thinking this, he felt as if the old gentleman must know it.

Long as all this takes to tell, it was not more than a couple of minutes in passing. As the stranger was moving away, Nicholas caught his eye again, and, in the awkwardness of the moment, stammered out an apology.

'No offence. Oh no offence!' said the old man.

This was said in such a hearty tone, and the voice was so exactly what it should have been from such a speaker, and there was such a cordiality in the manner, that Nicholas was emboldened to speak again.

'A great many opportunities here, sir,' he said, half smiling as he motioned towards the window.

'A great many people willing and anxious to be employed have seriously thought so very often, I dare say,' replied the old man. 'Poor fellows, poor fellows!'

He moved away as he said this; but seeing that Nicholas was about to speak, good-naturedly slackened his pace, as if he were unwilling to cut him short. After a little of that hesitation which may be sometimes observed between two people in the street who have exchanged a nod, and are both uncertain whether they shall turn back and speak, or not, Nicholas found himself at the old man's side.

'You were about to speak, young gentleman; what were you going to say?'

'Merely that I almost hoped—I mean to say, thought—you had some object in consulting those advertisements,' said Nicholas.

'Ay, ay? what object now—what object?' returned the old man, looking slyly at Nicholas. 'Did you think I wanted a situation now—eh? Did you think I did?'

Nicholas shook his head.

'Ha! ha!' laughed the old gentleman, rubbing his hands and wrists as if he were washing them. 'A very natural thought, at all events, after seeing me gazing at those bills. I thought the same of you, at first; upon my word I did.'

'If you had thought so at last, too, sir, you would not have been far from the truth,' rejoined Nicholas.

'Eh?' cried the old man, surveying him from head to foot. 'What! Dear me! No, no. Well-behaved young gentleman reduced to such a necessity! No no, no no.'

Nicholas bowed, and bidding him good-morning, turned upon his heel.

'Stay,' said the old man, beckoning him into a bye street, where they could converse with less interruption. 'What d'ye mean, eh?'

'Merely that your kind face and manner—both so unlike any I have ever seen—tempted me into an avowal, which, to any other stranger in this wilderness of London, I should not have dreamt of making,' returned Nicholas.

'Wilderness! Yes, it is, it is. Good! It is a wilderness,' said the old man with much animation. 'It was a wilderness to me once. I came here barefoot. I have never forgotten it. Thank God!' and he raised his hat from his head, and looked very grave.

'What's the matter? What is it? How did it all come about?' said the old man, laying his hand on the shoulder of Nicholas, and walking him up the street. 'You're—Eh?' laying his finger on the sleeve of his black coat. 'Who's it for, eh?'

'My father,' replied Nicholas.

'Ah!' said the old gentleman quickly. 'Bad thing for a young man to lose his father. Widowed mother, perhaps?'

Nicholas sighed.

'Brothers and sisters too? Eh?'

'One sister,' rejoined Nicholas.

'Poor thing, poor thing! You are a scholar too, I dare say?' said the old man, looking wistfully into the face of the young one.

'I have been tolerably well educated,' said Nicholas.

'Fine thing,' said the old gentleman, 'education a great thing: a very great thing! I never had any. I admire it the more in others. A very fine thing. Yes, yes. Tell me more of your history. Let me hear it all. No impertinent curiosity—no, no, no.'

There was something so earnest and guileless in the way in which all this was said, and such a complete disregard of all conventional restraints and coldnesses, that Nicholas could not resist it. Among men who have any sound and sterling qualities, there is nothing so contagious as pure openness of heart. Nicholas took the infection instantly, and ran over the main points of his little history without reserve: merely suppressing names, and touching as lightly as possible upon his uncle's treatment of Kate. The old man listened with great attention, and when he had concluded, drew his arm eagerly through his own.

'Don't say another word. Not another word' said he. 'Come along with me. We mustn't lose a minute.'

So saying, the old gentleman dragged him back into Oxford Street, and hailing an omnibus on its way to the city, pushed Nicholas in before him, and followed himself.

As he appeared in a most extraordinary condition of restless excitement, and whenever Nicholas offered to speak, immediately interposed with: 'Don't say another word, my dear sir, on any account—not another word,' the young man thought it better to attempt no further interruption. Into the city they journeyed accordingly, without interchanging any conversation; and the farther they went, the more Nicholas wondered what the end of the adventure could possibly be.

The old gentleman got out, with great alacrity, when they reached the Bank, and once more taking Nicholas by the arm, hurried him along Threadneedle Street, and through some lanes and passages on the right, until they, at length, emerged in a quiet shady little square. Into the oldest and cleanest-looking house of business in the square, he led the way. The only inscription on the door-post was 'Cheeryble, Brothers;' but from a hasty glance at the directions of some packages which were lying about, Nicholas supposed that the brothers Cheeryble were German merchants.

Passing through a warehouse which presented every indication of a thriving business, Mr. Cheeryble (for such Nicholas supposed him to be, from the respect which had been shown him by the warehousemen and porters whom they passed) led him into a little partitioned-off counting-house like a large glass case, in which counting-house there sat—as free from dust and blemish as if he had been fixed into the glass case before the top was put on, and had never come out since—a fat, elderly, large-faced clerk, with silver spectacles and a powdered head.

'Is my brother in his room, Tim?' said Mr. Cheeryble, with no less kindness of manner than he had shown to Nicholas.

'Yes, he is, sir,' replied the fat clerk, turning his spectacle-glasses towards his principal, and his eyes towards Nicholas, 'but Mr. Trimmers is with him.'

'Ay! And what has he come about, Tim?' said Mr. Cheeryble.

'He is getting up a subscription for the widow and family of a man who was killed in the East India Docks this morning, sir,' rejoined Tim. 'Smashed, sir, by a cask of sugar.'

'He is a good creature,' said Mr. Cheeryble, with great earnestness. 'He is a kind soul. I am very much obliged to Trimmers. Trimmers is one of the best friends we have. He makes a thousand cases known to us that we should never discover of ourselves. I am very much obliged to Trimmers.' Saying which, Mr. Cheeryble rubbed his hands with infinite delight, and Mr Trimmers happening to pass the door that instant, on his way out, shot out after him and caught him by the hand.

'I owe you a thousand thanks, Trimmers, ten thousand thanks. I take it very friendly of you, very friendly indeed,' said Mr. Cheeryble, dragging him into a corner to get out of hearing. 'How many children are there, and what has my brother Ned given, Trimmers?'

'There are six children,' replied the gentleman, 'and your brother has given us twenty pounds.'

'My brother Ned is a good fellow, and you're a good fellow too, Trimmers,' said the old man, shaking him by both hands with trembling eagerness. 'Put me down for another twenty—or—stop a minute, stop a minute. We mustn't look ostentatious; put me down ten pound, and Tim Linkinwater ten pound. A cheque for twenty pound for Mr. Trimmers, Tim. God bless you, Trimmers—and come and dine with us some day this week; you'll always find a knife and fork, and we shall be delighted. Now, my dear sir—cheque from Mr. Linkinwater, Tim. Smashed by a cask of sugar, and six poor children—oh dear, dear, dear!'

Talking on in this strain, as fast as he could, to prevent any friendly remonstrances from the collector of the subscription on the large amount of his donation, Mr. Cheeryble led Nicholas, equally astonished and affected by what he had seen and heard in this short space, to the half-opened door of another room.

'Brother Ned,' said Mr. Cheeryble, tapping with his knuckles, and stooping to listen, 'are you busy, my dear brother, or can you spare time for a word or two with me?'

'Brother Charles, my dear fellow,' replied a voice from the inside, so like in its tones to that which had just spoken, that Nicholas started, and almost thought it was the same, 'don't ask me such a question, but come in directly.'

They went in, without further parley. What was the amazement of Nicholas when his conductor advanced, and exchanged a warm greeting with another old gentleman, the very type and model of himself—the same face, the same figure, the same coat, waistcoat, and neckcloth, the same breeches and gaiters—nay, there was the very same white hat hanging against the wall!

As they shook each other by the hand: the face of each lighted up by beaming looks of affection, which would have been most delightful to behold in infants, and which, in men so old, was inexpressibly touching: Nicholas could observe that the last old gentleman was something stouter than his brother; this, and a slight additional shade of clumsiness in his gait and stature, formed the only perceptible difference between them. Nobody could have doubted their being twin brothers.

'Brother Ned,' said Nicholas's friend, closing the room-door, 'here is a young friend of mine whom we must assist. We must make proper inquiries into his statements, in justice to him as well as to ourselves, and if they are confirmed—as I feel assured they will be—we must assist him, we must assist him, brother Ned.'

'It is enough, my dear brother, that you say we should,' returned the other. 'When you say that, no further inquiries are needed. He shall be assisted. What are his necessities, and what does he require? Where is Tim Linkinwater? Let us have him here.'

Both the brothers, it may be here remarked, had a very emphatic and earnest delivery; both had lost nearly the same teeth, which imparted the same peculiarity to their speech; and both spoke as if, besides possessing the utmost serenity of mind that the kindliest and most unsuspecting nature could bestow, they had, in collecting the plums from Fortune's choicest pudding, retained a few for present use, and kept them in their mouths.

'Where is Tim Linkinwater?' said brother Ned.

'Stop, stop, stop!' said brother Charles, taking the other aside. 'I've a plan, my dear brother, I've a plan. Tim is getting old, and Tim has been a faithful servant, brother Ned; and I don't think pensioning Tim's mother and sister, and buying a little tomb for the family when his poor brother died, was a sufficient recompense for his faithful services.'

'No, no, no,' replied the other. 'Certainly not. Not half enough, not half.'

'If we could lighten Tim's duties,' said the old gentleman, 'and prevail upon him to go into the country, now and then, and sleep in the fresh air, besides, two or three times a week (which he could, if he began business an hour later in the morning), old Tim Linkinwater would grow young again in time; and he's three good years our senior now. Old Tim Linkinwater young again! Eh, brother Ned, eh? Why, I recollect old Tim Linkinwater quite a little boy, don't you? Ha, ha, ha! Poor Tim, poor Tim!'

And the fine old fellows laughed pleasantly together: each with a tear of regard for old Tim Linkinwater standing in his eye.

'But hear this first—hear this first, brother Ned,' said the old man, hastily, placing two chairs, one on each side of Nicholas: 'I'll tell it you myself, brother Ned, because the young gentleman is modest, and is a scholar, Ned, and I shouldn't feel it right that he should tell us his story over and over again as if he was a beggar, or as if we doubted him. No, no no.'

'No, no, no,' returned the other, nodding his head gravely. 'Very right, my dear brother, very right.'

'He will tell me I'm wrong, if I make a mistake,' said Nicholas's friend. 'But whether I do or not, you'll be very much affected, brother Ned, remembering the time when we were two friendless lads, and earned our first shilling in this great city.'

The twins pressed each other's hands in silence; and in his own homely manner, brother Charles related the particulars he had heard from Nicholas. The conversation which ensued was a long one, and when it was over, a secret conference of almost equal duration took place between brother Ned and Tim Linkinwater in another room. It is no disparagement to Nicholas to say, that before he had been closeted with the two brothers ten minutes, he could only wave his hand at every fresh expression of kindness and sympathy, and sob like a little child.

At length brother Ned and Tim Linkinwater came back together, when Tim instantly walked up to Nicholas and whispered in his ear in a very brief sentence (for Tim was ordinarily a man of few words), that he had taken down the address in the Strand, and would call upon him that evening, at eight. Having done which, Tim wiped his spectacles and put them on, preparatory to hearing what more the brothers Cheeryble had got to say.

'Tim,' said brother Charles, 'you understand that we have an intention of taking this young gentleman into the counting-house?'

Brother Ned remarked that Tim was aware of that intention, and quite approved of it; and Tim having nodded, and said he did, drew himself up and looked particularly fat, and very important. After which, there was a profound silence.

'I'm not coming an hour later in the morning, you know,' said Tim, breaking out all at once, and looking very resolute. 'I'm not going to sleep in the fresh air; no, nor I'm not going into the country either. A pretty thing at this time of day, certainly. Pho!'

'Damn your obstinacy, Tim Linkinwater,' said brother Charles, looking at him without the faintest spark of anger, and with a countenance radiant with attachment to the old clerk. 'Damn your obstinacy, Tim Linkinwater, what do you mean, sir?'

'It's forty-four year,' said Tim, making a calculation in the air with his pen, and drawing an imaginary line before he cast it up, 'forty-four year, next May, since I first kept the books of Cheeryble, Brothers. I've opened the safe every morning all that time (Sundays excepted) as the clock struck nine, and gone over the house every night at half-past ten (except on Foreign Post nights, and then twenty minutes before twelve) to see the doors fastened, and the fires out. I've never slept out of the back-attic one single night. There's the same mignonette box in the middle of the window, and the same four flower-pots, two on each side, that I brought with me when I first came. There an't—I've said it again and again, and I'll maintain it—there an't such a square as this in the world. I know there an't,' said Tim, with sudden energy, and looking sternly about him. 'Not one. For business or pleasure, in summer-time or winter—I don't care which—there's nothing like it. There's not such a spring in England as the pump under the archway. There's not such a view in England as the view out of my window; I've seen it every morning before I shaved, and I ought to know something about it. I have slept in that room,' added Tim, sinking his voice a little, 'for four-and-forty year; and if it wasn't inconvenient, and didn't interfere with business, I should request leave to die there.'

'Damn you, Tim Linkinwater, how dare you talk about dying?' roared the twins by one impulse, and blowing their old noses violently.

'That's what I've got to say, Mr. Edwin and Mr. Charles,' said Tim, squaring his shoulders again. 'This isn't the first time you've talked about superannuating me; but, if you please, we'll make it the last, and drop the subject for evermore.'

With these words, Tim Linkinwater stalked out, and shut himself up in his glass case, with the air of a man who had had his say, and was thoroughly resolved not to be put down.

The brothers interchanged looks, and coughed some half-dozen times without speaking.

'He must be done something with, brother Ned,' said the other, warmly; 'we must disregard his old scruples; they can't be tolerated, or borne. He must be made a partner, brother Ned; and if he won't submit to it peaceably, we must have recourse to violence.'

'Quite right,' replied brother Ned, nodding his head as a man thoroughly determined; 'quite right, my dear brother. If he won't listen to reason, we must do it against his will, and show him that we are determined to exert our authority. We must quarrel with him, brother Charles.'

'We must. We certainly must have a quarrel with Tim Linkinwater,' said the other. 'But in the meantime, my dear brother, we are keeping our young friend; and the poor lady and her daughter will be anxious for his return. So let us say goodbye for the present, and—there, there—take care of that box, my dear sir—and—no, no, not a word now; but be careful of the crossings and—'

And with any disjointed and unconnected words which would prevent Nicholas from pouring forth his thanks, the brothers hurried him out: shaking hands with him all the way, and affecting very unsuccessfully—they were poor hands at deception!—to be wholly unconscious of the feelings that completely mastered him.

Nicholas's heart was too full to allow of his turning into the street until he had recovered some composure. When he at last glided out of the dark doorway corner in which he had been compelled to halt, he caught a glimpse of the twins stealthily peeping in at one corner of the glass case, evidently undecided whether they should follow up their late attack without delay, or for the present postpone laying further siege to the inflexible Tim Linkinwater.

To recount all the delight and wonder which the circumstances just detailed awakened at Miss La Creevy's, and all the things that were done, said, thought, expected, hoped, and prophesied in consequence, is beside the present course and purpose of these adventures. It is sufficient to state, in brief, that Mr. Timothy Linkinwater arrived, punctual to his appointment; that, oddity as he was, and jealous, as he was bound to be, of the proper exercise of his employers' most comprehensive liberality, he reported strongly and warmly in favour of Nicholas; and that, next day, he was appointed to the vacant stool in the counting-house of Cheeryble, Brothers, with a present salary of one hundred and twenty pounds a year.

'And I think, my dear brother,' said Nicholas's first friend, 'that if we were to let them that little cottage at Bow which is empty, at something under the usual rent, now? Eh, brother Ned?'

'For nothing at all,' said brother Ned. 'We are rich, and should be ashamed to touch the rent under such circumstances as these. Where is Tim Linkinwater?—for nothing at all, my dear brother, for nothing at all.'

'Perhaps it would be better to say something, brother Ned,' suggested the other, mildly; 'it would help to preserve habits of frugality, you know, and remove any painful sense of overwhelming obligations. We might say fifteen pound, or twenty pound, and if it was punctually paid, make it up to them in some other way. And I might secretly advance a small loan towards a little furniture, and you might secretly advance another small loan, brother Ned; and if we find them doing well—as we shall; there's no fear, no fear—we can change the loans into gifts. Carefully, brother Ned, and by degrees, and without pressing upon them too much; what do you say now, brother?'

Brother Ned gave his hand upon it, and not only said it should be done, but had it done too; and, in one short week, Nicholas took possession of the stool, and Mrs. Nickleby and Kate took possession of the house, and all was hope, bustle, and light-heartedness.

There surely never was such a week of discoveries and surprises as the first week of that cottage. Every night when Nicholas came home, something new had been found out. One day it was a grapevine, and another day it was a boiler, and another day it was the key of the front-parlour closet at the bottom of the water-butt, and so on through a hundred items. Then, this room was embellished with a muslin curtain, and that room was rendered quite elegant by a window-blind, and such improvements were made, as no one would have supposed possible. Then there was Miss La Creevy, who had come out in the omnibus to stop a day or two and help, and who was perpetually losing a very small brown-paper parcel of tin tacks and a very large hammer, and running about with her sleeves tucked up at the wrists, and falling off pairs of steps and hurting herself very much—and Mrs Nickleby, who talked incessantly, and did something now and then, but not often—and Kate, who busied herself noiselessly everywhere, and was pleased with everything—and Smike, who made the garden a perfect wonder to look upon—and Nicholas, who helped and encouraged them every one—all the peace and cheerfulness of home restored, with such new zest imparted to every frugal pleasure, and such delight to every hour of meeting, as misfortune and separation alone could give!

In short, the poor Nicklebys were social and happy; while the rich Nickleby was alone and miserable.

CHAPTER 36
Private and confidential; relating to Family Matters. Showing how Mr Kenwigs underwent violent Agitation, and how Mrs. Kenwigs was as well as could be expected

It might have been seven o'clock in the evening, and it was growing dark in the narrow streets near Golden Square, when Mr. Kenwigs sent out for a pair of the cheapest white kid gloves—those at fourteen-pence—and selecting the strongest, which happened to be the right-hand one, walked downstairs with an air of pomp and much excitement, and proceeded to muffle the knob of the street-door knocker therein. Having executed this task with great nicety, Mr. Kenwigs pulled the door to, after him, and just stepped across the road to try the effect from the opposite side of the street. Satisfied that nothing could possibly look better in its way, Mr Kenwigs then stepped back again, and calling through the keyhole to Morleena to open the door, vanished into the house, and was seen no longer.

Now, considered as an abstract circumstance, there was no more obvious cause or reason why Mr. Kenwigs should take the trouble of muffling this particular knocker, than there would have been for his muffling the knocker of any nobleman or gentleman resident ten miles off; because, for the greater convenience of the numerous lodgers, the street-door always stood wide open, and the knocker was never used at all. The first floor, the second floor, and the third floor, had each a bell of its own. As to the attics, no one ever called on them; if anybody wanted the parlours, they were close at hand, and all he had to do was to walk straight into them; while the kitchen had a separate entrance down the area steps. As a question of mere necessity and usefulness, therefore, this muffling of the knocker was thoroughly incomprehensible.

But knockers may be muffled for other purposes than those of mere utilitarianism, as, in the present instance, was clearly shown. There are certain polite forms and ceremonies which must be observed in civilised life, or mankind relapse into their original barbarism. No genteel lady was ever yet confined—indeed, no genteel confinement can possibly take place— without the accompanying symbol of a muffled knocker. Mrs Kenwigs was a lady of some pretensions to gentility; Mrs. Kenwigs was confined. And, therefore, Mr. Kenwigs tied up the silent knocker on the premises in a white kid glove.

'I'm not quite certain neither,' said Mr. Kenwigs, arranging his shirt-collar, and walking slowly upstairs, 'whether, as it's a boy, I won't have it in the papers.'

Pondering upon the advisability of this step, and the sensation it was likely to create in the neighbourhood, Mr. Kenwigs betook himself to the sitting-room, where various extremely diminutive articles of clothing were airing on a horse before the fire, and Mr. Lumbey, the doctor, was dandling the baby—that is, the old baby—not the new one.

'It's a fine boy, Mr. Kenwigs,' said Mr. Lumbey, the doctor.

'You consider him a fine boy, do you, sir?' returned Mr. Kenwigs.

'It's the finest boy I ever saw in all my life,' said the doctor. 'I never saw such a baby.'

It is a pleasant thing to reflect upon, and furnishes a complete answer to those who contend for the gradual degeneration of the human species, that every baby born into the world is a finer one than the last.

'I ne—ver saw such a baby,' said Mr. Lumbey, the doctor.

'Morleena was a fine baby,' remarked Mr. Kenwigs; as if this were rather an attack, by implication, upon the family.

'They were all fine babies,' said Mr. Lumbey. And Mr. Lumbey went on nursing the baby with a thoughtful look. Whether he was considering under what head he could best charge the nursing in the bill, was best known to himself.

During this short conversation, Miss Morleena, as the eldest of the family, and natural representative of her mother during her indisposition, had been hustling and slapping the three younger Miss Kenwigses, without intermission; which considerate and affectionate conduct brought tears into the eyes of Mr. Kenwigs, and caused him to declare that, in understanding and behaviour, that child was a woman.

'She will be a treasure to the man she marries, sir,' said Mr. Kenwigs, half aside; 'I think she'll marry above her station, Mr. Lumbey.'

'I shouldn't wonder at all,' replied the doctor.

'You never see her dance, sir, did you?' asked Mr. Kenwigs.

The doctor shook his head.

'Ay!' said Mr. Kenwigs, as though he pitied him from his heart, 'then you don't know what she's capable of.'

All this time there had been a great whisking in and out of the other room; the door had been opened and shut very softly about twenty times a minute (for it was necessary to keep Mrs. Kenwigs quiet); and the baby had been exhibited to a score or two of deputations from a select body of female friends, who had assembled in the passage, and about the street-door, to discuss the event in all its bearings. Indeed, the excitement extended itself over the whole street, and groups of ladies might be seen standing at the doors, (some in the interesting condition in which Mrs. Kenwigs had last appeared in public,) relating their experiences of similar occurrences. Some few acquired great credit from having prophesied, the day before yesterday, exactly when it would come to pass; others, again, related, how that they guessed what it was, directly they saw Mr. Kenwigs turn pale and run up the street as hard as ever he could go. Some said one thing, and some another; but all talked together, and all agreed upon two points: first, that it was very meritorious and highly praiseworthy in Mrs. Kenwigs to do as she had done: and secondly, that there never was such a skilful and scientific doctor as that Dr Lumbey.

In the midst of this general hubbub, Dr Lumbey sat in the first-floor front, as before related, nursing the deposed baby, and talking to Mr Kenwigs. He was a stout bluff-looking gentleman, with no shirt-collar to speak of, and a beard that had been growing since yesterday morning; for Dr Lumbey was popular, and the neighbourhood was prolific; and there had been no less than three other knockers muffled, one after the other within the last forty-eight hours.

'Well, Mr. Kenwigs,' said Dr Lumbey, 'this makes six. You'll have a fine family in time, sir.'

'I think six is almost enough, sir,' returned Mr. Kenwigs.

'Pooh! pooh!' said the doctor. 'Nonsense! not half enough.'

With this, the doctor laughed; but he didn't laugh half as much as a married friend of Mrs. Kenwigs's, who had just come in from the sick chamber to report progress, and take a small sip of brandy-and-water: and who seemed to consider it one of the best jokes ever launched upon society.

'They're not altogether dependent upon good fortune, neither,' said Mr Kenwigs, taking his second daughter on his knee; 'they have expectations.'

'Oh, indeed!' said Mr. Lumbey, the doctor.

'And very good ones too, I believe, haven't they?' asked the married lady.

'Why, ma'am,' said Mr. Kenwigs, 'it's not exactly for me to say what they may be, or what they may not be. It's not for me to boast of any family with which I have the honour to be connected; at the same time, Mrs Kenwigs's is—I should say,' said Mr. Kenwigs, abruptly, and raising his voice as he spoke, 'that my children might come into a matter of a hundred pound apiece, perhaps. Perhaps more, but certainly that.'

'And a very pretty little fortune,' said the married lady.

'There are some relations of Mrs. Kenwigs's,' said Mr. Kenwigs, taking a pinch of snuff from the doctor's box, and then sneezing very hard, for he wasn't used to it, 'that might leave their hundred pound apiece to ten people, and yet not go begging when they had done it.'

'Ah! I know who you mean,' observed the married lady, nodding her head.

'I made mention of no names, and I wish to make mention of no names,' said Mr. Kenwigs, with a portentous look. 'Many of my friends have met a relation of Mrs. Kenwigs's in this very room, as would do honour to any company; that's all.'

'I've met him,' said the married lady, with a glance towards Dr Lumbey.

'It's naterally very gratifying to my feelings as a father, to see such a man as that, a kissing and taking notice of my children,' pursued Mr Kenwigs. 'It's naterally very gratifying to my feelings as a man, to know that man. It will be naterally very gratifying to my feelings as a husband, to make that man acquainted with this ewent.'

Having delivered his sentiments in this form of words, Mr. Kenwigs arranged his second daughter's flaxen tail, and bade her be a good girl and mind what her sister, Morleena, said.

'That girl grows more like her mother every day,' said Mr. Lumbey, suddenly stricken with an enthusiastic admiration of Morleena.

'There!' rejoined the married lady. 'What I always say; what I always did say! She's the very picter of her.' Having thus directed the general attention to the young lady in question, the married lady embraced the opportunity of taking another sip of the brandy-and-water—and a pretty long sip too.

'Yes! there is a likeness,' said Mr. Kenwigs, after some reflection. 'But such a woman as Mrs. Kenwigs was, afore she was married! Good gracious, such a woman!'

Mr. Lumbey shook his head with great solemnity, as though to imply that he supposed she must have been rather a dazzler.

'Talk of fairies!' cried Mr. Kenwigs 'I never see anybody so light to be alive, never. Such manners too; so playful, and yet so sewerely proper! As for her figure! It isn't generally known,' said Mr. Kenwigs, dropping his voice; 'but her figure was such, at that time, that the sign of the Britannia, over in the Holloway Road, was painted from it!'

'But only see what it is now,' urged the married lady. 'Does she look like the mother of six?'

'Quite ridiculous,' cried the doctor.

'She looks a deal more like her own daughter,' said the married lady.

'So she does,' assented Mr. Lumbey. 'A great deal more.'

Mr. Kenwigs was about to make some further observations, most probably in confirmation of this opinion, when another married lady, who had looked in to keep up Mrs. Kenwigs's spirits, and help to clear off anything in the eating and drinking way that might be going about, put in her head to announce that she had just been down to answer the bell, and that there was a gentleman at the door who wanted to see Mr. Kenwigs 'most particular.'

Shadowy visions of his distinguished relation flitted through the brain of Mr. Kenwigs, as this message was delivered; and under their influence, he dispatched Morleena to show the gentleman up straightway.

'Why, I do declare,' said Mr. Kenwigs, standing opposite the door so as to get the earliest glimpse of the visitor, as he came upstairs, 'it's Mr Johnson! How do you find yourself, sir?'

Nicholas shook hands, kissed his old pupils all round, intrusted a large parcel of toys to the guardianship of Morleena, bowed to the doctor and the married ladies, and inquired after Mrs. Kenwigs in a tone of interest, which went to the very heart and soul of the nurse, who had come in to warm some mysterious compound, in a little saucepan over the fire.

'I ought to make a hundred apologies to you for calling at such a season,' said Nicholas, 'but I was not aware of it until I had rung the bell, and my time is so fully occupied now, that I feared it might be some days before I could possibly come again.'

'No time like the present, sir,' said Mr. Kenwigs. 'The sitiwation of Mrs Kenwigs, sir, is no obstacle to a little conversation between you and me, I hope?'

'You are very good,' said Nicholas.

At this juncture, proclamation was made by another married lady, that the baby had begun to eat like anything; whereupon the two married ladies, already mentioned, rushed tumultuously into the bedroom to behold him in the act.

'The fact is,' resumed Nicholas, 'that before I left the country, where I have been for some time past, I undertook to deliver a message to you.'

'Ay, ay?' said Mr. Kenwigs.

'And I have been,' added Nicholas, 'already in town for some days, without having had an opportunity of doing so.'

'It's no matter, sir,' said Mr. Kenwigs. 'I dare say it's none the worse for keeping cold. Message from the country!' said Mr. Kenwigs, ruminating; 'that's curious. I don't know anybody in the country.'

'Miss Petowker,' suggested Nicholas.

'Oh! from her, is it?' said Mr. Kenwigs. 'Oh dear, yes. Ah! Mrs. Kenwigs will be glad to hear from her. Henrietta Petowker, eh? How odd things come about, now! That you should have met her in the country! Well!'

Hearing this mention of their old friend's name, the four Miss Kenwigses gathered round Nicholas, open eyed and mouthed, to hear more. Mr. Kenwigs looked a little curious too, but quite comfortable and unsuspecting.

'The message relates to family matters,' said Nicholas, hesitating.

'Oh, never mind,' said Kenwigs, glancing at Mr. Lumbey, who, having rashly taken charge of little Lillyvick, found nobody disposed to relieve him of his precious burden. 'All friends here.'

Nicholas hemmed once or twice, and seemed to have some difficulty in proceeding.

'At Portsmouth, Henrietta Petowker is,' observed Mr. Kenwigs.

'Yes,' said Nicholas, 'Mr. Lillyvick is there.'

Mr. Kenwigs turned pale, but he recovered, and said, that was an odd coincidence also.

'The message is from him,' said Nicholas.

Mr. Kenwigs appeared to revive. He knew that his niece was in a delicate state, and had, no doubt, sent word that they were to forward full particulars. Yes. That was very kind of him; so like him too!

'He desired me to give his kindest love,' said Nicholas.

'Very much obliged to him, I'm sure. Your great-uncle, Lillyvick, my dears!' interposed Mr. Kenwigs, condescendingly explaining it to the children.

'His kindest love,' resumed Nicholas; 'and to say that he had no time to write, but that he was married to Miss Petowker.'

Mr. Kenwigs started from his seat with a petrified stare, caught his second daughter by her flaxen tail, and covered his face with his pocket-handkerchief. Morleena fell, all stiff and rigid, into the baby's chair, as she had seen her mother fall when she fainted away, and the two remaining little Kenwigses shrieked in affright.

'My children, my defrauded, swindled infants!' cried Mr. Kenwigs, pulling so hard, in his vehemence, at the flaxen tail of his second daughter, that he lifted her up on tiptoe, and kept her, for some seconds, in that attitude. 'Villain, ass, traitor!'

'Drat the man!' cried the nurse, looking angrily around. 'What does he mean by making that noise here?'

'Silence, woman!' said Mr. Kenwigs, fiercely.

'I won't be silent,' returned the nurse. 'Be silent yourself, you wretch. Have you no regard for your baby?'

'No!' returned Mr. Kenwigs.

'More shame for you,' retorted the nurse. 'Ugh! you unnatural monster.'

'Let him die,' cried Mr. Kenwigs, in the torrent of his wrath. 'Let him die! He has no expectations, no property to come into. We want no babies here,' said Mr. Kenwigs recklessly. 'Take 'em away, take 'em away to the Fondling!'

With these awful remarks, Mr. Kenwigs sat himself down in a chair, and defied the nurse, who made the best of her way into the adjoining room, and returned with a stream of matrons: declaring that Mr. Kenwigs had spoken blasphemy against his family, and must be raving mad.

Appearances were certainly not in Mr. Kenwigs's favour, for the exertion of speaking with so much vehemence, and yet in such a tone as should prevent his lamentations reaching the ears of Mrs. Kenwigs, had made him very black in the face; besides which, the excitement of the occasion, and an unwonted indulgence in various strong cordials to celebrate it, had swollen and dilated his features to a most unusual extent. But, Nicholas and the doctor—who had been passive at first, doubting very much whether Mr. Kenwigs could be in earnest—interfering to explain the immediate cause of his condition, the indignation of the matrons was changed to pity, and they implored him, with much feeling, to go quietly to bed.

'The attention,' said Mr. Kenwigs, looking around with a plaintive air, 'the attention that I've shown to that man! The hyseters he has eat, and the pints of ale he has drank, in this house—!'

'It's very trying, and very hard to bear, we know,' said one of the married ladies; 'but think of your dear darling wife.'

'Oh yes, and what she's been a undergoing of, only this day,' cried a great many voices. 'There's a good man, do.'

'The presents that have been made to him,' said Mr. Kenwigs, reverting to his calamity, 'the pipes, the snuff-boxes—a pair of india-rubber goloshes, that cost six-and-six—'

'Ah! it won't bear thinking of, indeed,' cried the matrons generally; 'but it'll all come home to him, never fear.'

Mr. Kenwigs looked darkly upon the ladies, as if he would prefer its all coming home to him, as there was nothing to be got by it; but he said nothing, and resting his head upon his hand, subsided into a kind of doze.

Then, the matrons again expatiated on the expediency of taking the good gentleman to bed; observing that he would be better tomorrow, and that they knew what was the wear and tear of some men's minds when their wives were taken as Mrs. Kenwigs had been that day, and that it did him great credit, and there was nothing to be ashamed of in it; far from it; they liked to see it, they did, for it showed a good heart. And one lady observed, as a case bearing upon the present, that her husband was often quite light-headed from anxiety on similar occasions, and that once, when her little Johnny was born, it was nearly a week before he came to himself again, during the whole of which time he did nothing but cry 'Is it a boy, is it a boy?' in a manner which went to the hearts of all his hearers.

At length, Morleena (who quite forgot she had fainted, when she found she was not noticed) announced that a chamber was ready for her afflicted parent; and Mr. Kenwigs, having partially smothered his four daughters in the closeness of his embrace, accepted the doctor's arm on one side, and the support of Nicholas on the other, and was conducted upstairs to a bedroom which been secured for the occasion.

Having seen him sound asleep, and heard him snore most satisfactorily, and having further presided over the distribution of the toys, to the perfect contentment of all the little Kenwigses, Nicholas took his leave. The matrons dropped off one by one, with the exception of six or eight particular friends, who had determined to stop all night; the lights in the houses gradually disappeared; the last bulletin was issued that Mrs Kenwigs was as well as could be expected; and the whole family were left to their repose.

CHAPTER 37
Nicholas finds further Favour in the Eyes of the brothers Cheeryble and Mr Timothy Linkinwater. The brothers give a Banquet on a great Annual Occasion. Nicholas, on returning Home from it, receives a mysterious and important Disclosure from the Lips of Mrs. Nickleby

The square in which the counting-house of the brothers Cheeryble was situated, although it might not wholly realise the very sanguine expectations which a stranger would be disposed to form on hearing the fervent encomiums bestowed upon it by Tim Linkinwater, was, nevertheless, a sufficiently desirable nook in the heart of a busy town like London, and one which occupied a high place in the affectionate remembrances of several grave persons domiciled in the neighbourhood, whose recollections, however, dated from a much more recent period, and whose attachment to the spot was far less absorbing, than were the recollections and attachment of the enthusiastic Tim.

And let not those whose eyes have been accustomed to the aristocratic gravity of Grosvenor Square and Hanover Square, the dowager barrenness and frigidity of Fitzroy Square, or the gravel walks and garden seats of the Squares of Russell and Euston, suppose that the affections of Tim Linkinwater, or the inferior lovers of this particular locality, had been awakened and kept alive by any refreshing associations with leaves, however dingy, or grass, however bare and thin. The city square has no enclosure, save the lamp-post in the middle: and no grass, but the weeds which spring up round its base. It is a quiet, little-frequented, retired spot, favourable to melancholy and contemplation, and appointments of long-waiting; and up and down its every side the Appointed saunters idly by the hour together wakening the echoes with the monotonous sound of his footsteps on the smooth worn stones, and counting, first the windows, and then the very bricks of the tall silent houses that hem him round about. In winter-time, the snow will linger there, long after it has melted from the busy streets and highways. The summer's sun holds it in some respect, and while he darts his cheerful rays sparingly into the square, keeps his fiery heat and glare for noisier and less-imposing precincts. It is so quiet, that you can almost hear the ticking of your own watch when you stop to cool in its refreshing atmosphere. There is a distant hum—of coaches, not of insects—but no other sound disturbs the stillness of the square. The ticket porter leans idly against the post at the corner: comfortably warm, but not hot, although the day is broiling. His white apron flaps languidly in the air, his head gradually droops upon his breast, he takes very long winks with both eyes at once; even he is unable to withstand the soporific influence of the place, and is gradually falling asleep. But now, he starts into full wakefulness, recoils a step or two, and gazes out before him with eager wildness in his eye. Is it a job, or a boy at marbles? Does he see a ghost, or hear an organ? No; sight more unwonted still—there is a butterfly in the square—a real, live butterfly! astray from flowers and sweets, and fluttering among the iron heads of the dusty area railings.

But if there were not many matters immediately without the doors of Cheeryble Brothers, to engage the attention or distract the thoughts of the young clerk, there were not a few within, to interest and amuse him. There was scarcely an object in the place, animate or inanimate, which did not partake in some degree of the scrupulous method and punctuality of Mr Timothy Linkinwater. Punctual as the counting-house dial, which he maintained to be the best time-keeper in London next after the clock of some old, hidden, unknown church hard by, (for Tim held the fabled goodness of that at the Horse Guards to be a pleasant fiction, invented by jealous West-enders,) the old clerk performed the minutest actions of the day, and arranged the minutest articles in the little room, in a precise and regular order, which could not have been exceeded if it had actually been a real glass case, fitted with the choicest curiosities. Paper, pens, ink, ruler, sealing-wax, wafers, pounce-box, string-box, fire-box, Tim's hat, Tim's scrupulously-folded gloves, Tim's other coat—looking precisely like a back view of himself as it hung against the wall—all had their accustomed inches of space. Except the clock, there was not such an accurate and unimpeachable instrument in existence as the little thermometer which hung behind the door. There was not a bird of such methodical and business-like habits in all the world, as the blind blackbird, who dreamed and dozed away his days in a large snug cage, and had lost his voice, from old age, years before Tim first bought him. There was not such an eventful story in the whole range of anecdote, as Tim could tell concerning the acquisition of that very bird; how, compassionating his starved and suffering condition, he had purchased him, with the view of humanely terminating his wretched life; how he determined to wait three days and see whether the bird revived; how, before half the time was out, the bird did revive; and how he went on reviving and picking up his appetite and good looks until he gradually became what—'what you see him now, sir,'—Tim would say, glancing proudly at the cage. And with that, Tim would utter a melodious chirrup, and cry 'Dick;' and Dick, who, for any sign of life he had previously given, might have been a wooden or stuffed representation of a blackbird indifferently executed, would come to the side of the cage in three small jumps, and, thrusting his bill between the bars, turn his sightless head towards his old master—and at that moment it would be very difficult to determine which of the two was the happier, the bird or Tim Linkinwater.

Nor was this all. Everything gave back, besides, some reflection of the kindly spirit of the brothers. The warehousemen and porters were such sturdy, jolly fellows, that it was a treat to see them. Among the shipping announcements and steam-packet lists which decorated the counting-house wall, were designs for almshouses, statements of charities, and plans for new hospitals. A blunderbuss and two swords hung above the chimney-piece, for the terror of evil-doers, but the blunderbuss was rusty and shattered, and the swords were broken and edgeless. Elsewhere, their open display in such a condition would have realised a smile; but, there, it seemed as though even violent and offensive weapons partook of the reigning influence, and became emblems of mercy and forbearance.

Such thoughts as these occurred to Nicholas very strongly, on the morning when he first took possession of the vacant stool, and looked about him, more freely and at ease, than he had before enjoyed an opportunity of doing. Perhaps they encouraged and stimulated him to exertion, for, during the next two weeks, all his spare hours, late at night and early in the morning, were incessantly devoted to acquiring the mysteries of book-keeping and some other forms of mercantile account. To these, he applied himself with such steadiness and perseverance that, although he brought no greater amount of previous knowledge to the subject than certain dim recollections of two or three very long sums entered into a ciphering-book at school, and relieved for parental inspection by the effigy of a fat swan tastefully flourished by the writing-master's own hand, he found himself, at the end of a fortnight, in a condition to report his proficiency to Mr. Linkinwater, and to claim his promise that he, Nicholas Nickleby, should now be allowed to assist him in his graver labours.

It was a sight to behold Tim Linkinwater slowly bring out a massive ledger and day-book, and, after turning them over and over, and affectionately dusting their backs and sides, open the leaves here and there, and cast his eyes, half mournfully, half proudly, upon the fair and unblotted entries.

'Four-and-forty year, next May!' said Tim. 'Many new ledgers since then. Four-and-forty year!'

Tim closed the book again.

'Come, come,' said Nicholas, 'I am all impatience to begin.'

Tim Linkinwater shook his head with an air of mild reproof. Mr. Nickleby was not sufficiently impressed with the deep and awful nature of his undertaking. Suppose there should be any mistake—any scratching out!

Young men are adventurous. It is extraordinary what they will rush upon, sometimes. Without even taking the precaution of sitting himself down upon his stool, but standing leisurely at the desk, and with a smile upon his face—actually a smile—there was no mistake about it; Mr Linkinwater often mentioned it afterwards—Nicholas dipped his pen into the inkstand before him, and plunged into the books of Cheeryble Brothers!

Tim Linkinwater turned pale, and tilting up his stool on the two legs nearest Nicholas, looked over his shoulder in breathless anxiety. Brother Charles and brother Ned entered the counting-house together; but Tim Linkinwater, without looking round, impatiently waved his hand as a caution that profound silence must be observed, and followed the nib of the inexperienced pen with strained and eager eyes.

The brothers looked on with smiling faces, but Tim Linkinwater smiled not, nor moved for some minutes. At length, he drew a long slow breath, and still maintaining his position on the tilted stool, glanced at brother Charles, secretly pointed with the feather of his pen towards Nicholas, and nodded his head in a grave and resolute manner, plainly signifying 'He'll do.'

Brother Charles nodded again, and exchanged a laughing look with brother Ned; but, just then, Nicholas stopped to refer to some other page, and Tim Linkinwater, unable to contain his satisfaction any longer, descended from his stool, and caught him rapturously by the hand.

'He has done it!' said Tim, looking round at his employers and shaking his head triumphantly. 'His capital B's and D's are exactly like mine; he dots all his small i's and crosses every t as he writes it. There an't such a young man as this in all London,' said Tim, clapping Nicholas on the back; 'not one. Don't tell me! The city can't produce his equal. I challenge the city to do it!'

With this casting down of his gauntlet, Tim Linkinwater struck the desk such a blow with his clenched fist, that the old blackbird tumbled off his perch with the start it gave him, and actually uttered a feeble croak, in the extremity of his astonishment.

'Well said, Tim—well said, Tim Linkinwater!' cried brother Charles, scarcely less pleased than Tim himself, and clapping his hands gently as he spoke. 'I knew our young friend would take great pains, and I was quite certain he would succeed, in no time. Didn't I say so, brother Ned?'

'You did, my dear brother; certainly, my dear brother, you said so, and you were quite right,' replied Ned. 'Quite right. Tim Linkinwater is excited, but he is justly excited, properly excited. Tim is a fine fellow. Tim Linkinwater, sir—you're a fine fellow.'

'Here's a pleasant thing to think of!' said Tim, wholly regardless of this address to himself, and raising his spectacles from the ledger to the brothers. 'Here's a pleasant thing. Do you suppose I haven't often thought of what would become of these books when I was gone? Do you suppose I haven't often thought that things might go on irregular and untidy here, after I was taken away? But now,' said Tim, extending his forefinger towards Nicholas, 'now, when I've shown him a little more, I'm satisfied. The business will go on, when I'm dead, as well as it did when I was alive—just the same—and I shall have the satisfaction of knowing that there never were such books—never were such books! No, nor never will be such books—as the books of Cheeryble Brothers.'

Having thus expressed his sentiments, Mr. Linkinwater gave vent to a short laugh, indicative of defiance to the cities of London and Westminster, and, turning again to his desk, quietly carried seventy-six from the last column he had added up, and went on with his work.

'Tim Linkinwater, sir,' said brother Charles; 'give me your hand, sir. This is your birthday. How dare you talk about anything else till you have been wished many happy returns of the day, Tim Linkinwater? God bless you, Tim! God bless you!'

'My dear brother,' said the other, seizing Tim's disengaged fist, 'Tim Linkinwater looks ten years younger than he did on his last birthday.'

'Brother Ned, my dear boy,' returned the other old fellow, 'I believe that Tim Linkinwater was born a hundred and fifty years old, and is gradually coming down to five-and-twenty; for he's younger every birthday than he was the year before.'

'So he is, brother Charles, so he is,' replied brother Ned. 'There's not a doubt about it.'

'Remember, Tim,' said brother Charles, 'that we dine at half-past five today instead of two o'clock; we always depart from our usual custom on this anniversary, as you very well know, Tim Linkinwater. Mr. Nickleby, my dear sir, you will make one. Tim Linkinwater, give me your snuff-box as a remembrance to brother Charles and myself of an attached and faithful rascal, and take that, in exchange, as a feeble mark of our respect and esteem, and don't open it until you go to bed, and never say another word upon the subject, or I'll kill the blackbird. A dog! He should have had a golden cage half-a-dozen years ago, if it would have made him or his master a bit the happier. Now, brother Ned, my dear fellow, I'm ready. At half-past five, remember, Mr. Nickleby! Tim Linkinwater, sir, take care of Mr. Nickleby at half-past five. Now, brother Ned.'

Chattering away thus, according to custom, to prevent the possibility of any thanks or acknowledgment being expressed on the other side, the twins trotted off, arm-in-arm; having endowed Tim Linkinwater with a costly gold snuff-box, enclosing a bank note worth more than its value ten times told.

At a quarter past five o'clock, punctual to the minute, arrived, according to annual usage, Tim Linkinwater's sister; and a great to-do there was, between Tim Linkinwater's sister and the old housekeeper, respecting Tim Linkinwater's sister's cap, which had been dispatched, per boy, from the house of the family where Tim Linkinwater's sister boarded, and had not yet come to hand: notwithstanding that it had been packed up in a bandbox, and the bandbox in a handkerchief, and the handkerchief tied on to the boy's arm; and notwithstanding, too, that the place of its consignment had been duly set forth, at full length, on the back of an old letter, and the boy enjoined, under pain of divers horrible penalties, the full extent of which the eye of man could not foresee, to deliver the same with all possible speed, and not to loiter by the way. Tim Linkinwater's sister lamented; the housekeeper condoled; and both kept thrusting their heads out of the second-floor window to see if the boy was 'coming'—which would have been highly satisfactory, and, upon the whole, tantamount to his being come, as the distance to the corner was not quite five yards—when, all of a sudden, and when he was least expected, the messenger, carrying the bandbox with elaborate caution, appeared in an exactly opposite direction, puffing and panting for breath, and flushed with recent exercise; as well he might be; for he had taken the air, in the first instance, behind a hackney coach that went to Camberwell, and had followed two Punches afterwards and had seen the Stilts home to their own door. The cap was all safe, however—that was one comfort—and it was no use scolding him—that was another; so the boy went upon his way rejoicing, and Tim Linkinwater's sister presented herself to the company below-stairs, just five minutes after the half-hour had struck by Tim Linkinwater's own infallible clock.

The company consisted of the brothers Cheeryble, Tim Linkinwater, a ruddy-faced white-headed friend of Tim's (who was a superannuated bank clerk), and Nicholas, who was presented to Tim Linkinwater's sister with much gravity and solemnity. The party being now completed, brother Ned rang for dinner, and, dinner being shortly afterwards announced, led Tim Linkinwater's sister into the next room, where it was set forth with great preparation. Then, brother Ned took the head of the table, and brother Charles the foot; and Tim Linkinwater's sister sat on the left hand of brother Ned, and Tim Linkinwater himself on his right: and an ancient butler of apoplectic appearance, and with very short legs, took up his position at the back of brother Ned's armchair, and, waving his right arm preparatory to taking off the covers with a flourish, stood bolt upright and motionless.

'For these and all other blessings, brother Charles,' said Ned.

'Lord, make us truly thankful, brother Ned,' said Charles.

Whereupon the apoplectic butler whisked off the top of the soup tureen, and shot, all at once, into a state of violent activity.

There was abundance of conversation, and little fear of its ever flagging, for the good-humour of the glorious old twins drew everybody out, and Tim Linkinwater's sister went off into a long and circumstantial account of Tim Linkinwater's infancy, immediately after the very first glass of champagne—taking care to premise that she was very much Tim's junior, and had only become acquainted with the facts from their being preserved and handed down in the family. This history concluded, brother Ned related how that, exactly thirty-five years ago, Tim Linkinwater was suspected to have received a love-letter, and how that vague information had been brought to the counting-house of his having been seen walking down Cheapside with an uncommonly handsome spinster; at which there was a roar of laughter, and Tim Linkinwater being charged with blushing, and called upon to explain, denied that the accusation was true; and further, that there would have been any harm in it if it had been; which last position occasioned the superannuated bank clerk to laugh tremendously, and to declare that it was the very best thing he had ever heard in his life, and that Tim Linkinwater might say a great many things before he said anything which would beat that.

There was one little ceremony peculiar to the day, both the matter and manner of which made a very strong impression upon Nicholas. The cloth having been removed and the decanters sent round for the first time, a profound silence succeeded, and in the cheerful faces of the brothers there appeared an expression, not of absolute melancholy, but of quiet thoughtfulness very unusual at a festive table. As Nicholas, struck by this sudden alteration, was wondering what it could portend, the brothers rose together, and the one at the top of the table leaning forward towards the other, and speaking in a low voice as if he were addressing him individually, said:

'Brother Charles, my dear fellow, there is another association connected with this day which must never be forgotten, and never can be forgotten, by you and me. This day, which brought into the world a most faithful and excellent and exemplary fellow, took from it the kindest and very best of parents, the very best of parents to us both. I wish that she could have seen us in our prosperity, and shared it, and had the happiness of knowing how dearly we loved her in it, as we did when we were two poor boys; but that was not to be. My dear brother—The Memory of our Mother.'

'Good Lord!' thought Nicholas, 'and there are scores of people of their own station, knowing all this, and twenty thousand times more, who wouldn't ask these men to dinner because they eat with their knives and never went to school!'

But there was no time to moralise, for the joviality again became very brisk, and the decanter of port being nearly out, brother Ned pulled the bell, which was instantly answered by the apoplectic butler.

'David,' said brother Ned.

'Sir,' replied the butler.

'A magnum of the double-diamond, David, to drink the health of Mr Linkinwater.'

Instantly, by a feat of dexterity, which was the admiration of all the company, and had been, annually, for some years past, the apoplectic butler, bringing his left hand from behind the small of his back, produced the bottle with the corkscrew already inserted; uncorked it at a jerk; and placed the magnum and the cork before his master with the dignity of conscious cleverness.

'Ha!' said brother Ned, first examining the cork and afterwards filling his glass, while the old butler looked complacently and amiably on, as if it were all his own property, but the company were quite welcome to make free with it, 'this looks well, David.'

'It ought to, sir,' replied David. 'You'd be troubled to find such a glass of wine as is our double-diamond, and that Mr. Linkinwater knows very well. That was laid down when Mr. Linkinwater first come: that wine was, gentlemen.'

'Nay, David, nay,' interposed brother Charles.

'I wrote the entry in the cellar-book myself, sir, if you please,' said David, in the tone of a man, quite confident in the strength of his facts. 'Mr. Linkinwater had only been here twenty year, sir, when that pipe of double-diamond was laid down.'

'David is quite right, quite right, brother Charles,' said Ned: 'are the people here, David?'

'Outside the door, sir,' replied the butler.

'Show 'em in, David, show 'em in.'

At this bidding, the older butler placed before his master a small tray of clean glasses, and opening the door admitted the jolly porters and warehousemen whom Nicholas had seen below. They were four in all, and as they came in, bowing, and grinning, and blushing, the housekeeper, and cook, and housemaid, brought up the rear.

'Seven,' said brother Ned, filling a corresponding number of glasses with the double-diamond, 'and David, eight. There! Now, you're all of you to drink the health of your best friend Mr. Timothy Linkinwater, and wish him health and long life and many happy returns of this day, both for his own sake and that of your old masters, who consider him an inestimable treasure. Tim Linkinwater, sir, your health. Devil take you, Tim Linkinwater, sir, God bless you.'

With this singular contradiction of terms, brother Ned gave Tim Linkinwater a slap on the back, which made him look, for the moment, almost as apoplectic as the butler: and tossed off the contents of his glass in a twinkling.

The toast was scarcely drunk with all honour to Tim Linkinwater, when the sturdiest and jolliest subordinate elbowed himself a little in advance of his fellows, and exhibiting a very hot and flushed countenance, pulled a single lock of grey hair in the middle of his forehead as a respectful salute to the company, and delivered himself as follows—rubbing the palms of his hands very hard on a blue cotton handkerchief as he did so:

'We're allowed to take a liberty once a year, gen'lemen, and if you please we'll take it now; there being no time like the present, and no two birds in the hand worth one in the bush, as is well known—leastways in a contrairy sense, which the meaning is the same. (A pause—the butler unconvinced.) What we mean to say is, that there never was (looking at the butler)—such—(looking at the cook) noble—excellent—(looking everywhere and seeing nobody) free, generous-spirited masters as them as has treated us so handsome this day. And here's thanking of 'em for all their goodness as is so constancy a diffusing of itself over everywhere, and wishing they may live long and die happy!'

When the foregoing speech was over—and it might have been much more elegant and much less to the purpose—the whole body of subordinates under command of the apoplectic butler gave three soft cheers; which, to that gentleman's great indignation, were not very regular, inasmuch as the women persisted in giving an immense number of little shrill hurrahs among themselves, in utter disregard of the time. This done, they withdrew; shortly afterwards, Tim Linkinwater's sister withdrew; in reasonable time after that, the sitting was broken up for tea and coffee, and a round game of cards.

At half-past ten—late hours for the square—there appeared a little tray of sandwiches and a bowl of bishop, which bishop coming on the top of the double-diamond, and other excitements, had such an effect upon Tim Linkinwater, that he drew Nicholas aside, and gave him to understand, confidentially, that it was quite true about the uncommonly handsome spinster, and that she was to the full as good-looking as she had been described—more so, indeed—but that she was in too much of a hurry to change her condition, and consequently, while Tim was courting her and thinking of changing his, got married to somebody else. 'After all, I dare say it was my fault,' said Tim. 'I'll show you a print I have got upstairs, one of these days. It cost me five-and-twenty shillings. I bought it soon after we were cool to each other. Don't mention it, but it's the most extraordinary accidental likeness you ever saw—her very portrait, sir!'

By this time it was past eleven o'clock; and Tim Linkinwater's sister declaring that she ought to have been at home a full hour ago, a coach was procured, into which she was handed with great ceremony by brother Ned, while brother Charles imparted the fullest directions to the coachman, and besides paying the man a shilling over and above his fare, in order that he might take the utmost care of the lady, all but choked him with a glass of spirits of uncommon strength, and then nearly knocked all the breath out of his body in his energetic endeavours to knock it in again.

At length the coach rumbled off, and Tim Linkinwater's sister being now fairly on her way home, Nicholas and Tim Linkinwater's friend took their leaves together, and left old Tim and the worthy brothers to their repose.

As Nicholas had some distance to walk, it was considerably past midnight by the time he reached home, where he found his mother and Smike sitting up to receive him. It was long after their usual hour of retiring, and they had expected him, at the very latest, two hours ago; but the time had not hung heavily on their hands, for Mrs. Nickleby had entertained Smike with a genealogical account of her family by the mother's side, comprising biographical sketches of the principal members, and Smike had sat wondering what it was all about, and whether it was learnt from a book, or said out of Mrs. Nickleby's own head; so that they got on together very pleasantly.

Nicholas could not go to bed without expatiating on the excellences and munificence of the brothers Cheeryble, and relating the great success which had attended his efforts that day. But before he had said a dozen words, Mrs. Nickleby, with many sly winks and nods, observed, that she was sure Mr. Smike must be quite tired out, and that she positively must insist on his not sitting up a minute longer.

'A most biddable creature he is, to be sure,' said Mrs. Nickleby, when Smike had wished them good-night and left the room. 'I know you'll excuse me, Nicholas, my dear, but I don't like to do this before a third person; indeed, before a young man it would not be quite proper, though really, after all, I don't know what harm there is in it, except that to be sure it's not a very becoming thing, though some people say it is very much so, and really I don't know why it should not be, if it's well got up, and the borders are small-plaited; of course, a good deal depends upon that.'

With which preface, Mrs. Nickleby took her nightcap from between the leaves of a very large prayer-book where it had been folded up small, and proceeded to tie it on: talking away in her usual discursive manner, all the time.

'People may say what they like,' observed Mrs. Nickleby, 'but there's a great deal of comfort in a nightcap, as I'm sure you would confess, Nicholas my dear, if you would only have strings to yours, and wear it like a Christian, instead of sticking it upon the very top of your head like a blue-coat boy. You needn't think it an unmanly or quizzical thing to be particular about your nightcap, for I have often heard your poor dear papa, and the Reverend Mr. What's-his-name, who used to read prayers in that old church with the curious little steeple that the weathercock was blown off the night week before you were born,—I have often heard them say, that the young men at college are uncommonly particular about their nightcaps, and that the Oxford nightcaps are quite celebrated for their strength and goodness; so much so, indeed, that the young men never dream of going to bed without 'em, and I believe it's admitted on all hands that they know what's good, and don't coddle themselves.'

Nicholas laughed, and entering no further into the subject of this lengthened harangue, reverted to the pleasant tone of the little birthday party. And as Mrs. Nickleby instantly became very curious respecting it, and made a great number of inquiries touching what they had had for dinner, and how it was put on table, and whether it was overdone or underdone, and who was there, and what 'the Mr. Cherrybles' said, and what Nicholas said, and what the Mr. Cherrybles said when he said that; Nicholas described the festivities at full length, and also the occurrences of the morning.

'Late as it is,' said Nicholas, 'I am almost selfish enough to wish that Kate had been up to hear all this. I was all impatience, as I came along, to tell her.'

'Why, Kate,' said Mrs. Nickleby, putting her feet upon the fender, and drawing her chair close to it, as if settling herself for a long talk. 'Kate has been in bed—oh! a couple of hours—and I'm very glad, Nicholas my dear, that I prevailed upon her not to sit up, for I wished very much to have an opportunity of saying a few words to you. I am naturally anxious about it, and of course it's a very delightful and consoling thing to have a grown-up son that one can put confidence in, and advise with; indeed I don't know any use there would be in having sons at all, unless people could put confidence in them.'

Nicholas stopped in the middle of a sleepy yawn, as his mother began to speak: and looked at her with fixed attention.

'There was a lady in our neighbourhood,' said Mrs. Nickleby, 'speaking of sons puts me in mind of it—a lady in our neighbourhood when we lived near Dawlish, I think her name was Rogers; indeed I am sure it was if it wasn't Murphy, which is the only doubt I have—'

'Is it about her, mother, that you wished to speak to me?' said Nicholas quietly.

'About her!' cried Mrs. Nickleby. 'Good gracious, Nicholas, my dear, how can you be so ridiculous! But that was always the way with your poor dear papa,—just his way—always wandering, never able to fix his thoughts on any one subject for two minutes together. I think I see him now!' said Mrs. Nickleby, wiping her eyes, 'looking at me while I was talking to him about his affairs, just as if his ideas were in a state of perfect conglomeration! Anybody who had come in upon us suddenly, would have supposed I was confusing and distracting him instead of making things plainer; upon my word they would.'

'I am very sorry, mother, that I should inherit this unfortunate slowness of apprehension,' said Nicholas, kindly; 'but I'll do my best to understand you, if you'll only go straight on: indeed I will.'

'Your poor pa!' said Mrs. Nickleby, pondering. 'He never knew, till it was too late, what I would have had him do!'

This was undoubtedly the case, inasmuch as the deceased Mr. Nickleby had not arrived at the knowledge when he died. Neither had Mrs. Nickleby herself; which is, in some sort, an explanation of the circumstance.

'However,' said Mrs. Nickleby, drying her tears, 'this has nothing to do—certainly nothing whatever to do—with the gentleman in the next house.'

'I should suppose that the gentleman in the next house has as little to do with us,' returned Nicholas.

'There can be no doubt,' said Mrs. Nickleby, 'that he is a gentleman, and has the manners of a gentleman, and the appearance of a gentleman, although he does wear smalls and grey worsted stockings. That may be eccentricity, or he may be proud of his legs. I don't see why he shouldn't be. The Prince Regent was proud of his legs, and so was Daniel Lambert, who was also a fat man; he was proud of his legs. So was Miss Biffin: she was—no,' added Mrs. Nickleby, correcting, herself, 'I think she had only toes, but the principle is the same.'

Nicholas looked on, quite amazed at the introduction of this new theme. Which seemed just what Mrs. Nickleby had expected him to be.

'You may well be surprised, Nicholas, my dear,' she said, 'I am sure I was. It came upon me like a flash of fire, and almost froze my blood. The bottom of his garden joins the bottom of ours, and of course I had several times seen him sitting among the scarlet-beans in his little arbour, or working at his little hot-beds. I used to think he stared rather, but I didn't take any particular notice of that, as we were newcomers, and he might be curious to see what we were like. But when he began to throw his cucumbers over our wall—'

'To throw his cucumbers over our wall!' repeated Nicholas, in great astonishment.

'Yes, Nicholas, my dear,' replied Mrs. Nickleby in a very serious tone; 'his cucumbers over our wall. And vegetable marrows likewise.'

'Confound his impudence!' said Nicholas, firing immediately. 'What does he mean by that?'

'I don't think he means it impertinently at all,' replied Mrs. Nickleby.

'What!' said Nicholas, 'cucumbers and vegetable marrows flying at the heads of the family as they walk in their own garden, and not meant impertinently! Why, mother—'

Nicholas stopped short; for there was an indescribable expression of placid triumph, mingled with a modest confusion, lingering between the borders of Mrs. Nickleby's nightcap, which arrested his attention suddenly.

'He must be a very weak, and foolish, and inconsiderate man,' said Mrs Nickleby; 'blamable indeed—at least I suppose other people would consider him so; of course I can't be expected to express any opinion on that point, especially after always defending your poor dear papa when other people blamed him for making proposals to me; and to be sure there can be no doubt that he has taken a very singular way of showing it. Still at the same time, his attentions are—that is, as far as it goes, and to a certain extent of course—a flattering sort of thing; and although I should never dream of marrying again with a dear girl like Kate still unsettled in life—'

'Surely, mother, such an idea never entered your brain for an instant?' said Nicholas.

'Bless my heart, Nicholas my dear,' returned his mother in a peevish tone, 'isn't that precisely what I am saying, if you would only let me speak? Of course, I never gave it a second thought, and I am surprised and astonished that you should suppose me capable of such a thing. All I say is, what step is the best to take, so as to reject these advances civilly and delicately, and without hurting his feelings too much, and driving him to despair, or anything of that kind? My goodness me!' exclaimed Mrs Nickleby, with a half-simper, 'suppose he was to go doing anything rash to himself. Could I ever be happy again, Nicholas?'

Despite his vexation and concern, Nicholas could scarcely help smiling, as he rejoined, 'Now, do you think, mother, that such a result would be likely to ensue from the most cruel repulse?'

'Upon my word, my dear, I don't know,' returned Mrs. Nickleby; 'really, I don't know. I am sure there was a case in the day before yesterday's paper, extracted from one of the French newspapers, about a journeyman shoemaker who was jealous of a young girl in an adjoining village, because she wouldn't shut herself up in an air-tight three-pair-of-stairs, and charcoal herself to death with him; and who went and hid himself in a wood with a sharp-pointed knife, and rushed out, as she was passing by with a few friends, and killed himself first, and then all the friends, and then her—no, killed all the friends first, and then herself, and then himself—which it is quite frightful to think of. Somehow or other,' added Mrs. Nickleby, after a momentary pause, 'they always are journeyman shoemakers who do these things in France, according to the papers. I don't know how it is—something in the leather, I suppose.'

'But this man, who is not a shoemaker—what has he done, mother, what has he said?' inquired Nicholas, fretted almost beyond endurance, but looking nearly as resigned and patient as Mrs. Nickleby herself. 'You know, there is no language of vegetables, which converts a cucumber into a formal declaration of attachment.'

'My dear,' replied Mrs. Nickleby, tossing her head and looking at the ashes in the grate, 'he has done and said all sorts of things.'

'Is there no mistake on your part?' asked Nicholas.

'Mistake!' cried Mrs. Nickleby. 'Lord, Nicholas my dear, do you suppose I don't know when a man's in earnest?'

'Well, well!' muttered Nicholas.

'Every time I go to the window,' said Mrs. Nickleby, 'he kisses one hand, and lays the other upon his heart—of course it's very foolish of him to do so, and I dare say you'll say it's very wrong, but he does it very respectfully—very respectfully indeed—and very tenderly, extremely tenderly. So far, he deserves the greatest credit; there can be no doubt about that. Then, there are the presents which come pouring over the wall every day, and very fine they certainly are, very fine; we had one of the cucumbers at dinner yesterday, and think of pickling the rest for next winter. And last evening,' added Mrs. Nickleby, with increased confusion, 'he called gently over the wall, as I was walking in the garden, and proposed marriage, and an elopement. His voice is as clear as a bell or a musical glass—very like a musical glass indeed—but of course I didn't listen to it. Then, the question is, Nicholas my dear, what am I to do?'

'Does Kate know of this?' asked Nicholas.

'I have not said a word about it yet,' answered his mother.

'Then, for Heaven's sake,' rejoined Nicholas, rising, 'do not, for it would make her very unhappy. And with regard to what you should do, my dear mother, do what your good sense and feeling, and respect for my father's memory, would prompt. There are a thousand ways in which you can show your dislike of these preposterous and doting attentions. If you act as decidedly as you ought and they are still continued, and to your annoyance, I can speedily put a stop to them. But I should not interfere in a matter so ridiculous, and attach importance to it, until you have vindicated yourself. Most women can do that, but especially one of your age and condition, in circumstances like these, which are unworthy of a serious thought. I would not shame you by seeming to take them to heart, or treat them earnestly for an instant. Absurd old idiot!'

So saying, Nicholas kissed his mother, and bade her good-night, and they retired to their respective chambers.

To do Mrs. Nickleby justice, her attachment to her children would have prevented her seriously contemplating a second marriage, even if she could have so far conquered her recollections of her late husband as to have any strong inclinations that way. But, although there was no evil and little real selfishness in Mrs. Nickleby's heart, she had a weak head and a vain one; and there was something so flattering in being sought (and vainly sought) in marriage at this time of day, that she could not dismiss the passion of the unknown gentleman quite so summarily or lightly as Nicholas appeared to deem becoming.

'As to its being preposterous, and doting, and ridiculous,' thought Mrs Nickleby, communing with herself in her own room, 'I don't see that, at all. It's hopeless on his part, certainly; but why he should be an absurd old idiot, I confess I don't see. He is not to be supposed to know it's hopeless. Poor fellow! He is to be pitied, I think!'

Having made these reflections, Mrs. Nickleby looked in her little dressing-glass, and walking backward a few steps from it, tried to remember who it was who used to say that when Nicholas was one-and-twenty he would have more the appearance of her brother than her son. Not being able to call the authority to mind, she extinguished her candle, and drew up the window-blind to admit the light of morning, which had, by this time, begun to dawn.

'It's a bad light to distinguish objects in,' murmured Mrs. Nickleby, peering into the garden, 'and my eyes are not very good—I was short-sighted from a child—but, upon my word, I think there's another large vegetable marrow sticking, at this moment, on the broken glass bottles at the top of the wall!'

CHAPTER 38

Comprises certain Particulars arising out of a Visit of Condolence, which may prove important hereafter. Smike unexpectedly encounters a very old Friend, who invites him to his House, and will take no Denial

Quite unconscious of the demonstrations of their amorous neighbour, or their effects upon the susceptible bosom of her mama, Kate Nickleby had, by this time, begun to enjoy a settled feeling of tranquillity and happiness, to which, even in occasional and transitory glimpses, she had long been a stranger. Living under the same roof with the beloved brother from whom she had been so suddenly and hardly separated: with a mind at ease, and free from any persecutions which could call a blush into her cheek, or a pang into her heart, she seemed to have passed into a new state of being. Her former cheerfulness was restored, her step regained its elasticity and lightness, the colour which had forsaken her cheek visited it once again, and Kate Nickleby looked more beautiful than ever.

Such was the result to which Miss La Creevy's ruminations and observations led her, when the cottage had been, as she emphatically said, 'thoroughly got to rights, from the chimney-pots to the street-door scraper,' and the busy little woman had at length a moment's time to think about its inmates.

'Which I declare I haven't had since I first came down here,' said Miss La Creevy; 'for I have thought of nothing but hammers, nails, screwdrivers, and gimlets, morning, noon, and night.'

'You never bestowed one thought upon yourself, I believe,' returned Kate, smiling.

'Upon my word, my dear, when there are so many pleasanter things to think of, I should be a goose if I did,' said Miss La Creevy. 'By-the-bye, I have thought of somebody too. Do you know, that I observe a great change in one of this family—a very extraordinary change?'

'In whom?' asked Kate, anxiously. 'Not in—'

'Not in your brother, my dear,' returned Miss La Creevy, anticipating the close of the sentence, 'for he is always the same affectionate good-natured clever creature, with a spice of the—I won't say who—in him when there's any occasion, that he was when I first knew you. No. Smike, as he will be called, poor fellow! for he won't hear of a Mr before his name, is greatly altered, even in this short time.'

'How?' asked Kate. 'Not in health?'

'N—n—o; perhaps not in health exactly,' said Miss La Creevy, pausing to consider, 'although he is a worn and feeble creature, and has that in his face which it would wring my heart to see in yours. No; not in health.'

'How then?'

'I scarcely know,' said the miniature painter. 'But I have watched him, and he has brought the tears into my eyes many times. It is not a very difficult matter to do that, certainly, for I am easily melted; still I think these came with good cause and reason. I am sure that since he has been here, he has grown, from some strong cause, more conscious of his weak intellect. He feels it more. It gives him greater pain to know that he wanders sometimes, and cannot understand very simple things. I have watched him when you have not been by, my dear, sit brooding by himself, with such a look of pain as I could scarcely bear to see, and then get up and leave the room: so sorrowfully, and in such dejection, that I cannot tell you how it has hurt me. Not three weeks ago, he was a light-hearted busy creature, overjoyed to be in a bustle, and as happy as the day was long. Now, he is another being—the same willing, harmless, faithful, loving creature—but the same in nothing else.'

'Surely this will all pass off,' said Kate. 'Poor fellow!'

'I hope,' returned her little friend, with a gravity very unusual in her, 'it may. I hope, for the sake of that poor lad, it may. However,' said Miss La Creevy, relapsing into the cheerful, chattering tone, which was habitual to her, 'I have said my say, and a very long say it is, and a very wrong say too, I shouldn't wonder at all. I shall cheer him up tonight, at all events, for if he is to be my squire all the way to the Strand, I shall talk on, and on, and on, and never leave off, till I have roused him into a laugh at something. So the sooner he goes, the better for him, and the sooner I go, the better for me, I am sure, or else I shall have my maid gallivanting with somebody who may rob the house—though what there is to take away, besides tables and chairs, I don't know, except the miniatures: and he is a clever thief who can dispose of them to any great advantage, for I can't, I know, and that's the honest truth.'

So saying, little Miss La Creevy hid her face in a very flat bonnet, and herself in a very big shawl; and fixing herself tightly into the latter, by means of a large pin, declared that the omnibus might come as soon as it pleased, for she was quite ready.

But there was still Mrs. Nickleby to take leave of; and long before that good lady had concluded some reminiscences bearing upon, and appropriate to, the occasion, the omnibus arrived. This put Miss La Creevy in a great bustle, in consequence whereof, as she secretly rewarded the servant girl with eighteen-pence behind the street-door, she pulled out of her reticule ten-pennyworth of halfpence, which rolled into all possible corners of the passage, and occupied some considerable time in the picking up. This ceremony had, of course, to be succeeded by a second kissing of Kate and Mrs. Nickleby, and a gathering together of the little basket and the brown-paper parcel, during which proceedings, 'the omnibus,' as Miss La Creevy protested, 'swore so dreadfully, that it was quite awful to hear it.' At length and at last, it made a feint of going away, and then Miss La Creevy darted out, and darted in, apologising with great volubility to all the passengers, and declaring that she wouldn't purposely have kept them waiting on any account whatever. While she was looking about for a convenient seat, the conductor pushed Smike in, and cried that it was all right—though it wasn't—and away went the huge vehicle, with the noise of half-a-dozen brewers' drays at least.

Leaving it to pursue its journey at the pleasure of the conductor aforementioned, who lounged gracefully on his little shelf behind, smoking an odoriferous cigar; and leaving it to stop, or go on, or gallop, or crawl, as that gentleman deemed expedient and advisable; this narrative may embrace the opportunity of ascertaining the condition of Sir Mulberry Hawk, and to what extent he had, by this time, recovered from the injuries consequent on being flung violently from his cabriolet, under the circumstances already detailed.

With a shattered limb, a body severely bruised, a face disfigured by half-healed scars, and pallid from the exhaustion of recent pain and fever, Sir Mulberry Hawk lay stretched upon his back, on the couch to which he was doomed to be a prisoner for some weeks yet to come. Mr. Pyke and Mr. Pluck sat drinking hard in the next room, now and then varying the monotonous murmurs of their conversation with a half-smothered laugh, while the young lord—the only member of the party who was not thoroughly irredeemable, and who really had a kind heart—sat beside his Mentor, with a cigar in his mouth, and read to him, by the light of a lamp, such scraps of intelligence from a paper of the day, as were most likely to yield him interest or amusement.

'Curse those hounds!' said the invalid, turning his head impatiently towards the adjoining room; 'will nothing stop their infernal throats?'

Messrs Pyke and Pluck heard the exclamation, and stopped immediately: winking to each other as they did so, and filling their glasses to the brim, as some recompense for the deprivation of speech.

'Damn!' muttered the sick man between his teeth, and writhing impatiently in his bed. 'Isn't this mattress hard enough, and the room dull enough, and pain bad enough, but they must torture me? What's the time?'

'Half-past eight,' replied his friend.

'Here, draw the table nearer, and let us have the cards again,' said Sir Mulberry. 'More piquet. Come.'

It was curious to see how eagerly the sick man, debarred from any change of position save the mere turning of his head from side to side, watched every motion of his friend in the progress of the game; and with what eagerness and interest he played, and yet how warily and coolly. His address and skill were more than twenty times a match for his adversary, who could make little head against them, even when fortune favoured him with good cards, which was not often the case. Sir Mulberry won every game; and when his companion threw down the cards, and refused to play any longer, thrust forth his wasted arm and caught up the stakes with a boastful oath, and the same hoarse laugh, though considerably lowered in tone, that had resounded in Ralph Nickleby's dining-room, months before.

While he was thus occupied, his man appeared, to announce that Mr. Ralph Nickleby was below, and wished to know how he was, tonight.

'Better,' said Sir Mulberry, impatiently.

'Mr. Nickleby wishes to know, sir—'

'I tell you, better,' replied Sir Mulberry, striking his hand upon the table.

The man hesitated for a moment or two, and then said that Mr. Nickleby had requested permission to see Sir Mulberry Hawk, if it was not inconvenient.

'It is inconvenient. I can't see him. I can't see anybody,' said his master, more violently than before. 'You know that, you blockhead.'

'I am very sorry, sir,' returned the man. 'But Mr. Nickleby pressed so much, sir—'

The fact was, that Ralph Nickleby had bribed the man, who, being anxious to earn his money with a view to future favours, held the door in his hand, and ventured to linger still.

'Did he say whether he had any business to speak about?' inquired Sir Mulberry, after a little impatient consideration.

'No, sir. He said he wished to see you, sir. Particularly, Mr. Nickleby said, sir.'

'Tell him to come up. Here,' cried Sir Mulberry, calling the man back, as he passed his hand over his disfigured face, 'move that lamp, and put it on the stand behind me. Wheel that table away, and place a chair there—further off. Leave it so.'

The man obeyed these directions as if he quite comprehended the motive with which they were dictated, and left the room. Lord Frederick Verisopht, remarking that he would look in presently, strolled into the adjoining apartment, and closed the folding door behind him.

Then was heard a subdued footstep on the stairs; and Ralph Nickleby, hat in hand, crept softly into the room, with his body bent forward as if in profound respect, and his eyes fixed upon the face of his worthy client.

'Well, Nickleby,' said Sir Mulberry, motioning him to the chair by the couch side, and waving his hand in assumed carelessness, 'I have had a bad accident, you see.'

'I see,' rejoined Ralph, with the same steady gaze. 'Bad, indeed! I should not have known you, Sir Mulberry. Dear, dear! This is bad.'

Ralph's manner was one of profound humility and respect; and the low tone of voice was that, which the gentlest consideration for a sick man would have taught a visitor to assume. But the expression of his face, Sir Mulberry's being averted, was in extraordinary contrast; and as he stood, in his usual attitude, calmly looking on the prostrate form before him, all that part of his features which was not cast into shadow by his protruding and contracted brows, bore the impress of a sarcastic smile.

'Sit down,' said Sir Mulberry, turning towards him, as though by a violent effort. 'Am I a sight, that you stand gazing there?'

As he turned his face, Ralph recoiled a step or two, and making as though he were irresistibly impelled to express astonishment, but was determined not to do so, sat down with well-acted confusion.

'I have inquired at the door, Sir Mulberry, every day,' said Ralph, 'twice a day, indeed, at first—and tonight, presuming upon old acquaintance, and past transactions by which we have mutually benefited in some degree, I could not resist soliciting admission to your chamber. Have you—have you suffered much?' said Ralph, bending forward, and allowing the same harsh smile to gather upon his face, as the other closed his eyes.

'More than enough to please me, and less than enough to please some broken-down hacks that you and I know of, and who lay their ruin between us, I dare say,' returned Sir Mulberry, tossing his arm restlessly upon the coverlet.

Ralph shrugged his shoulders in deprecation of the intense irritation with which this had been said; for there was an aggravating, cold distinctness in his speech and manner which so grated on the sick man that he could scarcely endure it.

'And what is it in these "past transactions," that brought you here tonight?' asked Sir Mulberry.

'Nothing,' replied Ralph. 'There are some bills of my lord's which need renewal; but let them be till you are well. I—I—came,' said Ralph, speaking more slowly, and with harsher emphasis, 'I came to say how grieved I am that any relative of mine, although disowned by me, should have inflicted such punishment on you as—'

'Punishment!' interposed Sir Mulberry.

'I know it has been a severe one,' said Ralph, wilfully mistaking the meaning of the interruption, 'and that has made me the more anxious to tell you that I disown this vagabond— that I acknowledge him as no kin of mine—and that I leave him to take his deserts from you, and every man besides. You may wring his neck if you please. I shall not interfere.'

'This story that they tell me here, has got abroad then, has it?' asked Sir Mulberry, clenching his hands and teeth.

'Noised in all directions,' replied Ralph. 'Every club and gaming-room has rung with it. There has been a good song made about it, as I am told,' said Ralph, looking eagerly at his questioner. 'I have not heard it myself, not being in the way of such things, but I have been told it's even printed—for private circulation—but that's all over town, of course.'

'It's a lie!' said Sir Mulberry; 'I tell you it's all a lie. The mare took fright.'

'They say he frightened her,' observed Ralph, in the same unmoved and quiet manner. 'Some say he frightened you, but that's a lie, I know. I have said that boldly—oh, a score of times! I am a peaceable man, but I can't hear folks tell that of you. No, no.'

When Sir Mulberry found coherent words to utter, Ralph bent forward with his hand to his ear, and a face as calm as if its every line of sternness had been cast in iron.

'When I am off this cursed bed,' said the invalid, actually striking at his broken leg in the ecstasy of his passion, 'I'll have such revenge as never man had yet. By God, I will. Accident favouring him, he has marked me for a week or two, but I'll put a mark on him that he shall carry to his grave. I'll slit his nose and ears, flog him, maim him for life. I'll do more than that; I'll drag that pattern of chastity, that pink of prudery, the delicate sister, through—'

It might have been that even Ralph's cold blood tingled in his cheeks at that moment.

It might have been that Sir Mulberry remembered, that, knave and usurer as he was, he must, in some early time of infancy, have twined his arm about her father's neck. He stopped, and menacing with his hand, confirmed the unuttered threat with a tremendous oath.

'It is a galling thing,' said Ralph, after a short term of silence, during which he had eyed the sufferer keenly, 'to think that the man about town, the rake, the roue, the rook of twenty seasons should be brought to this pass by a mere boy!'

Sir Mulberry darted a wrathful look at him, but Ralph's eyes were bent upon the ground, and his face wore no other expression than one of thoughtfulness.

'A raw, slight stripling,' continued Ralph, 'against a man whose very weight might crush him; to say nothing of his skill in—I am right, I think,' said Ralph, raising his eyes, 'you were a patron of the ring once, were you not?'

The sick man made an impatient gesture, which Ralph chose to consider as one of acquiescence.

'Ha!' he said, 'I thought so. That was before I knew you, but I was pretty sure I couldn't be mistaken. He is light and active, I suppose. But those were slight advantages compared with yours. Luck, luck! These hang-dog outcasts have it.'

'He'll need the most he has, when I am well again,' said Sir Mulberry Hawk, 'let him fly where he will.'

'Oh!' returned Ralph quickly, 'he doesn't dream of that. He is here, good sir, waiting your pleasure, here in London, walking the streets at noonday; carrying it off jauntily; looking for you, I swear,' said Ralph, his face darkening, and his own hatred getting the upper hand of him, for the first time, as this gay picture of Nicholas presented itself; 'if we were only citizens of a country where it could be safely done, I'd give good money to have him stabbed to the heart and rolled into the kennel for the dogs to tear.'

As Ralph, somewhat to the surprise of his old client, vented this little piece of sound family feeling, and took up his hat preparatory to departing, Lord Frederick Verisopht looked in.

'Why what in the deyvle's name, Hawk, have you and Nickleby been talking about?' said the young man. 'I neyver heard such an insufferable riot. Croak, croak, croak. Bow, wow, wow. What has it all been about?'

'Sir Mulberry has been angry, my Lord,' said Ralph, looking towards the couch.

'Not about money, I hope? Nothing has gone wrong in business, has it, Nickleby?'

'No, my Lord, no,' returned Ralph. 'On that point we always agree. Sir Mulberry has been calling to mind the cause of—'

There was neither necessity nor opportunity for Ralph to proceed; for Sir Mulberry took up the theme, and vented his threats and oaths against Nicholas, almost as ferociously as before.

Ralph, who was no common observer, was surprised to see that as this tirade proceeded, the manner of Lord Frederick Verisopht, who at the commencement had been twirling his whiskers with a most dandified and listless air, underwent a complete alteration. He was still more surprised when, Sir Mulberry ceasing to speak, the young lord angrily, and almost unaffectedly, requested never to have the subject renewed in his presence.

'Mind that, Hawk!' he added, with unusual energy. 'I never will be a party to, or permit, if I can help it, a cowardly attack upon this young fellow.'

'Cowardly!' interrupted his friend.

'Ye-es,' said the other, turning full upon him. 'If you had told him who you were; if you had given him your card, and found out, afterwards, that his station or character prevented your fighting him, it would have been bad enough then; upon my soul it would have been bad enough then. As it is, you did wrong. I did wrong too, not to interfere, and I am sorry for it. What happened to you afterwards, was as much the consequence of accident as design, and more your fault than his; and it shall not, with my knowledge, be cruelly visited upon him, it shall not indeed.'

With this emphatic repetition of his concluding words, the young lord turned upon his heel; but before he had reached the adjoining room he turned back again, and said, with even greater vehemence than he had displayed before,

'I do believe, now; upon my honour I do believe, that the sister is as virtuous and modest a young lady as she is a handsome one; and of the brother, I say this, that he acted as her brother should, and in a manly and spirited manner. And I only wish, with all my heart and soul, that any one of us came out of this matter half as well as he does.'

So saying, Lord Frederick Verisopht walked out of the room, leaving Ralph Nickleby and Sir Mulberry in most unpleasant astonishment.

'Is this your pupil?' asked Ralph, softly, 'or has he come fresh from some country parson?'

'Green fools take these fits sometimes,' replied Sir Mulberry Hawk, biting his lip, and pointing to the door. 'Leave him to me.'

Ralph exchanged a familiar look with his old acquaintance; for they had suddenly grown confidential again in this alarming surprise; and took his way home, thoughtfully and slowly.

While these things were being said and done, and long before they were concluded, the omnibus had disgorged Miss La Creevy and her escort, and they had arrived at her own door. Now, the good-nature of the little miniature painter would by no means allow of Smike's walking back again, until he had been previously refreshed with just a sip of something comfortable and a mixed biscuit or so; and Smike, entertaining no objection either to the sip of something comfortable, or the mixed biscuit, but, considering on the contrary that they would be a very pleasant preparation for a walk to Bow, it fell out that he delayed much longer than he originally intended, and that it was some half-hour after dusk when he set forth on his journey home.

There was no likelihood of his losing his way, for it lay quite straight before him, and he had walked into town with Nicholas, and back alone, almost every day. So, Miss La Creevy and he shook hands with mutual confidence, and, being charged with more kind remembrances to Mrs. and Miss Nickleby, Smike started off.

At the foot of Ludgate Hill, he turned a little out of the road to satisfy his curiosity by having a look at Newgate. After staring up at the sombre walls, from the opposite side of the way, with great care and dread for some minutes, he turned back again into the old track, and walked briskly through the city; stopping now and then to gaze in at the window of some particularly attractive shop, then running for a little way, then stopping again, and so on, as any other country lad might do.

He had been gazing for a long time through a jeweller's window, wishing he could take some of the beautiful trinkets home as a present, and imagining what delight they would afford if he could, when the clocks struck three-quarters past eight; roused by the sound, he hurried on at a very quick pace, and was crossing the corner of a by-street when he felt himself violently brought to, with a jerk so sudden that he was obliged to cling to a lamp-post to save himself from falling. At the same moment, a small boy clung tight round his leg, and a shrill cry of 'Here he is, father! Hooray!' vibrated in his ears.

Smike knew that voice too well. He cast his despairing eyes downward towards the form from which it had proceeded, and, shuddering from head to foot, looked round. Mr. Squeers had hooked him in the coat collar with the handle of his umbrella, and was hanging on at the other end with all his might and main. The cry of triumph proceeded from Master Wackford, who, regardless of all his kicks and struggles, clung to him with the tenacity of a bull-dog!

One glance showed him this; and in that one glance the terrified creature became utterly powerless and unable to utter a sound.

'Here's a go!' cried Mr. Squeers, gradually coming hand-over-hand down the umbrella, and only unhooking it when he had got tight hold of the victim's collar. 'Here's a delicious go! Wackford, my boy, call up one of them coaches.'

'A coach, father!' cried little Wackford.

'Yes, a coach, sir,' replied Squeers, feasting his eyes upon the countenance of Smike. 'Damn the expense. Let's have him in a coach.'

'What's he been a doing of?' asked a labourer with a hod of bricks, against whom and a fellow-labourer Mr. Squeers had backed, on the first jerk of the umbrella.

'Everything!' replied Mr. Squeers, looking fixedly at his old pupil in a sort of rapturous trance. 'Everything—running away, sir—joining in bloodthirsty attacks upon his master— there's nothing that's bad that he hasn't done. Oh, what a delicious go is this here, good Lord!'

The man looked from Squeers to Smike; but such mental faculties as the poor fellow possessed, had utterly deserted him. The coach came up; Master Wackford entered; Squeers pushed in his prize, and following close at his heels, pulled up the glasses. The coachman mounted his box and drove slowly off, leaving the two bricklayers, and an old apple-woman, and a town-made little boy returning from an evening school, who had been the only witnesses of the scene, to meditate upon it at their leisure.

Mr. Squeers sat himself down on the opposite seat to the unfortunate Smike, and, planting his hands firmly on his knees, looked at him for some five minutes, when, seeming to recover from his trance, he uttered a loud laugh, and slapped his old pupil's face several times—taking the right and left sides alternately.

'It isn't a dream!' said Squeers. 'That's real flesh and blood! I know the feel of it!' and being quite assured of his good fortune by these experiments, Mr. Squeers administered a few boxes on the ear, lest the entertainments should seem to partake of sameness, and laughed louder and longer at every one.

'Your mother will be fit to jump out of her skin, my boy, when she hears of this,' said Squeers to his son.

'Oh, won't she though, father?' replied Master Wackford.

'To think,' said Squeers, 'that you and me should be turning out of a street, and come upon him at the very nick; and that I should have him tight, at only one cast of the umbrella, as if I had hooked him with a grappling-iron! Ha, ha!'

'Didn't I catch hold of his leg, neither, father?' said little Wackford.

'You did; like a good 'un, my boy,' said Mr. Squeers, patting his son's head, 'and you shall have the best button-over jacket and waistcoat that the next new boy brings down, as a reward of merit. Mind that. You always keep on in the same path, and do them things that you see your father do, and when you die you'll go right slap to Heaven and no questions asked.'

Improving the occasion in these words, Mr. Squeers patted his son's head again, and then patted Smike's—but harder; and inquired in a bantering tone how he found himself by this time.

'I must go home,' replied Smike, looking wildly round.

'To be sure you must. You're about right there,' replied Mr. Squeers. 'You'll go home very soon, you will. You'll find yourself at the peaceful village of Dotheboys, in Yorkshire, in something under a week's time, my young friend; and the next time you get away from there, I give you leave to keep away. Where's the clothes you run off in, you ungrateful robber?' said Mr. Squeers, in a severe voice.

Smike glanced at the neat attire which the care of Nicholas had provided for him; and wrung his hands.

'Do you know that I could hang you up, outside of the Old Bailey, for making away with them articles of property?' said Squeers. 'Do you know that it's a hanging matter—and I an't quite certain whether it an't an anatomy one besides—to walk off with up'ards of the valley of five pound from a dwelling-house? Eh? Do you know that? What do you suppose was the worth of them clothes you had? Do you know that that Wellington boot you wore, cost eight-and-twenty shillings when it was a pair, and the shoe seven-and-six? But you came to the right shop for mercy when you came to me, and thank your stars that it is me as has got to serve you with the article.'

Anybody not in Mr. Squeers's confidence would have supposed that he was quite out of the article in question, instead of having a large stock on hand ready for all comers; nor would the opinion of sceptical persons have undergone much alteration when he followed up the remark by poking Smike in the chest with the ferrule of his umbrella, and dealing a smart shower of blows, with the ribs of the same instrument, upon his head and shoulders.

'I never threshed a boy in a hackney coach before,' said Mr. Squeers, when he stopped to rest. 'There's inconveniency in it, but the novelty gives it a sort of relish, too!'

Poor Smike! He warded off the blows, as well as he could, and now shrunk into a corner of the coach, with his head resting on his hands, and his elbows on his knees; he was stunned and stupefied, and had no more idea that any act of his, would enable him to escape from the all-powerful Squeers, now that he had no friend to speak to or to advise with, than he had had in all the weary years of his Yorkshire life which preceded the arrival of Nicholas.

The journey seemed endless; street after street was entered and left behind; and still they went jolting on. At last Mr. Squeers began to thrust his head out of the widow every half-minute, and to bawl a variety of directions to the coachman; and after passing, with some difficulty, through several mean streets which the appearance of the houses and the bad state of the road denoted to have been recently built, Mr. Squeers suddenly tugged at the check string with all his might, and cried, 'Stop!'

'What are you pulling a man's arm off for?' said the coachman looking angrily down.

'That's the house,' replied Squeers. 'The second of them four little houses, one story high, with the green shutters. There's brass plate on the door, with the name of Snawley.'

'Couldn't you say that without wrenching a man's limbs off his body?' inquired the coachman.

'No!' bawled Mr. Squeers. 'Say another word, and I'll summons you for having a broken winder. Stop!'

Obedient to this direction, the coach stopped at Mr. Snawley's door. Mr Snawley may be remembered as the sleek and sanctified gentleman who confided two sons (in law) to the parental care of Mr. Squeers, as narrated in the fourth chapter of this history. Mr. Snawley's house was on the extreme borders of some new settlements adjoining Somers Town, and Mr Squeers had taken lodgings therein for a short time, as his stay was longer than usual, and the Saracen, having experience of Master Wackford's appetite, had declined to receive him on any other terms than as a full-grown customer.

'Here we are!' said Squeers, hurrying Smike into the little parlour, where Mr. Snawley and his wife were taking a lobster supper. 'Here's the vagrant—the felon—the rebel—the monster of unthankfulness.'

'What! The boy that run away!' cried Snawley, resting his knife and fork upright on the table, and opening his eyes to their full width.

'The very boy', said Squeers, putting his fist close to Smike's nose, and drawing it away again, and repeating the process several times, with a vicious aspect. 'If there wasn't a lady present, I'd fetch him such a—: never mind, I'll owe it him.'

And here Mr. Squeers related how, and in what manner, and when and where, he had picked up the runaway.

'It's clear that there has been a Providence in it, sir,' said Mr. Snawley, casting down his eyes with an air of humility, and elevating his fork, with a bit of lobster on the top of it, towards the ceiling.

'Providence is against him, no doubt,' replied Mr. Squeers, scratching his nose. 'Of course; that was to be expected. Anybody might have known that.'

'Hard-heartedness and evil-doing will never prosper, sir,' said Mr Snawley.

'Never was such a thing known,' rejoined Squeers, taking a little roll of notes from his pocket-book, to see that they were all safe.

'I have been, Mr. Snawley,' said Mr. Squeers, when he had satisfied himself upon this point, 'I have been that chap's benefactor, feeder, teacher, and clother. I have been that chap's classical, commercial, mathematical, philosophical, and trigonomical friend. My son—my only son, Wackford—has been his brother; Mrs. Squeers has been his mother, grandmother, aunt,—ah! and I may say uncle too, all in one. She never cottoned to anybody, except them two engaging and delightful boys of yours, as she cottoned to this chap. What's my return? What's come of my milk of human kindness? It turns into curds and whey when I look at him.'

'Well it may, sir,' said Mrs. Snawley. 'Oh! Well it may, sir.'

'Where has he been all this time?' inquired Snawley. 'Has he been living with—?'

'Ah, sir!' interposed Squeers, confronting him again. 'Have you been a living with that there devilish Nickleby, sir?'

But no threats or cuffs could elicit from Smike one word of reply to this question; for he had internally resolved that he would rather perish in the wretched prison to which he was again about to be consigned, than utter one syllable which could involve his first and true friend. He had already called to mind the strict injunctions of secrecy as to his past life, which Nicholas had laid upon him when they travelled from Yorkshire; and a confused and perplexed idea that his benefactor might have committed some terrible crime in bringing him away, which would render him liable to heavy punishment if detected, had contributed, in some degree, to reduce him to his present state of apathy and terror.

Such were the thoughts—if to visions so imperfect and undefined as those which wandered through his enfeebled brain, the term can be applied—which were present to the mind of Smike, and rendered him deaf alike to intimidation and persuasion. Finding every effort useless, Mr. Squeers conducted him to a little back room up-stairs, where he was to pass the night; and, taking the precaution of removing his shoes, and coat and waistcoat, and also of locking the door on the outside, lest he should muster up sufficient energy to make an attempt at escape, that worthy gentleman left him to his meditations.

What those meditations were, and how the poor creature's heart sunk within him when he thought—when did he, for a moment, cease to think?—of his late home, and the dear friends and familiar faces with which it was associated, cannot be told. To prepare the mind for such a heavy sleep, its growth must be stopped by rigour and cruelty in childhood; there must be years of misery and suffering, lightened by no ray of hope; the chords of the heart, which beat a quick response to the voice of gentleness and affection, must have rusted and broken in their secret places, and bear the lingering echo of no old word of love or kindness. Gloomy, indeed, must have been the short day, and dull the long, long twilight, preceding such a night of intellect as his.

There were voices which would have roused him, even then; but their welcome tones could not penetrate there; and he crept to bed the same listless, hopeless, blighted creature, that Nicholas had first found him at the Yorkshire school.

CHAPTER 39

In which another old Friend encounters Smike, very opportunely and to some Purpose

The night, fraught with so much bitterness to one poor soul, had given place to a bright and cloudless summer morning, when a north-country mail-coach traversed, with cheerful noise, the yet silent streets of Islington, and, giving brisk note of its approach with the lively winding of the guard's horn, clattered onward to its halting-place hard by the Post Office.

The only outside passenger was a burly, honest-looking countryman on the box, who, with his eyes fixed upon the dome of St Paul's Cathedral, appeared so wrapt in admiring wonder, as to be quite insensible to all the bustle of getting out the bags and parcels, until one of the coach windows being let sharply down, he looked round, and encountered a pretty female face which was just then thrust out.

'See there, lass!' bawled the countryman, pointing towards the object of his admiration. 'There be Paul's Church. 'Ecod, he be a soizable 'un, he be.'

'Goodness, John! I shouldn't have thought it could have been half the size. What a monster!'

'Monsther!—Ye're aboot right theer, I reckon, Mrs. Browdie,' said the countryman good-humouredly, as he came slowly down in his huge top-coat; 'and wa'at dost thee tak yon place to be noo—thot'un owor the wa'? Ye'd never coom near it 'gin you thried for twelve moonths. It's na' but a Poast Office! Ho! ho! They need to charge for dooble-latthers. A Poast Office! Wa'at dost thee think o' thot? 'Ecod, if thot's on'y a Poast Office, I'd loike to see where the Lord Mayor o' Lunnun lives.'

So saying, John Browdie—for he it was—opened the coach-door, and tapping Mrs. Browdie, late Miss Price, on the cheek as he looked in, burst into a boisterous fit of laughter.

'Weel!' said John. 'Dang my bootuns if she bean't asleep agean!'

'She's been asleep all night, and was, all yesterday, except for a minute or two now and then,' replied John Browdie's choice, 'and I was very sorry when she woke, for she has been so cross!'

The subject of these remarks was a slumbering figure, so muffled in shawl and cloak, that it would have been matter of impossibility to guess at its sex but for a brown beaver bonnet and green veil which ornamented the head, and which, having been crushed and flattened, for two hundred and fifty miles, in that particular angle of the vehicle from which the lady's snores now proceeded, presented an appearance sufficiently ludicrous to have moved less risible muscles than those of John Browdie's ruddy face.

'Hollo!' cried John, twitching one end of the dragged veil. 'Coom, wakken oop, will 'ee?'

After several burrowings into the old corner, and many exclamations of impatience and fatigue, the figure struggled into a sitting posture; and there, under a mass of crumpled beaver, and surrounded by a semicircle of blue curl-papers, were the delicate features of Miss Fanny Squeers.

'Oh, 'Tilda!' cried Miss Squeers, 'how you have been kicking of me through this blessed night!'

'Well, I do like that,' replied her friend, laughing, 'when you have had nearly the whole coach to yourself.'

'Don't deny it, 'Tilda,' said Miss Squeers, impressively, 'because you have, and it's no use to go attempting to say you haven't. You mightn't have known it in your sleep, 'Tilda, but I haven't closed my eyes for a single wink, and so I think I am to be believed.'

With which reply, Miss Squeers adjusted the bonnet and veil, which nothing but supernatural interference and an utter suspension of nature's laws could have reduced to any shape or form; and evidently flattering herself that it looked uncommonly neat, brushed off the sandwich-crumbs and bits of biscuit which had accumulated in her lap, and availing herself of John Browdie's proffered arm, descended from the coach.

'Noo,' said John, when a hackney coach had been called, and the ladies and the luggage hurried in, 'gang to the Sarah's Head, mun.'

'To the vere?' cried the coachman.

'Lawk, Mr. Browdie!' interrupted Miss Squeers. 'The idea! Saracen's Head.'

'Sure-ly,' said John, 'I know'd it was something aboot Sarah's Son's Head. Dost thou know thot?'

'Oh, ah! I know that,' replied the coachman gruffly, as he banged the door.

''Tilda, dear, really,' remonstrated Miss Squeers, 'we shall be taken for I don't know what.'

'Let them tak' us as they foind us,' said John Browdie; 'we dean't come to Lunnun to do nought but 'joy oursel, do we?'

'I hope not, Mr. Browdie,' replied Miss Squeers, looking singularly dismal.

'Well, then,' said John, 'it's no matther. I've only been a married man fower days, 'account of poor old feyther deein, and puttin' it off. Here be a weddin' party—broide and broide's-maid, and the groom—if a mun dean't 'joy himsel noo, when ought he, hey? Drat it all, thot's what I want to know.'

So, in order that he might begin to enjoy himself at once, and lose no time, Mr. Browdie gave his wife a hearty kiss, and succeeded in wresting another from Miss Squeers, after a maidenly resistance of scratching and struggling on the part of that young lady, which was not quite over when they reached the Saracen's Head.

Here, the party straightway retired to rest; the refreshment of sleep being necessary after so long a journey; and here they met again about noon, to a substantial breakfast, spread by direction of Mr. John Browdie, in a small private room upstairs commanding an uninterrupted view of the stables.

To have seen Miss Squeers now, divested of the brown beaver, the green veil, and the blue curl-papers, and arrayed in all the virgin splendour of a white frock and spencer, with a white muslin bonnet, and an imitative damask rose in full bloom on the inside thereof—her luxuriant crop of hair arranged in curls so tight that it was impossible they could come out by any accident, and her bonnet-cap trimmed with little damask roses, which might be supposed to be so many promising scions of the big rose—to have seen all this, and to have seen the broad damask belt, matching both the family rose and the little roses, which encircled her slender waist, and by a happy ingenuity took off from the shortness of the spencer behind,—to have beheld all this, and to have taken further into account the coral bracelets (rather short of beads, and with a very visible black string) which clasped her wrists, and the coral necklace which rested on her neck, supporting, outside her frock, a lonely cornelian heart, typical of her own disengaged affections—to have contemplated all these mute but expressive appeals to the purest feelings of our nature, might have thawed the frost of age, and added new and inextinguishable fuel to the fire of youth.

The waiter was touched. Waiter as he was, he had human passions and feelings, and he looked very hard at Miss Squeers as he handed the muffins.

'Is my pa in, do you know?' asked Miss Squeers with dignity.

'Beg your pardon, miss?'

'My pa,' repeated Miss Squeers; 'is he in?'

'In where, miss?'

'In here—in the house!' replied Miss Squeers. 'My pa—Mr Wackford Squeers—he's stopping here. Is he at home?'

'I didn't know there was any gen'l'man of that name in the house, miss' replied the waiter. 'There may be, in the coffee-room.'

May Be. Very pretty this, indeed! Here was Miss Squeers, who had been depending, all the way to London, upon showing her friends how much at home she would be, and how much respectful notice her name and connections would excite, told that her father might be there! 'As if he was a feller!' observed Miss Squeers, with emphatic indignation.

'Ye'd bether inquire, mun,' said John Browdie. 'An' hond up another pigeon-pie, will 'ee? Dang the chap,' muttered John, looking into the empty dish as the waiter retired; 'does he ca' this a pie—three yoong pigeons and a troifling matther o' steak, and a crust so loight that you doant know when it's in your mooth and when it's gane? I wonder hoo many pies goes to a breakfast!'

After a short interval, which John Browdie employed upon the ham and a cold round of beef, the waiter returned with another pie, and the information that Mr. Squeers was not stopping in the house, but that he came there every day and that directly he arrived, he should be shown upstairs. With this, he retired; and he had not retired two minutes, when he returned with Mr. Squeers and his hopeful son.

'Why, who'd have thought of this?' said Mr. Squeers, when he had saluted the party and received some private family intelligence from his daughter.

'Who, indeed, pa!' replied that young lady, spitefully. 'But you see 'Tilda is married at last.'

'And I stond threat for a soight o' Lunnun, schoolmeasther,' said John, vigorously attacking the pie.

'One of them things that young men do when they get married,' returned Squeers; 'and as runs through with their money like nothing at all! How much better wouldn't it be now, to save it up for the eddication of any little boys, for instance! They come on you,' said Mr. Squeers in a moralising way, 'before you're aware of it; mine did upon me.'

'Will 'ee pick a bit?' said John.

'I won't myself,' returned Squeers; 'but if you'll just let little Wackford tuck into something fat, I'll be obliged to you. Give it him in his fingers, else the waiter charges it on, and there's lot of profit on this sort of vittles without that. If you hear the waiter coming, sir, shove it in your pocket and look out of the window, d'ye hear?'

'I'm awake, father,' replied the dutiful Wackford.

'Well,' said Squeers, turning to his daughter, 'it's your turn to be married next. You must make haste.'

'Oh, I'm in no hurry,' said Miss Squeers, very sharply.

'No, Fanny?' cried her old friend with some archness.

'No, 'Tilda,' replied Miss Squeers, shaking her head vehemently. 'I can wait.'

'So can the young men, it seems, Fanny,' observed Mrs. Browdie.

'They an't draw'd into it by me, 'Tilda,' retorted Miss Squeers.

'No,' returned her friend; 'that's exceedingly true.'

The sarcastic tone of this reply might have provoked a rather acrimonious retort from Miss Squeers, who, besides being of a constitutionally vicious temper—aggravated, just now, by travel and recent jolting—was somewhat irritated by old recollections and the failure of her own designs upon Mr. Browdie; and the acrimonious retort might have led to a great many other retorts, which might have led to Heaven knows what, if the subject of conversation had not been, at that precise moment, accidentally changed by Mr. Squeers himself

'What do you think?' said that gentleman; 'who do you suppose we have laid hands on, Wackford and me?'

'Pa! not Mr—?' Miss Squeers was unable to finish the sentence, but Mrs. Browdie did it for her, and added, 'Nickleby?'

'No,' said Squeers. 'But next door to him though.'

'You can't mean Smike?' cried Miss Squeers, clapping her hands.

'Yes, I can though,' rejoined her father. 'I've got him, hard and fast.'

'Wa'at!' exclaimed John Browdie, pushing away his plate. 'Got that poor—dom'd scoondrel? Where?'

'Why, in the top back room, at my lodging,' replied Squeers, 'with him on one side, and the key on the other.'

'At thy loodgin'! Thee'st gotten him at thy loodgin'? Ho! ho! The schoolmeasther agin all England. Give us thee hond, mun; I'm darned but I must shak thee by the hond for thot.— Gotten him at thy loodgin'?'

'Yes,' replied Squeers, staggering in his chair under the congratulatory blow on the chest which the stout Yorkshireman dealt him; 'thankee. Don't do it again. You mean it kindly, I know, but it hurts rather. Yes, there he is. That's not so bad, is it?'

'Ba'ad!' repeated John Browdie. 'It's eneaf to scare a mun to hear tell on.'

'I thought it would surprise you a bit,' said Squeers, rubbing his hands. 'It was pretty neatly done, and pretty quick too.'

'Hoo wor it?' inquired John, sitting down close to him. 'Tell us all aboot it, mun; coom, quick!'

Although he could not keep pace with John Browdie's impatience, Mr. Squeers related the lucky chance by which Smike had fallen into his hands, as quickly as he could, and, except when he was interrupted by the admiring remarks of his auditors, paused not in the recital until he had brought it to an end.

'For fear he should give me the slip, by any chance,' observed Squeers, when he had finished, looking very cunning, 'I've taken three outsides for tomorrow morning—for Wackford and him and me—and have arranged to leave the accounts and the new boys to the agent, don't you see? So it's very lucky you come today, or you'd have missed us; and as it is, unless you could come and tea with me tonight, we shan't see anything more of you before we go away.'

'Dean't say anoother wurd,' returned the Yorkshireman, shaking him by the hand. 'We'd coom, if it was twenty mile.'

'No, would you though?' returned Mr. Squeers, who had not expected quite such a ready acceptance of his invitation, or he would have considered twice before he gave it.

John Browdie's only reply was another squeeze of the hand, and an assurance that they would not begin to see London till tomorrow, so that they might be at Mr. Snawley's at six o'clock without fail; and after some further conversation, Mr. Squeers and his son departed.

During the remainder of the day, Mr. Browdie was in a very odd and excitable state; bursting occasionally into an explosion of laughter, and then taking up his hat and running into the coach-yard to have it out by himself. He was very restless too, constantly walking in and out, and snapping his fingers, and dancing scraps of uncouth country dances, and, in short, conducting himself in such a very extraordinary manner, that Miss Squeers opined he was going mad, and, begging her dear 'Tilda not to distress herself, communicated her suspicions in so many words. Mrs Browdie, however, without discovering any great alarm, observed that she had seen him so once before, and that although he was almost sure to be ill after it, it would not be anything very serious, and therefore he was better left alone.

The result proved her to be perfectly correct for, while they were all sitting in Mr. Snawley's parlour that night, and just as it was beginning to get dusk, John Browdie was taken so ill, and seized with such an alarming dizziness in the head, that the whole company were thrown into the utmost consternation. His good lady, indeed, was the only person present, who retained presence of mind enough to observe that if he were allowed to lie down on Mr. Squeers's bed for an hour or so, and left entirely to himself, he would be sure to recover again almost as quickly as he had been taken ill. Nobody could refuse to try the effect of so reasonable a proposal, before sending for a surgeon. Accordingly, John was supported upstairs, with great difficulty; being a monstrous weight, and regularly tumbling down two steps every time they hoisted him up three; and, being laid on the bed, was left in charge of his wife, who, after a short interval, reappeared in the parlour, with the gratifying intelligence that he had fallen fast asleep.

Now, the fact was, that at that particular moment, John Browdie was sitting on the bed with the reddest face ever seen, cramming the corner of the pillow into his mouth, to prevent his roaring out loud with laughter. He had no sooner succeeded in suppressing this emotion, than he slipped off his shoes, and creeping to the adjoining room where the prisoner was confined, turned the key, which was on the outside, and darting in, covered Smike's mouth with his huge hand before he could utter a sound.

'Ods-bobs, dost thee not know me, mun?' whispered the Yorkshireman to the bewildered lad. 'Browdie. Chap as met thee efther schoolmeasther was banged?'

'Yes, yes,' cried Smike. 'Oh! help me.'

'Help thee!' replied John, stopping his mouth again, the instant he had said this much. 'Thee didn't need help, if thee warn't as silly yoongster as ever draw'd breath. Wa'at did 'ee come here for, then?'

'He brought me; oh! he brought me,' cried Smike.

'Brout thee!' replied John. 'Why didn't 'ee punch his head, or lay theeself doon and kick, and squeal out for the pollis? I'd ha' licked a doozen such as him when I was yoong as thee. But thee be'est a poor broken-doon chap,' said John, sadly, 'and God forgi' me for bragging ower yan o' his weakest creeturs!'

Smike opened his mouth to speak, but John Browdie stopped him.

'Stan' still,' said the Yorkshireman, 'and doant'ee speak a morsel o' talk till I tell'ee.'

With this caution, John Browdie shook his head significantly, and drawing a screwdriver from his pocket, took off the box of the lock in a very deliberate and workmanlike manner, and laid it, together with the implement, on the floor.

'See thot?' said John 'Thot be thy doin'. Noo, coot awa'!'

Smike looked vacantly at him, as if unable to comprehend his meaning.

'I say, coot awa',' repeated John, hastily. 'Dost thee know where thee livest? Thee dost? Weel. Are yon thy clothes, or schoolmeasther's?'

'Mine,' replied Smike, as the Yorkshireman hurried him to the adjoining room, and pointed out a pair of shoes and a coat which were lying on a chair.

'On wi' 'em,' said John, forcing the wrong arm into the wrong sleeve, and winding the tails of the coat round the fugitive's neck. 'Noo, foller me, and when thee get'st ootside door, turn to the right, and they wean't see thee pass.'

'But—but—he'll hear me shut the door,' replied Smike, trembling from head to foot.

'Then dean't shut it at all,' retorted John Browdie. 'Dang it, thee bean't afeard o' schoolmeasther's takkin cold, I hope?'

'N-no,' said Smike, his teeth chattering in his head. 'But he brought me back before, and will again. He will, he will indeed.'

'He wull, he wull!' replied John impatiently. 'He wean't, he wean't. Look'ee! I wont to do this neighbourly loike, and let them think thee's gotten awa' o' theeself, but if he cooms oot o' thot parlour awhiles theer't clearing off, he mun' have mercy on his oun boans, for I wean't. If he foinds it oot, soon efther, I'll put 'un on a wrong scent, I warrant 'ee. But if thee keep'st a good hart, thee'lt be at whoam afore they know thee'st gotten off. Coom!'

Smike, who comprehended just enough of this to know it was intended as encouragement, prepared to follow with tottering steps, when John whispered in his ear.

'Thee'lt just tell yoong Measther that I'm sploiced to 'Tilly Price, and to be heerd on at the Saracen by latther, and that I bean't jealous of 'un—dang it, I'm loike to boost when I think o' that neight! 'Cod, I think I see 'un now, a powderin' awa' at the thin bread an' butther!'

It was rather a ticklish recollection for John just then, for he was within an ace of breaking out into a loud guffaw. Restraining himself, however, just in time, by a great effort, he glided downstairs, hauling Smike behind him; and placing himself close to the parlour door, to confront the first person that might come out, signed to him to make off.

Having got so far, Smike needed no second bidding. Opening the house-door gently, and casting a look of mingled gratitude and terror at his deliverer, he took the direction which had been indicated to him, and sped away like the wind.

The Yorkshireman remained on his post for a few minutes, but, finding that there was no pause in the conversation inside, crept back again unheard, and stood, listening over the stair-rail, for a full hour. Everything remaining perfectly quiet, he got into Mr. Squeers's bed, once more, and drawing the clothes over his head, laughed till he was nearly smothered.

If there could only have been somebody by, to see how the bedclothes shook, and to see the Yorkshireman's great red face and round head appear above the sheets, every now and then, like some jovial monster coming to the surface to breathe, and once more dive down convulsed with the laughter which came bursting forth afresh—that somebody would have been scarcely less amused than John Browdie himself.

CHAPTER 40
In which Nicholas falls in Love. He employs a Mediator, whose Proceedings are crowned with unexpected Success, excepting in one solitary Particular

Once more out of the clutches of his old persecutor, it needed no fresh stimulation to call forth the utmost energy and exertion that Smike was capable of summoning to his aid. Without pausing for a moment to reflect upon the course he was taking, or the probability of its leading him homewards or the reverse, he fled away with surprising swiftness and constancy of purpose, borne upon such wings as only Fear can wear, and impelled by imaginary shouts in the well remembered voice of Squeers, who, with a host of pursuers, seemed to the poor fellow's disordered senses to press hard upon his track; now left at a greater distance in the rear, and now gaining faster and faster upon him, as the alternations of hope and terror agitated him by turns. Long after he had become assured that these sounds were but the creation of his excited brain, he still held on, at a pace which even weakness and exhaustion could scarcely retard. It was not until the darkness and quiet of a country road, recalled him to a sense of external objects, and the starry sky, above, warned him of the rapid flight of time, that, covered with dust and panting for breath, he stopped to listen and look about him.

All was still and silent. A glare of light in the distance, casting a warm glow upon the sky, marked where the huge city lay. Solitary fields, divided by hedges and ditches, through many of which he had crashed and scrambled in his flight, skirted the road, both by the way he had come and upon the opposite side. It was late now. They could scarcely trace him by such paths as he had taken, and if he could hope to regain his own dwelling, it must surely be at such a time as that, and under cover of the darkness. This, by degrees, became pretty plain, even to the mind of Smike. He had, at first, entertained some vague and childish idea of travelling into the country for ten or a dozen miles, and then returning homewards by a wide circuit, which should keep him clear of London—so great was his apprehension of traversing the streets alone, lest he should again encounter his dreaded enemy—but, yielding to the conviction which these thoughts inspired, he turned back, and taking the open road, though not without many fears and misgivings, made for London again, with scarcely less speed of foot than that with which he had left the temporary abode of Mr. Squeers.

By the time he re-entered it, at the western extremity, the greater part of the shops were closed. Of the throngs of people who had been tempted abroad after the heat of the day, but few remained in the streets, and they were lounging home. But of these he asked his way from time to time, and by dint of repeated inquiries, he at length reached the dwelling of Newman Noggs.

All that evening, Newman had been hunting and searching in byways and corners for the very person who now knocked at his door, while Nicholas had been pursuing the same inquiry in other directions. He was sitting, with a melancholy air, at his poor supper, when Smike's timorous and uncertain knock reached his ears. Alive to every sound, in his anxious and expectant state, Newman hurried downstairs, and, uttering a cry of joyful surprise, dragged the welcome visitor into the passage and up the stairs, and said not a word until he had him safe in his own garret and the door was shut behind them, when he mixed a great mug-full of gin-and-water, and holding it to Smike's mouth, as one might hold a bowl of medicine to the lips of a refractory child, commanded him to drain it to the last drop.

Newman looked uncommonly blank when he found that Smike did little more than put his lips to the precious mixture; he was in the act of raising the mug to his own mouth with a deep sigh of compassion for his poor friend's weakness, when Smike, beginning to relate the adventures which had befallen him, arrested him half-way, and he stood listening, with the mug in his hand.

It was odd enough to see the change that came over Newman as Smike proceeded. At first he stood, rubbing his lips with the back of his hand, as a preparatory ceremony towards composing himself for a draught; then, at the mention of Squeers, he took the mug under his arm, and opening his eyes very wide, looked on, in the utmost astonishment. When Smike came to the assault upon himself in the hackney coach, he hastily deposited the mug upon the table, and limped up and down the room in a state of the greatest excitement, stopping himself with a jerk, every now and then, as if to listen more attentively. When John Browdie came to be spoken of, he dropped, by slow and gradual degrees, into a chair, and rubbing his hands upon his knees—quicker and quicker as the story reached its climax—burst, at last, into a laugh composed of one loud sonorous 'Ha! ha!' having given vent to which, his countenance immediately fell again as he inquired, with the utmost anxiety, whether it was probable that John Browdie and Squeers had come to blows.

'No! I think not,' replied Smike. 'I don't think he could have missed me till I had got quite away.'

Newman scratched his head with a shout of great disappointment, and once more lifting up the mug, applied himself to the contents; smiling meanwhile, over the rim, with a grim and ghastly smile at Smike.

'You shall stay here,' said Newman; 'you're tired—fagged. I'll tell them you're come back. They have been half mad about you. Mr. Nicholas—'

'God bless him!' cried Smike.

'Amen!' returned Newman. 'He hasn't had a minute's rest or peace; no more has the old lady, nor Miss Nickleby.'

370

'No, no. Has she thought about me?' said Smike. 'Has she though? oh, has she, has she? Don't tell me so if she has not.'

'She has,' cried Newman. 'She is as noble-hearted as she is beautiful.'

'Yes, yes!' cried Smike. 'Well said!'

'So mild and gentle,' said Newman.

'Yes, yes!' cried Smike, with increasing eagerness.

'And yet with such a true and gallant spirit,' pursued Newman.

He was going on, in his enthusiasm, when, chancing to look at his companion, he saw that he had covered his face with his hands, and that tears were stealing out between his fingers.

A moment before, the boy's eyes were sparkling with unwonted fire, and every feature had been lighted up with an excitement which made him appear, for the moment, quite a different being.

'Well, well,' muttered Newman, as if he were a little puzzled. 'It has touched me, more than once, to think such a nature should have been exposed to such trials; this poor fellow— yes, yes,—he feels that too—it softens him—makes him think of his former misery. Hah! That's it? Yes, that's—hum!'

It was by no means clear, from the tone of these broken reflections, that Newman Noggs considered them as explaining, at all satisfactorily, the emotion which had suggested them. He sat, in a musing attitude, for some time, regarding Smike occasionally with an anxious and doubtful glance, which sufficiently showed that he was not very remotely connected with his thoughts.

At length he repeated his proposition that Smike should remain where he was for that night, and that he (Noggs) should straightway repair to the cottage to relieve the suspense of the family. But, as Smike would not hear of this—pleading his anxiety to see his friends again—they eventually sallied forth together; and the night being, by this time, far advanced, and Smike being, besides, so footsore that he could hardly crawl along, it was within an hour of sunrise when they reached their destination.

At the first sound of their voices outside the house, Nicholas, who had passed a sleepless night, devising schemes for the recovery of his lost charge, started from his bed, and joyfully admitted them. There was so much noisy conversation, and congratulation, and indignation, that the remainder of the family were soon awakened, and Smike received a warm and cordial welcome, not only from Kate, but from Mrs. Nickleby also, who assured him of her future favour and regard, and was so obliging as to relate, for his entertainment and that of the assembled circle, a most remarkable account extracted from some work the name of which she had never known, of a miraculous escape from some prison, but what one she couldn't remember, effected by an officer whose name she had forgotten, confined for some crime which she didn't clearly recollect.

At first Nicholas was disposed to give his uncle credit for some portion of this bold attempt (which had so nearly proved successful) to carry off Smike; but on more mature consideration, he was inclined to think that the full merit of it rested with Mr. Squeers. Determined to ascertain, if he could, through John Browdie, how the case really stood, he betook himself to his daily occupation: meditating, as he went, on a great variety of schemes for the punishment of the Yorkshire schoolmaster, all of which had their foundation in the strictest principles of retributive justice, and had but the one drawback of being wholly impracticable.

'A fine morning, Mr. Linkinwater!' said Nicholas, entering the office.

'Ah!' replied Tim, 'talk of the country, indeed! What do you think of this, now, for a day—a London day—eh?'

'It's a little clearer out of town,' said Nicholas.

'Clearer!' echoed Tim Linkinwater. 'You should see it from my bedroom window.'

'You should see it from mine,' replied Nicholas, with a smile.

'Pooh! pooh!' said Tim Linkinwater, 'don't tell me. Country!' (Bow was quite a rustic place to Tim.) 'Nonsense! What can you get in the country but new-laid eggs and flowers? I can buy new-laid eggs in Leadenhall Market, any morning before breakfast; and as to flowers, it's worth a run upstairs to smell my mignonette, or to see the double wallflower in the back-attic window, at No. 6, in the court.'

'There is a double wallflower at No. 6, in the court, is there?' said Nicholas.

'Yes, is there!' replied Tim, 'and planted in a cracked jug, without a spout. There were hyacinths there, this last spring, blossoming, in—but you'll laugh at that, of course.'

'At what?'

'At their blossoming in old blacking-bottles,' said Tim.

'Not I, indeed,' returned Nicholas.

Tim looked wistfully at him, for a moment, as if he were encouraged by the tone of this reply to be more communicative on the subject; and sticking behind his ear, a pen that he had been making, and shutting up his knife with a smart click, said,

'They belong to a sickly bedridden hump-backed boy, and seem to be the only pleasure, Mr. Nickleby, of his sad existence. How many years is it,' said Tim, pondering, 'since I first noticed him, quite a little child, dragging himself about on a pair of tiny crutches? Well! Well! Not many; but though they would appear nothing, if I thought of other things, they seem a long, long time, when I think of him. It is a sad thing,' said Tim, breaking off, 'to see a little deformed child sitting apart from other children, who are active and merry, watching the games he is denied the power to share in. He made my heart ache very often.'

'It is a good heart,' said Nicholas, 'that disentangles itself from the close avocations of every day, to heed such things. You were saying—'

'That the flowers belonged to this poor boy,' said Tim; 'that's all. When it is fine weather, and he can crawl out of bed, he draws a chair close to the window, and sits there, looking at them and arranging them, all day long. He used to nod, at first, and then we came to speak. Formerly, when I called to him of a morning, and asked him how he was, he would smile, and say, "Better!" but now he shakes his head, and only bends more closely over his old plants. It must be dull to watch the dark housetops and the flying clouds, for so many months; but he is very patient.'

'Is there nobody in the house to cheer or help him?' asked Nicholas.

'His father lives there, I believe,' replied Tim, 'and other people too; but no one seems to care much for the poor sickly cripple. I have asked him, very often, if I can do nothing for him; his answer is always the same. "Nothing." His voice is growing weak of late, but I can see that he makes the old reply. He can't leave his bed now, so they have moved it close beside the window, and there he lies, all day: now looking at the sky, and now at his flowers, which he still makes shift to trim and water, with his own thin hands. At night, when he sees my candle, he draws back his curtain, and leaves it so, till I am in bed. It seems such company to him to know that I am there, that I often sit at my window for an hour or more, that he may see I am still awake; and sometimes I get up in the night to look at the dull melancholy light in his little room, and wonder whether he is awake or sleeping.

'The night will not be long coming,' said Tim, 'when he will sleep, and never wake again on earth. We have never so much as shaken hands in all our lives; and yet I shall miss him like an old friend. Are there any country flowers that could interest me like these, do you think? Or do you suppose that the withering of a hundred kinds of the choicest flowers that blow, called by the hardest Latin names that were ever invented, would give me one fraction of the pain that I shall feel when these old jugs and bottles are swept away as lumber? Country!' cried Tim, with a contemptuous emphasis; 'don't you know that I couldn't have such a court under my bedroom window, anywhere, but in London?'

With which inquiry, Tim turned his back, and pretending to be absorbed in his accounts, took an opportunity of hastily wiping his eyes when he supposed Nicholas was looking another way.

Whether it was that Tim's accounts were more than usually intricate that morning, or whether it was that his habitual serenity had been a little disturbed by these recollections, it so happened that when Nicholas returned from executing some commission, and inquired whether Mr. Charles Cheeryble was alone in his room, Tim promptly, and without the smallest hesitation, replied in the affirmative, although somebody had passed into the room not ten minutes before, and Tim took especial and particular pride in preventing any intrusion on either of the brothers when they were engaged with any visitor whatever.

'I'll take this letter to him at once,' said Nicholas, 'if that's the case.' And with that, he walked to the room and knocked at the door.

No answer.

Another knock, and still no answer.

'He can't be here,' thought Nicholas. 'I'll lay it on his table.'

So, Nicholas opened the door and walked in; and very quickly he turned to walk out again, when he saw, to his great astonishment and discomfiture, a young lady upon her knees at Mr. Cheeryble's feet, and Mr. Cheeryble beseeching her to rise, and entreating a third person, who had the appearance of the young lady's female attendant, to add her persuasions to his to induce her to do so.

Nicholas stammered out an awkward apology, and was precipitately retiring, when the young lady, turning her head a little, presented to his view the features of the lovely girl whom he had seen at the register-office on his first visit long before. Glancing from her to the attendant, he recognised the same clumsy servant who had accompanied her then; and between his admiration of the young lady's beauty, and the confusion and surprise of this unexpected recognition, he stood stock-still, in such a bewildered state of surprise and embarrassment that, for the moment, he was quite bereft of the power either to speak or move.

'My dear ma'am—my dear young lady,' cried brother Charles in violent agitation, 'pray don't—not another word, I beseech and entreat you! I implore you—I beg of you—to rise. We—we—are not alone.'

As he spoke, he raised the young lady, who staggered to a chair and swooned away.

'She has fainted, sir,' said Nicholas, darting eagerly forward.

'Poor dear, poor dear!' cried brother Charles 'Where is my brother Ned? Ned, my dear brother, come here pray.'

'Brother Charles, my dear fellow,' replied his brother, hurrying into the room, 'what is the—ah! what—'

'Hush! hush!—not a word for your life, brother Ned,' returned the other. 'Ring for the housekeeper, my dear brother—call Tim Linkinwater! Here, Tim Linkinwater, sir—Mr. Nickleby, my dear sir, leave the room, I beg and beseech of you.'

'I think she is better now,' said Nicholas, who had been watching the patient so eagerly, that he had not heard the request.

'Poor bird!' cried brother Charles, gently taking her hand in his, and laying her head upon his arm. 'Brother Ned, my dear fellow, you will be surprised, I know, to witness this, in business hours; but—' here he was again reminded of the presence of Nicholas, and shaking him by the hand, earnestly requested him to leave the room, and to send Tim Linkinwater without an instant's delay.

Nicholas immediately withdrew and, on his way to the counting-house, met both the old housekeeper and Tim Linkinwater, jostling each other in the passage, and hurrying to the scene of action with extraordinary speed. Without waiting to hear his message, Tim Linkinwater darted into the room, and presently afterwards Nicholas heard the door shut and locked on the inside.

He had abundance of time to ruminate on this discovery, for Tim Linkinwater was absent during the greater part of an hour, during the whole of which time Nicholas thought of nothing but the young lady, and her exceeding beauty, and what could possibly have brought her there, and why they made such a mystery of it. The more he thought of all this, the more it perplexed him, and the more anxious he became to know who and what she was. 'I should have known her among ten thousand,' thought Nicholas. And with that he walked up and down the room, and recalling her face and figure (of which he had a peculiarly vivid remembrance), discarded all other subjects of reflection and dwelt upon that alone.

At length Tim Linkinwater came back—provokingly cool, and with papers in his hand, and a pen in his mouth, as if nothing had happened.

'Is she quite recovered?' said Nicholas, impetuously.

'Who?' returned Tim Linkinwater.

'Who!' repeated Nicholas. 'The young lady.'

'What do you make, Mr. Nickleby,' said Tim, taking his pen out of his mouth, 'what do you make of four hundred and twenty-seven times three thousand two hundred and thirty-eight?'

'Nay,' returned Nicholas, 'what do you make of my question first? I asked you—'

'About the young lady,' said Tim Linkinwater, putting on his spectacles. 'To be sure. Yes. Oh! she's very well.'

'Very well, is she?' returned Nicholas.

'Very well,' replied Mr. Linkinwater, gravely.

'Will she be able to go home today?' asked Nicholas.

'She's gone,' said Tim.

'Gone!'

'Yes.'

'I hope she has not far to go?' said Nicholas, looking earnestly at the other.

'Ay,' replied the immovable Tim, 'I hope she hasn't.'

Nicholas hazarded one or two further remarks, but it was evident that Tim Linkinwater had his own reasons for evading the subject, and that he was determined to afford no further information respecting the fair unknown, who had awakened so much curiosity in the breast of his young friend. Nothing daunted by this repulse, Nicholas returned to the charge next day, emboldened by the circumstance of Mr. Linkinwater being in a very talkative and communicative mood; but, directly he resumed the theme, Tim relapsed into a state of most provoking taciturnity, and from answering in monosyllables, came to returning no answers at all, save such as were to be inferred from several grave nods and shrugs, which only served to whet that appetite for intelligence in Nicholas, which had already attained a most unreasonable height.

Foiled in these attempts, he was fain to content himself with watching for the young lady's next visit, but here again he was disappointed. Day after day passed, and she did not return. He looked eagerly at the superscription of all the notes and letters, but there was not one among them which he could fancy to be in her handwriting. On two or three occasions he was employed on business which took him to a distance, and had formerly been transacted by Tim Linkinwater. Nicholas could not help suspecting that, for some reason or other, he was sent out of the way on purpose, and that the young lady was there in his absence. Nothing transpired, however, to confirm this suspicion, and Tim could not be entrapped into any confession or admission tending to support it in the smallest degree.

Mystery and disappointment are not absolutely indispensable to the growth of love, but they are, very often, its powerful auxiliaries. 'Out of sight, out of mind,' is well enough as a proverb applicable to cases of friendship, though absence is not always necessary to hollowness of heart, even between friends, and truth and honesty, like precious stones, are perhaps most easily imitated at a distance, when the counterfeits often pass for real. Love, however, is very materially assisted by a warm and active imagination: which has a long memory, and will thrive, for a considerable time, on very slight and sparing food. Thus it is, that it often attains its most luxuriant growth in separation and under circumstances of the utmost difficulty; and thus it was, that Nicholas, thinking of nothing but the unknown young lady, from day to day and from hour to hour, began, at last, to think that he was very desperately in love with her, and that never was such an ill-used and persecuted lover as he.

Still, though he loved and languished after the most orthodox models, and was only deterred from making a confidante of Kate by the slight considerations of having never, in all his life, spoken to the object of his passion, and having never set eyes upon her, except on two occasions, on both of which she had come and gone like a flash of lightning—or, as Nicholas himself said, in the numerous conversations he held with himself, like a vision of youth and beauty much too bright to last—his ardour and devotion remained without its reward. The young lady appeared no more; so there was a great deal of love wasted (enough indeed to have set up half-a-dozen young gentlemen, as times go, with the utmost decency), and nobody was a bit the wiser for it; not even Nicholas himself, who, on the contrary, became more dull, sentimental, and lackadaisical, every day.

While matters were in this state, the failure of a correspondent of the brothers Cheeryble, in Germany, imposed upon Tim Linkinwater and Nicholas the necessity of going through some very long and complicated accounts, extending over a considerable space of time. To get through them with the greater dispatch, Tim Linkinwater proposed that they should remain at the counting-house, for a week or so, until ten o'clock at night; to this, as nothing damped the zeal of Nicholas in the service of his kind patrons—not even romance, which has seldom business habits—he cheerfully assented. On the very first night of these later hours, at nine exactly, there came: not the young lady herself, but her servant, who, being closeted with brother Charles for some time, went away, and returned next night at the same hour, and on the next, and on the next again.

These repeated visits inflamed the curiosity of Nicholas to the very highest pitch. Tantalised and excited, beyond all bearing, and unable to fathom the mystery without neglecting his duty, he confided the whole secret to Newman Noggs, imploring him to be on the watch next night; to follow the girl home; to set on foot such inquiries relative to the name, condition, and history of her mistress, as he could, without exciting suspicion; and to report the result to him with the least possible delay.

Beyond all measure proud of this commission, Newman Noggs took up his post, in the square, on the following evening, a full hour before the needful time, and planting himself behind the pump and pulling his hat over his eyes, began his watch with an elaborate appearance of mystery, admirably calculated to excite the suspicion of all beholders. Indeed, divers servant girls who came to draw water, and sundry little boys who stopped to drink at the ladle, were almost scared out of their senses, by the apparition of Newman Noggs looking stealthily round the pump, with nothing of him visible but his face, and that wearing the expression of a meditative Ogre.

Punctual to her time, the messenger came again, and, after an interview of rather longer duration than usual, departed. Newman had made two appointments with Nicholas: one for the next evening, conditional on his success: and one the next night following, which was to be kept under all circumstances. The first night he was not at the place of meeting (a certain tavern about half-way between the city and Golden Square), but on the second night he was there before Nicholas, and received him with open arms.

'It's all right,' whispered Newman. 'Sit down. Sit down, there's a dear young man, and let me tell you all about it.'

Nicholas needed no second invitation, and eagerly inquired what was the news.

'There's a great deal of news,' said Newman, in a flutter of exultation. 'It's all right. Don't be anxious. I don't know where to begin. Never mind that. Keep up your spirits. It's all right.'

'Well?' said Nicholas eagerly. 'Yes?'

'Yes,' replied Newman. 'That's it.'

'What's it?' said Nicholas. 'The name—the name, my dear fellow!'

'The name's Bobster,' replied Newman.

'Bobster!' repeated Nicholas, indignantly.

'That's the name,' said Newman. 'I remember it by lobster.'

'Bobster!' repeated Nicholas, more emphatically than before. 'That must be the servant's name.'

'No, it an't,' said Newman, shaking his head with great positiveness. 'Miss Cecilia Bobster.'

'Cecilia, eh?' returned Nicholas, muttering the two names together over and over again in every variety of tone, to try the effect. 'Well, Cecilia is a pretty name.'

'Very. And a pretty creature too,' said Newman.

'Who?' said Nicholas.

'Miss Bobster.'

'Why, where have you seen her?' demanded Nicholas.

'Never mind, my dear boy,' retorted Noggs, clapping him on the shoulder. 'I have seen her. You shall see her. I've managed it all.'

'My dear Newman,' cried Nicholas, grasping his hand, 'are you serious?'

'I am,' replied Newman. 'I mean it all. Every word. You shall see her tomorrow night. She consents to hear you speak for yourself. I persuaded her. She is all affability, goodness, sweetness, and beauty.'

'I know she is; I know she must be, Newman!' said Nicholas, wringing his hand.

'You are right,' returned Newman.

'Where does she live?' cried Nicholas. 'What have you learnt of her history? Has she a father—mother—any brothers—sisters? What did she say? How came you to see her? Was she not very much surprised? Did you say how passionately I have longed to speak to her? Did you tell her where I had seen her? Did you tell her how, and when, and where, and how long, and how often, I have thought of that sweet face which came upon me in my bitterest distress like a glimpse of some better world—did you, Newman—did you?'

Poor Noggs literally gasped for breath as this flood of questions rushed upon him, and moved spasmodically in his chair at every fresh inquiry, staring at Nicholas meanwhile with a most ludicrous expression of perplexity.

'No,' said Newman, 'I didn't tell her that.'

'Didn't tell her which?' asked Nicholas.

'About the glimpse of the better world,' said Newman. 'I didn't tell her who you were, either, or where you'd seen her. I said you loved her to distraction.'

'That's true, Newman,' replied Nicholas, with his characteristic vehemence. 'Heaven knows I do!'

'I said too, that you had admired her for a long time in secret,' said Newman.

'Yes, yes. What did she say to that?' asked Nicholas.

'Blushed,' said Newman.

'To be sure. Of course she would,' said Nicholas approvingly. Newman then went on to say, that the young lady was an only child, that her mother was dead, that she resided with her father, and that she had been induced to allow her lover a secret interview, at the intercession of her servant, who had great influence with her. He further related how it required much moving and great eloquence to bring the young lady to this pass; how it was expressly understood that she merely afforded Nicholas an opportunity of declaring his passion; and how she by no means pledged herself to be favourably impressed with his attentions. The mystery of her visits to the brothers Cheeryble remained wholly unexplained, for Newman had not alluded to them, either in his preliminary conversations with the servant or his subsequent interview with the mistress, merely remarking that he had been instructed to watch the girl home and plead his young friend's cause, and not saying how far he had followed her, or from what point. But Newman hinted that from what had fallen from the confidante, he had been led to suspect that the young lady led a very miserable and unhappy life, under the strict control of her only parent, who was of a violent and brutal temper; a circumstance which he thought might in some degree account, both for her having sought the protection and friendship of the brothers, and her suffering herself to be prevailed upon to grant the promised interview. The last he held to be a very logical deduction from the premises, inasmuch as it was but natural to suppose that a young lady, whose present condition was so unenviable, would be more than commonly desirous to change it.

It appeared, on further questioning—for it was only by a very long and arduous process that all this could be got out of Newman Noggs—that Newman, in explanation of his shabby appearance, had represented himself as being, for certain wise and indispensable purposes connected with that intrigue, in disguise; and, being questioned how he had come to exceed his commission so far as to procure an interview, he responded, that the lady appearing willing to grant it, he considered himself bound, both in duty and gallantry, to avail himself of such a golden means of enabling Nicholas to prosecute his addresses. After these and all possible questions had been asked and answered twenty times over, they parted, undertaking to meet on the following night at half-past ten, for the purpose of fulfilling the appointment; which was for eleven o'clock.

'Things come about very strangely!' thought Nicholas, as he walked home. 'I never contemplated anything of this kind; never dreamt of the possibility of it. To know something of the life of one in whom I felt such interest; to see her in the street, to pass the house in which she lived, to meet her sometimes in her walks, to hope that a day might come when I might be in a condition to tell her of my love, this was the utmost extent of my thoughts. Now, however—but I should be a fool, indeed, to repine at my own good fortune!'

Still, Nicholas was dissatisfied; and there was more in the dissatisfaction than mere revulsion of feeling. He was angry with the young lady for being so easily won, 'because,' reasoned Nicholas, 'it is not as if she knew it was I, but it might have been anybody,'—which was certainly not pleasant. The next moment, he was angry with himself for entertaining such thoughts, arguing that nothing but goodness could dwell in such a temple, and that the behaviour of the brothers sufficiently showed the estimation in which they held her. 'The fact is, she's a mystery altogether,' said Nicholas. This was not more satisfactory than his previous course of reflection, and only drove him out upon a new sea of speculation and conjecture, where he tossed and tumbled, in great discomfort of mind, until the clock struck ten, and the hour of meeting drew nigh.

Nicholas had dressed himself with great care, and even Newman Noggs had trimmed himself up a little; his coat presenting the phenomenon of two consecutive buttons, and the supplementary pins being inserted at tolerably regular intervals. He wore his hat, too, in the newest taste, with a pocket-handkerchief in the crown, and a twisted end of it straggling out behind after the fashion of a pigtail, though he could scarcely lay claim to the ingenuity of inventing this latter decoration, inasmuch as he was utterly unconscious of it: being in a nervous and excited condition which rendered him quite insensible to everything but the great object of the expedition.

They traversed the streets in profound silence; and after walking at a round pace for some distance, arrived in one, of a gloomy appearance and very little frequented, near the Edgeware Road.

'Number twelve,' said Newman.

'Oh!' replied Nicholas, looking about him.

'Good street?' said Newman.

'Yes,' returned Nicholas. 'Rather dull.'

Newman made no answer to this remark, but, halting abruptly, planted Nicholas with his back to some area railings, and gave him to understand that he was to wait there, without moving hand or foot, until it was satisfactorily ascertained that the coast was clear. This done, Noggs limped away with great alacrity; looking over his shoulder every instant, to make quite certain that Nicholas was obeying his directions; and, ascending the steps of a house some half-dozen doors off, was lost to view.

After a short delay, he reappeared, and limping back again, halted midway, and beckoned Nicholas to follow him.

'Well?' said Nicholas, advancing towards him on tiptoe.

'All right,' replied Newman, in high glee. 'All ready; nobody at home. Couldn't be better. Ha! ha!'

With this fortifying assurance, he stole past a street-door, on which Nicholas caught a glimpse of a brass plate, with 'BOBSTER,' in very large letters; and, stopping at the area-gate, which was open, signed to his young friend to descend.

'What the devil!' cried Nicholas, drawing back. 'Are we to sneak into the kitchen, as if we came after the forks?'

'Hush!' replied Newman. 'Old Bobster—ferocious Turk. He'd kill 'em all—box the young lady's ears—he does—often.'

'What!' cried Nicholas, in high wrath, 'do you mean to tell me that any man would dare to box the ears of such a—'

He had no time to sing the praises of his mistress, just then, for Newman gave him a gentle push which had nearly precipitated him to the bottom of the area steps. Thinking it best to take the hint in good part, Nicholas descended, without further remonstrance, but with a countenance bespeaking anything rather than the hope and rapture of a passionate lover. Newman followed—he would have followed head first, but for the timely assistance of Nicholas—and, taking his hand, led him through a stone passage, profoundly dark, into a back-kitchen or cellar, of the blackest and most pitchy obscurity, where they stopped.

'Well!' said Nicholas, in a discontented whisper, 'this is not all, I suppose, is it?'

'No, no,' rejoined Noggs; 'they'll be here directly. It's all right.'

'I am glad to hear it,' said Nicholas. 'I shouldn't have thought it, I confess.'

They exchanged no further words, and there Nicholas stood, listening to the loud breathing of Newman Noggs, and imagining that his nose seemed to glow like a red-hot coal, even in the midst of the darkness which enshrouded them. Suddenly the sound of cautious footsteps attracted his ear, and directly afterwards a female voice inquired if the gentleman was there.

'Yes,' replied Nicholas, turning towards the corner from which the voice proceeded. 'Who is that?'

'Only me, sir,' replied the voice. 'Now if you please, ma'am.'

A gleam of light shone into the place, and presently the servant girl appeared, bearing a light, and followed by her young mistress, who seemed to be overwhelmed by modesty and confusion.

At sight of the young lady, Nicholas started and changed colour; his heart beat violently, and he stood rooted to the spot. At that instant, and almost simultaneously with her arrival and that of the candle, there was heard a loud and furious knocking at the street-door, which caused Newman Noggs to jump up, with great agility, from a beer-barrel on which he had been seated astride, and to exclaim abruptly, and with a face of ashy paleness, 'Bobster, by the Lord!'

The young lady shrieked, the attendant wrung her hands, Nicholas gazed from one to the other in apparent stupefaction, and Newman hurried to and fro, thrusting his hands into all his pockets successively, and drawing out the linings of every one in the excess of his irresolution. It was but a moment, but the confusion crowded into that one moment no imagination can exaggerate.

'Leave the house, for Heaven's sake! We have done wrong, we deserve it all,' cried the young lady. 'Leave the house, or I am ruined and undone for ever.'

'Will you hear me say but one word?' cried Nicholas. 'Only one. I will not detain you. Will you hear me say one word, in explanation of this mischance?'

But Nicholas might as well have spoken to the wind, for the young lady, with distracted looks, hurried up the stairs. He would have followed her, but Newman, twisting his hand in his coat collar, dragged him towards the passage by which they had entered.

'Let me go, Newman, in the Devil's name!' cried Nicholas. 'I must speak to her. I will! I will not leave this house without.'

'Reputation—character—violence—consider,' said Newman, clinging round him with both arms, and hurrying him away. 'Let them open the door. We'll go, as we came, directly it's shut. Come. This way. Here.'

Overpowered by the remonstrances of Newman, and the tears and prayers of the girl, and the tremendous knocking above, which had never ceased, Nicholas allowed himself to be hurried off; and, precisely as Mr. Bobster made his entrance by the street-door, he and Noggs made their exit by the area-gate.

They hurried away, through several streets, without stopping or speaking. At last, they halted and confronted each other with blank and rueful faces.

'Never mind,' said Newman, gasping for breath. 'Don't be cast down. It's all right. More fortunate next time. It couldn't be helped. I did my part.'

'Excellently,' replied Nicholas, taking his hand. 'Excellently, and like the true and zealous friend you are. Only—mind, I am not disappointed, Newman, and feel just as much indebted to you—only it was the wrong lady.'

'Eh?' cried Newman Noggs. 'Taken in by the servant?'

'Newman, Newman,' said Nicholas, laying his hand upon his shoulder: 'it was the wrong servant too.'

Newman's under-jaw dropped, and he gazed at Nicholas, with his sound eye fixed fast and motionless in his head.

'Don't take it to heart,' said Nicholas; 'it's of no consequence; you see I don't care about it; you followed the wrong person, that's all.'

That was all. Whether Newman Noggs had looked round the pump, in a slanting direction, so long, that his sight became impaired; or whether, finding that there was time to spare, he had recruited himself with a few drops of something stronger than the pump could yield—by whatsoever means it had come to pass, this was his mistake. And Nicholas went home to brood upon it, and to meditate upon the charms of the unknown young lady, now as far beyond his reach as ever.

CHAPTER 41

Containing some Romantic Passages between Mrs. Nickleby and the Gentleman in the Small-clothes next Door

Ever since her last momentous conversation with her son, Mrs. Nickleby had begun to display unusual care in the adornment of her person, gradually superadding to those staid and matronly habiliments, which had, up to that time, formed her ordinary attire, a variety of embellishments and decorations, slight perhaps in themselves, but, taken together, and considered with reference to the subject of her disclosure, of no mean importance. Even her black dress assumed something of a deadly-lively air from the jaunty style in which it was worn; and, eked out as its lingering attractions were; by a prudent disposal, here and there, of certain juvenile ornaments of little or no value, which had, for that reason alone, escaped the general wreck and been permitted to slumber peacefully in odd corners of old drawers and boxes where daylight seldom shone, her mourning garments assumed quite a new character. From being the outward tokens of respect and sorrow for the dead, they became converted into signals of very slaughterous and killing designs upon the living.

Mrs. Nickleby might have been stimulated to this proceeding by a lofty sense of duty, and impulses of unquestionable excellence. She might, by this time, have become impressed with the sinfulness of long indulgence in unavailing woe, or the necessity of setting a proper example of neatness and decorum to her blooming daughter. Considerations of duty and responsibility apart, the change might have taken its rise in feelings of the purest and most disinterested charity. The gentleman next door had been vilified by Nicholas; rudely stigmatised as a dotard and an idiot; and for these attacks upon his understanding, Mrs. Nickleby was, in some sort, accountable. She might have felt that it was the act of a good Christian to show by all means in her power, that the abused gentleman was neither the one nor the other. And what better means could she adopt, towards so virtuous and laudable an end, than proving to all men, in her own person, that his passion was the most rational and reasonable in the world, and just the very result, of all others, which discreet and thinking persons might have foreseen, from her incautiously displaying her matured charms, without reserve, under the very eye, as it were, of an ardent and too-susceptible man?

'Ah!' said Mrs. Nickleby, gravely shaking her head; 'if Nicholas knew what his poor dear papa suffered before we were engaged, when I used to hate him, he would have a little more feeling. Shall I ever forget the morning I looked scornfully at him when he offered to carry my parasol? Or that night, when I frowned at him? It was a mercy he didn't emigrate. It very nearly drove him to it.'

Whether the deceased might not have been better off if he had emigrated in his bachelor days, was a question which his relict did not stop to consider; for Kate entered the room, with her workbox, in this stage of her reflections; and a much slighter interruption, or no interruption at all, would have diverted Mrs. Nickleby's thoughts into a new channel at any time.

'Kate, my dear,' said Mrs. Nickleby; 'I don't know how it is, but a fine warm summer day like this, with the birds singing in every direction, always puts me in mind of roast pig, with sage and onion sauce, and made gravy.'

'That's a curious association of ideas, is it not, mama?'

'Upon my word, my dear, I don't know,' replied Mrs. Nickleby. 'Roast pig; let me see. On the day five weeks after you were christened, we had a roast—no, that couldn't have been a pig, either, because I recollect there were a pair of them to carve, and your poor papa and I could never have thought of sitting down to two pigs—they must have been partridges. Roast pig! I hardly think we ever could have had one, now I come to remember, for your papa could never bear the sight of them in the shops, and used to say that they always put him in mind of very little babies, only the pigs had much fairer complexions; and he had a horror of little babies, too, because he couldn't very well afford any increase to his family, and had a natural dislike to the subject. It's very odd now, what can have put that in my head! I recollect dining once at Mrs. Bevan's, in that broad street round the corner by the coachmaker's, where the tipsy man fell through the cellar-flap of an empty house nearly a week before the quarter-day, and wasn't found till the new tenant went in—and we had roast pig there. It must be that, I think, that reminds me of it, especially as there was a little bird in the room that would keep on singing all the time of dinner—at least, not a little bird, for it was a parrot, and he didn't sing exactly, for he talked and swore dreadfully: but I think it must be that. Indeed I am sure it must. Shouldn't you say so, my dear?'

'I should say there was not a doubt about it, mama,' returned Kate, with a cheerful smile.

'No; but do you think so, Kate?' said Mrs. Nickleby, with as much gravity as if it were a question of the most imminent and thrilling interest. 'If you don't, say so at once, you know; because it's just as well to be correct, particularly on a point of this kind, which is very curious and worth settling while one thinks about it.'

Kate laughingly replied that she was quite convinced; and as her mama still appeared undetermined whether it was not absolutely essential that the subject should be renewed, proposed that they should take their work into the summer-house, and enjoy the beauty of the afternoon. Mrs. Nickleby readily assented, and to the summer-house they repaired, without further discussion.

'Well, I will say,' observed Mrs. Nickleby, as she took her seat, 'that there never was such a good creature as Smike. Upon my word, the pains he has taken in putting this little arbour to rights, and training the sweetest flowers about it, are beyond anything I could have—I wish he wouldn't put all the gravel on your side, Kate, my dear, though, and leave nothing but mould for me.'

'Dear mama,' returned Kate, hastily, 'take this seat—do—to oblige me, mama.'

'No, indeed, my dear. I shall keep my own side,' said Mrs. Nickleby. 'Well! I declare!'

Kate looked up inquiringly.

'If he hasn't been,' said Mrs. Nickleby, 'and got, from somewhere or other, a couple of roots of those flowers that I said I was so fond of, the other night, and asked you if you were not—no, that you said you were so fond of, the other night, and asked me if I wasn't—it's the same thing. Now, upon my word, I take that as very kind and attentive indeed! I don't see,' added Mrs. Nickleby, looking narrowly about her, 'any of them on my side, but I suppose they grow best near the gravel. You may depend upon it they do, Kate, and that's the reason they are all near you, and he has put the gravel there, because it's the sunny side. Upon my word, that's very clever now! I shouldn't have had half as much thought myself!'

'Mama,' said Kate, bending over her work so that her face was almost hidden, 'before you were married—'

'Dear me, Kate,' interrupted Mrs. Nickleby, 'what in the name of goodness graciousness makes you fly off to the time before I was married, when I'm talking to you about his thoughtfulness and attention to me? You don't seem to take the smallest interest in the garden.'

'Oh! mama,' said Kate, raising her face again, 'you know I do.'

'Well then, my dear, why don't you praise the neatness and prettiness with which it's kept?' said Mrs. Nickleby. 'How very odd you are, Kate!'

'I do praise it, mama,' answered Kate, gently. 'Poor fellow!'

'I scarcely ever hear you, my dear,' retorted Mrs. Nickleby; 'that's all I've got to say.' By this time the good lady had been a long while upon one topic, so she fell at once into her daughter's little trap, if trap it were, and inquired what she had been going to say.

'About what, mama?' said Kate, who had apparently quite forgotten her diversion.

'Lor, Kate, my dear,' returned her mother, 'why, you're asleep or stupid! About the time before I was married.'

'Oh yes!' said Kate, 'I remember. I was going to ask, mama, before you were married, had you many suitors?'

'Suitors, my dear!' cried Mrs. Nickleby, with a smile of wonderful complacency. 'First and last, Kate, I must have had a dozen at least.'

'Mama!' returned Kate, in a tone of remonstrance.

'I had indeed, my dear,' said Mrs. Nickleby; 'not including your poor papa, or a young gentleman who used to go, at that time, to the same dancing school, and who would send gold watches and bracelets to our house in gilt-edged paper, (which were always returned,) and who afterwards unfortunately went out to Botany Bay in a cadet ship—a convict ship I mean—and escaped into a bush and killed sheep, (I don't know how they got there,) and was going to be hung, only he accidentally choked himself, and the government pardoned him. Then there was young Lukin,' said Mrs. Nickleby, beginning with her left thumb and checking off the names on her fingers—'Mogley—Tipslark—Cabbery—Smifser—'

Having now reached her little finger, Mrs. Nickleby was carrying the account over to the other hand, when a loud 'Hem!' which appeared to come from the very foundation of the garden-wall, gave both herself and her daughter a violent start.

'Mama! what was that?' said Kate, in a low tone of voice.

'Upon my word, my dear,' returned Mrs. Nickleby, considerably startled, 'unless it was the gentleman belonging to the next house, I don't know what it could possibly—'

'A—hem!' cried the same voice; and that, not in the tone of an ordinary clearing of the throat, but in a kind of bellow, which woke up all the echoes in the neighbourhood, and was prolonged to an extent which must have made the unseen bellower quite black in the face.

'I understand it now, my dear,' said Mrs. Nickleby, laying her hand on Kate's; 'don't be alarmed, my love, it's not directed to you, and is not intended to frighten anybody. Let us give everybody their due, Kate; I am bound to say that.'

So saying, Mrs. Nickleby nodded her head, and patted the back of her daughter's hand, a great many times, and looked as if she could tell something vastly important if she chose, but had self-denial, thank Heaven; and wouldn't do it.

'What do you mean, mama?' demanded Kate, in evident surprise.

'Don't be flurried, my dear,' replied Mrs. Nickleby, looking towards the garden-wall, 'for you see I'm not, and if it would be excusable in anybody to be flurried, it certainly would—under all the circumstances—be excusable in me, but I am not, Kate—not at all.'

'It seems designed to attract our attention, mama,' said Kate.

'It is designed to attract our attention, my dear; at least,' rejoined Mrs Nickleby, drawing herself up, and patting her daughter's hand more blandly than before, 'to attract the attention of one of us. Hem! you needn't be at all uneasy, my dear.'

Kate looked very much perplexed, and was apparently about to ask for further explanation, when a shouting and scuffling noise, as of an elderly gentleman whooping, and kicking up his legs on loose gravel, with great violence, was heard to proceed from the same direction as the former sounds; and before they had subsided, a large cucumber was seen to shoot up in the air with the velocity of a sky-rocket, whence it descended, tumbling over and over, until it fell at Mrs. Nickleby's feet.

This remarkable appearance was succeeded by another of a precisely similar description; then a fine vegetable marrow, of unusually large dimensions, was seen to whirl aloft, and come toppling down; then, several cucumbers shot up together; and, finally, the air was darkened by a shower of onions, turnip-radishes, and other small vegetables, which fell rolling and scattering, and bumping about, in all directions.

As Kate rose from her seat, in some alarm, and caught her mother's hand to run with her into the house, she felt herself rather retarded than assisted in her intention; and following the direction of Mrs. Nickleby's eyes, was quite terrified by the apparition of an old black velvet cap, which, by slow degrees, as if its wearer were ascending a ladder or pair of steps, rose above the wall dividing their garden from that of the next cottage, (which, like their own, was a detached building,) and was gradually followed by a very large head, and an old face, in which were a pair of most extraordinary grey eyes: very wild, very wide open, and rolling in their sockets, with a dull, languishing, leering look, most ugly to behold.

'Mama!' cried Kate, really terrified for the moment, 'why do you stop, why do you lose an instant? Mama, pray come in!'

'Kate, my dear,' returned her mother, still holding back, 'how can you be so foolish? I'm ashamed of you. How do you suppose you are ever to get through life, if you're such a coward as this? What do you want, sir?' said Mrs. Nickleby, addressing the intruder with a sort of simpering displeasure. 'How dare you look into this garden?'

'Queen of my soul,' replied the stranger, folding his hands together, 'this goblet sip!'

'Nonsense, sir,' said Mrs. Nickleby. 'Kate, my love, pray be quiet.'

'Won't you sip the goblet?' urged the stranger, with his head imploringly on one side, and his right hand on his breast. 'Oh, do sip the goblet!'

'I shall not consent to do anything of the kind, sir,' said Mrs. Nickleby. 'Pray, begone.'

'Why is it,' said the old gentleman, coming up a step higher, and leaning his elbows on the wall, with as much complacency as if he were looking out of window, 'why is it that beauty is always obdurate, even when admiration is as honourable and respectful as mine?' Here he smiled, kissed his hand, and made several low bows. 'Is it owing to the bees, who, when the honey season is over, and they are supposed to have been killed with brimstone, in reality fly to Barbary and lull the captive Moors to sleep with their drowsy songs? Or is it,' he added, dropping his voice almost to a whisper, 'in consequence of the statue at Charing Cross having been lately seen, on the Stock Exchange at midnight, walking arm-in-arm with the Pump from Aldgate, in a riding-habit?'

'Mama,' murmured Kate, 'do you hear him?'

'Hush, my dear!' replied Mrs. Nickleby, in the same tone of voice, 'he is very polite, and I think that was a quotation from the poets. Pray, don't worry me so—you'll pinch my arm black and blue. Go away, sir!'

'Quite away?' said the gentleman, with a languishing look. 'Oh! quite away?'

'Yes,' returned Mrs. Nickleby, 'certainly. You have no business here. This is private property, sir; you ought to know that.'

'I do know,' said the old gentleman, laying his finger on his nose, with an air of familiarity, most reprehensible, 'that this is a sacred and enchanted spot, where the most divine charms'— here he kissed his hand and bowed again—'waft mellifluousness over the neighbours' gardens, and force the fruit and vegetables into premature existence. That fact I am acquainted with. But will you permit me, fairest creature, to ask you one question, in the absence of the planet Venus, who has gone on business to the Horse Guards, and would otherwise—jealous of your superior charms—interpose between us?'

'Kate,' observed Mrs. Nickleby, turning to her daughter, 'it's very awkward, positively. I really don't know what to say to this gentleman. One ought to be civil, you know.'

'Dear mama,' rejoined Kate, 'don't say a word to him, but let us run away as fast as we can, and shut ourselves up till Nicholas comes home.'

Mrs. Nickleby looked very grand, not to say contemptuous, at this humiliating proposal; and, turning to the old gentleman, who had watched them during these whispers with absorbing eagerness, said:

'If you will conduct yourself, sir, like the gentleman I should imagine you to be, from your language and—and—appearance, (quite the counterpart of your grandpapa, Kate, my dear, in his best days,) and will put your question to me in plain words, I will answer it.'

If Mrs. Nickleby's excellent papa had borne, in his best days, a resemblance to the neighbour now looking over the wall, he must have been, to say the least, a very queer-looking old gentleman in his prime. Perhaps Kate thought so, for she ventured to glance at his living portrait with some attention, as he took off his black velvet cap, and, exhibiting a perfectly bald head, made a long series of bows, each accompanied with a fresh kiss of the hand. After exhausting himself, to all appearance, with this fatiguing performance, he covered his head once more, pulled the cap very carefully over the tips of his ears, and resuming his former attitude, said,

'The question is—'

Here he broke off to look round in every direction, and satisfy himself beyond all doubt that there were no listeners near. Assured that there were not, he tapped his nose several times, accompanying the action with a cunning look, as though congratulating himself on his caution; and stretching out his neck, said in a loud whisper,

'Are you a princess?'

'You are mocking me, sir,' replied Mrs. Nickleby, making a feint of retreating towards the house.

'No, but are you?' said the old gentleman.

'You know I am not, sir,' replied Mrs. Nickleby.

'Then are you any relation to the Archbishop of Canterbury?' inquired the old gentleman with great anxiety, 'or to the Pope of Rome? Or the Speaker of the House of Commons? Forgive me, if I am wrong, but I was told you were niece to the Commissioners of Paving, and daughter-in-law to the Lord Mayor and Court of Common Council, which would account for your relationship to all three.'

'Whoever has spread such reports, sir,' returned Mrs. Nickleby, with some warmth, 'has taken great liberties with my name, and one which I am sure my son Nicholas, if he was aware of it, would not allow for an instant. The idea!' said Mrs. Nickleby, drawing herself up, 'niece to the Commissioners of Paving!'

'Pray, mama, come away!' whispered Kate.

'"Pray mama!" Nonsense, Kate,' said Mrs. Nickleby, angrily, 'but that's just the way. If they had said I was niece to a piping bullfinch, what would you care? But I have no sympathy,' whimpered Mrs. Nickleby. 'I don't expect it, that's one thing.'

'Tears!' cried the old gentleman, with such an energetic jump, that he fell down two or three steps and grated his chin against the wall. 'Catch the crystal globules—catch 'em—bottle 'em up—cork 'em tight—put sealing wax on the top—seal 'em with a cupid—label 'em "Best quality"—and stow 'em away in the fourteen binn, with a bar of iron on the top to keep the thunder off!'

Issuing these commands, as if there were a dozen attendants all actively engaged in their execution, he turned his velvet cap inside out, put it on with great dignity so as to obscure his right eye and three-fourths of his nose, and sticking his arms a-kimbo, looked very fiercely at a sparrow hard by, till the bird flew away, when he put his cap in his pocket with an air of great satisfaction, and addressed himself with respectful demeanour to Mrs. Nickleby.

'Beautiful madam,' such were his words, 'if I have made any mistake with regard to your family or connections, I humbly beseech you to pardon me. If I supposed you to be related to Foreign Powers or Native Boards, it is because you have a manner, a carriage, a dignity, which you will excuse my saying that none but yourself (with the single exception perhaps of the tragic muse, when playing extemporaneously on the barrel organ before the East India Company) can parallel. I am not a youth, ma'am, as you see; and although beings like you can never grow old, I venture to presume that we are fitted for each other.'

'Really, Kate, my love!' said Mrs. Nickleby faintly, and looking another way.

'I have estates, ma'am,' said the old gentleman, flourishing his right hand negligently, as if he made very light of such matters, and speaking very fast; 'jewels, lighthouses, fish-ponds, a whalery of my own in the North Sea, and several oyster-beds of great profit in the Pacific Ocean. If you will have the kindness to step down to the Royal Exchange and to take the cocked-hat off the stoutest beadle's head, you will find my card in the lining of the crown, wrapped up in a piece of blue paper. My walking-stick is also to be seen on application to the chaplain of the House of Commons, who is strictly forbidden to take any money for showing it. I have enemies about me, ma'am,' he looked towards his house and spoke very low, 'who attack me on all occasions, and wish to secure my property. If you bless me with your hand and heart, you can apply to the Lord Chancellor or call out the military if necessary—sending my toothpick to the commander-in-chief will be sufficient—and so clear the house of them before the ceremony is performed. After that, love, bliss and rapture; rapture, love and bliss.

Be mine, be mine!'

Repeating these last words with great rapture and enthusiasm, the old gentleman put on his black velvet cap again, and looking up into the sky in a hasty manner, said something that was not quite intelligible concerning a balloon he expected, and which was rather after its time.

'Be mine, be mine!' repeated the old gentleman.

'Kate, my dear,' said Mrs. Nickleby, 'I have hardly the power to speak; but it is necessary for the happiness of all parties that this matter should be set at rest for ever.'

'Surely there is no necessity for you to say one word, mama?' reasoned Kate.

'You will allow me, my dear, if you please, to judge for myself,' said Mrs Nickleby.

'Be mine, be mine!' cried the old gentleman.

'It can scarcely be expected, sir,' said Mrs. Nickleby, fixing her eyes modestly on the ground, 'that I should tell a stranger whether I feel flattered and obliged by such proposals, or not. They certainly are made under very singular circumstances; still at the same time, as far as it goes, and to a certain extent of course' (Mrs. Nickleby's customary qualification), 'they must be gratifying and agreeable to one's feelings.'

'Be mine, be mine,' cried the old gentleman. 'Gog and Magog, Gog and Magog. Be mine, be mine!'

'It will be sufficient for me to say, sir,' resumed Mrs. Nickleby, with perfect seriousness— 'and I'm sure you'll see the propriety of taking an answer and going away—that I have made up my mind to remain a widow, and to devote myself to my children. You may not suppose I am the mother of two children—indeed many people have doubted it, and said that nothing on earth could ever make 'em believe it possible—but it is the case, and they are both grown up. We shall be very glad to have you for a neighbour—very glad; delighted, I'm sure—but in any other character it's quite impossible, quite. As to my being young enough to marry again, that perhaps may be so, or it may not be; but I couldn't think of it for an instant, not on any account whatever. I said I never would, and I never will. It's a very painful thing to have to reject proposals, and I would much rather that none were made; at the same time this is the answer that I determined long ago to make, and this is the answer I shall always give.'

These observations were partly addressed to the old gentleman, partly to Kate, and partly delivered in soliloquy. Towards their conclusion, the suitor evinced a very irreverent degree of inattention, and Mrs. Nickleby had scarcely finished speaking, when, to the great terror both of that lady and her daughter, he suddenly flung off his coat, and springing on the top of the wall, threw himself into an attitude which displayed his small-clothes and grey worsteds to the fullest advantage, and concluded by standing on one leg, and repeating his favourite bellow with increased vehemence.

While he was still dwelling on the last note, and embellishing it with a prolonged flourish, a dirty hand was observed to glide stealthily and swiftly along the top of the wall, as if in pursuit of a fly, and then to clasp with the utmost dexterity one of the old gentleman's ankles. This done, the companion hand appeared, and clasped the other ankle.

Thus encumbered the old gentleman lifted his legs awkwardly once or twice, as if they were very clumsy and imperfect pieces of machinery, and then looking down on his own side of the wall, burst into a loud laugh.

'It's you, is it?' said the old gentleman.

'Yes, it's me,' replied a gruff voice.

'How's the Emperor of Tartary?' said the old gentleman.

'Oh! he's much the same as usual,' was the reply. 'No better and no worse.'

'The young Prince of China,' said the old gentleman, with much interest. 'Is he reconciled to his father-in-law, the great potato salesman?'

'No,' answered the gruff voice; 'and he says he never will be, that's more.'

'If that's the case,' observed the old gentleman, 'perhaps I'd better come down.'

'Well,' said the man on the other side, 'I think you had, perhaps.'

One of the hands being then cautiously unclasped, the old gentleman dropped into a sitting posture, and was looking round to smile and bow to Mrs. Nickleby, when he disappeared with some precipitation, as if his legs had been pulled from below.

Very much relieved by his disappearance, Kate was turning to speak to her mama, when the dirty hands again became visible, and were immediately followed by the figure of a coarse squat man, who ascended by the steps which had been recently occupied by their singular neighbour.

'Beg your pardon, ladies,' said this new comer, grinning and touching his hat. 'Has he been making love to either of you?'

'Yes,' said Kate.

'Ah!' rejoined the man, taking his handkerchief out of his hat and wiping his face, 'he always will, you know. Nothing will prevent his making love.'

'I need not ask you if he is out of his mind, poor creature,' said Kate.

'Why no,' replied the man, looking into his hat, throwing his handkerchief in at one dab, and putting it on again. 'That's pretty plain, that is.'

'Has he been long so?' asked Kate.

'A long while.'

'And is there no hope for him?' said Kate, compassionately

'Not a bit, and don't deserve to be,' replied the keeper. 'He's a deal pleasanter without his senses than with 'em. He was the cruellest, wickedest, out-and-outerest old flint that ever drawed breath.'

'Indeed!' said Kate.

'By George!' replied the keeper, shaking his head so emphatically that he was obliged to frown to keep his hat on. 'I never come across such a vagabond, and my mate says the same. Broke his poor wife's heart, turned his daughters out of doors, drove his sons into the streets; it was a blessing he went mad at last, through evil tempers, and covetousness, and selfishness, and guzzling, and drinking, or he'd have drove many others so. Hope for him, an old rip! There isn't too much hope going, but I'll bet a crown that what there is, is saved for more deserving chaps than him, anyhow.'

With which confession of his faith, the keeper shook his head again, as much as to say that nothing short of this would do, if things were to go on at all; and touching his hat sulkily—not that he was in an ill humour, but that his subject ruffled him—descended the ladder, and took it away.

During this conversation, Mrs. Nickleby had regarded the man with a severe and steadfast look. She now heaved a profound sigh, and pursing up her lips, shook her head in a slow and doubtful manner.

'Poor creature!' said Kate.

'Ah! poor indeed!' rejoined Mrs. Nickleby. 'It's shameful that such things should be allowed. Shameful!'

'How can they be helped, mama?' said Kate, mournfully. 'The infirmities of nature—'

'Nature!' said Mrs. Nickleby. 'What! Do you suppose this poor gentleman is out of his mind?'

'Can anybody who sees him entertain any other opinion, mama?'

'Why then, I just tell you this, Kate,' returned Mrs. Nickleby, 'that, he is nothing of the kind, and I am surprised you can be so imposed upon. It's some plot of these people to possess themselves of his property—didn't he say so himself? He may be a little odd and flighty, perhaps, many of us are that; but downright mad! and express himself as he does, respectfully, and in quite poetical language, and making offers with so much thought, and care, and prudence—not as if he ran into the streets, and went down upon his knees to the first chit of a girl he met, as a madman would! No, no, Kate, there's a great deal too much method in his madness; depend upon that, my dear.'

CHAPTER 42
Illustrative of the convivial Sentiment, that the best of Friends must sometimes part

The pavement of Snow Hill had been baking and frying all day in the heat, and the twain Saracens' heads guarding the entrance to the hostelry of whose name and sign they are the duplicate presentments, looked—or seemed, in the eyes of jaded and footsore passers-by, to look—more vicious than usual, after blistering and scorching in the sun, when, in one of the inn's smallest sitting-rooms, through whose open window there rose, in a palpable steam, wholesome exhalations from reeking coach-horses, the usual furniture of a tea-table was displayed in neat and inviting order, flanked by large joints of roast and boiled, a tongue, a pigeon pie, a cold fowl, a tankard of ale, and other little matters of the like kind, which, in degenerate towns and cities, are generally understood to belong more particularly to solid lunches, stage-coach dinners, or unusually substantial breakfasts.

Mr. John Browdie, with his hands in his pockets, hovered restlessly about these delicacies, stopping occasionally to whisk the flies out of the sugar-basin with his wife's pocket-handkerchief, or to dip a teaspoon in the milk-pot and carry it to his mouth, or to cut off a little knob of crust, and a little corner of meat, and swallow them at two gulps like a couple of pills. After every one of these flirtations with the eatables, he pulled out his watch, and declared with an earnestness quite pathetic that he couldn't undertake to hold out two minutes longer.

'Tilly!' said John to his lady, who was reclining half awake and half asleep upon a sofa.

'Well, John!'

'Well, John!' retorted her husband, impatiently. 'Dost thou feel hoongry, lass?'

'Not very,' said Mrs. Browdie.

'Not vary!' repeated John, raising his eyes to the ceiling. 'Hear her say not vary, and us dining at three, and loonching off pasthry thot aggravates a mon 'stead of pacifying him! Not vary!'

'Here's a gen'l'man for you, sir,' said the waiter, looking in.

'A wa'at for me?' cried John, as though he thought it must be a letter, or a parcel.

'A gen'l'man, sir.'

'Stars and garthers, chap!' said John, 'wa'at dost thou coom and say thot for? In wi' 'un.'

'Are you at home, sir?'

'At whoam!' cried John, 'I wish I wur; I'd ha tea'd two hour ago. Why, I told t'oother chap to look sharp ootside door, and tell 'un d'rectly he coom, thot we war faint wi' hoonger. In wi' 'un. Aha! Thee hond, Misther Nickleby. This is nigh to be the proodest day o' my life, sir. Hoo be all wi' ye? Ding! But, I'm glod o' this!'

Quite forgetting even his hunger in the heartiness of his salutation, John Browdie shook Nicholas by the hand again and again, slapping his palm with great violence between each shake, to add warmth to the reception.

'Ah! there she be,' said John, observing the look which Nicholas directed towards his wife. 'There she be—we shan't quarrel about her noo—eh? Ecod, when I think o' thot—but thou want'st soom'at to eat. Fall to, mun, fall to, and for wa'at we're aboot to receive—'

No doubt the grace was properly finished, but nothing more was heard, for John had already begun to play such a knife and fork, that his speech was, for the time, gone.

'I shall take the usual licence, Mr. Browdie,' said Nicholas, as he placed a chair for the bride.

'Tak' whatever thou like'st,' said John, 'and when a's gane, ca' for more.'

Without stopping to explain, Nicholas kissed the blushing Mrs. Browdie, and handed her to her seat.

'I say,' said John, rather astounded for the moment, 'mak' theeself quite at whoam, will 'ee?'

'You may depend upon that,' replied Nicholas; 'on one condition.'

'And wa'at may thot be?' asked John.

'That you make me a godfather the very first time you have occasion for one.'

'Eh! d'ye hear thot?' cried John, laying down his knife and fork. 'A godfeyther! Ha! ha! ha! Tilly—hear till 'un—a godfeyther! Divn't say a word more, ye'll never beat thot. Occasion for 'un—a godfeyther! Ha! ha! ha!'

Never was man so tickled with a respectable old joke, as John Browdie was with this. He chuckled, roared, half suffocated himself by laughing large pieces of beef into his windpipe, roared again, persisted in eating at the same time, got red in the face and black in the forehead, coughed, cried, got better, went off again laughing inwardly, got worse, choked, had his back thumped, stamped about, frightened his wife, and at last recovered in a state of the last exhaustion and with the water streaming from his eyes, but still faintly ejaculating, 'A godfeyther—a godfeyther, Tilly!' in a tone bespeaking an exquisite relish of the sally, which no suffering could diminish.

'You remember the night of our first tea-drinking?' said Nicholas.

'Shall I e'er forget it, mun?' replied John Browdie.

'He was a desperate fellow that night though, was he not, Mrs. Browdie?' said Nicholas. 'Quite a monster!'

'If you had only heard him as we were going home, Mr. Nickleby, you'd have said so indeed,' returned the bride. 'I never was so frightened in all my life.'

'Coom, coom,' said John, with a broad grin; 'thou know'st betther than thot, Tilly.'

'So I was,' replied Mrs. Browdie. 'I almost made up my mind never to speak to you again.'

'A'most!' said John, with a broader grin than the last. 'A'most made up her mind! And she wur coaxin', and coaxin', and wheedlin', and wheedlin' a' the blessed wa'. "Wa'at didst thou let yon chap mak' oop tiv'ee for?" says I. "I deedn't, John," says she, a squeedgin my arm. "You deedn't?" says I. "Noa," says she, a squeedgin of me agean.'

'Lor, John!' interposed his pretty wife, colouring very much. 'How can you talk such nonsense? As if I should have dreamt of such a thing!'

'I dinnot know whether thou'd ever dreamt of it, though I think that's loike eneaf, mind,' retorted John; 'but thou didst it. "Ye're a feeckle, changeable weathercock, lass," says I. "Not feeckle, John," says she. "Yes," says I, "feeckle, dom'd feeckle. Dinnot tell me thou bean't, efther yon chap at schoolmeasther's," says I. "Him!" says she, quite screeching. "Ah! him!" says I. "Why, John," says she—and she coom a deal closer and squeedged a deal harder than she'd deane afore—"dost thou think it's nat'ral noo, that having such a proper mun as thou to keep company wi', I'd ever tak' opp wi' such a leetle scanty whipper-snapper as yon?" she says. Ha! ha! ha! She said whipper-snapper! "Ecod!" I says, "efther thot, neame the day, and let's have it ower!" Ha! ha! ha!'

Nicholas laughed very heartily at this story, both on account of its telling against himself, and his being desirous to spare the blushes of Mrs. Browdie, whose protestations were drowned in peals of laughter from her husband. His good-nature soon put her at her ease; and although she still denied the charge, she laughed so heartily at it, that Nicholas had the satisfaction of feeling assured that in all essential respects it was strictly true.

'This is the second time,' said Nicholas, 'that we have ever taken a meal together, and only third I have ever seen you; and yet it really seems to me as if I were among old friends.'

'Weel!' observed the Yorkshireman, 'so I say.'

'And I am sure I do,' added his young wife.

'I have the best reason to be impressed with the feeling, mind,' said Nicholas; 'for if it had not been for your kindness of heart, my good friend, when I had no right or reason to expect it, I know not what might have become of me or what plight I should have been in by this time.'

'Talk aboot soom'at else,' replied John, gruffly, 'and dinnot bother.'

'It must be a new song to the same tune then,' said Nicholas, smiling. 'I told you in my letter that I deeply felt and admired your sympathy with that poor lad, whom you released at the risk of involving yourself in trouble and difficulty; but I can never tell you how grateful he and I, and others whom you don't know, are to you for taking pity on him.'

'Ecod!' rejoined John Browdie, drawing up his chair; 'and I can never tell you hoo gratful soom folks that we do know would be loikewise, if they know'd I had takken pity on him.'

'Ah!' exclaimed Mrs. Browdie, 'what a state I was in that night!'

'Were they at all disposed to give you credit for assisting in the escape?' inquired Nicholas of John Browdie.

'Not a bit,' replied the Yorkshireman, extending his mouth from ear to ear. 'There I lay, snoog in schoolmeasther's bed long efther it was dark, and nobody coom nigh the pleace. "Weel!" thinks I, "he's got a pretty good start, and if he bean't whoam by noo, he never will be; so you may coom as quick as you loike, and foind us reddy"—that is, you know, schoolmeasther might coom.'

'I understand,' said Nicholas.

'Presently,' resumed John, 'he did coom. I heerd door shut doonstairs, and him a warking, oop in the daark. "Slow and steddy," I says to myself, "tak' your time, sir—no hurry." He cooms to the door, turns the key—turns the key when there warn't nothing to hoold the lock—and ca's oot "Hallo, there!"—"Yes," thinks I, "you may do thot agean, and not wakken anybody, sir." "Hallo, there," he says, and then he stops. "Thou'd betther not aggravate me," says schoolmeasther, efther a little time. "I'll brak' every boan in your boddy, Smike," he says, efther another little time. Then all of a soodden, he sings oot for a loight, and when it cooms— ecod, such a hoorly-boorly! "Wa'at's the matter?" says I. "He's gane," says he,—stark mad wi' vengeance. "Have you heerd nought?" "Ees," says I, "I heerd street-door shut, no time at a' ago. I heerd a person run doon there" (pointing t'other wa'—eh?) "Help!" he cries. "I'll help you," says I; and off we set—the wrong wa'! Ho! ho! ho!'

'Did you go far?' asked Nicholas.

'Far!' replied John; 'I run him clean off his legs in quarther of an hoor. To see old schoolmeasther wi'out his hat, skimming along oop to his knees in mud and wather, tumbling over fences, and rowling into ditches, and bawling oot like mad, wi' his one eye looking sharp out for the lad, and his coat-tails flying out behind, and him spattered wi' mud all ower, face and all! I tho't I should ha' dropped doon, and killed myself wi' laughing.'

John laughed so heartily at the mere recollection, that he communicated the contagion to both his hearers, and all three burst into peals of laughter, which were renewed again and again, until they could laugh no longer.

'He's a bad 'un,' said John, wiping his eyes; 'a very bad 'un, is schoolmeasther.'

'I can't bear the sight of him, John,' said his wife.

'Coom,' retorted John, 'thot's tidy in you, thot is. If it wa'nt along o' you, we shouldn't know nought aboot 'un. Thou know'd 'un first, Tilly, didn't thou?'

'I couldn't help knowing Fanny Squeers, John,' returned his wife; 'she was an old playmate of mine, you know.'

'Weel,' replied John, 'dean't I say so, lass? It's best to be neighbourly, and keep up old acquaintance loike; and what I say is, dean't quarrel if 'ee can help it. Dinnot think so, Mr. Nickleby?'

'Certainly,' returned Nicholas; 'and you acted upon that principle when I meet you on horseback on the road, after our memorable evening.'

'Sure-ly,' said John. 'Wa'at I say, I stick by.'

'And that's a fine thing to do, and manly too,' said Nicholas, 'though it's not exactly what we understand by "coming Yorkshire over us" in London. Miss Squeers is stopping with you, you said in your note.'

'Yes,' replied John, 'Tilly's bridesmaid; and a queer bridesmaid she be, too. She wean't be a bride in a hurry, I reckon.'

'For shame, John,' said Mrs. Browdie; with an acute perception of the joke though, being a bride herself.

'The groom will be a blessed mun,' said John, his eyes twinkling at the idea. 'He'll be in luck, he will.'

'You see, Mr. Nickleby,' said his wife, 'that it was in consequence of her being here, that John wrote to you and fixed tonight, because we thought that it wouldn't be pleasant for you to meet, after what has passed.'

'Unquestionably. You were quite right in that,' said Nicholas, interrupting.

'Especially,' observed Mrs. Browdie, looking very sly, 'after what we know about past and gone love matters.'

'We know, indeed!' said Nicholas, shaking his head. 'You behaved rather wickedly there, I suspect.'

'O' course she did,' said John Browdie, passing his huge forefinger through one of his wife's pretty ringlets, and looking very proud of her. 'She wur always as skittish and full o' tricks as a—'

'Well, as a what?' said his wife.

'As a woman,' returned John. 'Ding! But I dinnot know ought else that cooms near it.'

'You were speaking about Miss Squeers,' said Nicholas, with the view of stopping some slight connubialities which had begun to pass between Mr. and Mrs. Browdie, and which rendered the position of a third party in some degree embarrassing, as occasioning him to feel rather in the way than otherwise.

'Oh yes,' rejoined Mrs. Browdie. 'John ha' done. John fixed tonight, because she had settled that she would go and drink tea with her father. And to make quite sure of there being nothing amiss, and of your being quite alone with us, he settled to go out there and fetch her home.'

'That was a very good arrangement,' said Nicholas, 'though I am sorry to be the occasion of so much trouble.'

'Not the least in the world,' returned Mrs. Browdie; 'for we have looked forward to see you—John and I have—with the greatest possible pleasure. Do you know, Mr. Nickleby,' said Mrs. Browdie, with her archest smile, 'that I really think Fanny Squeers was very fond of you?'

'I am very much obliged to her,' said Nicholas; 'but upon my word, I never aspired to making any impression upon her virgin heart.'

'How you talk!' tittered Mrs. Browdie. 'No, but do you know that really—seriously now and without any joking—I was given to understand by Fanny herself, that you had made an offer to her, and that you two were going to be engaged quite solemn and regular.'

'Was you, ma'am—was you?' cried a shrill female voice, 'was you given to understand that I—I—was going to be engaged to an assassinating thief that shed the gore of my pa? Do you—do you think, ma'am—that I was very fond of such dirt beneath my feet, as I couldn't condescend to touch with kitchen tongs, without blacking and crocking myself by the contract? Do you, ma'am—do you? Oh! base and degrading 'Tilda!'

With these reproaches Miss Squeers flung the door wide open, and disclosed to the eyes of the astonished Browdies and Nicholas, not only her own symmetrical form, arrayed in the chaste white garments before described (a little dirtier), but the form of her brother and father, the pair of Wackfords.

'This is the hend, is it?' continued Miss Squeers, who, being excited, aspirated her h's strongly; 'this is the hend, is it, of all my forbearance and friendship for that double-faced thing—that viper, that—that—mermaid?' (Miss Squeers hesitated a long time for this last epithet, and brought it out triumphantly at last, as if it quite clinched the business.) 'This is the hend, is it, of all my bearing with her deceitfulness, her lowness, her falseness, her laying herself out to catch the admiration of vulgar minds, in a way which made me blush for my— for my—'

'Gender,' suggested Mr. Squeers, regarding the spectators with a malevolent eye—literally A malevolent eye.

'Yes,' said Miss Squeers; 'but I thank my stars that my ma is of the same—'

'Hear, hear!' remarked Mr. Squeers; 'and I wish she was here to have a scratch at this company.'

'This is the hend, is it,' said Miss Squeers, tossing her head, and looking contemptuously at the floor, 'of my taking notice of that rubbishing creature, and demeaning myself to patronise her?'

'Oh, come,' rejoined Mrs. Browdie, disregarding all the endeavours of her spouse to restrain her, and forcing herself into a front row, 'don't talk such nonsense as that.'

'Have I not patronised you, ma'am?' demanded Miss Squeers.

'No,' returned Mrs. Browdie.

'I will not look for blushes in such a quarter,' said Miss Squeers, haughtily, 'for that countenance is a stranger to everything but hignominiousness and red-faced boldness.'

'I say,' interposed John Browdie, nettled by these accumulated attacks on his wife, 'dra' it mild, dra' it mild.'

'You, Mr. Browdie,' said Miss Squeers, taking him up very quickly, 'I pity. I have no feeling for you, sir, but one of unliquidated pity.'

'Oh!' said John.

'No,' said Miss Squeers, looking sideways at her parent, 'although I am a queer bridesmaid, and SHAN'T be a bride in a hurry, and although my husband will be in luck, I entertain no sentiments towards you, sir, but sentiments of pity.'

Here Miss Squeers looked sideways at her father again, who looked sideways at her, as much as to say, 'There you had him.'

'I know what you've got to go through,' said Miss Squeers, shaking her curls violently. 'I know what life is before you, and if you was my bitterest and deadliest enemy, I could wish you nothing worse.'

'Couldn't you wish to be married to him yourself, if that was the case?' inquired Mrs. Browdie, with great suavity of manner.

'Oh, ma'am, how witty you are,' retorted Miss Squeers with a low curtsy, 'almost as witty, ma'am, as you are clever. How very clever it was in you, ma'am, to choose a time when I had gone to tea with my pa, and was sure not to come back without being fetched! What a pity you never thought that other people might be as clever as yourself and spoil your plans!'

'You won't vex me, child, with such airs as these,' said the late Miss Price, assuming the matron.

'Don't Missis me, ma'am, if you please,' returned Miss Squeers, sharply. 'I'll not bear it. Is this the hend—'

'Dang it a',' cried John Browdie, impatiently. 'Say thee say out, Fanny, and mak' sure it's the end, and dinnot ask nobody whether it is or not.'

'Thanking you for your advice which was not required, Mr. Browdie,' returned Miss Squeers, with laborious politeness, 'have the goodness not to presume to meddle with my Christian name. Even my pity shall never make me forget what's due to myself, Mr. Browdie. 'Tilda,' said Miss Squeers, with such a sudden accession of violence that John started in his boots, 'I throw you off for ever, miss. I abandon you. I renounce you. I wouldn't,' cried Miss Squeers in a solemn voice, 'have a child named 'Tilda, not to save it from its grave.'

'As for the matther o' that,' observed John, 'it'll be time eneaf to think aboot neaming of it when it cooms.'

'John!' interposed his wife, 'don't tease her.'

'Oh! Tease, indeed!' cried Miss Squeers, bridling up. 'Tease, indeed! He, he! Tease, too! No, don't tease her. Consider her feelings, pray!'

'If it's fated that listeners are never to hear any good of themselves,' said Mrs. Browdie, 'I can't help it, and I am very sorry for it. But I will say, Fanny, that times out of number I have spoken so kindly of you behind your back, that even you could have found no fault with what I said.'

'Oh, I dare say not, ma'am!' cried Miss Squeers, with another curtsy. 'Best thanks to you for your goodness, and begging and praying you not to be hard upon me another time!'

'I don't know,' resumed Mrs. Browdie, 'that I have said anything very bad of you, even now. At all events, what I did say was quite true; but if I have, I am very sorry for it, and I beg your pardon. You have said much worse of me, scores of times, Fanny; but I have never borne any malice to you, and I hope you'll not bear any to me.'

Miss Squeers made no more direct reply than surveying her former friend from top to toe, and elevating her nose in the air with ineffable disdain. But some indistinct allusions to a 'puss,' and a 'minx,' and a 'contemptible creature,' escaped her; and this, together with a severe biting of the lips, great difficulty in swallowing, and very frequent comings and goings of breath, seemed to imply that feelings were swelling in Miss Squeers's bosom too great for utterance.

While the foregoing conversation was proceeding, Master Wackford, finding himself unnoticed, and feeling his preponderating inclinations strong upon him, had by little and little sidled up to the table and attacked the food with such slight skirmishing as drawing his fingers round and round the inside of the plates, and afterwards sucking them with infinite relish; picking the bread, and dragging the pieces over the surface of the butter; pocketing lumps of sugar, pretending all the time to be absorbed in thought; and so forth. Finding that no interference was attempted with these small liberties, he gradually mounted to greater, and, after helping himself to a moderately good cold collation, was, by this time, deep in the pie.

Nothing of this had been unobserved by Mr. Squeers, who, so long as the attention of the company was fixed upon other objects, hugged himself to think that his son and heir should be fattening at the enemy's expense. But there being now an appearance of a temporary calm, in which the proceedings of little Wackford could scarcely fail to be observed, he feigned to be aware of the circumstance for the first time, and inflicted upon the face of that young gentleman a slap that made the very tea-cups ring.

'Eating!' cried Mr. Squeers, 'of what his father's enemies has left! It's fit to go and poison you, you unnat'ral boy.'

'It wean't hurt him,' said John, apparently very much relieved by the prospect of having a man in the quarrel; 'let' un eat. I wish the whole school was here. I'd give'em soom'at to stay their unfort'nate stomachs wi', if I spent the last penny I had!'

Squeers scowled at him with the worst and most malicious expression of which his face was capable—it was a face of remarkable capability, too, in that way—and shook his fist stealthily.

'Coom, coom, schoolmeasther,' said John, 'dinnot make a fool o' thyself; for if I was to sheake mine—only once—thou'd fa' doon wi' the wind o' it.'

'It was you, was it,' returned Squeers, 'that helped off my runaway boy? It was you, was it?'

'Me!' returned John, in a loud tone. 'Yes, it wa' me, coom; wa'at o' that? It wa' me. Noo then!'

'You hear him say he did it, my child!' said Squeers, appealing to his daughter. 'You hear him say he did it!'

'Did it!' cried John. 'I'll tell 'ee more; hear this, too. If thou'd got another roonaway boy, I'd do it agean. If thou'd got twenty roonaway boys, I'd do it twenty times ower, and twenty more to thot; and I tell thee more,' said John, 'noo my blood is oop, that thou'rt an old ra'ascal; and that it's weel for thou, thou be'est an old 'un, or I'd ha' poonded thee to flour when thou told an honest mun hoo thou'd licked that poor chap in t' coorch.'

'An honest man!' cried Squeers, with a sneer.

'Ah! an honest man,' replied John; 'honest in ought but ever putting legs under seame table wi' such as thou.'

'Scandal!' said Squeers, exultingly. 'Two witnesses to it; Wackford knows the nature of an oath, he does; we shall have you there, sir. Rascal, eh?' Mr. Squeers took out his pocketbook and made a note of it. 'Very good. I should say that was worth full twenty pound at the next assizes, without the honesty, sir.'

''Soizes,' cried John, 'thou'd bether not talk to me o' 'Soizes. Yorkshire schools have been shown up at 'Soizes afore noo, mun, and it's a ticklish soobjact to revive, I can tell ye.'

Mr. Squeers shook his head in a threatening manner, looking very white with passion; and taking his daughter's arm, and dragging little Wackford by the hand, retreated towards the door.

'As for you,' said Squeers, turning round and addressing Nicholas, who, as he had caused him to smart pretty soundly on a former occasion, purposely abstained from taking any part in the discussion, 'see if I ain't down upon you before long. You'll go a kidnapping of boys, will you? Take care their fathers don't turn up—mark that—take care their fathers don't turn up, and send 'em back to me to do as I like with, in spite of you.'

'I am not afraid of that,' replied Nicholas, shrugging his shoulders contemptuously, and turning away.

'Ain't you!' retorted Squeers, with a diabolical look. 'Now then, come along.'

'I leave such society, with my pa, for Hever,' said Miss Squeers, looking contemptuously and loftily round. 'I am defiled by breathing the air with such creatures. Poor Mr. Browdie! He! he! he! I do pity him, that I do; he's so deluded. He! he! he!—Artful and designing 'Tilda!'

With this sudden relapse into the sternest and most majestic wrath, Miss Squeers swept from the room; and having sustained her dignity until the last possible moment, was heard to sob and scream and struggle in the passage.

John Browdie remained standing behind the table, looking from his wife to Nicholas, and back again, with his mouth wide open, until his hand accidentally fell upon the tankard of ale, when he took it up, and having obscured his features therewith for some time, drew a long breath, handed it over to Nicholas, and rang the bell.

'Here, waither,' said John, briskly. 'Look alive here. Tak' these things awa', and let's have soomat broiled for sooper—vary comfortable and plenty o' it—at ten o'clock. Bring soom brandy and soom wather, and a pair o' slippers—the largest pair in the house—and be quick aboot it. Dash ma wig!' said John, rubbing his hands, 'there's no ganging oot to neeght, noo, to fetch anybody whoam, and ecod, we'll begin to spend the evening in airnest.'

CHAPTER 43

Officiates as a kind of Gentleman Usher, in bringing various People together

The storm had long given place to a calm the most profound, and the evening was pretty far advanced—indeed supper was over, and the process of digestion proceeding as favourably as, under the influence of complete tranquillity, cheerful conversation, and a moderate allowance of brandy-and-water, most wise men conversant with the anatomy and functions of the human frame will consider that it ought to have proceeded, when the three friends, or as one might say, both in a civil and religious sense, and with proper deference and regard to the holy state of matrimony, the two friends, (Mr. and Mrs. Browdie counting as no more than one,) were startled by the noise of loud and angry threatenings below stairs, which presently attained so high a pitch, and were conveyed besides in language so towering, sanguinary, and ferocious, that it could hardly have been surpassed, if there had actually been a Saracen's head then present in the establishment, supported on the shoulders and surmounting the trunk of a real, live, furious, and most unappeasable Saracen.

This turmoil, instead of quickly subsiding after the first outburst, (as turmoils not unfrequently do, whether in taverns, legislative assemblies, or elsewhere,) into a mere grumbling and growling squabble, increased every moment; and although the whole din appeared to be raised by but one pair of lungs, yet that one pair was of so powerful a quality, and repeated such words as 'scoundrel,' 'rascal,' 'insolent puppy,' and a variety of expletives no less flattering to the party addressed, with such great relish and strength of tone, that a dozen voices raised in concert under any ordinary circumstances would have made far less uproar and created much smaller consternation.

'Why, what's the matter?' said Nicholas, moving hastily towards the door.

John Browdie was striding in the same direction when Mrs. Browdie turned pale, and, leaning back in her chair, requested him with a faint voice to take notice, that if he ran into any danger it was her intention to fall into hysterics immediately, and that the consequences might be more serious than he thought for. John looked rather disconcerted by this intelligence, though there was a lurking grin on his face at the same time; but, being quite unable to keep out of the fray, he compromised the matter by tucking his wife's arm under his own, and, thus accompanied, following Nicholas downstairs with all speed.

The passage outside the coffee-room door was the scene of disturbance, and here were congregated the coffee-room customers and waiters, together with two or three coachmen and helpers from the yard. These had hastily assembled round a young man who from his appearance might have been a year or two older than Nicholas, and who, besides having given utterance to the defiances just now described, seemed to have proceeded to even greater lengths in his indignation, inasmuch as his feet had no other covering than a pair of stockings, while a couple of slippers lay at no great distance from the head of a prostrate figure in an opposite corner, who bore the appearance of having been shot into his present retreat by means of a kick, and complimented by having the slippers flung about his ears afterwards.

The coffee-room customers, and the waiters, and the coachmen, and the helpers—not to mention a barmaid who was looking on from behind an open sash window—seemed at that moment, if a spectator might judge from their winks, nods, and muttered exclamations, strongly disposed to take part against the young gentleman in the stockings. Observing this, and that the young gentleman was nearly of his own age and had in nothing the appearance of an habitual brawler, Nicholas, impelled by such feelings as will influence young men sometimes, felt a very strong disposition to side with the weaker party, and so thrust himself at once into the centre of the group, and in a more emphatic tone, perhaps, than circumstances might seem to warrant, demanded what all that noise was about.

'Hallo!' said one of the men from the yard, 'this is somebody in disguise, this is.'

'Room for the eldest son of the Emperor of Roosher, gen'l'men!' cried another fellow.

Disregarding these sallies, which were uncommonly well received, as sallies at the expense of the best-dressed persons in a crowd usually are, Nicholas glanced carelessly round, and addressing the young gentleman, who had by this time picked up his slippers and thrust his feet into them, repeated his inquiries with a courteous air.

'A mere nothing!' he replied.

At this a murmur was raised by the lookers-on, and some of the boldest cried, 'Oh, indeed!—Wasn't it though?—Nothing, eh?—He called that nothing, did he? Lucky for him if he found it nothing.' These and many other expressions of ironical disapprobation having been exhausted, two or three of the out-of-door fellows began to hustle Nicholas and the young gentleman who had made the noise: stumbling against them by accident, and treading on their toes, and so forth. But this being a round game, and one not necessarily limited to three or four players, was open to John Browdie too, who, bursting into the little crowd—to the great terror of his wife—and falling about in all directions, now to the right, now to the left, now forwards, now backwards, and accidentally driving his elbow through the hat of the tallest helper, who had been particularly active, speedily caused the odds to wear a very different appearance; while more than one stout fellow limped away to a respectful distance, anathematising with tears in his eyes the heavy tread and ponderous feet of the burly Yorkshireman.

'Let me see him do it again,' said he who had been kicked into the corner, rising as he spoke, apparently more from the fear of John Browdie's inadvertently treading upon him, than from any desire to place himself on equal terms with his late adversary. 'Let me see him do it again. That's all.'

'Let me hear you make those remarks again,' said the young man, 'and I'll knock that head of yours in among the wine-glasses behind you there.'

Here a waiter who had been rubbing his hands in excessive enjoyment of the scene, so long as only the breaking of heads was in question, adjured the spectators with great earnestness to fetch the police, declaring that otherwise murder would be surely done, and that he was responsible for all the glass and china on the premises.

'No one need trouble himself to stir,' said the young gentleman, 'I am going to remain in the house all night, and shall be found here in the morning if there is any assault to answer for.'

'What did you strike him for?' asked one of the bystanders.

'Ah! what did you strike him for?' demanded the others.

The unpopular gentleman looked coolly round, and addressing himself to Nicholas, said:

'You inquired just now what was the matter here. The matter is simply this. Yonder person, who was drinking with a friend in the coffee-room when I took my seat there for half an hour before going to bed, (for I have just come off a journey, and preferred stopping here tonight, to going home at this hour, where I was not expected until tomorrow,) chose to express himself in very disrespectful, and insolently familiar terms, of a young lady, whom I recognised from his description and other circumstances, and whom I have the honour to know. As he spoke loud enough to be overheard by the other guests who were present, I informed him most civilly that he was mistaken in his conjectures, which were of an offensive nature, and requested him to forbear. He did so for a little time, but as he chose to renew his conversation when leaving the room, in a more offensive strain than before, I could not refrain from making after him, and facilitating his departure by a kick, which reduced him to the posture in which you saw him just now. I am the best judge of my own affairs, I take it,' said the young man, who had certainly not quite recovered from his recent heat; 'if anybody here thinks proper to make this quarrel his own, I have not the smallest earthly objection, I do assure him.'

Of all possible courses of proceeding under the circumstances detailed, there was certainly not one which, in his then state of mind, could have appeared more laudable to Nicholas than this. There were not many subjects of dispute which at that moment could have come home to his own breast more powerfully, for having the unknown uppermost in his thoughts, it naturally occurred to him that he would have done just the same if any audacious gossiper durst have presumed in his hearing to speak lightly of her. Influenced by these considerations, he espoused the young gentleman's quarrel with great warmth, protesting that he had done quite right, and that he respected him for it; which John Browdie (albeit not quite clear as to the merits) immediately protested too, with not inferior vehemence.

'Let him take care, that's all,' said the defeated party, who was being rubbed down by a waiter, after his recent fall on the dusty boards. 'He don't knock me about for nothing, I can tell him that. A pretty state of things, if a man isn't to admire a handsome girl without being beat to pieces for it!'

This reflection appeared to have great weight with the young lady in the bar, who (adjusting her cap as she spoke, and glancing at a mirror) declared that it would be a very pretty state of things indeed; and that if people were to be punished for actions so innocent and natural as that, there would be more people to be knocked down than there would be people to knock them down, and that she wondered what the gentleman meant by it, that she did.

'My dear girl,' said the young gentleman in a low voice, advancing towards the sash window.

'Nonsense, sir!' replied the young lady sharply, smiling though as she turned aside, and biting her lip, (whereat Mrs. Browdie, who was still standing on the stairs, glanced at her with disdain, and called to her husband to come away).

'No, but listen to me,' said the young man. 'If admiration of a pretty face were criminal, I should be the most hopeless person alive, for I cannot resist one. It has the most extraordinary effect upon me, checks and controls me in the most furious and obstinate mood. You see what an effect yours has had upon me already.'

'Oh, that's very pretty,' replied the young lady, tossing her head, 'but—'

'Yes, I know it's very pretty,' said the young man, looking with an air of admiration in the barmaid's face; 'I said so, you know, just this moment. But beauty should be spoken of respectfully—respectfully, and in proper terms, and with a becoming sense of its worth and excellence, whereas this fellow has no more notion—'

The young lady interrupted the conversation at this point, by thrusting her head out of the bar-window, and inquiring of the waiter in a shrill voice whether that young man who had been knocked down was going to stand in the passage all night, or whether the entrance was to be left clear for other people. The waiters taking the hint, and communicating it to the hostlers, were not slow to change their tone too, and the result was, that the unfortunate victim was bundled out in a twinkling.

'I am sure I have seen that fellow before,' said Nicholas.

'Indeed!' replied his new acquaintance.

'I am certain of it,' said Nicholas, pausing to reflect. 'Where can I have—stop!—yes, to be sure—he belongs to a register-office up at the west end of the town. I knew I recollected the face.'

It was, indeed, Tom, the ugly clerk.

'That's odd enough!' said Nicholas, ruminating upon the strange manner in which the register-office seemed to start up and stare him in the face every now and then, and when he least expected it.

'I am much obliged to you for your kind advocacy of my cause when it most needed an advocate,' said the young man, laughing, and drawing a card from his pocket. 'Perhaps you'll do me the favour to let me know where I can thank you.'

Nicholas took the card, and glancing at it involuntarily as he returned the compliment, evinced very great surprise.

'Mr. Frank Cheeryble!' said Nicholas. 'Surely not the nephew of Cheeryble Brothers, who is expected tomorrow!'

'I don't usually call myself the nephew of the firm,' returned Mr. Frank, good-humouredly; 'but of the two excellent individuals who compose it, I am proud to say I am the nephew. And you, I see, are Mr. Nickleby, of whom I have heard so much! This is a most unexpected meeting, but not the less welcome, I assure you.'

Nicholas responded to these compliments with others of the same kind, and they shook hands warmly. Then he introduced John Browdie, who had remained in a state of great admiration ever since the young lady in the bar had been so skilfully won over to the right side. Then Mrs. John Browdie was introduced, and finally they all went upstairs together and spent the next half-hour with great satisfaction and mutual entertainment; Mrs. John Browdie beginning the conversation by declaring that of all the made-up things she ever saw, that young woman below-stairs was the vainest and the plainest.

This Mr. Frank Cheeryble, although, to judge from what had recently taken place, a hot-headed young man (which is not an absolute miracle and phenomenon in nature), was a sprightly, good-humoured, pleasant fellow, with much both in his countenance and disposition that reminded Nicholas very strongly of the kind-hearted brothers. His manner was as unaffected as theirs, and his demeanour full of that heartiness which, to most people who have anything generous in their composition, is peculiarly prepossessing. Add to this, that he was good-looking and intelligent, had a plentiful share of vivacity, was extremely cheerful, and accommodated himself in five minutes' time to all John Browdie's oddities with as much ease as if he had known him from a boy; and it will be a source of no great wonder that, when they parted for the night, he had produced a most favourable impression, not only upon the worthy Yorkshireman and his wife, but upon Nicholas also, who, revolving all these things in his mind as he made the best of his way home, arrived at the conclusion that he had laid the foundation of a most agreeable and desirable acquaintance.

'But it's a most extraordinary thing about that register-office fellow!' thought Nicholas. 'Is it likely that this nephew can know anything about that beautiful girl? When Tim Linkinwater gave me to understand the other day that he was coming to take a share in the business here, he said he had been superintending it in Germany for four years, and that during the last six months he had been engaged in establishing an agency in the north of England. That's four years and a half—four years and a half. She can't be more than seventeen—say eighteen at the outside. She was quite a child when he went away, then. I should say he knew nothing about her and had never seen her, so he can give me no information. At all events,' thought Nicholas, coming to the real point in his mind, 'there can be no danger of any prior occupation of her affections in that quarter; that's quite clear.'

Is selfishness a necessary ingredient in the composition of that passion called love, or does it deserve all the fine things which poets, in the exercise of their undoubted vocation, have said of it? There are, no doubt, authenticated instances of gentlemen having given up ladies and ladies having given up gentlemen to meritorious rivals, under circumstances of great high-mindedness; but is it quite established that the majority of such ladies and gentlemen have not made a virtue of necessity, and nobly resigned what was beyond their reach; as a private soldier might register a vow never to accept the order of the Garter, or a poor curate of great piety and learning, but of no family—save a very large family of children—might renounce a bishopric?

Here was Nicholas Nickleby, who would have scorned the thought of counting how the chances stood of his rising in favour or fortune with the brothers Cheeryble, now that their nephew had returned, already deep in calculations whether that same nephew was likely to rival him in the affections of the fair unknown—discussing the matter with himself too, as gravely as if, with that one exception, it were all settled; and recurring to the subject again and again, and feeling quite indignant and ill-used at the notion of anybody else making love to one with whom he had never exchanged a word in all his life. To be sure, he exaggerated rather than depreciated the merits of his new acquaintance; but still he took it as a kind of personal offence that he should have any merits at all—in the eyes of this particular young lady, that is; for elsewhere he was quite welcome to have as many as he pleased. There was undoubted selfishness in all this, and yet Nicholas was of a most free and generous nature, with as few mean or sordid thoughts, perhaps, as ever fell to the lot of any man; and there is no reason to suppose that, being in love, he felt and thought differently from other people in the like sublime condition.

He did not stop to set on foot an inquiry into his train of thought or state of feeling, however; but went thinking on all the way home, and continued to dream on in the same strain all night. For, having satisfied himself that Frank Cheeryble could have no knowledge of, or acquaintance with, the mysterious young lady, it began to occur to him that even he himself might never see her again; upon which hypothesis he built up a very ingenious succession of tormenting ideas which answered his purpose even better than the vision of Mr. Frank Cheeryble, and tantalised and worried him, waking and sleeping.

Notwithstanding all that has been said and sung to the contrary, there is no well-established case of morning having either deferred or hastened its approach by the term of an hour or so for the mere gratification of a splenetic feeling against some unoffending lover: the sun having, in the discharge of his public duty, as the books of precedent report, invariably risen according to the almanacs, and without suffering himself to be swayed by any private considerations. So, morning came as usual, and with it business-hours, and with them Mr. Frank Cheeryble, and with him a long train of smiles and welcomes from the worthy brothers, and a more grave and clerk-like, but scarcely less hearty reception from Mr. Timothy Linkinwater.

'That Mr. Frank and Mr. Nickleby should have met last night,' said Tim Linkinwater, getting slowly off his stool, and looking round the counting-house with his back planted against the desk, as was his custom when he had anything very particular to say: 'that those two young men should have met last night in that manner is, I say, a coincidence, a remarkable coincidence. Why, I don't believe now,' added Tim, taking off his spectacles, and smiling as with gentle pride, 'that there's such a place in all the world for coincidences as London is!'

'I don't know about that,' said Mr. Frank; 'but—'

'Don't know about it, Mr. Francis!' interrupted Tim, with an obstinate air. 'Well, but let us know. If there is any better place for such things, where is it? Is it in Europe? No, that it isn't. Is it in Asia? Why, of course it's not. Is it in Africa? Not a bit of it. Is it in America? you know better than that, at all events. Well, then,' said Tim, folding his arms resolutely, 'where is it?'

'I was not about to dispute the point, Tim,' said young Cheeryble, laughing. 'I am not such a heretic as that. All I was going to say was, that I hold myself under an obligation to the coincidence, that's all.'

'Oh! if you don't dispute it,' said Tim, quite satisfied, 'that's another thing. I'll tell you what though. I wish you had. I wish you or anybody would. I would so put that man down,' said Tim, tapping the forefinger of his left hand emphatically with his spectacles, 'so put that man down by argument—'

It was quite impossible to find language to express the degree of mental prostration to which such an adventurous wight would be reduced in the keen encounter with Tim Linkinwater, so Tim gave up the rest of his declaration in pure lack of words, and mounted his stool again.

'We may consider ourselves, brother Ned,' said Charles, after he had patted Tim Linkinwater approvingly on the back, 'very fortunate in having two such young men about us as our nephew Frank and Mr. Nickleby. It should be a source of great satisfaction and pleasure to us.'

'Certainly, Charles, certainly,' returned the other.

'Of Tim,' added brother Ned, 'I say nothing whatever, because Tim is a mere child—an infant—a nobody that we never think of or take into account at all. Tim, you villain, what do you say to that, sir?'

'I am jealous of both of 'em,' said Tim, 'and mean to look out for another situation; so provide yourselves, gentlemen, if you please.'

404

Tim thought this such an exquisite, unparalleled, and most extraordinary joke, that he laid his pen upon the inkstand, and rather tumbling off his stool than getting down with his usual deliberation, laughed till he was quite faint, shaking his head all the time so that little particles of powder flew palpably about the office. Nor were the brothers at all behind-hand, for they laughed almost as heartily at the ludicrous idea of any voluntary separation between themselves and old Tim. Nicholas and Mr Frank laughed quite boisterously, perhaps to conceal some other emotion awakened by this little incident, (and so, indeed, did the three old fellows after the first burst,) so perhaps there was as much keen enjoyment and relish in that laugh, altogether, as the politest assembly ever derived from the most poignant witticism uttered at any one person's expense.

'Mr. Nickleby,' said brother Charles, calling him aside, and taking him kindly by the hand, 'I—I—am anxious, my dear sir, to see that you are properly and comfortably settled in the cottage. We cannot allow those who serve us well to labour under any privation or discomfort that it is in our power to remove. I wish, too, to see your mother and sister: to know them, Mr. Nickleby, and have an opportunity of relieving their minds by assuring them that any trifling service we have been able to do them is a great deal more than repaid by the zeal and ardour you display.—Not a word, my dear sir, I beg. Tomorrow is Sunday. I shall make bold to come out at teatime, and take the chance of finding you at home; if you are not, you know, or the ladies should feel a delicacy in being intruded on, and would rather not be known to me just now, why I can come again another time, any other time would do for me. Let it remain upon that understanding. Brother Ned, my dear fellow, let me have a word with you this way.'

The twins went out of the office arm-in-arm, and Nicholas, who saw in this act of kindness, and many others of which he had been the subject that morning, only so many delicate renewals on the arrival of their nephew of the kind assurance which the brothers had given him in his absence, could scarcely feel sufficient admiration and gratitude for such extraordinary consideration.

The intelligence that they were to have a visitor—and such a visitor—next day, awakened in the breast of Mrs. Nickleby mingled feelings of exultation and regret; for whereas on the one hand she hailed it as an omen of her speedy restoration to good society and the almost-forgotten pleasures of morning calls and evening tea-drinkings, she could not, on the other, but reflect with bitterness of spirit on the absence of a silver teapot with an ivory knob on the lid, and a milk-jug to match, which had been the pride of her heart in days of yore, and had been kept from year's end to year's end wrapped up in wash-leather on a certain top shelf which now presented itself in lively colours to her sorrowing imagination.

'I wonder who's got that spice-box,' said Mrs. Nickleby, shaking her head. 'It used to stand in the left-hand corner, next but two to the pickled onions. You remember that spice-box, Kate?'

'Perfectly well, mama.'

'I shouldn't think you did, Kate,' returned Mrs. Nickleby, in a severe manner, 'talking about it in that cold and unfeeling way! If there is any one thing that vexes me in these losses more than the losses themselves, I do protest and declare,' said Mrs. Nickleby, rubbing her nose with an impassioned air, 'that it is to have people about me who take things with such provoking calmness.'

'My dear mama,' said Kate, stealing her arm round her mother's neck, 'why do you say what I know you cannot seriously mean or think, or why be angry with me for being happy and content? You and Nicholas are left to me, we are together once again, and what regard can I have for a few trifling things of which we never feel the want? When I have seen all the misery and desolation that death can bring, and known the lonesome feeling of being solitary and alone in crowds, and all the agony of separation in grief and poverty when we most needed comfort and support from each other, can you wonder that I look upon this as a place of such delicious quiet and rest, that with you beside me I have nothing to wish for or regret? There was a time, and not long since, when all the comforts of our old home did come back upon me, I own, very often—oftener than you would think perhaps—but I affected to care nothing for them, in the hope that you would so be brought to regret them the less. I was not insensible, indeed. I might have felt happier if I had been. Dear mama,' said Kate, in great agitation, 'I know no difference between this home and that in which we were all so happy for so many years, except that the kindest and gentlest heart that ever ached on earth has passed in peace to heaven.'

'Kate my dear, Kate,' cried Mrs. Nickleby, folding her in her arms.

'I have so often thought,' sobbed Kate, 'of all his kind words—of the last time he looked into my little room, as he passed upstairs to bed, and said "God bless you, darling." There was a paleness in his face, mama—the broken heart—I know it was—I little thought so—then—'

A gush of tears came to her relief, and Kate laid her head upon her mother's breast, and wept like a little child.

It is an exquisite and beautiful thing in our nature, that when the heart is touched and softened by some tranquil happiness or affectionate feeling, the memory of the dead comes over it most powerfully and irresistibly. It would almost seem as though our better thoughts and sympathies were charms, in virtue of which the soul is enabled to hold some vague and mysterious intercourse with the spirits of those whom we dearly loved in life. Alas! how often and how long may those patient angels hover above us, watching for the spell which is so seldom uttered, and so soon forgotten!

Poor Mrs. Nickleby, accustomed to give ready utterance to whatever came uppermost in her mind, had never conceived the possibility of her daughter's dwelling upon these thoughts in secret, the more especially as no hard trial or querulous reproach had ever drawn them from her. But now, when the happiness of all that Nicholas had just told them, and of their new and peaceful life, brought these recollections so strongly upon Kate that she could not suppress them, Mrs. Nickleby began to have a glimmering that she had been rather thoughtless now and then, and was conscious of something like self-reproach as she embraced her daughter, and yielded to the emotions which such a conversation naturally awakened.

There was a mighty bustle that night, and a vast quantity of preparation for the expected visitor, and a very large nosegay was brought from a gardener's hard by, and cut up into a number of very small ones, with which Mrs. Nickleby would have garnished the little sitting-room, in a style that certainly could not have failed to attract anybody's attention, if Kate had not offered to spare her the trouble, and arranged them in the prettiest and neatest manner possible. If the cottage ever looked pretty, it must have been on such a bright and sunshiny day as the next day was. But Smike's pride in the garden, or Mrs. Nickleby's in the condition of the furniture, or Kate's in everything, was nothing to the pride with which Nicholas looked at Kate herself; and surely the costliest mansion in all England might have found in her beautiful face and graceful form its most exquisite and peerless ornament.

About six o'clock in the afternoon Mrs. Nickleby was thrown into a great flutter of spirits by the long-expected knock at the door, nor was this flutter at all composed by the audible tread of two pair of boots in the passage, which Mrs. Nickleby augured, in a breathless state, must be 'the two Mr. Cheerybles;' as it certainly was, though not the two Mrs. Nickleby expected, because it was Mr. Charles Cheeryble, and his nephew, Mr. Frank, who made a thousand apologies for his intrusion, which Mrs. Nickleby (having tea-spoons enough and to spare for all) most graciously received. Nor did the appearance of this unexpected visitor occasion the least embarrassment, (save in Kate, and that only to the extent of a blush or two at first,) for the old gentleman was so kind and cordial, and the young gentleman imitated him in this respect so well, that the usual stiffness and formality of a first meeting showed no signs of appearing, and Kate really more than once detected herself in the very act of wondering when it was going to begin.

At the tea-table there was plenty of conversation on a great variety of subjects, nor were there wanting jocose matters of discussion, such as they were; for young Mr. Cheeryble's recent stay in Germany happening to be alluded to, old Mr. Cheeryble informed the company that the aforesaid young Mr. Cheeryble was suspected to have fallen deeply in love with the daughter of a certain German burgomaster. This accusation young Mr. Cheeryble most indignantly repelled, upon which Mrs. Nickleby slyly remarked, that she suspected, from the very warmth of the denial, there must be something in it. Young Mr. Cheeryble then earnestly entreated old Mr. Cheeryble to confess that it was all a jest, which old Mr. Cheeryble at last did, young Mr. Cheeryble being so much in earnest about it, that—as Mrs. Nickleby said many thousand times afterwards in recalling the scene—he 'quite coloured,' which she rightly considered a memorable circumstance, and one worthy of remark, young men not being as a class remarkable for modesty or self-denial, especially when there is a lady in the case, when, if they colour at all, it is rather their practice to colour the story, and not themselves.

After tea there was a walk in the garden, and the evening being very fine they strolled out at the garden-gate into some lanes and bye-roads, and sauntered up and down until it grew quite dark. The time seemed to pass very quickly with all the party. Kate went first, leaning upon her brother's arm, and talking with him and Mr. Frank Cheeryble; and Mrs Nickleby and the elder gentleman followed at a short distance, the kindness of the good merchant, his interest in the welfare of Nicholas, and his admiration of Kate, so operating upon the good lady's feelings, that the usual current of her speech was confined within very narrow and circumscribed limits. Smike (who, if he had ever been an object of interest in his life, had been one that day) accompanied them, joining sometimes one group and sometimes the other, as brother Charles, laying his hand upon his shoulder, bade him walk with him, or Nicholas, looking smilingly round, beckoned him to come and talk with the old friend who understood him best, and who could win a smile into his careworn face when none else could.

Pride is one of the seven deadly sins; but it cannot be the pride of a mother in her children, for that is a compound of two cardinal virtues—faith and hope. This was the pride which swelled Mrs. Nickleby's heart that night, and this it was which left upon her face, glistening in the light when they returned home, traces of the most grateful tears she had ever shed.

There was a quiet mirth about the little supper, which harmonised exactly with this tone of feeling, and at length the two gentlemen took their leave. There was one circumstance in the leave-taking which occasioned a vast deal of smiling and pleasantry, and that was, that Mr. Frank Cheeryble offered his hand to Kate twice over, quite forgetting that he had bade her adieu already. This was held by the elder Mr. Cheeryble to be a convincing proof that he was thinking of his German flame, and the jest occasioned immense laughter. So easy is it to move light hearts.

In short, it was a day of serene and tranquil happiness; and as we all have some bright day—many of us, let us hope, among a crowd of others—to which we revert with particular delight, so this one was often looked back to afterwards, as holding a conspicuous place in the calendar of those who shared it.

Was there one exception, and that one he who needed to have been most happy?

Who was that who, in the silence of his own chamber, sunk upon his knees to pray as his first friend had taught him, and folding his hands and stretching them wildly in the air, fell upon his face in a passion of bitter grief?

CHAPTER 44

Mr. Ralph Nickleby cuts an old Acquaintance. It would also appear from the Contents hereof, that a Joke, even between Husband and Wife, may be sometimes carried too far

There are some men who, living with the one object of enriching themselves, no matter by what means, and being perfectly conscious of the baseness and rascality of the means which they will use every day towards this end, affect nevertheless—even to themselves—a high tone of moral rectitude, and shake their heads and sigh over the depravity of the world. Some of the craftiest scoundrels that ever walked this earth, or rather—for walking implies, at least, an erect position and the bearing of a man—that ever crawled and crept through life by its dirtiest and narrowest ways, will gravely jot down in diaries the events of every day, and keep a regular debtor and creditor account with Heaven, which shall always show a floating balance in their own favour. Whether this is a gratuitous (the only gratuitous) part of the falsehood and trickery of such men's lives, or whether they really hope to cheat Heaven itself, and lay up treasure in the next world by the same process which has enabled them to lay up treasure in this—not to question how it is, so it is. And, doubtless, such book-keeping (like certain autobiographies which have enlightened the world) cannot fail to prove serviceable, in the one respect of sparing the recording Angel some time and labour.

Ralph Nickleby was not a man of this stamp. Stern, unyielding, dogged, and impenetrable, Ralph cared for nothing in life, or beyond it, save the gratification of two passions, avarice, the first and predominant appetite of his nature, and hatred, the second. Affecting to consider himself but a type of all humanity, he was at little pains to conceal his true character from the world in general, and in his own heart he exulted over and cherished every bad design as it had birth. The only scriptural admonition that Ralph Nickleby heeded, in the letter, was 'know thyself.' He knew himself well, and choosing to imagine that all mankind were cast in the same mould, hated them; for, though no man hates himself, the coldest among us having too much self-love for that, yet most men unconsciously judge the world from themselves, and it will be very generally found that those who sneer habitually at human nature, and affect to despise it, are among its worst and least pleasant samples.

But the present business of these adventures is with Ralph himself, who stood regarding Newman Noggs with a heavy frown, while that worthy took off his fingerless gloves, and spreading them carefully on the palm of his left hand, and flattening them with his right to take the creases out, proceeded to roll them up with an absent air as if he were utterly regardless of all things else, in the deep interest of the ceremonial.

'Gone out of town!' said Ralph, slowly. 'A mistake of yours. Go back again.'

'No mistake,' returned Newman. 'Not even going; gone.'

'Has he turned girl or baby?' muttered Ralph, with a fretful gesture.

'I don't know,' said Newman, 'but he's gone.'

The repetition of the word 'gone' seemed to afford Newman Noggs inexpressible delight, in proportion as it annoyed Ralph Nickleby. He uttered the word with a full round emphasis, dwelling upon it as long as he decently could, and when he could hold out no longer without attracting observation, stood gasping it to himself as if even that were a satisfaction.

'And where has he gone?' said Ralph.

'France,' replied Newman. 'Danger of another attack of erysipelas—a worse attack—in the head. So the doctors ordered him off. And he's gone.'

'And Lord Frederick—?' began Ralph.

'He's gone too,' replied Newman.

'And he carries his drubbing with him, does he?' said Ralph, turning away; 'pockets his bruises, and sneaks off without the retaliation of a word, or seeking the smallest reparation!'

'He's too ill,' said Newman.

'Too ill!' repeated Ralph. 'Why I would have it if I were dying; in that case I should only be the more determined to have it, and that without delay—I mean if I were he. But he's too ill! Poor Sir Mulberry! Too ill!'

Uttering these words with supreme contempt and great irritation of manner, Ralph signed hastily to Newman to leave the room; and throwing himself into his chair, beat his foot impatiently upon the ground.

'There is some spell about that boy,' said Ralph, grinding his teeth. 'Circumstances conspire to help him. Talk of fortune's favours! What is even money to such Devil's luck as this?'

He thrust his hands impatiently into his pockets, but notwithstanding his previous reflection there was some consolation there, for his face relaxed a little; and although there was still a deep frown upon the contracted brow, it was one of calculation, and not of disappointment.

'This Hawk will come back, however,' muttered Ralph; 'and if I know the man (and I should by this time) his wrath will have lost nothing of its violence in the meanwhile. Obliged to live in retirement—the monotony of a sick-room to a man of his habits—no life—no drink—no play—nothing that he likes and lives by. He is not likely to forget his obligations to the cause of all this. Few men would; but he of all others? No, no!'

He smiled and shook his head, and resting his chin upon his hand, fell a musing, and smiled again. After a time he rose and rang the bell.

'That Mr. Squeers; has he been here?' said Ralph.

'He was here last night. I left him here when I went home,' returned Newman.

'I know that, fool, do I not?' said Ralph, irascibly. 'Has he been here since? Was he here this morning?'

'No,' bawled Newman, in a very loud key.

'If he comes while I am out—he is pretty sure to be here by nine tonight—let him wait. And if there's another man with him, as there will be—perhaps,' said Ralph, checking himself, 'let him wait too.'

'Let 'em both wait?' said Newman.

'Ay,' replied Ralph, turning upon him with an angry look. 'Help me on with this spencer, and don't repeat after me, like a croaking parrot.'

'I wish I was a parrot,' Newman, sulkily.

'I wish you were,' rejoined Ralph, drawing his spencer on; 'I'd have wrung your neck long ago.'

Newman returned no answer to this compliment, but looked over Ralph's shoulder for an instant, (he was adjusting the collar of the spencer behind, just then,) as if he were strongly disposed to tweak him by the nose. Meeting Ralph's eye, however, he suddenly recalled his wandering fingers, and rubbed his own red nose with a vehemence quite astonishing.

Bestowing no further notice upon his eccentric follower than a threatening look, and an admonition to be careful and make no mistake, Ralph took his hat and gloves, and walked out.

He appeared to have a very extraordinary and miscellaneous connection, and very odd calls he made, some at great rich houses, and some at small poor ones, but all upon one subject: money. His face was a talisman to the porters and servants of his more dashing clients, and procured him ready admission, though he trudged on foot, and others, who were denied, rattled to the door in carriages. Here he was all softness and cringing civility; his step so light, that it scarcely produced a sound upon the thick carpets; his voice so soft that it was not audible beyond the person to whom it was addressed. But in the poorer habitations Ralph was another man; his boots creaked upon the passage floor as he walked boldly in; his voice was harsh and loud as he demanded the money that was overdue; his threats were coarse and angry. With another class of customers, Ralph was again another man. These were attorneys of more than doubtful reputation, who helped him to new business, or raised fresh profits upon old. With them Ralph was familiar and jocose, humorous upon the topics of the day, and especially pleasant upon bankruptcies and pecuniary difficulties that made good for trade. In short, it would have been difficult to have recognised the same man under these various aspects, but for the bulky leather case full of bills and notes which he drew from his pocket at every house, and the constant repetition of the same complaint, (varied only in tone and style of delivery,) that the world thought him rich, and that perhaps he might be if he had his own; but there was no getting money in when it was once out, either principal or interest, and it was a hard matter to live; even to live from day to day.

It was evening before a long round of such visits (interrupted only by a scanty dinner at an eating-house) terminated at Pimlico, and Ralph walked along St James's Park, on his way home.

There were some deep schemes in his head, as the puckered brow and firmly-set mouth would have abundantly testified, even if they had been unaccompanied by a complete indifference to, or unconsciousness of, the objects about him. So complete was his abstraction, however, that Ralph, usually as quick-sighted as any man, did not observe that he was followed by a shambling figure, which at one time stole behind him with noiseless footsteps, at another crept a few paces before him, and at another glided along by his side; at all times regarding him with an eye so keen, and a look so eager and attentive, that it was more like the expression of an intrusive face in some powerful picture or strongly marked dream, than the scrutiny even of a most interested and anxious observer.

The sky had been lowering and dark for some time, and the commencement of a violent storm of rain drove Ralph for shelter to a tree. He was leaning against it with folded arms, still buried in thought, when, happening to raise his eyes, he suddenly met those of a man who, creeping round the trunk, peered into his face with a searching look. There was something in the usurer's expression at the moment, which the man appeared to remember well, for it decided him; and stepping close up to Ralph, he pronounced his name.

Astonished for the moment, Ralph fell back a couple of paces and surveyed him from head to foot. A spare, dark, withered man, of about his own age, with a stooping body, and a very sinister face rendered more ill-favoured by hollow and hungry cheeks, deeply sunburnt, and thick black eyebrows, blacker in contrast with the perfect whiteness of his hair; roughly clothed in shabby garments, of a strange and uncouth make; and having about him an indefinable manner of depression and degradation—this, for a moment, was all he saw. But he looked again, and the face and person seemed gradually to grow less strange; to change as he looked, to subside and soften into lineaments that were familiar, until at last they resolved themselves, as if by some strange optical illusion, into those of one whom he had known for many years, and forgotten and lost sight of for nearly as many more.

The man saw that the recognition was mutual, and beckoning to Ralph to take his former place under the tree, and not to stand in the falling rain, of which, in his first surprise, he had been quite regardless, addressed him in a hoarse, faint tone.

'You would hardly have known me from my voice, I suppose, Mr. Nickleby?' he said.

'No,' returned Ralph, bending a severe look upon him. 'Though there is something in that, that I remember now.'

'There is little in me that you can call to mind as having been there eight years ago, I dare say?' observed the other.

'Quite enough,' said Ralph, carelessly, and averting his face. 'More than enough.'

'If I had remained in doubt about you, Mr. Nickleby,' said the other, 'this reception, and your manner, would have decided me very soon.'

'Did you expect any other?' asked Ralph, sharply.

'No!' said the man.

'You were right,' retorted Ralph; 'and as you feel no surprise, need express none.'

'Mr. Nickleby,' said the man, bluntly, after a brief pause, during which he had seemed to struggle with an inclination to answer him by some reproach, 'will you hear a few words that I have to say?'

'I am obliged to wait here till the rain holds a little,' said Ralph, looking abroad. 'If you talk, sir, I shall not put my fingers in my ears, though your talking may have as much effect as if I did.'

'I was once in your confidence—' thus his companion began. Ralph looked round, and smiled involuntarily.

'Well,' said the other, 'as much in your confidence as you ever chose to let anybody be.'

'Ah!' rejoined Ralph, folding his arms; 'that's another thing, quite another thing.'

'Don't let us play upon words, Mr. Nickleby, in the name of humanity.'

'Of what?' said Ralph.

'Of humanity,' replied the other, sternly. 'I am hungry and in want. If the change that you must see in me after so long an absence—must see, for I, upon whom it has come by slow and hard degrees, see it and know it well—will not move you to pity, let the knowledge that bread; not the daily bread of the Lord's Prayer, which, as it is offered up in cities like this, is understood to include half the luxuries of the world for the rich, and just as much coarse food as will support life for the poor—not that, but bread, a crust of dry hard bread, is beyond my reach today—let that have some weight with you, if nothing else has.'

'If this is the usual form in which you beg, sir,' said Ralph, 'you have studied your part well; but if you will take advice from one who knows something of the world and its ways, I should recommend a lower tone; a little lower tone, or you stand a fair chance of being starved in good earnest.'

As he said this, Ralph clenched his left wrist tightly with his right hand, and inclining his head a little on one side and dropping his chin upon his breast, looked at him whom he addressed with a frowning, sullen face. The very picture of a man whom nothing could move or soften.

'Yesterday was my first day in London,' said the old man, glancing at his travel-stained dress and worn shoes.

'It would have been better for you, I think, if it had been your last also,' replied Ralph.

'I have been seeking you these two days, where I thought you were most likely to be found,' resumed the other more humbly, 'and I met you here at last, when I had almost given up the hope of encountering you, Mr Nickleby.'

He seemed to wait for some reply, but Ralph giving him none, he continued:

'I am a most miserable and wretched outcast, nearly sixty years old, and as destitute and helpless as a child of six.'

'I am sixty years old, too,' replied Ralph, 'and am neither destitute nor helpless. Work. Don't make fine play-acting speeches about bread, but earn it.'

'How?' cried the other. 'Where? Show me the means. Will you give them to me—will you?'

'I did once,' replied Ralph, composedly; 'you scarcely need ask me whether I will again.'

'It's twenty years ago, or more,' said the man, in a suppressed voice, 'since you and I fell out. You remember that? I claimed a share in the profits of some business I brought to you, and, as I persisted, you arrested me for an old advance of ten pounds, odd shillings, including interest at fifty per cent, or so.'

'I remember something of it,' replied Ralph, carelessly. 'What then?'

'That didn't part us,' said the man. 'I made submission, being on the wrong side of the bolts and bars; and as you were not the made man then that you are now, you were glad enough to take back a clerk who wasn't over nice, and who knew something of the trade you drove.'

'You begged and prayed, and I consented,' returned Ralph. 'That was kind of me. Perhaps I did want you. I forget. I should think I did, or you would have begged in vain. You were useful; not too honest, not too delicate, not too nice of hand or heart; but useful.'

'Useful, indeed!' said the man. 'Come. You had pinched and ground me down for some years before that, but I had served you faithfully up to that time, in spite of all your dog's usage. Had I?'

Ralph made no reply.

'Had I?' said the man again.

'You had had your wages,' rejoined Ralph, 'and had done your work. We stood on equal ground so far, and could both cry quits.'

'Then, but not afterwards,' said the other.

'Not afterwards, certainly, nor even then, for (as you have just said) you owed me money, and do still,' replied Ralph.

'That's not all,' said the man, eagerly. 'That's not all. Mark that. I didn't forget that old sore, trust me. Partly in remembrance of that, and partly in the hope of making money someday by the scheme, I took advantage of my position about you, and possessed myself of a hold upon you, which you would give half of all you have to know, and never can know but through me. I left you—long after that time, remember—and, for some poor trickery that came within the law, but was nothing to what you money-makers daily practise just outside its bounds, was sent away a convict for seven years. I have returned what you see me. Now, Mr Nickleby,' said the man, with a strange mixture of humility and sense of power, 'what help and assistance will you give me; what bribe, to speak out plainly? My expectations are not monstrous, but I must live, and to live I must eat and drink. Money is on your side, and hunger and thirst on mine. You may drive an easy bargain.'

'Is that all?' said Ralph, still eyeing his companion with the same steady look, and moving nothing but his lips.

'It depends on you, Mr. Nickleby, whether that's all or not,' was the rejoinder.

'Why then, harkye, Mr—, I don't know by what name I am to call you,' said Ralph.

'By my old one, if you like.'

'Why then, harkye, Mr. Brooker,' said Ralph, in his harshest accents, 'and don't expect to draw another speech from me. Harkye, sir. I know you of old for a ready scoundrel, but you never had a stout heart; and hard work, with (maybe) chains upon those legs of yours, and shorter food than when I "pinched" and "ground" you, has blunted your wits, or you would not come with such a tale as this to me. You a hold upon me! Keep it, or publish it to the world, if you like.'

'I can't do that,' interposed Brooker. 'That wouldn't serve me.'

'Wouldn't it?' said Ralph. 'It will serve you as much as bringing it to me, I promise you. To be plain with you, I am a careful man, and know my affairs thoroughly. I know the world, and the world knows me. Whatever you gleaned, or heard, or saw, when you served me, the world knows and magnifies already. You could tell it nothing that would surprise it, unless, indeed, it redounded to my credit or honour, and then it would scout you for a liar. And yet I don't find business slack, or clients scrupulous. Quite the contrary. I am reviled or threatened every day by one man or another,' said Ralph; 'but things roll on just the same, and I don't grow poorer either.'

'I neither revile nor threaten,' rejoined the man. 'I can tell you of what you have lost by my act, what I only can restore, and what, if I die without restoring, dies with me, and never can be regained.'

'I tell my money pretty accurately, and generally keep it in my own custody,' said Ralph. 'I look sharply after most men that I deal with, and most of all I looked sharply after you. You are welcome to all you have kept from me.'

'Are those of your own name dear to you?' said the man emphatically. 'If they are—'

'They are not,' returned Ralph, exasperated at this perseverance, and the thought of Nicholas, which the last question awakened. 'They are not. If you had come as a common beggar, I might have thrown a sixpence to you in remembrance of the clever knave you used to be; but since you try to palm these stale tricks upon one you might have known better, I'll not part with a halfpenny—nor would I to save you from rotting. And remember this, 'scape-gallows,' said Ralph, menacing him with his hand, 'that if we meet again, and you so much as notice me by one begging gesture, you shall see the inside of a jail once more, and tighten this hold upon me in intervals of the hard labour that vagabonds are put to. There's my answer to your trash. Take it.'

With a disdainful scowl at the object of his anger, who met his eye but uttered not a word, Ralph walked away at his usual pace, without manifesting the slightest curiosity to see what became of his late companion, or indeed once looking behind him. The man remained on the same spot with his eyes fixed upon his retreating figure until it was lost to view, and then drawing his arm about his chest, as if the damp and lack of food struck coldly to him, lingered with slouching steps by the wayside, and begged of those who passed along.

Ralph, in no-wise moved by what had lately passed, further than as he had already expressed himself, walked deliberately on, and turning out of the Park and leaving Golden Square on his right, took his way through some streets at the west end of the town until he arrived in that particular one in which stood the residence of Madame Mantalini. The name of that lady no longer appeared on the flaming door-plate, that of Miss Knag being substituted in its stead; but the bonnets and dresses were still dimly visible in the first-floor windows by the decaying light of a summer's evening, and excepting this ostensible alteration in the proprietorship, the establishment wore its old appearance.

'Humph!' muttered Ralph, drawing his hand across his mouth with a connoisseur-like air, and surveying the house from top to bottom; 'these people look pretty well. They can't last long; but if I know of their going in good time, I am safe, and a fair profit too. I must keep them closely in view; that's all.'

So, nodding his head very complacently, Ralph was leaving the spot, when his quick ear caught the sound of a confused noise and hubbub of voices, mingled with a great running up and down stairs, in the very house which had been the subject of his scrutiny; and while he was hesitating whether to knock at the door or listen at the keyhole a little longer, a female servant of Madame Mantalini's (whom he had often seen) opened it abruptly and bounced out, with her blue cap-ribbons streaming in the air.

'Hallo here. Stop!' cried Ralph. 'What's the matter? Here am I. Didn't you hear me knock?'

'Oh! Mr. Nickleby, sir,' said the girl. 'Go up, for the love of Gracious. Master's been and done it again.'

'Done what?' said Ralph, tartly; 'what d'ye mean?'

'I knew he would if he was drove to it,' cried the girl. 'I said so all along.'

'Come here, you silly wench,' said Ralph, catching her by the wrist; 'and don't carry family matters to the neighbours, destroying the credit of the establishment. Come here; do you hear me, girl?'

Without any further expostulation, he led or rather pulled the frightened handmaid into the house, and shut the door; then bidding her walk upstairs before him, followed without more ceremony.

Guided by the noise of a great many voices all talking together, and passing the girl in his impatience, before they had ascended many steps, Ralph quickly reached the private sitting-room, when he was rather amazed by the confused and inexplicable scene in which he suddenly found himself.

There were all the young-lady workers, some with bonnets and some without, in various attitudes expressive of alarm and consternation; some gathered round Madame Mantalini, who was in tears upon one chair; and others round Miss Knag, who was in opposition tears upon another; and others round Mr Mantalini, who was perhaps the most striking figure in the whole group, for Mr. Mantalini's legs were extended at full length upon the floor, and his head and shoulders were supported by a very tall footman, who didn't seem to know what to do with them, and Mr. Mantalini's eyes were closed, and his face was pale and his hair was comparatively straight, and his whiskers and moustache were limp, and his teeth were clenched, and he had a little bottle in his right hand, and a little tea-spoon in his left; and his hands, arms, legs, and shoulders, were all stiff and powerless. And yet Madame Mantalini was not weeping upon the body, but was scolding violently upon her chair; and all this amidst a clamour of tongues perfectly deafening, and which really appeared to have driven the unfortunate footman to the utmost verge of distraction.

'What is the matter here?' said Ralph, pressing forward.

At this inquiry, the clamour was increased twenty-fold, and an astounding string of such shrill contradictions as 'He's poisoned himself'—'He hasn't'—'Send for a doctor'—'Don't'—'He's dying'—'He isn't, he's only pretending'—with various other cries, poured forth with bewildering volubility, until Madame Mantalini was seen to address herself to Ralph, when female curiosity to know what she would say, prevailed, and, as if by general consent, a dead silence, unbroken by a single whisper, instantaneously succeeded.

'Mr. Nickleby,' said Madame Mantalini; 'by what chance you came here, I don't know.'

Here a gurgling voice was heard to ejaculate, as part of the wanderings of a sick man, the words 'Demnition sweetness!' but nobody heeded them except the footman, who, being startled to hear such awful tones proceeding, as it were, from between his very fingers, dropped his master's head upon the floor with a pretty loud crash, and then, without an effort to lift it up, gazed upon the bystanders, as if he had done something rather clever than otherwise.

'I will, however,' continued Madame Mantalini, drying her eyes, and speaking with great indignation, 'say before you, and before everybody here, for the first time, and once for all, that I never will supply that man's extravagances and viciousness again. I have been a dupe and a fool to him long enough. In future, he shall support himself if he can, and then he may spend what money he pleases, upon whom and how he pleases; but it shall not be mine, and therefore you had better pause before you trust him further.'

Thereupon Madame Mantalini, quite unmoved by some most pathetic lamentations on the part of her husband, that the apothecary had not mixed the prussic acid strong enough, and that he must take another bottle or two to finish the work he had in hand, entered into a catalogue of that amiable gentleman's gallantries, deceptions, extravagances, and infidelities (especially the last), winding up with a protest against being supposed to entertain the smallest remnant of regard for him; and adducing, in proof of the altered state of her affections, the circumstance of his having poisoned himself in private no less than six times within the last fortnight, and her not having once interfered by word or deed to save his life.

'And I insist on being separated and left to myself,' said Madame Mantalini, sobbing. 'If he dares to refuse me a separation, I'll have one in law—I can—and I hope this will be a warning to all girls who have seen this disgraceful exhibition.'

Miss Knag, who was unquestionably the oldest girl in company, said with great solemnity, that it would be a warning to her, and so did the young ladies generally, with the exception of one or two who appeared to entertain some doubts whether such whispers could do wrong.

'Why do you say all this before so many listeners?' said Ralph, in a low voice. 'You know you are not in earnest.'

'I am in earnest,' replied Madame Mantalini, aloud, and retreating towards Miss Knag.

'Well, but consider,' reasoned Ralph, who had a great interest in the matter. 'It would be well to reflect. A married woman has no property.'

'Not a solitary single individual dem, my soul,' and Mr. Mantalini, raising himself upon his elbow.

'I am quite aware of that,' retorted Madame Mantalini, tossing her head; 'and I have none. The business, the stock, this house, and everything in it, all belong to Miss Knag.'

'That's quite true, Madame Mantalini,' said Miss Knag, with whom her late employer had secretly come to an amicable understanding on this point. 'Very true, indeed, Madame Mantalini—hem—very true. And I never was more glad in all my life, that I had strength of mind to resist matrimonial offers, no matter how advantageous, than I am when I think of my present position as compared with your most unfortunate and most undeserved one, Madame Mantalini.'

'Demmit!' cried Mr. Mantalini, turning his head towards his wife. 'Will it not slap and pinch the envious dowager, that dares to reflect upon its own delicious?'

But the day of Mr. Mantalini's blandishments had departed. 'Miss Knag, sir,' said his wife, 'is my particular friend;' and although Mr. Mantalini leered till his eyes seemed in danger of never coming back to their right places again, Madame Mantalini showed no signs of softening.

To do the excellent Miss Knag justice, she had been mainly instrumental in bringing about this altered state of things, for, finding by daily experience, that there was no chance of the business thriving, or even continuing to exist, while Mr. Mantalini had any hand in the expenditure, and having now a considerable interest in its well-doing, she had sedulously applied herself to the investigation of some little matters connected with that gentleman's private character, which she had so well elucidated, and artfully imparted to Madame Mantalini, as to open her eyes more effectually than the closest and most philosophical reasoning could have done in a series of years. To which end, the accidental discovery by Miss Knag of some tender correspondence, in which Madame Mantalini was described as 'old' and 'ordinary,' had most providentially contributed.

However, notwithstanding her firmness, Madame Mantalini wept very piteously; and as she leant upon Miss Knag, and signed towards the door, that young lady and all the other young ladies with sympathising faces, proceeded to bear her out.

'Nickleby,' said Mr. Mantalini in tears, 'you have been made a witness to this demnition cruelty, on the part of the demdest enslaver and captivator that never was, oh dem! I forgive that woman.'

'Forgive!' repeated Madame Mantalini, angrily.

'I do forgive her, Nickleby,' said Mr. Mantalini. 'You will blame me, the world will blame me, the women will blame me; everybody will laugh, and scoff, and smile, and grin most demnebly. They will say, "She had a blessing. She did not know it. He was too weak; he was too good; he was a dem'd fine fellow, but he loved too strong; he could not bear her to be cross, and call him wicked names. It was a dem'd case, there never was a demder." But I forgive her.'

With this affecting speech Mr. Mantalini fell down again very flat, and lay to all appearance without sense or motion, until all the females had left the room, when he came cautiously into a sitting posture, and confronted Ralph with a very blank face, and the little bottle still in one hand and the tea-spoon in the other.

'You may put away those fooleries now, and live by your wits again,' said Ralph, coolly putting on his hat.

'Demmit, Nickleby, you're not serious?'

'I seldom joke,' said Ralph. 'Good-night.'

'No, but Nickleby—' said Mantalini.

'I am wrong, perhaps,' rejoined Ralph. 'I hope so. You should know best. Good-night.'

Affecting not to hear his entreaties that he would stay and advise with him, Ralph left the crest-fallen Mr. Mantalini to his meditations, and left the house quietly.

'Oho!' he said, 'sets the wind that way so soon? Half knave and half fool, and detected in both characters? I think your day is over, sir.'

As he said this, he made some memorandum in his pocket-book in which Mr Mantalini's name figured conspicuously, and finding by his watch that it was between nine and ten o'clock, made all speed home.

'Are they here?' was the first question he asked of Newman.

Newman nodded. 'Been here half an hour.'

'Two of them? One a fat sleek man?'

'Ay,' said Newman. 'In your room now.'

'Good,' rejoined Ralph. 'Get me a coach.'

'A coach! What, you—going to—eh?' stammered Newman.

Ralph angrily repeated his orders, and Noggs, who might well have been excused for wondering at such an unusual and extraordinary circumstance (for he had never seen Ralph in a coach in his life) departed on his errand, and presently returned with the conveyance.

Into it went Mr. Squeers, and Ralph, and the third man, whom Newman Noggs had never seen. Newman stood upon the door-step to see them off, not troubling himself to wonder where or upon what business they were going, until he chanced by mere accident to hear Ralph name the address whither the coachman was to drive.

Quick as lightning and in a state of the most extreme wonder, Newman darted into his little office for his hat, and limped after the coach as if with the intention of getting up behind; but in this design he was balked, for it had too much the start of him and was soon hopelessly ahead, leaving him gaping in the empty street.

'I don't know though,' said Noggs, stopping for breath, 'any good that I could have done by going too. He would have seen me if I had. Drive there! What can come of this? If I had only known it yesterday I could have told—drive there! There's mischief in it. There must be.'

His reflections were interrupted by a grey-haired man of a very remarkable, though far from prepossessing appearance, who, coming stealthily towards him, solicited relief.

Newman, still cogitating deeply, turned away; but the man followed him, and pressed him with such a tale of misery that Newman (who might have been considered a hopeless person to beg from, and who had little enough to give) looked into his hat for some halfpence which he usually kept screwed up, when he had any, in a corner of his pocket-handkerchief.

While he was busily untwisting the knot with his teeth, the man said something which attracted his attention; whatever that something was, it led to something else, and in the end he and Newman walked away side by side—the strange man talking earnestly, and Newman listening.

CHAPTER 45
Containing Matter of a surprising Kind

'As we gang awa' fra' Lunnun tomorrow neeght, and as I dinnot know that I was e'er so happy in a' my days, Misther Nickleby, Ding! but I will tak' anoother glass to our next merry meeting!'

So said John Browdie, rubbing his hands with great joyousness, and looking round him with a ruddy shining face, quite in keeping with the declaration.

The time at which John found himself in this enviable condition was the same evening to which the last chapter bore reference; the place was the cottage; and the assembled company were Nicholas, Mrs. Nickleby, Mrs Browdie, Kate Nickleby, and Smike.

A very merry party they had been. Mrs. Nickleby, knowing of her son's obligations to the honest Yorkshireman, had, after some demur, yielded her consent to Mr. and Mrs. Browdie being invited out to tea; in the way of which arrangement, there were at first sundry difficulties and obstacles, arising out of her not having had an opportunity of 'calling' upon Mrs Browdie first; for although Mrs. Nickleby very often observed with much complacency (as most punctilious people do), that she had not an atom of pride or formality about her, still she was a great stickler for dignity and ceremonies; and as it was manifest that, until a call had been made, she could not be (politely speaking, and according to the laws of society) even cognisant of the fact of Mrs. Browdie's existence, she felt her situation to be one of peculiar delicacy and difficulty.

'The call must originate with me, my dear,' said Mrs. Nickleby, 'that's indispensable. The fact is, my dear, that it's necessary there should be a sort of condescension on my part, and that I should show this young person that I am willing to take notice of her. There's a very respectable-looking young man,' added Mrs. Nickleby, after a short consideration, 'who is conductor to one of the omnibuses that go by here, and who wears a glazed hat—your sister and I have noticed him very often—he has a wart upon his nose, Kate, you know, exactly like a gentleman's servant.'

'Have all gentlemen's servants warts upon their noses, mother?' asked Nicholas.

'Nicholas, my dear, how very absurd you are,' returned his mother; 'of course I mean that his glazed hat looks like a gentleman's servant, and not the wart upon his nose; though even that is not so ridiculous as it may seem to you, for we had a footboy once, who had not only a wart, but a wen also, and a very large wen too, and he demanded to have his wages raised in consequence, because he found it came very expensive. Let me see, what was I—oh yes, I know. The best way that I can think of would be to send a card, and my compliments, (I've no doubt he'd take 'em for a pot of porter,) by this young man, to the Saracen with Two Necks. If the waiter took him for a gentleman's servant, so much the better. Then all Mrs. Browdie would have to do would be to send her card back by the carrier (he could easily come with a double knock), and there's an end of it.'

'My dear mother,' said Nicholas, 'I don't suppose such unsophisticated people as these ever had a card of their own, or ever will have.'

'Oh that, indeed, Nicholas, my dear,' returned Mrs. Nickleby, 'that's another thing. If you put it upon that ground, why, of course, I have no more to say, than that I have no doubt they are very good sort of persons, and that I have no kind of objection to their coming here to tea if they like, and shall make a point of being very civil to them if they do.'

The point being thus effectually set at rest, and Mrs. Nickleby duly placed in the patronising and mildly-condescending position which became her rank and matrimonial years, Mr. and Mrs. Browdie were invited and came; and as they were very deferential to Mrs. Nickleby, and seemed to have a becoming appreciation of her greatness, and were very much pleased with everything, the good lady had more than once given Kate to understand, in a whisper, that she thought they were the very best-meaning people she had ever seen, and perfectly well behaved.

And thus it came to pass, that John Browdie declared, in the parlour after supper, to wit, and twenty minutes before eleven o'clock p.m., that he had never been so happy in all his days.

Nor was Mrs. Browdie much behind her husband in this respect, for that young matron, whose rustic beauty contrasted very prettily with the more delicate loveliness of Kate, and without suffering by the contrast either, for each served as it were to set off and decorate the other, could not sufficiently admire the gentle and winning manners of the young lady, or the engaging affability of the elder one. Then Kate had the art of turning the conversation to subjects upon which the country girl, bashful at first in strange company, could feel herself at home; and if Mrs. Nickleby was not quite so felicitous at times in the selection of topics of discourse, or if she did seem, as Mrs. Browdie expressed it, 'rather high in her notions,' still nothing could be kinder, and that she took considerable interest in the young couple was manifest from the very long lectures on housewifery with which she was so obliging as to entertain Mrs. Browdie's private ear, which were illustrated by various references to the domestic economy of the cottage, in which (those duties falling exclusively upon Kate) the good lady had about as much share, either in theory or practice, as any one of the statues of the Twelve Apostles which embellish the exterior of St Paul's Cathedral.

'Mr. Browdie,' said Kate, addressing his young wife, 'is the best-humoured, the kindest and heartiest creature I ever saw. If I were oppressed with I don't know how many cares, it would make me happy only to look at him.'

'He does seem indeed, upon my word, a most excellent creature, Kate,' said Mrs. Nickleby; 'most excellent. And I am sure that at all times it will give me pleasure—really pleasure now—to have you, Mrs. Browdie, to see me in this plain and homely manner. We make no display,' said Mrs Nickleby, with an air which seemed to insinuate that they could make a vast deal if they were so disposed; 'no fuss, no preparation; I wouldn't allow it. I said, "Kate, my dear, you will only make Mrs. Browdie feel uncomfortable, and how very foolish and inconsiderate that would be!"'

'I am very much obliged to you, I am sure, ma'am,' returned Mrs. Browdie, gratefully. 'It's nearly eleven o'clock, John. I am afraid we are keeping you up very late, ma'am.'

'Late!' cried Mrs. Nickleby, with a sharp thin laugh, and one little cough at the end, like a note of admiration expressed. 'This is quite early for us. We used to keep such hours! Twelve, one, two, three o'clock was nothing to us. Balls, dinners, card-parties! Never were such rakes as the people about where we used to live. I often think now, I am sure, that how we ever could go through with it is quite astonishing, and that is just the evil of having a large connection and being a great deal sought after, which I would recommend all young married people steadily to resist; though of course, and it's perfectly clear, and a very happy thing too, I think, that very few young married people can be exposed to such temptations. There was one family in particular, that used to live about a mile from us—not straight down the road, but turning sharp off to the left by the turnpike where the Plymouth mail ran over the donkey—that were quite extraordinary people for giving the most extravagant parties, with artificial flowers and champagne, and variegated lamps, and, in short, every delicacy of eating and drinking that the most singular epicure could possibly require. I don't think that there ever were such people as those Peltiroguses. You remember the Peltiroguses, Kate?'

Kate saw that for the ease and comfort of the visitors it was high time to stay this flood of recollection, so answered that she entertained of the Peltiroguses a most vivid and distinct remembrance; and then said that Mr Browdie had half promised, early in the evening, that he would sing a Yorkshire song, and that she was most impatient that he should redeem his promise, because she was sure it would afford her mama more amusement and pleasure than it was possible to express.

Mrs. Nickleby confirming her daughter with the best possible grace—for there was patronage in that too, and a kind of implication that she had a discerning taste in such matters, and was something of a critic—John Browdie proceeded to consider the words of some north-country ditty, and to take his wife's recollection respecting the same. This done, he made divers ungainly movements in his chair, and singling out one particular fly on the ceiling from the other flies there asleep, fixed his eyes upon him, and began to roar a meek sentiment (supposed to be uttered by a gentle swain fast pining away with love and despair) in a voice of thunder.

At the end of the first verse, as though some person without had waited until then to make himself audible, was heard a loud and violent knocking at the street-door; so loud and so violent, indeed, that the ladies started as by one accord, and John Browdie stopped.

'It must be some mistake,' said Nicholas, carelessly. 'We know nobody who would come here at this hour.'

Mrs. Nickleby surmised, however, that perhaps the counting-house was burnt down, or perhaps 'the Mr. Cheerybles' had sent to take Nicholas into partnership (which certainly appeared highly probable at that time of night), or perhaps Mr. Linkinwater had run away with the property, or perhaps Miss La Creevy was taken in, or perhaps—

But a hasty exclamation from Kate stopped her abruptly in her conjectures, and Ralph Nickleby walked into the room.

'Stay,' said Ralph, as Nicholas rose, and Kate, making her way towards him, threw herself upon his arm. 'Before that boy says a word, hear me.'

Nicholas bit his lip and shook his head in a threatening manner, but appeared for the moment unable to articulate a syllable. Kate clung closer to his arm, Smike retreated behind them, and John Browdie, who had heard of Ralph, and appeared to have no great difficulty in recognising him, stepped between the old man and his young friend, as if with the intention of preventing either of them from advancing a step further.

'Hear me, I say,' said Ralph, 'and not him.'

'Say what thou'st gotten to say then, sir,' retorted John; 'and tak' care thou dinnot put up angry bluid which thou'dst betther try to quiet.'

'I should know you,' said Ralph, 'by your tongue; and him' (pointing to Smike) 'by his looks.'

'Don't speak to him,' said Nicholas, recovering his voice. 'I will not have it. I will not hear him. I do not know that man. I cannot breathe the air that he corrupts. His presence is an insult to my sister. It is shame to see him. I will not bear it.'

'Stand!' cried John, laying his heavy hand upon his chest.

'Then let him instantly retire,' said Nicholas, struggling. 'I am not going to lay hands upon him, but he shall withdraw. I will not have him here. John, John Browdie, is this my house, am I a child? If he stands there,' cried Nicholas, burning with fury, 'looking so calmly upon those who know his black and dastardly heart, he'll drive me mad.'

To all these exclamations John Browdie answered not a word, but he retained his hold upon Nicholas; and when he was silent again, spoke.

'There's more to say and hear than thou think'st for,' said John. 'I tell'ee I ha' gotten scent o' thot already. Wa'at be that shadow ootside door there? Noo, schoolmeasther, show thyself, mun; dinnot be sheame-feaced. Noo, auld gen'l'man, let's have schoolmeasther, coom.'

Hearing this adjuration, Mr. Squeers, who had been lingering in the passage until such time as it should be expedient for him to enter and he could appear with effect, was fain to present himself in a somewhat undignified and sneaking way; at which John Browdie laughed with such keen and heartfelt delight, that even Kate, in all the pain, anxiety, and surprise of the scene, and though the tears were in her eyes, felt a disposition to join him.

'Have you done enjoying yourself, sir?' said Ralph, at length.

'Pratty nigh for the prasant time, sir,' replied John.

'I can wait,' said Ralph. 'Take your own time, pray.'

Ralph waited until there was a perfect silence, and then turning to Mrs Nickleby, but directing an eager glance at Kate, as if more anxious to watch his effect upon her, said:

'Now, ma'am, listen to me. I don't imagine that you were a party to a very fine tirade of words sent me by that boy of yours, because I don't believe that under his control, you have the slightest will of your own, or that your advice, your opinion, your wants, your wishes, anything which in nature and reason (or of what use is your great experience?) ought to weigh with him, has the slightest influence or weight whatever, or is taken for a moment into account.'

Mrs. Nickleby shook her head and sighed, as if there were a good deal in that, certainly.

'For this reason,' resumed Ralph, 'I address myself to you, ma'am. For this reason, partly, and partly because I do not wish to be disgraced by the acts of a vicious stripling whom I was obliged to disown, and who, afterwards, in his boyish majesty, feigns to—ha! ha!—to disown me, I present myself here tonight. I have another motive in coming: a motive of humanity. I come here,' said Ralph, looking round with a biting and triumphant smile, and gloating and dwelling upon the words as if he were loath to lose the pleasure of saying them, 'to restore a parent his child. Ay, sir,' he continued, bending eagerly forward, and addressing Nicholas, as he marked the change of his countenance, 'to restore a parent his child; his son, sir; trepanned, waylaid, and guarded at every turn by you, with the base design of robbing him some day of any little wretched pittance of which he might become possessed.'

'In that, you know you lie,' said Nicholas, proudly.

'In this, I know I speak the truth. I have his father here,' retorted Ralph.

'Here!' sneered Squeers, stepping forward. 'Do you hear that? Here! Didn't I tell you to be careful that his father didn't turn up and send him back to me? Why, his father's my friend; he's to come back to me directly, he is. Now, what do you say—eh!—now—come—what do you say to that—an't you sorry you took so much trouble for nothing? an't you? an't you?'

'You bear upon your body certain marks I gave you,' said Nicholas, looking quietly away, 'and may talk in acknowledgment of them as much as you please. You'll talk a long time before you rub them out, Mr. Squeers.'

The estimable gentleman last named cast a hasty look at the table, as if he were prompted by this retort to throw a jug or bottle at the head of Nicholas, but he was interrupted in this design (if such design he had) by Ralph, who, touching him on the elbow, bade him tell the father that he might now appear and claim his son.

This being purely a labour of love, Mr. Squeers readily complied, and leaving the room for the purpose, almost immediately returned, supporting a sleek personage with an oily face, who, bursting from him, and giving to view the form and face of Mr. Snawley, made straight up to Smike, and tucking that poor fellow's head under his arm in a most uncouth and awkward embrace, elevated his broad-brimmed hat at arm's length in the air as a token of devout thanksgiving, exclaiming, meanwhile, 'How little did I think of this here joyful meeting, when I saw him last! Oh, how little did I think it!'

'Be composed, sir,' said Ralph, with a gruff expression of sympathy, 'you have got him now.'

'Got him! Oh, haven't I got him! Have I got him, though?' cried Mr Snawley, scarcely able to believe it. 'Yes, here he is, flesh and blood, flesh and blood.'

'Vary little flesh,' said John Browdie.

Mr. Snawley was too much occupied by his parental feelings to notice this remark; and, to assure himself more completely of the restoration of his child, tucked his head under his arm again, and kept it there.

'What was it,' said Snawley, 'that made me take such a strong interest in him, when that worthy instructor of youth brought him to my house? What was it that made me burn all over with a wish to chastise him severely for cutting away from his best friends, his pastors and masters?'

'It was parental instinct, sir,' observed Squeers.

'That's what it was, sir,' rejoined Snawley; 'the elevated feeling, the feeling of the ancient Romans and Grecians, and of the beasts of the field and birds of the air, with the exception of rabbits and tom-cats, which sometimes devour their offspring. My heart yearned towards him. I could have—I don't know what I couldn't have done to him in the anger of a father.'

'It only shows what Natur is, sir,' said Mr. Squeers. 'She's rum 'un, is Natur.'

'She is a holy thing, sir,' remarked Snawley.

'I believe you,' added Mr. Squeers, with a moral sigh. 'I should like to know how we should ever get on without her. Natur,' said Mr. Squeers, solemnly, 'is more easier conceived than described. Oh what a blessed thing, sir, to be in a state of natur!'

Pending this philosophical discourse, the bystanders had been quite stupefied with amazement, while Nicholas had looked keenly from Snawley to Squeers, and from Squeers to Ralph, divided between his feelings of disgust, doubt, and surprise. At this juncture, Smike escaping from his father fled to Nicholas, and implored him, in most moving terms, never to give him up, but to let him live and die beside him.

'If you are this boy's father,' said Nicholas, 'look at the wreck he is, and tell me that you purpose to send him back to that loathsome den from which I brought him.'

'Scandal again!' cried Squeers. 'Recollect, you an't worth powder and shot, but I'll be even with you one way or another.'

'Stop,' interposed Ralph, as Snawley was about to speak. 'Let us cut this matter short, and not bandy words here with hare-brained profligates. This is your son, as you can prove. And you, Mr. Squeers, you know this boy to be the same that was with you for so many years under the name of Smike. Do you?'

'Do I!' returned Squeers. 'Don't I?'

'Good,' said Ralph; 'a very few words will be sufficient here. You had a son by your first wife, Mr. Snawley?'

'I had,' replied that person, 'and there he stands.'

'We'll show that presently,' said Ralph. 'You and your wife were separated, and she had the boy to live with her, when he was a year old. You received a communication from her, when you had lived apart a year or two, that the boy was dead; and you believed it?'

'Of course I did!' returned Snawley. 'Oh the joy of—'

'Be rational, sir, pray,' said Ralph. 'This is business, and transports interfere with it. This wife died a year and a half ago, or thereabouts—not more—in some obscure place, where she was housekeeper in a family. Is that the case?'

'That's the case,' replied Snawley.

'Having written on her death-bed a letter or confession to you, about this very boy, which, as it was not directed otherwise than in your name, only reached you, and that by a circuitous course, a few days since?'

'Just so,' said Snawley. 'Correct in every particular, sir.'

'And this confession,' resumed Ralph, 'is to the effect that his death was an invention of hers to wound you—was a part of a system of annoyance, in short, which you seem to have adopted towards each other—that the boy lived, but was of weak and imperfect intellect—that she sent him by a trusty hand to a cheap school in Yorkshire—that she had paid for his education for some years, and then, being poor, and going a long way off, gradually deserted him, for which she prayed forgiveness?'

Snawley nodded his head, and wiped his eyes; the first slightly, the last violently.

'The school was Mr. Squeers's,' continued Ralph; 'the boy was left there in the name of Smike; every description was fully given, dates tally exactly with Mr. Squeers's books, Mr. Squeers is lodging with you at this time; you have two other boys at his school: you communicated the whole discovery to him, he brought you to me as the person who had recommended to him the kidnapper of his child; and I brought you here. Is that so?'

'You talk like a good book, sir, that's got nothing in its inside but what's the truth,' replied Snawley.

'This is your pocket-book,' said Ralph, producing one from his coat; 'the certificates of your first marriage and of the boy's birth, and your wife's two letters, and every other paper that can support these statements directly or by implication, are here, are they?'

'Every one of 'em, sir.'

'And you don't object to their being looked at here, so that these people may be convinced of your power to substantiate your claim at once in law and reason, and you may resume your control over your own son without more delay. Do I understand you?'

'I couldn't have understood myself better, sir.'

'There, then,' said Ralph, tossing the pocket-book upon the table. 'Let them see them if they like; and as those are the original papers, I should recommend you to stand near while they are being examined, or you may chance to lose some.'

With these words Ralph sat down unbidden, and compressing his lips, which were for the moment slightly parted by a smile, folded his arms, and looked for the first time at his nephew.

Nicholas, stung by the concluding taunt, darted an indignant glance at him; but commanding himself as well as he could, entered upon a close examination of the documents, at which John Browdie assisted. There was nothing about them which could be called in question. The certificates were regularly signed as extracts from the parish books, the first letter had a genuine appearance of having been written and preserved for some years, the handwriting of the second tallied with it exactly, (making proper allowance for its having been written by a person in extremity,) and there were several other corroboratory scraps of entries and memoranda which it was equally difficult to question.

'Dear Nicholas,' whispered Kate, who had been looking anxiously over his shoulder, 'can this be really the case? Is this statement true?'

'I fear it is,' answered Nicholas. 'What say you, John?'

John scratched his head and shook it, but said nothing at all.

'You will observe, ma'am,' said Ralph, addressing himself to Mrs. Nickleby, 'that this boy being a minor and not of strong mind, we might have come here tonight, armed with the powers of the law, and backed by a troop of its myrmidons. I should have done so, ma'am, unquestionably, but for my regard for the feelings of yourself, and your daughter.'

'You have shown your regard for her feelings well,' said Nicholas, drawing his sister towards him.

'Thank you,' replied Ralph. 'Your praise, sir, is commendation, indeed.'

'Well,' said Squeers, 'what's to be done? Them hackney-coach horses will catch cold if we don't think of moving; there's one of 'em a sneezing now, so that he blows the street door right open. What's the order of the day? Is Master Snawley to come along with us?'

'No, no, no,' replied Smike, drawing back, and clinging to Nicholas.

'No. Pray, no. I will not go from you with him. No, no.'

'This is a cruel thing,' said Snawley, looking to his friends for support. 'Do parents bring children into the world for this?'

'Do parents bring children into the world for thot?' said John Browdie bluntly, pointing, as he spoke, to Squeers.

'Never you mind,' retorted that gentleman, tapping his nose derisively.

'Never I mind!' said John, 'no, nor never nobody mind, say'st thou, schoolmeasther. It's nobody's minding that keeps sike men as thou afloat. Noo then, where be'est thou coomin' to? Dang it, dinnot coom treadin' ower me, mun.'

Suiting the action to the word, John Browdie just jerked his elbow into the chest of Mr. Squeers who was advancing upon Smike; with so much dexterity that the schoolmaster reeled and staggered back upon Ralph Nickleby, and being unable to recover his balance, knocked that gentleman off his chair, and stumbled heavily upon him.

This accidental circumstance was the signal for some very decisive proceedings. In the midst of a great noise, occasioned by the prayers and entreaties of Smike, the cries and exclamations of the women, and the vehemence of the men, demonstrations were made of carrying off the lost son by violence. Squeers had actually begun to haul him out, when Nicholas (who, until then, had been evidently undecided how to act) took him by the collar, and shaking him so that such teeth as he had, chattered in his head, politely escorted him to the room-door, and thrusting him into the passage, shut it upon him.

'Now,' said Nicholas to the other two, 'have the goodness to follow your friend.'

'I want my son,' said Snawley.

'Your son,' replied Nicholas, 'chooses for himself. He chooses to remain here, and he shall.'

'You won't give him up?' said Snawley.

'I would not give him up against his will, to be the victim of such brutality as that to which you would consign him,' replied Nicholas, 'if he were a dog or a rat.'

'Knock that Nickleby down with a candlestick,' cried Mr. Squeers, through the keyhole, 'and bring out my hat, somebody, will you, unless he wants to steal it.'

'I am very sorry, indeed,' said Mrs. Nickleby, who, with Mrs. Browdie, had stood crying and biting her fingers in a corner, while Kate (very pale, but perfectly quiet) had kept as near her brother as she could. 'I am very sorry, indeed, for all this. I really don't know what would be best to do, and that's the truth. Nicholas ought to be the best judge, and I hope he is. Of course, it's a hard thing to have to keep other people's children, though young Mr. Snawley is certainly as useful and willing as it's possible for anybody to be; but, if it could be settled in any friendly manner—if old Mr. Snawley, for instance, would settle to pay something certain for his board and lodging, and some fair arrangement was come to, so that we undertook to have fish twice a week, and a pudding twice, or a dumpling, or something of that sort—I do think that it might be very satisfactory and pleasant for all parties.'

This compromise, which was proposed with abundance of tears and sighs, not exactly meeting the point at issue, nobody took any notice of it; and poor Mrs. Nickleby accordingly proceeded to enlighten Mrs. Browdie upon the advantages of such a scheme, and the unhappy results flowing, on all occasions, from her not being attended to when she proffered her advice.

'You, sir,' said Snawley, addressing the terrified Smike, 'are an unnatural, ungrateful, unlovable boy. You won't let me love you when I want to. Won't you come home, won't you?'

'No, no, no,' cried Smike, shrinking back.

'He never loved nobody,' bawled Squeers, through the keyhole. 'He never loved me; he never loved Wackford, who is next door but one to a cherubim. How can you expect that he'll love his father? He'll never love his father, he won't. He don't know what it is to have a father. He don't understand it. It an't in him.'

Mr. Snawley looked steadfastly at his son for a full minute, and then covering his eyes with his hand, and once more raising his hat in the air, appeared deeply occupied in deploring his black ingratitude. Then drawing his arm across his eyes, he picked up Mr. Squeers's hat, and taking it under one arm, and his own under the other, walked slowly and sadly out.

'Your romance, sir,' said Ralph, lingering for a moment, 'is destroyed, I take it. No unknown; no persecuted descendant of a man of high degree; but the weak, imbecile son of a poor, petty tradesman. We shall see how your sympathy melts before plain matter of fact.'

'You shall,' said Nicholas, motioning towards the door.

'And trust me, sir,' added Ralph, 'that I never supposed you would give him up tonight. Pride, obstinacy, reputation for fine feeling, were all against it. These must be brought down, sir, lowered, crushed, as they shall be soon. The protracted and wearing anxiety and expense of the law in its most oppressive form, its torture from hour to hour, its weary days and sleepless nights, with these I'll prove you, and break your haughty spirit, strong as you deem it now. And when you make this house a hell, and visit these trials upon yonder wretched object (as you will; I know you), and those who think you now a young-fledged hero, we'll go into old accounts between us two, and see who stands the debtor, and comes out best at last, even before the world.'

Ralph Nickleby withdrew. But Mr. Squeers, who had heard a portion of this closing address, and was by this time wound up to a pitch of impotent malignity almost unprecedented, could not refrain from returning to the parlour door, and actually cutting some dozen capers with various wry faces and hideous grimaces, expressive of his triumphant confidence in the downfall and defeat of Nicholas.

Having concluded this war-dance, in which his short trousers and large boots had borne a very conspicuous figure, Mr. Squeers followed his friends, and the family were left to meditate upon recent occurrences.

CHAPTER 46
Throws some Light upon Nicholas's Love; but whether for Good or Evil the Reader must determine

After an anxious consideration of the painful and embarrassing position in which he was placed, Nicholas decided that he ought to lose no time in frankly stating it to the kind brothers. Availing himself of the first opportunity of being alone with Mr. Charles Cheeryble at the close of next day, he accordingly related Smike's little history, and modestly but firmly expressed his hope that the good old gentleman would, under such circumstances as he described, hold him justified in adopting the extreme course of interfering between parent and child, and upholding the latter in his disobedience; even though his horror and dread of his father might seem, and would doubtless be represented as, a thing so repulsive and unnatural, as to render those who countenanced him in it, fit objects of general detestation and abhorrence.

'So deeply rooted does this horror of the man appear to be,' said Nicholas, 'that I can hardly believe he really is his son. Nature does not seem to have implanted in his breast one lingering feeling of affection for him, and surely she can never err.'

'My dear sir,' replied brother Charles, 'you fall into the very common mistake of charging upon Nature, matters with which she has not the smallest connection, and for which she is in no way responsible. Men talk of Nature as an abstract thing, and lose sight of what is natural while they do so. Here is a poor lad who has never felt a parent's care, who has scarcely known anything all his life but suffering and sorrow, presented to a man who he is told is his father, and whose first act is to signify his intention of putting an end to his short term of happiness, of consigning him to his old fate, and taking him from the only friend he has ever had—which is yourself. If Nature, in such a case, put into that lad's breast but one secret prompting which urged him towards his father and away from you, she would be a liar and an idiot.'

Nicholas was delighted to find that the old gentleman spoke so warmly, and in the hope that he might say something more to the same purpose, made no reply.

'The same mistake presents itself to me, in one shape or other, at every turn,' said brother Charles. 'Parents who never showed their love, complain of want of natural affection in their children; children who never showed their duty, complain of want of natural feeling in their parents; law-makers who find both so miserable that their affections have never had enough of life's sun to develop them, are loud in their moralisings over parents and children too, and cry that the very ties of nature are disregarded. Natural affections and instincts, my dear sir, are the most beautiful of the Almighty's works, but like other beautiful works of His, they must be reared and fostered, or it is as natural that they should be wholly obscured, and that new feelings should usurp their place, as it is that the sweetest productions of the earth, left untended, should be choked with weeds and briers. I wish we could be brought to consider this, and remembering natural obligations a little more at the right time, talk about them a little less at the wrong one.'

After this, brother Charles, who had talked himself into a great heat, stopped to cool a little, and then continued:

'I dare say you are surprised, my dear sir, that I have listened to your recital with so little astonishment. That is easily explained. Your uncle has been here this morning.'

Nicholas coloured, and drew back a step or two.

'Yes,' said the old gentleman, tapping his desk emphatically, 'here, in this room. He would listen neither to reason, feeling, nor justice. But brother Ned was hard upon him; brother Ned, sir, might have melted a paving-stone.'

'He came to—' said Nicholas.

'To complain of you,' returned brother Charles, 'to poison our ears with calumnies and falsehoods; but he came on a fruitless errand, and went away with some wholesome truths in his ear besides. Brother Ned, my dear Mr. Nickleby—brother Ned, sir, is a perfect lion. So is Tim Linkinwater; Tim is quite a lion. We had Tim in to face him at first, and Tim was at him, sir, before you could say "Jack Robinson."'

'How can I ever thank you for all the deep obligations you impose upon me every day?' said Nicholas.

'By keeping silence upon the subject, my dear sir,' returned brother Charles. 'You shall be righted. At least you shall not be wronged. Nobody belonging to you shall be wronged. They shall not hurt a hair of your head, or the boy's head, or your mother's head, or your sister's head. I have said it, brother Ned has said it, Tim Linkinwater has said it. We have all said it, and we'll all do it. I have seen the father—if he is the father—and I suppose he must be. He is a barbarian and a hypocrite, Mr. Nickleby. I told him, "You are a barbarian, sir." I did. I said, "You're a barbarian, sir." And I'm glad of it, I am very glad I told him he was a barbarian, very glad indeed!'

By this time brother Charles was in such a very warm state of indignation, that Nicholas thought he might venture to put in a word, but the moment he essayed to do so, Mr. Cheeryble laid his hand softly upon his arm, and pointed to a chair.

'The subject is at an end for the present,' said the old gentleman, wiping his face. 'Don't revive it by a single word. I am going to speak upon another subject, a confidential subject, Mr. Nickleby. We must be cool again, we must be cool.'

After two or three turns across the room he resumed his seat, and drawing his chair nearer to that on which Nicholas was seated, said:

'I am about to employ you, my dear sir, on a confidential and delicate mission.'

'You might employ many a more able messenger, sir,' said Nicholas, 'but a more trustworthy or zealous one, I may be bold to say, you could not find.'

'Of that I am well assured,' returned brother Charles, 'well assured. You will give me credit for thinking so, when I tell you that the object of this mission is a young lady.'

'A young lady, sir!' cried Nicholas, quite trembling for the moment with his eagerness to hear more.

'A very beautiful young lady,' said Mr. Cheeryble, gravely.

'Pray go on, sir,' returned Nicholas.

'I am thinking how to do so,' said brother Charles; sadly, as it seemed to his young friend, and with an expression allied to pain. 'You accidentally saw a young lady in this room one morning, my dear sir, in a fainting fit. Do you remember? Perhaps you have forgotten.'

'Oh no,' replied Nicholas, hurriedly. 'I—I—remember it very well indeed.'

'She is the lady I speak of,' said brother Charles. Like the famous parrot, Nicholas thought a great deal, but was unable to utter a word.

'She is the daughter,' said Mr. Cheeryble, 'of a lady who, when she was a beautiful girl herself, and I was very many years younger, I—it seems a strange word for me to utter now—I loved very dearly. You will smile, perhaps, to hear a grey-headed man talk about such things. You will not offend me, for when I was as young as you, I dare say I should have done the same.'

'I have no such inclination, indeed,' said Nicholas.

'My dear brother Ned,' continued Mr. Cheeryble, 'was to have married her sister, but she died. She is dead too now, and has been for many years. She married her choice; and I wish I could add that her after-life was as happy as God knows I ever prayed it might be!'

A short silence intervened, which Nicholas made no effort to break.

'If trial and calamity had fallen as lightly on his head, as in the deepest truth of my own heart I ever hoped (for her sake) it would, his life would have been one of peace and happiness,' said the old gentleman calmly. 'It will be enough to say that this was not the case; that she was not happy; that they fell into complicated distresses and difficulties; that she came, twelve months before her death, to appeal to my old friendship; sadly changed, sadly altered, broken-spirited from suffering and ill-usage, and almost broken-hearted. He readily availed himself of the money which, to give her but one hour's peace of mind, I would have poured out as freely as water—nay, he often sent her back for more—and yet even while he squandered it, he made the very success of these, her applications to me, the groundwork of cruel taunts and jeers, protesting that he knew she thought with bitter remorse of the choice she had made, that she had married him from motives of interest and vanity (he was a gay young man with great friends about him when she chose him for her husband), and venting in short upon her, by every unjust and unkind means, the bitterness of that ruin and disappointment which had been brought about by his profligacy alone. In those times this young lady was a mere child. I never saw her again until that morning when you saw her also, but my nephew, Frank—'

Nicholas started, and indistinctly apologising for the interruption, begged his patron to proceed.

'—My nephew, Frank, I say,' resumed Mr. Cheeryble, 'encountered her by accident, and lost sight of her almost in a minute afterwards, within two days after he returned to England. Her father lay in some secret place to avoid his creditors, reduced, between sickness and poverty, to the verge of death, and she, a child,—we might almost think, if we did not know the wisdom of all Heaven's decrees—who should have blessed a better man, was steadily braving privation, degradation, and everything most terrible to such a young and delicate creature's heart, for the purpose of supporting him. She was attended, sir,' said brother Charles, 'in these reverses, by one faithful creature, who had been, in old times, a poor kitchen wench in the family, who was then their solitary servant, but who might have been, for the truth and fidelity of her heart—who might have been—ah! the wife of Tim Linkinwater himself, sir!'

Pursuing this encomium upon the poor follower with such energy and relish as no words can describe, brother Charles leant back in his chair, and delivered the remainder of his relation with greater composure.

It was in substance this: That proudly resisting all offers of permanent aid and support from her late mother's friends, because they were made conditional upon her quitting the wretched man, her father, who had no friends left, and shrinking with instinctive delicacy from appealing in their behalf to that true and noble heart which he hated, and had, through its greatest and purest goodness, deeply wronged by misconstruction and ill report, this young girl had struggled alone and unassisted to maintain him by the labour of her hands. That through the utmost depths of poverty and affliction she had toiled, never turning aside for an instant from her task, never wearied by the petulant gloom of a sick man sustained by no consoling recollections of the past or hopes of the future; never repining for the comforts she had rejected, or bewailing the hard lot she had voluntarily incurred. That every little accomplishment she had acquired in happier days had been put into requisition for this purpose, and directed to this one end. That for two long years, toiling by day and often too by night, working at the needle, the pencil, and the pen, and submitting, as a daily governess, to such caprices and indignities as women (with daughters too) too often love to inflict upon their own sex when they serve in such capacities, as though in jealousy of the superior intelligence which they are necessitated to employ,—indignities, in ninety-nine cases out of every hundred, heaped upon persons immeasurably and incalculably their betters, but outweighing in comparison any that the most heartless blackleg would put upon his groom—that for two long years, by dint of labouring in all these capacities and wearying in none, she had not succeeded in the sole aim and object of her life, but that, overwhelmed by accumulated difficulties and disappointments, she had been compelled to seek out her mother's old friend, and, with a bursting heart, to confide in him at last.

'If I had been poor,' said brother Charles, with sparkling eyes; 'if I had been poor, Mr. Nickleby, my dear sir, which thank God I am not, I would have denied myself (of course anybody would under such circumstances) the commonest necessaries of life, to help her. As it is, the task is a difficult one. If her father were dead, nothing could be easier, for then she should share and cheer the happiest home that brother Ned and I could have, as if she were our child or sister. But he is still alive. Nobody can help him; that has been tried a thousand times; he was not abandoned by all without good cause, I know.'

'Cannot she be persuaded to—' Nicholas hesitated when he had got thus far.

'To leave him?' said brother Charles. 'Who could entreat a child to desert her parent? Such entreaties, limited to her seeing him occasionally, have been urged upon her—not by me—but always with the same result.'

'Is he kind to her?' said Nicholas. 'Does he requite her affection?'

'True kindness, considerate self-denying kindness, is not in his nature,' returned Mr. Cheeryble. 'Such kindness as he knows, he regards her with, I believe. The mother was a gentle, loving, confiding creature, and although he wounded her from their marriage till her death as cruelly and wantonly as ever man did, she never ceased to love him. She commended him on her death-bed to her child's care. Her child has never forgotten it, and never will.'

'Have you no influence over him?' asked Nicholas.

'I, my dear sir! The last man in the world. Such are his jealousy and hatred of me, that if he knew his daughter had opened her heart to me, he would render her life miserable with his reproaches; although—this is the inconsistency and selfishness of his character—although if he knew that every penny she had came from me, he would not relinquish one personal desire that the most reckless expenditure of her scanty stock could gratify.'

'An unnatural scoundrel!' said Nicholas, indignantly.

'We will use no harsh terms,' said brother Charles, in a gentle voice; 'but accommodate ourselves to the circumstances in which this young lady is placed. Such assistance as I have prevailed upon her to accept, I have been obliged, at her own earnest request, to dole out in the smallest portions, lest he, finding how easily money was procured, should squander it even more lightly than he is accustomed to do. She has come to and fro, to and fro, secretly and by night, to take even this; and I cannot bear that things should go on in this way, Mr. Nickleby, I really cannot bear it.'

Then it came out by little and little, how that the twins had been revolving in their good old heads manifold plans and schemes for helping this young lady in the most delicate and considerate way, and so that her father should not suspect the source whence the aid was derived; and how they had at last come to the conclusion, that the best course would be to make a feint of purchasing her little drawings and ornamental work at a high price, and keeping up a constant demand for the same. For the furtherance of which end and object it was necessary that somebody should represent the dealer in such commodities, and after great deliberation they had pitched upon Nicholas to support this character.

'He knows me,' said brother Charles, 'and he knows my brother Ned. Neither of us would do. Frank is a very good fellow—a very fine fellow—but we are afraid that he might be a little flighty and thoughtless in such a delicate matter, and that he might, perhaps—that he might, in short, be too susceptible (for she is a beautiful creature, sir; just what her poor mother was), and falling in love with her before he knew well his own mind, carry pain and sorrow into that innocent breast, which we would be the humble instruments of gradually making happy. He took an extraordinary interest in her fortunes when he first happened to encounter her; and we gather from the inquiries we have made of him, that it was she in whose behalf he made that turmoil which led to your first acquaintance.'

Nicholas stammered out that he had before suspected the possibility of such a thing; and in explanation of its having occurred to him, described when and where he had seen the young lady himself.

'Well; then you see,' continued brother Charles, 'that he wouldn't do. Tim Linkinwater is out of the question; for Tim, sir, is such a tremendous fellow, that he could never contain himself, but would go to loggerheads with the father before he had been in the place five minutes. You don't know what Tim is, sir, when he is aroused by anything that appeals to his feelings very strongly; then he is terrific, sir, is Tim Linkinwater, absolutely terrific. Now, in you we can repose the strictest confidence; in you we have seen—or at least I have seen, and that's the same thing, for there's no difference between me and my brother Ned, except that he is the finest creature that ever lived, and that there is not, and never will be, anybody like him in all the world—in you we have seen domestic virtues and affections, and delicacy of feeling, which exactly qualify you for such an office. And you are the man, sir.'

'The young lady, sir,' said Nicholas, who felt so embarrassed that he had no small difficulty in saying anything at all—'Does—is—is she a party to this innocent deceit?'

'Yes, yes,' returned Mr. Cheeryble; 'at least she knows you come from us; she does not know, however, but that we shall dispose of these little productions that you'll purchase from time to time; and, perhaps, if you did it very well (that is, very well indeed), perhaps she might be brought to believe that we—that we made a profit of them. Eh? Eh?'

In this guileless and most kind simplicity, brother Charles was so happy, and in this possibility of the young lady being led to think that she was under no obligation to him, he evidently felt so sanguine and had so much delight, that Nicholas would not breathe a doubt upon the subject.

All this time, however, there hovered upon the tip of his tongue a confession that the very same objections which Mr. Cheeryble had stated to the employment of his nephew in this commission applied with at least equal force and validity to himself, and a hundred times had he been upon the point of avowing the real state of his feelings, and entreating to be released from it. But as often, treading upon the heels of this impulse, came another which urged him to refrain, and to keep his secret to his own breast. 'Why should I,' thought Nicholas, 'why should I throw difficulties in the way of this benevolent and high-minded design? What if I do love and reverence this good and lovely creature. Should I not appear a most arrogant and shallow coxcomb if I gravely represented that there was any danger of her falling in love with me? Besides, have I no confidence in myself? Am I not now bound in honour to repress these thoughts? Has not this excellent man a right to my best and heartiest services, and should any considerations of self deter me from rendering them?'

Asking himself such questions as these, Nicholas mentally answered with great emphasis 'No!' and persuading himself that he was a most conscientious and glorious martyr, nobly resolved to do what, if he had examined his own heart a little more carefully, he would have found he could not resist. Such is the sleight of hand by which we juggle with ourselves, and change our very weaknesses into stanch and most magnanimous virtues!

Mr. Cheeryble, being of course wholly unsuspicious that such reflections were presenting themselves to his young friend, proceeded to give him the needful credentials and directions for his first visit, which was to be made next morning; and all preliminaries being arranged, and the strictest secrecy enjoined, Nicholas walked home for the night very thoughtfully indeed.

The place to which Mr. Cheeryble had directed him was a row of mean and not over-cleanly houses, situated within 'the Rules' of the King's Bench Prison, and not many hundred paces distant from the obelisk in St George's Fields. The Rules are a certain liberty adjoining the prison, and comprising some dozen streets in which debtors who can raise money to pay large fees, from which their creditors do not derive any benefit, are permitted to reside by the wise provisions of the same enlightened laws which leave the debtor who can raise no money to starve in jail, without the food, clothing, lodging, or warmth, which are provided for felons convicted of the most atrocious crimes that can disgrace humanity. There are many pleasant fictions of the law in constant operation, but there is not one so pleasant or practically humorous as that which supposes every man to be of equal value in its impartial eye, and the benefits of all laws to be equally attainable by all men, without the smallest reference to the furniture of their pockets.

To the row of houses indicated to him by Mr. Charles Cheeryble, Nicholas directed his steps, without much troubling his head with such matters as these; and at this row of houses—after traversing a very dirty and dusty suburb, of which minor theatricals, shell-fish, ginger-beer, spring vans, greengrocery, and brokers' shops, appeared to compose the main and most prominent features—he at length arrived with a palpitating heart. There were small gardens in front which, being wholly neglected in all other respects, served as little pens for the dust to collect in, until the wind came round the corner and blew it down the road. Opening the rickety gate which, dangling on its broken hinges before one of these, half admitted and half repulsed the visitor, Nicholas knocked at the street door with a faltering hand.

It was in truth a shabby house outside, with very dim parlour windows and very small show of blinds, and very dirty muslin curtains dangling across the lower panes on very loose and limp strings. Neither, when the door was opened, did the inside appear to belie the outward promise, as there was faded carpeting on the stairs and faded oil-cloth in the passage; in addition to which discomforts a gentleman Ruler was smoking hard in the front parlour (though it was not yet noon), while the lady of the house was busily engaged in turpentining the disjointed fragments of a tent-bedstead at the door of the back parlour, as if in preparation for the reception of some new lodger who had been fortunate enough to engage it.

Nicholas had ample time to make these observations while the little boy, who went on errands for the lodgers, clattered down the kitchen stairs and was heard to scream, as in some remote cellar, for Miss Bray's servant, who, presently appearing and requesting him to follow her, caused him to evince greater symptoms of nervousness and disorder than so natural a consequence of his having inquired for that young lady would seem calculated to occasion.

Upstairs he went, however, and into a front room he was shown, and there, seated at a little table by the window, on which were drawing materials with which she was occupied, sat the beautiful girl who had so engrossed his thoughts, and who, surrounded by all the new and strong interest which Nicholas attached to her story, seemed now, in his eyes, a thousand times more beautiful than he had ever yet supposed her.

But how the graces and elegancies which she had dispersed about the poorly-furnished room went to the heart of Nicholas! Flowers, plants, birds, the harp, the old piano whose notes had sounded so much sweeter in bygone times; how many struggles had it cost her to keep these two last links of that broken chain which bound her yet to home! With every slender ornament, the occupation of her leisure hours, replete with that graceful charm which lingers in every little tasteful work of woman's hands, how much patient endurance and how many gentle affections were entwined! He felt as though the smile of Heaven were on the little chamber; as though the beautiful devotion of so young and weak a creature had shed a ray of its own on the inanimate things around, and made them beautiful as itself; as though the halo with which old painters surround the bright angels of a sinless world played about a being akin in spirit to them, and its light were visibly before him.

And yet Nicholas was in the Rules of the King's Bench Prison! If he had been in Italy indeed, and the time had been sunset, and the scene a stately terrace! But, there is one broad sky over all the world, and whether it be blue or cloudy, the same heaven beyond it; so, perhaps, he had no need of compunction for thinking as he did.

It is not to be supposed that he took in everything at one glance, for he had as yet been unconscious of the presence of a sick man propped up with pillows in an easy-chair, who,

434

moving restlessly and impatiently in his seat, attracted his attention.

He was scarce fifty, perhaps, but so emaciated as to appear much older. His features presented the remains of a handsome countenance, but one in which the embers of strong and impetuous passions were easier to be traced than any expression which would have rendered a far plainer face much more prepossessing. His looks were very haggard, and his limbs and body literally worn to the bone, but there was something of the old fire in the large sunken eye notwithstanding, and it seemed to kindle afresh as he struck a thick stick, with which he seemed to have supported himself in his seat, impatiently on the floor twice or thrice, and called his daughter by her name.

'Madeline, who is this? What does anybody want here? Who told a stranger we could be seen? What is it?'

'I believe—' the young lady began, as she inclined her head with an air of some confusion, in reply to the salutation of Nicholas.

'You always believe,' returned her father, petulantly. 'What is it?'

By this time Nicholas had recovered sufficient presence of mind to speak for himself, so he said (as it had been agreed he should say) that he had called about a pair of hand-screens, and some painted velvet for an ottoman, both of which were required to be of the most elegant design possible, neither time nor expense being of the smallest consideration. He had also to pay for the two drawings, with many thanks, and, advancing to the little table, he laid upon it a bank note, folded in an envelope and sealed.

'See that the money is right, Madeline,' said the father. 'Open the paper, my dear.'

'It's quite right, papa, I'm sure.'

'Here!' said Mr. Bray, putting out his hand, and opening and shutting his bony fingers with irritable impatience. 'Let me see. What are you talking about, Madeline? You're sure? How can you be sure of any such thing? Five pounds—well, is that right?'

'Quite,' said Madeline, bending over him. She was so busily employed in arranging the pillows that Nicholas could not see her face, but as she stooped he thought he saw a tear fall.

'Ring the bell, ring the bell,' said the sick man, with the same nervous eagerness, and motioning towards it with such a quivering hand that the bank note rustled in the air. 'Tell her to get it changed, to get me a newspaper, to buy me some grapes, another bottle of the wine that I had last week—and—and—I forget half I want just now, but she can go out again. Let her get those first, those first. Now, Madeline, my love, quick, quick! Good God, how slow you are!'

'He remembers nothing that she wants!' thought Nicholas. Perhaps something of what he thought was expressed in his countenance, for the sick man, turning towards him with great asperity, demanded to know if he waited for a receipt.

'It is no matter at all,' said Nicholas.

'No matter! what do you mean, sir?' was the tart rejoinder. 'No matter! Do you think you bring your paltry money here as a favour or a gift; or as a matter of business, and in return for value received? D—n you, sir, because you can't appreciate the time and taste which are bestowed upon the goods you deal in, do you think you give your money away? Do you know that you are talking to a gentleman, sir, who at one time could have bought up fifty such men as you and all you have? What do you mean?'

'I merely mean that as I shall have many dealings with this lady, if she will kindly allow me, I will not trouble her with such forms,' said Nicholas.

'Then I mean, if you please, that we'll have as many forms as we can, returned the father. 'My daughter, sir, requires no kindness from you or anybody else. Have the goodness to confine your dealings strictly to trade and business, and not to travel beyond it. Every petty tradesman is to begin to pity her now, is he? Upon my soul! Very pretty. Madeline, my dear, give him a receipt; and mind you always do so.'

While she was feigning to write it, and Nicholas was ruminating upon the extraordinary but by no means uncommon character thus presented to his observation, the invalid, who appeared at times to suffer great bodily pain, sank back in his chair and moaned out a feeble complaint that the girl had been gone an hour, and that everybody conspired to goad him.

'When,' said Nicholas, as he took the piece of paper, 'when shall I call again?'

This was addressed to the daughter, but the father answered immediately.

'When you're requested to call, sir, and not before. Don't worry and persecute. Madeline, my dear, when is this person to call again?'

'Oh, not for a long time, not for three or four weeks; it is not necessary, indeed; I can do without,' said the young lady, with great eagerness.

'Why, how are we to do without?' urged her father, not speaking above his breath. 'Three or four weeks, Madeline! Three or four weeks!'

'Then sooner, sooner, if you please,' said the young lady, turning to Nicholas.

'Three or four weeks!' muttered the father. 'Madeline, what on earth—do nothing for three or four weeks!'

'It is a long time, ma'am,' said Nicholas.

'You think so, do you?' retorted the father, angrily. 'If I chose to beg, sir, and stoop to ask assistance from people I despise, three or four months would not be a long time; three or four years would not be a long time. Understand, sir, that is if I chose to be dependent; but as I don't, you may call in a week.'

Nicholas bowed low to the young lady and retired, pondering upon Mr. Bray's ideas of independence, and devoutly hoping that there might be few such independent spirits as he mingling with the baser clay of humanity.

He heard a light footstep above him as he descended the stairs, and looking round saw that the young lady was standing there, and glancing timidly towards him, seemed to hesitate whether she should call him back or no. The best way of settling the question was to turn back at once, which Nicholas did.

'I don't know whether I do right in asking you, sir,' said Madeline, hurriedly, 'but pray, pray, do not mention to my poor mother's dear friends what has passed here today. He has suffered much, and is worse this morning. I beg you, sir, as a boon, a favour to myself.'

'You have but to hint a wish,' returned Nicholas fervently, 'and I would hazard my life to gratify it.'

'You speak hastily, sir.'

'Truly and sincerely,' rejoined Nicholas, his lips trembling as he formed the words, 'if ever man spoke truly yet. I am not skilled in disguising my feelings, and if I were, I could not hide my heart from you. Dear madam, as I know your history, and feel as men and angels must who hear and see such things, I do entreat you to believe that I would die to serve you.'

The young lady turned away her head, and was plainly weeping.

'Forgive me,' said Nicholas, with respectful earnestness, 'if I seem to say too much, or to presume upon the confidence which has been intrusted to me. But I could not leave you as if my interest and sympathy expired with the commission of the day. I am your faithful servant, humbly devoted to you from this hour, devoted in strict truth and honour to him who sent me here, and in pure integrity of heart, and distant respect for you. If I meant more or less than this, I should be unworthy his regard, and false to the very nature that prompts the honest words I utter.'

She waved her hand, entreating him to be gone, but answered not a word. Nicholas could say no more, and silently withdrew. And thus ended his first interview with Madeline Bray.

CHAPTER 47

Mr. Ralph Nickleby has some confidential Intercourse with another old Friend. They concert between them a Project, which promises well for both

'There go the three-quarters past!' muttered Newman Noggs, listening to the chimes of some neighbouring church 'and my dinner time's two. He does it on purpose. He makes a point of it. It's just like him.'

It was in his own little den of an office and on the top of his official stool that Newman thus soliloquised; and the soliloquy referred, as Newman's grumbling soliloquies usually did, to Ralph Nickleby.

'I don't believe he ever had an appetite,' said Newman, 'except for pounds, shillings, and pence, and with them he's as greedy as a wolf. I should like to have him compelled to swallow one of every English coin. The penny would be an awkward morsel—but the crown—ha! ha!'

His good-humour being in some degree restored by the vision of Ralph Nickleby swallowing, perforce, a five-shilling piece, Newman slowly brought forth from his desk one of those portable bottles, currently known as pocket-pistols, and shaking the same close to his ear so as to produce a rippling sound very cool and pleasant to listen to, suffered his features to relax, and took a gurgling drink, which relaxed them still more. Replacing the cork, he smacked his lips twice or thrice with an air of great relish, and, the taste of the liquor having by this time evaporated, recurred to his grievance again.

'Five minutes to three,' growled Newman; 'it can't want more by this time; and I had my breakfast at eight o'clock, and such a breakfast! and my right dinner-time two! And I might have a nice little bit of hot roast meat spoiling at home all this time—how does he know I haven't? "Don't go till I come back," "Don't go till I come back," day after day. What do you always go out at my dinner-time for then—eh? Don't you know it's nothing but aggravation—eh?'

These words, though uttered in a very loud key, were addressed to nothing but empty air. The recital of his wrongs, however, seemed to have the effect of making Newman Noggs desperate; for he flattened his old hat upon his head, and drawing on the everlasting gloves, declared with great vehemence, that come what might, he would go to dinner that very minute.

Carrying this resolution into instant effect, he had advanced as far as the passage, when the sound of the latch-key in the street door caused him to make a precipitate retreat into his own office again.

'Here he is,' growled Newman, 'and somebody with him. Now it'll be "Stop till this gentleman's gone." But I won't. That's flat.'

So saying, Newman slipped into a tall empty closet which opened with two half doors, and shut himself up; intending to slip out directly Ralph was safe inside his own room.

'Noggs!' cried Ralph, 'where is that fellow, Noggs?'

But not a word said Newman.

'The dog has gone to his dinner, though I told him not,' muttered Ralph, looking into the office, and pulling out his watch. 'Humph!' You had better come in here, Gride. My man's out, and the sun is hot upon my room. This is cool and in the shade, if you don't mind roughing it.'

'Not at all, Mr. Nickleby, oh not at all! All places are alike to me, sir. Ah! very nice indeed. Oh! very nice!'

The parson who made this reply was a little old man, of about seventy or seventy-five years of age, of a very lean figure, much bent and slightly twisted. He wore a grey coat with a very narrow collar, an old-fashioned waistcoat of ribbed black silk, and such scanty trousers as displayed his shrunken spindle-shanks in their full ugliness. The only articles of display or ornament in his dress were a steel watch-chain to which were attached some large gold seals; and a black ribbon into which, in compliance with an old fashion scarcely ever observed in these days, his grey hair was gathered behind. His nose and chin were sharp and prominent, his jaws had fallen inwards from loss of teeth, his face was shrivelled and yellow, save where the cheeks were streaked with the colour of a dry winter apple; and where his beard had been, there lingered yet a few grey tufts which seemed, like the ragged eyebrows, to denote the badness of the soil from which they sprung. The whole air and attitude of the form was one of stealthy cat-like obsequiousness; the whole expression of the face was concentrated in a wrinkled leer, compounded of cunning, lecherousness, slyness, and avarice.

Such was old Arthur Gride, in whose face there was not a wrinkle, in whose dress there was not one spare fold or plait, but expressed the most covetous and griping penury, and sufficiently indicated his belonging to that class of which Ralph Nickleby was a member. Such was old Arthur Gride, as he sat in a low chair looking up into the face of Ralph Nickleby, who, lounging upon the tall office stool, with his arms upon his knees, looked down into his; a match for him on whatever errand he had come.

'And how have you been?' said Gride, feigning great interest in Ralph's state of health. 'I haven't seen you for—oh! not for—'

438

'Not for a long time,' said Ralph, with a peculiar smile, importing that he very well knew it was not on a mere visit of compliment that his friend had come. 'It was a narrow chance that you saw me now, for I had only just come up to the door as you turned the corner.'

'I am very lucky,' observed Gride.

'So men say,' replied Ralph, drily.

The older money-lender wagged his chin and smiled, but he originated no new remark, and they sat for some little time without speaking. Each was looking out to take the other at a disadvantage.

'Come, Gride,' said Ralph, at length; 'what's in the wind today?'

'Aha! you're a bold man, Mr. Nickleby,' cried the other, apparently very much relieved by Ralph's leading the way to business. 'Oh dear, dear, what a bold man you are!'

'Why, you have a sleek and slinking way with you that makes me seem so by contrast,' returned Ralph. 'I don't know but that yours may answer better, but I want the patience for it.'

'You were born a genius, Mr. Nickleby,' said old Arthur. 'Deep, deep, deep. Ah!'

'Deep enough,' retorted Ralph, 'to know that I shall need all the depth I have, when men like you begin to compliment. You know I have stood by when you fawned and flattered other people, and I remember pretty well what that always led to.'

'Ha, ha, ha!' rejoined Arthur, rubbing his hands. 'So you do, so you do, no doubt. Not a man knows it better. Well, it's a pleasant thing now to think that you remember old times. Oh dear!'

'Now then,' said Ralph, composedly; 'what's in the wind, I ask again? What is it?'

'See that now!' cried the other. 'He can't even keep from business while we're chatting over bygones. Oh dear, dear, what a man it is!'

'Which of the bygones do you want to revive?' said Ralph. 'One of them, I know, or you wouldn't talk about them.'

'He suspects even me!' cried old Arthur, holding up his hands. 'Even me! Oh dear, even me. What a man it is! Ha, ha, ha! What a man it is! Mr Nickleby against all the world. There's nobody like him. A giant among pigmies, a giant, a giant!'

Ralph looked at the old dog with a quiet smile as he chuckled on in this strain, and Newman Noggs in the closet felt his heart sink within him as the prospect of dinner grew fainter and fainter.

'I must humour him though,' cried old Arthur; 'he must have his way—a wilful man, as the Scotch say—well, well, they're a wise people, the Scotch. He will talk about business, and won't give away his time for nothing. He's very right. Time is money, time is money.'

'He was one of us who made that saying, I should think,' said Ralph. 'Time is money, and very good money too, to those who reckon interest by it. Time is money! Yes, and time costs money; it's rather an expensive article to some people we could name, or I forget my trade.'

In rejoinder to this sally, old Arthur again raised his hands, again chuckled, and again ejaculated 'What a man it is!' which done, he dragged the low chair a little nearer to Ralph's high stool, and looking upwards into his immovable face, said,

'What would you say to me, if I was to tell you that I was—that I was—going to be married?'

'I should tell you,' replied Ralph, looking coldly down upon him, 'that for some purpose of your own you told a lie, and that it wasn't the first time and wouldn't be the last; that I wasn't surprised and wasn't to be taken in.'

'Then I tell you seriously that I am,' said old Arthur.

'And I tell you seriously,' rejoined Ralph, 'what I told you this minute. Stay. Let me look at you. There's a liquorish devilry in your face. What is this?'

'I wouldn't deceive you, you know,' whined Arthur Gride; 'I couldn't do it, I should be mad to try. I, I, to deceive Mr. Nickleby! The pigmy to impose upon the giant. I ask again—he, he, he!—what should you say to me if I was to tell you that I was going to be married?'

'To some old hag?' said Ralph.

'No, No,' cried Arthur, interrupting him, and rubbing his hands in an ecstasy. 'Wrong, wrong again. Mr. Nickleby for once at fault; out, quite out! To a young and beautiful girl; fresh, lovely, bewitching, and not nineteen. Dark eyes, long eyelashes, ripe and ruddy lips that to look at is to long to kiss, beautiful clustering hair that one's fingers itch to play with, such a waist as might make a man clasp the air involuntarily, thinking of twining his arm about it, little feet that tread so lightly they hardly seem to walk upon the ground—to marry all this, sir, this—hey, hey!'

'This is something more than common drivelling,' said Ralph, after listening with a curled lip to the old sinner's raptures. 'The girl's name?'

'Oh deep, deep! See now how deep that is!' exclaimed old Arthur. 'He knows I want his help, he knows he can give it me, he knows it must all turn to his advantage, he sees the thing already. Her name—is there nobody within hearing?'

'Why, who the devil should there be?' retorted Ralph, testily.

'I didn't know but that perhaps somebody might be passing up or down the stairs,' said Arthur Gride, after looking out at the door and carefully reclosing it; 'or but that your man might have come back and might have been listening outside. Clerks and servants have a trick of listening, and I should have been very uncomfortable if Mr. Noggs—'

'Curse Mr. Noggs,' said Ralph, sharply, 'and go on with what you have to say.'

'Curse Mr. Noggs, by all means,' rejoined old Arthur; 'I am sure I have not the least objection to that. Her name is—'

'Well,' said Ralph, rendered very irritable by old Arthur's pausing again 'what is it?'

'Madeline Bray.'

Whatever reasons there might have been—and Arthur Gride appeared to have anticipated some—for the mention of this name producing an effect upon Ralph, or whatever effect it really did produce upon him, he permitted none to manifest itself, but calmly repeated the name several times, as if reflecting when and where he had heard it before.

'Bray,' said Ralph. 'Bray—there was young Bray of—no, he never had a daughter.'

'You remember Bray?' rejoined Arthur Gride.

'No,' said Ralph, looking vacantly at him.

'Not Walter Bray! The dashing man, who used his handsome wife so ill?'

'If you seek to recall any particular dashing man to my recollection by such a trait as that,' said Ralph, shrugging his shoulders, 'I shall confound him with nine-tenths of the dashing men I have ever known.'

'Tut, tut. That Bray who is now in the Rules of the Bench,' said old Arthur. 'You can't have forgotten Bray. Both of us did business with him. Why, he owes you money!'

'Oh him!' rejoined Ralph. 'Ay, ay. Now you speak. Oh! It's his daughter, is it?'

Naturally as this was said, it was not said so naturally but that a kindred spirit like old Arthur Gride might have discerned a design upon the part of Ralph to lead him on to much more explicit statements and explanations than he would have volunteered, or that Ralph could in all likelihood have obtained by any other means. Old Arthur, however, was so intent upon his own designs, that he suffered himself to be overreached, and had no suspicion but that his good friend was in earnest.

'I knew you couldn't forget him, when you came to think for a moment,' he said.

'You were right,' answered Ralph. 'But old Arthur Gride and matrimony is a most anomalous conjunction of words; old Arthur Gride and dark eyes and eyelashes, and lips that to look at is to long to kiss, and clustering hair that he wants to play with, and waists that he wants to span, and little feet that don't tread upon anything—old Arthur Gride and such things as these is more monstrous still; but old Arthur Gride marrying the daughter of a ruined "dashing man" in the Rules of the Bench, is the most monstrous and incredible of all. Plainly, friend Arthur Gride, if you want any help from me in this business (which of course you do, or you would not be here), speak out, and to the purpose. And, above all, don't talk to me of its turning to my advantage, for I know it must turn to yours also, and to a good round tune too, or you would have no finger in such a pie as this.'

There was enough acerbity and sarcasm not only in the matter of Ralph's speech, but in the tone of voice in which he uttered it, and the looks with which he eked it out, to have fired even the ancient usurer's cold blood and flushed even his withered cheek. But he gave vent to no demonstration of anger, contenting himself with exclaiming as before, 'What a man it is!' and rolling his head from side to side, as if in unrestrained enjoyment of his freedom and drollery. Clearly observing, however, from the expression in Ralph's features, that he had best come to the point as speedily as might be, he composed himself for more serious business, and entered upon the pith and marrow of his negotiation.

First, he dwelt upon the fact that Madeline Bray was devoted to the support and maintenance, and was a slave to every wish, of her only parent, who had no other friend on earth; to which Ralph rejoined that he had heard something of the kind before, and that if she had known a little more of the world, she wouldn't have been such a fool.

Secondly, he enlarged upon the character of her father, arguing, that even taking it for granted that he loved her in return with the utmost affection of which he was capable, yet he loved himself a great deal better; which Ralph said it was quite unnecessary to say anything more about, as that was very natural, and probable enough.

And, thirdly, old Arthur promised that the girl was a delicate and beautiful creature, and that he had really a hankering to have her for his wife. To this Ralph deigned no other rejoinder than a harsh smile, and a glance at the shrivelled old creature before him, which were, however, sufficiently expressive.

'Now,' said Gride, 'for the little plan I have in my mind to bring this about; because, I haven't offered myself even to the father yet, I should have told you. But that you have gathered already? Ah! oh dear, oh dear, what an edged tool you are!'

'Don't play with me then,' said Ralph impatiently. 'You know the proverb.'

'A reply always on the tip of his tongue!' cried old Arthur, raising his hands and eyes in admiration. 'He is always prepared! Oh dear, what a blessing to have such a ready wit, and so much ready money to back it!' Then, suddenly changing his tone, he went on: 'I have been backwards and forwards to Bray's lodgings several times within the last six months. It is just half a year since I first saw this delicate morsel, and, oh dear, what a delicate morsel it is! But that is neither here nor there. I am his detaining creditor for seventeen hundred pounds!'

'You talk as if you were the only detaining creditor,' said Ralph, pulling out his pocket-book. 'I am another for nine hundred and seventy-five pounds four and threepence.'

'The only other, Mr. Nickleby,' said old Arthur, eagerly. 'The only other. Nobody else went to the expense of lodging a detainer, trusting to our holding him fast enough, I warrant you. We both fell into the same snare; oh dear, what a pitfall it was; it almost ruined me! And lent him our money upon bills, with only one name besides his own, which to be sure everybody supposed to be a good one, and was as negotiable as money, but which turned out you know how. Just as we should have come upon him, he died insolvent. Ah! it went very nigh to ruin me, that loss did!'

'Go on with your scheme,' said Ralph. 'It's of no use raising the cry of our trade just now; there's nobody to hear us!'

'It's always as well to talk that way,' returned old Arthur, with a chuckle, 'whether there's anybody to hear us or not. Practice makes perfect, you know. Now, if I offer myself to Bray as his son-in-law, upon one simple condition that the moment I am fast married he shall be quietly released, and have an allowance to live just t'other side the water like a gentleman (he can't live long, for I have asked his doctor, and he declares that his complaint is one of the Heart and it is impossible), and if all the advantages of this condition are properly stated and dwelt upon to him, do you think he could resist me? And if he could not resist me, do you think his daughter could resist him? Shouldn't I have her Mrs. Arthur Gride—pretty Mrs. Arthur Gride—a tit-bit—a dainty chick—shouldn't I have her Mrs. Arthur Gride in a week, a month, a day—any time I chose to name?'

'Go on,' said Ralph, nodding his head deliberately, and speaking in a tone whose studied coldness presented a strange contrast to the rapturous squeak to which his friend had gradually mounted. 'Go on. You didn't come here to ask me that.'

'Oh dear, how you talk!' cried old Arthur, edging himself closer still to Ralph. 'Of course I didn't, I don't pretend I did! I came to ask what you would take from me, if I prospered with the father, for this debt of yours. Five shillings in the pound, six and-eightpence, ten shillings? I would go as far as ten for such a friend as you, we have always been on such good terms, but you won't be so hard upon me as that, I know. Now, will you?'

'There's something more to be told,' said Ralph, as stony and immovable as ever.

'Yes, yes, there is, but you won't give me time,' returned Arthur Gride. 'I want a backer in this matter; one who can talk, and urge, and press a point, which you can do as no man can. I can't do that, for I am a poor, timid, nervous creature. Now, if you get a good composition for this debt, which you long ago gave up for lost, you'll stand my friend, and help me. Won't you?'

'There's something more,' said Ralph.

'No, no, indeed,' cried Arthur Gride.

'Yes, yes, indeed. I tell you yes,' said Ralph.

'Oh!' returned old Arthur feigning to be suddenly enlightened. 'You mean something more, as concerns myself and my intention. Ay, surely, surely. Shall I mention that?'

'I think you had better,' rejoined Ralph, drily.

'I didn't like to trouble you with that, because I supposed your interest would cease with your own concern in the affair,' said Arthur Gride. 'That's kind of you to ask. Oh dear, how very kind of you! Why, supposing I had a knowledge of some property—some little property—very little—to which this pretty chick was entitled; which nobody does or can know of at this time, but which her husband could sweep into his pouch, if he knew as much as I do, would that account for—'

'For the whole proceeding,' rejoined Ralph, abruptly. 'Now, let me turn this matter over, and consider what I ought to have if I should help you to success.'

'But don't be hard,' cried old Arthur, raising his hands with an imploring gesture, and speaking, in a tremulous voice. 'Don't be too hard upon me. It's a very small property, it is indeed. Say the ten shillings, and we'll close the bargain. It's more than I ought to give, but you're so kind—shall we say the ten? Do now, do.'

Ralph took no notice of these supplications, but sat for three or four minutes in a brown study, looking thoughtfully at the person from whom they proceeded. After sufficient cogitation he broke silence, and it certainly could not be objected that he used any needless circumlocution, or failed to speak directly to the purpose.

'If you married this girl without me,' said Ralph, 'you must pay my debt in full, because you couldn't set her father free otherwise. It's plain, then, that I must have the whole amount, clear of all deduction or incumbrance, or I should lose from being honoured with your confidence, instead of gaining by it. That's the first article of the treaty. For the second, I shall stipulate that for my trouble in negotiation and persuasion, and helping you to this fortune, I have five hundred pounds. That's very little, because you have the ripe lips, and the clustering hair, and what not, all to yourself. For the third and last article, I require that you execute a bond to me, this day, binding yourself in the payment of these two sums, before noon of the day of your marriage with Madeline Bray. You have told me I can urge and press a point. I press this one, and will take nothing less than these terms. Accept them if you like. If not, marry her without me if you can. I shall still get my debt.'

To all entreaties, protestations, and offers of compromise between his own proposals and those which Arthur Gride had first suggested, Ralph was deaf as an adder. He would enter into no further discussion of the subject, and while old Arthur dilated upon the enormity of his demands and proposed modifications of them, approaching by degrees nearer and nearer to the terms he resisted, sat perfectly mute, looking with an air of quiet abstraction over the entries and papers in his pocket-book. Finding that it was impossible to make any impression upon his staunch friend, Arthur Gride, who had prepared himself for some such result before he came, consented with a heavy heart to the proposed treaty, and upon the spot filled up the bond required (Ralph kept such instruments handy), after exacting the condition that Mr. Nickleby should accompany him to Bray's lodgings that very hour, and open the negotiation at once, should circumstances appear auspicious and favourable to their designs.

In pursuance of this last understanding the worthy gentlemen went out together shortly afterwards, and Newman Noggs emerged, bottle in hand, from the cupboard, out of the upper door of which, at the imminent risk of detection, he had more than once thrust his red nose when such parts of the subject were under discussion as interested him most.

'I have no appetite now,' said Newman, putting the flask in his pocket. 'I've had my dinner.'

Having delivered this observation in a very grievous and doleful tone, Newman reached the door in one long limp, and came back again in another.

'I don't know who she may be, or what she may be,' he said: 'but I pity her with all my heart and soul; and I can't help her, nor can I any of the people against whom a hundred tricks, but none so vile as this, are plotted every day! Well, that adds to my pain, but not to theirs. The thing is no worse because I know it, and it tortures me as well as them. Gride and Nickleby! Good pair for a curricle. Oh roguery! roguery! roguery!'

With these reflections, and a very hard knock on the crown of his unfortunate hat at each repetition of the last word, Newman Noggs, whose brain was a little muddled by so much of the contents of the pocket-pistol as had found their way there during his recent concealment, went forth to seek such consolation as might be derivable from the beef and greens of some cheap eating-house.

Meanwhile the two plotters had betaken themselves to the same house whither Nicholas had repaired for the first time but a few mornings before, and having obtained access to Mr. Bray, and found his daughter from home, had by a train of the most masterly approaches that Ralph's utmost skill could frame, at length laid open the real object of their visit.

'There he sits, Mr. Bray,' said Ralph, as the invalid, not yet recovered from his surprise, reclined in his chair, looking alternately at him and Arthur Gride. 'What if he has had the ill-fortune to be one cause of your detention in this place? I have been another; men must live; you are too much a man of the world not to see that in its true light. We offer the best reparation in our power. Reparation! Here is an offer of marriage, that many a titled father would leap at, for his child. Mr. Arthur Gride, with the fortune of a prince. Think what a haul it is!'

'My daughter, sir,' returned Bray, haughtily, 'as I have brought her up, would be a rich recompense for the largest fortune that a man could bestow in exchange for her hand.'

'Precisely what I told you,' said the artful Ralph, turning to his friend, old Arthur. 'Precisely what made me consider the thing so fair and easy. There is no obligation on either side. You have money, and Miss Madeline has beauty and worth. She has youth, you have money. She has not money, you have not youth. Tit for tat, quits, a match of Heaven's own making!'

'Matches are made in Heaven, they say,' added Arthur Gride, leering hideously at the father-in-law he wanted. 'If we are married, it will be destiny, according to that.'

'Then think, Mr. Bray,' said Ralph, hastily substituting for this argument considerations more nearly allied to earth, 'think what a stake is involved in the acceptance or rejection of these proposals of my friend.'

'How can I accept or reject,' interrupted Mr. Bray, with an irritable consciousness that it really rested with him to decide. 'It is for my daughter to accept or reject; it is for my daughter. You know that.'

'True,' said Ralph, emphatically; 'but you have still the power to advise; to state the reasons for and against; to hint a wish.'

'To hint a wish, sir!' returned the debtor, proud and mean by turns, and selfish at all times. 'I am her father, am I not? Why should I hint, and beat about the bush? Do you suppose, like her mother's friends and my enemies—a curse upon them all!—that there is anything in what she has done for me but duty, sir, but duty? Or do you think that my having been unfortunate is a sufficient reason why our relative positions should be changed, and that she should command and I should obey? Hint a wish, too! Perhaps you think, because you see me in this place and scarcely able to leave this chair without assistance, that I am some broken-spirited dependent creature, without the courage or power to do what I may think best for my own child. Still the power to hint a wish! I hope so!'

'Pardon me,' returned Ralph, who thoroughly knew his man, and had taken his ground accordingly; 'you do not hear me out. I was about to say that your hinting a wish, even hinting a wish, would surely be equivalent to commanding.'

'Why, of course it would,' retorted Mr. Bray, in an exasperated tone. 'If you don't happen to have heard of the time, sir, I tell you that there was a time, when I carried every point in triumph against her mother's whole family, although they had power and wealth on their side, by my will alone.'

'Still,' rejoined Ralph, as mildly as his nature would allow him, 'you have not heard me out. You are a man yet qualified to shine in society, with many years of life before you; that is, if you lived in freer air, and under brighter skies, and chose your own companions. Gaiety is your element, you have shone in it before. Fashion and freedom for you. France, and an annuity that would support you there in luxury, would give you a new lease of life, would transfer you to a new existence. The town rang with your expensive pleasures once, and you could blaze up on a new scene again, profiting by experience, and living a little at others' cost, instead of letting others live at yours. What is there on the reverse side of the picture? What is there? I don't know which is the nearest churchyard, but a gravestone there, wherever it is, and a date, perhaps two years hence, perhaps twenty. That's all.'

Mr. Bray rested his elbow on the arm of his chair, and shaded his face with his hand.

'I speak plainly,' said Ralph, sitting down beside him, 'because I feel strongly. It's my interest that you should marry your daughter to my friend Gride, because then he sees me paid—in part, that is. I don't disguise it. I acknowledge it openly. But what interest have you in recommending her to such a step? Keep that in view. She might object, remonstrate, shed tears, talk of his being too old, and plead that her life would be rendered miserable. But what is it now?'

Several slight gestures on the part of the invalid showed that these arguments were no more lost upon him, than the smallest iota of his demeanour was upon Ralph.

'What is it now, I say,' pursued the wily usurer, 'or what has it a chance of being? If you died, indeed, the people you hate would make her happy. But can you bear the thought of that?'

'No!' returned Bray, urged by a vindictive impulse he could not repress.

'I should imagine not, indeed!' said Ralph, quietly. 'If she profits by anybody's death,' this was said in a lower tone, 'let it be by her husband's. Don't let her have to look back to yours, as the event from which to date a happier life. Where is the objection? Let me hear it stated. What is it? That her suitor is an old man? Why, how often do men of family and fortune, who haven't your excuse, but have all the means and superfluities of life within their reach, how often do they marry their daughters to old men, or (worse still) to young men without heads or hearts, to tickle some idle vanity, strengthen some family interest, or secure some seat in Parliament! Judge for her, sir, judge for her. You must know best, and she will live to thank you.'

'Hush! hush!' cried Mr. Bray, suddenly starting up, and covering Ralph's mouth with his trembling hand. 'I hear her at the door!'

There was a gleam of conscience in the shame and terror of this hasty action, which, in one short moment, tore the thin covering of sophistry from the cruel design, and laid it bare in all its meanness and heartless deformity. The father fell into his chair pale and trembling; Arthur Gride plucked and fumbled at his hat, and durst not raise his eyes from the floor; even Ralph crouched for the moment like a beaten hound, cowed by the presence of one young innocent girl!

The effect was almost as brief as sudden. Ralph was the first to recover himself, and observing Madeline's looks of alarm, entreated the poor girl to be composed, assuring her that there was no cause for fear.

'A sudden spasm,' said Ralph, glancing at Mr. Bray. 'He is quite well now.'

It might have moved a very hard and worldly heart to see the young and beautiful creature, whose certain misery they had been contriving but a minute before, throw her arms about her father's neck, and pour forth words of tender sympathy and love, the sweetest a father's ear can know, or child's lips form. But Ralph looked coldly on; and Arthur Gride, whose bleared eyes gloated only over the outward beauties, and were blind to the spirit which reigned within, evinced—a fantastic kind of warmth certainly, but not exactly that kind of warmth of feeling which the contemplation of virtue usually inspires.

'Madeline,' said her father, gently disengaging himself, 'it was nothing.'

'But you had that spasm yesterday, and it is terrible to see you in such pain. Can I do nothing for you?'

'Nothing just now. Here are two gentlemen, Madeline, one of whom you have seen before. She used to say,' added Mr. Bray, addressing Arthur Gride, 'that the sight of you always made me worse. That was natural, knowing what she did, and only what she did, of our connection and its results. Well, well. Perhaps she may change her mind on that point; girls have leave to change their minds, you know. You are very tired, my dear.'

'I am not, indeed.'

'Indeed you are. You do too much.'

'I wish I could do more.'

'I know you do, but you overtask your strength. This wretched life, my love, of daily labour and fatigue, is more than you can bear, I am sure it is. Poor Madeline!'

With these and many more kind words, Mr. Bray drew his daughter to him and kissed her cheek affectionately. Ralph, watching him sharply and closely in the meantime, made his way towards the door, and signed to Gride to follow him.

'You will communicate with us again?' said Ralph.

'Yes, yes,' returned Mr. Bray, hastily thrusting his daughter aside. 'In a week. Give me a week.'

'One week,' said Ralph, turning to his companion, 'from today. Good-morning. Miss Madeline, I kiss your hand.'

'We will shake hands, Gride,' said Mr. Bray, extending his, as old Arthur bowed. 'You mean well, no doubt. I am bound to say so now. If I owed you money, that was not your fault. Madeline, my love, your hand here.'

'Oh dear! If the young lady would condescent! Only the tips of her fingers,' said Arthur, hesitating and half retreating.

Madeline shrunk involuntarily from the goblin figure, but she placed the tips of her fingers in his hand and instantly withdrew them. After an ineffectual clutch, intended to detain and carry them to his lips, old Arthur gave his own fingers a mumbling kiss, and with many amorous distortions of visage went in pursuit of his friend, who was by this time in the street.

'What does he say, what does he say? What does the giant say to the pigmy?' inquired Arthur Gride, hobbling up to Ralph.

'What does the pigmy say to the giant?' rejoined Ralph, elevating his eyebrows and looking down upon his questioner.

'He doesn't know what to say,' replied Arthur Gride. 'He hopes and fears. But is she not a dainty morsel?'

'I have no great taste for beauty,' growled Ralph.

'But I have,' rejoined Arthur, rubbing his hands. 'Oh dear! How handsome her eyes looked when she was stooping over him! Such long lashes, such delicate fringe! She—she—looked at me so soft.'

'Not over-lovingly, I think,' said Ralph. 'Did she?'

'No, you think not?' replied old Arthur. 'But don't you think it can be brought about? Don't you think it can?'

Ralph looked at him with a contemptuous frown, and replied with a sneer, and between his teeth:

'Did you mark his telling her she was tired and did too much, and overtasked her strength?'

'Ay, ay. What of it?'

'When do you think he ever told her that before? The life is more than she can bear. Yes, yes. He'll change it for her.'

'D'ye think it's done?' inquired old Arthur, peering into his companion's face with half-closed eyes.

'I am sure it's done,' said Ralph. 'He is trying to deceive himself, even before our eyes, already. He is making believe that he thinks of her good and not his own. He is acting a virtuous part, and so considerate and affectionate, sir, that the daughter scarcely knew him. I saw a tear of surprise in her eye. There'll be a few more tears of surprise there before long, though of a different kind. Oh! we may wait with confidence for this day week.'

CHAPTER 48
Being for the Benefit of Mr. Vincent Crummles, and positively his last Appearance on this Stage

It was with a very sad and heavy heart, oppressed by many painful ideas, that Nicholas retraced his steps eastward and betook himself to the counting-house of Cheeryble Brothers. Whatever the idle hopes he had suffered himself to entertain, whatever the pleasant visions which had sprung up in his mind and grouped themselves round the fair image of Madeline Bray, they were now dispelled, and not a vestige of their gaiety and brightness remained.

It would be a poor compliment to Nicholas's better nature, and one which he was very far from deserving, to insinuate that the solution, and such a solution, of the mystery which had seemed to surround Madeline Bray, when he was ignorant even of her name, had damped his ardour or cooled the fervour of his admiration. If he had regarded her before, with such a passion as young men attracted by mere beauty and elegance may entertain, he was now conscious of much deeper and stronger feelings. But, reverence for the truth and purity of her heart, respect for the helplessness and loneliness of her situation, sympathy with the trials of one so young and fair and admiration of her great and noble spirit, all seemed to raise her far above his reach, and, while they imparted new depth and dignity to his love, to whisper that it was hopeless.

'I will keep my word, as I have pledged it to her,' said Nicholas, manfully. 'This is no common trust that I have to discharge, and I will perform the double duty that is imposed upon me most scrupulously and strictly. My secret feelings deserve no consideration in such a case as this, and they shall have none.'

Still, there were the secret feelings in existence just the same, and in secret Nicholas rather encouraged them than otherwise; reasoning (if he reasoned at all) that there they could do no harm to anybody but himself, and that if he kept them to himself from a sense of duty, he had an additional right to entertain himself with them as a reward for his heroism.

All these thoughts, coupled with what he had seen that morning and the anticipation of his next visit, rendered him a very dull and abstracted companion; so much so, indeed, that Tim Linkinwater suspected he must have made the mistake of a figure somewhere, which was preying upon his mind, and seriously conjured him, if such were the case, to make a clean breast and scratch it out, rather than have his whole life embittered by the tortures of remorse.

But in reply to these considerate representations, and many others both from Tim and Mr. Frank, Nicholas could only be brought to state that he was never merrier in his life; and so went on all day, and so went towards home at night, still turning over and over again the same subjects, thinking over and over again the same things, and arriving over and over again at the same conclusions.

In this pensive, wayward, and uncertain state, people are apt to lounge and loiter without knowing why, to read placards on the walls with great attention and without the smallest idea of one word of their contents, and to stare most earnestly through shop-windows at things which they don't see. It was thus that Nicholas found himself poring with the utmost interest over a large play-bill hanging outside a Minor Theatre which he had to pass on his way home, and reading a list of the actors and actresses who had promised to do honour to some approaching benefit, with as much gravity as if it had been a catalogue of the names of those ladies and gentlemen who stood highest upon the Book of Fate, and he had been looking anxiously for his own. He glanced at the top of the bill, with a smile at his own dulness, as he prepared to resume his walk, and there saw announced, in large letters with a large space between each of them, 'Positively the last appearance of Mr. Vincent Crummles of Provincial Celebrity!!!'

'Nonsense!' said Nicholas, turning back again. 'It can't be.'

But there it was. In one line by itself was an announcement of the first night of a new melodrama; in another line by itself was an announcement of the last six nights of an old one; a third line was devoted to the re-engagement of the unrivalled African Knife-swallower, who had kindly suffered himself to be prevailed upon to forego his country engagements for one week longer; a fourth line announced that Mr. Snittle Timberry, having recovered from his late severe indisposition, would have the honour of appearing that evening; a fifth line said that there were 'Cheers, Tears, and Laughter!' every night; a sixth, that that was positively the last appearance of Mr. Vincent Crummles of Provincial Celebrity.

'Surely it must be the same man,' thought Nicholas. 'There can't be two Vincent Crummleses.'

The better to settle this question he referred to the bill again, and finding that there was a Baron in the first piece, and that Roberto (his son) was enacted by one Master Crummles, and Spaletro (his nephew) by one Master Percy Crummles—their last appearances—and that, incidental to the piece, was a characteristic dance by the characters, and a castanet pas seul by the Infant Phenomenon—her last appearance—he no longer entertained any doubt; and presenting himself at the stage-door, and sending in a scrap of paper with 'Mr. Johnson' written thereon in pencil, was presently conducted by a Robber, with a very large belt and buckle round his waist, and very large leather gauntlets on his hands, into the presence of his former manager.

Mr. Crummles was unfeignedly glad to see him, and starting up from before a small dressing-glass, with one very bushy eyebrow stuck on crooked over his left eye, and the fellow eyebrow and the calf of one of his legs in his hand, embraced him cordially; at the same time observing, that it would do Mrs. Crummles's heart good to bid him goodbye before they went.

'You were always a favourite of hers, Johnson,' said Crummles, 'always were from the first. I was quite easy in my mind about you from that first day you dined with us. One that Mrs. Crummles took a fancy to, was sure to turn out right. Ah! Johnson, what a woman that is!'

'I am sincerely obliged to her for her kindness in this and all other respects,' said Nicholas. 'But where are you going, that you talk about bidding goodbye?'

'Haven't you seen it in the papers?' said Crummles, with some dignity.

'No,' replied Nicholas.

'I wonder at that,' said the manager. 'It was among the varieties. I had the paragraph here somewhere—but I don't know—oh, yes, here it is.'

So saying, Mr. Crummles, after pretending that he thought he must have lost it, produced a square inch of newspaper from the pocket of the pantaloons he wore in private life (which, together with the plain clothes of several other gentlemen, lay scattered about on a kind of dresser in the room), and gave it to Nicholas to read:

'The talented Vincent Crummles, long favourably known to fame as a country manager and actor of no ordinary pretensions, is about to cross the Atlantic on a histrionic expedition. Crummles is to be accompanied, we hear, by his lady and gifted family. We know no man superior to Crummles in his particular line of character, or one who, whether as a public or private individual, could carry with him the best wishes of a larger circle of friends. Crummles is certain to succeed.'

'Here's another bit,' said Mr. Crummles, handing over a still smaller scrap. 'This is from the notices to correspondents, this one.'

Nicholas read it aloud. '"Philo-Dramaticus. Crummles, the country manager and actor, cannot be more than forty-three, or forty-four years of age. Crummles is not a Prussian, having been born at Chelsea." Humph!' said Nicholas, 'that's an odd paragraph.'

'Very,' returned Crummles, scratching the side of his nose, and looking at Nicholas with an assumption of great unconcern. 'I can't think who puts these things in. I didn't.'

Still keeping his eye on Nicholas, Mr. Crummles shook his head twice or thrice with profound gravity, and remarking, that he could not for the life of him imagine how the newspapers found out the things they did, folded up the extracts and put them in his pocket again.

'I am astonished to hear this news,' said Nicholas. 'Going to America! You had no such thing in contemplation when I was with you.'

'No,' replied Crummles, 'I hadn't then. The fact is that Mrs. Crummles—most extraordinary woman, Johnson.' Here he broke off and whispered something in his ear.

'Oh!' said Nicholas, smiling. 'The prospect of an addition to your family?'

'The seventh addition, Johnson,' returned Mr. Crummles, solemnly. 'I thought such a child as the Phenomenon must have been a closer; but it seems we are to have another. She is a very remarkable woman.'

'I congratulate you,' said Nicholas, 'and I hope this may prove a phenomenon too.'

'Why, it's pretty sure to be something uncommon, I suppose,' rejoined Mr Crummles. 'The talent of the other three is principally in combat and serious pantomime. I should like this one to have a turn for juvenile tragedy; I understand they want something of that sort in America very much. However, we must take it as it comes. Perhaps it may have a genius for the tight-rope. It may have any sort of genius, in short, if it takes after its mother, Johnson, for she is an universal genius; but, whatever its genius is, that genius shall be developed.'

Expressing himself after these terms, Mr. Crummles put on his other eyebrow, and the calves of his legs, and then put on his legs, which were of a yellowish flesh-colour, and rather soiled about the knees, from frequent going down upon those joints, in curses, prayers, last struggles, and other strong passages.

While the ex-manager completed his toilet, he informed Nicholas that as he should have a fair start in America from the proceeds of a tolerably good engagement which he had been fortunate enough to obtain, and as he and Mrs Crummles could scarcely hope to act for ever (not being immortal, except in the breath of Fame and in a figurative sense) he had made up his mind to settle there permanently, in the hope of acquiring some land of his own which would support them in their old age, and which they could afterwards bequeath to their children. Nicholas, having highly commended the resolution, Mr. Crummles went on to impart such further intelligence relative to their mutual friends as he thought might prove interesting; informing Nicholas, among other things, that Miss Snevellicci was happily married to an affluent young wax-chandler who had supplied the theatre with candles, and that Mr. Lillyvick didn't dare to say his soul was his own, such was the tyrannical sway of Mrs. Lillyvick, who reigned paramount and supreme.

Nicholas responded to this confidence on the part of Mr. Crummles, by confiding to him his own name, situation, and prospects, and informing him, in as few general words as he could, of the circumstances which had led to their first acquaintance. After congratulating him with great heartiness on the improved state of his fortunes, Mr. Crummles gave him to understand that next morning he and his were to start for Liverpool, where the vessel lay which was to carry them from the shores of England, and that if Nicholas wished to take a last adieu of Mrs. Crummles, he must repair with him that night to a farewell supper, given in honour of the family at a neighbouring tavern; at which Mr. Snittle Timberry would preside, while the honours of the vice-chair would be sustained by the African Swallower.

The room being by this time very warm and somewhat crowded, in consequence of the influx of four gentlemen, who had just killed each other in the piece under representation, Nicholas accepted the invitation, and promised to return at the conclusion of the performances; preferring the cool air and twilight out of doors to the mingled perfume of gas, orange-peel, and gunpowder, which pervaded the hot and glaring theatre.

He availed himself of this interval to buy a silver snuff-box—the best his funds would afford—as a token of remembrance for Mr Crummles, and having purchased besides a pair of ear-rings for Mrs Crummles, a necklace for the Phenomenon, and a flaming shirt-pin for each of the young gentlemen, he refreshed himself with a walk, and returning a little after the appointed time, found the lights out, the theatre empty, the curtain raised for the night, and Mr. Crummles walking up and down the stage expecting his arrival.

'Timberry won't be long,' said Mr. Crummles. 'He played the audience out tonight. He does a faithful black in the last piece, and it takes him a little longer to wash himself.'

'A very unpleasant line of character, I should think?' said Nicholas.

'No, I don't know,' replied Mr. Crummles; 'it comes off easily enough, and there's only the face and neck. We had a first-tragedy man in our company once, who, when he played Othello, used to black himself all over. But that's feeling a part and going into it as if you meant it; it isn't usual; more's the pity.'

Mr. Snittle Timberry now appeared, arm-in-arm with the African Swallower, and, being introduced to Nicholas, raised his hat half a foot, and said he was proud to know him. The Swallower said the same, and looked and spoke remarkably like an Irishman.

'I see by the bills that you have been ill, sir,' said Nicholas to Mr Timberry. 'I hope you are none the worse for your exertions tonight?'

Mr. Timberry, in reply, shook his head with a gloomy air, tapped his chest several times with great significancy, and drawing his cloak more closely about him, said, 'But no matter, no matter. Come!'

It is observable that when people upon the stage are in any strait involving the very last extremity of weakness and exhaustion, they invariably perform feats of strength requiring great ingenuity and muscular power. Thus, a wounded prince or bandit chief, who is bleeding to death and too faint to move, except to the softest music (and then only upon his hands and knees), shall be seen to approach a cottage door for aid in such a series of writhings and twistings, and with such curlings up of the legs, and such rollings over and over, and such gettings up and tumblings down again, as could never be achieved save by a very strong man skilled in posture-making. And so natural did this sort of performance come to Mr. Snittle Timberry, that on their way out of the theatre and towards the tavern where the supper was to be holden, he testified the severity of his recent indisposition and its wasting effects upon the nervous system, by a series of gymnastic performances which were the admiration of all witnesses.

'Why this is indeed a joy I had not looked for!' said Mrs. Crummles, when Nicholas was presented.

'Nor I,' replied Nicholas. 'It is by a mere chance that I have this opportunity of seeing you, although I would have made a great exertion to have availed myself of it.'

'Here is one whom you know,' said Mrs. Crummles, thrusting forward the Phenomenon in a blue gauze frock, extensively flounced, and trousers of the same; 'and here another—and another,' presenting the Master Crummleses. 'And how is your friend, the faithful Digby?'

'Digby!' said Nicholas, forgetting at the instant that this had been Smike's theatrical name. 'Oh yes. He's quite—what am I saying?—he is very far from well.'

'How!' exclaimed Mrs. Crummles, with a tragic recoil.

'I fear,' said Nicholas, shaking his head, and making an attempt to smile, 'that your better-half would be more struck with him now than ever.'

'What mean you?' rejoined Mrs. Crummles, in her most popular manner. 'Whence comes this altered tone?'

'I mean that a dastardly enemy of mine has struck at me through him, and that while he thinks to torture me, he inflicts on him such agonies of terror and suspense as—You will excuse me, I am sure,' said Nicholas, checking himself. 'I should never speak of this, and never do, except to those who know the facts, but for a moment I forgot myself.'

With this hasty apology Nicholas stooped down to salute the Phenomenon, and changed the subject; inwardly cursing his precipitation, and very much wondering what Mrs. Crummles must think of so sudden an explosion.

That lady seemed to think very little about it, for the supper being by this time on table, she gave her hand to Nicholas and repaired with a stately step to the left hand of Mr. Snittle Timberry. Nicholas had the honour to support her, and Mr. Crummles was placed upon the chairman's right; the Phenomenon and the Master Crummleses sustained the vice.

The company amounted in number to some twenty-five or thirty, being composed of such members of the theatrical profession, then engaged or disengaged in London, as were numbered among the most intimate friends of Mr. and Mrs. Crummles. The ladies and gentlemen were pretty equally balanced; the expenses of the entertainment being defrayed by the latter, each of whom had the privilege of inviting one of the former as his guest.

It was upon the whole a very distinguished party, for independently of the lesser theatrical lights who clustered on this occasion round Mr. Snittle Timberry, there was a literary gentleman present who had dramatised in his time two hundred and forty-seven novels as fast as they had come out—some of them faster than they had come out—and who was a literary gentleman in consequence.

This gentleman sat on the left hand of Nicholas, to whom he was introduced by his friend the African Swallower, from the bottom of the table, with a high eulogium upon his fame and reputation.

'I am happy to know a gentleman of such great distinction,' said Nicholas, politely.

'Sir,' replied the wit, 'you're very welcome, I'm sure. The honour is reciprocal, sir, as I usually say when I dramatise a book. Did you ever hear a definition of fame, sir?'

'I have heard several,' replied Nicholas, with a smile. 'What is yours?'

'When I dramatise a book, sir,' said the literary gentleman, 'that's fame. For its author.'

'Oh, indeed!' rejoined Nicholas.

'That's fame, sir,' said the literary gentleman.

'So Richard Turpin, Tom King, and Jerry Abershaw have handed down to fame the names of those on whom they committed their most impudent robberies?' said Nicholas.

'I don't know anything about that, sir,' answered the literary gentleman.

'Shakespeare dramatised stories which had previously appeared in print, it is true,' observed Nicholas.

'Meaning Bill, sir?' said the literary gentleman. 'So he did. Bill was an adapter, certainly, so he was—and very well he adapted too—considering.'

'I was about to say,' rejoined Nicholas, 'that Shakespeare derived some of his plots from old tales and legends in general circulation; but it seems to me, that some of the gentlemen of your craft, at the present day, have shot very far beyond him—'

'You're quite right, sir,' interrupted the literary gentleman, leaning back in his chair and exercising his toothpick. 'Human intellect, sir, has progressed since his time, is progressing, will progress.'

'Shot beyond him, I mean,' resumed Nicholas, 'in quite another respect, for, whereas he brought within the magic circle of his genius, traditions peculiarly adapted for his purpose, and turned familiar things into constellations which should enlighten the world for ages, you drag within the magic circle of your dulness, subjects not at all adapted to the purposes of the stage, and debase as he exalted. For instance, you take the uncompleted books of living authors, fresh from their hands, wet from the press, cut, hack, and carve them to the powers and capacities of your actors, and the capability of your theatres, finish unfinished works, hastily and crudely vamp up ideas not yet worked out by their original projector, but which have doubtless cost him many thoughtful days and sleepless nights; by a comparison of incidents and dialogue, down to the very last word he may have written a fortnight before, do your utmost to anticipate his plot—all this without his permission, and against his will; and then, to crown the whole proceeding, publish in some mean pamphlet, an unmeaning farrago of garbled extracts from his work, to which your name as author, with the honourable distinction annexed, of having perpetrated a hundred other outrages of the same description. Now, show me the distinction between such pilfering as this, and picking a man's pocket in the street: unless, indeed, it be, that the legislature has a regard for pocket-handkerchiefs, and leaves men's brains, except when they are knocked out by violence, to take care of themselves.'

'Men must live, sir,' said the literary gentleman, shrugging his shoulders.

'That would be an equally fair plea in both cases,' replied Nicholas; 'but if you put it upon that ground, I have nothing more to say, than, that if I were a writer of books, and you a thirsty dramatist, I would rather pay your tavern score for six months, large as it might be, than have a niche in the Temple of Fame with you for the humblest corner of my pedestal, through six hundred generations.'

The conversation threatened to take a somewhat angry tone when it had arrived thus far, but Mrs. Crummles opportunely interposed to prevent its leading to any violent outbreak, by making some inquiries of the literary gentleman relative to the plots of the six new pieces which he had written by contract to introduce the African Knife-swallower in his various unrivalled performances. This speedily engaged him in an animated conversation with that lady, in the interest of which, all recollection of his recent discussion with Nicholas very quickly evaporated.

The board being now clear of the more substantial articles of food, and punch, wine, and spirits being placed upon it and handed about, the guests, who had been previously conversing in little groups of three or four, gradually fell off into a dead silence, while the majority of those present glanced from time to time at Mr. Snittle Timberry, and the bolder spirits did not even hesitate to strike the table with their knuckles, and plainly intimate their expectations, by uttering such encouragements as 'Now, Tim,' 'Wake up, Mr. Chairman,' 'All charged, sir, and waiting for a toast,' and so forth.

To these remonstrances Mr. Timberry deigned no other rejoinder than striking his chest and gasping for breath, and giving many other indications of being still the victim of indisposition—for a man must not make himself too cheap either on the stage or off—while Mr Crummles, who knew full well that he would be the subject of the forthcoming toast, sat gracefully in his chair with his arm thrown carelessly over the back, and now and then lifted his glass to his mouth and drank a little punch, with the same air with which he was accustomed to take long draughts of nothing, out of the pasteboard goblets in banquet scenes.

At length Mr. Snittle Timberry rose in the most approved attitude, with one hand in the breast of his waistcoat and the other on the nearest snuff-box, and having been received with great enthusiasm, proposed, with abundance of quotations, his friend Mr. Vincent Crummles: ending a pretty long speech by extending his right hand on one side and his left on the other, and severally calling upon Mr. and Mrs. Crummles to grasp the same. This done, Mr. Vincent Crummles returned thanks, and that done, the African Swallower proposed Mrs. Vincent Crummles, in affecting terms. Then were heard loud moans and sobs from Mrs. Crummles and the ladies, despite of which that heroic woman insisted upon returning thanks herself, which she did, in a manner and in a speech which has never been surpassed and seldom equalled. It then became the duty of Mr. Snittle Timberry to give the young Crummleses, which he did; after which Mr. Vincent Crummles, as their father, addressed the company in a supplementary speech, enlarging on their virtues, amiabilities, and excellences, and wishing that they were the sons and daughter of every lady and gentleman present. These solemnities having been succeeded by a decent interval, enlivened by musical and other entertainments, Mr. Crummles proposed that ornament of the profession, the African Swallower, his very dear friend, if he would allow him to call him so; which liberty (there being no particular reason why he should not allow it) the African Swallower graciously permitted. The literary gentleman was then about to be drunk, but it being discovered that he had been drunk for some time in another acceptation of the term, and was then asleep on the stairs, the intention was abandoned, and the honour transferred to the ladies. Finally, after a very long sitting, Mr Snittle Timberry vacated the chair, and the company with many adieux and embraces dispersed.

Nicholas waited to the last to give his little presents. When he had said goodbye all round and came to Mr. Crummles, he could not but mark the difference between their present separation and their parting at Portsmouth. Not a jot of his theatrical manner remained; he put out his hand with an air which, if he could have summoned it at will, would have made him the best actor of his day in homely parts, and when Nicholas shook it with the warmth he honestly felt, appeared thoroughly melted.

'We were a very happy little company, Johnson,' said poor Crummles. 'You and I never had a word. I shall be very glad tomorrow morning to think that I saw you again, but now I almost wish you hadn't come.'

Nicholas was about to return a cheerful reply, when he was greatly disconcerted by the sudden apparition of Mrs. Grudden, who it seemed had declined to attend the supper in order that she might rise earlier in the morning, and who now burst out of an adjoining bedroom, habited in very extraordinary white robes; and throwing her arms about his neck, hugged him with great affection.

'What! Are you going too?' said Nicholas, submitting with as good a grace as if she had been the finest young creature in the world.

'Going?' returned Mrs. Grudden. 'Lord ha' mercy, what do you think they'd do without me?'

Nicholas submitted to another hug with even a better grace than before, if that were possible, and waving his hat as cheerfully as he could, took farewell of the Vincent Crummleses.

CHAPTER 49
Chronicles the further Proceedings of the Nickleby Family, and the Sequel of the Adventure of the Gentleman in the Small-clothes

While Nicholas, absorbed in the one engrossing subject of interest which had recently opened upon him, occupied his leisure hours with thoughts of Madeline Bray, and in execution of the commissions which the anxiety of brother Charles in her behalf imposed upon him, saw her again and again, and each time with greater danger to his peace of mind and a more weakening effect upon the lofty resolutions he had formed, Mrs. Nickleby and Kate continued to live in peace and quiet, agitated by no other cares than those which were connected with certain harassing proceedings taken by Mr. Snawley for the recovery of his son, and their anxiety for Smike himself, whose health, long upon the wane, began to be so much affected by apprehension and uncertainty as sometimes to occasion both them and Nicholas considerable uneasiness, and even alarm.

It was no complaint or murmur on the part of the poor fellow himself that thus disturbed them. Ever eager to be employed in such slight services as he could render, and always anxious to repay his benefactors with cheerful and happy looks, less friendly eyes might have seen in him no cause for any misgiving. But there were times, and often too, when the sunken eye was too bright, the hollow cheek too flushed, the breath too thick and heavy in its course, the frame too feeble and exhausted, to escape their regard and notice.

There is a dread disease which so prepares its victim, as it were, for death; which so refines it of its grosser aspect, and throws around familiar looks unearthly indications of the coming change; a dread disease, in which the struggle between soul and body is so gradual, quiet, and solemn, and the result so sure, that day by day, and grain by grain, the mortal part wastes and withers away, so that the spirit grows light and sanguine with its lightening load, and, feeling immortality at hand, deems it but a new term of mortal life; a disease in which death and life are so strangely blended, that death takes the glow and hue of life, and life the gaunt and grisly form of death; a disease which medicine never cured, wealth never warded off, or poverty could boast exemption from; which sometimes moves in giant strides, and sometimes at a tardy sluggish pace, but, slow or quick, is ever sure and certain.

It was with some faint reference in his own mind to this disorder, though he would by no means admit it, even to himself, that Nicholas had already carried his faithful companion to a physician of great repute. There was no cause for immediate alarm, he said. There were no present symptoms which could be deemed conclusive. The constitution had been greatly tried and injured in childhood, but still it might not be—and that was all.

But he seemed to grow no worse, and, as it was not difficult to find a reason for these symptoms of illness in the shock and agitation he had recently undergone, Nicholas comforted himself with the hope that his poor friend would soon recover. This hope his mother and sister shared with him; and as the object of their joint solicitude seemed to have no uneasiness or despondency for himself, but each day answered with a quiet smile that he felt better than he had upon the day before, their fears abated, and the general happiness was by degrees restored.

Many and many a time in after years did Nicholas look back to this period of his life, and tread again the humble quiet homely scenes that rose up as of old before him. Many and many a time, in the twilight of a summer evening, or beside the flickering winter's fire—but not so often or so sadly then—would his thoughts wander back to these old days, and dwell with a pleasant sorrow upon every slight remembrance which they brought crowding home. The little room in which they had so often sat long after it was dark, figuring such happy futures; Kate's cheerful voice and merry laugh; how, if she were from home, they used to sit and watch for her return scarcely breaking silence but to say how dull it seemed without her; the glee with which poor Smike would start from the darkened corner where he used to sit, and hurry to admit her, and the tears they often saw upon his face, half wondering to see them too, and he so pleased and happy; every little incident, and even slight words and looks of those old days little heeded then, but well remembered when busy cares and trials were quite forgotten, came fresh and thick before him many and many a time, and, rustling above the dusty growth of years, came back green boughs of yesterday.

But there were other persons associated with these recollections, and many changes came about before they had being. A necessary reflection for the purposes of these adventures, which at once subside into their accustomed train, and shunning all flighty anticipations or wayward wanderings, pursue their steady and decorous course.

If the brothers Cheeryble, as they found Nicholas worthy of trust and confidence, bestowed upon him every day some new and substantial mark of kindness, they were not less mindful of those who depended on him. Various little presents to Mrs. Nickleby, always of the very things they most required, tended in no slight degree to the improvement and embellishment of the cottage. Kate's little store of trinkets became quite dazzling; and for company! If brother Charles and brother Ned failed to look in for at least a few minutes every Sunday, or one evening in the week, there was Mr Tim Linkinwater (who had never made half-a-dozen other acquaintances in all his life, and who took such delight in his new friends as no words can express) constantly coming and going in his evening walks, and stopping to rest; while Mr. Frank Cheeryble happened, by some strange conjunction of circumstances, to be passing the door on some business or other at least three nights in the week.

'He is the most attentive young man I ever saw, Kate,' said Mrs. Nickleby to her daughter one evening, when this last-named gentleman had been the subject of the worthy lady's eulogium for some time, and Kate had sat perfectly silent.

'Attentive, mama!' rejoined Kate.

'Bless my heart, Kate!' cried Mrs. Nickleby, with her wonted suddenness, 'what a colour you have got; why, you're quite flushed!'

'Oh, mama! what strange things you fancy!'

'It wasn't fancy, Kate, my dear, I'm certain of that,' returned her mother. 'However, it's gone now at any rate, so it don't much matter whether it was or not. What was it we were talking about? Oh! Mr. Frank. I never saw such attention in my life, never.'

'Surely you are not serious,' returned Kate, colouring again; and this time beyond all dispute.

'Not serious!' returned Mrs. Nickleby; 'why shouldn't I be serious? I'm sure I never was more serious. I will say that his politeness and attention to me is one of the most becoming, gratifying, pleasant things I have seen for a very long time. You don't often meet with such behaviour in young men, and it strikes one more when one does meet with it.'

'Oh! attention to you, mama,' rejoined Kate quickly—'oh yes.'

'Dear me, Kate,' retorted Mrs. Nickleby, 'what an extraordinary girl you are! Was it likely I should be talking of his attention to anybody else? I declare I'm quite sorry to think he should be in love with a German lady, that I am.'

'He said very positively that it was no such thing, mama,' returned Kate. 'Don't you remember his saying so that very first night he came here? Besides,' she added, in a more gentle tone, 'why should we be sorry if it is the case? What is it to us, mama?'

'Nothing to us, Kate, perhaps,' said Mrs. Nickleby, emphatically; 'but something to me, I confess. I like English people to be thorough English people, and not half English and half I don't know what. I shall tell him point-blank next time he comes, that I wish he would marry one of his own country-women; and see what he says to that.'

'Pray don't think of such a thing, mama,' returned Kate, hastily; 'not for the world. Consider. How very—'

'Well, my dear, how very what?' said Mrs. Nickleby, opening her eyes in great astonishment.

Before Kate had returned any reply, a queer little double knock announced that Miss La Creevy had called to see them; and when Miss La Creevy presented herself, Mrs. Nickleby, though strongly disposed to be argumentative on the previous question, forgot all about it in a gush of supposes about the coach she had come by; supposing that the man who drove must have been either the man in the shirt-sleeves or the man with the black eye; that whoever he was, he hadn't found that parasol she left inside last week; that no doubt they had stopped a long while at the Halfway House, coming down; or that perhaps being full, they had come straight on; and, lastly, that they, surely, must have passed Nicholas on the road.

'I saw nothing of him,' answered Miss La Creevy; 'but I saw that dear old soul Mr. Linkinwater.'

'Taking his evening walk, and coming on to rest here, before he turns back to the city, I'll be bound!' said Mrs. Nickleby.

'I should think he was,' returned Miss La Creevy; 'especially as young Mr Cheeryble was with him.'

'Surely that is no reason why Mr. Linkinwater should be coming here,' said Kate.

'Why I think it is, my dear,' said Miss La Creevy. 'For a young man, Mr Frank is not a very great walker; and I observe that he generally falls tired, and requires a good long rest, when he has come as far as this. But where is my friend?' said the little woman, looking about, after having glanced slyly at Kate. 'He has not been run away with again, has he?'

'Ah! where is Mr. Smike?' said Mrs. Nickleby; 'he was here this instant.'

Upon further inquiry, it turned out, to the good lady's unbounded astonishment, that Smike had, that moment, gone upstairs to bed.

'Well now,' said Mrs. Nickleby, 'he is the strangest creature! Last Tuesday—was it Tuesday? Yes, to be sure it was; you recollect, Kate, my dear, the very last time young Mr. Cheeryble was here—last Tuesday night he went off in just the same strange way, at the very moment the knock came to the door. It cannot be that he don't like company, because he is always fond of people who are fond of Nicholas, and I am sure young Mr. Cheeryble is. And the strangest thing is, that he does not go to bed; therefore it cannot be because he is tired. I know he doesn't go to bed, because my room is the next one, and when I went upstairs last Tuesday, hours after him, I found that he had not even taken his shoes off; and he had no candle, so he must have sat moping in the dark all the time. Now, upon my word,' said Mrs. Nickleby, 'when I come to think of it, that's very extraordinary!'

As the hearers did not echo this sentiment, but remained profoundly silent, either as not knowing what to say, or as being unwilling to interrupt, Mrs. Nickleby pursued the thread of her discourse after her own fashion.

'I hope,' said that lady, 'that this unaccountable conduct may not be the beginning of his taking to his bed and living there all his life, like the Thirsty Woman of Tutbury, or the Cock-lane Ghost, or some of those extraordinary creatures. One of them had some connection with our family. I forget, without looking back to some old letters I have upstairs, whether it was my great-grandfather who went to school with the Cock-lane Ghost, or the Thirsty Woman of Tutbury who went to school with my grandmother. Miss La Creevy, you know, of course. Which was it that didn't mind what the clergyman said? The Cock-lane Ghost or the Thirsty Woman of Tutbury?'

'The Cock-lane Ghost, I believe.'

'Then I have no doubt,' said Mrs. Nickleby, 'that it was with him my great-grandfather went to school; for I know the master of his school was a dissenter, and that would, in a great measure, account for the Cock-lane Ghost's behaving in such an improper manner to the clergyman when he grew up. Ah! Train up a Ghost—child, I mean—'

Any further reflections on this fruitful theme were abruptly cut short by the arrival of Tim Linkinwater and Mr. Frank Cheeryble; in the hurry of receiving whom, Mrs. Nickleby speedily lost sight of everything else.

'I am so sorry Nicholas is not at home,' said Mrs. Nickleby. 'Kate, my dear, you must be both Nicholas and yourself.'

'Miss Nickleby need be but herself,' said Frank. 'I—if I may venture to say so—oppose all change in her.'

'Then at all events she shall press you to stay,' returned Mrs. Nickleby. 'Mr. Linkinwater says ten minutes, but I cannot let you go so soon; Nicholas would be very much vexed, I am sure. Kate, my dear!'

In obedience to a great number of nods, and winks, and frowns of extra significance, Kate added her entreaties that the visitors would remain; but it was observable that she addressed them exclusively to Tim Linkinwater; and there was, besides, a certain embarrassment in her manner, which, although it was as far from impairing its graceful character as the tinge it communicated to her cheek was from diminishing her beauty, was obvious at a glance even to Mrs. Nickleby. Not being of a very speculative character, however, save under circumstances when her speculations could be put into words and uttered aloud, that discreet matron attributed the emotion to the circumstance of her daughter's not happening to have her best frock on: 'though I never saw her look better, certainly,' she reflected at the same time. Having settled the question in this way, and being most complacently satisfied that in this, and in all other instances, her conjecture could not fail to be the right one, Mrs Nickleby dismissed it from her thoughts, and inwardly congratulated herself on being so shrewd and knowing.

Nicholas did not come home nor did Smike reappear; but neither circumstance, to say the truth, had any great effect upon the little party, who were all in the best humour possible. Indeed, there sprung up quite a flirtation between Miss La Creevy and Tim Linkinwater, who said a thousand jocose and facetious things, and became, by degrees, quite gallant, not to say tender. Little Miss La Creevy, on her part, was in high spirits, and rallied Tim on having remained a bachelor all his life with so much success, that Tim was actually induced to declare, that if he could get anybody to have him, he didn't know but what he might change his condition even yet. Miss La Creevy earnestly recommended a lady she knew, who would exactly suit Mr. Linkinwater, and had a very comfortable property of her own; but this latter qualification had very little effect upon Tim, who manfully protested that fortune would be no object with him, but that true worth and cheerfulness of disposition were what a man should look for in a wife, and that if he had these, he could find money enough for the moderate wants of both. This avowal was considered so honourable to Tim, that neither Mrs. Nickleby nor Miss La Creevy could sufficiently extol it; and stimulated by their praises, Tim launched out into several other declarations also manifesting the disinterestedness of his heart, and a great devotion to the fair sex: which were received with no less approbation. This was done and said with a comical mixture of jest and earnest, and, leading to a great amount of laughter, made them very merry indeed.

Kate was commonly the life and soul of the conversation at home; but she was more silent than usual upon this occasion (perhaps because Tim and Miss La Creevy engrossed so much of it), and, keeping aloof from the talkers, sat at the window watching the shadows as the evening closed in, and enjoying the quiet beauty of the night, which seemed to have scarcely less attractions to Frank, who first lingered near, and then sat down beside, her. No doubt, there are a great many things to be said appropriate to a summer evening, and no doubt they are best said in a low voice, as being most suitable to the peace and serenity of the hour; long pauses, too, at times, and then an earnest word or so, and then another interval of silence which, somehow, does not seem like silence either, and perhaps now and then a hasty turning away of the head, or drooping of the eyes towards the ground, all these minor circumstances, with a disinclination to have candles introduced and a tendency to confuse hours with minutes, are doubtless mere influences of the time, as many lovely lips can clearly testify. Neither is there the slightest reason why Mrs Nickleby should have expressed surprise when, candles being at length brought in, Kate's bright eyes were unable to bear the light which obliged her to avert her face, and even to leave the room for some short time; because, when one has sat in the dark so long, candles are dazzling, and nothing can be more strictly natural than that such results should be produced, as all well-informed young people know. For that matter, old people know it too, or did know it once, but they forget these things sometimes, and more's the pity.

The good lady's surprise, however, did not end here. It was greatly increased when it was discovered that Kate had not the least appetite for supper: a discovery so alarming that there is no knowing in what unaccountable efforts of oratory Mrs. Nickleby's apprehensions might have been vented, if the general attention had not been attracted, at the moment, by a very strange and uncommon noise, proceeding, as the pale and trembling servant girl affirmed, and as everybody's sense of hearing seemed to affirm also, 'right down' the chimney of the adjoining room.

It being quite plain to the comprehension of all present that, however extraordinary and improbable it might appear, the noise did nevertheless proceed from the chimney in question; and the noise (which was a strange compound of various shuffling, sliding, rumbling, and struggling sounds, all muffled by the chimney) still continuing, Frank Cheeryble caught up a candle, and Tim Linkinwater the tongs, and they would have very quickly ascertained the cause of this disturbance if Mrs. Nickleby had not been taken very faint, and declined being left behind, on any account. This produced a short remonstrance, which terminated in their all proceeding to the troubled chamber in a body, excepting only Miss La Creevy, who, as the servant girl volunteered a confession of having been subject to fits in her infancy, remained with her to give the alarm and apply restoratives, in case of extremity.

Advancing to the door of the mysterious apartment, they were not a little surprised to hear a human voice, chanting with a highly elaborated expression of melancholy, and in tones of suffocation which a human voice might have produced from under five or six feather-beds of the best quality, the once popular air of 'Has she then failed in her truth, the beautiful maid I adore?' Nor, on bursting into the room without demanding a parley, was their astonishment lessened by the discovery that these romantic sounds certainly proceeded from the throat of some man up the chimney, of whom nothing was visible but a pair of legs, which were dangling above the grate; apparently feeling, with extreme anxiety, for the top bar whereon to effect a landing.

A sight so unusual and unbusiness-like as this, completely paralysed Tim Linkinwater, who, after one or two gentle pinches at the stranger's ankles, which were productive of no effect, stood clapping the tongs together, as if he were sharpening them for another assault, and did nothing else.

'This must be some drunken fellow,' said Frank. 'No thief would announce his presence thus.'

As he said this, with great indignation, he raised the candle to obtain a better view of the legs, and was darting forward to pull them down with very little ceremony, when Mrs. Nickleby, clasping her hands, uttered a sharp sound, something between a scream and an exclamation, and demanded to know whether the mysterious limbs were not clad in small-clothes and grey worsted stockings, or whether her eyes had deceived her.

'Yes,' cried Frank, looking a little closer. 'Small-clothes certainly, and—and—rough grey stockings, too. Do you know him, ma'am?'

'Kate, my dear,' said Mrs. Nickleby, deliberately sitting herself down in a chair with that sort of desperate resignation which seemed to imply that now matters had come to a crisis, and all disguise was useless, 'you will have the goodness, my love, to explain precisely how this matter stands. I have given him no encouragement—none whatever—not the least in the world. You know that, my dear, perfectly well. He was very respectful, exceedingly respectful, when he declared, as you were a witness to; still at the same time, if I am to be persecuted in this way, if vegetable what's-his-names and all kinds of garden-stuff are to strew my path out of doors, and gentlemen are to come choking up our chimneys at home, I really don't know—upon my word I do not know—what is to become of me. It's a very hard case—harder than anything I was ever exposed to, before I married your poor dear papa, though I suffered a good deal of annoyance then—but that, of course, I expected, and made up my mind for. When I was not nearly so old as you, my dear, there was a young gentleman who sat next us at church, who used, almost every Sunday, to cut my name in large letters in the front of his pew while the sermon was going on. It was gratifying, of course, naturally so, but still it was an annoyance, because the pew was in a very conspicuous place, and he was several times publicly taken out by the beadle for doing it. But that was nothing to this. This is a great deal worse, and a great deal more embarrassing. I would rather, Kate, my dear,' said Mrs. Nickleby, with great solemnity, and an effusion of tears: 'I would rather, I declare, have been a pig-faced lady, than be exposed to such a life as this!'

Frank Cheeryble and Tim Linkinwater looked, in irrepressible astonishment, first at each other and then at Kate, who felt that some explanation was necessary, but who, between her terror at the apparition of the legs, her fear lest their owner should be smothered, and her anxiety to give the least ridiculous solution of the mystery that it was capable of bearing, was quite unable to utter a single word.

'He gives me great pain,' continued Mrs. Nickleby, drying her eyes, 'great pain; but don't hurt a hair of his head, I beg. On no account hurt a hair of his head.'

It would not, under existing circumstances, have been quite so easy to hurt a hair of the gentleman's head as Mrs. Nickleby seemed to imagine, inasmuch as that part of his person was some feet up the chimney, which was by no means a wide one. But, as all this time he had never left off singing about the bankruptcy of the beautiful maid in respect of truth, and now began not only to croak very feebly, but to kick with great violence as if respiration became a task of difficulty, Frank Cheeryble, without further hesitation, pulled at the shorts and worsteds with such heartiness as to bring him floundering into the room with greater precipitation than he had quite calculated upon.

'Oh! yes, yes,' said Kate, directly the whole figure of this singular visitor appeared in this abrupt manner. 'I know who it is. Pray don't be rough with him. Is he hurt? I hope not. Oh, pray see if he is hurt.'

'He is not, I assure you,' replied Frank, handling the object of his surprise, after this appeal, with sudden tenderness and respect. 'He is not hurt in the least.'

'Don't let him come any nearer,' said Kate, retiring as far as she could.

'Oh, no, he shall not,' rejoined Frank. 'You see I have him secure here. But may I ask you what this means, and whether you expected this old gentleman?'

'Oh, no,' said Kate, 'of course not; but he—mama does not think so, I believe—but he is a mad gentleman who has escaped from the next house, and must have found an opportunity of secreting himself here.'

'Kate,' interposed Mrs. Nickleby with severe dignity, 'I am surprised at you.'

'Dear mama,' Kate gently remonstrated.

'I am surprised at you,' repeated Mrs. Nickleby; 'upon my word, Kate, I am quite astonished that you should join the persecutors of this unfortunate gentleman, when you know very well that they have the basest designs upon his property, and that that is the whole secret of it. It would be much kinder of you, Kate, to ask Mr. Linkinwater or Mr. Cheeryble to interfere in his behalf, and see him righted. You ought not to allow your feelings to influence you; it's not right, very far from it. What should my feelings be, do you suppose? If anybody ought to be indignant, who is it? I, of course, and very properly so. Still, at the same time, I wouldn't commit such an injustice for the world. No,' continued Mrs. Nickleby, drawing herself up, and looking another way with a kind of bashful stateliness; 'this gentleman will understand me when I tell him that I repeat the answer I gave him the other day; that I always will repeat it, though I do believe him to be sincere when I find him placing himself in such dreadful situations on my account; and that I request him to have the goodness to go away directly, or it will be impossible to keep his behaviour a secret from my son Nicholas. I am obliged to him, very much obliged to him, but I cannot listen to his addresses for a moment. It's quite impossible.'

While this address was in course of delivery, the old gentleman, with his nose and cheeks embellished with large patches of soot, sat upon the ground with his arms folded, eyeing the spectators in profound silence, and with a very majestic demeanour. He did not appear to take the smallest notice of what Mrs. Nickleby said, but when she ceased to speak he honoured her with a long stare, and inquired if she had quite finished.

'I have nothing more to say,' replied that lady modestly. 'I really cannot say anything more.'

'Very good,' said the old gentleman, raising his voice, 'then bring in the bottled lightning, a clean tumbler, and a corkscrew.'

Nobody executing this order, the old gentleman, after a short pause, raised his voice again and demanded a thunder sandwich. This article not being forthcoming either, he requested to be served with a fricassee of boot-tops and goldfish sauce, and then laughing heartily, gratified his hearers with a very long, very loud, and most melodious bellow.

But still Mrs. Nickleby, in reply to the significant looks of all about her, shook her head as though to assure them that she saw nothing whatever in all this, unless, indeed, it were a slight degree of eccentricity. She might have remained impressed with these opinions down to the latest moment of her life, but for a slight train of circumstances, which, trivial as they were, altered the whole complexion of the case.

It happened that Miss La Creevy, finding her patient in no very threatening condition, and being strongly impelled by curiosity to see what was going forward, bustled into the room while the old gentleman was in the very act of bellowing. It happened, too, that the instant the old gentleman saw her, he stopped short, skipped suddenly on his feet, and fell to kissing his hand violently: a change of demeanour which almost terrified the little portrait painter out of her senses, and caused her to retreat behind Tim Linkinwater with the utmost expedition.

'Aha!' cried the old gentleman, folding his hands, and squeezing them with great force against each other. 'I see her now; I see her now! My love, my life, my bride, my peerless beauty. She is come at last—at last—and all is gas and gaiters!'

Mrs. Nickleby looked rather disconcerted for a moment, but immediately recovering, nodded to Miss La Creevy and the other spectators several times, and frowned, and smiled gravely, giving them to understand that she saw where the mistake was, and would set it all to rights in a minute or two.

'She is come!' said the old gentleman, laying his hand upon his heart. 'Cormoran and Blunderbore! She is come! All the wealth I have is hers if she will take me for her slave. Where are grace, beauty, and blandishments, like those? In the Empress of Madagascar? No. In the Queen of Diamonds? No. In Mrs. Rowland, who every morning bathes in Kalydor for nothing? No. Melt all these down into one, with the three Graces, the nine Muses, and fourteen biscuit-bakers' daughters from Oxford Street, and make a woman half as lovely. Pho! I defy you.'

After uttering this rhapsody, the old gentleman snapped his fingers twenty or thirty times, and then subsided into an ecstatic contemplation of Miss La Creevy's charms. This affording Mrs. Nickleby a favourable opportunity of explanation, she went about it straight.

'I am sure,' said the worthy lady, with a prefatory cough, 'that it's a great relief, under such trying circumstances as these, to have anybody else mistaken for me—a very great relief; and it's a circumstance that never occurred before, although I have several times been mistaken for my daughter Kate. I have no doubt the people were very foolish, and perhaps ought to have known better, but still they did take me for her, and of course that was no fault of mine, and it would be very hard indeed if I was to be made responsible for it. However, in this instance, of course, I must feel that I should do exceedingly wrong if I suffered anybody—especially anybody that I am under great obligations to—to be made uncomfortable on my account. And therefore I think it my duty to tell that gentleman that he is mistaken, that I am the lady who he was told by some impertinent person was niece to the Council of Paving-stones, and that I do beg and entreat of him to go quietly away, if it's only for,' here Mrs. Nickleby simpered and hesitated, 'for my sake.'

It might have been expected that the old gentleman would have been penetrated to the heart by the delicacy and condescension of this appeal, and that he would at least have returned a courteous and suitable reply. What, then, was the shock which Mrs. Nickleby received, when, accosting her in the most unmistakable manner, he replied in a loud and sonorous voice: 'Avaunt! Cat!'

'Sir!' cried Mrs. Nickleby, in a faint tone.

'Cat!' repeated the old gentleman. 'Puss, Kit, Tit, Grimalkin, Tabby, Brindle! Whoosh!' with which last sound, uttered in a hissing manner between his teeth, the old gentleman swung his arms violently round and round, and at the same time alternately advanced on Mrs. Nickleby, and retreated from her, in that species of savage dance with which boys on market-days may be seen to frighten pigs, sheep, and other animals, when they give out obstinate indications of turning down a wrong street.

Mrs. Nickleby wasted no words, but uttered an exclamation of horror and surprise, and immediately fainted away.

'I'll attend to mama,' said Kate, hastily; 'I am not at all frightened. But pray take him away: pray take him away!'

Frank was not at all confident of his power of complying with this request, until he bethought himself of the stratagem of sending Miss La Creevy on a few paces in advance, and urging the old gentleman to follow her. It succeeded to a miracle; and he went away in a rapture of admiration, strongly guarded by Tim Linkinwater on one side, and Frank himself on the other.

'Kate,' murmured Mrs. Nickleby, reviving when the coast was clear, 'is he gone?'

She was assured that he was.

'I shall never forgive myself, Kate,' said Mrs. Nickleby. 'Never! That gentleman has lost his senses, and I am the unhappy cause.'

'You the cause!' said Kate, greatly astonished.

'I, my love,' replied Mrs. Nickleby, with a desperate calmness. 'You saw what he was the other day; you see what he is now. I told your brother, weeks and weeks ago, Kate, that I hoped a disappointment might not be too much for him. You see what a wreck he is. Making allowance for his being a little flighty, you know how rationally, and sensibly, and honourably he talked, when we saw him in the garden. You have heard the dreadful nonsense he has been guilty of this night, and the manner in which he has gone on with that poor unfortunate little old maid. Can anybody doubt how all this has been brought about?'

'I should scarcely think they could,' said Kate mildly.

'I should scarcely think so, either,' rejoined her mother. 'Well! if I am the unfortunate cause of this, I have the satisfaction of knowing that I am not to blame. I told Nicholas, I said to him, "Nicholas, my dear, we should be very careful how we proceed." He would scarcely hear me. If the matter had only been properly taken up at first, as I wished it to be! But you are both of you so like your poor papa. However, I have my consolation, and that should be enough for me!'

Washing her hands, thus, of all responsibility under this head, past, present, or to come, Mrs. Nickleby kindly added that she hoped her children might never have greater cause to reproach themselves than she had, and prepared herself to receive the escort, who soon returned with the intelligence that the old gentleman was safely housed, and that they found his custodians, who had been making merry with some friends, wholly ignorant of his absence.

Quiet being again restored, a delicious half-hour—so Frank called it, in the course of subsequent conversation with Tim Linkinwater as they were walking home—was spent in conversation, and Tim's watch at length apprising him that it was high time to depart, the ladies were left alone, though not without many offers on the part of Frank to remain until Nicholas arrived, no matter what hour of the night it might be, if, after the late neighbourly irruption, they entertained the least fear of being left to themselves. As their freedom from all further apprehension, however, left no pretext for his insisting on mounting guard, he was obliged to abandon the citadel, and to retire with the trusty Tim.

Nearly three hours of silence passed away. Kate blushed to find, when Nicholas returned, how long she had been sitting alone, occupied with her own thoughts.

'I really thought it had not been half an hour,' she said.

'They must have been pleasant thoughts, Kate,' rejoined Nicholas gaily, 'to make time pass away like that. What were they now?'

Kate was confused; she toyed with some trifle on the table, looked up and smiled, looked down and dropped a tear.

'Why, Kate,' said Nicholas, drawing his sister towards him and kissing her, 'let me see your face. No? Ah! that was but a glimpse; that's scarcely fair. A longer look than that, Kate. Come—and I'll read your thoughts for you.'

There was something in this proposition, albeit it was said without the slightest consciousness or application, which so alarmed his sister, that Nicholas laughingly changed the subject to domestic matters, and thus gathered, by degrees, as they left the room and went upstairs together, how lonely Smike had been all night—and by very slow degrees, too; for on this subject also, Kate seemed to speak with some reluctance.

'Poor fellow,' said Nicholas, tapping gently at his door, 'what can be the cause of all this?'

Kate was hanging on her brother's arm. The door being quickly opened, she had not time to disengage herself, before Smike, very pale and haggard, and completely dressed, confronted them.

'And have you not been to bed?' said Nicholas.

'N—n—no,' was the reply.

Nicholas gently detained his sister, who made an effort to retire; and asked, 'Why not?'

'I could not sleep,' said Smike, grasping the hand which his friend extended to him.

'You are not well?' rejoined Nicholas.

'I am better, indeed. A great deal better,' said Smike quickly.

'Then why do you give way to these fits of melancholy?' inquired Nicholas, in his kindest manner; 'or why not tell us the cause? You grow a different creature, Smike.'

'I do; I know I do,' he replied. 'I will tell you the reason one day, but not now. I hate myself for this; you are all so good and kind. But I cannot help it. My heart is very full; you do not know how full it is.'

He wrung Nicholas's hand before he released it; and glancing, for a moment, at the brother and sister as they stood together, as if there were something in their strong affection which touched him very deeply, withdrew into his chamber, and was soon the only watcher under that quiet roof.

CHAPTER 50
Involves a serious Catastrophe

The little race-course at Hampton was in the full tide and height of its gaiety; the day as dazzling as day could be; the sun high in the cloudless sky, and shining in its fullest splendour. Every gaudy colour that fluttered in the air from carriage seat and garish tent top, shone out in its gaudiest hues. Old dingy flags grew new again, faded gilding was re-burnished, stained rotten canvas looked a snowy white, the very beggars' rags were freshened up, and sentiment quite forgot its charity in its fervent admiration of poverty so picturesque.

It was one of those scenes of life and animation, caught in its very brightest and freshest moments, which can scarcely fail to please; for if the eye be tired of show and glare, or the ear be weary with a ceaseless round of noise, the one may repose, turn almost where it will, on eager, happy, and expectant faces, and the other deaden all consciousness of more annoying sounds in those of mirth and exhilaration. Even the sunburnt faces of gypsy children, half naked though they be, suggest a drop of comfort. It is a pleasant thing to see that the sun has been there; to know that the air and light are on them every day; to feel that they are children, and lead children's lives; that if their pillows be damp, it is with the dews of Heaven, and not with tears; that the limbs of their girls are free, and that they are not crippled by distortions, imposing an unnatural and horrible penance upon their sex; that their lives are spent, from day to day, at least among the waving trees, and not in the midst of dreadful engines which make young children old before they know what childhood is, and give them the exhaustion and infirmity of age, without, like age, the privilege to die. God send that old nursery tales were true, and that gypsies stole such children by the score!

The great race of the day had just been run; and the close lines of people, on either side of the course, suddenly breaking up and pouring into it, imparted a new liveliness to the scene, which was again all busy movement. Some hurried eagerly to catch a glimpse of the winning horse; others darted to and fro, searching, no less eagerly, for the carriages they had left in quest of better stations. Here, a little knot gathered round a pea and thimble table to watch the plucking of some unhappy greenhorn; and there, another proprietor with his confederates in various disguises—one man in spectacles; another, with an eyeglass and a stylish hat; a third, dressed as a farmer well to do in the world, with his top-coat over his arm and his flash notes in a large leathern pocket-book; and all with heavy-handled whips to represent most innocent country fellows who had trotted there on horseback—sought, by loud and noisy talk and pretended play, to entrap some unwary customer, while the gentlemen confederates (of more villainous aspect still, in clean linen and good clothes), betrayed their close interest in the concern by the anxious furtive glance they cast on all new comers. These would be hanging on the outskirts of a wide circle of people assembled round some itinerant juggler, opposed, in his turn, by a noisy band of music, or the classic game of 'Ring the Bull,' while ventriloquists holding dialogues with wooden dolls, and fortune-telling women smothering the cries of real babies, divided with them, and many more, the general attention of the company. Drinking-tents were full, glasses began to clink in carriages, hampers to be unpacked, tempting provisions to be set forth, knives and forks to rattle, champagne corks to fly, eyes to brighten that were not dull before, and pickpockets to count their gains during the last heat. The attention so recently strained on one object of interest, was now divided among a hundred; and look where you would, there was a motley assemblage of feasting, laughing, talking, begging, gambling, and mummery.

Of the gambling-booths there was a plentiful show, flourishing in all the splendour of carpeted ground, striped hangings, crimson cloth, pinnacled roofs, geranium pots, and livery servants. There were the Stranger's club-house, the Athenaeum club-house, the Hampton club-house, the St James's club-house, and half a mile of club-houses to play in; and there were Rouge-Et-Noir, French hazard, and other games to play at. It is into one of these booths that our story takes its way.

Fitted up with three tables for the purposes of play, and crowded with players and lookers on, it was, although the largest place of the kind upon the course, intensely hot, notwithstanding that a portion of the canvas roof was rolled back to admit more air, and there were two doors for a free passage in and out. Excepting one or two men who, each with a long roll of half-crowns, chequered with a few stray sovereigns, in his left hand, staked their money at every roll of the ball with a business-like sedateness which showed that they were used to it, and had been playing all day, and most probably all the day before, there was no very distinctive character about the players, who were chiefly young men, apparently attracted by curiosity, or staking small sums as part of the amusement of the day, with no very great interest in winning or losing. There were two persons present, however, who, as peculiarly good specimens of a class, deserve a passing notice.

Of these, one was a man of six or eight and fifty, who sat on a chair near one of the entrances of the booth, with his hands folded on the top of his stick, and his chin appearing above them. He was a tall, fat, long-bodied man, buttoned up to the throat in a light green coat, which made his body look still longer than it was. He wore, besides, drab breeches and gaiters, a white neckerchief, and a broad-brimmed white hat. Amid all the buzzing noise of the games, and the perpetual passing in and out of the people, he seemed perfectly calm and abstracted, without the smallest particle of excitement in his composition. He exhibited no indication of weariness, nor, to a casual observer, of interest either. There he sat, quite still and collected. Sometimes, but very rarely, he nodded to some passing face, or beckoned to a waiter to obey a call from one of the tables. The next instant he subsided into his old state. He might have been some profoundly deaf old gentleman, who had come in to take a rest, or he might have been patiently waiting for a friend, without the least consciousness of anybody's presence, or fixed in a trance, or under the influence of opium. People turned round and looked at him; he made no gesture, caught nobody's eye, let them pass away, and others come on and be succeeded by others, and took no notice. When he did move, it seemed wonderful how he could have seen anything to occasion it. And so, in truth, it was. But there was not a face that passed in or out, which this man failed to see; not a gesture at any one of the three tables that was lost upon him; not a word, spoken by the bankers, but reached his ear; not a winner or loser he could not have marked. And he was the proprietor of the place.

The other presided over the Rouge-Et-Noir table. He was probably some ten years younger, and was a plump, paunchy, sturdy-looking fellow, with his under-lip a little pursed, from a habit of counting money inwardly as he paid it, but with no decidedly bad expression in his face, which was rather an honest and jolly one than otherwise. He wore no coat, the weather being hot, and stood behind the table with a huge mound of crowns and half-crowns before him, and a cash-box for notes. This game was constantly playing. Perhaps twenty people would be staking at the same time. This man had to roll the ball, to watch the stakes as they were laid down, to gather them off the colour which lost, to pay those who won, to do it all with the utmost dispatch, to roll the ball again, and to keep this game perpetually alive. He did it all with a rapidity absolutely marvellous; never hesitating, never making a mistake, never stopping, and never ceasing to repeat such unconnected phrases as the following, which, partly from habit, and partly to have something appropriate and business-like to say, he constantly poured out with the same monotonous emphasis, and in nearly the same order, all day long:

'Rooge-a-nore from Paris! Gentlemen, make your game and back your own opinions—any time while the ball rolls—rooge-a-nore from Paris, gentlemen, it's a French game, gentlemen, I brought it over myself, I did indeed!—Rooge-a-nore from Paris—black wins—black—stop a minute, sir, and I'll pay you, directly—two there, half a pound there, three there—and one there—gentlemen, the ball's a rolling—any time, sir, while the ball rolls!—The beauty of this game is, that you can double your stakes or put down your money, gentlemen, any time while the ball rolls—black again—black wins—I never saw such a thing—I never did, in all my life, upon my word I never did; if any gentleman had been backing the black in the last five minutes he must have won five-and-forty pound in four rolls of the ball, he must indeed. Gentlemen, we've port, sherry, cigars, and most excellent champagne. Here, wai-ter, bring a bottle of champagne, and let's have a dozen or fifteen cigars here—and let's be comfortable, gentlemen—and bring some clean glasses—any time while the ball rolls!—I lost one hundred and thirty-seven pound yesterday, gentlemen, at one roll of the ball, I did indeed!—how do you do, sir?' (recognising some knowing gentleman without any halt or change of voice, and giving a wink so slight that it seems an accident), 'will you take a glass of sherry, sir?—here, wai-ter! bring a clean glass, and hand the sherry to this gentleman—and hand it round, will you, waiter?—this is the rooge-a-nore from Paris, gentlemen—any time while the ball rolls!— gentlemen, make your game, and back your own opinions—it's the rooge-a-nore from Paris— quite a new game, I brought it over myself, I did indeed—gentlemen, the ball's a-rolling!'

This officer was busily plying his vocation when half-a-dozen persons sauntered through the booth, to whom, but without stopping either in his speech or work, he bowed respectfully; at the same time directing, by a look, the attention of a man beside him to the tallest figure in the group, in recognition of whom the proprietor pulled off his hat. This was Sir Mulberry Hawk, with whom were his friend and pupil, and a small train of gentlemanly-dressed men, of characters more doubtful than obscure.

The proprietor, in a low voice, bade Sir Mulberry good-day. Sir Mulberry, in the same tone, bade the proprietor go to the devil, and turned to speak with his friends.

There was evidently an irritable consciousness about him that he was an object of curiosity, on this first occasion of showing himself in public after the accident that had befallen him; and it was easy to perceive that he appeared on the race-course, that day, more in the hope of meeting with a great many people who knew him, and so getting over as much as possible of the annoyance at once, than with any purpose of enjoying the sport. There yet remained a slight scar upon his face, and whenever he was recognised, as he was almost every minute by people sauntering in and out, he made a restless effort to conceal it with his glove; showing how keenly he felt the disgrace he had undergone.

'Ah! Hawk,' said one very sprucely-dressed personage in a Newmarket coat, a choice neckerchief, and all other accessories of the most unexceptionable kind. 'How d'ye do, old fellow?'

This was a rival trainer of young noblemen and gentlemen, and the person of all others whom Sir Mulberry most hated and dreaded to meet. They shook hands with excessive cordiality.

'And how are you now, old fellow, hey?'

'Quite well, quite well,' said Sir Mulberry.

'That's right,' said the other. 'How d'ye do, Verisopht? He's a little pulled down, our friend here. Rather out of condition still, hey?'

It should be observed that the gentleman had very white teeth, and that when there was no excuse for laughing, he generally finished with the same monosyllable, which he uttered so as to display them.

'He's in very good condition; there's nothing the matter with him,' said the young man carelessly.

'Upon my soul I'm glad to hear it,' rejoined the other. 'Have you just returned from Brussels?'

'We only reached town late last night,' said Lord Frederick. Sir Mulberry turned away to speak to one of his own party, and feigned not to hear.

'Now, upon my life,' said the friend, affecting to speak in a whisper, 'it's an uncommonly bold and game thing in Hawk to show himself so soon. I say it advisedly; there's a vast deal of courage in it. You see he has just rusticated long enough to excite curiosity, and not long enough for men to have forgotten that deuced unpleasant—by-the-bye—you know the rights of the affair, of course? Why did you never give those confounded papers the lie? I seldom read the papers, but I looked in the papers for that, and may I be—'

'Look in the papers,' interrupted Sir Mulberry, turning suddenly round, 'tomorrow—no, next day, will you?'

'Upon my life, my dear fellow, I seldom or never read the papers,' said the other, shrugging his shoulders, 'but I will, at your recommendation. What shall I look for?'

'Good day,' said Sir Mulberry, turning abruptly on his heel, and drawing his pupil with him. Falling, again, into the loitering, careless pace at which they had entered, they lounged out, arm in arm.

'I won't give him a case of murder to read,' muttered Sir Mulberry with an oath; 'but it shall be something very near it if whipcord cuts and bludgeons bruise.'

His companion said nothing, but there was something in his manner which galled Sir Mulberry to add, with nearly as much ferocity as if his friend had been Nicholas himself:

'I sent Jenkins to old Nickleby before eight o'clock this morning. He's a staunch one; he was back with me before the messenger. I had it all from him in the first five minutes. I know where this hound is to be met with; time and place both. But there's no need to talk; tomorrow will soon be here.'

'And wha-at's to be done tomorrow?' inquired Lord Frederick.

Sir Mulberry Hawk honoured him with an angry glance, but condescended to return no verbal answer to this inquiry. Both walked sullenly on, as though their thoughts were busily occupied, until they were quite clear of the crowd, and almost alone, when Sir Mulberry wheeled round to return.

'Stop,' said his companion, 'I want to speak to you in earnest. Don't turn back. Let us walk here, a few minutes.'

'What have you to say to me, that you could not say yonder as well as here?' returned his Mentor, disengaging his arm.

'Hawk,' rejoined the other, 'tell me; I must know.'

'Must know,' interrupted the other disdainfully. 'Whew! Go on. If you must know, of course there's no escape for me. Must know!'

'Must ask then,' returned Lord Frederick, 'and must press you for a plain and straightforward answer. Is what you have just said only a mere whim of the moment, occasioned by your being out of humour and irritated, or is it your serious intention, and one that you have actually contemplated?'

'Why, don't you remember what passed on the subject one night, when I was laid up with a broken limb?' said Sir Mulberry, with a sneer.

'Perfectly well.'

'Then take that for an answer, in the devil's name,' replied Sir Mulberry, 'and ask me for no other.'

Such was the ascendancy he had acquired over his dupe, and such the latter's general habit of submission, that, for the moment, the young man seemed half afraid to pursue the subject. He soon overcame this feeling, however, if it had restrained him at all, and retorted angrily:

'If I remember what passed at the time you speak of, I expressed a strong opinion on this subject, and said that, with my knowledge or consent, you never should do what you threaten now.'

'Will you prevent me?' asked Sir Mulberry, with a laugh.

'Ye-es, if I can,' returned the other, promptly.

'A very proper saving clause, that last,' said Sir Mulberry; 'and one you stand in need of. Oh! look to your own business, and leave me to look to mine.'

'This is mine,' retorted Lord Frederick. 'I make it mine; I will make it mine. It's mine already. I am more compromised than I should be, as it is.'

'Do as you please, and what you please, for yourself,' said Sir Mulberry, affecting an easy good-humour. 'Surely that must content you! Do nothing for me; that's all. I advise no man to interfere in proceedings that I choose to take. I am sure you know me better than to do so. The fact is, I see, you mean to offer me advice. It is well meant, I have no doubt, but I reject it. Now, if you please, we will return to the carriage. I find no entertainment here, but quite the reverse. If we prolong this conversation, we might quarrel, which would be no proof of wisdom in either you or me.'

With this rejoinder, and waiting for no further discussion, Sir Mulberry Hawk yawned, and very leisurely turned back.

There was not a little tact and knowledge of the young lord's disposition in this mode of treating him. Sir Mulberry clearly saw that if his dominion were to last, it must be established now. He knew that the moment he became violent, the young man would become violent too. He had, many times, been enabled to strengthen his influence, when any circumstance had occurred to weaken it, by adopting this cool and laconic style; and he trusted to it now, with very little doubt of its entire success.

But while he did this, and wore the most careless and indifferent deportment that his practised arts enabled him to assume, he inwardly resolved, not only to visit all the mortification of being compelled to suppress his feelings, with additional severity upon Nicholas, but also to make the young lord pay dearly for it, one day, in some shape or other. So long as he had been a passive instrument in his hands, Sir Mulberry had regarded him with no other feeling than contempt; but, now that he presumed to avow opinions in opposition to his, and even to turn upon him with a lofty tone and an air of superiority, he began to hate him. Conscious that, in the vilest and most worthless sense of the term, he was dependent upon the weak young lord, Sir Mulberry could the less brook humiliation at his hands; and when he began to dislike him he measured his dislike—as men often do—by the extent of the injuries he had inflicted upon its object. When it is remembered that Sir Mulberry Hawk had plundered, duped, deceived, and fooled his pupil in every possible way, it will not be wondered at, that, beginning to hate him, he began to hate him cordially.

On the other hand, the young lord having thought—which he very seldom did about anything—and seriously too, upon the affair with Nicholas, and the circumstances which led to it, had arrived at a manly and honest conclusion. Sir Mulberry's coarse and insulting behaviour on the occasion in question had produced a deep impression on his mind; a strong suspicion of his having led him on to pursue Miss Nickleby for purposes of his own, had been lurking there for some time; he was really ashamed of his share in the transaction, and deeply mortified by the misgiving that he had been gulled. He had had sufficient leisure to reflect upon these things, during their late retirement; and, at times, when his careless and indolent nature would permit, had availed himself of the opportunity. Slight circumstances, too, had occurred to increase his suspicion. It wanted but a very slight circumstance to kindle his wrath against Sir Mulberry. This his disdainful and insolent tone in their recent conversation (the only one they had held upon the subject since the period to which Sir Mulberry referred), effected.

Thus they rejoined their friends: each with causes of dislike against the other rankling in his breast: and the young man haunted, besides, with thoughts of the vindictive retaliation which was threatened against Nicholas, and the determination to prevent it by some strong step, if possible. But this was not all. Sir Mulberry, conceiving that he had silenced him effectually, could not suppress his triumph, or forbear from following up what he conceived to be his advantage. Mr. Pyke was there, and Mr. Pluck was there, and Colonel Chowser, and other gentlemen of the same caste, and it was a great point for Sir Mulberry to show them that he had not lost his influence. At first, the young lord contented himself with a silent determination to take measures for withdrawing himself from the connection immediately. By degrees, he grew more angry, and was exasperated by jests and familiarities which, a few hours before, would have been a source of amusement to him. This did not serve him; for, at such bantering or retort as suited the company, he was no match for Sir Mulberry. Still, no violent rupture took place. They returned to town; Messrs Pyke and Pluck and other gentlemen frequently protesting, on the way thither, that Sir Mulberry had never been in such tiptop spirits in all his life.

They dined together, sumptuously. The wine flowed freely, as indeed it had done all day. Sir Mulberry drank to recompense himself for his recent abstinence; the young lord, to drown his indignation; and the remainder of the party, because the wine was of the best and they had nothing to pay. It was nearly midnight when they rushed out, wild, burning with wine, their blood boiling, and their brains on fire, to the gaming-table.

Here, they encountered another party, mad like themselves. The excitement of play, hot rooms, and glaring lights was not calculated to allay the fever of the time. In that giddy whirl of noise and confusion, the men were delirious. Who thought of money, ruin, or the morrow, in the savage intoxication of the moment? More wine was called for, glass after glass was drained, their parched and scalding mouths were cracked with thirst. Down poured the wine like oil on blazing fire. And still the riot went on. The debauchery gained its height; glasses were dashed upon the floor by hands that could not carry them to lips; oaths were shouted out by lips which could scarcely form the words to vent them in; drunken losers cursed and roared; some mounted on the tables, waving bottles above their heads and bidding defiance to the rest; some danced, some sang, some tore the cards and raved. Tumult and frenzy reigned supreme; when a noise arose that drowned all others, and two men, seizing each other by the throat, struggled into the middle of the room.

A dozen voices, until now unheard, called aloud to part them. Those who had kept themselves cool, to win, and who earned their living in such scenes, threw themselves upon the combatants, and, forcing them asunder, dragged them some space apart.

'Let me go!' cried Sir Mulberry, in a thick hoarse voice; 'he struck me! Do you hear? I say, he struck me. Have I a friend here? Who is this? Westwood. Do you hear me say he struck me?'

'I hear, I hear,' replied one of those who held him. 'Come away for tonight!'

'I will not, by G—,' he replied. 'A dozen men about us saw the blow.'

'Tomorrow will be ample time,' said the friend.

'It will not be ample time!' cried Sir Mulberry. 'Tonight, at once, here!' His passion was so great, that he could not articulate, but stood clenching his fist, tearing his hair, and stamping upon the ground.

'What is this, my lord?' said one of those who surrounded him. 'Have blows passed?'

'One blow has,' was the panting reply. 'I struck him. I proclaim it to all here! I struck him, and he knows why. I say, with him, let this quarrel be adjusted now. Captain Adams,' said the young lord, looking hurriedly about him, and addressing one of those who had interposed, 'let me speak with you, I beg.'

The person addressed stepped forward, and taking the young man's arm, they retired together, followed shortly afterwards by Sir Mulberry and his friend.

It was a profligate haunt of the worst repute, and not a place in which such an affair was likely to awaken any sympathy for either party, or to call forth any further remonstrance or interposition. Elsewhere, its further progress would have been instantly prevented, and time allowed for sober and cool reflection; but not there. Disturbed in their orgies, the party broke up; some reeled away with looks of tipsy gravity; others withdrew noisily discussing what had just occurred; the gentlemen of honour who lived upon their winnings remarked to each other, as they went out, that Hawk was a good shot; and those who had been most noisy, fell fast asleep upon the sofas, and thought no more about it.

Meanwhile, the two seconds, as they may be called now, after a long conference, each with his principal, met together in another room. Both utterly heartless, both men upon town, both thoroughly initiated in its worst vices, both deeply in debt, both fallen from some higher estate, both addicted to every depravity for which society can find some genteel name and plead its most depraving conventionalities as an excuse, they were naturally gentlemen of most unblemished honour themselves, and of great nicety concerning the honour of other people.

These two gentlemen were unusually cheerful just now; for the affair was pretty certain to make some noise, and could scarcely fail to enhance their reputations.

'This is an awkward affair, Adams,' said Mr. Westwood, drawing himself up.

'Very,' returned the captain; 'a blow has been struck, and there is but one course, of course.'

'No apology, I suppose?' said Mr. Westwood.

'Not a syllable, sir, from my man, if we talk till doomsday,' returned the captain. 'The original cause of dispute, I understand, was some girl or other, to whom your principal applied certain terms, which Lord Frederick, defending the girl, repelled. But this led to a long recrimination upon a great many sore subjects, charges, and counter-charges. Sir Mulberry was sarcastic; Lord Frederick was excited, and struck him in the heat of provocation, and under circumstances of great aggravation. That blow, unless there is a full retraction on the part of Sir Mulberry, Lord Frederick is ready to justify.'

'There is no more to be said,' returned the other, 'but to settle the hour and the place of meeting. It's a responsibility; but there is a strong feeling to have it over. Do you object to say at sunrise?'

'Sharp work,' replied the captain, referring to his watch; 'however, as this seems to have been a long time breeding, and negotiation is only a waste of words, no.'

'Something may possibly be said, out of doors, after what passed in the other room, which renders it desirable that we should be off without delay, and quite clear of town,' said Mr. Westwood. 'What do you say to one of the meadows opposite Twickenham, by the river-side?'

The captain saw no objection.

'Shall we join company in the avenue of trees which leads from Petersham to Ham House, and settle the exact spot when we arrive there?' said Mr Westwood.

To this the captain also assented. After a few other preliminaries, equally brief, and having settled the road each party should take to avoid suspicion, they separated.

'We shall just have comfortable time, my lord,' said the captain, when he had communicated the arrangements, 'to call at my rooms for a case of pistols, and then jog coolly down. If you will allow me to dismiss your servant, we'll take my cab; for yours, perhaps, might be recognised.'

What a contrast, when they reached the street, to the scene they had just left! It was already daybreak. For the flaring yellow light within, was substituted the clear, bright, glorious morning; for a hot, close atmosphere, tainted with the smell of expiring lamps, and reeking with the steams of riot and dissipation, the free, fresh, wholesome air. But to the fevered head on which that cool air blew, it seemed to come laden with remorse for time misspent and countless opportunities neglected. With throbbing veins and burning skin, eyes wild and heavy, thoughts hurried and disordered, he felt as though the light were a reproach, and shrunk involuntarily from the day as if he were some foul and hideous thing.

'Shivering?' said the captain. 'You are cold.'

'Rather.'

'It does strike cool, coming out of those hot rooms. Wrap that cloak about you. So, so; now we're off.'

They rattled through the quiet streets, made their call at the captain's lodgings, cleared the town, and emerged upon the open road, without hindrance or molestation.

Fields, trees, gardens, hedges, everything looked very beautiful; the young man scarcely seemed to have noticed them before, though he had passed the same objects a thousand times.

There was a peace and serenity upon them all, strangely at variance with the bewilderment and confusion of his own half-sobered thoughts, and yet impressive and welcome. He had no fear upon his mind; but, as he looked about him, he had less anger; and though all old delusions, relative to his worthless late companion, were now cleared away, he rather wished he had never known him than thought of its having come to this.

The past night, the day before, and many other days and nights beside, all mingled themselves up in one unintelligible and senseless whirl; he could not separate the transactions of one time from those of another. Now, the noise of the wheels resolved itself into some wild tune in which he could recognise scraps of airs he knew; now, there was nothing in his ears but a stunning and bewildering sound, like rushing water. But his companion rallied him on being so silent, and they talked and laughed boisterously. When they stopped, he was a little surprised to find himself in the act of smoking; but, on reflection, he remembered when and where he had taken the cigar.

They stopped at the avenue gate and alighted, leaving the carriage to the care of the servant, who was a smart fellow, and nearly as well accustomed to such proceedings as his master. Sir Mulberry and his friend were already there. All four walked in profound silence up the aisle of stately elm trees, which, meeting far above their heads, formed a long green perspective of Gothic arches, terminating, like some old ruin, in the open sky.

After a pause, and a brief conference between the seconds, they, at length, turned to the right, and taking a track across a little meadow, passed Ham House and came into some fields beyond. In one of these, they stopped. The ground was measured, some usual forms gone through, the two principals were placed front to front at the distance agreed upon, and Sir Mulberry turned his face towards his young adversary for the first time. He was very pale, his eyes were bloodshot, his dress disordered, and his hair dishevelled. For the face, it expressed nothing but violent and evil passions. He shaded his eyes with his hand; grazed at his opponent, steadfastly, for a few moments; and, then taking the weapon which was tendered to him, bent his eyes upon that, and looked up no more until the word was given, when he instantly fired.

The two shots were fired, as nearly as possible, at the same instant. In that instant, the young lord turned his head sharply round, fixed upon his adversary a ghastly stare, and without a groan or stagger, fell down dead.

'He's gone!' cried Westwood, who, with the other second, had run up to the body, and fallen on one knee beside it.

'His blood on his own head,' said Sir Mulberry. 'He brought this upon himself, and forced it upon me.'

'Captain Adams,' cried Westwood, hastily, 'I call you to witness that this was fairly done. Hawk, we have not a moment to lose. We must leave this place immediately, push for Brighton, and cross to France with all speed. This has been a bad business, and may be worse, if we delay a moment. Adams, consult your own safety, and don't remain here; the living before the dead; goodbye!'

With these words, he seized Sir Mulberry by the arm, and hurried him away. Captain Adams—only pausing to convince himself, beyond all question, of the fatal result—sped off in the same direction, to concert measures with his servant for removing the body, and securing his own safety likewise.

So died Lord Frederick Verisopht, by the hand which he had loaded with gifts, and clasped a thousand times; by the act of him, but for whom, and others like him, he might have lived a happy man, and died with children's faces round his bed.

The sun came proudly up in all his majesty, the noble river ran its winding course, the leaves quivered and rustled in the air, the birds poured their cheerful songs from every tree, the short-lived butterfly fluttered its little wings; all the light and life of day came on; and, amidst it all, and pressing down the grass whose every blade bore twenty tiny lives, lay the dead man, with his stark and rigid face turned upwards to the sky.

CHAPTER 51

The Project of Mr. Ralph Nickleby and his Friend approaching a successful Issue, becomes unexpectedly known to another Party, not admitted into their Confidence

In an old house, dismal dark and dusty, which seemed to have withered, like himself, and to have grown yellow and shrivelled in hoarding him from the light of day, as he had in hoarding his money, lived Arthur Gride. Meagre old chairs and tables, of spare and bony make, and hard and cold as misers' hearts, were ranged, in grim array, against the gloomy walls; attenuated presses, grown lank and lantern-jawed in guarding the treasures they enclosed, and tottering, as though from constant fear and dread of thieves, shrunk up in dark corners, whence they cast no shadows on the ground, and seemed to hide and cower from observation. A tall grim clock upon the stairs, with long lean hands and famished face, ticked in cautious whispers; and when it struck the time, in thin and piping sounds, like an old man's voice, rattled, as if it were pinched with hunger.

No fireside couch was there, to invite repose and comfort. Elbow-chairs there were, but they looked uneasy in their minds, cocked their arms suspiciously and timidly, and kept upon their guard. Others, were fantastically grim and gaunt, as having drawn themselves up to their utmost height, and put on their fiercest looks to stare all comers out of countenance. Others, again, knocked up against their neighbours, or leant for support against the wall— somewhat ostentatiously, as if to call all men to witness that they were not worth the taking. The dark square lumbering bedsteads seemed built for restless dreams; the musty hangings seemed to creep in scanty folds together, whispering among themselves, when rustled by the wind, their trembling knowledge of the tempting wares that lurked within the dark and tight-locked closets.

From out the most spare and hungry room in all this spare and hungry house there came, one morning, the tremulous tones of old Gride's voice, as it feebly chirruped forth the fag end of some forgotten song, of which the burden ran:

Ta—ran—tan—too,

Throw the old shoe,

And may the wedding be lucky!

which he repeated, in the same shrill quavering notes, again and again, until a violent fit of coughing obliged him to desist, and to pursue in silence, the occupation upon which he was engaged.

This occupation was, to take down from the shelves of a worm-eaten wardrobe a quantity of frouzy garments, one by one; to subject each to a careful and minute inspection by holding it up against the light, and after folding it with great exactness, to lay it on one or other of two little heaps beside him. He never took two articles of clothing out together, but always brought them forth, singly, and never failed to shut the wardrobe door, and turn the key, between each visit to its shelves.

'The snuff-coloured suit,' said Arthur Gride, surveying a threadbare coat. 'Did I look well in snuff-colour? Let me think.'

The result of his cogitations appeared to be unfavourable, for he folded the garment once more, laid it aside, and mounted on a chair to get down another, chirping while he did so:

> Young, loving, and fair,
>
> Oh what happiness there!
>
> The wedding is sure to be lucky!

'They always put in "young,"' said old Arthur, 'but songs are only written for the sake of rhyme, and this is a silly one that the poor country-people sang, when I was a little boy. Though stop—young is quite right too—it means the bride—yes. He, he, he! It means the bride. Oh dear, that's good. That's very good. And true besides, quite true!'

In the satisfaction of this discovery, he went over the verse again, with increased expression, and a shake or two here and there. He then resumed his employment.

'The bottle-green,' said old Arthur; 'the bottle-green was a famous suit to wear, and I bought it very cheap at a pawnbroker's, and there was—he, he, he!—a tarnished shilling in the waistcoat pocket. To think that the pawnbroker shouldn't have known there was a shilling in it! I knew it! I felt it when I was examining the quality. Oh, what a dull dog of a pawnbroker! It was a lucky suit too, this bottle-green. The very day I put it on first, old Lord Mallowford was burnt to death in his bed, and all the post-obits fell in. I'll be married in the bottle-green. Peg. Peg Sliderskew—I'll wear the bottle-green!'

This call, loudly repeated twice or thrice at the room-door, brought into the apartment a short, thin, weasen, blear-eyed old woman, palsy-stricken and hideously ugly, who, wiping her shrivelled face upon her dirty apron, inquired, in that subdued tone in which deaf people commonly speak:

'Was that you a calling, or only the clock a striking? My hearing gets so bad, I never know which is which; but when I hear a noise, I know it must be one of you, because nothing else never stirs in the house.'

'Me, Peg, me,' said Arthur Gride, tapping himself on the breast to render the reply more intelligible.

'You, eh?' returned Peg. 'And what do you want?'

'I'll be married in the bottle-green,' cried Arthur Gride.

'It's a deal too good to be married in, master,' rejoined Peg, after a short inspection of the suit. 'Haven't you got anything worse than this?'

'Nothing that'll do,' replied old Arthur.

'Why not do?' retorted Peg. 'Why don't you wear your every-day clothes, like a man—eh?'

'They an't becoming enough, Peg,' returned her master.

'Not what enough?' said Peg.

'Becoming.'

'Becoming what?' said Peg, sharply. 'Not becoming too old to wear?'

Arthur Gride muttered an imprecation on his housekeeper's deafness, as he roared in her ear:

'Not smart enough! I want to look as well as I can.'

'Look?' cried Peg. 'If she's as handsome as you say she is, she won't look much at you, master, take your oath of that; and as to how you look yourself—pepper-and-salt, bottle-green, sky-blue, or tartan-plaid will make no difference in you.'

With which consolatory assurance, Peg Sliderskew gathered up the chosen suit, and folding her skinny arms upon the bundle, stood, mouthing, and grinning, and blinking her watery eyes, like an uncouth figure in some monstrous piece of carving.

'You're in a funny humour, an't you, Peg?' said Arthur, with not the best possible grace.

'Why, isn't it enough to make me?' rejoined the old woman. 'I shall, soon enough, be put out, though, if anybody tries to domineer it over me: and so I give you notice, master. Nobody shall be put over Peg Sliderskew's head, after so many years; you know that, and so I needn't tell you! That won't do for me—no, no, nor for you. Try that once, and come to ruin—ruin—ruin!'

'Oh dear, dear, I shall never try it,' said Arthur Gride, appalled by the mention of the word, 'not for the world. It would be very easy to ruin me; we must be very careful; more saving than ever, with another mouth to feed. Only we—we mustn't let her lose her good looks, Peg, because I like to see 'em.'

'Take care you don't find good looks come expensive,' returned Peg, shaking her forefinger.

'But she can earn money herself, Peg,' said Arthur Gride, eagerly watching what effect his communication produced upon the old woman's countenance: 'she can draw, paint, work all manner of pretty things for ornamenting stools and chairs: slippers, Peg, watch-guards, hair-chains, and a thousand little dainty trifles that I couldn't give you half the names of. Then she can play the piano, (and, what's more, she's got one), and sing like a little bird. She'll be very cheap to dress and keep, Peg; don't you think she will?'

'If you don't let her make a fool of you, she may,' returned Peg.

'A fool of me!' exclaimed Arthur. 'Trust your old master not to be fooled by pretty faces, Peg; no, no, no—nor by ugly ones neither, Mrs Sliderskew,' he softly added by way of soliloquy.

'You're a saying something you don't want me to hear,' said Peg; 'I know you are.'

'Oh dear! the devil's in this woman,' muttered Arthur; adding with an ugly leer, 'I said I trusted everything to you, Peg. That was all.'

'You do that, master, and all your cares are over,' said Peg approvingly.

'When I do that, Peg Sliderskew,' thought Arthur Gride, 'they will be.'

Although he thought this very distinctly, he durst not move his lips lest the old woman should detect him. He even seemed half afraid that she might have read his thoughts; for he leered coaxingly upon her, as he said aloud:

'Take up all loose stitches in the bottle-green with the best black silk. Have a skein of the best, and some new buttons for the coat, and—this is a good idea, Peg, and one you'll like, I know—as I have never given her anything yet, and girls like such attentions, you shall polish up a sparking necklace that I have got upstairs, and I'll give it her upon the wedding morning—clasp it round her charming little neck myself—and take it away again next day. He, he, he! I'll lock it up for her, Peg, and lose it. Who'll be made the fool of there, I wonder, to begin with—eh, Peg?'

Mrs. Sliderskew appeared to approve highly of this ingenious scheme, and expressed her satisfaction by various rackings and twitchings of her head and body, which by no means enhanced her charms. These she prolonged until she had hobbled to the door, when she exchanged them for a sour malignant look, and twisting her under-jaw from side to side, muttered hearty curses upon the future Mrs. Gride, as she crept slowly down the stairs, and paused for breath at nearly every one.

'She's half a witch, I think,' said Arthur Gride, when he found himself again alone. 'But she's very frugal, and she's very deaf. Her living costs me next to nothing; and it's no use her listening at keyholes; for she can't hear. She's a charming woman—for the purpose; a most discreet old housekeeper, and worth her weight in—copper.'

Having extolled the merits of his domestic in these high terms, old Arthur went back to the burden of his song. The suit destined to grace his approaching nuptials being now selected, he replaced the others with no less care than he had displayed in drawing them from the musty nooks where they had silently reposed for many years.

Startled by a ring at the door, he hastily concluded this operation, and locked the press; but there was no need for any particular hurry, as the discreet Peg seldom knew the bell was rung unless she happened to cast her dim eyes upwards, and to see it shaking against the kitchen ceiling. After a short delay, however, Peg tottered in, followed by Newman Noggs.

'Ah! Mr. Noggs!' cried Arthur Gride, rubbing his hands. 'My good friend, Mr Noggs, what news do you bring for me?'

Newman, with a steadfast and immovable aspect, and his fixed eye very fixed indeed, replied, suiting the action to the word, 'A letter. From Mr Nickleby. Bearer waits.'

'Won't you take a—a—'

Newman looked up, and smacked his lips.

'—A chair?' said Arthur Gride.

'No,' replied Newman. 'Thankee.'

Arthur opened the letter with trembling hands, and devoured its contents with the utmost greediness; chuckling rapturously over it, and reading it several times, before he could take it from before his eyes. So many times did he peruse and re-peruse it, that Newman considered it expedient to remind him of his presence.

'Answer,' said Newman. 'Bearer waits.'

'True,' replied old Arthur. 'Yes—yes; I almost forgot, I do declare.'

'I thought you were forgetting,' said Newman.

'Quite right to remind me, Mr. Noggs. Oh, very right indeed,' said Arthur. 'Yes. I'll write a line. I'm—I'm—rather flurried, Mr. Noggs. The news is—'

'Bad?' interrupted Newman.

'No, Mr. Noggs, thank you; good, good. The very best of news. Sit down. I'll get the pen and ink, and write a line in answer. I'll not detain you long. I know you're a treasure to your master, Mr. Noggs. He speaks of you in such terms, sometimes, that, oh dear! you'd be astonished. I may say that I do too, and always did. I always say the same of you.'

'That's "Curse Mr. Noggs with all my heart!" then, if you do,' thought Newman, as Gride hurried out.

The letter had fallen on the ground. Looking carefully about him for an instant, Newman, impelled by curiosity to know the result of the design he had overheard from his office closet, caught it up and rapidly read as follows:

'Gride.

'I saw Bray again this morning, and proposed the day after tomorrow (as you suggested) for the marriage. There is no objection on his part, and all days are alike to his daughter. We will go together, and you must be with me by seven in the morning. I need not tell you to be punctual.

'Make no further visits to the girl in the meantime. You have been there, of late, much oftener than you should. She does not languish for you, and it might have been dangerous. Restrain your youthful ardour for eight-and-forty hours, and leave her to the father. You only undo what he does, and does well.

'Yours,

'Ralph Nickleby.'

A footstep was heard without. Newman dropped the letter on the same spot again, pressed it with his foot to prevent its fluttering away, regained his seat in a single stride, and looked as vacant and unconscious as ever mortal looked. Arthur Gride, after peering nervously about him, spied it on the ground, picked it up, and sitting down to write, glanced at Newman Noggs, who was staring at the wall with an intensity so remarkable, that Arthur was quite alarmed.

'Do you see anything particular, Mr. Noggs?' said Arthur, trying to follow the direction of Newman's eyes—which was an impossibility, and a thing no man had ever done.

'Only a cobweb,' replied Newman.

'Oh! is that all?'

'No,' said Newman. 'There's a fly in it.'

'There are a good many cobwebs here,' observed Arthur Gride.

'So there are in our place,' returned Newman; 'and flies too.'

Newman appeared to derive great entertainment from this repartee, and to the great discomposure of Arthur Gride's nerves, produced a series of sharp cracks from his finger-joints, resembling the noise of a distant discharge of small artillery. Arthur succeeded in finishing his reply to Ralph's note, nevertheless, and at length handed it over to the eccentric messenger for delivery.

'That's it, Mr. Noggs,' said Gride.

Newman gave a nod, put it in his hat, and was shuffling away, when Gride, whose doting delight knew no bounds, beckoned him back again, and said, in a shrill whisper, and with a grin which puckered up his whole face, and almost obscured his eyes:

'Will you—will you take a little drop of something—just a taste?'

In good fellowship (if Arthur Gride had been capable of it) Newman would not have drunk with him one bubble of the richest wine that was ever made; but to see what he would be at, and to punish him as much as he could, he accepted the offer immediately.

Arthur Gride, therefore, again applied himself to the press, and from a shelf laden with tall Flemish drinking-glasses, and quaint bottles: some with necks like so many storks, and others with square Dutch-built bodies and short fat apoplectic throats: took down one dusty bottle of promising appearance, and two glasses of curiously small size.

'You never tasted this,' said Arthur. 'It's eau-d'or—golden water. I like it on account of its name. It's a delicious name. Water of gold, golden water! O dear me, it seems quite a sin to drink it!'

As his courage appeared to be fast failing him, and he trifled with the stopper in a manner which threatened the dismissal of the bottle to its old place, Newman took up one of the little glasses, and clinked it, twice or thrice, against the bottle, as a gentle reminder that he had not been helped yet. With a deep sigh, Arthur Gride slowly filled it—though not to the brim—and then filled his own.

'Stop, stop; don't drink it yet,' he said, laying his hand on Newman's; 'it was given to me, twenty years ago, and when I take a little taste, which is ve—ry seldom, I like to think of it beforehand, and tease myself. We'll drink a toast. Shall we drink a toast, Mr. Noggs?'

'Ah!' said Newman, eyeing his little glass impatiently. 'Look sharp. Bearer waits.'

'Why, then, I'll tell you what,' tittered Arthur, 'we'll drink—he, he, he!—we'll drink a lady.'

'The ladies?' said Newman.

'No, no, Mr. Noggs,' replied Gride, arresting his hand, 'A lady. You wonder to hear me say A lady. I know you do, I know you do. Here's little Madeline. That's the toast. Mr. Noggs. Little Madeline!'

'Madeline!' said Newman; inwardly adding, 'and God help her!'

The rapidity and unconcern with which Newman dismissed his portion of the golden water, had a great effect upon the old man, who sat upright in his chair, and gazed at him, open-mouthed, as if the sight had taken away his breath. Quite unmoved, however, Newman left him to sip his own at leisure, or to pour it back again into the bottle, if he chose, and departed; after greatly outraging the dignity of Peg Sliderskew by brushing past her, in the passage, without a word of apology or recognition.

Mr. Gride and his housekeeper, immediately on being left alone, resolved themselves into a committee of ways and means, and discussed the arrangements which should be made for the reception of the young bride. As they were, like some other committees, extremely dull and prolix in debate, this history may pursue the footsteps of Newman Noggs; thereby combining advantage with necessity; for it would have been necessary to do so under any circumstances, and necessity has no law, as all the world knows.

'You've been a long time,' said Ralph, when Newman returned.

'He was a long time,' replied Newman.

'Bah!' cried Ralph impatiently. 'Give me his note, if he gave you one: his message, if he didn't. And don't go away. I want a word with you, sir.'

Newman handed in the note, and looked very virtuous and innocent while his employer broke the seal, and glanced his eye over it.

'He'll be sure to come,' muttered Ralph, as he tore it to pieces; 'why of course, I know he'll be sure to come. What need to say that? Noggs! Pray, sir, what man was that, with whom I saw you in the street last night?'

'I don't know,' replied Newman.

'You had better refresh your memory, sir,' said Ralph, with a threatening look.

'I tell you,' returned Newman boldly, 'that I don't know. He came here twice, and asked for you. You were out. He came again. You packed him off, yourself. He gave the name of Brooker.'

'I know he did,' said Ralph; 'what then?'

'What then? Why, then he lurked about and dogged me in the street. He follows me, night after night, and urges me to bring him face to face with you; as he says he has been once, and not long ago either. He wants to see you face to face, he says, and you'll soon hear him out, he warrants.'

'And what say you to that?' inquired Ralph, looking keenly at his drudge.

'That it's no business of mine, and I won't. I told him he might catch you in the street, if that was all he wanted, but no! that wouldn't do. You wouldn't hear a word there, he said. He must have you alone in a room with the door locked, where he could speak without fear, and you'd soon change your tone, and hear him patiently.'

'An audacious dog!' Ralph muttered.

'That's all I know,' said Newman. 'I say again, I don't know what man he is. I don't believe he knows himself. You have seen him; perhaps you do.'

'I think I do,' replied Ralph.

'Well,' retored Newman, sulkily, 'don't expect me to know him too; that's all. You'll ask me, next, why I never told you this before. What would you say, if I was to tell you all that people say of you? What do you call me when I sometimes do? "Brute, ass!" and snap at me like a dragon.'

This was true enough; though the question which Newman anticipated, was, in fact, upon Ralph's lips at the moment.

'He is an idle ruffian,' said Ralph; 'a vagabond from beyond the sea where he travelled for his crimes; a felon let loose to run his neck into the halter; a swindler, who has the audacity to try his schemes on me who know him well. The next time he tampers with you, hand him over to the police, for attempting to extort money by lies and threats,—d'ye hear?—and leave the rest to me. He shall cool his heels in jail a little time, and I'll be bound he looks for other folks to fleece, when he comes out. You mind what I say, do you?'

'I hear,' said Newman.

'Do it then,' returned Ralph, 'and I'll reward you. Now, you may go.'

Newman readily availed himself of the permission, and, shutting himself up in his little office, remained there, in very serious cogitation, all day. When he was released at night, he proceeded, with all the expedition he could use, to the city, and took up his old position behind the pump, to watch for Nicholas. For Newman Noggs was proud in his way, and could not bear to appear as his friend, before the brothers Cheeryble, in the shabby and degraded state to which he was reduced.

He had not occupied this position many minutes, when he was rejoiced to see Nicholas approaching, and darted out from his ambuscade to meet him. Nicholas, on his part, was no less pleased to encounter his friend, whom he had not seen for some time; so, their greeting was a warm one.

'I was thinking of you, at that moment,' said Nicholas.

'That's right,' rejoined Newman, 'and I of you. I couldn't help coming up, tonight. I say, I think I am going to find out something.'

'And what may that be?' returned Nicholas, smiling at this odd communication.

'I don't know what it may be, I don't know what it may not be,' said Newman; 'it's some secret in which your uncle is concerned, but what, I've not yet been able to discover, although I have my strong suspicions. I'll not hint 'em now, in case you should be disappointed.'

'I disappointed!' cried Nicholas; 'am I interested?'

'I think you are,' replied Newman. 'I have a crotchet in my head that it must be so. I have found out a man, who plainly knows more than he cares to tell at once. And he has already dropped such hints to me as puzzle me—I say, as puzzle me,' said Newman, scratching his red nose into a state of violent inflammation, and staring at Nicholas with all his might and main meanwhile.

Admiring what could have wound his friend up to such a pitch of mystery, Nicholas endeavoured, by a series of questions, to elucidate the cause; but in vain. Newman could not be drawn into any more explicit statement than a repetition of the perplexities he had already thrown out, and a confused oration, showing, How it was necessary to use the utmost caution; how the lynx-eyed Ralph had already seen him in company with his unknown correspondent; and how he had baffled the said Ralph by extreme guardedness of manner and ingenuity of speech; having prepared himself for such a contingency from the first.

Remembering his companion's propensity,—of which his nose, indeed, perpetually warned all beholders like a beacon,—Nicholas had drawn him into a sequestered tavern. Here, they fell to reviewing the origin and progress of their acquaintance, as men sometimes do, and tracing out the little events by which it was most strongly marked, came at last to Miss Cecilia Bobster.

'And that reminds me,' said Newman, 'that you never told me the young lady's real name.'

'Madeline!' said Nicholas.

'Madeline!' cried Newman. 'What Madeline? Her other name. Say her other name.'

'Bray,' said Nicholas, in great astonishment.

'It's the same!' cried Newman. 'Sad story! Can you stand idly by, and let that unnatural marriage take place without one attempt to save her?'

'What do you mean?' exclaimed Nicholas, starting up; 'marriage! are you mad?'

'Are you? Is she? Are you blind, deaf, senseless, dead?' said Newman. 'Do you know that within one day, by means of your uncle Ralph, she will be married to a man as bad as he, and worse, if worse there is? Do you know that, within one day, she will be sacrificed, as sure as you stand there alive, to a hoary wretch—a devil born and bred, and grey in devils' ways?'

'Be careful what you say,' replied Nicholas. 'For Heaven's sake be careful! I am left here alone, and those who could stretch out a hand to rescue her are far away. What is it that you mean?'

'I never heard her name,' said Newman, choking with his energy. 'Why didn't you tell me? How was I to know? We might, at least, have had some time to think!'

'What is it that you mean?' cried Nicholas.

It was not an easy task to arrive at this information; but, after a great quantity of extraordinary pantomime, which in no way assisted it, Nicholas, who was almost as wild as Newman Noggs himself, forced the latter down upon his seat and held him down until he began his tale.

Rage, astonishment, indignation, and a storm of passions, rushed through the listener's heart, as the plot was laid bare. He no sooner understood it all, than with a face of ashy paleness, and trembling in every limb, he darted from the house.

'Stop him!' cried Newman, bolting out in pursuit. 'He'll be doing something desperate; he'll murder somebody. Hallo! there, stop him. Stop thief! stop thief!'

CHAPTER 52

Nicholas despairs of rescuing Madeline Bray, but plucks up his Spirits again, and determines to attempt it. Domestic Intelligence of the Kenwigses and Lillyvicks

Finding that Newman was determined to arrest his progress at any hazard, and apprehensive that some well-intentioned passenger, attracted by the cry of 'Stop thief,' might lay violent hands upon his person, and place him in a disagreeable predicament from which he might have some difficulty in extricating himself, Nicholas soon slackened his pace, and suffered Newman Noggs to come up with him: which he did, in so breathless a condition, that it seemed impossible he could have held out for a minute longer.

'I will go straight to Bray's,' said Nicholas. 'I will see this man. If there is a feeling of humanity lingering in his breast, a spark of consideration for his own child, motherless and friendless as she is, I will awaken it.'

'You will not,' replied Newman. 'You will not, indeed.'

'Then,' said Nicholas, pressing onward, 'I will act upon my first impulse, and go straight to Ralph Nickleby.'

'By the time you reach his house he will be in bed,' said Newman.

'I'll drag him from it,' cried Nicholas.

'Tut, tut,' said Noggs. 'Be yourself.'

'You are the best of friends to me, Newman,' rejoined Nicholas after a pause, and taking his hand as he spoke. 'I have made head against many trials; but the misery of another, and such misery, is involved in this one, that I declare to you I am rendered desperate, and know not how to act.'

In truth, it did seem a hopeless case. It was impossible to make any use of such intelligence as Newman Noggs had gleaned, when he lay concealed in the closet. The mere circumstance of the compact between Ralph Nickleby and Gride would not invalidate the marriage, or render Bray averse to it, who, if he did not actually know of the existence of some such understanding, doubtless suspected it. What had been hinted with reference to some fraud on Madeline, had been put, with sufficient obscurity by Arthur Gride, but coming from Newman Noggs, and obscured still further by the smoke of his pocket-pistol, it became wholly unintelligible, and involved in utter darkness.

'There seems no ray of hope,' said Nicholas.

'The greater necessity for coolness, for reason, for consideration, for thought,' said Newman, pausing at every alternate word, to look anxiously in his friend's face. 'Where are the brothers?'

'Both absent on urgent business, as they will be for a week to come.'

'Is there no way of communicating with them? No way of getting one of them here by tomorrow night?'

'Impossible!' said Nicholas, 'the sea is between us and them. With the fairest winds that ever blew, to go and return would take three days and nights.'

'Their nephew,' said Newman, 'their old clerk.'

'What could either do, that I cannot?' rejoined Nicholas. 'With reference to them, especially, I am enjoined to the strictest silence on this subject. What right have I to betray the confidence reposed in me, when nothing but a miracle can prevent this sacrifice?'

'Think,' urged Newman. 'Is there no way?'

'There is none,' said Nicholas, in utter dejection. 'Not one. The father urges, the daughter consents. These demons have her in their toils; legal right, might, power, money, and every influence are on their side. How can I hope to save her?'

'Hope to the last!' said Newman, clapping him on the back. 'Always hope; that's a dear boy. Never leave off hoping; it don't answer. Do you mind me, Nick? It don't answer. Don't leave a stone unturned. It's always something, to know you've done the most you could. But, don't leave off hoping, or it's of no use doing anything. Hope, hope, to the last!'

Nicholas needed encouragement. The suddenness with which intelligence of the two usurers' plans had come upon him, the little time which remained for exertion, the probability, almost amounting to certainty itself, that a few hours would place Madeline Bray for ever beyond his reach, consign her to unspeakable misery, and perhaps to an untimely death; all this quite stunned and overwhelmed him. Every hope connected with her that he had suffered himself to form, or had entertained unconsciously, seemed to fall at his feet, withered and dead. Every charm with which his memory or imagination had surrounded her, presented itself before him, only to heighten his anguish and add new bitterness to his despair. Every feeling of sympathy for her forlorn condition, and of admiration for her heroism and fortitude, aggravated the indignation which shook him in every limb, and swelled his heart almost to bursting.

But, if Nicholas's own heart embarrassed him, Newman's came to his relief. There was so much earnestness in his remonstrance, and such sincerity and fervour in his manner, odd and ludicrous as it always was, that it imparted to Nicholas new firmness, and enabled him to say, after he had walked on for some little way in silence:

'You read me a good lesson, Newman, and I will profit by it. One step, at least, I may take—am bound to take indeed—and to that I will apply myself tomorrow.'

'What is that?' asked Noggs wistfully. 'Not to threaten Ralph? Not to see the father?'

'To see the daughter, Newman,' replied Nicholas. 'To do what, after all, is the utmost that the brothers could do, if they were here, as Heaven send they were! To reason with her upon this hideous union, to point out to her all the horrors to which she is hastening; rashly, it may be, and without due reflection. To entreat her, at least, to pause. She can have had no counsellor for her good. Perhaps even I may move her so far yet, though it is the eleventh hour, and she upon the very brink of ruin.'

'Bravely spoken!' said Newman. 'Well done, well done! Yes. Very good.'

'And I do declare,' cried Nicholas, with honest enthusiasm, 'that in this effort I am influenced by no selfish or personal considerations, but by pity for her, and detestation and abhorrence of this scheme; and that I would do the same, were there twenty rivals in the field, and I the last and least favoured of them all.'

'You would, I believe,' said Newman. 'But where are you hurrying now?'

'Homewards,' answered Nicholas. 'Do you come with me, or I shall say good-night?'

'I'll come a little way, if you will but walk: not run,' said Noggs.

'I cannot walk tonight, Newman,' returned Nicholas, hurriedly. 'I must move rapidly, or I could not draw my breath. I'll tell you what I've said and done tomorrow.'

Without waiting for a reply, he darted off at a rapid pace, and, plunging into the crowds which thronged the street, was quickly lost to view.

'He's a violent youth at times,' said Newman, looking after him; 'and yet I like him for it. There's cause enough now, or the deuce is in it. Hope! I said hope, I think! Ralph Nickleby and Gride with their heads together! And hope for the opposite party! Ho! ho!'

It was with a very melancholy laugh that Newman Noggs concluded this soliloquy; and it was with a very melancholy shake of the head, and a very rueful countenance, that he turned about, and went plodding on his way.

This, under ordinary circumstances, would have been to some small tavern or dram-shop; that being his way, in more senses than one. But, Newman was too much interested, and too anxious, to betake himself even to this resource, and so, with many desponding and dismal reflections, went straight home.

It had come to pass, that afternoon, that Miss Morleena Kenwigs had received an invitation to repair next day, per steamer from Westminster Bridge, unto the Eel-pie Island at Twickenham: there to make merry upon a cold collation, bottled beer, shrub, and shrimps, and to dance in the open air to the music of a locomotive band, conveyed thither for the purpose: the steamer being specially engaged by a dancing-master of extensive connection for the accommodation of his numerous pupils, and the pupils displaying their appreciation of the dancing-master's services, by purchasing themselves, and inducing their friends to do the like, divers light-blue tickets, entitling them to join the expedition. Of these light-blue tickets, one had been presented by an ambitious neighbour to Miss Morleena Kenwigs, with an invitation to join her daughters; and Mrs Kenwigs, rightly deeming that the honour of the family was involved in Miss Morleena's making the most splendid appearance possible on so short a notice, and testifying to the dancing-master that there were other dancing-masters besides him, and to all fathers and mothers present that other people's children could learn to be genteel besides theirs, had fainted away twice under the magnitude of her preparations, but, upheld by a determination to sustain the family name or perish in the attempt, was still hard at work when Newman Noggs came home.

Now, between the italian-ironing of frills, the flouncing of trousers, the trimming of frocks, the faintings and the comings-to again, incidental to the occasion, Mrs. Kenwigs had been so entirely occupied, that she had not observed, until within half an hour before, that the flaxen tails of Miss Morleena's hair were, in a manner, run to seed; and that, unless she were put under the hands of a skilful hairdresser, she never could achieve that signal triumph over the daughters of all other people, anything less than which would be tantamount to defeat. This discovery drove Mrs. Kenwigs to despair; for the hairdresser lived three streets and eight dangerous crossings off; Morleena could not be trusted to go there alone, even if such a proceeding were strictly proper: of which Mrs. Kenwigs had her doubts; Mr. Kenwigs had not returned from business; and there was nobody to take her. So, Mrs. Kenwigs first slapped Miss Kenwigs for being the cause of her vexation, and then shed tears.

'You ungrateful child!' said Mrs. Kenwigs, 'after I have gone through what I have, this night, for your good.'

'I can't help it, ma,' replied Morleena, also in tears; 'my hair will grow.'

'Don't talk to me, you naughty thing!' said Mrs. Kenwigs, 'don't! Even if I was to trust you by yourself and you were to escape being run over, I know you'd run in to Laura Chopkins,' who was the daughter of the ambitious neighbour, 'and tell her what you're going to wear tomorrow, I know you would. You've no proper pride in yourself, and are not to be trusted out of sight for an instant.'

Deploring the evil-mindedness of her eldest daughter in these terms, Mrs Kenwigs distilled fresh drops of vexation from her eyes, and declared that she did believe there never was anybody so tried as she was. Thereupon, Morleena Kenwigs wept afresh, and they bemoaned themselves together.

Matters were at this point, as Newman Noggs was heard to limp past the door on his way upstairs; when Mrs. Kenwigs, gaining new hope from the sound of his footsteps, hastily removed from her countenance as many traces of her late emotion as were effaceable on so short a notice: and presenting herself before him, and representing their dilemma, entreated that he would escort Morleena to the hairdresser's shop.

'I wouldn't ask you, Mr. Noggs,' said Mrs. Kenwigs, 'if I didn't know what a good, kind-hearted creature you are; no, not for worlds. I am a weak constitution, Mr. Noggs, but my spirit would no more let me ask a favour where I thought there was a chance of its being refused, than it would let me submit to see my children trampled down and trod upon, by envy and lowness!'

Newman was too good-natured not to have consented, even without this avowal of confidence on the part of Mrs. Kenwigs. Accordingly, a very few minutes had elapsed, when he and Miss Morleena were on their way to the hairdresser's.

It was not exactly a hairdresser's; that is to say, people of a coarse and vulgar turn of mind might have called it a barber's; for they not only cut and curled ladies elegantly, and children carefully, but shaved gentlemen easily. Still, it was a highly genteel establishment—quite first-rate in fact—and there were displayed in the window, besides other elegancies, waxen busts of a light lady and a dark gentleman which were the admiration of the whole neighbourhood. Indeed, some ladies had gone so far as to assert, that the dark gentleman was actually a portrait of the spirted young proprietor; and the great similarity between their head-dresses—both wore very glossy hair, with a narrow walk straight down the middle, and a profusion of flat circular curls on both sides—encouraged the idea. The better informed among the sex, however, made light of this assertion, for however willing they were (and they were very willing) to do full justice to the handsome face and figure of the proprietor, they held the countenance of the dark gentleman in the window to be an exquisite and abstract idea of masculine beauty, realised sometimes, perhaps, among angels and military men, but very rarely embodied to gladden the eyes of mortals.

It was to this establishment that Newman Noggs led Miss Kenwigs in safety. The proprietor, knowing that Miss Kenwigs had three sisters, each with two flaxen tails, and all good for sixpence apiece, once a month at least, promptly deserted an old gentleman whom he had just lathered for shaving, and handing him over to the journeyman, (who was not very popular among the ladies, by reason of his obesity and middle age,) waited on the young lady himself.

Just as this change had been effected, there presented himself for shaving, a big, burly, good-humoured coal-heaver with a pipe in his mouth, who, drawing his hand across his chin, requested to know when a shaver would be disengaged.

The journeyman, to whom this question was put, looked doubtfully at the young proprietor, and the young proprietor looked scornfully at the coal-heaver: observing at the same time:

'You won't get shaved here, my man.'

'Why not?' said the coal-heaver.

'We don't shave gentlemen in your line,' remarked the young proprietor.

'Why, I see you a shaving of a baker, when I was a looking through the winder, last week,' said the coal-heaver.

'It's necessary to draw the line somewheres, my fine feller,' replied the principal. 'We draw the line there. We can't go beyond bakers. If we was to get any lower than bakers, our customers would desert us, and we might shut up shop. You must try some other establishment, sir. We couldn't do it here.'

The applicant stared; grinned at Newman Noggs, who appeared highly entertained; looked slightly round the shop, as if in depreciation of the pomatum pots and other articles of stock; took his pipe out of his mouth and gave a very loud whistle; and then put it in again, and walked out.

The old gentleman who had just been lathered, and who was sitting in a melancholy manner with his face turned towards the wall, appeared quite unconscious of this incident, and to be insensible to everything around him in the depth of a reverie—a very mournful one, to judge from the sighs he occasionally vented—in which he was absorbed. Affected by this example, the proprietor began to clip Miss Kenwigs, the journeyman to scrape the old gentleman, and Newman Noggs to read last Sunday's paper, all three in silence: when Miss Kenwigs uttered a shrill little scream, and Newman, raising his eyes, saw that it had been elicited by the circumstance of the old gentleman turning his head, and disclosing the features of Mr. Lillyvick the collector.

The features of Mr. Lillyvick they were, but strangely altered. If ever an old gentleman had made a point of appearing in public, shaved close and clean, that old gentleman was Mr. Lillyvick. If ever a collector had borne himself like a collector, and assumed, before all men, a solemn and portentous dignity as if he had the world on his books and it was all two quarters in arrear, that collector was Mr. Lillyvick. And now, there he sat, with the remains of a beard at least a week old encumbering his chin; a soiled and crumpled shirt-frill crouching, as it were, upon his breast, instead of standing boldly out; a demeanour so abashed and drooping, so despondent, and expressive of such humiliation, grief, and shame; that if the souls of forty unsubstantial housekeepers, all of whom had had their water cut off for non-payment of the rate, could have been concentrated in one body, that one body could hardly have expressed such mortification and defeat as were now expressed in the person of Mr. Lillyvick the collector.

Newman Noggs uttered his name, and Mr. Lillyvick groaned: then coughed to hide it. But the groan was a full-sized groan, and the cough was but a wheeze.

'Is anything the matter?' said Newman Noggs.

'Matter, sir!' cried Mr. Lillyvick. 'The plug of life is dry, sir, and but the mud is left.'

This speech—the style of which Newman attributed to Mr. Lillyvick's recent association with theatrical characters—not being quite explanatory, Newman looked as if he were about to ask another question, when Mr. Lillyvick prevented him by shaking his hand mournfully, and then waving his own.

'Let me be shaved!' said Mr. Lillyvick. 'It shall be done before Morleena; it is Morleena, isn't it?'

'Yes,' said Newman.

'Kenwigses have got a boy, haven't they?' inquired the collector.

Again Newman said 'Yes.'

'Is it a nice boy?' demanded the collector.

'It ain't a very nasty one,' returned Newman, rather embarrassed by the question.

'Susan Kenwigs used to say,' observed the collector, 'that if ever she had another boy, she hoped it might be like me. Is this one like me, Mr Noggs?'

This was a puzzling inquiry; but Newman evaded it, by replying to Mr Lillyvick, that he thought the baby might possibly come like him in time.

'I should be glad to have somebody like me, somehow,' said Mr. Lillyvick, 'before I die.'

'You don't mean to do that, yet awhile?' said Newman.

Unto which Mr. Lillyvick replied in a solemn voice, 'Let me be shaved!' and again consigning himself to the hands of the journeyman, said no more.

This was remarkable behaviour. So remarkable did it seem to Miss Morleena, that that young lady, at the imminent hazard of having her ear sliced off, had not been able to forbear looking round, some score of times, during the foregoing colloquy. Of her, however, Mr. Lillyvick took no notice: rather striving (so, at least, it seemed to Newman Noggs) to evade her observation, and to shrink into himself whenever he attracted her regards. Newman wondered very much what could have occasioned this altered behaviour on the part of the collector; but, philosophically reflecting that he would most likely know, sooner or later, and that he could perfectly afford to wait, he was very little disturbed by the singularity of the old gentleman's deportment.

The cutting and curling being at last concluded, the old gentleman, who had been some time waiting, rose to go, and, walking out with Newman and his charge, took Newman's arm, and proceeded for some time without making any observation. Newman, who in power of taciturnity was excelled by few people, made no attempt to break silence; and so they went on, until they had very nearly reached Miss Morleena's home, when Mr. Lillyvick said:

'Were the Kenwigses very much overpowered, Mr. Noggs, by that news?'

'What news?' returned Newman.

'That about—my—being—'

'Married?' suggested Newman.

'Ah!' replied Mr. Lillyvick, with another groan; this time not even disguised by a wheeze.

'It made ma cry when she knew it,' interposed Miss Morleena, 'but we kept it from her for a long time; and pa was very low in his spirits, but he is better now; and I was very ill, but I am better too.'

'Would you give your great-uncle Lillyvick a kiss if he was to ask you, Morleena?' said the collector, with some hesitation.

'Yes; uncle Lillyvick, I would,' returned Miss Morleena, with the energy of both her parents combined; 'but not aunt Lillyvick. She's not an aunt of mine, and I'll never call her one.'

Immediately upon the utterance of these words, Mr. Lillyvick caught Miss Morleena up in his arms, and kissed her; and, being by this time at the door of the house where Mr. Kenwigs lodged (which, as has been before mentioned, usually stood wide open), he walked straight up into Mr Kenwigs's sitting-room, and put Miss Morleena down in the midst. Mr. and Mrs. Kenwigs were at supper. At sight of their perjured relative, Mrs Kenwigs turned faint and pale, and Mr. Kenwigs rose majestically.

'Kenwigs,' said the collector, 'shake hands.'

'Sir,' said Mr. Kenwigs, 'the time has been, when I was proud to shake hands with such a man as that man as now surweys me. The time has been, sir,' said Mr. Kenwigs, 'when a wisit from that man has excited in me and my family's boozums sensations both nateral and awakening. But, now, I look upon that man with emotions totally surpassing everythink, and I ask myself where is his Honour, where is his straight-for'ardness, and where is his human natur?'

'Susan Kenwigs,' said Mr. Lillyvick, turning humbly to his niece, 'don't you say anything to me?'

'She is not equal to it, sir,' said Mr. Kenwigs, striking the table emphatically. 'What with the nursing of a healthy babby, and the reflections upon your cruel conduct, four pints of malt liquor a day is hardly able to sustain her.'

'I am glad,' said the poor collector meekly, 'that the baby is a healthy one. I am very glad of that.'

This was touching the Kenwigses on their tenderest point. Mrs. Kenwigs instantly burst into tears, and Mr. Kenwigs evinced great emotion.

'My pleasantest feeling, all the time that child was expected,' said Mr Kenwigs, mournfully, 'was a thinking, "If it's a boy, as I hope it may be; for I have heard its uncle Lillyvick say again and again he would prefer our having a boy next, if it's a boy, what will his uncle Lillyvick say? What will he like him to be called? Will he be Peter, or Alexander, or Pompey, or Diorgeenes, or what will he be?" And now when I look at him; a precious, unconscious, helpless infant, with no use in his little arms but to tear his little cap, and no use in his little legs but to kick his little self—when I see him a lying on his mother's lap, cooing and cooing, and, in his innocent state, almost a choking hisself with his little fist—when I see him such a infant as he is, and think that that uncle Lillyvick, as was once a-going to be so fond of him, has withdrawed himself away, such a feeling of wengeance comes over me as no language can depicter, and I feel as if even that holy babe was a telling me to hate him.'

This affecting picture moved Mrs. Kenwigs deeply. After several imperfect words, which vainly attempted to struggle to the surface, but were drowned and washed away by the strong tide of her tears, she spake.

'Uncle,' said Mrs. Kenwigs, 'to think that you should have turned your back upon me and my dear children, and upon Kenwigs which is the author of their being—you who was once so kind and affectionate, and who, if anybody had told us such a thing of, we should have withered with scorn like lightning—you that little Lillyvick, our first and earliest boy, was named after at the very altar! Oh gracious!'

'Was it money that we cared for?' said Mr. Kenwigs. 'Was it property that we ever thought of?'

'No,' cried Mrs. Kenwigs, 'I scorn it.'

'So do I,' said Mr. Kenwigs, 'and always did.'

'My feelings have been lancerated,' said Mrs. Kenwigs, 'my heart has been torn asunder with anguish, I have been thrown back in my confinement, my unoffending infant has been rendered uncomfortable and fractious, Morleena has pined herself away to nothing; all this I forget and forgive, and with you, uncle, I never can quarrel. But never ask me to receive her, never do it, uncle. For I will not, I will not, I won't, I won't, I won't!'

'Susan, my dear,' said Mr. Kenwigs, 'consider your child.'

'Yes,' shrieked Mrs. Kenwigs, 'I will consider my child! I will consider my child! My own child, that no uncles can deprive me of; my own hated, despised, deserted, cut-off little child.' And, here, the emotions of Mrs Kenwigs became so violent, that Mr. Kenwigs was fain to administer hartshorn internally, and vinegar externally, and to destroy a staylace, four petticoat strings, and several small buttons.

Newman had been a silent spectator of this scene; for Mr. Lillyvick had signed to him not to withdraw, and Mr. Kenwigs had further solicited his presence by a nod of invitation. When Mrs. Kenwigs had been, in some degree, restored, and Newman, as a person possessed of some influence with her, had remonstrated and begged her to compose herself, Mr. Lillyvick said in a faltering voice:

'I never shall ask anybody here to receive my—I needn't mention the word; you know what I mean. Kenwigs and Susan, yesterday was a week she eloped with a half-pay captain!'

Mr. and Mrs. Kenwigs started together.

'Eloped with a half-pay captain,' repeated Mr. Lillyvick, 'basely and falsely eloped with a half-pay captain. With a bottle-nosed captain that any man might have considered himself safe from. It was in this room,' said Mr. Lillyvick, looking sternly round, 'that I first see Henrietta Petowker. It is in this room that I turn her off, for ever.'

This declaration completely changed the whole posture of affairs. Mrs Kenwigs threw herself upon the old gentleman's neck, bitterly reproaching herself for her late harshness, and exclaiming, if she had suffered, what must his sufferings have been! Mr. Kenwigs grasped his hand, and vowed eternal friendship and remorse. Mrs. Kenwigs was horror-stricken to think that she should ever have nourished in her bosom such a snake, adder, viper, serpent, and base crocodile as Henrietta Petowker. Mr. Kenwigs argued that she must have been bad indeed not to have improved by so long a contemplation of Mrs. Kenwigs's virtue. Mrs. Kenwigs remembered that Mr Kenwigs had often said that he was not quite satisfied of the propriety of Miss Petowker's conduct, and wondered how it was that she could have been blinded by such a wretch. Mr. Kenwigs remembered that he had had his suspicions, but did not wonder why Mrs. Kenwigs had not had hers, as she was all chastity, purity, and truth, and Henrietta all baseness, falsehood, and deceit. And Mr. and Mrs. Kenwigs both said, with strong feelings and tears of sympathy, that everything happened for the best; and conjured the good collector not to give way to unavailing grief, but to seek consolation in the society of those affectionate relations whose arms and hearts were ever open to him.

492

'Out of affection and regard for you, Susan and Kenwigs,' said Mr Lillyvick, 'and not out of revenge and spite against her, for she is below it, I shall, tomorrow morning, settle upon your children, and make payable to the survivors of them when they come of age of marry, that money that I once meant to leave 'em in my will. The deed shall be executed tomorrow, and Mr. Noggs shall be one of the witnesses. He hears me promise this, and he shall see it done.'

Overpowered by this noble and generous offer, Mr. Kenwigs, Mrs. Kenwigs, and Miss Morleena Kenwigs, all began to sob together; and the noise of their sobbing, communicating itself to the next room, where the children lay a-bed, and causing them to cry too, Mr. Kenwigs rushed wildly in, and bringing them out in his arms, by two and two, tumbled them down in their nightcaps and gowns at the feet of Mr. Lillyvick, and called upon them to thank and bless him.

'And now,' said Mr. Lillyvick, when a heart-rending scene had ensued and the children were cleared away again, 'give me some supper. This took place twenty mile from town. I came up this morning, and have being lingering about all day, without being able to make up my mind to come and see you. I humoured her in everything, she had her own way, she did just as she pleased, and now she has done this. There was twelve teaspoons and twenty-four pound in sovereigns—I missed them first—it's a trial—I feel I shall never be able to knock a double knock again, when I go my rounds—don't say anything more about it, please—the spoons were worth—never mind—never mind!'

With such muttered outpourings as these, the old gentleman shed a few tears; but, they got him into the elbow-chair, and prevailed upon him, without much pressing, to make a hearty supper, and by the time he had finished his first pipe, and disposed of half-a-dozen glasses out of a crown bowl of punch, ordered by Mr. Kenwigs, in celebration of his return to the bosom of his family, he seemed, though still very humble, quite resigned to his fate, and rather relieved than otherwise by the flight of his wife.

'When I see that man,' said Mr. Kenwigs, with one hand round Mrs. Kenwigs's waist: his other hand supporting his pipe (which made him wink and cough very much, for he was no smoker): and his eyes on Morleena, who sat upon her uncle's knee, 'when I see that man as mingling, once again, in the spear which he adorns, and see his affections deweloping themselves in legitimate sitiwations, I feel that his nature is as elewated and expanded, as his standing afore society as a public character is unimpeached, and the woices of my infant children purvided for in life, seem to whisper to me softly, "This is an ewent at which Evins itself looks down!"'

CHAPTER 53
Containing the further Progress of the Plot contrived by Mr. Ralph Nickleby and Mr. Arthur Gride

With that settled resolution, and steadiness of purpose to which extreme circumstances so often give birth, acting upon far less excitable and more sluggish temperaments than that which was the lot of Madeline Bray's admirer, Nicholas started, at dawn of day, from the restless couch which no sleep had visited on the previous night, and prepared to make that last appeal, by whose slight and fragile thread her only remaining hope of escape depended.

Although, to restless and ardent minds, morning may be the fitting season for exertion and activity, it is not always at that time that hope is strongest or the spirit most sanguine and buoyant. In trying and doubtful positions, youth, custom, a steady contemplation of the difficulties which surround us, and a familiarity with them, imperceptibly diminish our apprehensions and beget comparative indifference, if not a vague and reckless confidence in some relief, the means or nature of which we care not to foresee. But when we come, fresh, upon such things in the morning, with that dark and silent gap between us and yesterday; with every link in the brittle chain of hope, to rivet afresh; our hot enthusiasm subdued, and cool calm reason substituted in its stead; doubt and misgiving revive. As the traveller sees farthest by day, and becomes aware of rugged mountains and trackless plains which the friendly darkness had shrouded from his sight and mind together, so, the wayfarer in the toilsome path of human life sees, with each returning sun, some new obstacle to surmount, some new height to be attained. Distances stretch out before him which, last night, were scarcely taken into account, and the light which gilds all nature with its cheerful beams, seems but to shine upon the weary obstacles that yet lie strewn between him and the grave.

So thought Nicholas, when, with the impatience natural to a situation like his, he softly left the house, and, feeling as though to remain in bed were to lose most precious time, and to be up and stirring were in some way to promote the end he had in view, wandered into London; perfectly well knowing that for hours to come he could not obtain speech with Madeline, and could do nothing but wish the intervening time away.

And, even now, as he paced the streets, and listlessly looked round on the gradually increasing bustle and preparation for the day, everything appeared to yield him some new occasion for despondency. Last night, the sacrifice of a young, affectionate, and beautiful creature, to such a wretch, and in such a cause, had seemed a thing too monstrous to succeed; and the warmer he grew, the more confident he felt that some interposition must save her from his clutches. But now, when he thought how regularly things went on, from day to day, in the same unvarying round; how youth and beauty died, and ugly griping age lived tottering on; how crafty avarice grew rich, and manly honest hearts were poor and sad; how few they were who tenanted the stately houses, and how many of those who lay in noisome pens, or rose each day and laid them down each night, and lived and died, father and son, mother and child, race upon race, and generation upon generation, without a home to shelter them or the energies of one single man directed to their aid; how, in seeking, not a luxurious and splendid life, but the bare means of a most wretched and inadequate subsistence, there were women and children in that one town, divided into classes, numbered and estimated as regularly as the noble families and folks of great degree, and reared from infancy to drive most criminal and dreadful trades; how ignorance was punished and never taught; how jail-doors gaped, and gallows loomed, for thousands urged towards them by circumstances darkly curtaining their very cradles' heads, and but for which they might have earned their honest bread and lived in peace; how many died in soul, and had no chance of life; how many who could scarcely go astray, be they vicious as they would, turned haughtily from the crushed and stricken wretch who could scarce do otherwise, and who would have been a greater wonder had he or she done well, than even they had they done ill; how much injustice, misery, and wrong, there was, and yet how the world rolled on, from year to year, alike careless and indifferent, and no man seeking to remedy or redress it; when he thought of all this, and selected from the mass the one slight case on which his thoughts were bent, he felt, indeed, that there was little ground for hope, and little reason why it should not form an atom in the huge aggregate of distress and sorrow, and add one small and unimportant unit to swell the great amount.

But youth is not prone to contemplate the darkest side of a picture it can shift at will. By dint of reflecting on what he had to do, and reviving the train of thought which night had interrupted, Nicholas gradually summoned up his utmost energy, and when the morning was sufficiently advanced for his purpose, had no thought but that of using it to the best advantage. A hasty breakfast taken, and such affairs of business as required prompt attention disposed of, he directed his steps to the residence of Madeline Bray: whither he lost no time in arriving.

It had occurred to him that, very possibly, the young lady might be denied, although to him she never had been; and he was still pondering upon the surest method of obtaining access to her in that case, when, coming to the door of the house, he found it had been left ajar—probably by the last person who had gone out. The occasion was not one upon which to observe the nicest ceremony; therefore, availing himself of this advantage, Nicholas walked gently upstairs and knocked at the door of the room into which he had been accustomed to be shown. Receiving permission to enter, from some person on the other side, he opened the door and walked in.

Bray and his daughter were sitting there alone. It was nearly three weeks since he had seen her last, but there was a change in the lovely girl before him which told Nicholas, in startling terms, how much mental suffering had been compressed into that short time. There are no words which can express, nothing with which can be compared, the perfect pallor, the clear transparent whiteness, of the beautiful face which turned towards him when he entered. Her hair was a rich deep brown, but shading that face, and straying upon a neck that rivalled it in whiteness, it seemed by the strong contrast raven black. Something of wildness and restlessness there was in the dark eye, but there was the same patient look, the same expression of gentle mournfulness which he well remembered, and no trace of a single tear. Most beautiful— more beautiful, perhaps, than ever—there was something in her face which quite unmanned him, and appeared far more touching than the wildest agony of grief. It was not merely calm and composed, but fixed and rigid, as though the violent effort which had summoned that composure beneath her father's eye, while it mastered all other thoughts, had prevented even the momentary expression they had communicated to the features from subsiding, and had fastened it there, as an evidence of its triumph.

The father sat opposite to her; not looking directly in her face, but glancing at her, as he talked with a gay air which ill disguised the anxiety of his thoughts. The drawing materials were not on their accustomed table, nor were any of the other tokens of her usual occupations to be seen. The little vases which Nicholas had always seen filled with fresh flowers were empty, or supplied only with a few withered stalks and leaves. The bird was silent. The cloth that covered his cage at night was not removed. His mistress had forgotten him.

There are times when, the mind being painfully alive to receive impressions, a great deal may be noted at a glance. This was one, for Nicholas had but glanced round him when he was recognised by Mr. Bray, who said impatiently:

'Now, sir, what do you want? Name your errand here, quickly, if you please, for my daughter and I are busily engaged with other and more important matters than those you come about. Come, sir, address yourself to your business at once.'

Nicholas could very well discern that the irritability and impatience of this speech were assumed, and that Bray, in his heart, was rejoiced at any interruption which promised to engage the attention of his daughter. He bent his eyes involuntarily upon the father as he spoke, and marked his uneasiness; for he coloured and turned his head away.

The device, however, so far as it was a device for causing Madeline to interfere, was successful. She rose, and advancing towards Nicholas paused half-way, and stretched out her hand as expecting a letter.

'Madeline,' said her father impatiently, 'my love, what are you doing?'

'Miss Bray expects an inclosure perhaps,' said Nicholas, speaking very distinctly, and with an emphasis she could scarcely misunderstand. 'My employer is absent from England, or I should have brought a letter with me. I hope she will give me time—a little time. I ask a very little time.'

'If that is all you come about, sir,' said Mr. Bray, 'you may make yourself easy on that head. Madeline, my dear, I didn't know this person was in your debt?'

'A—a trifle, I believe,' returned Madeline, faintly.

'I suppose you think now,' said Bray, wheeling his chair round and confronting Nicholas, 'that, but for such pitiful sums as you bring here, because my daughter has chosen to employ her time as she has, we should starve?'

'I have not thought about it,' returned Nicholas.

'You have not thought about it!' sneered the invalid. 'You know you have thought about it, and have thought that, and think so every time you come here. Do you suppose, young man, that I don't know what little purse-proud tradesmen are, when, through some fortunate circumstances, they get the upper hand for a brief day—or think they get the upper hand—of a gentleman?'

'My business,' said Nicholas respectfully, 'is with a lady.'

'With a gentleman's daughter, sir,' returned the sick man, 'and the pettifogging spirit is the same. But perhaps you bring orders, eh? Have you any fresh orders for my daughter, sir?'

Nicholas understood the tone of triumph in which this interrogatory was put; but remembering the necessity of supporting his assumed character, produced a scrap of paper purporting to contain a list of some subjects for drawings which his employer desired to have executed; and with which he had prepared himself in case of any such contingency.

'Oh!' said Mr. Bray. 'These are the orders, are they?'

'Since you insist upon the term, sir, yes,' replied Nicholas.

'Then you may tell your master,' said Bray, tossing the paper back again, with an exulting smile, 'that my daughter, Miss Madeline Bray, condescends to employ herself no longer in such labours as these; that she is not at his beck and call, as he supposes her to be; that we don't live upon his money, as he flatters himself we do; that he may give whatever he owes us, to the first beggar that passes his shop, or add it to his own profits next time he calculates them; and that he may go to the devil for me. That's my acknowledgment of his orders, sir!'

'And this is the independence of a man who sells his daughter as he has sold that weeping girl!' thought Nicholas.

The father was too much absorbed with his own exultation to mark the look of scorn which, for an instant, Nicholas could not have suppressed had he been upon the rack. 'There,' he continued, after a short silence, 'you have your message and can retire—unless you have any further—ha!—any further orders.'

'I have none,' said Nicholas; 'nor, in the consideration of the station you once held, have I used that or any other word which, however harmless in itself, could be supposed to imply authority on my part or dependence on yours. I have no orders, but I have fears—fears that I will express, chafe as you may—fears that you may be consigning that young lady to something worse than supporting you by the labour of her hands, had she worked herself dead. These are my fears, and these fears I found upon your own demeanour. Your conscience will tell you, sir, whether I construe it well or not.'

'For Heaven's sake!' cried Madeline, interposing in alarm between them. 'Remember, sir, he is ill.'

'Ill!' cried the invalid, gasping and catching for breath. 'Ill! Ill! I am bearded and bullied by a shop-boy, and she beseeches him to pity me and remember I am ill!'

He fell into a paroxysm of his disorder, so violent that for a few moments Nicholas was alarmed for his life; but finding that he began to recover, he withdrew, after signifying by a gesture to the young lady that he had something important to communicate, and would wait for her outside the room. He could hear that the sick man came gradually, but slowly, to himself, and that without any reference to what had just occurred, as though he had no distinct recollection of it as yet, he requested to be left alone.

'Oh!' thought Nicholas, 'that this slender chance might not be lost, and that I might prevail, if it were but for one week's time and reconsideration!'

'You are charged with some commission to me, sir,' said Madeline, presenting herself in great agitation. 'Do not press it now, I beg and pray you. The day after tomorrow; come here then.'

'It will be too late—too late for what I have to say,' rejoined Nicholas, 'and you will not be here. Oh, madam, if you have but one thought of him who sent me here, but one last lingering care for your own peace of mind and heart, I do for God's sake urge you to give me a hearing.'

She attempted to pass him, but Nicholas gently detained her.

'A hearing,' said Nicholas. 'I ask you but to hear me: not me alone, but him for whom I speak, who is far away and does not know your danger. In the name of Heaven hear me!'

The poor attendant, with her eyes swollen and red with weeping, stood by; and to her Nicholas appealed in such passionate terms that she opened a side-door, and, supporting her mistress into an adjoining room, beckoned Nicholas to follow them.

'Leave me, sir, pray,' said the young lady.

'I cannot, will not leave you thus,' returned Nicholas. 'I have a duty to discharge; and, either here, or in the room from which we have just now come, at whatever risk or hazard to Mr. Bray, I must beseech you to contemplate again the fearful course to which you have been impelled.'

'What course is this you speak of, and impelled by whom, sir?' demanded the young lady, with an effort to speak proudly.

'I speak of this marriage,' returned Nicholas, 'of this marriage, fixed for tomorrow, by one who never faltered in a bad purpose, or lent his aid to any good design; of this marriage, the history of which is known to me, better, far better, than it is to you. I know what web is wound about you. I know what men they are from whom these schemes have come. You are betrayed and sold for money; for gold, whose every coin is rusted with tears, if not red with the blood of ruined men, who have fallen desperately by their own mad hands.'

'You say you have a duty to discharge,' said Madeline, 'and so have I. And with the help of Heaven I will perform it.'

'Say rather with the help of devils,' replied Nicholas, 'with the help of men, one of them your destined husband, who are—'

'I must not hear this,' cried the young lady, striving to repress a shudder, occasioned, as it seemed, even by this slight allusion to Arthur Gride. 'This evil, if evil it be, has been of my own seeking. I am impelled to this course by no one, but follow it of my own free will. You see I am not constrained or forced. Report this,' said Madeline, 'to my dear friend and benefactor, and, taking with you my prayers and thanks for him and for yourself, leave me for ever!'

'Not until I have besought you, with all the earnestness and fervour by which I am animated,' cried Nicholas, 'to postpone this marriage for one short week. Not until I have besought you to think more deeply than you can have done, influenced as you are, upon the step you are about to take. Although you cannot be fully conscious of the villainy of this man to whom you are about to give your hand, some of his deeds you know. You have heard him speak, and have looked upon his face. Reflect, reflect, before it is too late, on the mockery of plighting to him at the altar, faith in which your heart can have no share—of uttering solemn words, against which nature and reason must rebel—of the degradation of yourself in your own esteem, which must ensue, and must be aggravated every day, as his detested character opens upon you more and more. Shrink from the loathsome companionship of this wretch as you would from corruption and disease. Suffer toil and labour if you will, but shun him, shun him, and be happy. For, believe me, I speak the truth; the most abject poverty, the most wretched condition of human life, with a pure and upright mind, would be happiness to that which you must undergo as the wife of such a man as this!'

Long before Nicholas ceased to speak, the young lady buried her face in her hands, and gave her tears free way. In a voice at first inarticulate with emotion, but gradually recovering strength as she proceeded, she answered him:

'I will not disguise from you, sir—though perhaps I ought—that I have undergone great pain of mind, and have been nearly broken-hearted since I saw you last. I do not love this gentleman. The difference between our ages, tastes, and habits, forbids it. This he knows, and knowing, still offers me his hand. By accepting it, and by that step alone, I can release my father who is dying in this place; prolong his life, perhaps, for many years; restore him to comfort—I may almost call it affluence; and relieve a generous man from the burden of assisting one, by whom, I grieve to say, his noble heart is little understood. Do not think so poorly of me as to believe that I feign a love I do not feel. Do not report so ill of me, for that I could not bear. If I cannot, in reason or in nature, love the man who pays this price for my poor hand, I can

498

discharge the duties of a wife: I can be all he seeks in me, and will. He is content to take me as I am. I have passed my word, and should rejoice, not weep, that it is so. I do. The interest you take in one so friendless and forlorn as I, the delicacy with which you have discharged your trust, the faith you have kept with me, have my warmest thanks: and, while I make this last feeble acknowledgment, move me to tears, as you see. But I do not repent, nor am I unhappy. I am happy in the prospect of all I can achieve so easily. I shall be more so when I look back upon it, and all is done, I know.'

'Your tears fall faster as you talk of happiness,' said Nicholas, 'and you shun the contemplation of that dark future which must be laden with so much misery to you. Defer this marriage for a week. For but one week!'

'He was talking, when you came upon us just now, with such smiles as I remember to have seen of old, and have not seen for many and many a day, of the freedom that was to come tomorrow,' said Madeline, with momentary firmness, 'of the welcome change, the fresh air: all the new scenes and objects that would bring fresh life to his exhausted frame. His eye grew bright, and his face lightened at the thought. I will not defer it for an hour.'

'These are but tricks and wiles to urge you on,' cried Nicholas.

'I'll hear no more,' said Madeline, hurriedly; 'I have heard too much—more than I should—already. What I have said to you, sir, I have said as to that dear friend to whom I trust in you honourably to repeat it. Some time hence, when I am more composed and reconciled to my new mode of life, if I should live so long, I will write to him. Meantime, all holy angels shower blessings on his head, and prosper and preserve him.'

She was hurrying past Nicholas, when he threw himself before her, and implored her to think, but once again, upon the fate to which she was precipitately hastening.

'There is no retreat,' said Nicholas, in an agony of supplication; 'no withdrawing! All regret will be unavailing, and deep and bitter it must be. What can I say, that will induce you to pause at this last moment? What can I do to save you?'

'Nothing,' she incoherently replied. 'This is the hardest trial I have had. Have mercy on me, sir, I beseech, and do not pierce my heart with such appeals as these. I—I hear him calling. I—I—must not, will not, remain here for another instant.'

'If this were a plot,' said Nicholas, with the same violent rapidity with which she spoke, 'a plot, not yet laid bare by me, but which, with time, I might unravel; if you were (not knowing it) entitled to fortune of your own, which, being recovered, would do all that this marriage can accomplish, would you not retract?'

'No, no, no! It is impossible; it is a child's tale. Time would bring his death. He is calling again!'

'It may be the last time we shall ever meet on earth,' said Nicholas, 'it may be better for me that we should never meet more.'

'For both, for both,' replied Madeline, not heeding what she said. 'The time will come when to recall the memory of this one interview might drive me mad. Be sure to tell them, that you left me calm and happy. And God be with you, sir, and my grateful heart and blessing!'

She was gone. Nicholas, staggering from the house, thought of the hurried scene which had just closed upon him, as if it were the phantom of some wild, unquiet dream. The day wore on; at night, having been enabled in some measure to collect his thoughts, he issued forth again.

That night, being the last of Arthur Gride's bachelorship, found him in tiptop spirits and great glee. The bottle-green suit had been brushed, ready for the morrow. Peg Sliderskew had rendered the accounts of her past housekeeping; the eighteen-pence had been rigidly accounted for (she was never trusted with a larger sum at once, and the accounts were not usually balanced more than twice a day); every preparation had been made for the coming festival; and Arthur might have sat down and contemplated his approaching happiness, but that he preferred sitting down and contemplating the entries in a dirty old vellum-book with rusty clasps.

'Well-a-day!' he chuckled, as sinking on his knees before a strong chest screwed down to the floor, he thrust in his arm nearly up to the shoulder, and slowly drew forth this greasy volume. 'Well-a-day now, this is all my library, but it's one of the most entertaining books that were ever written! It's a delightful book, and all true and real—that's the best of it—true as the Bank of England, and real as its gold and silver. Written by Arthur Gride. He, he, he! None of your storybook writers will ever make as good a book as this, I warrant me. It's composed for private circulation, for my own particular reading, and nobody else's. He, he, he!'

Muttering this soliloquy, Arthur carried his precious volume to the table, and, adjusting it upon a dusty desk, put on his spectacles, and began to pore among the leaves.

'It's a large sum to Mr. Nickleby,' he said, in a dolorous voice. 'Debt to be paid in full, nine hundred and seventy-five, four, three. Additional sum as per bond, five hundred pound. One thousand, four hundred and seventy-five pounds, four shillings, and threepence, tomorrow at twelve o'clock. On the other side, though, there's the per contra, by means of this pretty chick. But, again, there's the question whether I mightn't have brought all this about, myself. "Faint heart never won fair lady." Why was my heart so faint? Why didn't I boldly open it to Bray myself, and save one thousand four hundred and seventy-five, four, three?'

These reflections depressed the old usurer so much, as to wring a feeble groan or two from his breast, and cause him to declare, with uplifted hands, that he would die in a workhouse. Remembering on further cogitation, however, that under any circumstances he must have paid, or handsomely compounded for, Ralph's debt, and being by no means confident that he would have succeeded had he undertaken his enterprise alone, he regained his equanimity, and chattered and mowed over more satisfactory items, until the entrance of Peg Sliderskew interrupted him.

'Aha, Peg!' said Arthur, 'what is it? What is it now, Peg?'

'It's the fowl,' replied Peg, holding up a plate containing a little, a very little one. Quite a phenomenon of a fowl. So very small and skinny.

'A beautiful bird!' said Arthur, after inquiring the price, and finding it proportionate to the size. 'With a rasher of ham, and an egg made into sauce, and potatoes, and greens, and an apple pudding, Peg, and a little bit of cheese, we shall have a dinner for an emperor. There'll only be she and me—and you, Peg, when we've done.'

'Don't you complain of the expense afterwards,' said Mrs. Sliderskew, sulkily.

'I am afraid we must live expensively for the first week,' returned Arthur, with a groan, 'and then we must make up for it. I won't eat more than I can help, and I know you love your old master too much to eat more than you can help, don't you, Peg?'

'Don't I what?' said Peg.

'Love your old master too much—'

'No, not a bit too much,' said Peg.

'Oh, dear, I wish the devil had this woman!' cried Arthur: 'love him too much to eat more than you can help at his expense.'

'At his what?' said Peg.

'Oh dear! she can never hear the most important word, and hears all the others!' whined Gride. 'At his expense—you catamaran!'

The last-mentioned tribute to the charms of Mrs. Sliderskew being uttered in a whisper, that lady assented to the general proposition by a harsh growl, which was accompanied by a ring at the street-door.

'There's the bell,' said Arthur.

'Ay, ay; I know that,' rejoined Peg.

'Then why don't you go?' bawled Arthur.

'Go where?' retorted Peg. 'I ain't doing any harm here, am I?'

Arthur Gride in reply repeated the word 'bell' as loud as he could roar; and, his meaning being rendered further intelligible to Mrs. Sliderskew's dull sense of hearing by pantomime expressive of ringing at a street-door, Peg hobbled out, after sharply demanding why he hadn't said there was a ring before, instead of talking about all manner of things that had nothing to do with it, and keeping her half-pint of beer waiting on the steps.

'There's a change come over you, Mrs. Peg,' said Arthur, following her out with his eyes. 'What it means I don't quite know; but, if it lasts, we shan't agree together long I see. You are turning crazy, I think. If you are, you must take yourself off, Mrs. Peg—or be taken off. All's one to me.' Turning over the leaves of his book as he muttered this, he soon lighted upon something which attracted his attention, and forgot Peg Sliderskew and everything else in the engrossing interest of its pages.

The room had no other light than that which it derived from a dim and dirt-clogged lamp, whose lazy wick, being still further obscured by a dark shade, cast its feeble rays over a very little space, and left all beyond in heavy shadow. This lamp the money-lender had drawn so close to him, that there was only room between it and himself for the book over which he bent; and as he sat, with his elbows on the desk, and his sharp cheek-bones resting on his hands, it only served to bring out his ugly features in strong relief, together with the little table at which he sat, and to shroud all the rest of the chamber in a deep sullen gloom. Raising his eyes, and looking vacantly into this gloom as he made some mental calculation, Arthur Gride suddenly met the fixed gaze of a man.

'Thieves! thieves!' shrieked the usurer, starting up and folding his book to his breast. 'Robbers! Murder!'

'What is the matter?' said the form, advancing.

'Keep off!' cried the trembling wretch. 'Is it a man or a—a—'

'For what do you take me, if not for a man?' was the inquiry.

'Yes, yes,' cried Arthur Gride, shading his eyes with his hand, 'it is a man, and not a spirit. It is a man. Robbers! robbers!'

'For what are these cries raised? Unless indeed you know me, and have some purpose in your brain?' said the stranger, coming close up to him. 'I am no thief.'

'What then, and how come you here?' cried Gride, somewhat reassured, but still retreating from his visitor: 'what is your name, and what do you want?'

'My name you need not know,' was the reply. 'I came here, because I was shown the way by your servant. I have addressed you twice or thrice, but you were too profoundly engaged with your book to hear me, and I have been silently waiting until you should be less abstracted. What I want I will tell you, when you can summon up courage enough to hear and understand me.'

Arthur Gride, venturing to regard his visitor more attentively, and perceiving that he was a young man of good mien and bearing, returned to his seat, and muttering that there were bad characters about, and that this, with former attempts upon his house, had made him nervous, requested his visitor to sit down. This, however, he declined.

'Good God! I don't stand up to have you at an advantage,' said Nicholas (for Nicholas it was), as he observed a gesture of alarm on the part of Gride. 'Listen to me. You are to be married tomorrow morning.'

'N—n—no,' rejoined Gride. 'Who said I was? How do you know that?'

'No matter how,' replied Nicholas, 'I know it. The young lady who is to give you her hand hates and despises you. Her blood runs cold at the mention of your name; the vulture and the lamb, the rat and the dove, could not be worse matched than you and she. You see I know her.'

Gride looked at him as if he were petrified with astonishment, but did not speak; perhaps lacking the power.

'You and another man, Ralph Nickleby by name, have hatched this plot between you,' pursued Nicholas. 'You pay him for his share in bringing about this sale of Madeline Bray. You do. A lie is trembling on your lips, I see.'

He paused; but, Arthur making no reply, resumed again.

'You pay yourself by defrauding her. How or by what means—for I scorn to sully her cause by falsehood or deceit—I do not know; at present I do not know, but I am not alone or single-handed in this business. If the energy of man can compass the discovery of your fraud and treachery before your death; if wealth, revenge, and just hatred, can hunt and track you through your windings; you will yet be called to a dear account for this. We are on the scent already; judge you, who know what we do not, when we shall have you down!'

He paused again, and still Arthur Gride glared upon him in silence.

'If you were a man to whom I could appeal with any hope of touching his compassion or humanity,' said Nicholas, 'I would urge upon you to remember the helplessness, the innocence, the youth, of this lady; her worth and beauty, her filial excellence, and last, and more than all, as concerning you more nearly, the appeal she has made to your mercy and your manly feeling. But, I take the only ground that can be taken with men like you, and ask what money will buy you off. Remember the danger to which you are exposed. You see I know enough to know much more with very little help. Bate some expected gain for the risk you save, and say what is your price.'

Old Arthur Gride moved his lips, but they only formed an ugly smile and were motionless again.

'You think,' said Nicholas, 'that the price would not be paid. Miss Bray has wealthy friends who would coin their very hearts to save her in such a strait as this. Name your price, defer these nuptials for but a few days, and see whether those I speak of, shrink from the payment. Do you hear me?'

When Nicholas began, Arthur Gride's impression was, that Ralph Nickleby had betrayed him; but, as he proceeded, he felt convinced that however he had come by the knowledge he possessed, the part he acted was a genuine one, and that with Ralph he had no concern. All he seemed to know, for certain, was, that he, Gride, paid Ralph's debt; but that, to anybody who knew the circumstances of Bray's detention—even to Bray himself, on Ralph's own statement—must be perfectly notorious. As to the fraud on Madeline herself, his visitor knew so little about its nature or extent, that it might be a lucky guess, or a hap-hazard accusation. Whether or no, he had clearly no key to the mystery, and could not hurt him who kept it close within his own breast. The allusion to friends, and the offer of money, Gride held to be mere empty vapouring, for purposes of delay. 'And even if money were to be had,' thought Arthur Gride, as he glanced at Nicholas, and trembled with passion at his boldness and audacity, 'I'd have that dainty chick for my wife, and cheat you of her, young smooth-face!'

Long habit of weighing and noting well what clients said, and nicely balancing chances in his mind and calculating odds to their faces, without the least appearance of being so engaged, had rendered Gride quick in forming conclusions, and arriving, from puzzling, intricate, and often contradictory premises, at very cunning deductions. Hence it was that, as Nicholas went on, he followed him closely with his own constructions, and, when he ceased to speak, was as well prepared as if he had deliberated for a fortnight.

'I hear you,' he cried, starting from his seat, casting back the fastenings of the window-shutters, and throwing up the sash. 'Help here! Help! Help!'

'What are you doing?' said Nicholas, seizing him by the arm.

'I'll cry robbers, thieves, murder, alarm the neighbourhood, struggle with you, let loose some blood, and swear you came to rob me, if you don't quit my house,' replied Gride, drawing in his head with a frightful grin, 'I will!'

'Wretch!' cried Nicholas.

'You'll bring your threats here, will you?' said Gride, whom jealousy of Nicholas and a sense of his own triumph had converted into a perfect fiend. 'You, the disappointed lover? Oh dear! He! he! he! But you shan't have her, nor she you. She's my wife, my doting little wife. Do you think she'll miss you? Do you think she'll weep? I shall like to see her weep, I shan't mind it. She looks prettier in tears.'

'Villain!' said Nicholas, choking with his rage.

'One minute more,' cried Arthur Gride, 'and I'll rouse the street with such screams, as, if they were raised by anybody else, should wake me even in the arms of pretty Madeline.'

'You hound!' said Nicholas. 'If you were but a younger man—'

'Oh yes!' sneered Arthur Gride, 'If I was but a younger man it wouldn't be so bad; but for me, so old and ugly! To be jilted by little Madeline for me!'

'Hear me,' said Nicholas, 'and be thankful I have enough command over myself not to fling you into the street, which no aid could prevent my doing if I once grappled with you. I have been no lover of this lady's. No contract or engagement, no word of love, has ever passed between us. She does not even know my name.'

'I'll ask it for all that. I'll beg it of her with kisses,' said Arthur Gride. 'Yes, and she'll tell me, and pay them back, and we'll laugh together, and hug ourselves, and be very merry, when we think of the poor youth that wanted to have her, but couldn't because she was bespoke by me!'

This taunt brought such an expression into the face of Nicholas, that Arthur Gride plainly apprehended it to be the forerunner of his putting his threat of throwing him into the street in immediate execution; for he thrust his head out of the window, and holding tight on with both hands, raised a pretty brisk alarm. Not thinking it necessary to abide the issue of the noise, Nicholas gave vent to an indignant defiance, and stalked from the room and from the house. Arthur Gride watched him across the street, and then, drawing in his head, fastened the window as before, and sat down to take breath.

'If she ever turns pettish or ill-humoured, I'll taunt her with that spark,' he said, when he had recovered. 'She'll little think I know about him; and, if I manage it well, I can break her spirit by this means and have her under my thumb. I'm glad nobody came. I didn't call too loud. The audacity to enter my house, and open upon me! But I shall have a very good triumph tomorrow, and he'll be gnawing his fingers off: perhaps drown himself or cut his throat! I shouldn't wonder! That would make it quite complete, that would: quite.'

When he had become restored to his usual condition by these and other comments on his approaching triumph, Arthur Gride put away his book, and, having locked the chest with great caution, descended into the kitchen to warn Peg Sliderskew to bed, and scold her for having afforded such ready admission to a stranger.

The unconscious Peg, however, not being able to comprehend the offence of which she had been guilty, he summoned her to hold the light, while he made a tour of the fastenings, and secured the street-door with his own hands.

'Top bolt,' muttered Arthur, fastening as he spoke, 'bottom bolt, chain, bar, double lock, and key out to put under my pillow! So, if any more rejected admirers come, they may come through the keyhole. And now I'll go to sleep till half-past five, when I must get up to be married, Peg!'

With that, he jocularly tapped Mrs. Sliderskew under the chin, and appeared, for the moment, inclined to celebrate the close of his bachelor days by imprinting a kiss on her shrivelled lips. Thinking better of it, however, he gave her chin another tap, in lieu of that warmer familiarity, and stole away to bed.

CHAPTER 54
The Crisis of the Project and its Result

There are not many men who lie abed too late, or oversleep themselves, on their wedding morning. A legend there is of somebody remarkable for absence of mind, who opened his eyes upon the day which was to give him a young wife, and forgetting all about the matter, rated his servants for providing him with such fine clothes as had been prepared for the festival. There is also a legend of a young gentleman, who, not having before his eyes the fear of the canons of the church for such cases made and provided, conceived a passion for his grandmother. Both cases are of a singular and special kind and it is very doubtful whether either can be considered as a precedent likely to be extensively followed by succeeding generations.

Arthur Gride had enrobed himself in his marriage garments of bottle-green, a full hour before Mrs. Sliderskew, shaking off her more heavy slumbers, knocked at his chamber door; and he had hobbled downstairs in full array and smacked his lips over a scanty taste of his favourite cordial, ere that delicate piece of antiquity enlightened the kitchen with her presence.

'Faugh!' said Peg, grubbing, in the discharge of her domestic functions, among a scanty heap of ashes in the rusty grate. 'Wedding indeed! A precious wedding! He wants somebody better than his old Peg to take care of him, does he? And what has he said to me, many and many a time, to keep me content with short food, small wages, and little fire? "My will, Peg! my will!" says he: "I'm a bachelor—no friends—no relations, Peg." Lies! And now he's to bring home a new mistress, a baby-faced chit of a girl! If he wanted a wife, the fool, why couldn't he have one suitable to his age, and that knew his ways? She won't come in my way, he says. No, that she won't, but you little think why, Arthur boy!'

While Mrs. Sliderskew, influenced possibly by some lingering feelings of disappointment and personal slight, occasioned by her old master's preference for another, was giving loose to these grumblings below stairs, Arthur Gride was cogitating in the parlour upon what had taken place last night.

'I can't think how he can have picked up what he knows,' said Arthur, 'unless I have committed myself—let something drop at Bray's, for instance—which has been overheard. Perhaps I may. I shouldn't be surprised if that was it. Mr. Nickleby was often angry at my talking to him before we got outside the door. I mustn't tell him that part of the business, or he'll put me out of sorts, and make me nervous for the day.'

Ralph was universally looked up to, and recognised among his fellows as a superior genius, but upon Arthur Gride his stern unyielding character and consummate art had made so deep an impression, that he was actually afraid of him. Cringing and cowardly to the core by nature, Arthur Gride humbled himself in the dust before Ralph Nickleby, and, even when they had not this stake in common, would have licked his shoes and crawled upon the ground before him rather than venture to return him word for word, or retort upon him in any other spirit than one of the most slavish and abject sycophancy.

To Ralph Nickleby's, Arthur Gride now betook himself according to appointment; and to Ralph Nickleby he related how, last night, some young blustering blade, whom he had never seen, forced his way into his house, and tried to frighten him from the proposed nuptials. Told, in short, what Nicholas had said and done, with the slight reservation upon which he had determined.

'Well, and what then?' said Ralph.

'Oh! nothing more,' rejoined Gride.

'He tried to frighten you,' said Ralph, 'and you were frightened I suppose; is that it?'

'I frightened him by crying thieves and murder,' replied Gride. 'Once I was in earnest, I tell you that, for I had more than half a mind to swear he uttered threats, and demanded my life or my money.'

'Oho!' said Ralph, eyeing him askew. 'Jealous too!'

'Dear now, see that!' cried Arthur, rubbing his hands and affecting to laugh.

'Why do you make those grimaces, man?' said Ralph; 'you are jealous—and with good cause I think.'

'No, no, no; not with good cause, hey? You don't think with good cause, do you?' cried Arthur, faltering. 'Do you though, hey?'

'Why, how stands the fact?' returned Ralph. 'Here is an old man about to be forced in marriage upon a girl; and to this old man there comes a handsome young fellow—you said he was handsome, didn't you?'

'No!' snarled Arthur Gride.

'Oh!' rejoined Ralph, 'I thought you did. Well! Handsome or not handsome, to this old man there comes a young fellow who casts all manner of fierce defiances in his teeth—gums I should rather say—and tells him in plain terms that his mistress hates him. What does he do that for? Philanthropy's sake?'

'Not for love of the lady,' replied Gride, 'for he said that no word of love—his very words—had ever passed between 'em.'

'He said!' repeated Ralph, contemptuously. 'But I like him for one thing, and that is, his giving you this fair warning to keep your—what is it?—Tit-tit or dainty chick—which?— under lock and key. Be careful, Gride, be careful. It's a triumph, too, to tear her away from a gallant young rival: a great triumph for an old man! It only remains to keep her safe when you have her—that's all.'

'What a man it is!' cried Arthur Gride, affecting, in the extremity of his torture, to be highly amused. And then he added, anxiously, 'Yes; to keep her safe, that's all. And that isn't much, is it?'

'Much!' said Ralph, with a sneer. 'Why, everybody knows what easy things to understand and to control, women are. But come, it's very nearly time for you to be made happy. You'll pay the bond now, I suppose, to save us trouble afterwards.'

'Oh what a man you are!' croaked Arthur.

'Why not?' said Ralph. 'Nobody will pay you interest for the money, I suppose, between this and twelve o'clock; will they?'

'But nobody would pay you interest for it either, you know,' returned Arthur, leering at Ralph with all the cunning and slyness he could throw into his face.

'Besides which,' said Ralph, suffering his lip to curl into a smile, 'you haven't the money about you, and you weren't prepared for this, or you'd have brought it with you; and there's nobody you'd so much like to accommodate as me. I see. We trust each other in about an equal degree. Are you ready?'

Gride, who had done nothing but grin, and nod, and chatter, during this last speech of Ralph's, answered in the affirmative; and, producing from his hat a couple of large white favours, pinned one on his breast, and with considerable difficulty induced his friend to do the like. Thus accoutred, they got into a hired coach which Ralph had in waiting, and drove to the residence of the fair and most wretched bride.

Gride, whose spirits and courage had gradually failed him more and more as they approached nearer and nearer to the house, was utterly dismayed and cowed by the mournful silence which pervaded it. The face of the poor servant girl, the only person they saw, was disfigured with tears and want of sleep. There was nobody to receive or welcome them; and they stole upstairs into the usual sitting-room, more like two burglars than the bridegroom and his friend.

'One would think,' said Ralph, speaking, in spite of himself, in a low and subdued voice, 'that there was a funeral going on here, and not a wedding.'

'He, he!' tittered his friend, 'you are so—so very funny!'

'I need be,' remarked Ralph, drily, 'for this is rather dull and chilling. Look a little brisker, man, and not so hangdog like!'

'Yes, yes, I will,' said Gride. 'But—but—you don't think she's coming just yet, do you?'

'Why, I suppose she'll not come till she is obliged,' returned Ralph, looking at his watch, 'and she has a good half-hour to spare yet. Curb your impatience.'

'I—I—am not impatient,' stammered Arthur. 'I wouldn't be hard with her for the world. Oh dear, dear, not on any account. Let her take her time—her own time. Her time shall be ours by all means.'

While Ralph bent upon his trembling friend a keen look, which showed that he perfectly understood the reason of this great consideration and regard, a footstep was heard upon the stairs, and Bray himself came into the room on tiptoe, and holding up his hand with a cautious gesture, as if there were some sick person near, who must not be disturbed.

'Hush!' he said, in a low voice. 'She was very ill last night. I thought she would have broken her heart. She is dressed, and crying bitterly in her own room; but she's better, and quite quiet. That's everything!'

'She is ready, is she?' said Ralph.

'Quite ready,' returned the father.

'And not likely to delay us by any young-lady weaknesses—fainting, or so forth?' said Ralph.

'She may be safely trusted now,' returned Bray. 'I have been talking to her this morning. Here! Come a little this way.'

He drew Ralph Nickleby to the further end of the room, and pointed towards Gride, who sat huddled together in a corner, fumbling nervously with the buttons of his coat, and exhibiting a face, of which every skulking and base expression was sharpened and aggravated to the utmost by his anxiety and trepidation.

'Look at that man,' whispered Bray, emphatically. 'This seems a cruel thing, after all.'

'What seems a cruel thing?' inquired Ralph, with as much stolidity of face, as if he really were in utter ignorance of the other's meaning.

'This marriage,' answered Bray. 'Don't ask me what. You know as well as I do.'

Ralph shrugged his shoulders, in silent deprecation of Bray's impatience, and elevated his eyebrows, and pursed his lips, as men do when they are prepared with a sufficient answer to some remark, but wait for a more favourable opportunity of advancing it, or think it scarcely worth while to answer their adversary at all.

'Look at him. Does it not seem cruel?' said Bray.

'No!' replied Ralph, boldly.

'I say it does,' retorted Bray, with a show of much irritation. 'It is a cruel thing, by all that's bad and treacherous!'

When men are about to commit, or to sanction the commission of some injustice, it is not uncommon for them to express pity for the object either of that or some parallel proceeding, and to feel themselves, at the time, quite virtuous and moral, and immensely superior to those who express no pity at all. This is a kind of upholding of faith above works, and is very comfortable. To do Ralph Nickleby justice, he seldom practised this sort of dissimulation; but he understood those who did, and therefore suffered Bray to say, again and again, with great vehemence, that they were jointly doing a very cruel thing, before he again offered to interpose a word.

'You see what a dry, shrivelled, withered old chip it is,' returned Ralph, when the other was at length silent. 'If he were younger, it might be cruel, but as it is—harkee, Mr. Bray, he'll die soon, and leave her a rich young widow! Miss Madeline consults your tastes this time; let her consult her own next.'

'True, true,' said Bray, biting his nails, and plainly very ill at ease. 'I couldn't do anything better for her than advise her to accept these proposals, could I? Now, I ask you, Nickleby, as a man of the world; could I?'

'Surely not,' answered Ralph. 'I tell you what, sir; there are a hundred fathers, within a circuit of five miles from this place; well off; good, rich, substantial men; who would gladly give their daughters, and their own ears with them, to that very man yonder, ape and mummy as he looks.'

'So there are!' exclaimed Bray, eagerly catching at anything which seemed a justification of himself. 'And so I told her, both last night and today.'

'You told her truth,' said Ralph, 'and did well to do so; though I must say, at the same time, that if I had a daughter, and my freedom, pleasure, nay, my very health and life, depended on her taking a husband whom I pointed out, I should hope it would not be necessary to advance any other arguments to induce her to consent to my wishes.'

Bray looked at Ralph as if to see whether he spoke in earnest, and having nodded twice or thrice in unqualified assent to what had fallen from him, said:

'I must go upstairs for a few minutes, to finish dressing. When I come down, I'll bring

Madeline with me. Do you know, I had a very strange dream last night, which I have not remembered till this instant. I dreamt that it was this morning, and you and I had been talking as we have been this minute; that I went upstairs, for the very purpose for which I am going now; and that as I stretched out my hand to take Madeline's, and lead her down, the floor sunk with me, and after falling from such an indescribable and tremendous height as the imagination scarcely conceives, except in dreams, I alighted in a grave.'

'And you awoke, and found you were lying on your back, or with your head hanging over the bedside, or suffering some pain from indigestion?' said Ralph. 'Pshaw, Mr. Bray! Do as I do (you will have the opportunity, now that a constant round of pleasure and enjoyment opens upon you), and, occupying yourself a little more by day, have no time to think of what you dream by night.'

Ralph followed him, with a steady look, to the door; and, turning to the bridegroom, when they were again alone, said,

'Mark my words, Gride, you won't have to pay his annuity very long. You have the devil's luck in bargains, always. If he is not booked to make the long voyage before many months are past and gone, I wear an orange for a head!'

To this prophecy, so agreeable to his ears, Arthur returned no answer than a cackle of great delight. Ralph, throwing himself into a chair, they both sat waiting in profound silence. Ralph was thinking, with a sneer upon his lips, on the altered manner of Bray that day, and how soon their fellowship in a bad design had lowered his pride and established a familiarity between them, when his attentive ear caught the rustling of a female dress upon the stairs, and the footstep of a man.

'Wake up,' he said, stamping his foot impatiently upon the ground, 'and be something like life, man, will you? They are here. Urge those dry old bones of yours this way. Quick, man, quick!'

Gride shambled forward, and stood, leering and bowing, close by Ralph's side, when the door opened and there entered in haste—not Bray and his daughter, but Nicholas and his sister Kate.

If some tremendous apparition from the world of shadows had suddenly presented itself before him, Ralph Nickleby could not have been more thunder-stricken than he was by this surprise. His hands fell powerless by his side, he reeled back; and with open mouth, and a face of ashy paleness, stood gazing at them in speechless rage: his eyes so prominent, and his face so convulsed and changed by the passions which raged within him, that it would have been difficult to recognise in him the same stern, composed, hard-featured man he had been not a minute ago.

'The man that came to me last night,' whispered Gride, plucking at his elbow. 'The man that came to me last night!'

'I see,' muttered Ralph, 'I know! I might have guessed as much before. Across my every path, at every turn, go where I will, do what I may, he comes!'

The absence of all colour from the face; the dilated nostril; the quivering of the lips which, though set firmly against each other, would not be still; showed what emotions were struggling for the mastery with Nicholas. But he kept them down, and gently pressing Kate's arm to reassure her, stood erect and undaunted, front to front with his unworthy relative.

As the brother and sister stood side by side, with a gallant bearing which became them well, a close likeness between them was apparent, which many, had they only seen them apart, might have failed to remark. The air, carriage, and very look and expression of the brother were all reflected in the sister, but softened and refined to the nicest limit of feminine delicacy and attraction. More striking still was some indefinable resemblance, in the face of Ralph, to both. While they had never looked more handsome, nor he more ugly; while they had never held themselves more proudly, nor he shrunk half so low; there never had been a time when this resemblance was so perceptible, or when all the worst characteristics of a face rendered coarse and harsh by evil thoughts were half so manifest as now.

'Away!' was the first word he could utter as he literally gnashed his teeth. 'Away! What brings you here? Liar, scoundrel, dastard, thief!'

'I come here,' said Nicholas in a low deep voice, 'to save your victim if I can. Liar and scoundrel you are, in every action of your life; theft is your trade; and double dastard you must be, or you were not here today. Hard words will not move me, nor would hard blows. Here I stand, and will, till I have done my errand.'

'Girl!' said Ralph, 'retire! We can use force to him, but I would not hurt you if I could help it. Retire, you weak and silly wench, and leave this dog to be dealt with as he deserves.'

'I will not retire,' cried Kate, with flashing eyes and the red blood mantling in her cheeks. 'You will do him no hurt that he will not repay. You may use force with me; I think you will, for I am a girl, and that would well become you. But if I have a girl's weakness, I have a woman's heart, and it is not you who in a cause like this can turn that from its purpose.'

'And what may your purpose be, most lofty lady?' said Ralph.

'To offer to the unhappy subject of your treachery, at this last moment,' replied Nicholas, 'a refuge and a home. If the near prospect of such a husband as you have provided will not prevail upon her, I hope she may be moved by the prayers and entreaties of one of her own sex. At all events they shall be tried. I myself, avowing to her father from whom I come and by whom I am commissioned, will render it an act of greater baseness, meanness, and cruelty in him if he still dares to force this marriage on. Here I wait to see him and his daughter. For this I came and brought my sister even into your presence. Our purpose is not to see or speak with you; therefore to you we stoop to say no more.'

'Indeed!' said Ralph. 'You persist in remaining here, ma'am, do you?'

His niece's bosom heaved with the indignant excitement into which he had lashed her, but she gave him no reply.

'Now, Gride, see here,' said Ralph. 'This fellow—I grieve to say my brother's son: a reprobate and profligate, stained with every mean and selfish crime—this fellow, coming here today to disturb a solemn ceremony, and knowing that the consequence of his presenting himself in another man's house at such a time, and persisting in remaining there, must be his being kicked into the streets and dragged through them like the vagabond he is—this fellow, mark you, brings with him his sister as a protection, thinking we would not expose a silly girl to the degradation and indignity which is no novelty to him; and, even after I have warned her of what must ensue, he still keeps her by him, as you see, and clings to her apron-strings like a cowardly boy to his mother's. Is not this a pretty fellow to talk as big as you have heard him now?'

'And as I heard him last night,' said Arthur Gride; 'as I heard him last night when he sneaked into my house, and—he! he! he!—very soon sneaked out again, when I nearly frightened him to death. And he wanting to marry Miss Madeline too! Oh dear! Is there anything else he'd like? Anything else we can do for him, besides giving her up? Would he like his debts paid and his house furnished, and a few bank notes for shaving paper if he shaves at all? He! he! he!'

'You will remain, girl, will you?' said Ralph, turning upon Kate again, 'to be hauled downstairs like a drunken drab, as I swear you shall if you stop here? No answer! Thank your brother for what follows. Gride, call down Bray—and not his daughter. Let them keep her above.'

'If you value your head,' said Nicholas, taking up a position before the door, and speaking in the same low voice in which he had spoken before, and with no more outward passion than he had before displayed; 'stay where you are!'

'Mind me, and not him, and call down Bray,' said Ralph.

'Mind yourself rather than either of us, and stay where you are!' said Nicholas.

'Will you call down Bray?' cried Ralph.

'Remember that you come near me at your peril,' said Nicholas.

Gride hesitated. Ralph being, by this time, as furious as a baffled tiger, made for the door, and, attempting to pass Kate, clasped her arm roughly with his hand. Nicholas, with his eyes darting fire, seized him by the collar. At that moment, a heavy body fell with great violence on the floor above, and, in an instant afterwards, was heard a most appalling and terrific scream.

They all stood still, and gazed upon each other. Scream succeeded scream; a heavy pattering of feet succeeded; and many shrill voices clamouring together were heard to cry, 'He is dead!'

'Stand off!' cried Nicholas, letting loose all the passion he had restrained till now; 'if this is what I scarcely dare to hope it is, you are caught, villains, in your own toils.'

He burst from the room, and, darting upstairs to the quarter from whence the noise proceeded, forced his way through a crowd of persons who quite filled a small bed-chamber, and found Bray lying on the floor quite dead; his daughter clinging to the body.

'How did this happen?' he cried, looking wildly about him.

Several voices answered together, that he had been observed, through the half-opened door, reclining in a strange and uneasy position upon a chair; that he had been spoken to several times, and not answering, was supposed to be asleep, until some person going in and shaking him by the arm, he fell heavily to the ground and was discovered to be dead.

'Who is the owner of this house?' said Nicholas, hastily.

An elderly woman was pointed out to him; and to her he said, as he knelt down and gently unwound Madeline's arms from the lifeless mass round which they were entwined: 'I represent this lady's nearest friends, as her servant here knows, and must remove her from this dreadful scene. This is my sister to whose charge you confide her. My name and address are upon that card, and you shall receive from me all necessary directions for the arrangements that must be made. Stand aside, every one of you, and give me room and air for God's sake!'

The people fell back, scarce wondering more at what had just occurred, than at the excitement and impetuosity of him who spoke. Nicholas, taking the insensible girl in his arms, bore her from the chamber and downstairs into the room he had just quitted, followed by his sister and the faithful servant, whom he charged to procure a coach directly, while he and Kate bent over their beautiful charge and endeavoured, but in vain, to restore her to animation. The girl performed her office with such expedition, that in a very few minutes the coach was ready.

Ralph Nickleby and Gride, stunned and paralysed by the awful event which had so suddenly overthrown their schemes (it would not otherwise, perhaps, have made much impression on them), and carried away by the extraordinary energy and precipitation of Nicholas, which bore down all before him, looked on at these proceedings like men in a dream or trance. It was not until every preparation was made for Madeline's immediate removal that Ralph broke silence by declaring she should not be taken away.

'Who says so?' cried Nicholas, rising from his knee and confronting them, but still retaining Madeline's lifeless hand in his.

'I!' answered Ralph, hoarsely.

'Hush, hush!' cried the terrified Gride, catching him by the arm again. 'Hear what he says.'

'Ay!' said Nicholas, extending his disengaged hand in the air, 'hear what he says. That both your debts are paid in the one great debt of nature. That the bond, due today at twelve, is now waste paper. That your contemplated fraud shall be discovered yet. That your schemes are known to man, and overthrown by Heaven. Wretches, that he defies you both to do your worst.'

'This man,' said Ralph, in a voice scarcely intelligible, 'this man claims his wife, and he shall have her.'

'That man claims what is not his, and he should not have her if he were fifty men, with fifty more to back him,' said Nicholas.

'Who shall prevent him?'

'I will.'

'By what right I should like to know,' said Ralph. 'By what right I ask?'

'By this right. That, knowing what I do, you dare not tempt me further,' said Nicholas, 'and by this better right; that those I serve, and with whom you would have done me base wrong and injury, are her nearest and her dearest friends. In their name I bear her hence. Give way!'

'One word!' cried Ralph, foaming at the mouth.

'Not one,' replied Nicholas, 'I will not hear of one—save this. Look to yourself, and heed this warning that I give you! Your day is past, and night is comin' on.'

'My curse, my bitter, deadly curse, upon you, boy!'

'Whence will curses come at your command? Or what avails a curse or blessing from a man like you? I tell you, that misfortune and discovery are thickening about your head; that the structures you have raised, through all your ill-spent life, are crumbling into dust; that your path is beset with spies; that this very day, ten thousand pounds of your hoarded wealth have gone in one great crash!'

''Tis false!' cried Ralph, shrinking back.

''Tis true, and you shall find it so. I have no more words to waste. Stand from the door. Kate, do you go first. Lay not a hand on her, or on that woman, or on me, or so much a brush their garments as they pass you by!—You let them pass, and he blocks the door again!'

Arthur Gride happened to be in the doorway, but whether intentionally or from confusion was not quite apparent. Nicholas swung him away, with such violence as to cause him to spin round the room until he was caught by a sharp angle of the wall, and there knocked down; and then taking his beautiful burden in his arms rushed out. No one cared to stop him, if any were so disposed. Making his way through a mob of people, whom a report of the circumstances had attracted round the house, and carrying Madeline, in his excitement, as easily as if she were an infant, he reached the coach in which Kate and the girl were already waiting, and, confiding his charge to them, jumped up beside the coachman and bade him drive away.

CHAPTER 55
Of Family Matters, Cares, Hopes, Disappointments, and Sorrows

Although Mrs. Nickleby had been made acquainted by her son and daughter with every circumstance of Madeline Bray's history which was known to them; although the responsible situation in which Nicholas stood had been carefully explained to her, and she had been prepared, even for the possible contingency of having to receive the young lady in her own house, improbable as such a result had appeared only a few minutes before it came about, still, Mrs. Nickleby, from the moment when this confidence was first reposed in her, late on the previous evening, had remained in an unsatisfactory and profoundly mystified state, from which no explanations or arguments could relieve her, and which every fresh soliloquy and reflection only aggravated more and more.

'Bless my heart, Kate!' so the good lady argued; 'if the Mr. Cheerybles don't want this young lady to be married, why don't they file a bill against the Lord Chancellor, make her a Chancery ward, and shut her up in the Fleet prison for safety?—I have read of such things in the newspapers a hundred times. Or, if they are so very fond of her as Nicholas says they are, why don't they marry her themselves—one of them I mean? And even supposing they don't want her to be married, and don't want to marry her themselves, why in the name of wonder should Nicholas go about the world, forbidding people's banns?'

'I don't think you quite understand,' said Kate, gently.

'Well I am sure, Kate, my dear, you're very polite!' replied Mrs. Nickleby. 'I have been married myself I hope, and I have seen other people married. Not understand, indeed!'

'I know you have had great experience, dear mama,' said Kate; 'I mean that perhaps you don't quite understand all the circumstances in this instance. We have stated them awkwardly, I dare say.'

'That I dare say you have,' retorted her mother, briskly. 'That's very likely. I am not to be held accountable for that; though, at the same time, as the circumstances speak for themselves, I shall take the liberty, my love, of saying that I do understand them, and perfectly well too; whatever you and Nicholas may choose to think to the contrary. Why is such a great fuss made because this Miss Magdalen is going to marry somebody who is older than herself? Your poor papa was older than I was, four years and a half older. Jane Dibabs—the Dibabses lived in the beautiful little thatched white house one story high, covered all over with ivy and creeping plants, with an exquisite little porch with twining honysuckles and all sorts of things: where the earwigs used to fall into one's tea on a summer evening, and always fell upon their backs and kicked dreadfully, and where the frogs used to get into the rushlight shades when one stopped all night, and sit up and look through the little holes like Christians—Jane Dibabs, she married a man who was a great deal older than herself, and would marry him, notwithstanding all that could be said to the contrary, and she was so fond of him that nothing was ever equal to it. There was no fuss made about Jane Dibabs, and her husband was a most honourable and excellent man, and everybody spoke well of him. Then why should there by any fuss about this Magdalen?'

'Her husband is much older; he is not her own choice; his character is the very reverse of that which you have just described. Don't you see a broad destinction between the two cases?' said Kate.

To this, Mrs. Nickleby only replied that she durst say she was very stupid, indeed she had no doubt she was, for her own children almost as much as told her so, every day of her life; to be sure she was a little older than they, and perhaps some foolish people might think she ought reasonably to know best. However, no doubt she was wrong; of course she was; she always was, she couldn't be right, she couldn't be expected to be; so she had better not expose herself any more; and to all Kate's conciliations and concessions for an hour ensuing, the good lady gave no other replies than Oh, certainly, why did they ask her?, her opinion was of no consequence, it didn't matter what she said, with many other rejoinders of the same class.

In this frame of mind (expressed, when she had become too resigned for speech, by nods of the head, upliftings of the eyes, and little beginnings of groans, converted, as they attracted attention, into short coughs), Mrs Nickleby remained until Nicholas and Kate returned with the object of their solicitude; when, having by this time asserted her own importance, and becoming besides interested in the trials of one so young and beautiful, she not only displayed the utmost zeal and solicitude, but took great credit to herself for recommending the course of procedure which her son had adopted: frequently declaring, with an expressive look, that it was very fortunate things were as they were: and hinting, that but for great encouragement and wisdom on her own part, they never could have been brought to that pass.

Not to strain the question whether Mrs. Nickleby had or had not any great hand in bringing matters about, it is unquestionable that she had strong ground for exultation. The brothers, on their return, bestowed such commendations on Nicholas for the part he had taken, and evinced so much joy at the altered state of events and the recovery of their young friend from trials so great and dangers so threatening, that, as she more than once informed her daughter, she now considered the fortunes of the family 'as good as' made. Mr. Charles Cheeryble, indeed, Mrs. Nickleby positively asserted, had, in the first transports of his surprise and delight, 'as good as' said so. Without precisely explaining what this qualification meant, she subsided, whenever she mentioned the subject, into such a mysterious and important state, and had such visions of wealth and dignity in perspective, that (vague and clouded though they were) she was, at such times, almost as happy as if she had really been permanently provided for, on a scale of great splendour.

The sudden and terrible shock she had received, combined with the great affliction and anxiety of mind which she had, for a long time, endured, proved too much for Madeline's strength. Recovering from the state of stupefaction into which the sudden death of her father happily plunged her, she only exchanged that condition for one of dangerous and active illness. When the delicate physical powers which have been sustained by an unnatural strain upon the mental energies and a resolute determination not to yield, at last give way, their degree of prostration is usually proportionate to the strength of the effort which has previously upheld them. Thus it was that the illness which fell on Madeline was of no slight or temporary nature, but one which, for a time, threatened her reason, and—scarcely worse—her life itself.

Who, slowly recovering from a disorder so severe and dangerous, could be insensible to the unremitting attentions of such a nurse as gentle, tender, earnest Kate? On whom could the sweet soft voice, the light step, the delicate hand, the quiet, cheerful, noiseless discharge of those thousand little offices of kindness and relief which we feel so deeply when we are ill, and forget so lightly when we are well—on whom could they make so deep an impression as on a young heart stored with every pure and true affection that women cherish; almost a stranger to the endearments and devotion of its own sex, save as it learnt them from itself; and rendered, by calamity and suffering, keenly susceptible of the sympathy so long unknown and so long sought in vain? What wonder that days became as years in knitting them together! What wonder, if with every hour of returning health, there came some stronger and sweeter recognition of the praises which Kate, when they recalled old scenes—they seemed old now, and to have been acted years ago—would lavish on her brother! Where would have been the wonder, even, if those praises had found a quick response in the breast of Madeline, and if, with the image of Nicholas so constantly recurring in the features of his sister that she could scarcely separate the two, she had sometimes found it equally difficult to assign to each the feelings they had first inspired, and had imperceptibly mingled with her gratitude to Nicholas, some of that warmer feeling which she had assigned to Kate?

'My dear,' Mrs. Nickleby would say, coming into the room with an elaborate caution, calculated to discompose the nerves of an invalid rather more than the entry of a horse-soldier at full gallop; 'how do you find yourself tonight? I hope you are better.'

'Almost well, mama,' Kate would reply, laying down her work, and taking Madeline's hand in hers.

'Kate!' Mrs. Nickleby would say, reprovingly, 'don't talk so loud' (the worthy lady herself talking in a whisper that would have made the blood of the stoutest man run cold in his veins).

Kate would take this reproof very quietly, and Mrs. Nickleby, making every board creak and every thread rustle as she moved stealthily about, would add:

'My son Nicholas has just come home, and I have come, according to custom, my dear, to know, from your own lips, exactly how you are; for he won't take my account, and never will.'

'He is later than usual to-night,' perhaps Madeline would reply. 'Nearly half an hour.'

'Well, I never saw such people in all my life as you are, for time, up here!' Mrs. Nickleby would exclaim in great astonishment; 'I declare I never did! I had not the least idea that Nicholas was after his time, not the smallest. Mr. Nickleby used to say—your poor papa, I am speaking of, Kate my dear—used to say, that appetite was the best clock in the world, but you have no appetite, my dear Miss Bray, I wish you had, and upon my word I really think you ought to take something that would give you one. I am sure I don't know, but I have heard that two or three dozen native lobsters give an appetite, though that comes to the same thing after all, for I suppose you must have an appetite before you can take 'em. If I said lobsters, I meant oysters, but of course it's all the same, though really how you came to know about Nicholas—'

'We happened to be just talking about him, mama; that was it.'

'You never seem to me to be talking about anything else, Kate, and upon my word I am quite surprised at your being so very thoughtless. You can find subjects enough to talk about sometimes, and when you know how important it is to keep up Miss Bray's spirits, and interest her, and all that, it really is quite extraordinary to me what can induce you to keep on prose, prose, prose, din, din, din, everlastingly, upon the same theme. You are a very kind nurse, Kate, and a very good one, and I know you mean very well; but I will say this—that if it wasn't for me, I really don't know what would become of Miss Bray's spirits, and so I tell the doctor every day. He says he wonders how I sustain my own, and I am sure I very often wonder myself how I can contrive to keep up as I do. Of course it's an exertion, but still, when I know how much depends upon me in this house, I am obliged to make it. There's nothing praiseworthy in that, but it's necessary, and I do it.'

With that, Mrs. Nickleby would draw up a chair, and for some three-quarters of an hour run through a great variety of distracting topics in the most distracting manner possible; tearing herself away, at length, on the plea that she must now go and amuse Nicholas while he took his supper. After a preliminary raising of his spirits with the information that she considered the patient decidedly worse, she would further cheer him up by relating how dull, listless, and low-spirited Miss Bray was, because Kate foolishly talked about nothing else but him and family matters. When she had made Nicholas thoroughly comfortable with these and other inspiriting remarks, she would discourse at length on the arduous duties she had performed that day; and, sometimes, be moved to tears in wondering how, if anything were to happen to herself, the family would ever get on without her.

At other times, when Nicholas came home at night, he would be accompanied by Mr. Frank Cheeryble, who was commissioned by the brothers to inquire how Madeline was that evening. On such occasions (and they were of very frequent occurrence), Mrs. Nickleby deemed it of particular importance that she should have her wits about her; for, from certain signs and tokens which had attracted her attention, she shrewdly suspected that Mr. Frank, interested as his uncles were in Madeline, came quite as much to see Kate as to inquire after her; the more especially as the brothers were in constant communication with the medical man, came backwards and forwards very frequently themselves, and received a full report from Nicholas every morning. These were proud times for Mrs. Nickleby; never was anybody half so discreet and sage as she, or half so mysterious withal; and never were there such cunning generalship, and such unfathomable designs, as she brought to bear upon Mr. Frank, with the view of ascertaining whether her suspicions were well founded: and if so, of tantalising him into taking her into his confidence and throwing himself upon her merciful consideration. Extensive was the artillery, heavy and light, which Mrs Nickleby brought into play for the furtherance of these great schemes; various and opposite the means which she employed to bring about the end she had in view. At one time, she was all cordiality and ease; at another, all stiffness and frigidity. Now, she would seem to open her whole heart to her unhappy victim; the next time they met, she would receive him with the most distant and studious reserve, as if a new light had broken in upon her, and, guessing his intentions, she had resolved to check them in the bud; as if she felt it her bounden duty to act with Spartan firmness, and at once and for ever to discourage hopes which never could be realised. At other times, when Nicholas was not there to overhear, and Kate was upstairs busily tending her sick friend, the worthy lady would throw out dark hints of an intention to send her daughter to France for three or four years, or to Scotland for the improvement of her health impaired by her late fatigues, or to America on a visit, or anywhere that threatened a long and tedious separation. Nay, she even went so far as to hint, obscurely, at an attachment entertained for her daughter by the son of an old neighbour of theirs, one Horatio Peltirogus (a young gentleman who might have been, at that time, four years old, or thereabouts), and to represent it, indeed, as almost a settled thing between the families—only waiting for her daughter's final decision, to come off with the sanction of the church, and to the unspeakable happiness and content of all parties.

It was in the full pride and glory of having sprung this last mine one night with extraordinary success, that Mrs. Nickleby took the opportunity of being left alone with her son before retiring to rest, to sound him on the subject which so occupied her thoughts: not doubting that they could have but one opinion respecting it. To this end, she approached the question with divers laudatory and appropriate remarks touching the general amiability of Mr. Frank Cheeryble.

'You are quite right, mother,' said Nicholas, 'quite right. He is a fine fellow.'

'Good-looking, too,' said Mrs. Nickleby.

'Decidedly good-looking,' answered Nicholas.

'What may you call his nose, now, my dear?' pursued Mrs. Nickleby, wishing to interest Nicholas in the subject to the utmost.

'Call it?' repeated Nicholas.

'Ah!' returned his mother, 'what style of nose? What order of architecture, if one may say so. I am not very learned in noses. Do you call it a Roman or a Grecian?'

'Upon my word, mother,' said Nicholas, laughing, 'as well as I remember, I should call it a kind of Composite, or mixed nose. But I have no very strong recollection on the subject. If it will afford you any gratification, I'll observe it more closely, and let you know.'

'I wish you would, my dear,' said Mrs. Nickleby, with an earnest look.

'Very well,' returned Nicholas. 'I will.'

Nicholas returned to the perusal of the book he had been reading, when the dialogue had gone thus far. Mrs. Nickleby, after stopping a little for consideration, resumed.

'He is very much attached to you, Nicholas, my dear.'

Nicholas laughingly said, as he closed his book, that he was glad to hear it, and observed that his mother seemed deep in their new friend's confidence already.

'Hem!' said Mrs. Nickleby. 'I don't know about that, my dear, but I think it is very necessary that somebody should be in his confidence; highly necessary.'

Elated by a look of curiosity from her son, and the consciousness of possessing a great secret, all to herself, Mrs. Nickleby went on with great animation:

'I am sure, my dear Nicholas, how you can have failed to notice it, is, to me, quite extraordinary; though I don't know why I should say that, either, because, of course, as far as it goes, and to a certain extent, there is a great deal in this sort of thing, especially in this early stage, which, however clear it may be to females, can scarcely be expected to be so evident to men. I don't say that I have any particular penetration in such matters. I may have; those about me should know best about that, and perhaps do know. Upon that point I shall express no opinion, it wouldn't become me to do so, it's quite out of the question, quite.'

Nicholas snuffed the candles, put his hands in his pockets, and, leaning back in his chair, assumed a look of patient suffering and melancholy resignation.

'I think it my duty, Nicholas, my dear,' resumed his mother, 'to tell you what I know: not only because you have a right to know it too, and to know everything that happens in this family, but because you have it in your power to promote and assist the thing very much; and there is no doubt that the sooner one can come to a clear understanding on such subjects, it is always better, every way. There are a great many things you might do; such as taking a walk in the garden sometimes, or sitting upstairs in your own room for a little while, or making believe to fall asleep occasionally, or pretending that you recollected some business, and going out for an hour or so, and taking Mr. Smike with you. These seem very slight things, and I dare say you will be amused at my making them of so much importance; at the same time, my dear, I can assure you (and you'll find this out, Nicholas, for yourself one of these days, if you ever fall in love with anybody; as I trust and hope you will, provided she is respectable and well conducted, and of course you'd never dream of falling in love with anybody who was not), I say, I can assure you that a great deal more depends upon these little things than you would suppose possible. If your poor papa was alive, he would tell you how much depended on the parties being left alone. Of course, you are not to go out of the room as if you meant it and did it on purpose, but as if it was quite an accident, and to come back again in the same way. If you cough in the passage before you open the door, or whistle carelessly, or hum a tune, or something of that sort, to let them know you're coming, it's always better; because, of course, though it's not only natural but perfectly correct and proper under the circumstances, still it is very confusing if you interrupt young people when they are—when they are sitting on the sofa, and—and all that sort of thing: which is very nonsensical, perhaps, but still they will do it.'

The profound astonishment with which her son regarded her during this long address, gradually increasing as it approached its climax in no way discomposed Mrs. Nickleby, but rather exalted her opinion of her own cleverness; therefore, merely stopping to remark, with much complacency, that she had fully expected him to be surprised, she entered on a vast quantity of circumstantial evidence of a particularly incoherent and perplexing kind; the upshot of which was, to establish, beyond the possibility of doubt, that Mr. Frank Cheeryble had fallen desperately in love with Kate.

'With whom?' cried Nicholas.

Mrs. Nickleby repeated, with Kate.

'What! our Kate! My sister!'

'Lord, Nicholas!' returned Mrs. Nickleby, 'whose Kate should it be, if not ours; or what should I care about it, or take any interest in it for, if it was anybody but your sister?'

'Dear mother,' said Nicholas, 'surely it can't be!'

'Very good, my dear,' replied Mrs. Nickleby, with great confidence. 'Wait and see.'

Nicholas had never, until that moment, bestowed a thought upon the remote possibility of such an occurrence as that which was now communicated to him; for, besides that he had been much from home of late and closely occupied with other matters, his own jealous fears had prompted the suspicion that some secret interest in Madeline, akin to that which he felt himself, occasioned those visits of Frank Cheeryble which had recently become so frequent. Even now, although he knew that the observation of an anxious mother was much more likely to be correct in such a case than his own, and although she reminded him of many little circumstances which, taken together, were certainly susceptible of the construction she triumphantly put upon them, he was not quite convinced but that they arose from mere good-natured thoughtless gallantry, which would have dictated the same conduct towards any other girl who was young and pleasing. At all events, he hoped so, and therefore tried to believe it.

'I am very much disturbed by what you tell me,' said Nicholas, after a little reflection, 'though I yet hope you may be mistaken.'

'I don't understand why you should hope so,' said Mrs. Nickleby, 'I confess; but you may depend upon it I am not.'

'What of Kate?' inquired Nicholas.

'Why that, my dear,' returned Mrs. Nickleby, 'is just the point upon which I am not yet satisfied. During this sickness, she has been constantly at Madeline's bedside—never were two people so fond of each other as they have grown—and to tell you the truth, Nicholas, I have rather kept her away now and then, because I think it's a good plan, and urges a young man on. He doesn't get too sure, you know.'

She said this with such a mingling of high delight and self-congratulation, that it was inexpressibly painful to Nicholas to dash her hopes; but he felt that there was only one honourable course before him, and that he was bound to take it.

'Dear mother,' he said kindly, 'don't you see that if there were really any serious inclination on the part of Mr. Frank towards Kate, and we suffered ourselves for a moment to encourage it, we should be acting a most dishonourable and ungrateful part? I ask you if you don't see it, but I need not say that I know you don't, or you would have been more strictly on your guard. Let me explain my meaning to you. Remember how poor we are.'

Mrs. Nickleby shook her head, and said, through her tears, that poverty was not a crime.

'No,' said Nicholas, 'and for that reason poverty should engender an honest pride, that it may not lead and tempt us to unworthy actions, and that we may preserve the self-respect which a hewer of wood and drawer of water may maintain, and does better in maintaining than a monarch in preserving his. Think what we owe to these two brothers: remember what they have done, and what they do every day for us with a generosity and delicacy for which the devotion of our whole lives would be a most imperfect and inadequate return. What kind of return would that be which would be comprised in our permitting their nephew, their only relative, whom they regard as a son, and for whom it would be mere childishness to suppose they have not formed plans suitably adapted to the education he has had, and the fortune he will inherit—in our permitting him to marry a portionless girl: so closely connected with us, that the irresistible inference must be, that he was entrapped by a plot; that it was a deliberate scheme, and a speculation amongst us three? Bring the matter clearly before yourself, mother. Now, how would you feel, if they were married, and the brothers, coming here on one of those kind errands which bring them here so often, you had to break out to them the truth? Would you be at ease, and feel that you had played an open part?'

Poor Mrs. Nickleby, crying more and more, murmured that of course Mr. Frank would ask the consent of his uncles first.

'Why, to be sure, that would place him in a better situation with them,' said Nicholas, 'but we should still be open to the same suspicions; the distance between us would still be as great; the advantages to be gained would still be as manifest as now. We may be reckoning without our host in all this,' he added more cheerfully, 'and I trust, and almost believe we are. If it be otherwise, I have that confidence in Kate that I know she will feel as I do—and in you, dear mother, to be assured that after a little consideration you will do the same.'

After many more representations and entreaties, Nicholas obtained a promise from Mrs. Nickleby that she would try all she could to think as he did; and that if Mr. Frank persevered in his attentions she would endeavour to discourage them, or, at the least, would render him no countenance or assistance. He determined to forbear mentioning the subject to Kate until he was quite convinced that there existed a real necessity for his doing so; and resolved to assure himself, as well as he could by close personal observation, of the exact position of affairs. This was a very wise resolution, but he was prevented from putting it in practice by a new source of anxiety and uneasiness.

Smike became alarmingly ill; so reduced and exhausted that he could scarcely move from room to room without assistance; and so worn and emaciated, that it was painful to look upon him. Nicholas was warned, by the same medical authority to whom he had at first appealed, that the last chance and hope of his life depended on his being instantly removed from London. That part of Devonshire in which Nicholas had been himself bred was named as the most favourable spot; but this advice was cautiously coupled with the information, that whoever accompanied him thither must be prepared for the worst; for every token of rapid consumption had appeared, and he might never return alive.

The kind brothers, who were acquainted with the poor creature's sad history, dispatched old Tim to be present at this consultation. That same morning, Nicholas was summoned by brother Charles into his private room, and thus addressed:

'My dear sir, no time must be lost. This lad shall not die, if such human means as we can use can save his life; neither shall he die alone, and in a strange place. Remove him tomorrow morning, see that he has every comfort that his situation requires, and don't leave him; don't leave him, my dear sir, until you know that there is no longer any immediate danger. It would be hard, indeed, to part you now. No, no, no! Tim shall wait upon you tonight, sir; Tim shall wait upon you tonight with a parting word or two. Brother Ned, my dear fellow, Mr. Nickleby waits to shake hands and say goodbye; Mr. Nickleby won't be long gone; this poor chap will soon get better, very soon get better; and then he'll find out some nice homely country-people to leave him with, and will go backwards and forwards sometimes—backwards and forwards you know, Ned. And there's no cause to be downhearted, for he'll very soon get better, very soon. Won't he, won't he, Ned?'

What Tim Linkinwater said, or what he brought with him that night, needs not to be told. Next morning Nicholas and his feeble companion began their journey.

And who but one—and that one he who, but for those who crowded round him then, had never met a look of kindness, or known a word of pity—could tell what agony of mind, what blighted thoughts, what unavailing sorrow, were involved in that sad parting?

'See,' cried Nicholas eagerly, as he looked from the coach window, 'they are at the corner of the lane still! And now there's Kate, poor Kate, whom you said you couldn't bear to say goodbye to, waving her handkerchief. Don't go without one gesture of farewell to Kate!'

'I cannot make it!' cried his trembling companion, falling back in his seat and covering his eyes. 'Do you see her now? Is she there still?'

'Yes, yes!' said Nicholas earnestly. 'There! She waves her hand again! I have answered it for you—and now they are out of sight. Do not give way so bitterly, dear friend, don't. You will meet them all again.'

He whom he thus encouraged, raised his withered hands and clasped them fervently together.

'In heaven. I humbly pray to God in heaven.'

It sounded like the prayer of a broken heart.

CHAPTER 56

Ralph Nickleby, baffled by his Nephew in his late Design, hatches a Scheme of Retaliation which Accident suggests to him, and takes into his Counsels a tried Auxiliary

The course which these adventures shape out for themselves, and imperatively call upon the historian to observe, now demands that they should revert to the point they attained previously to the commencement of the last chapter, when Ralph Nickleby and Arthur Gride were left together in the house where death had so suddenly reared his dark and heavy banner.

With clenched hands, and teeth ground together so firm and tight that no locking of the jaws could have fixed and riveted them more securely, Ralph stood, for some minutes, in the attitude in which he had last addressed his nephew: breathing heavily, but as rigid and motionless in other respects as if he had been a brazen statue. After a time, he began, by slow degrees, as a man rousing himself from heavy slumber, to relax. For a moment he shook his clasped fist towards the door by which Nicholas had disappeared; and then thrusting it into his breast, as if to repress by force even this show of passion, turned round and confronted the less hardy usurer, who had not yet risen from the ground.

The cowering wretch, who still shook in every limb, and whose few grey hairs trembled and quivered on his head with abject dismay, tottered to his feet as he met Ralph's eye, and, shielding his face with both hands, protested, while he crept towards the door, that it was no fault of his.

'Who said it was, man?' returned Ralph, in a suppressed voice. 'Who said it was?'

'You looked as if you thought I was to blame,' said Gride, timidly.

'Pshaw!' Ralph muttered, forcing a laugh. 'I blame him for not living an hour longer. One hour longer would have been long enough. I blame no one else.'

'N—n—no one else?' said Gride.

'Not for this mischance,' replied Ralph. 'I have an old score to clear with that young fellow who has carried off your mistress; but that has nothing to do with his blustering just now, for we should soon have been quit of him, but for this cursed accident.'

There was something so unnatural in the calmness with which Ralph Nickleby spoke, when coupled with his face, the expression of the features, to which every nerve and muscle, as it twitched and throbbed with a spasm whose workings no effort could conceal, gave, every instant, some new and frightful aspect—there was something so unnatural and ghastly in the contrast between his harsh, slow, steady voice (only altered by a certain halting of the breath which made him pause between almost every word like a drunken man bent upon speaking plainly), and these evidences of the most intense and violent passion, and the struggle he made to keep them under; that if the dead body which lay above had stood, instead of him, before the cowering Gride, it could scarcely have presented a spectacle which would have terrified him more.

'The coach,' said Ralph after a time, during which he had struggled like some strong man against a fit. 'We came in a coach. Is it waiting?'

Gride gladly availed himself of the pretext for going to the window to see. Ralph, keeping his face steadily the other way, tore at his shirt with the hand which he had thrust into his breast, and muttered in a hoarse whisper:

'Ten thousand pounds! He said ten thousand! The precise sum paid in but yesterday for the two mortgages, and which would have gone out again, at heavy interest, tomorrow. If that house has failed, and he the first to bring the news!—Is the coach there?'

'Yes, yes,' said Gride, startled by the fierce tone of the inquiry. 'It's here. Dear, dear, what a fiery man you are!'

'Come here,' said Ralph, beckoning to him. 'We mustn't make a show of being disturbed. We'll go down arm in arm.'

'But you pinch me black and blue,' urged Gride.

Ralph let him go impatiently, and descending the stairs with his usual firm and heavy tread, got into the coach. Arthur Gride followed. After looking doubtfully at Ralph when the man asked where he was to drive, and finding that he remained silent, and expressed no wish upon the subject, Arthur mentioned his own house, and thither they proceeded.

On their way, Ralph sat in the furthest corner with folded arms, and uttered not a word. With his chin sunk upon his breast, and his downcast eyes quite hidden by the contraction of his knotted brows, he might have been asleep for any sign of consciousness he gave until the coach stopped, when he raised his head, and glancing through the window, inquired what place that was.

'My house,' answered the disconsolate Gride, affected perhaps by its loneliness. 'Oh dear!

my house.'

'True,' said Ralph 'I have not observed the way we came. I should like a glass of water. You have that in the house, I suppose?'

'You shall have a glass of—of anything you like,' answered Gride, with a groan. 'It's no use knocking, coachman. Ring the bell!'

The man rang, and rang, and rang again; then, knocked until the street re-echoed with the sounds; then, listened at the keyhole of the door. Nobody came. The house was silent as the grave.

'How's this?' said Ralph impatiently.

'Peg is so very deaf,' answered Gride with a look of anxiety and alarm. 'Oh dear! Ring again, coachman. She sees the bell.'

Again the man rang and knocked, and knocked and rang again. Some of the neighbours threw up their windows, and called across the street to each other that old Gride's housekeeper must have dropped down dead. Others collected round the coach, and gave vent to various surmises; some held that she had fallen asleep; some, that she had burnt herself to death; some, that she had got drunk; and one very fat man that she had seen something to eat which had frightened her so much (not being used to it) that she had fallen into a fit. This last suggestion particularly delighted the bystanders, who cheered it rather uproariously, and were, with some difficulty, deterred from dropping down the area and breaking open the kitchen door to ascertain the fact. Nor was this all. Rumours having gone abroad that Arthur was to be married that morning, very particular inquiries were made after the bride, who was held by the majority to be disguised in the person of Mr. Ralph Nickleby, which gave rise to much jocose indignation at the public appearance of a bride in boots and pantaloons, and called forth a great many hoots and groans. At length, the two money-lenders obtained shelter in a house next door, and, being accommodated with a ladder, clambered over the wall of the back-yard—which was not a high one—and descended in safety on the other side.

'I am almost afraid to go in, I declare,' said Arthur, turning to Ralph when they were alone. 'Suppose she should be murdered. Lying with her brains knocked out by a poker, eh?'

'Suppose she were,' said Ralph. 'I tell you, I wish such things were more common than they are, and more easily done. You may stare and shiver. I do!'

He applied himself to a pump in the yard; and, having taken a deep draught of water and flung a quantity on his head and face, regained his accustomed manner and led the way into the house: Gride following close at his heels.

It was the same dark place as ever: every room dismal and silent as it was wont to be, and every ghostly article of furniture in its customary place. The iron heart of the grim old clock, undisturbed by all the noise without, still beat heavily within its dusty case; the tottering presses slunk from the sight, as usual, in their melancholy corners; the echoes of footsteps returned the same dreary sound; the long-legged spider paused in his nimble run, and, scared by the sight of men in that his dull domain, hung motionless on the wall, counterfeiting death until they should have passed him by.

From cellar to garret went the two usurers, opening every creaking door and looking into every deserted room. But no Peg was there. At last, they sat them down in the apartment which

Arthur Gride usually inhabited, to rest after their search.

'The hag is out, on some preparation for your wedding festivities, I suppose,' said Ralph, preparing to depart. 'See here! I destroy the bond; we shall never need it now.'

Gride, who had been peering narrowly about the room, fell, at that moment, upon his knees before a large chest, and uttered a terrible yell.

'How now?' said Ralph, looking sternly round.

'Robbed! robbed!' screamed Arthur Gride.

'Robbed! of money?'

'No, no, no. Worse! far worse!'

'Of what then?' demanded Ralph.

'Worse than money, worse than money!' cried the old man, casting the papers out of the chest, like some beast tearing up the earth. 'She had better have stolen money—all my money—I haven't much! She had better have made me a beggar than have done this!'

'Done what?' said Ralph. 'Done what, you devil's dotard?'

Still Gride made no answer, but tore and scratched among the papers, and yelled and screeched like a fiend in torment.

'There is something missing, you say,' said Ralph, shaking him furiously by the collar. 'What is it?'

'Papers, deeds. I am a ruined man. Lost, lost! I am robbed, I am ruined! She saw me reading it—reading it of late—I did very often—She watched me, saw me put it in the box that fitted into this, the box is gone, she has stolen it. Damnation seize her, she has robbed me!'

'Of what?' cried Ralph, on whom a sudden light appeared to break, for his eyes flashed and his frame trembled with agitation as he clutched Gride by his bony arm. 'Of what?'

'She don't know what it is; she can't read!' shrieked Gride, not heeding the inquiry. 'There's only one way in which money can be made of it, and that is by taking it to her. Somebody will read it for her, and tell her what to do. She and her accomplice will get money for it and be let off besides; they'll make a merit of it—say they found it—knew it—and be evidence against me. The only person it will fall upon is me, me, me!'

'Patience!' said Ralph, clutching him still tighter and eyeing him with a sidelong look, so fixed and eager as sufficiently to denote that he had some hidden purpose in what he was about to say. 'Hear reason. She can't have been gone long. I'll call the police. Do you but give information of what she has stolen, and they'll lay hands upon her, trust me. Here! Help!'

'No, no, no!' screamed the old man, putting his hand on Ralph's mouth. 'I can't, I daren't.'

'Help! help!' cried Ralph.

'No, no, no!' shrieked the other, stamping on the ground with the energy of a madman. 'I tell you no. I daren't, I daren't!'

'Daren't make this robbery public?' said Ralph.

'No!' rejoined Gride, wringing his hands. 'Hush! Hush! Not a word of this; not a word must be said. I am undone. Whichever way I turn, I am undone. I am betrayed. I shall be given up. I shall die in Newgate!'

With frantic exclamations such as these, and with many others in which fear, grief, and rage, were strangely blended, the panic-stricken wretch gradually subdued his first loud outcry, until it had softened down into a low despairing moan, chequered now and then by a howl, as, going over such papers as were left in the chest, he discovered some new loss. With very little excuse for departing so abruptly, Ralph left him, and, greatly disappointing the loiterers outside the house by telling them there was nothing the matter, got into the coach, and was driven to his own home.

A letter lay on his table. He let it lie there for some time, as if he had not the courage to open it, but at length did so and turned deadly pale.

'The worst has happened,' he said; 'the house has failed. I see. The rumour was abroad in the city last night, and reached the ears of those merchants. Well, well!'

He strode violently up and down the room and stopped again.

'Ten thousand pounds! And only lying there for a day—for one day! How many anxious years, how many pinching days and sleepless nights, before I scraped together that ten thousand pounds!—Ten thousand pounds! How many proud painted dames would have fawned and smiled, and how many spendthrift blockheads done me lip-service to my face and cursed me in their hearts, while I turned that ten thousand pounds into twenty! While I ground, and pinched, and used these needy borrowers for my pleasure and profit, what smooth-tongued speeches, and courteous looks, and civil letters, they would have given me! The cant of the lying world is, that men like me compass our riches by dissimulation and treachery: by fawning, cringing, and stooping. Why, how many lies, what mean and abject evasions, what humbled behaviour from upstarts who, but for my money, would spurn me aside as they do their betters every day, would that ten thousand pounds have brought me in! Grant that I had doubled it—made cent. per cent.—for every sovereign told another—there would not be one piece of money in all the heap which wouldn't represent ten thousand mean and paltry lies, told, not by the money-lender, oh no! but by the money-borrowers, your liberal, thoughtless, generous, dashing folks, who wouldn't be so mean as save a sixpence for the world!'

Striving, as it would seem, to lose part of the bitterness of his regrets in the bitterness of these other thoughts, Ralph continued to pace the room. There was less and less of resolution in his manner as his mind gradually reverted to his loss; at length, dropping into his elbow-chair and grasping its sides so firmly that they creaked again, he said:

'The time has been when nothing could have moved me like the loss of this great sum. Nothing. For births, deaths, marriages, and all the events which are of interest to most men, have (unless they are connected with gain or loss of money) no interest for me. But now, I swear, I mix up with the loss, his triumph in telling it. If he had brought it about,—I almost feel as if he had,—I couldn't hate him more. Let me but retaliate upon him, by degrees, however slow—let me but begin to get the better of him, let me but turn the scale—and I can bear it.'

His meditations were long and deep. They terminated in his dispatching a letter by Newman, addressed to Mr. Squeers at the Saracen's Head, with instructions to inquire whether he had arrived in town, and, if so, to wait an answer. Newman brought back the information that Mr. Squeers had come by mail that morning, and had received the letter in bed; but that he sent his duty, and word that he would get up and wait upon Mr. Nickleby directly.

The interval between the delivery of this message, and the arrival of Mr Squeers, was very short; but, before he came, Ralph had suppressed every sign of emotion, and once more regained the hard, immovable, inflexible manner which was habitual to him, and to which, perhaps, was ascribable no small part of the influence which, over many men of no very strong prejudices on the score of morality, he could exert, almost at will.

'Well, Mr. Squeers,' he said, welcoming that worthy with his accustomed smile, of which a sharp look and a thoughtful frown were part and parcel: 'how do you do?'

'Why, sir,' said Mr. Squeers, 'I'm pretty well. So's the family, and so's the boys, except for a sort of rash as is a running through the school, and rather puts 'em off their feed. But it's a ill wind as blows no good to nobody; that's what I always say when them lads has a wisitation. A wisitation, sir, is the lot of mortality. Mortality itself, sir, is a wisitation. The world is chock full of wisitations; and if a boy repines at a wisitation and makes you uncomfortable with his noise, he must have his head punched. That's going according to the Scripter, that is.'

'Mr. Squeers,' said Ralph, drily.

'Sir.'

'We'll avoid these precious morsels of morality if you please, and talk of business.'

'With all my heart, sir,' rejoined Squeers, 'and first let me say—'

'First let me say, if you please.—Noggs!'

Newman presented himself when the summons had been twice or thrice repeated, and asked if his master called.

'I did. Go to your dinner. And go at once. Do you hear?'

'It an't time,' said Newman, doggedly.

'My time is yours, and I say it is,' returned Ralph.

'You alter it every day,' said Newman. 'It isn't fair.'

'You don't keep many cooks, and can easily apologise to them for the trouble,' retorted Ralph. 'Begone, sir!'

Ralph not only issued this order in his most peremptory manner, but, under pretence of fetching some papers from the little office, saw it obeyed, and, when Newman had left the house, chained the door, to prevent the possibility of his returning secretly, by means of his latch-key.

'I have reason to suspect that fellow,' said Ralph, when he returned to his own office. 'Therefore, until I have thought of the shortest and least troublesome way of ruining him, I hold it best to keep him at a distance.'

'It wouldn't take much to ruin him, I should think,' said Squeers, with a grin.

'Perhaps not,' answered Ralph. 'Nor to ruin a great many people whom I know. You were going to say—?'

Ralph's summary and matter-of-course way of holding up this example, and throwing out the hint that followed it, had evidently an effect (as doubtless it was designed to have) upon Mr. Squeers, who said, after a little hesitation and in a much more subdued tone:

'Why, what I was a-going to say, sir, is, that this here business regarding of that ungrateful and hard-hearted chap, Snawley senior, puts me out of my way, and occasions a inconveniency quite unparalleled, besides, as I may say, making, for whole weeks together, Mrs. Squeers a perfect widder. It's a pleasure to me to act with you, of course.'

'Of course,' said Ralph, drily.

'Yes, I say of course,' resumed Mr. Squeers, rubbing his knees, 'but at the same time, when one comes, as I do now, better than two hundred and fifty mile to take a afferdavid, it does put a man out a good deal, letting alone the risk.'

'And where may the risk be, Mr. Squeers?' said Ralph.

'I said, letting alone the risk,' replied Squeers, evasively.

'And I said, where was the risk?'

'I wasn't complaining, you know, Mr. Nickleby,' pleaded Squeers. 'Upon my word I never see such a—'

'I ask you where is the risk?' repeated Ralph, emphatically.

'Where the risk?' returned Squeers, rubbing his knees still harder. 'Why, it an't necessary to mention. Certain subjects is best awoided. Oh, you know what risk I mean.'

'How often have I told you,' said Ralph, 'and how often am I to tell you, that you run no risk? What have you sworn, or what are you asked to swear, but that at such and such a time a boy was left with you in the name of Smike; that he was at your school for a given number of years, was lost under such and such circumstances, is now found, and has been identified by you in such and such keeping? This is all true; is it not?'

'Yes,' replied Squeers, 'that's all true.'

'Well, then,' said Ralph, 'what risk do you run? Who swears to a lie but Snawley; a man whom I have paid much less than I have you?'

'He certainly did it cheap, did Snawley,' observed Squeers.

'He did it cheap!' retorted Ralph, testily; 'yes, and he did it well, and carries it off with a hypocritical face and a sanctified air, but you! Risk! What do you mean by risk? The certificates are all genuine, Snawley had another son, he HAS been married twice, his first wife is dead, none but her ghost could tell that she didn't write that letter, none but Snawley himself can tell that this is not his son, and that his son is food for worms! The only perjury is Snawley's, and I fancy he is pretty well used to it. Where's your risk?'

'Why, you know,' said Squeers, fidgeting in his chair, 'if you come to that, I might say where's yours?'

'You might say where's mine!' returned Ralph; 'you may say where's mine. I don't appear in the business, neither do you. All Snawley's interest is to stick well to the story he has told; and all his risk is, to depart from it in the least. Talk of your risk in the conspiracy!'

'I say,' remonstrated Squeers, looking uneasily round: 'don't call it that! Just as a favour, don't.'

'Call it what you like,' said Ralph, irritably, 'but attend to me. This tale was originally fabricated as a means of annoyance against one who hurt your trade and half cudgelled you to death, and to enable you to obtain repossession of a half-dead drudge, whom you wished to regain, because, while you wreaked your vengeance on him for his share in the business, you knew that the knowledge that he was again in your power would be the best punishment you could inflict upon your enemy. Is that so, Mr. Squeers?'

'Why, sir,' returned Squeers, almost overpowered by the determination which Ralph displayed to make everything tell against him, and by his stern unyielding manner, 'in a measure it was.'

'What does that mean?' said Ralph.

'Why, in a measure means,' returned Squeers, 'as it may be, that it wasn't all on my account, because you had some old grudge to satisfy, too.'

'If I had not had,' said Ralph, in no way abashed by the reminder, 'do you think I should have helped you?'

'Why no, I don't suppose you would,' Squeers replied. 'I only wanted that point to be all square and straight between us.'

'How can it ever be otherwise?' retorted Ralph. 'Except that the account is against me, for I spend money to gratify my hatred, and you pocket it, and gratify yours at the same time. You are, at least, as avaricious as you are revengeful. So am I. Which is best off? You, who win money and revenge, at the same time and by the same process, and who are, at all events, sure of money, if not of revenge; or I, who am only sure of spending money in any case, and can but win bare revenge at last?'

As Mr. Squeers could only answer this proposition by shrugs and smiles, Ralph bade him be silent, and thankful that he was so well off; and then, fixing his eyes steadily upon him, proceeded to say:

First, that Nicholas had thwarted him in a plan he had formed for the disposal in marriage of a certain young lady, and had, in the confusion attendant on her father's sudden death, secured that lady himself, and borne her off in triumph.

Secondly, that by some will or settlement—certainly by some instrument in writing, which must contain the young lady's name, and could be, therefore, easily selected from others, if access to the place where it was deposited were once secured—she was entitled to property which, if the existence of this deed ever became known to her, would make her husband (and Ralph represented that Nicholas was certain to marry her) a rich and prosperous man, and most formidable enemy.

Thirdly, that this deed had been, with others, stolen from one who had himself obtained or concealed it fraudulently, and who feared to take any steps for its recovery; and that he (Ralph) knew the thief.

To all this Mr. Squeers listened, with greedy ears that devoured every syllable, and with his one eye and his mouth wide open: marvelling for what special reason he was honoured with so much of Ralph's confidence, and to what it all tended.

'Now,' said Ralph, leaning forward, and placing his hand on Squeers's arm, 'hear the design which I have conceived, and which I must—I say, must, if I can ripen it—have carried into execution. No advantage can be reaped from this deed, whatever it is, save by the girl herself, or her husband; and the possession of this deed by one or other of them is indispensable to any advantage being gained. That I have discovered beyond the possibility of doubt. I want that deed brought here, that I may give the man who brings it fifty pounds in gold, and burn it to ashes before his face.'

Mr. Squeers, after following with his eye the action of Ralph's hand towards the fire-place as if he were at that moment consuming the paper, drew a long breath, and said:

'Yes; but who's to bring it?'

'Nobody, perhaps, for much is to be done before it can be got at,' said Ralph. 'But if anybody—you!'

Mr. Squeers's first tokens of consternation, and his flat relinquishment of the task, would have staggered most men, if they had not immediately occasioned an utter abandonment of the proposition. On Ralph they produced not the slightest effect. Resuming, when the schoolmaster had quite talked himself out of breath, as coolly as if he had never been interrupted, Ralph proceeded to expatiate on such features of the case as he deemed it most advisable to lay the greatest stress on.

These were, the age, decrepitude, and weakness of Mrs. Sliderskew; the great improbability of her having any accomplice or even acquaintance: taking into account her secluded habits, and her long residence in such a house as Gride's; the strong reason there was to suppose that the robbery was not the result of a concerted plan: otherwise she would have watched an opportunity of carrying off a sum of money; the difficulty she would be placed in when she began to think on what she had done, and found herself encumbered with documents of whose nature she was utterly ignorant; and the comparative ease with which somebody, with a full knowledge of her position, obtaining access to her, and working on her fears, if necessary, might worm himself into her confidence and obtain, under one pretence or another, free possession of the deed. To these were added such considerations as the constant residence of Mr. Squeers at a long distance from London, which rendered his association with Mrs. Sliderskew a mere masquerading frolic, in which nobody was likely to recognise him, either at the time or afterwards; the impossibility of Ralph's undertaking the task himself, he being already known to her by sight; and various comments on the uncommon tact and experience of Mr. Squeers: which would make his overreaching one old woman a mere matter of child's play and amusement. In addition to these influences and persuasions, Ralph drew, with his utmost skill and power, a vivid picture of the defeat which Nicholas would sustain, should they succeed, in linking himself to a beggar, where he expected to wed an heiress—glanced at the immeasurable importance it must be to a man situated as Squeers, to preserve such a friend as himself—dwelt on a long train of benefits, conferred since their first acquaintance, when he had reported favourably of his treatment of a sickly boy who had died under his hands (and whose death was very convenient to Ralph and his clients, but this he did not say), and finally hinted that the fifty pounds might be increased to seventy-five, or, in the event of very great success, even to a hundred.

These arguments at length concluded, Mr. Squeers crossed his legs, uncrossed them, scratched his head, rubbed his eye, examined the palms of his hands, and bit his nails, and after exhibiting many other signs of restlessness and indecision, asked 'whether one hundred pound was the highest that Mr. Nickleby could go.' Being answered in the affirmative, he became restless again, and, after some thought, and an unsuccessful inquiry 'whether he couldn't go another fifty,' said he supposed he must try and do the most he could for a friend: which was always his maxim, and therefore he undertook the job.

'But how are you to get at the woman?' he said; 'that's what it is as puzzles me.'

'I may not get at her at all,' replied Ralph, 'but I'll try. I have hunted people in this city, before now, who have been better hid than she; and I know quarters in which a guinea or two, carefully spent, will often solve darker riddles than this. Ay, and keep them close too, if need be! I hear my man ringing at the door. We may as well part. You had better not come to and fro, but wait till you hear from me.'

'Good!' returned Squeers. 'I say! If you shouldn't find her out, you'll pay expenses at the Saracen, and something for loss of time?'

'Well,' said Ralph, testily; 'yes! You have nothing more to say?'

Squeers shaking his head, Ralph accompanied him to the streetdoor, and audibly wondering, for the edification of Newman, why it was fastened as if it were night, let him in and Squeers out, and returned to his own room.

'Now!' he muttered, 'come what come may, for the present I am firm and unshaken. Let me but retrieve this one small portion of my loss and disgrace; let me but defeat him in this one hope, dear to his heart as I know it must be; let me but do this; and it shall be the first link in such a chain which I will wind about him, as never man forged yet.'

CHAPTER 57
How Ralph Nickleby's Auxiliary went about his Work, and how he prospered with it

It was a dark, wet, gloomy night in autumn, when in an upper room of a mean house situated in an obscure street, or rather court, near Lambeth, there sat, all alone, a one-eyed man grotesquely habited, either for lack of better garments or for purposes of disguise, in a loose greatcoat, with arms half as long again as his own, and a capacity of breadth and length which would have admitted of his winding himself in it, head and all, with the utmost ease, and without any risk of straining the old and greasy material of which it was composed.

So attired, and in a place so far removed from his usual haunts and occupations, and so very poor and wretched in its character, perhaps Mrs Squeers herself would have had some difficulty in recognising her lord: quickened though her natural sagacity doubtless would have been by the affectionate yearnings and impulses of a tender wife. But Mrs. Squeers's lord it was; and in a tolerably disconsolate mood Mrs. Squeers's lord appeared to be, as, helping himself from a black bottle which stood on the table beside him, he cast round the chamber a look, in which very slight regard for the objects within view was plainly mingled with some regretful and impatient recollection of distant scenes and persons.

There were, certainly, no particular attractions, either in the room over which the glance of Mr. Squeers so discontentedly wandered, or in the narrow street into which it might have penetrated, if he had thought fit to approach the window. The attic chamber in which he sat was bare and mean; the bedstead, and such few other articles of necessary furniture as it contained, were of the commonest description, in a most crazy state, and of a most uninviting appearance. The street was muddy, dirty, and deserted. Having but one outlet, it was traversed by few but the inhabitants at any time; and the night being one of those on which most people are glad to be within doors, it now presented no other signs of life than the dull glimmering of poor candles from the dirty windows, and few sounds but the pattering of the rain, and occasionally the heavy closing of some creaking door.

Mr. Squeers continued to look disconsolately about him, and to listen to these noises in profound silence, broken only by the rustling of his large coat, as he now and then moved his arm to raise his glass to his lips. Mr Squeers continued to do this for some time, until the increasing gloom warned him to snuff the candle. Seeming to be slightly roused by this exertion, he raised his eye to the ceiling, and fixing it upon some uncouth and fantastic figures, traced upon it by the wet and damp which had penetrated through the roof, broke into the following soliloquy:

'Well, this is a pretty go, is this here! An uncommon pretty go! Here have I been, a matter of how many weeks—hard upon six—a follering up this here blessed old dowager petty larcenerer,'—Mr. Squeers delivered himself of this epithet with great difficulty and effort,—'and Dotheboys Hall a-running itself regularly to seed the while! That's the worst of ever being in with a owdacious chap like that old Nickleby. You never know when he's done with you, and if you're in for a penny, you're in for a pound.'

This remark, perhaps, reminded Mr. Squeers that he was in for a hundred pound at any rate. His countenance relaxed, and he raised his glass to his mouth with an air of greater enjoyment of its contents than he had before evinced.

'I never see,' soliloquised Mr. Squeers in continuation, 'I never see nor come across such a file as that old Nickleby. Never! He's out of everybody's depth, he is. He's what you may call a rasper, is Nickleby. To see how sly and cunning he grubbed on, day after day, a-worming and plodding and tracing and turning and twining of hisself about, till he found out where this precious Mrs. Peg was hid, and cleared the ground for me to work upon. Creeping and crawling and gliding, like a ugly, old, bright-eyed, stagnation-blooded adder! Ah! He'd have made a good 'un in our line, but it would have been too limited for him; his genius would have busted all bonds, and coming over every obstacle, broke down all before it, till it erected itself into a monneyment of—Well, I'll think of the rest, and say it when conwenient.'

Making a halt in his reflections at this place, Mr. Squeers again put his glass to his lips, and drawing a dirty letter from his pocket, proceeded to con over its contents with the air of a man who had read it very often, and now refreshed his memory rather in the absence of better amusement than for any specific information.

'The pigs is well,' said Mr. Squeers, 'the cows is well, and the boys is bobbish. Young Sprouter has been a-winking, has he? I'll wink him when I get back. "Cobbey would persist in sniffing while he was a-eating his dinner, and said that the beef was so strong it made him."—Very good, Cobbey, we'll see if we can't make you sniff a little without beef. "Pitcher was took with another fever,"—of course he was—"and being fetched by his friends, died the day after he got home,"—of course he did, and out of aggravation; it's part of a deep-laid system. There an't another chap in the school but that boy as would have died exactly at the end of the quarter: taking it out of me to the very last, and then carrying his spite to the utmost extremity.

"The juniorest Palmer said he wished he was in Heaven." I really don't know, I do not know what's to be done with that young fellow; he's always a-wishing something horrid. He said once, he wished he was a donkey, because then he wouldn't have a father as didn't love him! Pretty wicious that for a child of six!'

Mr. Squeers was so much moved by the contemplation of this hardened nature in one so young, that he angrily put up the letter, and sought, in a new train of ideas, a subject of consolation.

'It's a long time to have been a-lingering in London,' he said; 'and this is a precious hole to come and live in, even if it has been only for a week or so. Still, one hundred pound is five boys, and five boys takes a whole year to pay one hundred pounds, and there's their keep to be substracted, besides. There's nothing lost, neither, by one's being here; because the boys' money comes in just the same as if I was at home, and Mrs. Squeers she keeps them in order. There'll be some lost time to make up, of course. There'll be an arrear of flogging as'll have to be gone through: still, a couple of days makes that all right, and one don't mind a little extra work for one hundred pound. It's pretty nigh the time to wait upon the old woman. From what she said last night, I suspect that if I'm to succeed at all, I shall succeed tonight; so I'll have half a glass more, to wish myself success, and put myself in spirits. Mrs. Squeers, my dear, your health!'

Leering with his one eye as if the lady to whom he drank had been actually present, Mr. Squeers—in his enthusiasm, no doubt—poured out a full glass, and emptied it; and as the liquor was raw spirits, and he had applied himself to the same bottle more than once already, it is not surprising that he found himself, by this time, in an extremely cheerful state, and quite enough excited for his purpose.

What this purpose was soon appeared; for, after a few turns about the room to steady himself, he took the bottle under his arm and the glass in his hand, and blowing out the candle as if he purposed being gone some time, stole out upon the staircase, and creeping softly to a door opposite his own, tapped gently at it.

'But what's the use of tapping?' he said, 'She'll never hear. I suppose she isn't doing anything very particular; and if she is, it don't much matter, that I see.'

With this brief preface, Mr. Squeers applied his hand to the latch of the door, and thrusting his head into a garret far more deplorable than that he had just left, and seeing that there was nobody there but an old woman, who was bending over a wretched fire (for although the weather was still warm, the evening was chilly), walked in, and tapped her on the shoulder.

'Well, my Slider,' said Mr. Squeers, jocularly.

'Is that you?' inquired Peg.

'Ah! it's me, and me's the first person singular, nominative case, agreeing with the verb "it's", and governed by Squeers understood, as a acorn, a hour; but when the h is sounded, the a only is to be used, as a and, a art, a ighway,' replied Mr. Squeers, quoting at random from the grammar. 'At least, if it isn't, you don't know any better, and if it is, I've done it accidentally.'

Delivering this reply in his accustomed tone of voice, in which of course it was inaudible to Peg, Mr. Squeers drew a stool to the fire, and placing himself over against her, and the bottle and glass on the floor between them, roared out again, very loud,

'Well, my Slider!'

'I hear you,' said Peg, receiving him very graciously.

'I've come according to promise,' roared Squeers.

'So they used to say in that part of the country I come from,' observed Peg, complacently, 'but I think oil's better.'

'Better than what?' roared Squeers, adding some rather strong language in an undertone.

'No,' said Peg, 'of course not.'

'I never saw such a monster as you are!' muttered Squeers, looking as amiable as he possibly could the while; for Peg's eye was upon him, and she was chuckling fearfully, as though in delight at having made a choice repartee, 'Do you see this? This is a bottle.'

'I see it,' answered Peg.

'Well, and do you see this?' bawled Squeers. 'This is a glass.' Peg saw that too.

'See here, then,' said Squeers, accompanying his remarks with appropriate action, 'I fill the glass from the bottle, and I say "Your health, Slider," and empty it; then I rinse it genteelly with a little drop, which I'm forced to throw into the fire—hallo! we shall have the chimbley alight next—fill it again, and hand it over to you.'

'Your health,' said Peg.

'She understands that, anyways,' muttered Squeers, watching Mrs. Sliderskew as she dispatched her portion, and choked and gasped in a most awful manner after so doing. 'Now then, let's have a talk. How's the rheumatics?'

Mrs. Sliderskew, with much blinking and chuckling, and with looks expressive of her strong admiration of Mr. Squeers, his person, manners, and conversation, replied that the rheumatics were better.

'What's the reason,' said Mr. Squeers, deriving fresh facetiousness from the bottle; 'what's the reason of rheumatics? What do they mean? What do people have'em for—eh?'

Mrs. Sliderskew didn't know, but suggested that it was possibly because they couldn't help it.

'Measles, rheumatics, hooping-cough, fevers, agers, and lumbagers,' said Mr. Squeers, 'is all philosophy together; that's what it is. The heavenly bodies is philosophy, and the earthly bodies is philosophy. If there's a screw loose in a heavenly body, that's philosophy; and if there's screw loose in a earthly body, that's philosophy too; or it may be that sometimes there's a little metaphysics in it, but that's not often. Philosophy's the chap for me. If a parent asks a question in the classical, commercial, or mathematical line, says I, gravely, "Why, sir, in the first place, are you a philosopher?"—"No, Mr. Squeers," he says, "I an't." "Then, sir," says I, "I am sorry for you, for I shan't be able to explain it." Naturally, the parent goes away and wishes he was a philosopher, and, equally naturally, thinks I'm one.'

Saying this, and a great deal more, with tipsy profundity and a serio-comic air, and keeping his eye all the time on Mrs. Sliderskew, who was unable to hear one word, Mr. Squeers concluded by helping himself and passing the bottle: to which Peg did becoming reverence.

'That's the time of day!' said Mr. Squeers. 'You look twenty pound ten better than you did.'

Again Mrs. Sliderskew chuckled, but modesty forbade her assenting verbally to the compliment.

'Twenty pound ten better,' repeated Mr. Squeers, 'than you did that day when I first introduced myself. Don't you know?'

'Ah!' said Peg, shaking her head, 'but you frightened me that day.'

'Did I?' said Squeers; 'well, it was rather a startling thing for a stranger to come and recommend himself by saying that he knew all about you, and what your name was, and why you were living so quiet here, and what you had boned, and who you boned it from, wasn't it?'

Peg nodded her head in strong assent.

'But I know everything that happens in that way, you see,' continued Squeers. 'Nothing takes place, of that kind, that I an't up to entirely. I'm a sort of a lawyer, Slider, of first-rate standing, and understanding too; I'm the intimate friend and confidential adwiser of pretty nigh every man, woman, and child that gets themselves into difficulties by being too nimble with their fingers, I'm—'

Mr. Squeers's catalogue of his own merits and accomplishments, which was partly the result of a concerted plan between himself and Ralph Nickleby, and flowed, in part, from the black bottle, was here interrupted by Mrs Sliderskew.

'Ha, ha, ha!' she cried, folding her arms and wagging her head; 'and so he wasn't married after all, wasn't he. Not married after all?'

'No,' replied Squeers, 'that he wasn't!'

'And a young lover come and carried off the bride, eh?' said Peg.

'From under his very nose,' replied Squeers; 'and I'm told the young chap cut up rough besides, and broke the winders, and forced him to swaller his wedding favour which nearly choked him.'

'Tell me all about it again,' cried Peg, with a malicious relish of her old master's defeat, which made her natural hideousness something quite fearful; 'let's hear it all again, beginning at the beginning now, as if you'd never told me. Let's have it every word—now—now—beginning at the very first, you know, when he went to the house that morning!'

Mr. Squeers, plying Mrs. Sliderskew freely with the liquor, and sustaining himself under the exertion of speaking so loud by frequent applications to it himself, complied with this request by describing the discomfiture of Arthur Gride, with such improvements on the truth as happened to occur to him, and the ingenious invention and application of which had been very instrumental in recommending him to her notice in the beginning of their acquaintance. Mrs. Sliderskew was in an ecstasy of delight, rolling her head about, drawing up her skinny shoulders, and wrinkling her cadaverous face into so many and such complicated forms of ugliness, as awakened the unbounded astonishment and disgust even of Mr. Squeers.

'He's a treacherous old goat,' said Peg, 'and cozened me with cunning tricks and lying promises, but never mind. I'm even with him. I'm even with him.'

'More than even, Slider,' returned Squeers; 'you'd have been even with him if he'd got married; but with the disappointment besides, you're a long way ahead. Out of sight, Slider, quite out of sight. And that reminds me,' he added, handing her the glass, 'if you want me to give you my opinion of them deeds, and tell you what you'd better keep and what you'd better burn, why, now's your time, Slider.'

'There an't no hurry for that,' said Peg, with several knowing looks and winks.

'Oh! very well!' observed Squeers, 'it don't matter to me; you asked me, you know. I shouldn't charge you nothing, being a friend. You're the best judge of course. But you're a bold woman, Slider.'

'How do you mean, bold?' said Peg.

'Why, I only mean that if it was me, I wouldn't keep papers as might hang me, littering about when they might be turned into money—them as wasn't useful made away with, and them as was, laid by somewheres, safe; that's all,' returned Squeers; 'but everybody's the best judge of their own affairs. All I say is, Slider, I wouldn't do it.'

'Come,' said Peg, 'then you shall see 'em.'

'I don't want to see 'em,' replied Squeers, affecting to be out of humour; 'don't talk as if it was a treat. Show 'em to somebody else, and take their advice.'

Mr. Squeers would, very likely, have carried on the farce of being offended a little longer, if Mrs. Sliderskew, in her anxiety to restore herself to her former high position in his good graces, had not become so extremely affectionate that he stood at some risk of being smothered by her caresses. Repressing, with as good a grace as possible, these little familiarities—for which, there is reason to believe, the black bottle was at least as much to blame as any constitutional infirmity on the part of Mrs. Sliderskew—he protested that he had only been joking: and, in proof of his unimpaired good-humour, that he was ready to examine the deeds at once, if, by so doing, he could afford any satisfaction or relief of mind to his fair friend.

'And now you're up, my Slider,' bawled Squeers, as she rose to fetch them, 'bolt the door.'

Peg trotted to the door, and after fumbling at the bolt, crept to the other end of the room, and from beneath the coals which filled the bottom of the cupboard, drew forth a small deal box. Having placed this on the floor at Squeers's feet, she brought, from under the pillow of her bed, a small key, with which she signed to that gentleman to open it. Mr. Squeers, who had eagerly followed her every motion, lost no time in obeying this hint: and, throwing back the lid, gazed with rapture on the documents which lay within.

'Now you see,' said Peg, kneeling down on the floor beside him, and staying his impatient hand; 'what's of no use we'll burn; what we can get any money by, we'll keep; and if there's any we could get him into trouble by, and fret and waste away his heart to shreds, those we'll take particular care of; for that's what I want to do, and what I hoped to do when I left him.'

'I thought,' said Squeers, 'that you didn't bear him any particular good-will. But, I say, why didn't you take some money besides?'

'Some what?' asked Peg.

'Some money,' roared Squeers. 'I do believe the woman hears me, and wants to make me break a wessel, so that she may have the pleasure of nursing me. Some money, Slider, money!'

'Why, what a man you are to ask!' cried Peg, with some contempt. 'If I had taken money from Arthur Gride, he'd have scoured the whole earth to find me—aye, and he'd have smelt it out, and raked it up, somehow, if I had buried it at the bottom of the deepest well in England.

No, no! I knew better than that. I took what I thought his secrets were hid in: and them he couldn't afford to make public, let'em be worth ever so much money. He's an old dog; a sly, old, cunning, thankless dog! He first starved, and then tricked me; and if I could I'd kill him.'

'All right, and very laudable,' said Squeers. 'But, first and foremost, Slider, burn the box. You should never keep things as may lead to discovery. Always mind that. So while you pull it to pieces (which you can easily do, for it's very old and rickety) and burn it in little bits, I'll look over the papers and tell you what they are.'

Peg, expressing her acquiescence in this arrangement, Mr. Squeers turned the box bottom upwards, and tumbling the contents upon the floor, handed it to her; the destruction of the box being an extemporary device for engaging her attention, in case it should prove desirable to distract it from his own proceedings.

'There!' said Squeers; 'you poke the pieces between the bars, and make up a good fire, and I'll read the while. Let me see, let me see.' And taking the candle down beside him, Mr. Squeers, with great eagerness and a cunning grin overspreading his face, entered upon his task of examination.

If the old woman had not been very deaf, she must have heard, when she last went to the door, the breathing of two persons close behind it: and if those two persons had been unacquainted with her infirmity, they must probably have chosen that moment either for presenting themselves or taking to flight. But, knowing with whom they had to deal, they remained quite still, and now, not only appeared unobserved at the door—which was not bolted, for the bolt had no hasp—but warily, and with noiseless footsteps, advanced into the room.

As they stole farther and farther in by slight and scarcely perceptible degrees, and with such caution that they scarcely seemed to breathe, the old hag and Squeers little dreaming of any such invasion, and utterly unconscious of there being any soul near but themselves, were busily occupied with their tasks. The old woman, with her wrinkled face close to the bars of the stove, puffing at the dull embers which had not yet caught the wood; Squeers stooping down to the candle, which brought out the full ugliness of his face, as the light of the fire did that of his companion; both intently engaged, and wearing faces of exultation which contrasted strongly with the anxious looks of those behind, who took advantage of the slightest sound to cover their advance, and, almost before they had moved an inch, and all was silent, stopped again. This, with the large bare room, damp walls, and flickering doubtful light, combined to form a scene which the most careless and indifferent spectator (could any have been present) could scarcely have failed to derive some interest from, and would not readily have forgotten.

Of the stealthy comers, Frank Cheeryble was one, and Newman Noggs the other. Newman had caught up, by the rusty nozzle, an old pair of bellows, which were just undergoing a flourish in the air preparatory to a descent upon the head of Mr. Squeers, when Frank, with an earnest gesture, stayed his arm, and, taking another step in advance, came so close behind the schoolmaster that, by leaning slightly forward, he could plainly distinguish the writing which he held up to his eye.

Mr. Squeers, not being remarkably erudite, appeared to be considerably puzzled by this first prize, which was in an engrossing hand, and not very legible except to a practised eye. Having tried it by reading from left to right, and from right to left, and finding it equally clear both ways, he turned it upside down with no better success.

'Ha, ha, ha!' chuckled Peg, who, on her knees before the fire, was feeding it with fragments of the box, and grinning in most devilish exultation. 'What's that writing about, eh?'

'Nothing particular,' replied Squeers, tossing it towards her. 'It's only an old lease, as well as I can make out. Throw it in the fire.'

Mrs. Sliderskew complied, and inquired what the next one was.

'This,' said Squeers, 'is a bundle of overdue acceptances and renewed bills of six or eight young gentlemen, but they're all MPs, so it's of no use to anybody. Throw it in the fire!' Peg did as she was bidden, and waited for the next.

'This,' said Squeers, 'seems to be some deed of sale of the right of presentation to the rectory of Purechurch, in the valley of Cashup. Take care of that, Slider, literally for God's sake. It'll fetch its price at the Auction Mart.'

'What's the next?' inquired Peg.

'Why, this,' said Squeers, 'seems, from the two letters that's with it, to be a bond from a curate down in the country, to pay half a year's wages of forty pound for borrowing twenty. Take care of that, for if he don't pay it, his bishop will very soon be down upon him. We know what the camel and the needle's eye means; no man as can't live upon his income, whatever it is, must expect to go to heaven at any price. It's very odd; I don't see anything like it yet.'

'What's the matter?' said Peg.

'Nothing,' replied Squeers, 'only I'm looking for—'

Newman raised the bellows again. Once more, Frank, by a rapid motion of his arm, unaccompanied by any noise, checked him in his purpose.

'Here you are,' said Squeers, 'bonds—take care of them. Warrant of attorney—take care of that. Two cognovits—take care of them. Lease and release—burn that. Ah! "Madeline Bray—come of age or marry—the said Madeline"—here, burn that!'

Eagerly throwing towards the old woman a parchment that he caught up for the purpose, Squeers, as she turned her head, thrust into the breast of his large coat, the deed in which these words had caught his eye, and burst into a shout of triumph.

'I've got it!' said Squeers. 'I've got it! Hurrah! The plan was a good one, though the chance was desperate, and the day's our own at last!'

Peg demanded what he laughed at, but no answer was returned. Newman's arm could no longer be restrained; the bellows, descending heavily and with unerring aim on the very centre of Mr. Squeers's head, felled him to the floor, and stretched him on it flat and senseless.

CHAPTER 58
In which one Scene of this History is closed

Dividing the distance into two days' journey, in order that his charge might sustain the less exhaustion and fatigue from travelling so far, Nicholas, at the end of the second day from their leaving home, found himself within a very few miles of the spot where the happiest years of his life had been passed, and which, while it filled his mind with pleasant and peaceful thoughts, brought back many painful and vivid recollections of the circumstances in which he and his had wandered forth from their old home, cast upon the rough world and the mercy of strangers.

It needed no such reflections as those which the memory of old days, and wanderings among scenes where our childhood has been passed, usually awaken in the most insensible minds, to soften the heart of Nicholas, and render him more than usually mindful of his drooping friend. By night and day, at all times and seasons: always watchful, attentive, and solicitous, and never varying in the discharge of his self-imposed duty to one so friendless and helpless as he whose sands of life were now fast running out and dwindling rapidly away: he was ever at his side. He never left him. To encourage and animate him, administer to his wants, support and cheer him to the utmost of his power, was now his constant and unceasing occupation.

They procured a humble lodging in a small farmhouse, surrounded by meadows where Nicholas had often revelled when a child with a troop of merry schoolfellows; and here they took up their rest.

At first, Smike was strong enough to walk about, for short distances at a time, with no other support or aid than that which Nicholas could afford him. At this time, nothing appeared to interest him so much as visiting those places which had been most familiar to his friend in bygone days. Yielding to this fancy, and pleased to find that its indulgence beguiled the sick boy of many tedious hours, and never failed to afford him matter for thought and conversation afterwards, Nicholas made such spots the scenes of their daily rambles: driving him from place to place in a little pony-chair, and supporting him on his arm while they walked slowly among these old haunts, or lingered in the sunlight to take long parting looks of those which were most quiet and beautiful.

It was on such occasions as these, that Nicholas, yielding almost unconsciously to the interest of old associations, would point out some tree that he had climbed, a hundred times, to peep at the young birds in their nest; and the branch from which he used to shout to little Kate, who stood below terrified at the height he had gained, and yet urging him higher still by the intensity of her admiration. There was the old house too, which they would pass every day, looking up at the tiny window through which the sun used to stream in and wake him on the summer mornings—they were all summer mornings then—and climbing up the garden-wall and looking over, Nicholas could see the very rose-bush which had come, a present to Kate, from some little lover, and she had planted with her own hands. There were the hedgerows where the brother and sister had so often gathered wild flowers together, and the green fields and shady paths where they had so often strayed. There was not a lane, or brook, or copse, or cottage near, with which some childish event was not entwined, and back it came upon the mind—as events of childhood do—nothing in itself: perhaps a word, a laugh, a look, some slight distress, a passing thought or fear: and yet more strongly and distinctly marked, and better remembered, than the hardest trials or severest sorrows of a year ago.

One of these expeditions led them through the churchyard where was his father's grave. 'Even here,' said Nicholas softly, 'we used to loiter before we knew what death was, and when we little thought whose ashes would rest beneath; and, wondering at the silence, sit down to rest and speak below our breath. Once, Kate was lost, and after an hour of fruitless search, they found her, fast asleep, under that tree which shades my father's grave. He was very fond of her, and said when he took her up in his arms, still sleeping, that whenever he died he would wish to be buried where his dear little child had laid her head. You see his wish was not forgotten.'

Nothing more passed at the time, but that night, as Nicholas sat beside his bed, Smike started from what had seemed to be a slumber, and laying his hand in his, prayed, as the tears coursed down his face, that he would make him one solemn promise.

'What is that?' said Nicholas, kindly. 'If I can redeem it, or hope to do so, you know I will.'

'I am sure you will,' was the reply. 'Promise me that when I die, I shall be buried near—as near as they can make my grave—to the tree we saw today.'

Nicholas gave the promise; he had few words to give it in, but they were solemn and earnest. His poor friend kept his hand in his, and turned as if to sleep. But there were stifled sobs; and the hand was pressed more than once, or twice, or thrice, before he sank to rest, and slowly loosed his hold.

In a fortnight's time, he became too ill to move about. Once or twice, Nicholas drove him out, propped up with pillows; but the motion of the chaise was painful to him, and brought on fits of fainting, which, in his weakened state, were dangerous. There was an old couch in the house, which was his favourite resting-place by day; and when the sun shone, and the weather was warm, Nicholas had this wheeled into a little orchard which was close at hand, and his charge being well wrapped up and carried out to it, they used to sit there sometimes for hours together.

It was on one of these occasions that a circumstance took place, which Nicholas, at the time, thoroughly believed to be the mere delusion of an imagination affected by disease; but which he had, afterwards, too good reason to know was of real and actual occurrence.

He had brought Smike out in his arms—poor fellow! a child might have carried him then—to see the sunset, and, having arranged his couch, had taken his seat beside it. He had been watching the whole of the night before, and being greatly fatigued both in mind and body, gradually fell asleep.

He could not have closed his eyes five minutes, when he was awakened by a scream, and starting up in that kind of terror which affects a person suddenly roused, saw, to his great astonishment, that his charge had struggled into a sitting posture, and with eyes almost starting from their sockets, cold dew standing on his forehead, and in a fit of trembling which quite convulsed his frame, was calling to him for help.

'Good Heaven, what is this?' said Nicholas, bending over him. 'Be calm; you have been dreaming.'

'No, no, no!' cried Smike, clinging to him. 'Hold me tight. Don't let me go. There, there. Behind the tree!'

Nicholas followed his eyes, which were directed to some distance behind the chair from which he himself had just risen. But, there was nothing there.

'This is nothing but your fancy,' he said, as he strove to compose him; 'nothing else, indeed.'

'I know better. I saw as plain as I see now,' was the answer. 'Oh! say you'll keep me with you. Swear you won't leave me for an instant!'

'Do I ever leave you?' returned Nicholas. 'Lie down again—there! You see I'm here. Now, tell me; what was it?'

'Do you remember,' said Smike, in a low voice, and glancing fearfully round, 'do you remember my telling you of the man who first took me to the school?'

'Yes, surely.'

'I raised my eyes, just now, towards that tree—that one with the thick trunk—and there, with his eyes fixed on me, he stood!'

'Only reflect for one moment,' said Nicholas; 'granting, for an instant, that it's likely he is alive and wandering about a lonely place like this, so far removed from the public road, do you think that at this distance of time you could possibly know that man again?'

'Anywhere—in any dress,' returned Smike; 'but, just now, he stood leaning upon his stick and looking at me, exactly as I told you I remembered him. He was dusty with walking, and poorly dressed—I think his clothes were ragged—but directly I saw him, the wet night, his face when he left me, the parlour I was left in, and the people that were there, all seemed to come back together. When he knew I saw him, he looked frightened; for he started, and shrunk away. I have thought of him by day, and dreamt of him by night. He looked in my sleep, when I was quite a little child, and has looked in my sleep ever since, as he did just now.'

Nicholas endeavoured, by every persuasion and argument he could think of, to convince the terrified creature that his imagination had deceived him, and that this close resemblance between the creation of his dreams and the man he supposed he had seen was but a proof of it; but all in vain. When he could persuade him to remain, for a few moments, in the care of the people to whom the house belonged, he instituted a strict inquiry whether any stranger had been seen, and searched himself behind the tree, and through the orchard, and upon the land immediately adjoining, and in every place near, where it was possible for a man to lie concealed; but all in vain. Satisfied that he was right in his original conjecture, he applied himself to calming the fears of Smike, which, after some time, he partially succeeded in doing, though not in removing the impression upon his mind; for he still declared, again and again, in the most solemn and fervid manner, that he had positively seen what he had described, and that nothing could ever remove his conviction of its reality.

And now, Nicholas began to see that hope was gone, and that, upon the partner of his poverty, and the sharer of his better fortune, the world was closing fast. There was little pain, little uneasiness, but there was no rallying, no effort, no struggle for life. He was worn and wasted to the last degree; his voice had sunk so low, that he could scarce be heard to speak. Nature was thoroughly exhausted, and he had lain him down to die.

On a fine, mild autumn day, when all was tranquil and at peace: when the soft sweet air crept in at the open window of the quiet room, and not a sound was heard but the gentle rustling of the leaves: Nicholas sat in his old place by the bedside, and knew that the time was nearly come. So very still it was, that, every now and then, he bent down his ear to listen for the breathing of him who lay asleep, as if to assure himself that life was still there, and that he had not fallen into that deep slumber from which on earth there is no waking.

While he was thus employed, the closed eyes opened, and on the pale face there came a placid smile.

'That's well!' said Nicholas. 'The sleep has done you good.'

'I have had such pleasant dreams,' was the answer. 'Such pleasant, happy dreams!'

'Of what?' said Nicholas.

The dying boy turned towards him, and, putting his arm about his neck, made answer, 'I shall soon be there!'

After a short silence, he spoke again.

'I am not afraid to die,' he said. 'I am quite contented. I almost think that if I could rise from this bed quite well I would not wish to do so, now. You have so often told me we shall meet again—so very often lately, and now I feel the truth of that so strongly—that I can even bear to part from you.'

The trembling voice and tearful eye, and the closer grasp of the arm which accompanied these latter words, showed how they filled the speaker's heart; nor were there wanting indications of how deeply they had touched the heart of him to whom they were addressed.

'You say well,' returned Nicholas at length, 'and comfort me very much, dear fellow. Let me hear you say you are happy, if you can.'

'I must tell you something, first. I should not have a secret from you. You would not blame me, at a time like this, I know.'

'I blame you!' exclaimed Nicholas.

'I am sure you would not. You asked me why I was so changed, and—and sat so much alone. Shall I tell you why?'

'Not if it pains you,' said Nicholas. 'I only asked that I might make you happier, if I could.'

'I know. I felt that, at the time.' He drew his friend closer to him. 'You will forgive me; I could not help it, but though I would have died to make her happy, it broke my heart to see—I know he loves her dearly—Oh! who could find that out so soon as I?'

The words which followed were feebly and faintly uttered, and broken by long pauses; but, from them, Nicholas learnt, for the first time, that the dying boy, with all the ardour of a nature concentrated on one absorbing, hopeless, secret passion, loved his sister Kate.

He had procured a lock of her hair, which hung at his breast, folded in one or two slight ribbons she had worn. He prayed that, when he was dead, Nicholas would take it off, so that no eyes but his might see it, and that when he was laid in his coffin and about to be placed in the earth, he would hang it round his neck again, that it might rest with him in the grave.

Upon his knees Nicholas gave him this pledge, and promised again that he should rest in the spot he had pointed out. They embraced, and kissed each other on the cheek.

'Now,' he murmured, 'I am happy.'

He fell into a light slumber, and waking smiled as before; then, spoke of beautiful gardens, which he said stretched out before him, and were filled with figures of men, women, and many children, all with light upon their faces; then, whispered that it was Eden—and so died.

CHAPTER 59
The Plots begin to fail, and Doubts and Dangers to disturb the Plotter

Ralph sat alone, in the solitary room where he was accustomed to take his meals, and to sit of nights when no profitable occupation called him abroad. Before him was an untasted breakfast, and near to where his fingers beat restlessly upon the table, lay his watch. It was long past the time at which, for many years, he had put it in his pocket and gone with measured steps downstairs to the business of the day, but he took as little heed of its monotonous warning, as of the meat and drink before him, and remained with his head resting on one hand, and his eyes fixed moodily on the ground.

This departure from his regular and constant habit, in one so regular and unvarying in all that appertained to the daily pursuit of riches, would almost of itself have told that the usurer was not well. That he laboured under some mental or bodily indisposition, and that it was one of no slight kind so to affect a man like him, was sufficiently shown by his haggard face, jaded air, and hollow languid eyes: which he raised at last with a start and a hasty glance around him, as one who suddenly awakes from sleep, and cannot immediately recognise the place in which he finds himself.

'What is this,' he said, 'that hangs over me, and I cannot shake off? I have never pampered myself, and should not be ill. I have never moped, and pined, and yielded to fancies; but what can a man do without rest?'

He pressed his hand upon his forehead.

'Night after night comes and goes, and I have no rest. If I sleep, what rest is that which is disturbed by constant dreams of the same detested faces crowding round me—of the same detested people, in every variety of action, mingling with all I say and do, and always to my defeat? Waking, what rest have I, constantly haunted by this heavy shadow of—I know not what—which is its worst character? I must have rest. One night's unbroken rest, and I should be a man again.'

Pushing the table from him while he spoke, as though he loathed the sight of food, he encountered the watch: the hands of which were almost upon noon.

'This is strange!' he said; 'noon, and Noggs not here! What drunken brawl keeps him away? I would give something now—something in money even after that dreadful loss—if he had stabbed a man in a tavern scuffle, or broken into a house, or picked a pocket, or done anything that would send him abroad with an iron ring upon his leg, and rid me of him. Better still, if I could throw temptation in his way, and lure him on to rob me. He should be welcome to what he took, so I brought the law upon him; for he is a traitor, I swear! How, or when, or where, I don't know, though I suspect.'

After waiting for another half-hour, he dispatched the woman who kept his house to Newman's lodging, to inquire if he were ill, and why he had not come or sent. She brought back answer that he had not been home all night, and that no one could tell her anything about him.

'But there is a gentleman, sir,' she said, 'below, who was standing at the door when I came in, and he says—'

'What says he?' demanded Ralph, turning angrily upon her. 'I told you I would see nobody.'

'He says,' replied the woman, abashed by his harshness, 'that he comes on very particular business which admits of no excuse; and I thought perhaps it might be about—'

'About what, in the devil's name?' said Ralph. 'You spy and speculate on people's business with me, do you?'

'Dear, no, sir! I saw you were anxious, and thought it might be about Mr Noggs; that's all.'

'Saw I was anxious!' muttered Ralph; 'they all watch me, now. Where is this person? You did not say I was not down yet, I hope?'

The woman replied that he was in the little office, and that she had said her master was engaged, but she would take the message.

'Well,' said Ralph, 'I'll see him. Go you to your kitchen, and keep there. Do you mind me?'

Glad to be released, the woman quickly disappeared. Collecting himself, and assuming as much of his accustomed manner as his utmost resolution could summon, Ralph descended the stairs. After pausing for a few moments, with his hand upon the lock, he entered Newman's room, and confronted Mr Charles Cheeryble.

Of all men alive, this was one of the last he would have wished to meet at any time; but, now that he recognised in him only the patron and protector of Nicholas, he would rather have seen a spectre. One beneficial effect, however, the encounter had upon him. It instantly roused all his dormant energies; rekindled in his breast the passions that, for many years, had found an improving home there; called up all his wrath, hatred, and malice; restored the sneer to his lip, and the scowl to his brow; and made him again, in all outward appearance, the same Ralph Nickleby whom so many had bitter cause to remember.

'Humph!' said Ralph, pausing at the door. 'This is an unexpected favour, sir.'

'And an unwelcome one,' said brother Charles; 'an unwelcome one, I know.'

'Men say you are truth itself, sir,' replied Ralph. 'You speak truth now, at all events, and I'll not contradict you. The favour is, at least, as unwelcome as it is unexpected. I can scarcely say more.'

'Plainly, sir—' began brother Charles.

'Plainly, sir,' interrupted Ralph, 'I wish this conference to be a short one, and to end where it begins. I guess the subject upon which you are about to speak, and I'll not hear you. You like plainness, I believe; there it is. Here is the door as you see. Our way lies in very different directions. Take yours, I beg of you, and leave me to pursue mine in quiet.'

'In quiet!' repeated brother Charles mildly, and looking at him with more of pity than reproach. 'To pursue his way in quiet!'

'You will scarcely remain in my house, I presume, sir, against my will,' said Ralph; 'or you can scarcely hope to make an impression upon a man who closes his ears to all that you can say, and is firmly and resolutely determined not to hear you.'

'Mr. Nickleby, sir,' returned brother Charles: no less mildly than before, but firmly too: 'I come here against my will, sorely and grievously against my will. I have never been in this house before; and, to speak my mind, sir, I don't feel at home or easy in it, and have no wish ever to be here again. You do not guess the subject on which I come to speak to you; you do not indeed. I am sure of that, or your manner would be a very different one.'

Ralph glanced keenly at him, but the clear eye and open countenance of the honest old merchant underwent no change of expression, and met his look without reserve.

'Shall I go on?' said Mr. Cheeryble.

'Oh, by all means, if you please,' returned Ralph drily. 'Here are walls to speak to, sir, a desk, and two stools: most attentive auditors, and certain not to interrupt you. Go on, I beg; make my house yours, and perhaps by the time I return from my walk, you will have finished what you have to say, and will yield me up possession again.'

So saying, he buttoned his coat, and turning into the passage, took down his hat. The old gentleman followed, and was about to speak, when Ralph waved him off impatiently, and said:

'Not a word. I tell you, sir, not a word. Virtuous as you are, you are not an angel yet, to appear in men's houses whether they will or no, and pour your speech into unwilling ears. Preach to the walls I tell you; not to me!'

'I am no angel, Heaven knows,' returned brother Charles, shaking his head, 'but an erring and imperfect man; nevertheless, there is one quality which all men have, in common with the angels, blessed opportunities of exercising, if they will; mercy. It is an errand of mercy that brings me here. Pray let me discharge it.'

'I show no mercy,' retorted Ralph with a triumphant smile, 'and I ask none. Seek no mercy from me, sir, in behalf of the fellow who has imposed upon your childish credulity, but let him expect the worst that I can do.'

'He ask mercy at your hands!' exclaimed the old merchant warmly; 'ask it at his, sir; ask it at his. If you will not hear me now, when you may, hear me when you must, or anticipate what I would say, and take measures to prevent our ever meeting again. Your nephew is a noble lad, sir, an honest, noble lad. What you are, Mr. Nickleby, I will not say; but what you have done, I know. Now, sir, when you go about the business in which you have been recently engaged, and find it difficult of pursuing, come to me and my brother Ned, and Tim Linkinwater, sir, and we'll explain it for you—and come soon, or it may be too late, and you may have it explained with a little more roughness, and a little less delicacy—and never forget, sir, that I came here this morning, in mercy to you, and am still ready to talk to you in the same spirit.'

With these words, uttered with great emphasis and emotion, brother Charles put on his broad-brimmed hat, and, passing Ralph Nickleby without any other remark, trotted nimbly into the street. Ralph looked after him, but neither moved nor spoke for some time: when he broke what almost seemed the silence of stupefaction, by a scornful laugh.

'This,' he said, 'from its wildness, should be another of those dreams that have so broken my rest of late. In mercy to me! Pho! The old simpleton has gone mad.'

Although he expressed himself in this derisive and contemptuous manner, it was plain that, the more Ralph pondered, the more ill at ease he became, and the more he laboured under some vague anxiety and alarm, which increased as the time passed on and no tidings of Newman Noggs arrived. After waiting until late in the afternoon, tortured by various apprehensions and misgivings, and the recollection of the warning which his nephew had given him when they last met: the further confirmation of which now presented itself in one shape of probability, now in another, and haunted him perpetually: he left home, and, scarcely knowing why, save that he was in a suspicious and agitated mood, betook himself to Snawley's house. His wife presented herself; and, of her, Ralph inquired whether her husband was at home.

'No,' she said sharply, 'he is not indeed, and I don't think he will be at home for a very long time; that's more.'

'Do you know who I am?' asked Ralph.

'Oh yes, I know you very well; too well, perhaps, and perhaps he does too, and sorry am I that I should have to say it.'

'Tell him that I saw him through the window-blind above, as I crossed the road just now, and that I would speak to him on business,' said Ralph. 'Do you hear?'

'I hear,' rejoined Mrs. Snawley, taking no further notice of the request.

'I knew this woman was a hypocrite, in the way of psalms and Scripture phrases,' said Ralph, passing quietly by, 'but I never knew she drank before.'

'Stop! You don't come in here,' said Mr. Snawley's better-half, interposing her person, which was a robust one, in the doorway. 'You have said more than enough to him on business, before now. I always told him what dealing with you and working out your schemes would come to. It was either you or the schoolmaster—one of you, or the two between you—that got the forged letter done; remember that! That wasn't his doing, so don't lay it at his door.'

'Hold your tongue, you Jezebel,' said Ralph, looking fearfully round.

'Ah, I know when to hold my tongue, and when to speak, Mr. Nickleby,' retorted the dame. 'Take care that other people know when to hold theirs.'

'You jade,' said Ralph, 'if your husband has been idiot enough to trust you with his secrets, keep them; keep them, she-devil that you are!'

'Not so much his secrets as other people's secrets, perhaps,' retorted the woman; 'not so much his secrets as yours. None of your black looks at me! You'll want 'em all, perhaps, for another time. You had better keep 'em.'

'Will you,' said Ralph, suppressing his passion as well as he could, and clutching her tightly by the wrist; 'will you go to your husband and tell him that I know he is at home, and that I must see him? And will you tell me what it is that you and he mean by this new style of behaviour?'

'No,' replied the woman, violently disengaging herself, 'I'll do neither.'

'You set me at defiance, do you?' said Ralph.

'Yes,' was the answer. 'I do.'

For an instant Ralph had his hand raised, as though he were about to strike her; but, checking himself, and nodding his head and muttering as though to assure her he would not forget this, walked away.

Thence, he went straight to the inn which Mr. Squeers frequented, and inquired when he had been there last; in the vague hope that, successful or unsuccessful, he might, by this time, have returned from his mission and be able to assure him that all was safe. But Mr. Squeers had not been there for ten days, and all that the people could tell about him was, that he had left his luggage and his bill.

Disturbed by a thousand fears and surmises, and bent upon ascertaining whether Squeers had any suspicion of Snawley, or was, in any way, a party to this altered behaviour, Ralph determined to hazard the extreme step of inquiring for him at the Lambeth lodging, and having an interview with him even there. Bent upon this purpose, and in that mood in which delay is insupportable, he repaired at once to the place; and being, by description, perfectly acquainted with the situation of his room, crept upstairs and knocked gently at the door.

Not one, nor two, nor three, nor yet a dozen knocks, served to convince Ralph, against his wish, that there was nobody inside. He reasoned that he might be asleep; and, listening, almost persuaded himself that he could hear him breathe. Even when he was satisfied that he could not be there, he sat patiently on a broken stair and waited; arguing, that he had gone out upon some slight errand, and must soon return.

Many feet came up the creaking stairs; and the step of some seemed to his listening ear so like that of the man for whom he waited, that Ralph often stood up to be ready to address him when he reached the top; but, one by one, each person turned off into some room short of the place where he was stationed: and at every such disappointment he felt quite chilled and lonely.

At length he felt it was hopeless to remain, and going downstairs again, inquired of one of the lodgers if he knew anything of Mr. Squeers's movements—mentioning that worthy by an assumed name which had been agreed upon between them. By this lodger he was referred to another, and by him to someone else, from whom he learnt, that, late on the previous night, he had gone out hastily with two men, who had shortly afterwards returned for the old woman who lived on the same floor; and that, although the circumstance had attracted the attention of the informant, he had not spoken to them at the time, nor made any inquiry afterwards.

This possessed him with the idea that, perhaps, Peg Sliderskew had been apprehended for the robbery, and that Mr. Squeers, being with her at the time, had been apprehended also, on suspicion of being a confederate. If this were so, the fact must be known to Gride; and to Gride's house he directed his steps; now thoroughly alarmed, and fearful that there were indeed plots afoot, tending to his discomfiture and ruin.

Arrived at the usurer's house, he found the windows close shut, the dingy blinds drawn down; all was silent, melancholy, and deserted. But this was its usual aspect. He knocked—gently at first—then loud and vigorously. Nobody came. He wrote a few words in pencil on a card, and having thrust it under the door was going away, when a noise above, as though a window-sash were stealthily raised, caught his ear, and looking up he could just discern the face of Gride himself, cautiously peering over the house parapet from the window of the garret. Seeing who was below, he drew it in again; not so quickly, however, but that Ralph let him know he was observed, and called to him to come down.

The call being repeated, Gride looked out again, so cautiously that no part of the old man's body was visible. The sharp features and white hair appearing alone, above the parapet, looked like a severed head garnishing the wall.

'Hush!' he cried. 'Go away, go away!'

'Come down,' said Ralph, beckoning him.

'Go a—way!' squeaked Gride, shaking his head in a sort of ecstasy of impatience. 'Don't speak to me, don't knock, don't call attention to the house, but go away.'

'I'll knock, I swear, till I have your neighbours up in arms,' said Ralph, 'if you don't tell me what you mean by lurking there, you whining cur.'

'I can't hear what you say—don't talk to me—it isn't safe—go away—go away!' returned Gride.

'Come down, I say. Will you come down?' said Ralph fiercely.

'No—o—o—oo,' snarled Gride. He drew in his head; and Ralph, left standing in the street, could hear the sash closed, as gently and carefully as it had been opened.

'How is this,' said he, 'that they all fall from me, and shun me like the plague, these men who have licked the dust from my feet? is my day past, and is this indeed the coming on of night? I'll know what it means! I will, at any cost. I am firmer and more myself, just now, than I have been these many days.'

Turning from the door, which, in the first transport of his rage, he had meditated battering upon until Gride's very fears should impel him to open it, he turned his face towards the city, and working his way steadily through the crowd which was pouring from it (it was by this time between five and six o'clock in the afternoon) went straight to the house of business of the brothers Cheeryble, and putting his head into the glass case, found Tim Linkinwater alone.

'My name's Nickleby,' said Ralph.

'I know it,' replied Tim, surveying him through his spectacles.

'Which of your firm was it who called on me this morning?' demanded Ralph.

'Mr. Charles.'

'Then, tell Mr. Charles I want to see him.'

'You shall see,' said Tim, getting off his stool with great agility, 'you shall see, not only Mr. Charles, but Mr. Ned likewise.'

Tim stopped, looked steadily and severely at Ralph, nodded his head once, in a curt manner which seemed to say there was a little more behind, and vanished. After a short interval, he returned, and, ushering Ralph into the presence of the two brothers, remained in the room himself.

'I want to speak to you, who spoke to me this morning,' said Ralph, pointing out with his finger the man whom he addressed.

'I have no secrets from my brother Ned, or from Tim Linkinwater,' observed brother Charles quietly.

'I have,' said Ralph.

'Mr. Nickleby, sir,' said brother Ned, 'the matter upon which my brother Charles called upon you this morning is one which is already perfectly well known to us three, and to others besides, and must unhappily soon become known to a great many more. He waited upon you, sir, this morning, alone, as a matter of delicacy and consideration. We feel, now, that further delicacy and consideration would be misplaced; and, if we confer together, it must be as we are or not at all.'

'Well, gentlemen,' said Ralph with a curl of the lip, 'talking in riddles would seem to be the peculiar forte of you two, and I suppose your clerk, like a prudent man, has studied the art also with a view to your good graces. Talk in company, gentlemen, in God's name. I'll humour you.'

'Humour!' cried Tim Linkinwater, suddenly growing very red in the face. 'He'll humour us! He'll humour Cheeryble Brothers! Do you hear that? Do you hear him? Do you hear him say he'll humour Cheeryble Brothers?'

'Tim,' said Charles and Ned together, 'pray, Tim, pray now, don't.'

Tim, taking the hint, stifled his indignation as well as he could, and suffered it to escape through his spectacles, with the additional safety-valve of a short hysterical laugh now and then, which seemed to relieve him mightily.

'As nobody bids me to a seat,' said Ralph, looking round, 'I'll take one, for I am fatigued with walking. And now, if you please, gentlemen, I wish to know—I demand to know; I have the right—what you have to say to me, which justifies such a tone as you have assumed, and that underhand interference in my affairs which, I have reason to suppose, you have been practising. I tell you plainly, gentlemen, that little as I care for the opinion of the world (as the slang goes), I don't choose to submit quietly to slander and malice. Whether you suffer yourselves to be imposed upon too easily, or wilfully make yourselves parties to it, the result to me is the same. In either case, you can't expect from a plain man like myself much consideration or forbearance.'

So coolly and deliberately was this said, that nine men out of ten, ignorant of the circumstances, would have supposed Ralph to be really an injured man. There he sat, with folded arms; paler than usual, certainly, and sufficiently ill-favoured, but quite collected—far more so than the brothers or the exasperated Tim—and ready to face out the worst.

'Very well, sir,' said brother Charles. 'Very well. Brother Ned, will you ring the bell?'

'Charles, my dear fellow! stop one instant,' returned the other. 'It will be better for Mr. Nickleby and for our object that he should remain silent, if he can, till we have said what we have to say. I wish him to understand that.'

'Quite right, quite right,' said brother Charles.

Ralph smiled, but made no reply. The bell was rung; the room-door opened; a man came in, with a halting walk; and, looking round, Ralph's eyes met those of Newman Noggs. From that moment, his heart began to fail him.

'This is a good beginning,' he said bitterly. 'Oh! this is a good beginning. You are candid, honest, open-hearted, fair-dealing men! I always knew the real worth of such characters as yours! To tamper with a fellow like this, who would sell his soul (if he had one) for drink, and whose every word is a lie. What men are safe if this is done? Oh, it's a good beginning!'

'I will speak,' cried Newman, standing on tiptoe to look over Tim's head, who had interposed to prevent him. 'Hallo, you sir—old Nickleby!—what do you mean when you talk of "a fellow like this"? Who made me "a fellow like this"? If I would sell my soul for drink, why wasn't I a thief, swindler, housebreaker, area sneak, robber of pence out of the trays of blind men's dogs, rather than your drudge and packhorse? If my every word was a lie, why wasn't I a pet and favourite of yours? Lie! When did I ever cringe and fawn to you. Tell me that! I served you faithfully. I did more work, because I was poor, and took more hard words from you because I despised you and them, than any man you could have got from the parish workhouse. I did. I served you because I was proud; because I was a lonely man with you, and there were no other drudges to see my degradation; and because nobody knew, better than you, that I was a ruined man: that I hadn't always been what I am: and that I might have been better off, if I hadn't been a fool and fallen into the hands of you and others who were knaves. Do you deny that?'

'Gently,' reasoned Tim; 'you said you wouldn't.'

'I said I wouldn't!' cried Newman, thrusting him aside, and moving his hand as Tim moved, so as to keep him at arm's length; 'don't tell me! Here, you Nickleby! Don't pretend not to mind me; it won't do; I know better. You were talking of tampering, just now. Who tampered with Yorkshire schoolmasters, and, while they sent the drudge out, that he shouldn't overhear, forgot that such great caution might render him suspicious, and that he might watch his master out at nights, and might set other eyes to watch the schoolmaster? Who tampered with a selfish father, urging him to sell his daughter to old Arthur Gride, and tampered with Gride too, and did so in the little office, with a closet in the room?'

Ralph had put a great command upon himself; but he could not have suppressed a slight start, if he had been certain to be beheaded for it next moment.

'Aha!' cried Newman, 'you mind me now, do you? What first set this fag to be jealous of his master's actions, and to feel that, if he hadn't crossed him when he might, he would have been as bad as he, or worse? That master's cruel treatment of his own flesh and blood, and vile designs upon a young girl who interested even his broken-down, drunken, miserable hack, and made him linger in his service, in the hope of doing her some good (as, thank God, he had done others once or twice before), when he would, otherwise, have relieved his feelings by pummelling his master soundly, and then going to the Devil. He would—mark that; and mark this—that I'm here now, because these gentlemen thought it best. When I sought them out (as I did; there was no tampering with me), I told them I wanted help to find you out, to trace you down, to go through with what I had begun, to help the right; and that when I had done it, I'd burst into your room and tell you all, face to face, man to man, and like a man. Now I've said my say, and let anybody else say theirs, and fire away!'

With this concluding sentiment, Newman Noggs, who had been perpetually sitting down and getting up again all through his speech, which he had delivered in a series of jerks; and who was, from the violent exercise and the excitement combined, in a state of most intense and fiery heat; became, without passing through any intermediate stage, stiff, upright, and motionless, and so remained, staring at Ralph Nickleby with all his might and main.

Ralph looked at him for an instant, and for an instant only; then, waved his hand, and beating the ground with his foot, said in a choking voice:

'Go on, gentlemen, go on! I'm patient, you see. There's law to be had, there's law. I shall call you to an account for this. Take care what you say; I shall make you prove it.'

'The proof is ready,' returned brother Charles, 'quite ready to our hands. The man Snawley, last night, made a confession.'

'Who may "the man Snawley" be,' returned Ralph, 'and what may his "confession" have to do with my affairs?'

To this inquiry, put with a dogged inflexibility of manner, the old gentleman returned no answer, but went on to say, that to show him how much they were in earnest, it would be necessary to tell him, not only what accusations were made against him, but what proof of them they had, and how that proof had been acquired. This laying open of the whole question brought up brother Ned, Tim Linkinwater, and Newman Noggs, all three at once; who, after a vast deal of talking together, and a scene of great confusion, laid before Ralph, in distinct terms, the following statement.

That, Newman, having been solemnly assured by one not then producible that Smike was not the son of Snawley, and this person having offered to make oath to that effect, if necessary, they had by this communication been first led to doubt the claim set up, which they would otherwise have seen no reason to dispute, supported as it was by evidence which they had no power of disproving. That, once suspecting the existence of a conspiracy, they had no difficulty in tracing back its origin to the malice of Ralph, and the vindictiveness and avarice of Squeers. That, suspicion and proof being two very different things, they had been advised by a lawyer, eminent for his sagacity and acuteness in such practice, to resist the proceedings taken on the other side for the recovery of the youth as slowly and artfully as possible, and meanwhile to beset Snawley (with whom it was clear the main falsehood must rest); to lead him, if possible, into contradictory and conflicting statements; to harass him by all available means; and so to practise on his fears, and regard for his own safety, as to induce him to divulge the whole scheme, and to give up his employer and whomsoever else he could implicate. That, all this had been skilfully done; but that Snawley, who was well practised in the arts of low cunning and intrigue, had successfully baffled all their attempts, until an unexpected circumstance had brought him, last night, upon his knees.

It thus arose. When Newman Noggs reported that Squeers was again in town, and that an interview of such secrecy had taken place between him and Ralph that he had been sent out of the house, plainly lest he should overhear a word, a watch was set upon the schoolmaster, in the hope that something might be discovered which would throw some light upon the suspected plot. It being found, however, that he held no further communication with Ralph, nor any with Snawley, and lived quite alone, they were completely at fault; the watch was withdrawn, and they would have observed his motions no longer, if it had not happened that, one night, Newman stumbled unobserved on him and Ralph in the street together. Following them, he discovered, to his surprise, that they repaired to various low lodging-houses, and taverns kept by broken gamblers, to more than one of whom Ralph was known, and that they were in pursuit—so he found by inquiries when they had left—of an old woman, whose description exactly tallied with that of deaf Mrs. Sliderskew. Affairs now appearing to assume a more serious complexion, the watch was renewed with increased vigilance; an officer was procured, who took up his abode in the same tavern with Squeers: and by him and Frank Cheeryble the footsteps of the unconscious schoolmaster were dogged, until he was safely housed in the lodging at Lambeth. Mr. Squeers having shifted his lodging, the officer shifted his, and lying concealed in the same street, and, indeed, in the opposite house, soon found that Mr. Squeers and Mrs. Sliderskew were in constant communication.

In this state of things, Arthur Gride was appealed to. The robbery, partly owing to the inquisitiveness of the neighbours, and partly to his own grief and rage, had, long ago, become known; but he positively refused to give his sanction or yield any assistance to the old woman's capture, and was seized with such a panic at the idea of being called upon to give evidence against her, that he shut himself up close in his house, and refused to hold communication with anybody. Upon this, the pursuers took counsel together, and, coming so near the truth as to arrive at the conclusion that Gride and Ralph, with Squeers for their instrument, were negotiating for the recovery of some of the stolen papers which would not bear the light, and might possibly explain the hints relative to Madeline which Newman had overheard, resolved that Mrs. Sliderskew should be taken into custody before she had parted with them: and Squeers too, if anything suspicious could be attached to him. Accordingly, a search-warrant being procured, and all prepared, Mr. Squeers's window was watched, until his light was put out, and the time arrived when, as had been previously ascertained, he usually visited Mrs. Sliderskew. This done, Frank Cheeryble and Newman stole upstairs to listen to their discourse, and to give the signal to the officer at the most favourable time. At what an opportune moment they arrived, how they listened, and what they heard, is already known to the reader. Mr. Squeers, still half stunned, was hurried off with a stolen deed in his possession, and Mrs. Sliderskew was apprehended likewise. The information being promptly carried to Snawley that Squeers was in custody—he was not told for what—that worthy, first extorting a promise that he should be kept harmless, declared the whole tale concerning Smike to be a fiction and forgery, and implicated Ralph Nickleby to the fullest extent. As to Mr. Squeers, he had, that morning, undergone a private examination before a magistrate; and, being unable to account satisfactorily for his possession of the deed or his companionship with Mrs. Sliderskew, had been, with her, remanded for a week.

All these discoveries were now related to Ralph, circumstantially, and in detail. Whatever impression they secretly produced, he suffered no sign of emotion to escape him, but sat perfectly still, not raising his frowning eyes from the ground, and covering his mouth with his hand. When the narrative was concluded; he raised his head hastily, as if about to speak, but on brother Charles resuming, fell into his old attitude again.

'I told you this morning,' said the old gentleman, laying his hand upon his brother's shoulder, 'that I came to you in mercy. How far you may be implicated in this last transaction, or how far the person who is now in custody may criminate you, you best know. But, justice must take its course against the parties implicated in the plot against this poor, unoffending, injured lad. It is not in my power, or in the power of my brother Ned, to save you from the consequences. The utmost we can do is, to warn you in time, and to give you an opportunity of escaping them. We would not have an old man like you disgraced and punished by your near relation; nor would we have him forget, like you, all ties of blood and nature. We entreat you—brother Ned, you join me, I know, in this entreaty, and so, Tim Linkinwater, do you, although you pretend to be an obstinate dog, sir, and sit there frowning as if you didn't—we entreat you to retire from London, to take shelter in some place where you will be safe from the consequences of these wicked designs, and where you may have time, sir, to atone for them, and to become a better man.'

'And do you think,' returned Ralph, rising, 'and do you think, you will so easily crush me? Do you think that a hundred well-arranged plans, or a hundred suborned witnesses, or a hundred false curs at my heels, or a hundred canting speeches full of oily words, will move me? I thank you for disclosing your schemes, which I am now prepared for. You have not the man to deal with that you think; try me! and remember that I spit upon your fair words and false dealings, and dare you—provoke you—taunt you—to do to me the very worst you can!'

Thus they parted, for that time; but the worst had not come yet.

CHAPTER 60
The Dangers thicken, and the Worst is Told

Instead of going home, Ralph threw himself into the first street cabriolet he could find, and, directing the driver towards the police-office of the district in which Mr. Squeers's misfortunes had occurred, alighted at a short distance from it, and, discharging the man, went the rest of his way thither on foot. Inquiring for the object of his solicitude, he learnt that he had timed his visit well; for Mr. Squeers was, in fact, at that moment waiting for a hackney coach he had ordered, and in which he purposed proceeding to his week's retirement, like a gentleman.

Demanding speech with the prisoner, he was ushered into a kind of waiting-room in which, by reason of his scholastic profession and superior respectability, Mr. Squeers had been permitted to pass the day. Here, by the light of a guttering and blackened candle, he could barely discern the schoolmaster, fast asleep on a bench in a remote corner. An empty glass stood on a table before him, which, with his somnolent condition and a very strong smell of brandy and water, forewarned the visitor that Mr Squeers had been seeking, in creature comforts, a temporary forgetfulness of his unpleasant situation.

It was not a very easy matter to rouse him: so lethargic and heavy were his slumbers. Regaining his faculties by slow and faint glimmerings, he at length sat upright; and, displaying a very yellow face, a very red nose, and a very bristly beard: the joint effect of which was considerably heightened by a dirty white handkerchief, spotted with blood, drawn over the crown of his head and tied under his chin: stared ruefully at Ralph in silence, until his feelings found a vent in this pithy sentence:

'I say, young fellow, you've been and done it now; you have!'

'What's the matter with your head?' asked Ralph.

'Why, your man, your informing kidnapping man, has been and broke it,' rejoined Squeers sulkily; 'that's what's the matter with it. You've come at last, have you?'

'Why have you not sent to me?' said Ralph. 'How could I come till I knew what had befallen you?'

'My family!' hiccuped Mr. Squeers, raising his eye to the ceiling: 'my daughter, as is at that age when all the sensibilities is a-coming out strong in blow—my son as is the young Norval of private life, and the pride and ornament of a doting willage—here's a shock for my family! The coat-of-arms of the Squeerses is tore, and their sun is gone down into the ocean wave!'

'You have been drinking,' said Ralph, 'and have not yet slept yourself sober.'

552

'I haven't been drinking your health, my codger,' replied Mr. Squeers; 'so you have nothing to do with that.'

Ralph suppressed the indignation which the schoolmaster's altered and insolent manner awakened, and asked again why he had not sent to him.

'What should I get by sending to you?' returned Squeers. 'To be known to be in with you wouldn't do me a deal of good, and they won't take bail till they know something more of the case, so here am I hard and fast: and there are you, loose and comfortable.'

'And so must you be in a few days,' retorted Ralph, with affected good-humour. 'They can't hurt you, man.'

'Why, I suppose they can't do much to me, if I explain how it was that I got into the good company of that there ca-daverous old Slider,' replied Squeers viciously, 'who I wish was dead and buried, and resurrected and dissected, and hung upon wires in a anatomical museum, before ever I'd had anything to do with her. This is what him with the powdered head says this morning, in so many words: "Prisoner! As you have been found in company with this woman; as you were detected in possession of this document; as you were engaged with her in fraudulently destroying others, and can give no satisfactory account of yourself; I shall remand you for a week, in order that inquiries may be made, and evidence got. And meanwhile I can't take any bail for your appearance." Well then, what I say now is, that I can give a satisfactory account of myself; I can hand in the card of my establishment and say, "I am the Wackford Squeers as is therein named, sir. I am the man as is guaranteed, by unimpeachable references, to be a out-and-outer in morals and uprightness of principle. Whatever is wrong in this business is no fault of mine. I had no evil design in it, sir. I was not aware that anything was wrong. I was merely employed by a friend, my friend Mr. Ralph Nickleby, of Golden Square. Send for him, sir, and ask him what he has to say; he's the man; not me!"'

'What document was it that you had?' asked Ralph, evading, for the moment, the point just raised.

'What document? Why, the document,' replied Squeers. 'The Madeline What's-her-name one. It was a will; that's what it was.'

'Of what nature, whose will, when dated, how benefiting her, to what extent?' asked Ralph hurriedly.

'A will in her favour; that's all I know,' rejoined Squeers, 'and that's more than you'd have known, if you'd had them bellows on your head. It's all owing to your precious caution that they got hold of it. If you had let me burn it, and taken my word that it was gone, it would have been a heap of ashes behind the fire, instead of being whole and sound, inside of my great-coat.'

'Beaten at every point!' muttered Ralph.

'Ah!' sighed Squeers, who, between the brandy and water and his broken head, wandered strangely, 'at the delightful village of Dotheboys near Greta Bridge in Yorkshire, youth are boarded, clothed, booked, washed, furnished with pocket-money, provided with all necessaries, instructed in all languages living and dead, mathematics, orthography, geometry, astronomy, trigonometry—this is a altered state of trigonomics, this is! A double l—all, everything—a cobbler's weapon. U-p-up, adjective, not down. S-q-u-double e-r-s-Squeers, noun substantive, a educator of youth. Total, all up with Squeers!'

His running on, in this way, had afforded Ralph an opportunity of recovering his presence of mind, which at once suggested to him the necessity of removing, as far as possible, the schoolmaster's misgivings, and leading him to believe that his safety and best policy lay in the preservation of a rigid silence.

'I tell you, once again,' he said, 'they can't hurt you. You shall have an action for false imprisonment, and make a profit of this, yet. We will devise a story for you that should carry you through twenty times such a trivial scrape as this; and if they want security in a thousand pounds for your reappearance in case you should be called upon, you shall have it. All you have to do is, to keep back the truth. You're a little fuddled tonight, and may not be able to see this as clearly as you would at another time; but this is what you must do, and you'll need all your senses about you; for a slip might be awkward.'

'Oh!' said Squeers, who had looked cunningly at him, with his head stuck on one side, like an old raven. 'That's what I'm to do, is it? Now then, just you hear a word or two from me. I an't a-going to have any stories made for me, and I an't a-going to stick to any. If I find matters going again me, I shall expect you to take your share, and I'll take care you do. You never said anything about danger. I never bargained for being brought into such a plight as this, and I don't mean to take it as quiet as you think. I let you lead me on, from one thing to another, because we had been mixed up together in a certain sort of a way, and if you had liked to be ill-natured you might perhaps have hurt the business, and if you liked to be good-natured you might throw a good deal in my way. Well; if all goes right now, that's quite correct, and I don't mind it; but if anything goes wrong, then times are altered, and I shall just say and do whatever I think may serve me most, and take advice from nobody. My moral influence with them lads,' added Mr. Squeers, with deeper gravity, 'is a tottering to its basis. The images of Mrs. Squeers, my daughter, and my son Wackford, all short of vittles, is perpetually before me; every other consideration melts away and vanishes, in front of these; the only number in all arithmetic that I know of, as a husband and a father, is number one, under this here most fatal go!'

How long Mr. Squeers might have declaimed, or how stormy a discussion his declamation might have led to, nobody knows. Being interrupted, at this point, by the arrival of the coach and an attendant who was to bear him company, he perched his hat with great dignity on the top of the handkerchief that bound his head; and, thrusting one hand in his pocket, and taking the attendant's arm with the other, suffered himself to be led forth.

'As I supposed from his not sending!' thought Ralph. 'This fellow, I plainly see through all his tipsy fooling, has made up his mind to turn upon me. I am so beset and hemmed in, that they are not only all struck with fear, but, like the beasts in the fable, have their fling at me now, though time was, and no longer ago than yesterday too, when they were all civility and compliance. But they shall not move me. I'll not give way. I will not budge one inch!'

He went home, and was glad to find his housekeeper complaining of illness, that he might have an excuse for being alone and sending her away to where she lived: which was hard by. Then, he sat down by the light of a single candle, and began to think, for the first time, on all that had taken place that day.

He had neither eaten nor drunk since last night, and, in addition to the anxiety of mind he had undergone, had been travelling about, from place to place almost incessantly, for many hours. He felt sick and exhausted, but could taste nothing save a glass of water, and continued to sit with his head upon his hand; not resting nor thinking, but laboriously trying to do both, and feeling that every sense but one of weariness and desolation, was for the time benumbed.

It was nearly ten o'clock when he heard a knocking at the door, and still sat quiet as before, as if he could not even bring his thoughts to bear upon that. It had been often repeated, and he had, several times, heard a voice outside, saying there was a light in the window (meaning, as he knew, his own candle), before he could rouse himself and go downstairs.

'Mr. Nickleby, there is terrible news for you, and I am sent to beg you will come with me directly,' said a voice he seemed to recognise. He held his hand above his eyes, and, looking out, saw Tim Linkinwater on the steps.

'Come where?' demanded Ralph.

'To our house, where you came this morning. I have a coach here.'

'Why should I go there?' said Ralph.

'Don't ask me why, but pray come with me.'

'Another edition of today!' returned Ralph, making as though he would shut the door.

'No, no!' cried Tim, catching him by the arm and speaking most earnestly; 'it is only that you may hear something that has occurred: something very dreadful, Mr. Nickleby, which concerns you nearly. Do you think I would tell you so or come to you like this, if it were not the case?'

Ralph looked at him more closely. Seeing that he was indeed greatly excited, he faltered, and could not tell what to say or think.

'You had better hear this now, than at any other time,' said Tim; 'it may have some influence with you. For Heaven's sake come!'

Perhaps, at, another time, Ralph's obstinacy and dislike would have been proof against any appeal from such a quarter, however emphatically urged; but now, after a moment's hesitation, he went into the hall for his hat, and returning, got into the coach without speaking a word.

Tim well remembered afterwards, and often said, that as Ralph Nickleby went into the house for this purpose, he saw him, by the light of the candle which he had set down upon a chair, reel and stagger like a drunken man. He well remembered, too, that when he had placed his foot upon the coach-steps, he turned round and looked upon him with a face so ashy pale and so very wild and vacant that it made him shudder, and for the moment almost afraid to follow. People were fond of saying that he had some dark presentiment upon him then, but his emotion might, perhaps, with greater show of reason, be referred to what he had undergone that day.

A profound silence was observed during the ride. Arrived at their place of destination, Ralph followed his conductor into the house, and into a room where the two brothers were. He was so astounded, not to say awed, by something of a mute compassion for himself which was visible in their manner and in that of the old clerk, that he could scarcely speak.

Having taken a seat, however, he contrived to say, though in broken words, 'What—what have you to say to me—more than has been said already?'

The room was old and large, very imperfectly lighted, and terminated in a bay window, about which hung some heavy drapery. Casting his eyes in this direction as he spoke, he thought he made out the dusky figure of a man. He was confirmed in this impression by seeing that the object moved, as if uneasy under his scrutiny.

'Who's that yonder?' he said.

'One who has conveyed to us, within these two hours, the intelligence which caused our sending to you,' replied brother Charles. 'Let him be, sir, let him be for the present.'

'More riddles!' said Ralph, faintly. 'Well, sir?'

In turning his face towards the brothers he was obliged to avert it from the window; but, before either of them could speak, he had looked round again. It was evident that he was rendered restless and uncomfortable by the presence of the unseen person; for he repeated this action several times, and at length, as if in a nervous state which rendered him positively unable to turn away from the place, sat so as to have it opposite him, muttering as an excuse that he could not bear the light.

The brothers conferred apart for a short time: their manner showing that they were agitated. Ralph glanced at them twice or thrice, and ultimately said, with a great effort to recover his self-possession, 'Now, what is this? If I am brought from home at this time of night, let it be for something. What have you got to tell me?' After a short pause, he added, 'Is my niece dead?'

He had struck upon a key which rendered the task of commencement an easier one. Brother Charles turned, and said that it was a death of which they had to tell him, but that his niece was well.

'You don't mean to tell me,' said Ralph, as his eyes brightened, 'that her brother's dead? No, that's too good. I'd not believe it, if you told me so. It would be too welcome news to be true.'

'Shame on you, you hardened and unnatural man,' cried the other brother, warmly. 'Prepare yourself for intelligence which, if you have any human feeling in your breast, will make even you shrink and tremble. What if we tell you that a poor unfortunate boy: a child in everything but never having known one of those tender endearments, or one of those lightsome hours which make our childhood a time to be remembered like a happy dream through all our after life: a warm-hearted, harmless, affectionate creature, who never offended you, or did you wrong, but on whom you have vented the malice and hatred you have conceived for your nephew, and whom you have made an instrument for wreaking your bad passions upon him: what if we tell you that, sinking under your persecution, sir, and the misery and ill-usage of a life short in years but long in suffering, this poor creature has gone to tell his sad tale where, for your part in it, you must surely answer?'

'If you tell me,' said Ralph; 'if you tell me that he is dead, I forgive you all else. If you tell me that he is dead, I am in your debt and bound to you for life. He is! I see it in your faces. Who triumphs now? Is this your dreadful news; this your terrible intelligence? You see how it moves me. You did well to send. I would have travelled a hundred miles afoot, through mud, mire, and darkness, to hear this news just at this time.'

Even then, moved as he was by this savage joy, Ralph could see in the faces of the two brothers, mingling with their look of disgust and horror, something of that indefinable compassion for himself which he had noticed before.

'And he brought you the intelligence, did he?' said Ralph, pointing with his finger towards the recess already mentioned; 'and sat there, no doubt, to see me prostrated and overwhelmed by it! Ha, ha, ha! But I tell him that I'll be a sharp thorn in his side for many a long day to come; and I tell you two, again, that you don't know him yet; and that you'll rue the day you took compassion on the vagabond.'

'You take me for your nephew,' said a hollow voice; 'it would be better for you, and for me too, if I were he indeed.'

The figure that he had seen so dimly, rose, and came slowly down. He started back, for he found that he confronted—not Nicholas, as he had supposed, but Brooker.

Ralph had no reason, that he knew, to fear this man; he had never feared him before; but the pallor which had been observed in his face when he issued forth that night, came upon him again. He was seen to tremble, and his voice changed as he said, keeping his eyes upon him,

'What does this fellow here? Do you know he is a convict, a felon, a common thief?'

'Hear what he has to tell you. Oh, Mr. Nickleby, hear what he has to tell you, be he what he may!' cried the brothers, with such emphatic earnestness, that Ralph turned to them in wonder. They pointed to Brooker. Ralph again gazed at him: as it seemed mechanically.

'That boy,' said the man, 'that these gentlemen have been talking of—'

'That boy,' repeated Ralph, looking vacantly at him.

'Whom I saw, stretched dead and cold upon his bed, and who is now in his grave—'

'Who is now in his grave,' echoed Ralph, like one who talks in his sleep.

The man raised his eyes, and clasped his hands solemnly together:

'—Was your only son, so help me God in heaven!'

In the midst of a dead silence, Ralph sat down, pressing his two hands upon his temples. He removed them, after a minute, and never was there seen, part of a living man undisfigured by any wound, such a ghastly face as he then disclosed. He looked at Brooker, who was by this time standing at a short distance from him; but did not say one word, or make the slightest sound or gesture.

'Gentlemen,' said the man, 'I offer no excuses for myself. I am long past that. If, in telling you how this has happened, I tell you that I was harshly used, and perhaps driven out of my real nature, I do it only as a necessary part of my story, and not to shield myself. I am a guilty man.'

He stopped, as if to recollect, and looking away from Ralph, and addressing himself to the brothers, proceeded in a subdued and humble tone:

'Among those who once had dealings with this man, gentlemen—that's from twenty to five-and-twenty years ago—there was one: a rough fox-hunting, hard-drinking gentleman, who had run through his own fortune, and wanted to squander away that of his sister: they were both orphans, and she lived with him and managed his house. I don't know whether it was, originally, to back his influence and try to over-persuade the young woman or not, but he,' pointing, to Ralph, 'used to go down to the house in Leicestershire pretty often, and stop there many days at a time. They had had a great many dealings together, and he may have gone on some of those, or to patch up his client's affairs, which were in a ruinous state; of course he went for profit. The gentlewoman was not a girl, but she was, I have heard say, handsome, and entitled to a pretty large property. In course of time, he married her. The same love of gain which led him to contract this marriage, led to its being kept strictly private; for a clause in her father's will declared that if she married without her brother's consent, the property, in which she had only some life interest while she remained single, should pass away altogether to another branch of the family. The brother would give no consent that the sister didn't buy, and pay for handsomely; Mr. Nickleby would consent to no such sacrifice; and so they went on, keeping their marriage secret, and waiting for him to break his neck or die of a fever. He did neither, and meanwhile the result of this private marriage was a son. The child was put out to nurse, a long way off; his mother never saw him but once or twice, and then by stealth; and his father—so eagerly did he thirst after the money which seemed to come almost within his grasp now, for his brother-in-law was very ill, and breaking more and more every day—never went near him, to avoid raising any suspicion. The brother lingered on; Mr Nickleby's wife constantly urged him to avow their marriage; he peremptorily refused. She remained alone in a dull country house: seeing little or no company but riotous, drunken sportsmen. He lived in London and clung to his business. Angry quarrels and recriminations took place, and when they had been married nearly seven years, and were within a few weeks of the time when the brother's death would have adjusted all, she eloped with a younger man, and left him.'

Here he paused, but Ralph did not stir, and the brothers signed to him to proceed.

'It was then that I became acquainted with these circumstances from his own lips. They were no secrets then; for the brother, and others, knew them; but they were communicated to me, not on this account, but because I was wanted. He followed the fugitives. Some said to make money of his wife's shame, but, I believe, to take some violent revenge, for that was as much his character as the other; perhaps more. He didn't find them, and she died not long after. I don't know whether he began to think he might like the child, or whether he wished to make sure that it should never fall into its mother's hands; but, before he went, he intrusted me with the charge of bringing it home. And I did so.'

He went on, from this point, in a still more humble tone, and spoke in a very low voice; pointing to Ralph as he resumed.

'He had used me ill—cruelly—I reminded him in what, not long ago when I met him in the street—and I hated him. I brought the child home to his own house, and lodged him in the front garret. Neglect had made him very sickly, and I was obliged to call in a doctor, who said he must be removed for change of air, or he would die. I think that first put it in my head. I did it then. He was gone six weeks, and when he came back, I told him—with every circumstance well planned and proved; nobody could have suspected me—that the child was dead and buried. He might have been disappointed in some intention he had formed, or he might have had some natural affection, but he was grieved at that, and I was confirmed in my design of opening up the secret one day, and making it a means of getting money from him. I had heard, like most other men, of Yorkshire schools. I took the child to one kept by a man named Squeers, and left it there. I gave him the name of Smike. Year by year, I paid twenty pounds a-year for him for six years; never breathing the secret all the time; for I had left his father's service after more hard usage, and quarrelled with him again. I was sent away from this country. I have been away nearly eight years. Directly I came home again, I travelled down into Yorkshire, and, skulking in the village of an evening-time, made inquiries about the boys at the school, and found that this one, whom I had placed there, had run away with a young man bearing the name of his own father. I sought his father out in London, and hinting at what I could tell him, tried for a little money to support life; but he repulsed me with threats. I then found out his clerk, and, going on from little to little, and showing him that there were good reasons for communicating with me, learnt what was going on; and it was I who told him that the boy was no son of the man who claimed to be his father. All this time I had never seen the boy. At length, I heard from this same source that he was very ill, and where he was. I travelled down there, that I might recall myself, if possible, to his recollection and confirm my story. I came upon him unexpectedly; but before I could speak he knew me—he had good cause to remember me, poor lad!—and I would have sworn to him if I had met him in the Indies. I knew the piteous face I had seen in the little child. After a few days' indecision, I applied to the young gentleman in whose care he was, and I found that he was dead. He knows how quickly he recognised me again, how often he had described me and my leaving him at the school, and how he told him of a garret he recollected: which is the one I have spoken of, and in his father's house to this day. This is my story. I demand to be brought face to face with the schoolmaster, and put to any possible proof of any part of it, and I will show that it's too true, and that I have this guilt upon my soul.'

'Unhappy man!' said the brothers. 'What reparation can you make for this?'

'None, gentlemen, none! I have none to make, and nothing to hope now. I am old in years, and older still in misery and care. This confession can bring nothing upon me but new suffering and punishment; but I make it, and will abide by it whatever comes. I have been made the instrument of working out this dreadful retribution upon the head of a man who, in the hot pursuit of his bad ends, has persecuted and hunted down his own child to death. It must descend upon me too. I know it must fall. My reparation comes too late; and, neither in this world nor in the next, can I have hope again!'

He had hardly spoken, when the lamp, which stood upon the table close to where Ralph was seated, and which was the only one in the room, was thrown to the ground, and left them in darkness. There was some trifling confusion in obtaining another light; the interval was a mere nothing; but when the light appeared, Ralph Nickleby was gone.

The good brothers and Tim Linkinwater occupied some time in discussing the probability of his return; and, when it became apparent that he would not come back, they hesitated whether or no to send after him. At length, remembering how strangely and silently he had sat in one immovable position during the interview, and thinking he might possibly be ill, they determined, although it was now very late, to send to his house on some pretence. Finding an excuse in the presence of Brooker, whom they knew not how to dispose of without consulting his wishes, they concluded to act upon this resolution before going to bed.

CHAPTER 61
Wherein Nicholas and his Sister forfeit the good Opinion of all worldly and prudent People

On the next morning after Brooker's disclosure had been made, Nicholas returned home. The meeting between him and those whom he had left there was not without strong emotion on both sides; for they had been informed by his letters of what had occurred: and, besides that his griefs were theirs, they mourned with him the death of one whose forlorn and helpless state had first established a claim upon their compassion, and whose truth of heart and grateful earnest nature had, every day, endeared him to them more and more.

'I am sure,' said Mrs. Nickleby, wiping her eyes, and sobbing bitterly, 'I have lost the best, the most zealous, and most attentive creature that has ever been a companion to me in my life—putting you, my dear Nicholas, and Kate, and your poor papa, and that well-behaved nurse who ran away with the linen and the twelve small forks, out of the question, of course. Of all the tractable, equal-tempered, attached, and faithful beings that ever lived, I believe he was the most so. To look round upon the garden, now, that he took so much pride in, or to go into his room and see it filled with so many of those little contrivances for our comfort that he was so fond of making, and made so well, and so little thought he would leave unfinished—I can't bear it, I cannot really. Ah! This is a great trial to me, a great trial. It will be comfort to you, my dear Nicholas, to the end of your life, to recollect how kind and good you always were to him—so it will be to me, to think what excellent terms we were always upon, and how fond he always was of me, poor fellow! It was very natural you should have been attached to him, my dear—very—and of course you were, and are very much cut up by this. I am sure it's only necessary to look at you and see how changed you are, to see that; but nobody knows what my feelings are—nobody can—it's quite impossible!'

While Mrs. Nickleby, with the utmost sincerity, gave vent to her sorrows after her own peculiar fashion of considering herself foremost, she was not the only one who indulged such feelings. Kate, although well accustomed to forget herself when others were to be considered, could not repress her grief; Madeline was scarcely less moved than she; and poor, hearty, honest little Miss La Creevy, who had come upon one of her visits while Nicholas was away, and had done nothing, since the sad news arrived, but console and cheer them all, no sooner beheld him coming in at the door, than she sat herself down upon the stairs, and bursting into a flood of tears, refused for a long time to be comforted.

'It hurts me so,' cried the poor body, 'to see him come back alone. I can't help thinking what he must have suffered himself. I wouldn't mind so much if he gave way a little more; but he bears it so manfully.'

'Why, so I should,' said Nicholas, 'should I not?'

'Yes, yes,' replied the little woman, 'and bless you for a good creature! but this does seem at first to a simple soul like me—I know it's wrong to say so, and I shall be sorry for it presently—this does seem such a poor reward for all you have done.'

'Nay,' said Nicholas gently, 'what better reward could I have, than the knowledge that his last days were peaceful and happy, and the recollection that I was his constant companion, and was not prevented, as I might have been by a hundred circumstances, from being beside him?'

'To be sure,' sobbed Miss La Creevy; 'it's very true, and I'm an ungrateful, impious, wicked little fool, I know.'

With that, the good soul fell to crying afresh, and, endeavouring to recover herself, tried to laugh. The laugh and the cry, meeting each other thus abruptly, had a struggle for the mastery; the result was, that it was a drawn battle, and Miss La Creevy went into hysterics.

Waiting until they were all tolerably quiet and composed again, Nicholas, who stood in need of some rest after his long journey, retired to his own room, and throwing himself, dressed as he was, upon the bed, fell into a sound sleep. When he awoke, he found Kate sitting by his bedside, who, seeing that he had opened his eyes, stooped down to kiss him.

'I came to tell you how glad I am to see you home again.'

'But I can't tell you how glad I am to see you, Kate.'

'We have been wearying so for your return,' said Kate, 'mama and I, and—and Madeline.'

'You said in your last letter that she was quite well,' said Nicholas, rather hastily, and colouring as he spoke. 'Has nothing been said, since I have been away, about any future arrangements that the brothers have in contemplation for her?'

'Oh, not a word,' replied Kate. 'I can't think of parting from her without sorrow; and surely, Nicholas, you don't wish it!'

Nicholas coloured again, and, sitting down beside his sister on a little couch near the window, said:

'No, Kate, no, I do not. I might strive to disguise my real feelings from anybody but you; but I will tell you that—briefly and plainly, Kate—that I love her.'

Kate's eyes brightened, and she was going to make some reply, when Nicholas laid his hand upon her arm, and went on:

'Nobody must know this but you. She, last of all.'

'Dear Nicholas!'

'Last of all; never, though never is a long day. Sometimes, I try to think that the time may come when I may honestly tell her this; but it is so far off; in such distant perspective, so many years must elapse before it comes, and when it does come (if ever) I shall be so unlike what I am now, and shall have so outlived my days of youth and romance—though not, I am sure, of love for her—that even I feel how visionary all such hopes must be, and try to crush them rudely myself, and have the pain over, rather than suffer time to wither them, and keep the disappointment in store. No, Kate! Since I have been absent, I have had, in that poor fellow who is gone, perpetually before my eyes, another instance of the munificent liberality of these noble brothers. As far as in me lies, I will deserve it, and if I have wavered in my bounden duty to them before, I am now determined to discharge it rigidly, and to put further delays and temptations beyond my reach.'

'Before you say another word, dear Nicholas,' said Kate, turning pale, 'you must hear what I have to tell you. I came on purpose, but I had not the courage. What you say now, gives me new heart.' She faltered, and burst into tears.

There was that in her manner which prepared Nicholas for what was coming. Kate tried to speak, but her tears prevented her.

'Come, you foolish girl,' said Nicholas; 'why, Kate, Kate, be a woman! I think I know what you would tell me. It concerns Mr. Frank, does it not?'

Kate sunk her head upon his shoulder, and sobbed out 'Yes.'

'And he has offered you his hand, perhaps, since I have been away,' said Nicholas; 'is that it? Yes. Well, well; it is not so difficult, you see, to tell me, after all. He offered you his hand?'

'Which I refused,' said Kate.

'Yes; and why?'

'I told him,' she said, in a trembling voice, 'all that I have since found you told mama; and while I could not conceal from him, and cannot from you, that—that it was a pang and a great trial, I did so firmly, and begged him not to see me any more.'

'That's my own brave Kate!' said Nicholas, pressing her to his breast. 'I knew you would.'

'He tried to alter my resolution,' said Kate, 'and declared that, be my decision what it might, he would not only inform his uncles of the step he had taken, but would communicate it to you also, directly you returned. I am afraid,' she added, her momentary composure forsaking her, 'I am afraid I may not have said, strongly enough, how deeply I felt such disinterested love, and how earnestly I prayed for his future happiness. If you do talk together, I should—I should like him to know that.'

'And did you suppose, Kate, when you had made this sacrifice to what you knew was right and honourable, that I should shrink from mine?' said Nicholas tenderly.

'Oh no! not if your position had been the same, but—'

'But it is the same,' interrupted Nicholas. 'Madeline is not the near relation of our benefactors, but she is closely bound to them by ties as dear; and I was first intrusted with her history, specially because they reposed unbounded confidence in me, and believed that I was as true as steel. How base would it be of me to take advantage of the circumstances which placed her here, or of the slight service I was happily able to render her, and to seek to engage her affections when the result must be, if I succeeded, that the brothers would be disappointed in their darling wish of establishing her as their own child, and that I must seem to hope to build my fortunes on their compassion for the young creature whom I had so meanly and unworthily entrapped: turning her very gratitude and warmth of heart to my own purpose and account, and trading in her misfortunes! I, too, whose duty, and pride, and pleasure, Kate, it is to have other claims upon me which I will never forget; and who have the means of a comfortable and happy life already, and have no right to look beyond it! I have determined to remove this weight from my mind. I doubt whether I have not done wrong, even now; and today I will, without reserve or equivocation, disclose my real reasons to Mr. Cherryble, and implore him to take immediate measures for removing this young lady to the shelter of some other roof.'

'Today? so very soon?'

'I have thought of this for weeks, and why should I postpone it? If the scene through which I have just passed has taught me to reflect, and has awakened me to a more anxious and careful sense of duty, why should I wait until the impression has cooled? You would not dissuade me, Kate; now would you?'

'You may grow rich, you know,' said Kate.

'I may grow rich!' repeated Nicholas, with a mournful smile, 'ay, and I may grow old! But rich or poor, or old or young, we shall ever be the same to each other, and in that our comfort lies. What if we have but one home? It can never be a solitary one to you and me. What if we were to remain so true to these first impressions as to form no others? It is but one more link to the strong chain that binds us together. It seems but yesterday that we were playfellows, Kate, and it will seem but tomorrow when we are staid old people, looking back to these cares as we look back, now, to those of our childish days: and recollecting with a melancholy pleasure that the time was, when they could move us. Perhaps then, when we are quaint old folks and talk of the times when our step was lighter and our hair not grey, we may be even thankful for the trials that so endeared us to each other, and turned our lives into that current, down which we shall have glided so peacefully and calmly. And having caught some inkling of our story, the young people about us—as young as you and I are now, Kate—may come to us for sympathy, and pour distresses which hope and inexperience could scarcely feel enough for, into the compassionate ears of the old bachelor brother and his maiden sister.'

Kate smiled through her tears as Nicholas drew this picture; but they were not tears of sorrow, although they continued to fall when he had ceased to speak.

'Am I not right, Kate?' he said, after a short silence.

'Quite, quite, dear brother; and I cannot tell you how happy I am that I have acted as you would have had me.'

'You don't regret?'

'N—n—no,' said Kate timidly, tracing some pattern upon the ground with her little foot. 'I don't regret having done what was honourable and right, of course; but I do regret that this should have ever happened—at least sometimes I regret it, and sometimes I—I don't know what I say; I am but a weak girl, Nicholas, and it has agitated me very much.'

It is no vaunt to affirm that if Nicholas had had ten thousand pounds at the minute, he would, in his generous affection for the owner of the blushing cheek and downcast eye, have bestowed its utmost farthing, in perfect forgetfulness of himself, to secure her happiness. But all he could do was to comfort and console her by kind words; and words they were of such love and kindness, and cheerful encouragement, that poor Kate threw her arms about his neck, and declared she would weep no more.

'What man,' thought Nicholas proudly, while on his way, soon afterwards, to the brothers' house, 'would not be sufficiently rewarded for any sacrifice of fortune by the possession of such a heart as Kate's, which, but that hearts weigh light, and gold and silver heavy, is beyond all praise? Frank has money, and wants no more. Where would it buy him such a treasure as Kate? And yet, in unequal marriages, the rich party is always supposed to make a great sacrifice, and the other to get a good bargain! But I am thinking like a lover, or like an ass: which I suppose is pretty nearly the same.'

Checking thoughts so little adapted to the business on which he was bound, by such self-reproofs as this and many others no less sturdy, he proceeded on his way and presented himself before Tim Linkinwater.

'Ah! Mr. Nickleby!' cried Tim, 'God bless you! how d'ye do? Well? Say you're quite well and never better. Do now.'

'Quite,' said Nicholas, shaking him by both hands.

'Ah!' said Tim, 'you look tired though, now I come to look at you. Hark! there he is, d'ye hear him? That was Dick, the blackbird. He hasn't been himself since you've been gone. He'd never get on without you, now; he takes as naturally to you as he does to me.'

'Dick is a far less sagacious fellow than I supposed him, if he thinks I am half so well worthy of his notice as you,' replied Nicholas.

'Why, I'll tell you what, sir,' said Tim, standing in his favourite attitude and pointing to the cage with the feather of his pen, 'it's a very extraordinary thing about that bird, that the only people he ever takes the smallest notice of, are Mr. Charles, and Mr. Ned, and you, and me.'

Here, Tim stopped and glanced anxiously at Nicholas; then unexpectedly catching his eye repeated, 'And you and me, sir, and you and me.' And then he glanced at Nicholas again, and, squeezing his hand, said, 'I am a bad one at putting off anything I am interested in. I didn't mean to ask you, but I should like to hear a few particulars about that poor boy. Did he mention Cheeryble Brothers at all?'

'Yes,' said Nicholas, 'many and many a time.'

'That was right of him,' returned Tim, wiping his eyes; 'that was very right of him.'

'And he mentioned your name a score of times,' said Nicholas, 'and often bade me carry back his love to Mr. Linkinwater.'

'No, no, did he though?' rejoined Tim, sobbing outright. 'Poor fellow! I wish we could have had him buried in town. There isn't such a burying-ground in all London as that little one on the other side of the square—there are counting-houses all round it, and if you go in there, on a fine day, you can see the books and safes through the open windows. And he sent his love to me, did he? I didn't expect he would have thought of me. Poor fellow, poor fellow! His love too!'

Tim was so completely overcome by this little mark of recollection, that he was quite unequal to any more conversation at the moment. Nicholas therefore slipped quietly out, and went to brother Charles's room.

If he had previously sustained his firmness and fortitude, it had been by an effort which had cost him no little pain; but the warm welcome, the hearty manner, the homely unaffected commiseration, of the good old man, went to his heart, and no inward struggle could prevent his showing it.

'Come, come, my dear sir,' said the benevolent merchant; 'we must not be cast down; no, no. We must learn to bear misfortune, and we must remember that there are many sources of consolation even in death. Every day that this poor lad had lived, he must have been less and less qualified for the world, and more and more unhappy in is own deficiencies. It is better as it is, my dear sir. Yes, yes, yes, it's better as it is.'

'I have thought of all that, sir,' replied Nicholas, clearing his throat. 'I feel it, I assure you.'

'Yes, that's well,' replied Mr. Cheeryble, who, in the midst of all his comforting, was quite as much taken aback as honest old Tim; 'that's well. Where is my brother Ned? Tim Linkinwater, sir, where is my brother Ned?'

'Gone out with Mr. Trimmers, about getting that unfortunate man into the hospital, and sending a nurse to his children,' said Tim.

'My brother Ned is a fine fellow, a great fellow!' exclaimed brother Charles as he shut the door and returned to Nicholas. 'He will be overjoyed to see you, my dear sir. We have been speaking of you every day.'

'To tell you the truth, sir, I am glad to find you alone,' said Nicholas, with some natural

564

hesitation; 'for I am anxious to say something to you. Can you spare me a very few minutes?'

'Surely, surely,' returned brother Charles, looking at him with an anxious countenance. 'Say on, my dear sir, say on.'

'I scarcely know how, or where, to begin,' said Nicholas. 'If ever one mortal had reason to be penetrated with love and reverence for another: with such attachment as would make the hardest service in his behalf a pleasure and delight: with such grateful recollections as must rouse the utmost zeal and fidelity of his nature: those are the feelings which I should entertain for you, and do, from my heart and soul, believe me!'

'I do believe you,' replied the old gentleman, 'and I am happy in the belief. I have never doubted it; I never shall. I am sure I never shall.'

'Your telling me that so kindly,' said Nicholas, 'emboldens me to proceed. When you first took me into your confidence, and dispatched me on those missions to Miss Bray, I should have told you that I had seen her long before; that her beauty had made an impression upon me which I could not efface; and that I had fruitlessly endeavoured to trace her, and become acquainted with her history. I did not tell you so, because I vainly thought I could conquer my weaker feelings, and render every consideration subservient to my duty to you.'

'Mr. Nickleby,' said brother Charles, 'you did not violate the confidence I placed in you, or take an unworthy advantage of it. I am sure you did not.'

'I did not,' said Nicholas, firmly. 'Although I found that the necessity for self-command and restraint became every day more imperious, and the difficulty greater, I never, for one instant, spoke or looked but as I would have done had you been by. I never, for one moment, deserted my trust, nor have I to this instant. But I find that constant association and companionship with this sweet girl is fatal to my peace of mind, and may prove destructive to the resolutions I made in the beginning, and up to this time have faithfully kept. In short, sir, I cannot trust myself, and I implore and beseech you to remove this young lady from under the charge of my mother and sister without delay. I know that to anyone but myself—to you, who consider the immeasurable distance between me and this young lady, who is now your ward, and the object of your peculiar care—my loving her, even in thought, must appear the height of rashness and presumption. I know it is so. But who can see her as I have seen, who can know what her life has been, and not love her? I have no excuse but that; and as I cannot fly from this temptation, and cannot repress this passion, with its object constantly before me, what can I do but pray and beseech you to remove it, and to leave me to forget her?'

'Mr. Nickleby,' said the old man, after a short silence, 'you can do no more. I was wrong to expose a young man like you to this trial. I might have foreseen what would happen. Thank you, sir, thank you. Madeline shall be removed.'

'If you would grant me one favour, dear sir, and suffer her to remember me with esteem, by never revealing to her this confession—'

'I will take care,' said Mr. Cheeryble. 'And now, is this all you have to tell me?'

'No!' returned Nicholas, meeting his eye, 'it is not.'

'I know the rest,' said Mr. Cheeryble, apparently very much relieved by this prompt reply. 'When did it come to your knowledge?'

'When I reached home this morning.'

'You felt it your duty immediately to come to me, and tell me what your sister no doubt acquainted you with?'

'I did,' said Nicholas, 'though I could have wished to have spoken to Mr Frank first.'

'Frank was with me last night,' replied the old gentleman. 'You have done well, Mr. Nickleby—very well, sir—and I thank you again.'

Upon this head, Nicholas requested permission to add a few words. He ventured to hope that nothing he had said would lead to the estrangement of Kate and Madeline, who had formed an attachment for each other, any interruption of which would, he knew, be attended with great pain to them, and, most of all, with remorse and pain to him, as its unhappy cause. When these things were all forgotten, he hoped that Frank and he might still be warm friends, and that no word or thought of his humble home, or of her who was well contented to remain there and share his quiet fortunes, would ever again disturb the harmony between them. He recounted, as nearly as he could, what had passed between himself and Kate that morning: speaking of her with such warmth of pride and affection, and dwelling so cheerfully upon the confidence they had of overcoming any selfish regrets and living contented and happy in each other's love, that few could have heard him unmoved. More moved himself than he had been yet, he expressed in a few hurried words—as expressive, perhaps, as the most eloquent phrases—his devotion to the brothers, and his hope that he might live and die in their service.

To all this, brother Charles listened in profound silence, and with his chair so turned from Nicholas that his face could not be seen. He had not spoken either, in his accustomed manner, but with a certain stiffness and embarrassment very foreign to it. Nicholas feared he had offended him. He said, 'No, no, he had done quite right,' but that was all.

'Frank is a heedless, foolish fellow,' he said, after Nicholas had paused for some time; 'a very heedless, foolish fellow. I will take care that this is brought to a close without delay. Let us say no more upon the subject; it's a very painful one to me. Come to me in half an hour; I have strange things to tell you, my dear sir, and your uncle has appointed this afternoon for your waiting upon him with me.'

'Waiting upon him! With you, sir!' cried Nicholas.

'Ay, with me,' replied the old gentleman. 'Return to me in half an hour, and I'll tell you more.'

Nicholas waited upon him at the time mentioned, and then learnt all that had taken place on the previous day, and all that was known of the appointment Ralph had made with the brothers; which was for that night; and for the better understanding of which it will be requisite to return and follow his own footsteps from the house of the twin brothers. Therefore, we leave Nicholas somewhat reassured by the restored kindness of their manner towards him, and yet sensible that it was different from what it had been (though he scarcely knew in what respect): so he was full of uneasiness, uncertainty, and disquiet.

CHAPTER 62
Ralph makes one last Appointment—and keeps it

Creeping from the house, and slinking off like a thief; groping with his hands, when first he got into the street, as if he were a blind man; and looking often over his shoulder while he hurried away, as though he were followed in imagination or reality by someone anxious to question or detain him; Ralph Nickleby left the city behind him, and took the road to his own home.

The night was dark, and a cold wind blew, driving the clouds, furiously and fast, before it. There was one black, gloomy mass that seemed to follow him: not hurrying in the wild chase with the others, but lingering sullenly behind, and gliding darkly and stealthily on. He often looked back at this, and, more than once, stopped to let it pass over; but, somehow, when he went forward again, it was still behind him, coming mournfully and slowly up, like a shadowy funeral train.

He had to pass a poor, mean burial-ground—a dismal place, raised a few feet above the level of the street, and parted from it by a low parapet-wall and an iron railing; a rank, unwholesome, rotten spot, where the very grass and weeds seemed, in their frouzy growth, to tell that they had sprung from paupers' bodies, and had struck their roots in the graves of men, sodden, while alive, in steaming courts and drunken hungry dens. And here, in truth, they lay, parted from the living by a little earth and a board or two—lay thick and close—corrupting in body as they had in mind—a dense and squalid crowd. Here they lay, cheek by jowl with life: no deeper down than the feet of the throng that passed there every day, and piled high as their throats. Here they lay, a grisly family, all these dear departed brothers and sisters of the ruddy clergyman who did his task so speedily when they were hidden in the ground!

As he passed here, Ralph called to mind that he had been one of a jury, long before, on the body of a man who had cut his throat; and that he was buried in this place. He could not tell how he came to recollect it now, when he had so often passed and never thought about him, or how it was that he felt an interest in the circumstance; but he did both; and stopping, and clasping the iron railings with his hands, looked eagerly in, wondering which might be his grave.

While he was thus engaged, there came towards him, with noise of shouts and singing, some fellows full of drink, followed by others, who were remonstrating with them and urging them to go home in quiet. They were in high good-humour; and one of them, a little, weazen, hump-backed man, began to dance. He was a grotesque, fantastic figure, and the few bystanders laughed. Ralph himself was moved to mirth, and echoed the laugh of one who stood near and who looked round in his face. When they had passed on, and he was left alone again, he resumed his speculation with a new kind of interest; for he recollected that the last person who had seen the suicide alive, had left him very merry, and he remembered how strange he and the other jurors had thought that at the time.

He could not fix upon the spot among such a heap of graves, but he conjured up a strong and vivid idea of the man himself, and how he looked, and what had led him to do it; all of which he recalled with ease. By dint of dwelling upon this theme, he carried the impression with him when he went away; as he remembered, when a child, to have had frequently before him the figure of some goblin he had once seen chalked upon a door. But as he drew nearer and nearer home he forgot it again, and began to think how very dull and solitary the house would be inside.

This feeling became so strong at last, that when he reached his own door, he could hardly make up his mind to turn the key and open it. When he had done that, and gone into the passage, he felt as though to shut it again would be to shut out the world. But he let it go, and it closed with a loud noise. There was no light. How very dreary, cold, and still it was!

Shivering from head to foot, he made his way upstairs into the room where he had been last disturbed. He had made a kind of compact with himself that he would not think of what had happened until he got home. He was at home now, and suffered himself to consider it.

His own child, his own child! He never doubted the tale; he felt it was true; knew it as well, now, as if he had been privy to it all along. His own child! And dead too. Dying beside Nicholas, loving him, and looking upon him as something like an angel. That was the worst!

They had all turned from him and deserted him in his very first need. Even money could not buy them now; everything must come out, and everybody must know all. Here was the young lord dead, his companion abroad and beyond his reach, ten thousand pounds gone at one blow, his plot with Gride overset at the very moment of triumph, his after-schemes discovered, himself in danger, the object of his persecution and Nicholas's love, his own wretched boy; everything crumbled and fallen upon him, and he beaten down beneath the ruins and grovelling in the dust.

If he had known his child to be alive; if no deceit had been ever practised, and he had grown up beneath his eye; he might have been a careless, indifferent, rough, harsh father—like enough—he felt that; but the thought would come that he might have been otherwise, and that his son might have been a comfort to him, and they two happy together. He began to think now, that his supposed death and his wife's flight had had some share in making him the morose, hard man he was. He seemed to remember a time when he was not quite so rough and obdurate; and almost thought that he had first hated Nicholas because he was young and gallant, and perhaps like the stripling who had brought dishonour and loss of fortune on his head.

But one tender thought, or one of natural regret, in his whirlwind of passion and remorse, was as a drop of calm water in a stormy maddened sea. His hatred of Nicholas had been fed upon his own defeat, nourished on his interference with his schemes, fattened upon his old defiance and success. There were reasons for its increase; it had grown and strengthened gradually. Now it attained a height which was sheer wild lunacy. That his, of all others, should have been the hands to rescue his miserable child; that he should have been his protector and faithful friend; that he should have shown him that love and tenderness which, from the wretched moment of his birth, he had never known; that he should have taught him to hate his own parent and execrate his very name; that he should now know and feel all this, and triumph in the recollection; was gall and madness to the usurer's heart. The dead boy's love for Nicholas, and the attachment of Nicholas to him, was insupportable agony. The picture of his deathbed, with Nicholas at his side, tending and supporting him, and he breathing out his thanks, and expiring in his arms, when he would have had them mortal enemies and hating each other to the last, drove him frantic. He gnashed his teeth and smote the air, and looking wildly round, with eyes which gleamed through the darkness, cried aloud:

'I am trampled down and ruined. The wretch told me true. The night has come! Is there no way to rob them of further triumph, and spurn their mercy and compassion? Is there no devil to help me?'

Swiftly, there glided again into his brain the figure he had raised that night. It seemed to lie before him. The head was covered now. So it was when he first saw it. The rigid, upturned, marble feet too, he remembered well. Then came before him the pale and trembling relatives who had told their tale upon the inquest—the shrieks of women—the silent dread of men—the consternation and disquiet—the victory achieved by that heap of clay, which, with one motion of its hand, had let out the life and made this stir among them—

He spoke no more; but, after a pause, softly groped his way out of the room, and up the echoing stairs—up to the top—to the front garret—where he closed the door behind him, and remained.

It was a mere lumber-room now, but it yet contained an old dismantled bedstead; the one on which his son had slept; for no other had ever been there. He avoided it hastily, and sat down as far from it as he could.

The weakened glare of the lights in the street below, shining through the window which had no blind or curtain to intercept it, was enough to show the character of the room, though not sufficient fully to reveal the various articles of lumber, old corded trunks and broken furniture, which were scattered about. It had a shelving roof; high in one part, and at another descending almost to the floor. It was towards the highest part that Ralph directed his eyes; and upon it he kept them fixed steadily for some minutes, when he rose, and dragging thither an old chest upon which he had been seated, mounted on it, and felt along the wall above his head with both hands. At length, they touched a large iron hook, firmly driven into one of the beams.

At that moment, he was interrupted by a loud knocking at the door below. After a little hesitation he opened the window, and demanded who it was.

'I want Mr. Nickleby,' replied a voice.

'What with him?'

'That's not Mr. Nickleby's voice, surely?' was the rejoinder.

It was not like it; but it was Ralph who spoke, and so he said.

The voice made answer that the twin brothers wished to know whether the man whom he had seen that night was to be detained; and that although it was now midnight they had sent, in their anxiety to do right.

'Yes,' cried Ralph, 'detain him till tomorrow; then let them bring him here—him and my nephew—and come themselves, and be sure that I will be ready to receive them.'

'At what hour?' asked the voice.

'At any hour,' replied Ralph fiercely. 'In the afternoon, tell them. At any hour, at any minute. All times will be alike to me.'

He listened to the man's retreating footsteps until the sound had passed, and then, gazing up into the sky, saw, or thought he saw, the same black cloud that had seemed to follow him home, and which now appeared to hover directly above the house.

'I know its meaning now,' he muttered, 'and the restless nights, the dreams, and why I have quailed of late. All pointed to this. Oh! if men by selling their own souls could ride rampant for a term, for how short a term would I barter mine tonight!'

The sound of a deep bell came along the wind. One.

'Lie on!' cried the usurer, 'with your iron tongue! Ring merrily for births that make expectants writhe, and marriages that are made in hell, and toll ruefully for the dead whose shoes are worn already! Call men to prayers who are godly because not found out, and ring chimes for the coming in of every year that brings this cursed world nearer to its end. No bell or book for me! Throw me on a dunghill, and let me rot there, to infect the air!'

With a wild look around, in which frenzy, hatred, and despair were horribly mingled, he shook his clenched hand at the sky above him, which was still dark and threatening, and closed the window.

The rain and hail pattered against the glass; the chimneys quaked and rocked; the crazy casement rattled with the wind, as though an impatient hand inside were striving to burst it open. But no hand was there, and it opened no more.

'How's this?' cried one. 'The gentleman say they can't make anybody hear, and have been trying these two hours.'

'And yet he came home last night,' said another; 'for he spoke to somebody out of that window upstairs.'

They were a little knot of men, and, the window being mentioned, went out into the road to look up at it. This occasioned their observing that the house was still close shut, as the housekeeper had said she had left it on the previous night, and led to a great many suggestions: which terminated in two or three of the boldest getting round to the back, and so entering by a window, while the others remained outside, in impatient expectation.

They looked into all the rooms below: opening the shutters as they went, to admit the fading light: and still finding nobody, and everything quiet and in its place, doubted whether they should go farther. One man, however, remarking that they had not yet been into the garret, and that it was there he had been last seen, they agreed to look there too, and went up softly; for the mystery and silence made them timid.

After they had stood for an instant, on the landing, eyeing each other, he who had proposed their carrying the search so far, turned the handle of the door, and, pushing it open, looked through the chink, and fell back directly.

'It's very odd,' he whispered, 'he's hiding behind the door! Look!'

They pressed forward to see; but one among them thrusting the others aside with a loud exclamation, drew a clasp-knife from his pocket, and dashing into the room, cut down the body.

He had torn a rope from one of the old trunks, and hung himself on an iron hook immediately below the trap-door in the ceiling—in the very place to which the eyes of his son, a lonely, desolate, little creature, had so often been directed in childish terror, fourteen years before.

CHAPTER 63

The Brothers Cheeryble make various Declarations for themselves and others. Tim Linkinwater makes a Declaration for himself

Some weeks had passed, and the first shock of these events had subsided. Madeline had been removed; Frank had been absent; and Nicholas and Kate had begun to try in good earnest to stifle their own regrets, and to live for each other and for their mother—who, poor lady, could in nowise be reconciled to this dull and altered state of affairs—when there came one evening, per favour of Mr. Linkinwater, an invitation from the brothers to dinner on the next day but one: comprehending, not only Mrs Nickleby, Kate, and Nicholas, but little Miss La Creevy, who was most particularly mentioned.

'Now, my dears,' said Mrs. Nickleby, when they had rendered becoming honour to the bidding, and Tim had taken his departure, 'what does this mean?'

'What do you mean, mother?' asked Nicholas, smiling.

'I say, my dear,' rejoined that lady, with a face of unfathomable mystery, 'what does this invitation to dinner mean? What is its intention and object?'

'I conclude it means, that on such a day we are to eat and drink in their house, and that its intent and object is to confer pleasure upon us,' said Nicholas.

'And that's all you conclude it is, my dear?'

'I have not yet arrived at anything deeper, mother.'

'Then I'll just tell you one thing,' said Mrs. Nickleby, 'you'll find yourself a little surprised; that's all. You may depend upon it that this means something besides dinner.'

'Tea and supper, perhaps,' suggested Nicholas.

'I wouldn't be absurd, my dear, if I were you,' replied Mrs. Nickleby, in a lofty manner, 'because it's not by any means becoming, and doesn't suit you at all. What I mean to say is, that the Mr. Cheerybles don't ask us to dinner with all this ceremony for nothing. Never mind; wait and see. You won't believe anything I say, of course. It's much better to wait; a great deal better; it's satisfactory to all parties, and there can be no disputing. All I say is, remember what I say now, and when I say I said so, don't say I didn't.'

With this stipulation, Mrs. Nickleby, who was troubled, night and day, with a vision of a hot messenger tearing up to the door to announce that Nicholas had been taken into partnership, quitted that branch of the subject, and entered upon a new one.

'It's a very extraordinary thing,' she said, 'a most extraordinary thing, that they should have invited Miss La Creevy. It quite astonishes me, upon my word it does. Of course it's very pleasant that she should be invited, very pleasant, and I have no doubt that she'll conduct herself extremely well; she always does. It's very gratifying to think that we should have been the means of introducing her into such society, and I'm quite glad of it—quite rejoiced—for she certainly is an exceedingly well-behaved and good-natured little person. I could wish that some friend would mention to her how very badly she has her cap trimmed, and what very preposterous bows those are, but of course that's impossible, and if she likes to make a fright of herself, no doubt she has a perfect right to do so. We never see ourselves—never do, and never did—and I suppose we never shall.'

This moral reflection reminding her of the necessity of being peculiarly smart on the occasion, so as to counterbalance Miss La Creevy, and be herself an effectual set-off and atonement, led Mrs. Nickleby into a consultation with her daughter relative to certain ribbons, gloves, and trimmings: which, being a complicated question, and one of paramount importance, soon routed the previous one, and put it to flight.

The great day arriving, the good lady put herself under Kate's hands an hour or so after breakfast, and, dressing by easy stages, completed her toilette in sufficient time to allow of her daughter's making hers, which was very simple, and not very long, though so satisfactory that she had never appeared more charming or looked more lovely. Miss La Creevy, too, arrived with two bandboxes (whereof the bottoms fell out as they were handed from the coach) and something in a newspaper, which a gentleman had sat upon, coming down, and which was obliged to be ironed again, before it was fit for service. At last, everybody was dressed, including Nicholas, who had come home to fetch them, and they went away in a coach sent by the brothers for the purpose: Mrs. Nickleby wondering very much what they would have for dinner, and cross-examining Nicholas as to the extent of his discoveries in the morning; whether he had smelt anything cooking at all like turtle, and if not, what he had smelt; and diversifying the conversation with reminiscences of dinners to which she had gone some twenty years ago, concerning which she particularised not only the dishes but the guests, in whom her hearers did not feel a very absorbing interest, as not one of them had ever chanced to hear their names before.

The old butler received them with profound respect and many smiles, and ushered them into the drawing-room, where they were received by the brothers with so much cordiality and kindness that Mrs. Nickleby was quite in a flutter, and had scarcely presence of mind enough, even to patronise Miss La Creevy. Kate was still more affected by the reception: for, knowing that the brothers were acquainted with all that had passed between her and Frank, she felt her position a most delicate and trying one, and was trembling on the arm of Nicholas, when Mr. Charles took her in his, and led her to another part of the room.

'Have you seen Madeline, my dear,' he said, 'since she left your house?'

'No, sir!' replied Kate. 'Not once.'

'And not heard from her, eh? Not heard from her?'

'I have only had one letter,' rejoined Kate, gently. 'I thought she would not have forgotten me quite so soon.'

'Ah,' said the old man, patting her on the head, and speaking as affectionately as if she had been his favourite child. 'Poor dear! what do you think of this, brother Ned? Madeline has only written to her once, only once, Ned, and she didn't think she would have forgotten her quite so soon, Ned.'

'Oh! sad, sad; very sad!' said Ned.

The brothers interchanged a glance, and looking at Kate for a little time without speaking, shook hands, and nodded as if they were congratulating each other on something very delightful.

'Well, well,' said brother Charles, 'go into that room, my dear—that door yonder—and see if there's not a letter for you from her. I think there's one upon the table. You needn't hurry back, my love, if there is, for we don't dine just yet, and there's plenty of time. Plenty of time.'

Kate retired as she was directed. Brother Charles, having followed her graceful figure with his eyes, turned to Mrs. Nickleby, and said:

'We took the liberty of naming one hour before the real dinner-time, ma'am, because we had a little business to speak about, which would occupy the interval. Ned, my dear fellow, will you mention what we agreed upon? Mr. Nickleby, sir, have the goodness to follow me.'

Without any further explanation, Mrs. Nickleby, Miss La Creevy, and brother Ned, were left alone together, and Nicholas followed brother Charles into his private room; where, to his great astonishment, he encountered Frank, whom he supposed to be abroad.

'Young men,' said Mr. Cheeryble, 'shake hands!'

'I need no bidding to do that,' said Nicholas, extending his.

'Nor I,' rejoined Frank, as he clasped it heartily.

The old gentleman thought that two handsomer or finer young fellows could scarcely stand side by side than those on whom he looked with so much pleasure. Suffering his eyes to rest upon them, for a short time in silence, he said, while he seated himself at his desk:

'I wish to see you friends—close and firm friends—and if I thought you otherwise, I should hesitate in what I am about to say. Frank, look here! Mr. Nickleby, will you come on the other side?'

The young men stepped up on either hand of brother Charles, who produced a paper from his desk, and unfolded it.

'This,' he said, 'is a copy of the will of Madeline's maternal grandfather, bequeathing her the sum of twelve thousand pounds, payable either upon her coming of age or marrying. It would appear that this gentleman, angry with her (his only relation) because she would not put herself under his protection, and detach herself from the society of her father, in compliance with his repeated overtures, made a will leaving this property (which was all he possessed) to a charitable institution. He would seem to have repented this determination, however, for three weeks afterwards, and in the same month, he executed this. By some fraud, it was abstracted immediately after his decease, and the other—the only will found—was proved and administered. Friendly negotiations, which have only just now terminated, have been proceeding since this instrument came into our hands, and, as there is no doubt of its authenticity, and the witnesses have been discovered (after some trouble), the money has been refunded. Madeline has therefore obtained her right, and is, or will be, when either of the contingencies which I have mentioned has arisen, mistress of this fortune. You understand me?'

Frank replied in the affirmative. Nicholas, who could not trust himself to speak lest his voice should be heard to falter, bowed his head.

'Now, Frank,' said the old gentleman, 'you were the immediate means of recovering this deed. The fortune is but a small one; but we love Madeline; and such as it is, we would rather see you allied to her with that, than to any other girl we know who has three times the money. Will you become a suitor to her for her hand?'

'No, sir. I interested myself in the recovery of that instrument, believing that her hand was already pledged to one who has a thousand times the claims upon her gratitude, and, if I mistake not, upon her heart, that I or any other man can ever urge. In this it seems I judged hastily.'

'As you always do, sir,' cried brother Charles, utterly forgetting his assumed dignity, 'as you always do. How dare you think, Frank, that we would have you marry for money, when

573

youth, beauty, and every amiable virtue and excellence were to be had for love? How dared you, Frank, go and make love to Mr. Nickleby's sister without telling us first what you meant to do, and letting us speak for you?'

'I hardly dared to hope—'

'You hardly dared to hope! Then, so much the greater reason for having our assistance! Mr. Nickleby, sir, Frank, although he judged hastily, judged, for once, correctly. Madeline's heart is occupied. Give me your hand, sir; it is occupied by you, and worthily and naturally. This fortune is destined to be yours, but you have a greater fortune in her, sir, than you would have in money were it forty times told. She chooses you, Mr Nickleby. She chooses as we, her dearest friends, would have her choose. Frank chooses as we would have him choose. He should have your sister's little hand, sir, if she had refused it a score of times; ay, he should, and he shall! You acted nobly, not knowing our sentiments, but now you know them, sir, you must do as you are bid. What! You are the children of a worthy gentleman! The time was, sir, when my dear brother Ned and I were two poor simple-hearted boys, wandering, almost barefoot, to seek our fortunes: are we changed in anything but years and worldly circumstances since that time? No, God forbid! Oh, Ned, Ned, Ned, what a happy day this is for you and me! If our poor mother had only lived to see us now, Ned, how proud it would have made her dear heart at last!'

Thus apostrophised, brother Ned, who had entered with Mrs. Nickleby, and who had been before unobserved by the young men, darted forward, and fairly hugged brother Charles in his arms.

'Bring in my little Kate,' said the latter, after a short silence. 'Bring her in, Ned. Let me see Kate, let me kiss her. I have a right to do so now; I was very near it when she first came; I have often been very near it. Ah! Did you find the letter, my bird? Did you find Madeline herself, waiting for you and expecting you? Did you find that she had not quite forgotten her friend and nurse and sweet companion? Why, this is almost the best of all!'

'Come, come,' said Ned, 'Frank will be jealous, and we shall have some cutting of throats before dinner.'

'Then let him take her away, Ned, let him take her away. Madeline's in the next room. Let all the lovers get out of the way, and talk among themselves, if they've anything to say. Turn 'em out, Ned, every one!'

Brother Charles began the clearance by leading the blushing girl to the door, and dismissing her with a kiss. Frank was not very slow to follow, and Nicholas had disappeared first of all. So there only remained Mrs Nickleby and Miss La Creevy, who were both sobbing heartily; the two brothers; and Tim Linkinwater, who now came in to shake hands with everybody: his round face all radiant and beaming with smiles.

'Well, Tim Linkinwater, sir,' said brother Charles, who was always spokesman, 'now the young folks are happy, sir.'

'You didn't keep 'em in suspense as long as you said you would, though,' returned Tim, archly. 'Why, Mr. Nickleby and Mr. Frank were to have been in your room for I don't know how long; and I don't know what you weren't to have told them before you came out with the truth.'

574

'Now, did you ever know such a villain as this, Ned?' said the old gentleman; 'did you ever know such a villain as Tim Linkinwater? He accusing me of being impatient, and he the very man who has been wearying us morning, noon, and night, and torturing us for leave to go and tell 'em what was in store, before our plans were half complete, or we had arranged a single thing. A treacherous dog!'

'So he is, brother Charles,' returned Ned; 'Tim is a treacherous dog. Tim is not to be trusted. Tim is a wild young fellow. He wants gravity and steadiness; he must sow his wild oats, and then perhaps he'll become in time a respectable member of society.'

This being one of the standing jokes between the old fellows and Tim, they all three laughed very heartily, and might have laughed much longer, but that the brothers, seeing that Mrs. Nickleby was labouring to express her feelings, and was really overwhelmed by the happiness of the time, took her between them, and led her from the room under pretence of having to consult her on some most important arrangements.

Now, Tim and Miss La Creevy had met very often, and had always been very chatty and pleasant together—had always been great friends—and consequently it was the most natural thing in the world that Tim, finding that she still sobbed, should endeavour to console her. As Miss La Creevy sat on a large old-fashioned window-seat, where there was ample room for two, it was also natural that Tim should sit down beside her; and as to Tim's being unusually spruce and particular in his attire that day, why it was a high festival and a great occasion, and that was the most natural thing of all.

Tim sat down beside Miss La Creevy, and, crossing one leg over the other so that his foot—he had very comely feet and happened to be wearing the neatest shoes and black silk stockings possible—should come easily within the range of her eye, said in a soothing way:

'Don't cry!'

'I must,' rejoined Miss La Creevy.

'No, don't,' said Tim. 'Please don't; pray don't.'

'I am so happy!' sobbed the little woman.

'Then laugh,' said Tim. 'Do laugh.'

What in the world Tim was doing with his arm, it is impossible to conjecture, but he knocked his elbow against that part of the window which was quite on the other side of Miss La Creevy; and it is clear that it could have no business there.

'Do laugh,' said Tim, 'or I'll cry.'

'Why should you cry?' asked Miss La Creevy, smiling.

'Because I'm happy too,' said Tim. 'We are both happy, and I should like to do as you do.'

Surely, there never was a man who fidgeted as Tim must have done then; for he knocked the window again—almost in the same place—and Miss La Creevy said she was sure he'd break it.

'I knew,' said Tim, 'that you would be pleased with this scene.'

'It was very thoughtful and kind to remember me,' returned Miss La Creevy. 'Nothing could have delighted me half so much.'

Why on earth should Miss La Creevy and Tim Linkinwater have said all this in a whisper? It was no secret. And why should Tim Linkinwater have looked so hard at Miss La Creevy, and why should Miss La Creevy have looked so hard at the ground?

'It's a pleasant thing,' said Tim, 'to people like us, who have passed all our lives in the world alone, to see young folks that we are fond of, brought together with so many years of happiness before them.'

'Ah!' cried the little woman with all her heart, 'that it is!'

'Although,' pursued Tim 'although it makes one feel quite solitary and cast away. Now don't it?'

Miss La Creevy said she didn't know. And why should she say she didn't know? Because she must have known whether it did or not.

'It's almost enough to make us get married after all, isn't it?' said Tim.

'Oh, nonsense!' replied Miss La Creevy, laughing. 'We are too old.'

'Not a bit,' said Tim; 'we are too old to be single. Why shouldn't we both be married, instead of sitting through the long winter evenings by our solitary firesides? Why shouldn't we make one fireside of it, and marry each other?'

'Oh, Mr. Linkinwater, you're joking!'

'No, no, I'm not. I'm not indeed,' said Tim. 'I will, if you will. Do, my dear!'

'It would make people laugh so.'

'Let 'em laugh,' cried Tim stoutly; 'we have good tempers I know, and we'll laugh too. Why, what hearty laughs we have had since we've known each other!'

'So we have,' cried Miss La Creevy—giving way a little, as Tim thought.

'It has been the happiest time in all my life; at least, away from the counting-house and Cheeryble Brothers,' said Tim. 'Do, my dear! Now say you will.'

'No, no, we mustn't think of it,' returned Miss La Creevy. 'What would the brothers say?'

'Why, God bless your soul!' cried Tim, innocently, 'you don't suppose I should think of such a thing without their knowing it! Why they left us here on purpose.'

'I can never look 'em in the face again!' exclaimed Miss La Creevy, faintly.

'Come,' said Tim, 'let's be a comfortable couple. We shall live in the old house here, where I have been for four-and-forty year; we shall go to the old church, where I've been, every Sunday morning, all through that time; we shall have all my old friends about us—Dick, the archway, the pump, the flower-pots, and Mr. Frank's children, and Mr. Nickleby's children, that we shall seem like grandfather and grandmother to. Let's be a comfortable couple, and take care of each other! And if we should get deaf, or lame, or blind, or bed-ridden, how glad we shall be that we have somebody we are fond of, always to talk to and sit with! Let's be a comfortable couple. Now, do, my dear!'

Five minutes after this honest and straightforward speech, little Miss La Creevy and Tim were talking as pleasantly as if they had been married for a score of years, and had never once quarrelled all the time; and five minutes after that, when Miss La Creevy had bustled out to see if her eyes were red and put her hair to rights, Tim moved with a stately step towards the drawing-room, exclaiming as he went, 'There an't such another woman in all London! I know there an't!'

By this time, the apoplectic butler was nearly in fits, in consequence of the unheard-of postponement of dinner. Nicholas, who had been engaged in a manner in which every reader may imagine for himself or herself, was hurrying downstairs in obedience to his angry summons, when he encountered a new surprise.

On his way down, he overtook, in one of the passages, a stranger genteelly dressed in black, who was also moving towards the dining-room. As he was rather lame, and walked slowly, Nicholas lingered behind, and was following him step by step, wondering who he was, when he suddenly turned round and caught him by both hands.

'Newman Noggs!' cried Nicholas joyfully

'Ah! Newman, your own Newman, your own old faithful Newman! My dear boy, my dear Nick, I give you joy—health, happiness, every blessing! I can't bear it—it's too much, my dear boy—it makes a child of me!'

'Where have you been?' said Nicholas. 'What have you been doing? How often have I inquired for you, and been told that I should hear before long!'

'I know, I know!' returned Newman. 'They wanted all the happiness to come together. I've been helping 'em. I—I—look at me, Nick, look at me!'

'You would never let me do that,' said Nicholas in a tone of gentle reproach.

'I didn't mind what I was, then. I shouldn't have had the heart to put on gentleman's clothes. They would have reminded me of old times and made me miserable. I am another man now, Nick. My dear boy, I can't speak. Don't say anything to me. Don't think the worse of me for these tears. You don't know what I feel today; you can't, and never will!'

They walked in to dinner arm-in-arm, and sat down side by side.

Never was such a dinner as that, since the world began. There was the superannuated bank clerk, Tim Linkinwater's friend; and there was the chubby old lady, Tim Linkinwater's sister; and there was so much attention from Tim Linkinwater's sister to Miss La Creevy, and there were so many jokes from the superannuated bank clerk, and Tim Linkinwater himself was in such tiptop spirits, and little Miss La Creevy was in such a comical state, that of themselves they would have composed the pleasantest party conceivable. Then, there was Mrs. Nickleby, so grand and complacent; Madeline and Kate, so blushing and beautiful; Nicholas and Frank, so devoted and proud; and all four so silently and tremblingly happy; there was Newman so subdued yet so overjoyed, and there were the twin brothers so delighted and interchanging such looks, that the old servant stood transfixed behind his master's chair, and felt his eyes grow dim as they wandered round the table.

When the first novelty of the meeting had worn off, and they began truly to feel how happy they were, the conversation became more general, and the harmony and pleasure if possible increased. The brothers were in a perfect ecstasy; and their insisting on saluting the ladies all round, before they would permit them to retire, gave occasion to the superannuated bank clerk to say so many good things, that he quite outshone himself, and was looked upon as a prodigy of humour.

'Kate, my dear,' said Mrs. Nickleby, taking her daughter aside, as soon as they got upstairs, 'you don't really mean to tell me that this is actually true about Miss La Creevy and Mr. Linkinwater?'

'Indeed it is, mama.'

'Why, I never heard such a thing in my life!' exclaimed Mrs. Nickleby.

'Mr. Linkinwater is a most excellent creature,' reasoned Kate, 'and, for his age, quite young still.'

'For his age, my dear!' returned Mrs. Nickleby, 'yes; nobody says anything against him, except that I think he is the weakest and most foolish man I ever knew. It's her age I speak of. That he should have gone and offered himself to a woman who must be—ah, half as old again as I am—and that she should have dared to accept him! It don't signify, Kate; I'm disgusted with her!'

Shaking her head very emphatically indeed, Mrs. Nickleby swept away; and all the evening, in the midst of the merriment and enjoyment that ensued, and in which with that exception she freely participated, conducted herself towards Miss La Creevy in a stately and distant manner, designed to mark her sense of the impropriety of her conduct, and to signify her extreme and cutting disapprobation of the misdemeanour she had so flagrantly committed.

CHAPTER 64
An old Acquaintance is recognised under melancholy Circumstances, and Dotheboys Hall breaks up for ever

Nicholas was one of those whose joy is incomplete unless it is shared by the friends of adverse and less fortunate days. Surrounded by every fascination of love and hope, his warm heart yearned towards plain John Browdie. He remembered their first meeting with a smile, and their second with a tear; saw poor Smike once again with the bundle on his shoulder trudging patiently by his side; and heard the honest Yorkshireman's rough words of encouragement as he left them on their road to London.

Madeline and he sat down, very many times, jointly to produce a letter which should acquaint John at full length with his altered fortunes, and assure him of his friendship and gratitude. It so happened, however, that the letter could never be written. Although they applied themselves to it with the best intentions in the world, it chanced that they always fell to talking about something else, and when Nicholas tried it by himself, he found it impossible to write one-half of what he wished to say, or to pen anything, indeed, which on reperusal did not appear cold and unsatisfactory compared with what he had in his mind. At last, after going on thus from day to day, and reproaching himself more and more, he resolved (the more readily as Madeline strongly urged him) to make a hasty trip into Yorkshire, and present himself before Mr. and Mrs. Browdie without a word of notice.

Thus it was that between seven and eight o'clock one evening, he and Kate found themselves in the Saracen's Head booking-office, securing a place to Greta Bridge by the next morning's coach. They had to go westward, to procure some little necessaries for his journey, and, as it was a fine night, they agreed to walk there, and ride home.

The place they had just been in called up so many recollections, and Kate had so many anecdotes of Madeline, and Nicholas so many anecdotes of Frank, and each was so interested in what the other said, and both were so happy and confiding, and had so much to talk about, that it was not until they had plunged for a full half-hour into that labyrinth of streets which lies between Seven Dials and Soho, without emerging into any large thoroughfare, that Nicholas began to think it just possible they might have lost their way.

The possibility was soon converted into a certainty; for, on looking about, and walking first to one end of the street and then to the other, he could find no landmark he could recognise, and was fain to turn back again in quest of some place at which he could seek a direction.

It was a by-street, and there was nobody about, or in the few wretched shops they passed. Making towards a faint gleam of light which streamed across the pavement from a cellar, Nicholas was about to descend two or three steps so as to render himself visible to those below and make his inquiry, when he was arrested by a loud noise of scolding in a woman's voice.

'Oh come away!' said Kate, 'they are quarrelling. You'll be hurt.'

'Wait one instant, Kate. Let us hear if there's anything the matter,' returned her brother. 'Hush!'

'You nasty, idle, vicious, good-for-nothing brute,' cried the woman, stamping on the ground, 'why don't you turn the mangle?'

'So I am, my life and soul!' replied the man's voice. 'I am always turning. I am perpetually turning, like a demd old horse in a demnition mill. My life is one demd horrid grind!'

'Then why don't you go and list for a soldier?' retorted the woman; 'you're welcome to.'

'For a soldier!' cried the man. 'For a soldier! Would his joy and gladness see him in a coarse red coat with a little tail? Would she hear of his being slapped and beat by drummers demnebly? Would she have him fire off real guns, and have his hair cut, and his whiskers shaved, and his eyes turned right and left, and his trousers pipeclayed?'

'Dear Nicholas,' whispered Kate, 'you don't know who that is. It's Mr Mantalini I am confident.'

'Do make sure! Peep at him while I ask the way,' said Nicholas. 'Come down a step or two. Come!'

Drawing her after him, Nicholas crept down the steps and looked into a small boarded cellar. There, amidst clothes-baskets and clothes, stripped up to his shirt-sleeves, but wearing still an old patched pair of pantaloons of superlative make, a once brilliant waistcoat, and moustache and whiskers as of yore, but lacking their lustrous dye—there, endeavouring to mollify the wrath of a buxom female—not the lawful Madame Mantalini, but the proprietress of the concern—and grinding meanwhile as if for very life at the mangle, whose creaking noise, mingled with her shrill tones, appeared almost to deafen him—there was the graceful, elegant, fascinating, and once dashing Mantalini.

'Oh you false traitor!' cried the lady, threatening personal violence on Mr. Mantalini's face.

'False! Oh dem! Now my soul, my gentle, captivating, bewitching, and most demnebly enslaving chick-a-biddy, be calm,' said Mr. Mantalini, humbly.

'I won't!' screamed the woman. 'I'll tear your eyes out!'

'Oh! What a demd savage lamb!' cried Mr. Mantalini.

'You're never to be trusted,' screamed the woman; 'you were out all day yesterday, and gallivanting somewhere I know. You know you were! Isn't it enough that I paid two pound fourteen for you, and took you out of prison and let you live here like a gentleman, but must you go on like this: breaking my heart besides?'

'I will never break its heart, I will be a good boy, and never do so any more; I will never be naughty again; I beg its little pardon,' said Mr Mantalini, dropping the handle of the mangle, and folding his palms together; 'it is all up with its handsome friend! He has gone to the demnition bow-wows. It will have pity? It will not scratch and claw, but pet and comfort? Oh, demmit!'

Very little affected, to judge from her action, by this tender appeal, the lady was on the point of returning some angry reply, when Nicholas, raising his voice, asked his way to Piccadilly.

Mr. Mantalini turned round, caught sight of Kate, and, without another word, leapt at one bound into a bed which stood behind the door, and drew the counterpane over his face: kicking meanwhile convulsively.

'Demmit,' he cried, in a suffocating voice, 'it's little Nickleby! Shut the door, put out the candle, turn me up in the bedstead! Oh, dem, dem, dem!'

The woman looked, first at Nicholas, and then at Mr. Mantalini, as if uncertain on whom to visit this extraordinary behaviour; but Mr. Mantalini happening by ill-luck to thrust his nose from under the bedclothes, in his anxiety to ascertain whether the visitors were gone, she suddenly, and with a dexterity which could only have been acquired by long practice, flung a pretty heavy clothes-basket at him, with so good an aim that he kicked more violently than before, though without venturing to make any effort to disengage his head, which was quite extinguished. Thinking this a favourable opportunity for departing before any of the torrent of her wrath discharged itself upon him, Nicholas hurried Kate off, and left the unfortunate subject of this unexpected recognition to explain his conduct as he best could.

The next morning he began his journey. It was now cold, winter weather: forcibly recalling to his mind under what circumstances he had first travelled that road, and how many vicissitudes and changes he had since undergone. He was alone inside the greater part of the way, and sometimes, when he had fallen into a doze, and, rousing himself, looked out of the window, and recognised some place which he well remembered as having passed, either on his journey down, or in the long walk back with poor Smike, he could hardly believe but that all which had since happened had been a dream, and that they were still plodding wearily on towards London, with the world before them.

To render these recollections the more vivid, it came on to snow as night set in; and, passing through Stamford and Grantham, and by the little alehouse where he had heard the story of the bold Baron of Grogzwig, everything looked as if he had seen it but yesterday, and not even a flake of the white crust on the roofs had melted away. Encouraging the train of ideas which flocked upon him, he could almost persuade himself that he sat again outside the coach, with Squeers and the boys; that he heard their voices in the air; and that he felt again, but with a mingled sensation of pain and pleasure now, that old sinking of the heart, and longing after home. While he was yet yielding himself up to these fancies he fell asleep, and, dreaming of Madeline, forgot them.

He slept at the inn at Greta Bridge on the night of his arrival, and, rising at a very early hour next morning, walked to the market town, and inquired for John Browdie's house. John lived in the outskirts, now he was a family man; and as everbody knew him, Nicholas had no difficulty in finding a boy who undertook to guide him to his residence.

Dismissing his guide at the gate, and in his impatience not even stopping to admire the thriving look of cottage or garden either, Nicholas made his way to the kitchen door, and knocked lustily with his stick.

'Halloa!' cried a voice inside. 'Wa'et be the matther noo? Be the toon a-fire? Ding, but thou mak'st noise eneaf!'

With these words, John Browdie opened the door himself, and opening his eyes too to their utmost width, cried, as he clapped his hands together, and burst into a hearty roar:

'Ecod, it be the godfeyther, it be the godfeyther! Tilly, here be Misther Nickleby. Gi' us thee hond, mun. Coom awa', coom awa'. In wi 'un, doon beside the fire; tak' a soop o' thot. Dinnot say a word till thou'st droonk it a'! Oop wi' it, mun. Ding! but I'm reeght glod to see thee.'

Adapting his action to his text, John dragged Nicholas into the kitchen, forced him down upon a huge settle beside a blazing fire, poured out from an enormous bottle about a quarter of a pint of spirits, thrust it into his hand, opened his mouth and threw back his head as a sign to him to drink it instantly, and stood with a broad grin of welcome overspreading his great red face like a jolly giant.

'I might ha' knowa'd,' said John, 'that nobody but thou would ha' coom wi' sike a knock as you. Thot was the wa' thou knocked at schoolmeasther's door, eh? Ha, ha, ha! But I say; wa'at be a' this aboot schoolmeasther?'

'You know it then?' said Nicholas.

'They were talking aboot it, doon toon, last neeght,' replied John, 'but neane on 'em seemed quite to un'erstan' it, loike.'

'After various shiftings and delays,' said Nicholas, 'he has been sentenced to be transported for seven years, for being in the unlawful possession of a stolen will; and, after that, he has to suffer the consequence of a conspiracy.'

'Whew!' cried John, 'a conspiracy! Soom'at in the pooder-plot wa'? Eh? Soom'at in the Guy Faux line?'

'No, no, no, a conspiracy connected with his school; I'll explain it presently.'

'Thot's reeght!' said John, 'explain it arter breakfast, not noo, for thou be'est hoongry, and so am I; and Tilly she mun' be at the bottom o' a' explanations, for she says thot's the mutual confidence. Ha, ha, ha! Ecod, it's a room start, is the mutual confidence!'

The entrance of Mrs. Browdie, with a smart cap on, and very many apologies for their having been detected in the act of breakfasting in the kitchen, stopped John in his discussion of this grave subject, and hastened the breakfast: which, being composed of vast mounds of toast, new-laid eggs, boiled ham, Yorkshire pie, and other cold substantials (of which heavy relays were constantly appearing from another kitchen under the direction of a very plump servant), was admirably adapted to the cold bleak morning, and received the utmost justice from all parties. At last, it came to a close; and the fire which had been lighted in the best parlour having by this time burnt up, they adjourned thither, to hear what Nicholas had to tell.

Nicholas told them all, and never was there a story which awakened so many emotions in the breasts of two eager listeners. At one time, honest John groaned in sympathy, and at another roared with joy; at one time he vowed to go up to London on purpose to get a sight of the brothers Cheeryble; and, at another, swore that Tim Linkinwater should receive such a ham by coach, and carriage free, as mortal knife had never carved. When Nicholas began to describe Madeline, he sat with his mouth wide open, nudging Mrs Browdie from time to time, and exclaiming under his breath that she must be 'raa'ther a tidy sart,' and when he heard at last that his young friend had come down purposely to communicate his good fortune, and to convey to him all those assurances of friendship which he could not state with sufficient warmth in writing—that the only object of his journey was to share his happiness with them, and to tell them that when he was married they must come up to see him, and that Madeline insisted on it as well as he—John could hold out no longer, but after looking indignantly at his wife, and demanding to know what she was whimpering for, drew his coat sleeve over his eyes and blubbered outright.

'Tell'ee wa'at though,' said John seriously, when a great deal had been said on both sides, 'to return to schoolmeasther. If this news aboot 'un has reached school today, the old 'ooman wean't have a whole boan in her boddy, nor Fanny neither.'

'Oh, John!' cried Mrs. Browdie.

'Ah! and Oh, John agean,' replied the Yorkshireman. 'I dinnot know what they lads mightn't do. When it first got aboot that schoolmeasther was in trouble, some feythers and moothers sent and took their young chaps awa'. If them as is left, should know waat's coom tiv'un, there'll be sike a revolution and rebel!—Ding! But I think they'll a' gang daft, and spill bluid like wather!'

In fact, John Browdie's apprehensions were so strong that he determined to ride over to the school without delay, and invited Nicholas to accompany him, which, however, he declined, pleading that his presence might perhaps aggravate the bitterness of their adversity.

'Thot's true!' said John; 'I should ne'er ha' thought o' thot.'

'I must return tomorrow,' said Nicholas, 'but I mean to dine with you today, and if Mrs. Browdie can give me a bed—'

'Bed!' cried John, 'I wish thou couldst sleep in fower beds at once. Ecod, thou shouldst have 'em a'. Bide till I coom back; on'y bide till I coom back, and ecod we'll make a day of it.'

Giving his wife a hearty kiss, and Nicholas a no less hearty shake of the hand, John mounted his horse and rode off: leaving Mrs. Browdie to apply herself to hospitable preparations, and his young friend to stroll about the neighbourhood, and revisit spots which were rendered familiar to him by many a miserable association.

John cantered away, and arriving at Dotheboys Hall, tied his horse to a gate and made his way to the schoolroom door, which he found locked on the inside. A tremendous noise and riot arose from within, and, applying his eye to a convenient crevice in the wall, he did not remain long in ignorance of its meaning.

The news of Mr. Squeers's downfall had reached Dotheboys; that was quite clear. To all appearance, it had very recently become known to the young gentlemen; for the rebellion had just broken out.

It was one of the brimstone-and-treacle mornings, and Mrs. Squeers had entered school according to custom with the large bowl and spoon, followed by Miss Squeers and the amiable Wackford: who, during his father's absence, had taken upon him such minor branches of the executive as kicking the pupils with his nailed boots, pulling the hair of some of the smaller boys, pinching the others in aggravating places, and rendering himself, in various similar ways, a great comfort and happiness to his mother. Their entrance, whether by premeditation or a simultaneous impulse, was the signal of revolt. While one detachment rushed to the door and locked it, and another mounted on the desks and forms, the stoutest (and consequently the newest) boy seized the cane, and confronting Mrs Squeers with a stern countenance, snatched off her cap and beaver bonnet, put them on his own head, armed himself with the wooden spoon, and bade her, on pain of death, go down upon her knees and take a dose directly. Before that estimable lady could recover herself, or offer the slightest retaliation, she was forced into a kneeling posture by a crowd of shouting tormentors, and compelled to swallow a spoonful of the odious mixture, rendered more than usually savoury by the immersion in the bowl of Master Wackford's head, whose ducking was intrusted to another rebel. The success of this first achievement prompted the malicious crowd, whose faces were clustered together in every variety of lank and half-starved ugliness, to further acts of outrage. The leader was insisting upon Mrs. Squeers repeating her dose, Master Squeers was undergoing another dip in the treacle, and a violent assault had been commenced on Miss Squeers, when John Browdie, bursting open the door with a vigorous kick, rushed to the rescue. The shouts, screams, groans, hoots, and clapping of hands, suddenly ceased, and a dead silence ensued.

'Ye be noice chaps,' said John, looking steadily round. 'What's to do here, thou yoong dogs?'

'Squeers is in prison, and we are going to run away!' cried a score of shrill voices. 'We won't stop, we won't stop!'

'Weel then, dinnot stop,' replied John; 'who waants thee to stop? Roon awa' loike men, but dinnot hurt the women.'

'Hurrah!' cried the shrill voices, more shrilly still.

'Hurrah?' repeated John. 'Weel, hurrah loike men too. Noo then, look out. Hip—hip,—hip—hurrah!'

'Hurrah!' cried the voices.

'Hurrah! Agean;' said John. 'Looder still.'

The boys obeyed.

'Anoother!' said John. 'Dinnot be afeared on it. Let's have a good 'un!'

'Hurrah!'

'Noo then,' said John, 'let's have yan more to end wi', and then coot off as quick as you loike. Tak' a good breath noo—Squeers be in jail—the school's brokken oop—it's a' ower—past and gane—think o' thot, and let it be a hearty 'un! Hurrah!'

Such a cheer arose as the walls of Dotheboys Hall had never echoed before, and were destined never to respond to again. When the sound had died away, the school was empty; and of the busy noisy crowd which had peopled it but five minutes before, not one remained.

'Very well, Mr. Browdie!' said Miss Squeers, hot and flushed from the recent encounter, but vixenish to the last; 'you've been and excited our boys to run away. Now see if we don't pay you out for that, sir! If my pa is unfortunate and trod down by henemies, we're not going to be basely crowed and conquered over by you and 'Tilda.'

'Noa!' replied John bluntly, 'thou bean't. Tak' thy oath o' thot. Think betther o' us, Fanny. I tell 'ee both, that I'm glod the auld man has been caught out at last—dom'd glod—but ye'll sooffer eneaf wi'out any crowin' fra' me, and I be not the mun to crow, nor be Tilly the lass, so I tell 'ee flat. More than thot, I tell 'ee noo, that if thou need'st friends to help thee awa' from this place—dinnot turn up thy nose, Fanny, thou may'st—thou'lt foind Tilly and I wi' a thout o' old times aboot us, ready to lend thee a hond. And when I say thot, dinnot think I be asheamed of waa't I've deane, for I say again, Hurrah! and dom the schoolmeasther. There!'

His parting words concluded, John Browdie strode heavily out, remounted his nag, put him once more into a smart canter, and, carolling lustily forth some fragments of an old song, to which the horse's hoofs rang a merry accompaniment, sped back to his pretty wife and to Nicholas.

For some days afterwards, the neighbouring country was overrun with boys, who, the report went, had been secretly furnished by Mr. and Mrs. Browdie, not only with a hearty meal of bread and meat, but with sundry shillings and sixpences to help them on their way. To this rumour John always returned a stout denial, which he accompanied, however, with a lurking grin, that rendered the suspicious doubtful, and fully confirmed all previous believers.

There were a few timid young children, who, miserable as they had been, and many as were the tears they had shed in the wretched school, still knew no other home, and had formed for it a sort of attachment, which made them weep when the bolder spirits fled, and cling to it as a refuge. Of these, some were found crying under hedges and in such places, frightened at the solitude. One had a dead bird in a little cage; he had wandered nearly twenty miles, and when his poor favourite died, lost courage, and lay down beside him. Another was discovered in a yard hard by the school, sleeping with a dog, who bit at those who came to remove him, and licked the sleeping child's pale face.

They were taken back, and some other stragglers were recovered, but by degrees they were claimed, or lost again; and, in course of time, Dotheboys Hall and its last breaking-up began to be forgotten by the neighbours, or to be only spoken of as among the things that had been.

CHAPTER 65
Conclusion

When her term of mourning had expired, Madeline gave her hand and fortune to Nicholas; and, on the same day and at the same time, Kate became Mrs Frank Cheeryble. It was expected that Tim Linkinwater and Miss La Creevy would have made a third couple on the occasion, but they declined, and two or three weeks afterwards went out together one morning before breakfast, and, coming back with merry faces, were found to have been quietly married that day.

The money which Nicholas acquired in right of his wife he invested in the firm of Cheeryble Brothers, in which Frank had become a partner. Before many years elapsed, the business began to be carried on in the names of 'Cheeryble and Nickleby,' so that Mrs. Nickleby's prophetic anticipations were realised at last.

The twin brothers retired. Who needs to be told that they were happy? They were surrounded by happiness of their own creation, and lived but to increase it.

Tim Linkinwater condescended, after much entreaty and brow-beating, to accept a share in the house; but he could never be prevailed upon to suffer the publication of his name as a partner, and always persisted in the punctual and regular discharge of his clerkly duties.

He and his wife lived in the old house, and occupied the very bedchamber in which he had slept for four-and-forty years. As his wife grew older, she became even a more cheerful and light-hearted little creature; and it was a common saying among their friends, that it was impossible to say which looked the happier, Tim as he sat calmly smiling in his elbow-chair on one side of the fire, or his brisk little wife chatting and laughing, and constantly bustling in and out of hers, on the other.

Dick, the blackbird, was removed from the counting-house and promoted to a warm corner in the common sitting-room. Beneath his cage hung two miniatures, of Mrs. Linkinwater's execution; one representing herself, and the other Tim; and both smiling very hard at all beholders. Tim's head being powdered like a twelfth cake, and his spectacles copied with great nicety, strangers detected a close resemblance to him at the first glance, and this leading them to suspect that the other must be his wife, and emboldening them to say so without scruple, Mrs. Linkinwater grew very proud of these achievements in time, and considered them among the most successful likenesses she had ever painted. Tim had the profoundest faith in them, likewise; for on this, as on all other subjects, they held but one opinion; and if ever there were a 'comfortable couple' in the world, it was Mr. and Mrs. Linkinwater.

Ralph, having died intestate, and having no relations but those with whom he had lived in such enmity, they would have become in legal course his heirs. But they could not bear the thought of growing rich on money so acquired, and felt as though they could never hope to prosper with it. They made no claim to his wealth; and the riches for which he had toiled all his days, and burdened his soul with so many evil deeds, were swept at last into the coffers of the state, and no man was the better or the happier for them.

Arthur Gride was tried for the unlawful possession of the will, which he had either procured to be stolen, or had dishonestly acquired and retained by other means as bad. By dint of an ingenious counsel, and a legal flaw, he escaped; but only to undergo a worse punishment; for, some years afterwards, his house was broken open in the night by robbers, tempted by the rumours of his great wealth, and he was found murdered in his bed.

Mrs. Sliderskew went beyond the seas at nearly the same time as Mr. Squeers, and in the course of nature never returned. Brooker died penitent. Sir Mulberry Hawk lived abroad for some years, courted and caressed, and in high repute as a fine dashing fellow. Ultimately, returning to this country, he was thrown into jail for debt, and there perished miserably, as such high spirits generally do.

The first act of Nicholas, when he became a rich and prosperous merchant, was to buy his father's old house. As time crept on, and there came gradually about him a group of lovely children, it was altered and enlarged; but none of the old rooms were ever pulled down, no old tree was ever rooted up, nothing with which there was any association of bygone times was ever removed or changed.

Within a stone's throw was another retreat, enlivened by children's pleasant voices too; and here was Kate, with many new cares and occupations, and many new faces courting her sweet smile (and one so like her own, that to her mother she seemed a child again), the same true gentle creature, the same fond sister, the same in the love of all about her, as in her girlish days.

Mrs. Nickleby lived, sometimes with her daughter, and sometimes with her son, accompanying one or other of them to London at those periods when the cares of business obliged both families to reside there, and always preserving a great appearance of dignity, and relating her experiences (especially on points connected with the management and bringing-up of children) with much solemnity and importance. It was a very long time before she could be induced to receive Mrs. Linkinwater into favour, and it is even doubtful whether she ever thoroughly forgave her.

There was one grey-haired, quiet, harmless gentleman, who, winter and summer, lived in a little cottage hard by Nicholas's house, and, when he was not there, assumed the superintendence of affairs. His chief pleasure and delight was in the children, with whom he was a child himself, and master of the revels. The little people could do nothing without dear Newman Noggs.

The grass was green above the dead boy's grave, and trodden by feet so small and light, that not a daisy drooped its head beneath their pressure. Through all the spring and summertime, garlands of fresh flowers, wreathed by infant hands, rested on the stone; and, when the children came to change them lest they should wither and be pleasant to him no longer, their eyes filled with tears, and they spoke low and softly of their poor dead cousin.

OLIVER TWIST

CHAPTER I. TREATS OF THE PLACE WHERE OLIVER TWIST WAS BORN AND OF THE CIRCUMSTANCES ATTENDING HIS BIRTH

Among other public buildings in a certain town, which for many reasons it will be prudent to refrain from mentioning, and to which I will assign no fictitious name, there is one anciently common to most towns, great or small: to wit, a workhouse; and in this workhouse was born; on a day and date which I need not trouble myself to repeat, inasmuch as it can be of no possible consequence to the reader, in this stage of the business at all events; the item of mortality whose name is prefixed to the head of this chapter.

For a long time after it was ushered into this world of sorrow and trouble, by the parish surgeon, it remained a matter of considerable doubt whether the child would survive to bear any name at all; in which case it is somewhat more than probable that these memoirs would never have appeared; or, if they had, that being comprised within a couple of pages, they would have possessed the inestimable merit of being the most concise and faithful specimen of biography, extant in the literature of any age or country.

Although I am not disposed to maintain that the being born in a workhouse, is in itself the most fortunate and enviable circumstance that can possibly befall a human being, I do mean to say that in this particular instance, it was the best thing for Oliver Twist that could by possibility have occurred. The fact is, that there was considerable difficulty in inducing Oliver to take upon himself the office of respiration,—a troublesome practice, but one which custom has rendered necessary to our easy existence; and for some time he lay gasping on a little flock mattress, rather unequally poised between this world and the next: the balance being decidedly in favour of the latter. Now, if, during this brief period, Oliver had been surrounded by careful grandmothers, anxious aunts, experienced nurses, and doctors of profound wisdom, he would most inevitably and indubitably have been killed in no time. There being nobody by, however, but a pauper old woman, who was rendered rather misty by an unwonted allowance of beer; and a parish surgeon who did such matters by contract; Oliver and Nature fought out the point between them. The result was, that, after a few struggles, Oliver breathed, sneezed, and proceeded to advertise to the inmates of the workhouse the fact of a new burden having been imposed upon the parish, by setting up as loud a cry as could reasonably have been expected from a male infant who had not been possessed of that very useful appendage, a voice, for a much longer space of time than three minutes and a quarter.

As Oliver gave this first proof of the free and proper action of his lungs, the patchwork coverlet which was carelessly flung over the iron bedstead, rustled; the pale face of a young woman was raised feebly from the pillow; and a faint voice imperfectly articulated the words, 'Let me see the child, and die.'

The surgeon had been sitting with his face turned towards the fire: giving the palms of his hands a warm and a rub alternately. As the young woman spoke, he rose, and advancing to the bed's head, said, with more kindness than might have been expected of him:

'Oh, you must not talk about dying yet.'

'Lor bless her dear heart, no!' interposed the nurse, hastily depositing in her pocket a green glass bottle, the contents of which she had been tasting in a corner with evident satisfaction.

'Lor bless her dear heart, when she has lived as long as I have, sir, and had thirteen children of her own, and all on 'em dead except two, and them in the wurkus with me, she'll know better than to take on in that way, bless her dear heart! Think what it is to be a mother, there's a dear young lamb do.'

Apparently this consolatory perspective of a mother's prospects failed in producing its due effect. The patient shook her head, and stretched out her hand towards the child.

The surgeon deposited it in her arms. She imprinted her cold white lips passionately on its forehead; passed her hands over her face; gazed wildly round; shuddered; fell back—and died. They chafed her breast, hands, and temples; but the blood had stopped forever. They talked of hope and comfort. They had been strangers too long.

'It's all over, Mrs. Thingummy!' said the surgeon at last.

'Ah, poor dear, so it is!' said the nurse, picking up the cork of the green bottle, which had fallen out on the pillow, as she stooped to take up the child. 'Poor dear!'

'You needn't mind sending up to me, if the child cries, nurse,' said the surgeon, putting on his gloves with great deliberation. 'It's very likely it will be troublesome. Give it a little gruel if it is.' He put on his hat, and, pausing by the bed-side on his way to the door, added, 'She was a good-looking girl, too; where did she come from?'

'She was brought here last night,' replied the old woman, 'by the overseer's order. She was found lying in the street. She had walked some distance, for her shoes were worn to pieces; but where she came from, or where she was going to, nobody knows.'

The surgeon leaned over the body, and raised the left hand. 'The old story,' he said, shaking his head: 'no wedding-ring, I see. Ah! Good-night!'

The medical gentleman walked away to dinner; and the nurse, having once more applied herself to the green bottle, sat down on a low chair before the fire, and proceeded to dress the infant.

What an excellent example of the power of dress, young Oliver Twist was! Wrapped in the blanket which had hitherto formed his only covering, he might have been the child of a nobleman or a beggar; it would have been hard for the haughtiest stranger to have assigned him his proper station in society. But now that he was enveloped in the old calico robes which had grown yellow in the same service, he was badged and ticketed, and fell into his place at once—a parish child—the orphan of a workhouse—the humble, half-starved drudge—to be cuffed and buffeted through the world—despised by all, and pitied by none.

Oliver cried lustily. If he could have known that he was an orphan, left to the tender mercies of church-wardens and overseers, perhaps he would have cried the louder.

CHAPTER II. TREATS OF OLIVER TWIST'S GROWTH, EDUCATION, AND BOARD

For the next eight or ten months, Oliver was the victim of a systematic course of treachery and deception. He was brought up by hand. The hungry and destitute situation of the infant orphan was duly reported by the workhouse authorities to the parish authorities. The parish authorities inquired with dignity of the workhouse authorities, whether there was no female then domiciled in 'the house' who was in a situation to impart to Oliver Twist, the consolation and nourishment of which he stood in need. The workhouse authorities replied with humility, that there was not. Upon this, the parish authorities magnanimously and humanely resolved, that Oliver should be 'farmed,' or, in other words, that he should be dispatched to a branch-workhouse some three miles off, where twenty or thirty other juvenile offenders against the poor-laws, rolled about the floor all day, without the inconvenience of too much food or too much clothing, under the parental superintendence of an elderly female, who received the culprits at and for the consideration of sevenpence-halfpenny per small head per week. Sevenpence-halfpenny's worth per week is a good round diet for a child; a great deal may be got for sevenpence-halfpenny, quite enough to overload its stomach, and make it uncomfortable. The elderly female was a woman of wisdom and experience; she knew what was good for children; and she had a very accurate perception of what was good for herself. So, she appropriated the greater part of the weekly stipend to her own use, and consigned the rising parochial generation to even a shorter allowance than was originally provided for them. Thereby finding in the lowest depth a deeper still; and proving herself a very great experimental philosopher.

Everybody knows the story of another experimental philosopher who had a great theory about a horse being able to live without eating, and who demonstrated it so well, that he had got his own horse down to a straw a day, and would unquestionably have rendered him a very spirited and rampacious animal on nothing at all, if he had not died, four-and-twenty hours before he was to have had his first comfortable bait of air. Unfortunately for, the experimental philosophy of the female to whose protecting care Oliver Twist was delivered over, a similar result usually attended the operation of her system; for at the very moment when the child had contrived to exist upon the smallest possible portion of the weakest possible food, it did perversely happen in eight and a half cases out of ten, either that it sickened from want and cold, or fell into the fire from neglect, or got half-smothered by accident; in any one of which cases, the miserable little being was usually summoned into another world, and there gathered to the fathers it had never known in this.

Occasionally, when there was some more than usually interesting inquest upon a parish child who had been overlooked in turning up a bedstead, or inadvertently scalded to death when there happened to be a washing—though the latter accident was very scarce, anything approaching to a washing being of rare occurrence in the farm—the jury would take it into their heads to ask troublesome questions, or the parishioners would rebelliously affix their signatures to a remonstrance. But these impertinences were speedily checked by the evidence of the surgeon, and the testimony of the beadle; the former of whom had always opened the body and found nothing inside (which was very probable indeed), and the latter of whom invariably swore whatever the parish wanted; which was very self-devotional. Besides, the board made periodical pilgrimages to the farm, and always sent the beadle the day before, to say they were going. The children were neat and clean to behold, when they went; and what more would the people have!

It cannot be expected that this system of farming would produce any very extraordinary or luxuriant crop. Oliver Twist's ninth birthday found him a pale thin child, somewhat diminutive in stature, and decidedly small in circumference. But nature or inheritance had implanted a good sturdy spirit in Oliver's breast. It had had plenty of room to expand, thanks to the spare diet of the establishment; and perhaps to this circumstance may be attributed his having any ninth birth-day at all. Be this as it may, however, it was his ninth birthday; and he was keeping it in the coal-cellar with a select party of two other young gentleman, who, after participating with him in a sound thrashing, had been locked up for atrociously presuming to be hungry, when Mrs. Mann, the good lady of the house, was unexpectedly startled by the apparition of Mr. Bumble, the beadle, striving to undo the wicket of the garden-gate.

'Goodness gracious! Is that you, Mr. Bumble, sir?' said Mrs. Mann, thrusting her head out of the window in well-affected ecstasies of joy. '(Susan, take Oliver and them two brats upstairs, and wash 'em directly.)—My heart alive! Mr. Bumble, how glad I am to see you, sure-ly!'

Now, Mr. Bumble was a fat man, and a choleric; so, instead of responding to this open-hearted salutation in a kindred spirit, he gave the little wicket a tremendous shake, and then bestowed upon it a kick which could have emanated from no leg but a beadle's.

'Lor, only think,' said Mrs. Mann, running out,—for the three boys had been removed by this time,—'only think of that! That I should have forgotten that the gate was bolted on the inside, on account of them dear children! Walk in sir; walk in, pray, Mr. Bumble, do, sir.'

Although this invitation was accompanied with a curtsey that might have softened the heart of a church-warden, it by no means mollified the beadle.

'Do you think this respectful or proper conduct, Mrs. Mann,' inquired Mr. Bumble, grasping his cane, 'to keep the parish officers a waiting at your garden-gate, when they come here upon porochial business with the porochial orphans? Are you aweer, Mrs. Mann, that you are, as I may say, a porochial delegate, and a stipendiary?'

'I'm sure Mr. Bumble, that I was only a telling one or two of the dear children as is so fond of you, that it was you a coming,' replied Mrs. Mann with great humility.

Mr. Bumble had a great idea of his oratorical powers and his importance. He had displayed the one, and vindicated the other. He relaxed.

'Well, well, Mrs. Mann,' he replied in a calmer tone; 'it may be as you say; it may be. Lead the way in, Mrs. Mann, for I come on business, and have something to say.'

Mrs. Mann ushered the beadle into a small parlour with a brick floor; placed a seat for him; and officiously deposited his cocked hat and cane on the table before him. Mr. Bumble wiped from his forehead the perspiration which his walk had engendered, glanced complacently at the cocked hat, and smiled. Yes, he smiled. Beadles are but men: and Mr. Bumble smiled.

'Now don't you be offended at what I'm a going to say,' observed Mrs. Mann, with captivating sweetness. 'You've had a long walk, you know, or I wouldn't mention it. Now, will you take a little drop of somethink, Mr. Bumble?'

'Not a drop. Nor a drop,' said Mr. Bumble, waving his right hand in a dignified, but placid manner.

'I think you will,' said Mrs. Mann, who had noticed the tone of the refusal, and the gesture that had accompanied it. 'Just a leetle drop, with a little cold water, and a lump of sugar.'

Mr. Bumble coughed.

'Now, just a leetle drop,' said Mrs. Mann persuasively.

'What is it?' inquired the beadle.

'Why, it's what I'm obliged to keep a little of in the house, to put into the blessed infants' Daffy, when they ain't well, Mr. Bumble,' replied Mrs. Mann as she opened a corner cupboard, and took down a bottle and glass. 'It's gin. I'll not deceive you, Mr. B. It's gin.'

'Do you give the children Daffy, Mrs. Mann?' inquired Bumble, following with his eyes the interesting process of mixing.

'Ah, bless 'em, that I do, dear as it is,' replied the nurse. 'I couldn't see 'em suffer before my very eyes, you know sir.'

'No'; said Mr. Bumble approvingly; 'no, you could not. You are a humane woman, Mrs. Mann.' (Here she set down the glass.) 'I shall take a early opportunity of mentioning it to the board, Mrs. Mann.' (He drew it towards him.) 'You feel as a mother, Mrs. Mann.' (He stirred the gin-and-water.) 'I—I drink your health with cheerfulness, Mrs. Mann'; and he swallowed half of it.

'And now about business,' said the beadle, taking out a leathern pocket-book. 'The child that was half-baptized Oliver Twist, is nine year old to-day.'

'Bless him!' interposed Mrs. Mann, inflaming her left eye with the corner of her apron.

'And notwithstanding a offered reward of ten pound, which was afterwards increased to twenty pound. Notwithstanding the most superlative, and, I may say, supernat'ral exertions on the part of this parish,' said Bumble, 'we have never been able to discover who is his father, or what was his mother's settlement, name, or condition.'

Mrs. Mann raised her hands in astonishment; but added, after a moment's reflection, 'How comes he to have any name at all, then?'

The beadle drew himself up with great pride, and said, 'I inwented it.'

'You, Mr. Bumble!'

'I, Mrs. Mann. We name our fondlings in alphabetical order. The last was a S,—Swubble, I named him. This was a T,—Twist, I named him. The next one comes will be Unwin, and the next Vilkins. I have got names ready made to the end of the alphabet, and all the way through it again, when we come to Z.'

'Why, you're quite a literary character, sir!' said Mrs. Mann.

'Well, well,' said the beadle, evidently gratified with the compliment; 'perhaps I may be. Perhaps I may be, Mrs. Mann.' He finished the gin-and-water, and added, 'Oliver being now too old to remain here, the board have determined to have him back into the house. I have come out myself to take him there. So let me see him at once.'

'I'll fetch him directly,' said Mrs. Mann, leaving the room for that purpose. Oliver, having had by this time as much of the outer coat of dirt which encrusted his face and hands, removed, as could be scrubbed off in one washing, was led into the room by his benevolent protectress.

'Make a bow to the gentleman, Oliver,' said Mrs. Mann.

Oliver made a bow, which was divided between the beadle on the chair, and the cocked hat on the table.

'Will you go along with me, Oliver?' said Mr. Bumble, in a majestic voice.

Oliver was about to say that he would go along with anybody with great readiness, when, glancing upward, he caught sight of Mrs. Mann, who had got behind the beadle's chair, and was shaking her fist at him with a furious countenance. He took the hint at once, for the fist had been too often impressed upon his body not to be deeply impressed upon his recollection.

'Will she go with me?' inquired poor Oliver.

'No, she can't,' replied Mr. Bumble. 'But she'll come and see you sometimes.'

This was no very great consolation to the child. Young as he was, however, he had sense enough to make a feint of feeling great regret at going away. It was no very difficult matter for the boy to call tears into his eyes. Hunger and recent ill-usage are great assistants if you want to cry; and Oliver cried very naturally indeed. Mrs. Mann gave him a thousand embraces, and what Oliver wanted a great deal more, a piece of bread and butter, less he should seem too hungry when he got to the workhouse. With the slice of bread in his hand, and the little brown-cloth parish cap on his head, Oliver was then led away by Mr. Bumble from the wretched home where one kind word or look had never lighted the gloom of his infant years. And yet he burst into an agony of childish grief, as the cottage-gate closed after him. Wretched as were the little companions in misery he was leaving behind, they were the only friends he had ever known; and a sense of his loneliness in the great wide world, sank into the child's heart for the first time.

Mr. Bumble walked on with long strides; little Oliver, firmly grasping his gold-laced cuff, trotted beside him, inquiring at the end of every quarter of a mile whether they were 'nearly there.' To these interrogations Mr. Bumble returned very brief and snappish replies; for the temporary blandness which gin-and-water awakens in some bosoms had by this time evaporated; and he was once again a beadle.

Oliver had not been within the walls of the workhouse a quarter of an hour, and had scarcely completed the demolition of a second slice of bread, when Mr. Bumble, who had handed him over to the care of an old woman, returned; and, telling him it was a board night, informed him that the board had said he was to appear before it forthwith.

Not having a very clearly defined notion of what a live board was, Oliver was rather astounded by this intelligence, and was not quite certain whether he ought to laugh or cry. He had no time to think about the matter, however; for Mr. Bumble gave him a tap on the head, with his cane, to wake him up: and another on the back to make him lively: and bidding him to follow, conducted him into a large white-washed room, where eight or ten fat gentlemen were sitting round a table. At the top of the table, seated in an arm-chair rather higher than the rest, was a particularly fat gentleman with a very round, red face.

'Bow to the board,' said Bumble. Oliver brushed away two or three tears that were lingering in his eyes; and seeing no board but the table, fortunately bowed to that.

'What's your name, boy?' said the gentleman in the high chair.

Oliver was frightened at the sight of so many gentlemen, which made him tremble: and the beadle gave him another tap behind, which made him cry. These two causes made him answer in a very low and hesitating voice; whereupon a gentleman in a white waistcoat said

594

he was a fool. Which was a capital way of raising his spirits, and putting him quite at his ease.

'Boy,' said the gentleman in the high chair, 'listen to me. You know you're an orphan, I suppose?'

'What's that, sir?' inquired poor Oliver.

'The boy is a fool—I thought he was,' said the gentleman in the white waistcoat.

'Hush!' said the gentleman who had spoken first. 'You know you've got no father or mother, and that you were brought up by the parish, don't you?'

'Yes, sir,' replied Oliver, weeping bitterly.

'What are you crying for?' inquired the gentleman in the white waistcoat. And to be sure it was very extraordinary. What could the boy be crying for?

'I hope you say your prayers every night,' said another gentleman in a gruff voice; 'and pray for the people who feed you, and take care of you—like a Christian.'

'Yes, sir,' stammered the boy. The gentleman who spoke last was unconsciously right. It would have been very like a Christian, and a marvellously good Christian too, if Oliver had prayed for the people who fed and took care of him. But he hadn't, because nobody had taught him.

'Well! You have come here to be educated, and taught a useful trade,' said the red-faced gentleman in the high chair.

'So you'll begin to pick oakum to-morrow morning at six o'clock,' added the surly one in the white waistcoat.

For the combination of both these blessings in the one simple process of picking oakum, Oliver bowed low by the direction of the beadle, and was then hurried away to a large ward; where, on a rough, hard bed, he sobbed himself to sleep. What a novel illustration of the tender laws of England! They let the paupers go to sleep!

Poor Oliver! He little thought, as he lay sleeping in happy unconsciousness of all around him, that the board had that very day arrived at a decision which would exercise the most material influence over all his future fortunes. But they had. And this was it:

The members of this board were very sage, deep, philosophical men; and when they came to turn their attention to the workhouse, they found out at once, what ordinary folks would never have discovered—the poor people liked it! It was a regular place of public entertainment for the poorer classes; a tavern where there was nothing to pay; a public breakfast, dinner, tea, and supper all the year round; a brick and mortar elysium, where it was all play and no work. 'Oho!' said the board, looking very knowing; 'we are the fellows to set this to rights; we'll stop it all, in no time.' So, they established the rule, that all poor people should have the alternative (for they would compel nobody, not they), of being starved by a gradual process in the house, or by a quick one out of it. With this view, they contracted with the water-works to lay on an unlimited supply of water; and with a corn-factor to supply periodically small quantities of oatmeal; and issued three meals of thin gruel a day, with an onion twice a week, and half a roll of Sundays. They made a great many other wise and humane regulations, having reference to the ladies, which it is not necessary to repeat; kindly undertook to divorce poor married people, in consequence of the great expense of a suit in Doctors' Commons; and, instead of compelling a man to support his family, as they had theretofore done, took his family away from him, and made him a bachelor! There is no saying how many applicants for relief, under these last two heads, might have started up in all classes of society, if it had not been coupled with the workhouse; but the board were long-headed men, and had provided for this difficulty. The relief was inseparable from the workhouse and the gruel; and that frightened people.

For the first six months after Oliver Twist was removed, the system was in full operation. It was rather expensive at first, in consequence of the increase in the undertaker's bill, and the necessity of taking in the clothes of all the paupers, which fluttered loosely on their wasted, shrunken forms, after a week or two's gruel. But the number of workhouse inmates got thin as well as the paupers; and the board were in ecstasies.

The room in which the boys were fed, was a large stone hall, with a copper at one end: out of which the master, dressed in an apron for the purpose, and assisted by one or two women, ladled the gruel at mealtimes. Of this festive composition each boy had one porringer, and no more—except on occasions of great public rejoicing, when he had two ounces and a quarter of bread besides.

The bowls never wanted washing. The boys polished them with their spoons till they shone again; and when they had performed this operation (which never took very long, the spoons being nearly as large as the bowls), they would sit staring at the copper, with such eager eyes, as if they could have devoured the very bricks of which it was composed; employing themselves, meanwhile, in sucking their fingers most assiduously, with the view of catching up any stray splashes of gruel that might have been cast thereon. Boys have generally excellent appetites. Oliver Twist and his companions suffered the tortures of slow starvation for three months: at last they got so voracious and wild with hunger, that one boy, who was tall for his age, and hadn't been used to that sort of thing (for his father had kept a small cook-shop), hinted darkly to his companions, that unless he had another basin of gruel per diem, he was afraid he might some night happen to eat the boy who slept next him, who happened to be a weakly youth of tender age. He had a wild, hungry eye; and they implicitly believed him. A council was held; lots were cast who should walk up to the master after supper that evening, and ask for more; and it fell to Oliver Twist.

The evening arrived; the boys took their places. The master, in his cook's uniform, stationed himself at the copper; his pauper assistants ranged themselves behind him; the gruel was served out; and a long grace was said over the short commons. The gruel disappeared; the boys whispered each other, and winked at Oliver; while his next neighbors nudged him. Child as he was, he was desperate with hunger, and reckless with misery. He rose from the table; and advancing to the master, basin and spoon in hand, said: somewhat alarmed at his own temerity:

'Please, sir, I want some more.'

The master was a fat, healthy man; but he turned very pale. He gazed in stupefied astonishment on the small rebel for some seconds, and then clung for support to the copper. The assistants were paralysed with wonder; the boys with fear.

'What!' said the master at length, in a faint voice.

'Please, sir,' replied Oliver, 'I want some more.'

The master aimed a blow at Oliver's head with the ladle; pinioned him in his arm; and

596

shrieked aloud for the beadle.

The board were sitting in solemn conclave, when Mr. Bumble rushed into the room in great excitement, and addressing the gentleman in the high chair, said,

'Mr. Limbkins, I beg your pardon, sir! Oliver Twist has asked for more!'

There was a general start. Horror was depicted on every countenance.

'For more!' said Mr. Limbkins. 'Compose yourself, Bumble, and answer me distinctly. Do I understand that he asked for more, after he had eaten the supper allotted by the dietary?'

'He did, sir,' replied Bumble.

'That boy will be hung,' said the gentleman in the white waistcoat. 'I know that boy will be hung.'

Nobody controverted the prophetic gentleman's opinion. An animated discussion took place. Oliver was ordered into instant confinement; and a bill was next morning pasted on the outside of the gate, offering a reward of five pounds to anybody who would take Oliver Twist off the hands of the parish. In other words, five pounds and Oliver Twist were offered to any man or woman who wanted an apprentice to any trade, business, or calling.

'I never was more convinced of anything in my life,' said the gentleman in the white waistcoat, as he knocked at the gate and read the bill next morning: 'I never was more convinced of anything in my life, than I am that that boy will come to be hung.'

As I purpose to show in the sequel whether the white waistcoated gentleman was right or not, I should perhaps mar the interest of this narrative (supposing it to possess any at all), if I ventured to hint just yet, whether the life of Oliver Twist had this violent termination or no.

CHAPTER III. RELATES HOW OLIVER TWIST WAS VERY NEAR GETTING A PLACE WHICH WOULD NOT HAVE BEEN A SINECURE

For a week after the commission of the impious and profane offence of asking for more, Oliver remained a close prisoner in the dark and solitary room to which he had been consigned by the wisdom and mercy of the board. It appears, at first sight not unreasonable to suppose, that, if he had entertained a becoming feeling of respect for the prediction of the gentleman in the white waistcoat, he would have established that sage individual's prophetic character, once and for ever, by tying one end of his pocket-handkerchief to a hook in the wall, and attaching himself to the other. To the performance of this feat, however, there was one obstacle: namely, that pocket-handkerchiefs being decided articles of luxury, had been, for all future times and ages, removed from the noses of paupers by the express order of the board, in council assembled: solemnly given and pronounced under their hands and seals. There was a still greater obstacle in Oliver's youth and childishness. He only cried bitterly all day; and, when the long, dismal night came on, spread his little hands before his eyes to shut out the darkness, and crouching in the corner, tried to sleep: ever and anon waking with a start and tremble, and drawing himself closer and closer to the wall, as if to feel even its cold hard surface were a protection in the gloom and loneliness which surrounded him.

Let it not be supposed by the enemies of 'the system,' that, during the period of his solitary incarceration, Oliver was denied the benefit of exercise, the pleasure of society, or the advantages of religious consolation. As for exercise, it was nice cold weather, and he was allowed to perform his ablutions every morning under the pump, in a stone yard, in the presence of Mr. Bumble, who prevented his catching cold, and caused a tingling sensation to pervade his frame, by repeated applications of the cane. As for society, he was carried every other day into the hall where the boys dined, and there sociably flogged as a public warning and example. And so far from being denied the advantages of religious consolation, he was kicked into the same apartment every evening at prayer-time, and there permitted to listen to, and console his mind with, a general supplication of the boys, containing a special clause, therein inserted by authority of the board, in which they entreated to be made good, virtuous, contented, and obedient, and to be guarded from the sins and vices of Oliver Twist: whom the supplication distinctly set forth to be under the exclusive patronage and protection of the powers of wickedness, and an article direct from the manufactory of the very Devil himself.

It chanced one morning, while Oliver's affairs were in this auspicious and comfortable state, that Mr. Gamfield, chimney-sweep, went his way down the High Street, deeply cogitating in his mind his ways and means of paying certain arrears of rent, for which his landlord had become rather pressing. Mr. Gamfield's most sanguine estimate of his finances could not raise them within full five pounds of the desired amount; and, in a species of arithmetical desperation, he was alternately cudgelling his brains and his donkey, when passing the workhouse, his eyes encountered the bill on the gate.

'Wo—o!' said Mr. Gamfield to the donkey.

The donkey was in a state of profound abstraction: wondering, probably, whether he was destined to be regaled with a cabbage-stalk or two when he had disposed of the two sacks of soot with which the little cart was laden; so, without noticing the word of command, he jogged onward.

Mr. Gamfield growled a fierce imprecation on the donkey generally, but more particularly on his eyes; and, running after him, bestowed a blow on his head, which would inevitably have beaten in any skull but a donkey's. Then, catching hold of the bridle, he gave his jaw a sharp wrench, by way of gentle reminder that he was not his own master; and by these means turned him round. He then gave him another blow on the head, just to stun him till he came back again. Having completed these arrangements, he walked up to the gate, to read the bill.

The gentleman with the white waistcoat was standing at the gate with his hands behind him, after having delivered himself of some profound sentiments in the board-room. Having witnessed the little dispute between Mr. Gamfield and the donkey, he smiled joyously when that person came up to read the bill, for he saw at once that Mr. Gamfield was exactly the sort of master Oliver Twist wanted. Mr. Gamfield smiled, too, as he perused the document; for five pounds was just the sum he had been wishing for; and, as to the boy with which it was encumbered, Mr. Gamfield, knowing what the dietary of the workhouse was, well knew he would be a nice small pattern, just the very thing for register stoves. So, he spelt the bill through again, from beginning to end; and then, touching his fur cap in token of humility, accosted the gentleman in the white waistcoat.

'This here boy, sir, wot the parish wants to 'prentis,' said Mr. Gamfield.

'Ay, my man,' said the gentleman in the white waistcoat, with a condescending smile. 'What of him?'

'If the parish vould like him to learn a right pleasant trade, in a good 'spectable chimbley-sweepin' bisness,' said Mr. Gamfield, 'I wants a 'prentis, and I am ready to take him.'

'Walk in,' said the gentleman in the white waistcoat. Mr. Gamfield having lingered behind, to give the donkey another blow on the head, and another wrench of the jaw, as a caution not to run away in his absence, followed the gentleman with the white waistcoat into the room where Oliver had first seen him.

'It's a nasty trade,' said Mr. Limbkins, when Gamfield had again stated his wish.

'Young boys have been smothered in chimneys before now,' said another gentleman.

'That's acause they damped the straw afore they lit it in the chimbley to make 'em come down again,' said Gamfield; 'that's all smoke, and no blaze; vereas smoke ain't o' no use at all in making a boy come down, for it only sinds him to sleep, and that's wot he likes. Boys is wery obstinit, and wery lazy, Gen'l'men, and there's nothink like a good hot blaze to make 'em come down with a run. It's humane too, gen'l'men, acause, even if they've stuck in the chimbley, roasting their feet makes 'em struggle to hextricate theirselves.'

The gentleman in the white waistcoat appeared very much amused by this explanation; but his mirth was speedily checked by a look from Mr. Limbkins. The board then proceeded to converse among themselves for a few minutes, but in so low a tone, that the words 'saving of expenditure,' 'looked well in the accounts,' 'have a printed report published,' were alone audible. These only chanced to be heard, indeed, or account of their being very frequently repeated with great emphasis.

At length the whispering ceased; and the members of the board, having resumed their seats and their solemnity, Mr. Limbkins said:

'We have considered your proposition, and we don't approve of it.'

'Not at all,' said the gentleman in the white waistcoat.

'Decidedly not,' added the other members.

As Mr. Gamfield did happen to labour under the slight imputation of having bruised three or four boys to death already, it occurred to him that the board had, perhaps, in some unaccountable freak, taken it into their heads that this extraneous circumstance ought to influence their proceedings. It was very unlike their general mode of doing business, if they had; but still, as he had no particular wish to revive the rumour, he twisted his cap in his hands, and walked slowly from the table.

'So you won't let me have him, gen'l'men?' said Mr. Gamfield, pausing near the door.

'No,' replied Mr. Limbkins; 'at least, as it's a nasty business, we think you ought to take something less than the premium we offered.'

Mr. Gamfield's countenance brightened, as, with a quick step, he returned to the table, and said,

'What'll you give, gen'l'men? Come! Don't be too hard on a poor man. What'll you give?'

'I should say, three pound ten was plenty,' said Mr. Limbkins.

'Ten shillings too much,' said the gentleman in the white waistcoat.

'Come!' said Gamfield; 'say four pound, gen'l'men. Say four pound, and you've got rid of him for good and all. There!'

'Three pound ten,' repeated Mr. Limbkins, firmly.

'Come! I'll split the diff'erence, gen'l'men,' urged Gamfield. 'Three pound fifteen.'

'Not a farthing more,' was the firm reply of Mr. Limbkins.

'You're desperate hard upon me, gen'l'men,' said Gamfield, wavering.

'Pooh! pooh! nonsense!' said the gentleman in the white waistcoat. 'He'd be cheap with nothing at all, as a premium. Take him, you silly fellow! He's just the boy for you. He wants the stick, now and then: it'll do him good; and his board needn't come very expensive, for he hasn't been overfed since he was born. Ha! ha! ha!'

Mr. Gamfield gave an arch look at the faces round the table, and, observing a smile on all of them, gradually broke into a smile himself. The bargain was made. Mr. Bumble, was at once instructed that Oliver Twist and his indentures were to be conveyed before the magistrate, for signature and approval, that very afternoon.

In pursuance of this determination, little Oliver, to his excessive astonishment, was released from bondage, and ordered to put himself into a clean shirt. He had hardly achieved this very unusual gymnastic performance, when Mr. Bumble brought him, with his own hands, a basin of gruel, and the holiday allowance of two ounces and a quarter of bread. At this tremendous sight, Oliver began to cry very piteously: thinking, not unnaturally, that the board must have determined to kill him for some useful purpose, or they never would have begun to fatten him up in that way.

'Don't make your eyes red, Oliver, but eat your food and be thankful,' said Mr. Bumble, in a tone of impressive pomposity. 'You're a going to be made a 'prentice of, Oliver.'

'A prentice, sir!' said the child, trembling.

'Yes, Oliver,' said Mr. Bumble. 'The kind and blessed gentleman which is so many parents to you, Oliver, when you have none of your own: are a going to 'prentice' you: and to set you up in life, and make a man of you: although the expense to the parish is three pound ten!—three pound ten, Oliver!—seventy shillins—one hundred and forty sixpences!—and all for a naughty orphan which nobody can't love.'

As Mr. Bumble paused to take breath, after delivering this address in an awful voice, the tears rolled down the poor child's face, and he sobbed bitterly.

'Come,' said Mr. Bumble, somewhat less pompously, for it was gratifying to his feelings to observe the effect his eloquence had produced; 'Come, Oliver! Wipe your eyes with the cuffs of your jacket, and don't cry into your gruel; that's a very foolish action, Oliver.' It certainly was, for there was quite enough water in it already.

On their way to the magistrate, Mr. Bumble instructed Oliver that all he would have to do, would be to look very happy, and say, when the gentleman asked him if he wanted to be apprenticed, that he should like it very much indeed; both of which injunctions Oliver promised to obey: the rather as Mr. Bumble threw in a gentle hint, that if he failed in either particular, there was no telling what would be done to him. When they arrived at the office, he was shut up in a little room by himself, and admonished by Mr. Bumble to stay there, until he came back to fetch him.

There the boy remained, with a palpitating heart, for half an hour. At the expiration of which time Mr. Bumble thrust in his head, unadorned with the cocked hat, and said aloud:

'Now, Oliver, my dear, come to the gentleman.' As Mr. Bumble said this, he put on a grim and threatening look, and added, in a low voice, 'Mind what I told you, you young rascal!'

Oliver stared innocently in Mr. Bumble's face at this somewhat contradictory style of address; but that gentleman prevented his offering any remark thereupon, by leading him at once into an adjoining room: the door of which was open. It was a large room, with a great window. Behind a desk, sat two old gentleman with powdered heads: one of whom was reading the newspaper; while the other was perusing, with the aid of a pair of tortoise-shell spectacles, a small piece of parchment which lay before him. Mr. Limbkins was standing in front of the desk on one side; and Mr. Gamfield, with a partially washed face, on the other; while two or three bluff-looking men, in top-boots, were lounging about.

The old gentleman with the spectacles gradually dozed off, over the little bit of parchment; and there was a short pause, after Oliver had been stationed by Mr. Bumble in front of the desk.

'This is the boy, your worship,' said Mr. Bumble.

The old gentleman who was reading the newspaper raised his head for a moment, and pulled the other old gentleman by the sleeve; whereupon, the last-mentioned old gentleman woke up.

'Oh, is this the boy?' said the old gentleman.

'This is him, sir,' replied Mr. Bumble. 'Bow to the magistrate, my dear.'

Oliver roused himself, and made his best obeisance. He had been wondering, with his eyes fixed on the magistrates' powder, whether all boards were born with that white stuff on their heads, and were boards from thenceforth on that account.

'Well,' said the old gentleman, 'I suppose he's fond of chimney-sweeping?'

'He doats on it, your worship,' replied Bumble; giving Oliver a sly pinch, to intimate that he had better not say he didn't.

'And he will be a sweep, will he?' inquired the old gentleman.

'If we was to bind him to any other trade to-morrow, he'd run away simultaneous, your worship,' replied Bumble.

'And this man that's to be his master—you, sir—you'll treat him well, and feed him, and do all that sort of thing, will you?' said the old gentleman.

'When I says I will, I means I will,' replied Mr. Gamfield doggedly.

'You're a rough speaker, my friend, but you look an honest, open-hearted man,' said the old gentleman: turning his spectacles in the direction of the candidate for Oliver's premium, whose villainous countenance was a regular stamped receipt for cruelty. But the magistrate was half blind and half childish, so he couldn't reasonably be expected to discern what other people did.

'I hope I am, sir,' said Mr. Gamfield, with an ugly leer.

'I have no doubt you are, my friend,' replied the old gentleman: fixing his spectacles more firmly on his nose, and looking about him for the inkstand.

It was the critical moment of Oliver's fate. If the inkstand had been where the old gentleman thought it was, he would have dipped his pen into it, and signed the indentures, and Oliver would have been straightway hurried off. But, as it chanced to be immediately under his nose, it followed, as a matter of course, that he looked all over his desk for it, without finding it; and happening in the course of his search to look straight before him, his gaze encountered the pale and terrified face of Oliver Twist: who, despite all the admonitory looks and pinches of Bumble, was regarding the repulsive countenance of his future master, with a mingled expression of horror and fear, too palpable to be mistaken, even by a half-blind magistrate.

The old gentleman stopped, laid down his pen, and looked from Oliver to Mr. Limbkins; who attempted to take snuff with a cheerful and unconcerned aspect.

'My boy!' said the old gentleman, 'you look pale and alarmed. What is the matter?'

'Stand a little away from him, Beadle,' said the other magistrate: laying aside the paper, and leaning forward with an expression of interest. 'Now, boy, tell us what's the matter: don't be afraid.'

Oliver fell on his knees, and clasping his hands together, prayed that they would order him back to the dark room—that they would starve him—beat him—kill him if they pleased—rather than send him away with that dreadful man.

'Well!' said Mr. Bumble, raising his hands and eyes with most impressive solemnity. 'Well! of all the artful and designing orphans that ever I see, Oliver, you are one of the most bare-facedest.'

'Hold your tongue, Beadle,' said the second old gentleman, when Mr. Bumble had given vent to this compound adjective.

'I beg your worship's pardon,' said Mr. Bumble, incredulous of having heard aright. 'Did your worship speak to me?'

'Yes. Hold your tongue.'

Mr. Bumble was stupefied with astonishment. A beadle ordered to hold his tongue! A moral revolution!

The old gentleman in the tortoise-shell spectacles looked at his companion, he nodded significantly.

'We refuse to sanction these indentures,' said the old gentleman: tossing aside the piece of parchment as he spoke.

'I hope,' stammered Mr. Limbkins: 'I hope the magistrates will not form the opinion that the authorities have been guilty of any improper conduct, on the unsupported testimony of a child.'

'The magistrates are not called upon to pronounce any opinion on the matter,' said the second old gentleman sharply. 'Take the boy back to the workhouse, and treat him kindly. He seems to want it.'

That same evening, the gentleman in the white waistcoat most positively and decidedly affirmed, not only that Oliver would be hung, but that he would be drawn and quartered into the bargain. Mr. Bumble shook his head with gloomy mystery, and said he wished he might come to good; whereunto Mr. Gamfield replied, that he wished he might come to him; which, although he agreed with the beadle in most matters, would seem to be a wish of a totally opposite description.

The next morning, the public were once informed that Oliver Twist was again To Let, and that five pounds would be paid to anybody who would take possession of him.

CHAPTER IV. OLIVER, BEING OFFERED ANOTHER PLACE, MAKES HIS FIRST ENTRY INTO PUBLIC LIFE

In great families, when an advantageous place cannot be obtained, either in possession, reversion, remainder, or expectancy, for the young man who is growing up, it is a very general custom to send him to sea. The board, in imitation of so wise and salutary an example, took counsel together on the expediency of shipping off Oliver Twist, in some small trading vessel bound to a good unhealthy port. This suggested itself as the very best thing that could possibly be done with him: the probability being, that the skipper would flog him to death, in a playful mood, some day after dinner, or would knock his brains out with an iron bar; both pastimes being, as is pretty generally known, very favourite and common recreations among gentleman of that class. The more the case presented itself to the board, in this point of view, the more manifold the advantages of the step appeared; so, they came to the conclusion that the only way of providing for Oliver effectually, was to send him to sea without delay.

Mr. Bumble had been despatched to make various preliminary inquiries, with the view of finding out some captain or other who wanted a cabin-boy without any friends; and was returning to the workhouse to communicate the result of his mission; when he encountered at the gate, no less a person than Mr. Sowerberry, the parochial undertaker.

Mr. Sowerberry was a tall gaunt, large-jointed man, attired in a suit of threadbare black, with darned cotton stockings of the same colour, and shoes to answer. His features were not naturally intended to wear a smiling aspect, but he was in general rather given to professional jocosity. His step was elastic, and his face betokened inward pleasantry, as he advanced to Mr. Bumble, and shook him cordially by the hand.

'I have taken the measure of the two women that died last night, Mr. Bumble,' said the undertaker.

'You'll make your fortune, Mr. Sowerberry,' said the beadle, as he thrust his thumb and forefinger into the proffered snuff-box of the undertaker: which was an ingenious little model of a patent coffin. 'I say you'll make your fortune, Mr. Sowerberry,' repeated Mr. Bumble, tapping the undertaker on the shoulder, in a friendly manner, with his cane.

'Think so?' said the undertaker in a tone which half admitted and half disputed the probability of the event. 'The prices allowed by the board are very small, Mr. Bumble.'

'So are the coffins,' replied the beadle: with precisely as near an approach to a laugh as a great official ought to indulge in.

Mr. Sowerberry was much tickled at this: as of course he ought to be; and laughed a long time without cessation. 'Well, well, Mr. Bumble,' he said at length, 'there's no denying that, since the new system of feeding has come in, the coffins are something narrower and more shallow than they used to be; but we must have some profit, Mr. Bumble. Well-seasoned timber is an expensive article, sir; and all the iron handles come, by canal, from Birmingham.'

'Well, well,' said Mr. Bumble, 'every trade has its drawbacks. A fair profit is, of course, allowable.'

'Of course, of course,' replied the undertaker; 'and if I don't get a profit upon this or that particular article, why, I make it up in the long-run, you see—he! he! he!'

'Just so,' said Mr. Bumble.

'Though I must say,' continued the undertaker, resuming the current of observations which the beadle had interrupted: 'though I must say, Mr. Bumble, that I have to contend against one very great disadvantage: which is, that all the stout people go off the quickest. The people who have been better off, and have paid rates for many years, are the first to sink when they come into the house; and let me tell you, Mr. Bumble, that three or four inches over one's calculation makes a great hole in one's profits: especially when one has a family to provide for, sir.'

As Mr. Sowerberry said this, with the becoming indignation of an ill-used man; and as Mr. Bumble felt that it rather tended to convey a reflection on the honour of the parish; the latter gentleman thought it advisable to change the subject. Oliver Twist being uppermost in his mind, he made him his theme.

'By the bye,' said Mr. Bumble, 'you don't know anybody who wants a boy, do you? A porochial 'prentis, who is at present a dead-weight; a millstone, as I may say, round the porochial throat? Liberal terms, Mr. Sowerberry, liberal terms?' As Mr. Bumble spoke, he raised his cane to the bill above him, and gave three distinct raps upon the words 'five pounds': which were printed thereon in Roman capitals of gigantic size.

'Gadso!' said the undertaker: taking Mr. Bumble by the gilt-edged lappel of his official coat; 'that's just the very thing I wanted to speak to you about. You know—dear me, what a very elegant button this is, Mr. Bumble! I never noticed it before.'

'Yes, I think it rather pretty,' said the beadle, glancing proudly downwards at the large brass buttons which embellished his coat. 'The die is the same as the porochial seal—the Good Samaritan healing the sick and bruised man. The board presented it to me on Newyear's morning, Mr. Sowerberry. I put it on, I remember, for the first time, to attend the inquest on that reduced tradesman, who died in a doorway at midnight.'

'I recollect,' said the undertaker. 'The jury brought it in, "Died from exposure to the cold, and want of the common necessaries of life," didn't they?'

Mr. Bumble nodded.

'And they made it a special verdict, I think,' said the undertaker, 'by adding some words to the effect, that if the relieving officer had—'

'Tush! Foolery!' interposed the beadle. 'If the board attended to all the nonsense that ignorant jurymen talk, they'd have enough to do.'

'Very true,' said the undertaker; 'they would indeed.'

'Juries,' said Mr. Bumble, grasping his cane tightly, as was his wont when working into a passion: 'juries is ineddicated, vulgar, grovelling wretches.'

'So they are,' said the undertaker.

'They haven't no more philosophy nor political economy about 'em than that,' said the beadle, snapping his fingers contemptuously.

'No more they have,' acquiesced the undertaker.

'I despise 'em,' said the beadle, growing very red in the face.

'So do I,' rejoined the undertaker.

'And I only wish we'd a jury of the independent sort, in the house for a week or two,' said the beadle; 'the rules and regulations of the board would soon bring their spirit down for 'em.'

'Let 'em alone for that,' replied the undertaker. So saying, he smiled, approvingly: to calm the rising wrath of the indignant parish officer.

Mr Bumble lifted off his cocked hat; took a handkerchief from the inside of the crown; wiped from his forehead the perspiration which his rage had engendered; fixed the cocked hat on again; and, turning to the undertaker, said in a calmer voice:

'Well; what about the boy?'

'Oh!' replied the undertaker; 'why, you know, Mr. Bumble, I pay a good deal towards the poor's rates.'

'Hem!' said Mr. Bumble. 'Well?'

'Well,' replied the undertaker, 'I was thinking that if I pay so much towards 'em, I've a right to get as much out of 'em as I can, Mr. Bumble; and so—I think I'll take the boy myself.'

Mr. Bumble grasped the undertaker by the arm, and led him into the building. Mr. Sowerberry was closeted with the board for five minutes; and it was arranged that Oliver should go to him that evening 'upon liking'—a phrase which means, in the case of a parish apprentice, that if the master find, upon a short trial, that he can get enough work out of a boy without putting too much food into him, he shall have him for a term of years, to do what he likes with.

When little Oliver was taken before 'the gentlemen' that evening; and informed that he was to go, that night, as general house-lad to a coffin-maker's; and that if he complained of his situation, or ever came back to the parish again, he would be sent to sea, there to be drowned, or knocked on the head, as the case might be, he evinced so little emotion, that they by common consent pronounced him a hardened young rascal, and ordered Mr. Bumble to remove him forthwith.

Now, although it was very natural that the board, of all people in the world, should feel in a great state of virtuous astonishment and horror at the smallest tokens of want of feeling on the part of anybody, they were rather out, in this particular instance. The simple fact was, that Oliver, instead of possessing too little feeling, possessed rather too much; and was in a fair way of being reduced, for life, to a state of brutal stupidity and sullenness by the ill usage he had received. He heard the news of his destination, in perfect silence; and, having had his luggage put into his hand—which was not very difficult to carry, inasmuch as it was all comprised within the limits of a brown paper parcel, about half a foot square by three inches deep—he pulled his cap over his eyes; and once more attaching himself to Mr. Bumble's coat cuff, was led away by that dignitary to a new scene of suffering.

For some time, Mr. Bumble drew Oliver along, without notice or remark; for the beadle carried his head very erect, as a beadle always should: and, it being a windy day, little Oliver was completely enshrouded by the skirts of Mr. Bumble's coat as they blew open, and disclosed to great advantage his flapped waistcoat and drab plush knee-breeches. As they drew near to their destination, however, Mr. Bumble thought it expedient to look down, and see that the boy was in good order for inspection by his new master: which he accordingly did, with a fit and becoming air of gracious patronage.

'Oliver!' said Mr. Bumble.

'Yes, sir,' replied Oliver, in a low, tremulous voice.

'Pull that cap off your eyes, and hold up your head, sir.'

Although Oliver did as he was desired, at once; and passed the back of his unoccupied hand briskly across his eyes, he left a tear in them when he looked up at his conductor. As Mr. Bumble gazed sternly upon him, it rolled down his cheek. It was followed by another, and another. The child made a strong effort, but it was an unsuccessful one. Withdrawing his other hand from Mr. Bumble's he covered his face with both; and wept until the tears sprung out from between his chin and bony fingers.

'Well!' exclaimed Mr. Bumble, stopping short, and darting at his little charge a look of intense malignity. 'Well! Of all the ungratefullest, and worst-disposed boys as ever I see, Oliver, you are the—'

'No, no, sir,' sobbed Oliver, clinging to the hand which held the well-known cane; 'no, no, sir; I will be good indeed; indeed, indeed I will, sir! I am a very little boy, sir; and it is so—so—'

'So what?' inquired Mr. Bumble in amazement.

'So lonely, sir! So very lonely!' cried the child. 'Everybody hates me. Oh! sir, don't, don't pray be cross to me!' The child beat his hand upon his heart; and looked in his companion's face, with tears of real agony.

Mr. Bumble regarded Oliver's piteous and helpless look, with some astonishment, for a few seconds; hemmed three or four times in a husky manner; and after muttering something about 'that troublesome cough,' bade Oliver dry his eyes and be a good boy. Then once more taking his hand, he walked on with him in silence.

The undertaker, who had just put up the shutters of his shop, was making some entries in his day-book by the light of a most appropriate dismal candle, when Mr. Bumble entered.

'Aha!' said the undertaker; looking up from the book, and pausing in the middle of a word; 'is that you, Bumble?'

'No one else, Mr. Sowerberry,' replied the beadle. 'Here! I've brought the boy.' Oliver made a bow.

'Oh! that's the boy, is it?' said the undertaker: raising the candle above his head, to get a better view of Oliver. 'Mrs. Sowerberry, will you have the goodness to come here a moment, my dear?'

Mrs. Sowerberry emerged from a little room behind the shop, and presented the form of a short, then, squeezed-up woman, with a vixenish countenance.

'My dear,' said Mr. Sowerberry, deferentially, 'this is the boy from the workhouse that I told you of.' Oliver bowed again.

'Dear me!' said the undertaker's wife, 'he's very small.'

'Why, he is rather small,' replied Mr. Bumble: looking at Oliver as if it were his fault that he was no bigger; 'he is small. There's no denying it. But he'll grow, Mrs. Sowerberry—he'll grow.'

'Ah! I dare say he will,' replied the lady pettishly, 'on our victuals and our drink. I see no saving in parish children, not I; for they always cost more to keep, than they're worth. However, men always think they know best. There! Get downstairs, little bag o' bones.' With this, the undertaker's wife opened a side door, and pushed Oliver down a steep flight of stairs into a stone cell, damp and dark: forming the ante-room to the coal-cellar, and denominated 'kitchen'; wherein sat a slatternly girl, in shoes down at heel, and blue worsted stockings very much out of repair.

'Here, Charlotte,' said Mr. Sowerberry, who had followed Oliver down, 'give this boy some of the cold bits that were put by for Trip. He hasn't come home since the morning, so he may go without 'em. I dare say the boy isn't too dainty to eat 'em—are you, boy?'

Oliver, whose eyes had glistened at the mention of meat, and who was trembling with eagerness to devour it, replied in the negative; and a plateful of coarse broken victuals was set before him.

I wish some well-fed philosopher, whose meat and drink turn to gall within him; whose blood is ice, whose heart is iron; could have seen Oliver Twist clutching at the dainty viands that the dog had neglected. I wish he could have witnessed the horrible avidity with which Oliver tore the bits asunder with all the ferocity of famine. There is only one thing I should like better; and that would be to see the Philosopher making the same sort of meal himself, with the same relish.

'Well,' said the undertaker's wife, when Oliver had finished his supper: which she had regarded in silent horror, and with fearful auguries of his future appetite: 'have you done?'

There being nothing eatable within his reach, Oliver replied in the affirmative.

'Then come with me,' said Mrs. Sowerberry: taking up a dim and dirty lamp, and leading the way upstairs; 'your bed's under the counter. You don't mind sleeping among the coffins, I suppose? But it doesn't much matter whether you do or don't, for you can't sleep anywhere else. Come; don't keep me here all night!'

Oliver lingered no longer, but meekly followed his new mistress.

CHAPTER V. OLIVER MINGLES WITH NEW ASSOCIATES. GOING TO A FUNERAL FOR THE FIRST TIME, HE FORMS AN UNFAVOURABLE NOTION OF HIS MASTER'S BUSINESS

Oliver, being left to himself in the undertaker's shop, set the lamp down on a workman's bench, and gazed timidly about him with a feeling of awe and dread, which many people a good deal older than he will be at no loss to understand. An unfinished coffin on black tressels, which stood in the middle of the shop, looked so gloomy and death-like that a cold tremble came over him, every time his eyes wandered in the direction of the dismal object: from which he almost expected to see some frightful form slowly rear its head, to drive him mad with terror. Against the wall were ranged, in regular array, a long row of elm boards cut in the same shape: looking in the dim light, like high-shouldered ghosts with their hands in their breeches pockets. Coffin-plates, elm-chips, bright-headed nails, and shreds of black cloth, lay scattered on the floor; and the wall behind the counter was ornamented with a lively representation of two mutes in very stiff neckcloths, on duty at a large private door, with a hearse drawn by four black steeds, approaching in the distance. The shop was close and hot. The atmosphere seemed tainted with the smell of coffins. The recess beneath the counter in which his flock mattress was thrust, looked like a grave.

Nor were these the only dismal feelings which depressed Oliver. He was alone in a strange place; and we all know how chilled and desolate the best of us will sometimes feel in such a situation. The boy had no friends to care for, or to care for him. The regret of no recent separation was fresh in his mind; the absence of no loved and well-remembered face sank heavily into his heart.

But his heart was heavy, notwithstanding; and he wished, as he crept into his narrow bed, that that were his coffin, and that he could be lain in a calm and lasting sleep in the churchyard ground, with the tall grass waving gently above his head, and the sound of the old deep bell to soothe him in his sleep.

Oliver was awakened in the morning, by a loud kicking at the outside of the shop-door: which, before he could huddle on his clothes, was repeated, in an angry and impetuous manner, about twenty-five times. When he began to undo the chain, the legs desisted, and a voice began.

'Open the door, will yer?' cried the voice which belonged to the legs which had kicked at the door.

'I will, directly, sir,' replied Oliver: undoing the chain, and turning the key.

'I suppose yer the new boy, ain't yer?' said the voice through the key-hole.

'Yes, sir,' replied Oliver.

'How old are yer?' inquired the voice.

'Ten, sir,' replied Oliver.

'Then I'll whop yer when I get in,' said the voice; 'you just see if I don't, that's all, my work'us brat!' and having made this obliging promise, the voice began to whistle.

Oliver had been too often subjected to the process to which the very expressive monosyllable just recorded bears reference, to entertain the smallest doubt that the owner of the voice, whoever he might be, would redeem his pledge, most honourably. He drew back the bolts with a trembling hand, and opened the door.

For a second or two, Oliver glanced up the street, and down the street, and over the way: impressed with the belief that the unknown, who had addressed him through the key-hole, had walked a few paces off, to warm himself; for nobody did he see but a big charity-boy, sitting on a post in front of the house, eating a slice of bread and butter: which he cut into wedges, the size of his mouth, with a clasp-knife, and then consumed with great dexterity.

'I beg your pardon, sir,' said Oliver at length: seeing that no other visitor made his appearance; 'did you knock?'

'I kicked,' replied the charity-boy.

'Did you want a coffin, sir?' inquired Oliver, innocently.

At this, the charity-boy looked monstrous fierce; and said that Oliver would want one before long, if he cut jokes with his superiors in that way.

'Yer don't know who I am, I suppose, Work'us?' said the charity-boy, in continuation: descending from the top of the post, meanwhile, with edifying gravity.

'No, sir,' rejoined Oliver.

'I'm Mister Noah Claypole,' said the charity-boy, 'and you're under me. Take down the shutters, yer idle young ruffian!' With this, Mr. Claypole administered a kick to Oliver, and entered the shop with a dignified air, which did him great credit. It is difficult for a large-headed, small-eyed youth, of lumbering make and heavy countenance, to look dignified under any circumstances; but it is more especially so, when superadded to these personal attractions are a red nose and yellow smalls.

Oliver, having taken down the shutters, and broken a pane of glass in his effort to stagger away beneath the weight of the first one to a small court at the side of the house in which they were kept during the day, was graciously assisted by Noah: who having consoled him with the assurance that 'he'd catch it,' condescended to help him. Mr. Sowerberry came down soon after. Shortly afterwards, Mrs. Sowerberry appeared. Oliver having 'caught it,' in fulfilment of Noah's prediction, followed that young gentleman down the stairs to breakfast.

'Come near the fire, Noah,' said Charlotte. 'I saved a nice little bit of bacon for you from master's breakfast. Oliver, shut that door at Mister Noah's back, and take them bits that I've put out on the cover of the bread-pan. There's your tea; take it away to that box, and drink it there, and make haste, for they'll want you to mind the shop. D'ye hear?'

'D'ye hear, Work'us?' said Noah Claypole.

'Lor, Noah!' said Charlotte, 'what a rum creature you are! Why don't you let the boy alone?'

'Let him alone!' said Noah. 'Why everybody lets him alone enough, for the matter of that. Neither his father nor his mother will ever interfere with him. All his relations let him have his own way pretty well. Eh, Charlotte? He! he! he!'

'Oh, you queer soul!' said Charlotte, bursting into a hearty laugh, in which she was joined by Noah; after which they both looked scornfully at poor Oliver Twist, as he sat shivering on the box in the coldest corner of the room, and ate the stale pieces which had been specially reserved for him.

Noah was a charity-boy, but not a workhouse orphan. No chance-child was he, for he could trace his genealogy all the way back to his parents, who lived hard by; his mother being a washerwoman, and his father a drunken soldier, discharged with a wooden leg, and a diurnal pension of twopence-halfpenny and an unstateable fraction. The shop-boys in the neighbourhood had long been in the habit of branding Noah in the public streets, with the ignominious epithets of 'leathers,' 'charity,' and the like; and Noah had bourne them without reply. But, now that fortune had cast in his way a nameless orphan, at whom even the meanest could point the finger of scorn, he retorted on him with interest. This affords charming food for contemplation. It shows us what a beautiful thing human nature may be made to be; and how impartially the same amiable qualities are developed in the finest lord and the dirtiest charity-boy.

Oliver had been sojourning at the undertaker's some three weeks or a month. Mr. and Mrs. Sowerberry—the shop being shut up—were taking their supper in the little back-parlour, when Mr. Sowerberry, after several deferential glances at his wife, said,

'My dear—' He was going to say more; but, Mrs. Sowerberry looking up, with a peculiarly unpropitious aspect, he stopped short.

'Well,' said Mrs. Sowerberry, sharply.

'Nothing, my dear, nothing,' said Mr. Sowerberry.

'Ugh, you brute!' said Mrs. Sowerberry.

'Not at all, my dear,' said Mr. Sowerberry humbly. 'I thought you didn't want to hear, my dear. I was only going to say—'

'Oh, don't tell me what you were going to say,' interposed Mrs. Sowerberry. 'I am nobody; don't consult me, pray. I don't want to intrude upon your secrets.' As Mrs. Sowerberry said this, she gave an hysterical laugh, which threatened violent consequences.

'But, my dear,' said Sowerberry, 'I want to ask your advice.'

'No, no, don't ask mine,' replied Mrs. Sowerberry, in an affecting manner: 'ask somebody else's.' Here, there was another hysterical laugh, which frightened Mr. Sowerberry very much. This is a very common and much-approved matrimonial course of treatment, which is often very effective. It at once reduced Mr. Sowerberry to begging, as a special favour, to be allowed to say what Mrs. Sowerberry was most curious to hear. After a short duration, the permission was most graciously conceded.

'It's only about young Twist, my dear,' said Mr. Sowerberry. 'A very good-looking boy, that, my dear.'

'He need be, for he eats enough,' observed the lady.

'There's an expression of melancholy in his face, my dear,' resumed Mr. Sowerberry, 'which is very interesting. He would make a delightful mute, my love.'

Mrs. Sowerberry looked up with an expression of considerable wonderment. Mr. Sowerberry remarked it and, without allowing time for any observation on the good lady's part, proceeded.

'I don't mean a regular mute to attend grown-up people, my dear, but only for children's practice. It would be very new to have a mute in proportion, my dear. You may depend upon it, it would have a superb effect.'

Mrs. Sowerberry, who had a good deal of taste in the undertaking way, was much struck by the novelty of this idea; but, as it would have been compromising her dignity to have said so, under existing circumstances, she merely inquired, with much sharpness, why such an obvious suggestion had not presented itself to her husband's mind before? Mr. Sowerberry rightly construed this, as an acquiescence in his proposition; it was speedily determined, therefore, that Oliver should be at once initiated into the mysteries of the trade; and, with this view, that he should accompany his master on the very next occasion of his services being required.

The occasion was not long in coming. Half an hour after breakfast next morning, Mr. Bumble entered the shop; and supporting his cane against the counter, drew forth his large leathern pocket-book: from which he selected a small scrap of paper, which he handed over to Sowerberry.

'Aha!' said the undertaker, glancing over it with a lively countenance; 'an order for a coffin, eh?'

'For a coffin first, and a porochial funeral afterwards,' replied Mr. Bumble, fastening the strap of the leathern pocket-book: which, like himself, was very corpulent.

'Bayton,' said the undertaker, looking from the scrap of paper to Mr. Bumble. 'I never heard the name before.'

Bumble shook his head, as he replied, 'Obstinate people, Mr. Sowerberry; very obstinate. Proud, too, I'm afraid, sir.'

'Proud, eh?' exclaimed Mr. Sowerberry with a sneer. 'Come, that's too much.'

'Oh, it's sickening,' replied the beadle. 'Antimonial, Mr. Sowerberry!'

'So it is,' acquiesced the undertaker.

'We only heard of the family the night before last,' said the beadle; 'and we shouldn't have known anything about them, then, only a woman who lodges in the same house made an application to the porochial committee for them to send the porochial surgeon to see a woman as was very bad. He had gone out to dinner; but his 'prentice (which is a very clever lad) sent 'em some medicine in a blacking-bottle, offhand.'

'Ah, there's promptness,' said the undertaker.

'Promptness, indeed!' replied the beadle. 'But what's the consequence; what's the ungrateful behaviour of these rebels, sir? Why, the husband sends back word that the medicine won't suit his wife's complaint, and so she shan't take it—says she shan't take it, sir! Good, strong, wholesome medicine, as was given with great success to two Irish labourers and a coal-heaver, only a week before—sent 'em for nothing, with a blackin'-bottle in,—and he sends back word that she shan't take it, sir!'

As the atrocity presented itself to Mr. Bumble's mind in full force, he struck the counter sharply with his cane, and became flushed with indignation.

'Well,' said the undertaker, 'I ne—ver—did—'

'Never did, sir!' ejaculated the beadle. 'No, nor nobody never did; but now she's dead, we've got to bury her; and that's the direction; and the sooner it's done, the better.'

Thus saying, Mr. Bumble put on his cocked hat wrong side first, in a fever of parochial excitement; and flounced out of the shop.

'Why, he was so angry, Oliver, that he forgot even to ask after you!' said Mr. Sowerberry, looking after the beadle as he strode down the street.

'Yes, sir,' replied Oliver, who had carefully kept himself out of sight, during the interview; and who was shaking from head to foot at the mere recollection of the sound of Mr. Bumble's voice.

He needn't haven taken the trouble to shrink from Mr. Bumble's glance, however; for that functionary, on whom the prediction of the gentleman in the white waistcoat had made a very strong impression, thought that now the undertaker had got Oliver upon trial the subject was better avoided, until such time as he should be firmly bound for seven years, and all danger of his being returned upon the hands of the parish should be thus effectually and legally overcome.

'Well,' said Mr. Sowerberry, taking up his hat, 'the sooner this job is done, the better. Noah, look after the shop. Oliver, put on your cap, and come with me.' Oliver obeyed, and followed his master on his professional mission.

They walked on, for some time, through the most crowded and densely inhabited part of the town; and then, striking down a narrow street more dirty and miserable than any they had yet passed through, paused to look for the house which was the object of their search. The houses on either side were high and large, but very old, and tenanted by people of the poorest class: as their neglected appearance would have sufficiently denoted, without the concurrent testimony afforded by the squalid looks of the few men and women who, with folded arms and bodies half doubled, occasionally skulked along. A great many of the tenements had shop-fronts; but these were fast closed, and mouldering away; only the upper rooms being inhabited. Some houses which had become insecure from age and decay, were prevented from falling into the street, by huge beams of wood reared against the walls, and firmly planted in the road; but even these crazy dens seemed to have been selected as the nightly haunts of some houseless wretches, for many of the rough boards which supplied the place of door and window, were wrenched from their positions, to afford an aperture wide enough for the passage of a human body. The kennel was stagnant and filthy. The very rats, which here and there lay putrefying in its rottenness, were hideous with famine.

There was neither knocker nor bell-handle at the open door where Oliver and his master stopped; so, groping his way cautiously through the dark passage, and bidding Oliver keep close to him and not be afraid the undertaker mounted to the top of the first flight of stairs. Stumbling against a door on the landing, he rapped at it with his knuckles.

It was opened by a young girl of thirteen or fourteen. The undertaker at once saw enough of what the room contained, to know it was the apartment to which he had been directed. He stepped in; Oliver followed him.

There was no fire in the room; but a man was crouching, mechanically, over the empty stove. An old woman, too, had drawn a low stool to the cold hearth, and was sitting beside him. There were some ragged children in another corner; and in a small recess, opposite the door, there lay upon the ground, something covered with an old blanket. Oliver shuddered as he cast his eyes toward the place, and crept involuntarily closer to his master; for though it was covered up, the boy felt that it was a corpse.

The man's face was thin and very pale; his hair and beard were grizzly; his eyes were bloodshot. The old woman's face was wrinkled; her two remaining teeth protruded over her under lip; and her eyes were bright and piercing. Oliver was afraid to look at either her or the man. They seemed so like the rats he had seen outside.

'Nobody shall go near her,' said the man, starting fiercely up, as the undertaker approached the recess. 'Keep back! Damn you, keep back, if you've a life to lose!'

'Nonsense, my good man,' said the undertaker, who was pretty well used to misery in all its shapes. 'Nonsense!'

'I tell you,' said the man: clenching his hands, and stamping furiously on the floor,—'I tell you I won't have her put into the ground. She couldn't rest there. The worms would worry her—not eat her—she is so worn away.'

The undertaker offered no reply to this raving; but producing a tape from his pocket, knelt down for a moment by the side of the body.

'Ah!' said the man: bursting into tears, and sinking on his knees at the feet of the dead woman; 'kneel down, kneel down—kneel round her, every one of you, and mark my words! I say she was starved to death. I never knew how bad she was, till the fever came upon her; and then her bones were starting through the skin. There was neither fire nor candle; she died in the dark—in the dark! She couldn't even see her children's faces, though we heard her gasping out their names. I begged for her in the streets: and they sent me to prison. When I came back, she was dying; and all the blood in my heart has dried up, for they starved her to death. I swear it before the God that saw it! They starved her!' He twined his hands in his hair; and, with a loud scream, rolled grovelling upon the floor: his eyes fixed, and the foam covering his lips.

The terrified children cried bitterly; but the old woman, who had hitherto remained as quiet as if she had been wholly deaf to all that passed, menaced them into silence. Having unloosened the cravat of the man who still remained extended on the ground, she tottered towards the undertaker.

'She was my daughter,' said the old woman, nodding her head in the direction of the corpse; and speaking with an idiotic leer, more ghastly than even the presence of death in such a place. 'Lord, Lord! Well, it is strange that I who gave birth to her, and was a woman then, should be alive and merry now, and she lying there: so cold and stiff! Lord, Lord!—to think of it; it's as good as a play—as good as a play!'

As the wretched creature mumbled and chuckled in her hideous merriment, the undertaker turned to go away.

'Stop, stop!' said the old woman in a loud whisper. 'Will she be buried to-morrow, or next day, or to-night? I laid her out; and I must walk, you know. Send me a large cloak: a good warm one: for it is bitter cold. We should have cake and wine, too, before we go! Never mind; send some bread—only a loaf of bread and a cup of water. Shall we have some bread, dear?' she said eagerly: catching at the undertaker's coat, as he once more moved towards the door.

'Yes, yes,' said the undertaker,'of course. Anything you like!' He disengaged himself from the old woman's grasp; and, drawing Oliver after him, hurried away.

The next day, (the family having been meanwhile relieved with a half-quartern loaf and a piece of cheese, left with them by Mr. Bumble himself,) Oliver and his master returned to the miserable abode; where Mr. Bumble had already arrived, accompanied by four men from the workhouse, who were to act as bearers. An old black cloak had been thrown over the rags of the old woman and the man; and the bare coffin having been screwed down, was hoisted on the shoulders of the bearers, and carried into the street.

'Now, you must put your best leg foremost, old lady!' whispered Sowerberry in the old woman's ear; 'we are rather late; and it won't do, to keep the clergyman waiting. Move on, my men,—as quick as you like!'

Thus directed, the bearers trotted on under their light burden; and the two mourners kept as near them, as they could. Mr. Bumble and Sowerberry walked at a good smart pace in front; and Oliver, whose legs were not so long as his master's, ran by the side.

There was not so great a necessity for hurrying as Mr. Sowerberry had anticipated, however; for when they reached the obscure corner of the churchyard in which the nettles grew, and where the parish graves were made, the clergyman had not arrived; and the clerk, who was sitting by the vestry-room fire, seemed to think it by no means improbable that it might be an hour or so, before he came. So, they put the bier on the brink of the grave; and the two mourners waited patiently in the damp clay, with a cold rain drizzling down, while the ragged boys whom the spectacle had attracted into the churchyard played a noisy game at hide-and-seek among the tombstones, or varied their amusements by jumping backwards and forwards over the coffin. Mr. Sowerberry and Bumble, being personal friends of the clerk, sat by the fire with him, and read the paper.

At length, after a lapse of something more than an hour, Mr. Bumble, and Sowerberry, and the clerk, were seen running towards the grave. Immediately afterwards, the clergyman appeared: putting on his surplice as he came along. Mr. Bumble then thrashed a boy or two, to keep up appearances; and the reverend gentleman, having read as much of the burial service as could be compressed into four minutes, gave his surplice to the clerk, and walked away again.

'Now, Bill!' said Sowerberry to the grave-digger. 'Fill up!'

It was no very difficult task, for the grave was so full, that the uppermost coffin was within a few feet of the surface. The grave-digger shovelled in the earth; stamped it loosely down with his feet: shouldered his spade; and walked off, followed by the boys, who murmured very loud complaints at the fun being over so soon.

'Come, my good fellow!' said Bumble, tapping the man on the back. 'They want to shut up the yard.'

The man who had never once moved, since he had taken his station by the grave side, started, raised his head, stared at the person who had addressed him, walked forward for a few paces; and fell down in a swoon. The crazy old woman was too much occupied in bewailing the loss of her cloak (which the undertaker had taken off), to pay him any attention; so they threw a can of cold water over him; and when he came to, saw him safely out of the churchyard, locked the gate, and departed on their different ways.

'Well, Oliver,' said Sowerberry, as they walked home, 'how do you like it?'

'Pretty well, thank you, sir' replied Oliver, with considerable hesitation. 'Not very much, sir.'

'Ah, you'll get used to it in time, Oliver,' said Sowerberry. 'Nothing when you are used to it, my boy.'

Oliver wondered, in his own mind, whether it had taken a very long time to get Mr. Sowerberry used to it. But he thought it better not to ask the question; and walked back to the shop: thinking over all he had seen and heard.

CHAPTER VI. OLIVER, BEING GOADED BY THE TAUNTS OF NOAH, ROUSES INTO ACTION, AND RATHER ASTONISHES HIM

The month's trial over, Oliver was formally apprenticed. It was a nice sickly season just at this time. In commercial phrase, coffins were looking up; and, in the course of a few weeks, Oliver acquired a great deal of experience. The success of Mr. Sowerberry's ingenious speculation, exceeded even his most sanguine hopes. The oldest inhabitants recollected no period at which measles had been so prevalent, or so fatal to infant existence; and many were the mournful processions which little Oliver headed, in a hat-band reaching down to his knees, to the indescribable admiration and emotion of all the mothers in the town. As Oliver accompanied his master in most of his adult expeditions too, in order that he might acquire that equanimity of demeanour and full command of nerve which was essential to a finished undertaker, he had many opportunities of observing the beautiful resignation and fortitude with which some strong-minded people bear their trials and losses.

For instance; when Sowerberry had an order for the burial of some rich old lady or gentleman, who was surrounded by a great number of nephews and nieces, who had been perfectly inconsolable during the previous illness, and whose grief had been wholly irrepressible even on the most public occasions, they would be as happy among themselves as need be— quite cheerful and contented—conversing together with as much freedom and gaiety, as if nothing whatever had happened to disturb them. Husbands, too, bore the loss of their wives with the most heroic calmness. Wives, again, put on weeds for their husbands, as if, so far from grieving in the garb of sorrow, they had made up their minds to render it as becoming and attractive as possible. It was observable, too, that ladies and gentlemen who were in passions of anguish during the ceremony of interment, recovered almost as soon as they reached home, and became quite composed before the tea-drinking was over. All this was very pleasant and improving to see; and Oliver beheld it with great admiration.

That Oliver Twist was moved to resignation by the example of these good people, I cannot, although I am his biographer, undertake to affirm with any degree of confidence; but I can most distinctly say, that for many months he continued meekly to submit to the domination and ill-treatment of Noah Claypole: who used him far worse than before, now that his jealousy was roused by seeing the new boy promoted to the black stick and hatband, while he, the old one, remained stationary in the muffin-cap and leathers. Charlotte treated him ill, because Noah did; and Mrs. Sowerberry was his decided enemy, because Mr. Sowerberry was disposed to be his friend; so, between these three on one side, and a glut of funerals on the other, Oliver was not altogether as comfortable as the hungry pig was, when he was shut up, by mistake, in the grain department of a brewery.

And now, I come to a very important passage in Oliver's history; for I have to record an act, slight and unimportant perhaps in appearance, but which indirectly produced a material change in all his future prospects and proceedings.

One day, Oliver and Noah had descended into the kitchen at the usual dinner-hour, to banquet upon a small joint of mutton—a pound and a half of the worst end of the neck— when Charlotte being called out of the way, there ensued a brief interval of time, which Noah Claypole, being hungry and vicious, considered he could not possibly devote to a worthier purpose than aggravating and tantalising young Oliver Twist.

Intent upon this innocent amusement, Noah put his feet on the table-cloth; and pulled Oliver's hair; and twitched his ears; and expressed his opinion that he was a 'sneak'; and furthermore announced his intention of coming to see him hanged, whenever that desirable event should take place; and entered upon various topics of petty annoyance, like a malicious and ill-conditioned charity-boy as he was. But, making Oliver cry, Noah attempted to be more facetious still; and in his attempt, did what many sometimes do to this day, when they want to be funny. He got rather personal.

'Work'us,' said Noah, 'how's your mother?'

'She's dead,' replied Oliver; 'don't you say anything about her to me!'

Oliver's colour rose as he said this; he breathed quickly; and there was a curious working of the mouth and nostrils, which Mr. Claypole thought must be the immediate precursor of a violent fit of crying. Under this impression he returned to the charge.

'What did she die of, Work'us?' said Noah.

'Of a broken heart, some of our old nurses told me,' replied Oliver: more as if he were talking to himself, than answering Noah. 'I think I know what it must be to die of that!'

'Tol de rol lol lol, right fol lairy, Work'us,' said Noah, as a tear rolled down Oliver's cheek. 'What's set you a snivelling now?'

'Not you,' replied Oliver, sharply. 'There; that's enough. Don't say anything more to me about her; you'd better not!'

'Better not!' exclaimed Noah. 'Well! Better not! Work'us, don't be impudent. Your mother, too! She was a nice 'un she was. Oh, Lor!' And here, Noah nodded his head expressively; and curled up as much of his small red nose as muscular action could collect together, for the occasion.

'Yer know, Work'us,' continued Noah, emboldened by Oliver's silence, and speaking in a jeering tone of affected pity: of all tones the most annoying: 'Yer know, Work'us, it can't be helped now; and of course yer couldn't help it then; and I am very sorry for it; and I'm sure we all are, and pity yer very much. But yer must know, Work'us, yer mother was a regular right-down bad 'un.'

'What did you say?' inquired Oliver, looking up very quickly.

'A regular right-down bad 'un, Work'us,' replied Noah, coolly. 'And it's a great deal better, Work'us, that she died when she did, or else she'd have been hard labouring in Bridewell, or transported, or hung; which is more likely than either, isn't it?'

Crimson with fury, Oliver started up; overthrew the chair and table; seized Noah by the throat; shook him, in the violence of his rage, till his teeth chattered in his head; and collecting his whole force into one heavy blow, felled him to the ground.

A minute ago, the boy had looked the quiet child, mild, dejected creature that harsh treatment had made him. But his spirit was roused at last; the cruel insult to his dead mother had set his blood on fire. His breast heaved; his attitude was erect; his eye bright and vivid; his whole person changed; as he stood glaring over the cowardly tormentor who now lay crouching at his feet; and defied him with an energy he had never known before.

'He'll murder me!' blubbered Noah. 'Charlotte! missis! Here's the new boy a murdering of me! Help! help! Oliver's gone mad! Char—lotte!'

Noah's shouts were responded to, by a loud scream from Charlotte, and a louder from Mrs. Sowerberry; the former of whom rushed into the kitchen by a side-door, while the latter paused on the staircase till she was quite certain that it was consistent with the preservation of human life, to come further down.

'Oh, you little wretch!' screamed Charlotte: seizing Oliver with her utmost force, which was about equal to that of a moderately strong man in particularly good training. 'Oh, you little un-grate-ful, mur-de-rous, hor-rid villain!' And between every syllable, Charlotte gave Oliver a blow with all her might: accompanying it with a scream, for the benefit of society.

Charlotte's fist was by no means a light one; but, lest it should not be effectual in calming Oliver's wrath, Mrs. Sowerberry plunged into the kitchen, and assisted to hold him with one hand, while she scratched his face with the other. In this favourable position of affairs, Noah rose from the ground, and pommelled him behind.

This was rather too violent exercise to last long. When they were all wearied out, and could tear and beat no longer, they dragged Oliver, struggling and shouting, but nothing daunted, into the dust-cellar, and there locked him up. This being done, Mrs. Sowerberry sunk into a chair, and burst into tears.

'Bless her, she's going off!' said Charlotte. 'A glass of water, Noah, dear. Make haste!'

'Oh! Charlotte,' said Mrs. Sowerberry: speaking as well as she could, through a deficiency of breath, and a sufficiency of cold water, which Noah had poured over her head and shoulders. 'Oh! Charlotte, what a mercy we have not all been murdered in our beds!'

'Ah! mercy indeed, ma'am,' was the reply. 'I only hope this'll teach master not to have any more of these dreadful creatures, that are born to be murderers and robbers from their very cradle. Poor Noah! He was all but killed, ma'am, when I come in.'

'Poor fellow!' said Mrs. Sowerberry: looking piteously on the charity-boy.

Noah, whose top waistcoat-button might have been somewhere on a level with the crown of Oliver's head, rubbed his eyes with the inside of his wrists while this commiseration was bestowed upon him, and performed some affecting tears and sniffs.

'What's to be done!' exclaimed Mrs. Sowerberry. 'Your master's not at home; there's not a man in the house, and he'll kick that door down in ten minutes.' Oliver's vigorous plunges against the bit of timber in question, rendered this occurance highly probable.

'Dear, dear! I don't know, ma'am,' said Charlotte, 'unless we send for the police-officers.'

'Or the millingtary,' suggested Mr. Claypole.

'No, no,' said Mrs. Sowerberry: bethinking herself of Oliver's old friend. 'Run to Mr. Bumble, Noah, and tell him to come here directly, and not to lose a minute; never mind your cap! Make haste! You can hold a knife to that black eye, as you run along. It'll keep the swelling down.'

Noah stopped to make no reply, but started off at his fullest speed; and very much it astonished the people who were out walking, to see a charity-boy tearing through the streets pell-mell, with no cap on his head, and a clasp-knife at his eye.

CHAPTER VII. OLIVER CONTINUES REFRACTORY

Noah Claypole ran along the streets at his swiftest pace, and paused not once for breath, until he reached the workhouse-gate. Having rested here, for a minute or so, to collect a good burst of sobs and an imposing show of tears and terror, he knocked loudly at the wicket; and presented such a rueful face to the aged pauper who opened it, that even he, who saw nothing but rueful faces about him at the best of times, started back in astonishment.

'Why, what's the matter with the boy!' said the old pauper.

'Mr. Bumble! Mr. Bumble!' cried Noah, with well-affected dismay: and in tones so loud and agitated, that they not only caught the ear of Mr. Bumble himself, who happened to be hard by, but alarmed him so much that he rushed into the yard without his cocked hat,—which is a very curious and remarkable circumstance: as showing that even a beadle, acted upon a sudden and powerful impulse, may be afflicted with a momentary visitation of loss of self-possession, and forgetfulness of personal dignity.

'Oh, Mr. Bumble, sir!' said Noah: 'Oliver, sir,—Oliver has—'

'What? What?' interposed Mr. Bumble: with a gleam of pleasure in his metallic eyes. 'Not run away; he hasn't run away, has he, Noah?'

'No, sir, no. Not run away, sir, but he's turned wicious,' replied Noah. 'He tried to murder me, sir; and then he tried to murder Charlotte; and then missis. Oh! what dreadful pain it is!

Such agony, please, sir!' And here, Noah writhed and twisted his body into an extensive variety of eel-like positions; thereby giving Mr. Bumble to understand that, from the violent and sanguinary onset of Oliver Twist, he had sustained severe internal injury and damage, from which he was at that moment suffering the acutest torture.

When Noah saw that the intelligence he communicated perfectly paralysed Mr. Bumble, he imparted additional effect thereunto, by bewailing his dreadful wounds ten times louder than before; and when he observed a gentleman in a white waistcoat crossing the yard, he was more tragic in his lamentations than ever: rightly conceiving it highly expedient to attract the notice, and rouse the indignation, of the gentleman aforesaid.

The gentleman's notice was very soon attracted; for he had not walked three paces, when he turned angrily round, and inquired what that young cur was howling for, and why Mr. Bumble did not favour him with something which would render the series of vocular exclamations so designated, an involuntary process?

'It's a poor boy from the free-school, sir,' replied Mr. Bumble, 'who has been nearly murdered—all but murdered, sir,—by young Twist.'

'By Jove!' exclaimed the gentleman in the white waistcoat, stopping short. 'I knew it! I felt a strange presentiment from the very first, that that audacious young savage would come to be hung!'

'He has likewise attempted, sir, to murder the female servant,' said Mr. Bumble, with a face of ashy paleness.

'And his missis,' interposed Mr. Claypole.

'And his master, too, I think you said, Noah?' added Mr. Bumble.

'No! he's out, or he would have murdered him,' replied Noah. 'He said he wanted to.'

'Ah! Said he wanted to, did he, my boy?' inquired the gentleman in the white waistcoat.

'Yes, sir,' replied Noah. 'And please, sir, missis wants to know whether Mr. Bumble can spare time to step up there, directly, and flog him—'cause master's out.'

'Certainly, my boy; certainly,' said the gentleman in the white waistcoat: smiling benignly, and patting Noah's head, which was about three inches higher than his own. 'You're a good boy—a very good boy. Here's a penny for you. Bumble, just step up to Sowerberry's with your cane, and see what's best to be done. Don't spare him, Bumble.'

'No, I will not, sir,' replied the beadle. And the cocked hat and cane having been, by this time, adjusted to their owner's satisfaction, Mr. Bumble and Noah Claypole betook themselves with all speed to the undertaker's shop.

Here the position of affairs had not at all improved. Sowerberry had not yet returned, and Oliver continued to kick, with undiminished vigour, at the cellar-door. The accounts of his ferocity as related by Mrs. Sowerberry and Charlotte, were of so startling a nature, that Mr. Bumble judged it prudent to parley, before opening the door. With this view he gave a kick at the outside, by way of prelude; and, then, applying his mouth to the keyhole, said, in a deep and impressive tone:

'Oliver!'

'Come; you let me out!' replied Oliver, from the inside.

'Do you know this here voice, Oliver?' said Mr. Bumble.

'Yes,' replied Oliver.

'Ain't you afraid of it, sir? Ain't you a-trembling while I speak, sir?' said Mr. Bumble.

'No!' replied Oliver, boldly.

An answer so different from the one he had expected to elicit, and was in the habit of receiving, staggered Mr. Bumble not a little. He stepped back from the keyhole; drew himself up to his full height; and looked from one to another of the three bystanders, in mute astonishment.

'Oh, you know, Mr. Bumble, he must be mad,' said Mrs. Sowerberry.

'No boy in half his senses could venture to speak so to you.'

'It's not Madness, ma'am,' replied Mr. Bumble, after a few moments of deep meditation. 'It's Meat.'

'What?' exclaimed Mrs. Sowerberry.

'Meat, ma'am, meat,' replied Bumble, with stern emphasis. 'You've over-fed him, ma'am. You've raised a artificial soul and spirit in him, ma'am unbecoming a person of his condition: as the board, Mrs. Sowerberry, who are practical philosophers, will tell you. What have paupers to do with soul or spirit? It's quite enough that we let 'em have live bodies. If you had kept the boy on gruel, ma'am, this would never have happened.'

'Dear, dear!' ejaculated Mrs. Sowerberry, piously raising her eyes to the kitchen ceiling: 'this comes of being liberal!'

The liberality of Mrs. Sowerberry to Oliver, had consisted of a profuse bestowal upon him of all the dirty odds and ends which nobody else would eat; so there was a great deal of meekness and self-devotion in her voluntarily remaining under Mr. Bumble's heavy accusation. Of which, to do her justice, she was wholly innocent, in thought, word, or deed.

'Ah!' said Mr. Bumble, when the lady brought her eyes down to earth again; 'the only thing that can be done now, that I know of, is to leave him in the cellar for a day or so, till he's a little starved down; and then to take him out, and keep him on gruel all through the apprenticeship. He comes of a bad family. Excitable natures, Mrs. Sowerberry! Both the nurse and doctor said, that that mother of his made her way here, against difficulties and pain that would have killed any well-disposed woman, weeks before.'

At this point of Mr. Bumble's discourse, Oliver, just hearing enough to know that some allusion was being made to his mother, recommenced kicking, with a violence that rendered every other sound inaudible. Sowerberry returned at this juncture. Oliver's offence having been explained to him, with such exaggerations as the ladies thought best calculated to rouse his ire, he unlocked the cellar-door in a twinkling, and dragged his rebellious apprentice out, by the collar.

Oliver's clothes had been torn in the beating he had received; his face was bruised and scratched; and his hair scattered over his forehead. The angry flush had not disappeared, however; and when he was pulled out of his prison, he scowled boldly on Noah, and looked quite undismayed.

'Now, you are a nice young fellow, ain't you?' said Sowerberry; giving Oliver a shake, and a box on the ear.

'He called my mother names,' replied Oliver.

'Well, and what if he did, you little ungrateful wretch?' said Mrs. Sowerberry. 'She deserved what he said, and worse.'

'She didn't' said Oliver.

'She did,' said Mrs. Sowerberry.

'It's a lie!' said Oliver.

Mrs. Sowerberry burst into a flood of tears.

This flood of tears left Mr. Sowerberry no alternative. If he had hesitated for one instant to punish Oliver most severely, it must be quite clear to every experienced reader that he would have been, according to all precedents in disputes of matrimony established, a brute, an unnatural husband, an insulting creature, a base imitation of a man, and various other agreeable characters too numerous for recital within the limits of this chapter. To do him justice, he was, as far as his power went—it was not very extensive—kindly disposed towards the boy; perhaps, because it was his interest to be so; perhaps, because his wife disliked him. The flood of tears, however, left him no resource; so he at once gave him a drubbing, which satisfied even Mrs. Sowerberry herself, and rendered Mr. Bumble's subsequent application of the parochial cane, rather unnecessary. For the rest of the day, he was shut up in the back kitchen, in company with a pump and a slice of bread; and at night, Mrs. Sowerberry, after making various remarks outside the door, by no means complimentary to the memory of his mother, looked into the room, and, amidst the jeers and pointings of Noah and Charlotte, ordered him upstairs to his dismal bed.

It was not until he was left alone in the silence and stillness of the gloomy workshop of the undertaker, that Oliver gave way to the feelings which the day's treatment may be supposed likely to have awakened in a mere child. He had listened to their taunts with a look of contempt; he had borne the lash without a cry: for he felt that pride swelling in his heart which would have kept down a shriek to the last, though they had roasted him alive. But now, when there were none to see or hear him, he fell upon his knees on the floor; and, hiding his face in his hands, wept such tears as, God send for the credit of our nature, few so young may ever have cause to pour out before him!

For a long time, Oliver remained motionless in this attitude. The candle was burning low in the socket when he rose to his feet. Having gazed cautiously round him, and listened intently, he gently undid the fastenings of the door, and looked abroad.

It was a cold, dark night. The stars seemed, to the boy's eyes, farther from the earth than he had ever seen them before; there was no wind; and the sombre shadows thrown by the trees upon the ground, looked sepulchral and death-like, from being so still. He softly reclosed the door. Having availed himself of the expiring light of the candle to tie up in a handkerchief the few articles of wearing apparel he had, sat himself down upon a bench, to wait for morning.

With the first ray of light that struggled through the crevices in the shutters, Oliver arose, and again unbarred the door. One timid look around—one moment's pause of hesitation—he had closed it behind him, and was in the open street.

He looked to the right and to the left, uncertain whither to fly.

He remembered to have seen the waggons, as they went out, toiling up the hill. He took the same route; and arriving at a footpath across the fields: which he knew, after some distance, led out again into the road; struck into it, and walked quickly on.

Along this same footpath, Oliver well-remembered he had trotted beside Mr. Bumble, when he first carried him to the workhouse from the farm. His way lay directly in front of the cottage. His heart beat quickly when he bethought himself of this; and he half resolved to turn back. He had come a long way though, and should lose a great deal of time by doing so. Besides, it was so early that there was very little fear of his being seen; so he walked on.

He reached the house. There was no appearance of its inmates stirring at that early hour. Oliver stopped, and peeped into the garden. A child was weeding one of the little beds; as he stopped, he raised his pale face and disclosed the features of one of his former companions. Oliver felt glad to see him, before he went; for, though younger than himself, he had been his little friend and playmate. They had been beaten, and starved, and shut up together, many and many a time.

'Hush, Dick!' said Oliver, as the boy ran to the gate, and thrust his thin arm between the rails to greet him. 'Is any one up?'

'Nobody but me,' replied the child.

'You musn't say you saw me, Dick,' said Oliver. 'I am running away. They beat and ill-use me, Dick; and I am going to seek my fortune, some long way off. I don't know where. How pale you are!'

'I heard the doctor tell them I was dying,' replied the child with a faint smile. 'I am very glad to see you, dear; but don't stop, don't stop!'

'Yes, yes, I will, to say good-b'ye to you,' replied Oliver. 'I shall see you again, Dick. I know I shall! You will be well and happy!'

'I hope so,' replied the child. 'After I am dead, but not before. I know the doctor must be right, Oliver, because I dream so much of Heaven, and Angels, and kind faces that I never see when I am awake. Kiss me,' said the child, climbing up the low gate, and flinging his little arms round Oliver's neck. 'Good-b'ye, dear! God bless you!'

The blessing was from a young child's lips, but it was the first that Oliver had ever heard invoked upon his head; and through the struggles and sufferings, and troubles and changes, of his after life, he never once forgot it.

CHAPTER VIII. OLIVER WALKS TO LONDON. HE ENCOUNTERS ON THE ROAD A STRANGE SORT OF YOUNG GENTLEMAN

Oliver reached the stile at which the by-path terminated; and once more gained the high-road. It was eight o'clock now. Though he was nearly five miles away from the town, he ran, and hid behind the hedges, by turns, till noon: fearing that he might be pursued and overtaken. Then he sat down to rest by the side of the milestone, and began to think, for the first time, where he had better go and try to live.

The stone by which he was seated, bore, in large characters, an intimation that it was just seventy miles from that spot to London. The name awakened a new train of ideas in the boy's mind.

London!—that great place!—nobody—not even Mr. Bumble—could ever find him there! He had often heard the old men in the workhouse, too, say that no lad of spirit need want in London; and that there were ways of living in that vast city, which those who had been bred up in country parts had no idea of. It was the very place for a homeless boy, who must die in the streets unless some one helped him. As these things passed through his thoughts, he jumped upon his feet, and again walked forward.

He had diminished the distance between himself and London by full four miles more, before he recollected how much he must undergo ere he could hope to reach his place of destination. As this consideration forced itself upon him, he slackened his pace a little, and meditated upon his means of getting there. He had a crust of bread, a coarse shirt, and two pairs of stockings, in his bundle. He had a penny too—a gift of Sowerberry's after some funeral in which he had acquitted himself more than ordinarily well—in his pocket. 'A clean shirt,' thought Oliver, 'is a very comfortable thing; and so are two pairs of darned stockings; and so is a penny; but they are small helps to a sixty-five miles' walk in winter time.' But Oliver's thoughts, like those of most other people, although they were extremely ready and active to point out his difficulties, were wholly at a loss to suggest any feasible mode of surmounting them; so, after a good deal of thinking to no particular purpose, he changed his little bundle over to the other shoulder, and trudged on.

Oliver walked twenty miles that day; and all that time tasted nothing but the crust of dry bread, and a few draughts of water, which he begged at the cottage-doors by the road-side. When the night came, he turned into a meadow; and, creeping close under a hay-rick, determined to lie there, till morning. He felt frightened at first, for the wind moaned dismally over the empty fields: and he was cold and hungry, and more alone than he had ever felt before. Being very tired with his walk, however, he soon fell asleep and forgot his troubles.

He felt cold and stiff, when he got up next morning, and so hungry that he was obliged to exchange the penny for a small loaf, in the very first village through which he passed. He had walked no more than twelve miles, when night closed in again. His feet were sore, and his legs so weak that they trembled beneath him. Another night passed in the bleak damp air, made him worse; when he set forward on his journey next morning he could hardly crawl along.

He waited at the bottom of a steep hill till a stage-coach came up, and then begged of the outside passengers; but there were very few who took any notice of him: and even those told him to wait till they got to the top of the hill, and then let them see how far he could run for a halfpenny. Poor Oliver tried to keep up with the coach a little way, but was unable to do it, by reason of his fatigue and sore feet. When the outsides saw this, they put their halfpence back into their pockets again, declaring that he was an idle young dog, and didn't deserve anything; and the coach rattled away and left only a cloud of dust behind.

In some villages, large painted boards were fixed up: warning all persons who begged within the district, that they would be sent to jail. This frightened Oliver very much, and made him glad to get out of those villages with all possible expedition. In others, he would stand about the inn-yards, and look mournfully at every one who passed: a proceeding which generally terminated in the landlady's ordering one of the post-boys who were lounging about, to drive that strange boy out of the place, for she was sure he had come to steal something. If he begged at a farmer's house, ten to one but they threatened to set the dog on him; and when he showed his nose in a shop, they talked about the beadle—which brought Oliver's heart into his mouth,—very often the only thing he had there, for many hours together.

In fact, if it had not been for a good-hearted turnpike-man, and a benevolent old lady, Oliver's troubles would have been shortened by the very same process which had put an end to his mother's; in other words, he would most assuredly have fallen dead upon the king's highway. But the turnpike-man gave him a meal of bread and cheese; and the old lady, who had a shipwrecked grandson wandering barefoot in some distant part of the earth, took pity upon the poor orphan, and gave him what little she could afford—and more—with such kind and gentle words, and such tears of sympathy and compassion, that they sank deeper into Oliver's soul, than all the sufferings he had ever undergone.

Early on the seventh morning after he had left his native place, Oliver limped slowly into the little town of Barnet. The window-shutters were closed; the street was empty; not a soul had awakened to the business of the day. The sun was rising in all its splendid beauty; but the light only served to show the boy his own lonesomeness and desolation, as he sat, with bleeding feet and covered with dust, upon a door-step.

By degrees, the shutters were opened; the window-blinds were drawn up; and people began passing to and fro. Some few stopped to gaze at Oliver for a moment or two, or turned round to stare at him as they hurried by; but none relieved him, or troubled themselves to inquire how he came there. He had no heart to beg. And there he sat.

He had been crouching on the step for some time: wondering at the great number of public-houses (every other house in Barnet was a tavern, large or small), gazing listlessly at the coaches as they passed through, and thinking how strange it seemed that they could do, with ease, in a few hours, what it had taken him a whole week of courage and determination beyond his years to accomplish: when he was roused by observing that a boy, who had passed him carelessly some minutes before, had returned, and was now surveying him most earnestly from the opposite side of the way. He took little heed of this at first; but the boy remained in the same attitude of close observation so long, that Oliver raised his head, and returned his steady look. Upon this, the boy crossed over; and walking close up to Oliver, said,

'Hullo, my covey! What's the row?'

The boy who addressed this inquiry to the young wayfarer, was about his own age: but one of the queerest looking boys that Oliver had even seen. He was a snub-nosed, flat-browed, common-faced boy enough; and as dirty a juvenile as one would wish to see; but he had about him all the airs and manners of a man. He was short of his age: with rather bow-legs, and little, sharp, ugly eyes. His hat was stuck on the top of his head so lightly, that it threatened to fall off every moment—and would have done so, very often, if the wearer had not had a knack of every now and then giving his head a sudden twitch, which brought it back to its old place again. He wore a man's coat, which reached nearly to his heels. He had turned the cuffs back, half-way up his arm, to get his hands out of the sleeves: apparently with the ultimate view of thrusting them into the pockets of his corduroy trousers; for there he kept them. He was, altogether, as roystering and swaggering a young gentleman as ever stood four feet six, or something less, in the bluchers.

'Hullo, my covey! What's the row?' said this strange young gentleman to Oliver.

'I am very hungry and tired,' replied Oliver: the tears standing in his eyes as he spoke. 'I have walked a long way. I have been walking these seven days.'

'Walking for sivin days!' said the young gentleman. 'Oh, I see. Beak's order, eh? But,' he added, noticing Oliver's look of surprise, 'I suppose you don't know what a beak is, my flash com-pan-i-on.'

Oliver mildly replied, that he had always heard a bird's mouth described by the term in question.

'My eyes, how green!' exclaimed the young gentleman. 'Why, a beak's a madgst'rate; and when you walk by a beak's order, it's not straight forerd, but always agoing up, and niver a coming down agin. Was you never on the mill?'

'What mill?' inquired Oliver.

'What mill! Why, the mill—the mill as takes up so little room that it'll work inside a Stone Jug; and always goes better when the wind's low with people, than when it's high; acos then they can't get workmen. But come,' said the young gentleman; 'you want grub, and you shall have it. I'm at low-water-mark myself—only one bob and a magpie; but, as far as it goes, I'll fork out and stump. Up with you on your pins. There! Now then! 'Morrice!'

Assisting Oliver to rise, the young gentleman took him to an adjacent chandler's shop, where he purchased a sufficiency of ready-dressed ham and a half-quartern loaf, or, as he himself expressed it, 'a fourpenny bran!' the ham being kept clean and preserved from dust, by the ingenious expedient of making a hole in the loaf by pulling out a portion of the crumb, and stuffing it therein. Taking the bread under his arm, the young gentlman turned into a small public-house, and led the way to a tap-room in the rear of the premises. Here, a pot of beer was brought in, by direction of the mysterious youth; and Oliver, falling to, at his new friend's bidding, made a long and hearty meal, during the progress of which the strange boy eyed him from time to time with great attention.

'Going to London?' said the strange boy, when Oliver had at length concluded.

'Yes.'

'Got any lodgings?'

'No.'

'Money?'

'No.'

The strange boy whistled; and put his arms into his pockets, as far as the big coat-sleeves would let them go.

'Do you live in London?' inquired Oliver.

'Yes. I do, when I'm at home,' replied the boy. 'I suppose you want some place to sleep in to-night, don't you?'

'I do, indeed,' answered Oliver. 'I have not slept under a roof since I left the country.'

'Don't fret your eyelids on that score,' said the young gentleman. 'I've got to be in London to-night; and I know a 'spectable old gentleman as lives there, wot'll give you lodgings for nothink, and never ask for the change—that is, if any genelman he knows interduces you. And don't he know me? Oh, no! Not in the least! By no means. Certainly not!'

The young gentleman smiled, as if to intimate that the latter fragments of discourse were playfully ironical; and finished the beer as he did so.

This unexpected offer of shelter was too tempting to be resisted; especially as it was immediately followed up, by the assurance that the old gentleman referred to, would doubtless provide Oliver with a comfortable place, without loss of time. This led to a more friendly and confidential dialogue; from which Oliver discovered that his friend's name was Jack Dawkins, and that he was a peculiar pet and protege of the elderly gentleman before mentioned.

Mr. Dawkin's appearance did not say a vast deal in favour of the comforts which his patron's interest obtained for those whom he took under his protection; but, as he had a rather flighty and dissolute mode of conversing, and furthermore avowed that among his intimate friends he was better known by the sobriquet of 'The Artful Dodger,' Oliver concluded that, being of a dissipated and careless turn, the moral precepts of his benefactor had hitherto been thrown away upon him. Under this impression, he secretly resolved to cultivate the good opinion of the old gentleman as quickly as possible; and, if he found the Dodger incorrigible, as he more than half suspected he should, to decline the honour of his farther acquaintance.

As John Dawkins objected to their entering London before nightfall, it was nearly eleven o'clock when they reached the turnpike at Islington. They crossed from the Angel into St. John's Road; struck down the small street which terminates at Sadler's Wells Theatre; through Exmouth Street and Coppice Row; down the little court by the side of the workhouse; across the classic ground which once bore the name of Hockley-in-the-Hole; thence into Little Saffron Hill; and so into Saffron Hill the Great: along which the Dodger scudded at a rapid pace, directing Oliver to follow close at his heels.

Although Oliver had enough to occupy his attention in keeping sight of his leader, he could not help bestowing a few hasty glances on either side of the way, as he passed along. A dirtier or more wretched place he had never seen. The street was very narrow and muddy, and the air was impregnated with filthy odours.

There were a good many small shops; but the only stock in trade appeared to be heaps of children, who, even at that time of night, were crawling in and out at the doors, or screaming from the inside. The sole places that seemed to prosper amid the general blight of the place, were the public-houses; and in them, the lowest orders of Irish were wrangling with might and main. Covered ways and yards, which here and there diverged from the main street, disclosed little knots of houses, where drunken men and women were positively wallowing in filth; and from several of the door-ways, great ill-looking fellows were cautiously emerging, bound, to all appearance, on no very well-disposed or harmless errands.

Oliver was just considering whether he hadn't better run away, when they reached the bottom of the hill. His conductor, catching him by the arm, pushed open the door of a house near Field Lane; and drawing him into the passage, closed it behind them.

'Now, then!' cried a voice from below, in reply to a whistle from the Dodger.

'Plummy and slam!' was the reply.

This seemed to be some watchword or signal that all was right; for the light of a feeble candle gleamed on the wall at the remote end of the passage; and a man's face peeped out, from where a balustrade of the old kitchen staircase had been broken away.

'There's two on you,' said the man, thrusting the candle farther out, and shielding his eyes with his hand. 'Who's the t'other one?'

'A new pal,' replied Jack Dawkins, pulling Oliver forward.

'Where did he come from?'

'Greenland. Is Fagin upstairs?'

'Yes, he's a sortin' the wipes. Up with you!' The candle was drawn back, and the face disappeared.

Oliver, groping his way with one hand, and having the other firmly grasped by his companion, ascended with much difficulty the dark and broken stairs: which his conductor mounted with an ease and expedition that showed he was well acquainted with them.

He threw open the door of a back-room, and drew Oliver in after him.

The walls and ceiling of the room were perfectly black with age and dirt. There was a deal table before the fire: upon which were a candle, stuck in a ginger-beer bottle, two or three pewter pots, a loaf and butter, and a plate. In a frying-pan, which was on the fire, and which was secured to the mantelshelf by a string, some sausages were cooking; and standing over them, with a toasting-fork in his hand, was a very old shrivelled Jew, whose villainous-looking and repulsive face was obscured by a quantity of matted red hair. He was dressed in a greasy flannel gown, with his throat bare; and seemed to be dividing his attention between the frying-pan and the clothes-horse, over which a great number of silk handkerchiefs were hanging. Several rough beds made of old sacks, were huddled side by side on the floor. Seated round the table were four or five boys, none older than the Dodger, smoking long clay pipes, and drinking spirits with the air of middle-aged men. These all crowded about their associate as he whispered a few words to the Jew; and then turned round and grinned at Oliver. So did the Jew himself, toasting-fork in hand.

'This is him, Fagin,' said Jack Dawkins;'my friend Oliver Twist.'

The Jew grinned; and, making a low obeisance to Oliver, took him by the hand, and hoped he should have the honour of his intimate acquaintance. Upon this, the young gentleman with the pipes came round him, and shook both his hands very hard—especially the one in which he held his little bundle. One young gentleman was very anxious to hang up his cap for him; and another was so obliging as to put his hands in his pockets, in order that, as he was very tired, he might not have the trouble of emptying them, himself, when he went to bed. These civilities would probably be extended much farther, but for a liberal exercise of the Jew's toasting-fork on the heads and shoulders of the affectionate youths who offered them.

'We are very glad to see you, Oliver, very,' said the Jew. 'Dodger, take off the sausages; and draw a tub near the fire for Oliver. Ah, you're a-staring at the pocket-handkerchiefs! eh, my dear. There are a good many of 'em, ain't there? We've just looked 'em out, ready for the wash; that's all, Oliver; that's all. Ha! ha! ha!'

The latter part of this speech, was hailed by a boisterous shout from all the hopeful pupils of the merry old gentleman. In the midst of which they went to supper.

Oliver ate his share, and the Jew then mixed him a glass of hot gin-and-water: telling him he must drink it off directly, because another gentleman wanted the tumbler. Oliver did as he was desired. Immediately afterwards he felt himself gently lifted on to one of the sacks; and then he sunk into a deep sleep.

CHAPTER IX. CONTAINING FURTHER PARTICULARS CONCERNING THE PLEASANT OLD GENTLEMAN, AND HIS HOPEFUL PUPILS

It was late next morning when Oliver awoke, from a sound, long sleep. There was no other person in the room but the old Jew, who was boiling some coffee in a saucepan for breakfast, and whistling softly to himself as he stirred it round and round, with an iron spoon. He would stop every now and then to listen when there was the least noise below: and when he had satisfied himself, he would go on whistling and stirring again, as before.

Although Oliver had roused himself from sleep, he was not thoroughly awake. There is a drowsy state, between sleeping and waking, when you dream more in five minutes with your eyes half open, and yourself half conscious of everything that is passing around you, than you would in five nights with your eyes fast closed, and your senses wrapt in perfect unconsciousness. At such time, a mortal knows just enough of what his mind is doing, to form some glimmering conception of its mighty powers, its bounding from earth and spurning time and space, when freed from the restraint of its corporeal associate.

Oliver was precisely in this condition. He saw the Jew with his half-closed eyes; heard his low whistling; and recognised the sound of the spoon grating against the saucepan's sides: and yet the self-same senses were mentally engaged, at the same time, in busy action with almost everybody he had ever known.

When the coffee was done, the Jew drew the saucepan to the hob. Standing, then in an irresolute attitude for a few minutes, as if he did not well know how to employ himself, he turned round and looked at Oliver, and called him by his name. He did not answer, and was to all appearances asleep.

After satisfying himself upon this head, the Jew stepped gently to the door: which he fastened. He then drew forth: as it seemed to Oliver, from some trap in the floor: a small box, which he placed carefully on the table. His eyes glistened as he raised the lid, and looked in. Dragging an old chair to the table, he sat down; and took from it a magnificent gold watch, sparkling with jewels.

'Aha!' said the Jew, shrugging up his shoulders, and distorting every feature with a hideous grin. 'Clever dogs! Clever dogs! Staunch to the last! Never told the old parson where they were. Never poached upon old Fagin! And why should they? It wouldn't have loosened the knot, or kept the drop up, a minute longer. No, no, no! Fine fellows! Fine fellows!'

With these, and other muttered reflections of the like nature, the Jew once more deposited the watch in its place of safety. At least half a dozen more were severally drawn forth from the same box, and surveyed with equal pleasure; besides rings, brooches, bracelets, and other articles of jewellery, of such magnificent materials, and costly workmanship, that Oliver had no idea, even of their names.

Having replaced these trinkets, the Jew took out another: so small that it lay in the palm of his hand. There seemed to be some very minute inscription on it; for the Jew laid it flat upon the table, and shading it with his hand, pored over it, long and earnestly. At length he put it down, as if despairing of success; and, leaning back in his chair, muttered:

'What a fine thing capital punishment is! Dead men never repent; dead men never bring awkward stories to light. Ah, it's a fine thing for the trade! Five of 'em strung up in a row, and none left to play booty, or turn white-livered!'

As the Jew uttered these words, his bright dark eyes, which had been staring vacantly before him, fell on Oliver's face; the boy's eyes were fixed on his in mute curiousity; and although the recognition was only for an instant—for the briefest space of time that can possibly be conceived—it was enough to show the old man that he had been observed.

He closed the lid of the box with a loud crash; and, laying his hand on a bread knife which was on the table, started furiously up. He trembled very much though; for, even in his terror, Oliver could see that the knife quivered in the air.

'What's that?' said the Jew. 'What do you watch me for? Why are you awake? What have you seen? Speak out, boy! Quick—quick! for your life.'

'I wasn't able to sleep any longer, sir,' replied Oliver, meekly. 'I am very sorry if I have disturbed you, sir.'

'You were not awake an hour ago?' said the Jew, scowling fiercely on the boy.

'No! No, indeed!' replied Oliver.

'Are you sure?' cried the Jew: with a still fiercer look than before: and a threatening attitude.

'Upon my word I was not, sir,' replied Oliver, earnestly. 'I was not, indeed, sir.'

'Tush, tush, my dear!' said the Jew, abruptly resuming his old manner, and playing with

628

the knife a little, before he laid it down; as if to induce the belief that he had caught it up, in mere sport. 'Of course I know that, my dear. I only tried to frighten you. You're a brave boy. Ha! ha! you're a brave boy, Oliver.' The Jew rubbed his hands with a chuckle, but glanced uneasily at the box, notwithstanding.

'Did you see any of these pretty things, my dear?' said the Jew, laying his hand upon it after a short pause.

'Yes, sir,' replied Oliver.

'Ah!' said the Jew, turning rather pale. 'They—they're mine, Oliver; my little property. All I have to live upon, in my old age. The folks call me a miser, my dear. Only a miser; that's all.'

Oliver thought the old gentleman must be a decided miser to live in such a dirty place, with so many watches; but, thinking that perhaps his fondness for the Dodger and the other boys, cost him a good deal of money, he only cast a deferential look at the Jew, and asked if he might get up.

'Certainly, my dear, certainly,' replied the old gentleman. 'Stay. There's a pitcher of water in the corner by the door. Bring it here; and I'll give you a basin to wash in, my dear.'

Oliver got up; walked across the room; and stooped for an instant to raise the pitcher. When he turned his head, the box was gone.

He had scarcely washed himself, and made everything tidy, by emptying the basin out of the window, agreeably to the Jew's directions, when the Dodger returned: accompanied by a very sprightly young friend, whom Oliver had seen smoking on the previous night, and who was now formally introduced to him as Charley Bates. The four sat down, to breakfast, on the coffee, and some hot rolls and ham which the Dodger had brought home in the crown of his hat.

'Well,' said the Jew, glancing slyly at Oliver, and addressing himself to the Dodger, 'I hope you've been at work this morning, my dears?'

'Hard,' replied the Dodger.

'As nails,' added Charley Bates.

'Good boys, good boys!' said the Jew. 'What have you got, Dodger?'

'A couple of pocket-books,' replied that young gentleman.

'Lined?' inquired the Jew, with eagerness.

'Pretty well,' replied the Dodger, producing two pocket-books; one green, and the other red.

'Not so heavy as they might be,' said the Jew, after looking at the insides carefully; 'but very neat and nicely made. Ingenious workman, ain't he, Oliver?'

'Very indeed, sir,' said Oliver. At which Mr. Charles Bates laughed uproariously; very much to the amazement of Oliver, who saw nothing to laugh at, in anything that had passed.

'And what have you got, my dear?' said Fagin to Charley Bates.

'Wipes,' replied Master Bates; at the same time producing four pocket-handkerchiefs.

'Well,' said the Jew, inspecting them closely; 'they're very good ones, very. You haven't marked them well, though, Charley; so the marks shall be picked out with a needle, and we'll teach Oliver how to do it. Shall us, Oliver, eh? Ha! ha! ha!'

'If you please, sir,' said Oliver.

'You'd like to be able to make pocket-handkerchiefs as easy as Charley Bates, wouldn't you, my dear?' said the Jew.

'Very much, indeed, if you'll teach me, sir,' replied Oliver.

Master Bates saw something so exquisitely ludicrous in this reply, that he burst into another laugh; which laugh, meeting the coffee he was drinking, and carrying it down some wrong channel, very nearly terminated in his premature suffocation.

'He is so jolly green!' said Charley when he recovered, as an apology to the company for his unpolite behaviour.

The Dodger said nothing, but he smoothed Oliver's hair over his eyes, and said he'd know better, by and by; upon which the old gentleman, observing Oliver's colour mounting, changed the subject by asking whether there had been much of a crowd at the execution that morning? This made him wonder more and more; for it was plain from the replies of the two boys that they had both been there; and Oliver naturally wondered how they could possibly have found time to be so very industrious.

When the breakfast was cleared away; the merry old gentlman and the two boys played at a very curious and uncommon game, which was performed in this way. The merry old gentleman, placing a snuff-box in one pocket of his trousers, a note-case in the other, and a watch in his waistcoat pocket, with a guard-chain round his neck, and sticking a mock diamond pin in his shirt: buttoned his coat tight round him, and putting his spectacle-case and handkerchief in his pockets, trotted up and down the room with a stick, in imitation of the manner in which old gentlemen walk about the streets any hour in the day. Sometimes he stopped at the fire-place, and sometimes at the door, making believe that he was staring with all his might into shop-windows. At such times, he would look constantly round him, for fear of thieves, and would keep slapping all his pockets in turn, to see that he hadn't lost anything, in such a very funny and natural manner, that Oliver laughed till the tears ran down his face. All this time, the two boys followed him closely about: getting out of his sight, so nimbly, every time he turned round, that it was impossible to follow their motions. At last, the Dodger trod upon his toes, or ran upon his boot accidently, while Charley Bates stumbled up against him behind; and in that one moment they took from him, with the most extraordinary rapidity, snuff-box, note-case, watch-guard, chain, shirt-pin, pocket-handkerchief, even the spectacle-case. If the old gentlman felt a hand in any one of his pockets, he cried out where it was; and then the game began all over again.

When this game had been played a great many times, a couple of young ladies called to see the young gentleman; one of whom was named Bet, and the other Nancy. They wore a good deal of hair, not very neatly turned up behind, and were rather untidy about the shoes and stockings. They were not exactly pretty, perhaps; but they had a great deal of colour in their faces, and looked quite stout and hearty. Being remarkably free and agreeable in their manners, Oliver thought them very nice girls indeed. As there is no doubt they were.

The visitors stopped a long time. Spirits were produced, in consequence of one of the young ladies complaining of a coldness in her inside; and the conversation took a very convivial and improving turn. At length, Charley Bates expressed his opinion that it was time to pad the hoof. This, it occurred to Oliver, must be French for going out; for directly afterwards, the Dodger, and Charley, and the two young ladies, went away together, having been kindly furnished by the amiable old Jew with money to spend.

'There, my dear,' said Fagin. 'That's a pleasant life, isn't it? They have gone out for the day.'

'Have they done work, sir?' inquired Oliver.

'Yes,' said the Jew; 'that is, unless they should unexpectedly come across any, when they are out; and they won't neglect it, if they do, my dear, depend upon it. Make 'em your models, my dear. Make 'em your models,' tapping the fire-shovel on the hearth to add force to his words; 'do everything they bid you, and take their advice in all matters—especially the Dodger's, my dear. He'll be a great man himself, and will make you one too, if you take pattern by him.—Is my handkerchief hanging out of my pocket, my dear?' said the Jew, stopping short.

'Yes, sir,' said Oliver.

'See if you can take it out, without my feeling it; as you saw them do, when we were at play this morning.'

Oliver held up the bottom of the pocket with one hand, as he had seen the Dodger hold it, and drew the handkerchief lightly out of it with the other.

'Is it gone?' cried the Jew.

'Here it is, sir,' said Oliver, showing it in his hand.

'You're a clever boy, my dear,' said the playful old gentleman, patting Oliver on the head approvingly. 'I never saw a sharper lad. Here's a shilling for you. If you go on, in this way, you'll be the greatest man of the time. And now come here, and I'll show you how to take the marks out of the handkerchiefs.'

Oliver wondered what picking the old gentleman's pocket in play, had to do with his chances of being a great man. But, thinking that the Jew, being so much his senior, must know best, he followed him quietly to the table, and was soon deeply involved in his new study.

CHAPTER X. OLIVER BECOMES BETTER ACQUAINTED WITH THE CHARACTERS OF HIS NEW ASSOCIATES; AND PURCHASES EXPERIENCE AT A HIGH PRICE. BEING A SHORT, BUT VERY IMPORTANT CHAPTER, IN THIS HISTORY

For many days, Oliver remained in the Jew's room, picking the marks out of the pocket-handkerchief, (of which a great number were brought home,) and sometimes taking part in the game already described: which the two boys and the Jew played, regularly, every morning. At length, he began to languish for fresh air, and took many occasions of earnestly entreating the old gentleman to allow him to go out to work with his two companions.

Oliver was rendered the more anxious to be actively employed, by what he had seen of the stern morality of the old gentleman's character. Whenever the Dodger or Charley Bates came home at night, empty-handed, he would expatiate with great vehemence on the misery of idle and lazy habits; and would enforce upon them the necessity of an active life, by sending them supperless to bed. On one occasion, indeed, he even went so far as to knock them both down a flight of stairs; but this was carrying out his virtuous precepts to an unusual extent.

At length, one morning, Oliver obtained the permission he had so eagerly sought. There had been no handkerchiefs to work upon, for two or three days, and the dinners had been rather meagre. Perhaps these were reasons for the old gentleman's giving his assent; but, whether they were or no, he told Oliver he might go, and placed him under the joint guardianship of Charley Bates, and his friend the Dodger.

The three boys sallied out; the Dodger with his coat-sleeves tucked up, and his hat cocked, as usual; Master Bates sauntering along with his hands in his pockets; and Oliver between them, wondering where they were going, and what branch of manufacture he would be instructed in, first.

The pace at which they went, was such a very lazy, ill-looking saunter, that Oliver soon began to think his companions were going to deceive the old gentleman, by not going to work at all. The Dodger had a vicious propensity, too, of pulling the caps from the heads of small boys and tossing them down areas; while Charley Bates exhibited some very loose notions concerning the rights of property, by pilfering divers apples and onions from the stalls at the kennel sides, and thrusting them into pockets which were so surprisingly capacious, that they seemed to undermine his whole suit of clothes in every direction. These things looked so bad, that Oliver was on the point of declaring his intention of seeking his way back, in the best way he could; when his thoughts were suddenly directed into another channel, by a very mysterious change of behaviour on the part of the Dodger.

They were just emerging from a narrow court not far from the open square in Clerkenwell, which is yet called, by some strange perversion of terms, 'The Green': when the Dodger made a sudden stop; and, laying his finger on his lip, drew his companions back again, with the greatest caution and circumspection.

'What's the matter?' demanded Oliver.

'Hush!' replied the Dodger. 'Do you see that old cove at the book-stall?'

'The old gentleman over the way?' said Oliver. 'Yes, I see him.'

'He'll do,' said the Dodger.

'A prime plant,' observed Master Charley Bates.

Oliver looked from one to the other, with the greatest surprise; but he was not permitted to make any inquiries; for the two boys walked stealthily across the road, and slunk close behind the old gentleman towards whom his attention had been directed. Oliver walked a few paces after them; and, not knowing whether to advance or retire, stood looking on in silent amazement.

The old gentleman was a very respectable-looking personage, with a powdered head and gold spectacles. He was dressed in a bottle-green coat with a black velvet collar; wore white trousers; and carried a smart bamboo cane under his arm. He had taken up a book from the stall, and there he stood, reading away, as hard as if he were in his elbow-chair, in his own study. It is very possible that he fancied himself there, indeed; for it was plain, from his abstraction, that he saw not the book-stall, nor the street, nor the boys, nor, in short, anything but the book itself: which he was reading straight through: turning over the leaf when he got to the bottom of a page, beginning at the top line of the next one, and going regularly on, with the greatest interest and eagerness.

What was Oliver's horror and alarm as he stood a few paces off, looking on with his eyelids as wide open as they would possibly go, to see the Dodger plunge his hand into the old gentleman's pocket, and draw from thence a handkerchief! To see him hand the same to Charley Bates; and finally to behold them, both running away round the corner at full speed!

In an instant the whole mystery of the hankerchiefs, and the watches, and the jewels, and the Jew, rushed upon the boy's mind.

He stood, for a moment, with the blood so tingling through all his veins from terror, that he felt as if he were in a burning fire; then, confused and frightened, he took to his heels; and, not knowing what he did, made off as fast as he could lay his feet to the ground.

This was all done in a minute's space. In the very instant when Oliver began to run, the old gentleman, putting his hand to his pocket, and missing his handkerchief, turned sharp round. Seeing the boy scudding away at such a rapid pace, he very naturally concluded him to be the depredator; and shouting 'Stop thief!' with all his might, made off after him, book in hand.

But the old gentleman was not the only person who raised the hue-and-cry. The Dodger and Master Bates, unwilling to attract public attention by running down the open street, had merely retired into the very first doorway round the corner. They no sooner heard the cry, and saw Oliver running, than, guessing exactly how the matter stood, they issued forth with great promptitude; and, shouting 'Stop thief!' too, joined in the pursuit like good citizens.

Although Oliver had been brought up by philosophers, he was not theoretically acquainted with the beautiful axiom that self-preservation is the first law of nature. If he had been, perhaps he would have been prepared for this. Not being prepared, however, it alarmed him the more; so away he went like the wind, with the old gentleman and the two boys roaring and shouting behind him.

'Stop thief! Stop thief!' There is a magic in the sound. The tradesman leaves his counter, and the car-man his waggon; the butcher throws down his tray; the baker his basket; the milkman his pail; the errand-boy his parcels; the school-boy his marbles; the paviour his pickaxe; the child his battledore. Away they run, pell-mell, helter-skelter, slap-dash: tearing, yelling, screaming, knocking down the passengers as they turn the corners, rousing up the dogs, and astonishing the fowls: and streets, squares, and courts, re-echo with the sound.

'Stop thief! Stop thief!' The cry is taken up by a hundred voices, and the crowd accumulate at every turning. Away they fly, splashing through the mud, and rattling along the pavements: up go the windows, out run the people, onward bear the mob, a whole audience desert Punch in the very thickest of the plot, and, joining the rushing throng, swell the shout, and lend fresh vigour to the cry, 'Stop thief! Stop thief!'

'Stop thief! Stop thief!' There is a passion FOR hunting something deeply implanted in the human breast. One wretched breathless child, panting with exhaustion; terror in his looks; agony in his eyes; large drops of perspiration streaming down his face; strains every nerve to make head upon his pursuers; and as they follow on his track, and gain upon him every instant, they hail his decreasing strength with joy. 'Stop thief!' Ay, stop him for God's sake, were it only in mercy!

Stopped at last! A clever blow. He is down upon the pavement; and the crowd eagerly gather round him: each new comer, jostling and struggling with the others to catch a glimpse. 'Stand aside!' 'Give him a little air!' 'Nonsense! he don't deserve it.' 'Where's the gentleman?' 'Here his is, coming down the street.' 'Make room there for the gentleman!' 'Is this the boy, sir!' 'Yes.'

Oliver lay, covered with mud and dust, and bleeding from the mouth, looking wildly round upon the heap of faces that surrounded him, when the old gentleman was officiously dragged and pushed into the circle by the foremost of the pursuers.

'Yes,' said the gentleman, 'I am afraid it is the boy.'

'Afraid!' murmured the crowd. 'That's a good 'un!'

'Poor fellow!' said the gentleman, 'he has hurt himself.'

'I did that, sir,' said a great lubberly fellow, stepping forward; 'and preciously I cut my knuckle agin' his mouth. I stopped him, sir.'

The fellow touched his hat with a grin, expecting something for his pains; but, the old gentleman, eyeing him with an expression of dislike, look anxiously round, as if he contemplated running away himself: which it is very possible he might have attempted to do, and thus have afforded another chase, had not a police officer (who is generally the last person to arrive in such cases) at that moment made his way through the crowd, and seized Oliver by the collar.

'Come, get up,' said the man, roughly.

'It wasn't me indeed, sir. Indeed, indeed, it was two other boys,' said Oliver, clasping his hands passionately, and looking round. 'They are here somewhere.'

'Oh no, they ain't,' said the officer. He meant this to be ironical, but it was true besides; for the Dodger and Charley Bates had filed off down the first convenient court they came to.

'Come, get up!'

'Don't hurt him,' said the old gentleman, compassionately.

'Oh no, I won't hurt him,' replied the officer, tearing his jacket half off his back, in proof thereof. 'Come, I know you; it won't do. Will you stand upon your legs, you young devil?'

Oliver, who could hardly stand, made a shift to raise himself on his feet, and was at once lugged along the streets by the jacket-collar, at a rapid pace. The gentleman walked on with them by the officer's side; and as many of the crowd as could achieve the feat, got a little ahead, and stared back at Oliver from time to time. The boys shouted in triumph; and on they went.

CHAPTER XI. TREATS OF MR. FANG THE POLICE MAGISTRATE; AND FURNISHES A SLIGHT SPECIMEN OF HIS MODE OF ADMINISTERING JUSTICE

The offence had been committed within the district, and indeed in the immediate neighborhood of, a very notorious metropolitan police office. The crowd had only the satisfaction of accompanying Oliver through two or three streets, and down a place called Mutton Hill, when he was led beneath a low archway, and up a dirty court, into this dispensary of summary justice, by the back way. It was a small paved yard into which they turned; and here they encountered a stout man with a bunch of whiskers on his face, and a bunch of keys in his hand.

'What's the matter now?' said the man carelessly.

'A young fogle-hunter,' replied the man who had Oliver in charge.

'Are you the party that's been robbed, sir?' inquired the man with the keys.

'Yes, I am,' replied the old gentleman; 'but I am not sure that this boy actually took the handkerchief. I—I would rather not press the case.'

'Must go before the magistrate now, sir,' replied the man. 'His worship will be disengaged in half a minute. Now, young gallows!'

This was an invitation for Oliver to enter through a door which he unlocked as he spoke, and which led into a stone cell. Here he was searched; and nothing being found upon him, locked up.

This cell was in shape and size something like an area cellar, only not so light. It was most intolerably dirty; for it was Monday morning; and it had been tenanted by six drunken people, who had been locked up, elsewhere, since Saturday night. But this is little. In our station-houses, men and women are every night confined on the most trivial charges—the word is worth noting—in dungeons, compared with which, those in Newgate, occupied by the most atrocious felons, tried, found guilty, and under sentence of death, are palaces. Let any one who doubts this, compare the two.

The old gentleman looked almost as rueful as Oliver when the key grated in the lock. He turned with a sigh to the book, which had been the innocent cause of all this disturbance.

'There is something in that boy's face,' said the old gentleman to himself as he walked slowly away, tapping his chin with the cover of the book, in a thoughtful manner; 'something that touches and interests me. Can he be innocent? He looked like—Bye the bye,' exclaimed the old gentleman, halting very abruptly, and staring up into the sky, 'Bless my soul!—where have I seen something like that look before?'

After musing for some minutes, the old gentleman walked, with the same meditative face, into a back anteroom opening from the yard; and there, retiring into a corner, called up before his mind's eye a vast amphitheatre of faces over which a dusky curtain had hung for many years. 'No,' said the old gentleman, shaking his head; 'it must be imagination.'

He wandered over them again. He had called them into view, and it was not easy to replace the shroud that had so long concealed them. There were the faces of friends, and foes, and of many that had been almost strangers peering intrusively from the crowd; there were the faces of young and blooming girls that were now old women; there were faces that the grave had changed and closed upon, but which the mind, superior to its power, still dressed in their old freshness and beauty, calling back the lustre of the eyes, the brightness of the smile, the beaming of the soul through its mask of clay, and whispering of beauty beyond the tomb, changed but to be heightened, and taken from earth only to be set up as a light, to shed a soft and gentle glow upon the path to Heaven.

But the old gentleman could recall no one countenance of which Oliver's features bore a trace. So, he heaved a sigh over the recollections he awakened; and being, happily for himself, an absent old gentleman, buried them again in the pages of the musty book.

He was roused by a touch on the shoulder, and a request from the man with the keys to follow him into the office. He closed his book hastily; and was at once ushered into the imposing presence of the renowned Mr. Fang.

The office was a front parlour, with a panelled wall. Mr. Fang sat behind a bar, at the upper end; and on one side the door was a sort of wooden pen in which poor little Oliver was already deposited; trembling very much at the awfulness of the scene.

Mr. Fang was a lean, long-backed, stiff-necked, middle-sized man, with no great quantity of hair, and what he had, growing on the back and sides of his head. His face was stern, and much flushed. If he were really not in the habit of drinking rather more than was exactly good for him, he might have brought action against his countenance for libel, and have recovered heavy damages.

The old gentleman bowed respectfully; and advancing to the magistrate's desk, said, suiting the action to the word, 'That is my name and address, sir.' He then withdrew a pace or two; and, with another polite and gentlemanly inclination of the head, waited to be questioned.

Now, it so happened that Mr. Fang was at that moment perusing a leading article in a newspaper of the morning, adverting to some recent decision of his, and commending him, for the three hundred and fiftieth time, to the special and particular notice of the Secretary of State for the Home Department. He was out of temper; and he looked up with an angry scowl.

'Who are you?' said Mr. Fang.

The old gentleman pointed, with some surprise, to his card.

'Officer!' said Mr. Fang, tossing the card contemptuously away with the newspaper. 'Who is this fellow?'

'My name, sir,' said the old gentleman, speaking like a gentleman, 'my name, sir, is Brownlow. Permit me to inquire the name of the magistrate who offers a gratuitous and unprovoked insult to a respectable person, under the protection of the bench.' Saying this, Mr. Brownlow looked around the office as if in search of some person who would afford him the required information.

'Officer!' said Mr. Fang, throwing the paper on one side, 'what's this fellow charged with?'

'He's not charged at all, your worship,' replied the officer. 'He appears against this boy, your worship.'

His worship knew this perfectly well; but it was a good annoyance, and a safe one.

'Appears against the boy, does he?' said Mr. Fang, surveying Mr. Brownlow contemptuously from head to foot. 'Swear him!'

'Before I am sworn, I must beg to say one word,' said Mr. Brownlow; 'and that is, that I really never, without actual experience, could have believed—'

'Hold your tongue, sir!' said Mr. Fang, peremptorily.

'I will not, sir!' replied the old gentleman.

'Hold your tongue this instant, or I'll have you turned out of the office!' said Mr. Fang. 'You're an insolent impertinent fellow. How dare you bully a magistrate!'

'What!' exclaimed the old gentleman, reddening.

'Swear this person!' said Fang to the clerk. 'I'll not hear another word. Swear him.'

Mr. Brownlow's indignation was greatly roused; but reflecting perhaps, that he might only injure the boy by giving vent to it, he suppressed his feelings and submitted to be sworn at once.

'Now,' said Fang, 'what's the charge against this boy? What have you got to say, sir?'

'I was standing at a bookstall—' Mr. Brownlow began.

'Hold your tongue, sir,' said Mr. Fang. 'Policeman! Where's the policeman? Here, swear this policeman. Now, policeman, what is this?'

The policeman, with becoming humility, related how he had taken the charge; how he had searched Oliver, and found nothing on his person; and how that was all he knew about it.

'Are there any witnesses?' inquired Mr. Fang.

'None, your worship,' replied the policeman.

Mr. Fang sat silent for some minutes, and then, turning round to the prosecutor, said in a towering passion.

'Do you mean to state what your complaint against this boy is, man, or do you not? You have been sworn. Now, if you stand there, refusing to give evidence, I'll punish you for disrespect to the bench; I will, by—'

By what, or by whom, nobody knows, for the clerk and jailor coughed very loud, just at the right moment; and the former dropped a heavy book upon the floor, thus preventing the word from being heard—accidently, of course.

With many interruptions, and repeated insults, Mr. Brownlow contrived to state his case; observing that, in the surprise of the moment, he had run after the boy because he had saw him running away; and expressing his hope that, if the magistrate should believe him, although not actually the thief, to be connected with the thieves, he would deal as leniently with him as justice would allow.

'He has been hurt already,' said the old gentleman in conclusion. 'And I fear,' he added, with great energy, looking towards the bar, 'I really fear that he is ill.'

'Oh! yes, I dare say!' said Mr. Fang, with a sneer. 'Come, none of your tricks here, you young vagabond; they won't do. What's your name?'

Oliver tried to reply but his tongue failed him. He was deadly pale; and the whole place seemed turning round and round.

'What's your name, you hardened scoundrel?' demanded Mr. Fang. 'Officer, what's his name?'

This was addressed to a bluff old fellow, in a striped waistcoat, who was standing by the bar. He bent over Oliver, and repeated the inquiry; but finding him really incapable of understanding the question; and knowing that his not replying would only infuriate the magistrate the more, and add to the severity of his sentence; he hazarded a guess.

'He says his name's Tom White, your worship,' said the kind-hearted thief-taker.

'Oh, he won't speak out, won't he?' said Fang. 'Very well, very well. Where does he live?'

'Where he can, your worship,' replied the officer; again pretending to receive Oliver's answer.

'Has he any parents?' inquired Mr. Fang.

'He says they died in his infancy, your worship,' replied the officer: hazarding the usual reply.

At this point of the inquiry, Oliver raised his head; and, looking round with imploring eyes, murmured a feeble prayer for a draught of water.

'Stuff and nonsense!' said Mr. Fang: 'don't try to make a fool of me.'

'I think he really is ill, your worship,' remonstrated the officer.

'I know better,' said Mr. Fang.

'Take care of him, officer,' said the old gentleman, raising his hands instinctively; 'he'll fall down.'

'Stand away, officer,' cried Fang; 'let him, if he likes.'

Oliver availed himself of the kind permission, and fell to the floor in a fainting fit. The men in the office looked at each other, but no one dared to stir.

'I knew he was shamming,' said Fang, as if this were incontestable proof of the fact. 'Let him lie there; he'll soon be tired of that.'

'How do you propose to deal with the case, sir?' inquired the clerk in a low voice.

'Summarily,' replied Mr. Fang. 'He stands committed for three months—hard labour of course. Clear the office.'

The door was opened for this purpose, and a couple of men were preparing to carry the insensible boy to his cell; when an elderly man of decent but poor appearance, clad in an old suit of black, rushed hastily into the office, and advanced towards the bench.

'Stop, stop! don't take him away! For Heaven's sake stop a moment!' cried the new comer, breathless with haste.

Although the presiding Genii in such an office as this, exercise a summary and arbitrary power over the liberties, the good name, the character, almost the lives, of Her Majesty's subjects, especially of the poorer class; and although, within such walls, enough fantastic tricks are daily played to make the angels blind with weeping; they are closed to the public, save through the medium of the daily press.[Footnote: Or were virtually, then.] Mr. Fang was consequently not a little indignant to see an unbidden guest enter in such irreverent disorder.

'What is this? Who is this? Turn this man out. Clear the office!' cried Mr. Fang.

'I will speak,' cried the man; 'I will not be turned out. I saw it all. I keep the book-stall. I demand to be sworn. I will not be put down. Mr. Fang, you must hear me. You must not refuse, sir.'

The man was right. His manner was determined; and the matter was growing rather too serious to be hushed up.

'Swear the man,' growled Mr. Fang, with a very ill grace. 'Now, man, what have you got to say?'

'This,' said the man: 'I saw three boys: two others and the prisoner here: loitering on the opposite side of the way, when this gentleman was reading. The robbery was committed by another boy. I saw it done; and I saw that this boy was perfectly amazed and stupified by it.' Having by this time recovered a little breath, the worthy book-stall keeper proceeded to relate, in a more coherent manner the exact circumstances of the robbery.

'Why didn't you come here before?' said Fang, after a pause.

'I hadn't a soul to mind the shop,' replied the man. 'Everybody who could have helped me, had joined in the pursuit. I could get nobody till five minutes ago; and I've run here all the way.'

'The prosecutor was reading, was he?' inquired Fang, after another pause.

'Yes,' replied the man. 'The very book he has in his hand.'

'Oh, that book, eh?' said Fang. 'Is it paid for?'

'No, it is not,' replied the man, with a smile.

'Dear me, I forgot all about it!' exclaimed the absent old gentleman, innocently.

'A nice person to prefer a charge against a poor boy!' said Fang, with a comical effort to look humane. 'I consider, sir, that you have obtained possession of that book, under very suspicious and disreputable circumstances; and you may think yourself very fortunate that the owner of the property declines to prosecute. Let this be a lesson to you, my man, or the law will overtake you yet. The boy is discharged. Clear the office!'

'D—n me!' cried the old gentleman, bursting out with the rage he had kept down so long, 'd—n me! I'll—'

'Clear the office!' said the magistrate. 'Officers, do you hear? Clear the office!'

The mandate was obeyed; and the indignant Mr. Brownlow was conveyed out, with the book in one hand, and the bamboo cane in the other: in a perfect phrenzy of rage and defiance. He reached the yard; and his passion vanished in a moment. Little Oliver Twist lay on his back on the pavement, with his shirt unbuttoned, and his temples bathed with water; his face a deadly white; and a cold tremble convulsing his whole frame.

'Poor boy, poor boy!' said Mr. Brownlow, bending over him. 'Call a coach, somebody, pray. Directly!'

A coach was obtained, and Oliver having been carefully laid on the seat, the old gentleman got in and sat himself on the other.

'May I accompany you?' said the book-stall keeper, looking in.

'Bless me, yes, my dear sir,' said Mr. Brownlow quickly. 'I forgot you. Dear, dear! I have this unhappy book still! Jump in. Poor fellow! There's no time to lose.'

The book-stall keeper got into the coach; and away they drove.

CHAPTER XII. IN WHICH OLIVER IS TAKEN BETTER CARE OF THAN HE EVER WAS BEFORE. AND IN WHICH THE NARRATIVE REVERTS TO THE MERRY OLD GENTLEMAN AND HIS YOUTHFUL FRIENDS.

The coach rattled away, over nearly the same ground as that which Oliver had traversed when he first entered London in company with the Dodger; and, turning a different way when it reached the Angel at Islington, stopped at length before a neat house, in a quiet shady street near Pentonville. Here, a bed was prepared, without loss of time, in which Mr. Brownlow saw his young charge carefully and comfortably deposited; and here, he was tended with a kindness and solicitude that knew no bounds.

But, for many days, Oliver remained insensible to all the goodness of his new friends. The sun rose and sank, and rose and sank again, and many times after that; and still the boy lay stretched on his uneasy bed, dwindling away beneath the dry and wasting heat of fever. The worm does not work more surely on the dead body, than does this slow creeping fire upon the living frame.

Weak, and thin, and pallid, he awoke at last from what seemed to have been a long and troubled dream. Feebly raising himself in the bed, with his head resting on his trembling arm, he looked anxiously around.

'What room is this? Where have I been brought to?' said Oliver. 'This is not the place I went to sleep in.'

He uttered these words in a feeble voice, being very faint and weak; but they were overheard at once. The curtain at the bed's head was hastily drawn back, and a motherly old lady, very neatly and precisely dressed, rose as she undrew it, from an arm-chair close by, in which she had been sitting at needle-work.

'Hush, my dear,' said the old lady softly. 'You must be very quiet, or you will be ill again; and you have been very bad,—as bad as bad could be, pretty nigh. Lie down again; there's a dear!' With those words, the old lady very gently placed Oliver's head upon the pillow; and, smoothing back his hair from his forehead, looked so kindly and loving in his face, that he could not help placing his little withered hand in hers, and drawing it round his neck.

'Save us!' said the old lady, with tears in her eyes. 'What a grateful little dear it is. Pretty creetur! What would his mother feel if she had sat by him as I have, and could see him now!'

'Perhaps she does see me,' whispered Oliver, folding his hands together; 'perhaps she has sat by me. I almost feel as if she had.'

'That was the fever, my dear,' said the old lady mildly.

'I suppose it was,' replied Oliver, 'because heaven is a long way off; and they are too happy there, to come down to the bedside of a poor boy. But if she knew I was ill, she must have pitied me, even there; for she was very ill herself before she died. She can't know anything about me though,' added Oliver after a moment's silence. 'If she had seen me hurt, it would have made her sorrowful; and her face has always looked sweet and happy, when I have dreamed of her.'

The old lady made no reply to this; but wiping her eyes first, and her spectacles, which lay on the counterpane, afterwards, as if they were part and parcel of those features, brought

640

some cool stuff for Oliver to drink; and then, patting him on the cheek, told him he must lie very quiet, or he would be ill again.

So, Oliver kept very still; partly because he was anxious to obey the kind old lady in all things; and partly, to tell the truth, because he was completely exhausted with what he had already said. He soon fell into a gentle doze, from which he was awakened by the light of a candle: which, being brought near the bed, showed him a gentleman with a very large and loud-ticking gold watch in his hand, who felt his pulse, and said he was a great deal better.

'You are a great deal better, are you not, my dear?' said the gentleman.

'Yes, thank you, sir,' replied Oliver.

'Yes, I know you are,' said the gentleman: 'You're hungry too, an't you?'

'No, sir,' answered Oliver.

'Hem!' said the gentleman. 'No, I know you're not. He is not hungry, Mrs. Bedwin,' said the gentleman: looking very wise.

The old lady made a respectful inclination of the head, which seemed to say that she thought the doctor was a very clever man. The doctor appeared much of the same opinion himself.

'You feel sleepy, don't you, my dear?' said the doctor.

'No, sir,' replied Oliver.

'No,' said the doctor, with a very shrewd and satisfied look. 'You're not sleepy. Nor thirsty. Are you?'

'Yes, sir, rather thirsty,' answered Oliver.

'Just as I expected, Mrs. Bedwin,' said the doctor. 'It's very natural that he should be thirsty. You may give him a little tea, ma'am, and some dry toast without any butter. Don't keep him too warm, ma'am; but be careful that you don't let him be too cold; will you have the goodness?'

The old lady dropped a curtsey. The doctor, after tasting the cool stuff, and expressing a qualified approval of it, hurried away: his boots creaking in a very important and wealthy manner as he went downstairs.

Oliver dozed off again, soon after this; when he awoke, it was nearly twelve o'clock. The old lady tenderly bade him good-night shortly afterwards, and left him in charge of a fat old woman who had just come: bringing with her, in a little bundle, a small Prayer Book and a large nightcap. Putting the latter on her head and the former on the table, the old woman, after telling Oliver that she had come to sit up with him, drew her chair close to the fire and went off into a series of short naps, chequered at frequent intervals with sundry tumblings forward, and divers moans and chokings. These, however, had no worse effect than causing her to rub her nose very hard, and then fall asleep again.

And thus the night crept slowly on. Oliver lay awake for some time, counting the little circles of light which the reflection of the rushlight-shade threw upon the ceiling; or tracing with his languid eyes the intricate pattern of the paper on the wall. The darkness and the deep stillness of the room were very solemn; as they brought into the boy's mind the thought that death had been hovering there, for many days and nights, and might yet fill it with the gloom and dread of his awful presence, he turned his face upon the pillow, and fervently prayed to Heaven.

Gradually, he fell into that deep tranquil sleep which ease from recent suffering alone imparts; that calm and peaceful rest which it is pain to wake from. Who, if this were death, would be roused again to all the struggles and turmoils of life; to all its cares for the present; its anxieties for the future; more than all, its weary recollections of the past!

It had been bright day, for hours, when Oliver opened his eyes; he felt cheerful and happy. The crisis of the disease was safely past. He belonged to the world again.

In three days' time he was able to sit in an easy-chair, well propped up with pillows; and, as he was still too weak to walk, Mrs. Bedwin had him carried downstairs into the little housekeeper's room, which belonged to her. Having him set, here, by the fire-side, the good old lady sat herself down too; and, being in a state of considerable delight at seeing him so much better, forthwith began to cry most violently.

'Never mind me, my dear,' said the old lady; 'I'm only having a regular good cry. There; it's all over now; and I'm quite comfortable.'

'You're very, very kind to me, ma'am,' said Oliver.

'Well, never you mind that, my dear,' said the old lady; 'that's got nothing to do with your broth; and it's full time you had it; for the doctor says Mr. Brownlow may come in to see you this morning; and we must get up our best looks, because the better we look, the more he'll be pleased.' And with this, the old lady applied herself to warming up, in a little saucepan, a basin full of broth: strong enough, Oliver thought, to furnish an ample dinner, when reduced to the regulation strength, for three hundred and fifty paupers, at the lowest computation.

'Are you fond of pictures, dear?' inquired the old lady, seeing that Oliver had fixed his eyes, most intently, on a portrait which hung against the wall; just opposite his chair.

'I don't quite know, ma'am,' said Oliver, without taking his eyes from the canvas; 'I have seen so few that I hardly know. What a beautiful, mild face that lady's is!'

'Ah!' said the old lady, 'painters always make ladies out prettier than they are, or they wouldn't get any custom, child. The man that invented the machine for taking likenesses might have known that would never succeed; it's a deal too honest. A deal,' said the old lady, laughing very heartily at her own acuteness.

'Is—is that a likeness, ma'am?' said Oliver.

'Yes,' said the old lady, looking up for a moment from the broth; 'that's a portrait.'

'Whose, ma'am?' asked Oliver.

'Why, really, my dear, I don't know,' answered the old lady in a good-humoured manner. 'It's not a likeness of anybody that you or I know, I expect. It seems to strike your fancy, dear.'

'It is so pretty,' replied Oliver.

'Why, sure you're not afraid of it?' said the old lady: observing in great surprise, the look of awe with which the child regarded the painting.

'Oh no, no,' returned Oliver quickly; 'but the eyes look so sorrowful; and where I sit, they seem fixed upon me. It makes my heart beat,' added Oliver in a low voice, 'as if it was alive, and wanted to speak to me, but couldn't.'

'Lord save us!' exclaimed the old lady, starting; 'don't talk in that way, child. You're weak and nervous after your illness. Let me wheel your chair round to the other side; and then you won't see it. There!' said the old lady, suiting the action to the word; 'you don't see it now, at all events.'

Oliver did see it in his mind's eye as distinctly as if he had not altered his position; but he thought it better not to worry the kind old lady; so he smiled gently when she looked at him; and Mrs. Bedwin, satisfied that he felt more comfortable, salted and broke bits of toasted bread into the broth, with all the bustle befitting so solemn a preparation. Oliver got through it with extraordinary expedition. He had scarcely swallowed the last spoonful, when there came a soft rap at the door. 'Come in,' said the old lady; and in walked Mr. Brownlow.

Now, the old gentleman came in as brisk as need be; but, he had no sooner raised his spectacles on his forehead, and thrust his hands behind the skirts of his dressing-gown to take a good long look at Oliver, than his countenance underwent a very great variety of odd contortions. Oliver looked very worn and shadowy from sickness, and made an ineffectual attempt to stand up, out of respect to his benefactor, which terminated in his sinking back into the chair again; and the fact is, if the truth must be told, that Mr. Brownlow's heart, being large enough for any six ordinary old gentlemen of humane disposition, forced a supply of tears into his eyes, by some hydraulic process which we are not sufficiently philosophical to be in a condition to explain.

'Poor boy, poor boy!' said Mr. Brownlow, clearing his throat. 'I'm rather hoarse this morning, Mrs. Bedwin. I'm afraid I have caught cold.'

'I hope not, sir,' said Mrs. Bedwin. 'Everything you have had, has been well aired, sir.'

'I don't know, Bedwin. I don't know,' said Mr. Brownlow; 'I rather think I had a damp napkin at dinner-time yesterday; but never mind that. How do you feel, my dear?'

'Very happy, sir,' replied Oliver. 'And very grateful indeed, sir, for your goodness to me.'

'Good by,' said Mr. Brownlow, stoutly. 'Have you given him any nourishment, Bedwin? Any slops, eh?'

'He has just had a basin of beautiful strong broth, sir,' replied Mrs. Bedwin: drawing herself up slightly, and laying strong emphasis on the last word: to intimate that between slops, and broth will compounded, there existed no affinity or connection whatsoever.

'Ugh!' said Mr. Brownlow, with a slight shudder; 'a couple of glasses of port wine would have done him a great deal more good. Wouldn't they, Tom White, eh?'

'My name is Oliver, sir,' replied the little invalid: with a look of great astonishment.

'Oliver,' said Mr. Brownlow; 'Oliver what? Oliver White, eh?'

'No, sir, Twist, Oliver Twist.'

'Queer name!' said the old gentleman. 'What made you tell the magistrate your name was White?'

'I never told him so, sir,' returned Oliver in amazement.

This sounded so like a falsehood, that the old gentleman looked somewhat sternly in

Oliver's face. It was impossible to doubt him; there was truth in every one of its thin and sharpened lineaments.

'Some mistake,' said Mr. Brownlow. But, although his motive for looking steadily at Oliver no longer existed, the old idea of the resemblance between his features and some familiar face came upon him so strongly, that he could not withdraw his gaze.

'I hope you are not angry with me, sir?' said Oliver, raising his eyes beseechingly.

'No, no,' replied the old gentleman. 'Why! what's this? Bedwin, look there!'

As he spoke, he pointed hastily to the picture over Oliver's head, and then to the boy's face. There was its living copy. The eyes, the head, the mouth; every feature was the same. The expression was, for the instant, so precisely alike, that the minutest line seemed copied with startling accuracy!

Oliver knew not the cause of this sudden exclamation; for, not being strong enough to bear the start it gave him, he fainted away. A weakness on his part, which affords the narrative an opportunity of relieving the reader from suspense, in behalf of the two young pupils of the Merry Old Gentleman; and of recording—

That when the Dodger, and his accomplished friend Master Bates, joined in the hue-and-cry which was raised at Oliver's heels, in consequence of their executing an illegal conveyance of Mr. Brownlow's personal property, as has been already described, they were actuated by a very laudable and becoming regard for themselves; and forasmuch as the freedom of the subject and the liberty of the individual are among the first and proudest boasts of a true-hearted Englishman, so, I need hardly beg the reader to observe, that this action should tend to exalt them in the opinion of all public and patriotic men, in almost as great a degree as this strong proof of their anxiety for their own preservation and safety goes to corroborate and confirm the little code of laws which certain profound and sound-judging philosophers have laid down as the main-springs of all Nature's deeds and actions: the said philosophers very wisely reducing the good lady's proceedings to matters of maxim and theory: and, by a very neat and pretty compliment to her exalted wisdom and understanding, putting entirely out of sight any considerations of heart, or generous impulse and feeling. For, these are matters totally beneath a female who is acknowledged by universal admission to be far above the numerous little foibles and weaknesses of her sex.

If I wanted any further proof of the strictly philosophical nature of the conduct of these young gentlemen in their very delicate predicament, I should at once find it in the fact (also recorded in a foregoing part of this narrative), of their quitting the pursuit, when the general attention was fixed upon Oliver; and making immediately for their home by the shortest possible cut. Although I do not mean to assert that it is usually the practice of renowned and learned sages, to shorten the road to any great conclusion (their course indeed being rather to lengthen the distance, by various circumlocutions and discursive staggerings, like unto those in which drunken men under the pressure of a too mighty flow of ideas, are prone to indulge); still, I do mean to say, and do say distinctly, that it is the invariable practice of many mighty philosophers, in carrying out their theories, to evince great wisdom and foresight in providing against every possible contingency which can be supposed at all likely to affect themselves. Thus, to do a great right, you may do a little wrong; and you may take any means which the end to be attained, will justify; the amount of the right, or the amount of the wrong, or indeed the distinction between the two, being left entirely to the philosopher concerned, to be settled and determined by his clear, comprehensive, and impartial view of his own particular case.

It was not until the two boys had scoured, with great rapidity, through a most intricate maze of narrow streets and courts, that they ventured to halt beneath a low and dark archway. Having remained silent here, just long enough to recover breath to speak, Master Bates uttered an exclamation of amusement and delight; and, bursting into an uncontrollable fit of laughter, flung himself upon a doorstep, and rolled thereon in a transport of mirth.

'What's the matter?' inquired the Dodger.

'Ha! ha! ha!' roared Charley Bates.

'Hold your noise,' remonstrated the Dodger, looking cautiously round. 'Do you want to be grabbed, stupid?'

'I can't help it,' said Charley, 'I can't help it! To see him splitting away at that pace, and cutting round the corners, and knocking up again' the posts, and starting on again as if he was made of iron as well as them, and me with the wipe in my pocket, singing out arter him—oh, my eye!' The vivid imagination of Master Bates presented the scene before him in too strong colours. As he arrived at this apostrophe, he again rolled upon the door-step, and laughed louder than before.

'What'll Fagin say?' inquired the Dodger; taking advantage of the next interval of breathlessness on the part of his friend to propound the question.

'What?' repeated Charley Bates.

'Ah, what?' said the Dodger.

'Why, what should he say?' inquired Charley: stopping rather suddenly in his merriment; for the Dodger's manner was impressive. 'What should he say?'

Mr. Dawkins whistled for a couple of minutes; then, taking off his hat, scratched his head, and nodded thrice.

'What do you mean?' said Charley.

'Toor rul lol loo, gammon and spinnage, the frog he wouldn't, and high cockolorum,' said the Dodger: with a slight sneer on his intellectual countenance.

This was explanatory, but not satisfactory. Master Bates felt it so; and again said, 'What do you mean?'

The Dodger made no reply; but putting his hat on again, and gathering the skirts of his long-tailed coat under his arm, thrust his tongue into his cheek, slapped the bridge of his nose some half-dozen times in a familiar but expressive manner, and turning on his heel, slunk down the court. Master Bates followed, with a thoughtful countenance.

The noise of footsteps on the creaking stairs, a few minutes after the occurrence of this conversation, roused the merry old gentleman as he sat over the fire with a saveloy and a small loaf in his hand; a pocket-knife in his right; and a pewter pot on the trivet. There was a rascally smile on his white face as he turned round, and looking sharply out from under his thick red eyebrows, bent his ear towards the door, and listened.

'Why, how's this?' muttered the Jew: changing countenance; 'only two of 'em? Where's the third? They can't have got into trouble. Hark!'

The footsteps approached nearer; they reached the landing. The door was slowly opened; and the Dodger and Charley Bates entered, closing it behind them.

CHAPTER XIII. SOME NEW ACQUAINTANCES ARE INTRODUCED TO THE INTELLIGENT READER, CONNECTED WITH WHOM VARIOUS PLEASANT MATTERS ARE RELATED, APPERTAINING TO THIS HISTORY

'Where's Oliver?' said the Jew, rising with a menacing look. 'Where's the boy?'

The young thieves eyed their preceptor as if they were alarmed at his violence; and looked uneasily at each other. But they made no reply.

'What's become of the boy?' said the Jew, seizing the Dodger tightly by the collar, and threatening him with horrid imprecations. 'Speak out, or I'll throttle you!'

Mr. Fagin looked so very much in earnest, that Charley Bates, who deemed it prudent in all cases to be on the safe side, and who conceived it by no means improbable that it might be his turn to be throttled second, dropped upon his knees, and raised a loud, well-sustained, and continuous roar—something between a mad bull and a speaking trumpet.

'Will you speak?' thundered the Jew: shaking the Dodger so much that his keeping in the big coat at all, seemed perfectly miraculous.

'Why, the traps have got him, and that's all about it,' said the Dodger, sullenly. 'Come, let go o' me, will you!' And, swinging himself, at one jerk, clean out of the big coat, which he left in the Jew's hands, the Dodger snatched up the toasting fork, and made a pass at the merry old gentleman's waistcoat; which, if it had taken effect, would have let a little more merriment out than could have been easily replaced.

The Jew stepped back in this emergency, with more agility than could have been anticipated in a man of his apparent decrepitude; and, seizing up the pot, prepared to hurl it at his assailant's head. But Charley Bates, at this moment, calling his attention by a perfectly terrific howl, he suddenly altered its destination, and flung it full at that young gentleman.

'Why, what the blazes is in the wind now!' growled a deep voice. 'Who pitched that 'ere at me? It's well it's the beer, and not the pot, as hit me, or I'd have settled somebody. I might have know'd, as nobody but an infernal, rich, plundering, thundering old Jew could afford to throw away any drink but water—and not that, unless he done the River Company every quarter. Wot's it all about, Fagin? D—me, if my neck-handkercher an't lined with beer! Come in, you sneaking warmint; wot are you stopping outside for, as if you was ashamed of your master! Come in!'

The man who growled out these words, was a stoutly-built fellow of about five-and-thirty, in a black velveteen coat, very soiled drab breeches, lace-up half boots, and grey cotton stockings which inclosed a bulky pair of legs, with large swelling calves;—the kind of legs, which in such costume, always look in an unfinished and incomplete state without a set of fetters to garnish them. He had a brown hat on his head, and a dirty belcher handkerchief round his neck: with the long frayed ends of which he smeared the beer from his face as he spoke. He disclosed, when he had done so, a broad heavy countenance with a beard of three days' growth, and two scowling eyes; one of which displayed various parti-coloured symptoms of having been recently damaged by a blow.

'Come in, d'ye hear?' growled this engaging ruffian.

A white shaggy dog, with his face scratched and torn in twenty different places, skulked into the room.

'Why didn't you come in afore?' said the man. 'You're getting too proud to own me afore company, are you? Lie down!'

This command was accompanied with a kick, which sent the animal to the other end of the room. He appeared well used to it, however; for he coiled himself up in a corner very quietly, without uttering a sound, and winking his very ill-looking eyes twenty times in a minute, appeared to occupy himself in taking a survey of the apartment.

'What are you up to? Ill-treating the boys, you covetous, avaricious, in-sa-ti-a-ble old fence?' said the man, seating himself deliberately. 'I wonder they don't murder you! I would if I was them. If I'd been your 'prentice, I'd have done it long ago, and—no, I couldn't have sold you afterwards, for you're fit for nothing but keeping as a curiosity of ugliness in a glass bottle, and I suppose they don't blow glass bottles large enough.'

'Hush! hush! Mr. Sikes,' said the Jew, trembling; 'don't speak so loud!'

'None of your mistering,' replied the ruffian; 'you always mean mischief when you come that. You know my name: out with it! I shan't disgrace it when the time comes.'

'Well, well, then—Bill Sikes,' said the Jew, with abject humility. 'You seem out of humour, Bill.'

'Perhaps I am,' replied Sikes; 'I should think you was rather out of sorts too, unless you mean as little harm when you throw pewter pots about, as you do when you blab and—'

'Are you mad?' said the Jew, catching the man by the sleeve, and pointing towards the boys.

Mr. Sikes contented himself with tying an imaginary knot under his left ear, and jerking his head over on the right shoulder; a piece of dumb show which the Jew appeared to understand perfectly. He then, in cant terms, with which his whole conversation was plentifully besprinkled, but which would be quite unintelligible if they were recorded here, demanded a glass of liquor.

'And mind you don't poison it,' said Mr. Sikes, laying his hat upon the table.

This was said in jest; but if the speaker could have seen the evil leer with which the Jew bit his pale lip as he turned round to the cupboard, he might have thought the caution not wholly unnecessary, or the wish (at all events) to improve upon the distiller's ingenuity not very far from the old gentleman's merry heart.

After swallowing two of three glasses of spirits, Mr. Sikes condescended to take some notice of the young gentlemen; which gracious act led to a conversation, in which the cause and manner of Oliver's capture were circumstantially detailed, with such alterations and improvements on the truth, as to the Dodger appeared most advisable under the circumstances.

'I'm afraid,' said the Jew, 'that he may say something which will get us into trouble.'

'That's very likely,' returned Sikes with a malicious grin. 'You're blowed upon, Fagin.'

'And I'm afraid, you see,' added the Jew, speaking as if he had not noticed the interruption; and regarding the other closely as he did so,—'I'm afraid that, if the game was up with us, it might be up with a good many more, and that it would come out rather worse for you than it would for me, my dear.'

The man started, and turned round upon the Jew. But the old gentleman's shoulders were shrugged up to his ears; and his eyes were vacantly staring on the opposite wall.

There was a long pause. Every member of the respectable coterie appeared plunged in his own reflections; not excepting the dog, who by a certain malicious licking of his lips seemed to be meditating an attack upon the legs of the first gentleman or lady he might encounter in the streets when he went out.

'Somebody must find out wot's been done at the office,' said Mr. Sikes in a much lower tone than he had taken since he came in.

The Jew nodded assent.

'If he hasn't peached, and is committed, there's no fear till he comes out again,' said Mr. Sikes, 'and then he must be taken care on. You must get hold of him somehow.'

Again the Jew nodded.

The prudence of this line of action, indeed, was obvious; but, unfortunately, there was one very strong objection to its being adopted. This was, that the Dodger, and Charley Bates, and Fagin, and Mr. William Sikes, happened, one and all, to entertain a violent and deeply-rooted antipathy to going near a police-office on any ground or pretext whatever.

How long they might have sat and looked at each other, in a state of uncertainty not the most pleasant of its kind, it is difficult to guess. It is not necessary to make any guesses on the subject, however; for the sudden entrance of the two young ladies whom Oliver had seen on a former occasion, caused the conversation to flow afresh.

'The very thing!' said the Jew. 'Bet will go; won't you, my dear?'

'Wheres?' inquired the young lady.

'Only just up to the office, my dear,' said the Jew coaxingly.

It is due to the young lady to say that she did not positively affirm that she would not, but that she merely expressed an emphatic and earnest desire to be 'blessed' if she would; a polite and delicate evasion of the request, which shows the young lady to have been possessed of that natural good breeding which cannot bear to inflict upon a fellow-creature, the pain of a direct and pointed refusal.

The Jew's countenance fell. He turned from this young lady, who was gaily, not to say gorgeously attired, in a red gown, green boots, and yellow curl-papers, to the other female.

'Nancy, my dear,' said the Jew in a soothing manner, 'what do YOU say?'

'That it won't do; so it's no use a-trying it on, Fagin,' replied Nancy.

'What do you mean by that?' said Mr. Sikes, looking up in a surly manner.

'What I say, Bill,' replied the lady collectedly.

'Why, you're just the very person for it,' reasoned Mr. Sikes: 'nobody about here knows anything of you.'

'And as I don't want 'em to, neither,' replied Nancy in the same composed manner, 'it's rather more no than yes with me, Bill.'

'She'll go, Fagin,' said Sikes.

'No, she won't, Fagin,' said Nancy.

'Yes, she will, Fagin,' said Sikes.

And Mr. Sikes was right. By dint of alternate threats, promises, and bribes, the lady in question was ultimately prevailed upon to undertake the commission. She was not, indeed, withheld by the same considerations as her agreeable friend; for, having recently removed into the neighborhood of Field Lane from the remote but genteel suburb of Ratcliffe, she was not under the same apprehension of being recognised by any of her numerous acquaintances.

Accordingly, with a clean white apron tied over her gown, and her curl-papers tucked up under a straw bonnet,—both articles of dress being provided from the Jew's inexhaustible stock,—Miss Nancy prepared to issue forth on her errand.

'Stop a minute, my dear,' said the Jew, producing, a little covered basket. 'Carry that in one hand. It looks more respectable, my dear.'

'Give her a door-key to carry in her t'other one, Fagin,' said Sikes; 'it looks real and genivine like.'

'Yes, yes, my dear, so it does,' said the Jew, hanging a large street-door key on the forefinger of the young lady's right hand.

'There; very good! Very good indeed, my dear!' said the Jew, rubbing his hands.

'Oh, my brother! My poor, dear, sweet, innocent little brother!' exclaimed Nancy, bursting into tears, and wringing the little basket and the street-door key in an agony of distress. 'What has become of him! Where have they taken him to! Oh, do have pity, and tell me what's been done with the dear boy, gentlemen; do, gentlemen, if you please, gentlemen!'

Having uttered those words in a most lamentable and heart-broken tone: to the immeasurable delight of her hearers: Miss Nancy paused, winked to the company, nodded smilingly round, and disappeared.

'Ah, she's a clever girl, my dears,' said the Jew, turning round to his young friends, and shaking his head gravely, as if in mute admonition to them to follow the bright example they had just beheld.

'She's a honour to her sex,' said Mr. Sikes, filling his glass, and smiting the table with his enormous fist. 'Here's her health, and wishing they was all like her!'

While these, and many other encomiums, were being passed on the accomplished Nancy, that young lady made the best of her way to the police-office; whither, notwithstanding a little natural timidity consequent upon walking through the streets alone and unprotected, she arrived in perfect safety shortly afterwards.

Entering by the back way, she tapped softly with the key at one of the cell-doors, and listened. There was no sound within: so she coughed and listened again. Still there was no reply: so she spoke.

'Nolly, dear?' murmured Nancy in a gentle voice; 'Nolly?'

There was nobody inside but a miserable shoeless criminal, who had been taken up for playing the flute, and who, the offence against society having been clearly proved, had been very properly committed by Mr. Fang to the House of Correction for one month; with the appropriate and amusing remark that since he had so much breath to spare, it would be more wholesomely expended on the treadmill than in a musical instrument. He made no answer: being occupied mentally bewailing the loss of the flute, which had been confiscated for the use of the county: so Nancy passed on to the next cell, and knocked there.

'Well!' cried a faint and feeble voice.

'Is there a little boy here?' inquired Nancy, with a preliminary sob.

'No,' replied the voice; 'God forbid.'

This was a vagrant of sixty-five, who was going to prison for not playing the flute; or, in other words, for begging in the streets, and doing nothing for his livelihood. In the next cell was another man, who was going to the same prison for hawking tin saucepans without license; thereby doing something for his living, in defiance of the Stamp-office.

But, as neither of these criminals answered to the name of Oliver, or knew anything about him, Nancy made straight up to the bluff officer in the striped waistcoat; and with the most piteous wailings and lamentations, rendered more piteous by a prompt and efficient use of the street-door key and the little basket, demanded her own dear brother.

'I haven't got him, my dear,' said the old man.

'Where is he?' screamed Nancy, in a distracted manner.

'Why, the gentleman's got him,' replied the officer.

'What gentleman! Oh, gracious heavens! What gentleman?' exclaimed Nancy.

In reply to this incoherent questioning, the old man informed the deeply affected sister that Oliver had been taken ill in the office, and discharged in consequence of a witness having proved the robbery to have been committed by another boy, not in custody; and that the prosecutor had carried him away, in an insensible condition, to his own residence: of and concerning which, all the informant knew was, that it was somewhere in Pentonville, he having heard that word mentioned in the directions to the coachman.

In a dreadful state of doubt and uncertainty, the agonised young woman staggered to the gate, and then, exchanging her faltering walk for a swift run, returned by the most devious and complicated route she could think of, to the domicile of the Jew.

Mr. Bill Sikes no sooner heard the account of the expedition delivered, than he very hastily called up the white dog, and, putting on his hat, expeditiously departed: without devoting any time to the formality of wishing the company good-morning.

'We must know where he is, my dears; he must be found,' said the Jew greatly excited. 'Charley, do nothing but skulk about, till you bring home some news of him! Nancy, my dear, I must have him found. I trust to you, my dear,—to you and the Artful for everything! Stay, stay,' added the Jew, unlocking a drawer with a shaking hand; 'there's money, my dears. I shall shut up this shop to-night. You'll know where to find me! Don't stop here a minute. Not an instant, my dears!'

With these words, he pushed them from the room: and carefully double-locking and barring the door behind them, drew from its place of concealment the box which he had unintentionally disclosed to Oliver. Then, he hastily proceeded to dispose the watches and jewellery beneath his clothing.

A rap at the door startled him in this occupation. 'Who's there?' he cried in a shrill tone.

'Me!' replied the voice of the Dodger, through the key-hole.

'What now?' cried the Jew impatiently.

'Is he to be kidnapped to the other ken, Nancy says?' inquired the Dodger.

'Yes,' replied the Jew, 'wherever she lays hands on him. Find him, find him out, that's all. I shall know what to do next; never fear.'

The boy murmured a reply of intelligence: and hurried downstairs after his companions.

'He has not peached so far,' said the Jew as he pursued his occupation. 'If he means to blab us among his new friends, we may stop his mouth yet.'

CHAPTER XIV. COMPRISING FURTHER PARTICULARS OF OLIVER'S STAY AT MR. BROWNLOW'S, WITH THE REMARKABLE PREDICTION WHICH ONE MR. GRIMWIG UTTERED CONCERNING HIM, WHEN HE WENT OUT ON AN ERRAND

Oliver soon recovering from the fainting-fit into which Mr. Brownlow's abrupt exclamation had thrown him, the subject of the picture was carefully avoided, both by the old gentleman and Mrs. Bedwin, in the conversation that ensued: which indeed bore no reference to Oliver's history or prospects, but was confined to such topics as might amuse without exciting him. He was still too weak to get up to breakfast; but, when he came down into the housekeeper's room next day, his first act was to cast an eager glance at the wall, in the hope of again looking on the face of the beautiful lady. His expectations were disappointed, however, for the picture had been removed.

'Ah!' said the housekeeper, watching the direction of Oliver's eyes. 'It is gone, you see.'

'I see it is ma'am,' replied Oliver. 'Why have they taken it away?'

'It has been taken down, child, because Mr. Brownlow said, that as it seemed to worry you, perhaps it might prevent your getting well, you know,' rejoined the old lady.

'Oh, no, indeed. It didn't worry me, ma'am,' said Oliver. 'I liked to see it. I quite loved it.'

'Well, well!' said the old lady, good-humouredly; 'you get well as fast as ever you can, dear, and it shall be hung up again. There! I promise you that! Now, let us talk about something else.'

This was all the information Oliver could obtain about the picture at that time. As the old lady had been so kind to him in his illness, he endeavoured to think no more of the subject just then; so he listened attentively to a great many stories she told him, about an amiable and handsome daughter of hers, who was married to an amiable and handsome man, and lived in the country; and about a son, who was clerk to a merchant in the West Indies; and who was, also, such a good young man, and wrote such dutiful letters home four times a-year, that it brought the tears into her eyes to talk about them. When the old lady had expatiated, a long time, on the excellences of her children, and the merits of her kind good husband besides, who had been dead and gone, poor dear soul! just six-and-twenty years, it was time to have tea. After tea she began to teach Oliver cribbage: which he learnt as quickly as she could teach: and at which game they played, with great interest and gravity, until it was time for the invalid to have some warm wine and water, with a slice of dry toast, and then to go cosily to bed.

They were happy days, those of Oliver's recovery. Everything was so quiet, and neat, and orderly; everybody so kind and gentle; that after the noise and turbulence in the midst of which he had always lived, it seemed like Heaven itself. He was no sooner strong enough to put his clothes on, properly, than Mr. Brownlow caused a complete new suit, and a new cap, and a new pair of shoes, to be provided for him. As Oliver was told that he might do what he liked with the old clothes, he gave them to a servant who had been very kind to him, and asked her to sell them to a Jew, and keep the money for herself. This she very readily did; and, as Oliver looked out of the parlour window, and saw the Jew roll them up in his bag and walk away, he felt quite delighted to think that they were safely gone, and that there was now no possible danger of his ever being able to wear them again. They were sad rags, to tell the truth; and Oliver had never had a new suit before.

One evening, about a week after the affair of the picture, as he was sitting talking to Mrs. Bedwin, there came a message down from Mr. Brownlow, that if Oliver Twist felt pretty well, he should like to see him in his study, and talk to him a little while.

'Bless us, and save us! Wash your hands, and let me part your hair nicely for you, child,' said Mrs. Bedwin. 'Dear heart alive! If we had known he would have asked for you, we would have put you a clean collar on, and made you as smart as sixpence!'

Oliver did as the old lady bade him; and, although she lamented grievously, meanwhile, that there was not even time to crimp the little frill that bordered his shirt-collar; he looked so delicate and handsome, despite that important personal advantage, that she went so far as to say: looking at him with great complacency from head to foot, that she really didn't think it would have been possible, on the longest notice, to have made much difference in him for the better.

Thus encouraged, Oliver tapped at the study door. On Mr. Brownlow calling to him to come in, he found himself in a little back room, quite full of books, with a window, looking into some pleasant little gardens. There was a table drawn up before the window, at which Mr. Brownlow was seated reading. When he saw Oliver, he pushed the book away from him, and told him to come near the table, and sit down. Oliver complied; marvelling where the people could be found to read such a great number of books as seemed to be written to make the world wiser. Which is still a marvel to more experienced people than Oliver Twist, every day of their lives.

'There are a good many books, are there not, my boy?' said Mr. Brownlow, observing the curiosity with which Oliver surveyed the shelves that reached from the floor to the ceiling.

'A great number, sir,' replied Oliver. 'I never saw so many.'

'You shall read them, if you behave well,' said the old gentleman kindly; 'and you will like that, better than looking at the outsides,—that is, some cases; because there are books of which the backs and covers are by far the best parts.'

'I suppose they are those heavy ones, sir,' said Oliver, pointing to some large quartos, with a good deal of gilding about the binding.

'Not always those,' said the old gentleman, patting Oliver on the head, and smiling as he did so; 'there are other equally heavy ones, though of a much smaller size. How should you like to grow up a clever man, and write books, eh?'

'I think I would rather read them, sir,' replied Oliver.

'What! wouldn't you like to be a book-writer?' said the old gentleman.

Oliver considered a little while; and at last said, he should think it would be a much better thing to be a book-seller; upon which the old gentleman laughed heartily, and declared he had said a very good thing. Which Oliver felt glad to have done, though he by no means knew what it was.

'Well, well,' said the old gentleman, composing his features. 'Don't be afraid! We won't make an author of you, while there's an honest trade to be learnt, or brick-making to turn to.'

'Thank you, sir,' said Oliver. At the earnest manner of his reply, the old gentleman laughed again; and said something about a curious instinct, which Oliver, not understanding, paid no very great attention to.

'Now,' said Mr. Brownlow, speaking if possible in a kinder, but at the same time in a much more serious manner, than Oliver had ever known him assume yet, 'I want you to pay great attention, my boy, to what I am going to say. I shall talk to you without any reserve; because I am sure you are well able to understand me, as many older persons would be.'

'Oh, don't tell you are going to send me away, sir, pray!' exclaimed Oliver, alarmed at the serious tone of the old gentleman's commencement! 'Don't turn me out of doors to wander in the streets again. Let me stay here, and be a servant. Don't send me back to the wretched place I came from. Have mercy upon a poor boy, sir!'

'My dear child,' said the old gentleman, moved by the warmth of Oliver's sudden appeal; 'you need not be afraid of my deserting you, unless you give me cause.'

'I never, never will, sir,' interposed Oliver.

'I hope not,' rejoined the old gentleman. 'I do not think you ever will. I have been deceived, before, in the objects whom I have endeavoured to benefit; but I feel strongly disposed to trust you, nevertheless; and I am more interested in your behalf than I can well account for, even to myself. The persons on whom I have bestowed my dearest love, lie deep in their graves; but, although the happiness and delight of my life lie buried there too, I have not made a coffin of my heart, and sealed it up, forever, on my best affections. Deep affliction has but strengthened and refined them.'

As the old gentleman said this in a low voice: more to himself than to his companion: and as he remained silent for a short time afterwards: Oliver sat quite still.

'Well, well!' said the old gentleman at length, in a more cheerful tone, 'I only say this, because you have a young heart; and knowing that I have suffered great pain and sorrow, you will be more careful, perhaps, not to wound me again. You say you are an orphan, without a friend in the world; all the inquiries I have been able to make, confirm the statement. Let me hear your story; where you come from; who brought you up; and how you got into the company in which I found you. Speak the truth, and you shall not be friendless while I live.'

Oliver's sobs checked his utterance for some minutes; when he was on the point of beginning to relate how he had been brought up at the farm, and carried to the workhouse by Mr. Bumble, a peculiarly impatient little double-knock was heard at the street-door: and the servant, running upstairs, announced Mr. Grimwig.

'Is he coming up?' inquired Mr. Brownlow.

'Yes, sir,' replied the servant. 'He asked if there were any muffins in the house; and, when I told him yes, he said he had come to tea.'

Mr. Brownlow smiled; and, turning to Oliver, said that Mr. Grimwig was an old friend of his, and he must not mind his being a little rough in his manners; for he was a worthy creature at bottom, as he had reason to know.

'Shall I go downstairs, sir?' inquired Oliver.

'No,' replied Mr. Brownlow, 'I would rather you remained here.'

At this moment, there walked into the room: supporting himself by a thick stick: a stout old gentleman, rather lame in one leg, who was dressed in a blue coat, striped waistcoat, nankeen breeches and gaiters, and a broad-brimmed white hat, with the sides turned up with green. A very small-plaited shirt frill stuck out from his waistcoat; and a very long steel watch-chain, with nothing but a key at the end, dangled loosely below it. The ends of his white neckerchief were twisted into a ball about the size of an orange; the variety of shapes into which his countenance was twisted, defy description. He had a manner of screwing his head on one side when he spoke; and of looking out of the corners of his eyes at the same time: which irresistibly reminded the beholder of a parrot. In this attitude, he fixed himself, the moment he made his appearance; and, holding out a small piece of orange-peel at arm's length, exclaimed, in a growling, discontented voice.

'Look here! do you see this! Isn't it a most wonderful and extraordinary thing that I can't call at a man's house but I find a piece of this poor surgeon's friend on the staircase? I've been lamed with orange-peel once, and I know orange-peel will be my death, or I'll be content to eat my own head, sir!'

This was the handsome offer with which Mr. Grimwig backed and confirmed nearly every assertion he made; and it was the more singular in his case, because, even admitting for the sake of argument, the possibility of scientific improvements being brought to that pass which will enable a gentleman to eat his own head in the event of his being so disposed, Mr. Grimwig's head was such a particularly large one, that the most sanguine man alive could hardly entertain a hope of being able to get through it at a sitting—to put entirely out of the question, a very thick coating of powder.

'I'll eat my head, sir,' repeated Mr. Grimwig, striking his stick upon the ground. 'Hallo! what's that!' looking at Oliver, and retreating a pace or two.

'This is young Oliver Twist, whom we were speaking about,' said Mr. Brownlow.

Oliver bowed.

'You don't mean to say that's the boy who had the fever, I hope?' said Mr. Grimwig, recoiling a little more. 'Wait a minute! Don't speak! Stop—' continued Mr. Grimwig, abruptly, losing all dread of the fever in his triumph at the discovery; 'that's the boy who had the orange! If that's not the boy, sir, who had the orange, and threw this bit of peel upon the staircase, I'll eat my head, and his too.'

'No, no, he has not had one,' said Mr. Brownlow, laughing. 'Come! Put down your hat; and speak to my young friend.'

'I feel strongly on this subject, sir,' said the irritable old gentleman, drawing off his gloves. 'There's always more or less orange-peel on the pavement in our street; and I know it's put there by the surgeon's boy at the corner. A young woman stumbled over a bit last night, and fell against my garden-railings; directly she got up I saw her look towards his infernal red lamp with the pantomime-light. "Don't go to him," I called out of the window, "he's an assassin! A man-trap!" So he is. If he is not—' Here the irascible old gentleman gave a great knock on the ground with his stick; which was always understood, by his friends, to imply the customary offer, whenever it was not expressed in words. Then, still keeping his stick in his hand, he sat down; and, opening a double eye-glass, which he wore attached to a broad black riband, took a view of Oliver: who, seeing that he was the object of inspection, coloured, and bowed again.

'That's the boy, is it?' said Mr. Grimwig, at length.

'That's the boy,' replied Mr. Brownlow.

'How are you, boy?' said Mr. Grimwig.

'A great deal better, thank you, sir,' replied Oliver.

Mr. Brownlow, seeming to apprehend that his singular friend was about to say something disagreeable, asked Oliver to step downstairs and tell Mrs. Bedwin they were ready for tea; which, as he did not half like the visitor's manner, he was very happy to do.

'He is a nice-looking boy, is he not?' inquired Mr. Brownlow.

'I don't know,' replied Mr. Grimwig, pettishly.

'Don't know?'

'No. I don't know. I never see any difference in boys. I only knew two sort of boys. Mealy boys, and beef-faced boys.'

'And which is Oliver?'

'Mealy. I know a friend who has a beef-faced boy; a fine boy, they call him; with a round head, and red cheeks, and glaring eyes; a horrid boy; with a body and limbs that appear to be swelling out of the seams of his blue clothes; with the voice of a pilot, and the appetite of a wolf. I know him! The wretch!'

'Come,' said Mr. Brownlow, 'these are not the characteristics of young Oliver Twist; so he needn't excite your wrath.'

'They are not,' replied Mr. Grimwig. 'He may have worse.'

Here, Mr. Brownlow coughed impatiently; which appeared to afford Mr. Grimwig the most exquisite delight.

'He may have worse, I say,' repeated Mr. Grimwig. 'Where does he come from! Who is he? What is he? He has had a fever. What of that? Fevers are not peculiar to good people; are they? Bad people have fevers sometimes; haven't they, eh? I knew a man who was hung in

Jamaica for murdering his master. He had had a fever six times; he wasn't recommended to mercy on that account. Pooh! nonsense!'

Now, the fact was, that in the inmost recesses of his own heart, Mr. Grimwig was strongly disposed to admit that Oliver's appearance and manner were unusually prepossessing; but he had a strong appetite for contradiction, sharpened on this occasion by the finding of the orange-peel; and, inwardly determining that no man should dictate to him whether a boy was well-looking or not, he had resolved, from the first, to oppose his friend. When Mr. Brownlow admitted that on no one point of inquiry could he yet return a satisfactory answer; and that he had postponed any investigation into Oliver's previous history until he thought the boy was strong enough to hear it; Mr. Grimwig chuckled maliciously. And he demanded, with a sneer, whether the housekeeper was in the habit of counting the plate at night; because if she didn't find a table-spoon or two missing some sunshiny morning, why, he would be content to—and so forth.

All this, Mr. Brownlow, although himself somewhat of an impetuous gentleman: knowing his friend's peculiarities, bore with great good humour; as Mr. Grimwig, at tea, was graciously pleased to express his entire approval of the muffins, matters went on very smoothly; and Oliver, who made one of the party, began to feel more at his ease than he had yet done in the fierce old gentleman's presence.

'And when are you going to hear a full, true, and particular account of the life and adventures of Oliver Twist?' asked Grimwig of Mr. Brownlow, at the conclusion of the meal; looking sideways at Oliver, as he resumed his subject.

'To-morrow morning,' replied Mr. Brownlow. 'I would rather he was alone with me at the time. Come up to me to-morrow morning at ten o'clock, my dear.'

'Yes, sir,' replied Oliver. He answered with some hesitation, because he was confused by Mr. Grimwig's looking so hard at him.

'I'll tell you what,' whispered that gentleman to Mr. Brownlow; 'he won't come up to you to-morrow morning. I saw him hesitate. He is deceiving you, my good friend.'

'I'll swear he is not,' replied Mr. Brownlow, warmly.

'If he is not,' said Mr. Grimwig, 'I'll—' and down went the stick.

'I'll answer for that boy's truth with my life!' said Mr. Brownlow, knocking the table.

'And I for his falsehood with my head!' rejoined Mr. Grimwig, knocking the table also.

'We shall see,' said Mr. Brownlow, checking his rising anger.

'We will,' replied Mr. Grimwig, with a provoking smile; 'we will.'

As fate would have it, Mrs. Bedwin chanced to bring in, at this moment, a small parcel of books, which Mr. Brownlow had that morning purchased of the identical bookstall-keeper, who has already figured in this history; having laid them on the table, she prepared to leave the room.

'Stop the boy, Mrs. Bedwin!' said Mr. Brownlow; 'there is something to go back.'

'He has gone, sir,' replied Mrs. Bedwin.

'Call after him,' said Mr. Brownlow; 'it's particular. He is a poor man, and they are not paid for. There are some books to be taken back, too.'

The street-door was opened. Oliver ran one way; and the girl ran another; and Mrs. Bedwin stood on the step and screamed for the boy; but there was no boy in sight. Oliver and the girl returned, in a breathless state, to report that there were no tidings of him.

'Dear me, I am very sorry for that,' exclaimed Mr. Brownlow; 'I particularly wished those books to be returned to-night.'

'Send Oliver with them,' said Mr. Grimwig, with an ironical smile; 'he will be sure to deliver them safely, you know.'

'Yes; do let me take them, if you please, sir,' said Oliver. 'I'll run all the way, sir.'

The old gentleman was just going to say that Oliver should not go out on any account; when a most malicious cough from Mr. Grimwig determined him that he should; and that, by his prompt discharge of the commission, he should prove to him the injustice of his suspicions: on this head at least: at once.

'You shall go, my dear,' said the old gentleman. 'The books are on a chair by my table. Fetch them down.'

Oliver, delighted to be of use, brought down the books under his arm in a great bustle; and waited, cap in hand, to hear what message he was to take.

'You are to say,' said Mr. Brownlow, glancing steadily at Grimwig; 'you are to say that you have brought those books back; and that you have come to pay the four pound ten I owe him. This is a five-pound note, so you will have to bring me back, ten shillings change.'

'I won't be ten minutes, sir,' said Oliver, eagerly. Having buttoned up the bank-note in his jacket pocket, and placed the books carefully under his arm, he made a respectful bow, and left the room. Mrs. Bedwin followed him to the street-door, giving him many directions about the nearest way, and the name of the bookseller, and the name of the street: all of which Oliver said he clearly understood. Having superadded many injunctions to be sure and not take cold, the old lady at length permitted him to depart.

'Bless his sweet face!' said the old lady, looking after him. 'I can't bear, somehow, to let him go out of my sight.'

At this moment, Oliver looked gaily round, and nodded before he turned the corner. The old lady smilingly returned his salutation, and, closing the door, went back to her own room.

'Let me see; he'll be back in twenty minutes, at the longest,' said Mr. Brownlow, pulling out his watch, and placing it on the table. 'It will be dark by that time.'

'Oh! you really expect him to come back, do you?' inquired Mr. Grimwig.

'Don't you?' asked Mr. Brownlow, smiling.

The spirit of contradiction was strong in Mr. Grimwig's breast, at the moment; and it was rendered stronger by his friend's confident smile.

'No,' he said, smiting the table with his fist, 'I do not. The boy has a new suit of clothes on his back, a set of valuable books under his arm, and a five-pound note in his pocket. He'll join his old friends the thieves, and laugh at you. If ever that boy returns to this house, sir, I'll eat my head.'

With these words he drew his chair closer to the table; and there the two friends sat, in silent expectation, with the watch between them.

It is worthy of remark, as illustrating the importance we attach to our own judgments, and the pride with which we put forth our most rash and hasty conclusions, that, although Mr. Grimwig was not by any means a bad-hearted man, and though he would have been unfeignedly sorry to see his respected friend duped and deceived, he really did most earnestly and strongly hope at that moment, that Oliver Twist might not come back.

It grew so dark, that the figures on the dial-plate were scarcely discernible; but there the two old gentlemen continued to sit, in silence, with the watch between them.

CHAPTER XV. SHOWING HOW VERY FOND OF OLIVER TWIST, THE MERRY OLD JEW AND MISS NANCY WERE

In the obscure parlour of a low public-house, in the filthiest part of Little Saffron Hill; a dark and gloomy den, where a flaring gas-light burnt all day in the winter-time; and where no ray of sun ever shone in the summer: there sat, brooding over a little pewter measure and a small glass, strongly impregnated with the smell of liquor, a man in a velveteen coat, drab shorts, half-boots and stockings, whom even by that dim light no experienced agent of the police would have hesitated to recognise as Mr. William Sikes. At his feet, sat a white-coated, red-eyed dog; who occupied himself, alternately, in winking at his master with both eyes at the same time; and in licking a large, fresh cut on one side of his mouth, which appeared to be the result of some recent conflict.

'Keep quiet, you warmint! Keep quiet!' said Mr. Sikes, suddenly breaking silence. Whether his meditations were so intense as to be disturbed by the dog's winking, or whether his feelings were so wrought upon by his reflections that they required all the relief derivable from kicking an unoffending animal to allay them, is matter for argument and consideration. Whatever was the cause, the effect was a kick and a curse, bestowed upon the dog simultaneously.

Dogs are not generally apt to revenge injuries inflicted upon them by their masters; but Mr. Sikes's dog, having faults of temper in common with his owner, and labouring, perhaps, at this moment, under a powerful sense of injury, made no more ado but at once fixed his teeth in one of the half-boots. Having given in a hearty shake, he retired, growling, under a form; just escaping the pewter measure which Mr. Sikes levelled at his head.

'You would, would you?' said Sikes, seizing the poker in one hand, and deliberately opening with the other a large clasp-knife, which he drew from his pocket. 'Come here, you born devil! Come here! D'ye hear?'

The dog no doubt heard; because Mr. Sikes spoke in the very harshest key of a very harsh voice; but, appearing to entertain some unaccountable objection to having his throat cut, he remained where he was, and growled more fiercely than before: at the same time grasping the end of the poker between his teeth, and biting at it like a wild beast.

This resistance only infuriated Mr. Sikes the more; who, dropping on his knees, began to assail the animal most furiously. The dog jumped from right to left, and from left to right; snapping, growling, and barking; the man thrust and swore, and struck and blasphemed; and the struggle was reaching a most critical point for one or other; when, the door suddenly opening, the dog darted out: leaving Bill Sikes with the poker and the clasp-knife in his hands.

There must always be two parties to a quarrel, says the old adage. Mr. Sikes, being disappointed of the dog's participation, at once transferred his share in the quarrel to the new comer.

'What the devil do you come in between me and my dog for?' said Sikes, with a fierce gesture.

'I didn't know, my dear, I didn't know,' replied Fagin, humbly; for the Jew was the new comer.

'Didn't know, you white-livered thief!' growled Sikes. 'Couldn't you hear the noise?'

'Not a sound of it, as I'm a living man, Bill,' replied the Jew.

'Oh no! You hear nothing, you don't,' retorted Sikes with a fierce sneer. 'Sneaking in and out, so as nobody hears how you come or go! I wish you had been the dog, Fagin, half a minute ago.'

'Why?' inquired the Jew with a forced smile.

'Cause the government, as cares for the lives of such men as you, as haven't half the pluck of curs, lets a man kill a dog how he likes,' replied Sikes, shutting up the knife with a very expressive look; 'that's why.'

The Jew rubbed his hands; and, sitting down at the table, affected to laugh at the pleasantry of his friend. He was obviously very ill at ease, however.

'Grin away,' said Sikes, replacing the poker, and surveying him with savage contempt; 'grin away. You'll never have the laugh at me, though, unless it's behind a nightcap. I've got the upper hand over you, Fagin; and, d—me, I'll keep it. There! If I go, you go; so take care of me.'

'Well, well, my dear,' said the Jew, 'I know all that; we—we—have a mutual interest, Bill,—a mutual interest.'

'Humph,' said Sikes, as if he thought the interest lay rather more on the Jew's side than on his. 'Well, what have you got to say to me?'

'It's all passed safe through the melting-pot,' replied Fagin, 'and this is your share. It's rather more than it ought to be, my dear; but as I know you'll do me a good turn another time, and—'

'Stow that gammon,' interposed the robber, impatiently. 'Where is it? Hand over!'

'Yes, yes, Bill; give me time, give me time,' replied the Jew, soothingly. 'Here it is! All safe!' As he spoke, he drew forth an old cotton handkerchief from his breast; and untying a large knot in one corner, produced a small brown-paper packet. Sikes, snatching it from him, hastily opened it; and proceeded to count the sovereigns it contained.

'This is all, is it?' inquired Sikes.

'All,' replied the Jew.

'You haven't opened the parcel and swallowed one or two as you come along, have you?' inquired Sikes, suspiciously. 'Don't put on an injured look at the question; you've done it many a time. Jerk the tinkler.'

These words, in plain English, conveyed an injunction to ring the bell. It was answered by another Jew: younger than Fagin, but nearly as vile and repulsive in appearance.

Bill Sikes merely pointed to the empty measure. The Jew, perfectly understanding the hint, retired to fill it: previously exchanging a remarkable look with Fagin, who raised his eyes for an instant, as if in expectation of it, and shook his head in reply; so slightly that the action would have been almost imperceptible to an observant third person. It was lost upon Sikes, who was stooping at the moment to tie the boot-lace which the dog had torn. Possibly, if he had observed the brief interchange of signals, he might have thought that it boded no good to him.

'Is anybody here, Barney?' inquired Fagin; speaking, now that that Sikes was looking on, without raising his eyes from the ground.

'Dot a shoul,' replied Barney; whose words: whether they came from the heart or not: made their way through the nose.

'Nobody?' inquired Fagin, in a tone of surprise: which perhaps might mean that Barney was at liberty to tell the truth.

'Dobody but Biss Dadsy,' replied Barney.

'Nancy!' exclaimed Sikes. 'Where? Strike me blind, if I don't honour that 'ere girl, for her native talents.'

'She's bid havid a plate of boiled beef id the bar,' replied Barney.

'Send her here,' said Sikes, pouring out a glass of liquor. 'Send her here.'

Barney looked timidly at Fagin, as if for permission; the Jew remaining silent, and not lifting his eyes from the ground, he retired; and presently returned, ushering in Nancy; who was decorated with the bonnet, apron, basket, and street-door key, complete.

'You are on the scent, are you, Nancy?' inquired Sikes, proffering the glass.

'Yes, I am, Bill,' replied the young lady, disposing of its contents; 'and tired enough of it I am, too. The young brat's been ill and confined to the crib; and—'

'Ah, Nancy, dear!' said Fagin, looking up.

Now, whether a peculiar contraction of the Jew's red eye-brows, and a half closing of his deeply-set eyes, warned Miss Nancy that she was disposed to be too communicative, is not a matter of much importance. The fact is all we need care for here; and the fact is, that she suddenly checked herself, and with several gracious smiles upon Mr. Sikes, turned the conversation to other matters. In about ten minutes' time, Mr. Fagin was seized with a fit of coughing; upon which Nancy pulled her shawl over her shoulders, and declared it was time to go. Mr. Sikes, finding that he was walking a short part of her way himself, expressed his intention of accompanying her; they went away together, followed, at a little distant, by the dog, who slunk out of a back-yard as soon as his master was out of sight.

The Jew thrust his head out of the room door when Sikes had left it; looked after him as he walked up the dark passage; shook his clenched fist; muttered a deep curse; and then, with a horrible grin, reseated himself at the table; where he was soon deeply absorbed in the interesting pages of the Hue-and-Cry.

Meanwhile, Oliver Twist, little dreaming that he was within so very short a distance of the merry old gentleman, was on his way to the book-stall. When he got into Clerkenwell, he accidently turned down a by-street which was not exactly in his way; but not discovering his mistake until he had got half-way down it, and knowing it must lead in the right direction, he did not think it worth while to turn back; and so marched on, as quickly as he could, with the books under his arm.

He was walking along, thinking how happy and contented he ought to feel; and how much he would give for only one look at poor little Dick, who, starved and beaten, might be weeping bitterly at that very moment; when he was startled by a young woman screaming out very loud. 'Oh, my dear brother!' And he had hardly looked up, to see what the matter was, when he was stopped by having a pair of arms thrown tight round his neck.

'Don't,' cried Oliver, struggling. 'Let go of me. Who is it? What are you stopping me for?'

The only reply to this, was a great number of loud lamentations from the young woman who had embraced him; and who had a little basket and a street-door key in her hand.

'Oh my gracious!' said the young woman, 'I have found him! Oh! Oliver! Oliver! Oh you naughty boy, to make me suffer such distress on your account! Come home, dear, come. Oh, I've found him. Thank gracious goodness heavins, I've found him!' With these incoherent exclamations, the young woman burst into another fit of crying, and got so dreadfully hysterical, that a couple of women who came up at the moment asked a butcher's boy with a shiny head of hair anointed with suet, who was also looking on, whether he didn't think he had better run for the doctor. To which, the butcher's boy: who appeared of a lounging, not to say indolent disposition: replied, that he thought not.

'Oh, no, no, never mind,' said the young woman, grasping Oliver's hand; 'I'm better now. Come home directly, you cruel boy! Come!'

'Oh, ma'am,' replied the young woman, 'he ran away, near a month ago, from his parents, who are hard-working and respectable people; and went and joined a set of thieves and bad characters; and almost broke his mother's heart.'

'Young wretch!' said one woman.

'Go home, do, you little brute,' said the other.

'I am not,' replied Oliver, greatly alarmed. 'I don't know her. I haven't any sister, or father and mother either. I'm an orphan; I live at Pentonville.'

'Only hear him, how he braves it out!' cried the young woman.

'Why, it's Nancy!' exclaimed Oliver; who now saw her face for the first time; and started back, in irrepressible astonishment.

'You see he knows me!' cried Nancy, appealing to the bystanders. 'He can't help himself. Make him come home, there's good people, or he'll kill his dear mother and father, and break my heart!'

'What the devil's this?' said a man, bursting out of a beer-shop, with a white dog at his heels; 'young Oliver! Come home to your poor mother, you young dog! Come home directly.'

'I don't belong to them. I don't know them. Help! help!' cried Oliver, struggling in the man's powerful grasp.

'Help!' repeated the man. 'Yes; I'll help you, you young rascal!

What books are these? You've been a stealing 'em, have you? Give 'em here.' With these words, the man tore the volumes from his grasp, and struck him on the head.

'That's right!' cried a looker-on, from a garret-window. 'That's the only way of bringing him to his senses!'

'To be sure!' cried a sleepy-faced carpenter, casting an approving look at the garret-window.

'It'll do him good!' said the two women.

'And he shall have it, too!' rejoined the man, administering another blow, and seizing Oliver by the collar. 'Come on, you young villain! Here, Bull's-eye, mind him, boy! Mind him!'

Weak with recent illness; stupified by the blows and the suddenness of the attack; terrified by the fierce growling of the dog, and the brutality of the man; overpowered by the conviction of the bystanders that he really was the hardened little wretch he was described to be; what could one poor child do! Darkness had set in; it was a low neighborhood; no help was near; resistance was useless. In another moment he was dragged into a labyrinth of dark narrow courts, and was forced along them at a pace which rendered the few cries he dared to give utterance to, unintelligible. It was of little moment, indeed, whether they were intelligible or no; for there was nobody to care for them, had they been ever so plain.

The gas-lamps were lighted; Mrs. Bedwin was waiting anxiously at the open door; the servant had run up the street twenty times to see if there were any traces of Oliver; and still the two old gentlemen sat, perseveringly, in the dark parlour, with the watch between them.

CHAPTER XVI. RELATES WHAT BECAME OF OLIVER TWIST, AFTER HE HAD BEEN CLAIMED BY NANCY

The narrow streets and courts, at length, terminated in a large open space; scattered about which, were pens for beasts, and other indications of a cattle-market. Sikes slackened his pace when they reached this spot: the girl being quite unable to support any longer, the rapid rate at which they had hitherto walked. Turning to Oliver, he roughly commanded him to take hold of Nancy's hand.

'Do you hear?' growled Sikes, as Oliver hesitated, and looked round.

They were in a dark corner, quite out of the track of passengers.

Oliver saw, but too plainly, that resistance would be of no avail. He held out his hand, which Nancy clasped tight in hers.

'Give me the other,' said Sikes, seizing Oliver's unoccupied hand. 'Here, Bull's-Eye!'

The dog looked up, and growled.

'See here, boy!' said Sikes, putting his other hand to Oliver's throat; 'if he speaks ever so soft a word, hold him! D'ye mind!'

The dog growled again; and licking his lips, eyed Oliver as if he were anxious to attach himself to his windpipe without delay.

'He's as willing as a Christian, strike me blind if he isn't!' said Sikes, regarding the animal with a kind of grim and ferocious approval. 'Now, you know what you've got to expect, master, so call away as quick as you like; the dog will soon stop that game. Get on, young'un!'

Bull's-eye wagged his tail in acknowledgment of this unusually endearing form of speech; and, giving vent to another admonitory growl for the benefit of Oliver, led the way onward.

It was Smithfield that they were crossing, although it might have been Grosvenor Square, for anything Oliver knew to the contrary. The night was dark and foggy. The lights in the shops could scarcely struggle through the heavy mist, which thickened every moment and shrouded the streets and houses in gloom; rendering the strange place still stranger in Oliver's eyes; and making his uncertainty the more dismal and depressing.

They had hurried on a few paces, when a deep church-bell struck the hour. With its first stroke, his two conductors stopped, and turned their heads in the direction whence the sound proceeded.

'Eight o' clock, Bill,' said Nancy, when the bell ceased.

'What's the good of telling me that; I can hear it, can't I!' replied Sikes.

'I wonder whether THEY can hear it,' said Nancy.

'Of course they can,' replied Sikes. 'It was Bartlemy time when I was shopped; and there warn't a penny trumpet in the fair, as I couldn't hear the squeaking on. Arter I was locked up for the night, the row and din outside made the thundering old jail so silent, that I could almost have beat my brains out against the iron plates of the door.'

'Poor fellow!' said Nancy, who still had her face turned towards the quarter in which the bell had sounded. 'Oh, Bill, such fine young chaps as them!'

'Yes; that's all you women think of,' answered Sikes. 'Fine young chaps! Well, they're as good as dead, so it don't much matter.'

With this consolation, Mr. Sikes appeared to repress a rising tendency to jealousy, and, clasping Oliver's wrist more firmly, told him to step out again.

'Wait a minute!' said the girl: 'I wouldn't hurry by, if it was you that was coming out to be hung, the next time eight o'clock struck, Bill. I'd walk round and round the place till I dropped, if the snow was on the ground, and I hadn't a shawl to cover me.'

'And what good would that do?' inquired the unsentimental Mr. Sikes. 'Unless you could pitch over a file and twenty yards of good stout rope, you might as well be walking fifty mile off, or not walking at all, for all the good it would do me. Come on, and don't stand preaching there.'

The girl burst into a laugh; drew her shawl more closely round her; and they walked away. But Oliver felt her hand tremble, and, looking up in her face as they passed a gas-lamp, saw that it had turned a deadly white.

They walked on, by little-frequented and dirty ways, for a full half-hour: meeting very few people, and those appearing from their looks to hold much the same position in society as Mr. Sikes himself. At length they turned into a very filthy narrow street, nearly full of old-clothes shops; the dog running forward, as if conscious that there was no further occasion for his keeping on guard, stopped before the door of a shop that was closed and apparently untenanted; the house was in a ruinous condition, and on the door was nailed a board, intimating that it was to let: which looked as if it had hung there for many years.

'All right,' cried Sikes, glancing cautiously about.

Nancy stooped below the shutters, and Oliver heard the sound of a bell. They crossed to the opposite side of the street, and stood for a few moments under a lamp. A noise, as if a sash window were gently raised, was heard; and soon afterwards the door softly opened. Mr. Sikes then seized the terrified boy by the collar with very little ceremony; and all three were quickly inside the house.

The passage was perfectly dark. They waited, while the person who had let them in, chained and barred the door.

'Anybody here?' inquired Sikes.

'No,' replied a voice, which Oliver thought he had heard before.

'Is the old 'un here?' asked the robber.

'Yes,' replied the voice, 'and precious down in the mouth he has been. Won't he be glad to see you? Oh, no!'

The style of this reply, as well as the voice which delivered it, seemed familiar to Oliver's ears: but it was impossible to distinguish even the form of the speaker in the darkness.

'Let's have a glim,' said Sikes, 'or we shall go breaking our necks, or treading on the dog. Look after your legs if you do!'

'Stand still a moment, and I'll get you one,' replied the voice. The receding footsteps of the speaker were heard; and, in another minute, the form of Mr. John Dawkins, otherwise the Artful Dodger, appeared. He bore in his right hand a tallow candle stuck in the end of a cleft stick.

The young gentleman did not stop to bestow any other mark of recognition upon Oliver than a humourous grin; but, turning away, beckoned the visitors to follow him down a flight of stairs. They crossed an empty kitchen; and, opening the door of a low earthy-smelling room, which seemed to have been built in a small back-yard, were received with a shout of laughter.

'Oh, my wig, my wig!' cried Master Charles Bates, from whose lungs the laughter had proceeded: 'here he is! oh, cry, here he is! Oh, Fagin, look at him! Fagin, do look at him! I can't bear it; it is such a jolly game, I cant' bear it. Hold me, somebody, while I laugh it out.'

With this irrepressible ebullition of mirth, Master Bates laid himself flat on the floor: and kicked convulsively for five minutes, in an ectasy of facetious joy. Then jumping to his feet, he snatched the cleft stick from the Dodger; and, advancing to Oliver, viewed him round and round; while the Jew, taking off his nightcap, made a great number of low bows to the bewildered boy. The Artful, meantime, who was of a rather saturnine disposition, and seldom gave way to merriment when it interfered with business, rifled Oliver's pockets with steady assiduity.

'Look at his togs, Fagin!' said Charley, putting the light so close to his new jacket as nearly to set him on fire. 'Look at his togs! Superfine cloth, and the heavy swell cut! Oh, my eye, what a game! And his books, too! Nothing but a gentleman, Fagin!'

'Delighted to see you looking so well, my dear,' said the Jew, bowing with mock humility. 'The Artful shall give you another suit, my dear, for fear you should spoil that Sunday one. Why didn't you write, my dear, and say you were coming? We'd have got something warm for supper.'

At his, Master Bates roared again: so loud, that Fagin himself relaxed, and even the Dodger smiled; but as the Artful drew forth the five-pound note at that instant, it is doubtful whether the sally of the discovery awakened his merriment.

'Hallo, what's that?' inquired Sikes, stepping forward as the Jew seized the note. 'That's mine, Fagin.'

'No, no, my dear,' said the Jew. 'Mine, Bill, mine. You shall have the books.'

'If that ain't mine!' said Bill Sikes, putting on his hat with a determined air; 'mine and Nancy's that is; I'll take the boy back again.'

The Jew started. Oliver started too, though from a very different cause; for he hoped that the dispute might really end in his being taken back.

'Come! Hand over, will you?' said Sikes.

'This is hardly fair, Bill; hardly fair, is it, Nancy?' inquired the Jew.

'Fair, or not fair,' retorted Sikes, 'hand over, I tell you! Do you think Nancy and me has got nothing else to do with our precious time but to spend it in scouting arter, and kidnapping, every young boy as gets grabbed through you? Give it here, you avaricious old skeleton, give it here!'

With this gentle remonstrance, Mr. Sikes plucked the note from between the Jew's finger and thumb; and looking the old man coolly in the face, folded it up small, and tied it in his neckerchief.

'That's for our share of the trouble,' said Sikes; 'and not half enough, neither. You may keep the books, if you're fond of reading. If you ain't, sell 'em.'

'They're very pretty,' said Charley Bates: who, with sundry grimaces, had been affecting to read one of the volumes in question; 'beautiful writing, isn't is, Oliver?' At sight of the dismayed look with which Oliver regarded his tormentors, Master Bates, who was blessed with a lively sense of the ludicrous, fell into another ectasy, more boisterous than the first.

'They belong to the old gentleman,' said Oliver, wringing his hands; 'to the good, kind, old gentleman who took me into his house, and had me nursed, when I was near dying of the fever. Oh, pray send them back; send him back the books and money. Keep me here all my life long; but pray, pray send them back. He'll think I stole them; the old lady: all of them who were so kind to me: will think I stole them. Oh, do have mercy upon me, and send them back!'

With these words, which were uttered with all the energy of passionate grief, Oliver fell upon his knees at the Jew's feet; and beat his hands together, in perfect desperation.

'The boy's right,' remarked Fagin, looking covertly round, and knitting his shaggy eyebrows into a hard knot. 'You're right, Oliver, you're right; they WILL think you have stolen 'em. Ha! ha!' chuckled the Jew, rubbing his hands, 'it couldn't have happened better, if we had chosen our time!'

'Of course it couldn't,' replied Sikes; 'I know'd that, directly I see him coming through Clerkenwell, with the books under his arm. It's all right enough. They're soft-hearted psalm-singers, or they wouldn't have taken him in at all; and they'll ask no questions after him, fear they should be obliged to prosecute, and so get him lagged. He's safe enough.'

Oliver had looked from one to the other, while these words were being spoken, as if he were bewildered, and could scarecely understand what passed; but when Bill Sikes concluded, he jumped suddenly to his feet, and tore wildly from the room: uttering shrieks for help, which made the bare old house echo to the roof.

'Keep back the dog, Bill!' cried Nancy, springing before the door, and closing it, as the Jew and his two pupils darted out in pursuit. 'Keep back the dog; he'll tear the boy to pieces.'

'Serve him right!' cried Sikes, struggling to disengage himself from the girl's grasp. 'Stand off from me, or I'll split your head against the wall.'

'I don't care for that, Bill, I don't care for that,' screamed the girl, struggling violently with the man, 'the child shan't be torn down by the dog, unless you kill me first.'

'Shan't he!' said Sikes, setting his teeth. 'I'll soon do that, if you don't keep off.'

The housebreaker flung the girl from him to the further end of the room, just as the Jew and the two boys returned, dragging Oliver among them.

'What's the matter here!' said Fagin, looking round.

'The girl's gone mad, I think,' replied Sikes, savagely.

'No, she hasn't,' said Nancy, pale and breathless from the scuffle; 'no, she hasn't, Fagin; don't think it.'

'Then keep quiet, will you?' said the Jew, with a threatening look.

'No, I won't do that, neither,' replied Nancy, speaking very loud. 'Come! What do you think of that?'

Mr. Fagin was sufficiently well acquainted with the manners and customs of that particular species of humanity to which Nancy belonged, to feel tolerably certain that it would be rather unsafe to prolong any conversation with her, at present. With the view of diverting the attention of the company, he turned to Oliver.

'So you wanted to get away, my dear, did you?' said the Jew, taking up a jagged and knotted club which law in a corner of the fireplace; 'eh?'

Oliver made no reply. But he watched the Jew's motions, and breathed quickly.

'Wanted to get assistance; called for the police; did you?' sneered the Jew, catching the boy by the arm. 'We'll cure you of that, my young master.'

The Jew inflicted a smart blow on Oliver's shoulders with the club; and was raising it for a second, when the girl, rushing forward, wrested it from his hand. She flung it into the fire, with a force that brought some of the glowing coals whirling out into the room.

'I won't stand by and see it done, Fagin,' cried the girl. 'You've got the boy, and what more would you have?—Let him be—let him be—or I shall put that mark on some of you, that will bring me to the gallows before my time.'

The girl stamped her foot violently on the floor as she vented this threat; and with her lips compressed, and her hands clenched, looked alternately at the Jew and the other robber: her face quite colourless from the passion of rage into which she had gradually worked herself.

'Why, Nancy!' said the Jew, in a soothing tone; after a pause, during which he and Mr. Sikes had stared at one another in a disconcerted manner; 'you,—you're more clever than ever to-night. Ha! ha! my dear, you are acting beautifully.'

'Am I!' said the girl. 'Take care I don't overdo it. You will be the worse for it, Fagin, if I do; and so I tell you in good time to keep clear of me.'

There is something about a roused woman: especially if she add to all her other strong passions, the fierce impulses of recklessness and despair; which few men like to provoke. The Jew saw that it would be hopeless to affect any further mistake regarding the reality of Miss Nancy's rage; and, shrinking involuntarily back a few paces, cast a glance, half imploring and half cowardly, at Sikes: as if to hint that he was the fittest person to pursue the dialogue.

Mr. Sikes, thus mutely appealed to; and possibly feeling his personal pride and influence interested in the immediate reduction of Miss Nancy to reason; gave utterance to about a couple of score of curses and threats, the rapid production of which reflected great credit on the fertility of his invention. As they produced no visible effect on the object against whom they were discharged, however, he resorted to more tangible arguments.

'What do you mean by this?' said Sikes; backing the inquiry with a very common imprecation concerning the most beautiful of human features: which, if it were heard above, only once out of every fifty thousand times that it is uttered below, would render blindness as common a disorder as measles: 'what do you mean by it? Burn my body! Do you know who you are, and what you are?'

'Oh, yes, I know all about it,' replied the girl, laughing hysterically; and shaking her head from side to side, with a poor assumption of indifference.

'Well, then, keep quiet,' rejoined Sikes, with a growl like that he was accustomed to use when addressing his dog, 'or I'll quiet you for a good long time to come.'

The girl laughed again: even less composedly than before; and, darting a hasty look at Sikes, turned her face aside, and bit her lip till the blood came.

'You're a nice one,' added Sikes, as he surveyed her with a contemptuous air, 'to take up the humane and gen—teel side! A pretty subject for the child, as you call him, to make a friend of!'

'God Almighty help me, I am!' cried the girl passionately; 'and I wish I had been struck dead in the street, or had changed places with them we passed so near to-night, before I had lent a hand in bringing him here. He's a thief, a liar, a devil, all that's bad, from this night forth. Isn't that enough for the old wretch, without blows?'

'Come, come, Sikes,' said the Jew appealing to him in a remonstratory tone, and motioning towards the boys, who were eagerly attentive to all that passed; 'we must have civil words; civil words, Bill.'

'Civil words!' cried the girl, whose passion was frightful to see. 'Civil words, you villain! Yes, you deserve 'em from me. I thieved for you when I was a child not half as old as this!' pointing to Oliver. 'I have been in the same trade, and in the same service, for twelve years since. Don't you know it? Speak out! Don't you know it?'

'Well, well,' replied the Jew, with an attempt at pacification; 'and, if you have, it's your living!'

'Aye, it is!' returned the girl; not speaking, but pouring out the words in one continuous and vehement scream. 'It is my living; and the cold, wet, dirty streets are my home; and you're the wretch that drove me to them long ago, and that'll keep me there, day and night, day and night, till I die!'

'I shall do you a mischief!' interposed the Jew, goaded by these reproaches; 'a mischief worse than that, if you say much more!'

The girl said nothing more; but, tearing her hair and dress in a transport of passion, made such a rush at the Jew as would probably have left signal marks of her revenge upon him, had not her wrists been seized by Sikes at the right moment; upon which, she made a few ineffectual struggles, and fainted.

'She's all right now,' said Sikes, laying her down in a corner. 'She's uncommon strong in the arms, when she's up in this way.'

The Jew wiped his forehead: and smiled, as if it were a relief to have the disturbance over; but neither he, nor Sikes, nor the dog, nor the boys, seemed to consider it in any other light than a common occurance incidental to business.

'It's the worst of having to do with women,' said the Jew, replacing his club; 'but they're clever, and we can't get on, in our line, without 'em. Charley, show Oliver to bed.'

'I suppose he'd better not wear his best clothes tomorrow, Fagin, had he?' inquired Charley Bates.

'Certainly not,' replied the Jew, reciprocating the grin with which Charley put the question.

Master Bates, apparently much delighted with his commission, took the cleft stick: and led Oliver into an adjacent kitchen, where there were two or three of the beds on which he had slept before; and here, with many uncontrollable bursts of laughter, he produced the identical old suit of clothes which Oliver had so much congratulated himself upon leaving off at Mr. Brownlow's; and the accidental display of which, to Fagin, by the Jew who purchased them, had been the very first clue received, of his whereabout.

'Put off the smart ones,' said Charley, 'and I'll give 'em to Fagin to take care of. What fun it is!'

Poor Oliver unwillingly complied. Master Bates rolling up the new clothes under his arm, departed from the room, leaving Oliver in the dark, and locking the door behind him.

The noise of Charley's laughter, and the voice of Miss Betsy, who opportunely arrived to throw water over her friend, and perform other feminine offices for the promotion of her recovery, might have kept many people awake under more happy circumstances than those in which Oliver was placed. But he was sick and weary; and he soon fell sound asleep.

CHAPTER XVII. OLIVER'S DESTINY CONTINUING UNPROPITIOUS, BRINGS A GREAT MAN TO LONDON TO INJURE HIS REPUTATION

It is the custom on the stage, in all good murderous melodramas, to present the tragic and the comic scenes, in as regular alternation, as the layers of red and white in a side of streaky bacon. The hero sinks upon his straw bed, weighed down by fetters and misfortunes; in the next scene, his faithful but unconscious squire regales the audience with a comic song. We behold, with throbbing bosoms, the heroine in the grasp of a proud and ruthless baron: her virtue and her life alike in danger, drawing forth her dagger to preserve the one at the cost of the other; and just as our expectations are wrought up to the highest pitch, a whistle is heard, and we are straightway transported to the great hall of the castle; where a grey-headed seneschal sings a funny chorus with a funnier body of vassals, who are free of all sorts of places, from church vaults to palaces, and roam about in company, carolling perpetually.

Such changes appear absurd; but they are not so unnatural as they would seem at first sight. The transitions in real life from well-spread boards to death-beds, and from mourning-weeds to holiday garments, are not a whit less startling; only, there, we are busy actors, instead of passive lookers-on, which makes a vast difference. The actors in the mimic life of the theatre, are blind to violent transitions and abrupt impulses of passion or feeling, which, presented before the eyes of mere spectators, are at once condemned as outrageous and preposterous.

As sudden shiftings of the scene, and rapid changes of time and place, are not only sanctioned in books by long usage, but are by many considered as the great art of authorship: an author's skill in his craft being, by such critics, chiefly estimated with relation to the dilemmas in which he leaves his characters at the end of every chapter: this brief introduction to the present one may perhaps be deemed unnecessary. If so, let it be considered a delicate intimation on the part of the historian that he is going back to the town in which Oliver Twist was born; the reader taking it for granted that there are good and substantial reasons for making the journey, or he would not be invited to proceed upon such an expedition.

Mr. Bumble emerged at early morning from the workhouse-gate, and walked with portly carriage and commanding steps, up the High Street. He was in the full bloom and pride of beadlehood; his cocked hat and coat were dazzling in the morning sun; he clutched his cane with the vigorous tenacity of health and power. Mr. Bumble always carried his head high; but this morning it was higher than usual. There was an abstraction in his eye, an elevation in his air, which might have warned an observant stranger that thoughts were passing in the beadle's mind, too great for utterance.

Mr. Bumble stopped not to converse with the small shopkeepers and others who spoke to him, deferentially, as he passed along. He merely returned their salutations with a wave of his hand, and relaxed not in his dignified pace, until he reached the farm where Mrs. Mann tended the infant paupers with parochial care.

'Drat that beadle!' said Mrs. Mann, hearing the well-known shaking at the garden-gate. 'If it isn't him at this time in the morning! Lauk, Mr. Bumble, only think of its being you! Well, dear me, it IS a pleasure, this is! Come into the parlour, sir, please.'

The first sentence was addressed to Susan; and the exclamations of delight were uttered to Mr. Bumble: as the good lady unlocked the garden-gate: and showed him, with great attention and respect, into the house.

'Mrs. Mann,' said Mr. Bumble; not sitting upon, or dropping himself into a seat, as any common jackanapes would: but letting himself gradually and slowly down into a chair; 'Mrs. Mann, ma'am, good morning.'

'Well, and good morning to you, sir,' replied Mrs. Mann, with many smiles; 'and hoping you find yourself well, sir!'

'So-so, Mrs. Mann,' replied the beadle. 'A porochial life is not a bed of roses, Mrs. Mann.'

'Ah, that it isn't indeed, Mr. Bumble,' rejoined the lady. And all the infant paupers might have chorussed the rejoinder with great propriety, if they had heard it.

'A porochial life, ma'am,' continued Mr. Bumble, striking the table with his cane, 'is a life of worrit, and vexation, and hardihood; but all public characters, as I may say, must suffer prosecution.'

Mrs. Mann, not very well knowing what the beadle meant, raised her hands with a look of sympathy, and sighed.

'Ah! You may well sigh, Mrs. Mann!' said the beadle.

Finding she had done right, Mrs. Mann sighed again: evidently to the satisfaction of the public character: who, repressing a complacent smile by looking sternly at his cocked hat, said,

'Mrs. Mann, I am going to London.'

'Lauk, Mr. Bumble!' cried Mrs. Mann, starting back.

'To London, ma'am,' resumed the inflexible beadle, 'by coach. I and two paupers, Mrs. Mann! A legal action is a coming on, about a settlement; and the board has appointed me— me, Mrs. Mann—to dispose to the matter before the quarter-sessions at Clerkinwell.

And I very much question,' added Mr. Bumble, drawing himself up, 'whether the Clerkinwell Sessions will not find themselves in the wrong box before they have done with me.'

'Oh! you mustn't be too hard upon them, sir,' said Mrs. Mann, coaxingly.

'The Clerkinwell Sessions have brought it upon themselves, ma'am,' replied Mr. Bumble; 'and if the Clerkinwell Sessions find that they come off rather worse than they expected, the Clerkinwell Sessions have only themselves to thank.'

There was so much determination and depth of purpose about the menacing manner in which Mr. Bumble delivered himself of these words, that Mrs. Mann appeared quite awed by them. At length she said,

'You're going by coach, sir? I thought it was always usual to send them paupers in carts.'

'That's when they're ill, Mrs. Mann,' said the beadle. 'We put the sick paupers into open carts in the rainy weather, to prevent their taking cold.'

'Oh!' said Mrs. Mann.

'The opposition coach contracts for these two; and takes them cheap,' said Mr. Bumble. 'They are both in a very low state, and we find it would come two pound cheaper to move 'em than to bury 'em—that is, if we can throw 'em upon another parish, which I think we shall be able to do, if they don't die upon the road to spite us. Ha! ha! ha!'

When Mr. Bumble had laughed a little while, his eyes again encountered the cocked hat; and he became grave.

'We are forgetting business, ma'am,' said the beadle; 'here is your porochial stipend for the month.'

Mr. Bumble produced some silver money rolled up in paper, from his pocket-book; and requested a receipt: which Mrs. Mann wrote.

'It's very much blotted, sir,' said the farmer of infants; 'but it's formal enough, I dare say.

Thank you, Mr. Bumble, sir, I am very much obliged to you, I'm sure.'

Mr. Bumble nodded, blandly, in acknowledgment of Mrs. Mann's curtsey; and inquired how the children were.

'Bless their dear little hearts!' said Mrs. Mann with emotion, 'they're as well as can be, the dears! Of course, except the two that died last week. And little Dick.'

'Isn't that boy no better?' inquired Mr. Bumble.

Mrs. Mann shook her head.

'He's a ill-conditioned, wicious, bad-disposed porochial child that,' said Mr. Bumble angrily. 'Where is he?'

'I'll bring him to you in one minute, sir,' replied Mrs. Mann. 'Here, you Dick!'

After some calling, Dick was discovered. Having had his face put under the pump, and dried upon Mrs. Mann's gown, he was led into the awful presence of Mr. Bumble, the beadle.

The child was pale and thin; his cheeks were sunken; and his eyes large and bright. The scanty parish dress, the livery of his misery, hung loosely on his feeble body; and his young limbs had wasted away, like those of an old man.

Such was the little being who stood trembling beneath Mr. Bumble's glance; not daring to lift his eyes from the floor; and dreading even to hear the beadle's voice.

'Can't you look at the gentleman, you obstinate boy?' said Mrs. Mann.

The child meekly raised his eyes, and encountered those of Mr. Bumble.

'What's the matter with you, porochial Dick?' inquired Mr. Bumble, with well-timed jocularity.

'Nothing, sir,' replied the child faintly.

'I should think not,' said Mrs. Mann, who had of course laughed very much at Mr. Bumble's humour.

'You want for nothing, I'm sure.'

'I should like—' faltered the child.

'Hey-day!' interposed Mr. Mann, 'I suppose you're going to say that you DO want for something, now? Why, you little wretch—'

'Stop, Mrs. Mann, stop!' said the beadle, raising his hand with a show of authority. 'Like what, sir, eh?'

'I should like,' faltered the child, 'if somebody that can write, would put a few words down for me on a piece of paper, and fold it up and seal it, and keep it for me, after I am laid in the ground.'

'Why, what does the boy mean?' exclaimed Mr. Bumble, on whom the earnest manner and wan aspect of the child had made some impression: accustomed as he was to such things. 'What do you mean, sir?'

'I should like,' said the child, 'to leave my dear love to poor Oliver Twist; and to let him know how often I have sat by myself and cried to think of his wandering about in the dark nights with nobody to help him. And I should like to tell him,' said the child pressing his small hands together, and speaking with great fervour, 'that I was glad to die when I was very young; for, perhaps, if I had lived to be a man, and had grown old, my little sister who is in Heaven, might forget me, or be unlike me; and it would be so much happier if we were both children there together.'

Mr. Bumble surveyed the little speaker, from head to foot, with indescribable astonishment; and, turning to his companion, said, 'They're all in one story, Mrs. Mann. That out-dacious Oliver had demogalized them all!'

'I couldn't have believed it, sir' said Mrs Mann, holding up her hands, and looking malignantly at Dick. 'I never see such a hardened little wretch!'

'Take him away, ma'am!' said Mr. Bumble imperiously. 'This must be stated to the board, Mrs. Mann.

'I hope the gentleman will understand that it isn't my fault, sir?' said Mrs. Mann, whimpering pathetically.

'They shall understand that, ma'am; they shall be acquainted with the true state of the case,' said Mr. Bumble. 'There; take him away, I can't bear the sight on him.'

Dick was immediately taken away, and locked up in the coal-cellar. Mr. Bumble shortly afterwards took himself off, to prepare for his journey.

At six o'clock next morning, Mr. Bumble: having exchanged his cocked hat for a round one, and encased his person in a blue great-coat with a cape to it: took his place on the outside of the coach, accompanied by the criminals whose settlement was disputed; with whom, in due course of time, he arrived in London.

He experienced no other crosses on the way, than those which originated in the perverse behaviour of the two paupers, who persisted in shivering, and complaining of the cold, in a manner which, Mr. Bumble declared, caused his teeth to chatter in his head, and made him feel quite uncomfortable; although he had a great-coat on.

Having disposed of these evil-minded persons for the night, Mr. Bumble sat himself down in the house at which the coach stopped; and took a temperate dinner of steaks, oyster sauce, and porter. Putting a glass of hot gin-and-water on the chimney-piece, he drew his chair to the fire; and, with sundry moral reflections on the too-prevalent sin of discontent and complaining, composed himself to read the paper.

The very first paragraph upon which Mr. Bumble's eye rested, was the following advertisement.

'FIVE GUINEAS REWARD

'Whereas a young boy, named Oliver Twist, absconded, or was enticed, on Thursday evening last, from his home, at Pentonville; and has not since been heard of. The above reward will be paid to any person who will give such information as will lead to the discovery of the said Oliver Twist, or tend to throw any light upon his previous history, in which the advertiser is, for many reasons, warmly interested.'

And then followed a full description of Oliver's dress, person, appearance, and disappearance: with the name and address of Mr. Brownlow at full length.

Mr. Bumble opened his eyes; read the advertisement, slowly and carefully, three several times; and in something more than five minutes was on his way to Pentonville: having actually, in his excitement, left the glass of hot gin-and-water, untasted.

'Is Mr. Brownlow at home?' inquired Mr. Bumble of the girl who opened the door.

To this inquiry the girl returned the not uncommon, but rather evasive reply of 'I don't know; where do you come from?'

Mr. Bumble no sooner uttered Oliver's name, in explanation of his errand, than Mrs. Bedwin, who had been listening at the parlour door, hastened into the passage in a breathless state.

'Come in, come in,' said the old lady: 'I knew we should hear of him. Poor dear! I knew we should! I was certain of it. Bless his heart! I said so all along.'

Having heard this, the worthy old lady hurried back into the parlour again; and seating herself on a sofa, burst into tears. The girl, who was not quite so susceptible, had run upstairs meanwhile; and now returned with a request that Mr. Bumble would follow her immediately: which he did.

He was shown into the little back study, where sat Mr. Brownlow and his friend Mr. Grimwig, with decanters and glasses before them. The latter gentleman at once burst into the exclamation:

'A beadle. A parish beadle, or I'll eat my head.'

'Pray don't interrupt just now,' said Mr. Brownlow. 'Take a seat, will you?'

Mr. Bumble sat himself down; quite confounded by the oddity of Mr. Grimwig's manner. Mr. Brownlow moved the lamp, so as to obtain an uninterrupted view of the beadle's countenance; and said, with a little impatience,

'Now, sir, you come in consequence of having seen the advertisement?'

'Yes, sir,' said Mr. Bumble.

'And you ARE a beadle, are you not?' inquired Mr. Grimwig.

'I am a porochial beadle, gentlemen,' rejoined Mr. Bumble proudly.

'Of course,' observed Mr. Grimwig aside to his friend, 'I knew he was. A beadle all over!'

Mr. Brownlow gently shook his head to impose silence on his friend, and resumed:

'Do you know where this poor boy is now?'

'No more than nobody,' replied Mr. Bumble.

'Well, what DO you know of him?' inquired the old gentleman. 'Speak out, my friend, if you have anything to say. What DO you know of him?'

'You don't happen to know any good of him, do you?' said Mr. Grimwig, caustically; after an attentive perusal of Mr. Bumble's features.

Mr. Bumble, catching at the inquiry very quickly, shook his head with portentous solemnity.

'You see?' said Mr. Grimwig, looking triumphantly at Mr. Brownlow.

Mr. Brownlow looked apprehensively at Mr. Bumble's pursed-up countenance; and requested him to communicate what he knew regarding Oliver, in as few words as possible.

Mr. Bumble put down his hat; unbuttoned his coat; folded his arms; inclined his head in a retrospective manner; and, after a few moments' reflection, commenced his story.

It would be tedious if given in the beadle's words: occupying, as it did, some twenty minutes in the telling; but the sum and substance of it was, that Oliver was a foundling, born of low and vicious parents. That he had, from his birth, displayed no better qualities than treachery, ingratitude, and malice. That he had terminated his brief career in the place of his birth, by making a sanguinary and cowardly attack on an unoffending lad, and running away in the night-time from his master's house. In proof of his really being the person he represented himself, Mr. Bumble laid upon the table the papers he had brought to town. Folding his arms again, he then awaited Mr. Brownlow's observations.

'I fear it is all too true,' said the old gentleman sorrowfully, after looking over the papers. 'This is not much for your intelligence; but I would gladly have given you treble the money, if it had been favourable to the boy.'

It is not improbable that if Mr. Bumble had been possessed of this information at an earlier period of the interview, he might have imparted a very different colouring to his little history. It was too late to do it now, however; so he shook his head gravely, and, pocketing the five guineas, withdrew.

Mr. Brownlow paced the room to and fro for some minutes; evidently so much disturbed by the beadle's tale, that even Mr. Grimwig forbore to vex him further.

At length he stopped, and rang the bell violently.

'Mrs. Bedwin,' said Mr. Brownlow, when the housekeeper appeared; 'that boy, Oliver, is an imposter.'

'It can't be, sir. It cannot be,' said the old lady energetically.

'I tell you he is,' retorted the old gentleman. 'What do you mean by can't be? We have just heard a full account of him from his birth; and he has been a thorough-paced little villain, all his life.'

'I never will believe it, sir,' replied the old lady, firmly. 'Never!'

'You old women never believe anything but quack-doctors, and lying story-books,' growled Mr. Grimwig. 'I knew it all along. Why didn't you take my advise in the beginning; you would if he hadn't had a fever, I suppose, eh? He was interesting, wasn't he? Interesting! Bah!' And Mr. Grimwig poked the fire with a flourish.

'He was a dear, grateful, gentle child, sir,' retorted Mrs. Bedwin, indignantly. 'I know what children are, sir; and have done these forty years; and people who can't say the same, shouldn't say anything about them. That's my opinion!'

This was a hard hit at Mr. Grimwig, who was a bachelor. As it extorted nothing from that gentleman but a smile, the old lady tossed her head, and smoothed down her apron preparatory to another speech, when she was stopped by Mr. Brownlow.

'Silence!' said the old gentleman, feigning an anger he was far from feeling. 'Never let me hear the boy's name again. I rang to tell you that. Never. Never, on any pretence, mind! You may leave the room, Mrs. Bedwin. Remember! I am in earnest.'

There were sad hearts at Mr. Brownlow's that night.

Oliver's heart sank within him, when he thought of his good friends; it was well for him that he could not know what they had heard, or it might have broken outright.

CHAPTER XVIII. HOW OLIVER PASSED HIS TIME IN THE IMPROVING SOCIETY OF HIS REPUTABLE FRIENDS

About noon next day, when the Dodger and Master Bates had gone out to pursue their customary avocations, Mr. Fagin took the opportunity of reading Oliver a long lecture on the crying sin of ingratitude; of which he clearly demonstrated he had been guilty, to no ordinary extent, in wilfully absenting himself from the society of his anxious friends; and, still more, in endeavouring to escape from them after so much trouble and expense had been incurred in his recovery. Mr. Fagin laid great stress on the fact of his having taken Oliver in, and cherished him, when, without his timely aid, he might have perished with hunger; and he related the dismal and affecting history of a young lad whom, in his philanthropy, he had succoured under parallel circumstances, but who, proving unworthy of his confidence and evincing a desire to communicate with the police, had unfortunately come to be hanged at the Old Bailey one morning. Mr. Fagin did not seek to conceal his share in the catastrophe, but lamented with tears in his eyes that the wrong-headed and treacherous behaviour of the young person in question, had rendered it necessary that he should become the victim of certain evidence for the crown: which, if it were not precisely true, was indispensably necessary for the safety of him (Mr. Fagin) and a few select friends. Mr. Fagin concluded by drawing a rather disagreeable picture of the discomforts of hanging; and, with great friendliness and politeness of manner, expressed his anxious hopes that he might never be obliged to submit Oliver Twist to that unpleasant operation.

Little Oliver's blood ran cold, as he listened to the Jew's words, and imperfectly comprehended the dark threats conveyed in them. That it was possible even for justice itself to confound the innocent with the guilty when they were in accidental companionship, he knew already; and that deeply-laid plans for the destruction of inconveniently knowing or over-communicative persons, had been really devised and carried out by the Jew on more occasions than one, he thought by no means unlikely, when he recollected the general nature of the altercations between that gentleman and Mr. Sikes: which seemed to bear reference to some foregone conspiracy of the kind. As he glanced timidly up, and met the Jew's searching look, he felt that his pale face and trembling limbs were neither unnoticed nor unrelished by that wary old gentleman.

The Jew, smiling hideously, patted Oliver on the head, and said, that if he kept himself quiet, and applied himself to business, he saw they would be very good friends yet. Then, taking his hat, and covering himself with an old patched great-coat, he went out, and locked the room-door behind him.

And so Oliver remained all that day, and for the greater part of many subsequent days, seeing nobody, between early morning and midnight, and left during the long hours to commune with his own thoughts. Which, never failing to revert to his kind friends, and the opinion they must long ago have formed of him, were sad indeed.

After the lapse of a week or so, the Jew left the room-door unlocked; and he was at liberty to wander about the house.

It was a very dirty place. The rooms upstairs had great high wooden chimney-pieces and large doors, with panelled walls and cornices to the ceiling; which, although they were black with neglect and dust, were ornamented in various ways. From all of these tokens Oliver concluded that a long time ago, before the old Jew was born, it had belonged to better people, and had perhaps been quite gay and handsome: dismal and dreary as it looked now.

Spiders had built their webs in the angles of the walls and ceilings; and sometimes, when Oliver walked softly into a room, the mice would scamper across the floor, and run back terrified to their holes. With these exceptions, there was neither sight nor sound of any living thing; and often, when it grew dark, and he was tired of wandering from room to room, he would crouch in the corner of the passage by the street-door, to be as near living people as he could; and would remain there, listening and counting the hours, until the Jew or the boys returned.

In all the rooms, the mouldering shutters were fast closed: the bars which held them were screwed tight into the wood; the only light which was admitted, stealing its way through round holes at the top: which made the rooms more gloomy, and filled them with strange shadows. There was a back-garret window with rusty bars outside, which had no shutter; and out of this, Oliver often gazed with a melancholy face for hours together; but nothing was to be descried from it but a confused and crowded mass of housetops, blackened chimneys, and gable-ends. Sometimes, indeed, a grizzly head might be seen, peering over the parapet-wall of a distant house; but it was quickly withdrawn again; and as the window of Oliver's observatory was nailed down, and dimmed with the rain and smoke of years, it was as much as he could do to make out the forms of the different objects beyond, without making any attempt to be seen or heard,—which he had as much chance of being, as if he had lived inside the ball of St. Paul's Cathedral.

One afternoon, the Dodger and Master Bates being engaged out that evening, the first-named young gentleman took it into his head to evince some anxiety regarding the decoration of his person (to do him justice, this was by no means an habitual weakness with him); and, with this end and aim, he condescendingly commanded Oliver to assist him in his toilet, straightway.

Oliver was but too glad to make himself useful; too happy to have some faces, however bad, to look upon; too desirous to conciliate those about him when he could honestly do so; to throw any objection in the way of this proposal. So he at once expressed his readiness; and, kneeling on the floor, while the Dodger sat upon the table so that he could take his foot in his laps, he applied himself to a process which Mr. Dawkins designated as 'japanning his trotter-cases.' The phrase, rendered into plain English, signifieth, cleaning his boots.

Whether it was the sense of freedom and independence which a rational animal may be supposed to feel when he sits on a table in an easy attitude smoking a pipe, swinging one leg carelessly to and fro, and having his boots cleaned all the time, without even the past trouble of having taken them off, or the prospective misery of putting them on, to disturb his reflections; or whether it was the goodness of the tobacco that soothed the feelings of the Dodger, or the mildness of the beer that mollified his thoughts; he was evidently tinctured, for the nonce, with a spice of romance and enthusiasm, foreign to his general nature. He looked down on Oliver, with a thoughtful countenance, for a brief space; and then, raising his head, and heaving a gentle sign, said, half in abstraction, and half to Master Bates:

'What a pity it is he isn't a prig!'

'Ah!' said Master Charles Bates; 'he don't know what's good for him.'

The Dodger sighed again, and resumed his pipe: as did Charley Bates. They both smoked, for some seconds, in silence.

'I suppose you don't even know what a prig is?' said the Dodger mournfully.

'I think I know that,' replied Oliver, looking up. 'It's a the—; you're one, are you not?' inquired Oliver, checking himself.

'I am,' replied the Dodger. 'I'd scorn to be anything else.' Mr. Dawkins gave his hat a ferocious cock, after delivering this sentiment, and looked at Master Bates, as if to denote that he would feel obliged by his saying anything to the contrary.

'I am,' repeated the Dodger. 'So's Charley. So's Fagin. So's Sikes. So's Nancy. So's Bet. So we all are, down to the dog. And he's the downiest one of the lot!'

'And the least given to peaching,' added Charley Bates.

'He wouldn't so much as bark in a witness-box, for fear of committing himself; no, not if you tied him up in one, and left him there without wittles for a fortnight,' said the Dodger.

'Not a bit of it,' observed Charley.

'He's a rum dog. Don't he look fierce at any strange cove that laughs or sings when he's in company!' pursued the Dodger. 'Won't he growl at all, when he hears a fiddle playing! And don't he hate other dogs as ain't of his breed! Oh, no!'

'He's an out-and-out Christian,' said Charley.

This was merely intended as a tribute to the animal's abilities, but it was an appropriate remark in another sense, if Master Bates had only known it; for there are a good many ladies and gentlemen, claiming to be out-and-out Christians, between whom, and Mr. Sikes' dog, there exist strong and singular points of resemblance.

'Well, well,' said the Dodger, recurring to the point from which they had strayed: with that mindfulness of his profession which influenced all his proceedings. 'This hasn't go anything to do with young Green here.'

'No more it has,' said Charley. 'Why don't you put yourself under Fagin, Oliver?'

'And make your fortun' out of hand?' added the Dodger, with a grin.

'And so be able to retire on your property, and do the gen-teel: as I mean to, in the very next leap-year but four that ever comes, and the forty-second Tuesday in Trinity-week,' said Charley Bates.

'I don't like it,' rejoined Oliver, timidly; 'I wish they would let me go. I—I—would rather go.'

'And Fagin would RATHER not!' rejoined Charley.

Oliver knew this too well; but thinking it might be dangerous to express his feelings more openly, he only sighed, and went on with his boot-cleaning.

'Go!' exclaimed the Dodger. 'Why, where's your spirit?' Don't you take any pride out of yourself? Would you go and be dependent on your friends?'

'Oh, blow that!' said Master Bates: drawing two or three silk handkerchiefs from his pocket, and tossing them into a cupboard, 'that's too mean; that is.'

'I couldn't do it,' said the Dodger, with an air of haughty disgust.

'You can leave your friends, though,' said Oliver with a half smile; 'and let them be punished for what you did.'

'That,' rejoined the Dodger, with a wave of his pipe, 'That was all out of consideration for Fagin, 'cause the traps know that we work together, and he might have got into trouble if we hadn't made our lucky; that was the move, wasn't it, Charley?'

Master Bates nodded assent, and would have spoken, but the recollection of Oliver's flight came so suddenly upon him, that the smoke he was inhaling got entangled with a laugh, and went up into his head, and down into his throat: and brought on a fit of coughing and stamping, about five minutes long.

'Look here!' said the Dodger, drawing forth a handful of shillings and halfpence. 'Here's a jolly life! What's the odds where it comes from? Here, catch hold; there's plenty more where they were took from. You won't, won't you? Oh, you precious flat!'

'It's naughty, ain't it, Oliver?' inquired Charley Bates. 'He'll come to be scragged, won't he?'

'I don't know what that means,' replied Oliver.

'Something in this way, old feller,' said Charly. As he said it, Master Bates caught up an end of his neckerchief; and, holding it erect in the air, dropped his head on his shoulder, and jerked a curious sound through his teeth; thereby indicating, by a lively pantomimic representation, that scragging and hanging were one and the same thing.

'That's what it means,' said Charley. 'Look how he stares, Jack!

I never did see such prime company as that 'ere boy; he'll be the death of me, I know he will.' Master Charley Bates, having laughed heartily again, resumed his pipe with tears in his eyes.

'You've been brought up bad,' said the Dodger, surveying his boots with much satisfaction when Oliver had polished them. 'Fagin will make something of you, though, or you'll be the first he ever had that turned out unprofitable. You'd better begin at once; for you'll come to the trade long before you think of it; and you're only losing time, Oliver.'

Master Bates backed this advice with sundry moral admonitions of his own: which, being exhausted, he and his friend Mr. Dawkins launched into a glowing description of the numerous pleasures incidental to the life they led, interspersed with a variety of hints to Oliver that the best thing he could do, would be to secure Fagin's favour without more delay, by the means which they themselves had employed to gain it.

'And always put this in your pipe, Nolly,' said the Dodger, as the Jew was heard unlocking the door above, 'if you don't take fogels and tickers—'

'What's the good of talking in that way?' interposed Master Bates; 'he don't know what you mean.'

'If you don't take pocket-handkechers and watches,' said the Dodger, reducing his conversation to the level of Oliver's capacity, 'some other cove will; so that the coves that lose 'em will be all the worse, and you'll be all the worse, too, and nobody half a ha'p'orth the better, except the chaps wot gets them—and you've just as good a right to them as they have.'

'To be sure, to be sure!' said the Jew, who had entered unseen by Oliver. 'It all lies in a nutshell my dear; in a nutshell, take the Dodger's word for it. Ha! ha! ha! He understands the catechism of his trade.'

The old man rubbed his hands gleefully together, as he corroborated the Dodger's reasoning in these terms; and chuckled with delight at his pupil's proficiency.

The conversation proceeded no farther at this time, for the Jew had returned home accompanied by Miss Betsy, and a gentleman whom Oliver had never seen before, but who was accosted by the Dodger as Tom Chitling; and who, having lingered on the stairs to exchange a few gallantries with the lady, now made his appearance.

Mr. Chitling was older in years than the Dodger: having perhaps numbered eighteen winters; but there was a degree of deference in his deportment towards that young gentleman which seemed to indicate that he felt himself conscious of a slight inferiority in point of genius and professional aquirements. He had small twinkling eyes, and a pock-marked face; wore a fur cap, a dark corduroy jacket, greasy fustian trousers, and an apron. His wardrobe was, in truth, rather out of repair; but he excused himself to the company by stating that his 'time' was only out an hour before; and that, in consequence of having worn the regimentals for six weeks past, he had not been able to bestow any attention on his private clothes. Mr. Chitling added, with strong marks of irritation, that the new way of fumigating clothes up yonder was infernal unconstitutional, for it burnt holes in them, and there was no remedy against the County. The same remark he considered to apply to the regulation mode of cutting the hair: which he held to be decidedly unlawful. Mr. Chitling wound up his observations by stating that he had not touched a drop of anything for forty-two moral long hard-working days; and that he 'wished he might be busted if he warn't as dry as a lime-basket.'

'Where do you think the gentleman has come from, Oliver?' inquired the Jew, with a grin, as the other boys put a bottle of spirits on the table.

'I—I—don't know, sir,' replied Oliver.

'Who's that?' inquired Tom Chitling, casting a contemptuous look at Oliver.

'A young friend of mine, my dear,' replied the Jew.

'He's in luck, then,' said the young man, with a meaning look at Fagin. 'Never mind where I came from, young 'un; you'll find your way there, soon enough, I'll bet a crown!'

At this sally, the boys laughed. After some more jokes on the same subject, they exchanged a few short whispers with Fagin; and withdrew.

After some words apart between the last comer and Fagin, they drew their chairs towards the fire; and the Jew, telling Oliver to come and sit by him, led the conversation to the topics most calculated to interest his hearers. These were, the great advantages of the trade, the proficiency of the Dodger, the amiability of Charley Bates, and the liberality of the Jew himself. At length these subjects displayed signs of being thoroughly exhausted; and Mr. Chitling did the same: for the house of correction becomes fatiguing after a week or two. Miss

Betsy accordingly withdrew; and left the party to their repose.

From this day, Oliver was seldom left alone; but was placed in almost constant communication with the two boys, who played the old game with the Jew every day: whether for their own improvement or Oliver's, Mr. Fagin best knew. At other times the old man would tell them stories of robberies he had committed in his younger days: mixed up with so much that was droll and curious, that Oliver could not help laughing heartily, and showing that he was amused in spite of all his better feelings.

In short, the wily old Jew had the boy in his toils. Having prepared his mind, by solitude and gloom, to prefer any society to the companionship of his own sad thoughts in such a dreary place, he was now slowly instilling into his soul the poison which he hoped would blacken it, and change its hue for ever.

CHAPTER XIX. IN WHICH A NOTABLE PLAN IS DISCUSSED AND DETERMINED ON

It was a chill, damp, windy night, when the Jew: buttoning his great-coat tight round his shrivelled body, and pulling the collar up over his ears so as completely to obscure the lower part of his face: emerged from his den. He paused on the step as the door was locked and chained behind him; and having listened while the boys made all secure, and until their retreating footsteps were no longer audible, slunk down the street as quickly as he could.

The house to which Oliver had been conveyed, was in the neighborhood of Whitechapel. The Jew stopped for an instant at the corner of the street; and, glancing suspiciously round, crossed the road, and struck off in the direction of the Spitalfields.

The mud lay thick upon the stones, and a black mist hung over the streets; the rain fell sluggishly down, and everything felt cold and clammy to the touch. It seemed just the night when it befitted such a being as the Jew to be abroad. As he glided stealthily along, creeping beneath the shelter of the walls and doorways, the hideous old man seemed like some loathsome reptile, engendered in the slime and darkness through which he moved: crawling forth, by night, in search of some rich offal for a meal.

He kept on his course, through many winding and narrow ways, until he reached Bethnal Green; then, turning suddenly off to the left, he soon became involved in a maze of the mean and dirty streets which abound in that close and densely-populated quarter.

The Jew was evidently too familiar with the ground he traversed to be at all bewildered, either by the darkness of the night, or the intricacies of the way. He hurried through several alleys and streets, and at length turned into one, lighted only by a single lamp at the farther end. At the door of a house in this street, he knocked; having exchanged a few muttered words with the person who opened it, he walked upstairs.

A dog growled as he touched the handle of a room-door; and a man's voice demanded who was there.

'Only me, Bill; only me, my dear,' said the Jew looking in.

'Bring in your body then,' said Sikes. 'Lie down, you stupid brute! Don't you know the devil when he's got a great-coat on?'

Apparently, the dog had been somewhat deceived by Mr. Fagin's outer garment; for as the

Jew unbuttoned it, and threw it over the back of a chair, he retired to the corner from which he had risen: wagging his tail as he went, to show that he was as well satisfied as it was in his nature to be.

'Well!' said Sikes.

'Well, my dear,' replied the Jew.—'Ah! Nancy.'

The latter recognition was uttered with just enough of embarrassment to imply a doubt of its reception; for Mr. Fagin and his young friend had not met, since she had interfered in behalf of Oliver. All doubts upon the subject, if he had any, were speedily removed by the young lady's behaviour. She took her feet off the fender, pushed back her chair, and bade Fagin draw up his, without saying more about it: for it was a cold night, and no mistake.

'It is cold, Nancy dear,' said the Jew, as he warmed his skinny hands over the fire. 'It seems to go right through one,' added the old man, touching his side.

'It must be a piercer, if it finds its way through your heart,' said Mr. Sikes. 'Give him something to drink, Nancy. Burn my body, make haste! It's enough to turn a man ill, to see his lean old carcase shivering in that way, like a ugly ghost just rose from the grave.'

Nancy quickly brought a bottle from a cupboard, in which there were many: which, to judge from the diversity of their appearance, were filled with several kinds of liquids. Sikes pouring out a glass of brandy, bade the Jew drink it off.

'Quite enough, quite, thankye, Bill,' replied the Jew, putting down the glass after just setting his lips to it.

'What! You're afraid of our getting the better of you, are you?' inquired Sikes, fixing his eyes on the Jew. 'Ugh!'

With a hoarse grunt of contempt, Mr. Sikes seized the glass, and threw the remainder of its contents into the ashes: as a preparatory ceremony to filling it again for himself: which he did at once.

The Jew glanced round the room, as his companion tossed down the second glassful; not in curiosity, for he had seen it often before; but in a restless and suspicious manner habitual to him. It was a meanly furnished apartment, with nothing but the contents of the closet to induce the belief that its occupier was anything but a working man; and with no more suspicious articles displayed to view than two or three heavy bludgeons which stood in a corner, and a 'life-preserver' that hung over the chimney-piece.

'There,' said Sikes, smacking his lips. 'Now I'm ready.'

'For business?' inquired the Jew.

'For business,' replied Sikes; 'so say what you've got to say.'

'About the crib at Chertsey, Bill?' said the Jew, drawing his chair forward, and speaking in a very low voice.

'Yes. Wot about it?' inquired Sikes.

'Ah! you know what I mean, my dear,' said the Jew. 'He knows what I mean, Nancy; don't he?'

'No, he don't,' sneered Mr. Sikes. 'Or he won't, and that's the same thing. Speak out, and call things by their right names; don't sit there, winking and blinking, and talking to me in hints, as if you warn't the very first that thought about the robbery. Wot d'ye mean?'

'Hush, Bill, hush!' said the Jew, who had in vain attempted to stop this burst of indignation; 'somebody will hear us, my dear. Somebody will hear us.'

'Let 'em hear!' said Sikes; 'I don't care.' But as Mr. Sikes DID care, on reflection, he dropped his voice as he said the words, and grew calmer.

'There, there,' said the Jew, coaxingly. 'It was only my caution, nothing more. Now, my dear, about that crib at Chertsey; when is it to be done, Bill, eh? When is it to be done? Such plate, my dear, such plate!' said the Jew: rubbing his hands, and elevating his eyebrows in a rapture of anticipation.

'Not at all,' replied Sikes coldly.

'Not to be done at all!' echoed the Jew, leaning back in his chair.

'No, not at all,' rejoined Sikes. 'At least it can't be a put-up job, as we expected.'

'Then it hasn't been properly gone about,' said the Jew, turning pale with anger. 'Don't tell me!'

'But I will tell you,' retorted Sikes. 'Who are you that's not to be told? I tell you that Toby Crackit has been hanging about the place for a fortnight, and he can't get one of the servants in line.'

'Do you mean to tell me, Bill,' said the Jew: softening as the other grew heated: 'that neither of the two men in the house can be got over?'

'Yes, I do mean to tell you so,' replied Sikes. 'The old lady has had 'em these twenty years; and if you were to give 'em five hundred pound, they wouldn't be in it.'

'But do you mean to say, my dear,' remonstrated the Jew, 'that the women can't be got over?'

'Not a bit of it,' replied Sikes.

'Not by flash Toby Crackit?' said the Jew incredulously. 'Think what women are, Bill,'

'No; not even by flash Toby Crackit,' replied Sikes. 'He says he's worn sham whiskers, and a canary waistcoat, the whole blessed time he's been loitering down there, and it's all of no use.'

'He should have tried mustachios and a pair of military trousers, my dear,' said the Jew.

'So he did,' rejoined Sikes, 'and they warn't of no more use than the other plant.'

The Jew looked blank at this information. After ruminating for some minutes with his chin sunk on his breast, he raised his head and said, with a deep sigh, that if flash Toby Crackit reported aright, he feared the game was up.

'And yet,' said the old man, dropping his hands on his knees, 'it's a sad thing, my dear, to lose so much when we had set our hearts upon it.'

'So it is,' said Mr. Sikes. 'Worse luck!'

A long silence ensued; during which the Jew was plunged in deep thought, with his face wrinkled into an expression of villainy perfectly demoniacal. Sikes eyed him furtively from time to time. Nancy, apparently fearful of irritating the housebreaker, sat with her eyes fixed upon the fire, as if she had been deaf to all that passed.

'Fagin,' said Sikes, abruptly breaking the stillness that prevailed; 'is it worth fifty shiners extra, if it's safely done from the outside?'

'Yes,' said the Jew, as suddenly rousing himself.

'Is it a bargain?' inquired Sikes.

'Yes, my dear, yes,' rejoined the Jew; his eyes glistening, and every muscle in his face working, with the excitement that the inquiry had awakened.

'Then,' said Sikes, thrusting aside the Jew's hand, with some disdain, 'let it come off as soon as you like. Toby and me were over the garden-wall the night afore last, sounding the panels of the door and shutters. The crib's barred up at night like a jail; but there's one part we can crack, safe and softly.'

'Which is that, Bill?' asked the Jew eagerly.

'Why,' whispered Sikes, 'as you cross the lawn—'

'Yes?' said the Jew, bending his head forward, with his eyes almost starting out of it.

'Umph!' cried Sikes, stopping short, as the girl, scarcely moving her head, looked suddenly round, and pointed for an instant to the Jew's face. 'Never mind which part it is. You can't do it without me, I know; but it's best to be on the safe side when one deals with you.'

'As you like, my dear, as you like' replied the Jew. 'Is there no help wanted, but yours and Toby's?'

'None,' said Sikes. 'Cept a centre-bit and a boy. The first we've both got; the second you must find us.'

'A boy!' exclaimed the Jew. 'Oh! then it's a panel, eh?'

'Never mind wot it is!' replied Sikes. 'I want a boy, and he musn't be a big 'un. Lord!' said Mr. Sikes, reflectively, 'if I'd only got that young boy of Ned, the chimbley-sweeper's! He kept him small on purpose, and let him out by the job. But the father gets lagged; and then the Juvenile Delinquent Society comes, and takes the boy away from a trade where he was earning money, teaches him to read and write, and in time makes a 'prentice of him. And so they go on,' said Mr. Sikes, his wrath rising with the recollection of his wrongs, 'so they go on; and, if they'd got money enough (which it's a Providence they haven't,) we shouldn't have half a dozen boys left in the whole trade, in a year or two.'

'No more we should,' acquiesced the Jew, who had been considering during this speech, and had only caught the last sentence. 'Bill!'

'What now?' inquired Sikes.

The Jew nodded his head towards Nancy, who was still gazing at the fire; and intimated, by a sign, that he would have her told to leave the room. Sikes shrugged his shoulders impatiently, as if he thought the precaution unnecessary; but complied, nevertheless, by requesting Miss Nancy to fetch him a jug of beer.

'You don't want any beer,' said Nancy, folding her arms, and retaining her seat very composedly.

'I tell you I do!' replied Sikes.

'Nonsense,' rejoined the girl coolly, 'Go on, Fagin. I know what he's going to say, Bill; he needn't mind me.'

The Jew still hesitated. Sikes looked from one to the other in some surprise.

'Why, you don't mind the old girl, do you, Fagin?' he asked at length. 'You've known her long enough to trust her, or the Devil's in it. She ain't one to blab. Are you Nancy?'

'I should think not!' replied the young lady: drawing her chair up to the table, and putting her elbows upon it.

'No, no, my dear, I know you're not,' said the Jew; 'but—' and again the old man paused.

'But wot?' inquired Sikes.

'I didn't know whether she mightn't p'r'aps be out of sorts, you know, my dear, as she was the other night,' replied the Jew.

At this confession, Miss Nancy burst into a loud laugh; and, swallowing a glass of brandy, shook her head with an air of defiance, and burst into sundry exclamations of 'Keep the game a-going!' 'Never say die!' and the like. These seemed to have the effect of re-assuring both gentlemen; for the Jew nodded his head with a satisfied air, and resumed his seat: as did Mr. Sikes likewise.

'Now, Fagin,' said Nancy with a laugh. 'Tell Bill at once, about Oliver!'

'Ha! you're a clever one, my dear: the sharpest girl I ever saw!' said the Jew, patting her on the neck. 'It WAS about Oliver I was going to speak, sure enough. Ha! ha! ha!'

'What about him?' demanded Sikes.

'He's the boy for you, my dear,' replied the Jew in a hoarse whisper; laying his finger on the side of his nose, and grinning frightfully.

'He!' exclaimed Sikes.

'Have him, Bill!' said Nancy. 'I would, if I was in your place. He mayn't be so much up, as any of the others; but that's not what you want, if he's only to open a door for you. Depend upon it he's a safe one, Bill.'

'I know he is,' rejoined Fagin. 'He's been in good training these last few weeks, and it's time he began to work for his bread. Besides, the others are all too big.'

'Well, he is just the size I want,' said Mr. Sikes, ruminating.

'And will do everything you want, Bill, my dear,' interposed the Jew; 'he can't help himself. That is, if you frighten him enough.'

'Frighten him!' echoed Sikes. 'It'll be no sham frightening, mind you. If there's anything queer about him when we once get into the work; in for a penny, in for a pound. You won't see him alive again, Fagin. Think of that, before you send him. Mark my words!' said the robber, poising a crowbar, which he had drawn from under the bedstead.

'I've thought of it all,' said the Jew with energy. 'I've—I've had my eye upon him, my dears, close—close. Once let him feel that he is one of us; once fill his mind with the idea that he has been a thief; and he's ours! Ours for his life. Oho! It couldn't have come about better!

The old man crossed his arms upon his breast; and, drawing his head and shoulders into a heap, literally hugged himself for joy.

'Ours!' said Sikes. 'Yours, you mean.'

'Perhaps I do, my dear,' said the Jew, with a shrill chuckle. 'Mine, if you like, Bill.'

'And wot,' said Sikes, scowling fiercely on his agreeable friend, 'wot makes you take so much pains about one chalk-faced kid, when you know there are fifty boys snoozing about Common Garden every night, as you might pick and choose from?'

'Because they're of no use to me, my dear,' replied the Jew, with some confusion, 'not worth the taking. Their looks convict 'em when they get into trouble, and I lose 'em all. With this boy, properly managed, my dears, I could do what I couldn't with twenty of them. Besides,' said the Jew, recovering his self-possession, 'he has us now if he could only give us leg-bail again; and he must be in the same boat with us. Never mind how he came there; it's quite enough for my power over him that he was in a robbery; that's all I want. Now, how much better this is, than being obliged to put the poor leetle boy out of the way—which would be dangerous, and we should lose by it besides.'

'When is it to be done?' asked Nancy, stopping some turbulent exclamation on the part of Mr. Sikes, expressive of the disgust with which he received Fagin's affectation of humanity.

'Ah, to be sure,' said the Jew; 'when is it to be done, Bill?'

'I planned with Toby, the night arter to-morrow,' rejoined Sikes in a surly voice, 'if he heerd nothing from me to the contrairy.'

'Good,' said the Jew; 'there's no moon.'

'No,' rejoined Sikes.

'It's all arranged about bringing off the swag, is it?' asked the Jew.

Sikes nodded.

'And about—'

'Oh, ah, it's all planned,' rejoined Sikes, interrupting him. 'Never mind particulars. You'd better bring the boy here to-morrow night. I shall get off the stone an hour arter daybreak. Then you hold your tongue, and keep the melting-pot ready, and that's all you'll have to do.'

After some discussion, in which all three took an active part, it was decided that Nancy should repair to the Jew's next evening when the night had set in, and bring Oliver away with her; Fagin craftily observing, that, if he evinced any disinclination to the task, he would be more willing to accompany the girl who had so recently interfered in his behalf, than anybody else. It was also solemnly arranged that poor Oliver should, for the purposes of the contemplated expedition, be unreservedly consigned to the care and custody of Mr. William Sikes; and further, that the said Sikes should deal with him as he thought fit; and should not be held responsible by the Jew for any mischance or evil that might be necessary to visit him: it being understood that, to render the compact in this respect binding, any representations made by Mr. Sikes on his return should be required to be confirmed and corroborated, in all important particulars, by the testimony of flash Toby Crackit.

These preliminaries adjusted, Mr. Sikes proceeded to drink brandy at a furious rate, and to flourish the crowbar in an alarming manner; yelling forth, at the same time, most unmusical snatches of song, mingled with wild execrations. At length, in a fit of professional enthusiasm, he insisted upon producing his box of housebreaking tools: which he had no sooner stumbled in with, and opened for the purpose of explaining the nature and properties of the various implements it contained, and the peculiar beauties of their construction, than he fell over the box upon the floor, and went to sleep where he fell.

'Good-night, Nancy,' said the Jew, muffling himself up as before.

'Good-night.'

Their eyes met, and the Jew scrutinised her, narrowly. There was no flinching about the girl. She was as true and earnest in the matter as Toby Crackit himself could be.

The Jew again bade her good-night, and, bestowing a sly kick upon the prostrate form of Mr. Sikes while her back was turned, groped downstairs.

'Always the way!' muttered the Jew to himself as he turned homeward. 'The worst of these women is, that a very little thing serves to call up some long-forgotten feeling; and, the best of them is, that it never lasts. Ha! ha! The man against the child, for a bag of gold!'

Beguiling the time with these pleasant reflections, Mr. Fagin wended his way, through mud and mire, to his gloomy abode: where the Dodger was sitting up, impatiently awaiting his return.

'Is Oliver a-bed? I want to speak to him,' was his first remark as they descended the stairs.

'Hours ago,' replied the Dodger, throwing open a door. 'Here he is!'

The boy was lying, fast asleep, on a rude bed upon the floor; so pale with anxiety, and sadness, and the closeness of his prison, that he looked like death; not death as it shows in shroud and coffin, but in the guise it wears when life has just departed; when a young and gentle spirit has, but an instant, fled to Heaven, and the gross air of the world has not had time to breathe upon the changing dust it hallowed.

'Not now,' said the Jew, turning softly away. 'To-morrow. To-morrow.'

CHAPTER XX. WHEREIN OLIVER IS DELIVERED OVER TO MR. WILLIAM SIKES

When Oliver awoke in the morning, he was a good deal surprised to find that a new pair of shoes, with strong thick soles, had been placed at his bedside; and that his old shoes had been removed. At first, he was pleased with the discovery: hoping that it might be the forerunner of his release; but such thoughts were quickly dispelled, on his sitting down to breakfast along with the Jew, who told him, in a tone and manner which increased his alarm, that he was to be taken to the residence of Bill Sikes that night.

'To—to—stop there, sir?' asked Oliver, anxiously.

'No, no, my dear. Not to stop there,' replied the Jew. 'We shouldn't like to lose you. Don't be afraid, Oliver, you shall come back to us again. Ha! ha! ha! We won't be so cruel as to send you away, my dear. Oh no, no!'

The old man, who was stooping over the fire toasting a piece of bread, looked round as he bantered Oliver thus; and chuckled as if to show that he knew he would still be very glad to get away if he could.

'I suppose,' said the Jew, fixing his eyes on Oliver, 'you want to know what you're going to Bill's for——eh, my dear?'

Oliver coloured, involuntarily, to find that the old thief had been reading his thoughts; but boldly said, Yes, he did want to know.

'Why, do you think?' inquired Fagin, parrying the question.

'Indeed I don't know, sir,' replied Oliver.

'Bah!' said the Jew, turning away with a disappointed countenance from a close perusal of the boy's face. 'Wait till Bill tells you, then.'

The Jew seemed much vexed by Oliver's not expressing any greater curiosity on the subject; but the truth is, that, although Oliver felt very anxious, he was too much confused by the earnest cunning of Fagin's looks, and his own speculations, to make any further inquiries just then. He had no other opportunity: for the Jew remained very surly and silent till night: when he prepared to go abroad.

'You may burn a candle,' said the Jew, putting one upon the table. 'And here's a book for you to read, till they come to fetch you. Good-night!'

'Good-night!' replied Oliver, softly.

The Jew walked to the door: looking over his shoulder at the boy as he went. Suddenly stopping, he called him by his name.

Oliver looked up; the Jew, pointing to the candle, motioned him to light it. He did so; and, as he placed the candlestick upon the table, saw that the Jew was gazing fixedly at him, with lowering and contracted brows, from the dark end of the room.

'Take heed, Oliver! take heed!' said the old man, shaking his right hand before him in a warning manner. 'He's a rough man, and thinks nothing of blood when his own is up. Whatever falls out, say nothing; and do what he bids you. Mind!' Placing a strong emphasis on the last word, he suffered his features gradually to resolve themselves into a ghastly grin, and, nodding his head, left the room.

Oliver leaned his head upon his hand when the old man disappeared, and pondered, with a trembling heart, on the words he had just heard. The more he thought of the Jew's admonition, the more he was at a loss to divine its real purpose and meaning.

He could think of no bad object to be attained by sending him to Sikes, which would not be equally well answered by his remaining with Fagin; and after meditating for a long time, concluded that he had been selected to perform some ordinary menial offices for the housebreaker, until another boy, better suited for his purpose could be engaged. He was too well accustomed to suffering, and had suffered too much where he was, to bewail the prospect of change very severely. He remained lost in thought for some minutes; and then, with a heavy sigh, snuffed the candle, and, taking up the book which the Jew had left with him, began to read.

He turned over the leaves. Carelessly at first; but, lighting on a passage which attracted his attention, he soon became intent upon the volume. It was a history of the lives and trials of great criminals; and the pages were soiled and thumbed with use. Here, he read of dreadful crimes that made the blood run cold; of secret murders that had been committed by the lonely wayside; of bodies hidden from the eye of man in deep pits and wells: which would not keep them down, deep as they were, but had yielded them up at last, after many years, and so maddened the murderers with the sight, that in their horror they had confessed their guilt, and yelled for the gibbet to end their agony. Here, too, he read of men who, lying in their beds at dead of night, had been tempted (so they said) and led on, by their own bad thoughts, to such dreadful bloodshed as it made the flesh creep, and the limbs quail, to think of. The terrible descriptions were so real and vivid, that the sallow pages seemed to turn red with gore; and the words upon them, to be sounded in his ears, as if they were whispered, in hollow murmurs, by the spirits of the dead.

In a paroxysm of fear, the boy closed the book, and thrust it from him. Then, falling upon his knees, he prayed Heaven to spare him from such deeds; and rather to will that he should die at once, than be reserved for crimes, so fearful and appalling. By degrees, he grew more calm, and besought, in a low and broken voice, that he might be rescued from his present dangers; and that if any aid were to be raised up for a poor outcast boy who had never known the love of friends or kindred, it might come to him now, when, desolate and deserted, he stood alone in the midst of wickedness and guilt.

He had concluded his prayer, but still remained with his head buried in his hands, when a rustling noise aroused him.

'What's that!' he cried, starting up, and catching sight of a figure standing by the door. 'Who's there?'

'Me. Only me,' replied a tremulous voice.

Oliver raised the candle above his head: and looked towards the door. It was Nancy.

'Put down the light,' said the girl, turning away her head. 'It hurts my eyes.'

Oliver saw that she was very pale, and gently inquired if she were ill. The girl threw herself into a chair, with her back towards him: and wrung her hands; but made no reply.

'God forgive me!' she cried after a while, 'I never thought of this.'

'Has anything happened?' asked Oliver. 'Can I help you? I will if I can. I will, indeed.'

She rocked herself to and fro; caught her throat; and, uttering a gurgling sound, gasped for breath.

'Nancy!' cried Oliver, 'What is it?'

The girl beat her hands upon her knees, and her feet upon the ground; and, suddenly stopping, drew her shawl close round her: and shivered with cold.

Oliver stirred the fire. Drawing her chair close to it, she sat there, for a little time, without speaking; but at length she raised her head, and looked round.

'I don't know what comes over me sometimes,' said she, affecting to busy herself in arranging her dress; 'it's this damp dirty room, I think. Now, Nolly, dear, are you ready?'

'Am I to go with you?' asked Oliver.

'Yes. I have come from Bill,' replied the girl. 'You are to go with me.'

'What for?' asked Oliver, recoiling.

'What for?' echoed the girl, raising her eyes, and averting them again, the moment they encountered the boy's face. 'Oh! For no harm.'

'I don't believe it,' said Oliver: who had watched her closely.

'Have it your own way,' rejoined the girl, affecting to laugh. 'For no good, then.'

Oliver could see that he had some power over the girl's better feelings, and, for an instant, thought of appealing to her compassion for his helpless state. But, then, the thought darted across his mind that it was barely eleven o'clock; and that many people were still in the streets: of whom surely some might be found to give credence to his tale. As the reflection occured to him, he stepped forward: and said, somewhat hastily, that he was ready.

Neither his brief consideration, nor its purport, was lost on his companion. She eyed him narrowly, while he spoke; and cast upon him a look of intelligence which sufficiently showed that she guessed what had been passing in his thoughts.

'Hush!' said the girl, stooping over him, and pointing to the door as she looked cautiously round. 'You can't help yourself. I have tried hard for you, but all to no purpose. You are hedged round and round. If ever you are to get loose from here, this is not the time.'

Struck by the energy of her manner, Oliver looked up in her face with great surprise. She seemed to speak the truth; her countenance was white and agitated; and she trembled with very earnestness.

'I have saved you from being ill-used once, and I will again, and I do now,' continued the girl aloud; 'for those who would have fetched you, if I had not, would have been far more rough than me. I have promised for your being quiet and silent; if you are not, you will only do harm to yourself and me too, and perhaps be my death. See here! I have borne all this for you already, as true as God sees me show it.'

She pointed, hastily, to some livid bruises on her neck and arms; and continued, with great rapidity:

'Remember this! And don't let me suffer more for you, just now. If I could help you, I would; but I have not the power. They don't mean to harm you; whatever they make you do, is no fault of yours. Hush! Every word from you is a blow for me. Give me your hand. Make haste! Your hand!'

She caught the hand which Oliver instinctively placed in hers, and, blowing out the light, drew him after her up the stairs. The door was opened, quickly, by some one shrouded in the darkness, and was as quickly closed, when they had passed out. A hackney-cabriolet was in waiting; with the same vehemence which she had exhibited in addressing Oliver, the girl pulled him in with her, and drew the curtains close. The driver wanted no directions, but lashed his horse into full speed, without the delay of an instant.

The girl still held Oliver fast by the hand, and continued to pour into his ear, the warnings and assurances she had already imparted. All was so quick and hurried, that he had scarcely time to recollect where he was, or how he came there, when the carriage stopped at the house to which the Jew's steps had been directed on the previous evening.

For one brief moment, Oliver cast a hurried glance along the empty street, and a cry for help hung upon his lips. But the girl's voice was in his ear, beseeching him in such tones of agony to remember her, that he had not the heart to utter it. While he hesitated, the opportunity was gone; he was already in the house, and the door was shut.

'This way,' said the girl, releasing her hold for the first time. 'Bill!'

'Hallo!' replied Sikes: appearing at the head of the stairs, with a candle. 'Oh! That's the time of day. Come on!'

This was a very strong expression of approbation, an uncommonly hearty welcome, from a person of Mr. Sikes' temperament. Nancy, appearing much gratified thereby, saluted him cordially.

'Bull's-eye's gone home with Tom,' observed Sikes, as he lighted them up. 'He'd have been in the way.'

'That's right,' rejoined Nancy.

'So you've got the kid,' said Sikes when they had all reached the room: closing the door as he spoke.

'Yes, here he is,' replied Nancy.

'Did he come quiet?' inquired Sikes.

'Like a lamb,' rejoined Nancy.

'I'm glad to hear it,' said Sikes, looking grimly at Oliver; 'for the sake of his young carcase: as would otherways have suffered for it. Come here, young 'un; and let me read you a lectur', which is as well got over at once.'

Thus addressing his new pupil, Mr. Sikes pulled off Oliver's cap and threw it into a corner; and then, taking him by the shoulder, sat himself down by the table, and stood the boy in front of him.

'Now, first: do you know wot this is?' inquired Sikes, taking up a pocket-pistol which lay on the table.

Oliver replied in the affirmative.

'Well, then, look here,' continued Sikes. 'This is powder; that 'ere's a bullet; and this is a little bit of a old hat for waddin'.'

Oliver murmured his comprehension of the different bodies referred to; and Mr. Sikes proceeded to load the pistol, with great nicety and deliberation.

'Now it's loaded,' said Mr. Sikes, when he had finished.

'Yes, I see it is, sir,' replied Oliver.

'Well,' said the robber, grasping Oliver's wrist, and putting the barrel so close to his temple that they touched; at which moment the boy could not repress a start; 'if you speak a word when you're out o'doors with me, except when I speak to you, that loading will be in your head without notice. So, if you do make up your mind to speak without leave, say your prayers first.'

Having bestowed a scowl upon the object of this warning, to increase its effect, Mr. Sikes continued.

'As near as I know, there isn't anybody as would be asking very partickler arter you, if you was disposed of; so I needn't take this devil-and-all of trouble to explain matters to you, if it warn't for your own good. D'ye hear me?'

'The short and the long of what you mean,' said Nancy: speaking very emphatically, and slightly frowning at Oliver as if to bespeak his serious attention to her words: 'is, that if you're crossed by him in this job you have on hand, you'll prevent his ever telling tales afterwards, by shooting him through the head, and will take your chance of swinging for it, as you do for a great many other things in the way of business, every month of your life.'

'That's it!' observed Mr. Sikes, approvingly; 'women can always put things in fewest words.—Except when it's blowing up; and then they lengthens it out. And now that he's thoroughly up to it, let's have some supper, and get a snooze before starting.'

In pursuance of this request, Nancy quickly laid the cloth; disappearing for a few minutes, she presently returned with a pot of porter and a dish of sheep's heads: which gave occasion to several pleasant witticisms on the part of Mr. Sikes, founded upon the singular coincidence of 'jemmies' being a can name, common to them, and also to an ingenious implement much used in his profession. Indeed, the worthy gentleman, stimulated perhaps by the immediate prospect of being on active service, was in great spirits and good humour; in proof whereof, it may be here remarked, that he humourously drank all the beer at a draught, and did not utter, on a rough calculation, more than four-score oaths during the whole progress of the meal.

Supper being ended—it may be easily conceived that Oliver had no great appetite for it—Mr. Sikes disposed of a couple of glasses of spirits and water, and threw himself on the bed; ordering Nancy, with many imprecations in case of failure, to call him at five precisely. Oliver stretched himself in his clothes, by command of the same authority, on a mattress upon the floor; and the girl, mending the fire, sat before it, in readiness to rouse them at the appointed time.

For a long time Oliver lay awake, thinking it not impossible that Nancy might seek that opportunity of whispering some further advice; but the girl sat brooding over the fire, without moving, save now and then to trim the light. Weary with watching and anxiety, he at length fell asleep.

When he awoke, the table was covered with tea-things, and Sikes was thrusting various articles into the pockets of his great-coat, which hung over the back of a chair. Nancy was busily engaged in preparing breakfast. It was not yet daylight; for the candle was still burning, and it was quite dark outside. A sharp rain, too, was beating against the window-panes; and the sky looked black and cloudy.

'Now, then!' growled Sikes, as Oliver started up; 'half-past five! Look sharp, or you'll get no breakfast; for it's late as it is.'

Oliver was not long in making his toilet; having taken some breakfast, he replied to a surly inquiry from Sikes, by saying that he was quite ready.

Nancy, scarcely looking at the boy, threw him a handkerchief to tie round his throat; Sikes gave him a large rough cape to button over his shoulders. Thus attired, he gave his hand to the robber, who, merely pausing to show him with a menacing gesture that he had that same pistol in a side-pocket of his great-coat, clasped it firmly in his, and, exchanging a farewell with Nancy, led him away.

Oliver turned, for an instant, when they reached the door, in the hope of meeting a look from the girl. But she had resumed her old seat in front of the fire, and sat, perfectly motionless before it.

CHAPTER XXI. THE EXPEDITION

It was a cheerless morning when they got into the street; blowing and raining hard; and the clouds looking dull and stormy. The night had been very wet: large pools of water had collected in the road: and the kennels were overflowing. There was a faint glimmering of the coming day in the sky; but it rather aggravated than relieved the gloom of the scene: the sombre light only serving to pale that which the street lamps afforded, without shedding any warmer or brighter tints upon the wet house-tops, and dreary streets. There appeared to be nobody stirring in that quarter of the town; the windows of the houses were all closely shut; and the streets through which they passed, were noiseless and empty.

By the time they had turned into the Bethnal Green Road, the day had fairly begun to break. Many of the lamps were already extinguished; a few country waggons were slowly toiling on, towards London; now and then, a stage-coach, covered with mud, rattled briskly by: the driver bestowing, as he passed, an admonitory lash upon the heavy waggoner who, by keeping on the wrong side of the road, had endangered his arriving at the office, a quarter of a minute after his time. The public-houses, with gas-lights burning inside, were already open. By degrees, other shops began to be unclosed, and a few scattered people were met with. Then, came straggling groups of labourers going to their work; then, men and women with fish-baskets on their heads; donkey-carts laden with vegetables; chaise-carts filled with live-stock or whole carcasses of meat; milk-women with pails; an unbroken concourse of people, trudging out with various supplies to the eastern suburbs of the town. As they approached the City, the noise and traffic gradually increased; when they threaded the streets between Shoreditch and Smithfield, it had swelled into a roar of sound and bustle. It was as light as it was likely to be, till night came on again, and the busy morning of half the London population had begun.

Turning down Sun Street and Crown Street, and crossing Finsbury square, Mr. Sikes struck, by way of Chiswell Street, into Barbican: thence into Long Lane, and so into Smithfield; from which latter place arose a tumult of discordant sounds that filled Oliver Twist with amazement.

It was market-morning. The ground was covered, nearly ankle-deep, with filth and mire; a thick steam, perpetually rising from the reeking bodies of the cattle, and mingling with the fog, which seemed to rest upon the chimney-tops, hung heavily above. All the pens in the centre of the large area, and as many temporary pens as could be crowded into the vacant space, were filled with sheep; tied up to posts by the gutter side were long lines of beasts and oxen, three or four deep. Countrymen, butchers, drovers, hawkers, boys, thieves, idlers, and vagabonds of every low grade, were mingled together in a mass; the whistling of drovers, the barking dogs, the bellowing and plunging of the oxen, the bleating of sheep, the grunting and squeaking of pigs, the cries of hawkers, the shouts, oaths, and quarrelling on all sides; the ringing of bells and roar of voices, that issued from every public-house; the crowding, pushing, driving, beating, whooping and yelling; the hideous and discordant dim that resounded from every corner of the market; and the unwashed, unshaven, squalid, and dirty figures constantly running to and fro, and bursting in and out of the throng; rendered it a stunning and bewildering scene, which quite confounded the senses.

Mr. Sikes, dragging Oliver after him, elbowed his way through the thickest of the crowd, and bestowed very little attention on the numerous sights and sounds, which so astonished the boy. He nodded, twice or thrice, to a passing friend; and, resisting as many invitations to take a morning dram, pressed steadily onward, until they were clear of the turmoil, and had made their way through Hosier Lane into Holborn.

'Now, young 'un!' said Sikes, looking up at the clock of St. Andrew's Church, 'hard upon seven! you must step out. Come, don't lag behind already, Lazy-legs!'

Mr. Sikes accompanied this speech with a jerk at his little companion's wrist; Oliver, quickening his pace into a kind of trot between a fast walk and a run, kept up with the rapid strides of the house-breaker as well as he could.

They held their course at this rate, until they had passed Hyde Park corner, and were on their way to Kensington: when Sikes relaxed his pace, until an empty cart which was at some little distance behind, came up. Seeing 'Hounslow' written on it, he asked the driver with as much civility as he could assume, if he would give them a lift as far as Isleworth.

'Jump up,' said the man. 'Is that your boy?'

'Yes; he's my boy,' replied Sikes, looking hard at Oliver, and putting his hand abstractedly into the pocket where the pistol was.

'Your father walks rather too quick for you, don't he, my man?' inquired the driver: seeing that Oliver was out of breath.

'Not a bit of it,' replied Sikes, interposing. 'He's used to it.

Here, take hold of my hand, Ned. In with you!'

Thus addressing Oliver, he helped him into the cart; and the driver, pointing to a heap of sacks, told him to lie down there, and rest himself.

As they passed the different mile-stones, Oliver wondered, more and more, where his companion meant to take him. Kensington, Hammersmith, Chiswick, Kew Bridge, Brentford, were all passed; and yet they went on as steadily as if they had only just begun their journey. At length, they came to a public-house called the Coach and Horses; a little way beyond which, another road appeared to run off. And here, the cart stopped.

Sikes dismounted with great precipitation, holding Oliver by the hand all the while; and lifting him down directly, bestowed a furious look upon him, and rapped the side-pocket with his fist, in a significant manner.

'Good-bye, boy,' said the man.

'He's sulky,' replied Sikes, giving him a shake; 'he's sulky. A young dog! Don't mind him.'

'Not I!' rejoined the other, getting into his cart. 'It's a fine day, after all.' And he drove away.

Sikes waited until he had fairly gone; and then, telling Oliver he might look about him if he wanted, once again led him onward on his journey.

They turned round to the left, a short way past the public-house; and then, taking a right-hand road, walked on for a long time: passing many large gardens and gentlemen's houses on both sides of the way, and stopping for nothing but a little beer, until they reached a town. Here against the wall of a house, Oliver saw written up in pretty large letters, 'Hampton.' They lingered about, in the fields, for some hours. At length they came back into the town; and, turning into an old public-house with a defaced sign-board, ordered some dinner by the kitchen fire.

The kitchen was an old, low-roofed room; with a great beam across the middle of the ceiling, and benches, with high backs to them, by the fire; on which were seated several rough men in smock-frocks, drinking and smoking. They took no notice of Oliver; and very little of Sikes; and, as Sikes took very little notice of them, he and his young comrade sat in a corner by themselves, without being much troubled by their company.

They had some cold meat for dinner, and sat so long after it, while Mr. Sikes indulged himself with three or four pipes, that Oliver began to feel quite certain they were not going any further. Being much tired with the walk, and getting up so early, he dozed a little at first; then, quite overpowered by fatigue and the fumes of the tobacco, fell asleep.

It was quite dark when he was awakened by a push from Sikes. Rousing himself sufficiently to sit up and look about him, he found that worthy in close fellowship and communication with a labouring man, over a pint of ale.

'So, you're going on to Lower Halliford, are you?' inquired Sikes.

'Yes, I am,' replied the man, who seemed a little the worse—or better, as the case might be—for drinking; 'and not slow about it neither. My horse hasn't got a load behind him going back, as he had coming up in the mornin'; and he won't be long a-doing of it. Here's luck to him. Ecod! he's a good 'un!'

'Could you give my boy and me a lift as far as there?' demanded Sikes, pushing the ale towards his new friend.

'If you're going directly, I can,' replied the man, looking out of the pot. 'Are you going to Halliford?'

'Going on to Shepperton,' replied Sikes.

'I'm your man, as far as I go,' replied the other. 'Is all paid, Becky?'

'Yes, the other gentleman's paid,' replied the girl.

'I say!' said the man, with tipsy gravity; 'that won't do, you know.'

'Why not?' rejoined Sikes. 'You're a-going to accommodate us, and wot's to prevent my standing treat for a pint or so, in return?'

The stranger reflected upon this argument, with a very profound face; having done so, he seized Sikes by the hand: and declared he was a real good fellow. To which Mr. Sikes replied, he was joking; as, if he had been sober, there would have been strong reason to suppose he was.

After the exchange of a few more compliments, they bade the company good-night, and went out; the girl gathering up the pots and glasses as they did so, and lounging out to the door, with her hands full, to see the party start.

The horse, whose health had been drunk in his absence, was standing outside: ready harnessed to the cart. Oliver and Sikes got in without any further ceremony; and the man to whom he belonged, having lingered for a minute or two 'to bear him up,' and to defy the hostler and the world to produce his equal, mounted also. Then, the hostler was told to give the horse his head; and, his head being given him, he made a very unpleasant use of it: tossing it into the air with great disdain, and running into the parlour windows over the way; after performing those feats, and supporting himself for a short time on his hind-legs, he started off at great speed, and rattled out of the town right gallantly.

The night was very dark. A damp mist rose from the river, and the marshy ground about; and spread itself over the dreary fields. It was piercing cold, too; all was gloomy and black. Not a word was spoken; for the driver had grown sleepy; and Sikes was in no mood to lead him into conversation. Oliver sat huddled together, in a corner of the cart; bewildered with alarm and apprehension; and figuring strange objects in the gaunt trees, whose branches waved grimly to and fro, as if in some fantastic joy at the desolation of the scene.

As they passed Sunbury Church, the clock struck seven. There was a light in the ferry-house window opposite: which streamed across the road, and threw into more sombre shadow a dark yew-tree with graves beneath it. There was a dull sound of falling water not far off; and the leaves of the old tree stirred gently in the night wind. It seemed like quiet music for the repose of the dead.

Sunbury was passed through, and they came again into the lonely road. Two or three miles more, and the cart stopped. Sikes alighted, took Oliver by the hand, and they once again walked on.

They turned into no house at Shepperton, as the weary boy had expected; but still kept walking on, in mud and darkness, through gloomy lanes and over cold open wastes, until they came within sight of the lights of a town at no great distance. On looking intently forward, Oliver saw that the water was just below them, and that they were coming to the foot of a bridge.

Sikes kept straight on, until they were close upon the bridge; then turned suddenly down a bank upon the left.

'The water!' thought Oliver, turning sick with fear. 'He has brought me to this lonely place to murder me!'

He was about to throw himself on the ground, and make one struggle for his young life, when he saw that they stood before a solitary house: all ruinous and decayed. There was a window on each side of the dilapidated entrance; and one story above; but no light was visible. The house was dark, dismantled: and the all appearance, uninhabited.

Sikes, with Oliver's hand still in his, softly approached the low porch, and raised the latch. The door yielded to the pressure, and they passed in together.

CHAPTER XXII. THE BURGLARY

'Hallo!' cried a loud, hoarse voice, as soon as they set foot in the passage.

'Don't make such a row,' said Sikes, bolting the door. 'Show a glim, Toby.'

'Aha! my pal!' cried the same voice. 'A glim, Barney, a glim! Show the gentleman in, Barney; wake up first, if convenient.'

The speaker appeared to throw a boot-jack, or some such article, at the person he addressed, to rouse him from his slumbers: for the noise of a wooden body, falling violently, was heard; and then an indistinct muttering, as of a man between sleep and awake.

'Do you hear?' cried the same voice. 'There's Bill Sikes in the passage with nobody to do the civil to him; and you sleeping there, as if you took laudanum with your meals, and nothing stronger. Are you any fresher now, or do you want the iron candlestick to wake you thoroughly?'

A pair of slipshod feet shuffled, hastily, across the bare floor of the room, as this interrogatory was put; and there issued, from a door on the right hand; first, a feeble candle: and next, the form of the same individual who has been heretofore described as labouring under the infirmity of speaking through his nose, and officiating as waiter at the public-house on Saffron Hill.

'Bister Sikes!' exclaimed Barney, with real or counterfeit joy; 'cub id, sir; cub id.'

'Here! you get on first,' said Sikes, putting Oliver in front of him. 'Quicker! or I shall tread upon your heels.'

Muttering a curse upon his tardiness, Sikes pushed Oliver before him; and they entered a low dark room with a smoky fire, two or three broken chairs, a table, and a very old couch: on which, with his legs much higher than his head, a man was reposing at full length, smoking a long clay pipe. He was dressed in a smartly-cut snuff-coloured coat, with large brass buttons; an orange neckerchief; a coarse, staring, shawl-pattern waistcoat; and drab breeches. Mr. Crackit (for he it was) had no very great quantity of hair, either upon his head or face; but what he had, was of a reddish dye, and tortured into long corkscrew curls, through which he occasionally thrust some very dirty fingers, ornamented with large common rings. He was a trifle above the middle size, and apparently rather weak in the legs; but this circumstance by no means detracted from his own admiration of his top-boots, which he contemplated, in their elevated situation, with lively satisfaction.

'Bill, my boy!' said this figure, turning his head towards the door, 'I'm glad to see you. I was almost afraid you'd given it up: in which case I should have made a personal wentur. Hallo!'

Uttering this exclamation in a tone of great surprise, as his eyes rested on Oliver, Mr. Toby Crackit brought himself into a sitting posture, and demanded who that was.

'The boy. Only the boy!' replied Sikes, drawing a chair towards the fire.

'Wud of Bister Fagid's lads,' exclaimed Barney, with a grin.

'Fagin's, eh!' exclaimed Toby, looking at Oliver. 'Wot an inwalable boy that'll make, for the old ladies' pockets in chapels! His mug is a fortin' to him.'

'There—there's enough of that,' interposed Sikes, impatiently; and stooping over his recumbant friend, he whispered a few words in his ear: at which Mr. Crackit laughed immensely, and honoured Oliver with a long stare of astonishment.

'Now,' said Sikes, as he resumed his seat, 'if you'll give us something to eat and drink while we're waiting, you'll put some heart in us; or in me, at all events. Sit down by the fire, younker, and rest yourself; for you'll have to go out with us again to-night, though not very far off.'

Oliver looked at Sikes, in mute and timid wonder; and drawing a stool to the fire, sat with his aching head upon his hands, scarecely knowing where he was, or what was passing around him.

'Here,' said Toby, as the young Jew placed some fragments of food, and a bottle upon the table, 'Success to the crack!' He rose to honour the toast; and, carefully depositing his empty pipe in a corner, advanced to the table, filled a glass with spirits, and drank off its contents. Mr. Sikes did the same.

'A drain for the boy,' said Toby, half-filling a wine-glass. 'Down with it, innocence.'

'Indeed,' said Oliver, looking piteously up into the man's face; 'indeed, I—'

'Down with it!' echoed Toby. 'Do you think I don't know what's good for you? Tell him to drink it, Bill.'

'He had better!' said Sikes clapping his hand upon his pocket. 'Burn my body, if he isn't more trouble than a whole family of Dodgers. Drink it, you perwerse imp; drink it!'

Frightened by the menacing gestures of the two men, Oliver hastily swallowed the contents of the glass, and immediately fell into a violent fit of coughing: which delighted Toby Crackit and Barney, and even drew a smile from the surly Mr. Sikes.

This done, and Sikes having satisfied his appetite (Oliver could eat nothing but a small crust of bread which they made him swallow), the two men laid themselves down on chairs for a short nap. Oliver retained his stool by the fire; Barney wrapped in a blanket, stretched himself on the floor: close outside the fender.

They slept, or appeared to sleep, for some time; nobody stirring but Barney, who rose once or twice to throw coals on the fire. Oliver fell into a heavy doze: imagining himself straying along the gloomy lanes, or wandering about the dark churchyard, or retracing some one or other of the scenes of the past day: when he was roused by Toby Crackit jumping up and declaring it was half-past one.

In an instant, the other two were on their legs, and all were actively engaged in busy preparation. Sikes and his companion enveloped their necks and chins in large dark shawls, and drew on their great-coats; Barney, opening a cupboard, brought forth several articles, which he hastily crammed into the pockets.

'Barkers for me, Barney,' said Toby Crackit.

'Here they are,' replied Barney, producing a pair of pistols. 'You loaded them yourself.'

'All right!' replied Toby, stowing them away. 'The persuaders?'

'I've got 'em,' replied Sikes.

'Crape, keys, centre-bits, darkies—nothing forgotten?' inquired Toby: fastening a small crowbar to a loop inside the skirt of his coat.

'All right,' rejoined his companion. 'Bring them bits of timber, Barney. That's the time of day.'

With these words, he took a thick stick from Barney's hands, who, having delivered another to Toby, busied himself in fastening on Oliver's cape.

'Now then!' said Sikes, holding out his hand.

Oliver: who was completely stupified by the unwonted exercise, and the air, and the drink which had been forced upon him: put his hand mechanically into that which Sikes extended for the purpose.

'Take his other hand, Toby,' said Sikes. 'Look out, Barney.'

The man went to the door, and returned to announce that all was quiet. The two robbers issued forth with Oliver between them. Barney, having made all fast, rolled himself up as before, and was soon asleep again.

It was now intensely dark. The fog was much heavier than it had been in the early part of the night; and the atmosphere was so damp, that, although no rain fell, Oliver's hair and eyebrows, within a few minutes after leaving the house, had become stiff with the half-frozen moisture that was floating about. They crossed the bridge, and kept on towards the lights which he had seen before. They were at no great distance off; and, as they walked pretty briskly, they soon arrived at Chertsey.

'Slap through the town,' whispered Sikes; 'there'll be nobody in the way, to-night, to see us.'

Toby acquiesced; and they hurried through the main street of the little town, which at that late hour was wholly deserted. A dim light shone at intervals from some bed-room window; and the hoarse barking of dogs occasionally broke the silence of the night. But there was nobody abroad. They had cleared the town, as the church-bell struck two.

Quickening their pace, they turned up a road upon the left hand. After walking about a quarter of a mile, they stopped before a detached house surrounded by a wall: to the top of which, Toby Crackit, scarcely pausing to take breath, climbed in a twinkling.

'The boy next,' said Toby. 'Hoist him up; I'll catch hold of him.'

Before Oliver had time to look round, Sikes had caught him under the arms; and in three or four seconds he and Toby were lying on the grass on the other side. Sikes followed directly. And they stole cautiously towards the house.

And now, for the first time, Oliver, well-nigh mad with grief and terror, saw that housebreaking and robbery, if not murder, were the objects of the expedition. He clasped his hands together, and involuntarily uttered a subdued exclamation of horror. A mist came before his eyes; the cold sweat stood upon his ashy face; his limbs failed him; and he sank upon his knees.

'Get up!' murmured Sikes, trembling with rage, and drawing the pistol from his pocket; 'Get up, or I'll strew your brains upon the grass.'

'Oh! for God's sake let me go!' cried Oliver; 'let me run away and die in the fields. I will never come near London; never, never! Oh! pray have mercy on me, and do not make me steal. For the love of all the bright Angels that rest in Heaven, have mercy upon me!'

The man to whom this appeal was made, swore a dreadful oath, and had cocked the pistol, when Toby, striking it from his grasp, placed his hand upon the boy's mouth, and dragged him to the house.

'Hush!' cried the man; 'it won't answer here. Say another word, and I'll do your business myself with a crack on the head. That makes no noise, and is quite as certain, and more genteel. Here, Bill, wrench the shutter open. He's game enough now, I'll engage. I've seen older hands of his age took the same way, for a minute or two, on a cold night.'

Sikes, invoking terrific imprecations upon Fagin's head for sending Oliver on such an errand, plied the crowbar vigorously, but with little noise. After some delay, and some assistance from Toby, the shutter to which he had referred, swung open on its hinges.

It was a little lattice window, about five feet and a half above the ground, at the back of the house: which belonged to a scullery, or small brewing-place, at the end of the passage. The aperture was so small, that the inmates had probably not thought it worth while to defend it more securely; but it was large enough to admit a boy of Oliver's size, nevertheless. A very brief exercise of Mr. Sike's art, sufficed to overcome the fastening of the lattice; and it soon stood wide open also.

'Now listen, you young limb,' whispered Sikes, drawing a dark lantern from his pocket, and throwing the glare full on Oliver's face; 'I'm a going to put you through there. Take this light; go softly up the steps straight afore you, and along the little hall, to the street door; unfasten it, and let us in.'

'There's a bolt at the top, you won't be able to reach,' interposed Toby. 'Stand upon one of the hall chairs. There are three there, Bill, with a jolly large blue unicorn and gold pitchfork on 'em: which is the old lady's arms.'

'Keep quiet, can't you?' replied Sikes, with a threatening look. 'The room-door is open, is it?'

'Wide,' replied Toby, after peeping in to satisfy himself. 'The game of that is, that they always leave it open with a catch, so that the dog, who's got a bed in here, may walk up and down the passage when he feels wakeful. Ha! ha! Barney 'ticed him away to-night. So neat!'

Although Mr. Crackit spoke in a scarcely audible whisper, and laughed without noise, Sikes imperiously commanded him to be silent, and to get to work. Toby complied, by first producing his lantern, and placing it on the ground; then by planting himself firmly with his head against the wall beneath the window, and his hands upon his knees, so as to make a step of his back. This was no sooner done, than Sikes, mounting upon him, put Oliver gently through the window with his feet first; and, without leaving hold of his collar, planted him safely on the floor inside.

'Take this lantern,' said Sikes, looking into the room. 'You see the stairs afore you?'

Oliver, more dead than alive, gasped out, 'Yes.' Sikes, pointing to the street-door with the pistol-barrel, briefly advised him to take notice that he was within shot all the way; and that if he faltered, he would fall dead that instant.

'It's done in a minute,' said Sikes, in the same low whisper. 'Directly I leave go of you, do your work. Hark!'

'What's that?' whispered the other man.

They listened intently.

'Nothing,' said Sikes, releasing his hold of Oliver. 'Now!'

In the short time he had had to collect his senses, the boy had firmly resolved that, whether he died in the attempt or not, he would make one effort to dart upstairs from the hall, and alarm the family. Filled with this idea, he advanced at once, but stealthily.

'Come back!' suddenly cried Sikes aloud. 'Back! back!'

Scared by the sudden breaking of the dead stillness of the place, and by a loud cry which followed it, Oliver let his lantern fall, and knew not whether to advance or fly.

The cry was repeated—a light appeared—a vision of two terrified half-dressed men at the top of the stairs swam before his eyes—a flash—a loud noise—a smoke—a crash somewhere, but where he knew not,—and he staggered back.

Sikes had disappeared for an instant; but he was up again, and had him by the collar before the smoke had cleared away. He fired his own pistol after the men, who were already retreating; and dragged the boy up.

'Clasp your arm tighter,' said Sikes, as he drew him through the window. 'Give me a shawl here. They've hit him. Quick! How the boy bleeds!'

Then came the loud ringing of a bell, mingled with the noise of fire-arms, and the shouts of men, and the sensation of being carried over uneven ground at a rapid pace. And then, the noises grew confused in the distance; and a cold deadly feeling crept over the boy's heart; and he saw or heard no more.

CHAPTER XXIII. WHICH CONTAINS THE SUBSTANCE OF A PLEASANT CONVERSATION BETWEEN MR. BUMBLE AND A LADY; AND SHOWS THAT EVEN A BEADLE MAY BE SUSCEPTIBLE ON SOME POINTS

The night was bitter cold. The snow lay on the ground, frozen into a hard thick crust, so that only the heaps that had drifted into byways and corners were affected by the sharp wind that howled abroad: which, as if expending increased fury on such prey as it found, caught it savagely up in clouds, and, whirling it into a thousand misty eddies, scattered it in air. Bleak, dark, and piercing cold, it was a night for the well-housed and fed to draw round the bright fire and thank God they were at home; and for the homeless, starving wretch to lay him down and die. Many hunger-worn outcasts close their eyes in our bare streets, at such times, who, let their crimes have been what they may, can hardly open them in a more bitter world.

Such was the aspect of out-of-doors affairs, when Mrs. Corney, the matron of the workhouse to which our readers have been already introduced as the birthplace of Oliver Twist, sat herself down before a cheerful fire in her own little room, and glanced, with no small degree of complacency, at a small round table: on which stood a tray of corresponding size, furnished with all necessary materials for the most grateful meal that matrons enjoy. In fact, Mrs. Corney was about to solace herself with a cup of tea. As she glanced from the table to the fireplace, where the smallest of all possible kettles was singing a small song in a small voice, her inward satisfaction evidently increased,—so much so, indeed, that Mrs. Corney smiled.

'Well!' said the matron, leaning her elbow on the table, and looking reflectively at the fire; 'I'm sure we have all on us a great deal to be grateful for! A great deal, if we did but know it. Ah!'

Mrs. Corney shook her head mournfully, as if deploring the mental blindness of those paupers who did not know it; and thrusting a silver spoon (private property) into the inmost recesses of a two-ounce tin tea-caddy, proceeded to make the tea.

How slight a thing will disturb the equanimity of our frail minds! The black teapot, being very small and easily filled, ran over while Mrs. Corney was moralising; and the water slightly scalded Mrs. Corney's hand.

'Drat the pot!' said the worthy matron, setting it down very hastily on the hob; 'a little stupid thing, that only holds a couple of cups! What use is it of, to anybody! Except,' said Mrs. Corney, pausing, 'except to a poor desolate creature like me. Oh dear!'

With these words, the matron dropped into her chair, and, once more resting her elbow on the table, thought of her solitary fate. The small teapot, and the single cup, had awakened in her mind sad recollections of Mr. Corney (who had not been dead more than five-and-twenty years); and she was overpowered.

'I shall never get another!' said Mrs. Corney, pettishly; 'I shall never get another—like him.'

Whether this remark bore reference to the husband, or the teapot, is uncertain. It might have been the latter; for Mrs. Corney looked at it as she spoke; and took it up afterwards. She had just tasted her first cup, when she was disturbed by a soft tap at the room-door.

'Oh, come in with you!' said Mrs. Corney, sharply. 'Some of the old women dying, I suppose. They always die when I'm at meals. Don't stand there, letting the cold air in, don't. What's amiss now, eh?'

'Nothing, ma'am, nothing,' replied a man's voice.

'Dear me!' exclaimed the matron, in a much sweeter tone, 'is that Mr. Bumble?'

'At your service, ma'am,' said Mr. Bumble, who had been stopping outside to rub his shoes clean, and to shake the snow off his coat; and who now made his appearance, bearing the cocked hat in one hand and a bundle in the other. 'Shall I shut the door, ma'am?'

The lady modestly hesitated to reply, lest there should be any impropriety in holding an interview with Mr. Bumble, with closed doors. Mr. Bumble taking advantage of the hesitation, and being very cold himself, shut it without permission.

'Hard weather, Mr. Bumble,' said the matron.

'Hard, indeed, ma'am,' replied the beadle. 'Anti-porochial weather this, ma'am. We have given away, Mrs. Corney, we have given away a matter of twenty quartern loaves and a cheese and a half, this very blessed afternoon; and yet them paupers are not contented.'

'Of course not. When would they be, Mr. Bumble?' said the matron, sipping her tea.

'When, indeed, ma'am!' rejoined Mr. Bumble. 'Why here's one man that, in consideration of his wife and large family, has a quartern loaf and a good pound of cheese, full weight. Is he grateful, ma'am? Is he grateful? Not a copper farthing's worth of it! What does he do, ma'am, but ask for a few coals; if it's only a pocket handkerchief full, he says! Coals! What would he do with coals? Toast his cheese with 'em and then come back for more. That's the way with these people, ma'am; give 'em a apron full of coals to-day, and they'll come back for another, the day after to-morrow, as brazen as alabaster.'

The matron expressed her entire concurrence in this intelligible simile; and the beadle went on.

'I never,' said Mr. Bumble, 'see anything like the pitch it's got to. The day afore yesterday, a man—you have been a married woman, ma'am, and I may mention it to you—a man, with hardly a rag upon his back (here Mrs. Corney looked at the floor), goes to our overseer's door when he has got company coming to dinner; and says, he must be relieved, Mrs. Corney. As he wouldn't go away, and shocked the company very much, our overseer sent him out a pound of potatoes and half a pint of oatmeal. "My heart!" says the ungrateful villain, "what's the use of this to me? You might as well give me a pair of iron spectacles!" "Very good," says our overseer, taking 'em away again, "you won't get anything else here." "Then I'll die in the streets!" says the vagrant. "Oh no, you won't," says our overseer.'

'Ha! ha! That was very good! So like Mr. Grannett, wasn't it?' interposed the matron. 'Well, Mr. Bumble?'

'Well, ma'am,' rejoined the beadle, 'he went away; and he did die in the streets. There's a obstinate pauper for you!'

'It beats anything I could have believed,' observed the matron emphatically. 'But don't you think out-of-door relief a very bad thing, any way, Mr. Bumble? You're a gentleman of experience, and ought to know. Come.'

'Mrs. Corney,' said the beadle, smiling as men smile who are conscious of superior information, 'out-of-door relief, properly managed: properly managed, ma'am: is the porochial safeguard. The great principle of out-of-door relief is, to give the paupers exactly what they don't want; and then they get tired of coming.'

'Dear me!' exclaimed Mrs. Corney. 'Well, that is a good one, too!'

'Yes. Betwixt you and me, ma'am,' returned Mr. Bumble, 'that's the great principle; and that's the reason why, if you look at any cases that get into them owdacious newspapers, you'll always observe that sick families have been relieved with slices of cheese. That's the rule now, Mrs. Corney, all over the country. But, however,' said the beadle, stopping to unpack his bundle, 'these are official secrets, ma'am; not to be spoken of; except, as I may say, among the porochial officers, such as ourselves. This is the port wine, ma'am, that the board ordered for the infirmary; real, fresh, genuine port wine; only out of the cask this forenoon; clear as a bell, and no sediment!'

Having held the first bottle up to the light, and shaken it well to test its excellence, Mr. Bumble placed them both on top of a chest of drawers; folded the handkerchief in which they had been wrapped; put it carefully in his pocket; and took up his hat, as if to go.

'You'll have a very cold walk, Mr. Bumble,' said the matron.

'It blows, ma'am,' replied Mr. Bumble, turning up his coat-collar, 'enough to cut one's ears off.'

The matron looked, from the little kettle, to the beadle, who was moving towards the door; and as the beadle coughed, preparatory to bidding her good-night, bashfully inquired whether—whether he wouldn't take a cup of tea?

Mr. Bumble instantaneously turned back his collar again; laid his hat and stick upon a chair; and drew another chair up to the table. As he slowly seated himself, he looked at the lady. She fixed her eyes upon the little teapot. Mr. Bumble coughed again, and slightly smiled.

Mrs. Corney rose to get another cup and saucer from the closet. As she sat down, her eyes once again encountered those of the gallant beadle; she coloured, and applied herself to the task of making his tea. Again Mr. Bumble coughed—louder this time than he had coughed yet.

'Sweet? Mr. Bumble?' inquired the matron, taking up the sugar-basin.

'Very sweet, indeed, ma'am,' replied Mr. Bumble. He fixed his eyes on Mrs. Corney as he said this; and if ever a beadle looked tender, Mr. Bumble was that beadle at that moment.

The tea was made, and handed in silence. Mr. Bumble, having spread a handkerchief over his knees to prevent the crumbs from sullying the splendour of his shorts, began to eat and drink; varying these amusements, occasionally, by fetching a deep sigh; which, however, had no injurious effect upon his appetite, but, on the contrary, rather seemed to facilitate his operations in the tea and toast department.

'You have a cat, ma'am, I see,' said Mr. Bumble, glancing at one who, in the centre of her family, was basking before the fire; 'and kittens too, I declare!'

'I am so fond of them, Mr. Bumble, you can't think,' replied the matron. 'They're so happy, so frolicsome, and so cheerful, that they are quite companions for me.'

'Very nice animals, ma'am,' replied Mr. Bumble, approvingly; 'so very domestic.'

'Oh, yes!' rejoined the matron with enthusiasm; 'so fond of their home too, that it's quite a pleasure, I'm sure.'

'Mrs. Corney, ma'am,' said Mr. Bumble, slowly, and marking the time with his teaspoon, 'I mean to say this, ma'am; that any cat, or kitten, that could live with you, ma'am, and not be fond of its home, must be a ass, ma'am.'

'Oh, Mr. Bumble!' remonstrated Mrs. Corney.

'It's of no use disguising facts, ma'am,' said Mr. Bumble, slowly flourishing the teaspoon with a kind of amorous dignity which made him doubly impressive; 'I would drown it myself, with pleasure.'

'Then you're a cruel man,' said the matron vivaciously, as she held out her hand for the beadle's cup; 'and a very hard-hearted man besides.'

'Hard-hearted, ma'am?' said Mr. Bumble. 'Hard?' Mr. Bumble resigned his cup without another word; squeezed Mrs. Corney's little finger as she took it; and inflicting two open-handed slaps upon his laced waistcoat, gave a mighty sigh, and hitched his chair a very little morsel farther from the fire.

It was a round table; and as Mrs. Corney and Mr. Bumble had been sitting opposite each other, with no great space between them, and fronting the fire, it will be seen that Mr. Bumble, in receding from the fire, and still keeping at the table, increased the distance between himself and Mrs. Corney; which proceeding, some prudent readers will doubtless be disposed to admire, and to consider an act of great heroism on Mr. Bumble's part: he being in some sort tempted by time, place, and opportunity, to give utterance to certain soft nothings, which however well they may become the lips of the light and thoughtless, do seem immeasurably beneath the dignity of judges of the land, members of parliament, ministers of state, lord mayors, and other great public functionaries, but more particularly beneath the stateliness and gravity of a beadle: who (as is well known) should be the sternest and most inflexible among them all.

Whatever were Mr. Bumble's intentions, however (and no doubt they were of the best): it unfortunately happened, as has been twice before remarked, that the table was a round one; consequently Mr. Bumble, moving his chair by little and little, soon began to diminish the distance between himself and the matron; and, continuing to travel round the outer edge of the circle, brought his chair, in time, close to that in which the matron was seated.

Indeed, the two chairs touched; and when they did so, Mr. Bumble stopped.

Now, if the matron had moved her chair to the right, she would have been scorched by the fire; and if to the left, she must have fallen into Mr. Bumble's arms; so (being a discreet matron, and no doubt foreseeing these consequences at a glance) she remained where she was, and handed Mr. Bumble another cup of tea.

'Hard-hearted, Mrs. Corney?' said Mr. Bumble, stirring his tea, and looking up into the matron's face; 'are you hard-hearted, Mrs. Corney?'

'Dear me!' exclaimed the matron, 'what a very curious question from a single man. What can you want to know for, Mr. Bumble?'

The beadle drank his tea to the last drop; finished a piece of toast; whisked the crumbs off his knees; wiped his lips; and deliberately kissed the matron.

'Mr. Bumble!' cried that discreet lady in a whisper; for the fright was so great, that she had quite lost her voice, 'Mr. Bumble, I shall scream!' Mr. Bumble made no reply; but in a slow and dignified manner, put his arm round the matron's waist.

As the lady had stated her intention of screaming, of course she would have screamed at this additional boldness, but that the exertion was rendered unnecessary by a hasty knocking at the door: which was no sooner heard, than Mr. Bumble darted, with much agility, to the wine bottles, and began dusting them with great violence: while the matron sharply demanded who was there.

It is worthy of remark, as a curious physical instance of the efficacy of a sudden surprise in counteracting the effects of extreme fear, that her voice had quite recovered all its official asperity.

'If you please, mistress,' said a withered old female pauper, hideously ugly: putting her head in at the door, 'Old Sally is a-going fast.'

'Well, what's that to me?' angrily demanded the matron. 'I can't keep her alive, can I?'

'No, no, mistress,' replied the old woman, 'nobody can; she's far beyond the reach of help. I've seen a many people die; little babes and great strong men; and I know when death's a-coming, well enough. But she's troubled in her mind: and when the fits are not on her,—and that's not often, for she is dying very hard,—she says she has got something to tell, which you must hear. She'll never die quiet till you come, mistress.'

At this intelligence, the worthy Mrs. Corney muttered a variety of invectives against old women who couldn't even die without purposely annoying their betters; and, muffling herself in a thick shawl which she hastily caught up, briefly requested Mr. Bumble to stay till she came back, lest anything particular should occur. Bidding the messenger walk fast, and not be all night hobbling up the stairs, she followed her from the room with a very ill grace, scolding all the way.

Mr. Bumble's conduct on being left to himself, was rather inexplicable. He opened the closet, counted the teaspoons, weighed the sugar-tongs, closely inspected a silver milk-pot to ascertain that it was of the genuine metal, and, having satisfied his curiosity on these points, put on his cocked hat corner-wise, and danced with much gravity four distinct times round the table.

Having gone through this very extraordinary performance, he took off the cocked hat again, and, spreading himself before the fire with his back towards it, seemed to be mentally engaged in taking an exact inventory of the furniture.

CHAPTER XXIV. TREATS ON A VERY POOR SUBJECT. BUT IS A SHORT ONE, AND MAY BE FOUND OF IMPORTANCE IN THIS HISTORY

It was no unfit messenger of death, who had disturbed the quiet of the matron's room. Her body was bent by age; her limbs trembled with palsy; her face, distorted into a mumbling leer, resembled more the grotesque shaping of some wild pencil, than the work of Nature's hand.

Alas! How few of Nature's faces are left alone to gladden us with their beauty! The cares, and sorrows, and hungerings, of the world, change them as they change hearts; and it is only when those passions sleep, and have lost their hold for ever, that the troubled clouds pass off, and leave Heaven's surface clear. It is a common thing for the countenances of the dead, even in that fixed and rigid state, to subside into the long-forgotten expression of sleeping infancy, and settle into the very look of early life; so calm, so peaceful, do they grow again, that those who knew them in their happy childhood, kneel by the coffin's side in awe, and see the Angel even upon earth.

The old crone tottered along the passages, and up the stairs, muttering some indistinct answers to the chidings of her companion; being at length compelled to pause for breath, she gave the light into her hand, and remained behind to follow as she might: while the more nimble superior made her way to the room where the sick woman lay.

It was a bare garret-room, with a dim light burning at the farther end. There was another old woman watching by the bed; the parish apothecary's apprentice was standing by the fire, making a toothpick out of a quill.

'Cold night, Mrs. Corney,' said this young gentleman, as the matron entered.

'Very cold, indeed, sir,' replied the mistress, in her most civil tones, and dropping a curtsey as she spoke.

'You should get better coals out of your contractors,' said the apothecary's deputy, breaking a lump on the top of the fire with the rusty poker; 'these are not at all the sort of thing for a cold night.'

'They're the board's choosing, sir,' returned the matron. 'The least they could do, would be to keep us pretty warm: for our places are hard enough.'

The conversation was here interrupted by a moan from the sick woman.

'Oh!' said the young mag, turning his face towards the bed, as if he had previously quite forgotten the patient, 'it's all U.P. there, Mrs. Corney.'

'It is, is it, sir?' asked the matron.

'If she lasts a couple of hours, I shall be surprised,' said the apothecary's apprentice, intent upon the toothpick's point. 'It's a break-up of the system altogether. Is she dozing, old lady?'

The attendant stooped over the bed, to ascertain; and nodded in the affirmative.

'Then perhaps she'll go off in that way, if you don't make a row,' said the young man. 'Put the light on the floor. She won't see it there.'

The attendant did as she was told: shaking her head meanwhile, to intimate that the woman would not die so easily; having done so, she resumed her seat by the side of the other nurse, who had by this time returned. The mistress, with an expression of impatience, wrapped herself in her shawl, and sat at the foot of the bed.

The apothecary's apprentice, having completed the manufacture of the toothpick, planted himself in front of the fire and made good use of it for ten minutes or so: when apparently growing rather dull, he wished Mrs. Corney joy of her job, and took himself off on tiptoe.

When they had sat in silence for some time, the two old women rose from the bed, and crouching over the fire, held out their withered hands to catch the heat. The flame threw a ghastly light on their shrivelled faces, and made their ugliness appear terrible, as, in this position, they began to converse in a low voice.

'Did she say any more, Anny dear, while I was gone?' inquired the messenger.

'Not a word,' replied the other. 'She plucked and tore at her arms for a little time; but I held her hands, and she soon dropped off. She hasn't much strength in her, so I easily kept her quiet. I ain't so weak for an old woman, although I am on parish allowance; no, no!'

'Did she drink the hot wine the doctor said she was to have?' demanded the first.

'I tried to get it down,' rejoined the other. 'But her teeth were tight set, and she clenched the mug so hard that it was as much as I could do to get it back again. So I drank it; and it did me good!'

Looking cautiously round, to ascertain that they were not overheard, the two hags cowered nearer to the fire, and chuckled heartily.

'I mind the time,' said the first speaker, 'when she would have done the same, and made rare fun of it afterwards.'

'Ay, that she would,' rejoined the other; 'she had a merry heart. 'A many, many, beautiful corpses she laid out, as nice and neat as waxwork. My old eyes have seen them—ay, and those old hands touched them too; for I have helped her, scores of times.'

Stretching forth her trembling fingers as she spoke, the old creature shook them exultingly before her face, and fumbling in her pocket, brought out an old time-discoloured tin snuff-box, from which she shook a few grains into the outstretched palm of her companion, and a few more into her own. While they were thus employed, the matron, who had been impatiently watching until the dying woman should awaken from her stupor, joined them by the fire, and sharply asked how long she was to wait?

'Not long, mistress,' replied the second woman, looking up into her face. 'We have none of us long to wait for Death. Patience, patience! He'll be here soon enough for us all.'

'Hold your tongue, you doting idiot!' said the matron sternly. 'You, Martha, tell me; has she been in this way before?'

'Often,' answered the first woman.

'But will never be again,' added the second one; 'that is, she'll never wake again but once—and mind, mistress, that won't be for long!'

'Long or short,' said the matron, snappishly, 'she won't find me here when she does wake; take care, both of you, how you worry me again for nothing. It's no part of my duty to see all the old women in the house die, and I won't—that's more. Mind that, you impudent old harridans. If you make a fool of me again, I'll soon cure you, I warrant you!'

She was bouncing away, when a cry from the two women, who had turned towards the bed, caused her to look round. The patient had raised herself upright, and was stretching her arms towards them.

'Who's that?' she cried, in a hollow voice.

'Hush, hush!' said one of the women, stooping over her. 'Lie down, lie down!'

'I'll never lie down again alive!' said the woman, struggling. 'I will tell her! Come here! Nearer! Let me whisper in your ear.'

She clutched the matron by the arm, and forcing her into a chair by the bedside, was about to speak, when looking round, she caught sight of the two old women bending forward in the attitude of eager listeners.

'Turn them away,' said the woman, drowsily; 'make haste! make haste!'

The two old crones, chiming in together, began pouring out many piteous lamentations that the poor dear was too far gone to know her best friends; and were uttering sundry protestations that they would never leave her, when the superior pushed them from the room, closed the door, and returned to the bedside. On being excluded, the old ladies changed their tone, and cried through the keyhole that old Sally was drunk; which, indeed, was not unlikely; since, in addition to a moderate dose of opium prescribed by the apothecary, she was labouring under the effects of a final taste of gin-and-water which had been privily administered, in the openness of their hearts, by the worthy old ladies themselves.

'Now listen to me,' said the dying woman aloud, as if making a great effort to revive one latent spark of energy. 'In this very room—in this very bed—I once nursed a pretty young creetur', that was brought into the house with her feet cut and bruised with walking, and all soiled with dust and blood. She gave birth to a boy, and died. Let me think—what was the year again!'

'Never mind the year,' said the impatient auditor; 'what about her?'

'Ay,' murmured the sick woman, relapsing into her former drowsy state, 'what about her?—what about—I know!' she cried, jumping fiercely up: her face flushed, and her eyes starting from her head—'I robbed her, so I did! She wasn't cold—I tell you she wasn't cold, when I stole it!'

'Stole what, for God's sake?' cried the matron, with a gesture as if she would call for help.

'It!' replied the woman, laying her hand over the other's mouth. 'The only thing she had. She wanted clothes to keep her warm, and food to eat; but she had kept it safe, and had it in her bosom. It was gold, I tell you! Rich gold, that might have saved her life!'

'Gold!' echoed the matron, bending eagerly over the woman as she fell back. 'Go on, go on—yes—what of it? Who was the mother? When was it?'

'She charged me to keep it safe,' replied the woman with a groan, 'and trusted me as the only woman about her. I stole it in my heart when she first showed it me hanging round her neck; and the child's death, perhaps, is on me besides! They would have treated him better, if they had known it all!'

'Known what?' asked the other. 'Speak!'

'The boy grew so like his mother,' said the woman, rambling on, and not heeding the question, 'that I could never forget it when I saw his face. Poor girl! poor girl! She was so young, too! Such a gentle lamb! Wait; there's more to tell. I have not told you all, have I?'

'No, no,' replied the matron, inclining her head to catch the words, as they came more faintly from the dying woman. 'Be quick, or it may be too late!'

'The mother,' said the woman, making a more violent effort than before; 'the mother, when the pains of death first came upon her, whispered in my ear that if her baby was born alive, and thrived, the day might come when it would not feel so much disgraced to hear its poor young mother named. "And oh, kind Heaven!" she said, folding her thin hands together, "whether it be boy or girl, raise up some friends for it in this troubled world, and take pity upon a lonely desolate child, abandoned to its mercy!"'

'The boy's name?' demanded the matron.

'They called him Oliver,' replied the woman, feebly. 'The gold I stole was—'

'Yes, yes—what?' cried the other.

She was bending eagerly over the woman to hear her reply; but drew back, instinctively, as she once again rose, slowly and stiffly, into a sitting posture; then, clutching the coverlid with both hands, muttered some indistinct sounds in her throat, and fell lifeless on the bed.

'Stone dead!' said one of the old women, hurrying in as soon as the door was opened.

'And nothing to tell, after all,' rejoined the matron, walking carelessly away.

The two crones, to all appearance, too busily occupied in the preparations for their dreadful duties to make any reply, were left alone, hovering about the body.

CHAPTER XXV. WHEREIN THIS HISTORY REVERTS TO MR. FAGIN AND COMPANY

While these things were passing in the country workhouse, Mr. Fagin sat in the old den—the same from which Oliver had been removed by the girl—brooding over a dull, smoky fire. He held a pair of bellows upon his knee, with which he had apparently been endeavouring to rouse it into more cheerful action; but he had fallen into deep thought; and with his arms folded on them, and his chin resting on his thumbs, fixed his eyes, abstractedly, on the rusty bars.

At a table behind him sat the Artful Dodger, Master Charles Bates, and Mr. Chitling: all intent upon a game of whist; the Artful taking dummy against Master Bates and Mr. Chitling. The countenance of the first-named gentleman, peculiarly intelligent at all times, acquired great additional interest from his close observance of the game, and his attentive perusal of Mr. Chitling's hand; upon which, from time to time, as occasion served, he bestowed a variety of earnest glances: wisely regulating his own play by the result of his observations upon his neighbour's cards. It being a cold night, the Dodger wore his hat, as, indeed, was often his custom within doors. He also sustained a clay pipe between his teeth, which he only removed for a brief space when he deemed it necessary to apply for refreshment to a quart pot upon the table, which stood ready filled with gin-and-water for the accommodation of the company.

Master Bates was also attentive to the play; but being of a more excitable nature than his accomplished friend, it was observable that he more frequently applied himself to the gin-and-water, and moreover indulged in many jests and irrelevant remarks, all highly unbecoming a scientific rubber. Indeed, the Artful, presuming upon their close attachment, more than once took occasion to reason gravely with his companion upon these improprieties; all of which remonstrances, Master Bates received in extremely good part; merely requesting his friend to be 'blowed,' or to insert his head in a sack, or replying with some other neatly-turned witticism of a similar kind, the happy application of which, excited considerable admiration in the mind of Mr. Chitling. It was remarkable that the latter gentleman and his partner invariably lost; and that the circumstance, so far from angering Master Bates, appeared to afford him the highest amusement, inasmuch as he laughed most uproariously at the end of every deal, and protested that he had never seen such a jolly game in all his born days.

'That's two doubles and the rub,' said Mr. Chitling, with a very long face, as he drew half-a-crown from his waistcoat-pocket. 'I never see such a feller as you, Jack; you win everything. Even when we've good cards, Charley and I can't make nothing of 'em.'

Either the master or the manner of this remark, which was made very ruefully, delighted Charley Bates so much, that his consequent shout of laughter roused the Jew from his reverie, and induced him to inquire what was the matter.

'Matter, Fagin!' cried Charley. 'I wish you had watched the play. Tommy Chitling hasn't won a point; and I went partners with him against the Artfull and dumb.'

'Ay, ay!' said the Jew, with a grin, which sufficiently demonstrated that he was at no loss to understand the reason. 'Try 'em again, Tom; try 'em again.'

'No more of it for me, thank 'ee, Fagin,' replied Mr. Chitling; 'I've had enough. That 'ere Dodger has such a run of luck that there's no standing again' him.'

'Ha! ha! my dear,' replied the Jew, 'you must get up very early in the morning, to win against the Dodger.'

'Morning!' said Charley Bates; 'you must put your boots on over-night, and have a telescope at each eye, and a opera-glass between your shoulders, if you want to come over him.'

Mr. Dawkins received these handsome compliments with much philosophy, and offered to cut any gentleman in company, for the first picture-card, at a shilling at a time. Nobody accepting the challenge, and his pipe being by this time smoked out, he proceeded to amuse himself by sketching a ground-plan of Newgate on the table with the piece of chalk which had served him in lieu of counters; whistling, meantime, with peculiar shrillness.

'How precious dull you are, Tommy!' said the Dodger, stopping short when there had been a long silence; and addressing Mr. Chitling. 'What do you think he's thinking of, Fagin?'

'How should I know, my dear?' replied the Jew, looking round as he plied the bellows. 'About his losses, maybe; or the little retirement in the country that he's just left, eh? Ha! ha! Is that it, my dear?'

'Not a bit of it,' replied the Dodger, stopping the subject of discourse as Mr. Chitling was about to reply. 'What do you say, Charley?'

'I should say,' replied Master Bates, with a grin, 'that he was uncommon sweet upon Betsy. See how he's a-blushing! Oh, my eye! here's a merry-go-rounder! Tommy Chitling's in love! Oh, Fagin, Fagin! what a spree!'

Thoroughly overpowered with the notion of Mr. Chitling being the victim of the tender passion, Master Bates threw himself back in his chair with such violence, that he lost his balance, and pitched over upon the floor; where (the accident abating nothing of his merriment) he lay at full length until his laugh was over, when he resumed his former position, and began another laugh.

'Never mind him, my dear,' said the Jew, winking at Mr. Dawkins, and giving Master Bates a reproving tap with the nozzle of the bellows. 'Betsy's a fine girl. Stick up to her, Tom. Stick up to her.'

'What I mean to say, Fagin,' replied Mr. Chitling, very red in the face, 'is, that that isn't anything to anybody here.'

'No more it is,' replied the Jew; 'Charley will talk. Don't mind him, my dear; don't mind him. Betsy's a fine girl. Do as she bids you, Tom, and you will make your fortune.'

'So I do do as she bids me,' replied Mr. Chitling; 'I shouldn't have been milled, if it hadn't been for her advice. But it turned out a good job for you; didn't it, Fagin! And what's six weeks of it? It must come, some time or another, and why not in the winter time when you don't want to go out a-walking so much; eh, Fagin?'

'Ah, to be sure, my dear,' replied the Jew.

'You wouldn't mind it again, Tom, would you,' asked the Dodger, winking upon Charley and the Jew, 'if Bet was all right?'

'I mean to say that I shouldn't,' replied Tom, angrily. 'There, now. Ah! Who'll say as much as that, I should like to know; eh, Fagin?'

'Nobody, my dear,' replied the Jew; 'not a soul, Tom. I don't know one of 'em that would do it besides you; not one of 'em, my dear.'

'I might have got clear off, if I'd split upon her; mightn't I, Fagin?' angrily pursued the poor half-witted dupe. 'A word from me would have done it; wouldn't it, Fagin?'

'To be sure it would, my dear,' replied the Jew.

'But I didn't blab it; did I, Fagin?' demanded Tom, pouring question upon question with great volubility.

'No, no, to be sure,' replied the Jew; 'you were too stout-hearted for that. A deal too stout, my dear!'

'Perhaps I was,' rejoined Tom, looking round; 'and if I was, what's to laugh at, in that; eh, Fagin?'

The Jew, perceiving that Mr. Chitling was considerably roused, hastened to assure him that nobody was laughing; and to prove the gravity of the company, appealed to Master Bates, the principal offender. But, unfortunately, Charley, in opening his mouth to reply that he was never more serious in his life, was unable to prevent the escape of such a violent roar, that the abused Mr. Chitling, without any preliminary ceremonies, rushed across the room and aimed a blow at the offender; who, being skilful in evading pursuit, ducked to avoid it, and chose his time so well that it lighted on the chest of the merry old gentleman, and caused him to stagger to the wall, where he stood panting for breath, while Mr. Chitling looked on in intense dismay.

'Hark!' cried the Dodger at this moment, 'I heard the tinkler.' Catching up the light, he crept softly upstairs.

The bell was rung again, with some impatience, while the party were in darkness. After a short pause, the Dodger reappeared, and whispered Fagin mysteriously.

'What!' cried the Jew, 'alone?'

The Dodger nodded in the affirmative, and, shading the flame of the candle with his hand, gave Charley Bates a private intimation, in dumb show, that he had better not be funny just then. Having performed this friendly office, he fixed his eyes on the Jew's face, and awaited his directions.

The old man bit his yellow fingers, and meditated for some seconds; his face working with agitation the while, as if he dreaded something, and feared to know the worst. At length he raised his head.

'Where is he?' he asked.

The Dodger pointed to the floor above, and made a gesture, as if to leave the room.

'Yes,' said the Jew, answering the mute inquiry; 'bring him down. Hush! Quiet, Charley! Gently, Tom! Scarce, scarce!'

This brief direction to Charley Bates, and his recent antagonist, was softly and immediately obeyed. There was no sound of their whereabout, when the Dodger descended the stairs, bearing the light in his hand, and followed by a man in a coarse smock-frock; who, after casting a hurried glance round the room, pulled off a large wrapper which had concealed the lower portion of his face, and disclosed: all haggard, unwashed, and unshorn: the features of flash Toby Crackit.

'How are you, Faguey?' said this worthy, nodding to the Jew. 'Pop that shawl away in my castor, Dodger, so that I may know where to find it when I cut; that's the time of day! You'll be a fine young cracksman afore the old file now.'

With these words he pulled up the smock-frock; and, winding it round his middle, drew a chair to the fire, and placed his feet upon the hob.

'See there, Faguey,' he said, pointing disconsolately to his top boots; 'not a drop of Day and Martin since you know when; not a bubble of blacking, by Jove! But don't look at me in that way, man. All in good time. I can't talk about business till I've eat and drank; so produce the sustenance, and let's have a quiet fill-out for the first time these three days!'

The Jew motioned to the Dodger to place what eatables there were, upon the table; and, seating himself opposite the housebreaker, waited his leisure.

To judge from appearances, Toby was by no means in a hurry to open the conversation. At first, the Jew contented himself with patiently watching his countenance, as if to gain from its expression some clue to the intelligence he brought; but in vain.

He looked tired and worn, but there was the same complacent repose upon his features that they always wore: and through dirt, and beard, and whisker, there still shone, unimpaired, the self-satisfied smirk of flash Toby Crackit. Then the Jew, in an agony of impatience, watched every morsel he put into his mouth; pacing up and down the room, meanwhile, in irrepressible excitement. It was all of no use. Toby continued to eat with the utmost outward indifference, until he could eat no more; then, ordering the Dodger out, he closed the door, mixed a glass of spirits and water, and composed himself for talking.

'First and foremost, Faguey,' said Toby.

'Yes, yes!' interposed the Jew, drawing up his chair.

Mr. Crackit stopped to take a draught of spirits and water, and to declare that the gin was excellent; then placing his feet against the low mantelpiece, so as to bring his boots to about the level of his eye, he quietly resumed.

'First and foremost, Faguey,' said the housebreaker, 'how's Bill?'

'What!' screamed the Jew, starting from his seat.

'Why, you don't mean to say—' began Toby, turning pale.

'Mean!' cried the Jew, stamping furiously on the ground. 'Where are they? Sikes and the boy! Where are they? Where have they been? Where are they hiding? Why have they not been here?'

'The crack failed,' said Toby faintly.

'I know it,' replied the Jew, tearing a newspaper from his pocket and pointing to it. 'What more?'

'They fired and hit the boy. We cut over the fields at the back, with him between us—straight as the crow flies—through hedge and ditch. They gave chase. Damme! the whole country was awake, and the dogs upon us.'

'The boy!'

'Bill had him on his back, and scudded like the wind. We stopped to take him between us; his head hung down, and he was cold. They were close upon our heels; every man for himself, and each from the gallows! We parted company, and left the youngster lying in a ditch. Alive or dead, that's all I know about him.'

The Jew stopped to hear no more; but uttering a loud yell, and twining his hands in his hair, rushed from the room, and from the house.

CHAPTER XXVI. IN WHICH A MYSTERIOUS CHARACTER APPEARS UPON THE SCENE; AND MANY THINGS, INSEPARABLE FROM THIS HISTORY, ARE DONE AND PERFORMED

The old man had gained the street corner, before he began to recover the effect of Toby Crackit's intelligence. He had relaxed nothing of his unusual speed; but was still pressing onward, in the same wild and disordered manner, when the sudden dashing past of a carriage:

712

and a boisterous cry from the foot passengers, who saw his danger: drove him back upon the pavement. Avoiding, as much as was possible, all the main streets, and skulking only through the by-ways and alleys, he at length emerged on Snow Hill. Here he walked even faster than before; nor did he linger until he had again turned into a court; when, as if conscious that he was now in his proper element, he fell into his usual shuffling pace, and seemed to breathe more freely.

Near to the spot on which Snow Hill and Holborn Hill meet, opens, upon the right hand as you come out of the City, a narrow and dismal alley, leading to Saffron Hill. In its filthy shops are exposed for sale huge bunches of second-hand silk handkerchiefs, of all sizes and patterns; for here reside the traders who purchase them from pick-pockets. Hundreds of these handkerchiefs hang dangling from pegs outside the windows or flaunting from the door-posts; and the shelves, within, are piled with them. Confined as the limits of Field Lane are, it has its barber, its coffee-shop, its beer-shop, and its fried-fish warehouse. It is a commercial colony of itself: the emporium of petty larceny: visited at early morning, and setting-in of dusk, by silent merchants, who traffic in dark back-parlours, and who go as strangely as they come. Here, the clothesman, the shoe-vamper, and the rag-merchant, display their goods, as sign-boards to the petty thief; here, stores of old iron and bones, and heaps of mildewy fragments of woollen-stuff and linen, rust and rot in the grimy cellars.

It was into this place that the Jew turned. He was well known to the sallow denizens of the lane; for such of them as were on the look-out to buy or sell, nodded, familiarly, as he passed along. He replied to their salutations in the same way; but bestowed no closer recognition until he reached the further end of the alley; when he stopped, to address a salesman of small stature, who had squeezed as much of his person into a child's chair as the chair would hold, and was smoking a pipe at his warehouse door.

'Why, the sight of you, Mr. Fagin, would cure the hoptalmy!' said this respectable trader, in acknowledgment of the Jew's inquiry after his health.

'The neighbourhood was a little too hot, Lively,' said Fagin, elevating his eyebrows, and crossing his hands upon his shoulders.

'Well, I've heerd that complaint of it, once or twice before,' replied the trader; 'but it soon cools down again; don't you find it so?'

Fagin nodded in the affirmative. Pointing in the direction of Saffron Hill, he inquired whether any one was up yonder to-night.

'At the Cripples?' inquired the man.

The Jew nodded.

'Let me see,' pursued the merchant, reflecting.

'Yes, there's some half-dozen of 'em gone in, that I knows. I don't think your friend's there.'

'Sikes is not, I suppose?' inquired the Jew, with a disappointed countenance.

'Non istwentus, as the lawyers say,' replied the little man, shaking his head, and looking amazingly sly. 'Have you got anything in my line to-night?'

'Nothing to-night,' said the Jew, turning away.

'Are you going up to the Cripples, Fagin?' cried the little man, calling after him. 'Stop! I don't mind if I have a drop there with you!'

But as the Jew, looking back, waved his hand to intimate that he preferred being alone; and, moreover, as the little man could not very easily disengage himself from the chair; the sign of the Cripples was, for a time, bereft of the advantage of Mr. Lively's presence. By the time he had got upon his legs, the Jew had disappeared; so Mr. Lively, after ineffectually standing on tiptoe, in the hope of catching sight of him, again forced himself into the little chair, and, exchanging a shake of the head with a lady in the opposite shop, in which doubt and mistrust were plainly mingled, resumed his pipe with a grave demeanour.

The Three Cripples, or rather the Cripples; which was the sign by which the establishment was familiarly known to its patrons: was the public-house in which Mr. Sikes and his dog have already figured. Merely making a sign to a man at the bar, Fagin walked straight upstairs, and opening the door of a room, and softly insinuating himself into the chamber, looked anxiously about: shading his eyes with his hand, as if in search of some particular person.

The room was illuminated by two gas-lights; the glare of which was prevented by the barred shutters, and closely-drawn curtains of faded red, from being visible outside. The ceiling was blackened, to prevent its colour from being injured by the flaring of the lamps; and the place was so full of dense tobacco smoke, that at first it was scarcely possible to discern anything more. By degrees, however, as some of it cleared away through the open door, an assemblage of heads, as confused as the noises that greeted the ear, might be made out; and as the eye grew more accustomed to the scene, the spectator gradually became aware of the presence of a numerous company, male and female, crowded round a long table: at the upper end of which, sat a chairman with a hammer of office in his hand; while a professional gentleman with a bluish nose, and his face tied up for the benefit of a toothache, presided at a jingling piano in a remote corner.

As Fagin stepped softly in, the professional gentleman, running over the keys by way of prelude, occasioned a general cry of order for a song; which having subsided, a young lady proceeded to entertain the company with a ballad in four verses, between each of which the accompanyist played the melody all through, as loud as he could. When this was over, the chairman gave a sentiment, after which, the professional gentleman on the chairman's right and left volunteered a duet, and sang it, with great applause.

It was curious to observe some faces which stood out prominently from among the group. There was the chairman himself, (the landlord of the house,) a coarse, rough, heavy built fellow, who, while the songs were proceeding, rolled his eyes hither and thither, and, seeming to give himself up to joviality, had an eye for everything that was done, and an ear for everything that was said—and sharp ones, too. Near him were the singers: receiving, with professional indifference, the compliments of the company, and applying themselves, in turn, to a dozen proffered glasses of spirits and water, tendered by their more boisterous admirers; whose countenances, expressive of almost every vice in almost every grade, irresistibly attracted the attention, by their very repulsiveness. Cunning, ferocity, and drunkeness in all its stages, were there, in their strongest aspect; and women: some with the last lingering tinge of their early freshness almost fading as you looked: others with every mark and stamp of their sex utterly beaten out, and presenting but one loathsome blank of profligacy and crime; some mere girls, others but young women, and none past the prime of life; formed the darkest and saddest portion of this dreary picture.

Fagin, troubled by no grave emotions, looked eagerly from face to face while these proceedings were in progress; but apparently without meeting that of which he was in search. Succeeding, at length, in catching the eye of the man who occupied the chair, he beckoned to him slightly, and left the room, as quietly as he had entered it.

'What can I do for you, Mr. Fagin?' inquired the man, as he followed him out to the landing. 'Won't you join us? They'll be delighted, every one of 'em.'

The Jew shook his head impatiently, and said in a whisper, 'Is he here?'

'No,' replied the man.

'And no news of Barney?' inquired Fagin.

'None,' replied the landlord of the Cripples; for it was he. 'He won't stir till it's all safe. Depend on it, they're on the scent down there; and that if he moved, he'd blow upon the thing at once. He's all right enough, Barney is, else I should have heard of him. I'll pound it, that Barney's managing properly. Let him alone for that.'

'Will he be here to-night?' asked the Jew, laying the same emphasis on the pronoun as before.

'Monks, do you mean?' inquired the landlord, hesitating.

'Hush!' said the Jew. 'Yes.'

'Certain,' replied the man, drawing a gold watch from his fob; 'I expected him here before now. If you'll wait ten minutes, he'll be—'

'No, no,' said the Jew, hastily; as though, however desirous he might be to see the person in question, he was nevertheless relieved by his absence. 'Tell him I came here to see him; and that he must come to me to-night. No, say to-morrow. As he is not here, to-morrow will be time enough.'

'Good!' said the man. 'Nothing more?'

'Not a word now,' said the Jew, descending the stairs.

'I say,' said the other, looking over the rails, and speaking in a hoarse whisper; 'what a time this would be for a sell! I've got Phil Barker here: so drunk, that a boy might take him!'

'Ah! But it's not Phil Barker's time,' said the Jew, looking up.

'Phil has something more to do, before we can afford to part with him; so go back to the company, my dear, and tell them to lead merry lives—while they last. Ha! ha! ha!'

The landlord reciprocated the old man's laugh; and returned to his guests. The Jew was no sooner alone, than his countenance resumed its former expression of anxiety and thought. After a brief reflection, he called a hack-cabriolet, and bade the man drive towards Bethnal Green. He dismissed him within some quarter of a mile of Mr. Sikes's residence, and performed the short remainder of the distance, on foot.

'Now,' muttered the Jew, as he knocked at the door, 'if there is any deep play here, I shall have it out of you, my girl, cunning as you are.'

She was in her room, the woman said. Fagin crept softly upstairs, and entered it without any previous ceremony. The girl was alone; lying with her head upon the table, and her hair straggling over it.

'She has been drinking,' thought the Jew, cooly, 'or perhaps she is only miserable.'

The old man turned to close the door, as he made this reflection; the noise thus occasioned, roused the girl. She eyed his crafty face narrowly, as she inquired to his recital of Toby Crackit's story. When it was concluded, she sank into her former attitude, but spoke not a word. She pushed the candle impatiently away; and once or twice as she feverishly changed her position, shuffled her feet upon the ground; but this was all.

During the silence, the Jew looked restlessly about the room, as if to assure himself that there were no appearances of Sikes having covertly returned. Apparently satisfied with his inspection, he coughed twice or thrice, and made as many efforts to open a conversation; but the girl heeded him no more than if he had been made of stone. At length he made another attempt; and rubbing his hands together, said, in his most conciliatory tone,

'And where should you think Bill was now, my dear?'

The girl moaned out some half intelligible reply, that she could not tell; and seemed, from the smothered noise that escaped her, to be crying.

'And the boy, too,' said the Jew, straining his eyes to catch a glimpse of her face. 'Poor leetle child! Left in a ditch, Nance; only think!'

'The child,' said the girl, suddenly looking up, 'is better where he is, than among us; and if no harm comes to Bill from it, I hope he lies dead in the ditch and that his young bones may rot there.'

'What!' cried the Jew, in amazement.

'Ay, I do,' returned the girl, meeting his gaze. 'I shall be glad to have him away from my eyes, and to know that the worst is over. I can't bear to have him about me. The sight of him turns me against myself, and all of you.'

'Pooh!' said the Jew, scornfully. 'You're drunk.'

'Am I?' cried the girl bitterly. 'It's no fault of yours, if I am not! You'd never have me anything else, if you had your will, except now;—the humour doesn't suit you, doesn't it?'

'No!' rejoined the Jew, furiously. 'It does not.'

'Change it, then!' responded the girl, with a laugh.

'Change it!' exclaimed the Jew, exasperated beyond all bounds by his companion's unexpected obstinacy, and the vexation of the night, 'I will change it! Listen to me, you drab. Listen to me, who with six words, can strangle Sikes as surely as if I had his bull's throat between my fingers now. If he comes back, and leaves the boy behind him; if he gets off free, and dead or alive, fails to restore him to me; murder him yourself if you would have him escape Jack Ketch. And do it the moment he sets foot in this room, or mind me, it will be too late!'

'What is all this?' cried the girl involuntarily.

'What is it?' pursued Fagin, mad with rage. 'When the boy's worth hundreds of pounds to me, am I to lose what chance threw me in the way of getting safely, through the whims of a drunken gang that I could whistle away the lives of! And me bound, too, to a born devil that only wants the will, and has the power to, to—'

Panting for breath, the old man stammered for a word; and in that instant checked the torrent of his wrath, and changed his whole demeanour. A moment before, his clenched hands had grasped the air; his eyes had dilated; and his face grown livid with passion; but now, he shrunk into a chair, and, cowering together, trembled with the apprehension of having himself disclosed some hidden villainy. After a short silence, he ventured to look round at his companion. He appeared somewhat reassured, on beholding her in the same listless attitude from which he had first roused her.

'Nancy, dear!' croaked the Jew, in his usual voice. 'Did you mind me, dear?'

'Don't worry me now, Fagin!' replied the girl, raising her head languidly. 'If Bill has not done it this time, he will another. He has done many a good job for you, and will do many more when he can; and when he can't he won't; so no more about that.'

'Regarding this boy, my dear?' said the Jew, rubbing the palms of his hands nervously together.

'The boy must take his chance with the rest,' interrupted Nancy, hastily; 'and I say again, I hope he is dead, and out of harm's way, and out of yours,—that is, if Bill comes to no harm. And if Toby got clear off, Bill's pretty sure to be safe; for Bill's worth two of Toby any time.'

'And about what I was saying, my dear?' observed the Jew, keeping his glistening eye steadily upon her.

'You must say it all over again, if it's anything you want me to do,' rejoined Nancy; 'and if it is, you had better wait till to-morrow. You put me up for a minute; but now I'm stupid again.'

Fagin put several other questions: all with the same drift of ascertaining whether the girl had profited by his unguarded hints; but, she answered them so readily, and was withal so utterly unmoved by his searching looks, that his original impression of her being more than a trifle in liquor, was confirmed. Nancy, indeed, was not exempt from a failing which was very common among the Jew's female pupils; and in which, in their tenderer years, they were rather encouraged than checked. Her disordered appearance, and a wholesale perfume of Geneva which pervaded the apartment, afforded strong confirmatory evidence of the justice of the Jew's supposition; and when, after indulging in the temporary display of violence above described, she subsided, first into dullness, and afterwards into a compound of feelings: under the influence of which she shed tears one minute, and in the next gave utterance to various exclamations of 'Never say die!' and divers calculations as to what might be the amount of the odds so long as a lady or gentleman was happy, Mr. Fagin, who had had considerable experience of such matters in his time, saw, with great satisfaction, that she was very far gone indeed.

Having eased his mind by this discovery; and having accomplished his twofold object of imparting to the girl what he had, that night, heard, and of ascertaining, with his own eyes, that Sikes had not returned, Mr. Fagin again turned his face homeward: leaving his young friend asleep, with her head upon the table.

It was within an hour of midnight. The weather being dark, and piercing cold, he had no great temptation to loiter. The sharp wind that scoured the streets, seemed to have cleared them of passengers, as of dust and mud, for few people were abroad, and they were to all appearance hastening fast home. It blew from the right quarter for the Jew, however, and straight before it he went: trembling, and shivering, as every fresh gust drove him rudely on his way.

He had reached the corner of his own street, and was already fumbling in his pocket for the door-key, when a dark figure emerged from a projecting entrance which lay in deep shadow, and, crossing the road, glided up to him unperceived.

'Fagin!' whispered a voice close to his ear.

'Ah!' said the Jew, turning quickly round, 'is that—'

'Yes!' interrupted the stranger. 'I have been lingering here these two hours. Where the devil have you been?'

'On your business, my dear,' replied the Jew, glancing uneasily at his companion, and slackening his pace as he spoke. 'On your business all night.'

'Oh, of course!' said the stranger, with a sneer. 'Well; and what's come of it?'

'Nothing good,' said the Jew.

'Nothing bad, I hope?' said the stranger, stopping short, and turning a startled look on his companion.

The Jew shook his head, and was about to reply, when the stranger, interrupting him, motioned to the house, before which they had by this time arrived: remarking, that he had better say what he had got to say, under cover: for his blood was chilled with standing about so long, and the wind blew through him.

Fagin looked as if he could have willingly excused himself from taking home a visitor at that unseasonable hour; and, indeed, muttered something about having no fire; but his companion repeating his request in a peremptory manner, he unlocked the door, and requested him to close it softly, while he got a light.

'It's as dark as the grave,' said the man, groping forward a few steps. 'Make haste!'

'Shut the door,' whispered Fagin from the end of the passage. As he spoke, it closed with a loud noise.

'That wasn't my doing,' said the other man, feeling his way. 'The wind blew it to, or it shut of its own accord: one or the other. Look sharp with the light, or I shall knock my brains out against something in this confounded hole.'

Fagin stealthily descended the kitchen stairs. After a short absence, he returned with a lighted candle, and the intelligence that Toby Crackit was asleep in the back room below, and that the boys were in the front one. Beckoning the man to follow him, he led the way upstairs.

'We can say the few words we've got to say in here, my dear,' said the Jew, throwing open a door on the first floor; 'and as there are holes in the shutters, and we never show lights to our neighbours, we'll set the candle on the stairs. There!'

With those words, the Jew, stooping down, placed the candle on an upper flight of stairs, exactly opposite to the room door. This done, he led the way into the apartment; which was destitute of all movables save a broken arm-chair, and an old couch or sofa without covering, which stood behind the door. Upon this piece of furniture, the stranger sat himself with the air of a weary man; and the Jew, drawing up the arm-chair opposite, they sat face to face. It was not quite dark; the door was partially open; and the candle outside, threw a feeble reflection on the opposite wall.

They conversed for some time in whispers. Though nothing of the conversation was distinguishable beyond a few disjointed words here and there, a listener might easily have perceived that Fagin appeared to be defending himself against some remarks of the stranger; and that the latter was in a state of considerable irritation. They might have been talking, thus, for a quarter of an hour or more, when Monks—by which name the Jew had designated the strange man several times in the course of their colloquy—said, raising his voice a little,

'I tell you again, it was badly planned. Why not have kept him here among the rest, and made a sneaking, snivelling pickpocket of him at once?'

'Only hear him!' exclaimed the Jew, shrugging his shoulders.

'Why, do you mean to say you couldn't have done it, if you had chosen?' demanded Monks, sternly. 'Haven't you done it, with other boys, scores of times? If you had had patience for a twelvemonth, at most, couldn't you have got him convicted, and sent safely out of the kingdom; perhaps for life?'

'Whose turn would that have served, my dear?' inquired the Jew humbly.

'Mine,' replied Monks.

'But not mine,' said the Jew, submissively. 'He might have become of use to me. When there are two parties to a bargain, it is only reasonable that the interests of both should be consulted; is it, my good friend?'

'What then?' demanded Monks.

'I saw it was not easy to train him to the business,' replied the Jew; 'he was not like other boys in the same circumstances.'

'Curse him, no!' muttered the man, 'or he would have been a thief, long ago.'

'I had no hold upon him to make him worse,' pursued the Jew, anxiously watching the countenance of his companion. 'His hand was not in. I had nothing to frighten him with; which we always must have in the beginning, or we labour in vain. What could I do? Send him out with the Dodger and Charley? We had enough of that, at first, my dear; I trembled for us all.'

'That was not my doing,' observed Monks.

'No, no, my dear!' renewed the Jew. 'And I don't quarrel with it now; because, if it had never happened, you might never have clapped eyes on the boy to notice him, and so led to the discovery that it was him you were looking for. Well! I got him back for you by means of the girl; and then she begins to favour him.'

'Throttle the girl!' said Monks, impatiently.

'Why, we can't afford to do that just now, my dear,' replied the Jew, smiling; 'and, besides, that sort of thing is not in our way; or, one of these days, I might be glad to have it done. I know what these girls are, Monks, well. As soon as the boy begins to harden, she'll care no more for him, than for a block of wood. You want him made a thief. If he is alive, I can make him one from this time; and, if—if—' said the Jew, drawing nearer to the other,—'it's not likely, mind,—but if the worst comes to the worst, and he is dead—'

'It's no fault of mine if he is!' interposed the other man, with a look of terror, and clasping the Jew's arm with trembling hands. 'Mind that. Fagin! I had no hand in it. Anything but his death, I told you from the first. I won't shed blood; it's always found out, and haunts a man besides. If they shot him dead, I was not the cause; do you hear me? Fire this infernal den! What's that?'

'What!' cried the Jew, grasping the coward round the body, with both arms, as he sprung to his feet. 'Where?'

'Yonder!' replied the man, glaring at the opposite wall. 'The shadow! I saw the shadow of a woman, in a cloak and bonnet, pass along the wainscot like a breath!'

The Jew released his hold, and they rushed tumultuously from the room. The candle, wasted by the draught, was standing where it had been placed. It showed them only the empty staircase, and their own white faces. They listened intently: a profound silence reigned throughout the house.

'It's your fancy,' said the Jew, taking up the light and turning to his companion.

'I'll swear I saw it!' replied Monks, trembling. 'It was bending forward when I saw it first; and when I spoke, it darted away.'

The Jew glanced contemptuously at the pale face of his associate, and, telling him he could follow, if he pleased, ascended the stairs. They looked into all the rooms; they were cold, bare, and empty. They descended into the passage, and thence into the cellars below. The green damp hung upon the low walls; the tracks of the snail and slug glistened in the light of the candle; but all was still as death.

'What do you think now?' said the Jew, when they had regained the passage. 'Besides ourselves, there's not a creature in the house except Toby and the boys; and they're safe enough. See here!'

As a proof of the fact, the Jew drew forth two keys from his pocket; and explained, that when he first went downstairs, he had locked them in, to prevent any intrusion on the conference.

This accumulated testimony effectually staggered Mr. Monks. His protestations had gradually become less and less vehement as they proceeded in their search without making any discovery; and, now, he gave vent to several very grim laughs, and confessed it could only have been his excited imagination. He declined any renewal of the conversation, however, for that night: suddenly remembering that it was past one o'clock. And so the amiable couple parted.

CHAPTER XXVII. ATONES FOR THE UNPOLITENESS OF A FORMER CHAPTER; WHICH DESERTED A LADY, MOST UNCEREMONIOUSLY

As it would be, by no means, seemly in a humble author to keep so mighty a personage as a beadle waiting, with his back to the fire, and the skirts of his coat gathered up under his arms, until such time as it might suit his pleasure to relieve him; and as it would still less become his station, or his gallantry to involve in the same neglect a lady on whom that beadle had looked with an eye of tenderness and affection, and in whose ear he had whispered sweet words, which, coming from such a quarter, might well thrill the bosom of maid or matron of whatsoever degree; the historian whose pen traces these words—trusting that he knows his place, and that he entertains a becoming reverence for those upon earth to whom high and important authority is delegated—hastens to pay them that respect which their position demands, and to treat them with all that duteous ceremony which their exalted rank, and (by consequence) great virtues, imperatively claim at his hands. Towards this end, indeed, he had purposed to introduce, in this place, a dissertation touching the divine right of beadles, and elucidative of the position, that a beadle can do no wrong: which could not fail to have been both pleasurable and profitable to the right-minded reader but which he is unfortunately compelled, by want of time and space, to postpone to some more convenient and fitting opportunity; on the arrival of which, he will be prepared to show, that a beadle properly constituted: that is to say, a parochial beadle, attached to a parochial workhouse, and attending in his official capacity the parochial church: is, in right and virtue of his office, possessed of all the excellences and best qualities of humanity; and that to none of those excellences, can mere companies' beadles, or court-of-law beadles, or even chapel-of-ease beadles (save the last, and they in a very lowly and inferior degree), lay the remotest sustainable claim.

Mr. Bumble had re-counted the teaspoons, re-weighed the sugar-tongs, made a closer inspection of the milk-pot, and ascertained to a nicety the exact condition of the furniture, down to the very horse-hair seats of the chairs; and had repeated each process full half a dozen times; before he began to think that it was time for Mrs. Corney to return. Thinking begets thinking; as there were no sounds of Mrs. Corney's approach, it occured to Mr. Bumble that it would be an innocent and virtuous way of spending the time, if he were further to allay his curiosity by a cursory glance at the interior of Mrs. Corney's chest of drawers.

Having listened at the keyhole, to assure himself that nobody was approaching the chamber, Mr. Bumble, beginning at the bottom, proceeded to make himself acquainted with the contents of the three long drawers: which, being filled with various garments of good fashion and texture, carefully preserved between two layers of old newspapers, speckled with dried lavender: seemed to yield him exceeding satisfaction. Arriving, in course of time, at the right-hand corner drawer (in which was the key), and beholding therein a small padlocked box, which, being shaken, gave forth a pleasant sound, as of the chinking of coin, Mr. Bumble returned with a stately walk to the fireplace; and, resuming his old attitude, said, with a grave and determined air, 'I'll do it!' He followed up this remarkable declaration, by shaking his head in a waggish manner for ten minutes, as though he were remonstrating with himself for being such a pleasant dog; and then, he took a view of his legs in profile, with much seeming pleasure and interest.

He was still placidly engaged in this latter survey, when Mrs. Corney, hurrying into the room, threw herself, in a breathless state, on a chair by the fireside, and covering her eyes with one hand, placed the other over her heart, and gasped for breath.

'Mrs. Corney,' said Mr. Bumble, stooping over the matron, 'what is this, ma'am? Has anything happened, ma'am? Pray answer me: I'm on—on—' Mr. Bumble, in his alarm, could not immediately think of the word 'tenterhooks,' so he said 'broken bottles.'

'Oh, Mr. Bumble!' cried the lady, 'I have been so dreadfully put out!'

'Put out, ma'am!' exclaimed Mr. Bumble; 'who has dared to—? I know!' said Mr. Bumble, checking himself, with native majesty, 'this is them wicious paupers!'

'It's dreadful to think of!' said the lady, shuddering.

'Then don't think of it, ma'am,' rejoined Mr. Bumble.

'I can't help it,' whimpered the lady.

'Then take something, ma'am,' said Mr. Bumble soothingly. 'A little of the wine?'

'Not for the world!' replied Mrs. Corney. 'I couldn't,—oh! The top shelf in the right-hand corner—oh!' Uttering these words, the good lady pointed, distractedly, to the cupboard, and underwent a convulsion from internal spasms. Mr. Bumble rushed to the closet; and, snatching a pint green-glass bottle from the shelf thus incoherently indicated, filled a tea-cup with its contents, and held it to the lady's lips.

'I'm better now,' said Mrs. Corney, falling back, after drinking half of it.

Mr. Bumble raised his eyes piously to the ceiling in thankfulness; and, bringing them down again to the brim of the cup, lifted it to his nose.

'Peppermint,' exclaimed Mrs. Corney, in a faint voice, smiling gently on the beadle as she spoke. 'Try it! There's a little—a little something else in it.'

Mr. Bumble tasted the medicine with a doubtful look; smacked his lips; took another taste; and put the cup down empty.

'It's very comforting,' said Mrs. Corney.

'Very much so indeed, ma'am,' said the beadle. As he spoke, he drew a chair beside the matron, and tenderly inquired what had happened to distress her.

'Nothing,' replied Mrs. Corney. 'I am a foolish, excitable, weak creetur.'

'Not weak, ma'am,' retorted Mr. Bumble, drawing his chair a little closer. 'Are you a weak creetur, Mrs. Corney?'

'We are all weak creeturs,' said Mrs. Corney, laying down a general principle.

'So we are,' said the beadle.

Nothing was said on either side, for a minute or two afterwards. By the expiration of that time, Mr. Bumble had illustrated the position by removing his left arm from the back of Mrs. Corney's chair, where it had previously rested, to Mrs. Corney's apron-string, round which it gradually became entwined.

'We are all weak creeturs,' said Mr. Bumble.

Mrs. Corney sighed.

'Don't sigh, Mrs. Corney,' said Mr. Bumble.

'I can't help it,' said Mrs. Corney. And she sighed again.

'This is a very comfortable room, ma'am,' said Mr. Bumble looking round. 'Another room, and this, ma'am, would be a complete thing.'

'It would be too much for one,' murmured the lady.

'But not for two, ma'am,' rejoined Mr. Bumble, in soft accents. 'Eh, Mrs. Corney?'

Mrs. Corney drooped her head, when the beadle said this; the beadle drooped his, to get a view of Mrs. Corney's face. Mrs. Corney, with great propriety, turned her head away, and released her hand to get at her pocket-handkerchief; but insensibly replaced it in that of Mr. Bumble.

'The board allows you coals, don't they, Mrs. Corney?' inquired the beadle, affectionately pressing her hand.

'And candles,' replied Mrs. Corney, slightly returning the pressure.

'Coals, candles, and house-rent free,' said Mr. Bumble. 'Oh, Mrs. Corney, what an Angel you are!'

The lady was not proof against this burst of feeling. She sank into Mr. Bumble's arms; and that gentleman in his agitation, imprinted a passionate kiss upon her chaste nose.

'Such porochial perfection!' exclaimed Mr. Bumble, rapturously. 'You know that Mr. Slout is worse to-night, my fascinator?'

'Yes,' replied Mrs. Corney, bashfully.

'He can't live a week, the doctor says,' pursued Mr. Bumble. 'He is the master of this establishment; his death will cause a wacancy; that wacancy must be filled up. Oh, Mrs. Corney, what a prospect this opens! What a opportunity for a jining of hearts and housekeepings!'

Mrs. Corney sobbed.

'The little word?' said Mr. Bumble, bending over the bashful beauty. 'The one little, little, little word, my blessed Corney?'

'Ye—ye—yes!' sighed out the matron.

'One more,' pursued the beadle; 'compose your darling feelings for only one more. When is it to come off?'

Mrs. Corney twice essayed to speak: and twice failed. At length summoning up courage, she threw her arms around Mr. Bumble's neck, and said, it might be as soon as ever he pleased, and that he was 'a irresistible duck.'

Matters being thus amicably and satisfactorily arranged, the contract was solemnly ratified in another teacupful of the peppermint mixture; which was rendered the more necessary, by the flutter and agitation of the lady's spirits. While it was being disposed of, she acquainted Mr. Bumble with the old woman's decease.

'Very good,' said that gentleman, sipping his peppermint; 'I'll call at Sowerberry's as I go home, and tell him to send to-morrow morning. Was it that as frightened you, love?'

'It wasn't anything particular, dear,' said the lady evasively.

'It must have been something, love,' urged Mr. Bumble. 'Won't you tell your own B.?'

'Not now,' rejoined the lady; 'one of these days. After we're married, dear.'

'After we're married!' exclaimed Mr. Bumble. 'It wasn't any impudence from any of them male paupers as—'

'No, no, love!' interposed the lady, hastily.

'If I thought it was,' continued Mr. Bumble; 'if I thought as any one of 'em had dared to lift his wulgar eyes to that lovely countenance—'

'They wouldn't have dared to do it, love,' responded the lady.

'They had better not!' said Mr. Bumble, clenching his fist. 'Let me see any man, porochial or extra-porochial, as would presume to do it; and I can tell him that he wouldn't do it a second time!'

Unembellished by any violence of gesticulation, this might have seemed no very high compliment to the lady's charms; but, as Mr. Bumble accompanied the threat with many warlike gestures, she was much touched with this proof of his devotion, and protested, with great admiration, that he was indeed a dove.

The dove then turned up his coat-collar, and put on his cocked hat; and, having exchanged a long and affectionate embrace with his future partner, once again braved the cold wind of the night: merely pausing, for a few minutes, in the male paupers' ward, to abuse them a little, with the view of satisfying himself that he could fill the office of workhouse-master with needful acerbity. Assured of his qualifications, Mr. Bumble left the building with a light heart, and bright visions of his future promotion: which served to occupy his mind until he reached the shop of the undertaker.

Now, Mr. and Mrs. Sowerberry having gone out to tea and supper: and Noah Claypole not being at any time disposed to take upon himself a greater amount of physical exertion than is necessary to a convenient performance of the two functions of eating and drinking, the shop was not closed, although it was past the usual hour of shutting-up. Mr. Bumble tapped with his cane on the counter several times; but, attracting no attention, and beholding a light shining through the glass-window of the little parlour at the back of the shop, he made bold to peep in and see what was going forward; and when he saw what was going forward, he was not a little surprised.

The cloth was laid for supper; the table was covered with bread and butter, plates and glasses; a porter-pot and a wine-bottle. At the upper end of the table, Mr. Noah Claypole lolled negligently in an easy-chair, with his legs thrown over one of the arms: an open clasp-knife in one hand, and a mass of buttered bread in the other. Close beside him stood Charlotte, opening oysters from a barrel: which Mr. Claypole condescended to swallow, with remarkable avidity. A more than ordinary redness in the region of the young gentleman's nose, and a kind of fixed wink in his right eye, denoted that he was in a slight degree intoxicated; these symptoms were confirmed by the intense relish with which he took his oysters, for which nothing but a strong appreciation of their cooling properties, in cases of internal fever, could have sufficiently accounted.

'Here's a delicious fat one, Noah, dear!' said Charlotte; 'try him, do; only this one.'

'What a delicious thing is a oyster!' remarked Mr. Claypole, after he had swallowed it. 'What a pity it is, a number of 'em should ever make you feel uncomfortable; isn't it, Charlotte?'

'It's quite a cruelty,' said Charlotte.

'So it is,' acquiesced Mr. Claypole. 'An't yer fond of oysters?'

'Not overmuch,' replied Charlotte. 'I like to see you eat 'em, Noah dear, better than eating 'em myself.'

'Lor!' said Noah, reflectively; 'how queer!'

'Have another,' said Charlotte. 'Here's one with such a beautiful, delicate beard!'

'I can't manage any more,' said Noah. 'I'm very sorry. Come here, Charlotte, and I'll kiss yer.'

'What!' said Mr. Bumble, bursting into the room. 'Say that again, sir.'

Charlotte uttered a scream, and hid her face in her apron. Mr. Claypole, without making any further change in his position than suffering his legs to reach the ground, gazed at the beadle in drunken terror.

'Say it again, you wile, owdacious fellow!' said Mr. Bumble. 'How dare you mention such a thing, sir? And how dare you encourage him, you insolent minx? Kiss her!' exclaimed Mr. Bumble, in strong indignation. 'Faugh!'

'I didn't mean to do it!' said Noah, blubbering. 'She's always a-kissing of me, whether I like it, or not.'

'Oh, Noah,' cried Charlotte, reproachfully.

'Yer are; yer know yer are!' retorted Noah. 'She's always a-doin' of it, Mr. Bumble, sir; she chucks me under the chin, please, sir; and makes all manner of love!'

'Silence!' cried Mr. Bumble, sternly. 'Take yourself downstairs, ma'am. Noah, you shut up the shop; say another word till your master comes home, at your peril; and, when he does come home, tell him that Mr. Bumble said he was to send a old woman's shell after breakfast to-morrow morning. Do you hear sir? Kissing!' cried Mr. Bumble, holding up his hands. 'The sin and wickedness of the lower orders in this porochial district is frightful! If Parliament don't take their abominable courses under consideration, this country's ruined, and the character of the peasantry gone for ever!' With these words, the beadle strode, with a lofty and gloomy air, from the undertaker's premises.

And now that we have accompanied him so far on his road home, and have made all necessary preparations for the old woman's funeral, let us set on foot a few inquires after young Oliver Twist, and ascertain whether he be still lying in the ditch where Toby Crackit left him.

CHAPTER XXVIII. LOOKS AFTER OLIVER, AND PROCEEDS WITH HIS ADVENTURES

'Wolves tear your throats!' muttered Sikes, grinding his teeth. 'I wish I was among some of you; you'd howl the hoarser for it.'

As Sikes growled forth this imprecation, with the most desperate ferocity that his desperate nature was capable of, he rested the body of the wounded boy across his bended knee; and turned his head, for an instant, to look back at his pursuers.

There was little to be made out, in the mist and darkness; but the loud shouting of men vibrated through the air, and the barking of the neighbouring dogs, roused by the sound of the alarm bell, resounded in every direction.

'Stop, you white-livered hound!' cried the robber, shouting after Toby Crackit, who, making the best use of his long legs, was already ahead. 'Stop!'

The repetition of the word, brought Toby to a dead stand-still. For he was not quite satisfied that he was beyond the range of pistol-shot; and Sikes was in no mood to be played with.

'Bear a hand with the boy,' cried Sikes, beckoning furiously to his confederate. 'Come back!'

Toby made a show of returning; but ventured, in a low voice, broken for want of breath, to intimate considerable reluctance as he came slowly along.

'Quicker!' cried Sikes, laying the boy in a dry ditch at his feet, and drawing a pistol from his pocket. 'Don't play booty with me.'

At this moment the noise grew louder. Sikes, again looking round, could discern that the men who had given chase were already climbing the gate of the field in which he stood; and that a couple of dogs were some paces in advance of them.

'It's all up, Bill!' cried Toby; 'drop the kid, and show 'em your heels.' With this parting advice, Mr. Crackit, preferring the chance of being shot by his friend, to the certainty of being taken by his enemies, fairly turned tail, and darted off at full speed. Sikes clenched his teeth; took one look around; threw over the prostrate form of Oliver, the cape in which he had been hurriedly muffled; ran along the front of the hedge, as if to distract the attention of those behind, from the spot where the boy lay; paused, for a second, before another hedge which met it at right angles; and whirling his pistol high into the air, cleared it at a bound, and was gone.

'Ho, ho, there!' cried a tremulous voice in the rear. 'Pincher! Neptune! Come here, come here!'

The dogs, who, in common with their masters, seemed to have no particular relish for the sport in which they were engaged, readily answered to the command. Three men, who had by this time advanced some distance into the field, stopped to take counsel together.

'My advice, or, leastways, I should say, my orders, is,' said the fattest man of the party, 'that we 'mediately go home again.'

'I am agreeable to anything which is agreeable to Mr. Giles,' said a shorter man; who was by no means of a slim figure, and who was very pale in the face, and very polite: as frightened men frequently are.

'I shouldn't wish to appear ill-mannered, gentlemen,' said the third, who had called the dogs back, 'Mr. Giles ought to know.'

'Certainly,' replied the shorter man; 'and whatever Mr. Giles says, it isn't our place to contradict him. No, no, I know my sitiwation! Thank my stars, I know my sitiwation.' To tell the truth, the little man did seem to know his situation, and to know perfectly well that it was by no means a desirable one; for his teeth chattered in his head as he spoke.

'You are afraid, Brittles,' said Mr. Giles.

'I an't,' said Brittles.

'You are,' said Giles.

'You're a falsehood, Mr. Giles,' said Brittles.

'You're a lie, Brittles,' said Mr. Giles.

Now, these four retorts arose from Mr. Giles's taunt; and Mr. Giles's taunt had arisen from his indignation at having the responsibility of going home again, imposed upon himself under cover of a compliment. The third man brought the dispute to a close, most philosophically.

'I'll tell you what it is, gentlemen,' said he, 'we're all afraid.'

'Speak for yourself, sir,' said Mr. Giles, who was the palest of the party.

'So I do,' replied the man. 'It's natural and proper to be afraid, under such circumstances. I am.'

'So am I,' said Brittles; 'only there's no call to tell a man he is, so bounceably.'

These frank admissions softened Mr. Giles, who at once owned that he was afraid; upon which, they all three faced about, and ran back again with the completest unanimity, until Mr. Giles (who had the shortest wind of the party, as was encumbered with a pitchfork) most handsomely insisted on stopping, to make an apology for his hastiness of speech.

'But it's wonderful,' said Mr. Giles, when he had explained, 'what a man will do, when his blood is up. I should have committed murder—I know I should—if we'd caught one of them rascals.'

As the other two were impressed with a similar presentiment; and as their blood, like his, had all gone down again; some speculation ensued upon the cause of this sudden change in their temperament.

'I know what it was,' said Mr. Giles; 'it was the gate.'

'I shouldn't wonder if it was,' exclaimed Brittles, catching at the idea.

'You may depend upon it,' said Giles, 'that that gate stopped the flow of the excitement. I felt all mine suddenly going away, as I was climbing over it.'

By a remarkable coincidence, the other two had been visited with the same unpleasant sensation at that precise moment. It was quite obvious, therefore, that it was the gate; especially as there was no doubt regarding the time at which the change had taken place, because all three remembered that they had come in sight of the robbers at the instant of its occurance.

This dialogue was held between the two men who had surprised the burglars, and a travelling tinker who had been sleeping in an outhouse, and who had been roused, together with his two mongrel curs, to join in the pursuit. Mr. Giles acted in the double capacity of butler and steward to the old lady of the mansion; Brittles was a lad of all-work: who, having entered her service a mere child, was treated as a promising young boy still, though he was something past thirty.

Encouraging each other with such converse as this; but, keeping very close together, notwithstanding, and looking apprehensively round, whenever a fresh gust rattled through the boughs; the three men hurried back to a tree, behind which they had left their lantern, lest its light should inform the thieves in what direction to fire. Catching up the light, they made the best of their way home, at a good round trot; and long after their dusky forms had ceased to be discernible, the light might have been seen twinkling and dancing in the distance, like some exhalation of the damp and gloomy atmosphere through which it was swiftly borne.

The air grew colder, as day came slowly on; and the mist rolled along the ground like a dense cloud of smoke. The grass was wet; the pathways, and low places, were all mire and water; the damp breath of an unwholesome wind went languidly by, with a hollow moaning. Still, Oliver lay motionless and insensible on the spot where Sikes had left him.

Morning drew on apace. The air become more sharp and piercing, as its first dull hue—

the death of night, rather than the birth of day—glimmered faintly in the sky. The objects which had looked dim and terrible in the darkness, grew more and more defined, and gradually resolved into their familiar shapes. The rain came down, thick and fast, and pattered noisily among the leafless bushes. But, Oliver felt it not, as it beat against him; for he still lay stretched, helpless and unconscious, on his bed of clay.

At length, a low cry of pain broke the stillness that prevailed; and uttering it, the boy awoke. His left arm, rudely bandaged in a shawl, hung heavy and useless at his side; the bandage was saturated with blood. He was so weak, that he could scarcely raise himself into a sitting posture; when he had done so, he looked feebly round for help, and groaned with pain. Trembling in every joint, from cold and exhaustion, he made an effort to stand upright; but, shuddering from head to foot, fell prostrate on the ground.

After a short return of the stupor in which he had been so long plunged, Oliver: urged by a creeping sickness at his heart, which seemed to warn him that if he lay there, he must surely die: got upon his feet, and essayed to walk. His head was dizzy, and he staggered to and fro like a drunken man. But he kept up, nevertheless, and, with his head drooping languidly on his breast, went stumbling onward, he knew not whither.

And now, hosts of bewildering and confused ideas came crowding on his mind. He seemed to be still walking between Sikes and Crackit, who were angrily disputing—for the very words they said, sounded in his ears; and when he caught his own attention, as it were, by making some violent effort to save himself from falling, he found that he was talking to them. Then, he was alone with Sikes, plodding on as on the previous day; and as shadowy people passed them, he felt the robber's grasp upon his wrist. Suddenly, he started back at the report of firearms; there rose into the air, loud cries and shouts; lights gleamed before his eyes; all was noise and tumult, as some unseen hand bore him hurriedly away. Through all these rapid visions, there ran an undefined, uneasy consciousness of pain, which wearied and tormented him incessantly.

Thus he staggered on, creeping, almost mechanically, between the bars of gates, or through hedge-gaps as they came in his way, until he reached a road. Here the rain began to fall so heavily, that it roused him.

He looked about, and saw that at no great distance there was a house, which perhaps he could reach. Pitying his condition, they might have compassion on him; and if they did not, it would be better, he thought, to die near human beings, than in the lonely open fields. He summoned up all his strength for one last trial, and bent his faltering steps towards it.

As he drew nearer to this house, a feeling come over him that he had seen it before. He remembered nothing of its details; but the shape and aspect of the building seemed familiar to him.

That garden wall! On the grass inside, he had fallen on his knees last night, and prayed the two men's mercy. It was the very house they had attempted to rob.

Oliver felt such fear come over him when he recognised the place, that, for the instant, he forgot the agony of his wound, and thought only of flight. Flight! He could scarcely stand: and if he were in full possession of all the best powers of his slight and youthful frame, whither could he fly? He pushed against the garden-gate; it was unlocked, and swung open on its hinges. He tottered across the lawn; climbed the steps; knocked faintly at the door; and, his whole strength failing him, sunk down against one of the pillars of the little portico.

It happened that about this time, Mr. Giles, Brittles, and the tinker, were recruiting themselves, after the fatigues and terrors of the night, with tea and sundries, in the kitchen. Not that it was Mr. Giles's habit to admit to too great familiarity the humbler servants: towards whom it was rather his wont to deport himself with a lofty affability, which, while it gratified, could not fail to remind them of his superior position in society. But, death, fires, and burglary, make all men equals; so Mr. Giles sat with his legs stretched out before the kitchen fender, leaning his left arm on the table, while, with his right, he illustrated a circumstantial and minute account of the robbery, to which his bearers (but especially the cook and housemaid, who were of the party) listened with breathless interest.

'It was about half-past two,' said Mr. Giles, 'or I wouldn't swear that it mightn't have been a little nearer three, when I woke up, and, turning round in my bed, as it might be so, (here Mr. Giles turned round in his chair, and pulled the corner of the table-cloth over him to imitate bed-clothes,) I fancied I heerd a noise.'

At this point of the narrative the cook turned pale, and asked the housemaid to shut the door: who asked Brittles, who asked the tinker, who pretended not to hear.

'—Heerd a noise,' continued Mr. Giles. 'I says, at first, "This is illusion"; and was composing myself off to sleep, when I heerd the noise again, distinct.'

'What sort of a noise?' asked the cook.

'A kind of a busting noise,' replied Mr. Giles, looking round him.

'More like the noise of powdering a iron bar on a nutmeg-grater,' suggested Brittles.

'It was, when you heerd it, sir,' rejoined Mr. Giles; 'but, at this time, it had a busting sound. I turned down the clothes'; continued Giles, rolling back the table-cloth, 'sat up in bed; and listened.'

The cook and housemaid simultaneously ejaculated 'Lor!' and drew their chairs closer together.

'I heerd it now, quite apparent,' resumed Mr. Giles. '"Somebody," I says, "is forcing of a door, or window; what's to be done? I'll call up that poor lad, Brittles, and save him from being murdered in his bed; or his throat," I says, "may be cut from his right ear to his left, without his ever knowing it."'

Here, all eyes were turned upon Brittles, who fixed his upon the speaker, and stared at him, with his mouth wide open, and his face expressive of the most unmitigated horror.

'I tossed off the clothes,' said Giles, throwing away the table-cloth, and looking very hard at the cook and housemaid, 'got softly out of bed; drew on a pair of—'

'Ladies present, Mr. Giles,' murmured the tinker.

'—Of shoes, sir,' said Giles, turning upon him, and laying great emphasis on the word; 'seized the loaded pistol that always goes upstairs with the plate-basket; and walked on tiptoes to his room. "Brittles," I says, when I had woke him, "don't be frightened!"'

'So you did,' observed Brittles, in a low voice.

'"We're dead men, I think, Brittles," I says,' continued Giles; '"but don't be frightened."'

'Was he frightened?' asked the cook.

'Not a bit of it,' replied Mr. Giles. 'He was as firm—ah! pretty near as firm as I was.'

'I should have died at once, I'm sure, if it had been me,' observed the housemaid.

'You're a woman,' retorted Brittles, plucking up a little.

'Brittles is right,' said Mr. Giles, nodding his head, approvingly; 'from a woman, nothing else was to be expected. We, being men, took a dark lantern that was standing on Brittle's hob, and groped our way downstairs in the pitch dark,—as it might be so.'

Mr. Giles had risen from his seat, and taken two steps with his eyes shut, to accompany his description with appropriate action, when he started violently, in common with the rest of the company, and hurried back to his chair. The cook and housemaid screamed.

'It was a knock,' said Mr. Giles, assuming perfect serenity. 'Open the door, somebody.'

Nobody moved.

'It seems a strange sort of a thing, a knock coming at such a time in the morning,' said Mr. Giles, surveying the pale faces which surrounded him, and looking very blank himself; 'but the door must be opened. Do you hear, somebody?'

Mr. Giles, as he spoke, looked at Brittles; but that young man, being naturally modest, probably considered himself nobody, and so held that the inquiry could not have any application to him; at all events, he tendered no reply. Mr. Giles directed an appealing glance at the tinker; but he had suddenly fallen asleep. The women were out of the question.

'If Brittles would rather open the door, in the presence of witnesses,' said Mr. Giles, after a short silence, 'I am ready to make one.'

'So am I,' said the tinker, waking up, as suddenly as he had fallen asleep.

Brittles capitulated on these terms; and the party being somewhat re-assured by the discovery (made on throwing open the shutters) that it was now broad day, took their way upstairs; with the dogs in front. The two women, who were afraid to stay below, brought up the rear. By the advice of Mr. Giles, they all talked very loud, to warn any evil-disposed person outside, that they were strong in numbers; and by a master-stoke of policy, originating in the brain of the same ingenious gentleman, the dogs' tails were well pinched, in the hall, to make them bark savagely.

These precautions having been taken, Mr. Giles held on fast by the tinker's arm (to prevent his running away, as he pleasantly said), and gave the word of command to open the door. Brittles obeyed; the group, peeping timorously over each other's shoulders, beheld no more formidable object than poor little Oliver Twist, speechless and exhausted, who raised his heavy eyes, and mutely solicited their compassion.

'A boy!' exclaimed Mr. Giles, valiantly, pushing the tinker into the background. 'What's the matter with the—eh?—Why—Brittles—look here—don't you know?'

Brittles, who had got behind the door to open it, no sooner saw Oliver, than he uttered a loud cry. Mr. Giles, seizing the boy by one leg and one arm (fortunately not the broken limb) lugged him straight into the hall, and deposited him at full length on the floor thereof.

'Here he is!' bawled Giles, calling in a state of great excitement, up the staircase; 'here's one of the thieves, ma'am! Here's a thief, miss! Wounded, miss! I shot him, miss; and Brittles held the light.'

'—In a lantern, miss,' cried Brittles, applying one hand to the side of his mouth, so that his voice might travel the better.

The two women-servants ran upstairs to carry the intelligence that Mr. Giles had captured a robber; and the tinker busied himself in endeavouring to restore Oliver, lest he should die before he could be hanged. In the midst of all this noise and commotion, there was heard a sweet female voice, which quelled it in an instant.

'Giles!' whispered the voice from the stair-head.

'I'm here, miss,' replied Mr. Giles. 'Don't be frightened, miss; I ain't much injured. He didn't make a very desperate resistance, miss! I was soon too many for him.'

'Hush!' replied the young lady; 'you frighten my aunt as much as the thieves did. Is the poor creature much hurt?'

'Wounded desperate, miss,' replied Giles, with indescribable complacency.

'He looks as if he was a-going, miss,' bawled Brittles, in the same manner as before. 'Wouldn't you like to come and look at him, miss, in case he should?'

'Hush, pray; there's a good man!' rejoined the lady. 'Wait quietly only one instant, while I speak to aunt.'

With a footstep as soft and gentle as the voice, the speaker tripped away. She soon returned, with the direction that the wounded person was to be carried, carefully, upstairs to Mr. Giles's room; and that Brittles was to saddle the pony and betake himself instantly to Chertsey: from which place, he was to despatch, with all speed, a constable and doctor.

'But won't you take one look at him, first, miss?' asked Mr. Giles, with as much pride as if Oliver were some bird of rare plumage, that he had skilfully brought down. 'Not one little peep, miss?'

'Not now, for the world,' replied the young lady. 'Poor fellow! Oh! treat him kindly, Giles for my sake!'

The old servant looked up at the speaker, as she turned away, with a glance as proud and admiring as if she had been his own child. Then, bending over Oliver, he helped to carry him upstairs, with the care and solicitude of a woman.

CHAPTER XXIX. HAS AN INTRODUCTORY ACCOUNT OF THE INMATES OF THE HOUSE, TO WHICH OLIVER RESORTED

In a handsome room: though its furniture had rather the air of old-fashioned comfort, than of modern elegance: there sat two ladies at a well-spread breakfast-table. Mr. Giles, dressed with scrupulous care in a full suit of black, was in attendance upon them. He had taken his station some half-way between the side-board and the breakfast-table; and, with his body drawn up to its full height, his head thrown back, and inclined the merest trifle on one side, his left leg advanced, and his right hand thrust into his waist-coat, while his left hung down by his side, grasping a waiter, looked like one who laboured under a very agreeable sense of his own merits and importance.

Of the two ladies, one was well advanced in years; but the high-backed oaken chair in which she sat, was not more upright than she. Dressed with the utmost nicety and precision, in a quaint mixture of by-gone costume, with some slight concessions to the prevailing taste, which rather served to point the old style pleasantly than to impair its effect, she sat, in a stately manner, with her hands folded on the table before her. Her eyes (and age had dimmed but little of their brightness) were attentively upon her young companion.

The younger lady was in the lovely bloom and spring-time of womanhood; at that age, when, if ever angels be for God's good purposes enthroned in mortal forms, they may be, without impiety, supposed to abide in such as hers.

She was not past seventeen. Cast in so slight and exquisite a mould; so mild and gentle; so pure and beautiful; that earth seemed not her element, nor its rough creatures her fit companions. The very intelligence that shone in her deep blue eye, and was stamped upon her noble head, seemed scarcely of her age, or of the world; and yet the changing expression of sweetness and good humour, the thousand lights that played about the face, and left no shadow there; above all, the smile, the cheerful, happy smile, were made for Home, and fireside peace and happiness.

She was busily engaged in the little offices of the table. Chancing to raise her eyes as the elder lady was regarding her, she playfully put back her hair, which was simply braided on her forehead; and threw into her beaming look, such an expression of affection and artless loveliness, that blessed spirits might have smiled to look upon her.

'And Brittles has been gone upwards of an hour, has he?' asked the old lady, after a pause.

'An hour and twelve minutes, ma'am,' replied Mr. Giles, referring to a silver watch, which he drew forth by a black ribbon.

'He is always slow,' remarked the old lady.

'Brittles always was a slow boy, ma'am,' replied the attendant. And seeing, by the bye, that Brittles had been a slow boy for upwards of thirty years, there appeared no great probability of his ever being a fast one.

'He gets worse instead of better, I think,' said the elder lady.

'It is very inexcusable in him if he stops to play with any other boys,' said the young lady, smiling.

Mr. Giles was apparently considering the propriety of indulging in a respectful smile himself, when a gig drove up to the garden-gate: out of which there jumped a fat gentleman, who ran straight up to the door: and who, getting quickly into the house by some mysterious process, burst into the room, and nearly overturned Mr. Giles and the breakfast-table together.

'I never heard of such a thing!' exclaimed the fat gentleman. 'My dear Mrs. Maylie— bless my soul—in the silence of the night, too—I never heard of such a thing!'

With these expressions of condolence, the fat gentleman shook hands with both ladies, and drawing up a chair, inquired how they found themselves.

'You ought to be dead; positively dead with the fright,' said the fat gentleman. 'Why didn't you send? Bless me, my man should have come in a minute; and so would I; and my assistant would have been delighted; or anybody, I'm sure, under such circumstances. Dear,

dear! So unexpected! In the silence of the night, too!'

The doctor seemed especially troubled by the fact of the robbery having been unexpected, and attempted in the night-time; as if it were the established custom of gentlemen in the housebreaking way to transact business at noon, and to make an appointment, by post, a day or two previous.

'And you, Miss Rose,' said the doctor, turning to the young lady, 'I—'

'Oh! very much so, indeed,' said Rose, interrupting him; 'but there is a poor creature upstairs, whom aunt wishes you to see.'

'Ah! to be sure,' replied the doctor, 'so there is. That was your handiwork, Giles, I understand.'

Mr. Giles, who had been feverishly putting the tea-cups to rights, blushed very red, and said that he had had that honour.

'Honour, eh?' said the doctor; 'well, I don't know; perhaps it's as honourable to hit a thief in a back kitchen, as to hit your man at twelve paces. Fancy that he fired in the air, and you've fought a duel, Giles.'

Mr. Giles, who thought this light treatment of the matter an unjust attempt at diminishing his glory, answered respectfully, that it was not for the like of him to judge about that; but he rather thought it was no joke to the opposite party.

'Gad, that's true!' said the doctor. 'Where is he? Show me the way. I'll look in again, as I come down, Mrs. Maylie. That's the little window that he got in at, eh? Well, I couldn't have believed it!'

Talking all the way, he followed Mr. Giles upstairs; and while he is going upstairs, the reader may be informed, that Mr. Losberne, a surgeon in the neighbourhood, known through a circuit of ten miles round as 'the doctor,' had grown fat, more from good-humour than from good living: and was as kind and hearty, and withal as eccentric an old bachelor, as will be found in five times that space, by any explorer alive.

The doctor was absent, much longer than either he or the ladies had anticipated. A large flat box was fetched out of the gig; and a bedroom bell was rung very often; and the servants ran up and down stairs perpetually; from which tokens it was justly concluded that something important was going on above. At length he returned; and in reply to an anxious inquiry after his patient; looked very mysterious, and closed the door, carefully.

'This is a very extraordinary thing, Mrs. Maylie,' said the doctor, standing with his back to the door, as if to keep it shut.

'He is not in danger, I hope?' said the old lady.

'Why, that would not be an extraordinary thing, under the circumstances,' replied the doctor; 'though I don't think he is. Have you seen the thief?'

'No,' rejoined the old lady.

'Nor heard anything about him?'

'No.'

'I beg your pardon, ma'am, interposed Mr. Giles; 'but I was going to tell you about him when Doctor Losberne came in.'

The fact was, that Mr. Giles had not, at first, been able to bring his mind to the avowal, that he had only shot a boy. Such commendations had been bestowed upon his bravery, that he could not, for the life of him, help postponing the explanation for a few delicious minutes; during which he had flourished, in the very zenith of a brief reputation for undaunted courage.

'Rose wished to see the man,' said Mrs. Maylie, 'but I wouldn't hear of it.'

'Humph!' rejoined the doctor. 'There is nothing very alarming in his appearance. Have you any objection to see him in my presence?'

'If it be necessary,' replied the old lady, 'certainly not.'

'Then I think it is necessary,' said the doctor; 'at all events, I am quite sure that you would deeply regret not having done so, if you postponed it. He is perfectly quiet and comfortable now. Allow me—Miss Rose, will you permit me? Not the slightest fear, I pledge you my honour!'

CHAPTER XXX. RELATES WHAT OLIVER'S NEW VISITORS THOUGHT OF HIM

With many loquacious assurances that they would be agreeably surprised in the aspect of the criminal, the doctor drew the young lady's arm through one of his; and offering his disengaged hand to Mrs. Maylie, led them, with much ceremony and stateliness, upstairs.

'Now,' said the doctor, in a whisper, as he softly turned the handle of a bedroom-door, 'let us hear what you think of him. He has not been shaved very recently, but he don't look at all ferocious notwithstanding. Stop, though! Let me first see that he is in visiting order.'

Stepping before them, he looked into the room. Motioning them to advance, he closed the door when they had entered; and gently drew back the curtains of the bed. Upon it, in lieu of the dogged, black-visaged ruffian they had expected to behold, there lay a mere child: worn with pain and exhaustion, and sunk into a deep sleep. His wounded arm, bound and splintered up, was crossed upon his breast; his head reclined upon the other arm, which was half hidden by his long hair, as it streamed over the pillow.

The honest gentleman held the curtain in his hand, and looked on, for a minute or so, in silence. Whilst he was watching the patient thus, the younger lady glided softly past, and seating herself in a chair by the bedside, gathered Oliver's hair from his face. As she stooped over him, her tears fell upon his forehead.

The boy stirred, and smiled in his sleep, as though these marks of pity and compassion had awakened some pleasant dream of a love and affection he had never known. Thus, a strain of gentle music, or the rippling of water in a silent place, or the odour of a flower, or the mention of a familiar word, will sometimes call up sudden dim remembrances of scenes that never were, in this life; which vanish like a breath; which some brief memory of a happier existence, long gone by, would seem to have awakened; which no voluntary exertion of the mind can ever recall.

'What can this mean?' exclaimed the elder lady. 'This poor child can never have been the pupil of robbers!'

734

'Vice,' said the surgeon, replacing the curtain, 'takes up her abode in many temples; and who can say that a fair outside shell not enshrine her?'

'But at so early an age!' urged Rose.

'My dear young lady,' rejoined the surgeon, mournfully shaking his head; 'crime, like death, is not confined to the old and withered alone. The youngest and fairest are too often its chosen victims.'

'But, can you—oh! can you really believe that this delicate boy has been the voluntary associate of the worst outcasts of society?' said Rose.

The surgeon shook his head, in a manner which intimated that he feared it was very possible; and observing that they might disturb the patient, led the way into an adjoining apartment.

'But even if he has been wicked,' pursued Rose, 'think how young he is; think that he may never have known a mother's love, or the comfort of a home; that ill-usage and blows, or the want of bread, may have driven him to herd with men who have forced him to guilt. Aunt, dear aunt, for mercy's sake, think of this, before you let them drag this sick child to a prison, which in any case must be the grave of all his chances of amendment. Oh! as you love me, and know that I have never felt the want of parents in your goodness and affection, but that I might have done so, and might have been equally helpless and unprotected with this poor child, have pity upon him before it is too late!'

'My dear love,' said the elder lady, as she folded the weeping girl to her bosom, 'do you think I would harm a hair of his head?'

'Oh, no!' replied Rose, eagerly.

'No, surely,' said the old lady; 'my days are drawing to their close: and may mercy be shown to me as I show it to others! What can I do to save him, sir?'

'Let me think, ma'am,' said the doctor; 'let me think.'

Mr. Losberne thrust his hands into his pockets, and took several turns up and down the room; often stopping, and balancing himself on his toes, and frowning frightfully. After various exclamations of 'I've got it now' and 'no, I haven't,' and as many renewals of the walking and frowning, he at length made a dead halt, and spoke as follows:

'I think if you give me a full and unlimited commission to bully Giles, and that little boy, Brittles, I can manage it. Giles is a faithful fellow and an old servant, I know; but you can make it up to him in a thousand ways, and reward him for being such a good shot besides. You don't object to that?'

'Unless there is some other way of preserving the child,' replied Mrs. Maylie.

'There is no other,' said the doctor. 'No other, take my word for it.'

'Then my aunt invests you with full power,' said Rose, smiling through her tears; 'but pray don't be harder upon the poor fellows than is indispensably necessary.'

'You seem to think,' retorted the doctor, 'that everybody is disposed to be hard-hearted to-day, except yourself, Miss Rose. I only hope, for the sake of the rising male sex generally, that you may be found in as vulnerable and soft-hearted a mood by the first eligible young fellow who appeals to your compassion; and I wish I were a young fellow, that I might avail myself, on the spot, of such a favourable opportunity for doing so, as the present.'

'You are as great a boy as poor Brittles himself,' returned Rose, blushing.

'Well,' said the doctor, laughing heartily, 'that is no very difficult matter. But to return to this boy. The great point of our agreement is yet to come. He will wake in an hour or so, I dare say; and although I have told that thick-headed constable-fellow downstairs that he musn't be moved or spoken to, on peril of his life, I think we may converse with him without danger. Now I make this stipulation—that I shall examine him in your presence, and that, if, from what he says, we judge, and I can show to the satisfaction of your cool reason, that he is a real and thorough bad one (which is more than possible), he shall be left to his fate, without any farther interference on my part, at all events.'

'Oh no, aunt!' entreated Rose.

'Oh yes, aunt!' said the doctor. 'Is is a bargain?'

'He cannot be hardened in vice,' said Rose; 'It is impossible.'

'Very good,' retorted the doctor; 'then so much the more reason for acceding to my proposition.'

Finally the treaty was entered into; and the parties thereunto sat down to wait, with some impatience, until Oliver should awake.

The patience of the two ladies was destined to undergo a longer trial than Mr. Losberne had led them to expect; for hour after hour passed on, and still Oliver slumbered heavily. It was evening, indeed, before the kind-hearted doctor brought them the intelligence, that he was at length sufficiently restored to be spoken to. The boy was very ill, he said, and weak from the loss of blood; but his mind was so troubled with anxiety to disclose something, that he deemed it better to give him the opportunity, than to insist upon his remaining quiet until next morning: which he should otherwise have done.

The conference was a long one. Oliver told them all his simple history, and was often compelled to stop, by pain and want of strength. It was a solemn thing, to hear, in the darkened room, the feeble voice of the sick child recounting a weary catalogue of evils and calamities which hard men had brought upon him. Oh! if when we oppress and grind our fellow-creatures, we bestowed but one thought on the dark evidences of human error, which, like dense and heavy clouds, are rising, slowly it is true, but not less surely, to Heaven, to pour their after-vengeance on our heads; if we heard but one instant, in imagination, the deep testimony of dead men's voices, which no power can stifle, and no pride shut out; where would be the injury and injustice, the suffering, misery, cruelty, and wrong, that each day's life brings with it!

Oliver's pillow was smoothed by gentle hands that night; and loveliness and virtue watched him as he slept. He felt calm and happy, and could have died without a murmur.

The momentous interview was no sooner concluded, and Oliver composed to rest again, than the doctor, after wiping his eyes, and condemning them for being weak all at once, betook himself downstairs to open upon Mr. Giles. And finding nobody about the parlours, it occurred to him, that he could perhaps originate the proceedings with better effect in the kitchen; so into the kitchen he went.

There were assembled, in that lower house of the domestic parliament, the women-servants, Mr. Brittles, Mr. Giles, the tinker (who had received a special invitation to regale himself for the remainder of the day, in consideration of his services), and the constable. The latter gentleman had a large staff, a large head, large features, and large half-boots; and he looked as if he had been taking a proportionate allowance of ale—as indeed he had.

The adventures of the previous night were still under discussion; for Mr. Giles was expatiating upon his presence of mind, when the doctor entered; Mr. Brittles, with a mug of ale in his hand, was corroborating everything, before his superior said it.

'Sit still!' said the doctor, waving his hand.

'Thank you, sir,' said Mr. Giles. 'Misses wished some ale to be given out, sir; and as I felt no ways inclined for my own little room, sir, and was disposed for company, I am taking mine among 'em here.'

Brittles headed a low murmur, by which the ladies and gentlemen generally were understood to express the gratification they derived from Mr. Giles's condescension. Mr. Giles looked round with a patronising air, as much as to say that so long as they behaved properly, he would never desert them.

'How is the patient to-night, sir?' asked Giles.

'So-so'; returned the doctor. 'I am afraid you have got yourself into a scrape there, Mr. Giles.'

'I hope you don't mean to say, sir,' said Mr. Giles, trembling, 'that he's going to die. If I thought it, I should never be happy again. I wouldn't cut a boy off: no, not even Brittles here; not for all the plate in the county, sir.'

'That's not the point,' said the doctor, mysteriously. 'Mr. Giles, are you a Protestant?'

'Yes, sir, I hope so,' faltered Mr. Giles, who had turned very pale.

'And what are you, boy?' said the doctor, turning sharply upon Brittles.

'Lord bless me, sir!' replied Brittles, starting violently; 'I'm the same as Mr. Giles, sir.'

'Then tell me this,' said the doctor, 'both of you, both of you! Are you going to take upon yourselves to swear, that that boy upstairs is the boy that was put through the little window last night? Out with it! Come! We are prepared for you!'

The doctor, who was universally considered one of the best-tempered creatures on earth, made this demand in such a dreadful tone of anger, that Giles and Brittles, who were considerably muddled by ale and excitement, stared at each other in a state of stupefaction.

'Pay attention to the reply, constable, will you?' said the doctor, shaking his forefinger with great solemnity of manner, and tapping the bridge of his nose with it, to bespeak the exercise of that worthy's utmost acuteness. 'Something may come of this before long.'

The constable looked as wise as he could, and took up his staff of office: which had been reclining indolently in the chimney-corner.

'It's a simple question of identity, you will observe,' said the doctor.

'That's what it is, sir,' replied the constable, coughing with great violence; for he had finished his ale in a hurry, and some of it had gone the wrong way.

'Here's the house broken into,' said the doctor, 'and a couple of men catch one moment's glimpse of a boy, in the midst of gunpowder smoke, and in all the distraction of alarm and darkness. Here's a boy comes to that very same house, next morning, and because he happens to have his arm tied up, these men lay violent hands upon him—by doing which, they place his life in great danger—and swear he is the thief. Now, the question is, whether these men are justified by the fact; if not, in what situation do they place themselves?'

The constable nodded profoundly. He said, if that wasn't law, he would be glad to know what was.

'I ask you again,' thundered the doctor, 'are you, on your solemn oaths, able to identify that boy?'

Brittles looked doubtfully at Mr. Giles; Mr. Giles looked doubtfully at Brittles; the constable put his hand behind his ear, to catch the reply; the two women and the tinker leaned forward to listen; the doctor glanced keenly round; when a ring was heard at the gate, and at the same moment, the sound of wheels.

'It's the runners!' cried Brittles, to all appearance much relieved.

'The what?' exclaimed the doctor, aghast in his turn.

'The Bow Street officers, sir,' replied Brittles, taking up a candle; 'me and Mr. Giles sent for 'em this morning.'

'What?' cried the doctor.

'Yes,' replied Brittles; 'I sent a message up by the coachman, and I only wonder they weren't here before, sir.'

'You did, did you? Then confound your—slow coaches down here; that's all,' said the doctor, walking away.

CHAPTER XXXI. INVOLVES A CRITICAL POSITION

'Who's that?' inquired Brittles, opening the door a little way, with the chain up, and peeping out, shading the candle with his hand.

'Open the door,' replied a man outside; 'it's the officers from Bow Street, as was sent to to-day.'

Much comforted by this assurance, Brittles opened the door to its full width, and confronted a portly man in a great-coat; who walked in, without saying anything more, and wiped his shoes on the mat, as coolly as if he lived there.

'Just send somebody out to relieve my mate, will you, young man?' said the officer; 'he's in the gig, a-minding the prad. Have you got a coach 'us here, that you could put it up in, for five or ten minutes?'

Brittles replying in the affirmative, and pointing out the building, the portly man stepped back to the garden-gate, and helped his companion to put up the gig: while Brittles lighted them, in a state of great admiration. This done, they returned to the house, and, being shown into a parlour, took off their great-coats and hats, and showed like what they were.

The man who had knocked at the door, was a stout personage of middle height, aged about fifty: with shiny black hair, cropped pretty close; half-whiskers, a round face, and sharp eyes. The other was a red-headed, bony man, in top-boots; with a rather ill-favoured countenance, and a turned-up sinister-looking nose.

'Tell your governor that Blathers and Duff is here, will you?' said the stouter man, smoothing down his hair, and laying a pair of handcuffs on the table. 'Oh! Good-evening, master. Can I have a word or two with you in private, if you please?'

This was addressed to Mr. Losberne, who now made his appearance; that gentleman, motioning Brittles to retire, brought in the two ladies, and shut the door.

'This is the lady of the house,' said Mr. Losberne, motioning towards Mrs. Maylie.

Mr. Blathers made a bow. Being desired to sit down, he put his hat on the floor, and taking a chair, motioned to Duff to do the same. The latter gentleman, who did not appear quite so much accustomed to good society, or quite so much at his ease in it—one of the two—seated himself, after undergoing several muscular affections of the limbs, and the head of his stick into his mouth, with some embarrassment.

'Now, with regard to this here robbery, master,' said Blathers. 'What are the circumstances?'

Mr. Losberne, who appeared desirous of gaining time, recounted them at great length, and with much circumlocution. Messrs. Blathers and Duff looked very knowing meanwhile, and occasionally exchanged a nod.

'I can't say, for certain, till I see the work, of course,' said Blathers; 'but my opinion at once is,—I don't mind committing myself to that extent,—that this wasn't done by a yokel; eh, Duff?'

'Certainly not,' replied Duff.

'And, translating the word yokel for the benefit of the ladies, I apprehend your meaning to be, that this attempt was not made by a countryman?' said Mr. Losberne, with a smile.

'That's it, master,' replied Blathers. 'This is all about the robbery, is it?'

'All,' replied the doctor.

'Now, what is this, about this here boy that the servants are a-talking on?' said Blathers.

'Nothing at all,' replied the doctor. 'One of the frightened servants chose to take it into his head, that he had something to do with this attempt to break into the house; but it's nonsense: sheer absurdity.'

'Wery easy disposed of, if it is,' remarked Duff.

'What he says is quite correct,' observed Blathers, nodding his head in a confirmatory way, and playing carelessly with the handcuffs, as if they were a pair of castanets. 'Who is the boy? What account does he give of himself? Where did he come from? He didn't drop out of the clouds, did he, master?'

'Of course not,' replied the doctor, with a nervous glance at the two ladies. 'I know his whole history: but we can talk about that presently. You would like, first, to see the place where the thieves made their attempt, I suppose?'

'Certainly,' rejoined Mr. Blathers. 'We had better inspect the premises first, and examine the servants afterwards. That's the usual way of doing business.'

Lights were then procured; and Messrs. Blathers and Duff, attended by the native constable, Brittles, Giles, and everybody else in short, went into the little room at the end of the passage and looked out at the window; and afterwards went round by way of the lawn, and looked in at the window; and after that, had a candle handed out to inspect the shutter with; and after that, a lantern to trace the footsteps with; and after that, a pitchfork to poke the bushes with. This done, amidst the breathless interest of all beholders, they came in again; and Mr. Giles and Brittles were put through a melodramatic representation of their share in the previous night's adventures: which they performed some six times over: contradicting each other, in not more than one important respect, the first time, and in not more than a dozen the last. This consummation being arrived at, Blathers and Duff cleared the room, and held a long council together, compared with which, for secrecy and solemnity, a consultation of great doctors on the knottiest point in medicine, would be mere child's play.

Meanwhile, the doctor walked up and down the next room in a very uneasy state; and Mrs. Maylie and Rose looked on, with anxious faces.

'Upon my word,' he said, making a halt, after a great number of very rapid turns, 'I hardly know what to do.'

'Surely,' said Rose, 'the poor child's story, faithfully repeated to these men, will be sufficient to exonerate him.'

'I doubt it, my dear young lady,' said the doctor, shaking his head. 'I don't think it would exonerate him, either with them, or with legal functionaries of a higher grade. What is he, after all, they would say? A runaway. Judged by mere worldly considerations and probabilities, his story is a very doubtful one.'

'You believe it, surely?' interrupted Rose.

'I believe it, strange as it is; and perhaps I may be an old fool for doing so,' rejoined the doctor; 'but I don't think it is exactly the tale for a practical police-officer, nevertheless.'

'Why not?' demanded Rose.

'Because, my pretty cross-examiner,' replied the doctor: 'because, viewed with their eyes, there are many ugly points about it; he can only prove the parts that look ill, and none of those that look well. Confound the fellows, they will have the why and the wherefore, and will take nothing for granted. On his own showing, you see, he has been the companion of thieves for some time past; he has been carried to a police-officer, on a charge of picking a gentleman's pocket; he has been taken away, forcibly, from that gentleman's house, to a place which he cannot describe or point out, and of the situation of which he has not the remotest idea. He is brought down to Chertsey, by men who seem to have taken a violent fancy to him, whether he will or no; and is put through a window to rob a house; and then, just at the very moment when he is going to alarm the inmates, and so do the very thing that would set him all to rights, there rushes into the way, a blundering dog of a half-bred butler, and shoots him! As if on purpose to prevent his doing any good for himself! Don't you see all this?'

'I see it, of course,' replied Rose, smiling at the doctor's impetuosity; 'but still I do not see anything in it, to criminate the poor child.'

'No,' replied the doctor; 'of course not! Bless the bright eyes of your sex! They never see, whether for good or bad, more than one side of any question; and that is, always, the one which first presents itself to them.'

Having given vent to this result of experience, the doctor put his hands into his pockets, and walked up and down the room with even greater rapidity than before.

'The more I think of it,' said the doctor, 'the more I see that it will occasion endless trouble and difficulty if we put these men in possession of the boy's real story. I am certain it will not be believed; and even if they can do nothing to him in the end, still the dragging it forward, and giving publicity to all the doubts that will be cast upon it, must interfere, materially, with your benevolent plan of rescuing him from misery.'

'Oh! what is to be done?' cried Rose. 'Dear, dear! why did they send for these people?'

'Why, indeed!' exclaimed Mrs. Maylie. 'I would not have had them here, for the world.'

'All I know is,' said Mr. Losberne, at last: sitting down with a kind of desperate calmness, 'that we must try and carry it off with a bold face. The object is a good one, and that must be our excuse. The boy has strong symptoms of fever upon him, and is in no condition to be talked to any more; that's one comfort. We must make the best of it; and if bad be the best, it is no fault of ours. Come in!'

'Well, master,' said Blathers, entering the room followed by his colleague, and making the door fast, before he said any more. 'This warn't a put-up thing.'

'And what the devil's a put-up thing?' demanded the doctor, impatiently.

'We call it a put-up robbery, ladies,' said Blathers, turning to them, as if he pitied their ignorance, but had a contempt for the doctor's, 'when the servants is in it.'

'Nobody suspected them, in this case,' said Mrs. Maylie.

'Wery likely not, ma'am,' replied Blathers; 'but they might have been in it, for all that.'

'More likely on that wery account,' said Duff.

'We find it was a town hand,' said Blathers, continuing his report; 'for the style of work is first-rate.'

'Wery pretty indeed it is,' remarked Duff, in an undertone.

'There was two of 'em in it,' continued Blathers; 'and they had a boy with 'em; that's plain from the size of the window. That's all to be said at present. We'll see this lad that you've got upstairs at once, if you please.'

'Perhaps they will take something to drink first, Mrs. Maylie?' said the doctor: his face brightening, as if some new thought had occurred to him.

'Oh! to be sure!' exclaimed Rose, eagerly. 'You shall have it immediately, if you will.'

'Why, thank you, miss!' said Blathers, drawing his coat-sleeve across his mouth; 'it's dry work, this sort of duty. Anythink that's handy, miss; don't put yourself out of the way, on our accounts.'

'What shall it be?' asked the doctor, following the young lady to the sideboard.

'A little drop of spirits, master, if it's all the same,' replied Blathers. 'It's a cold ride from London, ma'am; and I always find that spirits comes home warmer to the feelings.'

This interesting communication was addressed to Mrs. Maylie, who received it very graciously. While it was being conveyed to her, the doctor slipped out of the room.

'Ah!' said Mr. Blathers: not holding his wine-glass by the stem, but grasping the bottom between the thumb and forefinger of his left hand: and placing it in front of his chest; 'I have seen a good many pieces of business like this, in my time, ladies.'

'That crack down in the back lane at Edmonton, Blathers,' said Mr. Duff, assisting his colleague's memory.

'That was something in this way, warn't it?' rejoined Mr. Blathers; 'that was done by Conkey Chickweed, that was.'

'You always gave that to him' replied Duff. 'It was the Family Pet, I tell you. Conkey hadn't any more to do with it than I had.'

'Get out!' retorted Mr. Blathers; 'I know better. Do you mind that time when Conkey was robbed of his money, though? What a start that was! Better than any novel-book I ever see!'

'What was that?' inquired Rose: anxious to encourage any symptoms of good-humour in the unwelcome visitors.

'It was a robbery, miss, that hardly anybody would have been down upon,' said Blathers. 'This here Conkey Chickweed—'

'Conkey means Nosey, ma'am,' interposed Duff.

'Of course the lady knows that, don't she?' demanded Mr. Blathers. 'Always interrupting, you are, partner! This here Conkey Chickweed, miss, kept a public-house over Battlebridge way, and he had a cellar, where a good many young lords went to see cock-fighting, and badger-drawing, and that; and a wery intellectual manner the sports was conducted in, for I've seen 'em off en. He warn't one of the family, at that time; and one night he was robbed of three hundred and twenty-seven guineas in a canvas bag, that was stole out of his bedroom in the dead of night, by a tall man with a black patch over his eye, who had concealed himself under the bed, and after committing the robbery, jumped slap out of window: which was only a story high. He was wery quick about it. But Conkey was quick, too; for he fired a blunderbuss arter him, and roused the neighbourhood. They set up a hue-and-cry, directly, and when they came to look about 'em, found that Conkey had hit the robber; for there was traces of blood, all the way to some palings a good distance off; and there they lost 'em. However, he had made off with the blunt; and, consequently, the name of Mr. Chickweed, licensed witler, appeared in the Gazette among the other bankrupts; and all manner of benefits and subscriptions, and I don't know what all, was got up for the poor man, who was in a wery low state of mind about his loss, and went up and down the streets, for three or four days, a pulling his hair off in such a desperate manner that many people was afraid he might be going to make away with himself. One day he came up to the office, all in a hurry, and had a private interview with the magistrate, who, after a deal of talk, rings the bell, and orders Jem Spyers in (Jem was a active officer), and tells him to go and assist Mr. Chickweed in apprehending the man as robbed his house. "I see him, Spyers," said Chickweed, "pass my house yesterday morning," "Why didn't you up, and collar him!" says Spyers. "I was so struck all of a heap, that you might have fractured my skull with a toothpick," says the poor man; "but we're sure to have him; for between ten and eleven o'clock at night he passed again." Spyers no sooner heard this, than he put some clean linen and a comb, in his pocket, in case he should have to stop a day or two; and away he goes, and sets himself down at one of the public-house windows behind the little red curtain, with his hat on, all ready to bolt out, at a moment's notice. He was smoking his pipe here, late at night, when all of a sudden Chickweed roars out, "Here he is! Stop thief! Murder!" Jem Spyers dashes out; and there he sees Chickweed, a-tearing down the street full cry. Away goes Spyers; on goes Chickweed; round turns the people; everybody roars out, "Thieves!" and Chickweed himself keeps on shouting, all the time, like mad. Spyers loses sight of him a minute as he turns a corner; shoots round; sees a little crowd; dives in; "Which is the man?" "D—me!" says Chickweed, "I've lost him again!" It was a remarkable occurrence, but he warn't to be seen nowhere, so they went back to the public-house. Next morning, Spyers took his old place, and looked out, from behind the curtain, for a tall man with a black patch over his eye, till his own two eyes ached again. At last, he couldn't help shutting 'em, to ease 'em a minute; and the very moment he did so, he hears Chickweed a-roaring out, "Here he is!" Off he starts once more, with Chickweed half-way down the street ahead of him; and after twice as long a run as the yesterday's one, the man's lost again! This was done, once or twice more, till one-half the neighbours gave out that Mr. Chickweed had been robbed by the devil, who was playing tricks with him arterwards; and the other half, that poor Mr. Chickweed had gone mad with grief.'

'What did Jem Spyers say?' inquired the doctor; who had returned to the room shortly after the commencement of the story.

'Jem Spyers,' resumed the officer, 'for a long time said nothing at all, and listened to everything without seeming to, which showed he understood his business. But, one morning, he walked into the bar, and taking out his snuffbox, says "Chickweed, I've found out who done this here robbery." "Have you?" said Chickweed. "Oh, my dear Spyers, only let me have wengeance, and I shall die contented! Oh, my dear Spyers, where is the villain!" "Come!" said Spyers, offering him a pinch of snuff, "none of that gammon! You did it yourself." So he had; and a good bit of money he had made by it, too; and nobody would never have found it out, if he hadn't been so precious anxious to keep up appearances!' said Mr. Blathers, putting down his wine-glass, and clinking the handcuffs together.

'Very curious, indeed,' observed the doctor. 'Now, if you please, you can walk upstairs.'

'If you please, sir,' returned Mr. Blathers. Closely following Mr. Losberne, the two officers ascended to Oliver's bedroom; Mr. Giles preceding the party, with a lighted candle.

Oliver had been dozing; but looked worse, and was more feverish than he had appeared yet. Being assisted by the doctor, he managed to sit up in bed for a minute or so; and looked at the strangers without at all understanding what was going forward—in fact, without seeming to recollect where he was, or what had been passing.

'This,' said Mr. Losberne, speaking softly, but with great vehemence notwithstanding, 'this is the lad, who, being accidently wounded by a spring-gun in some boyish trespass on Mr. What-d' ye-call-him's grounds, at the back here, comes to the house for assistance this morning, and is immediately laid hold of and maltreated, by that ingenious gentleman with the candle in his hand: who has placed his life in considerable danger, as I can professionally certify.'

Messrs. Blathers and Duff looked at Mr. Giles, as he was thus recommended to their notice. The bewildered butler gazed from them towards Oliver, and from Oliver towards Mr. Losberne, with a most ludicrous mixture of fear and perplexity.

'You don't mean to deny that, I suppose?' said the doctor, laying Oliver gently down again.

'It was all done for the—for the best, sir,' answered Giles. 'I am sure I thought it was the boy, or I wouldn't have meddled with him. I am not of an inhuman disposition, sir.'

'Thought it was what boy?' inquired the senior officer.

'The housebreaker's boy, sir!' replied Giles. 'They—they certainly had a boy.'

'Well? Do you think so now?' inquired Blathers.

'Think what, now?' replied Giles, looking vacantly at his questioner.

'Think it's the same boy, Stupid-head?' rejoined Blathers, impatiently.

'I don't know; I really don't know,' said Giles, with a rueful countenance. 'I couldn't swear to him.'

'What do you think?' asked Mr. Blathers.

'I don't know what to think,' replied poor Giles. 'I don't think it is the boy; indeed, I'm almost certain that it isn't. You know it can't be.'

'Has this man been a-drinking, sir?' inquired Blathers, turning to the doctor.

'What a precious muddle-headed chap you are!' said Duff, addressing Mr. Giles, with supreme contempt.

Mr. Losberne had been feeling the patient's pulse during this short dialogue; but he now rose from the chair by the bedside, and remarked, that if the officers had any doubts upon the subject, they would perhaps like to step into the next room, and have Brittles before them.

Acting upon this suggestion, they adjourned to a neighbouring apartment, where Mr. Brittles, being called in, involved himself and his respected superior in such a wonderful maze of fresh contradictions and impossibilities, as tended to throw no particular light on anything, but the fact of his own strong mystification; except, indeed, his declarations that he shouldn't know the real boy, if he were put before him that instant; that he had only taken Oliver to be he, because Mr. Giles had said he was; and that Mr. Giles had, five minutes previously, admitted in the kitchen, that he began to be very much afraid he had been a little too hasty.

Among other ingenious surmises, the question was then raised, whether Mr. Giles had really hit anybody; and upon examination of the fellow pistol to that which he had fired, it turned out to have no more destructive loading than gunpowder and brown paper: a discovery which made a considerable impression on everybody but the doctor, who had drawn the ball about ten minutes before. Upon no one, however, did it make a greater impression than on Mr. Giles himself; who, after labouring, for some hours, under the fear of having mortally wounded a fellow-creature, eagerly caught at this new idea, and favoured it to the utmost. Finally, the officers, without troubling themselves very much about Oliver, left the Chertsey constable in the house, and took up their rest for that night in the town; promising to return the next morning.

With the next morning, there came a rumour, that two men and a boy were in the cage at Kingston, who had been apprehended over night under suspicious circumstances; and to Kingston Messrs. Blathers and Duff journeyed accordingly. The suspicious circumstances, however, resolving themselves, on investigation, into the one fact, that they had been discovered sleeping under a haystack; which, although a great crime, is only punishable by imprisonment, and is, in the merciful eye of the English law, and its comprehensive love of all the King's subjects, held to be no satisfactory proof, in the absence of all other evidence, that the sleeper, or sleepers, have committed burglary accompanied with violence, and have therefore rendered themselves liable to the punishment of death; Messrs. Blathers and Duff came back again, as wise as they went.

In short, after some more examination, and a great deal more conversation, a neighbouring magistrate was readily induced to take the joint bail of Mrs. Maylie and Mr. Losberne for Oliver's appearance if he should ever be called upon; and Blathers and Duff, being rewarded with a couple of guineas, returned to town with divided opinions on the subject of their expedition: the latter gentleman on a mature consideration of all the circumstances, inclining to the belief that the burglarious attempt had originated with the Family Pet; and the former being equally disposed to concede the full merit of it to the great Mr. Conkey Chickweed.

Meanwhile, Oliver gradually throve and prospered under the united care of Mrs. Maylie, Rose, and the kind-hearted Mr. Losberne. If fervent prayers, gushing from hearts overcharged with gratitude, be heard in heaven—and if they be not, what prayers are!—the blessings which the orphan child called down upon them, sunk into their souls, diffusing peace and happiness.

CHAPTER XXXII. OF THE HAPPY LIFE OLIVER BEGAN TO LEAD WITH HIS KIND FRIENDS

Oliver's ailings were neither slight nor few. In addition to the pain and delay attendant on a broken limb, his exposure to the wet and cold had brought on fever and ague: which hung about him for many weeks, and reduced him sadly. But, at length, he began, by slow degrees, to get better, and to be able to say sometimes, in a few tearful words, how deeply he felt the goodness of the two sweet ladies, and how ardently he hoped that when he grew strong and well again, he could do something to show his gratitude; only something, which would let them see the love and duty with which his breast was full; something, however slight, which would prove to them that their gentle kindness had not been cast away; but that the poor boy whom their charity had rescued from misery, or death, was eager to serve them with his whole heart and soul.

'Poor fellow!' said Rose, when Oliver had been one day feebly endeavouring to utter the words of thankfulness that rose to his pale lips; 'you shall have many opportunities of serving us, if you will. We are going into the country, and my aunt intends that you shall accompany us. The quiet place, the pure air, and all the pleasure and beauties of spring, will restore you in a few days. We will employ you in a hundred ways, when you can bear the trouble.'

'The trouble!' cried Oliver. 'Oh! dear lady, if I could but work for you; if I could only give you pleasure by watering your flowers, or watching your birds, or running up and down the whole day long, to make you happy; what would I give to do it!'

'You shall give nothing at all,' said Miss Maylie, smiling; 'for, as I told you before, we shall employ you in a hundred ways; and if you only take half the trouble to please us, that you promise now, you will make me very happy indeed.'

'Happy, ma'am!' cried Oliver; 'how kind of you to say so!'

'You will make me happier than I can tell you,' replied the young lady. 'To think that my dear good aunt should have been the means of rescuing any one from such sad misery as you have described to us, would be an unspeakable pleasure to me; but to know that the object of her goodness and compassion was sincerely grateful and attached, in consequence, would delight me, more than you can well imagine. Do you understand me?' she inquired, watching Oliver's thoughtful face.

'Oh yes, ma'am, yes!' replied Oliver eagerly; 'but I was thinking that I am ungrateful now.'

'To whom?' inquired the young lady.

'To the kind gentleman, and the dear old nurse, who took so much care of me before,' rejoined Oliver. 'If they knew how happy I am, they would be pleased, I am sure.'

'I am sure they would,' rejoined Oliver's benefactress; 'and Mr. Losberne has already been kind enough to promise that when you are well enough to bear the journey, he will carry you to see them.'

'Has he, ma'am?' cried Oliver, his face brightening with pleasure. 'I don't know what I shall do for joy when I see their kind faces once again!'

In a short time Oliver was sufficiently recovered to undergo the fatigue of this expedition. One morning he and Mr. Losberne set out, accordingly, in a little carriage which belonged to Mrs. Maylie. When they came to Chertsey Bridge, Oliver turned very pale, and uttered a loud exclamation.

'What's the matter with the boy?' cried the doctor, as usual, all in a bustle. 'Do you see anything—hear anything—feel anything—eh?'

'That, sir,' cried Oliver, pointing out of the carriage window. 'That house!'

'Yes; well, what of it? Stop coachman. Pull up here,' cried the doctor. 'What of the house, my man; eh?'

'The thieves—the house they took me to!' whispered Oliver.

'The devil it is!' cried the doctor. 'Hallo, there! let me out!'

But, before the coachman could dismount from his box, he had tumbled out of the coach, by some means or other; and, running down to the deserted tenement, began kicking at the door like a madman.

'Halloa?' said a little ugly hump-backed man: opening the door so suddenly, that the doctor, from the very impetus of his last kick, nearly fell forward into the passage. 'What's the matter here?'

'Matter!' exclaimed the other, collaring him, without a moment's reflection. 'A good deal. Robbery is the matter.'

'There'll be Murder the matter, too,' replied the hump-backed man, coolly, 'if you don't take your hands off. Do you hear me?'

'I hear you,' said the doctor, giving his captive a hearty shake.

'Where's—confound the fellow, what's his rascally name—Sikes; that's it. Where's Sikes, you thief?'

The hump-backed man stared, as if in excess of amazement and indignation; then, twisting himself, dexterously, from the doctor's grasp, growled forth a volley of horrid oaths, and retired into the house. Before he could shut the door, however, the doctor had passed into the parlour, without a word of parley.

He looked anxiously round; not an article of furniture; not a vestige of anything, animate or inanimate; not even the position of the cupboards; answered Oliver's description!

'Now!' said the hump-backed man, who had watched him keenly, 'what do you mean by coming into my house, in this violent way? Do you want to rob me, or to murder me? Which is it?'

'Did you ever know a man come out to do either, in a chariot and pair, you ridiculous old vampire?' said the irritable doctor.

'What do you want, then?' demanded the hunchback. 'Will you take yourself off, before I do you a mischief? Curse you!'

'As soon as I think proper,' said Mr. Losberne, looking into the other parlour; which, like the first, bore no resemblance whatever to Oliver's account of it. 'I shall find you out, some day, my friend.'

'Will you?' sneered the ill-favoured cripple. 'If you ever want me, I'm here. I haven't lived here mad and all alone, for five-and-twenty years, to be scared by you. You shall pay for this; you shall pay for this.' And so saying, the mis-shapen little demon set up a yell, and danced upon the ground, as if wild with rage.

'Stupid enough, this,' muttered the doctor to himself; 'the boy must have made a mistake. Here! Put that in your pocket, and shut yourself up again.' With these words he flung the hunchback a piece of money, and returned to the carriage.

The man followed to the chariot door, uttering the wildest imprecations and curses all the way; but as Mr. Losberne turned to speak to the driver, he looked into the carriage, and eyed Oliver for an instant with a glance so sharp and fierce and at the same time so furious and vindictive, that, waking or sleeping, he could not forget it for months afterwards. He continued to utter the most fearful imprecations, until the driver had resumed his seat; and when they were once more on their way, they could see him some distance behind: beating his feet upon the ground, and tearing his hair, in transports of real or pretended rage.

'I am an ass!' said the doctor, after a long silence. 'Did you know that before, Oliver?'

'No, sir.'

'Then don't forget it another time.'

'An ass,' said the doctor again, after a further silence of some minutes. 'Even if it had been the right place, and the right fellows had been there, what could I have done, single-handed? And if I had had assistance, I see no good that I should have done, except leading to my own exposure, and an unavoidable statement of the manner in which I have hushed up this business. That would have served me right, though. I am always involving myself in some scrape or other, by acting on impulse. It might have done me good.'

Now, the fact was that the excellent doctor had never acted upon anything but impulse all through his life, and it was no bad compliment to the nature of the impulses which governed him, that so far from being involved in any peculiar troubles or misfortunes, he had the warmest respect and esteem of all who knew him. If the truth must be told, he was a little out of temper, for a minute or two, at being disappointed in procuring corroborative evidence of Oliver's story on the very first occasion on which he had a chance of obtaining any. He soon came round again, however; and finding that Oliver's replies to his questions, were still as straightforward and consistent, and still delivered with as much apparent sincerity and truth, as they had ever been, he made up his mind to attach full credence to them, from that time forth.

As Oliver knew the name of the street in which Mr. Brownlow resided, they were enabled to drive straight thither. When the coach turned into it, his heart beat so violently, that he could scarcely draw his breath.

'Now, my boy, which house is it?' inquired Mr. Losberne.

'That! That!' replied Oliver, pointing eagerly out of the window. 'The white house. Oh! make haste! Pray make haste! I feel as if I should die: it makes me tremble so.'

'Come, come!' said the good doctor, patting him on the shoulder. 'You will see them directly, and they will be overjoyed to find you safe and well.'

'Oh! I hope so!' cried Oliver. 'They were so good to me; so very, very good to me.'

The coach rolled on. It stopped. No; that was the wrong house; the next door. It went on a few paces, and stopped again. Oliver looked up at the windows, with tears of happy expectation coursing down his face.

Alas! the white house was empty, and there was a bill in the window. 'To Let.'

'Knock at the next door,' cried Mr. Losberne, taking Oliver's arm in his. 'What has become of Mr. Brownlow, who used to live in the adjoining house, do you know?'

The servant did not know; but would go and inquire. She presently returned, and said, that Mr. Brownlow had sold off his goods, and gone to the West Indies, six weeks before. Oliver clasped his hands, and sank feebly backward.

'Has his housekeeper gone too?' inquired Mr. Losberne, after a moment's pause.

'Yes, sir'; replied the servant. 'The old gentleman, the housekeeper, and a gentleman who was a friend of Mr. Brownlow's, all went together.'

'Then turn towards home again,' said Mr. Losberne to the driver; 'and don't stop to bait the horses, till you get out of this confounded London!'

'The book-stall keeper, sir?' said Oliver. 'I know the way there. See him, pray, sir! Do see him!'

'My poor boy, this is disappointment enough for one day,' said the doctor. 'Quite enough for both of us. If we go to the book-stall keeper's, we shall certainly find that he is dead, or has set his house on fire, or run away. No; home again straight!' And in obedience to the doctor's impulse, home they went.

This bitter disappointment caused Oliver much sorrow and grief, even in the midst of his happiness; for he had pleased himself, many times during his illness, with thinking of all that Mr. Brownlow and Mrs. Bedwin would say to him: and what delight it would be to tell them how many long days and nights he had passed in reflecting on what they had done for him, and in bewailing his cruel separation from them. The hope of eventually clearing himself with them, too, and explaining how he had been forced away, had buoyed him up, and sustained him, under many of his recent trials; and now, the idea that they should have gone so far, and carried with them the belief that he was an impostor and a robber—a belief which might remain uncontradicted to his dying day—was almost more than he could bear.

The circumstance occasioned no alteration, however, in the behaviour of his benefactors. After another fortnight, when the fine warm weather had fairly begun, and every tree and flower was putting forth its young leaves and rich blossoms, they made preparations for quitting the house at Chertsey, for some months.

Sending the plate, which had so excited Fagin's cupidity, to the banker's; and leaving Giles and another servant in care of the house, they departed to a cottage at some distance in the country, and took Oliver with them.

Who can describe the pleasure and delight, the peace of mind and soft tranquillity, the sickly boy felt in the balmy air, and among the green hills and rich woods, of an inland village! Who can tell how scenes of peace and quietude sink into the minds of pain-worn dwellers in close and noisy places, and carry their own freshness, deep into their jaded hearts! Men who have lived in crowded, pent-up streets, through lives of toil, and who have never wished for change; men, to whom custom has indeed been second nature, and who have come almost to love each brick and stone that formed the narrow boundaries of their daily walks; even they, with the hand of death upon them, have been known to yearn at last for one short glimpse of Nature's face; and, carried far from the scenes of their old pains and pleasures, have seemed to pass at once into a new state of being. Crawling forth, from day to day, to some green sunny spot, they have had such memories wakened up within them by the sight of the sky, and hill and plain, and glistening water, that a foretaste of heaven itself has soothed their quick decline, and they have sunk into their tombs, as peacefully as the sun whose setting they watched from their lonely chamber window but a few hours before, faded from their dim and feeble sight! The memories which peaceful country scenes call up, are not of this world, nor of its thoughts and hopes. Their gentle influence may teach us how to weave fresh garlands for the graves of those we loved: may purify our thoughts, and bear down before it old enmity and hatred; but beneath all this, there lingers, in the least reflective mind, a vague and half-formed consciousness of having held such feelings long before, in some remote and distant time, which calls up solemn thoughts of distant times to come, and bends down pride and worldliness beneath it.

It was a lovely spot to which they repaired. Oliver, whose days had been spent among squalid crowds, and in the midst of noise and brawling, seemed to enter on a new existence there. The rose and honeysuckle clung to the cottage walls; the ivy crept round the trunks of the trees; and the garden-flowers perfumed the air with delicious odours. Hard by, was a little churchyard; not crowded with tall unsightly gravestones, but full of humble mounds, covered with fresh turf and moss: beneath which, the old people of the village lay at rest. Oliver often wandered here; and, thinking of the wretched grave in which his mother lay, would sometimes sit him down and sob unseen; but, when he raised his eyes to the deep sky overhead, he would cease to think of her as lying in the ground, and would weep for her, sadly, but without pain.

It was a happy time. The days were peaceful and serene; the nights brought with them neither fear nor care; no languishing in a wretched prison, or associating with wretched men;

nothing but pleasant and happy thoughts. Every morning he went to a white-headed old gentleman, who lived near the little church: who taught him to read better, and to write: and who spoke so kindly, and took such pains, that Oliver could never try enough to please him. Then, he would walk with Mrs. Maylie and Rose, and hear them talk of books; or perhaps sit near them, in some shady place, and listen whilst the young lady read: which he could have done, until it grew too dark to see the letters. Then, he had his own lesson for the next day to prepare; and at this, he would work hard, in a little room which looked into the garden, till evening came slowly on, when the ladies would walk out again, and he with them: listening with such pleasure to all they said: and so happy if they wanted a flower that he could climb to reach, or had forgotten anything he could run to fetch: that he could never be quick enough about it. When it became quite dark, and they returned home, the young lady would sit down to the piano, and play some pleasant air, or sing, in a low and gentle voice, some old song which it pleased her aunt to hear. There would be no candles lighted at such times as these; and Oliver would sit by one of the windows, listening to the sweet music, in a perfect rapture.

And when Sunday came, how differently the day was spent, from any way in which he had ever spent it yet! and how happily too; like all the other days in that most happy time! There was the little church, in the morning, with the green leaves fluttering at the windows: the birds singing without: and the sweet-smelling air stealing in at the low porch, and filling the homely building with its fragrance. The poor people were so neat and clean, and knelt so reverently in prayer, that it seemed a pleasure, not a tedious duty, their assembling there together; and though the singing might be rude, it was real, and sounded more musical (to Oliver's ears at least) than any he had ever heard in church before. Then, there were the walks as usual, and many calls at the clean houses of the labouring men; and at night, Oliver read a chapter or two from the Bible, which he had been studying all the week, and in the performance of which duty he felt more proud and pleased, than if he had been the clergyman himself.

In the morning, Oliver would be a-foot by six o'clock, roaming the fields, and plundering the hedges, far and wide, for nosegays of wild flowers, with which he would return laden, home; and which it took great care and consideration to arrange, to the best advantage, for the embellishment of the breakfast-table. There was fresh groundsel, too, for Miss Maylie's birds, with which Oliver, who had been studying the subject under the able tuition of the village clerk, would decorate the cages, in the most approved taste. When the birds were made all spruce and smart for the day, there was usually some little commission of charity to execute in the village; or, failing that, there was rare cricket-playing, sometimes, on the green; or, failing that, there was always something to do in the garden, or about the plants, to which Oliver (who had studied this science also, under the same master, who was a gardener by trade,) applied himself with hearty good-will, until Miss Rose made her appearance: when there were a thousand commendations to be bestowed on all he had done.

So three months glided away; three months which, in the life of the most blessed and favoured of mortals, might have been unmingled happiness, and which, in Oliver's were true felicity. With the purest and most amiable generosity on one side; and the truest, warmest, soul-felt gratitude on the other; it is no wonder that, by the end of that short time, Oliver Twist had become completely domesticated with the old lady and her niece, and that the fervent attachment of his young and sensitive heart, was repaid by their pride in, and attachment to, himself.

CHAPTER XXXIII. WHEREIN THE HAPPINESS OF OLIVER AND HIS FRIENDS, EXPERIENCES A SUDDEN CHECK

Spring flew swiftly by, and summer came. If the village had been beautiful at first it was now in the full glow and luxuriance of its richness. The great trees, which had looked shrunken and bare in the earlier months, had now burst into strong life and health; and stretching forth their green arms over the thirsty ground, converted open and naked spots into choice nooks, where was a deep and pleasant shade from which to look upon the wide prospect, steeped in sunshine, which lay stretched beyond. The earth had donned her mantle of brightest green; and shed her richest perfumes abroad. It was the prime and vigour of the year; all things were glad and flourishing.

Still, the same quiet life went on at the little cottage, and the same cheerful serenity prevailed among its inmates. Oliver had long since grown stout and healthy; but health or sickness made no difference in his warm feelings of a great many people. He was still the same gentle, attached, affectionate creature that he had been when pain and suffering had wasted his strength, and when he was dependent for every slight attention, and comfort on those who tended him.

One beautiful night, when they had taken a longer walk than was customary with them: for the day had been unusually warm, and there was a brilliant moon, and a light wind had sprung up, which was unusually refreshing. Rose had been in high spirits, too, and they had walked on, in merry conversation, until they had far exceeded their ordinary bounds. Mrs. Maylie being fatigued, they returned more slowly home. The young lady merely throwing off her simple bonnet, sat down to the piano as usual. After running abstractedly over the keys for a few minutes, she fell into a low and very solemn air; and as she played it, they heard a sound as if she were weeping.

'Rose, my dear!' said the elder lady.

Rose made no reply, but played a little quicker, as though the words had roused her from some painful thoughts.

'Rose, my love!' cried Mrs. Maylie, rising hastily, and bending over her. 'What is this? In tears! My dear child, what distresses you?'

'Nothing, aunt; nothing,' replied the young lady. 'I don't know what it is; I can't describe it; but I feel—'

'Not ill, my love?' interposed Mrs. Maylie.

'No, no! Oh, not ill!' replied Rose: shuddering as though some deadly chillness were passing over her, while she spoke; 'I shall be better presently. Close the window, pray!'

Oliver hastened to comply with her request. The young lady, making an effort to recover her cheerfulness, strove to play some livelier tune; but her fingers dropped powerless over the keys. Covering her face with her hands, she sank upon a sofa, and gave vent to the tears which she was now unable to repress.

'My child!' said the elderly lady, folding her arms about her, 'I never saw you so before.'

'I would not alarm you if I could avoid it,' rejoined Rose; 'but indeed I have tried very hard, and cannot help this. I fear I am ill, aunt.'

She was, indeed; for, when candles were brought, they saw that in the very short time which had elapsed since their return home, the hue of her countenance had changed to a marble whiteness. Its expression had lost nothing of its beauty; but it was changed; and there was an anxious haggard look about the gentle face, which it had never worn before. Another minute, and it was suffused with a crimson flush: and a heavy wildness came over the soft blue eye. Again this disappeared, like the shadow thrown by a passing cloud; and she was once more deadly pale.

Oliver, who watched the old lady anxiously, observed that she was alarmed by these appearances; and so in truth, was he; but seeing that she affected to make light of them, he endeavoured to do the same, and they so far succeeded, that when Rose was persuaded by her aunt to retire for the night, she was in better spirits; and appeared even in better health: assuring them that she felt certain she should rise in the morning, quite well.

'I hope,' said Oliver, when Mrs. Maylie returned, 'that nothing is the matter? She don't look well to-night, but—'

The old lady motioned to him not to speak; and sitting herself down in a dark corner of the room, remained silent for some time. At length, she said, in a trembling voice:

'I hope not, Oliver. I have been very happy with her for some years: too happy, perhaps. It may be time that I should meet with some misfortune; but I hope it is not this.'

'What?' inquired Oliver.

'The heavy blow,' said the old lady, 'of losing the dear girl who has so long been my comfort and happiness.'

'Oh! God forbid!' exclaimed Oliver, hastily.

'Amen to that, my child!' said the old lady, wringing her hands.

'Surely there is no danger of anything so dreadful?' said Oliver. 'Two hours ago, she was quite well.'

'She is very ill now,' rejoined Mrs. Maylies; 'and will be worse, I am sure. My dear, dear Rose! Oh, what shall I do without her!'

She gave way to such great grief, that Oliver, suppressing his own emotion, ventured to remonstrate with her; and to beg, earnestly, that, for the sake of the dear young lady herself, she would be more calm.

'And consider, ma'am,' said Oliver, as the tears forced themselves into his eyes, despite of his efforts to the contrary. 'Oh! consider how young and good she is, and what pleasure and comfort she gives to all about her. I am sure—certain—quite certain—that, for your sake, who are so good yourself; and for her own; and for the sake of all she makes so happy; she will not die. Heaven will never let her die so young.'

'Hush!' said Mrs. Maylie, laying her hand on Oliver's head. 'You think like a child, poor boy. But you teach me my duty, notwithstanding. I had forgotten it for a moment, Oliver, but I hope I may be pardoned, for I am old, and have seen enough of illness and death to know the agony of separation from the objects of our love. I have seen enough, too, to know that it is not always the youngest and best who are spared to those that love them; but this should give us comfort in our sorrow; for Heaven is just; and such things teach us, impressively, that there is a brighter world than this; and that the passage to it is speedy. God's will be done! I love her; and He knows how well!'

Oliver was surprised to see that as Mrs. Maylie said these words, she checked her lamentations as though by one effort; and drawing herself up as she spoke, became composed and firm. He was still more astonished to find that this firmness lasted; and that, under all the care and watching which ensued, Mrs. Maylie was ever ready and collected: performing all the duties which had devolved upon her, steadily, and, to all external appearances, even cheerfully. But he was young, and did not know what strong minds are capable of, under trying circumstances. How should he, when their possessors so seldom know themselves?

An anxious night ensued. When morning came, Mrs. Maylie's predictions were but too well verified. Rose was in the first stage of a high and dangerous fever.

'We must be active, Oliver, and not give way to useless grief,' said Mrs. Maylie, laying her finger on her lip, as she looked steadily into his face; 'this letter must be sent, with all possible expedition, to Mr. Losberne. It must be carried to the market-town: which is not more than four miles off, by the footpath across the field: and thence dispatched, by an express on horseback, straight to Chertsey. The people at the inn will undertake to do this: and I can trust to you to see it done, I know.'

Oliver could make no reply, but looked his anxiety to be gone at once.

'Here is another letter,' said Mrs. Maylie, pausing to reflect; 'but whether to send it now, or wait until I see how Rose goes on, I scarcely know. I would not forward it, unless I feared the worst.'

'Is it for Chertsey, too, ma'am?' inquired Oliver; impatient to execute his commission, and holding out his trembling hand for the letter.

'No,' replied the old lady, giving it to him mechanically. Oliver glanced at it, and saw that it was directed to Harry Maylie, Esquire, at some great lord's house in the country; where, he could not make out.

'Shall it go, ma'am?' asked Oliver, looking up, impatiently.

'I think not,' replied Mrs. Maylie, taking it back. 'I will wait until to-morrow.'

With these words, she gave Oliver her purse, and he started off, without more delay, at the greatest speed he could muster.

Swiftly he ran across the fields, and down the little lanes which sometimes divided them: now almost hidden by the high corn on either side, and now emerging on an open field, where the mowers and haymakers were busy at their work: nor did he stop once, save now and then, for a few seconds, to recover breath, until he came, in a great heat, and covered with dust, on the little market-place of the market-town.

Here he paused, and looked about for the inn. There were a white bank, and a red brewery, and a yellow town-hall; and in one corner there was a large house, with all the wood about it painted green: before which was the sign of 'The George.' To this he hastened, as soon as it caught his eye.

He spoke to a postboy who was dozing under the gateway; and who, after hearing what he wanted, referred him to the ostler; who after hearing all he had to say again, referred him to the landlord; who was a tall gentleman in a blue neckcloth, a white hat, drab breeches, and boots with tops to match, leaning against a pump by the stable-door, picking his teeth with a silver toothpick.

This gentleman walked with much deliberation into the bar to make out the bill: which took a long time making out: and after it was ready, and paid, a horse had to be saddled, and a man to be dressed, which took up ten good minutes more. Meanwhile Oliver was in such a desperate state of impatience and anxiety, that he felt as if he could have jumped upon the horse himself, and galloped away, full tear, to the next stage. At length, all was ready; and the little parcel having been handed up, with many injunctions and entreaties for its speedy delivery, the man set spurs to his horse, and rattling over the uneven paving of the market-place, was out of the town, and galloping along the turnpike-road, in a couple of minutes.

As it was something to feel certain that assistance was sent for, and that no time had been lost, Oliver hurried up the inn-yard, with a somewhat lighter heart. He was turning out of the gateway when he accidently stumbled against a tall man wrapped in a cloak, who was at that moment coming out of the inn door.

'Hah!' cried the man, fixing his eyes on Oliver, and suddenly recoiling. 'What the devil's this?'

'I beg your pardon, sir,' said Oliver; 'I was in a great hurry to get home, and didn't see you were coming.'

'Death!' muttered the man to himself, glaring at the boy with his large dark eyes. 'Who would have thought it! Grind him to ashes! He'd start up from a stone coffin, to come in my way!'

'I am sorry,' stammered Oliver, confused by the strange man's wild look. 'I hope I have not hurt you!'

'Rot you!' murmured the man, in a horrible passion; between his clenched teeth; 'if I had only had the courage to say the word, I might have been free of you in a night. Curses on your head, and black death on your heart, you imp! What are you doing here?'

The man shook his fist, as he uttered these words incoherently. He advanced towards Oliver, as if with the intention of aiming a blow at him, but fell violently on the ground: writhing and foaming, in a fit.

Oliver gazed, for a moment, at the struggles of the madman (for such he supposed him to be); and then darted into the house for help. Having seen him safely carried into the hotel, he turned his face homewards, running as fast as he could, to make up for lost time: and recalling with a great deal of astonishment and some fear, the extraordinary behaviour of the person from whom he had just parted.

The circumstance did not dwell in his recollection long, however: for when he reached the cottage, there was enough to occupy his mind, and to drive all considerations of self completely from his memory.

Rose Maylie had rapidly grown worse; before mid-night she was delirious. A medical practitioner, who resided on the spot, was in constant attendance upon her; and after first seeing the patient, he had taken Mrs. Maylie aside, and pronounced her disorder to be one of a most alarming nature. 'In fact,' he said, 'it would be little short of a miracle, if she recovered.'

How often did Oliver start from his bed that night, and stealing out, with noiseless footstep, to the staircase, listen for the slightest sound from the sick chamber! How often did a tremble shake his frame, and cold drops of terror start upon his brow, when a sudden trampling of feet caused him to fear that something too dreadful to think of, had even then occurred! And what had been the fervency of all the prayers he had ever muttered, compared with those he poured forth, now, in the agony and passion of his supplication for the life and health of the gentle creature, who was tottering on the deep grave's verge!

Oh! the suspense, the fearful, acute suspense, of standing idly by while the life of one we dearly love, is trembling in the balance! Oh! the racking thoughts that crowd upon the mind, and make the heart beat violently, and the breath come thick, by the force of the images they conjure up before it; the desperate anxiety to be doing something to relieve the pain, or lessen the danger, which we have no power to alleviate; the sinking of soul and spirit, which the sad remembrance of our helplessness produces; what tortures can equal these; what reflections or endeavours can, in the full tide and fever of the time, allay them!

Morning came; and the little cottage was lonely and still. People spoke in whispers; anxious faces appeared at the gate, from time to time; women and children went away in tears. All the livelong day, and for hours after it had grown dark, Oliver paced softly up and down the garden, raising his eyes every instant to the sick chamber, and shuddering to see the darkened window, looking as if death lay stretched inside. Late that night, Mr. Losberne arrived. 'It is hard,' said the good doctor, turning away as he spoke; 'so young; so much beloved; but there is very little hope.'

Another morning. The sun shone brightly; as brightly as if it looked upon no misery or care; and, with every leaf and flower in full bloom about her; with life, and health, and sounds and sights of joy, surrounding her on every side: the fair young creature lay, wasting fast. Oliver crept away to the old churchyard, and, sitting down on one of the green mounds, wept and prayed for her, in silence.

There was such peace and beauty in the scene; so much of brightness and mirth in the sunny landscape; such blithesome music in the songs of the summer birds; such freedom in the rapid flight of the rook, careering overhead; so much of life and joyousness in all; that, when the boy raised his aching eyes, and looked about, the thought instinctively occurred to him, that this was not a time for death; that Rose could surely never die when humbler things were all so glad and gay; that graves were for cold and cheerless winter: not for sunlight and fragrance. He almost thought that shrouds were for the old and shrunken; and that they never wrapped the young and graceful form in their ghastly folds.

A knell from the church bell broke harshly on these youthful thoughts. Another! Again! It was tolling for the funeral service. A group of humble mourners entered the gate: wearing white favours; for the corpse was young. They stood uncovered by a grave; and there was a mother—a mother once—among the weeping train. But the sun shone brightly, and the birds sang on.

Oliver turned homeward, thinking on the many kindnesses he had received from the young lady, and wishing that the time could come again, that he might never cease showing her how grateful and attached he was. He had no cause for self-reproach on the score of neglect, or want of thought, for he had been devoted to her service; and yet a hundred little occasions rose up before him, on which he fancied he might have been more zealous, and more earnest, and wished he had been. We need be careful how we deal with those about us, when every death carries to some small circle of survivors, thoughts of so much omitted, and so little done—of so many things forgotten, and so many more which might have been repaired! There is no remorse so deep as that which is unavailing; if we would be spared its tortures, let us remember this, in time.

When he reached home Mrs. Maylie was sitting in the little parlour. Oliver's heart sank at sight of her; for she had never left the bedside of her niece; and he trembled to think what change could have driven her away. He learnt that she had fallen into a deep sleep, from which she would waken, either to recovery and life, or to bid them farewell, and die.

They sat, listening, and afraid to speak, for hours. The untasted meal was removed, with looks which showed that their thoughts were elsewhere, they watched the sun as he sank lower and lower, and, at length, cast over sky and earth those brilliant hues which herald his departure. Their quick ears caught the sound of an approaching footstep. They both involuntarily darted to the door, as Mr. Losberne entered.

'What of Rose?' cried the old lady. 'Tell me at once! I can bear it; anything but suspense! Oh, tell me! in the name of Heaven!'

'You must compose yourself,' said the doctor supporting her. 'Be calm, my dear ma'am, pray.'

'Let me go, in God's name! My dear child! She is dead! She is dying!'

'No!' cried the doctor, passionately. 'As He is good and merciful, she will live to bless us all, for years to come.'

The lady fell upon her knees, and tried to fold her hands together; but the energy which had supported her so long, fled up to Heaven with her first thanksgiving; and she sank into the friendly arms which were extended to receive her.

CHAPTER XXXIV. CONTAINS SOME INTRODUCTORY PARTICULARS RELATIVE TO A YOUNG GENTLEMAN WHO NOW ARRIVES UPON THE SCENE; AND A NEW ADVENTURE WHICH HAPPENED TO OLIVER

It was almost too much happiness to bear. Oliver felt stunned and stupefied by the unexpected intelligence; he could not weep, or speak, or rest. He had scarcely the power of understanding anything that had passed, until, after a long ramble in the quiet evening air, a burst of tears came to his relief, and he seemed to awaken, all at once, to a full sense of the joyful change that had occurred, and the almost insupportable load of anguish which had been taken from his breast.

The night was fast closing in, when he returned homeward: laden with flowers which he had culled, with peculiar care, for the adornment of the sick chamber. As he walked briskly along the road, he heard behind him, the noise of some vehicle, approaching at a furious pace. Looking round, he saw that it was a post-chaise, driven at great speed; and as the horses were galloping, and the road was narrow, he stood leaning against a gate until it should have passed him.

As it dashed on, Oliver caught a glimpse of a man in a white nightcap, whose face seemed familiar to him, although his view was so brief that he could not identify the person. In another second or two, the nightcap was thrust out of the chaise-window, and a stentorian voice bellowed to the driver to stop: which he did, as soon as he could pull up his horses. Then, the nightcap once again appeared: and the same voice called Oliver by his name.

'Here!' cried the voice. 'Oliver, what's the news? Miss Rose! Master O-li-ver!'

'Is it you, Giles?' cried Oliver, running up to the chaise-door.

Giles popped out his nightcap again, preparatory to making some reply, when he was suddenly pulled back by a young gentleman who occupied the other corner of the chaise, and who eagerly demanded what was the news.

'In a word!' cried the gentleman, 'Better or worse?'

'Better—much better!' replied Oliver, hastily.

'Thank Heaven!' exclaimed the gentleman. 'You are sure?'

'Quite, sir,' replied Oliver. 'The change took place only a few hours ago; and Mr. Losberne says, that all danger is at an end.'

The gentleman said not another word, but, opening the chaise-door, leaped out, and taking Oliver hurriedly by the arm, led him aside.

'You are quite certain? There is no possibility of any mistake on your part, my boy, is there?' demanded the gentleman in a tremulous voice. 'Do not deceive me, by awakening hopes that are not to be fulfilled.'

'I would not for the world, sir,' replied Oliver. 'Indeed you may believe me. Mr. Losberne's words were, that she would live to bless us all for many years to come. I heard him say so.'

The tears stood in Oliver's eyes as he recalled the scene which was the beginning of so much happiness; and the gentleman turned his face away, and remained silent, for some minutes. Oliver thought he heard him sob, more than once; but he feared to interrupt him by any fresh remark—for he could well guess what his feelings were—and so stood apart, feigning to be occupied with his nosegay.

All this time, Mr. Giles, with the white nightcap on, had been sitting on the steps of the chaise, supporting an elbow on each knee, and wiping his eyes with a blue cotton pocket-handkerchief dotted with white spots. That the honest fellow had not been feigning emotion, was abundantly demonstrated by the very red eyes with which he regarded the young gentleman, when he turned round and addressed him.

'I think you had better go on to my mother's in the chaise, Giles,' said he. 'I would rather walk slowly, so as to gain a little time before I see her. You can say I am coming.'

'I beg your pardon, Mr. Harry,' said Giles: giving a final polish to his ruffled countenance with the handkerchief; 'but if you would leave the postboy to say that, I should be very much obliged to you. It wouldn't be proper for the maids to see me in this state, sir; I should never have any more authority with them if they did.'

'Well,' rejoined Harry Maylie, smiling, 'you can do as you like. Let him go on with the luggage, if you wish it, and do you follow with us. Only first exchange that nightcap for some more appropriate covering, or we shall be taken for madmen.'

Mr. Giles, reminded of his unbecoming costume, snatched off and pocketed his nightcap; and substituted a hat, of grave and sober shape, which he took out of the chaise. This done, the postboy drove off; Giles, Mr. Maylie, and Oliver, followed at their leisure.

As they walked along, Oliver glanced from time to time with much interest and curiosity at the new comer. He seemed about five-and-twenty years of age, and was of the middle height; his countenance was frank and handsome; and his demeanor easy and prepossessing. Notwithstanding the difference between youth and age, he bore so strong a likeness to the old lady, that Oliver would have had no great difficulty in imagining their relationship, if he had not already spoken of her as his mother.

Mrs. Maylie was anxiously waiting to receive her son when he reached the cottage. The meeting did not take place without great emotion on both sides.

'Mother!' whispered the young man; 'why did you not write before?'

'I did,' replied Mrs. Maylie; 'but, on reflection, I determined to keep back the letter until I had heard Mr. Losberne's opinion.'

'But why,' said the young man, 'why run the chance of that occurring which so nearly happened? If Rose had—I cannot utter that word now—if this illness had terminated differently, how could you ever have forgiven yourself! How could I ever have know happiness again!'

'If that had been the case, Harry,' said Mrs. Maylie, 'I fear your happiness would have been effectually blighted, and that your arrival here, a day sooner or a day later, would have been of very, very little import.'

'And who can wonder if it be so, mother?' rejoined the young man; 'or why should I say, if?—It is—it is—you know it, mother—you must know it!'

'I know that she deserves the best and purest love the heart of man can offer,' said Mrs. Maylie; 'I know that the devotion and affection of her nature require no ordinary return, but one that shall be deep and lasting. If I did not feel this, and know, besides, that a changed behaviour in one she loved would break her heart, I should not feel my task so difficult of performance, or have to encounter so many struggles in my own bosom, when I take what seems to me to be the strict line of duty.'

'This is unkind, mother,' said Harry. 'Do you still suppose that I am a boy ignorant of my own mind, and mistaking the impulses of my own soul?'

'I think, my dear son,' returned Mrs. Maylie, laying her hand upon his shoulder, 'that youth has many generous impulses which do not last; and that among them are some, which, being gratified, become only the more fleeting. Above all, I think' said the lady, fixing her eyes on her son's face, 'that if an enthusiastic, ardent, and ambitious man marry a wife on whose name there is a stain, which, though it originate in no fault of hers, may be visited by cold and sordid people upon her, and upon his children also: and, in exact proportion to his success in the world, be cast in his teeth, and made the subject of sneers against him: he may, no matter how generous and good his nature, one day repent of the connection he formed in early life. And she may have the pain of knowing that he does so.'

'Mother,' said the young man, impatiently, 'he would be a selfish brute, unworthy alike of the name of man and of the woman you describe, who acted thus.'

'You think so now, Harry,' replied his mother.

'And ever will!' said the young man. 'The mental agony I have suffered, during the last two days, wrings from me the avowal to you of a passion which, as you well know, is not one of yesterday, nor one I have lightly formed. On Rose, sweet, gentle girl! my heart is set, as firmly as ever heart of man was set on woman. I have no thought, no view, no hope in life, beyond her; and if you oppose me in this great stake, you take my peace and happiness in your hands, and cast them to the wind. Mother, think better of this, and of me, and do not disregard the happiness of which you seem to think so little.'

'Harry,' said Mrs. Maylie, 'it is because I think so much of warm and sensitive hearts, that I would spare them from being wounded. But we have said enough, and more than enough, on this matter, just now.'

'Let it rest with Rose, then,' interposed Harry. 'You will not press these overstrained opinions of yours, so far, as to throw any obstacle in my way?'

'I will not,' rejoined Mrs. Maylie; 'but I would have you consider—'

'I have considered!' was the impatient reply; 'Mother, I have considered, years and years. I have considered, ever since I have been capable of serious reflection. My feelings remain unchanged, as they ever will; and why should I suffer the pain of a delay in giving them vent, which can be productive of no earthly good? No! Before I leave this place, Rose shall hear me.'

'She shall,' said Mrs. Maylie.

'There is something in your manner, which would almost imply that she will hear me coldly, mother,' said the young man.

'Not coldly,' rejoined the old lady; 'far from it.'

'How then?' urged the young man. 'She has formed no other attachment?'

'No, indeed,' replied his mother; 'you have, or I mistake, too strong a hold on her affections already. What I would say,' resumed the old lady, stopping her son as he was about to speak, 'is this. Before you stake your all on this chance; before you suffer yourself to be carried to the highest point of hope; reflect for a few moments, my dear child, on Rose's history, and consider what effect the knowledge of her doubtful birth may have on her decision: devoted as she is to us, with all the intensity of her noble mind, and with that perfect sacrifice of self which, in all matters, great or trifling, has always been her characteristic.'

'What do you mean?'

'That I leave you to discover,' replied Mrs. Maylie. 'I must go back to her. God bless you!'

'I shall see you again to-night?' said the young man, eagerly.

'By and by,' replied the lady; 'when I leave Rose.'

'You will tell her I am here?' said Harry.

'Of course,' replied Mrs. Maylie.

'And say how anxious I have been, and how much I have suffered, and how I long to see her. You will not refuse to do this, mother?'

'No,' said the old lady; 'I will tell her all.' And pressing her son's hand, affectionately, she hastened from the room.

Mr. Losberne and Oliver had remained at another end of the apartment while this hurried conversation was proceeding. The former now held out his hand to Harry Maylie; and hearty salutations were exchanged between them. The doctor then communicated, in reply to multifarious questions from his young friend, a precise account of his patient's situation; which was quite as consolatory and full of promise, as Oliver's statement had encouraged him to hope; and to the whole of which, Mr. Giles, who affected to be busy about the luggage, listened with greedy ears.

'Have you shot anything particular, lately, Giles?' inquired the doctor, when he had concluded.

'Nothing particular, sir,' replied Mr. Giles, colouring up to the eyes.

'Nor catching any thieves, nor identifying any house-breakers?' said the doctor.

'None at all, sir,' replied Mr. Giles, with much gravity.

'Well,' said the doctor, 'I am sorry to hear it, because you do that sort of thing admirably. Pray, how is Brittles?'

'The boy is very well, sir,' said Mr. Giles, recovering his usual tone of patronage; 'and sends his respectful duty, sir.'

'That's well,' said the doctor. 'Seeing you here, reminds me, Mr. Giles, that on the day before that on which I was called away so hurriedly, I executed, at the request of your good mistress, a small commission in your favour. Just step into this corner a moment, will you?'

Mr. Giles walked into the corner with much importance, and some wonder, and was honoured with a short whispering conference with the doctor, on the termination of which, he made a great many bows, and retired with steps of unusual stateliness. The subject matter of this conference was not disclosed in the parlour, but the kitchen was speedily enlightened concerning it; for Mr. Giles walked straight thither, and having called for a mug of ale, announced, with an air of majesty, which was highly effective, that it had pleased his mistress, in consideration of his gallant behaviour on the occasion of that attempted robbery, to deposit, in the local savings-bank, the sum of five-and-twenty pounds, for his sole use and benefit. At this, the two women-servants lifted up their hands and eyes, and supposed that Mr. Giles, pulling out his shirt-frill, replied, 'No, no'; and that if they observed that he was at all haughty to his inferiors, he would thank them to tell him so. And then he made a great many other remarks, no less illustrative of his humility, which were received with equal favour and applause, and were, withal, as original and as much to the purpose, as the remarks of great men commonly are.

Above stairs, the remainder of the evening passed cheerfully away; for the doctor was in high spirits; and however fatigued or thoughtful Harry Maylie might have been at first, he was not proof against the worthy gentleman's good humour, which displayed itself in a great variety of sallies and professional recollections, and an abundance of small jokes, which struck Oliver as being the drollest things he had ever heard, and caused him to laugh proportionately; to the evident satisfaction of the doctor, who laughed immoderately at himself, and made Harry laugh almost as heartily, by the very force of sympathy. So, they were as pleasant a party as, under the circumstances, they could well have been; and it was late before they retired, with light and thankful hearts, to take that rest of which, after the doubt and suspense they had recently undergone, they stood much in need.

Oliver rose next morning, in better heart, and went about his usual occupations, with more hope and pleasure than he had known for many days. The birds were once more hung out, to sing, in their old places; and the sweetest wild flowers that could be found, were once more gathered to gladden Rose with their beauty. The melancholy which had seemed to the sad eyes of the anxious boy to hang, for days past, over every object, beautiful as all were, was dispelled by magic. The dew seemed to sparkle more brightly on the green leaves; the air to rustle among them with a sweeter music; and the sky itself to look more blue and bright. Such is the influence which the condition of our own thoughts, exercise, even over the appearance of external objects. Men who look on nature, and their fellow-men, and cry that all is dark and gloomy, are in the right; but the sombre colours are reflections from their own jaundiced eyes and hearts. The real hues are delicate, and need a clearer vision.

It is worthy of remark, and Oliver did not fail to note it at the time, that his morning expeditions were no longer made alone. Harry Maylie, after the very first morning when he met Oliver coming laden home, was seized with such a passion for flowers, and displayed such a taste in their arrangement, as left his young companion far behind. If Oliver were behindhand in these respects, he knew where the best were to be found; and morning after morning they scoured the country together, and brought home the fairest that blossomed. The window of the young lady's chamber was opened now; for she loved to feel the rich summer air stream in, and revive her with its freshness; but there always stood in water, just inside the lattice, one particular little bunch, which was made up with great care, every morning. Oliver could not help noticing that the withered flowers were never thrown away, although the little vase was regularly replenished; nor, could he help observing, that whenever the doctor came into the garden, he invariably cast his eyes up to that particular corner, and nodded his head most expressively, as he set forth on his morning's walk. Pending these observations, the days were flying by; and Rose was rapidly recovering.

Nor did Oliver's time hang heavy on his hands, although the young lady had not yet left her chamber, and there were no evening walks, save now and then, for a short distance, with Mrs. Maylie. He applied himself, with redoubled assiduity, to the instructions of the white-headed old gentleman, and laboured so hard that his quick progress surprised even himself. It was while he was engaged in this pursuit, that he was greatly startled and distressed by a most unexpected occurrence.

The little room in which he was accustomed to sit, when busy at his books, was on the ground-floor, at the back of the house. It was quite a cottage-room, with a lattice-window: around which were clusters of jessamine and honeysuckle, that crept over the casement, and filled the place with their delicious perfume. It looked into a garden, whence a wicket-gate opened into a small paddock; all beyond, was fine meadow-land and wood. There was no other dwelling near, in that direction; and the prospect it commanded was very extensive.

One beautiful evening, when the first shades of twilight were beginning to settle upon the earth, Oliver sat at this window, intent upon his books. He had been poring over them for some time; and, as the day had been uncommonly sultry, and he had exerted himself a great deal, it is no disparagement to the authors, whoever they may have been, to say, that gradually and by slow degrees, he fell asleep.

There is a kind of sleep that steals upon us sometimes, which, while it holds the body prisoner, does not free the mind from a sense of things about it, and enable it to ramble at its pleasure. So far as an overpowering heaviness, a prostration of strength, and an utter inability to control our thoughts or power of motion, can be called sleep, this is it; and yet, we have a consciousness of all that is going on about us, and, if we dream at such a time, words which are really spoken, or sounds which really exist at the moment, accommodate themselves with surprising readiness to our visions, until reality and imagination become so strangely blended that it is afterwards almost matter of impossibility to separate the two. Nor is this, the most striking phenomenon incidental to such a state. It is an undoubted fact, that although our senses of touch and sight be for the time dead, yet our sleeping thoughts, and the visionary scenes that pass before us, will be influenced and materially influenced, by the mere silent presence of some external object; which may not have been near us when we closed our eyes: and of whose vicinity we have had no waking consciousness.

Oliver knew, perfectly well, that he was in his own little room; that his books were lying on the table before him; that the sweet air was stirring among the creeping plants outside. And yet he was asleep. Suddenly, the scene changed; the air became close and confined; and he thought, with a glow of terror, that he was in the Jew's house again. There sat the hideous old man, in his accustomed corner, pointing at him, and whispering to another man, with his face averted, who sat beside him.

'Hush, my dear!' he thought he heard the Jew say; 'it is he, sure enough. Come away.'

'He!' the other man seemed to answer; 'could I mistake him, think you? If a crowd of ghosts were to put themselves into his exact shape, and he stood amongst them, there is something that would tell me how to point him out. If you buried him fifty feet deep, and took me across his grave, I fancy I should know, if there wasn't a mark above it, that he lay buried there?'

The man seemed to say this, with such dreadful hatred, that Oliver awoke with the fear, and started up.

Good Heaven! what was that, which sent the blood tingling to his heart, and deprived him of his voice, and of power to move! There—there—at the window—close before him—so close, that he could have almost touched him before he started back: with his eyes peering into the room, and meeting his: there stood the Jew! And beside him, white with rage or fear, or both, were the scowling features of the man who had accosted him in the inn-yard.

It was but an instant, a glance, a flash, before his eyes; and they were gone. But they had recognised him, and he them; and their look was as firmly impressed upon his memory, as if it had been deeply carved in stone, and set before him from his birth. He stood transfixed for a moment; then, leaping from the window into the garden, called loudly for help.

CHAPTER XXXV. CONTAINING THE UNSATISFACTORY RESULT OF OLIVER'S ADVENTURE; AND A CONVERSATION OF SOME IMPORTANCE BETWEEN HARRY MAYLIE AND ROSE

When the inmates of the house, attracted by Oliver's cries, hurried to the spot from which they proceeded, they found him, pale and agitated, pointing in the direction of the meadows behind the house, and scarcely able to articulate the words, 'The Jew! the Jew!'

Mr. Giles was at a loss to comprehend what this outcry meant; but Harry Maylie, whose perceptions were something quicker, and who had heard Oliver's history from his mother, understood it at once.

'What direction did he take?' he asked, catching up a heavy stick which was standing in a corner.

'That,' replied Oliver, pointing out the course the man had taken; 'I missed them in an instant.'

'Then, they are in the ditch!' said Harry. 'Follow! And keep as near me, as you can.' So saying, he sprang over the hedge, and darted off with a speed which rendered it matter of exceeding difficulty for the others to keep near him.

Giles followed as well as he could; and Oliver followed too; and in the course of a minute or two, Mr. Losberne, who had been out walking, and just then returned, tumbled over the hedge after them, and picking himself up with more agility than he could have been supposed to possess, struck into the same course at no contemptible speed, shouting all the while, most prodigiously, to know what was the matter.

On they all went; nor stopped they once to breathe, until the leader, striking off into an angle of the field indicated by Oliver, began to search, narrowly, the ditch and hedge adjoining; which afforded time for the remainder of the party to come up; and for Oliver to communicate to Mr. Losberne the circumstances that had led to so vigorous a pursuit.

The search was all in vain. There were not even the traces of recent footsteps, to be seen. They stood now, on the summit of a little hill, commanding the open fields in every direction for three or four miles. There was the village in the hollow on the left; but, in order to gain that, after pursuing the track Oliver had pointed out, the men must have made a circuit of open ground, which it was impossible they could have accomplished in so short a time. A thick wood skirted the meadow-land in another direction; but they could not have gained that covert for the same reason.

'It must have been a dream, Oliver,' said Harry Maylie.

'Oh no, indeed, sir,' replied Oliver, shuddering at the very recollection of the old wretch's countenance; 'I saw him too plainly for that. I saw them both, as plainly as I see you now.'

'Who was the other?' inquired Harry and Mr. Losberne, together.

'The very same man I told you of, who came so suddenly upon me at the inn,' said Oliver. 'We had our eyes fixed full upon each other; and I could swear to him.'

'They took this way?' demanded Harry: 'are you sure?'

'As I am that the men were at the window,' replied Oliver, pointing down, as he spoke, to the hedge which divided the cottage-garden from the meadow. 'The tall man leaped over, just there; and the Jew, running a few paces to the right, crept through that gap.'

The two gentlemen watched Oliver's earnest face, as he spoke, and looking from him to each other, seemed to feel satisfied of the accuracy of what he said. Still, in no direction were there any appearances of the trampling of men in hurried flight. The grass was long; but it was trodden down nowhere, save where their own feet had crushed it. The sides and brinks of the ditches were of damp clay; but in no one place could they discern the print of men's shoes, or the slightest mark which would indicate that any feet had pressed the ground for hours before.

'This is strange!' said Harry.

'Strange?' echoed the doctor. 'Blathers and Duff, themselves, could make nothing of it.'

Notwithstanding the evidently useless nature of their search, they did not desist until the coming on of night rendered its further prosecution hopeless; and even then, they gave it up with reluctance. Giles was dispatched to the different ale-houses in the village, furnished with the best description Oliver could give of the appearance and dress of the strangers. Of these, the Jew was, at all events, sufficiently remarkable to be remembered, supposing he had been seen drinking, or loitering about; but Giles returned without any intelligence, calculated to dispel or lessen the mystery.

On the next day, fresh search was made, and the inquiries renewed; but with no better success. On the day following, Oliver and Mr. Maylie repaired to the market-town, in the hope of seeing or hearing something of the men there; but this effort was equally fruitless. After a few days, the affair began to be forgotten, as most affairs are, when wonder, having no fresh food to support it, dies away of itself.

Meanwhile, Rose was rapidly recovering. She had left her room: was able to go out; and mixing once more with the family, carried joy into the hearts of all.

But, although this happy change had a visible effect on the little circle; and although cheerful voices and merry laughter were once more heard in the cottage; there was at times, an unwonted restraint upon some there: even upon Rose herself: which Oliver could not fail to remark. Mrs. Maylie and her son were often closeted together for a long time; and more than once Rose appeared with traces of tears upon her face. After Mr. Losberne had fixed a day for his departure to Chertsey, these symptoms increased; and it became evident that something was in progress which affected the peace of the young lady, and of somebody else besides.

At length, one morning, when Rose was alone in the breakfast-parlour, Harry Maylie entered; and, with some hesitation, begged permission to speak with her for a few moments.

'A few—a very few—will suffice, Rose,' said the young man, drawing his chair towards her. 'What I shall have to say, has already presented itself to your mind; the most cherished hopes of my heart are not unknown to you, though from my lips you have not heard them stated.'

Rose had been very pale from the moment of his entrance; but that might have been the effect of her recent illness. She merely bowed; and bending over some plants that stood near, waited in silence for him to proceed.

'I—I—ought to have left here, before,' said Harry.

'You should, indeed,' replied Rose. 'Forgive me for saying so, but I wish you had.'

'I was brought here, by the most dreadful and agonising of all apprehensions,' said the young man; 'the fear of losing the one dear being on whom my every wish and hope are fixed. You had been dying; trembling between earth and heaven. We know that when the young, the beautiful, and good, are visited with sickness, their pure spirits insensibly turn towards their bright home of lasting rest; we know, Heaven help us! that the best and fairest of our kind, too often fade in blooming.'

There were tears in the eyes of the gentle girl, as these words were spoken; and when one fell upon the flower over which she bent, and glistened brightly in its cup, making it more beautiful, it seemed as though the outpouring of her fresh young heart, claimed kindred naturally, with the loveliest things in nature.

'A creature,' continued the young man, passionately, 'a creature as fair and innocent of guile as one of God's own angels, fluttered between life and death. Oh! who could hope, when the distant world to which she was akin, half opened to her view, that she would return to the sorrow and calamity of this! Rose, Rose, to know that you were passing away like some soft shadow, which a light from above, casts upon the earth; to have no hope that you would be spared to those who linger here; hardly to know a reason why you should be; to feel that you belonged to that bright sphere whither so many of the fairest and the best have winged their early flight; and yet to pray, amid all these consolations, that you might be restored to those who loved you—these were distractions almost too great to bear. They were mine, by day and night; and with them, came such a rushing torrent of fears, and apprehensions, and selfish regrets, lest you should die, and never know how devotedly I loved you, as almost bore down sense and reason in its course. You recovered. Day by day, and almost hour by hour, some drop of health came back, and mingling with the spent and feeble stream of life which circulated languidly within you, swelled it again to a high and rushing tide. I have watched you change almost from death, to life, with eyes that turned blind with their eagerness and deep affection. Do not tell me that you wish I had lost this; for it has softened my heart to all mankind.'

'I did not mean that,' said Rose, weeping; 'I only wish you had left here, that you might have turned to high and noble pursuits again; to pursuits well worthy of you.'

'There is no pursuit more worthy of me: more worthy of the highest nature that exists: than the struggle to win such a heart as yours,' said the young man, taking her hand. 'Rose, my own dear Rose! For years—for years—I have loved you; hoping to win my way to fame, and then come proudly home and tell you it had been pursued only for you to share; thinking, in my daydreams, how I would remind you, in that happy moment, of the many silent tokens I had given of a boy's attachment, and claim your hand, as in redemption of some old mute contract that had been sealed between us! That time has not arrived; but here, with not fame won, and no young vision realised, I offer you the heart so long your own, and stake my all upon the words with which you greet the offer.'

'Your behaviour has ever been kind and noble.' said Rose, mastering the emotions by which she was agitated. 'As you believe that I am not insensible or ungrateful, so hear my answer.'

'It is, that I may endeavour to deserve you; it is, dear Rose?'

'It is,' replied Rose, 'that you must endeavour to forget me; not as your old and dearly-attached companion, for that would wound me deeply; but, as the object of your love. Look into the world; think how many hearts you would be proud to gain, are there. Confide some other passion to me, if you will; I will be the truest, warmest, and most faithful friend you have.'

There was a pause, during which, Rose, who had covered her face with one hand, gave free vent to her tears. Harry still retained the other.

'And your reasons, Rose,' he said, at length, in a low voice; 'your reasons for this decision?'

'You have a right to know them,' rejoined Rose. 'You can say nothing to alter my resolution. It is a duty that I must perform. I owe it, alike to others, and to myself.'

'To yourself?'

'Yes, Harry. I owe it to myself, that I, a friendless, portionless, girl, with a blight upon my name, should not give your friends reason to suspect that I had sordidly yielded to your first passion, and fastened myself, a clog, on all your hopes and projects. I owe it to you and yours, to prevent you from opposing, in the warmth of your generous nature, this great obstacle to your progress in the world.'

'If your inclinations chime with your sense of duty—' Harry began.

'They do not,' replied Rose, colouring deeply.

'Then you return my love?' said Harry. 'Say but that, dear Rose; say but that; and soften the bitterness of this hard disappointment!'

'If I could have done so, without doing heavy wrong to him I loved,' rejoined Rose, 'I could have—'

'Have received this declaration very differently?' said Harry. 'Do not conceal that from me, at least, Rose.'

'I could,' said Rose. 'Stay!' she added, disengaging her hand, 'why should we prolong this painful interview? Most painful to me, and yet productive of lasting happiness, notwithstanding; for it will be happiness to know that I once held the high place in your regard which I now occupy, and every triumph you achieve in life will animate me with new fortitude and firmness. Farewell, Harry! As we have met to-day, we meet no more; but in other relations than those in which this conversation have placed us, we may be long and happily entwined; and may every blessing that the prayers of a true and earnest heart can call down from the source of all truth and sincerity, cheer and prosper you!'

'Another word, Rose,' said Harry. 'Your reason in your own words. From your own lips, let me hear it!'

'The prospect before you,' answered Rose, firmly, 'is a brilliant one. All the honours to which great talents and powerful connections can help men in public life, are in store for you. But those connections are proud; and I will neither mingle with such as may hold in scorn the mother who gave me life; nor bring disgrace or failure on the son of her who has so well supplied that mother's place. In a word,' said the young lady, turning away, as her temporary firmness forsook her, 'there is a stain upon my name, which the world visits on innocent heads. I will carry it into no blood but my own; and the reproach shall rest alone on me.'

'One word more, Rose. Dearest Rose! one more!' cried Harry, throwing himself before her. 'If I had been less—less fortunate, the world would call it—if some obscure and peaceful life had been my destiny—if I had been poor, sick, helpless—would you have turned from me then? Or has my probable advancement to riches and honour, given this scruple birth?'

'Do not press me to reply,' answered Rose. 'The question does not arise, and never will. It is unfair, almost unkind, to urge it.'

'If your answer be what I almost dare to hope it is,' retorted Harry, 'it will shed a gleam of happiness upon my lonely way, and light the path before me. It is not an idle thing to do so much, by the utterance of a few brief words, for one who loves you beyond all else. Oh, Rose: in the name of my ardent and enduring attachment; in the name of all I have suffered for you, and all you doom me to undergo; answer me this one question!'

'Then, if your lot had been differently cast,' rejoined Rose; 'if you had been even a little, but not so far, above me; if I could have been a help and comfort to you in any humble scene of peace and retirement, and not a blot and drawback in ambitious and distinguished crowds; I should have been spared this trial. I have every reason to be happy, very happy, now; but then, Harry, I own I should have been happier.'

Busy recollections of old hopes, cherished as a girl, long ago, crowded into the mind of Rose, while making this avowal; but they brought tears with them, as old hopes will when they come back withered; and they relieved her.

'I cannot help this weakness, and it makes my purpose stronger,' said Rose, extending her hand. 'I must leave you now, indeed.'

'I ask one promise,' said Harry. 'Once, and only once more,—say within a year, but it may be much sooner,—I may speak to you again on this subject, for the last time.'

'Not to press me to alter my right determination,' replied Rose, with a melancholy smile; 'it will be useless.'

'No,' said Harry; 'to hear you repeat it, if you will—finally repeat it! I will lay at your feet, whatever of station of fortune I may possess; and if you still adhere to your present resolution, will not seek, by word or act, to change it.'

'Then let it be so,' rejoined Rose; 'it is but one pang the more, and by that time I may be enabled to bear it better.'

She extended her hand again. But the young man caught her to his bosom; and imprinting one kiss on her beautiful forehead, hurried from the room.

CHAPTER XXXVI. IS A VERY SHORT ONE, AND MAY APPEAR OF NO GREAT IMPORTANCE IN ITS PLACE, BUT IT SHOULD BE READ NOTWITHSTANDING, AS A SEQUEL TO THE LAST, AND A KEY TO ONE THAT WILL FOLLOW WHEN ITS TIME ARRIVES

'And so you are resolved to be my travelling companion this morning; eh?' said the doctor, as Harry Maylie joined him and Oliver at the breakfast-table. 'Why, you are not in the same mind or intention two half-hours together!'

'You will tell me a different tale one of these days,' said Harry, colouring without any perceptible reason.

'I hope I may have good cause to do so,' replied Mr. Losberne; 'though I confess I don't think I shall. But yesterday morning you had made up your mind, in a great hurry, to stay here, and to accompany your mother, like a dutiful son, to the sea-side. Before noon, you announce that you are going to do me the honour of accompanying me as far as I go, on your road to London. And at night, you urge me, with great mystery, to start before the ladies are stirring; the consequence of which is, that young Oliver here is pinned down to his breakfast when he ought to be ranging the meadows after botanical phenomena of all kinds. Too bad, isn't it, Oliver?'

'I should have been very sorry not to have been at home when you and Mr. Maylie went away, sir,' rejoined Oliver.

'That's a fine fellow,' said the doctor; 'you shall come and see me when you return. But, to speak seriously, Harry; has any communication from the great nobs produced this sudden anxiety on your part to be gone?'

'The great nobs,' replied Harry, 'under which designation, I presume, you include my most stately uncle, have not communicated with me at all, since I have been here; nor, at this time of the year, is it likely that anything would occur to render necessary my immediate attendance among them.'

'Well,' said the doctor, 'you are a queer fellow. But of course they will get you into parliament at the election before Christmas, and these sudden shiftings and changes are no bad preparation for political life. There's something in that. Good training is always desirable, whether the race be for place, cup, or sweepstakes.'

Harry Maylie looked as if he could have followed up this short dialogue by one or two remarks that would have staggered the doctor not a little; but he contented himself with saying, 'We shall see,' and pursued the subject no farther. The post-chaise drove up to the door shortly afterwards; and Giles coming in for the luggage, the good doctor bustled out, to see it packed.

'Oliver,' said Harry Maylie, in a low voice, 'let me speak a word with you.'

Oliver walked into the window-recess to which Mr. Maylie beckoned him; much surprised at the mixture of sadness and boisterous spirits, which his whole behaviour displayed.

'You can write well now?' said Harry, laying his hand upon his arm.

'I hope so, sir,' replied Oliver.

'I shall not be at home again, perhaps for some time; I wish you would write to me—say once a fort-night: every alternate Monday: to the General Post Office in London. Will you?'

'Oh! certainly, sir; I shall be proud to do it,' exclaimed Oliver, greatly delighted with the commission.

'I should like to know how—how my mother and Miss Maylie are,' said the young man; 'and you can fill up a sheet by telling me what walks you take, and what you talk about, and whether she—they, I mean—seem happy and quite well. You understand me?'

'Oh! quite, sir, quite,' replied Oliver.

'I would rather you did not mention it to them,' said Harry, hurrying over his words; 'because it might make my mother anxious to write to me oftener, and it is a trouble and worry to her. Let it be a secret between you and me; and mind you tell me everything! I depend upon you.'

Oliver, quite elated and honoured by a sense of his importance, faithfully promised to be secret and explicit in his communications. Mr. Maylie took leave of him, with many assurances of his regard and protection.

The doctor was in the chaise; Giles (who, it had been arranged, should be left behind) held the door open in his hand; and the women-servants were in the garden, looking on. Harry cast one slight glance at the latticed window, and jumped into the carriage.

'Drive on!' he cried, 'hard, fast, full gallop! Nothing short of flying will keep pace with me, to-day.'

'Halloa!' cried the doctor, letting down the front glass in a great hurry, and shouting to the postillion; 'something very short of flying will keep pace with me. Do you hear?'

Jingling and clattering, till distance rendered its noise inaudible, and its rapid progress only perceptible to the eye, the vehicle wound its way along the road, almost hidden in a cloud of dust: now wholly disappearing, and now becoming visible again, as intervening objects, or the intricacies of the way, permitted. It was not until even the dusty cloud was no longer to be seen, that the gazers dispersed.

And there was one looker-on, who remained with eyes fixed upon the spot where the carriage had disappeared, long after it was many miles away; for, behind the white curtain which had shrouded her from view when Harry raised his eyes towards the window, sat Rose herself.

'He seems in high spirits and happy,' she said, at length. 'I feared for a time he might be otherwise. I was mistaken. I am very, very glad.'

Tears are signs of gladness as well as grief; but those which coursed down Rose's face, as she sat pensively at the window, still gazing in the same direction, seemed to tell more of sorrow than of joy.

CHAPTER XXXVII. IN WHICH THE READER MAY PERCEIVE A CONTRAST, NOT UNCOMMON IN MATRIMONIAL CASES

Mr. Bumble sat in the workhouse parlour, with his eyes moodily fixed on the cheerless grate, whence, as it was summer time, no brighter gleam proceeded, than the reflection of certain sickly rays of the sun, which were sent back from its cold and shining surface. A paper fly-cage dangled from the ceiling, to which he occasionally raised his eyes in gloomy thought; and, as the heedless insects hovered round the gaudy net-work, Mr. Bumble would heave a deep sigh, while a more gloomy shadow overspread his countenance. Mr. Bumble was meditating; it might be that the insects brought to mind, some painful passage in his own past life.

Nor was Mr. Bumble's gloom the only thing calculated to awaken a pleasing melancholy in the bosom of a spectator. There were not wanting other appearances, and those closely connected with his own person, which announced that a great change had taken place in the position of his affairs. The laced coat, and the cocked hat; where were they? He still wore knee-breeches, and dark cotton stockings on his nether limbs; but they were not the breeches. The coat was wide-skirted; and in that respect like the coat, but, oh how different! The mighty cocked hat was replaced by a modest round one. Mr. Bumble was no longer a beadle.

There are some promotions in life, which, independent of the more substantial rewards they offer, require peculiar value and dignity from the coats and waistcoats connected with them. A field-marshal has his uniform; a bishop his silk apron; a counsellor his silk gown; a beadle his cocked hat. Strip the bishop of his apron, or the beadle of his hat and lace; what are they? Men. Mere men. Dignity, and even holiness too, sometimes, are more questions of coat and waistcoat than some people imagine.

Mr. Bumble had married Mrs. Corney, and was master of the workhouse. Another beadle had come into power. On him the cocked hat, gold-laced coat, and staff, had all three descended.

'And to-morrow two months it was done!' said Mr. Bumble, with a sigh. 'It seems a age.'

Mr. Bumble might have meant that he had concentrated a whole existence of happiness into the short space of eight weeks; but the sigh—there was a vast deal of meaning in the sigh.

'I sold myself,' said Mr. Bumble, pursuing the same train of relection, 'for six teaspoons, a pair of sugar-tongs, and a milk-pot; with a small quantity of second-hand furniture, and twenty pound in money. I went very reasonable. Cheap, dirt cheap!'

'Cheap!' cried a shrill voice in Mr. Bumble's ear: 'you would have been dear at any price; and dear enough I paid for you, Lord above knows that!'

Mr. Bumble turned, and encountered the face of his interesting consort, who, imperfectly comprehending the few words she had overheard of his complaint, had hazarded the foregoing remark at a venture.

'Mrs. Bumble, ma'am!' said Mr. Bumble, with a sentimental sternness.

'Well!' cried the lady.

'Have the goodness to look at me,' said Mr. Bumble, fixing his eyes upon her. (If she stands such a eye as that,' said Mr. Bumble to himself, 'she can stand anything. It is a eye I never knew to fail with paupers. If it fails with her, my power is gone.')

Whether an exceedingly small expansion of eye be sufficient to quell paupers, who, being lightly fed, are in no very high condition; or whether the late Mrs. Corney was particularly proof against eagle glances; are matters of opinion. The matter of fact, is, that the matron was in no way overpowered by Mr. Bumble's scowl, but, on the contrary, treated it with great disdain, and even raised a laugh thereat, which sounded as though it were genuine.

On hearing this most unexpected sound, Mr. Bumble looked, first incredulous, and afterwards amazed. He then relapsed into his former state; nor did he rouse himself until his attention was again awakened by the voice of his partner.

'Are you going to sit snoring there, all day?' inquired Mrs. Bumble.

'I am going to sit here, as long as I think proper, ma'am,' rejoined Mr. Bumble; 'and although I was not snoring, I shall snore, gape, sneeze, laugh, or cry, as the humour strikes me; such being my prerogative.'

'Your prerogative!' sneered Mrs. Bumble, with ineffable contempt.

'I said the word, ma'am,' said Mr. Bumble. 'The prerogative of a man is to command.'

'And what's the prerogative of a woman, in the name of Goodness?' cried the relict of Mr. Corney deceased.

'To obey, ma'am,' thundered Mr. Bumble. 'Your late unfortunate husband should have taught it you; and then, perhaps, he might have been alive now. I wish he was, poor man!'

Mrs. Bumble, seeing at a glance, that the decisive moment had now arrived, and that a blow struck for the mastership on one side or other, must necessarily be final and conclusive, no sooner heard this allusion to the dead and gone, than she dropped into a chair, and with a loud scream that Mr. Bumble was a hard-hearted brute, fell into a paroxysm of tears.

But, tears were not the things to find their way to Mr. Bumble's soul; his heart was waterproof. Like washable beaver hats that improve with rain, his nerves were rendered stouter and more vigorous, by showers of tears, which, being tokens of weakness, and so far tacit admissions of his own power, pleased and exalted him. He eyed his good lady with looks of great satisfaction, and begged, in an encouraging manner, that she should cry her hardest: the exercise being looked upon, by the faculty, as strongly conducive to health.

'It opens the lungs, washes the countenance, exercises the eyes, and softens down the temper,' said Mr. Bumble. 'So cry away.'

As he discharged himself of this pleasantry, Mr. Bumble took his hat from a peg, and putting it on, rather rakishly, on one side, as a man might, who felt he had asserted his superiority in a becoming manner, thrust his hands into his pockets, and sauntered towards the door, with much ease and waggishness depicted in his whole appearance.

Now, Mrs. Corney that was, had tried the tears, because they were less troublesome than a manual assault; but, she was quite prepared to make trial of the latter mode of proceeding, as Mr. Bumble was not long in discovering.

The first proof he experienced of the fact, was conveyed in a hollow sound, immediately succeeded by the sudden flying off of his hat to the opposite end of the room. This preliminary proceeding laying bare his head, the expert lady, clasping him tightly round the throat with one hand, inflicted a shower of blows (dealt with singular vigour and dexterity) upon it with the other. This done, she created a little variety by scratching his face, and tearing his hair; and, having, by this time, inflicted as much punishment as she deemed necessary for the offence, she pushed him over a chair, which was luckily well situated for the purpose: and defied him to talk about his prerogative again, if he dared.

'Get up!' said Mrs. Bumble, in a voice of command. 'And take yourself away from here, unless you want me to do something desperate.'

Mr. Bumble rose with a very rueful countenance: wondering much what something desperate might be. Picking up his hat, he looked towards the door.

'Are you going?' demanded Mrs. Bumble.

'Certainly, my dear, certainly,' rejoined Mr. Bumble, making a quicker motion towards the door. 'I didn't intend to—I'm going, my dear! You are so very violent, that really I—'

At this instant, Mrs. Bumble stepped hastily forward to replace the carpet, which had been kicked up in the scuffle. Mr. Bumble immediately darted out of the room, without bestowing another thought on his unfinished sentence: leaving the late Mrs. Corney in full possession of the field.

Mr. Bumble was fairly taken by surprise, and fairly beaten. He had a decided propensity for bullying: derived no inconsiderable pleasure from the exercise of petty cruelty; and, consequently, was (it is needless to say) a coward. This is by no means a disparagement to his character; for many official personages, who are held in high respect and admiration, are the victims of similar infirmities. The remark is made, indeed, rather in his favour than otherwise, and with a view of impressing the reader with a just sense of his qualifications for office.

But, the measure of his degradation was not yet full. After making a tour of the house, and thinking, for the first time, that the poor-laws really were too hard on people; and that men who ran away from their wives, leaving them chargeable to the parish, ought, in justice to be visited with no punishment at all, but rather rewarded as meritorious individuals who had suffered much; Mr. Bumble came to a room where some of the female paupers were usually employed in washing the parish linen: when the sound of voices in conversation, now proceeded.

'Hem!' said Mr. Bumble, summoning up all his native dignity. 'These women at least shall continue to respect the prerogative. Hallo! hallo there! What do you mean by this noise, you hussies?'

With these words, Mr. Bumble opened the door, and walked in with a very fierce and angry manner: which was at once exchanged for a most humiliated and cowering air, as his eyes unexpectedly rested on the form of his lady wife.

'My dear,' said Mr. Bumble, 'I didn't know you were here.'

'Didn't know I was here!' repeated Mrs. Bumble. 'What do you do here?'

'I thought they were talking rather too much to be doing their work properly, my dear,' replied Mr. Bumble: glancing distractedly at a couple of old women at the wash-tub, who were comparing notes of admiration at the workhouse-master's humility.

'You thought they were talking too much?' said Mrs. Bumble. 'What business is it of yours?'

'Why, my dear—' urged Mr. Bumble submissively.

'What business is it of yours?' demanded Mrs. Bumble, again.

'It's very true, you're matron here, my dear,' submitted Mr. Bumble; 'but I thought you mightn't be in the way just then.'

'I'll tell you what, Mr. Bumble,' returned his lady. 'We don't want any of your interference. You're a great deal too fond of poking your nose into things that don't concern you, making everybody in the house laugh, the moment your back is turned, and making yourself look like a fool every hour in the day. Be off; come!'

Mr. Bumble, seeing with excruciating feelings, the delight of the two old paupers, who were tittering together most rapturously, hesitated for an instant. Mrs. Bumble, whose patience brooked no delay, caught up a bowl of soap-suds, and motioning him towards the door, ordered him instantly to depart, on pain of receiving the contents upon his portly person.

What could Mr. Bumble do? He looked dejectedly round, and slunk away; and, as he reached the door, the titterings of the paupers broke into a shrill chuckle of irrepressible delight. It wanted but this. He was degraded in their eyes; he had lost caste and station before the very paupers; he had fallen from all the height and pomp of beadleship, to the lowest depth of the most snubbed hen-peckery.

'All in two months!' said Mr. Bumble, filled with dismal thoughts. 'Two months! No more than two months ago, I was not only my own master, but everybody else's, so far as the porochial workhouse was concerned, and now!—'

It was too much. Mr. Bumble boxed the ears of the boy who opened the gate for him (for he had reached the portal in his reverie); and walked, distractedly, into the street.

He walked up one street, and down another, until exercise had abated the first passion of his grief; and then the revulsion of feeling made him thirsty. He passed a great many public-houses; but, at length paused before one in a by-way, whose parlour, as he gathered from a hasty peep over the blinds, was deserted, save by one solitary customer. It began to rain, heavily, at the moment. This determined him. Mr. Bumble stepped in; and ordering something to drink, as he passed the bar, entered the apartment into which he had looked from the street.

The man who was seated there, was tall and dark, and wore a large cloak. He had the air of a stranger; and seemed, by a certain haggardness in his look, as well as by the dusty soils on his dress, to have travelled some distance. He eyed Bumble askance, as he entered, but scarcely deigned to nod his head in acknowledgment of his salutation.

Mr. Bumble had quite dignity enough for two; supposing even that the stranger had been more familiar: so he drank his gin-and-water in silence, and read the paper with great show of pomp and circumstance.

It so happened, however: as it will happen very often, when men fall into company under such circumstances: that Mr. Bumble felt, every now and then, a powerful inducement, which he could not resist, to steal a look at the stranger: and that whenever he did so, he withdrew his eyes, in some confusion, to find that the stranger was at that moment stealing a look at him. Mr. Bumble's awkwardness was enhanced by the very remarkable expression of the stranger's eye, which was keen and bright, but shadowed by a scowl of distrust and suspicion, unlike anything he had ever observed before, and repulsive to behold.

When they had encountered each other's glance several times in this way, the stranger, in a harsh, deep voice, broke silence.

'Were you looking for me,' he said, 'when you peered in at the window?'

'Not that I am aware of, unless you're Mr.—' Here Mr. Bumble stopped short; for he was curious to know the stranger's name, and thought in his impatience, he might supply the blank.

'I see you were not,' said the stranger; an expression of quiet sarcasm playing about his mouth; 'or you have known my name. You don't know it. I would recommend you not to ask for it.'

'I meant no harm, young man,' observed Mr. Bumble, majestically.

'And have done none,' said the stranger.

Another silence succeeded this short dialogue: which was again broken by the stranger.

'I have seen you before, I think?' said he. 'You were differently dressed at that time, and I only passed you in the street, but I should know you again. You were beadle here, once; were you not?'

'I was,' said Mr. Bumble, in some surprise; 'porochial beadle.'

'Just so,' rejoined the other, nodding his head. 'It was in that character I saw you. What are you now?'

'Master of the workhouse,' rejoined Mr. Bumble, slowly and impressively, to check any undue familiarity the stranger might otherwise assume. 'Master of the workhouse, young man!'

'You have the same eye to your own interest, that you always had, I doubt not?' resumed the stranger, looking keenly into Mr. Bumble's eyes, as he raised them in astonishment at the question.

'Don't scruple to answer freely, man. I know you pretty well, you see.'

'I suppose, a married man,' replied Mr. Bumble, shading his eyes with his hand, and surveying the stranger, from head to foot, in evident perplexity, 'is not more averse to turning an honest penny when he can, than a single one. Porochial officers are not so well paid that they can afford to refuse any little extra fee, when it comes to them in a civil and proper manner.'

The stranger smiled, and nodded his head again: as much to say, he had not mistaken his man; then rang the bell.

'Fill this glass again,' he said, handing Mr. Bumble's empty tumbler to the landlord. 'Let it be strong and hot. You like it so, I suppose?'

'Not too strong,' replied Mr. Bumble, with a delicate cough.

'You understand what that means, landlord!' said the stranger, drily.

The host smiled, disappeared, and shortly afterwards returned with a steaming jorum: of which, the first gulp brought the water into Mr. Bumble's eyes.

'Now listen to me,' said the stranger, after closing the door and window. 'I came down to this place, to-day, to find you out; and, by one of those chances which the devil throws in the way of his friends sometimes, you walked into the very room I was sitting in, while you were uppermost in my mind. I want some information from you. I don't ask you to give it for nothing, slight as it is. Put up that, to begin with.'

As he spoke, he pushed a couple of sovereigns across the table to his companion, carefully, as though unwilling that the chinking of money should be heard without. When Mr. Bumble had scrupulously examined the coins, to see that they were genuine, and had put them up, with much satisfaction, in his waistcoat-pocket, he went on:

'Carry your memory back—let me see—twelve years, last winter.'

'It's a long time,' said Mr. Bumble. 'Very good. I've done it.'

'The scene, the workhouse.'

'Good!'

'And the time, night.'

'Yes.'

'And the place, the crazy hole, wherever it was, in which miserable drabs brought forth the life and health so often denied to themselves—gave birth to puling children for the parish to rear; and hid their shame, rot 'em in the grave!'

'The lying-in room, I suppose?' said Mr. Bumble, not quite following the stranger's excited description.

'Yes,' said the stranger. 'A boy was born there.'

'A many boys,' observed Mr. Bumble, shaking his head, despondingly.

'A murrain on the young devils!' cried the stranger; 'I speak of one; a meek-looking, pale-faced boy, who was apprenticed down here, to a coffin-maker—I wish he had made his coffin, and screwed his body in it—and who afterwards ran away to London, as it was supposed.'

'Why, you mean Oliver! Young Twist!' said Mr. Bumble; 'I remember him, of course. There wasn't a obstinater young rascal—'

'It's not of him I want to hear; I've heard enough of him,' said the stranger, stopping Mr. Bumble in the outset of a tirade on the subject of poor Oliver's vices. 'It's of a woman; the hag that nursed his mother. Where is she?'

'Where is she?' said Mr. Bumble, whom the gin-and-water had rendered facetious. 'It would be hard to tell. There's no midwifery there, whichever place she's gone to; so I suppose she's out of employment, anyway.'

'What do you mean?' demanded the stranger, sternly.

'That she died last winter,' rejoined Mr. Bumble.

The man looked fixedly at him when he had given this information, and although he did not withdraw his eyes for some time afterwards, his gaze gradually became vacant and abstracted, and he seemed lost in thought. For some time, he appeared doubtful whether he ought to be relieved or disappointed by the intelligence; but at length he breathed more freely; and withdrawing his eyes, observed that it was no great matter. With that he rose, as if to depart.

But Mr. Bumble was cunning enough; and he at once saw that an opportunity was opened, for the lucrative disposal of some secret in the possession of his better half. He well remembered the night of old Sally's death, which the occurrences of that day had given him good reason to recollect, as the occasion on which he had proposed to Mrs. Corney; and although that lady had never confided to him the disclosure of which she had been the solitary witness, he had heard enough to know that it related to something that had occurred in the old woman's attendance, as workhouse nurse, upon the young mother of Oliver Twist. Hastily calling this circumstance to mind, he informed the stranger, with an air of mystery, that one woman had been closeted with the old harridan shortly before she died; and that she could, as he had reason to believe, throw some light on the subject of his inquiry.

'How can I find her?' said the stranger, thrown off his guard; and plainly showing that all his fears (whatever they were) were aroused afresh by the intelligence.

'Only through me,' rejoined Mr. Bumble.

'When?' cried the stranger, hastily.

'To-morrow,' rejoined Bumble.

'At nine in the evening,' said the stranger, producing a scrap of paper, and writing down upon it, an obscure address by the water-side, in characters that betrayed his agitation; 'at nine in the evening, bring her to me there. I needn't tell you to be secret. It's your interest.'

With these words, he led the way to the door, after stopping to pay for the liquor that had been drunk. Shortly remarking that their roads were different, he departed, without more ceremony than an emphatic repetition of the hour of appointment for the following night.

On glancing at the address, the parochial functionary observed that it contained no name. The stranger had not gone far, so he made after him to ask it.

'What do you want?' cried the man, turning quickly round, as Bumble touched him on the arm. 'Following me?'

'Only to ask a question,' said the other, pointing to the scrap of paper. 'What name am I to ask for?'

'Monks!' rejoined the man; and strode hastily, away.

CHAPTER XXXVIII. CONTAINING AN ACCOUNT OF WHAT PASSED BETWEEN MR. AND MRS. BUMBLE, AND MR. MONKS, AT THEIR NOCTURNAL INTERVIEW

It was a dull, close, overcast summer evening. The clouds, which had been threatening all day, spread out in a dense and sluggish mass of vapour, already yielded large drops of rain, and seemed to presage a violent thunder-storm, when Mr. and Mrs. Bumble, turning out of the main street of the town, directed their course towards a scattered little colony of ruinous houses, distant from it some mile and a-half, or thereabouts, and erected on a low unwholesome swamp, bordering upon the river.

They were both wrapped in old and shabby outer garments, which might, perhaps, serve the double purpose of protecting their persons from the rain, and sheltering them from observation. The husband carried a lantern, from which, however, no light yet shone; and trudged on, a few paces in front, as though—the way being dirty—to give his wife the benefit of treading in his heavy footprints. They went on, in profound silence; every now and then, Mr. Bumble relaxed his pace, and turned his head as if to make sure that his helpmate was following; then, discovering that she was close at his heels, he mended his rate of walking, and proceeded, at a considerable increase of speed, towards their place of destination.

This was far from being a place of doubtful character; for it had long been known as the residence of none but low ruffians, who, under various pretences of living by their labour, subsisted chiefly on plunder and crime. It was a collection of mere hovels: some, hastily built with loose bricks: others, of old worm-eaten ship-timber: jumbled together without any attempt at order or arrangement, and planted, for the most part, within a few feet of the river's bank. A few leaky boats drawn up on the mud, and made fast to the dwarf wall which skirted it: and here and there an oar or coil of rope: appeared, at first, to indicate that the inhabitants of these miserable cottages pursued some avocation on the river; but a glance at the shattered and useless condition of the articles thus displayed, would have led a passer-by, without much difficulty, to the conjecture that they were disposed there, rather for the preservation of appearances, than with any view to their being actually employed.

In the heart of this cluster of huts; and skirting the river, which its upper stories overhung; stood a large building, formerly used as a manufactory of some kind. It had, in its day, probably furnished employment to the inhabitants of the surrounding tenements. But it had long since gone to ruin. The rat, the worm, and the action of the damp, had weakened and rotted the piles on which it stood; and a considerable portion of the building had already sunk down into the water; while the remainder, tottering and bending over the dark stream, seemed to wait a favourable opportunity of following its old companion, and involving itself in the same fate.

It was before this ruinous building that the worthy couple paused, as the first peal of distant thunder reverberated in the air, and the rain commenced pouring violently down.

'The place should be somewhere here,' said Bumble, consulting a scrap of paper he held in his hand.

'Halloa there!' cried a voice from above.

Following the sound, Mr. Bumble raised his head and descried a man looking out of a door, breast-high, on the second story.

'Stand still, a minute,' cried the voice; 'I'll be with you directly.' With which the head disappeared, and the door closed.

'Is that the man?' asked Mr. Bumble's good lady.

Mr. Bumble nodded in the affirmative.

'Then, mind what I told you,' said the matron: 'and be careful to say as little as you can, or you'll betray us at once.'

Mr. Bumble, who had eyed the building with very rueful looks, was apparently about to express some doubts relative to the advisability of proceeding any further with the enterprise just then, when he was prevented by the appearance of Monks: who opened a small door, near which they stood, and beckoned them inwards.

'Come in!' he cried impatiently, stamping his foot upon the ground. 'Don't keep me here!'

The woman, who had hesitated at first, walked boldly in, without any other invitation. Mr. Bumble, who was ashamed or afraid to lag behind, followed: obviously very ill at ease and with scarcely any of that remarkable dignity which was usually his chief characteristic.

'What the devil made you stand lingering there, in the wet?' said Monks, turning round, and addressing Bumble, after he had bolted the door behind them.

'We—we were only cooling ourselves,' stammered Bumble, looking apprehensively about him.

'Cooling yourselves!' retorted Monks. 'Not all the rain that ever fell, or ever will fall, will put as much of hell's fire out, as a man can carry about with him. You won't cool yourself so easily; don't think it!'

With this agreeable speech, Monks turned short upon the matron, and bent his gaze upon her, till even she, who was not easily cowed, was fain to withdraw her eyes, and turn them towards the ground.

'This is the woman, is it?' demanded Monks.

'Hem! That is the woman,' replied Mr. Bumble, mindful of his wife's caution.

'You think women never can keep secrets, I suppose?' said the matron, interposing, and returning, as she spoke, the searching look of Monks.

'I know they will always keep one till it's found out,' said Monks.

'And what may that be?' asked the matron.

'The loss of their own good name,' replied Monks. 'So, by the same rule, if a woman's a party to a secret that might hang or transport her, I'm not afraid of her telling it to anybody;

not I! Do you understand, mistress?'

'No,' rejoined the matron, slightly colouring as she spoke.

'Of course you don't!' said Monks. 'How should you?'

Bestowing something half-way between a smile and a frown upon his two companions, and again beckoning them to follow him, the man hastened across the apartment, which was of considerable extent, but low in the roof. He was preparing to ascend a steep staircase, or rather ladder, leading to another floor of warehouses above: when a bright flash of lightning streamed down the aperture, and a peal of thunder followed, which shook the crazy building to its centre.

'Hear it!' he cried, shrinking back. 'Hear it! Rolling and crashing on as if it echoed through a thousand caverns where the devils were hiding from it. I hate the sound!'

He remained silent for a few moments; and then, removing his hands suddenly from his face, showed, to the unspeakable discomposure of Mr. Bumble, that it was much distorted and discoloured.

'These fits come over me, now and then,' said Monks, observing his alarm; 'and thunder sometimes brings them on. Don't mind me now; it's all over for this once.'

Thus speaking, he led the way up the ladder; and hastily closing the window-shutter of the room into which it led, lowered a lantern which hung at the end of a rope and pulley passed through one of the heavy beams in the ceiling: and which cast a dim light upon an old table and three chairs that were placed beneath it.

'Now,' said Monks, when they had all three seated themselves, 'the sooner we come to our business, the better for all. The woman know what it is, does she?'

The question was addressed to Bumble; but his wife anticipated the reply, by intimating that she was perfectly acquainted with it.

'He is right in saying that you were with this hag the night she died; and that she told you something—'

'About the mother of the boy you named,' replied the matron interrupting him. 'Yes.'

'The first question is, of what nature was her communication?' said Monks.

'That's the second,' observed the woman with much deliberation. 'The first is, what may the communication be worth?'

'Who the devil can tell that, without knowing of what kind it is?' asked Monks.

'Nobody better than you, I am persuaded,' answered Mrs. Bumble: who did not want for spirit, as her yoke-fellow could abundantly testify.

'Humph!' said Monks significantly, and with a look of eager inquiry; 'there may be money's worth to get, eh?'

'Perhaps there may,' was the composed reply.

'Something that was taken from her,' said Monks. 'Something that she wore. Something that—'

'You had better bid,' interrupted Mrs. Bumble. 'I have heard enough, already, to assure me that you are the man I ought to talk to.'

Mr. Bumble, who had not yet been admitted by his better half into any greater share of the secret than he had originally possessed, listened to this dialogue with outstretched neck and distended eyes: which he directed towards his wife and Monks, by turns, in undisguised astonishment; increased, if possible, when the latter sternly demanded, what sum was required for the disclosure.

'What's it worth to you?' asked the woman, as collectedly as before.

'It may be nothing; it may be twenty pounds,' replied Monks. 'Speak out, and let me know which.'

'Add five pounds to the sum you have named; give me five-and-twenty pounds in gold,' said the woman; 'and I'll tell you all I know. Not before.'

'Five-and-twenty pounds!' exclaimed Monks, drawing back.

'I spoke as plainly as I could,' replied Mrs. Bumble. 'It's not a large sum, either.'

'Not a large sum for a paltry secret, that may be nothing when it's told!' cried Monks impatiently; 'and which has been lying dead for twelve years past or more!'

'Such matters keep well, and, like good wine, often double their value in course of time,' answered the matron, still preserving the resolute indifference she had assumed. 'As to lying dead, there are those who will lie dead for twelve thousand years to come, or twelve million, for anything you or I know, who will tell strange tales at last!'

'What if I pay it for nothing?' asked Monks, hesitating.

'You can easily take it away again,' replied the matron. 'I am but a woman; alone here; and unprotected.'

'Not alone, my dear, nor unprotected, neither,' submitted Mr. Bumble, in a voice tremulous with fear: 'I am here, my dear. And besides,' said Mr. Bumble, his teeth chattering as he spoke, 'Mr. Monks is too much of a gentleman to attempt any violence on porochial persons. Mr. Monks is aware that I am not a young man, my dear, and also that I am a little run to seed, as I may say; bu he has heerd: I say I have no doubt Mr. Monks has heerd, my dear: that I am a very determined officer, with very uncommon strength, if I'm once roused. I only want a little rousing; that's all.'

As Mr. Bumble spoke, he made a melancholy feint of grasping his lantern with fierce determination; and plainly showed, by the alarmed expression of every feature, that he did want a little rousing, and not a little, prior to making any very warlike demonstration: unless, indeed, against paupers, or other person or persons trained down for the purpose.

'You are a fool,' said Mrs. Bumble, in reply; 'and had better hold your tongue.'

'He had better have cut it out, before he came, if he can't speak in a lower tone,' said Monks, grimly. 'So! He's your husband, eh?'

'He my husband!' tittered the matron, parrying the question.

'I thought as much, when you came in,' rejoined Monks, marking the angry glance which the lady darted at her spouse as she spoke. 'So much the better; I have less hesitation in dealing with two people, when I find that there's only one will between them. I'm in earnest.

See here!'

He thrust his hand into a side-pocket; and producing a canvas bag, told out twenty-five sovereigns on the table, and pushed them over to the woman.

'Now,' he said, 'gather them up; and when this cursed peal of thunder, which I feel is coming up to break over the house-top, is gone, let's hear your story.'

The thunder, which seemed in fact much nearer, and to shiver and break almost over their heads, having subsided, Monks, raising his face from the table, bent forward to listen to what the woman should say. The faces of the three nearly touched, as the two men leant over the small table in their eagerness to hear, and the woman also leant forward to render her whisper audible. The sickly rays of the suspended lantern falling directly upon them, aggravated the paleness and anxiety of their countenances: which, encircled by the deepest gloom and darkness, looked ghastly in the extreme.

'When this woman, that we called old Sally, died,' the matron began, 'she and I were alone.'

'Was there no one by?' asked Monks, in the same hollow whisper; 'No sick wretch or idiot in some other bed? No one who could hear, and might, by possibility, understand?'

'Not a soul,' replied the woman; 'we were alone. I stood alone beside the body when death came over it.'

'Good,' said Monks, regarding her attentively. 'Go on.'

'She spoke of a young creature,' resumed the matron, 'who had brought a child into the world some years before; not merely in the same room, but in the same bed, in which she then lay dying.'

'Ay?' said Monks, with quivering lip, and glancing over his shoulder, 'Blood! How things come about!'

'The child was the one you named to him last night,' said the matron, nodding carelessly towards her husband; 'the mother this nurse had robbed.'

'In life?' asked Monks.

'In death,' replied the woman, with something like a shudder. 'She stole from the corpse, when it had hardly turned to one, that which the dead mother had prayed her, with her last breath, to keep for the infant's sake.'

'She sold it,' cried Monks, with desperate eagerness; 'did she sell it? Where? When? To whom? How long before?'

'As she told me, with great difficulty, that she had done this,' said the matron, 'she fell back and died.'

'Without saying more?' cried Monks, in a voice which, from its very suppression, seemed only the more furious. 'It's a lie! I'll not be played with. She said more. I'll tear the life out of you both, but I'll know what it was.'

'She didn't utter another word,' said the woman, to all appearance unmoved (as Mr. Bumble was very far from being) by the strange man's violence; 'but she clutched my gown, violently, with one hand, which was partly closed; and when I saw that she was dead, and so removed the hand by force, I found it clasped a scrap of dirty paper.'

'Which contained—' interposed Monks, stretching forward.

'Nothing,' replied the woman; 'it was a pawnbroker's duplicate.'

'For what?' demanded Monks.

'In good time I'll tell you.' said the woman. 'I judge that she had kept the trinket, for some time, in the hope of turning it to better account; and then had pawned it; and had saved or scraped together money to pay the pawnbroker's interest year by year, and prevent its running out; so that if anything came of it, it could still be redeemed. Nothing had come of it; and, as I tell you, she died with the scrap of paper, all worn and tattered, in her hand. The time was out in two days; I thought something might one day come of it too; and so redeemed the pledge.'

'Where is it now?' asked Monks quickly.

'There,' replied the woman. And, as if glad to be relieved of it, she hastily threw upon the table a small kid bag scarcely large enough for a French watch, which Monks pouncing upon, tore open with trembling hands. It contained a little gold locket: in which were two locks of hair, and a plain gold wedding-ring.

'It has the word "Agnes" engraved on the inside,' said the woman.

'There is a blank left for the surname; and then follows the date; which is within a year before the child was born. I found out that.'

'And this is all?' said Monks, after a close and eager scrutiny of the contents of the little packet.

'All,' replied the woman.

Mr. Bumble drew a long breath, as if he were glad to find that the story was over, and no mention made of taking the five-and-twenty pounds back again; and now he took courage to wipe the perspiration which had been trickling over his nose, unchecked, during the whole of the previous dialogue.

'I know nothing of the story, beyond what I can guess at,' said his wife addressing Monks, after a short silence; 'and I want to know nothing; for it's safer not. But I may ask you two questions, may I?'

'You may ask,' said Monks, with some show of surprise; 'but whether I answer or not is another question.'

'—Which makes three,' observed Mr. Bumble, essaying a stroke of facetiousness.

'Is that what you expected to get from me?' demanded the matron.

'It is,' replied Monks. 'The other question?'

'What do you propose to do with it? Can it be used against me?'

'Never,' rejoined Monks; 'nor against me either. See here! But don't move a step forward, or your life is not worth a bulrush.'

With these words, he suddenly wheeled the table aside, and pulling an iron ring in the boarding, threw back a large trap-door which opened close at Mr. Bumble's feet, and caused that gentleman to retire several paces backward, with great precipitation.

'Look down,' said Monks, lowering the lantern into the gulf. 'Don't fear me. I could have let you down, quietly enough, when you were seated over it, if that had been my game.'

Thus encouraged, the matron drew near to the brink; and even Mr. Bumble himself, impelled by curiousity, ventured to do the same. The turbid water, swollen by the heavy rain, was rushing rapidly on below; and all other sounds were lost in the noise of its plashing and eddying against the green and slimy piles. There had once been a water-mill beneath; the tide foaming and chafing round the few rotten stakes, and fragments of machinery that yet remained, seemed to dart onward, with a new impulse, when freed from the obstacles which had unavailingly attempted to stem its headlong course.

'If you flung a man's body down there, where would it be to-morrow morning?' said Monks, swinging the lantern to and fro in the dark well.

'Twelve miles down the river, and cut to pieces besides,' replied Bumble, recoiling at the thought.

Monks drew the little packet from his breast, where he had hurriedly thrust it; and tying it to a leaden weight, which had formed a part of some pulley, and was lying on the floor, dropped it into the stream. It fell straight, and true as a die; clove the water with a scarcely audible splash; and was gone.

The three looking into each other's faces, seemed to breathe more freely.

'There!' said Monks, closing the trap-door, which fell heavily back into its former position. 'If the sea ever gives up its dead, as books say it will, it will keep its gold and silver to itself, and that trash among it. We have nothing more to say, and may break up our pleasant party.'

'By all means,' observed Mr. Bumble, with great alacrity.

'You'll keep a quiet tongue in your head, will you?' said Monks, with a threatening look. 'I am not afraid of your wife.'

'You may depend upon me, young man,' answered Mr. Bumble, bowing himself gradually towards the ladder, with excessive politeness. 'On everybody's account, young man; on my own, you know, Mr. Monks.'

'I am glad, for your sake, to hear it,' remarked Monks. 'Light your lantern! And get away from here as fast as you can.'

It was fortunate that the conversation terminated at this point, or Mr. Bumble, who had bowed himself to within six inches of the ladder, would infallibly have pitched headlong into the room below. He lighted his lantern from that which Monks had detached from the rope, and now carried in his hand; and making no effort to prolong the discourse, descended in silence, followed by his wife. Monks brought up the rear, after pausing on the steps to satisfy himself that there were no other sounds to be heard than the beating of the rain without, and the rushing of the water.

They traversed the lower room, slowly, and with caution; for Monks started at every shadow; and Mr. Bumble, holding his lantern a foot above the ground, walked not only with remarkable care, but with a marvellously light step for a gentleman of his figure: looking nervously about him for hidden trap-doors. The gate at which they had entered, was softly unfastened and opened by Monks; merely exchanging a nod with their mysterious acquaintance, the married couple emerged into the wet and darkness outside.

They were no sooner gone, than Monks, who appeared to entertain an invincible repugnance to being left alone, called to a boy who had been hidden somewhere below. Bidding him go first, and bear the light, he returned to the chamber he had just quitted.

CHAPTER XXXIX. INTRODUCES SOME RESPECTABLE CHARACTERS WITH WHOM THE READER IS ALREADY ACQUAINTED, AND SHOWS HOW MONKS AND THE JEW LAID THEIR WORTHY HEADS TOGETHER

On the evening following that upon which the three worthies mentioned in the last chapter, disposed of their little matter of business as therein narrated, Mr. William Sikes, awakening from a nap, drowsily growled forth an inquiry what time of night it was.

The room in which Mr. Sikes propounded this question, was not one of those he had tenanted, previous to the Chertsey expedition, although it was in the same quarter of the town, and was situated at no great distance from his former lodgings. It was not, in appearance, so desirable a habitation as his old quarters: being a mean and badly-furnished apartment, of very limited size; lighted only by one small window in the shelving roof, and abutting on a close and dirty lane. Nor were there wanting other indications of the good gentleman's having gone down in the world of late: for a great scarcity of furniture, and total absence of comfort, together with the disappearance of all such small moveables as spare clothes and linen, bespoke a state of extreme poverty; while the meagre and attenuated condition of Mr. Sikes himself would have fully confirmed these symptoms, if they had stood in any need of corroboration.

The housebreaker was lying on the bed, wrapped in his white great-coat, by way of dressing-gown, and displaying a set of features in no degree improved by the cadaverous hue of illness, and the addition of a soiled nightcap, and a stiff, black beard of a week's growth. The dog sat at the bedside: now eyeing his master with a wistful look, and now pricking his ears, and uttering a low growl as some noise in the street, or in the lower part of the house, attracted his attention. Seated by the window, busily engaged in patching an old waistcoat which formed a portion of the robber's ordinary dress, was a female: so pale and reduced with watching and privation, that there would have been considerable difficulty in recognising her as the same Nancy who has already figured in this tale, but for the voice in which she replied to Mr. Sikes's question.

'Not long gone seven,' said the girl. 'How do you feel to-night, Bill?'

'As weak as water,' replied Mr. Sikes, with an imprecation on his eyes and limbs. 'Here; lend us a hand, and let me get off this thundering bed anyhow.'

Illness had not improved Mr. Sikes's temper; for, as the girl raised him up and led him to a chair, he muttered various curses on her awkwardness, and struck her.

'Whining are you?' said Sikes. 'Come! Don't stand snivelling there. If you can't do anything better than that, cut off altogether. D'ye hear me?'

'I hear you,' replied the girl, turning her face aside, and forcing a laugh. 'What fancy have you got in your head now?'

'Oh! you've thought better of it, have you?' growled Sikes, marking the tear which trembled in her eye. 'All the better for you, you have.'

'Why, you don't mean to say, you'd be hard upon me to-night, Bill,' said the girl, laying her hand upon his shoulder.

'No!' cried Mr. Sikes. 'Why not?'

'Such a number of nights,' said the girl, with a touch of woman's tenderness, which communicated something like sweetness of tone, even to her voice: 'such a number of nights as I've been patient with you, nursing and caring for you, as if you had been a child: and this the first that I've seen you like yourself; you wouldn't have served me as you did just now, if you'd thought of that, would you? Come, come; say you wouldn't.'

'Well, then,' rejoined Mr. Sikes, 'I wouldn't. Why, damme, now, the girls's whining again!'

'It's nothing,' said the girl, throwing herself into a chair. 'Don't you seem to mind me. It'll soon be over.'

'What'll be over?' demanded Mr. Sikes in a savage voice. 'What foolery are you up to, now, again? Get up and bustle about, and don't come over me with your woman's nonsense.'

At any other time, this remonstrance, and the tone in which it was delivered, would have had the desired effect; but the girl being really weak and exhausted, dropped her head over the back of the chair, and fainted, before Mr. Sikes could get out a few of the appropriate oaths with which, on similar occasions, he was accustomed to garnish his threats. Not knowing, very well, what to do, in this uncommon emergency; for Miss Nancy's hysterics were usually of that violent kind which the patient fights and struggles out of, without much assistance; Mr. Sikes tried a little blasphemy: and finding that mode of treatment wholly ineffectual, called for assistance.

'What's the matter here, my dear?' said Fagin, looking in.

'Lend a hand to the girl, can't you?' replied Sikes impatiently. 'Don't stand chattering and grinning at me!'

With an exclamation of surprise, Fagin hastened to the girl's assistance, while Mr. John Dawkins (otherwise the Artful Dodger), who had followed his venerable friend into the room, hastily deposited on the floor a bundle with which he was laden; and snatching a bottle from the grasp of Master Charles Bates who came close at his heels, uncorked it in a twinkling with his teeth, and poured a portion of its contents down the patient's throat: previously taking a taste, himself, to prevent mistakes.

'Give her a whiff of fresh air with the bellows, Charley,' said Mr. Dawkins; 'and you slap her hands, Fagin, while Bill undoes the petticuts.'

These united restoratives, administered with great energy: especially that department consigned to Master Bates, who appeared to consider his share in the proceedings, a piece of unexampled pleasantry: were not long in producing the desired effect. The girl gradually recovered her senses; and, staggering to a chair by the bedside, hid her face upon the pillow: leaving Mr. Sikes to confront the new comers, in some astonishment at their unlooked-for appearance.

'Why, what evil wind has blowed you here?' he asked Fagin.

'No evil wind at all, my dear, for evil winds blow nobody any good; and I've brought something good with me, that you'll be glad to see. Dodger, my dear, open the bundle; and give Bill the little trifles that we spent all our money on, this morning.'

In compliance with Mr. Fagin's request, the Artful untied this bundle, which was of large size, and formed of an old table-cloth; and handed the articles it contained, one by one, to Charley Bates: who placed them on the table, with various encomiums on their rarity and excellence.

'Sitch a rabbit pie, Bill,' exclaimed that young gentleman, disclosing to view a huge pasty; 'sitch delicate creeturs, with sitch tender limbs, Bill, that the wery bones melt in your mouth, and there's no occasion to pick 'em; half a pound of seven and six-penny green, so precious strong that if you mix it with biling water, it'll go nigh to blow the lid of the tea-pot off; a pound and a half of moist sugar that the niggers didn't work at all at, afore they got it up to sitch a pitch of goodness,—oh no! Two half-quartern brans; pound of best fresh; piece of double Glo'ster; and, to wind up all, some of the richest sort you ever lushed!'

Uttering this last panegyric, Master Bates produced, from one of his extensive pockets, a full-sized wine-bottle, carefully corked; while Mr. Dawkins, at the same instant, poured out a wine-glassful of raw spirits from the bottle he carried: which the invalid tossed down his throat without a moment's hesitation.

'Ah!' said Fagin, rubbing his hands with great satisfaction. 'You'll do, Bill; you'll do now.'

'Do!' exclaimed Mr. Sikes; 'I might have been done for, twenty times over, afore you'd have done anything to help me. What do you mean by leaving a man in this state, three weeks and more, you false-hearted wagabond?'

'Only hear him, boys!' said Fagin, shrugging his shoulders. 'And us come to bring him all these beau-ti-ful things.'

'The things is well enough in their way,' observed Mr. Sikes: a little soothed as he glanced over the table; 'but what have you got to say for yourself, why you should leave me here, down in the mouth, health, blunt, and everything else; and take no more notice of me, all this mortal time, than if I was that 'ere dog.—Drive him down, Charley!'

'I never see such a jolly dog as that,' cried Master Bates, doing as he was desired. 'Smelling the grub like a old lady a going to market! He'd make his fortun' on the stage that dog would, and rewive the drayma besides.'

'Hold your din,' cried Sikes, as the dog retreated under the bed: still growling angrily. 'What have you got to say for yourself, you withered old fence, eh?'

'I was away from London, a week and more, my dear, on a plant,' replied the Jew.

'And what about the other fortnight?' demanded Sikes. 'What about the other fortnight that you've left me lying here, like a sick rat in his hole?'

'I couldn't help it, Bill. I can't go into a long explanation before company; but I couldn't help it, upon my honour.'

'Upon your what?' growled Sikes, with excessive disgust. 'Here! Cut me off a piece of that pie, one of you boys, to take the taste of that out of my mouth, or it'll choke me dead.'

'Don't be out of temper, my dear,' urged Fagin, submissively. 'I have never forgot you, Bill; never once.'

'No! I'll pound it that you han't,' replied Sikes, with a bitter grin. 'You've been scheming and plotting away, every hour that I have laid shivering and burning here; and Bill was to do this; and Bill was to do that; and Bill was to do it all, dirt cheap, as soon as he got well: and was quite poor enough for your work. If it hadn't been for the girl, I might have died.'

'There now, Bill,' remonstrated Fagin, eagerly catching at the word. 'If it hadn't been for the girl! Who but poor ould Fagin was the means of your having such a handy girl about you?'

'He says true enough there!' said Nancy, coming hastily forward. 'Let him be; let him be.'

Nancy's appearance gave a new turn to the conversation; for the boys, receiving a sly wink from the wary old Jew, began to ply her with liquor: of which, however, she took very sparingly; while Fagin, assuming an unusual flow of spirits, gradually brought Mr. Sikes into a better temper, by affecting to regard his threats as a little pleasant banter; and, moreover, by laughing very heartily at one or two rough jokes, which, after repeated applications to the spirit-bottle, he condescended to make.

'It's all very well,' said Mr. Sikes; 'but I must have some blunt from you to-night.'

'I haven't a piece of coin about me,' replied the Jew.

'Then you've got lots at home,' retorted Sikes; 'and I must have some from there.'

'Lots!' cried Fagin, holding up is hands. 'I haven't so much as would—'

'I don't know how much you've got, and I dare say you hardly know yourself, as it would take a pretty long time to count it,' said Sikes; 'but I must have some to-night; and that's flat.'

'Well, well,' said Fagin, with a sigh, 'I'll send the Artful round presently.'

'You won't do nothing of the kind,' rejoined Mr. Sikes. 'The Artful's a deal too artful, and would forget to come, or lose his way, or get dodged by traps and so be perwented, or anything for an excuse, if you put him up to it. Nancy shall go to the ken and fetch it, to make all sure; and I'll lie down and have a snooze while she's gone.'

After a great deal of haggling and squabbling, Fagin beat down the amount of the required advance from five pounds to three pounds four and sixpence: protesting with many solemn asseverations that that would only leave him eighteen-pence to keep house with; Mr. Sikes sullenly remarking that if he couldn't get any more he must accompany him home; with the Dodger and Master Bates put the eatables in the cupboard. The Jew then, taking leave of his affectionate friend, returned homeward, attended by Nancy and the boys: Mr. Sikes, meanwhile, flinging himself on the bed, and composing himself to sleep away the time until the young lady's return.

In due course, they arrived at Fagin's abode, where they found Toby Crackit and Mr. Chitling intent upon their fifteenth game at cribbage, which it is scarcely necessary to say the latter gentleman lost, and with it, his fifteenth and last sixpence: much to the amusement of his young friends. Mr. Crackit, apparently somewhat ashamed at being found relaxing himself with a gentleman so much his inferior in station and mental endowments, yawned, and inquiring after Sikes, took up his hat to go.

'Has nobody been, Toby?' asked Fagin.

'Not a living leg,' answered Mr. Crackit, pulling up his collar; 'it's been as dull as swipes. You ought to stand something handsome, Fagin, to recompense me for keeping house so long. Damme, I'm as flat as a juryman; and should have gone to sleep, as fast as Newgate, if I hadn't had the good natur' to amuse this youngster. Horrid dull, I'm blessed if I an't!'

With these and other ejaculations of the same kind, Mr. Toby Crackit swept up his winnings, and crammed them into his waistcoat pocket with a haughty air, as though such small pieces of silver were wholly beneath the consideration of a man of his figure; this done, he swaggered out of the room, with so much elegance and gentility, that Mr. Chitling, bestowing numerous admiring glances on his legs and boots till they were out of sight, assured the company that he considered his acquaintance cheap at fifteen sixpences an interview, and that he didn't value his losses the snap of his little finger.

'Wot a rum chap you are, Tom!' said Master Bates, highly amused by this declaration.

'Not a bit of it,' replied Mr. Chitling. 'Am I, Fagin?'

'A very clever fellow, my dear,' said Fagin, patting him on the shoulder, and winking to his other pupils.

'And Mr. Crackit is a heavy swell; an't he, Fagin?' asked Tom.

'No doubt at all of that, my dear.'

'And it is a creditable thing to have his acquaintance; an't it, Fagin?' pursued Tom.

'Very much so, indeed, my dear. They're only jealous, Tom, because he won't give it to them.'

'Ah!' cried Tom, triumphantly, 'that's where it is! He has cleaned me out. But I can go and earn some more, when I like; can't I, Fagin?'

'To be sure you can, and the sooner you go the better, Tom; so make up your loss at once, and don't lose any more time. Dodger! Charley! It's time you were on the lay. Come! It's near ten, and nothing done yet.'

In obedience to this hint, the boys, nodding to Nancy, took up their hats, and left the room; the Dodger and his vivacious friend indulging, as they went, in many witticisms at the expense of Mr. Chitling; in whose conduct, it is but justice to say, there was nothing very conspicuous or peculiar: inasmuch as there are a great number of spirited young bloods upon town, who pay a much higher price than Mr. Chitling for being seen in good society: and a great number of fine gentlemen (composing the good society aforesaid) who established their reputation upon very much the same footing as flash Toby Crackit.

'Now,' said Fagin, when they had left the room, 'I'll go and get you that cash, Nancy. This is only the key of a little cupboard where I keep a few odd things the boys get, my dear. I never lock up my money, for I've got none to lock up, my dear—ha! ha! ha!—none to lock up. It's a poor trade, Nancy, and no thanks; but I'm fond of seeing the young people about me; and I bear it all, I bear it all. Hush!' he said, hastily concealing the key in his breast; 'who's that? Listen!'

The girl, who was sitting at the table with her arms folded, appeared in no way interested in the arrival: or to care whether the person, whoever he was, came or went: until the murmur of a man's voice reached her ears. The instant she caught the sound, she tore off her bonnet and shawl, with the rapidity of lightning, and thrust them under the table. The Jew, turning round immediately afterwards, she muttered a complaint of the heat: in a tone of languor that contrasted, very remarkably, with the extreme haste and violence of this action: which, however, had been unobserved by Fagin, who had his back towards her at the time.

'Bah!' he whispered, as though nettled by the interruption; 'it's the man I expected before; he's coming downstairs. Not a word about the money while he's here, Nance. He won't stop long. Not ten minutes, my dear.'

Laying his skinny forefinger upon his lip, the Jew carried a candle to the door, as a man's step was heard upon the stairs without. He reached it, at the same moment as the visitor, who, coming hastily into the room, was close upon the girl before he observed her.

It was Monks.

'Only one of my young people,' said Fagin, observing that Monks drew back, on beholding a stranger. 'Don't move, Nancy.'

The girl drew closer to the table, and glancing at Monks with an air of careless levity, withdrew her eyes; but as he turned towards Fagin, she stole another look; so keen and searching, and full of purpose, that if there had been any bystander to observe the change, he could hardly have believed the two looks to have proceeded from the same person.

'Any news?' inquired Fagin.

'Great.'

'And—and—good?' asked Fagin, hesitating as though he feared to vex the other man by being too sanguine.

'Not bad, any way,' replied Monks with a smile. 'I have been prompt enough this time. Let me have a word with you.'

The girl drew closer to the table, and made no offer to leave the room, although she could see that Monks was pointing to her. The Jew: perhaps fearing she might say something aloud about the money, if he endeavoured to get rid of her: pointed upward, and took Monks out of the room.

'Not that infernal hole we were in before,' she could hear the man say as they went upstairs. Fagin laughed; and making some reply which did not reach her, seemed, by the creaking of the boards, to lead his companion to the second story.

Before the sound of their footsteps had ceased to echo through the house, the girl had slipped off her shoes; and drawing her gown loosely over her head, and muffling her arms in it, stood at the door, listening with breathless interest. The moment the noise ceased, she glided from the room; ascended the stairs with incredible softness and silence; and was lost in the gloom above.

The room remained deserted for a quarter of an hour or more; the girl glided back with the same unearthly tread; and, immediately afterwards, the two men were heard descending. Monks went at once into the street; and the Jew crawled upstairs again for the money. When he returned, the girl was adjusting her shawl and bonnet, as if preparing to be gone.

'Why, Nance!' exclaimed the Jew, starting back as he put down the candle, 'how pale you are!'

'Pale!' echoed the girl, shading her eyes with her hands, as if to look steadily at him.

'Quite horrible. What have you been doing to yourself?'

'Nothing that I know of, except sitting in this close place for I don't know how long and all,' replied the girl carelessly. 'Come! Let me get back; that's a dear.'

With a sigh for every piece of money, Fagin told the amount into her hand. They parted without more conversation, merely interchanging a 'good-night.'

When the girl got into the open street, she sat down upon a doorstep; and seemed, for a few moments, wholly bewildered and unable to pursue her way. Suddenly she arose; and hurrying on, in a direction quite opposite to that in which Sikes was awaiting her returned, quickened her pace, until it gradually resolved into a violent run. After completely exhausting herself, she stopped to take breath: and, as if suddenly recollecting herself, and deploring her inability to do something she was bent upon, wrung her hands, and burst into tears.

It might be that her tears relieved her, or that she felt the full hopelessness of her condition; but she turned back; and hurrying with nearly as great rapidity in the contrary direction; partly to recover lost time, and partly to keep pace with the violent current of her own thoughts: soon reached the dwelling where she had left the housebreaker.

If she betrayed any agitation, when she presented herself to Mr. Sikes, he did not observe it; for merely inquiring if she had brought the money, and receiving a reply in the affirmative, he uttered a growl of satisfaction, and replacing his head upon the pillow, resumed the slumbers which her arrival had interrupted.

It was fortunate for her that the possession of money occasioned him so much employment next day in the way of eating and drinking; and withal had so beneficial an effect in smoothing down the asperities of his temper; that he had neither time nor inclination to be very critical upon her behaviour and deportment. That she had all the abstracted and nervous manner of one who is on the eve of some bold and hazardous step, which it has required no common struggle to resolve upon, would have been obvious to the lynx-eyed Fagin, who would most probably have taken the alarm at once; but Mr. Sikes lacking the niceties of discrimination, and being troubled with no more subtle misgivings than those which resolve themselves into a dogged roughness of behaviour towards everybody; and being, furthermore, in an unusually amiable condition, as has been already observed; saw nothing unusual in her demeanor, and indeed, troubled himself so little about her, that, had her agitation been far more perceptible than it was, it would have been very unlikely to have awakened his suspicions.

As that day closed in, the girl's excitement increased; and, when night came on, and she sat by, watching until the housebreaker should drink himself asleep, there was an unusual paleness in her cheek, and a fire in her eye, that even Sikes observed with astonishment.

Mr. Sikes being weak from the fever, was lying in bed, taking hot water with his gin to render it less inflammatory; and had pushed his glass towards Nancy to be replenished for the third or fourth time, when these symptoms first struck him.

'Why, burn my body!' said the man, raising himself on his hands as he stared the girl in the face. 'You look like a corpse come to life again. What's the matter?'

'Matter!' replied the girl. 'Nothing. What do you look at me so hard for?'

'What foolery is this?' demanded Sikes, grasping her by the arm, and shaking her roughly.

'What is it? What do you mean? What are you thinking of?'

'Of many things, Bill,' replied the girl, shivering, and as she did so, pressing her hands upon her eyes. 'But, Lord! What odds in that?'

The tone of forced gaiety in which the last words were spoken, seemed to produce a deeper impression on Sikes than the wild and rigid look which had preceded them.

'I tell you wot it is,' said Sikes; 'if you haven't caught the fever, and got it comin' on, now, there's something more than usual in the wind, and something dangerous too. You're not a-going to—. No, damme! you wouldn't do that!'

'Do what?' asked the girl.

'There ain't,' said Sikes, fixing his eyes upon her, and muttering the words to himself; 'there ain't a stauncher-hearted gal going, or I'd have cut her throat three months ago. She's got the fever coming on; that's it.'

Fortifying himself with this assurance, Sikes drained the glass to the bottom, and then, with many grumbling oaths, called for his physic. The girl jumped up, with great alacrity; poured it quickly out, but with her back towards him; and held the vessel to his lips, while he drank off the contents.

'Now,' said the robber, 'come and sit aside of me, and put on your own face; or I'll alter it so, that you won't know it agin when you do want it.'

The girl obeyed. Sikes, locking her hand in his, fell back upon the pillow: turning his eyes upon her face. They closed; opened again; closed once more; again opened. He shifted his position restlessly; and, after dozing again, and again, for two or three minutes, and as often springing up with a look of terror, and gazing vacantly about him, was suddenly stricken, as it were, while in the very attitude of rising, into a deep and heavy sleep. The grasp of his hand relaxed; the uplifted arm fell languidly by his side; and he lay like one in a profound trance.

'The laudanum has taken effect at last,' murmured the girl, as she rose from the bedside. 'I may be too late, even now.'

She hastily dressed herself in her bonnet and shawl: looking fearfully round, from time to time, as if, despite the sleeping draught, she expected every moment to feel the pressure of Sikes's heavy hand upon her shoulder; then, stooping softly over the bed, she kissed the robber's lips; and then opening and closing the room-door with noiseless touch, hurried from the house.

A watchman was crying half-past nine, down a dark passage through which she had to pass, in gaining the main thoroughfare.

'Has it long gone the half-hour?' asked the girl.

'It'll strike the hour in another quarter,' said the man: raising his lantern to her face.

'And I cannot get there in less than an hour or more,' muttered Nancy: brushing swiftly past him, and gliding rapidly down the street.

Many of the shops were already closing in the back lanes and avenues through which she tracked her way, in making from Spitalfields towards the West-End of London. The clock struck ten, increasing her impatience. She tore along the narrow pavement: elbowing the passengers from side to side; and darting almost under the horses' heads, crossed crowded streets, where clusters of persons were eagerly watching their opportunity to do the like.

'The woman is mad!' said the people, turning to look after her as she rushed away.

When she reached the more wealthy quarter of the town, the streets were comparatively deserted; and here her headlong progress excited a still greater curiosity in the stragglers whom she hurried past. Some quickened their pace behind, as though to see whither she was hastening at such an unusual rate; and a few made head upon her, and looked back, surprised at her undiminished speed; but they fell off one by one; and when she neared her place of destination, she was alone.

It was a family hotel in a quiet but handsome street near Hyde Park. As the brilliant light of the lamp which burnt before its door, guided her to the spot, the clock struck eleven. She had loitered for a few paces as though irresolute, and making up her mind to advance; but the sound determined her, and she stepped into the hall. The porter's seat was vacant. She looked round with an air of incertitude, and advanced towards the stairs.

'Now, young woman!' said a smartly-dressed female, looking out from a door behind her, 'who do you want here?'

'A lady who is stopping in this house,' answered the girl.

'A lady!' was the reply, accompanied with a scornful look. 'What lady?'

'Miss Maylie,' said Nancy.

The young woman, who had by this time, noted her appearance, replied only by a look of virtuous disdain; and summoned a man to answer her. To him, Nancy repeated her request.

'What name am I to say?' asked the waiter.

'It's of no use saying any,' replied Nancy.

'Nor business?' said the man.

'No, nor that neither,' rejoined the girl. 'I must see the lady.'

'Come!' said the man, pushing her towards the door. 'None of this. Take yourself off.'

'I shall be carried out if I go!' said the girl violently; 'and I can make that a job that two of you won't like to do. Isn't there anybody here,' she said, looking round, 'that will see a simple message carried for a poor wretch like me?'

This appeal produced an effect on a good-tempered-faced man-cook, who with some of the other servants was looking on, and who stepped forward to interfere.

'Take it up for her, Joe; can't you?' said this person.

'What's the good?' replied the man. 'You don't suppose the young lady will see such as her; do you?'

This allusion to Nancy's doubtful character, raised a vast quantity of chaste wrath in the bosoms of four housemaids, who remarked, with great fervour, that the creature was a disgrace to her sex; and strongly advocated her being thrown, ruthlessly, into the kennel.

'Do what you like with me,' said the girl, turning to the men again; 'but do what I ask you first, and I ask you to give this message for God Almighty's sake.'

The soft-hearted cook added his intercession, and the result was that the man who had first appeared undertook its delivery.

'What's it to be?' said the man, with one foot on the stairs.

'That a young woman earnestly asks to speak to Miss Maylie alone,' said Nancy; 'and that if the lady will only hear the first word she has to say, she will know whether to hear her business, or to have her turned out of doors as an impostor.'

'I say,' said the man, 'you're coming it strong!'

'You give the message,' said the girl firmly; 'and let me hear the answer.'

The man ran upstairs. Nancy remained, pale and almost breathless, listening with quivering lip to the very audible expressions of scorn, of which the chaste housemaids were very prolific; and of which they became still more so, when the man returned, and said the young woman was to walk upstairs.

'It's no good being proper in this world,' said the first housemaid.

'Brass can do better than the gold what has stood the fire,' said the second.

The third contented herself with wondering 'what ladies was made of'; and the fourth took the first in a quartette of 'Shameful!' with which the Dianas concluded.

Regardless of all this: for she had weightier matters at heart: Nancy followed the man, with trembling limbs, to a small ante-chamber, lighted by a lamp from the ceiling. Here he left her, and retired.

CHAPTER XL. A STRANGE INTERVIEW, WHICH IS A SEQUEL TO THE LAST CHAMBER

The girl's life had been squandered in the streets, and among the most noisome of the stews and dens of London, but there was something of the woman's original nature left in her still; and when she heard a light step approaching the door opposite to that by which she had entered, and thought of the wide contrast which the small room would in another moment contain, she felt burdened with the sense of her own deep shame, and shrunk as though she could scarcely bear the presence of her with whom she had sought this interview.

But struggling with these better feelings was pride,—the vice of the lowest and most debased creatures no less than of the high and self-assured. The miserable companion of thieves and ruffians, the fallen outcast of low haunts, the associate of the scourings of the jails and hulks, living within the shadow of the gallows itself,—even this degraded being felt too proud to betray a feeble gleam of the womanly feeling which she thought a weakness, but which alone connected her with that humanity, of which her wasting life had obliterated so many, many traces when a very child.

She raised her eyes sufficiently to observe that the figure which presented itself was that of a slight and beautiful girl; then, bending them on the ground, she tossed her head with affected carelessness as she said:

'It's a hard matter to get to see you, lady. If I had taken offence, and gone away, as many would have done, you'd have been sorry for it one day, and not without reason either.'

'I am very sorry if any one has behaved harshly to you,' replied Rose. 'Do not think of that. Tell me why you wished to see me. I am the person you inquired for.'

The kind tone of this answer, the sweet voice, the gentle manner, the absence of any accent of haughtiness or displeasure, took the girl completely by surprise, and she burst into tears.

'Oh, lady, lady!' she said, clasping her hands passionately before her face, 'if there was more like you, there would be fewer like me,—there would—there would!'

'Sit down,' said Rose, earnestly. 'If you are in poverty or affliction I shall be truly glad to relieve you if I can,—I shall indeed. Sit down.'

'Let me stand, lady,' said the girl, still weeping, 'and do not speak to me so kindly till you know me better. It is growing late. Is—is—that door shut?'

'Yes,' said Rose, recoiling a few steps, as if to be nearer assistance in case she should require it. 'Why?'

'Because,' said the girl, 'I am about to put my life and the lives of others in your hands. I am the girl that dragged little Oliver back to old Fagin's on the night he went out from the house in Pentonville.'

'You!' said Rose Maylie.

'I, lady!' replied the girl. 'I am the infamous creature you have heard of, that lives among the thieves, and that never from the first moment I can recollect my eyes and senses opening on London streets have known any better life, or kinder words than they have given me, so help me God! Do not mind shrinking openly from me, lady. I am younger than you would think, to look at me, but I am well used to it. The poorest women fall back, as I make my way along the crowded pavement.'

'What dreadful things are these!' said Rose, involuntarily falling from her strange companion.

'Thank Heaven upon your knees, dear lady,' cried the girl, 'that you had friends to care for and keep you in your childhood, and that you were never in the midst of cold and hunger, and riot and drunkenness, and—and—something worse than all—as I have been from my cradle. I may use the word, for the alley and the gutter were mine, as they will be my deathbed.'

'I pity you!' said Rose, in a broken voice. 'It wrings my heart to hear you!'

'Heaven bless you for your goodness!' rejoined the girl. 'If you knew what I am sometimes, you would pity me, indeed. But I have stolen away from those who would surely murder me, if they knew I had been here, to tell you what I have overheard. Do you know a man named Monks?'

'No,' said Rose.

'He knows you,' replied the girl; 'and knew you were here, for it was by hearing him tell the place that I found you out.'

'I never heard the name,' said Rose.

'Then he goes by some other amongst us,' rejoined the girl, 'which I more than thought before. Some time ago, and soon after Oliver was put into your house on the night of the robbery, I—suspecting this man—listened to a conversation held between him and Fagin in the dark. I found out, from what I heard, that Monks—the man I asked you about, you know—'

'Yes,' said Rose, 'I understand.'

'—That Monks,' pursued the girl, 'had seen him accidently with two of our boys on the day we first lost him, and had known him directly to be the same child that he was watching for, though I couldn't make out why. A bargain was struck with Fagin, that if Oliver was got back he should have a certain sum; and he was to have more for making him a thief, which this Monks wanted for some purpose of his own.'

'For what purpose?' asked Rose.

'He caught sight of my shadow on the wall as I listened, in the hope of finding out,' said the girl; 'and there are not many people besides me that could have got out of their way in time to escape discovery. But I did; and I saw him no more till last night.'

'And what occurred then?'

'I'll tell you, lady. Last night he came again. Again they went upstairs, and I, wrapping myself up so that my shadow would not betray me, again listened at the door. The first words I heard Monks say were these: "So the only proofs of the boy's identity lie at the bottom of the river, and the old hag that received them from the mother is rotting in her coffin." They laughed, and talked of his success in doing this; and Monks, talking on about the boy, and getting very wild, said that though he had got the young devil's money safely now, he'd rather have had it the other way; for, what a game it would have been to have brought down the boast of the father's will, by driving him through every jail in town, and then hauling him up for some capital felony which Fagin could easily manage, after having made a good profit of him besides.'

'What is all this!' said Rose.

'The truth, lady, though it comes from my lips,' replied the girl. 'Then, he said, with oaths common enough in my ears, but strange to yours, that if he could gratify his hatred by taking the boy's life without bringing his own neck in danger, he would; but, as he couldn't, he'd be upon the watch to meet him at every turn in life; and if he took advantage of his birth and history, he might harm him yet. "In short, Fagin," he says, "Jew as you are, you never laid such snares as I'll contrive for my young brother, Oliver."'

'His brother!' exclaimed Rose.

'Those were his words,' said Nancy, glancing uneasily round, as she had scarcely ceased to do, since she began to speak, for a vision of Sikes haunted her perpetually. 'And more. When he spoke of you and the other lady, and said it seemed contrived by Heaven, or the devil, against him, that Oliver should come into your hands, he laughed, and said there was some comfort in that too, for how many thousands and hundreds of thousands of pounds would you not give, if you had them, to know who your two-legged spaniel was.'

'You do not mean,' said Rose, turning very pale, 'to tell me that this was said in earnest?'

'He spoke in hard and angry earnest, if a man ever did,' replied the girl, shaking her head. 'He is an earnest man when his hatred is up. I know many who do worse things; but I'd rather listen to them all a dozen times, than to that Monks once. It is growing late, and I have to reach home without suspicion of having been on such an errand as this. I must get back quickly.'

'But what can I do?' said Rose. 'To what use can I turn this communication without you? Back! Why do you wish to return to companions you paint in such terrible colors? If you repeat this information to a gentleman whom I can summon in an instant from the next room, you can be consigned to some place of safety without half an hour's delay.'

'I wish to go back,' said the girl. 'I must go back, because—how can I tell such things to an innocent lady like you?—because among the men I have told you of, there is one: the most desperate among them all; that I can't leave: no, not even to be saved from the life I am leading now.'

'Your having interfered in this dear boy's behalf before,' said Rose; 'your coming here, at so great a risk, to tell me what you have heard; your manner, which convinces me of the truth of what you say; your evident contrition, and sense of shame; all lead me to believe that you might yet be reclaimed. Oh!' said the earnest girl, folding her hands as the tears coursed down her face, 'do not turn a deaf ear to the entreaties of one of your own sex; the first—the first, I do believe, who ever appealed to you in the voice of pity and compassion. Do hear my words, and let me save you yet, for better things.'

'Lady,' cried the girl, sinking on her knees, 'dear, sweet, angel lady, you are the first that ever blessed me with such words as these, and if I had heard them years ago, they might have turned me from a life of sin and sorrow; but it is too late, it is too late!'

'It is never too late,' said Rose, 'for penitence and atonement.'

'It is,' cried the girl, writhing in agony of her mind; 'I cannot leave him now! I could not be his death.'

'Why should you be?' asked Rose.

'Nothing could save him,' cried the girl. 'If I told others what I have told you, and led to their being taken, he would be sure to die. He is the boldest, and has been so cruel!'

'Is it possible,' cried Rose, 'that for such a man as this, you can resign every future hope, and the certainty of immediate rescue? It is madness.'

'I don't know what it is,' answered the girl; 'I only know that it is so, and not with me alone, but with hundreds of others as bad and wretched as myself. I must go back. Whether it is God's wrath for the wrong I have done, I do not know; but I am drawn back to him through every suffering and ill usage; and I should be, I believe, if I knew that I was to die by his hand at last.'

'What am I to do?' said Rose. 'I should not let you depart from me thus.'

'You should, lady, and I know you will,' rejoined the girl, rising. 'You will not stop my going because I have trusted in your goodness, and forced no promise from you, as I might have done.'

'Of what use, then, is the communication you have made?' said Rose. 'This mystery must be investigated, or how will its disclosure to me, benefit Oliver, whom you are anxious to serve?'

'You must have some kind gentleman about you that will hear it as a secret, and advise you what to do,' rejoined the girl.

'But where can I find you again when it is necessary?' asked Rose. 'I do not seek to know where these dreadful people live, but where will you be walking or passing at any settled period from this time?'

'Will you promise me that you will have my secret strictly kept, and come alone, or with the only other person that knows it; and that I shall not be watched or followed?' asked the girl.

'I promise you solemnly,' answered Rose.

'Every Sunday night, from eleven until the clock strikes twelve,' said the girl without hesitation, 'I will walk on London Bridge if I am alive.'

'Stay another moment,' interposed Rose, as the girl moved hurriedly towards the door. 'Think once again on your own condition, and the opportunity you have of escaping from it. You have a claim on me: not only as the voluntary bearer of this intelligence, but as a woman lost almost beyond redemption. Will you return to this gang of robbers, and to this man, when a word can save you? What fascination is it that can take you back, and make you cling to wickedness and misery? Oh! is there no chord in your heart that I can touch! Is there nothing left, to which I can appeal against this terrible infatuation!'

'When ladies as young, and good, and beautiful as you are,' replied the girl steadily, 'give away your hearts, love will carry you all lengths—even such as you, who have home, friends, other admirers, everything, to fill them. When such as I, who have no certain roof but the coffinlid, and no friend in sickness or death but the hospital nurse, set our rotten hearts on any man, and let him fill the place that has been a blank through all our wretched lives, who can hope to cure us? Pity us, lady—pity us for having only one feeling of the woman left, and for having that turned, by a heavy judgment, from a comfort and a pride, into a new means of violence and suffering.'

'You will,' said Rose, after a pause, 'take some money from me, which may enable you to live without dishonesty—at all events until we meet again?'

'Not a penny,' replied the girl, waving her hand.

'Do not close your heart against all my efforts to help you,' said Rose, stepping gently forward. 'I wish to serve you indeed.'

'You would serve me best, lady,' replied the girl, wringing her hands, 'if you could take my life at once; for I have felt more grief to think of what I am, to-night, than I ever did before, and it would be something not to die in the hell in which I have lived. God bless you, sweet lady, and send as much happiness on your head as I have brought shame on mine!'

Thus speaking, and sobbing aloud, the unhappy creature turned away; while Rose Maylie, overpowered by this extraordinary interview, which had more the semblance of a rapid dream than an actual occurrence, sank into a chair, and endeavoured to collect her wandering thoughts.

CHAPTER XLI. CONTAINING FRESH DISCOVERIES, AND SHOWING THAT SUPRISES, LIKE MISFORTUNES, SELDOM COME ALONE

Her situation was, indeed, one of no common trial and difficulty. While she felt the most eager and burning desire to penetrate the mystery in which Oliver's history was enveloped, she could not but hold sacred the confidence which the miserable woman with whom she had just conversed, had reposed in her, as a young and guileless girl. Her words and manner had touched Rose Maylie's heart; and, mingled with her love for her young charge, and scarcely less intense in its truth and fervour, was her fond wish to win the outcast back to repentance and hope.

They purposed remaining in London only three days, prior to departing for some weeks to a distant part of the coast. It was now midnight of the first day. What course of action could she determine upon, which could be adopted in eight-and-forty hours? Or how could she postpone the journey without exciting suspicion?

Mr. Losberne was with them, and would be for the next two days; but Rose was too well acquainted with the excellent gentleman's impetuosity, and foresaw too clearly the wrath with which, in the first explosion of his indignation, he would regard the instrument of Oliver's recapture, to trust him with the secret, when her representations in the girl's behalf could be seconded by no experienced person. These were all reasons for the greatest caution and most circumspect behaviour in communicating it to Mrs. Maylie, whose first impulse would infallibly be to hold a conference with the worthy doctor on the subject. As to resorting to any legal adviser, even if she had known how to do so, it was scarcely to be thought of, for the same reason. Once the thought occurred to her of seeking assistance from Harry; but this awakened the recollection of their last parting, and it seemed unworthy of her to call him back, when— the tears rose to her eyes as she pursued this train of reflection—he might have by this time learnt to forget her, and to be happier away.

Disturbed by these different reflections; inclining now to one course and then to another, and again recoiling from all, as each successive consideration presented itself to her mind; Rose passed a sleepless and anxious night. After more communing with herself next day, she arrived at the desperate conclusion of consulting Harry.

'If it be painful to him,' she thought, 'to come back here, how painful it will be to me! But perhaps he will not come; he may write, or he may come himself, and studiously abstain from meeting me—he did when he went away. I hardly thought he would; but it was better for us both.' And here Rose dropped the pen, and turned away, as though the very paper which was to be her messenger should not see her weep.

She had taken up the same pen, and laid it down again fifty times, and had considered and reconsidered the first line of her letter without writing the first word, when Oliver, who had been walking in the streets, with Mr. Giles for a body-guard, entered the room in such breathless haste and violent agitation, as seemed to betoken some new cause of alarm.

'What makes you look so flurried?' asked Rose, advancing to meet him.

'I hardly know how; I feel as if I should be choked,' replied the boy. 'Oh dear! To think that I should see him at last, and you should be able to know that I have told you the truth!'

'I never thought you had told us anything but the truth,' said Rose, soothing him. 'But what is this?—of whom do you speak?'

'I have seen the gentleman,' replied Oliver, scarcely able to articulate, 'the gentleman who was so good to me—Mr. Brownlow, that we have so often talked about.'

'Where?' asked Rose.

'Getting out of a coach,' replied Oliver, shedding tears of delight, 'and going into a house. I didn't speak to him—I couldn't speak to him, for he didn't see me, and I trembled so, that I was not able to go up to him. But Giles asked, for me, whether he lived there, and they said he did. Look here,' said Oliver, opening a scrap of paper, 'here it is; here's where he lives—I'm going there directly! Oh, dear me, dear me! What shall I do when I come to see him and hear him speak again!'

With her attention not a little distracted by these and a great many other incoherent exclamations of joy, Rose read the address, which was Craven Street, in the Strand. She very soon determined upon turning the discovery to account.

'Quick!' she said. 'Tell them to fetch a hackney-coach, and be ready to go with me. I will take you there directly, without a minute's loss of time. I will only tell my aunt that we are going out for an hour, and be ready as soon as you are.'

Oliver needed no prompting to despatch, and in little more than five minutes they were on their way to Craven Street. When they arrived there, Rose left Oliver in the coach, under pretence of preparing the old gentleman to receive him; and sending up her card by the servant, requested to see Mr. Brownlow on very pressing business. The servant soon returned, to beg that she would walk upstairs; and following him into an upper room, Miss Maylie was presented to an elderly gentleman of benevolent appearance, in a bottle-green coat. At no great distance from whom, was seated another old gentleman, in nankeen breeches and gaiters; who did not look particularly benevolent, and who was sitting with his hands clasped on the top of a thick stick, and his chin propped thereupon.

'Dear me,' said the gentleman, in the bottle-green coat, hastily rising with great politeness, 'I beg your pardon, young lady—I imagined it was some importunate person who—I beg you will excuse me. Be seated, pray.'

'Mr. Brownlow, I believe, sir?' said Rose, glancing from the other gentleman to the one who had spoken.

'That is my name,' said the old gentleman. 'This is my friend, Mr. Grimwig. Grimwig, will you leave us for a few minutes?'

'I believe,' interposed Miss Maylie, 'that at this period of our interview, I need not give that gentleman the trouble of going away. If I am correctly informed, he is cognizant of the business on which I wish to speak to you.'

Mr. Brownlow inclined his head. Mr. Grimwig, who had made one very stiff bow, and risen from his chair, made another very stiff bow, and dropped into it again.

'I shall surprise you very much, I have no doubt,' said Rose, naturally embarrassed; 'but you once showed great benevolence and goodness to a very dear young friend of mine, and I am sure you will take an interest in hearing of him again.'

'Indeed!' said Mr. Brownlow.

'Oliver Twist you knew him as,' replied Rose.

The words no sooner escaped her lips, than Mr. Grimwig, who had been affecting to dip into a large book that lay on the table, upset it with a great crash, and falling back in his chair, discharged from his features every expression but one of unmitigated wonder, and indulged in a prolonged and vacant stare; then, as if ashamed of having betrayed so much emotion, he jerked himself, as it were, by a convulsion into his former attitude, and looking out straight before him emitted a long deep whistle, which seemed, at last, not to be discharged on empty air, but to die away in the innermost recesses of his stomach.

Mr. Browlow was no less surprised, although his astonishment was not expressed in the same eccentric manner. He drew his chair nearer to Miss Maylie's, and said,

'Do me the favour, my dear young lady, to leave entirely out of the question that goodness and benevolence of which you speak, and of which nobody else knows anything; and if you have it in your power to produce any evidence which will alter the unfavourable opinion I was once induced to entertain of that poor child, in Heaven's name put me in possession of it.'

'A bad one! I'll eat my head if he is not a bad one,' growled Mr. Grimwig, speaking by some ventriloquial power, without moving a muscle of his face.

'He is a child of a noble nature and a warm heart,' said Rose, colouring; 'and that Power which has thought fit to try him beyond his years, has planted in his breast affections and feelings which would do honour to many who have numbered his days six times over.'

'I'm only sixty-one,' said Mr. Grimwig, with the same rigid face. 'And, as the devil's in it if this Oliver is not twelve years old at least, I don't see the application of that remark.'

'Do not heed my friend, Miss Maylie,' said Mr. Brownlow; 'he does not mean what he says.'

'Yes, he does,' growled Mr. Grimwig.

'No, he does not,' said Mr. Brownlow, obviously rising in wrath as he spoke.

'He'll eat his head, if he doesn't,' growled Mr. Grimwig.

'He would deserve to have it knocked off, if he does,' said Mr. Brownlow.

'And he'd uncommonly like to see any man offer to do it,' responded Mr. Grimwig, knocking his stick upon the floor.

Having gone thus far, the two old gentlemen severally took snuff, and afterwards shook hands, according to their invariable custom.

'Now, Miss Maylie,' said Mr. Brownlow, 'to return to the subject in which your humanity is so much interested. Will you let me know what intelligence you have of this poor child: allowing me to promise that I exhausted every means in my power of discovering him, and that since I have been absent from this country, my first impression that he had imposed upon me, and had been persuaded by his former associates to rob me, has been considerably shaken.'

Rose, who had had time to collect her thoughts, at once related, in a few natural words, all that had befallen Oliver since he left Mr. Brownlow's house; reserving Nancy's information for that gentleman's private ear, and concluding with the assurance that his only sorrow, for some months past, had been not being able to meet with his former benefactor and friend.

'Thank God!' said the old gentleman. 'This is great happiness to me, great happiness. But you have not told me where he is now, Miss Maylie. You must pardon my finding fault with you,—but why not have brought him?'

'He is waiting in a coach at the door,' replied Rose.

'At this door!' cried the old gentleman. With which he hurried out of the room, down the stairs, up the coachsteps, and into the coach, without another word.

When the room-door closed behind him, Mr. Grimwig lifted up his head, and converting one of the hind legs of his chair into a pivot, described three distinct circles with the assistance of his stick and the table; sitting in it all the time. After performing this evolution, he rose and limped as fast as he could up and down the room at least a dozen times, and then stopping suddenly before Rose, kissed her without the slightest preface.

'Hush!' he said, as the young lady rose in some alarm at this unusual proceeding. 'Don't be afraid. I'm old enough to be your grandfather. You're a sweet girl. I like you. Here they are!'

In fact, as he threw himself at one dexterous dive into his former seat, Mr. Brownlow returned, accompanied by Oliver, whom Mr. Grimwig received very graciously; and if the gratification of that moment had been the only reward for all her anxiety and care in Oliver's behalf, Rose Maylie would have been well repaid.

'There is somebody else who should not be forgotten, by the bye,' said Mr. Brownlow, ringing the bell. 'Send Mrs. Bedwin here, if you please.'

The old housekeeper answered the summons with all dispatch; and dropping a curtsey at the door, waited for orders.

'Why, you get blinder every day, Bedwin,' said Mr. Brownlow, rather testily.

'Well, that I do, sir,' replied the old lady. 'People's eyes, at my time of life, don't improve with age, sir.'

'I could have told you that,' rejoined Mr. Brownlow; 'but put on your glasses, and see if you can't find out what you were wanted for, will you?'

The old lady began to rummage in her pocket for her spectacles. But Oliver's patience was not proof against this new trial; and yielding to his first impulse, he sprang into her arms.

'God be good to me!' cried the old lady, embracing him; 'it is my innocent boy!'

'My dear old nurse!' cried Oliver.

'He would come back—I knew he would,' said the old lady, holding him in her arms. 'How well he looks, and how like a gentleman's son he is dressed again! Where have you been, this long, long while? Ah! the same sweet face, but not so pale; the same soft eye, but not so sad. I have never forgotten them or his quiet smile, but have seen them every day, side by side with those of my own dear children, dead and gone since I was a lightsome young creature.' Running on thus, and now holding Oliver from her to mark how he had grown, now clasping him to her and passing her fingers fondly through his hair, the good soul laughed and wept upon his neck by turns.

Leaving her and Oliver to compare notes at leisure, Mr. Brownlow led the way into another room; and there, heard from Rose a full narration of her interview with Nancy, which occasioned him no little surprise and perplexity. Rose also explained her reasons for not confiding in her friend Mr. Losberne in the first instance. The old gentleman considered that she had acted prudently, and readily undertook to hold solemn conference with the worthy doctor himself. To afford him an early opportunity for the execution of this design, it was arranged that he should call at the hotel at eight o'clock that evening, and that in the meantime Mrs. Maylie should be cautiously informed of all that had occurred. These preliminaries adjusted, Rose and Oliver returned home.

Rose had by no means overrated the measure of the good doctor's wrath. Nancy's history was no sooner unfolded to him, than he poured forth a shower of mingled threats and execrations; threatened to make her the first victim of the combined ingenuity of Messrs. Blathers and Duff; and actually put on his hat preparatory to sallying forth to obtain the assistance of those worthies. And, doubtless, he would, in this first outbreak, have carried the intention into effect without a moment's consideration of the consequences, if he had not been restrained, in part, by corresponding violence on the side of Mr. Brownlow, who was himself of an irascible temperament, and party by such arguments and representations as seemed best calculated to dissuade him from his hotbrained purpose.

'Then what the devil is to be done?' said the impetuous doctor, when they had rejoined the two ladies. 'Are we to pass a vote of thanks to all these vagabonds, male and female, and beg them to accept a hundred pounds, or so, apiece, as a trifling mark of our esteem, and some slight acknowledgment of their kindness to Oliver?'

'Not exactly that,' rejoined Mr. Brownlow, laughing; 'but we must proceed gently and with great care.'

'Gentleness and care,' exclaimed the doctor. 'I'd send them one and all to—'

'Never mind where,' interposed Mr. Brownlow. 'But reflect whether sending them anywhere is likely to attain the object we have in view.'

'What object?' asked the doctor.

'Simply, the discovery of Oliver's parentage, and regaining for him the inheritance of which, if this story be true, he has been fraudulently deprived.'

'Ah!' said Mr. Losberne, cooling himself with his pocket-handkerchief; 'I almost forgot that.'

'You see,' pursued Mr. Brownlow; 'placing this poor girl entirely out of the question, and supposing it were possible to bring these scoundrels to justice without compromising her safety, what good should we bring about?'

'Hanging a few of them at least, in all probability,' suggested the doctor, 'and transporting the rest.'

'Very good,' replied Mr. Brownlow, smiling; 'but no doubt they will bring that about for themselves in the fulness of time, and if we step in to forestall them, it seems to me that we shall be performing a very Quixotic act, in direct opposition to our own interest—or at least to Oliver's, which is the same thing.'

'How?' inquired the doctor.

'Thus. It is quite clear that we shall have extreme difficulty in getting to the bottom of this mystery, unless we can bring this man, Monks, upon his knees. That can only be done by stratagem, and by catching him when he is not surrounded by these people. For, suppose he were apprehended, we have no proof against him. He is not even (so far as we know, or as the facts appear to us) concerned with the gang in any of their robberies. If he were not discharged, it is very unlikely that he could receive any further punishment than being committed to prison as a rogue and vagabond; and of course ever afterwards his mouth would be so obstinately closed that he might as well, for our purposes, be deaf, dumb, blind, and an idiot.'

'Then,' said the doctor impetuously, 'I put it to you again, whether you think it reasonable that this promise to the girl should be considered binding; a promise made with the best and kindest intentions, but really—'

'Do not discuss the point, my dear young lady, pray,' said Mr. Brownlow, interrupting Rose as she was about to speak. 'The promise shall be kept. I don't think it will, in the slightest degree, interfere with our proceedings. But, before we can resolve upon any precise course of action, it will be necessary to see the girl; to ascertain from her whether she will point out this Monks, on the understanding that he is to be dealt with by us, and not by the law; or, if she will not, or cannot do that, to procure from her such an account of his haunts and description of his person, as will enable us to identify him. She cannot be seen until next Sunday night; this is Tuesday. I would suggest that in the meantime, we remain perfectly quiet, and keep these matters secret even from Oliver himself.'

Although Mr. Losberne received with many wry faces a proposal involving a delay of five whole days, he was fain to admit that no better course occurred to him just then; and as both Rose and Mrs. Maylie sided very strongly with Mr. Brownlow, that gentleman's proposition was carried unanimously.

'I should like,' he said, 'to call in the aid of my friend Grimwig. He is a strange creature, but a shrewd one, and might prove of material assistance to us; I should say that he was bred a lawyer, and quitted the Bar in disgust because he had only one brief and a motion of course, in twenty years, though whether that is recommendation or not, you must determine for yourselves.'

'I have no objection to your calling in your friend if I may call in mine,' said the doctor.

'We must put it to the vote,' replied Mr. Brownlow, 'who may he be?'

'That lady's son, and this young lady's—very old friend,' said the doctor, motioning towards Mrs. Maylie, and concluding with an expressive glance at her niece.

Rose blushed deeply, but she did not make any audible objection to this motion (possibly she felt in a hopeless minority); and Harry Maylie and Mr. Grimwig were accordingly added to the committee.

'We stay in town, of course,' said Mrs. Maylie, 'while there remains the slightest prospect of prosecuting this inquiry with a chance of success. I will spare neither trouble nor expense in behalf of the object in which we are all so deeply interested, and I am content to remain here, if it be for twelve months, so long as you assure me that any hope remains.'

'Good!' rejoined Mr. Brownlow. 'And as I see on the faces about me, a disposition to inquire how it happened that I was not in the way to corroborate Oliver's tale, and had so suddenly left the kingdom, let me stipulate that I shall be asked no questions until such time as I may deem it expedient to forestall them by telling my own story. Believe me, I make this request with good reason, for I might otherwise excite hopes destined never to be realised, and only increase difficulties and disappointments already quite numerous enough. Come! Supper has been announced, and young Oliver, who is all alone in the next room, will have begun to think, by this time, that we have wearied of his company, and entered into some dark conspiracy to thrust him forth upon the world.'

With these words, the old gentleman gave his hand to Mrs. Maylie, and escorted her into the supper-room. Mr. Losberne followed, leading Rose; and the council was, for the present, effectually broken up.

CHAPTER XLII. AN OLD ACQUAINTANCE OF OLIVER'S, EXHIBITING DECIDED MARKS OF GENIUS, BECOMES A PUBLIC CHARACTER IN THE METROPOLIS

Upon the night when Nancy, having lulled Mr. Sikes to sleep, hurried on her self-imposed mission to Rose Maylie, there advanced towards London, by the Great North Road, two persons, upon whom it is expedient that this history should bestow some attention.

They were a man and woman; or perhaps they would be better described as a male and female: for the former was one of those long-limbed, knock-kneed, shambling, bony people, to whom it is difficult to assign any precise age,—looking as they do, when they are yet boys, like undergrown men, and when they are almost men, like overgrown boys. The woman was young, but of a robust and hardy make, as she need have been to bear the weight of the heavy bundle which was strapped to her back. Her companion was not encumbered with much luggage, as there merely dangled from a stick which he carried over his shoulder, a small parcel wrapped in a common handkerchief, and apparently light enough. This circumstance, added to the length of his legs, which were of unusual extent, enabled him with much ease to keep some half-dozen paces in advance of his companion, to whom he occasionally turned with an impatient jerk of the head: as if reproaching her tardiness, and urging her to greater exertion.

Thus, they had toiled along the dusty road, taking little heed of any object within sight, save when they stepped aside to allow a wider passage for the mail-coaches which were whirling out of town, until they passed through Highgate archway; when the foremost traveller stopped and called impatiently to his companion,

'Come on, can't yer? What a lazybones yer are, Charlotte.'

'It's a heavy load, I can tell you,' said the female, coming up, almost breathless with fatigue.

'Heavy! What are yer talking about? What are yer made for?' rejoined the male traveller, changing his own little bundle as he spoke, to the other shoulder. 'Oh, there yer are, resting again! Well, if yer ain't enough to tire anybody's patience out, I don't know what is!'

'Is it much farther?' asked the woman, resting herself against a bank, and looking up with the perspiration streaming from her face.

'Much farther! Yer as good as there,' said the long-legged tramper, pointing out before him. 'Look there! Those are the lights of London.'

'They're a good two mile off, at least,' said the woman despondingly.

'Never mind whether they're two mile off, or twenty,' said Noah Claypole; for he it was; 'but get up and come on, or I'll kick yer, and so I give yer notice.'

As Noah's red nose grew redder with anger, and as he crossed the road while speaking, as if fully prepared to put his threat into execution, the woman rose without any further remark, and trudged onward by his side.

'Where do you mean to stop for the night, Noah?' she asked, after they had walked a few hundred yards.

'How should I know?' replied Noah, whose temper had been considerably impaired by walking.

'Near, I hope,' said Charlotte.

'No, not near,' replied Mr. Claypole. 'There! Not near; so don't think it.'

'Why not?'

'When I tell yer that I don't mean to do a thing, that's enough, without any why or because either,' replied Mr. Claypole with dignity.

'Well, you needn't be so cross,' said his companion.

'A pretty thing it would be, wouldn't it to go and stop at the very first public-house outside the town, so that Sowerberry, if he come up after us, might poke in his old nose, and have us taken back in a cart with handcuffs on,' said Mr. Claypole in a jeering tone. 'No! I shall go and lose myself among the narrowest streets I can find, and not stop till we come to the very out-of-the-wayest house I can set eyes on. 'Cod, yer may thanks yer stars I've got a head; for if we hadn't gone, at first, the wrong road a purpose, and come back across country, yer'd have been locked up hard and fast a week ago, my lady. And serve yer right for being a fool.'

'I know I ain't as cunning as you are,' replied Charlotte; 'but don't put all the blame on me, and say I should have been locked up. You would have been if I had been, any way.'

'Yer took the money from the till, yer know yer did,' said Mr. Claypole.

'I took it for you, Noah, dear,' rejoined Charlotte.

'Did I keep it?' asked Mr. Claypole.

'No; you trusted in me, and let me carry it like a dear, and so you are,' said the lady, chucking him under the chin, and drawing her arm through his.

This was indeed the case; but as it was not Mr. Claypole's habit to repose a blind and foolish confidence in anybody, it should be observed, in justice to that gentleman, that he had trusted Charlotte to this extent, in order that, if they were pursued, the money might be found on her: which would leave him an opportunity of asserting his innocence of any theft, and would greatly facilitate his chances of escape. Of course, he entered at this juncture, into no explanation of his motives, and they walked on very lovingly together.

In pursuance of this cautious plan, Mr. Claypole went on, without halting, until he arrived at the Angel at Islington, where he wisely judged, from the crowd of passengers and numbers of vehicles, that London began in earnest. Just pausing to observe which appeared the most crowded streets, and consequently the most to be avoided, he crossed into Saint John's Road, and was soon deep in the obscurity of the intricate and dirty ways, which, lying between Gray's Inn Lane and Smithfield, render that part of the town one of the lowest and worst that improvement has left in the midst of London.

Through these streets, Noah Claypole walked, dragging Charlotte after him; now stepping into the kennel to embrace at a glance the whole external character of some small public-house; now jogging on again, as some fancied appearance induced him to believe it too public for his purpose. At length, he stopped in front of one, more humble in appearance and more dirty than any he had yet seen; and, having crossed over and surveyed it from the opposite pavement, graciously announced his intention of putting up there, for the night.

'So give us the bundle,' said Noah, unstrapping it from the woman's shoulders, and slinging it over his own; 'and don't yer speak, except when yer spoke to. What's the name of the house—t-h-r—three what?'

'Cripples,' said Charlotte.

'Three Cripples,' repeated Noah, 'and a very good sign too. Now, then! Keep close at my heels, and come along.' With these injunctions, he pushed the rattling door with his shoulder, and entered the house, followed by his companion.

There was nobody in the bar but a young Jew, who, with his two elbows on the counter, was reading a dirty newspaper. He stared very hard at Noah, and Noah stared very hard at him.

If Noah had been attired in his charity-boy's dress, there might have been some reason for the Jew opening his eyes so wide; but as he had discarded the coat and badge, and wore a short smock-frock over his leathers, there seemed no particular reason for his appearance exciting so much attention in a public-house.

'Is this the Three Cripples?' asked Noah.

'That is the dabe of this 'ouse,' replied the Jew.

'A gentleman we met on the road, coming up from the country, recommended us here,' said Noah, nudging Charlotte, perhaps to call her attention to this most ingenious device for attracting respect, and perhaps to warn her to betray no surprise. 'We want to sleep here to-night.'

'I'b dot certaid you cad,' said Barney, who was the attendant sprite; 'but I'll idquire.'

'Show us the tap, and give us a bit of cold meat and a drop of beer while yer inquiring, will yer?' said Noah.

Barney complied by ushering them into a small back-room, and setting the required viands before them; having done which, he informed the travellers that they could be lodged that night, and left the amiable couple to their refreshment.

Now, this back-room was immediately behind the bar, and some steps lower, so that any person connected with the house, undrawing a small curtain which concealed a single pane of glass fixed in the wall of the last-named apartment, about five feet from its flooring, could not only look down upon any guests in the back-room without any great hazard of being observed (the glass being in a dark angle of the wall, between which and a large upright beam the observer had to thrust himself), but could, by applying his ear to the partition, ascertain with tolerable distinctness, their subject of conversation. The landlord of the house had not withdrawn his eye from this place of espial for five minutes, and Barney had only just returned from making the communication above related, when Fagin, in the course of his evening's business, came into the bar to inquire after some of his young pupils.

'Hush!' said Barney: 'stradegers id the next roob.'

'Strangers!' repeated the old man in a whisper.

'Ah! Ad rub uds too,' added Barney. 'Frob the cuttry, but subthig in your way, or I'b bistaked.'

Fagin appeared to receive this communication with great interest.

Mounting a stool, he cautiously applied his eye to the pane of glass, from which secret post he could see Mr. Claypole taking cold beef from the dish, and porter from the pot, and administering homeopathic doses of both to Charlotte, who sat patiently by, eating and drinking at his pleasure.

'Aha!' he whispered, looking round to Barney, 'I like that fellow's looks. He'd be of use to us; he knows how to train the girl already. Don't make as much noise as a mouse, my dear, and let me hear 'em talk—let me hear 'em.'

He again applied his eye to the glass, and turning his ear to the partition, listened attentively: with a subtle and eager look upon his face, that might have appertained to some old goblin.

'So I mean to be a gentleman,' said Mr. Claypole, kicking out his legs, and continuing a conversation, the commencement of which Fagin had arrived too late to hear. 'No more jolly old coffins, Charlotte, but a gentleman's life for me: and, if yer like, yer shall be a lady.'

'I should like that well enough, dear,' replied Charlotte; 'but tills ain't to be emptied every day, and people to get clear off after it.'

'Tills be blowed!' said Mr. Claypole; 'there's more things besides tills to be emptied.'

'What do you mean?' asked his companion.

'Pockets, women's ridicules, houses, mail-coaches, banks!' said Mr. Claypole, rising with the porter.

'But you can't do all that, dear,' said Charlotte.

'I shall look out to get into company with them as can,' replied Noah. 'They'll be able to make us useful some way or another. Why, you yourself are worth fifty women; I never see such a precious sly and deceitful creetur as yer can be when I let yer.'

'Lor, how nice it is to hear yer say so!' exclaimed Charlotte, imprinting a kiss upon his ugly face.

'There, that'll do: don't yer be too affectionate, in case I'm cross with yer,' said Noah, disengaging himself with great gravity. 'I should like to be the captain of some band, and have the whopping of 'em, and follering 'em about, unbeknown to themselves. That would suit me, if there was good profit; and if we could only get in with some gentleman of this sort, I say it would be cheap at that twenty-pound note you've got,—especially as we don't very well know how to get rid of it ourselves.'

After expressing this opinion, Mr. Claypole looked into the porter-pot with an aspect of deep wisdom; and having well shaken its contents, nodded condescendingly to Charlotte, and took a draught, wherewith he appeared greatly refreshed. He was meditating another, when the sudden opening of the door, and the appearance of a stranger, interrupted him.

The stranger was Mr. Fagin. And very amiable he looked, and a very low bow he made, as he advanced, and setting himself down at the nearest table, ordered something to drink of the grinning Barney.

'A pleasant night, sir, but cool for the time of year,' said Fagin, rubbing his hands. 'From the country, I see, sir?'

'How do yer see that?' asked Noah Claypole.

'We have not so much dust as that in London,' replied Fagin, pointing from Noah's shoes to those of his companion, and from them to the two bundles.

'Yer a sharp feller,' said Noah. 'Ha! ha! only hear that, Charlotte!'

'Why, one need be sharp in this town, my dear,' replied the Jew, sinking his voice to a confidential whisper; 'and that's the truth.'

Fagin followed up this remark by striking the side of his nose with his right forefinger,—a gesture which Noah attempted to imitate, though not with complete success, in consequence of his own nose not being large enough for the purpose. However, Mr. Fagin seemed to interpret the endeavour as expressing a perfect coincidence with his opinion, and put about the liquor which Barney reappeared with, in a very friendly manner.

'Good stuff that,' observed Mr. Claypole, smacking his lips.

'Dear!' said Fagin. 'A man need be always emptying a till, or a pocket, or a woman's reticule, or a house, or a mail-coach, or a bank, if he drinks it regularly.'

Mr. Claypole no sooner heard this extract from his own remarks than he fell back in his chair, and looked from the Jew to Charlotte with a countenance of ashy paleness and excessive terror.

'Don't mind me, my dear,' said Fagin, drawing his chair closer. 'Ha! ha! it was lucky it was only me that heard you by chance. It was very lucky it was only me.'

'I didn't take it,' stammered Noah, no longer stretching out his legs like an independent gentleman, but coiling them up as well as he could under his chair; 'it was all her doing; yer've got it now, Charlotte, yer know yer have.'

'No matter who's got it, or who did it, my dear,' replied Fagin, glancing, nevertheless, with a hawk's eye at the girl and the two bundles. 'I'm in that way myself, and I like you for it.'

'In what way?' asked Mr. Claypole, a little recovering.

'In that way of business,' rejoined Fagin; 'and so are the people of the house. You've hit the right nail upon the head, and are as safe here as you could be. There is not a safer place in all this town than is the Cripples; that is, when I like to make it so. And I have taken a fancy to you and the young woman; so I've said the word, and you may make your minds easy.'

Noah Claypole's mind might have been at ease after this assurance, but his body certainly was not; for he shuffled and writhed about, into various uncouth positions: eyeing his new friend meanwhile with mingled fear and suspicion.

'I'll tell you more,' said Fagin, after he had reassured the girl, by dint of friendly nods and muttered encouragements. 'I have got a friend that I think can gratify your darling wish, and put you in the right way, where you can take whatever department of the business you think will suit you best at first, and be taught all the others.'

'Yer speak as if yer were in earnest,' replied Noah.

'What advantage would it be to me to be anything else?' inquired Fagin, shrugging his shoulders. 'Here! Let me have a word with you outside.'

'There's no occasion to trouble ourselves to move,' said Noah, getting his legs by gradual degrees abroad again. 'She'll take the luggage upstairs the while. Charlotte, see to them bundles.'

This mandate, which had been delivered with great majesty, was obeyed without the slightest demur; and Charlotte made the best of her way off with the packages while Noah held the door open and watched her out.

'She's kept tolerably well under, ain't she?' he asked as he resumed his seat: in the tone of a keeper who had tamed some wild animal.

'Quite perfect,' rejoined Fagin, clapping him on the shoulder. 'You're a genius, my dear.'

'Why, I suppose if I wasn't, I shouldn't be here,' replied Noah. 'But, I say, she'll be back if yer lose time.'

'Now, what do you think?' said Fagin. 'If you was to like my friend, could you do better than join him?'

'Is he in a good way of business; that's where it is!' responded Noah, winking one of his little eyes.

'The top of the tree; employs a power of hands; has the very best society in the profession.'

'Regular town-maders?' asked Mr. Claypole.

'Not a countryman among 'em; and I don't think he'd take you, even on my recommendation, if he didn't run rather short of assistants just now,' replied Fagin.

'Should I have to hand over?' said Noah, slapping his breeches-pocket.

'It couldn't possibly be done without,' replied Fagin, in a most decided manner.

'Twenty pound, though—it's a lot of money!'

'Not when it's in a note you can't get rid of,' retorted Fagin. 'Number and date taken, I suppose? Payment stopped at the Bank? Ah! It's not worth much to him. It'll have to go abroad, and he couldn't sell it for a great deal in the market.'

'When could I see him?' asked Noah doubtfully.

'To-morrow morning.'

'Where?'

'Here.'

'Um!' said Noah. 'What's the wages?'

'Live like a gentleman—board and lodging, pipes and spirits free—half of all you earn, and half of all the young woman earns,' replied Mr. Fagin.

Whether Noah Claypole, whose rapacity was none of the least comprehensive, would have acceded even to these glowing terms, had he been a perfectly free agent, is very doubtful; but as he recollected that, in the event of his refusal, it was in the power of his new acquaintance to give him up to justice immediately (and more unlikely things had come to pass), he gradually relented, and said he thought that would suit him.

'But, yer see,' observed Noah, 'as she will be able to do a good deal, I should like to take something very light.'

'A little fancy work?' suggested Fagin.

'Ah! something of that sort,' replied Noah. 'What do you think would suit me now? Something not too trying for the strength, and not very dangerous, you know. That's the sort of thing!'

'I heard you talk of something in the spy way upon the others, my dear,' said Fagin. 'My friend wants somebody who would do that well, very much.'

'Why, I did mention that, and I shouldn't mind turning my hand to it sometimes,' rejoined Mr. Claypole slowly; 'but it wouldn't pay by itself, you know.'

'That's true!' observed the Jew, ruminating or pretending to ruminate. 'No, it might not.'

'What do you think, then?' asked Noah, anxiously regarding him. 'Something in the sneaking way, where it was pretty sure work, and not much more risk than being at home.'

'What do you think of the old ladies?' asked Fagin. 'There's a good deal of money made in snatching their bags and parcels, and running round the corner.'

'Don't they holler out a good deal, and scratch sometimes?' asked Noah, shaking his head. 'I don't think that would answer my purpose. Ain't there any other line open?'

'Stop!' said Fagin, laying his hand on Noah's knee. 'The kinchin lay.'

'What's that?' demanded Mr. Claypole.

'The kinchins, my dear,' said Fagin, 'is the young children that's sent on errands by their mothers, with sixpences and shillings; and the lay is just to take their money away—they've always got it ready in their hands,—then knock 'em into the kennel, and walk off very slow, as if there were nothing else the matter but a child fallen down and hurt itself. Ha! ha! ha!'

'Ha! ha!' roared Mr. Claypole, kicking up his legs in an ecstasy. 'Lord, that's the very thing!'

'To be sure it is,' replied Fagin; 'and you can have a few good beats chalked out in Camden Town, and Battle Bridge, and neighborhoods like that, where they're always going errands; and you can upset as many kinchins as you want, any hour in the day. Ha! ha! ha!'

With this, Fagin poked Mr. Claypole in the side, and they joined in a burst of laughter both long and loud.

'Well, that's all right!' said Noah, when he had recovered himself, and Charlotte had returned. 'What time to-morrow shall we say?'

'Will ten do?' asked Fagin, adding, as Mr. Claypole nodded assent, 'What name shall I tell my good friend.'

'Mr. Bolter,' replied Noah, who had prepared himself for such emergency. 'Mr. Morris Bolter. This is Mrs. Bolter.'

'Mrs. Bolter's humble servant,' said Fagin, bowing with grotesque politeness. 'I hope I shall know her better very shortly.'

'Do you hear the gentleman, Charlotte?' thundered Mr. Claypole.

'Yes, Noah, dear!' replied Mrs. Bolter, extending her hand.

'She calls me Noah, as a sort of fond way of talking,' said Mr. Morris Bolter, late Claypole, turning to Fagin. 'You understand?'

'Oh yes, I understand—perfectly,' replied Fagin, telling the truth for once. 'Good-night! Good-night!'

With many adieus and good wishes, Mr. Fagin went his way. Noah Claypole, bespeaking his good lady's attention, proceeded to enlighten her relative to the arrangement he had made, with all that haughtiness and air of superiority, becoming, not only a member of the sterner sex, but a gentleman who appreciated the dignity of a special appointment on the kinchin lay, in London and its vicinity.

CHAPTER XLIII. WHEREIN IS SHOWN HOW THE ARTFUL DODGER GOT INTO TROUBLE

'And so it was you that was your own friend, was it?' asked Mr. Claypole, otherwise Bolter, when, by virtue of the compact entered into between them, he had removed next day to Fagin's house. ''Cod, I thought as much last night!'

'Every man's his own friend, my dear,' replied Fagin, with his most insinuating grin. 'He hasn't as good a one as himself anywhere.'

'Except sometimes,' replied Morris Bolter, assuming the air of a man of the world. 'Some people are nobody's enemies but their own, yer know.'

'Don't believe that,' said Fagin. 'When a man's his own enemy, it's only because he's too much his own friend; not because he's careful for everybody but himself. Pooh! pooh! There ain't such a thing in nature.'

'There oughn't to be, if there is,' replied Mr. Bolter.

'That stands to reason. Some conjurers say that number three is the magic number, and some say number seven. It's neither, my friend, neither. It's number one.

'Ha! ha!' cried Mr. Bolter. 'Number one for ever.'

'In a little community like ours, my dear,' said Fagin, who felt it necessary to qualify this position, 'we have a general number one, without considering me too as the same, and all the other young people.'

'Oh, the devil!' exclaimed Mr. Bolter.

'You see,' pursued Fagin, affecting to disregard this interruption, 'we are so mixed up together, and identified in our interests, that it must be so. For instance, it's your object to take care of number one—meaning yourself.'

'Certainly,' replied Mr. Bolter. 'Yer about right there.'

'Well! You can't take care of yourself, number one, without taking care of me, number one.'

'Number two, you mean,' said Mr. Bolter, who was largely endowed with the quality of selfishness.

'No, I don't!' retorted Fagin. 'I'm of the same importance to you, as you are to yourself.'

'I say,' interrupted Mr. Bolter, 'yer a very nice man, and I'm very fond of yer; but we ain't quite so thick together, as all that comes to.'

'Only think,' said Fagin, shrugging his shoulders, and stretching out his hands; 'only consider. You've done what's a very pretty thing, and what I love you for doing; but what at the same time would put the cravat round your throat, that's so very easily tied and so very difficult to unloose—in plain English, the halter!'

Mr. Bolter put his hand to his neckerchief, as if he felt it inconveniently tight; and murmured an assent, qualified in tone but not in substance.

'The gallows,' continued Fagin, 'the gallows, my dear, is an ugly finger-post, which points out a very short and sharp turning that has stopped many a bold fellow's career on the broad highway. To keep in the easy road, and keep it at a distance, is object number one with you.'

'Of course it is,' replied Mr. Bolter. 'What do yer talk about such things for?'

'Only to show you my meaning clearly,' said the Jew, raising his eyebrows. 'To be able to do that, you depend upon me. To keep my little business all snug, I depend upon you. The first is your number one, the second my number one. The more you value your number one, the more careful you must be of mine; so we come at last to what I told you at first—that a regard for number one holds us all together, and must do so, unless we would all go to pieces in company.'

'That's true,' rejoined Mr. Bolter, thoughtfully. 'Oh! yer a cunning old codger!'

Mr. Fagin saw, with delight, that this tribute to his powers was no mere compliment, but that he had really impressed his recruit with a sense of his wily genius, which it was most important that he should entertain in the outset of their acquaintance. To strengthen an impression so desirable and useful, he followed up the blow by acquainting him, in some detail, with the magnitude and extent of his operations; blending truth and fiction together, as best served his purpose; and bringing both to bear, with so much art, that Mr. Bolter's respect visibly increased, and became tempered, at the same time, with a degree of wholesome fear, which it was highly desirable to awaken.

'It's this mutual trust we have in each other that consoles me under heavy losses,' said Fagin. 'My best hand was taken from me, yesterday morning.'

'You don't mean to say he died?' cried Mr. Bolter.

'No, no,' replied Fagin, 'not so bad as that. Not quite so bad.'

'What, I suppose he was—'

'Wanted,' interposed Fagin. 'Yes, he was wanted.'

'Very particular?' inquired Mr. Bolter.

'No,' replied Fagin, 'not very. He was charged with attempting to pick a pocket, and they found a silver snuff-box on him,—his own, my dear, his own, for he took snuff himself, and was very fond of it. They remanded him till to-day, for they thought they knew the owner. Ah! he was worth fifty boxes, and I'd give the price of as many to have him back. You should have known the Dodger, my dear; you should have known the Dodger.'

'Well, but I shall know him, I hope; don't yer think so?' said Mr. Bolter.

'I'm doubtful about it,' replied Fagin, with a sigh. 'If they don't get any fresh evidence, it'll only be a summary conviction, and we shall have him back again after six weeks or so; but, if they do, it's a case of lagging. They know what a clever lad he is; he'll be a lifer. They'll make the Artful nothing less than a lifer.'

'What do you mean by lagging and a lifer?' demanded Mr. Bolter. 'What's the good of talking in that way to me; why don't yer speak so as I can understand yer?'

Fagin was about to translate these mysterious expressions into the vulgar tongue; and, being interpreted, Mr. Bolter would have been informed that they represented that combination of words, 'transportation for life,' when the dialogue was cut short by the entry of Master Bates, with his hands in his breeches-pockets, and his face twisted into a look of semi-comical woe.

'It's all up, Fagin,' said Charley, when he and his new companion had been made known to each other.

'What do you mean?'

'They've found the gentleman as owns the box; two or three more's a coming to 'dentify him; and the Artful's booked for a passage out,' replied Master Bates. 'I must have a full suit of mourning, Fagin, and a hatband, to wisit him in, afore he sets out upon his travels. To think of Jack Dawkins—lummy Jack—the Dodger—the Artful Dodger—going abroad for a common twopenny-halfpenny sneeze-box! I never thought he'd a done it under a gold watch, chain, and seals, at the lowest. Oh, why didn't he rob some rich old gentleman of all his walables, and go out as a gentleman, and not like a common prig, without no honour nor glory!'

With this expression of feeling for his unfortunate friend, Master Bates sat himself on the nearest chair with an aspect of chagrin and despondency.

'What do you talk about his having neither honour nor glory for!' exclaimed Fagin, darting an angry look at his pupil. 'Wasn't he always the top-sawyer among you all! Is there one of you that could touch him or come near him on any scent! Eh?'

'Not one,' replied Master Bates, in a voice rendered husky by regret; 'not one.'

'Then what do you talk of?' replied Fagin angrily; 'what are you blubbering for?'

''Cause it isn't on the rec-ord, is it?' said Charley, chafed into perfect defiance of his venerable friend by the current of his regrets; ''cause it can't come out in the 'dictment; 'cause nobody will never know half of what he was. How will he stand in the Newgate Calendar? P'raps not be there at all. Oh, my eye, my eye, wot a blow it is!'

'Ha! ha!' cried Fagin, extending his right hand, and turning to Mr. Bolter in a fit of chuckling which shook him as though he had the palsy; 'see what a pride they take in their profession, my dear. Ain't it beautiful?'

Mr. Bolter nodded assent, and Fagin, after contemplating the grief of Charley Bates for some seconds with evident satisfaction, stepped up to that young gentleman and patted him on the shoulder.

'Never mind, Charley,' said Fagin soothingly; 'it'll come out, it'll be sure to come out. They'll all know what a clever fellow he was; he'll show it himself, and not disgrace his old pals and teachers. Think how young he is too! What a distinction, Charley, to be lagged at his time of life!'

'Well, it is a honour that is!' said Charley, a little consoled.

'He shall have all he wants,' continued the Jew. 'He shall be kept in the Stone Jug, Charley, like a gentleman. Like a gentleman! With his beer every day, and money in his pocket to pitch and toss with, if he can't spend it.'

'No, shall he though?' cried Charley Bates.

'Ay, that he shall,' replied Fagin, 'and we'll have a big-wig, Charley: one that's got the greatest gift of the gab: to carry on his defence; and he shall make a speech for himself too, if he likes; and we'll read it all in the papers—"Artful Dodger—shrieks of laughter—here the court was convulsed"—eh, Charley, eh?'

'Ha! ha!' laughed Master Bates, 'what a lark that would be, wouldn't it, Fagin? I say, how the Artful would bother 'em wouldn't he?'

'Would!' cried Fagin. 'He shall—he will!'

'Ah, to be sure, so he will,' repeated Charley, rubbing his hands.

'I think I see him now,' cried the Jew, bending his eyes upon his pupil.

'So do I,' cried Charley Bates. 'Ha! ha! ha! so do I. I see it all afore me, upon my soul I do, Fagin. What a game! What a regular game! All the big-wigs trying to look solemn, and Jack Dawkins addressing of 'em as intimate and comfortable as if he was the judge's own son making a speech arter dinner—ha! ha! ha!'

In fact, Mr. Fagin had so well humoured his young friend's eccentric disposition, that Master Bates, who had at first been disposed to consider the imprisoned Dodger rather in the light of a victim, now looked upon him as the chief actor in a scene of most uncommon and exquisite humour, and felt quite impatient for the arrival of the time when his old companion should have so favourable an opportunity of displaying his abilities.

'We must know how he gets on to-day, by some handy means or other,' said Fagin. 'Let me think.'

'Shall I go?' asked Charley.

'Not for the world,' replied Fagin. 'Are you mad, my dear, stark mad, that you'd walk into the very place where—No, Charley, no. One is enough to lose at a time.'

'You don't mean to go yourself, I suppose?' said Charley with a humorous leer.

'That wouldn't quite fit,' replied Fagin shaking his head.

'Then why don't you send this new cove?' asked Master Bates, laying his hand on Noah's arm. 'Nobody knows him.'

'Why, if he didn't mind—' observed Fagin.

'Mind!' interposed Charley. 'What should he have to mind?'

'Really nothing, my dear,' said Fagin, turning to Mr. Bolter, 'really nothing.'

'Oh, I dare say about that, yer know,' observed Noah, backing towards the door, and shaking his head with a kind of sober alarm. 'No, no—none of that. It's not in my department, that ain't.'

'Wot department has he got, Fagin?' inquired Master Bates, surveying Noah's lank form with much disgust. 'The cutting away when there's anything wrong, and the eating all the wittles when there's everything right; is that his branch?'

'Never mind,' retorted Mr. Bolter; 'and don't yer take liberties with yer superiors, little boy, or yer'll find yerself in the wrong shop.'

Master Bates laughed so vehemently at this magnificent threat, that it was some time before Fagin could interpose, and represent to Mr. Bolter that he incurred no possible danger in visiting the police-office; that, inasmuch as no account of the little affair in which he had engaged, nor any description of his person, had yet been forwarded to the metropolis, it was very probable that he was not even suspected of having resorted to it for shelter; and that, if he were properly disguised, it would be as safe a spot for him to visit as any in London, inasmuch as it would be, of all places, the very last, to which he could be supposed likely to resort of his own free will.

Persuaded, in part, by these representations, but overborne in a much greater degree by his fear of Fagin, Mr. Bolter at length consented, with a very bad grace, to undertake the expedition. By Fagin's directions, he immediately substituted for his own attire, a waggoner's frock, velveteen breeches, and leather leggings: all of which articles the Jew had at hand. He was likewise furnished with a felt hat well garnished with turnpike tickets; and a carter's whip. Thus equipped, he was to saunter into the office, as some country fellow from Covent Garden market might be supposed to do for the gratification of his curiousity; and as he was as awkward, ungainly, and raw-boned a fellow as need be, Mr. Fagin had no fear but that he would look the part to perfection.

These arrangements completed, he was informed of the necessary signs and tokens by which to recognise the Artful Dodger, and was conveyed by Master Bates through dark and winding ways to within a very short distance of Bow Street. Having described the precise situation of the office, and accompanied it with copious directions how he was to walk straight up the passage, and when he got into the side, and pull off his hat as he went into the room, Charley Bates bade him hurry on alone, and promised to bide his return on the spot of their parting.

Noah Claypole, or Morris Bolter as the reader pleases, punctually followed the directions he had received, which—Master Bates being pretty well acquainted with the locality—were so exact that he was enabled to gain the magisterial presence without asking any question, or meeting with any interruption by the way.

He found himself jostled among a crowd of people, chiefly women, who were huddled together in a dirty frowsy room, at the upper end of which was a raised platform railed off from the rest, with a dock for the prisoners on the left hand against the wall, a box for the witnesses in the middle, and a desk for the magistrates on the right; the awful locality last named, being screened off by a partition which concealed the bench from the common gaze, and left the vulgar to imagine (if they could) the full majesty of justice.

There were only a couple of women in the dock, who were nodding to their admiring friends, while the clerk read some depositions to a couple of policemen and a man in plain clothes who leant over the table. A jailer stood reclining against the dock-rail, tapping his nose listlessly with a large key, except when he repressed an undue tendency to conversation among the idlers, by proclaiming silence; or looked sternly up to bid some woman 'Take that baby out,' when the gravity of justice was disturbed by feeble cries, half-smothered in the mother's shawl, from some meagre infant. The room smelt close and unwholesome; the walls were dirt-discoloured; and the ceiling blackened. There was an old smoky bust over the mantel-shelf, and a dusty clock above the dock—the only thing present, that seemed to go on as it ought; for depravity, or poverty, or an habitual acquaintance with both, had left a taint on all the animate matter, hardly less unpleasant than the thick greasy scum on every inanimate object that frowned upon it.

Noah looked eagerly about him for the Dodger; but although there were several women who would have done very well for that distinguished character's mother or sister, and more than one man who might be supposed to bear a strong resemblance to his father, nobody at all answering the description given him of Mr. Dawkins was to be seen. He waited in a state of much suspense and uncertainty until the women, being committed for trial, went flaunting out; and then was quickly relieved by the appearance of another prisoner who he felt at once could be no other than the object of his visit.

It was indeed Mr. Dawkins, who, shuffling into the office with the big coat sleeves tucked up as usual, his left hand in his pocket, and his hat in his right hand, preceded the jailer, with a rolling gait altogether indescribable, and, taking his place in the dock, requested in an audible voice to know what he was placed in that 'ere disgraceful sitivation for.

'Hold your tongue, will you?' said the jailer.

'I'm an Englishman, ain't I?' rejoined the Dodger. 'Where are my priwileges?'

'You'll get your privileges soon enough,' retorted the jailer, 'and pepper with 'em.'

'We'll see wot the Secretary of State for the Home Affairs has got to say to the beaks, if I don't,' replied Mr. Dawkins. 'Now then! Wot is this here business? I shall thank the madg'strates to dispose of this here little affair, and not to keep me while they read the paper, for I've got an appointment with a genelman in the City, and as I am a man of my word and wery punctual in business matters, he'll go away if I ain't there to my time, and then pr'aps ther won't be an action for damage against them as kep me away. Oh no, certainly not!'

At this point, the Dodger, with a show of being very particular with a view to proceedings to be had thereafter, desired the jailer to communicate 'the names of them two files as was on the bench.' Which so tickled the spectators, that they laughed almost as heartily as Master Bates could have done if he had heard the request.

'Silence there!' cried the jailer.

'What is this?' inquired one of the magistrates.

'A pick-pocketing case, your worship.'

'Has the boy ever been here before?'

'He ought to have been, a many times,' replied the jailer. 'He has been pretty well everywhere else. I know him well, your worship.'

'Oh! you know me, do you?' cried the Artful, making a note of the statement. 'Wery good. That's a case of deformation of character, any way.'

Here there was another laugh, and another cry of silence.

'Now then, where are the witnesses?' said the clerk.

'Ah! that's right,' added the Dodger. 'Where are they? I should like to see 'em.'

This wish was immediately gratified, for a policeman stepped forward who had seen the prisoner attempt the pocket of an unknown gentleman in a crowd, and indeed take a handkerchief therefrom, which, being a very old one, he deliberately put back again, after trying it on his own countenance. For this reason, he took the Dodger into custody as soon as he could get near him, and the said Dodger, being searched, had upon his person a silver snuff-box, with the owner's name engraved upon the lid. This gentleman had been discovered on reference to the Court Guide, and being then and there present, swore that the snuff-box was his, and that he had missed it on the previous day, the moment he had disengaged himself from the crowd before referred to. He had also remarked a young gentleman in the throng, particularly active in making his way about, and that young gentleman was the prisoner before him.

'Have you anything to ask this witness, boy?' said the magistrate.

'I wouldn't abase myself by descending to hold no conversation with him,' replied the Dodger.

'Have you anything to say at all?'

'Do you hear his worship ask if you've anything to say?' inquired the jailer, nudging the silent Dodger with his elbow.

'I beg your pardon,' said the Dodger, looking up with an air of abstraction. 'Did you redress yourself to me, my man?'

'I never see such an out-and-out young wagabond, your worship,' observed the officer with a grin. 'Do you mean to say anything, you young shaver?'

'No,' replied the Dodger, 'not here, for this ain't the shop for justice: besides which, my attorney is a-breakfasting this morning with the Wice President of the House of Commons; but I shall have something to say elsewhere, and so will he, and so will a wery numerous and 'spectable circle of acquaintance as'll make them beaks wish they'd never been born, or that they'd got their footmen to hang 'em up to their own hat-pegs, afore they let 'em come out this morning to try it on upon me. I'll—'

'There! He's fully committed!' interposed the clerk. 'Take him away.'

'Come on,' said the jailer.

'Oh ah! I'll come on,' replied the Dodger, brushing his hat with the palm of his hand. 'Ah! (to the Bench) it's no use your looking frightened; I won't show you no mercy, not a ha'porth of it. You'll pay for this, my fine fellers. I wouldn't be you for something! I wouldn't go free, now, if you was to fall down on your knees and ask me. Here, carry me off to prison! Take me away!'

With these last words, the Dodger suffered himself to be led off by the collar; threatening, till he got into the yard, to make a parliamentary business of it; and then grinning in the officer's face, with great glee and self-approval.

Having seen him locked up by himself in a little cell, Noah made the best of his way back to where he had left Master Bates. After waiting here some time, he was joined by that young gentleman, who had prudently abstained from showing himself until he had looked carefully abroad from a snug retreat, and ascertained that his new friend had not been followed by any impertinent person.

The two hastened back together, to bear to Mr. Fagin the animating news that the Dodger was doing full justice to his bringing-up, and establishing for himself a glorious reputation.

CHAPTER XLIV. THE TIME ARRIVES FOR NANCY TO REDEEM HER PLEDGE TO ROSE MAYLIE. SHE FAILS.

Adept as she was, in all the arts of cunning and dissimulation, the girl Nancy could not wholly conceal the effect which the knowledge of the step she had taken, wrought upon her mind. She remembered that both the crafty Jew and the brutal Sikes had confided to her schemes, which had been hidden from all others: in the full confidence that she was trustworthy and beyond the reach of their suspicion. Vile as those schemes were, desperate as were their originators, and bitter as were her feelings towards Fagin, who had led her, step by step, deeper and deeper down into an abyss of crime and misery, whence was no escape; still, there were times when, even towards him, she felt some relenting, lest her disclosure should bring him within the iron grasp he had so long eluded, and he should fall at last—richly as he merited such a fate—by her hand.

But, these were the mere wanderings of a mind unable wholly to detach itself from old companions and associations, though enabled to fix itself steadily on one object, and resolved not to be turned aside by any consideration. Her fears for Sikes would have been more powerful inducements to recoil while there was yet time; but she had stipulated that her secret should be rigidly kept, she had dropped no clue which could lead to his discovery, she had refused, even for his sake, a refuge from all the guilt and wretchedness that encompasses her—and what more could she do! She was resolved.

Though all her mental struggles terminated in this conclusion, they forced themselves upon her, again and again, and left their traces too. She grew pale and thin, even within a few days. At times, she took no heed of what was passing before her, or no part in conversations where once, she would have been the loudest. At other times, she laughed without merriment, and was noisy without a moment afterwards—she sat silent and dejected, brooding with her head upon her hands, while the very effort by which she roused herself, told, more forcibly than even these indications, that she was ill at ease, and that her thoughts were occupied with matters very different and distant from those in the course of discussion by her companions.

It was Sunday night, and the bell of the nearest church struck the hour. Sikes and the Jew were talking, but they paused to listen. The girl looked up from the low seat on which she crouched, and listened too. Eleven.

'An hour this side of midnight,' said Sikes, raising the blind to look out and returning to his seat. 'Dark and heavy it is too. A good night for business this.'

'Ah!' replied Fagin. 'What a pity, Bill, my dear, that there's none quite ready to be done.'

'You're right for once,' replied Sikes gruffly. 'It is a pity, for I'm in the humour too.'

Fagin sighed, and shook his head despondingly.

'We must make up for lost time when we've got things into a good train. That's all I know,' said Sikes.

'That's the way to talk, my dear,' replied Fagin, venturing to pat him on the shoulder. 'It does me good to hear you.'

'Does you good, does it!' cried Sikes. 'Well, so be it.'

'Ha! ha! ha!' laughed Fagin, as if he were relieved by even this concession. 'You're like yourself to-night, Bill. Quite like yourself.'

'I don't feel like myself when you lay that withered old claw on my shoulder, so take it away,' said Sikes, casting off the Jew's hand.

'It make you nervous, Bill,—reminds you of being nabbed, does it?' said Fagin, determined not to be offended.

'Reminds me of being nabbed by the devil,' returned Sikes. 'There never was another man with such a face as yours, unless it was your father, and I suppose he is singeing his grizzled red beard by this time, unless you came straight from the old 'un without any father at all betwixt you; which I shouldn't wonder at, a bit.'

Fagin offered no reply to this compliment: but, pulling Sikes by the sleeve, pointed his finger towards Nancy, who had taken advantage of the foregoing conversation to put on her bonnet, and was now leaving the room.

'Hallo!' cried Sikes. 'Nance. Where's the gal going to at this time of night?'

'Not far.'

'What answer's that?' retorted Sikes. 'Do you hear me?'

'I don't know where,' replied the girl.

'Then I do,' said Sikes, more in the spirit of obstinacy than because he had any real objection to the girl going where she listed. 'Nowhere. Sit down.'

'I'm not well. I told you that before,' rejoined the girl. 'I want a breath of air.'

'Put your head out of the winder,' replied Sikes.

'There's not enough there,' said the girl. 'I want it in the street.'

'Then you won't have it,' replied Sikes. With which assurance he rose, locked the door, took the key out, and pulling her bonnet from her head, flung it up to the top of an old press. 'There,' said the robber. 'Now stop quietly where you are, will you?'

'It's not such a matter as a bonnet would keep me,' said the girl turning very pale. 'What do you mean, Bill? Do you know what you're doing?'

'Know what I'm—Oh!' cried Sikes, turning to Fagin, 'she's out of her senses, you know, or she daren't talk to me in that way.'

'You'll drive me on the something desperate,' muttered the girl placing both hands upon her breast, as though to keep down by force some violent outbreak. 'Let me go, will you,—this minute—this instant.'

'No!' said Sikes.

'Tell him to let me go, Fagin. He had better. It'll be better for him. Do you hear me?' cried Nancy stamping her foot upon the ground.

'Hear you!' repeated Sikes turning round in his chair to confront her. 'Aye! And if I hear you for half a minute longer, the dog shall have such a grip on your throat as'll tear some of that screaming voice out. Wot has come over you, you jade! Wot is it?'

'Let me go,' said the girl with great earnestness; then sitting herself down on the floor, before the door, she said, 'Bill, let me go; you don't know what you are doing. You don't, indeed. For only one hour—do—do!'

'Cut my limbs off one by one!' cried Sikes, seizing her roughly by the arm, 'If I don't think the gal's stark raving mad. Get up.'

'Not till you let me go—not till you let me go—Never—never!' screamed the girl. Sikes looked on, for a minute, watching his opportunity, and suddenly pinioning her hands dragged her, struggling and wrestling with him by the way, into a small room adjoining, where he sat himself on a bench, and thrusting her into a chair, held her down by force. She struggled and implored by turns until twelve o'clock had struck, and then, wearied and exhausted, ceased to contest the point any further. With a caution, backed by many oaths, to make no more efforts to go out that night, Sikes left her to recover at leisure and rejoined Fagin.

'Whew!' said the housebreaker wiping the perspiration from his face. 'Wot a precious strange gal that is!'

'You may say that, Bill,' replied Fagin thoughtfully. 'You may say that.'

'Wot did she take it into her head to go out to-night for, do you think?' asked Sikes. 'Come; you should know her better than me. Wot does it mean?'

'Obstinacy; woman's obstinacy, I suppose, my dear.'

'Well, I suppose it is,' growled Sikes. 'I thought I had tamed her, but she's as bad as ever.'

'Worse,' said Fagin thoughtfully. 'I never knew her like this, for such a little cause.'

'Nor I,' said Sikes. 'I think she's got a touch of that fever in her blood yet, and it won't come out—eh?'

'Like enough.'

'I'll let her a little blood, without troubling the doctor, if she's took that way again,' said Sikes.

Fagin nodded an expressive approval of this mode of treatment.

'She was hanging about me all day, and night too, when I was stretched on my back; and you, like a blackhearted wolf as you are, kept yourself aloof,' said Sikes. 'We was poor too, all the time, and I think, one way or other, it's worried and fretted her; and that being shut up here so long has made her restless—eh?'

'That's it, my dear,' replied the Jew in a whisper. 'Hush!'

As he uttered these words, the girl herself appeared and resumed her former seat. Her eyes were swollen and red; she rocked herself to and fro; tossed her head; and, after a little time, burst out laughing.

'Why, now she's on the other tack!' exclaimed Sikes, turning a look of excessive surprise on his companion.

Fagin nodded to him to take no further notice just then; and, in a few minutes, the girl subsided into her accustomed demeanour. Whispering Sikes that there was no fear of her relapsing, Fagin took up his hat and bade him good-night. He paused when he reached the room-door, and looking round, asked if somebody would light him down the dark stairs.

'Light him down,' said Sikes, who was filling his pipe. 'It's a pity he should break his neck himself, and disappoint the sight-seers. Show him a light.'

Nancy followed the old man downstairs, with a candle. When they reached the passage, he laid his finger on his lip, and drawing close to the girl, said, in a whisper.

'What is it, Nancy, dear?'

'What do you mean?' replied the girl, in the same tone.

'The reason of all this,' replied Fagin. 'If he'—he pointed with his skinny fore-finger up the stairs—'is so hard with you (he's a brute, Nance, a brute-beast), why don't you—'

'Well?' said the girl, as Fagin paused, with his mouth almost touching her ear, and his eyes looking into hers.

'No matter just now. We'll talk of this again. You have a friend in me, Nance; a staunch friend. I have the means at hand, quiet and close. If you want revenge on those that treat you like a dog—like a dog! worse than his dog, for he humours him sometimes—come to me. I say, come to me. He is the mere hound of a day, but you know me of old, Nance.'

'I know you well,' replied the girl, without manifesting the least emotion. 'Good-night.'

She shrank back, as Fagin offered to lay his hand on hers, but said good-night again, in a steady voice, and, answering his parting look with a nod of intelligence, closed the door between them.

Fagin walked towards his home, intent upon the thoughts that were working within his brain. He had conceived the idea—not from what had just passed though that had tended to confirm him, but slowly and by degrees—that Nancy, wearied of the housebreaker's brutality, had conceived an attachment for some new friend. Her altered manner, her repeated absences from home alone, her comparative indifference to the interests of the gang for which she had once been so zealous, and, added to these, her desperate impatience to leave home that night at a particular hour, all favoured the supposition, and rendered it, to him at least, almost matter of certainty. The object of this new liking was not among his myrmidons. He would be a valuable acquisition with such an assistant as Nancy, and must (thus Fagin argued) be secured without delay.

There was another, and a darker object, to be gained. Sikes knew too much, and his ruffian taunts had not galled Fagin the less, because the wounds were hidden. The girl must know, well, that if she shook him off, she could never be safe from his fury, and that it would be surely wreaked—to the maiming of limbs, or perhaps the loss of life—on the object of her more recent fancy.

'With a little persuasion,' thought Fagin, 'what more likely than that she would consent to poison him? Women have done such things, and worse, to secure the same object before now. There would be the dangerous villain: the man I hate: gone; another secured in his place; and my influence over the girl, with a knowledge of this crime to back it, unlimited.'

These things passed through the mind of Fagin, during the short time he sat alone, in the housebreaker's room; and with them uppermost in his thoughts, he had taken the opportunity afterwards afforded him, of sounding the girl in the broken hints he threw out at parting. There was no expression of surprise, no assumption of an inability to understand his meaning. The girl clearly comprehended it. Her glance at parting showed that.

But perhaps she would recoil from a plot to take the life of Sikes, and that was one of the chief ends to be attained. 'How,' thought Fagin, as he crept homeward, 'can I increase my influence with her? What new power can I acquire?'

Such brains are fertile in expedients. If, without extracting a confession from herself, he laid a watch, discovered the object of her altered regard, and threatened to reveal the whole history to Sikes (of whom she stood in no common fear) unless she entered into his designs, could he not secure her compliance?

'I can,' said Fagin, almost aloud. 'She durst not refuse me then. Not for her life, not for her life! I have it all. The means are ready, and shall be set to work. I shall have you yet!'

He cast back a dark look, and a threatening motion of the hand, towards the spot where he had left the bolder villain; and went on his way: busying his bony hands in the folds of his tattered garment, which he wrenched tightly in his grasp, as though there were a hated enemy crushed with every motion of his fingers.

CHAPTER XLV. NOAH CLAYPOLE IS EMPLOYED BY FAGIN ON A SECRET MISSION

The old man was up, betimes, next morning, and waited impatiently for the appearance of his new associate, who after a delay that seemed interminable, at length presented himself, and commenced a voracious assault on the breakfast.

'Bolter,' said Fagin, drawing up a chair and seating himself opposite Morris Bolter.

'Well, here I am,' returned Noah. 'What's the matter? Don't yer ask me to do anything till I have done eating. That's a great fault in this place. Yer never get time enough over yer meals.'

'You can talk as you eat, can't you?' said Fagin, cursing his dear young friend's greediness from the very bottom of his heart.

'Oh yes, I can talk. I get on better when I talk,' said Noah, cutting a monstrous slice of bread. 'Where's Charlotte?'

'Out,' said Fagin. 'I sent her out this morning with the other young woman, because I wanted us to be alone.'

'Oh!' said Noah. 'I wish yer'd ordered her to make some buttered toast first. Well. Talk away. Yer won't interrupt me.'

There seemed, indeed, no great fear of anything interrupting him, as he had evidently sat down with a determination to do a great deal of business.

'You did well yesterday, my dear,' said Fagin. 'Beautiful! Six shillings and ninepence halfpenny on the very first day! The kinchin lay will be a fortune to you.'

'Don't you forget to add three pint-pots and a milk-can,' said Mr. Bolter.

'No, no, my dear. The pint-pots were great strokes of genius: but the milk-can was a perfect masterpiece.'

'Pretty well, I think, for a beginner,' remarked Mr. Bolter complacently. 'The pots I took off airy railings, and the milk-can was standing by itself outside a public-house. I thought it might get rusty with the rain, or catch cold, yer know. Eh? Ha! ha! ha!'

Fagin affected to laugh very heartily; and Mr. Bolter having had his laugh out, took a series of large bites, which finished his first hunk of bread and butter, and assisted himself to a second.

'I want you, Bolter,' said Fagin, leaning over the table, 'to do a piece of work for me, my dear, that needs great care and caution.'

'I say,' rejoined Bolter, 'don't yer go shoving me into danger, or sending me any more o' yer police-offices. That don't suit me, that don't; and so I tell yer.'

'That's not the smallest danger in it—not the very smallest,' said the Jew; 'it's only to dodge a woman.'

'An old woman?' demanded Mr. Bolter.

'A young one,' replied Fagin.

'I can do that pretty well, I know,' said Bolter. 'I was a regular cunning sneak when I was at school. What am I to dodge her for? Not to—'

'Not to do anything, but to tell me where she goes, who she sees, and, if possible, what she says; to remember the street, if it is a street, or the house, if it is a house; and to bring me back all the information you can.'

'What'll yer give me?' asked Noah, setting down his cup, and looking his employer, eagerly, in the face.

'If you do it well, a pound, my dear. One pound,' said Fagin, wishing to interest him in the scent as much as possible. 'And that's what I never gave yet, for any job of work where there wasn't valuable consideration to be gained.'

'Who is she?' inquired Noah.

'One of us.'

'Oh Lor!' cried Noah, curling up his nose. 'Yer doubtful of her, are yer?'

'She has found out some new friends, my dear, and I must know who they are,' replied Fagin.

'I see,' said Noah. 'Just to have the pleasure of knowing them, if they're respectable people, eh? Ha! ha! ha! I'm your man.'

'I knew you would be,' cried Fagin, elated by the success of his proposal.

'Of course, of course,' replied Noah. 'Where is she? Where am I to wait for her? Where am I to go?'

'All that, my dear, you shall hear from me. I'll point her out at the proper time,' said Fagin. 'You keep ready, and leave the rest to me.'

That night, and the next, and the next again, the spy sat booted and equipped in his carter's dress: ready to turn out at a word from Fagin. Six nights passed—six long weary nights—and on each, Fagin came home with a disappointed face, and briefly intimated that it was not yet time. On the seventh, he returned earlier, and with an exultation he could not conceal. It was Sunday.

'She goes abroad to-night,' said Fagin, 'and on the right errand, I'm sure; for she has been alone all day, and the man she is afraid of will not be back much before daybreak. Come with me. Quick!'

Noah started up without saying a word; for the Jew was in a state of such intense excitement that it infected him. They left the house stealthily, and hurrying through a labyrinth of streets, arrived at length before a public-house, which Noah recognised as the same in which he had slept, on the night of his arrival in London.

It was past eleven o'clock, and the door was closed. It opened softly on its hinges as Fagin gave a low whistle. They entered, without noise; and the door was closed behind them.

Scarcely venturing to whisper, but substituting dumb show for words, Fagin, and the young Jew who had admitted them, pointed out the pane of glass to Noah, and signed to him to climb up and observe the person in the adjoining room.

'Is that the woman?' he asked, scarcely above his breath.

Fagin nodded yes.

'I can't see her face well,' whispered Noah. 'She is looking down, and the candle is behind her.'

'Stay there,' whispered Fagin. He signed to Barney, who withdrew. In an instant, the lad entered the room adjoining, and, under pretence of snuffing the candle, moved it in the required position, and, speaking to the girl, caused her to raise her face.

'I see her now,' cried the spy.

'Plainly?'

'I should know her among a thousand.'

He hastily descended, as the room-door opened, and the girl came out. Fagin drew him behind a small partition which was curtained off, and they held their breaths as she passed within a few feet of their place of concealment, and emerged by the door at which they had entered.

'Hist!' cried the lad who held the door. 'Dow.'

Noah exchanged a look with Fagin, and darted out.

'To the left,' whispered the lad; 'take the left had, and keep od the other side.'

He did so; and, by the light of the lamps, saw the girl's retreating figure, already at some distance before him. He advanced as near as he considered prudent, and kept on the opposite side of the street, the better to observe her motions. She looked nervously round, twice or thrice, and once stopped to let two men who were following close behind her, pass on. She seemed to gather courage as she advanced, and to walk with a steadier and firmer step. The spy preserved the same relative distance between them, and followed: with his eye upon her.

CHAPTER XLVI. THE APPOINTMENT KEPT

The church clocks chimed three quarters past eleven, as two figures emerged on London Bridge. One, which advanced with a swift and rapid step, was that of a woman who looked eagerly about her as though in quest of some expected object; the other figure was that of a man, who slunk along in the deepest shadow he could find, and, at some distance, accommodated his pace to hers: stopping when she stopped: and as she moved again, creeping stealthily on:

but never allowing himself, in the ardour of his pursuit, to gain upon her footsteps. Thus, they crossed the bridge, from the Middlesex to the Surrey shore, when the woman, apparently disappointed in her anxious scrutiny of the foot-passengers, turned back. The movement was sudden; but he who watched her, was not thrown off his guard by it; for, shrinking into one of the recesses which surmount the piers of the bridge, and leaning over the parapet the better to conceal his figure, he suffered her to pass on the opposite pavement. When she was about the same distance in advance as she had been before, he slipped quietly down, and followed her again. At nearly the centre of the bridge, she stopped. The man stopped too.

It was a very dark night. The day had been unfavourable, and at that hour and place there were few people stirring. Such as there were, hurried quickly past: very possibly without seeing, but certainly without noticing, either the woman, or the man who kept her in view. Their appearance was not calculated to attract the importunate regards of such of London's destitute population, as chanced to take their way over the bridge that night in search of some cold arch or doorless hovel wherein to lay their heads; they stood there in silence: neither speaking nor spoken to, by any one who passed.

A mist hung over the river, deepening the red glare of the fires that burnt upon the small craft moored off the different wharfs, and rendering darker and more indistinct the murky buildings on the banks. The old smoke-stained storehouses on either side, rose heavy and dull from the dense mass of roofs and gables, and frowned sternly upon water too black to reflect even their lumbering shapes. The tower of old Saint Saviour's Church, and the spire of Saint Magnus, so long the giant-warders of the ancient bridge, were visible in the gloom; but the forest of shipping below bridge, and the thickly scattered spires of churches above, were nearly all hidden from sight.

The girl had taken a few restless turns to and fro—closely watched meanwhile by her hidden observer—when the heavy bell of St. Paul's tolled for the death of another day. Midnight had come upon the crowded city. The palace, the night-cellar, the jail, the madhouse: the chambers of birth and death, of health and sickness, the rigid face of the corpse and the calm sleep of the child: midnight was upon them all.

The hour had not struck two minutes, when a young lady, accompanied by a grey-haired gentleman, alighted from a hackney-carriage within a short distance of the bridge, and, having dismissed the vehicle, walked straight towards it. They had scarcely set foot upon its pavement, when the girl started, and immediately made towards them.

They walked onward, looking about them with the air of persons who entertained some very slight expectation which had little chance of being realised, when they were suddenly joined by this new associate. They halted with an exclamation of surprise, but suppressed it immediately; for a man in the garments of a countryman came close up—brushed against them, indeed—at that precise moment.

'Not here,' said Nancy hurriedly, 'I am afraid to speak to you here. Come away—out of the public road—down the steps yonder!'

As she uttered these words, and indicated, with her hand, the direction in which she wished them to proceed, the countryman looked round, and roughly asking what they took up the whole pavement for, passed on.

The steps to which the girl had pointed, were those which, on the Surrey bank, and on the same side of the bridge as Saint Saviour's Church, form a landing-stairs from the river. To this spot, the man bearing the appearance of a countryman, hastened unobserved; and after a moment's survey of the place, he began to descend.

These stairs are a part of the bridge; they consist of three flights. Just below the end of the second, going down, the stone wall on the left terminates in an ornamental pilaster facing towards the Thames. At this point the lower steps widen: so that a person turning that angle of the wall, is necessarily unseen by any others on the stairs who chance to be above him, if only a step. The countryman looked hastily round, when he reached this point; and as there seemed no better place of concealment, and, the tide being out, there was plenty of room, he slipped aside, with his back to the pilaster, and there waited: pretty certain that they would come no lower, and that even if he could not hear what was said, he could follow them again, with safety.

So tardily stole the time in this lonely place, and so eager was the spy to penetrate the motives of an interview so different from what he had been led to expect, that he more than once gave the matter up for lost, and persuaded himself, either that they had stopped far above, or had resorted to some entirely different spot to hold their mysterious conversation. He was on the point of emerging from his hiding-place, and regaining the road above, when he heard the sound of footsteps, and directly afterwards of voices almost close at his ear.

He drew himself straight upright against the wall, and, scarcely breathing, listened attentively.

'This is far enough,' said a voice, which was evidently that of the gentleman. 'I will not suffer the young lady to go any farther. Many people would have distrusted you too much to have come even so far, but you see I am willing to humour you.'

'To humour me!' cried the voice of the girl whom he had followed. 'You're considerate, indeed, sir. To humour me! Well, well, it's no matter.'

'Why, for what,' said the gentleman in a kinder tone, 'for what purpose can you have brought us to this strange place? Why not have let me speak to you, above there, where it is light, and there is something stirring, instead of bringing us to this dark and dismal hole?'

'I told you before,' replied Nancy, 'that I was afraid to speak to you there. I don't know why it is,' said the girl, shuddering, 'but I have such a fear and dread upon me to-night that I can hardly stand.'

'A fear of what?' asked the gentleman, who seemed to pity her.

'I scarcely know of what,' replied the girl. 'I wish I did. Horrible thoughts of death, and shrouds with blood upon them, and a fear that has made me burn as if I was on fire, have been upon me all day. I was reading a book to-night, to wile the time away, and the same things came into the print.'

'Imagination,' said the gentleman, soothing her.

'No imagination,' replied the girl in a hoarse voice. 'I'll swear I saw "coffin" written in every page of the book in large black letters,—aye, and they carried one close to me, in the streets to-night.'

'There is nothing unusual in that,' said the gentleman. 'They have passed me often.'

'Real ones,' rejoined the girl. 'This was not.'

There was something so uncommon in her manner, that the flesh of the concealed listener crept as he heard the girl utter these words, and the blood chilled within him. He had never experienced a greater relief than in hearing the sweet voice of the young lady as she begged her to be calm, and not allow herself to become the prey of such fearful fancies.

'Speak to her kindly,' said the young lady to her companion. 'Poor creature! She seems to need it.'

'Your haughty religious people would have held their heads up to see me as I am to-night, and preached of flames and vengeance,' cried the girl. 'Oh, dear lady, why ar'n't those who claim to be God's own folks as gentle and as kind to us poor wretches as you, who, having youth, and beauty, and all that they have lost, might be a little proud instead of so much humbler?'

'Ah!' said the gentleman. 'A Turk turns his face, after washing it well, to the East, when he says his prayers; these good people, after giving their faces such a rub against the World as to take the smiles off, turn with no less regularity, to the darkest side of Heaven. Between the Mussulman and the Pharisee, commend me to the first!'

These words appeared to be addressed to the young lady, and were perhaps uttered with the view of affording Nancy time to recover herself. The gentleman, shortly afterwards, addressed himself to her.

'You were not here last Sunday night,' he said.

'I couldn't come,' replied Nancy; 'I was kept by force.'

'By whom?'

'Him that I told the young lady of before.'

'You were not suspected of holding any communication with anybody on the subject which has brought us here to-night, I hope?' asked the old gentleman.

'No,' replied the girl, shaking her head. 'It's not very easy for me to leave him unless he knows why; I couldn't give him a drink of laudanum before I came away.'

'Did he awake before you returned?' inquired the gentleman.

'No; and neither he nor any of them suspect me.'

'Good,' said the gentleman. 'Now listen to me.'

'I am ready,' replied the girl, as he paused for a moment.

'This young lady,' the gentleman began, 'has communicated to me, and to some other friends who can be safely trusted, what you told her nearly a fortnight since. I confess to you that I had doubts, at first, whether you were to be implicitly relied upon, but now I firmly believe you are.'

'I am,' said the girl earnestly.

'I repeat that I firmly believe it. To prove to you that I am disposed to trust you, I tell you without reserve, that we propose to extort the secret, whatever it may be, from the fear of this man Monks. But if—if—' said the gentleman, 'he cannot be secured, or, if secured, cannot be acted upon as we wish, you must deliver up the Jew.'

'Fagin,' cried the girl, recoiling.

'That man must be delivered up by you,' said the gentleman.

'I will not do it! I will never do it!' replied the girl. 'Devil that he is, and worse than devil as he has been to me, I will never do that.'

'You will not?' said the gentleman, who seemed fully prepared for this answer.

'Never!' returned the girl.

'Tell me why?'

'For one reason,' rejoined the girl firmly, 'for one reason, that the lady knows and will stand by me in, I know she will, for I have her promise: and for this other reason, besides, that, bad life as he has led, I have led a bad life too; there are many of us who have kept the same courses together, and I'll not turn upon them, who might—any of them—have turned upon me, but didn't, bad as they are.'

'Then,' said the gentleman, quickly, as if this had been the point he had been aiming to attain; 'put Monks into my hands, and leave him to me to deal with.'

'What if he turns against the others?'

'I promise you that in that case, if the truth is forced from him, there the matter will rest; there must be circumstances in Oliver's little history which it would be painful to drag before the public eye, and if the truth is once elicited, they shall go scot free.'

'And if it is not?' suggested the girl.

'Then,' pursued the gentleman, 'this Fagin shall not be brought to justice without your consent. In such a case I could show you reasons, I think, which would induce you to yield it.'

'Have I the lady's promise for that?' asked the girl.

'You have,' replied Rose. 'My true and faithful pledge.'

'Monks would never learn how you knew what you do?' said the girl, after a short pause.

'Never,' replied the gentleman. 'The intelligence should be brought to bear upon him, that he could never even guess.'

'I have been a liar, and among liars from a little child,' said the girl after another interval of silence, 'but I will take your words.'

After receiving an assurance from both, that she might safely do so, she proceeded in a voice so low that it was often difficult for the listener to discover even the purport of what she said, to describe, by name and situation, the public-house whence she had been followed that night. From the manner in which she occasionally paused, it appeared as if the gentleman were making some hasty notes of the information she communicated. When she had thoroughly explained the localities of the place, the best position from which to watch it without exciting observation, and the night and hour on which Monks was most in the habit of frequenting it, she seemed to consider for a few moments, for the purpose of recalling his features and appearances more forcibly to her recollection.

'He is tall,' said the girl, 'and a strongly made man, but not stout; he has a lurking walk; and as he walks, constantly looks over his shoulder, first on one side, and then on the other. Don't forget that, for his eyes are sunk in his head so much deeper than any other man's, that you might almost tell him by that alone. His face is dark, like his hair and eyes; and, although he can't be more than six or eight and twenty, withered and haggard. His lips are often discoloured and disfigured with the marks of teeth; for he has desperate fits, and sometimes even bites his hands and covers them with wounds—why did you start?' said the girl, stopping suddenly.

The gentleman replied, in a hurried manner, that he was not conscious of having done so, and begged her to proceed.

'Part of this,' said the girl, 'I have drawn out from other people at the house I tell you of, for I have only seen him twice, and both times he was covered up in a large cloak. I think that's all I can give you to know him by. Stay though,' she added. 'Upon his throat: so high that you can see a part of it below his neckerchief when he turns his face: there is—'

'A broad red mark, like a burn or scald?' cried the gentleman.

'How's this?' said the girl. 'You know him!'

The young lady uttered a cry of surprise, and for a few moments they were so still that the listener could distinctly hear them breathe.

'I think I do,' said the gentleman, breaking silence. 'I should by your description. We shall see. Many people are singularly like each other. It may not be the same.'

As he expressed himself to this effect, with assumed carelessness, he took a step or two nearer the concealed spy, as the latter could tell from the distinctness with which he heard him mutter, 'It must be he!'

'Now,' he said, returning: so it seemed by the sound: to the spot where he had stood before, 'you have given us most valuable assistance, young woman, and I wish you to be the better for it. What can I do to serve you?'

'Nothing,' replied Nancy.

'You will not persist in saying that,' rejoined the gentleman, with a voice and emphasis of kindness that might have touched a much harder and more obdurate heart. 'Think now. Tell me.'

'Nothing, sir,' rejoined the girl, weeping. 'You can do nothing to help me. I am past all hope, indeed.'

'You put yourself beyond its pale,' said the gentleman. 'The past has been a dreary waste with you, of youthful energies mis-spent, and such priceless treasures lavished, as the Creator bestows but once and never grants again, but, for the future, you may hope. I do not say that it is in our power to offer you peace of heart and mind, for that must come as you seek it; but a quiet asylum, either in England, or, if you fear to remain here, in some foreign country, it is not only within the compass of our ability but our most anxious wish to secure you. Before the dawn of morning, before this river wakes to the first glimpse of day-light, you shall be placed as entirely beyond the reach of your former associates, and leave as utter an absence of all trace behind you, as if you were to disappear from the earth this moment. Come! I would not have you go back to exchange one word with any old companion, or take one look at any old haunt, or breathe the very air which is pestilence and death to you. Quit them all, while there is time and opportunity!'

'She will be persuaded now,' cried the young lady. 'She hesitates, I am sure.'

'I fear not, my dear,' said the gentleman.

'No sir, I do not,' replied the girl, after a short struggle. 'I am chained to my old life. I loathe and hate it now, but I cannot leave it. I must have gone too far to turn back,—and yet I don't know, for if you had spoken to me so, some time ago, I should have laughed it off. But,' she said, looking hastily round, 'this fear comes over me again. I must go home.'

'Home!' repeated the young lady, with great stress upon the word.

'Home, lady,' rejoined the girl. 'To such a home as I have raised for myself with the work of my whole life. Let us part. I shall be watched or seen. Go! Go! If I have done you any service all I ask is, that you leave me, and let me go my way alone.'

'It is useless,' said the gentleman, with a sigh. 'We compromise her safety, perhaps, by staying here. We may have detained her longer than she expected already.'

'Yes, yes,' urged the girl. 'You have.'

'What,' cried the young lady, 'can be the end of this poor creature's life!'

'What!' repeated the girl. 'Look before you, lady. Look at that dark water. How many times do you read of such as I who spring into the tide, and leave no living thing, to care for, or bewail them. It may be years hence, or it may be only months, but I shall come to that at last.'

'Do not speak thus, pray,' returned the young lady, sobbing.

'It will never reach your ears, dear lady, and God forbid such horrors should!' replied the girl. 'Good-night, good-night!'

The gentleman turned away.

'This purse,' cried the young lady. 'Take it for my sake, that you may have some resource in an hour of need and trouble.'

'No!' replied the girl. 'I have not done this for money. Let me have that to think of. And yet—give me something that you have worn: I should like to have something—no, no, not a ring—your gloves or handkerchief—anything that I can keep, as having belonged to you, sweet lady. There. Bless you! God bless you. Good-night, good-night!'

The violent agitation of the girl, and the apprehension of some discovery which would subject her to ill-usage and violence, seemed to determine the gentleman to leave her, as she requested.

The sound of retreating footsteps were audible and the voices ceased.

The two figures of the young lady and her companion soon afterwards appeared upon the bridge. They stopped at the summit of the stairs.

'Hark!' cried the young lady, listening. 'Did she call! I thought I heard her voice.'

'No, my love,' replied Mr. Brownlow, looking sadly back. 'She has not moved, and will not till we are gone.'

Rose Maylie lingered, but the old gentleman drew her arm through his, and led her, with gentle force, away. As they disappeared, the girl sunk down nearly at her full length upon one of the stone stairs, and vented the anguish of her heart in bitter tears.

After a time she arose, and with feeble and tottering steps ascended the street. The astonished listener remained motionless on his post for some minutes afterwards, and having ascertained, with many cautious glances round him, that he was again alone, crept slowly from his hiding-place, and returned, stealthily and in the shade of the wall, in the same manner as he had descended.

Peeping out, more than once, when he reached the top, to make sure that he was unobserved, Noah Claypole darted away at his utmost speed, and made for the Jew's house as fast as his legs would carry him.

CHAPTER XLVII. FATAL CONSEQUENCES

It was nearly two hours before day-break; that time which in the autumn of the year, may be truly called the dead of night; when the streets are silent and deserted; when even sounds appear to slumber, and profligacy and riot have staggered home to dream; it was at this still and silent hour, that Fagin sat watching in his old lair, with face so distorted and pale, and eyes so red and blood-shot, that he looked less like a man, than like some hideous phantom, moist from the grave, and worried by an evil spirit.

He sat crouching over a cold hearth, wrapped in an old torn coverlet, with his face turned towards a wasting candle that stood upon a table by his side. His right hand was raised to his lips, and as, absorbed in thought, he hit his long black nails, he disclosed among his toothless gums a few such fangs as should have been a dog's or rat's.

Stretched upon a mattress on the floor, lay Noah Claypole, fast asleep. Towards him the old man sometimes directed his eyes for an instant, and then brought them back again to the candle; which with a long-burnt wick drooping almost double, and hot grease falling down in clots upon the table, plainly showed that his thoughts were busy elsewhere.

Indeed they were. Mortification at the overthrow of his notable scheme; hatred of the girl who had dared to palter with strangers; and utter distrust of the sincerity of her refusal to yield him up; bitter disappointment at the loss of his revenge on Sikes; the fear of detection, and ruin, and death; and a fierce and deadly rage kindled by all; these were the passionate considerations which, following close upon each other with rapid and ceaseless whirl, shot through the brain of Fagin, as every evil thought and blackest purpose lay working at his heart.

He sat without changing his attitude in the least, or appearing to take the smallest heed of time, until his quick ear seemed to be attracted by a footstep in the street.

'At last,' he muttered, wiping his dry and fevered mouth. 'At last!'

The bell rang gently as he spoke. He crept upstairs to the door, and presently returned accompanied by a man muffled to the chin, who carried a bundle under one arm. Sitting down and throwing back his outer coat, the man displayed the burly frame of Sikes.

'There!' he said, laying the bundle on the table. 'Take care of that, and do the most you can with it. It's been trouble enough to get; I thought I should have been here, three hours ago.'

Fagin laid his hand upon the bundle, and locking it in the cupboard, sat down again without speaking. But he did not take his eyes off the robber, for an instant, during this action; and now that they sat over against each other, face to face, he looked fixedly at him, with his lips quivering so violently, and his face so altered by the emotions which had mastered him, that the housebreaker involuntarily drew back his chair, and surveyed him with a look of real affright.

'Wot now?' cried Sikes. 'Wot do you look at a man so for?'

Fagin raised his right hand, and shook his trembling forefinger in the air; but his passion was so great, that the power of speech was for the moment gone.

'Damme!' said Sikes, feeling in his breast with a look of alarm. 'He's gone mad. I must look to myself here.'

'No, no,' rejoined Fagin, finding his voice. 'It's not—you're not the person, Bill. I've no—no fault to find with you.'

'Oh, you haven't, haven't you?' said Sikes, looking sternly at him, and ostentatiously passing a pistol into a more convenient pocket. 'That's lucky—for one of us. Which one that is, don't matter.'

'I've got that to tell you, Bill,' said Fagin, drawing his chair nearer, 'will make you worse than me.'

'Aye?' returned the robber with an incredulous air. 'Tell away! Look sharp, or Nance will think I'm lost.'

'Lost!' cried Fagin. 'She has pretty well settled that, in her own mind, already.'

Sikes looked with an aspect of great perplexity into the Jew's face, and reading no satisfactory explanation of the riddle there, clenched his coat collar in his huge hand and shook him soundly.

'Speak, will you!' he said; 'or if you don't, it shall be for want of breath. Open your mouth and say wot you've got to say in plain words. Out with it, you thundering old cur, out with it!'

'Suppose that lad that's laying there—' Fagin began.

Sikes turned round to where Noah was sleeping, as if he had not previously observed him. 'Well!' he said, resuming his former position.

'Suppose that lad,' pursued Fagin, 'was to peach—to blow upon us all—first seeking out the right folks for the purpose, and then having a meeting with 'em in the street to paint our likenesses, describe every mark that they might know us by, and the crib where we might be most easily taken. Suppose he was to do all this, and besides to blow upon a plant we've all been in, more or less—of his own fancy; not grabbed, trapped, tried, earwigged by the parson and brought to it on bread and water,—but of his own fancy; to please his own taste; stealing out at nights to find those most interested against us, and peaching to them. Do you hear me?' cried the Jew, his eyes flashing with rage. 'Suppose he did all this, what then?'

'What then!' replied Sikes; with a tremendous oath. 'If he was left alive till I came, I'd grind his skull under the iron heel of my boot into as many grains as there are hairs upon his head.'

'What if I did it!' cried Fagin almost in a yell. 'I, that knows so much, and could hang so many besides myself!'

'I don't know,' replied Sikes, clenching his teeth and turning white at the mere suggestion. 'I'd do something in the jail that 'ud get me put in irons; and if I was tried along with you, I'd fall upon you with them in the open court, and beat your brains out afore the people. I should have such strength,' muttered the robber, poising his brawny arm, 'that I could smash your head as if a loaded waggon had gone over it.'

'You would?'

'Would I!' said the housebreaker. 'Try me.'

'If it was Charley, or the Dodger, or Bet, or—'

'I don't care who,' replied Sikes impatiently. 'Whoever it was, I'd serve them the same.'

Fagin looked hard at the robber; and, motioning him to be silent, stooped over the bed upon the floor, and shook the sleeper to rouse him. Sikes leant forward in his chair: looking on with his hands upon his knees, as if wondering much what all this questioning and preparation was to end in.

'Bolter, Bolter! Poor lad!' said Fagin, looking up with an expression of devilish anticipation, and speaking slowly and with marked emphasis. 'He's tired—tired with watching for her so long,—watching for her, Bill.'

'Wot d'ye mean?' asked Sikes, drawing back.

Fagin made no answer, but bending over the sleeper again, hauled him into a sitting posture. When his assumed name had been repeated several times, Noah rubbed his eyes, and, giving a heavy yawn, looked sleepily about him.

'Tell me that again—once again, just for him to hear,' said the Jew, pointing to Sikes as he spoke.

'Tell yer what?' asked the sleepy Noah, shaking himself pettishly.

'That about— Nancy,' said Fagin, clutching Sikes by the wrist, as if to prevent his leaving the house before he had heard enough. 'You followed her?'

'Yes.'

'To London Bridge?'

'Yes.'

'Where she met two people.'

'So she did.'

'A gentleman and a lady that she had gone to of her own accord before, who asked her to give up all her pals, and Monks first, which she did—and to describe him, which she did—and to tell her what house it was that we meet at, and go to, which she did—and where it could be best watched from, which she did—and what time the people went there, which she did. She did all this. She told it all every word without a threat, without a murmur—she did—did she not?' cried Fagin, half mad with fury.

'All right,' replied Noah, scratching his head. 'That's just what it was!'

'What did they say, about last Sunday?'

'About last Sunday!' replied Noah, considering. 'Why I told yer that before.'

'Again. Tell it again!' cried Fagin, tightening his grasp on Sikes, and brandishing his other hand aloft, as the foam flew from his lips.

'They asked her,' said Noah, who, as he grew more wakeful, seemed to have a dawning perception who Sikes was, 'they asked her why she didn't come, last Sunday, as she promised. She said she couldn't.'

'Why—why? Tell him that.'

'Because she was forcibly kept at home by Bill, the man she had told them of before,' replied Noah.

'What more of him?' cried Fagin. 'What more of the man she had told them of before? Tell him that, tell him that.'

'Why, that she couldn't very easily get out of doors unless he knew where she was going to,' said Noah; 'and so the first time she went to see the lady, she—ha! ha! ha! it made me laugh when she said it, that it did—she gave him a drink of laudanum.'

'Hell's fire!' cried Sikes, breaking fiercely from the Jew. 'Let me go!'

Flinging the old man from him, he rushed from the room, and darted, wildly and furiously, up the stairs.

'Bill, Bill!' cried Fagin, following him hastily. 'A word. Only a word.'

The word would not have been exchanged, but that the housebreaker was unable to open the door: on which he was expending fruitless oaths and violence, when the Jew came panting up.

'Let me out,' said Sikes. 'Don't speak to me; it's not safe. Let me out, I say!'

'Hear me speak a word,' rejoined Fagin, laying his hand upon the lock. 'You won't be—'

'Well,' replied the other.

'You won't be—too—violent, Bill?'

The day was breaking, and there was light enough for the men to see each other's faces. They exchanged one brief glance; there was a fire in the eyes of both, which could not be mistaken.

'I mean,' said Fagin, showing that he felt all disguise was now useless, 'not too violent for safety. Be crafty, Bill, and not too bold.'

Sikes made no reply; but, pulling open the door, of which Fagin had turned the lock, dashed into the silent streets.

Without one pause, or moment's consideration; without once turning his head to the right or left, or raising his eyes to the sky, or lowering them to the ground, but looking straight before him with savage resolution: his teeth so tightly compressed that the strained jaw seemed starting through his skin; the robber held on his headlong course, nor muttered a word, nor relaxed a muscle, until he reached his own door. He opened it, softly, with a key; strode lightly up the stairs; and entering his own room, double-locked the door, and lifting a heavy table against it, drew back the curtain of the bed.

The girl was lying, half-dressed, upon it. He had roused her from her sleep, for she raised herself with a hurried and startled look.

'Get up!' said the man.

'It is you, Bill!' said the girl, with an expression of pleasure at his return.

'It is,' was the reply. 'Get up.'

There was a candle burning, but the man hastily drew it from the candlestick, and hurled it under the grate. Seeing the faint light of early day without, the girl rose to undraw the curtain.

'Let it be,' said Sikes, thrusting his hand before her. 'There's enough light for wot I've got to do.'

'Bill,' said the girl, in the low voice of alarm, 'why do you look like that at me!'

The robber sat regarding her, for a few seconds, with dilated nostrils and heaving breast; and then, grasping her by the head and throat, dragged her into the middle of the room, and looking once towards the door, placed his heavy hand upon her mouth.

'Bill, Bill!' gasped the girl, wrestling with the strength of mortal fear,—'I—I won't scream or cry—not once—hear me—speak to me—tell me what I have done!'

'You know, you she devil!' returned the robber, suppressing his breath. 'You were watched to-night; every word you said was heard.'

'Then spare my life for the love of Heaven, as I spared yours,' rejoined the girl, clinging to him. 'Bill, dear Bill, you cannot have the heart to kill me. Oh! think of all I have given up, only this one night, for you. You shall have time to think, and save yourself this crime; I will not loose my hold, you cannot throw me off. Bill, Bill, for dear God's sake, for your own, for mine, stop before you spill my blood! I have been true to you, upon my guilty soul I have!'

The man struggled violently, to release his arms; but those of the girl were clasped round his, and tear her as he would, he could not tear them away.

'Bill,' cried the girl, striving to lay her head upon his breast, 'the gentleman and that dear lady, told me to-night of a home in some foreign country where I could end my days in solitude and peace. Let me see them again, and beg them, on my knees, to show the same mercy and goodness to you; and let us both leave this dreadful place, and far apart lead better lives, and forget how we have lived, except in prayers, and never see each other more. It is never too late to repent. They told me so—I feel it now—but we must have time—a little, little time!'

The housebreaker freed one arm, and grasped his pistol. The certainty of immediate detection if he fired, flashed across his mind even in the midst of his fury; and he beat it twice with all the force he could summon, upon the upturned face that almost touched his own.

She staggered and fell: nearly blinded with the blood that rained down from a deep gash in her forehead; but raising herself, with difficulty, on her knees, drew from her bosom a white handkerchief—Rose Maylie's own—and holding it up, in her folded hands, as high towards Heaven as her feeble strength would allow, breathed one prayer for mercy to her Maker.

It was a ghastly figure to look upon. The murderer staggering backward to the wall, and shutting out the sight with his hand, seized a heavy club and struck her down.

CHAPTER XLVIII. THE FLIGHT OF SIKES

Of all bad deeds that, under cover of the darkness, had been committed within wide London's bounds since night hung over it, that was the worst. Of all the horrors that rose with an ill scent upon the morning air, that was the foulest and most cruel.

The sun—the bright sun, that brings back, not light alone, but new life, and hope, and freshness to man—burst upon the crowded city in clear and radiant glory. Through costly-coloured glass and paper-mended window, through cathedral dome and rotten crevice, it shed its equal ray. It lighted up the room where the murdered woman lay. It did. He tried to shut it out, but it would stream in. If the sight had been a ghastly one in the dull morning, what was it, now, in all that brilliant light!

He had not moved; he had been afraid to stir. There had been a moan and motion of the hand; and, with terror added to rage, he had struck and struck again. Once he threw a rug over it; but it was worse to fancy the eyes, and imagine them moving towards him, than to see them glaring upward, as if watching the reflection of the pool of gore that quivered and danced in the sunlight on the ceiling. He had plucked it off again. And there was the body—mere flesh and blood, no more—but such flesh, and so much blood!

He struck a light, kindled a fire, and thrust the club into it. There was hair upon the end, which blazed and shrunk into a light cinder, and, caught by the air, whirled up the chimney. Even that frightened him, sturdy as he was; but he held the weapon till it broke, and then piled it on the coals to burn away, and smoulder into ashes. He washed himself, and rubbed his clothes; there were spots that would not be removed, but he cut the pieces out, and burnt them. How those stains were dispersed about the room! The very feet of the dog were bloody.

All this time he had, never once, turned his back upon the corpse; no, not for a moment. Such preparations completed, he moved, backward, towards the door: dragging the dog with him, lest he should soil his feet anew and carry out new evidence of the crime into the streets. He shut the door softly, locked it, took the key, and left the house.

He crossed over, and glanced up at the window, to be sure that nothing was visible from the outside. There was the curtain still drawn, which she would have opened to admit the light she never saw again. It lay nearly under there. He knew that. God, how the sun poured down upon the very spot!

The glance was instantaneous. It was a relief to have got free of the room. He whistled on the dog, and walked rapidly away.

He went through Islington; strode up the hill at Highgate on which stands the stone in honour of Whittington; turned down to Highgate Hill, unsteady of purpose, and uncertain where to go; struck off to the right again, almost as soon as he began to descend it; and taking the foot-path across the fields, skirted Caen Wood, and so came on Hampstead Heath. Traversing the hollow by the Vale of Heath, he mounted the opposite bank, and crossing the road which joins the villages of Hampstead and Highgate, made along the remaining portion of the heath to the fields at North End, in one of which he laid himself down under a hedge, and slept.

Soon he was up again, and away,—not far into the country, but back towards London by the high-road—then back again—then over another part of the same ground as he already traversed—then wandering up and down in fields, and lying on ditches' brinks to rest, and starting up to make for some other spot, and do the same, and ramble on again.

Where could he go, that was near and not too public, to get some meat and drink? Hendon. That was a good place, not far off, and out of most people's way. Thither he directed his steps,—running sometimes, and sometimes, with a strange perversity, loitering at a snail's pace, or stopping altogether and idly breaking the hedges with a stick. But when he got there, all the people he met—the very children at the doors—seemed to view him with suspicion. Back he turned again, without the courage to purchase bit or drop, though he had tasted no food for many hours; and once more he lingered on the Heath, uncertain where to go.

He wandered over miles and miles of ground, and still came back to the old place. Morning and noon had passed, and the day was on the wane, and still he rambled to and fro, and up and down, and round and round, and still lingered about the same spot. At last he got away, and shaped his course for Hatfield.

It was nine o'clock at night, when the man, quite tired out, and the dog, limping and lame from the unaccustomed exercise, turned down the hill by the church of the quiet village, and plodding along the little street, crept into a small public-house, whose scanty light had guided them to the spot. There was a fire in the tap-room, and some country-labourers were drinking before it.

They made room for the stranger, but he sat down in the furthest corner, and ate and drank alone, or rather with his dog: to whom he cast a morsel of food from time to time.

The conversation of the men assembled here, turned upon the neighbouring land, and farmers; and when those topics were exhausted, upon the age of some old man who had been buried on the previous Sunday; the young men present considering him very old, and the old men present declaring him to have been quite young—not older, one white-haired grandfather said, than he was—with ten or fifteen year of life in him at least—if he had taken care; if he had taken care.

There was nothing to attract attention, or excite alarm in this. The robber, after paying his reckoning, sat silent and unnoticed in his corner, and had almost dropped asleep, when he was half wakened by the noisy entrance of a new comer.

This was an antic fellow, half pedlar and half mountebank, who travelled about the country on foot to vend hones, strops, razors, washballs, harness-paste, medicine for dogs and horses, cheap perfumery, cosmetics, and such-like wares, which he carried in a case slung to his back. His entrance was the signal for various homely jokes with the countrymen, which slackened not until he had made his supper, and opened his box of treasures, when he ingeniously contrived to unite business with amusement.

'And what be that stoof? Good to eat, Harry?' asked a grinning countryman, pointing to some composition-cakes in one corner.

'This,' said the fellow, producing one, 'this is the infallible and invaluable composition for removing all sorts of stain, rust, dirt, mildew, spick, speck, spot, or spatter, from silk, satin, linen, cambric, cloth, crape, stuff, carpet, merino, muslin, bombazeen, or woollen stuff. Wine-stains, fruit-stains, beer-stains, water-stains, paint-stains, pitch-stains, any stains, all come out at one rub with the infallible and invaluable composition. If a lady stains her honour, she has only need to swallow one cake and she's cured at once—for it's poison. If a gentleman wants to prove this, he has only need to bolt one little square, and he has put it beyond question—for it's quite as satisfactory as a pistol-bullet, and a great deal nastier in the flavour, consequently the more credit in taking it. One penny a square. With all these virtues, one penny a square!'

There were two buyers directly, and more of the listeners plainly hesitated. The vendor observing this, increased in loquacity.

'It's all bought up as fast as it can be made,' said the fellow. 'There are fourteen water-mills, six steam-engines, and a galvanic battery, always a-working upon it, and they can't make it fast enough, though the men work so hard that they die off, and the widows is pensioned directly, with twenty pound a-year for each of the children, and a premium of fifty for twins. One penny a square! Two half-pence is all the same, and four farthings is received with joy. One penny a square! Wine-stains, fruit-stains, beer-stains, water-stains, paint-stains, pitch-stains, mud-stains, blood-stains! Here is a stain upon the hat of a gentleman in company, that I'll take clean out, before he can order me a pint of ale.'

'Hah!' cried Sikes starting up. 'Give that back.'

'I'll take it clean out, sir,' replied the man, winking to the company, 'before you can come across the room to get it. Gentlemen all, observe the dark stain upon this gentleman's hat, no wider than a shilling, but thicker than a half-crown. Whether it is a wine-stain, fruit-stain, beer-stain, water-stain, paint-stain, pitch-stain, mud-stain, or blood-stain—'

The man got no further, for Sikes with a hideous imprecation overthrew the table, and tearing the hat from him, burst out of the house.

With the same perversity of feeling and irresolution that had fastened upon him, despite himself, all day, the murderer, finding that he was not followed, and that they most probably considered him some drunken sullen fellow, turned back up the town, and getting out of the glare of the lamps of a stage-coach that was standing in the street, was walking past, when he recognised the mail from London, and saw that it was standing at the little post-office. He almost knew what was to come; but he crossed over, and listened.

The guard was standing at the door, waiting for the letter-bag. A man, dressed like a game-keeper, came up at the moment, and he handed him a basket which lay ready on the pavement.

'That's for your people,' said the guard. 'Now, look alive in there, will you. Damn that 'ere bag, it warn't ready night afore last; this won't do, you know!'

'Anything new up in town, Ben?' asked the game-keeper, drawing back to the window-shutters, the better to admire the horses.

'No, nothing that I knows on,' replied the man, pulling on his gloves. 'Corn's up a little. I heerd talk of a murder, too, down Spitalfields way, but I don't reckon much upon it.'

'Oh, that's quite true,' said a gentleman inside, who was looking out of the window. 'And a dreadful murder it was.'

'Was it, sir?' rejoined the guard, touching his hat. 'Man or woman, pray, sir?'

'A woman,' replied the gentleman. 'It is supposed—'

'Now, Ben,' replied the coachman impatiently.

'Damn that 'ere bag,' said the guard; 'are you gone to sleep in there?'

'Coming!' cried the office keeper, running out.

'Coming,' growled the guard. 'Ah, and so's the young 'ooman of property that's going to take a fancy to me, but I don't know when. Here, give hold. All ri—ight!'

The horn sounded a few cheerful notes, and the coach was gone.

Sikes remained standing in the street, apparently unmoved by what he had just heard, and agitated by no stronger feeling than a doubt where to go. At length he went back again, and took the road which leads from Hatfield to St. Albans.

He went on doggedly; but as he left the town behind him, and plunged into the solitude and darkness of the road, he felt a dread and awe creeping upon him which shook him to the core. Every object before him, substance or shadow, still or moving, took the semblance of some fearful thing; but these fears were nothing compared to the sense that haunted him of that morning's ghastly figure following at his heels. He could trace its shadow in the gloom, supply the smallest item of the outline, and note how stiff and solemn it seemed to stalk along. He could hear its garments rustling in the leaves, and every breath of wind came laden with that last low cry. If he stopped it did the same. If he ran, it followed—not running too: that would have been a relief: but like a corpse endowed with the mere machinery of life, and borne on one slow melancholy wind that never rose or fell.

At times, he turned, with desperate determination, resolved to beat this phantom off, though it should look him dead; but the hair rose on his head, and his blood stood still, for it had turned with him and was behind him then. He had kept it before him that morning, but it was behind now—always. He leaned his back against a bank, and felt that it stood above him, visibly out against the cold night-sky. He threw himself upon the road—on his back upon the road. At his head it stood, silent, erect, and still—a living grave-stone, with its epitaph in blood.

Let no man talk of murderers escaping justice, and hint that Providence must sleep. There were twenty score of violent deaths in one long minute of that agony of fear.

There was a shed in a field he passed, that offered shelter for the night. Before the door, were three tall poplar trees, which made it very dark within; and the wind moaned through them with a dismal wail. He could not walk on, till daylight came again; and here he stretched himself close to the wall—to undergo new torture.

For now, a vision came before him, as constant and more terrible than that from which he had escaped. Those widely staring eyes, so lustreless and so glassy, that he had better borne to see them than think upon them, appeared in the midst of the darkness: light in themselves, but giving light to nothing. There were but two, but they were everywhere. If he shut out the sight, there came the room with every well-known object—some, indeed, that he would have forgotten, if he had gone over its contents from memory—each in its accustomed place. The body was in its place, and its eyes were as he saw them when he stole away. He got up, and rushed into the field without. The figure was behind him. He re-entered the shed, and shrunk down once more. The eyes were there, before he had laid himself along.

And here he remained in such terror as none but he can know, trembling in every limb, and the cold sweat starting from every pore, when suddenly there arose upon the night-wind the noise of distant shouting, and the roar of voices mingled in alarm and wonder. Any sound of men in that lonely place, even though it conveyed a real cause of alarm, was something to him. He regained his strength and energy at the prospect of personal danger; and springing to his feet, rushed into the open air.

The broad sky seemed on fire. Rising into the air with showers of sparks, and rolling one above the other, were sheets of flame, lighting the atmosphere for miles round, and driving clouds of smoke in the direction where he stood. The shouts grew louder as new voices swelled the roar, and he could hear the cry of Fire! mingled with the ringing of an alarm-bell, the fall of heavy bodies, and the crackling of flames as they twined round some new obstacle, and shot aloft as though refreshed by food. The noise increased as he looked. There were people there— men and women—light, bustle. It was like new life to him. He darted onward—straight, headlong—dashing through brier and brake, and leaping gate and fence as madly as his dog, who careered with loud and sounding bark before him.

He came upon the spot. There were half-dressed figures tearing to and fro, some endeavouring to drag the frightened horses from the stables, others driving the cattle from the yard and out-houses, and others coming laden from the burning pile, amidst a shower of falling sparks, and the tumbling down of red-hot beams. The apertures, where doors and windows stood an hour ago, disclosed a mass of raging fire; walls rocked and crumbled into the burning well; the molten lead and iron poured down, white hot, upon the ground. Women and children shrieked, and men encouraged each other with noisy shouts and cheers. The clanking of the engine-pumps, and the spirting and hissing of the water as it fell upon the blazing wood, added to the tremendous roar. He shouted, too, till he was hoarse; and flying from memory and himself, plunged into the thickest of the throng. Hither and thither he dived that night: now working at the pumps, and now hurrying through the smoke and flame, but never ceasing to engage himself wherever noise and men were thickest. Up and down the ladders, upon the roofs of buildings, over floors that quaked and trembled with his weight, under the lee of falling bricks and stones, in every part of that great fire was he; but he bore a charmed life, and had neither scratch nor bruise, nor weariness nor thought, till morning dawned again, and only smoke and blackened ruins remained.

This mad excitement over, there returned, with ten-fold force, the dreadful consciousness of his crime. He looked suspiciously about him, for the men were conversing in groups, and he feared to be the subject of their talk. The dog obeyed the significant beck of his finger, and they drew off, stealthily, together. He passed near an engine where some men were seated, and they called to him to share in their refreshment. He took some bread and meat; and as he drank a draught of beer, heard the firemen, who were from London, talking about the murder. 'He has gone to Birmingham, they say,' said one: 'but they'll have him yet, for the scouts are out, and by to-morrow night there'll be a cry all through the country.'

He hurried off, and walked till he almost dropped upon the ground; then lay down in a lane, and had a long, but broken and uneasy sleep. He wandered on again, irresolute and undecided, and oppressed with the fear of another solitary night.

Suddenly, he took the desperate resolution to going back to London.

'There's somebody to speak to there, at all event,' he thought. 'A good hiding-place, too. They'll never expect to nab me there, after this country scent. Why can't I lie by for a week or so, and, forcing blunt from Fagin, get abroad to France? Damme, I'll risk it.'

He acted upon this impulse without delay, and choosing the least frequented roads began his journey back, resolved to lie concealed within a short distance of the metropolis, and, entering it at dusk by a circuitous route, to proceed straight to that part of it which he had fixed on for his destination.

The dog, though. If any description of him were out, it would not be forgotten that the dog was missing, and had probably gone with him. This might lead to his apprehension as he passed along the streets. He resolved to drown him, and walked on, looking about for a pond: picking up a heavy stone and tying it to his handkerchief as he went.

The animal looked up into his master's face while these preparations were making; whether his instinct apprehended something of their purpose, or the robber's sidelong look at him was sterner than ordinary, he skulked a little farther in the rear than usual, and cowered as he came more slowly along. When his master halted at the brink of a pool, and looked round to call him, he stopped outright.

'Do you hear me call? Come here!' cried Sikes.

The animal came up from the very force of habit; but as Sikes stooped to attach the handkerchief to his throat, he uttered a low growl and started back.

'Come back!' said the robber.

The dog wagged his tail, but moved not. Sikes made a running noose and called him again.

The dog advanced, retreated, paused an instant, and scoured away at his hardest speed.

The man whistled again and again, and sat down and waited in the expectation that he would return. But no dog appeared, and at length he resumed his journey.

CHAPTER XLIX. MONKS AND MR. BROWNLOW AT LENGTH MEET. THEIR CONVERSATION, AND THE INTELLIGENCE THAT INTERRUPTS IT

The twilight was beginning to close in, when Mr. Brownlow

alighted from a hackney-coach at his own door, and knocked softly. The door being opened, a sturdy man got out of the coach and stationed himself on one side of the steps, while another man, who had been seated on the box, dismounted too, and stood upon the other side. At a sign from Mr. Brownlow, they helped out a third man, and taking him between them, hurried him into the house. This man was Monks.

They walked in the same manner up the stairs without speaking, and Mr. Brownlow, preceding them, led the way into a back-room. At the door of this apartment, Monks, who had ascended with evident reluctance, stopped. The two men looked at the old gentleman as if for instructions.

'He knows the alternative,' said Mr. Browlow. 'If he hesitates or moves a finger but as you bid him, drag him into the street, call for the aid of the police, and impeach him as a felon in my name.'

'How dare you say this of me?' asked Monks.

'How dare you urge me to it, young man?' replied Mr. Brownlow, confronting him with a steady look. 'Are you mad enough to leave this house? Unhand him. There, sir. You are free to go, and we to follow. But I warn you, by all I hold most solemn and most sacred, that instant will have you apprehended on a charge of fraud and robbery. I am resolute and immoveable. If you are determined to be the same, your blood be upon your own head!'

'By what authority am I kidnapped in the street, and brought here by these dogs?' asked

Monks, looking from one to the other of the men who stood beside him.

'By mine,' replied Mr. Brownlow. 'Those persons are indemnified by me. If you complain of being deprived of your liberty—you had power and opportunity to retrieve it as you came along, but you deemed it advisable to remain quiet—I say again, throw yourself for protection on the law. I will appeal to the law too; but when you have gone too far to recede, do not sue to me for leniency, when the power will have passed into other hands; and do not say I plunged you down the gulf into which you rushed, yourself.'

Monks was plainly disconcerted, and alarmed besides. He hesitated.

'You will decide quickly,' said Mr. Brownlow, with perfect firmness and composure. 'If you wish me to prefer my charges publicly, and consign you to a punishment the extent of which, although I can, with a shudder, foresee, I cannot control, once more, I say, for you know the way. If not, and you appeal to my forbearance, and the mercy of those you have deeply injured, seat yourself, without a word, in that chair. It has waited for you two whole days.'

Monks muttered some unintelligible words, but wavered still.

'You will be prompt,' said Mr. Brownlow. 'A word from me, and the alternative has gone for ever.'

Still the man hesitated.

'I have not the inclination to parley,' said Mr. Brownlow, 'and, as I advocate the dearest interests of others, I have not the right.'

'Is there—' demanded Monks with a faltering tongue,—'is there—no middle course?'

'None.'

Monks looked at the old gentleman, with an anxious eye; but, reading in his countenance nothing but severity and determination, walked into the room, and, shrugging his shoulders, sat down.

'Lock the door on the outside,' said Mr. Brownlow to the attendants, 'and come when I ring.'

The men obeyed, and the two were left alone together.

'This is pretty treatment, sir,' said Monks, throwing down his hat and cloak, 'from my father's oldest friend.'

'It is because I was your father's oldest friend, young man,' returned Mr. Brownlow; 'it is because the hopes and wishes of young and happy years were bound up with him, and that fair creature of his blood and kindred who rejoined her God in youth, and left me here a solitary, lonely man: it is because he knelt with me beside his only sisters's death-bed when he was yet a boy, on the morning that would—but Heaven willed otherwise—have made her my young wife; it is because my seared heart clung to him, from that time forth, through all his trials and errors, till he died; it is because old recollections and associations filled my heart, and even the sight of you brings with it old thoughts of him; it is because of all these things that I am moved to treat you gently now—yes, Edward Leeford, even now—and blush for your unworthiness who bear the name.'

'What has the name to do with it?' asked the other, after contemplating, half in silence, and half in dogged wonder, the agitation of his companion. 'What is the name to me?'

'Nothing,' replied Mr. Brownlow, 'nothing to you. But it was hers, and even at this distance of time brings back to me, an old man, the glow and thrill which I once felt, only to hear it repeated by a stranger. I am very glad you have changed it—very—very.'

'This is all mighty fine,' said Monks (to retain his assumed designation) after a long silence, during which he had jerked himself in sullen defiance to and fro, and Mr. Brownlow had sat, shading his face with his hand. 'But what do you want with me?'

'You have a brother,' said Mr. Brownlow, rousing himself: 'a brother, the whisper of whose name in your ear when I came behind you in the street, was, in itself, almost enough to make you accompany me hither, in wonder and alarm.'

'I have no brother,' replied Monks. 'You know I was an only child. Why do you talk to me of brothers? You know that, as well as I.'

'Attend to what I do know, and you may not,' said Mr. Brownlow. 'I shall interest you by and by. I know that of the wretched marriage, into which family pride, and the most sordid and narrowest of all ambition, forced your unhappy father when a mere boy, you were the sole and most unnatural issue.'

'I don't care for hard names,' interrupted Monks with a jeering laugh. 'You know the fact, and that's enough for me.'

'But I also know,' pursued the old gentleman, 'the misery, the slow torture, the protracted anguish of that ill-assorted union. I know how listlessly and wearily each of that wretched pair dragged on their heavy chain through a world that was poisoned to them both. I know how cold formalities were succeeded by open taunts; how indifference gave place to dislike, dislike to hate, and hate to loathing, until at last they wrenched the clanking bond asunder, and retiring a wide space apart, carried each a galling fragment, of which nothing but death could break the rivets, to hide it in new society beneath the gayest looks they could assume. Your mother succeeded; she forgot it soon. But it rusted and cankered at your father's heart for years.'

'Well, they were separated,' said Monks, 'and what of that?'

'When they had been separated for some time,' returned Mr. Brownlow, 'and your mother, wholly given up to continental frivolities, had utterly forgotten the young husband ten good years her junior, who, with prospects blighted, lingered on at home, he fell among new friends. This circumstance, at least, you know already.'

'Not I,' said Monks, turning away his eyes and beating his foot upon the ground, as a man who is determined to deny everything. 'Not I.'

'Your manner, no less than your actions, assures me that you have never forgotten it, or ceased to think of it with bitterness,' returned Mr. Brownlow. 'I speak of fifteen years ago, when you were not more than eleven years old, and your father but one-and-thirty—for he was, I repeat, a boy, when his father ordered him to marry. Must I go back to events which cast a shade upon the memory of your parent, or will you spare it, and disclose to me the truth?'

'I have nothing to disclose,' rejoined Monks. 'You must talk on if you will.'

'These new friends, then,' said Mr. Brownlow, 'were a naval officer retired from active service, whose wife had died some half-a-year before, and left him with two children—there had been more, but, of all their family, happily but two survived. They were both daughters; one a beautiful creature of nineteen, and the other a mere child of two or three years old.'

'What's this to me?' asked Monks.

'They resided,' said Mr. Brownlow, without seeming to hear the interruption, 'in a part of the country to which your father in his wandering had repaired, and where he had taken up his abode. Acquaintance, intimacy, friendship, fast followed on each other. Your father was gifted as few men are. He had his sister's soul and person. As the old officer knew him more and more, he grew to love him. I would that it had ended there. His daughter did the same.'

The old gentleman paused; Monks was biting his lips, with his eyes fixed upon the floor; seeing this, he immediately resumed:

'The end of a year found him contracted, solemnly contracted, to that daughter; the object of the first, true, ardent, only passion of a guileless girl.'

'Your tale is of the longest,' observed Monks, moving restlessly in his chair.

'It is a true tale of grief and trial, and sorrow, young man,' returned Mr. Brownlow, 'and such tales usually are; if it were one of unmixed joy and happiness, it would be very brief. At length one of those rich relations to strengthen whose interest and importance your father had been sacrificed, as others are often—it is no uncommon case—died, and to repair the misery he had been instrumental in occasioning, left him his panacea for all griefs—Money. It was necessary that he should immediately repair to Rome, whither this man had sped for health, and where he had died, leaving his affairs in great confusion. He went; was seized with mortal illness there; was followed, the moment the intelligence reached Paris, by your mother who carried you with her; he died the day after her arrival, leaving no will—no will—so that the whole property fell to her and you.'

At this part of the recital Monks held his breath, and listened with a face of intense eagerness, though his eyes were not directed towards the speaker. As Mr. Brownlow paused, he changed his position with the air of one who has experienced a sudden relief, and wiped his hot face and hands.

'Before he went abroad, and as he passed through London on his way,' said Mr. Brownlow, slowly, and fixing his eyes upon the other's face, 'he came to me.'

'I never heard of that,' interrupted Monks in a tone intended to appear incredulous, but savouring more of disagreeable surprise.

'He came to me, and left with me, among some other things, a picture—a portrait painted by himself—a likeness of this poor girl—which he did not wish to leave behind, and could not carry forward on his hasty journey. He was worn by anxiety and remorse almost to a shadow; talked in a wild, distracted way, of ruin and dishonour worked by himself; confided to me his intention to convert his whole property, at any loss, into money, and, having settled on his wife and you a portion of his recent acquisition, to fly the country—I guessed too well he would not fly alone—and never see it more. Even from me, his old and early friend, whose strong attachment had taken root in the earth that covered one most dear to both—even from me he withheld any more particular confession, promising to write and tell me all, and after that to see me once again, for the last time on earth. Alas! That was the last time. I had no letter, and I never saw him more.'

'I went,' said Mr. Brownlow, after a short pause, 'I went, when all was over, to the scene of his—I will use the term the world would freely use, for worldly harshness or favour are now alike to him—of his guilty love, resolved that if my fears were realised that erring child should find one heart and home to shelter and compassionate her. The family had left that part a week before; they had called in such trifling debts as were outstanding, discharged them, and left the place by night. Why, or whither, none can tell.'

Monks drew his breath yet more freely, and looked round with a smile of triumph.

'When your brother,' said Mr. Brownlow, drawing nearer to the other's chair, 'When your brother: a feeble, ragged, neglected child: was cast in my way by a stronger hand than chance, and rescued by me from a life of vice and infamy—'

'What?' cried Monks.

'By me,' said Mr. Brownlow. 'I told you I should interest you before long. I say by me—I see that your cunning associate suppressed my name, although for ought he knew, it would be quite strange to your ears. When he was rescued by me, then, and lay recovering from sickness in my house, his strong resemblance to this picture I have spoken of, struck me with astonishment. Even when I first saw him in all his dirt and misery, there was a lingering expression in his face that came upon me like a glimpse of some old friend flashing on one in a vivid dream. I need not tell you he was snared away before I knew his history—'

'Why not?' asked Monks hastily.

'Because you know it well.'

'I!'

'Denial to me is vain,' replied Mr. Brownlow. 'I shall show you that I know more than that.'

'You—you—can't prove anything against me,' stammered Monks. 'I defy you to do it!'

'We shall see,' returned the old gentleman with a searching glance. 'I lost the boy, and no efforts of mine could recover him. Your mother being dead, I knew that you alone could solve the mystery if anybody could, and as when I had last heard of you-you were on your own estate in the West Indies—whither, as you well know, you retired upon your mother's death to escape the consequences of vicious courses here—I made the voyage. You had left it, months before, and were supposed to be in London, but no one could tell where. I returned. Your agents had no clue to your residence. You came and went, they said, as strangely as you had ever done: sometimes for days together and sometimes not for months: keeping to all appearance the same low haunts and mingling with the same infamous herd who had been your associates when a fierce ungovernable boy. I wearied them with new applications. I paced the streets by night and day, but until two hours ago, all my efforts were fruitless, and I never saw you for an instant.'

'And now you do see me,' said Monks, rising boldly, 'what then? Fraud and robbery are high-sounding words—justified, you think, by a fancied resemblance in some young imp to an idle daub of a dead man's Brother! You don't even know that a child was born of this maudlin pair; you don't even know that.'

844

'I did not,' replied Mr. Brownlow, rising too; 'but within the last fortnight I have learnt it all. You have a brother; you know it, and him. There was a will, which your mother destroyed, leaving the secret and the gain to you at her own death. It contained a reference to some child likely to be the result of this sad connection, which child was born, and accidentally encountered by you, when your suspicions were first awakened by his resemblance to your father. You repaired to the place of his birth. There existed proofs—proofs long suppressed— of his birth and parentage. Those proofs were destroyed by you, and now, in your own words to your accomplice the Jew, "the only proofs of the boy's identity lie at the bottom of the river, and the old hag that received them from the mother is rotting in her coffin." Unworthy son, coward, liar,—you, who hold your councils with thieves and murderers in dark rooms at night,—you, whose plots and wiles have brought a violent death upon the head of one worth millions such as you,—you, who from your cradle were gall and bitterness to your own father's heart, and in whom all evil passions, vice, and profligacy, festered, till they found a vent in a hideous disease which had made your face an index even to your mind—you, Edward Leeford, do you still brave me!'

'No, no, no!' returned the coward, overwhelmed by these accumulated charges.

'Every word!' cried the gentleman, 'every word that has passed between you and this detested villain, is known to me. Shadows on the wall have caught your whispers, and brought them to my ear; the sight of the persecuted child has turned vice itself, and given it the courage and almost the attributes of virtue. Murder has been done, to which you were morally if not really a party.'

'No, no,' interposed Monks. 'I—I knew nothing of that; I was going to inquire the truth of the story when you overtook me. I didn't know the cause. I thought it was a common quarrel.'

'It was the partial disclosure of your secrets,' replied Mr. Brownlow. 'Will you disclose the whole?'

'Yes, I will.'

'Set your hand to a statement of truth and facts, and repeat it before witnesses?'

'That I promise too.'

'Remain quietly here, until such a document is drawn up, and proceed with me to such a place as I may deem most advisable, for the purpose of attesting it?'

'If you insist upon that, I'll do that also,' replied Monks.

'You must do more than that,' said Mr. Brownlow. 'Make restitution to an innocent and unoffending child, for such he is, although the offspring of a guilty and most miserable love. You have not forgotten the provisions of the will. Carry them into execution so far as your brother is concerned, and then go where you please. In this world you need meet no more.'

While Monks was pacing up and down, meditating with dark and evil looks on this proposal and the possibilities of evading it: torn by his fears on the one hand and his hatred on the other: the door was hurriedly unlocked, and a gentleman (Mr. Losberne) entered the room in violent agitation.

'The man will be taken,' he cried. 'He will be taken to-night!'

'The murderer?' asked Mr. Brownlow.

'Yes, yes,' replied the other. 'His dog has been seen lurking about some old haunt, and there seems little doubt that his master either is, or will be, there, under cover of the darkness. Spies are hovering about in every direction. I have spoken to the men who are charged with his capture, and they tell me he cannot escape. A reward of a hundred pounds is proclaimed by Government to-night.'

'I will give fifty more,' said Mr. Brownlow, 'and proclaim it with my own lips upon the spot, if I can reach it. Where is Mr. Maylie?'

'Harry? As soon as he had seen your friend here, safe in a coach with you, he hurried off to where he heard this,' replied the doctor, 'and mounting his horse sallied forth to join the first party at some place in the outskirts agreed upon between them.'

'Fagin,' said Mr. Brownlow; 'what of him?'

'When I last heard, he had not been taken, but he will be, or is, by this time. They're sure of him.'

'Have you made up your mind?' asked Mr. Brownlow, in a low voice, of Monks.

'Yes,' he replied. 'You—you—will be secret with me?'

'I will. Remain here till I return. It is your only hope of safety.'

They left the room, and the door was again locked.

'What have you done?' asked the doctor in a whisper.

'All that I could hope to do, and even more. Coupling the poor girl's intelligence with my previous knowledge, and the result of our good friend's inquiries on the spot, I left him no loophole of escape, and laid bare the whole villainy which by these lights became plain as day. Write and appoint the evening after to-morrow, at seven, for the meeting. We shall be down there, a few hours before, but shall require rest: especially the young lady, who may have greater need of firmness than either you or I can quite foresee just now. But my blood boils to avenge this poor murdered creature. Which way have they taken?'

'Drive straight to the office and you will be in time,' replied Mr. Losberne. 'I will remain here.'

The two gentlemen hastily separated; each in a fever of excitement wholly uncontrollable.

CHAPTER L. THE PURSUIT AND ESCAPE

Near to that part of the Thames on which the church at Rotherhithe abuts, where the buildings on the banks are dirtiest and the vessels on the river blackest with the dust of colliers and the smoke of close-built low-roofed houses, there exists the filthiest, the strangest, the most extraordinary of the many localities that are hidden in London, wholly unknown, even by name, to the great mass of its inhabitants.

To reach this place, the visitor has to penetrate through a maze of close, narrow, and muddy streets, thronged by the roughest and poorest of waterside people, and devoted to the traffic they may be supposed to occasion. The cheapest and least delicate provisions are heaped in the shops; the coarsest and commonest articles of wearing apparel dangle at the salesman's door, and stream from the house-parapet and windows. Jostling with unemployed labourers of the lowest class, ballast-heavers, coal-whippers, brazen women, ragged children, and the raff and refuse of the river, he makes his way with difficulty along, assailed by offensive sights and smells from the narrow alleys which branch off on the right and left, and deafened by the clash of ponderous waggons that bear great piles of merchandise from the stacks of warehouses that rise from every corner. Arriving, at length, in streets remoter and less-frequented than those through which he has passed, he walks beneath tottering house-fronts projecting over the pavement, dismantled walls that seem to totter as he passes, chimneys half crushed half hesitating to fall, windows guarded by rusty iron bars that time and dirt have almost eaten away, every imaginable sign of desolation and neglect.

In such a neighborhood, beyond Dockhead in the Borough of Southwark, stands Jacob's Island, surrounded by a muddy ditch, six or eight feet deep and fifteen or twenty wide when the tide is in, once called Mill Pond, but known in the days of this story as Folly Ditch. It is a creek or inlet from the Thames, and can always be filled at high water by opening the sluices at the Lead Mills from which it took its old name. At such times, a stranger, looking from one of the wooden bridges thrown across it at Mill Lane, will see the inhabitants of the houses on either side lowering from their back doors and windows, buckets, pails, domestic utensils of all kinds, in which to haul the water up; and when his eye is turned from these operations to the houses themselves, his utmost astonishment will be excited by the scene before him. Crazy wooden galleries common to the backs of half a dozen houses, with holes from which to look upon the slime beneath; windows, broken and patched, with poles thrust out, on which to dry the linen that is never there; rooms so small, so filthy, so confined, that the air would seem too tainted even for the dirt and squalor which they shelter; wooden chambers thrusting themselves out above the mud, and threatening to fall into it—as some have done; dirt-besmeared walls and decaying foundations; every repulsive lineament of poverty, every loathsome indication of filth, rot, and garbage; all these ornament the banks of Folly Ditch.

In Jacob's Island, the warehouses are roofless and empty; the walls are crumbling down; the windows are windows no more; the doors are falling into the streets; the chimneys are blackened, but they yield no smoke. Thirty or forty years ago, before losses and chancery suits came upon it, it was a thriving place; but now it is a desolate island indeed. The houses have no owners; they are broken open, and entered upon by those who have the courage; and there they live, and there they die. They must have powerful motives for a secret residence, or be reduced to a destitute condition indeed, who seek a refuge in Jacob's Island.

In an upper room of one of these houses—a detached house of fair size, ruinous in other respects, but strongly defended at door and window: of which house the back commanded the ditch in manner already described—there were assembled three men, who, regarding each other every now and then with looks expressive of perplexity and expectation, sat for some time in profound and gloomy silence. One of these was Toby Crackit, another Mr. Chitling, and the third a robber of fifty years, whose nose had been almost beaten in, in some old scuffle, and whose face bore a frightful scar which might probably be traced to the same occasion. This man was a returned transport, and his name was Kags.

'I wish,' said Toby turning to Mr. Chitling, 'that you had picked out some other crib when the two old ones got too warm, and had not come here, my fine feller.'

'Why didn't you, blunder-head!' said Kags.

'Well, I thought you'd have been a little more glad to see me than this,' replied Mr. Chitling, with a melancholy air.

'Why, look'e, young gentleman,' said Toby, 'when a man keeps himself so very exclusive as I have done, and by that means has a snug house over his head with nobody a prying and smelling about it, it's rather a startling thing to have the honour of a wisit from a young gentleman (however respectable and pleasant a person he may be to play cards with at conweniency) circumstanced as you are.'

'Especially, when the exclusive young man has got a friend stopping with him, that's arrived sooner than was expected from foreign parts, and is too modest to want to be presented to the Judges on his return,' added Mr. Kags.

There was a short silence, after which Toby Crackit, seeming to abandon as hopeless any further effort to maintain his usual devil-may-care swagger, turned to Chitling and said,

'When was Fagin took then?'

'Just at dinner-time—two o'clock this afternoon. Charley and I made our lucky up the wash-us chimney, and Bolter got into the empty water-butt, head downwards; but his legs were so precious long that they stuck out at the top, and so they took him too.'

'And Bet?'

'Poor Bet! She went to see the Body, to speak to who it was,' replied Chitling, his countenance falling more and more, 'and went off mad, screaming and raving, and beating her head against the boards; so they put a strait-weskut on her and took her to the hospital—and there she is.'

'Wot's come of young Bates?' demanded Kags.

'He hung about, not to come over here afore dark, but he'll be here soon,' replied Chitling. 'There's nowhere else to go to now, for the people at the Cripples are all in custody, and the bar of the ken—I went up there and see it with my own eyes—is filled with traps.'

'This is a smash,' observed Toby, biting his lips. 'There's more than one will go with this.'

'The sessions are on,' said Kags: 'if they get the inquest over, and Bolter turns King's evidence: as of course he will, from what he's said already: they can prove Fagin an accessory before the fact, and get the trial on on Friday, and he'll swing in six days from this, by G—!'

'You should have heard the people groan,' said Chitling; 'the officers fought like devils, or they'd have torn him away. He was down once, but they made a ring round him, and fought their way along. You should have seen how he looked about him, all muddy and bleeding, and clung to them as if they were his dearest friends. I can see 'em now, not able to stand upright with the pressing of the mob, and draggin him along amongst 'em; I can see the people jumping up, one behind another, and snarling with their teeth and making at him; I can see the blood upon his hair and beard, and hear the cries with which the women worked themselves into the centre of the crowd at the street corner, and swore they'd tear his heart out!'

The horror-stricken witness of this scene pressed his hands upon his ears, and with his eyes closed got up and paced violently to and fro, like one distracted.

While he was thus engaged, and the two men sat by in silence with their eyes fixed upon the floor, a pattering noise was heard upon the stairs, and Sikes's dog bounded into the room.

They ran to the window, downstairs, and into the street. The dog had jumped in at an open window; he made no attempt to follow them, nor was his master to be seen.

'What's the meaning of this?' said Toby when they had returned. 'He can't be coming here. I—I—hope not.'

'If he was coming here, he'd have come with the dog,' said Kags, stooping down to examine the animal, who lay panting on the floor. 'Here! Give us some water for him; he has run himself faint.'

'He's drunk it all up, every drop,' said Chitling after watching the dog some time in silence. 'Covered with mud—lame—half blind—he must have come a long way.'

'Where can he have come from!' exclaimed Toby. 'He's been to the other kens of course, and finding them filled with strangers come on here, where he's been many a time and often. But where can he have come from first, and how comes he here alone without the other!'

'He'—(none of them called the murderer by his old name)—'He can't have made away with himself. What do you think?' said Chitling.

Toby shook his head.

'If he had,' said Kags, 'the dog 'ud want to lead us away to where he did it. No. I think he's got out of the country, and left the dog behind. He must have given him the slip somehow, or he wouldn't be so easy.'

This solution, appearing the most probable one, was adopted as the right; the dog, creeping under a chair, coiled himself up to sleep, without more notice from anybody.

It being now dark, the shutter was closed, and a candle lighted and placed upon the table. The terrible events of the last two days had made a deep impression on all three, increased by the danger and uncertainty of their own position. They drew their chairs closer together, starting at every sound. They spoke little, and that in whispers, and were as silent and awe-stricken as if the remains of the murdered woman lay in the next room.

They had sat thus, some time, when suddenly was heard a hurried knocking at the door below.

'Young Bates,' said Kags, looking angrily round, to check the fear he felt himself.

The knocking came again. No, it wasn't he. He never knocked like that.

Crackit went to the window, and shaking all over, drew in his head. There was no need to tell them who it was; his pale face was enough. The dog too was on the alert in an instant, and ran whining to the door.

'We must let him in,' he said, taking up the candle.

'Isn't there any help for it?' asked the other man in a hoarse voice.

'None. He must come in.'

'Don't leave us in the dark,' said Kags, taking down a candle from the chimney-piece, and lighting it, with such a trembling hand that the knocking was twice repeated before he had finished.

Crackit went down to the door, and returned followed by a man with the lower part of his face buried in a handkerchief, and another tied over his head under his hat. He drew them slowly off. Blanched face, sunken eyes, hollow cheeks, beard of three days' growth, wasted flesh, short thick breath; it was the very ghost of Sikes.

He laid his hand upon a chair which stood in the middle of the room, but shuddering as he was about to drop into it, and seeming to glance over his shoulder, dragged it back close to the wall—as close as it would go—and ground it against it—and sat down.

Not a word had been exchanged. He looked from one to another in silence. If an eye were furtively raised and met his, it was instantly averted. When his hollow voice broke silence, they all three started. They seemed never to have heard its tones before.

'How came that dog here?' he asked.

'Alone. Three hours ago.'

'To-night's paper says that Fagin's took. Is it true, or a lie?'

'True.'

They were silent again.

'Damn you all!' said Sikes, passing his hand across his forehead.

'Have you nothing to say to me?'

There was an uneasy movement among them, but nobody spoke.

'You that keep this house,' said Sikes, turning his face to Crackit, 'do you mean to sell me, or to let me lie here till this hunt is over?'

'You may stop here, if you think it safe,' returned the person addressed, after some hesitation.

Sikes carried his eyes slowly up the wall behind him: rather trying to turn his head than actually doing it: and said, 'Is—it—the body—is it buried?'

They shook their heads.

'Why isn't it!' he retorted with the same glance behind him. 'Wot do they keep such ugly things above the ground for?—Who's that knocking?'

Crackit intimated, by a motion of his hand as he left the room, that there was nothing to fear; and directly came back with Charley Bates behind him. Sikes sat opposite the door, so that the moment the boy entered the room he encountered his figure.

'Toby,' said the boy falling back, as Sikes turned his eyes towards him, 'why didn't you tell me this, downstairs?'

There had been something so tremendous in the shrinking off of the three, that the wretched man was willing to propitiate even this lad. Accordingly he nodded, and made as though he would shake hands with him.

'Let me go into some other room,' said the boy, retreating still farther.

'Charley!' said Sikes, stepping forward. 'Don't you—don't you know me?'

'Don't come nearer me,' answered the boy, still retreating, and looking, with horror in his eyes, upon the murderer's face. 'You monster!'

The man stopped half-way, and they looked at each other; but Sikes's eyes sunk gradually to the ground.

'Witness you three,' cried the boy shaking his clenched fist, and becoming more and more excited as he spoke. 'Witness you three—I'm not afraid of him—if they come here after him, I'll give him up; I will. I tell you out at once. He may kill me for it if he likes, or if he dares, but if I am here I'll give him up. I'd give him up if he was to be boiled alive. Murder! Help! If there's the pluck of a man among you three, you'll help me. Murder! Help! Down with him!'

Pouring out these cries, and accompanying them with violent gesticulation, the boy actually threw himself, single-handed, upon the strong man, and in the intensity of his energy and the suddenness of his surprise, brought him heavily to the ground.

The three spectators seemed quite stupefied. They offered no interference, and the boy and man rolled on the ground together; the former, heedless of the blows that showered upon him, wrenching his hands tighter and tighter in the garments about the murderer's breast, and never ceasing to call for help with all his might.

The contest, however, was too unequal to last long. Sikes had him down, and his knee was on his throat, when Crackit pulled him back with a look of alarm, and pointed to the window. There were lights gleaming below, voices in loud and earnest conversation, the tramp of hurried footsteps—endless they seemed in number—crossing the nearest wooden bridge. One man on horseback seemed to be among the crowd; for there was the noise of hoofs rattling on the uneven pavement. The gleam of lights increased; the footsteps came more thickly and noisily on. Then, came a loud knocking at the door, and then a hoarse murmur from such a multitude of angry voices as would have made the boldest quail.

'Help!' shrieked the boy in a voice that rent the air.

'He's here! Break down the door!'

'In the King's name,' cried the voices without; and the hoarse cry arose again, but louder.

'Break down the door!' screamed the boy. 'I tell you they'll never open it. Run straight to the room where the light is. Break down the door!'

Strokes, thick and heavy, rattled upon the door and lower window-shutters as he ceased to speak, and a loud huzzah burst from the crowd; giving the listener, for the first time, some adequate idea of its immense extent.

'Open the door of some place where I can lock this screeching Hell-babe,' cried Sikes fiercely; running to and fro, and dragging the boy, now, as easily as if he were an empty sack. 'That door. Quick!' He flung him in, bolted it, and turned the key. 'Is the downstairs door fast?'

'Double-locked and chained,' replied Crackit, who, with the other two men, still remained quite helpless and bewildered.

'The panels—are they strong?'

'Lined with sheet-iron.'

'And the windows too?'

'Yes, and the windows.'

'Damn you!' cried the desperate ruffian, throwing up the sash and menacing the crowd.

'Do your worst! I'll cheat you yet!'

Of all the terrific yells that ever fell on mortal ears, none could exceed the cry of the infuriated throng. Some shouted to those who were nearest to set the house on fire; others roared to the officers to shoot him dead. Among them all, none showed such fury as the man on horseback, who, throwing himself out of the saddle, and bursting through the crowd as if he were parting water, cried, beneath the window, in a voice that rose above all others, 'Twenty guineas to the man who brings a ladder!'

The nearest voices took up the cry, and hundreds echoed it. Some called for ladders, some for sledge-hammers; some ran with torches to and fro as if to seek them, and still came back and roared again; some spent their breath in impotent curses and execrations; some pressed forward with the ecstasy of madmen, and thus impeded the progress of those below; some among the boldest attempted to climb up by the water-spout and crevices in the wall; and all waved to and fro, in the darkness beneath, like a field of corn moved by an angry wind: and joined from time to time in one loud furious roar.

'The tide,' cried the murderer, as he staggered back into the room, and shut the faces out, 'the tide was in as I came up. Give me a rope, a long rope. They're all in front. I may drop into the Folly Ditch, and clear off that way. Give me a rope, or I shall do three more murders and kill myself.'

The panic-stricken men pointed to where such articles were kept; the murderer, hastily selecting the longest and strongest cord, hurried up to the house-top.

All the window in the rear of the house had been long ago bricked up, except one small trap in the room where the boy was locked, and that was too small even for the passage of his body. But, from this aperture, he had never ceased to call on those without, to guard the back; and thus, when the murderer emerged at last on the house-top by the door in the roof, a loud shout proclaimed the fact to those in front, who immediately began to pour round, pressing upon each other in an unbroken stream.

He planted a board, which he had carried up with him for the purpose, so firmly against the door that it must be matter of great difficulty to open it from the inside; and creeping over the tiles, looked over the low parapet.

The water was out, and the ditch a bed of mud.

The crowd had been hushed during these few moments, watching his motions and doubtful of his purpose, but the instant they perceived it and knew it was defeated, they raised a cry of triumphant execration to which all their previous shouting had been whispers. Again and again it rose. Those who were at too great a distance to know its meaning, took up the sound; it echoed and re-echoed; it seemed as though the whole city had poured its population out to curse him.

On pressed the people from the front—on, on, on, in a strong struggling current of angry faces, with here and there a glaring torch to lighten them up, and show them out in all their wrath and passion. The houses on the opposite side of the ditch had been entered by the mob; sashes were thrown up, or torn bodily out; there were tiers and tiers of faces in every window; cluster upon cluster of people clinging to every house-top. Each little bridge (and there were three in sight) bent beneath the weight of the crowd upon it. Still the current poured on to find some nook or hole from which to vent their shouts, and only for an instant see the wretch.

'They have him now,' cried a man on the nearest bridge. 'Hurrah!'

The crowd grew light with uncovered heads; and again the shout uprose.

'I will give fifty pounds,' cried an old gentleman from the same quarter, 'to the man who takes him alive. I will remain here, till he come to ask me for it.'

There was another roar. At this moment the word was passed among the crowd that the door was forced at last, and that he who had first called for the ladder had mounted into the room. The stream abruptly turned, as this intelligence ran from mouth to mouth; and the people at the windows, seeing those upon the bridges pouring back, quitted their stations, and running into the street, joined the concourse that now thronged pell-mell to the spot they had left: each man crushing and striving with his neighbor, and all panting with impatience to get near the door, and look upon the criminal as the officers brought him out. The cries and shrieks of those who were pressed almost to suffocation, or trampled down and trodden under foot in the confusion, were dreadful; the narrow ways were completely blocked up; and at this time, between the rush of some to regain the space in front of the house, and the unavailing struggles of others to extricate themselves from the mass, the immediate attention was distracted from the murderer, although the universal eagerness for his capture was, if possible, increased.

The man had shrunk down, thoroughly quelled by the ferocity of the crowd, and the impossibility of escape; but seeing this sudden change with no less rapidity than it had occurred, he sprang upon his feet, determined to make one last effort for his life by dropping into the ditch, and, at the risk of being stifled, endeavouring to creep away in the darkness and confusion.

Roused into new strength and energy, and stimulated by the noise within the house which announced that an entrance had really been effected, he set his foot against the stack of chimneys, fastened one end of the rope tightly and firmly round it, and with the other made a strong running noose by the aid of his hands and teeth almost in a second. He could let himself down by the cord to within a less distance of the ground than his own height, and had his knife ready in his hand to cut it then and drop.

At the very instant when he brought the loop over his head previous to slipping it beneath his arm-pits, and when the old gentleman before-mentioned (who had clung so tight to the railing of the bridge as to resist the force of the crowd, and retain his position) earnestly warned those about him that the man was about to lower himself down—at that very instant the murderer, looking behind him on the roof, threw his arms above his head, and uttered a yell of terror.

'The eyes again!' he cried in an unearthly screech.

Staggering as if struck by lightning, he lost his balance and tumbled over the parapet. The noose was on his neck. It ran up with his weight, tight as a bow-string, and swift as the arrow it speeds. He fell for five-and-thirty feet. There was a sudden jerk, a terrific convulsion of the limbs; and there he hung, with the open knife clenched in his stiffening hand.

The old chimney quivered with the shock, but stood it bravely. The murderer swung lifeless against the wall; and the boy, thrusting aside the dangling body which obscured his view, called to the people to come and take him out, for God's sake.

A dog, which had lain concealed till now, ran backwards and forwards on the parapet with a dismal howl, and collecting himself for a spring, jumped for the dead man's shoulders. Missing his aim, he fell into the ditch, turning completely over as he went; and striking his head against a stone, dashed out his brains.

CHAPTER LI. AFFORDING AN EXPLANATION OF MORE MYSTERIES THAN ONE, AND COMPREHENDING A PROPOSAL OF MARRIAGE WITH NO WORD OF SETTLEMENT OR PIN-MONEY

The events narrated in the last chapter were yet but two days old, when Oliver found himself, at three o'clock in the afternoon, in a travelling-carriage rolling fast towards his native town. Mrs. Maylie, and Rose, and Mrs. Bedwin, and the good doctor were with him: and Mr. Brownlow followed in a post-chaise, accompanied by one other person whose name had not been mentioned.

They had not talked much upon the way; for Oliver was in a flutter of agitation and uncertainty which deprived him of the power of collecting his thoughts, and almost of speech, and appeared to have scarcely less effect on his companions, who shared it, in at least an equal degree. He and the two ladies had been very carefully made acquainted by Mr. Brownlow with the nature of the admissions which had been forced from Monks; and although they knew that the object of their present journey was to complete the work which had been so well begun, still the whole matter was enveloped in enough of doubt and mystery to leave them in endurance of the most intense suspense.

The same kind friend had, with Mr. Losberne's assistance, cautiously stopped all channels of communication through which they could receive intelligence of the dreadful occurrences that so recently taken place. 'It was quite true,' he said, 'that they must know them before long, but it might be at a better time than the present, and it could not be at a worse.' So, they travelled on in silence: each busied with reflections on the object which had brought them together: and no one disposed to give utterance to the thoughts which crowded upon all.

But if Oliver, under these influences, had remained silent while they journeyed towards his birth-place by a road he had never seen, how the whole current of his recollections ran back to old times, and what a crowd of emotions were wakened up in his breast, when they turned into that which he had traversed on foot: a poor houseless, wandering boy, without a friend to help him, or a roof to shelter his head.

'See there, there!' cried Oliver, eagerly clasping the hand of Rose, and pointing out at the carriage window; 'that's the stile I came over; there are the hedges I crept behind, for fear any one should overtake me and force me back! Yonder is the path across the fields, leading to the old house where I was a little child! Oh Dick, Dick, my dear old friend, if I could only see you now!'

'You will see him soon,' replied Rose, gently taking his folded hands between her own. 'You shall tell him how happy you are, and how rich you have grown, and that in all your happiness you have none so great as the coming back to make him happy too.'

'Yes, yes,' said Oliver, 'and we'll—we'll take him away from here, and have him clothed and taught, and send him to some quiet country place where he may grow strong and well,—shall we?'

Rose nodded 'yes,' for the boy was smiling through such happy tears that she could not speak.

'You will be kind and good to him, for you are to every one,' said Oliver. 'It will make you cry, I know, to hear what he can tell; but never mind, never mind, it will be all over, and you will smile again—I know that too—to think how changed he is; you did the same with me. He said "God bless you" to me when I ran away,' cried the boy with a burst of affectionate emotion; 'and I will say "God bless you" now, and show him how I love him for it!'

As they approached the town, and at length drove through its narrow streets, it became matter of no small difficulty to restrain the boy within reasonable bounds. There was Sowerberry's the undertaker's just as it used to be, only smaller and less imposing in appearance than he remembered it—there were all the well-known shops and houses, with almost every one of which he had some slight incident connected—there was Gamfield's cart, the very cart he used to have, standing at the old public-house door—there was the workhouse, the dreary prison of his youthful days, with its dismal windows frowning on the street—there was the same lean porter standing at the gate, at sight of whom Oliver involuntarily shrunk back, and then laughed at himself for being so foolish, then cried, then laughed again—there were scores of faces at the doors and windows that he knew quite well—there was nearly everything as if he had left it but yesterday, and all his recent life had been but a happy dream.

But it was pure, earnest, joyful reality. They drove straight to the door of the chief hotel (which Oliver used to stare up at, with awe, and think a mighty palace, but which had somehow fallen off in grandeur and size); and here was Mr. Grimwig all ready to receive them, kissing the young lady, and the old one too, when they got out of the coach, as if he were the grandfather of the whole party, all smiles and kindness, and not offering to eat his head—no, not once; not even when he contradicted a very old postboy about the nearest road to London, and maintained he knew it best, though he had only come that way once, and that time fast asleep. There was dinner prepared, and there were bedrooms ready, and everything was arranged as if by magic.

Notwithstanding all this, when the hurry of the first half-hour was over, the same silence and constraint prevailed that had marked their journey down. Mr. Brownlow did not join them at dinner, but remained in a separate room. The two other gentlemen hurried in and out with anxious faces, and, during the short intervals when they were present, conversed apart. Once, Mrs. Maylie was called away, and after being absent for nearly an hour, returned with eyes swollen with weeping. All these things made Rose and Oliver, who were not in any new secrets, nervous and uncomfortable. They sat wondering, in silence; or, if they exchanged a few words, spoke in whispers, as if they were afraid to hear the sound of their own voices.

At length, when nine o'clock had come, and they began to think they were to hear no more that night, Mr. Losberne and Mr. Grimwig entered the room, followed by Mr. Brownlow and a man whom Oliver almost shrieked with surprise to see; for they told him it was his brother, and it was the same man he had met at the market-town, and seen looking in with Fagin at the window of his little room. Monks cast a look of hate, which, even then, he could not dissemble, at the astonished boy, and sat down near the door. Mr. Brownlow, who had papers in his hand, walked to a table near which Rose and Oliver were seated.

'This is a painful task,' said he, 'but these declarations, which have been signed in London before many gentlemen, must be in substance repeated here. I would have spared you the degradation, but we must hear them from your own lips before we part, and you know why.'

'Go on,' said the person addressed, turning away his face. 'Quick. I have almost done enough, I think. Don't keep me here.'

'This child,' said Mr. Brownlow, drawing Oliver to him, and laying his hand upon his head, 'is your half-brother; the illegitimate son of your father, my dear friend Edwin Leeford, by poor young Agnes Fleming, who died in giving him birth.'

'Yes,' said Monks, scowling at the trembling boy: the beating of whose heart he might have heard. 'That is the bastard child.'

'The term you use,' said Mr. Brownlow, sternly, 'is a reproach to those long since passed beyond the feeble censure of the world. It reflects disgrace on no one living, except you who use it. Let that pass. He was born in this town.'

'In the workhouse of this town,' was the sullen reply. 'You have the story there.' He pointed impatiently to the papers as he spoke.

'I must have it here, too,' said Mr. Brownlow, looking round upon the listeners.

'Listen then! You!' returned Monks. 'His father being taken ill at Rome, was joined by his wife, my mother, from whom he had been long separated, who went from Paris and took me with her—to look after his property, for what I know, for she had no great affection for him, nor he for her. He knew nothing of us, for his senses were gone, and he slumbered on till next day, when he died. Among the papers in his desk, were two, dated on the night his illness first came on, directed to yourself'; he addressed himself to Mr. Brownlow; 'and enclosed in a few short lines to you, with an intimation on the cover of the package that it was not to be forwarded till after he was dead. One of these papers was a letter to this girl Agnes; the other a will.'

'What of the letter?' asked Mr. Brownlow.

'The letter?—A sheet of paper crossed and crossed again, with a penitent confession, and prayers to God to help her. He had palmed a tale on the girl that some secret mystery—to be explained one day—prevented his marrying her just then; and so she had gone on, trusting patiently to him, until she trusted too far, and lost what none could ever give her back. She was, at that time, within a few months of her confinement. He told her all he had meant to do, to hide her shame, if he had lived, and prayed her, if he died, not to curse his memory, or think the consequences of their sin would be visited on her or their young child; for all the guilt was his. He reminded her of the day he had given her the little locket and the ring with her christian name engraved upon it, and a blank left for that which he hoped one day to have bestowed upon her—prayed her yet to keep it, and wear it next her heart, as she had done before—and then ran on, wildly, in the same words, over and over again, as if he had gone distracted. I believe he had.'

'The will,' said Mr. Brownlow, as Oliver's tears fell fast.

Monks was silent.

'The will,' said Mr. Brownlow, speaking for him, 'was in the same spirit as the letter. He talked of miseries which his wife had brought upon him; of the rebellious disposition, vice, malice, and premature bad passions of you his only son, who had been trained to hate him; and left you, and your mother, each an annuity of eight hundred pounds. The bulk of his property he divided into two equal portions—one for Agnes Fleming, and the other for their child, if it should be born alive, and ever come of age. If it were a girl, it was to inherit the money unconditionally; but if a boy, only on the stipulation that in his minority he should never have stained his name with any public act of dishonour, meanness, cowardice, or wrong. He did this, he said, to mark his confidence in the other, and his conviction—only strengthened by approaching death—that the child would share her gentle heart, and noble nature. If he were disappointed in this expectation, then the money was to come to you: for then, and not till then, when both children were equal, would he recognise your prior claim upon his purse, who had none upon his heart, but had, from an infant, repulsed him with coldness and aversion.'

'My mother,' said Monks, in a louder tone, 'did what a woman should have done. She burnt this will. The letter never reached its destination; but that, and other proofs, she kept, in case they ever tried to lie away the blot. The girl's father had the truth from her with every aggravation that her violent hate—I love her for it now—could add. Goaded by shame and dishonour he fled with his children into a remote corner of Wales, changing his very name that his friends might never know of his retreat; and here, no great while afterwards, he was found dead in his bed. The girl had left her home, in secret, some weeks before; he had searched for her, on foot, in every town and village near; it was on the night when he returned home, assured that she had destroyed herself, to hide her shame and his, that his old heart broke.'

There was a short silence here, until Mr. Brownlow took up the thread of the narrative.

'Years after this,' he said, 'this man's—Edward Leeford's—mother came to me. He had left her, when only eighteen; robbed her of jewels and money; gambled, squandered, forged, and fled to London: where for two years he had associated with the lowest outcasts. She was sinking under a painful and incurable disease, and wished to recover him before she died. Inquiries were set on foot, and strict searches made. They were unavailing for a long time, but ultimately successful; and he went back with her to France.'

'There she died,' said Monks, 'after a lingering illness; and, on her death-bed, she bequeathed these secrets to me, together with her unquenchable and deadly hatred of all whom they involved—though she need not have left me that, for I had inherited it long before. She would not believe that the girl had destroyed herself, and the child too, but was filled with the impression that a male child had been born, and was alive. I swore to her, if ever it crossed my path, to hunt it down; never to let it rest; to pursue it with the bitterest and most unrelenting animosity; to vent upon it the hatred that I deeply felt, and to spit upon the empty vaunt of that insulting will by draggin it, if I could, to the very gallows-foot. She was right. He came in my way at last. I began well; and, but for babbling drabs, I would have finished as I began!'

As the villain folded his arms tight together, and muttered curses on himself in the impotence of baffled malice, Mr. Brownlow turned to the terrified group beside him, and explained that the Jew, who had been his old accomplice and confidant, had a large reward for keeping Oliver ensnared: of which some part was to be given up, in the event of his being rescued: and that a dispute on this head had led to their visit to the country house for the purpose of identifying him.

'The locket and ring?' said Mr. Brownlow, turning to Monks.

'I bought them from the man and woman I told you of, who stole them from the nurse, who stole them from the corpse,' answered Monks without raising his eyes. 'You know what became of them.'

Mr. Brownlow merely nodded to Mr. Grimwig, who disappearing with great alacrity, shortly returned, pushing in Mrs. Bumble, and dragging her unwilling consort after him.

'Do my hi's deceive me!' cried Mr. Bumble, with ill-feigned enthusiasm, 'or is that little Oliver? Oh O-li-ver, if you know'd how I've been a-grieving for you—'

'Hold your tongue, fool,' murmured Mrs. Bumble.

'Isn't natur, natur, Mrs. Bumble?' remonstrated the workhouse master. 'Can't I be supposed to feel—I as brought him up porochially—when I see him a-setting here among ladies and gentlemen of the very affablest description! I always loved that boy as if he'd been my—my—my own grandfather,' said Mr. Bumble, halting for an appropriate comparison. 'Master Oliver, my dear, you remember the blessed gentleman in the white waistcoat? Ah! he went to heaven last week, in a oak coffin with plated handles, Oliver.'

'Come, sir,' said Mr. Grimwig, tartly; 'suppress your feelings.'

'I will do my endeavours, sir,' replied Mr. Bumble. 'How do you do, sir? I hope you are very well.'

This salutation was addressed to Mr. Brownlow, who had stepped up to within a short distance of the respectable couple. He inquired, as he pointed to Monks,

'Do you know that person?'

'No,' replied Mrs. Bumble flatly.

'Perhaps you don't?' said Mr. Brownlow, addressing her spouse.

'I never saw him in all my life,' said Mr. Bumble.

'Nor sold him anything, perhaps?'

'No,' replied Mrs. Bumble.

'You never had, perhaps, a certain gold locket and ring?' said Mr. Brownlow.

'Certainly not,' replied the matron. 'Why are we brought here to answer to such nonsense as this?'

Again Mr. Brownlow nodded to Mr. Grimwig; and again that gentleman limped away with extraordinary readiness. But not again did he return with a stout man and wife; for this time, he led in two palsied women, who shook and tottered as they walked.

'You shut the door the night old Sally died,' said the foremost one, raising her shrivelled hand, 'but you couldn't shut out the sound, nor stop the chinks.'

'No, no,' said the other, looking round her and wagging her toothless jaws. 'No, no, no.'

'We heard her try to tell you what she'd done, and saw you take a paper from her hand, and watched you too, next day, to the pawnbroker's shop,' said the first.

'Yes,' added the second, 'and it was a "locket and gold ring." We found out that, and saw it given you. We were by. Oh! we were by.'

'And we know more than that,' resumed the first, 'for she told us often, long ago, that the young mother had told her that, feeling she should never get over it, she was on her way, at the time that she was taken ill, to die near the grave of the father of the child.'

'Would you like to see the pawnbroker himself?' asked Mr. Grimwig with a motion towards the door.

'No,' replied the woman; 'if he'—she pointed to Monks—'has been coward enough to confess, as I see he has, and you have sounded all these hags till you have found the right ones, I have nothing more to say. I did sell them, and they're where you'll never get them. What then?'

'Nothing,' replied Mr. Brownlow, 'except that it remains for us to take care that neither of you is employed in a situation of trust again. You may leave the room.'

'I hope,' said Mr. Bumble, looking about him with great ruefulness, as Mr. Grimwig disappeared with the two old women: 'I hope that this unfortunate little circumstance will not deprive me of my porochial office?'

'Indeed it will,' replied Mr. Brownlow. 'You may make up your mind to that, and think yourself well off besides.'

'It was all Mrs. Bumble. She would do it,' urged Mr. Bumble; first looking round to ascertain that his partner had left the room.

'That is no excuse,' replied Mr. Brownlow. 'You were present on the occasion of the destruction of these trinkets, and indeed are the more guilty of the two, in the eye of the law; for the law supposes that your wife acts under your direction.'

'If the law supposes that,' said Mr. Bumble, squeezing his hat emphatically in both hands, 'the law is a ass—a idiot. If that's the eye of the law, the law is a bachelor; and the worst I wish the law is, that his eye may be opened by experience—by experience.'

Laying great stress on the repetition of these two words, Mr. Bumble fixed his hat on very tight, and putting his hands in his pockets, followed his helpmate downstairs.

'Young lady,' said Mr. Brownlow, turning to Rose, 'give me your hand. Do not tremble. You need not fear to hear the few remaining words we have to say.'

'If they have—I do not know how they can, but if they have—any reference to me,' said Rose, 'pray let me hear them at some other time. I have not strength or spirits now.'

'Nay,' returned the old gentleman, drawing her arm through his; 'you have more fortitude than this, I am sure. Do you know this young lady, sir?'

'Yes,' replied Monks.

'I never saw you before,' said Rose faintly.

'I have seen you often,' returned Monks.

'The father of the unhappy Agnes had two daughters,' said Mr. Brownlow. 'What was the fate of the other—the child?'

'The child,' replied Monks, 'when her father died in a strange place, in a strange name, without a letter, book, or scrap of paper that yielded the faintest clue by which his friends or relatives could be traced—the child was taken by some wretched cottagers, who reared it as their own.'

'Go on,' said Mr. Brownlow, signing to Mrs. Maylie to approach. 'Go on!'

'You couldn't find the spot to which these people had repaired,' said Monks, 'but where friendship fails, hatred will often force a way. My mother found it, after a year of cunning search—ay, and found the child.'

'She took it, did she?'

'No. The people were poor and began to sicken—at least the man did—of their fine humanity; so she left it with them, giving them a small present of money which would not last long, and promised more, which she never meant to send. She didn't quite rely, however, on their discontent and poverty for the child's unhappiness, but told the history of the sister's shame, with such alterations as suited her; bade them take good heed of the child, for she came of bad blood; and told them she was illegitimate, and sure to go wrong at one time or other. The circumstances countenanced all this; the people believed it; and there the child dragged on an existence, miserable enough even to satisfy us, until a widow lady, residing, then, at Chester, saw the girl by chance, pitied her, and took her home. There was some cursed spell, I think, against us; for in spite of all our efforts she remained there and was happy. I lost sight of her, two or three years ago, and saw her no more until a few months back.'

'Do you see her now?'

'Yes. Leaning on your arm.'

'But not the less my niece,' cried Mrs. Maylie, folding the fainting girl in her arms; 'not the less my dearest child. I would not lose her now, for all the treasures of the world. My sweet companion, my own dear girl!'

'The only friend I ever had,' cried Rose, clinging to her. 'The kindest, best of friends. My heart will burst. I cannot bear all this.'

'You have borne more, and have been, through all, the best and gentlest creature that ever shed happiness on every one she knew,' said Mrs. Maylie, embracing her tenderly. 'Come, come, my love, remember who this is who waits to clasp you in his arms, poor child! See here—look, look, my dear!'

'Not aunt,' cried Oliver, throwing his arms about her neck; 'I'll never call her aunt—sister, my own dear sister, that something taught my heart to love so dearly from the first! Rose, dear, darling Rose!'

Let the tears which fell, and the broken words which were exchanged in the long close embrace between the orphans, be sacred. A father, sister, and mother, were gained, and lost, in that one moment. Joy and grief were mingled in the cup; but there were no bitter tears: for even grief itself arose so softened, and clothed in such sweet and tender recollections, that it became a solemn pleasure, and lost all character of pain.

They were a long, long time alone. A soft tap at the door, at length announced that some one was without. Oliver opened it, glided away, and gave place to Harry Maylie.

'I know it all,' he said, taking a seat beside the lovely girl. 'Dear Rose, I know it all.'

'I am not here by accident,' he added after a lengthened silence; 'nor have I heard all this to-night, for I knew it yesterday—only yesterday. Do you guess that I have come to remind you of a promise?'

'Stay,' said Rose. 'You do know all.'

'All. You gave me leave, at any time within a year, to renew the subject of our last discourse.'

'I did.'

'Not to press you to alter your determination,' pursued the young man, 'but to hear you repeat it, if you would. I was to lay whatever of station or fortune I might possess at your feet, and if you still adhered to your former determination, I pledged myself, by no word or act, to seek to change it.'

'The same reasons which influenced me then, will influence me now,' said Rose firmly. 'If I ever owed a strict and rigid duty to her, whose goodness saved me from a life of indigence and suffering, when should I ever feel it, as I should to-night? It is a struggle,' said Rose, 'but one I am proud to make; it is a pang, but one my heart shall bear.'

'The disclosure of to-night,'—Harry began.

'The disclosure of to-night,' replied Rose softly, 'leaves me in the same position, with reference to you, as that in which I stood before.'

'You harden your heart against me, Rose,' urged her lover.

'Oh Harry, Harry,' said the young lady, bursting into tears; 'I wish I could, and spare myself this pain.'

'Then why inflict it on yourself?' said Harry, taking her hand. 'Think, dear Rose, think what you have heard to-night.'

'And what have I heard! What have I heard!' cried Rose. 'That a sense of his deep disgrace so worked upon my own father that he shunned all—there, we have said enough, Harry, we have said enough.'

'Not yet, not yet,' said the young man, detaining her as she rose. 'My hopes, my wishes, prospects, feeling: every thought in life except my love for you: have undergone a change. I offer you, now, no distinction among a bustling crowd; no mingling with a world of malice and detraction, where the blood is called into honest cheeks by aught but real disgrace and shame; but a home—a heart and home—yes, dearest Rose, and those, and those alone, are all I have to offer.'

'What do you mean!' she faltered.

'I mean but this—that when I left you last, I left you with a firm determination to level all fancied barriers between yourself and me; resolved that if my world could not be yours, I would make yours mine; that no pride of birth should curl the lip at you, for I would turn from it. This I have done. Those who have shrunk from me because of this, have shrunk from you, and proved you so far right. Such power and patronage: such relatives of influence and rank: as smiled upon me then, look coldly now; but there are smiling fields and waving trees in England's richest county; and by one village church—mine, Rose, my own!—there stands a rustic dwelling which you can make me prouder of, than all the hopes I have renounced, measured a thousandfold. This is my rank and station now, and here I lay it down!'

'It's a trying thing waiting supper for lovers,' said Mr. Grimwig, waking up, and pulling his pocket-handkerchief from over his head.

Truth to tell, the supper had been waiting a most unreasonable time. Neither Mrs. Maylie, nor Harry, nor Rose (who all came in together), could offer a word in extenuation.

'I had serious thoughts of eating my head to-night,' said Mr. Grimwig, 'for I began to think I should get nothing else. I'll take the liberty, if you'll allow me, of saluting the bride that is to be.'

Mr. Grimwig lost no time in carrying this notice into effect upon the blushing girl; and the example, being contagious, was followed both by the doctor and Mr. Brownlow: some people affirm that Harry Maylie had been observed to set it, originally, in a dark room adjoining; but the best authorities consider this downright scandal: he being young and a clergyman.

'Oliver, my child,' said Mrs. Maylie, 'where have you been, and why do you look so sad? There are tears stealing down your face at this moment. What is the matter?'

It is a world of disappointment: often to the hopes we most cherish, and hopes that do our nature the greatest honour.

Poor Dick was dead!

CHAPTER LII. FAGIN'S LAST NIGHT ALIVE

The court was paved, from floor to roof, with human faces. Inquisitive and eager eyes peered from every inch of space. From the rail before the dock, away into the sharpest angle of the smallest corner in the galleries, all looks were fixed upon one man—Fagin. Before him and behind: above, below, on the right and on the left: he seemed to stand surrounded by a firmament, all bright with gleaming eyes.

He stood there, in all this glare of living light, with one hand resting on the wooden slab before him, the other held to his ear, and his head thrust forward to enable him to catch with greater distinctness every word that fell from the presiding judge, who was delivering his charge to the jury. At times, he turned his eyes sharply upon them to observe the effect of the slightest featherweight in his favour; and when the points against him were stated with terrible distinctness, looked towards his counsel, in mute appeal that he would, even then, urge something in his behalf. Beyond these manifestations of anxiety, he stirred not hand or foot. He had scarcely moved since the trial began; and now that the judge ceased to speak, he still remained in the same strained attitude of close attention, with his gaze bent on him, as though he listened still.

A slight bustle in the court, recalled him to himself. Looking round, he saw that the juryman had turned together, to consider their verdict. As his eyes wandered to the gallery, he could see the people rising above each other to see his face: some hastily applying their glasses to their eyes: and others whispering their neighbours with looks expressive of abhorrence. A few there were, who seemed unmindful of him, and looked only to the jury, in impatient wonder how they could delay. But in no one face—not even among the women, of whom there were many there—could he read the faintest sympathy with himself, or any feeling but one of all-absorbing interest that he should be condemned.

As he saw all this in one bewildered glance, the deathlike stillness came again, and looking back he saw that the jurymen had turned towards the judge. Hush!

They only sought permission to retire.

He looked, wistfully, into their faces, one by one when they passed out, as though to see which way the greater number leant; but that was fruitless. The jailer touched him on the shoulder. He followed mechanically to the end of the dock, and sat down on a chair. The man pointed it out, or he would not have seen it.

He looked up into the gallery again. Some of the people were eating, and some fanning themselves with handkerchiefs; for the crowded place was very hot. There was one young man sketching his face in a little note-book. He wondered whether it was like, and looked on when the artist broke his pencil-point, and made another with his knife, as any idle spectator might have done.

In the same way, when he turned his eyes towards the judge, his mind began to busy itself with the fashion of his dress, and what it cost, and how he put it on. There was an old fat gentleman on the bench, too, who had gone out, some half an hour before, and now come back. He wondered within himself whether this man had been to get his dinner, what he had had, and where he had had it; and pursued this train of careless thought until some new object caught his eye and roused another.

Not that, all this time, his mind was, for an instant, free from one oppressive overwhelming sense of the grave that opened at his feet; it was ever present to him, but in a vague and general way, and he could not fix his thoughts upon it. Thus, even while he trembled, and turned burning hot at the idea of speedy death, he fell to counting the iron spikes before him, and wondering how the head of one had been broken off, and whether they would mend it, or leave it as it was. Then, he thought of all the horrors of the gallows and the scaffold—and stopped to watch a man sprinkling the floor to cool it—and then went on to think again.

At length there was a cry of silence, and a breathless look from all towards the door. The jury returned, and passed him close. He could glean nothing from their faces; they might as well have been of stone. Perfect stillness ensued—not a rustle—not a breath—Guilty.

The building rang with a tremendous shout, and another, and another, and then it echoed loud groans, that gathered strength as they swelled out, like angry thunder. It was a peal of joy from the populace outside, greeting the news that he would die on Monday.

The noise subsided, and he was asked if he had anything to say why sentence of death should not be passed upon him. He had resumed his listening attitude, and looked intently at his questioner while the demand was made; but it was twice repeated before he seemed to hear it, and then he only muttered that he was an old man—an old man—and so, dropping into a whisper, was silent again.

The judge assumed the black cap, and the prisoner still stood with the same air and gesture. A woman in the gallery, uttered some exclamation, called forth by this dread solemnity; he looked hastily up as if angry at the interruption, and bent forward yet more attentively. The address was solemn and impressive; the sentence fearful to hear. But he stood, like a marble figure, without the motion of a nerve. His haggard face was still thrust forward, his under-jaw hanging down, and his eyes staring out before him, when the jailer put his hand upon his arm, and beckoned him away. He gazed stupidly about him for an instant, and obeyed.

They led him through a paved room under the court, where some prisoners were waiting till their turns came, and others were talking to their friends, who crowded round a grate which looked into the open yard. There was nobody there to speak to him; but, as he passed, the prisoners fell back to render him more visible to the people who were clinging to the bars: and they assailed him with opprobrious names, and screeched and hissed. He shook his fist, and would have spat upon them; but his conductors hurried him on, through a gloomy passage lighted by a few dim lamps, into the interior of the prison.

Here, he was searched, that he might not have about him the means of anticipating the law; this ceremony performed, they led him to one of the condemned cells, and left him there—alone.

He sat down on a stone bench opposite the door, which served for seat and bedstead; and casting his blood-shot eyes upon the ground, tried to collect his thoughts. After awhile, he began to remember a few disjointed fragments of what the judge had said: though it had seemed to him, at the time, that he could not hear a word. These gradually fell into their proper places, and by degrees suggested more: so that in a little time he had the whole, almost as it was delivered. To be hanged by the neck, till he was dead—that was the end. To be hanged by the neck till he was dead.

As it came on very dark, he began to think of all the men he had known who had died upon the scaffold; some of them through his means. They rose up, in such quick succession, that he could hardly count them. He had seen some of them die,—and had joked too, because they died with prayers upon their lips. With what a rattling noise the drop went down; and how suddenly they changed, from strong and vigorous men to dangling heaps of clothes!

Some of them might have inhabited that very cell—sat upon that very spot. It was very dark; why didn't they bring a light? The cell had been built for many years. Scores of men must have passed their last hours there. It was like sitting in a vault strewn with dead bodies—the cap, the noose, the pinioned arms, the faces that he knew, even beneath that hideous veil.— Light, light!

At length, when his hands were raw with beating against the heavy door and walls, two men appeared: one bearing a candle, which he thrust into an iron candlestick fixed against the wall: the other dragging in a mattress on which to pass the night; for the prisoner was to be left alone no more.

Then came the night—dark, dismal, silent night. Other watchers are glad to hear this church-clock strike, for they tell of life and coming day. To him they brought despair. The boom of every iron bell came laden with the one, deep, hollow sound—Death. What availed the noise and bustle of cheerful morning, which penetrated even there, to him? It was another form of knell, with mockery added to the warning.

The day passed off. Day? There was no day; it was gone as soon as come—and night came on again; night so long, and yet so short; long in its dreadful silence, and short in its fleeting hours. At one time he raved and blasphemed; and at another howled and tore his hair. Venerable men of his own persuasion had come to pray beside him, but he had driven them away with curses. They renewed their charitable efforts, and he beat them off.

Saturday night. He had only one night more to live. And as he thought of this, the day broke—Sunday.

It was not until the night of this last awful day, that a withering sense of his helpless, desperate state came in its full intensity upon his blighted soul; not that he had ever held any defined or positive hope of mercy, but that he had never been able to consider more than the dim probability of dying so soon. He had spoken little to either of the two men, who relieved each other in their attendance upon him; and they, for their parts, made no effort to rouse his attention. He had sat there, awake, but dreaming. Now, he started up, every minute, and with gasping mouth and burning skin, hurried to and fro, in such a paroxysm of fear and wrath that even they—used to such sights—recoiled from him with horror. He grew so terrible, at last, in all the tortures of his evil conscience, that one man could not bear to sit there, eyeing him alone; and so the two kept watch together.

He cowered down upon his stone bed, and thought of the past. He had been wounded with some missiles from the crowd on the day of his capture, and his head was bandaged with a linen cloth. His red hair hung down upon his bloodless face; his beard was torn, and twisted into knots; his eyes shone with a terrible light; his unwashed flesh crackled with the fever that burnt him up. Eight—nine—then. If it was not a trick to frighten him, and those were the real hours treading on each other's heels, where would he be, when they came round again! Eleven! Another struck, before the voice of the previous hour had ceased to vibrate. At eight, he would be the only mourner in his own funeral train; at eleven—

Those dreadful walls of Newgate, which have hidden so much misery and such unspeakable anguish, not only from the eyes, but, too often, and too long, from the thoughts, of men, never held so dread a spectacle as that. The few who lingered as they passed, and wondered what the man was doing who was to be hanged to-morrow, would have slept but ill that night, if they could have seen him.

From early in the evening until nearly midnight, little groups of two and three presented themselves at the lodge-gate, and inquired, with anxious faces, whether any reprieve had been received. These being answered in the negative, communicated the welcome intelligence to clusters in the street, who pointed out to one another the door from which he must come out, and showed where the scaffold would be built, and, walking with unwilling steps away, turned back to conjure up the scene. By degrees they fell off, one by one; and, for an hour, in the dead of night, the street was left to solitude and darkness.

The space before the prison was cleared, and a few strong barriers, painted black, had been already thrown across the road to break the pressure of the expected crowd, when Mr. Brownlow and Oliver appeared at the wicket, and presented an order of admission to the prisoner, signed by one of the sheriffs. They were immediately admitted into the lodge.

'Is the young gentleman to come too, sir?' said the man whose duty it was to conduct them. 'It's not a sight for children, sir.'

'It is not indeed, my friend,' rejoined Mr. Brownlow; 'but my business with this man is intimately connected with him; and as this child has seen him in the full career of his success and villainy, I think it as well—even at the cost of some pain and fear—that he should see him now.'

These few words had been said apart, so as to be inaudible to Oliver. The man touched his hat; and glancing at Oliver with some curiousity, opened another gate, opposite to that by which they had entered, and led them on, through dark and winding ways, towards the cells.

'This,' said the man, stopping in a gloomy passage where a couple of workmen were making some preparations in profound silence—'this is the place he passes through. If you step this way, you can see the door he goes out at.'

He led them into a stone kitchen, fitted with coppers for dressing the prison food, and pointed to a door. There was an open grating above it, through which came the sound of men's voices, mingled with the noise of hammering, and the throwing down of boards. They were putting up the scaffold.

From this place, they passed through several strong gates, opened by other turnkeys from the inner side; and, having entered an open yard, ascended a flight of narrow steps, and came into a passage with a row of strong doors on the left hand. Motioning them to remain where they were, the turnkey knocked at one of these with his bunch of keys. The two attendants, after a little whispering, came out into the passage, stretching themselves as if glad of the temporary relief, and motioned the visitors to follow the jailer into the cell. They did so.

The condemned criminal was seated on his bed, rocking himself from side to side, with a countenance more like that of a snared beast than the face of a man. His mind was evidently wandering to his old life, for he continued to mutter, without appearing conscious of their presence otherwise than as a part of his vision.

'Good boy, Charley—well done—' he mumbled. 'Oliver, too, ha! ha! ha! Oliver too—quite the gentleman now—quite the—take that boy away to bed!'

The jailer took the disengaged hand of Oliver; and, whispering him not to be alarmed, looked on without speaking.

'Take him away to bed!' cried Fagin. 'Do you hear me, some of you? He has been the—the—somehow the cause of all this. It's worth the money to bring him up to it—Bolter's throat, Bill; never mind the girl—Bolter's throat as deep as you can cut. Saw his head off!'

'Fagin,' said the jailer.

'That's me!' cried the Jew, falling instantly, into the attitude of listening he had assumed upon his trial. 'An old man, my Lord; a very old, old man!'

'Here,' said the turnkey, laying his hand upon his breast to keep him down. 'Here's somebody wants to see you, to ask you some questions, I suppose. Fagin, Fagin! Are you a man?'

'I shan't be one long,' he replied, looking up with a face retaining no human expression but rage and terror. 'Strike them all dead! What right have they to butcher me?'

As he spoke he caught sight of Oliver and Mr. Brownlow. Shrinking to the furthest corner of the seat, he demanded to know what they wanted there.

'Steady,' said the turnkey, still holding him down. 'Now, sir, tell him what you want. Quick, if you please, for he grows worse as the time gets on.'

'You have some papers,' said Mr. Brownlow advancing, 'which were placed in your hands, for better security, by a man called Monks.'

'It's all a lie together,' replied Fagin. 'I haven't one—not one.'

'For the love of God,' said Mr. Brownlow solemnly, 'do not say that now, upon the very verge of death; but tell me where they are. You know that Sikes is dead; that Monks has confessed; that there is no hope of any further gain. Where are those papers?'

'Oliver,' cried Fagin, beckoning to him. 'Here, here! Let me whisper to you.'

'I am not afraid,' said Oliver in a low voice, as he relinquished Mr. Brownlow's hand.

'The papers,' said Fagin, drawing Oliver towards him, 'are in a canvas bag, in a hole a little way up the chimney in the top front-room. I want to talk to you, my dear. I want to talk to you.'

'Yes, yes,' returned Oliver. 'Let me say a prayer. Do! Let me say one prayer. Say only one, upon your knees, with me, and we will talk till morning.'

'Outside, outside,' replied Fagin, pushing the boy before him towards the door, and looking vacantly over his head. 'Say I've gone to sleep—they'll believe you. You can get me out, if you take me so. Now then, now then!'

'Oh! God forgive this wretched man!' cried the boy with a burst of tears.

'That's right, that's right,' said Fagin. 'That'll help us on. This door first. If I shake and tremble, as we pass the gallows, don't you mind, but hurry on. Now, now, now!'

'Have you nothing else to ask him, sir?' inquired the turnkey.

'No other question,' replied Mr. Brownlow. 'If I hoped we could recall him to a sense of his position—'

'Nothing will do that, sir,' replied the man, shaking his head. 'You had better leave him.'

The door of the cell opened, and the attendants returned.

'Press on, press on,' cried Fagin. 'Softly, but not so slow. Faster, faster!'

The men laid hands upon him, and disengaging Oliver from his grasp, held him back. He struggled with the power of desperation, for an instant; and then sent up cry upon cry that penetrated even those massive walls, and rang in their ears until they reached the open yard.

It was some time before they left the prison. Oliver nearly swooned after this frightful scene, and was so weak that for an hour or more, he had not the strength to walk.

Day was dawning when they again emerged. A great multitude had already assembled; the windows were filled with people, smoking and playing cards to beguile the time; the crowd were pushing, quarrelling, joking. Everything told of life and animation, but one dark cluster of objects in the centre of all—the black stage, the cross-beam, the rope, and all the hideous apparatus of death.

CHAPTER LIII. AND LAST

The fortunes of those who have figured in this tale are nearly closed. The little that remains to their historian to relate, is told in few and simple words.

Before three months had passed, Rose Fleming and Harry Maylie were married in the village church which was henceforth to be the scene of the young clergyman's labours; on the same day they entered into possession of their new and happy home.

Mrs. Maylie took up her abode with her son and daughter-in-law, to enjoy, during the tranquil remainder of her days, the greatest felicity that age and worth can know—the contemplation of the happiness of those on whom the warmest affections and tenderest cares of a well-spent life, have been unceasingly bestowed.

It appeared, on full and careful investigation, that if the wreck of property remaining in the custody of Monks (which had never prospered either in his hands or in those of his mother) were equally divided between himself and Oliver, it would yield, to each, little more than three thousand pounds. By the provisions of his father's will, Oliver would have been entitled to the whole; but Mr. Brownlow, unwilling to deprive the elder son of the opportunity of retrieving his former vices and pursuing an honest career, proposed this mode of distribution, to which his young charge joyfully acceded.

Monks, still bearing that assumed name, retired with his portion to a distant part of the New World; where, having quickly squandered it, he once more fell into his old courses, and, after undergoing a long confinement for some fresh act of fraud and knavery, at length sunk under an attack of his old disorder, and died in prison. As far from home, died the chief remaining members of his friend Fagin's gang.

Mr. Brownlow adopted Oliver as his son. Removing with him and the old housekeeper to within a mile of the parsonage-house, where his dear friends resided, he gratified the only remaining wish of Oliver's warm and earnest heart, and thus linked together a little society, whose condition approached as nearly to one of perfect happiness as can ever be known in this changing world.

Soon after the marriage of the young people, the worthy doctor returned to Chertsey, where, bereft of the presence of his old friends, he would have been discontented if his temperament had admitted of such a feeling; and would have turned quite peevish if he had known how. For two or three months, he contented himself with hinting that he feared the air began to disagree with him; then, finding that the place really no longer was, to him, what it had been, he settled his business on his assistant, took a bachelor's cottage outside the village of which his young friend was pastor, and instantaneously recovered. Here he took to gardening, planting, fishing, carpentering, and various other pursuits of a similar kind: all undertaken with his characteristic impetuosity. In each and all he has since become famous throughout the neighborhood, as a most profound authority.

Before his removal, he had managed to contract a strong friendship for Mr. Grimwig, which that eccentric gentleman cordially reciprocated. He is accordingly visited by Mr. Grimwig a great many times in the course of the year. On all such occasions, Mr. Grimwig plants, fishes, and carpenters, with great ardour; doing everything in a very singular and unprecedented manner, but always maintaining with his favourite asseveration, that his mode is the right one. On Sundays, he never fails to criticise the sermon to the young clergyman's face: always informing Mr. Losberne, in strict confidence afterwards, that he considers it an excellent performance, but deems it as well not to say so. It is a standing and very favourite joke, for Mr. Brownlow to rally him on his old prophecy concerning Oliver, and to remind him of the night on which they sat with the watch between them, waiting his return; but Mr. Grimwig contends that he was right in the main, and, in proof thereof, remarks that Oliver did not come back after all; which always calls forth a laugh on his side, and increases his good humour.

Mr. Noah Claypole: receiving a free pardon from the Crown in consequence of being admitted approver against Fagin: and considering his profession not altogether as safe a one as he could wish: was, for some little time, at a loss for the means of a livelihood, not burdened with too much work. After some consideration, he went into business as an informer, in which calling he realises a genteel subsistence. His plan is, to walk out once a week during church time attended by Charlotte in respectable attire. The lady faints away at the doors of charitable publicans, and the gentleman being accommodated with three-penny worth of brandy to restore her, lays an information next day, and pockets half the penalty. Sometimes Mr. Claypole faints himself, but the result is the same.

Mr. and Mrs. Bumble, deprived of their situations, were gradually reduced to great indigence and misery, and finally became paupers in that very same workhouse in which they had once lorded it over others. Mr. Bumble has been heard to say, that in this reverse and degradation, he has not even spirits to be thankful for being separated from his wife.

As to Mr. Giles and Brittles, they still remain in their old posts, although the former is bald, and the last-named boy quite grey. They sleep at the parsonage, but divide their attentions so equally among its inmates, and Oliver and Mr. Brownlow, and Mr. Losberne, that to this day the villagers have never been able to discover to which establishment they properly belong.

Master Charles Bates, appalled by Sikes's crime, fell into a train of reflection whether an honest life was not, after all, the best. Arriving at the conclusion that it certainly was, he turned his back upon the scenes of the past, resolved to amend it in some new sphere of action. He struggled hard, and suffered much, for some time; but, having a contented disposition, and a good purpose, succeeded in the end; and, from being a farmer's drudge, and a carrier's lad, he is now the merriest young grazier in all Northamptonshire.

And now, the hand that traces these words, falters, as it approaches the conclusion of its task; and would weave, for a little longer space, the thread of these adventures.

I would fain linger yet with a few of those among whom I have so long moved, and share their happiness by endeavouring to depict it. I would show Rose Maylie in all the bloom and grace of early womanhood, shedding on her secluded path in life soft and gentle light, that fell on all who trod it with her, and shone into their hearts. I would paint her the life and joy of the fire-side circle and the lively summer group; I would follow her through the sultry fields at noon, and hear the low tones of her sweet voice in the moonlit evening walk; I would watch her in all her goodness and charity abroad, and the smiling untiring discharge of domestic duties at home; I would paint her and her dead sister's child happy in their love for one another, and passing whole hours together in picturing the friends whom they had so sadly lost; I would summon before me, once again, those joyous little faces that clustered round her knee, and listen to their merry prattle; I would recall the tones of that clear laugh, and conjure up the sympathising tear that glistened in the soft blue eye. These, and a thousand looks and smiles, and turns of thought and speech—I would fain recall them every one.

How Mr. Brownlow went on, from day to day, filling the mind of his adopted child with stores of knowledge, and becoming attached to him, more and more, as his nature developed itself, and showed the thriving seeds of all he wished him to become—how he traced in him new traits of his early friend, that awakened in his own bosom old remembrances, melancholy and yet sweet and soothing—how the two orphans, tried by adversity, remembered its lessons in mercy to others, and mutual love, and fervent thanks to Him who had protected and preserved them—these are all matters which need not to be told. I have said that they were truly happy; and without strong affection and humanity of heart, and gratitude to that Being whose code is Mercy, and whose great attribute is Benevolence to all things that breathe, happiness can never be attained.

Within the altar of the old village church there stands a white marble tablet, which bears as yet but one word: 'AGNES.' There is no coffin in that tomb; and may it be many, many years, before another name is placed above it! But, if the spirits of the Dead ever come back to earth, to visit spots hallowed by the love—the love beyond the grave—of those whom they knew in life, I believe that the shade of Agnes sometimes hovers round that solemn nook. I believe it none the less because that nook is in a Church, and she was weak and erring.

About Author

Dickens's literary success began with the 1836 serial publication of The Pickwick Papers. Within a few years he had become an international literary celebrity, famous for his humour, satire, and keen observation of character and society. His novels, most published in monthly or weekly instalments, pioneered the serial publication of narrative fiction, which became the dominant Victorian mode for novel publication. Cliffhanger endings in his serial publications kept readers in suspense. The instalment format allowed Dickens to evaluate his audience's reaction, and he often modified his plot and character development based on such feedback. For example, when his wife's chiropodist expressed distress at the way Miss Mowcher in David Copperfield seemed to reflect her disabilities, Dickens improved the character with positive features. His plots were carefully constructed, and he often wove elements from topical events into his narratives. Masses of the illiterate poor chipped in ha'pennies to have each new monthly episode read to them, opening up and inspiring a new class of readers.

Dickens was regarded as the literary colossus of his age. His 1843 novella, A Christmas Carol, remains popular and continues to inspire adaptations in every artistic genre. Oliver Twist and Great Expectations are also frequently adapted, and, like many of his novels, evoke images of early Victorian London. His 1859 novel, A Tale of Two Cities, set in London and Paris, is his best-known work of historical fiction. Dickens has been praised by fellow writers—from Leo Tolstoy to George Orwell, G. K. Chesterton and Tom Wolfe—for his realism, comedy, prose style, unique characterisations, and social criticism. On the other hand, Oscar Wilde, Henry James, and Virginia Woolf complained of a lack of psychological depth, loose writing, and a vein of sentimentalism. The term Dickensian is used to describe something that is reminiscent of Dickens and his writings, such as poor social conditions or comically repulsive characters.

Early years

Charles John Huffam Dickens was born on 7 February 1812, at 1 Mile End Terrace (now 393 Commercial Road), Landport in Portsea Island (Portsmouth), the second of eight children of Elizabeth Dickens (née Barrow; 1789–1863) and John Dickens (1785–1851). His father was a clerk in the Navy Pay Office and was temporarily stationed in the district. He asked Christopher Huffam, rigger to His Majesty's Navy, gentleman, and head of an established firm, to act as godfather to Charles. Huffam is thought to be the inspiration for Paul Dombey, the owner of a shipping company in Dickens's novel Dombey and Son (1848).

In January 1815, John Dickens was called back to London, and the family moved to Norfolk Street, Fitzrovia. When Charles was four, they relocated to Sheerness, and thence to Chatham, Kent, where he spent his formative years until the age of 11. His early life seems to have been idyllic, though he thought himself a "very small and not-over-particularly-taken-care-of boy".

Charles spent time outdoors, but also read voraciously, including the picaresque novels of Tobias Smollett and Henry Fielding, as well as Robinson Crusoe and Gil Blas. He read and reread The Arabian Nights and the Collected Farces of Elizabeth Inchbald. He retained poignant memories of childhood, helped by an excellent memory of people and events, which he used in his writing. His father's brief work as a clerk in the Navy Pay Office afforded him a few years of private education, first at a dame school, and then at a school run by William Giles, a dissenter, in Chatham.

This period came to an end in June 1822, when John Dickens was recalled to Navy Pay Office headquarters at Somerset House, and the family (except for Charles, who stayed behind to finish his final term of work) moved to Camden Town in London. The family had left Kent amidst rapidly mounting debts, and, living beyond his means, John Dickens was forced by his creditors into the Marshalsea debtors' prison in Southwark, London in 1824. His wife and youngest children joined him there, as was the practice at the time. Charles, then 12 years old, boarded with Elizabeth Roylance, a family friend, at 112 College Place, Camden Town. Roylance was "a reduced [impoverished] old lady, long known to our family", whom Dickens later immortalised, "with a few alterations and embellishments", as "Mrs Pipchin" in Dombey and Son. Later, he lived in a back-attic in the house of an agent for the Insolvent Court, Archibald Russell, "a fat, good-natured, kind old gentleman... with a quiet old wife" and lame son, in Lant Street in Southwark. They provided the inspiration for the Garlands in The Old Curiosity Shop.

On Sundays—with his sister Frances, free from her studies at the Royal Academy of Music—he spent the day at the Marshalsea. Dickens later used the prison as a setting in Little Dorrit. To pay for his board and to help his family, Dickens was forced to leave school and work ten-hour days at Warren's Blacking Warehouse, on Hungerford Stairs, near the present Charing Cross railway station, where he earned six shillings a week pasting labels on pots of boot blacking. The strenuous and often harsh working conditions made a lasting impression on Dickens and later influenced his fiction and essays, becoming the foundation of his interest in the reform of socio-economic and labour conditions, the rigours of which he believed were unfairly borne by the poor. He later wrote that he wondered "how I could have been so easily cast away at such an age". As he recalled to John Forster (from The Life of Charles Dickens):

The blacking-warehouse was the last house on the left-hand side of the way, at old Hungerford Stairs. It was a crazy, tumble-down old house, abutting of course on the river, and literally overrun with rats. Its wainscoted rooms, and its rotten floors and staircase, and the old grey rats swarming down in the cellars, and the sound of their squeaking and scuffling coming up the stairs at all times, and the dirt and decay of the place, rise up visibly before me, as if I were there again. The counting-house was on the first floor, looking over the coal-barges and the river. There was a recess in it, in which I was to sit and work. My work was to cover the pots of paste-blacking; first with a piece of oil-paper, and then with a piece of blue paper; to tie them round with a string; and then to clip the paper close and neat, all round, until it looked as smart as a pot of ointment from an apothecary's shop. When a certain number of grosses of pots had attained this pitch of perfection, I was to paste on each a printed label, and then go on again with more pots. Two or three other boys were kept at similar duty down-stairs on similar wages. One of them came up, in a ragged apron and a paper cap, on the first Monday morning, to show me the trick of using the string and tying the knot. His name was Bob Fagin; and I took the liberty of using his name, long afterwards, in Oliver Twist.

When the warehouse was moved to Chandos Street in the smart, busy district of Covent Garden the boys worked in a room in which the window gave onto the street and little audiences gathered and watched them at work—in Dickens biographer Simon Callow's estimation, the public display was "a new refinement added to his misery".

A few months after his imprisonment, John Dickens's mother, Elizabeth Dickens, died and bequeathed him £450. On the expectation of this legacy, Dickens was released from prison. Under the Insolvent Debtors Act, Dickens arranged for payment of his creditors, and he and his family left Marshalsea, for the home of Mrs Roylance.

Charles's mother, Elizabeth Dickens, did not immediately support his removal from the boot-blacking warehouse. This influenced Dickens's view that a father should rule the family, and a mother find her proper sphere inside the home: "I never afterwards forgot, I never shall forget, I never can forget, that my mother was warm for my being sent back". His mother's failure to request his return was a factor in his dissatisfied attitude towards women.

Righteous indignation stemming from his own situation and the conditions under which working-class people lived became major themes of his works, and it was this unhappy period in his youth to which he alluded in his favourite, and most autobiographical, novel, David Copperfield: "I had no advice, no counsel, no encouragement, no consolation, no assistance, no support, of any kind, from anyone, that I can call to mind, as I hope to go to heaven!"

Dickens was eventually sent to the Wellington House Academy in Camden Town, where he remained until March 1827, having spent about two years there. He did not consider it to be a good school: "Much of the haphazard, desultory teaching, poor discipline punctuated by the headmaster's sadistic brutality, the seedy ushers and general run-down atmosphere, are embodied in Mr Creakle's Establishment in David Copperfield."

Dickens worked at the law office of Ellis and Blackmore, attorneys, of Holborn Court, Gray's Inn, as a junior clerk from May 1827 to November 1828. He was a gifted mimic and impersonated those around him: clients, lawyers, and clerks. He went to theatres obsessively—he claimed that for at least three years he went to the theatre every single day. His favourite actor was Charles Mathews, and Dickens learnt his monopolylogues, (farces in which Mathews played every character), by heart. Then, having learned Gurney's system of shorthand in his spare time, he left to become a freelance reporter. A distant relative, Thomas Charlton, was a freelance reporter at Doctors' Commons, and Dickens was able to share his box there to report the legal proceedings for nearly four years. This education was to inform works such as Nicholas Nickleby, Dombey and Son, and especially Bleak House—whose vivid portrayal of the machinations and bureaucracy of the legal system did much to enlighten the general public and served as a vehicle for dissemination of Dickens's own views regarding, particularly, the heavy burden on the poor who were forced by circumstances to "go to law".

In 1830, Dickens met his first love, Maria Beadnell, thought to have been the model for the character Dora in David Copperfield. Maria's parents disapproved of the courtship and ended the relationship by sending her to school in Paris.

Journalism and early novels

In 1832, at age 20, Dickens was energetic and increasingly self-confident. He enjoyed mimicry and popular entertainment, lacked a clear, specific sense of what he wanted to become, and yet knew he wanted fame. Drawn to the theatre—he became an early member of the Garrick — he landed an acting audition at Covent Garden, where the manager George Bartley and the actor Charles Kemble were to see him. Dickens prepared meticulously and decided to imitate the comedian Charles Mathews, but ultimately he missed the audition because of a cold. Before another opportunity arose, he had set out on his career as a writer.

In 1833, he submitted his first story, "A Dinner at Poplar Walk", to the London periodical Monthly Magazine. William Barrow, a brother of his mother, offered him a job on The Mirror of Parliament and he worked in the House of Commons for the first time early in 1832. He rented rooms at Furnival's Inn and worked as a political journalist, reporting on Parliamentary debates, and he travelled across Britain to cover election campaigns for the Morning Chronicle. His journalism, in the form of sketches in periodicals, formed his first collection of pieces, published in 1836: Sketches by Boz—Boz being a family nickname he employed as a pseudonym for some years. Dickens apparently adopted it from the nickname "Moses", which he had given to his youngest brother Augustus Dickens, after a character in Oliver Goldsmith's The Vicar of Wakefield. When pronounced by anyone with a head cold, "Moses" became "Boses"—later shortened to Boz. Dickens's own name was considered "queer" by a contemporary critic, who wrote in 1849: "Mr Dickens, as if in revenge for his own queer name, does bestow still queerer ones upon his fictitious creations." He contributed to and edited journals throughout his literary career. In January 1835, the Morning Chronicle launched an evening edition, under the editorship of the Chronicle's music critic, George Hogarth. Hogarth invited Dickens to contribute Street Sketches and Dickens became a regular visitor to his Fulham house, excited by Hogarth's friendship with a hero of his, Walter Scott, and enjoying the company of Hogarth's three daughters—Georgina, Mary, and nineteen-year-old Catherine.

Dickens made rapid progress both professionally and socially. He began a friendship with William Harrison Ainsworth, the author of the highwayman novel Rookwood (1834), whose bachelor salon in Harrow Road had become the meeting place for a set that included Daniel Maclise, Benjamin Disraeli, Edward Bulwer-Lytton, and George Cruikshank. All these became his friends and collaborators, with the exception of Disraeli, and he met his first publisher, John Macrone, at the house. The success of Sketches by Boz led to a proposal from publishers Chapman and Hall for Dickens to supply text to match Robert Seymour's engraved illustrations in a monthly letterpress. Seymour committed suicide after the second instalment, and Dickens, who wanted to write a connected series of sketches, hired "Phiz" to provide the engravings (which were reduced from four to two per instalment) for the story. The resulting story became The Pickwick Papers, and though the first few episodes were not successful, the introduction of the Cockney character Sam Weller in the fourth episode (the first to be illustrated by Phiz) marked a sharp climb in its popularity. The final instalment sold 40,000 copies.

In November 1836, Dickens accepted the position of editor of Bentley's Miscellany, a position he held for three years, until he fell out with the owner. In 1836 as he finished the last instalments of The Pickwick Papers, he began writing the beginning instalments of Oliver Twist—writing as many as 90 pages a month—while continuing work on Bentley's and also writing four plays, the production of which he oversaw. Oliver Twist, published in 1838, became one of Dickens's better known stories, and was the first Victorian novel with a child protagonist.

On 2 April 1836, after a one-year engagement, and between episodes two and three of The Pickwick Papers, Dickens married Catherine Thomson Hogarth (1816–1879), the daughter of George Hogarth, editor of the Evening Chronicle. They were married in St. Luke's Church, Chelsea, London. After a brief honeymoon in Chalk in Kent, the couple returned to lodgings at Furnival's Inn. The first of their ten children, Charley, was born in January 1837, and a few months later the family set up home in Bloomsbury at 48 Doughty Street, London, (on which Charles had a three-year lease at £80 a year) from 25 March 1837 until December 1839. Dickens's younger brother Frederick and Catherine's 17-year-old sister Mary, moved in with them. Dickens became very attached to Mary, and she died in his arms after a brief illness in 1837. Unusually for Dickens, as a consequence of his shock, he stopped working, and he and Kate stayed at a little farm on Hampstead Heath for a fortnight. Dickens idealised Mary—the character he fashioned after her, Rose Maylie, he found he could not now kill, as he had planned, in his fiction, and, according to Ackroyd, he drew on memories of her for his later descriptions of Little Nell and Florence Dombey. His grief was so great that he was unable to meet the deadline for the June instalment of Pickwick Papers and had to cancel the Oliver Twist instalment that month as well. The time in Hampstead was the occasion for a growing bond between Dickens and John Forster to develop and Forster soon became his unofficial business manager, and the first to read his work.

His success as a novelist continued. The young Queen Victoria read both Oliver Twist and Pickwick, staying up until midnight to discuss them. Nicholas Nickleby (1838–39), The Old Curiosity Shop (1840–41) and, finally, his first historical novel, Barnaby Rudge: A Tale of the Riots of 'Eighty, as part of the Master Humphrey's Clock series (1840–41), were all published in monthly instalments before being made into books.

In the midst of all his activity during this period, there was discontent with his publishers and John Macrone was bought off, while Richard Bentley signed over all his rights in Oliver Twist. Other signs of a certain restlessness and discontent emerge—in Broadstairs he flirted with Eleanor Picken, the young fiancée of his solicitor's best friend, and one night grabbed her and ran with her down to the sea. He declared they were both to drown there in the "sad sea waves". She finally got free but afterwards kept her distance. In June 1841 he precipitously set out on a two-month tour of Scotland and then, in September 1841, telegraphed Forster that he had decided to go to America. Master Humphrey's Clock was shut down, though Dickens was still keen on the idea of the weekly magazine, a form he liked, a liking that had begun with his childhood reading of the eighteenth-century magazines Tatler and The Spectator.

Dickens was perturbed by the return to power of the Tories, whom Dickens described as "people whom, politically, I despise and abhor." He had been tempted to stand for the Liberals in Reading, but decided against it due to financial straits. He wrote three anti-Tory verse satires ("The Fine Old English Gentleman", "The Quack Doctor's Proclamation", and "Subjects for Painters") which were published in The Examiner.

First visit to the United States

On 22 January 1842, Dickens and his wife arrived in Boston, Massachusetts aboard the RMS Britannia during their first trip to the United States and Canada. At this time Georgina Hogarth, another sister of Catherine, joined the Dickens household, now living at Devonshire Terrace, Marylebone, to care for the young family they had left behind. She remained with them as housekeeper, organiser, adviser, and friend until Dickens's death in 1870. Dickens modeled the character of Agnes Wickfield after Georgina and Mary.

He described his impressions in a travelogue, American Notes for General Circulation. Dickens includes in Notes a powerful condemnation of slavery, which he had attacked as early as

The Pickwick Papers, correlating the emancipation of the poor in England with the abolition of slavery abroad citing newspaper accounts of runaway slaves disfigured by their masters. In spite of the abolitionist sentiments gleaned from his trip to America, some modern commentators have pointed out inconsistencies in Dickens's views on racial inequality, for instance, he has been criticized for his subsequent acquiescence in Governor Eyre's harsh crackdown during the 1860s Morant Bay rebellion in Jamaica and his failure to join other British progressives in condemning it. From Richmond, Virginia, Dickens returned to Washington, D.C., and started a trek westward to St. Louis, Missouri. While there, he expressed a desire to see an American prairie before returning east. A group of 13 men then set out with Dickens to visit Looking Glass Prairie, a trip 30 miles into Illinois.

During his American visit, Dickens spent a month in New York City, giving lectures, raising the question of international copyright laws and the pirating of his work in America. He persuaded a group of twenty-five writers, headed by Washington Irving, to sign a petition for him to take to Congress, but the press were generally hostile to this, saying that he should be grateful for his popularity and that it was mercenary to complain about his work being pirated.

The popularity he gained caused a shift in his self-perception according to critic Kate Flint, who writes that he "found himself a cultural commodity, and its circulation had passed out his control", causing him to become interested in and delve into themes of public and personal personas in the next novels. She writes that he assumed a role of "influential commentator", publicly and in his fiction, evident in his next few books. His trip to the U.S. ended with a trip to Canada: Niagara Falls, Toronto, Kingston and Montreal where he appeared on stage in light comedies.

Soon after his return to England, Dickens began work on the first of his Christmas stories, A Christmas Carol, written in 1843, which was followed by The Chimes in 1844 and The Cricket on the Hearth in 1845. Of these, A Christmas Carol was most popular and, tapping into an old tradition, did much to promote a renewed enthusiasm for the joys of Christmas in Britain and America. The seeds for the story became planted in Dickens's mind during a trip to Manchester to witness the conditions of the manufacturing workers there. This, along with scenes he had recently witnessed at the Field Lane Ragged School, caused Dickens to resolve to "strike a sledge hammer blow" for the poor. As the idea for the story took shape and the writing began in earnest, Dickens became engrossed in the book. He later wrote that as the tale unfolded he "wept and laughed, and wept again" as he "walked about the black streets of London fifteen or twenty miles many a night when all sober folks had gone to bed."

After living briefly in Italy (1844), Dickens travelled to Switzerland (1846), where he began work on Dombey and Son (1846–48). This and David Copperfield (1849–50) mark a significant artistic break in Dickens's career as his novels became more serious in theme and more carefully planned than his early works.

At about this time, he was made aware of a large embezzlement at the firm where his brother, Augustus, worked (John Chapman & Co.). It had been carried out by Thomas Powell, a clerk, who was on friendly terms with Dickens and who had acted as mentor to Augustus when he started work. Powell was also an author and poet and knew many of the famous writers of the day. After further fraudulent activities, Powell fled to New York and published a book called The Living Authors of England with a chapter on Charles Dickens, who was not amused by what Powell had written. One item that seemed to have annoyed him was the assertion that he had based the character of Paul Dombey (Dombey and Son) on Thomas Chapman, one of the principal partners at John Chapman & Co. Dickens immediately sent a letter to Lewis Gaylord Clark, editor of the New York literary magazine The Knickerbocker, saying that Powell was a forger and thief. Clark published the letter in the New-York Tribune, and several other papers picked up on the story. Powell began proceedings to sue these publications, and Clark was arrested. Dickens, realising that he had acted in haste, contacted John Chapman & Co. to seek written confirmation of Powell's guilt. Dickens did receive a reply confirming Powell's embezzlement, but once the directors realised this information might have to be produced in court, they refused to make further disclosures. Owing to the difficulties of providing evidence in America to support his accusations, Dickens eventually made a private settlement with Powell out of court.

Philanthropy

Angela Burdett Coutts, heir to the Coutts banking fortune, approached Dickens in May 1846 about setting up a home for the redemption of fallen women of the working class. Coutts envisioned a home that would replace the punitive regimes of existing institutions with a reformative environment conducive to education and proficiency in domestic household chores. After initially resisting, Dickens eventually founded the home, named "Urania Cottage", in the Lime Grove section of Shepherds Bush, which he managed for ten years, setting the house rules, reviewing the accounts and interviewing prospective residents. Emigration and marriage were central to Dickens's agenda for the women on leaving Urania Cottage, from which it is estimated that about 100 women graduated between 1847 and 1859.

Death

On 8 June 1870, Dickens suffered another stroke at his home after a full day's work on Edwin Drood. He never regained consciousness, and the next day, five years to the day after the Staplehurst rail crash, he died at Gads Hill Place. Biographer Claire Tomalin has suggested Dickens was actually in Peckham when he suffered the stroke, and his mistress Ellen Ternan and her maids had him taken back to Gad's Hill so the public would not know the truth about their relationship. Contrary to his wish to be buried at Rochester Cathedral "in an inexpensive, unostentatious, and strictly private manner", he was laid to rest in the Poets' Corner of Westminster Abbey. A printed epitaph circulated at the time of the funeral reads:

To the Memory of Charles Dickens (England's most popular author) who died at his residence, Higham, near Rochester, Kent, 9 June 1870, aged 58 years. He was a sympathiser with the poor, the suffering, and the oppressed; and by his death, one of England's greatest writers is lost to the world.

His last words were: "On the ground", in response to his sister-in-law Georgina's request that he lie down. On Sunday, 19 June 1870, five days after Dickens was buried in the Abbey, Dean Arthur Penrhyn Stanley delivered a memorial elegy, lauding "the genial and loving humorist whom we now mourn", for showing by his own example "that even in dealing with the darkest scenes and the most degraded characters, genius could still be clean, and mirth could be innocent". Pointing to the fresh flowers that adorned the novelist's grave, Stanley assured those present that "the spot would thenceforth be a sacred one with both the New World and the Old, as that of the representative of literature, not of this island only, but of all who speak our English tongue."

In his will, drafted more than a year before his death, Dickens left the care of his £80,000 estate to his longtime colleague John Forster and his "best and truest friend" Georgina Hogarth who, along with Dickens's two sons, also received a tax-free sum of £8,000 (about £800,000 in present terms). Although Dickens and his wife had been separated for several years at the time of his death, he provided her with an annual income of £600 and made her similar allowances in his will. He also bequeathed £19 19s to each servant in his employment at the time of his death. (Source: Wikipedia)

CPSIA information can be obtained
at www.ICGtesting.com
Printed in the USA
LVHW091231240320
650924LV00009BA/107